The Jack Harvey Novels

Also by Ian Rankin

The Inspector Rebus Series

Knots & Crosses
Hide & Seek
Tooth & Nail (previously published as Wolfman)
A Good Hanging and Other Stories
Strip Jack
The Black Book
Mortal Causes
Let It Bleed
Black & Blue
The Hanging Garden
Death Is Not The End (a novella)
Dead Souls
Rebus: The Early Years
Set In Darkness

Other Novels

The Flood
Watchman
Westwind

The Jack Harvey Novels

■

Witch Hunt
Bleeding Hearts
Blood Hunt

■

Ian Rankin
Writing as Jack Harvey

ORION

This edition first published in Great Britain in 2000 by
Orion, an imprint of the Orion Publishing Group Ltd.

Second Impression October 2000

A CIP catalogue record for this book
is available from the British Library.

Typeset by Deltatype Ltd, Birkenhead, Merseyside

Printed in Great Britain by
Clays Ltd, St Ives plc

The Orion Publishing Group Ltd
Orion House
5 Upper St Martin's Lane
London WC2H 9EA

Contents

Foreword

In 1990 my wife and I took a fairly momentous decision. We would give up our jobs in London and move to rural France. Miranda's reasoning went thus: we could buy a house with a plot of land, become self-sufficient, and this would mean I could write full-time. Certainly, it was hard to imagine existing as a full-time writer in London. My meagre earnings from the Inspector Rebus novels wouldn't cover the mortgage, let alone buy us the occasional tin of food. So we found a place in the least sought-after corner of the Dordogne, bought it, and upped sticks. I was suddenly in deepest France, not a word of the language to my name. Miranda started sorting out the garden and soon our fridge overflowed with lettuce, peas and cabbage. We were, however, finding it hard to resist the charms of the many inexpensive restaurants around us, and the house was proving costly to renovate. (We certainly needed help in this department, if my own efforts were anything to go by. I managed to lay a tongue-and-groove floor without realising I should be nailing the planks down as I went. The result would have compared well with any world-class trampoline.)

I had time on my hands. The Rebus books were still at this time relatively short and uncomplicated affairs, and took about three months to write. Meantime I was filing away lots of ideas for non-Rebus projects. My agent came up with a plan: a pseudonymous series of mainstream thrillers. Publishers, I was told, don't like to put out more than one book a year by any particular author (though something tells me J.K. Rowling wouldn't have too many problems). The hunt for a suitable name commenced. Miranda had just given birth to our first son, Jack. Her own surname was Harvey. I mulled over 'Jack Harvey' and liked it. Maybe fans of Jack Higgins would be tricked into buying my titles instead of his. I'd already been informed of the psychology of author surnames: you want one in the middle of the alphabet, because most of the time this will ensure you a spot in the middle of the shelves at a bookshop, where the book can be more easily spotted by the casual eye. Jack Harvey seemed to fit the bill.

The first Jack Harvey novel (I'd signed a contract for three) was to be called *Witch Hunt*. Actually, the original title was *Witch*, but everyone said it would be mistaken for a horror novel. I'd already faced similar criticism with my Rebus novel *Wolfman* (latterly renamed *Tooth & Nail*) and didn't argue when *Witch Hunt* was suggested. I've always had a keen interest in comic books, and loved the 'Elektra: Assassin' series. I liked the notion of a female assassin, and wanted to know if I could write a book with a female heroine (or anti-heroine). I suppose *Witch Hunt* was an experiment; in fact all the Jack Harvey books were: they were ways of playing with ideas and structural problems outside the scope of my detective series.

After *Witch Hunt* came *Bleeding Hearts*. Here, I wanted to play tricks with the reader's mind. I would use first-person narration for the apparent 'baddie' – another professional assassin, but this time with a potentially fatal flaw (haemophilia) – and third-person for the apparent 'good guy', a slimy private detective hired to locate and destroy the hitman. I was hoping readers would come to empathise with the baddie, and be on his side against the private eye. I think it worked. It wasn't until afterwards that a friend (hiya, Sandy) remarked that my private eye, in his habits, lifestyle and personal hygiene, bore a strong resemblance to John Self in Martin Amis's *Money*. Amis's book was one of my favourite novels, and I think my friend was right. I was either paying homage, or else was trying to write that seductive narrative voice of John Self's out of my system.

For a long time, I didn't have an idea for book three. I wanted some sense of 'closure'. The books weren't selling, and it was unlikely any publisher would wish to prolong Jack Harvey's life. This was going to be my last book. I had plenty of ideas for plots, but none of them seemed quite right. And then two things happened. One was that I became interested in what I saw as a large-scale conspiracy concerning BSE and the prion proteins responsible for CJD. People who had been trying to uncover or promote the truth had been subject to assaults, threats, and so on. Papers had been ransacked, phones tapped, and at least one person had met an untimely and suspicious end. The other thing was, I went back to my novel *Knots & Crosses* and started imagining a parallel life for its villain. I started playing with his life, taking John Rebus out of the equation. I decided he'd been to the Falklands, had played an active part in that campaign. I decided he now ran a survival-training course in Scotland. He became the hero of the story, and I made sure his name was unchanged from *Knots & Crosses*. All I needed was a title, and it came by combining aspects of books one and two. *Witch Hunt* and *Bleeding Hearts* became *Blood Hunt*. I was pretty sure Neil Gunn had used the title before me, but that wasn't a problem. Actually, I liked that. His book was set in Scotland, too, and involved a cat and mouse game between hero and nemesis. Perfect.

The Jack Harvey books had come to the end of their natural life. A few people had bought and enjoyed them. They told me as much at readings and signings, and then asked when there would be more. But I was finding by this time that the Rebus books were growing in length and complexity. They were taking seven, eight, nine months to write. They were becoming more popular. They were pushing Jack Harvey aside. I had to concentrate on John Rebus. My days as a 'two-book-a-year' author were numbered.

I'm thrilled to see the books back in print, because I know how frustrating it has been for fans and completists who could not track them down these past few years. Maybe the collectors' market will be a bit calmer now.

And the Rebus fans among you may even spot the occasional in-joke.

Ian Rankin
Edinburgh, 2000

Witch Hunt

For Peter Robinson

Contents

'The female of the species is more deadly than the male'

— Rudyard Kipling, *The Female of the Species*

'If a woman had no existence save in the fiction written by men, one would imagine her a person of the utmost importance; very various; heroic and mean; splendid and sordid; infinitely beautiful and hideous in the extreme; as great as a man, some think even greater'

— Virginia Woolf, *A Room of One's Own*

'A woman's desire for revenge outlasts all her other emotions'

— Cyril Connolly

Arrival

Monday 1 June

It was a pleasure boat.

At least, that's how owner and skipper George Crane would have described it. It had been bought for pleasure back in the late-1980s when business was thriving, money both plentiful and cheap. He'd bought it to indulge himself. His wife had nagged about the waste of money, but then she suffered from chronic sea-sickness and wouldn't set foot on it. *She* wouldn't set foot on it, but there were plenty of women who would. Plenty of women for George Crane and his friends. There was Liza, for example, who liked to stand on deck clad only in her bikini bottom, waving at passing vessels. God, Liza, Siren of the South Coast. Where was she now? And all the others: Gail, Tracy, Debbie, Francesca . . . He smiled at the memories: of routes to France, Portugal, Spain; of trips taken around the treacherous British Isles. Trips taken with women aboard, or with women picked up en route. Wine and good food and perhaps a few lines of coke at the end of the evening. Good days, good memories. Memories of the pleasure boat *Cassandra Christa*.

But no pleasure tonight, the boat gliding across a calm British Channel. This was a business trip, the client below decks. Crane hadn't caught much more than a glimpse of her as she'd clambered aboard with her rucksack. Brian had gone to help her, but she hadn't needed any. She was tall, he was certain of that. Dark maybe, as in dark-haired, not dark-skinned. European? He couldn't say. Brian hadn't been able to add much either.

'Just asked if she could go below. Better down there than up here getting in the way.'

'She said that?'

Brian shook his head. 'All she said was "I'm going below". Not even a question, more like an order.'

'Did she sound English?'

Brian shrugged. He was a good and honest soul, unburdened by intellect. Still, he would keep his mouth shut about tonight's work. And he came cheap, since he was already one of George Crane's employees, one of that dwindling band. The business had overextended itself, that was the problem. Too big a loan to push the business into new areas, areas drying up just as George Crane arrived. More loans to cover the earlier loan . . . It was bad luck. Still, the business would weather it.

Cassandra Christa, however, might not. He'd put word out that she was for sale, and an ad had been placed in a couple of newspapers: one quality Sunday, one daily. There had been just the one phone call so far but it was early days, besides which maybe he wouldn't have to sell after all. He glanced at his watch. Five minutes short of three in the morning. Crane stifled a yawn.

'Want me to check the cargo?' Brian asked. Crane smiled.

'You stay where you are, you randy little sod. The cargo can look after itself.'

Crane had been told – had been *ordered* – not to be interested, not to be nosy. No chit-chat, no questions. It was just a delivery, that was all. He didn't know quite what he'd expected. Some chisel-chinned IRA bastard or ex-pat felon. He certainly hadn't expected a young woman. Young? Well, she *moved* like a young woman. He had to admit he was intrigued, despite the warning. The worst part would be coming up soon: the landing on the coast. But she spoke English, so that shouldn't pose any problem even if they were stopped. A midnight cruise, take the boat out, breathe in the ozone, that sort of thing. A nod and a wink to Customs or whoever. They understood these things. The pleasure of making love on the deck of a boat, sky above, water all around. He shivered slightly. It had been a long time. The good days seemed an awful long time ago. But maybe they'd return. A few more runs like this wouldn't go amiss. Money for old rope. And to think he'd worried about it for weeks. Shame really that he was selling the boat. But if he did a good job, a smooth job of work, they might employ his talents again. Another job or two would save the *Cassandra Christa*. Another couple of jobs like this one and he'd be home and dry.

'Shoreline, Skip.'

'I told you I don't like "Skip". Skipper's okay.'

'Sorry, Skipper.'

Crane nodded. Brian's attributes included sharp night vision. Yes, there it was now. The coastline. Hythe and Sandgate probably. Folkestone just a little to the east, their destination. Folkestone was the drop-off, the danger point. Then they'd turn the boat back towards Sandgate where it had its mooring. More instructions: after depositing the cargo, head back out to sea before making for final mooring. Do not hug the coastline as this would make them more likely to be spotted.

A silly order really, but he'd been told at the start: you either follow the orders to the letter or you don't take the job.

'I'll take the job,' he'd said. But the man had shaken his head.

'Don't make up your mind so quickly, Mr Grane.' That was the way he'd said it – Grane. He had trouble with consonants. Danish? Something Scandinavian? Or Dutch maybe? 'Take your time. You need to be sure for yourself. I'll telephone you next week. Meantime, happy sailing.'

Happy sailing? Well, plain sailing anyway. Crane didn't expect trouble. There was no Customs activity to speak of round here these days. Cutbacks. The British coastline was like a net – full of holes through which you could push unseen anything you liked. Crane had been definite about that.

'Not if it's drugs. I won't have anything to do with drugs.'

The foreigner had shaken his head slowly. 'Nothing like that. It's just a body.'

'A body?'

'A *live* body, Mr Grane. Very much alive. Someone who wants to see England but finds themself stranded on the Continent without a passport.'

'Ah.' Crane had nodded at that. He had his ideas: missing peers, runaways, crooks from the Costa Del Sol who'd decided they'd pay anything for the pleasure of an afternoon in a British boozer. 'What about a name then?'

Another shake of the head. 'No names, Mr Grane.'

'So how will I know I've got the right person?'

An indulgent smile. 'How many people do you think will be in the middle of the English Channel at midnight, waiting to meet a boat?'

Crane had laughed. 'Not many, I suppose. Any night in particular?'

'I'll let you know. I must warn you now, you won't get much notice, a few hours at most. So make sure you are home every evening. Make sure you remain available. And Mr Grane . . . ?'

'Yes?'

'Better think up a story to tell your wife.'

His wife! Least of his problems, he'd assured the man. But the man had seemed to know quite a lot about his problems, hadn't he? The way he'd approached Crane that early morning outside the office, telling him he might have some work for him. But he hadn't wanted to discuss it in Crane's office. They'd arranged to meet in a pub instead, that lunchtime.

With nothing to lose, but suspecting some kind of trap, Crane had gone along. What he hadn't told the man was that one of his own men, Mike McKillip, was in the bar too. First sign of trouble, Mike's orders were to wade in. Mike liked a bit of a barney, and Crane had slipped him a twenty as drinking money.

But there'd been no barney, no trap, just a muted conversation, mostly one way. A business proposition . . . believe you own a boat . . . financial difficulties . . . would like to hire your services. That was the way he'd put it: 'I would like to hire your services.' Like George Crane was some tugboat skipper. But then the man had started to talk serious money. He offered £1,000 on acceptance of the contract – he'd called it that too, making it sound like 'gontrag' – £2,000 on delivery, and a further and final £2,000 twelve weeks after delivery.

'Three months? How do I know you won't . . . I mean, I'm not suggesting . . . but all the same.' Crane's head spun with thoughts of money. He gulped a mouthful of whisky.

Cue the smile. 'You are a businessman, Mr Grane. Cautious, prudent, and suspicious. You are quite right. But the time-lag is so we can assure ourselves of your silence. If we don't pay, you could go to the police with your story.'

'Hardly! I'd be an accomplice.'

'Nevertheless, you could tell your story. We would rather pay for your silence. Two thousand seems to me a small price to pay for the gift of silence.'

George Crane still wasn't sure about that. What story could he possibly tell? Still, he'd have done the job for three grand in any case, and three grand was what he'd have by the end of tonight's little adventure. Three thousand beautiful pounds, a thousand of which had already been lodged in what he called his 'Number Four Account', one of several he'd managed to keep hidden from Inland Revenue's sniffer-dogs (the same sniffer-dogs he'd suspected of laying a trap for him in the first place). There was fifty quid to pay Brian, of course. It didn't seem much, but anything higher and he might start to get suspicious. Fifty was just right for Brian: enough to buy his fidelity, but not enough to get him excited.

There were lights along the coast, welcoming lights. He turned to Brian now. 'Better tell her we're home.'

'I think she already knows.'

And here she was, coming in a crouch through the small doorway and on to deck, pulling her rucksack behind her. She stood up straight, stretching her back. She was tall, five-ten or thereabouts. Tall and thin. Hard to tell much more through the waterproof she was wearing. She had a package with her which she held out to Crane. He accepted it.

'Brian,' he said, 'take over here for a sec.'

'Right, Skipper.'

Crane made his way to the side of the boat, nearest to the land. There was enough light to see by. He didn't want Brian to see how much money was involved. He tore open the package and flipped through the wad of notes. Fifties. Looked like about forty of them. Well, he wasn't going to stand here counting them out like Shylock. He stuffed them into his inside jacket pocket, creating a comfortable bulge, and returned to the wheel. The woman was looking at him, so he nodded towards her. Only towards her, not *at* her. It was difficult to meet her eyes, difficult to hold their gaze. It wasn't that she was beautiful or anything (though she might be in daylight). But she was . . . intense. And almost scowling, like she was spoiling for a fight.

'Round the coast a little way yet, Brian,' Crane said. 'Just outside the town, that's the drop.'

'How much longer?' she asked. Yes, European, thought Crane. Probably British, but she looked as if she'd been away for a while.

'Five minutes,' he said. He produced a hip flask from his pocket and unscrewed the top. 'A drop of malt,' he explained. 'Care for a tot?'

She shook her head, but as he drank deep she said: 'Good health.'

He exhaled noisily. 'Thank you. And here's to yours.' Then he passed the depleted flask to Brian, who finished it off in a mouthful.

'We've got a dinghy,' Crane announced. It was good policy to look helpful if he wanted future contracts. 'We can row you ashore.'

'I'll swim. Just get me close.'

'The water's freezing,' Brian protested. 'You'll catch your death.'

But she was shaking her head.

'And what about your bag?'

'It's waterproof, and so am I.'

'It'll sink like a—'

She was taking off the waterproof, slipping out of her shoes, undoing her jeans. The two men watched. Underneath, she was wearing a one-piece black bathing costume.

'I must get one of those for the wife,' Crane muttered.

She was stuffing her clothes into the rucksack. 'I'll change back when I reach shore.'

Brian, staring at her long white legs, seemed to be picturing this. Truth be told, Crane was picturing it too. She might not be beautiful, but she had a body. Christ, she had a body.

'Thanks for the thought,' she said finally, with a slight twist of her lips. It was as if she'd been reading their minds.

'It's been a pleasure,' said Crane. 'A pleasure.'

They dropped her off and watched for a few moments as she struck for shore. She swam strongly, dragging the rucksack after her. They were no more than a hundred yards from land. It looked like she'd make it with ease. Then Crane remembered his orders.

'Back out to sea with her, Brian. We'll come around to Sandgate. Home before dawn with a bit of luck.'

'She was something, wasn't she, Skip?' Brian was still gazing towards shore.

'Yes, son,' admitted Crane. 'She was something.'

She changed quickly. The rucksack contained quite a lot, including several changes of clothes and shoes. It also contained air pockets to help keep it afloat. She deflated these. The rucksack had been heavier early on in the evening. She smiled at the memory. Wrapped in polythene in an already waterproofed pocket was a diary, and beside it some odds and ends of make-up. The make-up was like a talisman to her. Make-up was the beginning of disguise. What else was in the rucksack? You could tell a lot about a woman from the contents of her bag. If you tried hard, this rucksack would tell you a lot too. Passport, driving licence, money. A few small tools. Some packages of what looked like plasticine. A tarot pack. A handgun. That was about it.

She didn't look out to sea, but she listened to it. The steady clash of waves, the whistling wind. Exhilarating. Her hair, pinned back, was still drying quickly, her scalp chilled by the wind. A sharp salt smell clung to her. Her eyes were closed slightly as she listened. Then, in the distance, she heard a loudish pop, there and then not there. Like the meeting of balloon and pin at a children's party. She knew she had measured the amount of the charge well, and had placed it well too, down in the bowels of the boat. The hole blown in the hull would be a couple of metres in diameter. The vessel would sink in seconds, seconds of shock and horror for its crew. And if the explosion didn't kill the two men outright . . . well, what chance of their reaching land? No chance for the older man, minimal for the younger. Minimal was as much as she liked to leave to chance. But she hung around for a while anyway, just in case anyone did reach shore. There was a certain amount of shelter so she did not freeze. In fact, the breeze was growing almost warm. Or perhaps she was just getting used to being back.

No sign of the two men. She waited seventy-five minutes, then unpinned her long hair, letting it fall forwards over her face. A simple trick, but one which reduced her age by several years, especially when she was not wearing make-up. She thought of the boat a final time. It would be a mere oil slick now. Perhaps banknotes were floating on the tide. Useless things anyway.

She made her way to the main road and began to walk. Hitching along the south coast. Going to visit a friend in Margate. (Or Cliftonville: dare she say Cliftonville?) Didn't get a lift out of Folkestone, so spent the night there, sleeping rough by the roadside . . .

That was the story she would tell to whichever motorist picked her up. Someone *would* pick her up. Some man, most probably. She was a single woman, young. They might lecture her about the dangers of hitching alone. She would listen. She was a good listener. A lorry driver might even go out of his way and take her to Margate or Cliftonville in a single run. Of course, he would expect a favour in return, something more than her good ear. Her good mouth maybe. But that was all right. That wasn't a problem for her. She was someone else after all, wasn't she? And tomorrow she would be someone else again . . .

Cassandra

Tuesday 2 June

Everyone in the Collator's Office had what might be termed a 'clerical mind'. Which is to say that they were scrupulous in their filing. They were, in fact, a kind of pre-information technology production line, feeding data into the central computer. This was their purpose in the Collator's Office. It was up to the computer to decide whether some news item or other might be important. The computer was capable of taking a petrol station hold-up in Kelso, the abduction of a girl in Doncaster and the finding of a body in rural Wales, and making of them a pattern.

But most of the time it didn't. Most of the time it just sat wherever it sat, a glutton's bottomless stomach, ingesting story after story, item after item, without excreting anything in return. A lot of false roads were taken, a lot of palpable nonsense spewed up by the computer. And occasionally a nugget of truth, but not often. No, not very often.

There were times when Collator's Assistant Jack Constant thought that the only things keeping him sane were the editions of French newspapers which he brought into work with him. Constant thought he'd plumbed the depths of boredom and futility during his year-long stint as Clerical Assistant in the office of Her Majesty's Collector of Taxes. He'd spent the year sending out demands and reminders and final notices, noting payments and passing the non-payers on to his boss. A year of ledgers, producing in him a ledger mentality. But then computerisation had 'saved' him by taking over his most onerous tasks, and a series of shuffles between departments had seen him dropped finally into the Collator's Office. The pit.

'So how goes the Font of All Knowledge?' asked Cynthia Crockett, a fellow CA. Each day, sometimes in the morning, sometimes after the lunch break, she asked this question with the same quizzical smile. Maybe she thought it was funny.

'Foak knows,' replied Constant, FOAK being the Font of All Knowledge, the central computer. Another CA, Jim Wilson, had another name for it. He called it the Fat Controller, or, when in a bad temper, even the Fat Bastard. He'd once come into work wearing a T-shirt printed with the legend WHO'S THAT FAT BASTARD? Mr Grayson, the office head, had summoned him into the inner sanctum for a quiet, disciplined word about dress code.

Afterwards, Wilson had not been mollified. 'Wants us wearing suits and bloody ties. I mean, it's not like we're dealing with the public, is it? We never *see* anyone. Nobody except old Grayskull himself.'

But he hadn't worn the T-shirt again.

Constant suffered his colleagues, even 'old Grayskull' of the shiny head and tweed-knit ties, drifting towards his pension. Mr Grayson's wife packed him exactly two salmon paste sandwiches, one apple, and one small chocolate biscuit for his lunch every day. Yvette would never do that. It would be a fresh baguette and some Camembert, maybe with pickles or a small salad with vinaigrette. The French took their food seriously, and Yvette, Constant's girlfriend, was French. She lived in Le Mans, which meant that they met only for holidays and occasional frantic weekends (trips barely sustainable on a CA's salary, not when his phone bill was so big). Yvette was still studying, but would soon come to England for good. She'd get a job as French assistant in some school. They would be together.

Meantime, he had his newspapers. Usually *Le Monde* but occasionally one of the others. He read them to improve his French, and also because Yvette didn't seem so far away while he was reading. So whenever a break was due, Jack would reach into his desk drawer and bring out his French newspaper, something to digest with the unspeakable coffee.

He read the snippet of news again. It was squeezed on to the front page below a much longer story about forest fires in the Mediterranean. A boat had sunk in the Channel, barely twenty kilometres from its home port of Calais. There were no survivors. Four sailors dead. The story jogged Jack Constant's memory. He'd filed a story earlier in the day, something about a boat sinking off the south coast of England. Coincidence? He wondered if he should mention it to someone. He looked up from the paper and saw that Mr Grayson had appeared from his inner sanctum. He was looking around as though bewildered to find himself there. He saw Constant looking at him and decided to approach for a conversation. Another day, someone else would suffer. Past the computer screens and the brown file-cases and the newspaper cuttings and the print-outs and the fax sheets he came. Past the clack of keyboard and the sizzle of disk-memory. Towards Jack Constant.

'Jack.'

Constant confirmed this with a nod.

'Everything quiet?'

'Quiet as it gets, sir.'

Grayson nodded seriously. 'Good.' His breath smelt of salmon paste. With a sad half-smile, he began to turn away.

Why not? thought Constant. It might pep the old bugger up a bit. 'Oh, sir?' he said. 'I've got a story here might be of interest.'

Mr Grayson seemed to doubt this. To be honest, Constant was doubting it too.

Wednesday 3 June

In the service, there was always someone above you. But the information ladder could splinter – a missing rung. The information ladder depended on people like Jack Constant reporting something to someone like Mr Grayson. And it depended on Grayson's instinct or 'nose', his ability to weed out what was interesting from what really was mere coincidence. The information was then passed up the ladder to his superior, who might make further inquiries before either filing the piece or passing it on to someone more senior yet.

These were lofty heights now. Working from his own small office Grayson had never met his superior's superior. He'd once received an inquiry from that person. The inquiry had been dealt with as a priority. Mr Grayson's office had never had to deal with inquiries from yet higher officials.

The item, the bare comparison of two sinkings on a single night, was passed quickly from rung to rung until it reached an office somewhere in central London where a twenty-five-year-old man, only two years older than Jack Constant himself, read it. He was humming an aria and chewing a pencil and had his legs stretched out in front of him, one foot crossed over the other. He had pushed his seat out from his desk to facilitate this, his legs being too long to stretch beneath the desk itself. There was a wall immediately in front of the desk, with memos and postcards and fire instructions pinned to it.

He read the item through three times. Spotted in *Le Monde* of all places. Either somebody was on the ball or this man . . . what was the name, Grayson? Yes, this man Grayson ran a tight ship. Poor metaphor under the circumstances. The item had grown unwieldy by now, attached as it was to notes from the various offices through which it had passed. But though unwieldy it was also irritatingly flimsy, constructed from thin sheets of fax paper. It had been faxed (standard practice) by the last office to see it. The real thing would turn up here eventually, but the fax was supposed to save valuable time. Michael Barclay did not like faxes. For a start, no matter how often the Engineering Section explained it to him, he couldn't see how they were safe from a tap. Tap into a fax line with your own fax, and you'd get a copy of anything sent to the original machine. Codes could be decoded, scramblers unscrambled. As he'd told his colleague from Engineering, 'If you can make something, you can unmake it.' To prove his point, he'd rigged up his own interception device. It had worked, just, proving his point if nothing else. After all, GCHQ made a living from information intercepts, as did the listening posts dotted around the UK. If anything there was an intelligence overload these days. Too much information to assimilate.

Assimilate? There was too much to *sift*, never mind taking any of it in. Which was why this little story interested him. It was a fluke that it had come this far. The image that popped into his head was of a particular sperm breaching an egg. A fluke. This fluke called life: those very words were printed on a memo above his desk.

Well, this particular fluke did have its curiosity aspect. It would bear investigation. There was only one thing for it. Barclay would have to show it to his superior.

Michael Barclay did not think of himself as a spy. Nor would he even say he belonged to the secret service or the security service – though he'd agree security was at the root of much of his work. If pressed, he might nod towards the word Intelligence. He liked the word. It meant knowing a lot. And 'Intelligence' meant knowing at least as much as and preferably more than anyone else. This was the problem with the word 'spy'. It belonged to the old days, the Cold War days and before. Breaking and entering, sleeping with the enemy, microfilm and microphones in ties and tunnels under embassies.

These days there was no black and white: everyone spied on everyone else. This was no revelation, it had always been the case, but it was more open now. More open and more closed. Spy satellites were toys only the very rich and the very paranoid could play with. The spying community had grown larger, all-encompassing, but it had also grown smaller, forming itself into an elite. All change.

He'd actually used the word 'paranoid' in one of his selection board interviews. A calculated risk. If the service didn't want to think of itself as paranoid, it would have to recruit those who suspected it of paranoia. Well, he'd passed the exams and the tests and the interviews. He'd passed the initiation and the regular assessments. He'd begun his own slow crawl up the ladder. And he'd seen that the world was changing.

No spies any more. Now there were only the technicians. Take telemetry for example. Who the hell knew what all that garble of information meant? Who knew how to ungarble it? Only the technicians. Machines might talk to machines, but it took a wonderful human mind to listen in and comprehend. Barclay had done his bit. He'd studied electronic engineering. He'd been a dab hand with a few microchips and LEDs ever since his early teens, when he'd constructed his own digital clock. At sixteen he'd been building loudspeakers and amplifiers. And at seventeen he'd bugged the girls' showers at his school.

At university he'd been 'noticed': that was the way they'd phrased it. His work on long-range surveillance had been noticed. His grasp of geostationary satellite technology had been noticed. His special project on miniaturisation had been noticed. Fortunately, nobody *noticed* that he'd cribbed a lot of the project from early R&D done by Japanese hi-fi companies. A career path lay ahead of him, full of interest and variety and opportunities for further learning. A career in Intelligence.

Michael Barclay, Intelligence Technician. Except that he'd ended up here instead.

He didn't need to knock at Joyce Parry's door. It was kept wide open. There was some argument in the office as to why. Was it to keep an eye on them? Or to show solidarity with them? Or to show them how hard she worked? Most of the theories bubbled to the surface on Friday evenings in the Bull by the Horns, the frankly dreadful pub across the road from the office block. The Bull was a 1960s creation which looked no better for its 1980s refitting. In the 80s, refitting had meant a lot of fake wood, eccentric ornaments and books by the yard. The effect was kitsch Edwardian Steptoe and Son, with sad beer and sad graffiti in the gents'. But on the occasional Friday night, they managed somehow to turn the Bull into a cosy local, full of laughter and colour. It was amazing what a few drinks could do.

Joyce Parry's door was closed.

Unexpected refusal at first hurdle. Barclay, who had rolled the fax sheets into a scroll the better to brandish them, now tapped the scroll against his chin. Well, no matter. She was in conference perhaps. Or out of the office. (That was one thing: when Mrs Parry wasn't at home, her office door stayed firmly locked.) Barclay might do a little work meantime, so he could present her with not only the original item but with his notes and additions. Yes, why not show willing?

John Greenleaf had the feeling that somewhere in the world, every second of the day, someone was having a laugh at his expense. It stood to reason, didn't it? He'd seen it happen with jokes. You made up a joke, told it to someone in a pub, and three months later while on holiday in Ecuador some native told the joke back to you. Because all it took was one person to tell two or three people, and for them to tell their friends. Like chain letters, or was it chain mail? All it took was that first person, that someone who might say: 'I know a man called Greenleaf. Guess who he works for? Special Branch! Greenleaf of the Branch!' Three months later they were laughing about it in Ecuador.

Inspector John Greenleaf, ex-Met and now – but for how long? – working for Special Branch. So what? There were plenty of butchers called Lamb. It shouldn't bother him. He knows Greenleaf is a nice name, women keep telling him so. But he can't shift the memory of last weekend out of his mind. Doyle's party. If you could call twenty men, two hundred pints of beer and a stripper, a 'party'. Greenleaf had debated skipping it altogether, then had decided he'd only get a slagging from Doyle if he didn't go. So along he went, along to a gym and boxing school in the East End. That was typical of Hardman Doyle who fancied himself with the fists. Raw animal smell to the place, and the beer piled high on a trestle table. No food: a curry house was booked for afterwards. There had been five or six of them in front of the table, and others spread out across the gym. Some were puffing on the parallel bars or half-vaulting the horse. Two took wild swings at punch-bags. And the five or six of them in front of the table . . . They all muttered their greetings as he arrived, but he'd heard the words that preceded him:

'. . . eenleaf of the Branch, geddit?'

He got it. Nothing was said. Doyle, his smile that of a double glazing salesman, slapped him on the back and handed over a can of beer.

'Glad you could make it, John. Party's been a bit lacklustre without you.' Doyle took another can from the table, shook it mightily, veins bulging above both eyes, then tapped the shoulder of some unsuspecting guest.

'Here you go, Dave.'

'Cheers, Doyle.'

Doyle winked at Greenleaf and waited for Dave to unhook the ring-pull . . .

And Greenleaf, Greenleaf of the Branch, he laughed as hard as any of them, and drank as much, and whistled at the stripper, and ate lime chutney with his madras . . . And felt nothing. As he feels nothing now.

New Scotland Yard . . . Special Branch . . . this is supposed to be Big Time for a copper. But Greenleaf has noticed something curious. He has noticed the truth of the saying, 'It takes a thief to catch a thief.' Some of his present colleagues don't seem so different from the villains they pull in. As narrow-minded as terrorists, as devious as smugglers. Doyle was a good example, though effective at his job. He just didn't mind cutting corners. Doyle refused to see the world in black and white, as a sharply defined Us and Them, while Greenleaf did. For him there were the good guys and then there was the enemy. The enemy was out there and was not to be suffered. If it was useful as an informant, then fine, use it. But don't reward it afterwards. Don't let it slink away. Lock it up.

'John?'

'Sir?'

'My office.'

Oh hell, now what? His last big job had been putting together a report on aspects of security at the forthcoming London summit. It had taken him a fortnight, working weekends and nights. He'd been proud of the finished result, but no one had commented on it – yet. Now here was the Old Man himself, the Chief, the Boss, here was Commander Bill Trilling summoning him into the office which smelt perpetually of peppermint.

'Sit down, John. Mint?'

'No thanks, sir.'

Trilling took out a sweet and slipped it into his mouth. It was seven months since he'd given up smoking and he was up to four packs of mints a day. His teeth were in ruins and he'd gained half a stone – half a stone he could ill afford. Seated in his chair, with its high armrests, it looked as though it would take a crowbar to get him out again. There was a sheet of paper on the notoriously tidy desk in front of him but no sign of Greenleaf's report. He picked up the paper.

'Bit of a job for you, John. May be something or nothing. A sinking off Folkestone. We've been asked to look into it. Happened a couple of days ago. Can't say I saw anything about it.'

It was well known that Trilling only ever looked at two newspapers, the *Financial Times* and the *Sporting Life*. He was a betting man, sometimes putting his money on a sure-fire stock or share, sometimes a horse or dog. Nobody really knew how successful he was since he didn't share information, even when goaded by Doyle.

'I think I read about it in my paper, sir.'

'Did you? Good, well . . .' Trilling handed over the sheet. 'Report back when you've got anything.'

'How far do I take it, sir?'

'As far as a day-trip to Folkestone. Better liaise with Doyle.'

'Doyle, sir?'

'I've put him on to the French end.' Greenleaf looked puzzled. 'Didn't I say? Another boat sank the same night off Calais. We're to look for a connection. Doyle speaks passable French apparently.'

A day out in Calais for Doyle, an afternoon in Folkestone for Greenleaf. Typical.

'As I say, liaise with Doyle. You might even consider travelling down together. But see what you can do by telephone first. We don't want expensive outings on office time if we can avoid it, not with *them* counting how many paper clips we use. Like the man says, John, value for money. Maybe you should write a letter rather than use the phone.'

The Commander was smiling. This was how people knew he'd made a joke.

Thursday 4 June

His first 'liaison' with Doyle was at eleven the next morning.

'Bring your chair over,' Doyle said, thereby seizing the initiative: the meeting would take place at Doyle's desk, in Doyle's territory. Greenleaf lifted his heavy metal-framed chair with both hands, first resting his notes on the seat of the chair itself. But as he was placing it in front of Doyle's desk, the notes slewed floorwards. Doyle affected not to notice. His own notes, Greenleaf noticed, were neatly word-processed: not because he'd laboured hard, but because he had a 'close friend' in the typing pool. No doubt she'd ignored more important work this morning so she could prepare these sheets for Doyle. It all looked efficient, a single paperclip holding the whole lot together. Doyle now slid the paperclip from the corner of the sheets and let it fall to the floor. He spread the sheets in front of him.

'Right,' he said, 'what have you got?'

'A small touring boat,' Greenleaf said from memory. 'Must have sunk about two miles off the coast, just south of Folkestone. There was an automatic alarm system on board which alerted the coastguard. The system only operates in two situations: when set off by a crew member or when it's exposed to water. No sign of the boat itself, just some debris and oil and the two bodies.'

'Post mortems?'

'I'm waiting for the reports.'

'What time did all this happen?'

'The alarm went off at three twenty-seven.'

'The French boat sank around three,' Doyle added. 'So who was on board?'

'Two men, George Crane and Brian Perch.'

'Crane and Perch?' Greenleaf nodded, and Doyle produced a gust of laughter. 'Were they out fishing?'

'Not fishing. If anything, the boat was a pleasure cruiser. You know, a sort of motorised yacht. I don't know much about sailing but that's what they tell me.'

'So what were they doing out at that time of night?'

'Nobody knows.'

'Where had they been?'

Greenleaf shook his head. 'Crane's widow didn't even know he was taking the boat out. He told her he was going for a drive. He suffered from insomnia, she says. All Perch's family know is that he was doing a job for Crane. The boat's mooring is along the coast from Folkestone, a place called Sandgate.'

'But the boat itself was nearer Folkestone when it went down?'

'Other side of Folkestone from Sandgate.'

Doyle tapped his fingers against the edge of the desk. His suit looked crumpled but comfortable. Greenleaf, on the other hand, felt as if he was wearing a restraint of some kind. Time to buy a new jacket or start a diet. 'What did Crane do?' Doyle asked.

'Had his own building firm.'

Doyle stopped tapping and reached into his jacket, scratching slowly. 'Figures with a name like that. Do you know why the boat sank?'

'They're going to try to recover it this afternoon, for what it's worth.'

Doyle brought his hand out of his jacket. 'I can tell you what they'll find.'

'What?'

Doyle smiled and looked down at the sheets spread across the desk in front of him. Eventually he looked up. 'They're a bit quicker off the mark than us across the Channel. They haven't quite got the boat up yet, but the post mortem's been done. I spoke to the *pathologiste* this morning.' He smiled again. Greenleaf hated him for the way he'd dropped the French pronunciation into his speech. '*Docteur* Lagarde had some interesting things to say. Incidentally, they reckon there were four on board the vessel. It was a fishing boat, registered in Calais.'

'So what does the doctor say?'

Doyle smiled at Greenleaf's impatience. 'Well, for a start the bodies suffered some puncture wounds.'

'What sort?'

'Splinters of wood, metal, glass. Lagarde took a nine-incher out of some poor sod. Embedded itself in the stomach and punctured the heart.'

'Meaning there was force behind it?'

'Oh, yes, there was force all right. *Upward* force. And burn marks too. One of the bodies in particular was badly scorched.'

'An explosion,' Greenleaf commented.

'Absolutely.'

'Anything else?'

'Only what they found floating around in the surface oil. Hundred-dollar bills. Fifteen of them, not in very good nick. They got a couple of serial numbers. The Americans are checking.'

'Fifteen hundred dollars. What do you reckon, drugs?'

'Drugs or arms, but probably drugs.'

'You think the two boats met mid-Channel?'

'It's an idea. There's only one way to tell for sure. We need the PM results from Folkestone. Want me to give you a lift?'

'What?'

Doyle leaned down behind his desk and raised a bulging holdall high. 'I'm off to Calais on the evening ferry. Spending the night there, do a bit of sniffing tomorrow, then hit the *hypermarché* before heading back. I got the nod from Trilling an hour ago.'

'The luck of the Irish.'

Doyle's face darkened a little. What had he said? Ah, Doyle was touchy about his name's Irishness, was he? Got you, thought Greenleaf, got you!

When Doyle spoke, he was still subdued. 'I've got to alter my headlights, dip them the right way, but after that I'm ready to leave. So if you're heading for Folkestone . . .'

'I'll take my own car, thanks.'

'Suit yourself,' said Doyle. He seemed to be staring at Greenleaf's straining suit as he said it.

'I wish you'd come to me with this earlier, Michael.'

It wasn't quite the opening line Michael Barclay had expected from his boss. Joyce Parry sat there, invulnerable behind thick-rimmed spectacles, his report held up in front of her. Having glanced at it for effect, she laid it back down and slipped off her glasses. They hung around her neck by a string, and she let them dangle against her chest. From time to time, they grazed the triple-string of Ciro pearls resting just below her throat. Her throat, thought Barclay, was the oldest part of her, permanently lined and stretched. Her good legs, face and hair might say early-40s, but the neck gave the lie to this. Late-40s, the neck said to Barclay.

'Sit down,' Joyce Parry's mouth told him.

Barclay had always believed that he was attractive to women. To women *and* to men actually. He had used his good looks and steady unblinking gaze to good effect both socially and professionally. He felt that he'd always got on well with Joyce Parry, being at his charming best in her office and at meetings where she was present. So much so in fact that someone had sent him an anonymous Valentine addressed: 'To a creeping, slimy, boss-loving toad'. The card was pinned above his desk, its sender still a mystery.

Barclay didn't mind it. He didn't mind envy in the workplace. He didn't mind that others thought he was getting on well with the boss. He'd always imagined that there was something *special* between Mrs Parry and him. He might almost have called it a 'special relationship'.

And now this.

'I really wish you'd shown me this earlier, Michael.' She used his first name softly, the sentence fading away, to show that she was disappointed in him. As he sat in front of her, his legs felt overlong and clumsy. He rested his hands on his knees, hiding them.

'I did try, but you were—'

'You should have tried later. Any news from Commander Trilling?'

'Just that he has two men working on it. One of them's off to France, the other to Folkestone.'

'A bit too early for Special Branch,' she said. 'You should have done some digging of your own first. You should have spoken to *me* first.' Now the endings of her sentences were like stabs at him. 'You jumped the gun.' She nodded slowly towards him, letting this sink in, then wheeled her chair to the corner of her desk where it met with another in an L-shape. Her main desk was all paperwork, but on the side desk stood a computer, the screen angled just enough so that no one sitting where Barclay was could see it. This large desk also hosted printer and modem, while in a far corner of the room sat a fax machine and document shredder. There were three telephones on the main desk. One of them rang just as she was accessing the computer. She pushed her chair back into place and, instead of lifting the receiver, hit one of the buttons.

'Mrs Parry here,' she said, swivelling back to her computer screen.

A small female voice came from the telephone's loudspeaker. 'I checked the computer files—'

'I *told* you not to bother, didn't I?'

'Yes, but I—'

'Mr Elder belongs to the pre-microchip days. He believed in *paper* files.'

Sensible man, thought Barclay. Elder . . . the name was familiar. The voice was speaking again.

'Yes, well, I've got those files too.'

'Good,' said Joyce Parry. 'All I need to know is . . . no, on second thoughts, bring them in here.'

Once more she wheeled back, this time to cut the connection. Then forwards again, her fingers fast on the keyboard. Barclay knew that his superior had computer clearance far above his own. He knew too that he could beat the computer system, given time and the will. If he wanted to, he could access anything. If he wanted to.

'Ah, here we are,' said Joyce Parry. He studied her profile. Classically English, whatever that meant. The way she raised her chin as she read from the screen. A long straightish nose, thin lips, short well-kept hair, showing just a little grey. Grey eyes too. She was one of those women who grow better looking as they get older. She pressed a few more keys, checked that the printer was on, then pressed two more keys. The laser printer began its quick quiet work. She swivelled back to the main desk and handed the first sheet to him. He had to rise from his chair to take it. The paper was still warm from the machine.

There was a sudden tapping on the wide-open door. Parry signalled for the secretary to come in. She was carrying two bulging folders, tied securely with what looked like shoelaces.

'Thanks, Angela, leave them on the desk.' Joyce Parry extracted two more sheets from the printer. Barclay tried to concentrate on the piece of paper he was holding but it was difficult not to stare at those two files, the files of someone called Elder. The name definitely stirred a memory, but this wasn't the time for reflection. Joyce Parry began untying the shoelaces while Barclay read from the laser-printed page.

The report was dated six years before, and had been filed originally by the CIA before being passed along 'for information' to the British authorities. What Barclay now held was formed as a precis, as abridged by D. Elder.

'On 16 May,' he read, 'a small fishing boat left the South Korean port of Pusan. Crew of six. Known and well liked in the port. No hint that the crew were involved in any illegal activities prior to this time, though most boatmen in the area regard smuggling as above the law anyway.

'On 17 May, debris and bodies (six) washed up on the island of Mishima, off the Japanese mainland. Earlier reported sighting of the boat near the Japanese coastal town of Susa. No reason why boat should have been in this area. Skipper/owner an experienced sailor. Scale of damage to vessel suggested an explosion rather than collision, grounding, etc. However, no report of anyone seeing or hearing a blast. (Southern-Asian ears and eyes not always fully functional. Remember, to them pirates are still an occupational hazard rather than a 1930s Errol Flynn film.)'

Barclay smiled and started on the second sheet.

'Investigation undertaken by Japanese and South Korean authorities. No further evidence uncovered up to date of this report. However, there was talk in Pusan of a young woman who had been seen talking with the boat's owner in a bar a few days prior to the final voyage. She is described as being tall with short dark hair, probably speaking English.

'From 18–20 May, International Conference for World Peace (ICWP) based at various locations in Hiroshima, Japan. Conference attended by 240 delegates from forty-six countries, supplemented by invited guests (e.g.: from Japanese universities, media) and, to some events, general public. World media invited to attend. Four intelligence agents among those accepting. (See file no. CI/46377/J/DE.) Six keynote speeches given prominence during conference. Other activities included film shows, art exhibition, theatre events, and concert by Music for Peace (the latter with its HQ in London, investigated 1984: see file no. UK/0/223660/L/JP).'

JP: Joyce Parry's initials. Barclay was beginning to sense what this was all about. His hands grew clammy, sticking to the sheet as he read on.

'On closing day, 20 May, final keynote address was to be given by international peace activist Jerome Hassan (CI/38225/USP/DG). However, Mr Hassan was taken ill with suspected food poisoning and his speech (much abbreviated – Hassan was known to work by improvisation) was delivered by a colleague, Dr Danielle Brecht.

'Mr Hassan died in hospital on evening of 20 May, just as live telecast at closing concert was beaming messages by pop and film luminaries into Japan.

'Post mortem was carried out on morning of 21 May, with Mr Hassan's hotel (and over 100 diners from the previous day) keenly awaiting findings. Laboratory analysis showed atropine poisoning. (Atropine is an alkaline found in Deadly Nightshade. From the Greek *atropos*, "the Fate that cuts the thread of life".)

'While still conscious, but thought to be delirious, Hassan spoke of a girl, a student probably. He spoke of her "beauty and generosity". Hotel staff when interviewed acknowledged that on the night of 19 May, a young woman had accompanied Mr Hassan to his room. No one saw her leave, despite a twenty-four-hour reception area. Descriptions given varied. One assessed her height at nearly six foot, another at only five foot six. One said black hair, another brown. Hair was probably cropped short, and woman was fair-skinned though tanned. European perhaps, or Asian. No one heard her speak. She had crossed the lobby with Mr Hassan and entered the lift with him. She was dressed in black denims, light T-shirt, light-coloured jacket. Mr Hassan was carrying a plastic carrier bag, weighted down with books. Reception staff got the impression the bag belonged to the woman.

'Woman has never been traced. Hassan's previous sexual history questioned. (Widow not forthcoming.) As a footnote, woman's entry to the country was clumsy, creating immediate suspicion. And her use of atropine, or at least the dosage used, was also clumsy, since it allowed the victim time to talk before dying. Pity is, he did not say anything useful.

'See: WITCH file.

'Final footnote: Susa is c. fifty miles from Hiroshima.'

Barclay turned to the third and final sheet, expecting more. But all he read were edited newspaper reports of Jerome Hassan's murder, mentioning poison and the mysterious young woman. A jealous lover was hinted at. He looked up and saw that Joyce Parry was immersed in the contents of one of the Elder files. He glanced through his own sheets again, quite liking Elder's tone – the explanation of the word atropine; the mention of the final night's rock concert; that nice late mention that Hassan was a married man.

'You see the coincidence,' Parry said without warning. She was looking at him now. 'An assassin is dropped off on the Japanese mainland and then destroys the boat which landed her. Now, six years later, something similar occurs.'

Barclay considered this. 'Special Branch are thinking more along the lines of drugs or arms.'

'Exactly. And that's why I'd rather you hadn't alerted them this early on. They may be off on half a dozen wild goose chases. Then, if we approach them with new information, they'll wonder why we didn't come up with it sooner. Do you see what I mean?' Her glasses glinted. Barclay was nodding.

'It makes us look bad.'

'It makes *me* look bad.' She wet two fingers with the tip of her tongue and turned a page.

'What's the Witch file?' Barclay asked.

But she was busy reading, too busy to answer. She seemed to be suppressing an occasional smile, as though reminiscing. Eventually she glanced up at him again.

'The Witch file doesn't exist. It was an idea of Mr Elder's.'

'So what *is* Witch?'

She closed the file carefully, and thought for a moment before speaking. 'I think it would be best if you asked Dominic Elder that, don't you?'

Once a year, the fairground came to Cliftonville.

Cliftonville liked to think itself the genteel equivalent to next-door neighbour Margate. It attracted coach tours, retired people. The younger holidaymakers usually made for Margate. So did the weekenders, down from London for a spot of seaside mayhem. But Cliftonville was struggling with a different problem, a crisis of identity. Afternoon bingo and a deckchair in front of the promenade organist just weren't enough. Candy floss and an arcade of one-armed bandits weren't enough. Too much of the town lingered in the 1950s. Few wanted the squeal and glitter of the 90s, yet without them the town would surely die, just as its clientele was dying.

If the town council had wanted to ask about survival, they might have consulted someone at the travelling fairground. It had changed too. The rides had become a little more 'daring' and more expensive. Barnaby's Gun Stall was a good example. The original Barnaby (whose real name had been Eric) had used rifles which fired air-propelled corks at painted tins. But Barnaby had died in 1978. His brother Randolph had replaced the cork-guns with proper pellet-firing rifles, using circular targets attached to silhouette human figures. But then Randolph had succumbed to alcohol and the charms of a woman who hated the fair, so his son Keith – the present Barnaby – had taken over. Nowadays the Gun Stall boasted *serious* entertainment in the form of an automatic-firing airgun rigged up to a compression pump. This machine-gun could fire one hundred large-bore pellets every minute. You just had to keep your finger on the trigger. The young men paid their money gladly, just to feel the sheer exhilaration of that minute's lethal action. Afterwards, the target would be brought forward. Keith still used cardboard circles marked off from the outer to the small black bullseye, and attached to the heart of a human silhouette. The thing about the automatic was, it couldn't be said to be accurate. If enough pellets hit the target, the cardboard was reduced to tatters. But more often than not the kids missed, dazed by the recoil and the noise and the speed.

The more dazed they were, the more likely they were to come back for more. It was a living. And yet in other ways the fair was very much an old-fashioned place. It had its ghost train and its waltzers, though this evening the ghost train was closed. There were smells of spun sugar and diesel, and the scratchy sounds of the next-to-latest pop records. Onions, the roar of machinery, and three-balls-for-fifty-pee at the kiddie stalls.

Gypsy Rose Pellengro's small caravan was still attached to its Volvo estate car, as though she was thinking of heading off. On a board outside the caravan door were letters of thanks from grateful clients. These letters were looking rather frail, and none of them seemed to include the date on which it had been written. Beside them was a scrawled note announcing 'Gypsy Rose back in an hour'.

The two windows of the caravan were tightly closed, and covered with thick net curtains. Inside, it was much like any holiday caravan. The small sink still held two unwashed plates, and on the table sat not a crystal ball but a portable black and white television, hooked up to the battery of the Volvo estate. The interior was lit by calor gas, the wall-mounted lamps roaring away. A woman was watching TV.

There was a knock at the door.

'Come in, sir, please,' she called, rising to switch off the set. The door was pulled open and a man climbed into the caravan. He was so tall that he had to stoop to avoid the ceiling. He was quite young, very thin, and dark-skinned.

'How did you know it was a man?' he asked, taking in the scene around him.

'I saw you peering in through the window.'

The man smiled at this, and Gypsy Rose Pellengro laughed, showing the four gold teeth in her mouth. 'What can I do for you, sir? Didn't you see the notice outside?'

'Yes. But I really would like my fortune told.' He paused, stroking a thick black moustache, before adding meaningfully: 'I think I have a lucky future ahead of me.'

Gypsy Rose nodded, not that she'd been in any doubt. 'Then you've come to the right place,' she said. 'I'm in the futures market myself. Would you like to sit down?'

'No, thank you. I'll just leave this . . .' He reached inside his jacket and brought out a large brown envelope. As he made to place it on the table in front of the woman, she snatched at his wrist and turned his hand palm upwards.

'Yes,' she said, releasing it after a moment. 'I can see you've been disappointed in love, but don't worry. The right woman isn't so very far away.'

He seemed scandalised that she had dared to touch him. He rubbed at his wrist, standing over her, his black pupils shadowed by his eyebrows. For a moment, violence was very close. But the woman just sat there with her old, stubborn look. Weary, too. There was nothing he could do to her that hadn't already been done. So instead he turned and, muttering foreign sounds, pushed open the caravan door, slamming it shut behind him so hard that it bounced back open again. Now Gypsy Rose could see out on to the slow procession of fairground visitors, some of whom stared back.

Slowly, she rose from the table, closed and locked the door, and returned to her seat, switching on the television. From time to time she fingered the large brown envelope. Eventually, when enough time had passed, she got up and pulled her shawl around her. She left the lamps burning in the caravan, but locked the door behind her when she left. The air was hot, the night sticky. She moved quickly, expertly, through the crowds, occasionally slipping between two stalls and behind the vans and the lorries, picking her way over cables, looking behind her to see if anyone was following. Then back between two more stalls and into the crowd again. Her path seemed to lack coordination, so that at one point she'd almost doubled back to her starting point before striking off in another direction. In all, she walked for nearly fifteen tiring minutes. Fifteen minutes for a journey of less than four hundred yards.

Darkness had fallen, and the atmosphere of the fair had grown darker and more restless, too. The children were home in bed, still excited and not asleep, but safe. Tough-speaking teenagers had taken over the fair now, swilling cheap beer from tins, stopping now and then for passionate kisses or to let off some shots at an unmoving target. Yells broke the night-time air. No longer the sounds of fun but feral sounds, the sounds of trouble. Gypsy Rose remembered one leather-jacketed boy, cradled in a friend's arms.

Jesus, missus, he's been stabbed. He didn't die, but it was touch and go.

Less than four hundred yards from her caravan was the ghost train. On the narrow set of tracks between the two double-doors sat the parked carriages. The sign on the kiosk said simply CLOSED. Well, there wouldn't have been many people using it at this time of night anyway. A chain prevented anyone gaining access to the wooden-slatted running boards in front of the ride. She lifted her skirt and stepped over the chain, winning a cheer and a wolf whistle from somewhere behind her. With a final glance over her shoulder, she pushed open one of the double-doors, on which was painted the grinning face of the devil himself, and stepped inside.

She stood for a moment, her eyes adjusting to the newer darkness. The doors muffled much of the sound from outside. Eventually, she felt confident enough to walk on, moving past the spindly mechanisms of ghost and goblin, the wires and pulleys which lowered shreds of raffia on to young heads, the skeleton, at rest now, which would spring to its feet at the approach of a carriage.

It was all so cheap, so obvious. She couldn't recall ever having been scared of the ghost train, even as a tot. Now she was moving further into the cramped construction, off the rails, away from the papier mâché Frankenstein and the strings that were supposed to be cobwebs, until she saw a glimmer of light behind a piece of black cloth. She made for the cloth and pulled it aside, stepping into the soft light of the tiny makeshift room.

The young woman who sat there, sucking her thumb and humming to herself, looked up. She sat crosslegged on the floor, rocking slightly, in her lap a small armless teddy bear, and spread out on the floor a tarot pack.

'He's been,' Gypsy Rose said. She fished the envelope out from under her skirt. It was slightly creased from where she had climbed over the chain. 'I didn't open it,' she said.

The thumb slipped wetly out of the mouth. The young woman nodded, then arched back her neck and twisted it to one side slowly, mouth open wide, until a loud sound like breaking twigs was heard. She ran her fingers through her long black hair. There were two streaks of dyed white above her temples. She wasn't sure about them. She thought they made her look mysterious but old. She didn't want to look old.

'Sit down,' she said. She nodded towards a low stool, the only seat in the room. Gypsy Rose sat down. The young woman gathered the tarot cards together carefully, edging them off the tarpaulin floor with long nails. She was wearing a long black skirt, tasselled at the hem, and a white open-necked blouse beneath a black waistcoat. She *knew* she looked mysterious. That was why she was playing with the tarot. She had rolled her sleeping bag into the shape of a log against the far wall. Having gathered up the cards and slipped them back into their box, she tossed the box over towards the sleeping bag and took the envelope from the older woman, slitting it open with one of her fingernails.

'Work,' she said, spilling the contents out on to the ground. There were sheets of typed paper, black and white five-by-eight photographs with notes written in pencil on their backs, and the money. The banknotes were held together with two paper rings. She slit them open and fanned the money in front of her. 'I've got to go away again,' she said.

Gypsy Rose Pellengro, who had seemed mesmerised by the money, now began to protest.

'But I won't be gone for long this time. A day or two. Will you still be here?'

'We pack up Sunday afternoon.'

'Headed where?'

'Brighton.' A pause. 'You'll take care, won't you?'

'Oh, yes,' said the young woman. 'I'll take care. I *always* take care.' She turned one of the photographs towards the woman. 'What do you think?'

'He's nice-looking,' said Gypsy Rose. 'An Asian gentleman.'

'Asian, yes.'

'The man who made the delivery was Asian, too.'

Witch nodded then read through the notes, taking her time. Gypsy Rose sat quite still, not wanting to disturb her, happy just to be here. She looked at the money again. Eventually, the young woman placed everything back in the envelope. She got up and lifted the tarot from where it lay, tossing it into Gypsy Rose Pellengro's lap.

'Here,' she said, 'take the cards.' There was a scream from outside. A girl's scream. Maybe a fight was starting. It might be the first tonight; it wouldn't be the last. 'Now, Rosa, tell me. Tell me what you see. Tell me about my mother.'

Gypsy Rose stared at the tarot pack, unwilling to lift it. The young woman slipped her thumb into her mouth again and began to hum, rocking backwards and forwards with the teddy bear on her lap. Outside, someone was still screaming. Gypsy Rose touched the box, pushed its flap open with her thumb. Slowly, she eased out the cards.

Friday 5 June

Greenleaf was in the office early. He'd spent the previous late-afternoon and evening in Folkestone, getting in the way, bothering people, not making any friends, but finally gathering all the information he needed, information he just couldn't get by telephone alone. He'd spoken to George Crane's widow, Brian Perch's parents, Crane's accountants, to people who knew the men, to other boatmen. He'd asked questions of the coastguard, the local police, forensics, and the pathologist. He'd been busy – so busy that he hadn't left Folkestone until ten o'clock, arriving home in Edmonton at close on midnight, thanks to a jam on the M20 and the Blackwall Tunnel being closed. Shirley was pretending to be asleep with the bedside lamp off but still hot to the touch, and her book pushed under her pillow.

'What time is it?' she'd muttered.

'Ten past ten.'

'Bloody liar.'

'Then stop trying to make me feel guilty.'

The hour was too late for an argument, really. The neighbours had complained in the past. So they kept it jokey and low-key. Just.

He'd taken her toast and tea in bed this morning as penance, despite feeling dead on his feet. And the drive into work hadn't helped. A car smash at Finsbury Park and a defunct bus holding everybody up between Oxford Street and Warren Street. There was nothing he could do about it except consult the *A–Z* for useless shortcuts and swear that he'd start travelling to work by tube. Good old public transport: a brisk morning walk to the bus stop, bus straight to Seven Sisters, and hop on to a Victoria Line tube which would rush him to Victoria and the short final walk to his office. Good old public transport.

Only he'd tried the trip a few times and it didn't work like that. From the half dozen crammed buses that glided past his stop without slowing, right to the crushed and sweaty tube compartment and the feeling that he would kill the next person who jammed their elbow into him . . . Good old public transport. London transportation. He'd stick to the car. At least in the car you had a *choice*. Stuck in a jam, you could park and wait it out in a cafe, or try another route. But stuck in a tunnel in a tube train . . . well, that was a tiny rehearsal for hell.

He thought of Doyle, dawdling over croissants and coffee at some French bar, making ready to stock up on cheap beer and duty free. Bastard. But Doyle was useful. Or rather, Greenleaf's dislike of Doyle was useful: it goaded him. It made him want his work to be efficient, and that included his reports. Which was why he was here so early. He wanted to get his notes typed up into presentable shape, so he could hand them to Trilling before lunchtime.

Basically Doyle had been right. The pathologist noted burns, scorch marks, on both men. A razor-sharp section of plastic had almost taken off Crane's head. And there were splinters and shards – of wood, glass, metal, perspex – embedded in both bodies. Definite signs of an explosion.

'Somewhere beneath them,' the pathologist added. 'Below decks. The two men were probably on deck at the time. The various angles of penetration are all consistent with a blast from below, sending the shrapnel upwards. For example, one splinter enters above the left knee and makes its way up the leg towards the groin, the exit wound appearing on the inside upper-thigh.'

There were photographs to go with the doctor's various graphic descriptions. What couldn't be shown, and might possibly never be shown, was what had caused the explosion in the first place. That was all down to deduction and supposition. Greenleaf guessed that a bomb wouldn't be too far out. One of those simple IRA jobs with timer attached. Messy though, blowing the whole caboodle up like that. Why not shoot the men and dump the bodies with weights attached? That way the bodies disappeared, and the boat remained: a mystery, but without the certainty that murder had been done. Yes, a loud and messy way to enter the country. In trying to cover their tracks they'd left a calling-card: no forwarding address, but a sure sign they'd been there.

And could now be anywhere, planning or doing anything, with a cache of drugs or of arms. It had to be a sizeable haul to merit killing two men. Six if you included the French . . .

Well, so much for the doctor. The local police were on the ball, too. Inside George Crane's jacket they'd discovered a wad of bank notes, £2,000 or thereabouts. The wad had been pierced by a chunk of metal, but the notes were still recognisable. More important, some of the serial numbers remained intact. Steeped in blood, but intact.

There were ways of checking these things, and Greenleaf knew all of them. He'd faxed details that evening to the Bank of England, and to the Counterfeit Currency Department inside New Scotland Yard, supplying photocopies of several of the cleaner notes. The photocopies weren't great, but the serial numbers were the crucial thing anyway. The notes themselves he was careful not to handle, except with the use of polythene gloves and tweezers. After all, it was unlikely that Crane carried so much money around with him on every boating trip (unless he was planning to bribe some customs officials). It was much more likely that the money had been a payment made to him by whomever he'd transported from mid-Channel to the English coast.

As such, the notes might well boast the odd fingerprint. The corpse of George Crane had already been fingerprinted – on Greenleaf's orders – so that the dead man's prints could be eliminated. Somehow, Greenleaf didn't think George Crane would have let Brian Perch near the money, but his body was being fingerprinted too. Best to be rigorous.

Perch was an employee, a no-questions-asked hired-hand who would, as a fellow worker had put it, 'go to the end of the earth' for Crane, so long as there was overtime in it. Why had Crane taken him along? For protection?

Because he didn't trust whomever he was carrying? Maybe just for company on the voyage out to mid-Channel? Whatever, Brian Perch didn't really interest Greenleaf, while George Crane did.

The accountant to the building business wasn't about to say that Crane's company was in terminal trouble, but he agreed that times were hard and that the company was 'overstretched financially'. Which meant there were bigger loan repayments than there were cheques from satisfied and solvent customers. For example, a larger than usual contract had gone unfinished and unpaid when the company employing Crane's firm had themselves gone broke. Crane just managed to hold his head above water. Well, in the financial sense anyway. He still had the big house outside Folkestone with the swimming pool and sauna. He still had a Porsche. He still had his boat. But Greenleaf knew that often the more prosperous a man tried to look, the deeper he was sinking.

He'd considered an insurance scam. Take the boat out at dead of night and blow it up, then claim the money. But it didn't add up. Why not just sell the boat? One reason might be that no one was buying. Okay, so why did *he* have to die too? A miscalculation with the timer or the amount of explosive used? Possible. But Greenleaf still didn't rate it. Why take someone else along? And besides, there was the French sinking to consider. It *had* to be tied in with the British sinking; too much of a coincidence otherwise.

Bringing him back to murder.

Crane's wife didn't know anything about anything. She knew nothing about her husband's movements that night, nothing about his business affairs, nothing about any of his meetings. All she knew was that she should wear black and deserve sympathy. She seemed to find his questions in particularly bad taste. Crane's secretary, when tracked down, had been no more forthcoming. No, no meetings with strangers. No sudden 'appointments' out of the office which couldn't be squared with his diary. No mysterious telephone calls.

So what was Greenleaf left with? A man in debt, needing a few thousand (well, fifteen or so actually) to see him back on dry land. Personal financial affairs which had yet to be disentangled (it seemed Crane had been a bit naughty, stashing his cash in several accounts kept hidden from the prying taxman). A midnight boat trip which ends with him two grand in pocket but not in any position to spend it. It all came back to smuggling, didn't it? Just as Doyle had said. Arms or dope or someone creeping back into the country unannounced. Well, hardly unannounced. Whatever it was, it had cost six lives so far, which was too high a price to pay, whatever the payoff.

Most of these thoughts Greenleaf kept to himself. On paper, he stuck to the facts and the procedures followed. It still looked like a tidy bit of work, scrupulous and unstinting. He began to feel quite pleased with himself. He'd get it to Trilling before lunchtime. Definite. When would Doyle file *his* findings? Not before tomorrow. He was due back tomorrow morning. Say tomorrow afternoon then. Giving Greenleaf over a day clear, a day during which he'd be ahead of his nemesis. He breathed deeply and decided to pause for another cup of coffee.

When he got back from the machine, his phone was ringing. He almost spilled hot coffee all down his shirt as he lunged for the receiver.

'Yes? Greenleaf here.'

'John? Terry Willard at CC.'

'Morning, Terry.' Good. Terry Willard was one of Counterfeit Currency's best workers. 'What can you do for me?'

'You sound chirpy for a man who must've been in – where was it? Folkestone? – till all hours last night. We're not used to getting faxes after six.'

Greenleaf laughed and relaxed into his chair. 'Just conscientious, Terry. So you've got some news, have you?'

'The notes aren't counterfeit. I'm pretty sure of that.'

'Oh.' Greenleaf tried not to sound disappointed.

'Better than that, really,' said Willard. 'I've already traced them.'

'What?' Greenleaf sat forward in his chair. 'Terry, you're a genius. Christ, it's not even ten o'clock yet.'

'To be honest, it wasn't the hardest work I've done. The computer picked the numbers out inside a couple of minutes. Those notes are ancient history. You probably wouldn't have noticed that last night, the state most of them must have been in, but take it from me they are *old* banknotes. And they've been out of circulation for some time. We were beginning to doubt we'd ever see them again.'

'What do you mean?'

'I mean they're marked. The serial numbers are on record. They're part of a kidnap pay-off.'

'A *kidnap*?'

'Best part of five years ago. In Italy. A British businessman's daughter was kidnapped by some gang . . . It's a bit of a long story. Want me to send you over what I've got?'

'Christ, yes. A *kidnap*?' Greenleaf's head was reeling. 'Yes, send me what you've got. And Terry . . . ?'

'Yes?'

'I owe you a beer.'

'No sweat.'

Commander Trilling showed no emotion as Greenleaf told his, or rather Willard's, story. Greenleaf's report was in front of Trilling, as was the file sent over from Willard, and he glanced at them from time to time as the Special Branch officer recapped.

'The father's name is Gibson, sir. At the time he was an executive with the Gironi chemicals company in Turin. The daughter, Christina, was in a private school near Genoa. She disappeared during a visit to an art gallery. She was missing two days before Mr Gibson received a telephone call from the kidnappers.

'By that time the Italian police were already involved. They know that when a rich businessman's daughter goes missing, there's usually a ransom demand somewhere at the back of it. They'd set up telephone taps at the Gibson home and the Gironi headquarters before the first call came.'

Trilling crunched down hard on a mint and nodded.

'The problem was timing,' Greenleaf went on. 'The gang telephoned on four occasions that first day, but never for more than eight seconds, not long enough for any tracing system to work. The first call merely stated that

Christina had been kidnapped, the second identified the terrorist gang responsible, the third stated how much of a ransom was required, and the fourth was a plea from Christina herself.

'Another two days passed before the gang got in touch again.'

Trilling interrupted. 'Was the caller male or female?'

'Male, sir.' Greenleaf had studied the case file well over the previous hour. He knew that he was leaving just enough out so that the Commander would ask him questions. He already knew the answers to those questions. It was an old trick which made you look not-quite-perfect but not too far off it either.

'And the gang?'

'La Croix Jaune: Yellow Cross. Nothing much about them on the files. Probably a splinter group from one of the other terrorist organisations. The name may be some obscure joke to do with the Red Brigade. They came on the scene in '85 and seemed to disappear again in '88. In fact, there are doubts they ever existed at all as a group. The name may just be a cover for two or three criminals working together. Two kidnaps and two armed bank robberies. They were never identified, let alone captured. The only time a bank camera caught them they were masked.'

'You say two or three members?'

'That's all Christina Gibson saw. They kept her blindfolded most of the time, and at others they were dressed in balaclavas and sunglasses. But she was fairly sure there were two men, one taller than the other, and one woman, as tall as the men but slimmer.'

Trilling nodded thoughtfully. 'So what happened?'

'Mr Gibson cooperated throughout with the police. It was an international effort by then, as far as these things go. Two Special Branch men were flown out to assist. Matt Duncan and Iain Campbell. The kidnappers—'

'Anyone else?'

'Sorry, sir?'

'The British contingent: did it include anyone else?'

'Not on record, sir.' Greenleaf frowned. This was the first question to have stumped him. But Trilling was smiling, nodding to himself.

'That means nothing,' he said quietly. 'Go on.'

'Well, sir, the kidnappers wanted dollars, but we asked Mr Gibson to persuade them to take sterling. He told them dollars would take some time, while he had the sterling to hand. They agreed. So we put together thirty grand's worth of notes. The intention was to catch them cold, but there was a shoot-out and they got away. The girl was released, but the money had flown with the gang.'

'Clumsy.'

'Agreed. The Italians reckoned they wounded one of the gang, but nothing came of it. And the money disappeared, despite a check by all clearing banks. The notes on Crane's body are the first to have surfaced.'

'Poor choice of word,' commented Trilling. 'Still, good work, John.'

'Thank you, sir.'

'Yes, very good work. So, what do we make of it?'

'Well, it links Crane to a terrorist group, which indicates arms smuggling rather than drugs.'

'All it links him to, John, is dirty money. You can buy dirty money for fivepence in the pound. It's a cheap way of paying someone a large sum when you're not bothered what happens to the person afterwards.' Trilling thought for a moment. 'You know, I'm not at all sure that we've been given a level playing field here.'

'Sir?'

'It all smacks of the cloak-and-dagger brigade. Who did you say contacted us in the first place?'

Christ, what was his name? Barrow . . . Beardsley . . . Barkworth . . . 'Barclay, sir.'

'Barclay. Never heard of him. But he's one of Joyce Parry's. I wonder what Joyce is playing at? I think I'd better have a word with her.'

He was about to pick up his receiver when there was a knock at the door. Greenleaf rubbed his stomach to stop it from rumbling. It was quarter to one, and so far today all he'd had was five cups of coffee.

'Come in.'

It was Trilling's secretary. She was holding two sheets of paper, stapled together. 'Mr Doyle's report, sir.'

'Thank you, Celia.' Trilling held out his hand, took the report and laid it on his desk, on top of Greenleaf's own report. Greenleaf stared at the closely typed top sheet. He was oblivious to Celia's smile, or the closing of the door after she left. He kept hearing her words: Mr Doyle's report . . . Mr Doyle's report. When Greenleaf looked up from the desk, he saw Commander Trilling studying him.

'Efficient, isn't he?' Trilling mused.

'Very, sir. But how . . . ?'

'Oh, quite simple really. Doyle requested a laptop computer. He's taken it with him. Clever devices, they work on rechargeable batteries you know. Sizeable memory, too. I can never get on with the screens on them, but some people can.'

'So Doyle's writing his report as he goes?'

'That's it. Then he plugs the laptop into a modem, presses a few buttons, and his copy arrives at a computer here. All we have to do is run off a hard copy.' He patted Doyle's report, then lifted it up. 'Now, let's see what he's got to say for himself.' But instead of reading, he looked at Greenleaf over the paper. '*If* there's a case to investigate, John, I want you and Doyle to work on it together. Understand? *Together*. Do you think you can manage that?'

'Of course, sir.'

Trilling continued to look at him. 'Good,' he said, before turning his attention to the report.

Dominic Elder was a large man, larger than Barclay had expected. That surname, Elder, had put him on the wrong track. He'd expected a hunched, defeated figure, the sort who had been elders at his mother's Presbyterian church. But Dominic Elder was large and fit and strong. He'd be about fifty, a year or two older than Joyce Parry. His face had been handsome once, but time had done things to it. He looked out of place in the garden of the pretty cottage, on his knees and planting out seedlings in a well-kept vegetable-bed.

'Mr Elder?' Barclay had driven slowly down the lane, and had parked right outside the gate before ejecting *Il Trovatore* from the cassette player. But, even as he pushed open the gate, the man in the garden seemed not to acknowledge his presence.

'Mr Elder?' Barclay repeated. 'Dominic Elder?'

'That's me, Mr Barclay,' the figure said, rising stiffly to its feet and brushing soil from its hands. 'Who did you expect to find?'

'There's no number or name on the gate,' Barclay explained. 'I wasn't sure I had the right house.'

Elder looked around him slowly. 'You may not have noticed,' he said in his quiet, deep voice, 'but this is the only house there is.' He said it slowly, as if he were explaining something to a child. His eyes fixed on Barclay's as he spoke. He was massaging his back with the knuckles of one hand. 'I suppose you were recruited straight from university, yes?'

Barclay made a non-committal gesture. He wasn't sure where this was leading. He'd had a long drive, and an exasperating one. Roadworks, wrong turnings, and trouble with the car's third gear. It kept slipping back into neutral. On top of which it was twenty-eight degrees, and he needed a drink.

'Yes,' Elder was saying, 'straight from university. What did you study?'

'Electronics.'

'"Oh, brave new world."' Elder chuckled. 'So they put you into surveillance first, did they?'

'Yes, but—'

'But it was routine and boring. You wanted out.'

Barclay shuffled his feet. Maybe Elder was astute, but then again maybe he'd learned all this from Joyce Parry. Barclay wasn't impressed by tricks.

'And eventually you got your transfer.' Elder checked the dirt beneath his gardener's fingernails. 'What school did you go to?'

'I really don't see what . . .' Barclay sighed. Losing his patience wouldn't do any good. Besides, this man was an old friend of Mrs Parry's. It might pay to humour him. 'It was a comprehensive,' he conceded. 'I *suppose* that's what you want to know.'

'Scottish?'

'I was born there.'

'But you moved away when you were young. The name's right, but there's not much of an accent left. Father in the armed forces?'

'RAF.'

Elder nodded. He checked his fingernails again, then stretched a hand out towards Barclay. 'Pleased to meet you, Mr Barclay.'

Barclay thought about refusing the handshake, but eventually gave in. Elder's grip was a lot firmer than he'd expected. He did his best to squeeze back.

'A rough journey, eh?' Elder commented. 'I was expecting you three-quarters of an hour ago, allowing for one stop at motorway services.'

'Roadworks,' Barclay explained. 'And my gearbox is playing up.'

'Been to Wales before?' Elder was walking back towards the cottage. Barclay followed him.

'Only to Llandudno.'

'Strange choice.'

'It was a day trip. We were on holiday in Southport.'

'Strange choice. This was when you were younger?'

'Eleven or twelve, yes. Why do you say "strange"?'

'Most families with children would choose Blackpool or Morecambe. I've always thought Southport very . . . reserved. Was there much to do there?'

They were at the front door now. It was already open, and Elder wandered inside and along the narrow hall. 'I don't remember,' Barclay said. 'Some would say there's not a lot to do in rural Wales either.'

'They'd be right.' At the end of the hall, Elder entered the kitchen and stood in front of the sink, rinsing his hands. Barclay, who had followed, felt awkward standing in the doorway. 'That's why I'm here,' said Elder. 'To enjoy my twilight years.'

'Twilight? But you're only—'

'Fifty. Like I say, twilight. In our profession.'

Our. For the first time, Barclay felt a little of his hostility fall away.

'Take my advice, Mr Barclay, set your sights on retirement at fifty. Maybe even at forty-five. I know, it all seems a long way off. What are you . . . late-twenties?'

'Twenty-five.'

'Twenty-five then. In a few more years, you'll begin to notice things. You'll notice your reactions slowing – almost imperceptibly, but with the proper equipment you can measure the decline. You'll start to feel aches and pains, twinges. Try testing your memory, speed and accuracy of recall. Do it every six months or so and chart your decline.'

'Very comforting.'

Elder, drying his hands on a teatowel, shook his head. 'Not comforting, no. But by being aware of your limitations, you may save your own life. More important still, you might just save other people's. Think about it. Think about our profession. That's all I'm saying.' He reached a hand behind his back and rubbed at it slowly, thoughtfully. 'Tea? Or would you prefer a beer?'

'Something cold would be gratefully received.'

'I think I've some bottles in the fridge. We can take a couple into the living room. It's cooler in there.'

Cooler and darker. There were windows only to the back and side of the cottage, and these were part-overgrown with ivy. The room was small and comfortable. It had a messy, lived-in look, like a favourite pullover. The walls were whitewashed stone, and against one stretched a series of chipboard and melamine bookcases, standing at crazy angles due to the weight of books pressing down on them over the years. On a low tile-topped table sat a range of bottles – gin, Pimm's, whisky, vodka – full or nearly full. Various knick-knacks filled the window ledges and a few of the spare shelves. The room also contained TV, video, a hi-fi, half a wall of classical LPs, a sofa, and two armchairs. Elder made for one of these. Again, he made no motion, no gesture to help Barclay decide what to do. Should he opt for the other chair or the sofa? He decided on the chair, and sank slowly into it, looking round appreciatively at the room. Yes, comfortable. But dusty, too. There were edges of fluff where the carpet met a chair or a bookcase. There was a layer of dust on the video recorder, and another covering the front of the hi-fi.

Well, thought Barclay, let's try playing him at his own game. He swallowed a mouthful of cold beer and said: 'You're not married, Mr Elder?'

But Elder was nodding. He waved his left hand towards Barclay. There was a ring on the wedding finger. 'Didn't you notice? I suppose you've got computers to do that sort of thing for you.'

Barclay knew now what Joyce Parry had been getting at when she'd talked of Elder as though he were some dinosaur from the ancient past. He'd retired only two years ago, yet his ideas were Stone Age. Barclay had come across them before, these troglodytes who thought the Enigma code-breaker was a bit too high-tech to deal with. They belonged to old spy novels, left unread in second-hand bookshops.

'A penny for them,' Elder said, startling Barclay.

'Oh, I was just wondering about your wife.'

'Why?'

'Curious, I suppose.'

'We're separated. Have been for years. No plans for divorce. Funny, we get on fine when we're not living together. We can meet for dinner or the theatre.'

'And you still wear your ring.'

'No reason not to.'

Barclay noticed a small framed photograph on one of the shelves. He got up the better to study it. A young girl dressed in pale colours. A big gap-toothed grin and short black hair. It looked like an old photo. He waited for Elder to say something, but Elder was ignoring him.

'Your daughter?' Barclay offered.

Elder nodded. 'Deceased.'

Barclay put the photograph back carefully. 'I'm sorry,' he said. 'How did she—'

'So,' Elder interrupted, 'how's Joyce Parry?'

'Fine.' Barclay sat down again.

'It was nice to hear from her. We haven't really kept in touch.' A pause. 'We should have. Have you worked out yet?'

'Worked out what?'

Elder smiled. 'Something we all used to wonder: whether she's an iron fist in a velvet glove, or a velvet fist in an iron one.'

Barclay smiled back. 'Both have the same effect, surely?'

'Not when the gloves are off.' Elder took another mouthful of beer. 'So,' he said, sounding suddenly businesslike, 'you're here to tell me something.'

'Well, yes.'

'Something about Witch.'

'We don't know that yet, even supposing Witch exists . . .'

'She exists.'

'She?'

'She, Mr Barclay. One woman.'

'I thought it was a group.'

Elder shook his head. 'That's what the department thought at the time. It's what Joyce believes to this day. It's not a gang, Mr Barclay, it's an individual, an assassin.'

'And female?'

'Female.'

'Because of the Hiroshima murder?'

'No, not just that. Hiroshima was merely her entrance. And now something similar has happened?'

'Two boats, one either side of the Channel—'

'Yes, so Joyce said. One off Calais, the other near Folkestone . . .'

'The *Cassandra Christa*.'

'What?'

'The English boat, it was called the *Cassandra Christa*.'

'Cassandra . . . extraordinary.'

Barclay didn't follow. 'You know it?'

But Elder shook his head. 'I meant the parallel. You didn't have a classical education, Mr Barclay?'

Barclay's voice was as cold as his drink. 'Apparently not.'

'Cassandra,' Elder was saying, 'was the daughter of Priam, King of Troy. The god Apollo endowed her with the gift of prophecy . . . but not of being believed.'

Barclay nodded slowly, smiling. 'And you're Cassandra, Mr Elder?'

His eyes twinkled. 'In the present case, yes, perhaps I am.' He paused. 'Mr Barclay, do you know *why* Joyce has sent you here?'

Barclay took a deep breath. 'To be honest, off the record, no.'

'Me neither. I admit I'm intrigued. Are Special Branch investigating the sinkings?'

'Yes.'

'They'll probably plump for an arms shipment. Believable scenario. Strange, if it *is* Witch . . .'

'Yes?'

'She's a quick learner, Mr Barclay. That's why she's survived so long. We haven't seen hide or hair of her for a couple of years. I thought maybe she'd retired. Yet here she is, announcing herself loud and clear. You see, she didn't use that particular trick again. She tends not to use the same trick twice, ever. She enters and leaves countries in different ways, using different disguises, different means of killing her victims. Now she seems to have returned to her original calling-card. Why?'

'Maybe she's run out of ideas, gone back to square one.'

'Maybe.'

'Mr Elder, you say this group . . . you say *she's* an assassin.'

'Yes.'

'For money, or for an ideal?'

'Both. Having an ideal costs money.'

'And what is her ideal?'

Elder shook his head. 'If I knew that, I might have caught her by now.' He sat up suddenly. 'There are two ways of doing this, the fast and the slow. I'd prefer the slow. Do you have any plans for this evening?'

'No.' This was a lie, but Barclay was intrigued.

'Then I'll cook some supper. Come on.' He rose to his feet. 'Let's see what needs picking in the garden.'

The evening stayed balmy, and they were able to eat at a picnic table in the back garden. Apart from the immaculate vegetable plot, the garden itself had been left wild. But there was order in the wilderness. The phrase that sprang to Barclay's mind was: the organisation of chaos.

He didn't know what to make of Elder. Partly, he thought the man intelligent, cautious, impressive; partly, he thought him just another old service crank. The story he told seemed harshly at odds with the scenery surrounding them as they sat into the twilight and beyond.

'Hiroshima was the first,' Elder said, almost drowsily. 'Except that it wasn't. That sounds like a riddle, but I'll explain it as I go along. I filed the report on the Hassan killing.'

'Yes, I read it.'

'But of course, I couldn't know then . . . well, nobody could know about Witch. Then there were other incidents, other operations. Most of them terrorist-related. I like to imagine Witch as a *pure* terrorist.' He smiled. 'I'm sure she isn't though.' He seemed to be drifting away. Barclay feared the man was about to fall asleep.

'And after Hassan?' he asked.

Elder stirred himself. 'After Hassan . . . well, there was an Italian kidnapping. A British businessman, working for some chemical conglomerate. They took his daughter. I was sent over there to liaise with police. It was an utter farce. The gang got away, *and* with the ransom.'

'The daughter?'

'Oh, freed. But she's been a nervous wreck ever since, poor child.'

'You said a gang: not Witch then?'

'Not just Witch, no. Two men and a woman. You see, this was her training period, a term of probation on the one hand and learning on the other. She didn't work alone in the early days.'

'And since?'

'Since?' Elder shrugged. 'The problem is that there's so little evidence. Seven armed robberies on the Continent . . . three assassinations. Many more assassination attempts, either foiled or botched. And always a woman mentioned afterwards, maybe just a passing note in somebody's report, but always a woman, a tall young woman. The most extraordinary story concerns a NATO General.' Elder toyed with his fork. 'It was hushed-up at the time, for reasons you will appreciate. He was an American based in Europe, but had to fly out to . . . let's just say Asia . . . as part of a very sensitive delegation. This General, however, had a taste for violent, forced sex. Oh, he was willing to pay. He'd made several pimps and madams very wealthy in his time. He was intrigued by stories of a very special prostitute. The rougher things got, the better she liked it. That was the story.' Elder paused and glanced around his garden, either appraising it or else playing for time, wondering how to phrase what came next. 'He was discovered lying naked on a bed with his head severed from its body at the neck. The head had been placed between his legs. In effect, the corpse was giving itself a blow-job.'

Now Elder looked towards Barclay. He was smiling.

'I never said Witch didn't have a sense of humour,' he said. Then he rose from his chair and walked into the house.

Barclay found that his hand was shaking just a little as he picked up his glass. This was his third glass of wine, on top of two beers. His third and last glass, otherwise the trip back would be fraught. He looked at his watch. It was getting late. He'd have to start off in the next hour or so anyway. He still didn't know what he was doing here. He was still intrigued.

Something exploded on the table. Looking round, he saw Elder standing just behind him. The man had approached in absolute silence. And on the table sat a fat document wallet, its flap open, spewing paper and glossy photographs across the table-top.

'The Witch Report,' Elder said, sitting down again.

'I was told there wasn't a file on Witch.'

'Joyce told you that? Well, here's one I made earlier.' Elder slapped the file. 'What I've been telling you so far are the facts, such as they are. *This* is the supposition. And it begins several years before the Hassan killing. It begins in 1982, when the Pope visited Scotland.' Elder was reaching into the file. He drew out three large black and white photographs. 'There was another tourist in Edinburgh that summer. Wolf Bandorff.' Elder handed the photo over. It was a close-up of a crowd scene, picking out three or four people, focusing on two of them. A young couple. The man had a long thick mane of hair and wore circular spectacles. He was looking over the person in front of his shoulder. He looked to Barclay like a postgraduate student. Beside him was a girl with long straight black hair and dark eye make-up. In the 60s, she might have passed for a model.

'You won't have heard of Wolf,' Elder was saying. But he waited until Barclay had shaken his head. 'No, thought not. He'll be in some computer, and that excuses us our bad memories and failure to learn. He was a West German terrorist. I say "West" because this was in the days before glorious unification, and I say "was" because he's currently serving a sentence in a maximum security prison outside Hanover. German intelligence tipped us off that he was in the UK. There were a few false starts before we found him in Edinburgh. As soon as he knew we were on to him, he disappeared, along with his girlfriend there. These photos are the slim prize for our time and effort.'

Barclay put the photographs down and waited for more. Elder dug into the file again and produced a single photograph of similar size. 'The girlfriend was Wolf's acolyte. You know what acolyte means?'

'Someone who's learning, isn't it?'

Elder's eyes seemed to sparkle in the disappearing light. The garden was illuminated now chiefly by lights from inside the cottage. 'That's right,' he said softly. 'Someone who's learning. In the early days, she attached herself to men, to the leaders of the various groups. That way she learned all the quicker, and gained power and influence too. That way, she gained *contacts*.' Now he handed over the photograph. 'This was taken just under four years ago, after the Hassan killing and the Italian kidnap. It was taken during Operation Warlock.'

Barclay looked up. 'Warlock?'

'Named by someone with an interest in role-playing games. And not very apt, since we soon found we were dealing not with a man but with a woman, apparently working alone. If there's any pattern to the way she works, I'd say she joins or puts together a group, then plans something with some financial reward – a bank robbery or kidnap or paid assassination. Then she uses her share to finance her . . . other activities. For example, the NATO General. No group ever claimed responsibility. There's no information that any group wanted him dead specifically.'

'A feminist assassin,' mused Barclay.

'That may not be so far from the truth.'

'And this is her?' Barclay waved the photograph.

'*I* think so. Others aren't convinced. I know Joyce thinks Witch is a group, and I know others think that too. Sticking to facts, this picture was taken at a rally by the opposition leader in one of the least stable South American countries.'

It was another crowd picture, focusing on a young woman with a dark tanned face but bleached and cropped blonde hair. Her cheeks were plump, her eyes small, her eyebrows almost non-existent.

'We knew there was a plot to assassinate him. It would have been against everyone's interests if such a plot had succeeded. There was concerted effort to stop the attempt taking place.'

'Operation Warlock.'

'Yes, Operation Warlock. After this rally and despite all our warnings, there was a motorcade. He died a few hours later. Poison. A pin-prick was found on the back of his hand. Among those who "pressed the flesh", so to speak, was a young supporter with bleached hair. Despite those distinctive looks, she was never seen again.'

Barclay turned the photo towards Elder, who nodded slowly back at him before sliding the Wolf Bandorff photo across the table.

'Look again, Mr Barclay. Look at Wolf's acolyte.'

'You think they're the same person?'

'I'm sure of it.' Elder watched as Barclay compared the two photographs. 'I see you're not convinced.'

'I can't really see any resemblance.'

Elder took the photos from him and stared at them. Barclay got the impression the older man had done this many times over the years. 'No, maybe you're right. The resemblance is *below* the skin. And the eyes of course. That look in the eyes . . . I know it's her. It's Witch.'

'Is that how she got her name? Operation Warlock?'

'Yes. From warlock to witch, once we knew the sex.'

'But there's no proof it was the woman who killed the—'

'Not a shred of proof. I never said there was. Suppositions, Mr Barclay.'

'Then we're no further forward really, are we?' Barclay was in a mood to wind things up. What had he learned here tonight? Stories, that's all. Merely stories.

'Perhaps not,' Elder said ruefully. 'You know best.'

'I didn't mean—'

'No, no, I know what you meant, Mr Barclay. You think this file represents the most tenuous speculation. Maybe you're right.' He stared at Barclay. 'Maybe I'm being paranoid, a symptom of the whole organisation.'

There was silence between them, Elder still staring. Barclay had heard those words before. Suddenly he realised they were *his* words, the ones he'd used at his selection-board.

'You,' he said. 'You were on my interview panel, weren't you?' Elder smiled, bowing his head a little. 'You didn't say a word the whole time, not one.'

'And that unsettled you,' Elder stated.

'Of course it did.'

'But it did not stop you making your little speech. And as you can see, I was listening.'

'I thought I knew your name, I wasn't sure how.'

Elder had begun slotting the photos back in their proper places inside the file. Barclay realised suddenly just how much this file meant to Elder.

'Mr Elder, could I take your report with me to look at?'

Elder considered this. 'I don't think so,' he said. 'You're not ready yet.' He rose and tucked the file beneath his arm. 'You've got a long drive ahead. We'd better have some coffee. Come on, it's too dark out here. Let's go inside where it's light.'

Over coffee, Elder would speak only of opera, of *Il Trovatore*, of performances seen and performances heard. Barclay tried consistently to bring the conversation back to Witch, but Elder was having none of it. Eventually, Barclay gave up. They moved from opera to the cricket season. And then it was time for Barclay to leave. He drove back to London in silence, wondering what else was in Dominic Elder's file on Witch, wondering what was in Joyce Parry's files on Elder. The word acolyte bounced around in his head. *You're not ready yet.* Was Elder inviting him to . . . to what? To learn? He wasn't sure.

He brightened when he remembered that this was Friday night. The weekend stretched ahead of him. He wondered if he'd be able to put Witch, Elder, and the American General out of his mind. Then he recalled that he himself had set these wheels in motion. *He* had noticed the original report on the sinkings. *He* had contacted Special Branch.

'What have I let myself in for?' he wondered as the overhead sodium arc came into view, the light emanating from London.

The Operating Theatre

Friday, Saturday, Sunday

Idres Salaam-Khan – known to everyone simply as Khan – had a good life. Khan knew it, and Khan's chauffeur-cum-bodyguard knew it. A good life. As a senior official (though not a director) of a small, anonymous bank, his salary was kept undisclosed. It managed to bury itself amidst still larger figures on the yearly accounting sheet. But whatever it was, it was enough to bring to Khan the simple and not so simple pleasures of life, such as his Belgravia mews house (a converted stables) and his country house in Scotland, his BMW 7-Series (so much less conspicuous than a Rolls-Royce) and, for when conspicuousness was the whole point, his Ferrari. These days, though, he did not use the Ferrari much, since there wasn't really room in it for his bodyguard. These were uncomfortable times, against which luxury proved a flimsy barrier. A bodyguard was some comfort. But Khan did not look upon Henrik as a luxury; he looked upon him as a necessity.

The small anonymous bank's small anonymous headquarters (Europe) was in London. The clients came to it precisely because it *was* small and anonymous. It was discreet, and it was generous in its interest rates. High players only though: there were no sterling accounts of less than six figures. Few of the customers using the bank in the UK actually ever borrowed from it. They tended to be depositors. The borrowers were elsewhere. In truth, the largest depositors were elsewhere too, but none of this bothered the UK operation.

Certainly, none of it bothered Khan, whose role at the bank was, to many, such a mystery. He seemed to spend three days there each week – Tuesday, Wednesday, Thursday – with Friday to Monday being spent elsewhere, most often these days in Scotland. He liked Scotland, finding it, like the bank, small and anonymous. The only thing missing, really, was nightlife. Which was why he'd decided, this trip, to bring his own nightlife with him. She was called either Shari or Sherri, he'd never really worked it out. She seemed to respond to both names as easily as she responded to questions like 'More champagne?', 'More smoked salmon?', and 'Another line?'

Khan had effortless access to the most exotic drugs. There were those in the London clubs who would have given their eye-teeth for his contacts. But Khan merely smiled with lips tightly shut, heightening the mystique around him. To have answered 'diplomatic baggage' would have burst the bubble after all, wouldn't it?

In the clubs he frequented, Khan was always 'Khan the banker'. Few knew more about his life than that simple three-word statement. He always either brought with him, or else ended the evening with, the most beautiful woman around. He always ordered either Krug or Roederer Cristal. And he always paid in cash. Cash was his currency, crisp new Bank of England notes, and because of this he found favour with every club owner and restaurateur.

He was an acknowledged creature of the night. There were stories of champagne at dawn in Hyde Park, of designer dresses being delivered out of the blue to Kensington flats – and fitting the recipient perfectly. There were gold taps in his Belgravia house, and breakfast was actually *delivered* from a nearby five-star hotel. But Shari or Sherri was the first person to take the trip to Scotland with him. She was an agency model, with no bookings all week. She was, with a name like that, naturally American – from Cincinnati. Her skin was soft and very lightly tanned, and she just loved what Khan did to her in bed.

There was a problem though. It was a long and tiring drive to the Scottish residence, situated just outside Auchterarder and not a ten-minute drive from Gleneagles Hotel. Henrik and Khan had driven it in the past, but recently Khan had opted for the bank's private twelve-seater plane which was kept at an airfield to the south-west of London. It could be flown to a small airfield adjoining Edinburgh Airport, from where it was an hour by hired car to Auchterarder. The plane usually stood idle anyway, with a pilot on permanent contract, and Khan reckoned all he was costing his employers were some fuel and the pilot's expenses in Edinburgh. But this week, the plane was booked. Two of the bank's South-East Asia personnel were in Britain, and the plane was required for trips to Manchester, Newcastle, and Glasgow.

However, the airfield's owner, recognising valued custom, asked if he might be of assistance to Khan. There was an eight-seater available which could be hired for fifteen hundred pounds a day, the fee to include a pilot's services. The airfield owner stressed that fifteen hundred was cheap these days, and Khan knew this to be the case. All the same. He would be charged per day, and staying in Scotland from Friday through Monday . . .

'Would the pilot be willing to fly us up there then bring the plane back the same day, and return to Edinburgh to collect us on the Monday?' Khan listened to the silence on the other end of his car-phone. The airfield owner was considering this proposition.

'I suppose that'd be all right,' the man answered at last.

'And the charge would be for the two days only?'

'I don't know about that, Mr Khan. See, if he's got to pick you up on the Monday, that means he's tied up. He can't take any other work.'

'I see,' said Khan. 'I'll get back to you.' And he terminated the call. He considered for a moment, then placed another call, this time to the Edinburgh airfield. 'It's Mr Khan here. Would it be possible to hire a small plane, a six-seater would suffice, to bring some people back from Edinburgh to London on Monday?' He listened to the answer. 'And how much would it cost?' he asked. 'Two thousand? Yes, thank you. That's a definite booking. It's Khan. K-h-a-n. I'll be arriving in Edinburgh this afternoon. I can pay the deposit then, if that's all right. I don't suppose there would be a cash discount?'

As he said this, he tried to make it sound like a joke. But it was certainly not taken as a joke at the other end of the line. There was an agreement. A ten percent discount for cash, and no receipts issued. Khan rang off, and rang the English airfield again. 'I'll take the plane and pilot for today only. One way. Fifteen hundred pounds as agreed.' Again, he terminated the call and sat back in his seat. The BMW was entering Jermyn Street. Khan needed some shirts.

Rich people are often those who are most canny with their money. At least, the people who stay rich are, and Khan had every intention of both him and his bank remaining wealthy. He was a born haggler, but only when it mattered. It was not, for example, worth asking for a cash discount on a bottle of Krug or a club membership. This would merely make one look cheap. But in business, haggling was an ancient and honourable adjunct. He didn't really understand the British reserve in this matter. He enjoyed the London markets, where stall-holders would cajole people into buying by adding another bunch of bananas to the box they were already holding. And another bunch . . . and another . . . until suddenly some invisible, unspoken point was reached, and several hands shot out holding money. Of course, only one of them was chosen.

Londoners, native Londoners, working-class Londoners, were excellent hagglers. Often it was trained out of them, but many retained the habit and the skill. Just look at the City, at the young brokers who were just as likely to come from the East End as from Eton. These people were a pleasure to do business with. Khan totted up that he had just saved £2,300, either for the bank or for himself (depending on how it swung). He was pleased. But then, what was £2,300? The cost of a single bottle of Petrus at some wine merchants. The cost of an adequate vintage in several London restaurants. The cost of thirty shirts: a scant month's worth. Of course, because the Edinburgh end of the deal involved no receipts, there could be no allowances against tax either . . . but then Khan and his bank were not worried by UK taxation laws.

'The parking looks difficult,' Henrik called from the driver's seat. 'Shall I drop you off and drive around the block?'

'Okay. I shouldn't be more than twenty minutes.'

'Yes, sir.'

The car stopped, blocking the narrow street. Behind it, a taxi sounded its horn. Khan stepped slowly from the back of the BMW and gave the taxi-driver a cool gaze. The pavements were wet, but drying fast. The summer shower was over, and the sun had appeared again. Steam rose into the sky. Khan walked on leather soles and heels through the steam and into the shop. The shop was another saving. He had found that, due to his 'regular shape', tailored shirts fitted him no better than a decent ready-made. There were four customers in the shop, each busy with an assistant.

'With you in a moment, sir,' someone said to Khan, who bowed his head in acknowledgement. He was in no hurry. He slipped his hands into his trouser pockets and examined the collar-sizes on the rows of wooden shelves. The hand in his left pocket touched something small and cold: an alarm. If he pressed its round red button, Henrik would arrive with all speed. This, too, Khan did not perceive as a luxury.

They flew up to Scotland over the west coast. The plane's interior was cramped yet somehow comfortable. There was something reassuring about the closeness of proximity. Henrik shifted seats half a dozen times, when he was not dispensing drinks. There was a cool-box on board, in which had been placed two bottles of champagne, several rounds of smoked salmon sandwiches, and small cocktail packets of pistachios and almonds. Plastic cups for the champagne though: an obvious oversight. Khan handed two cups to Henrik.

'Ask the pilot if he'd like one.'

'Yes, sir.'

The pilot could be seen, there being no curtain between cockpit and passenger deck. This annoyed Khan, too, though it could hardly be said to be the pilot's fault. Henrik returned with the two beakers. He was grinning.

'Not while he's driving, Mr Khan, but he thanks you for the thought.'

Khan nodded. Sensible, really, but then some of the pilots he'd had in the past were not what one would call top-flight. They were getting old and getting fat. Fat pilots worried Khan. They should be full of nervous energy, wiry as a result. He'd waited until well into the flight before offering the champagne, just to see if the pilot's will would crack. It hadn't.

Khan looked across to Henrik. He too was showing signs of the good, easy life. He was paid well for his services, and those services so far had not exactly taxed him, either physically or mentally. When Khan had hired him, Henrik had been muscular; almost musclebound. Working weights and hoping to turn pro, paying his way by acting as bouncer for a West End club owner. Khan had asked the club owner's permission before approaching Henrik with an offer of a job. The chauffeur's role hadn't appealed to the Dane, but he'd taken the job anyway. He was not stupid. He knew that as bodyguard he would have to accompany Khan just about everywhere: everywhere glamorous, everywhere expensive, everywhere that was Somewhere.

But too many hours in the driving seat were taking their toll. Henrik was still big, still strong, but there was excess flesh now, too. Khan, who worked out each day, appreciated Henrik's problem; it was one of mental application. The Dane was no longer hungry. Look at him, champagne in both hands, sipping from one cup then from the other, gazing out of the window down on to the visible landscape. Khan was aware that Henrik might have to go. There might be a termination of contract, the hiring of someone new, someone strong but hungry. Would he perhaps keep Henrik on as driver? He was a good, safe driver after all. But no, that would be to denigrate the man, to humble him. More importantly, it might well make Henrik bitter. And a bitter man was an enemy. It didn't do to employ potential spies, potential adversaries. No, Henrik would have to go. Soon. There was that new doorman at the Dorica Club . . .

'This is great, really great.' Shari or Sherri slumped her head against Khan's shoulder. She was dressed well. He'd been relieved when they'd stopped the car outside her block and she'd opened the door and started down the steps, smiling, waving, carrying two large holdalls . . . and above all dressed well. Discreetly sensual. Not too much make-up, not too much perfume. A clinging red dress which just met her knees. Her tanned legs did not need covering. Her shoes were red too. She knew how well her blonde hair and high cheekbones suited red.

'You're very special,' he told her now, rubbing one smooth knee. It was true: they were *all* very special.

'Touching down in ten minutes,' called the pilot. One bottle of champagne was still unopened, the sandwiches barely touched.

'You're special too, Khan,' said Shari or Sherri.

'Thank you, my dear.' He patted the back of her hand, which lay on his right thigh. 'I'm sure we're going to have a wonderful time.'

'Yes,' she said. 'Me too.'

Across the aisle from them, Henrik drained first one beaker and then the other. His chin dropped against his neck as he stifled a belch.

A wonderful time. Well, yes, at first it was. But it struck Khan that there was something not quite right. The time was wonderful but not perfect. It wasn't that he was worrying about bank business. The bank was always in and on his mind, even on these trips north. Scotland was not a refuge. There were computers and modems and faxes and telephones in his house. A call might come on his portable phone during lunch or dinner, or to his bedside telephone in the middle of the night. New York might call to warn of an incoming fax, for his eyes only. Seoul might need information. Karachi, Lahore, Patna, Bombay, Bangkok, George Town, Shanghai . . . not everyone appreciated what the local hour was when they called. If it was the middle or the beginning or the end of their banking day, then it was Khan's banking day too.

But no, it was nothing to do with business. Business was not a problem. Was the problem Shari or Sherri? Ah, yes, maybe. Maybe that was it. She did love what he did to her in bed . . . and elsewhere in and out of the house. Her American accent grated, but only a little. She was not over-talkative, which was a relief to him. And she looked good all the time. She made herself presentable. What then?

Well . . . There came a time when, sated, he liked his women to open themselves up a little to him, to tell him about their lives. Normally, he was uninterested in pasts, but there was something about the aftermath of the sexual act. He liked to listen to their stories then, and file them away. So that he could assure himself he had been fucking someone's history, a real flesh and blood human, and not just a beautiful dummy.

And it was here that Shari or Sherri had disappointed him. She had disappointed him by being at first vague, and then by making obvious mistakes. For instance, she told him about a childhood incident when a boy neighbour had lifted up her skirt and slipped his hot little hand inside her pants. She told the story twice, and the first time the boy's hand had gone down the front of her pants, the second time the back. Khan hadn't commented, but it had made him wonder. He made her work harder, recalling more and more of her past for him. He got her to go over the same story twice, once at breakfast and once over dinner, checking for mistakes in the retelling. There were one or two, not significant in themselves.

He remembered how he met her. In a club. She'd been with a friend, a male friend, an admirer perhaps. She'd caught Khan's eye several times, and he'd held her glances, until eye contact between them became more prolonged and meaningful. He was a sucker for this kind of conquest, the kind where he almost literally tore a woman from another man's arms. By the end of the evening she was at his table, and the other suitor had vanished. It had been easy, and she'd been ravishing, and he'd felt the sweet, warm glow of success.

He knew she worked as a model. Well, he knew she *said* she worked as a model. He'd once picked her up outside a prestigious model agency off Oxford Street, but then when his car had arrived she'd already been waiting on the pavement, hadn't she? How was he to know that she'd ever actually been inside the building? What really did he *know* about her? Precious little, it suddenly seemed to him. He'd liked that in the past, had preferred it. Keeping things casual, no hint of a more meaningful, a more lasting relationship. But now . . . Suddenly he wanted to know more about her. What was her last name? Kazowski? Kaprinski? Something East European. She told him she'd changed it to Capri for modelling purposes. Shari Capri or Sherri Capri. Stupid name. Stupid names.

And another thing, wasn't she overfriendly towards Henrik? With her 'Thank you, Henrik' whenever she stepped into or out of the car. Her smiles to him. The way she lightly touched his arm if she wanted to ask him something. Checking that she was in the bath, Khan strode quickly to his study, unlocked the door (he was never so foolish, so trusting as to leave it unlocked, but then locks were easy to pick, weren't they?), and made for his desk. He glanced at it, looking for signs that things had been moved, pages turned over. Nothing. He checked his computer for a certain phone number, then picked up the telephone and dialled London. An 081 number, Outer London. There was a young firm used by the bank sometimes. They were dynamic, and they got results. Nobody wanted to know *how* they got results, but they got them. There was no one in the office, but as he'd expected a recording gave him another phone number where he could reach one of the partners. He entered this number onto his computer for future reference, then dialled it. The call was answered almost immediately.

'Hello, is that Mr Allison? It's Khan here. I'm calling from Scotland. There's a job I'd like done. Private, not on the bank's account. I want you to check on a Miss Sherri S-h-e-r-r-i or Shari S-h-a-r-i Capri C-a-p-r-i. I'll give you her home address and where she says she works. I want anything on her you can find. Oh, and Mr Allison, she's up here with me, so there should be no problems. I mean, you won't bump into her should you happen to . . . well, you know what I mean. Her home address? Yes, of course . . .'

Afterwards, he felt a little relieved. Allison was *extremely* capable, ex-CID. And his partner Crichton had a pedigree which took in both the Parachute Regiment and the SAS. Yes, a trouble shared *was* a trouble halved. Khan felt better. So much so that he was able to put his troubles out of his mind for quarter of an hour, time spent in the bathroom with a wet and so very slippery Shari or Sherri Capri . . .

On their last evening, they dined in. There was a local chef who, on days off, could occasionally be persuaded to cook for Khan and his guests.

Usually, Khan reserved this treat for larger dinner parties. But on Sunday morning news came through of a spectacular deal which had been concluded by the South-East Asia personnel during their whistlestop tour of the British Isles. A great deal of money would be travelling from the UK to the bank's South-East Asia office, and it would travel via the London office where a certain amount, as always, would be held back in the name of handling fees. A sum slightly in excess of one million sterling.

It was a job well done, and Khan, who had played no part in it, felt a little of its success rub off on him. A quick call to the chef, Gordon Sinclair, had secured his services, and when all was said and done it was practically as cheap as eating out since this way Khan would drink champagne, wine and spirits from his own well-stocked cellar. And at the end of the evening it was always pleasant to share a malt with Gordon and talk about food and the appreciation of food. Gordon knew that Khan had contacts in London, that he had eaten in all the top restaurants and was on first-name terms with many of the restaurateurs and chefs – not merely in London but, it seemed, all over. And Khan knew that Gordon had itchy feet, that the only thing tying him to Scotland was his Scottishness. He would have to flee soon if he were really to start – the term came to Khan with a smile – *cooking*: a quality London restaurant, where he could make a name for himself, and then his own restaurant under his own name. That was the route to success.

They would talk about these things and more. Perhaps Shari would be listening, or perhaps she would have retired for the night, to be joined by Khan later.

Yes, it was Shari, not Sherri. Shari Capri. Allison had phoned with this information, and with a few other snippets. But as he pointed out, weekends weren't the best time to track down information, especially not from places of employment. Come Monday, he could work on the model agency, but not before. It was half in Khan's mind to ask if he'd considered breaking and entering, but such a question would have been in considerable bad taste besides which, if his phone were bugged, he could be accused of incitement to commit a criminal act. That would never do. So he had to accept what scant information Allison had gleaned, and wait until Monday. By Monday he would be back in London, he would have said goodbye to Shari, with promises of phone calls and meetings for dinner – promises he seldom kept as a rule. But it might be that he'd have to keep tabs on her for a little while longer, just until he knew the truth.

'More wine, Shari?'

They were alone in the dining room. The kitchen was a long way away. Henrik, dismissed for the evening, would be in one of the bars in Auchterarder. He'd told Khan about a barmaid with whom he'd become friendly. So it was just Shari and Khan, and, his presence no more than a distant clang of pots and sizzle of fat, Gordon Sinclair. And Gordon's girlfriend, who had come to help him in the kitchen. She would leave before dessert was served, while Gordon would linger, clearing up a little and loading his excess ingredients back into the boot of his small sports car. Khan hadn't met the girlfriend before. She was attractive, if a bit red in the cheeks. Very Scottish: shy, elusive even. Plump too, or at least well-rounded. Khan had the idea that Gordon and she might make a go of a restaurant together. Perhaps she was the knot which tied him to the area. Khan was beginning to form an idea about a restaurant, financed by him and run by Gordon and his girlfriend . . .

'Yes, please,' said Shari. 'This is delicious.'

Trout in almonds. Local trout, naturally, with the cream sauce flavoured by a little island malt. The sauce succeeded in not overpowering the delicate fish. The julienne of vegetables remained a little overcooked for Khan's tastes, but he knew Shari liked them soft almost to the point of mush. She retained the annoying American habit of cutting and spooning everything up with the use of just her fork.

'Delicious,' she said again.

He looked at her and smiled. Maybe he was becoming paranoid. Maybe there was nothing to worry about. Look at her – beautiful, fragile. Everything about her was surface. She couldn't possibly be hiding anything from him. No, he was being stupid. He should forget everything and just enjoy this final night with her.

'Yes, it is delicious, isn't it?' he said, pouring a little more Meursault. Meursault was a little rich for trout on its own, but the sauce both deserved and could cope with it. He knew Gordon liked to surprise him, but Khan guessed some prime beef would be next (albeit in a sauce of exotic provenance), followed by an Orkney cheese and freshly made crannachan. And the beauty was that all the mess in the kitchen and the plates and things in the dining-room could be left just as they were. Mrs MacArthur would come in on Monday afternoon and tidy the lot up.

Before he'd employed her, and again twice since, Khan had had Mrs MacArthur checked over by a detective agency in Dundee. The agency reckoned that not only was she clean, she was practically unbribable. So Khan didn't mind that she held a set of keys to the house and to the alarm system. Besides, she never entered the study, which was kept on a separate alarm circuit anyway (to which Khan and the local police held the only keys).

'Delicious,' he said, raising his glass as if in a toast.

It was one of those special pubs where at weekends after closing time the lights are turned off and the regulars drink on in darkness. But not on a Sunday. Some traditions held fast on a Sunday, and the pub closed at ten-thirty sharp. Which suited Henrik really, since he'd offered to drive Nessa home and she had laughingly accepted.

'Though it's only a five-minute walk,' she'd added.

'Well, we can always drive home the long way.'

She'd said nothing at that. He'd been waiting outside in the rented Ford Scorpio, the stereo playing, engine running. She said goodnight to the barman, who was locking up, then walked smartly to the edge of the kerb. Henrik was already out of the car, so he could hold the passenger door open for her. She gave him a funny look.

'Thank you, kind sir,' she said.

He got back into the driver's seat. 'Where to?' he asked her.

'Home, of course.'

'*Straight* home?'

She gave him the look again. 'Not necessarily.'

They stopped by a field just off the dual carriageway to the south of the town, and stayed there half an hour or so, chatting, kissing. They were as clumsy as teenagers, even with the seats tilted back. Eventually she laughed again and loosed herself from him.

'I'd better get back. My mum'll be getting worried.'

He nodded. 'Okay.' They drove more or less in silence after that, except for her few directions. Until eventually they arrived at the stone bungalow.

'This is it. Thanks for the lift.'

'I'll be back again next week probably. What about dinner?'
'Dinner?'
'At the hotel if you like.'
'Depends on my shifts really.'
'Maybe I can phone you at the pub?'
She thought this over. 'Yes, okay,' she said. 'Do that.'
'Goodnight, Nessa.' He pulled her to him for a final kiss, but she wriggled free and glanced out of the window.
'My mother might be watching. Night, Henrik.' And she relented, pecking him on the cheek. He watched her as she opened and closed her gate, gave him a final wave, and climbed the steps to her front door. He thought he saw a curtain twitch in one of the unlit windows. The hall light was on. She closed the door softly behind her. Henrik slipped the gear lever into the Drive position and started off. At the end of her road, he ejected Barry Manilow from the tape-player and pushed home some heavy metal, turning the volume all the way up. He drove through Auchterarder's dark deserted streets for some time with the driver's window down, grinning to himself. Then he headed home. No doubt he would have to lie in bed and put up with all that squealing and squawking from Khan's room, all the grunting and puffing. He wondered if it was a put-on, maybe a recording or something. Was it supposed to impress him? Or did neither party realise he had ears?
Mind you, she was a particular beauty, this present catch. And the way she looked at Henrik himself . . . the way she touched him, as though wanting to assure herself that his build was a fact and not some fantasy. Yes, maybe when Khan had finished with her, maybe there'd be room for Henrik to move in. He knew where she worked in London. He knew where she lived. He might just happen to be passing. He was pretty sure she'd make even more noise with him than she did with Khan. Yes, pretty damned sure. His grin was even wider as he drove through the gates of the walled and detached house.
He locked the high metal gates behind him. The chef would be long gone. There was no sign of another car. A short gravel driveway led to the front of the house. The place looked to be in darkness. It was only ten to twelve. Maybe they'd finished and were asleep. Maybe he wouldn't have to resort to vodka to send him into oblivion. He left the car at the top of the drive rather than parking it in the small garage. He stood for a moment, leaning against the cooling body of the car, listening to the silence. A rustling of trees, a bird in the distance, maybe even some frogs. But that was all. And it was so dark. So utterly dark, with the stars shining high in the sky. So different from London, so quiet and isolated. Certainly isolated. They'd talked of keeping guard dogs which could prowl the garden around the house, but then who would feed them and look after them? So instead there was the alarm system, linked to the local station *and* to Perth constabulary (the latter for times when the former was closed or unmanned).
His eyes having adjusted to the dark, Henrik walked to the front door and opened it, then locked it behind him, using the mortice deadlock as well as the Yale. The light was on at the far end of the hall, where the central alarm system was contained in a metal box secured to the wall beside the door to the kitchen. He used one key to open the box, and another to turn on the

system. The bedrooms upstairs were en suite, so he set the pressure-pad alarm for the whole house. No need for anyone to leave their rooms before morning. In the morning, the first person up would have a minute to deactivate the alarm system before the bells started ringing both outside the house itself and inside the police station.

Now, having turned on the system, he had a minute to get to his room, a minute before it was fully operational. He headed for the stairs. There was a soft buzzing from the alarm box which told him it was working. When the buzzing stopped, the various window devices and movement-sensitive beams and pressure-pads woke up for the evening. Silence upstairs, and no light from Khan's bedroom. Henrik switched off the hall lights and closed his door behind him.

She knows the house almost as well as she knows the surrounding area. In the past two days she's been here half a dozen times, and twice at the dead of night, the witching hour.

She's been in the grounds, and has peered through windows into rooms, through the letterbox into the hall. She has seen that the alarm box sits at the end of the hall, attached to the wall. She knows the kind of alarm it will be. She has checked door and window locks. She has even gone so far as to pass an angled mirror on the end of a stick through the letterbox, the better to see the locks from the inside. All has proven very satisfactory. The nearest house is half a mile away. There are no alarms in the garden, no infra red beams which, when broken, would turn on floodlights. No lights at all to complicate her approach. No cameras. No dogs. She is especially pleased that there are no dogs.

The gates are high and topped with spikes, but the wall is a pathetic affair with broken bottle-glass cemented to its top. Too pathetic for it to have been Khan's work. It must already have been in place when he bought the house. The glass has been worn smooth over the years. She won't even bother to cover it with a blanket before she climbs into the garden.

But first, there is the alarm system. She straps on a special climbing-belt – the sort known to every telephone engineer – and attaches spiked soles to her shoes. The spiked soles are for wear by gardeners so they can aerate their lawns. She has modified the spikes only a little. She drove to a garden centre outside Perth for the spike-shoes, and bought a lot of other stuff as well, stuff she didn't need, bought solely to disguise this singular purchase. She passed two garden centres before reaching Perth. Police might investigate one or two garden centres, but she doubts they would go much further afield.

She is now standing beside a telegraph-pole in a field across the lane from Khan's house. She knows this is a dangerous period. She will soon be visible from the house. She checks her watch. Two. The bodyguard locked up two hours ago. They will rise early tomorrow to catch their plane back south. Or rather, if things go as intended, they won't.

She waits another minute. What moon there is disappears behind a hefty bank of cloud. She ties her belt around the pole as well as herself, grips the pole, hugging herself to it, and begins to climb. Eventually, she knows, twenty-odd feet up, there will be foot-holds to help her. But for now she has only her own strength. She knows it will be enough. She does not hesitate.

At the top of the pole, beneath the wires themselves, sits a large junction box containing the thinner wires running back to homes in the area. She thinks Khan's alarm system works via telephone lines. From what she's seen of it, it looks just the type. If it doesn't . . . Well, she will fall back on other plans, other options. But for now she has to keep busy, working fast while the moon stays hidden. She slips a pencil-thin torch into her mouth, holding it as she would a cigarette, and, by its light, begins to unscrew the front from the junction box.

Terrorists aren't just people who terrorise. They are people who hunger for knowledge, the knowledge of how things work. In knowing how things work, you discover how society works, and that knowledge can help cripple society. She knows she can disrupt communications, bring transport systems to a halt, generate mayhem by computer. Given the knowledge, anything can be achieved. The junction box holds no surprises for her, only a certain measure of relief. She stares at the confusion of wires for a moment, and knows that she can stay with plan one.

There is a distinct colour-coding for the wires from Khan's alarm system. The puzzle is that there seem to be two sets. One for the main house . . . The other? A room inside the house, perhaps, or a garage or workshop. She decides to take both sets out with her neat rubber-handled wire-clippers. It was a good alarm system, but not a great one. A great alarm system would send a constant pulse to the outside world. And if that pulse were interrupted, *then* the alarm bells would ring. Cutting the wires would cause the alarm to sound in the distant police station. But such systems are unreliable and seldom used. They are nuisances, sounding whenever a fluctuation in current occurs, or a phone-line momentarily breaks up. Society demands alarms not be a nuisance.

There were times when Witch worried about society.

The job done, she slipped slowly back down the pole and untied her harness at the bottom, putting it back in her heavy black holdall along with the spikes and her tools. Now for the wall. She clambered up and sat on the top for a second, studying the windows in the house, then fell into the dark garden. She had climbed the wall precisely twelve feet to the left of the gate, so that she fell on to grass and not into shrubbery. She'd decided to enter the way most burglars would – by the back entrance – not that she was intending to make this look like a burglary. No, this was to be messy. Her employers wanted her to leave a message, a clear statement of their feelings.

The kitchen then, its door bolted top and bottom with a mortice lock beside the handle. The bedrooms are to the front of the house. She can make a certain amount of noise here. Silence, of course, would be best. Silence is the ideal. In her holdall is a carefully measured and cut piece of Fablon, purchased at a department store in Perth. Ghastly pattern and colour, though the assistant had praised it as though it were an Impressionist painting. Witch is surprised people still use it. She measured the kitchen windows yesterday, and chose the smaller for her purpose. Slowly, carefully, she unpeels the Fablon and presses it against the smaller window, covering it exactly. In the department store she also purchased some good-quality yellow dusters, while at a small hardware shop the keen young assistant was only too pleased to sell some garden twine and a hammer to a lady keen to stake out her future vegetable plots.

She takes the hammer from her holdall. She has used some twine to tie a duster around the head. Out of the spare cuts of Fablon she has made some makeshift handles, which she attaches to the sheet of Fablon stuck to the window. She grips one of these handles as, softly, near soundlessly, she begins to tap away at the glass, which falls away from the window-frame but stays attached to the Fablon. Within three minutes she is lifting the whole window out from its frame, laying it on the ground. The alarm is just outside the kitchen door. If she'd set it off, it would probably be buzzing by now. But she can't hear it. She can't hear anything, not even her heart.

Upstairs, Henrik is asleep and dreaming in Danish. He's dreaming of barmaids with pumps attached to their breasts, and of flying champagne bottles, and of winning a bodybuilding contest against Khan and the pre-movie star Schwarzenegger. He drank one glass of neat vodka before retiring, and watched ten minutes of the satellite movie on his eighteen-inch television before falling asleep, waking half an hour later just long enough to switch off the television.

He sleeps and he dreams with one hand tight between his legs, something he's done since childhood. Girlfriends have commented on it, laughed at it even. If he catches himself doing it, he shoves the hand under a pillow, but it always seems to creep south again of its own volition.

The barmaids are singing. Topless for some reason, and singing in a language he doesn't understand. His name? His name? Can they possibly be singing . . . his name?

'Wake up!' A whisper. A woman's urgent hiss. His eyes open to blackness and he tries to sit up, but a feminine hand pushes at his chest, and he sinks back down again. The hand remains against his chest, rubbing it. A silky-smooth hand.

Shari's hand.

'What is it?' he hisses back. 'What's the matter, Shari?'

Her face seems very close to him. 'It's Khan. He's sound asleep . . . as usual. He just doesn't . . . I don't want to put him down or anything, but he just doesn't *satisfy* me.'

Topless barmaids . . . breasts. Henrik gives a groggy half-smile in the dark. He reaches a hand to where he imagines her chest is. He's not sure whether he finds it or not. She's wearing her clothes . . . maybe some sort of nightdress, a baby-doll or something.

'I knew you'd come,' he whispers. 'I was going to call on you when we got back to London. Khan's a shit, he'll dump you the minute the plane lands.'

'I know.' Her hand rubbing him, rubbing in wider circles, taking in shoulders and down over his stomach. Feels good. 'He doesn't understand how I like it.'

'Like it?'

'Sex.' A low guttural sound, more moan than whisper. 'I love it.' Still rubbing, smooth hand. 'I like it tied up. Khan doesn't like that, but it's such a turn on. What about you, huh? Is it a turn on for you?'

'Sure.' He's waking up now. *Tied up?*

'Want to try? I've got some of Khan's ties. Want to try it with *his* ties?'

'Why not?' Her hand is insistent on him now. She moves one of his arms, then the other, until his hands are behind him, grasping at the bedposts. He realises now that *she* wants to tie *him* up . . . not what he had in mind, but all the same . . . And in fact she's already busy. It's easy for her to slip the ties around his wrists.

'Not too tight are they?'

'No.' Lying. His wrists feel like the circulation's been cut.

And around his feet too, so he is splayed and naked on the bed. He knows he's in good shape, but sucks his gut in a little anyway. He's stiff as a beer-pump himself now. Damn, he'll make her bells ring, little Shari's bells ring. Oh Christ, but if she calls out . . . what if Khan hears? He's a pretty light sleeper, what if he bursts in while he's lying here all trussed . . .

Bells . . . make her bells ring . . .

How come she hasn't set off the alarm system?

He's forming the question when he hears tape being torn, and next thing her hand is over his face, wrapping tape around his mouth, around the back of his head, mouth again, and again, and again. Jesus fucking Christ! He grunts, struggles. But then he hears a cli-chick, and another, and another, and another. Four. And he's not being held by ties any more. Something cold instead. And then the light goes on.

It takes his eyes a second or two to deal with the difference. He sees himself naked, and the handcuffs around his ankles. They're around his wrists too, pinning him to the bedposts top and bottom. No problem. He can contract himself and snap the goddamned bedposts off if he has to. Idiot that he was in the first place. Khan'll kill him for this. But who is the woman? The woman dressed in black, who's standing there at the foot of the bed. He hasn't been able to focus on her yet, but now she's stepping forwards and

Thwock!

One blow to the right temple with her hammer, and it's back to the barmaids for Henrik. Witch looks down on him and smiles. Well, what's the point of working if you can't have a little fun?

Across the corridor and down the hall, two people are asleep in a large rumpled bed. The whole room smells of perfume and bath-soap and sex. Their clothes are distributed across the floor without any discernible pattern or progress. The man is naked and lies on his side without any covering. The woman lies on her front, hair tangled across the pillow. She is covered by a white sheet, and her left arm hangs limply down from the edge of the bed, fingernails grazing the carpet. No fun and games here. Now the work begins in earnest. The arm is actually a bonus, lying bulging-veined like that. She uses the pencil-thin torch to help her prepare and test the syringe, which she then jabs home into one of Shari Capri's veins, just where the forearm meets the elbow. Not merely asleep now but unconscious. An explosion wouldn't wake her. Gunshots would cause no flickering of her eyelids. She'll wake up in the morning, gluey-mouthed, thirsty, with a sore head most probably.

These will be the least of her problems.

Now only Khan remains. He seems to be sleeping peacefully. She wonders what he's dreaming of. What *do* you dream of when you have everything? You dream of more. Or else the terror of losing everything you've got. Either would be appropriate, considering what is about to happen, and *why* it's about to happen. Witch squats on the floor, her face in line with Khan's. She's not six feet from him – not quite close enough for him to take a waking, desperate lunge at her, but close enough so that she can study him. And studying him, he becomes less human to her, and less human still. He becomes a motive, a deal, a set of crooked figures on an accounting sheet. He becomes her pay-off.

'Mr Khan,' she says softly. 'Mr Khan.' An eye opens to a slit. Her voice is as casual as any nurse's would be to the patient who's come out of the operating theatre. 'Time to wake up now, Mr Khan.'

The difference being, of course, that now Khan is awake, the operating theatre waits for him. Witch, smiling, already has the good sharp knife in her hand. It flashes through her mind that she has been in Britain exactly a week.

Happy anniversary.

The Protean Self

Monday 8 June

'So how was France then?' Greenleaf was smiling. Some might have called it a grimace.

Doyle smiled too: with pleasure. '*Mag-ni-fique*, John. Just *mag-ni-fique*. Here . . .' He reached into a carrier bag. 'Have a bottle of beer. I've another 199 of them in the garage at home.'

Greenleaf accepted the small green bottle. 'Thanks,' he said. 'I'll savour it.'

'You do that, John. That's one franc's worth of best Alsace lager in there. Four-point-nine alcohol, so take it slow, eh?' And Doyle gave Greenleaf a big wink.

I don't really hate him, Greenleaf thought suddenly. He's smarmy all right, but I wonder how seriously he takes himself. Maybe the whole thing is just him sending himself up. I don't really hate him. It's just gentle loathing.

'So,' Doyle was saying, looking around him at the office. 'The place didn't crumble in my absence? I'm hurt. I used to think I was the only thing holding this place together.'

'We do our best, Doyle. It's not easy, but we do our best.'

'Good man. So, what did you get in Folkestone?'

'Some cod and a couple of bloaters.'

Doyle laughed for a full fifteen seconds. 'Christ, John, I think a bit of me's rubbing off on you. Don't ask me which bit, mind.'

'As long as I don't catch anything.'

'There you go again! Catch anything. You're pinching all my best lines.'

'Lines, eh?' Even Greenleaf was smiling now: also with pleasure. 'Can I take it I'm part of a running gag about fish?'

'Bear in mind one of the poor sods who got blown up was called Perch.'

'Yes, I met his mother.'

The smile vanished from Doyle's face. 'Yes, doesn't do to joke, does it? So, what did you *really* find in Folkestone?'

'Haven't you read the report?'

Doyle wrinkled his nose. 'Give me the details. I'll read it later.'

'Well, I found pretty much what you said I would. Looks like it was an explosion all right. Guy's business was in trouble, he was open to any kind of offer. They found two grand on him. I managed to trace the notes.'

Doyle's eyes opened wide. 'Yeah?' Greenleaf nodded. 'Well, good for you, John. Good for you. And?'

'Old notes. Part of a ransom paid to some kidnappers in Italy five years ago.'

'What?'

'It's all in my report.'

'Maybe I'd better read it after all.'

'So what about Calais?'

'Not a lot to tell really.'

'I saw the stuff you sent through by modem on Friday.'

Doyle shrugged. 'Something to impress the old man. A bit of technology. There wasn't much substance to what I sent.'

Greenleaf nodded. This was true. What's more, it was a shrewd observation of Trilling, who had slavered over the print-out more for what it *was*, the manner of its transmission, than for what it contained.

'Still,' said Doyle, 'sending it as it happened meant I had the weekend clear. I found this great restaurant, five courses for a tenner. You should nip over for—'

'Doyle! Greenleaf! In my office!'

They looked at one another for a silent moment. Greenleaf spoke first. 'Sounds like the headmaster wants to see us.'

'John,' said Doyle, 'you took the words right out of my mouth.'

It occurred to Greenleaf that the reason he was feeling so . . . so damned *mellow* this morning was the weekend he'd just spent with Shirley. A glorious weekend. On Saturday they'd gone shopping at Brent Cross and bought a new dining-room suite, the one she'd been nagging him about for months. The summer sales had suddenly seen it reduced in price by twenty-five percent, and Greenleaf, seeing this as a reward for his previous prudence, had agreed they should buy the thing. They'd celebrated with dinner at an Indian place near their home, then watched half a video before going to bed. And on Sunday, waking late, they'd taken a picnic to Trent Park . . . All very different to Doyle's weekend, he was sure, but he felt the better for it.

'Sit down, please,' said Commander Trilling, himself already seated. He didn't look in the best of humours. His *Financial Times* sat folded, apparently unread, on a corner of his desk. 'I've just had a long chat with Mrs Parry over at Spook City. It seems I was right. She's been holding out on us.'

'Tut tut,' commented Doyle.

'Yes,' said Trilling. 'This double sinking is, apparently, a near copycat of a sinking several years ago off Japan.'

'Japan?' This from Greenleaf.

'Japan,' said the Commander. 'A terrorist entered Japan and then blew up the boat which had taken her there.'

'*Her?*' From Doyle.

'Her,' said Trilling.

'Which group, sir?' asked Greenleaf.

'Mrs Parry's more than a bit vague on that. She's sending over a courier with what information there is. The pair of you'd better study it. Makes sense if you think about it. Terrorists kidnap a girl, then the ransom money turns up after the Folkestone explosion. Simplest explanation is that someone from the original terrorist group has entered Britain.'

'And,' added Doyle, 'the "someone" in question also carried out an assassination in Japan.'

'Quite so.'

'Political?'

'Not entirely. A peace campaigner. The rumour, according to Mrs Parry, is that some arms dealers might have chipped in to hire a killer.'

'Nice people to do business with,' said Doyle.

Greenleaf said nothing. He was noting how Trilling harped on that *Mrs*. He really *was* pissed off with Parry.

'So now,' the Commander was saying, 'there's a good possibility that a terrorist, a hired assassin, is somewhere in the country. Maybe a woman. And she's been here for a few days now, while Mrs Parry has withheld vital information from us.'

Greenleaf: 'So by now she could be anywhere.'

'Anywhere.'

'And her target?'

Trilling shrugged. 'That's our next line of inquiry. Always supposing we *are* dealing with an individual – of whatever sex. Parry herself only sounds half-convinced, but the original theory starts with a retired agent called Dominic Elder. I know Elder of old. He's prone to exaggeration but basically sound.'

'So what do we do, sir?'

'I want you to put together a list of possible targets, political or otherwise. Including peace campaigners, journalists, judges, anyone of influence really. A lot of it will already be in the files, it's just a matter of collation.'

'The summit's the obvious contender,' said Doyle.

'Unfortunately that's true.'

'Do we have a description of the woman?'

'Not one that would help.'

'It's not much to go on, is it?'

'No,' said Trilling, 'it's not. But we've got the point of landing, and that's a start.'

'Depends, sir,' said Greenleaf. 'She may have left the boat at any point along the coast.'

'Well, let's take it that she . . . or *he* . . . or *they* . . . didn't. Let's start with a three-mile strip either side of Folkestone. Either there was a car waiting, which would make sense, or else the terrorist walked into town.'

'Or away from it.'

'Or away from it,' agreed Trilling. 'Whatever, it was well past midnight. At that time of night, anything arouses interest. A parked car on a deserted road . . . someone walking along that road . . . maybe even someone coming ashore. Let's get men on to it, asking questions, stopping drivers. Put up checkpoints on all the roads into Folkestone, and especially after midnight. Stop every driver and ask them if they saw anything suspicious. Most vehicles that time of night will be lorries, so check haulage firms, delivery vans, the lot.'

'That's a ton of work, sir.'

'I know it is. Would you rather we let this person take a pot-shot at a visiting dignitary? Think what it would do to the tourist trade.'

'It'd make the roads a bit quieter,' commented Doyle, and received a filthy look from Trilling.

'Maximum effort, gentlemen, starting now. As soon as the courier arrives,

I'll let you have copies of whatever there is. Remember, maximum effort. Whatever it takes.'

'Whatever it takes, sir,' agreed Doyle.

'Sir, what about a name for the operation?'

'For what it's worth, Parry and her crew used the name Witch.'

'But that's not the name of the gang?'

'No, it's just something Dominic Elder thought up.'

'What about Operation Bedknobs then?' Doyle suggested. 'You know, *Bedknobs and Broomsticks*.'

'Or just Witch Hunt,' Greenleaf added.

'I don't like the connotations of witch hunt,' commented Trilling. 'And Bedknobs is merely stupid. Let's go with Broomstick. Operation Broomstick. Now, both of you, get sweeping!'

In unison: 'Yes, sir.'

She sat staring from her desk, staring towards and out of her open door. It had been an uncomfortable conversation, and thinking back on it Joyce Parry realised that she might have phrased things differently; that she might, unusually for her, have played it all wrong. There were strong ties between her department and Special Branch. The secret services held no powers of arrest, and depended on Special Branch help in that, as in many other things. It didn't do to fall out. Especially not with Bill Trilling, who was a crotchety sod at the best of times, and not the easiest person either to work or merely to liaise with.

No, she'd played him all wrong. She'd tried to soothe things, to work *around* the problem. Best just to have dived in, admitting a cock-up, giving assurances that it wouldn't happen again. A little bit of grovelling and Trilling would have been satisfied. But having seen her grovel once, wouldn't he have demanded more? She didn't like to look weak. She certainly didn't like to look weak to people like Trilling. No, in the long run she'd probably done the right thing. She'd been strong and she'd tried to be diplomatic, and he would remember that. Always supposing one or both of them kept their present jobs . . .

If the woman Dominic Elder called Witch had entered the country, and *if* she carried out an assassination, then questions would be asked of the security and intelligence services. There could be no doubting where the buck would stop: it would stop with Bill Trilling and with her. But Trilling had a trump card. His men had been sent to investigate the double sinking without knowing of the possible link with the Japanese sinking six years before. So the buck came, finally, to Joyce Parry. In her defence, she could point out that it was six years ago, that it was merely a notion that had come into her head. There was nothing to prove that Witch was in Britain. Probably, there would be no proof until she or he or they made her or his or their move. But by then it would be too late. Of course, Barclay should have spoken to her before contacting Special Branch. He'd take a certain portion of the blame, but not enough to save her from forced resignation . . . She shivered at the thought. She'd worked so hard to get here, harder than any man would have had to work to achieve the same high office.

She didn't need Bill Trilling as an enemy; she needed him as a friend. But she was damned if she'd crawl or beg or even simper. She'd be herself. If he helped, he would help because it was in everyone's interests for him to and not because she'd asked him 'please'. Yes, she was stubborn. Dominic had always said it was her least alluring attribute.

He was one to talk.

Did Dominic hold the key? She should talk to him anyway about his meeting with Barclay. She wondered what he'd made of Michael Barclay . . . She thought she knew the answer, but it would be interesting to hear it. Besides, Dominic knew such a lot – or thought he did – about Witch. She needed friends. She needed people working *for* her rather than against her. If Witch was in the country, and if Witch was going to be caught, she could ignore nobody.

She picked up her receiver and, from memory, dialled his number. For her efforts, she got a constant tone: number unobtainable. She checked his phone number on the computer: she'd transposed the last two numbers. She dialled again. This time, he picked up the telephone on the first ring.

'Hello, Dominic, it's Joyce.'

'Yes, hello. I thought you'd call. I've been thinking about you.'

'Oh?'

'You just can't get the staff these days, can you?'

'I take it Barclay didn't meet with your approval?'

'Let's say he strikes me as . . . naive.'

'Weren't we all once?'

He ignored this. 'I blame computers. People sit in front of them all day thinking they're the answer.' Joyce, staring at his phone number on her computer screen, smiled at this. 'They're just the *tools*. People don't go out into the world any more.'

'I don't remember going out into the world.'

'Oh come on, Joyce, you were a field agent for – what? – five years?'

'And much good did it do me.'

'It broadened your mind.'

'I had to be broad-minded, Dominic, working with you.'

'That joke's a decade old, Joyce.'

'Then let's change the subject. I take it you weren't able to help Barclay?'

'He wasn't able to focus on what I was telling him.'

'So you did tell him about Witch?'

'I told him *all* about Witch. Much good will it do any of us. Joyce, if you need my help, I'm here. But I can be anywhere you want, just say the word.'

'I may take you up on that, Dominic.'

'Do.'

'I'm not sure there's funding for a freelancer.'

'I don't want money, Joyce. I want *her*.'

Joyce Parry smiled. Yes, he was committed all right. More, he was obsessed. Was she merely opening an old wound, or could she help him exorcise the ghost?

'I'll call you,' she said merely. 'Meantime, any suggestions?'

'I take it Special Branch are covering this end of things?'

'At the moment, yes.'

'Then at the moment, I'd leave them to it. What about sending someone to Calais?'

'Why?'

'It was her leaping-off point this trip. Someone may know something.'

'Special Branch already sent someone.'

'What? Some detective from New Scotland Yard? Spoke French did he? What was he looking for? How long was he there?'

Still sharp, Dominic. Maybe this *will* be good for you. God knows, you're not old enough for the cottage-and-garden routine, she thought. 'I believe he stayed there overnight, and he spoke a little French.'

'One night? Dinner at his hotel and a few gifts for his mistress. He'll have listened to what the local *gendarmes* tell him, then reported it back verbatim. It's hardly what you'd call Intelligence.'

'So you think we should send one of our own?'

'Yes.' A pause. 'Send Barclay.'

'Barclay?'

'Why not? He speaks French, and travel *does* broaden the mind.'

'I thought you said you didn't like him?'

'I don't recall saying anything of the kind. Remind me to play back the tape I'm making of our conversation, just to check. No, but let's say I think he could do with some . . . training. On his feet, so to speak, rather than with them stuck beneath a terminal screen. Terminal being the operative word.'

Joyce Parry smiled at the pun, whether it was intended or not. 'I'll think about it,' she said. 'I hope you're not up to your old tricks, Dominic.'

'Old tricks?'

'Using people, getting them to run your errands.'

'I don't know what you mean.'

She saw that Barclay himself was standing in her doorway, ready to report on his meeting with Elder. 'I'd better go. Talk to you later.'

'Joyce, I'm serious about wanting to help. You know that.'

'I know. Bye.' She put down the receiver. '*Bonjour*, Michael,' she said. '*Comment ça va?*'

Greenleaf was back at his desk barely quarter of an hour when the phone call came from Folkestone. It was Chief Inspector Rennie.

'Inspector Greenleaf?'

'Yes, Chief Inspector. What can I do for you, sir?'

'Might be nothing. We've been talking with Mr Crane's employees, present and past.'

'Yes?'

'One man, a Mr McKillip, said something quite interesting. I thought you might like to talk to him yourself . . .'

It was a slow drive to Folkestone. Roadworks and holiday caravans. But Trilling had been adamant: Greenleaf should go straight away. God knew, they'd been moving through treacle these past few days, ever since the original phone call from Michael Barclay.

Mike McKillip wasn't at the police station. He'd got tired of waiting and had gone home. It took Greenleaf a further twenty minutes to locate McKillip's house from the directions given him at the police station's front desk. You take a left here, then a right at the chip shop, then third on the left past the postbox . . . What chip shop? What postbox? McKillip was watching TV when Greenleaf finally arrived, hungry and parched. McKillip lay slumped along the sagging sofa, guzzling beer from the tin. He did not offer the policeman any, nor did he bother switching off the TV, or even turning the sound down. He just kept complaining about how the firm was going to the wall now that Crane was dead, and what was he supposed to do for work around these parts, and who'd have him at his age anyway when there were younger men out there?

Mike McKillip was thirty-seven. About six foot two tall, Greenleaf would guess, and probably fifteen stones. It wasn't a *fit* fifteen stones, but it was weight, weight to be thrown about, imposing weight. Which was why George Crane had paid him twenty quid to drink in a pub one lunchtime.

'What did he tell you, Mr McKillip?'

'Just that he had to talk business with some geezer, and the geezer might turn nasty. He didn't say why or anything, just that it might turn nasty. I was supposed to stand at the bar and have a drink, not stare at them or anything, just casual like. But if anything happened . . .' McKillip punched a meaty fist down into the soft fabric of the sofa.

'And did anything happen?'

'Nah. Soon as I saw the geezer I thought, *He's* not going to give any trouble. Big . . . tall, I mean. Though I've seen more meat on a butcher's pencil.' Another huge slurp of beer. Christ, Greenleaf would murder for a drink.

'Anything else about the man?'

'Fair hair, I think. Youngish, early-thirties. Going a bit thin on top. *Seriously* thin on top, now that I think about it. They had one drink, bit of a natter. I wasn't watching particularly. The geezer wasn't to know I was there. I just did me drinking. Easiest score I've ever made, I can tell you.' A low throaty chuckle. The can was empty. He crushed it and placed it on the carpet beside three other derelict cans, then gave a belch.

'Did Mr Crane say anything afterwards?'

McKillip shook his head. 'Looked pleased as punch though, so I asked him if it had all gone off all right after all. He said yeah, it was fine. That was the end of it, far as I was concerned.' He shrugged. 'That's all.'

'Which pub was this?'

'The Wheatsheaf.'

'At lunchtime, you say?'

'That's right.'

'Would you know the man again, Mr McKillip?'

'No sweat. I've got a memory for faces.'

Greenleaf nodded, not that he believed McKillip . . . not as far as he could throw him. He was desperate to be out of here, desperate to assuage both thirst and hunger. He swallowed drily. 'You hadn't seen him before?'

'Nor since.'

'How was the meeting arranged?'

'I don't know. Christ, man, I was just the muscle. I wasn't the boss's lawyer or anything.'

'And you didn't see anything change hands between Mr Crane and this other man?'

'Like what?'

'Anything. A parcel, a bag, some money maybe . . .?'

'Nah, nothing. They'd cooked something up all right though. The gaffer was chipper all that afternoon and the next day.'

'When was this meeting exactly, Mr McKillip?'

'God, now you're asking . . . No idea. Weeks ago.'

'Weeks?'

'Well, a couple of weeks anyway, maybe more like a month.'

'Between a fortnight and a month. I see. Thank you.'

'I told them down the station. I said, it's not much. Not worth bothering about. But they had to report it, they said. You come down from London?' Greenleaf nodded. McKillip shook his head. 'That's my taxes, you know, paying for all this farting about. Not that I'll be paying taxes much longer. *You'll* be paying my dole instead. That wife of his is winding the company up. Bloody shame that. If there'd been a son . . . maybe he could have made a go of it, but not her. Bloody women, you can't trust them. Soon as your pocket's empty, they're off. I'm speaking from experience, mind. Wife took the kids with her, back to her mum's in Croydon. Good luck to her. I like it fine here . . .'

'Yes,' said Greenleaf, rising from the tactile surface of his armchair, 'I'm sure you do, Mr McKillip.'

McKillip wished him a good drive back as Greenleaf made his exit. He got back in his car but stopped at the first pub he saw and drank several orange juices, using them to wash down a cheese and onion sandwich. Too late, he remembered that Shirley hated it when his mouth tasted of onion. Afterwards, he headed back to the police station where he made arrangements for an artist to make an appointment with McKillip. They'd get a sketch of the stranger in the pub. It might come in handy. Then again . . . Still, best to be thorough. Christ knows, if Doyle had come down here, he'd return to London with an oil painting of the man.

In his flat, Michael Barclay was busy packing for the trip to Calais. He'd pack one item, then have to sit for a while to ponder the same question: why me? Those two words bounced around in his brain like cursors gone mad. Why me? He couldn't figure it out. He tried not to think about it. If he continued to think about it, he'd be sure to forget something. He switched on the radio to take his mind off it. There was music, not very good music, and then there was news. It included a story about some banker murdered in his bed. Barclay caught mentions of handcuffs and glamorous models. Well, you could tell what *that* particular dirty banker had been up to, couldn't you? Handcuffs and models . . . some guys had all the luck.

Michael Barclay went on with his packing. He decided to take his personal cassette-player and some opera tapes. It might be a long crossing. And he tried out a few sentences in French, desperately recalling the work he'd done for A Level (C grade pass). Christ, that had been seven years ago. Then he had a brainwave. On the bookshelves in his study, he eventually tracked down an old French grammar book and a pocket French-English dictionary, both unused since schooldays. They, too, went into his case. He was pausing for coffee when he caught the next lot of news headlines. It seemed the banker had been found *handcuffed* to the model, that she'd been hysterical and was now under heavy sedation. Michael Barclay whistled.

Then he zipped up his case.

Tuesday 9 June

When Greenleaf arrived in the office that morning, Doyle was waiting to pounce.

'You are not going to believe this,' he said. 'I could give you five thousand guesses and you still wouldn't guess.'

'What?'

Doyle just leered and tapped the side of his nose. 'The Commander wants us in his office in five minutes. You'll find out then.'

Greenleaf suffered a moment's panic. He was going to be carpeted for something, something he either hadn't done or didn't know he had done. What? But then he relaxed. Doyle would have said something, something more than he'd hinted at. And besides, they hadn't put a foot wrong so far, had they? They'd set up the Folkestone operation, and they'd made good progress with the list of possible assassination hits. They'd started with 1,612 names on the list: 790 individuals (MPs, military chiefs, senior civil servants, prominent businessmen, etc.), 167 organisations or events (such as the summit meeting), and 655 buildings and other landmarks, everything from Stonehenge to the Old Man of Hoy.

This was an extensive, but not an exhaustive, list. It had been designed by the Intelligence department known as 'Profiling' to encompass the most likely terrorist targets in the UK. The details of Witch sent by Joyce Parry to Special Branch had also gone to Profiling, and they'd used these details to begin whittling the list down. Events and individuals were Witch's specialities; even at that she usually targeted an individual at an event rather than the event itself. Profiling had spoken by phone with Dominic Elder, who had agreed with their assessment. They were looking for an event, where a specific individual would be targeted.

Usually, a sitting of Parliament would be top of the list. But not this month. This month London was hosting something even bigger, and Greenleaf himself had compiled a report on its security.

Doyle had pointed out though that they couldn't know there was an assassin actually at large until *after* a hit had been attempted, successful or not. All they had so far was theory, supposition, and precious little fact. All they had was coincidence. Joyce Parry and her department had been at their cagiest. What reports had been sent over were full of 'might haves' and 'could bes' and 'ifs'. Riddled, in other words, with get-out clauses. Only Elder seemed sure of his ground, but then it was all right for him, he was out of the game.

Greenleaf mentioned this again as he waited with Doyle outside Commander Trilling's door. Doyle turned to him and grinned.

'Don't worry, John. We've got confirmation.'

'What?'

But Doyle was already knocking on and simultaneously opening the door.

'Come in, gentlemen,' said Commander Trilling. 'Sit down. Has Doyle told you, John?'

Greenleaf cast a glance towards his 'partner'. 'No, sir,' he said coldly. 'He's not seen fit to let me into the secret.'

'No secret,' said Trilling. 'It was on last night's news and it'll be on today's. Well, the bare facts will be. We've got a little more than that.' He glanced over a sheet of fax paper on his desk. 'A man's been murdered. A banker, based in London.'

'Murdered, sir?'

'Assassinated, if you like. No other motive, certainly not burglary. And the world of business espionage doesn't usually encompass slaughter.'

'Killed to order then.'

'You could say that,' Doyle said. He sat well back on his chair, with legs apart and arms folded. He looked like he was having a good time.

'Who was he exactly, sir?' asked Greenleaf.

'A Mr Khan, senior banking official for a small foreign bank based in London.'

Greenleaf nodded. 'I heard it on the radio. Killed up in Scotland, wasn't he?'

'Yes, he has a house up there, near . . .' Trilling examined the fax sheet again. 'Auchterarder,' he said, and looked up at Greenleaf. 'Gleneagles, that sort of area.'

'"Senior banking official" you said. What precisely does that mean, sir?'

Trilling sighed, exhaling peppermint. 'We're not sure. Nobody seems to know what Mr Khan's role was in this bank of his. Serious Fraud Office investigated the bank, but even they're not sure.'

'He was a fixer,' said Doyle bluntly.

'I'm not sure that description takes us much further,' Trilling complained. 'Whatever his job entailed, it seems to have made him enemies.'

'How professional was the hit, sir?'

'Very.'

'But not without its funny side,' added Doyle.

Greenleaf looked at Trilling. 'Funny?'

'Doyle has a strange sense of humour,' muttered Trilling. 'The murder took place sometime during Sunday night. Mr Khan was due to fly back to London yesterday morning. He has a cleaning lady tidy up after him—'

'Wiping the leftover coke off the hand-mirror, that sort of thing,' said Doyle.

Trilling ignored the interruption. 'A Mrs MacArthur tidies for him. She has her own key. But she was surprised to arrive at the house yesterday afternoon and find Mr Khan's car still in the drive. She went inside. There was no noise, but as she climbed the stairs she could hear sounds of a struggle in the room occupied by Mr Khan's chauffeur—'

'Bodyguard,' said Doyle.

'—a Danish gentleman. She went into his room and found him handcuffed to his bed, and trying desperately to free himself. He'd been gagged.'

'*And* he was stark bollock naked,' added Doyle.

'She didn't have any way of freeing him, so she went in search of Mr Khan. She suspected a robbery, and there was a phone in Mr Khan's bedroom. When she arrived, she found Mr Khan's girlfriend weeping and frantic. One of her wrists had been chained to the bedpost. The other was handcuffed to one of Mr Khan's wrists. Mr Khan himself was dead, tongue cut out and throat cut. The poor girl had to wait for police to release her. She's under sedation in hospital.'

'Christ,' said Greenleaf.

Doyle was chuckling. 'Isn't it a beauty? It'll be all over the papers. You couldn't keep it quiet if you tried. Blonde beauty driven mad in corpse-chaining horror. That's what the assassin wants, of course.'

'Why?' Greenleaf asked numbly.

'Easy,' said Doyle. 'It's a message, isn't it? Like sticking a horse's head in somebody's bed. Shock value. It scares people off.'

'But scares them off what?'

Trilling cleared his throat. 'I heard from Mrs Parry earlier this morning. It seems that her organisation had been . . . using Mr Khan.'

'Using him?'

'As a source of information. Mr Khan was skimming a certain amount from his bank without anyone's knowledge. Parry's agents found out and Khan was . . . persuaded to exchange information for silence.'

'Complicity,' corrected Doyle.

'That's a long word for you, Doyle,' warned Trilling. 'I'd be careful of long words, they can get you into trouble.'

'Come on, sir, it's the oldest blackmail scam in the book. Sex and money, the two persuaders.' Doyle turned to Greenleaf. 'Khan's bank's been laundering money for years. Terrorist money, drug money, all kinds of money. Parry's lot have known about it for just about as long as it's been going on. But it's *convenient* to have a dirty bank, just so long as you can keep tabs on its business. That way you know who's doing what to whom, how much it's making them, and where the money's going. They've had Khan in their pocket for over a year.'

'So Khan feeds titbits of information . . .'

'In return for Parry's lot keeping quiet about his skim. Nice and easy, and nobody gets hurt.'

'Unless you're found out,' said Greenleaf.

'Unless you're found out,' agreed Trilling. 'If you're discovered – or even simply *believed* – to be an informant, suddenly you've got a lot of enemies. Ruthless enemies, who will pay not only for your elimination, but will demand something more.'

'A very public execution,' said Doyle.

'To scare off other potential informers,' Greenleaf added, completing the deductive process.

'Exactly,' said Trilling. 'We can't know which particular group of investors ordered the assassination, but we can be pretty sure that they wanted it to be newsworthy, and newsworthy they got.'

'And we think the assassin is Witch?' Greenleaf surmised. Trilling shrugged his shoulders.

'There's no modus operandi for us to identify the present hit against. The killer was clever and well informed. An alarm and a window were taken out, a fit young man overpowered. What we do know, from the Dane, is that we're looking for a woman.'

'Description?'

Trilling shook his head. 'It was dark. He didn't see anything.'

Doyle leered again. 'She didn't chain two wrists and two ankles to bedposts in the dark without him waking up. It was a sucker-punch, sir.'

'That's not what the Dane says.'

'With respect, sir, bollocks to what the Dane says. He was awake, and she suckered him.'

'How?' asked Greenleaf. Doyle turned towards him so suddenly, Greenleaf knew he'd been waiting for the question to be asked.

'A woman comes into your bedroom and says she wants to tie you up. You fall for it. Why? Because you think she's got some rumpy in mind. The stupid bugger's supposed to be a bodyguard, and he lets some bird he's never seen before tie him to a bed. Sucker punch. Maybe she slipped him a couple of thousand on the side, make the whole thing more . . . palatable.'

'There you go again, Doyle. Stick to *short* words.' Trilling shifted in his chair. 'But we're checking him anyway. We don't think he was in on it, but you can never be sure. He did receive a nasty blow to the head, not far off being fatal according to the hospital.'

'What else have we got, sir?'

'Not much. Not yet. But the assassin did leave some clues behind.'

'What sorts of clue?'

'Things required to do the job. The handcuffs for a start, six pairs. You don't just place an order for six pairs of handcuffs without someone raising an eyebrow. Then there was some . . .'

'Sticky-backed plastic,' offered Doyle helpfully. 'That's what they used to call it on *Blue Peter*.'

'Probably bought locally. There's a murder team busy at the scene. They'll do what they can, ask around, check the various shops . . .'

'You don't sound too hopeful, sir.'

'I'll admit, John, I'm not. This was a pro, albeit one with a warped sense of humour. She won't have left many *real* clues, though Christ knows how many red herrings we'll find. And even if we trace the stuff back to a shop, what will we get? A general description of a female. She can change her looks in minutes: wig, hair-dye, make-up, new clothes . . .'

Shape-changer, thought Greenleaf. What did you call them? Proteus? Now that he thought of it, why weren't there more women con artists around? So easy for them to chop and change disguises: high heels and low heels, padding round the waist or in the bra, hair-dye . . . yes, a complete identity change in minutes. Trilling was right.

'But at least now, sir,' he offered, 'we know we *are* dealing with a woman, and we know she *did* land in the country. At least now we've got two facts where before we only had guesses.'

'True,' agreed Commander Trilling.

'But at the same time,' added Doyle, 'she's finished her job before we've even had half a chance. She could already be back out of the country.'

'I don't think so,' Greenleaf said quietly. Doyle and Trilling looked at him, seeking further explanation. He obliged. 'You don't hire an outside contractor for a single hit like this. And nobody's going to blow up two boats just because they're on a job to bump off a solitary banker. It has to be bigger, don't you think?'

'You've got a point,' said Trilling.

'I've trained him well, sir,' added Doyle. 'Yes, doesn't make much sense, does it? Unless the whole thing is one *huge* red herring, keeping us busy up in Jockland while Witch is busy elsewhere.'

'Could be,' said Greenleaf. 'But there's something else in one of those reports, the ones Mrs Parry sent over. Something said by that man Elder. He points out that Witch often kills for money in order to finance another operation. What is it he says?' Greenleaf threw his head back, quoting from memory. 'To finance her "pursuit of a pure terrorism, untainted by monetary, political or propaganda gain".' He shrugged self-effacingly. 'Something like that.'

'As I say, sir,' Doyle said to Trilling with a wink, 'I've trained him well.' And turning to Greenleaf: 'You're doing fine, John. Just remember who it was taught you everything you know.'

'How can I forget?' said Greenleaf.

The final edition of the day's *Evening Standard* ran with the story, as did other evening papers throughout the country. In Edinburgh and Glasgow, copies of those cities' evening offerings were snapped up. Radio news expanded on their previous day's coverage of the murder. Nor did television show much restraint as more details were leaked. Diversions had to be set up either end of the lane, to stop the curious blocking the road outside Khan's house.

In the field across from the house, a sky-platform, the sort used by firemen tackling fires and by council workers changing the lightbulbs in street-lamps, stood parked beneath a telegraph pole. The platform had been elevated to the height of the top of the pole, so that two CID men (afraid of heights and gripping on to the safety bar) could be shown by a British Telecom engineer just how the alarm wires from Khan's house had been severed. Prior to this, forensic scientists had taken the juddering trip to the top of the pole, dusting the junction box and photographing sections of the wooden pole itself, picking out the holes made by climbing-spikes and the chafing of the wood made by some sort of harness. The engineer was clear in his own mind.

'It was another telephone engineer,' he told the murder squad detectives. 'Had to be. He had all the gear, and he knew just what he was doing.' The detectives didn't bother telling him that he'd even got the sex wrong. They were keen to get back to Dundee, back to their watering holes where ears would be keen to hear the details. They pitied their poor colleagues who'd been sent to track down Fablon and garden twine, leaving no general store or garden centre unturned. But at least garden centres were sited on terra firma, and not forty feet up in the air . . .

In London, Joyce Parry sat in a railway station buffet, drinking tea and deep in thought. During her many telephone conversations that day and the evening before, no one had uttered much by way of condolence regarding Khan. He was a loss, but only as a merchantable item, not as a human being. His information had been useful, of course, but it could be gained in other ways. GCHQ already provided a lot of data – Khan's snippets had often served only to confirm or consolidate what was already known. Intelligence services in other countries, for example, passed on information about the bank's operations abroad. Joyce Parry hoped the bank would not find itself in trouble because of Khan. One bad apple shouldn't be allowed to . . . She'd already had to divert the attention of the Serious Fraud Office. If the drug barons and crime cartels moved their money out of the bank . . . well, then the security services would have to start all over again, locating the new bank, shifting spheres of operation so that the new bank was part of the orbit. Time-consuming, expensive, and prone to losses.

No, Joyce Parry hoped things would stay as they were. She hoped upon hope.

And she drank her tea, though 'tea' was not the most suitable description for the liquid in front of her. On the menu the drink was described as fresh-leaf tea. Well, it had been fresh once upon a time, she supposed, in some other country.

After her hectic morning – so many people who needed to be notified of Khan's demise and of the manner of his dying – she'd found time in her office for a moment's reflection . . . again, curiously enough, over a cup of tea. She'd reflected, then she'd made yet another call.

To Dominic Elder.

'Dominic, it's Joyce.'

'Ah, Joyce, I was beginning to wonder . . . Can I assume something has happened?'

'A killing.'

'Someone important?'

'No.'

'Someone murdered to order?'

'Yes.'

'I thought that's how it would be. She's just earned the money she needs for her own future hit.'

'What makes you so sure it was Witch?'

'You wouldn't have phoned otherwise.'

She'd smiled at that. So simple. 'Of course,' she'd said. 'Well, it was a woman. We don't have a description.'

'It wouldn't matter if you did,' he said calmly.

'No.'

'So what now?'

'Special Branch are checking—'

'Yes, fine, but what now?' The voice not so calm any more. 'The police can check till Doomsday. They'll find only as much as she wants them to.'

'You don't think Witch's job is finished?'

'Joyce, I don't *think* it's even begun . . .'

The door of the buffet opened, interrupting her reverie. He was carrying a suitcase which he placed on the floor beside her booth before sliding on to the seat opposite her.

'Hello, Joyce. I was expecting more of a welcome.'

'Your train's early. I was going to wait for you on the platform.'

He smiled. 'I was being ironic.'

'Oh.' She looked down at her hands. They lay palms down on the tabletop, either side of her cup. Then she slid one of them across the table towards him and lightly touched his fingers. 'It's nice to see you again, Dominic.'

'Nice to be here. How's the tea?'

She laughed. 'Terrible.'

'Thought as much. What about a drink?'

'A drink?'

'It's what people do in pubs.'

'A drink.' She thought for a moment. 'Yes, all right.'

'You can even treat me to dinner if you like.'

She almost winced. 'Sorry, Dominic, previous engagement.'

'Oh.'

'Official business. I can't worm out of it this late on.'

'No problem. I shall dine alone in the teeming city. Is Delpuy's still open?'

'Delpuy's? God, I don't know. I mean, I haven't been there in – well, since well, not for ages.'

'I'll give it a try. Did you find me a room?'

'Yes. Quite central, quite reasonable. I can drop you off if you like.'

'Is there time for that drink?'

'Just about.'

'Then what are we waiting for?' He slid back out of the booth. She pushed the tea aside and stood up too. For a moment they were inches apart, facing one another. He leaned towards her and pecked her on the cheek before picking up his case. 'After you,' he said.

Making to unlock her car-boot, she dropped her keys and had to bend to pick them up. Elder was asking her a question, but she didn't catch it.

'Sorry?' she said.

'I said, who's my contact at Special Branch?'

'Contacts. There are two of them, Doyle and . . . Greenleaf, I think the other one's called.' She thought again of the tea, fresh-leaf. A bit like green-leaf . . . She unlocked the boot and opened it. Elder heaved in his case.

'I've heard of Doyle. He's pretty good, isn't he?'

'I wouldn't know. They both work for Trilling.' She slammed shut the boot.

'Bill Trilling? Jesus, is he still around?'

'Very much so. I should warn you, he's not best pleased with us just at the minute. I'll tell you about it en route.' She unlocked the car and eased herself into the driver's seat, fumbling in her bag for her glasses. As they fastened their seatbelts, their hands touched. She started as though from a static shock. She couldn't help it. She'd thought she could handle this with her usual . . . well, whatever it was. But it was turning stupid. Meantime, Elder had asked another question.

'Sorry?' she said.

'Trouble with your ears, Joyce? That's twice I've had to repeat myself. I said, how's young Barclay getting on?'

'I don't know. Okay, I suppose.' She started the car. The sooner she'd delivered him to his hotel room, the better.

Better for all concerned.

'You sent him, didn't you?' He framed it as a question, but really it was a statement.

'Yes,' she said, reversing the car out of its parking space. 'I sent him.'

'Good.'

'Let's get one thing straight from the start, Dominic. You're here in a consultative capacity. I don't want you going rogue, and I don't want you . . .'

'Manipulating others to serve my needs? Dumping them afterwards?' He was quoting from memory; she'd given him this speech before. 'You're prejudging me, Joyce.'

'On past experience.' She felt more confident now, more like herself. She knew that given free rein Dominic would have the whole department looking for ghosts. He'd tried it before. 'Why the interest in Barclay?'

'*Am* I interested?'

'You wanted him sent to France. That smacks of the old Dominic Elder.'

'Maybe he reminds me of someone.'

'Who?'

'I'm not sure. Tell me about our friend Khan.'

Elder listened as she spoke, his eyes on the world outside the car. A tedious evening might lie ahead, and he had grown to loathe London, yet he felt quite calm, quite satisfied for the moment. He rubbed against the back of the seat. When Joyce had finished talking he was thoughtful for a moment.

'The model interests me,' he said.

'How so?'

'Witch must have had inside information. She knew where Khan was going to be, and she seems to have known he'd have company. It can't have been the bodyguard, she damned near killed him. We should be asking questions about the model.'

'Okay. Anything else?'

'Just the obvious question really.'

'And what's that?'

He turned to her. 'Where exactly did they find Khan's tongue?'

Calais was grim. Bloody French. They waited, seemingly with infinite patience, while he tried in his stumbling French to ask his questions, then it turned out half of them spoke English anyway. They would stare at him and explain slowly and carefully that an English policeman had already asked them these questions before. One of them had even had the gall to ask, at the end of a particularly fraught session, if Barclay wasn't going to ask him about the financial affairs of the sunken boat's skipper.

'The other policeman,' explained the Frenchman, 'he thought this was a very important question to ask.'

'Yes,' said Barclay through gritted teeth, 'I was just getting round to it.'

'Ah,' said the Frenchman, sitting back, hands resting easily on thighs. There could be no doubt in anyone's mind: this young man was a tyro, sent here for some mysterious reason but certainly not to gain any new information. There was no new information. Monsieur Doyle, the boisterous drinks-buying Englishman, had covered the ground before. Barclay didn't feel like a tyro. He felt like a remould tyre – all the miles had been covered before he'd appeared on the scene. He was driving an old circuit, a loop. No one could understand why. Not even Barclay.

Well, maybe that wasn't exactly true. At first, despite his puzzlement, he'd felt pleased. He was being trusted on a foreign mission, trusted with expenses and with back-up. He was going 'into the field'. He couldn't help feeling that Dominic Elder was somewhere at the back of it. Then he saw what it was, saw what was behind the whole thing.

He was being punished.

Joyce Parry was punishing him for having gone behind her back to Special Branch in the first place. He had blotted his copybook. And his punishment? He would follow in the footsteps of a Special Branch officer, unable to find fresh or missed information, expendable.

Yes, there was no doubt about it. This was the penance expected of him. So he kept his teeth gritted as he went about his business.

'But the other policeman, Monsieur Doyle, he already ask this!'

'Yes, but if you could just tell me again what it was that made you . . .'

All day. A long and exhausting day. And not a single grain of evidence or even supposition to show for it. There wasn't much to the centre of Calais. It had taken him an hour to explore what there was. There wasn't much to the centre, but the place stretched along the coast, a maze of docks and landing bays, quaysides, jetties and chaotic buildings, either smelling of fish or of engine oil.

That's why it had taken him so long to track down the people he wanted to question: the boatmen, the port authorities, people who'd been around and about that evening when the boat carrying Witch had chugged out to sea. It was no wonder the men he spoke to weren't enthusiastic, when he himself showed about as much enthusiasm as a netted cod. In short, he'd completed a poor day's work, and still with a number of people on his list, not yet found. He'd try to wrap it up tomorrow morning. Before lunchtime. The sooner the better.

It was six now. He'd been warned that the French did not eat dinner before eight o'clock. Time for a shower and a change of clothes back at his hotel. Really, he should head back out to the docks after dinner: there were a couple of names on his list who worked only after dark and whose home addresses no one seemed willing to divulge.

'*Sur le bleu,*' one man had told him, tapping finger against nose. On the blue: the French equivalent of the black economy. These men would work for cash, no questions asked or taxes paid. Maybe they had daytime jobs. But they were on the sidelines. Doyle had spoken with them and learnt nothing. How could men working '*sur le bleu*' afford to see anything or hear anything? They didn't exist officially. They were non-persons at the docks. All of this Doyle had put in his report, a report Barclay had read. It was a thorough report, certainly as good as the one Barclay himself would write. But it was also a bit pleased with itself, a bit smug: I've covered everything, it seemed to suggest, what did you expect me to find?

Barclay's hotel lay in a dark, narrow street near the bus terminus. There was a small piece of waste ground nearby which served as a car park (at each car owner's risk). Barclay had taken out European insurance before crossing the Channel, and he half-hoped someone *would* steal his creaky Fiesta with its malfunctioning gearbox. To this end, he gathered together his opera tapes and carried them in a plastic bag. He didn't mind losing the car, but he didn't want his tapes stolen too . . .

His hotel was in fact the two floors over a bar, but with a separate smoked-glass door taking residents up the steep staircase to the rooms. He'd been given a key to this door and told that meals were served in the bar. Between the smoked-glass door and the stairs there was another door of solid wood, leading into the bar. He paused, having pressed the time-controlled light-switch, illuminating the staircase with its grey vinyl wallpaper. He could nip into the bar for a drink: a cognac or a pastis. He could, but he wouldn't. He could hear locals in there, shouting the odds about something, their voices echoing. Two or three of them, the bar empty apart from them. He started to climb the stairs, and was halfway up when the lights went off.

He wasn't in complete darkness. A little light came from the downstairs door. But not much. There was another light-switch on the landing, just beside the huge potted plant and the framed painting of some anthropomorphic dogs playing pool. He climbed slowly, hand brushing against the horrible wallpaper with bristly vertical stripes, more like carpeting than anything else. The sort of carpeting that gave you an electric shock if you wore the wrong kind of shoes. Just along the wall a little . . . light-switch somewhere around here . . . ah, yes, just . . .

His fingers pressed against something. But it wasn't the switch. It was warm, soft, yielding. It was a hand. He started and almost fell back down the stairs, but another hand grabbed his arm and pulled him upright. At the same time, the lights came back on. The hand his own hand had touched had already been resting on the light-switch. He found himself facing a young woman, small, with short black hair and very red lips. Her face was round and mischievous. She smiled wryly.

'Pardon,' she said: the French word, not the English. He attempted a light laugh which came out as a strangled snuffle. Then she brushed past him and descended the staircase. He watched her go. She was wearing baggy trousers and a sort of cotton blouson, the trousers dark blue and the blouson sky blue. And lace-up shoes, quite rugged things. Her fingers touched the stair-rail as she went. At the bottom, unexpectedly, she turned back and caught him looking at her, then opened not the door to the street but the one leading into the bar. The voices from inside were amplified for a moment, then the door closed again, muffling them.

'Christ,' he said to himself. He walked unsteadily along the corridor and was just trying to fit his room-key into the lock when the lights went out yet again.

Inside the room, he threw his bag of cassettes on to the carpet and sat down on the springy bed. Then he lay back across it, left hand gripping right wrist and both resting on his forehead. He should make a start on his report, at least get his notes in order. But he kept seeing the girl in his mind. Why had she given him such a start? He managed to smile about it after a bit, rearranging his memory of the incident so that he came out of it in a better light. Well, at least he hadn't tried to say anything in his inimitable French.

He had a shower, humming to himself all the time, then dried himself briskly and lay back down on the bed again. After a moment's thought, he reached down beneath the bed and pulled out a bulging cardboard document wallet marked in thick felt pen with the single word WITCH. It had arrived by motorbike courier at his flat in London, less than half an hour before he'd been due to leave to catch the ferry. A large padded envelope, and the helmeted rider saying: 'Sign here.' He'd torn the envelope open, not knowing what to expect – certainly not expecting Dominic Elder's crammed but meticulously organised obsession. There was a note pinned to the dog-eared flap: 'I have the feeling your need will be greater than mine. Besides, I know it by heart. I'll be in touch. Good luck. Elder.'

Biked all the way from deepest south Wales to London. The bike charges must have been phenomenal, but then Barclay surmised that the department would be paying.

He'd read through the file on the trip across the Channel. It contained plenty of detail; the only thing missing was factual evidence that any of the operations and incidents outlined in two dozen separate reports had anything to do with an individual codenamed 'Witch'. It seemed to Barclay that Dominic Elder had latched onto any unsolved assassination, any unclaimed terrorist outrage, and had placed the name Witch beside it. A woman seen fleeing the scene . . . a telephone call made by a female . . . a prostitute visited . . . a girl student who disappeared afterwards . . . these shadowy, ephemeral figures all turned into the same person in Elder's mind. It smacked of psychosis.

Barclay wondered why. He wondered what had spurred Elder on, why had the mere *idea* of Witch gripped him in the first place? He got the feeling Elder knew more than he was saying. Flicking through the file for a second time, he caught a single mention of Operation Silverfish. It was noted in passing, no more. Operation Silverfish. No clue as to what it was, just that it had occurred two years before. The year, in fact, that Elder had 'retired' from the department. The year, too, that Barclay had joined: they'd missed one another by a little over five weeks. A slender gap between the old and the new. He would ask someone about Silverfish when he got back. Joyce Parry perhaps, or Elder. It might be that he could access the operation file without prior consent anyway. He'd be back tomorrow, back to the reality of technology, back to his role as Intelligence Technician.

His phone buzzed. This in itself was surprising: the apparatus looked too old to be functional. He picked up the receiver.

'Hello?'

'Barclay? It's Dominic Elder. I said I'd be in touch.'

'How did you get my . . . ?'

'Joyce passed it along. I'm in London now. Anything to report?'

'Nothing Special Branch haven't already found.'

'Flagging already, eh?'

Barclay bristled. 'Not at all.'

'Good. Listen, Special Branch are policemen, they've got policemen's minds. Don't get stuck in their rut.'

Barclay smiled at the image, remembering his retread tyre. 'You'd advise lateral thinking then?'

'No, just *deep* thinking. Follow every idea through. All right?'

'All right.'

'I'll call again tomorrow. And listen, don't tell Mrs Parry. It would only get us both into trouble.'

'I thought you said she'd given you this number?'

'Well, she told me which hotel you were in. I found the number for myself.'

Barclay smiled again. Then he remembered something. 'I've been reading the file, I wanted to ask you about Operation Silver—'

'Talk to you soon then. 'Bye.'

The connection was dead. It was as though Elder simply hadn't heard him. Barclay put the receiver back. He was quite getting to like Dominic Elder.

He had brought a couple of paperbacks with him, expecting to have time to kill. He'd been struggling with one of them for weeks, Thomas Pynchon's *Gravity's Rainbow*. A computer buff friend had recommended it. He'd unpacked the book and left it on the bedside cabinet, beside his French Grammar and travel alarm. He picked up the book now. He still had an hour before wandering off in search of dinner. Maybe he could pick up the thread of Pynchon.

He opened it where his leather bookmark rested. Jesus, was he really only up to page forty-nine? He read halfway down the page, sure that he'd read this before. He was much further on . . . page sixty-five or seventy at least. What was the bookmark doing left at a page he'd read before? He thought for a couple of minutes. Then he examined the corners of the book. There was a slight dent to the bottom right hand corner of the cover, and to a few of the pages after it. The book had been bought new, pristine. The dent was the kind made by dropping a book. Picking it up to flip through it . . . dropping it . . . the bookmark falling out . . . replaced at random . . .

'Jesus,' he said, for the second time in an hour.

Dressed for dinner, in lightweight cream suit and brown brogues, white shirt and red paisley tie, Barclay opened the door to the bar. It was busier, five men leaning against the bar itself and deep in discussion with the hotelier who filled glasses as he spoke. Barclay smiled and nodded towards him, then made for a table. There was only one other person seated, the young woman from the landing. He pulled out a chair from opposite her and sat down.

'Do you mind if I join you?' he asked.

'*Comment? Vous êtes anglais, monsieur?*'

'*Anglais, oui.*' He stared at her without blinking. 'Are you staying here, *mademoiselle? Restez-vous ici?*'

She appeared not to understand. The hotelier had come to the table to take Barclay's order. '*Une pression, s'il vous plaît.*' Barclay's eyes were still on her. 'Would you like another?' She had an empty glass in front of her. She shook her head. The hotelier moved back to the bar.

'So,' said Barclay quietly, 'did you find anything interesting in my room?'

A tinge of red came to her cheekbones and stayed there. She found that she could speak English after all. 'I did not mean to . . . I thought I would wait there for you. Then I changed my mind.'

'But we bumped into one another on the stairs. Why not introduce yourself then?'

She shrugged. 'It did not seem the right moment.'

He nodded. 'Because I would know you'd been to my room?'

'It was the book, yes?' She needed no affirmation. 'Yes, the book was stupid. I thought it would . . . pass time.'

'It was clumsy certainly.' His beer arrived. He waited till the hotelier had returned once again to the bar before asking, 'How much did you give him?'

'Nothing.' She dug into the pocket of her blouson. 'I had only to show him some identification.' She handed him a small laminated card, carrying a photograph of her with her hair longer and permed into tight curls. Her name was Dominique Herault. As she handed the card to him, he checked her fingers. She wore four ornate but cheap-looking rings; there was no ring on her wedding-finger.

'DST,' he read from the card, and nodded to himself. Direction de la Surveillance du Territoire, the French equivalent of MI5. Parry had warned him that once DST knew a British agent was on his way to France (and she would have to inform them – it was a matter of protocol) they would almost certainly send one of their agents to 'assist' him. He handed back her card. 'You're not quite what I had in mind,' he said.

'You were expecting perhaps Peter Sellers?'

He smiled. 'No, no, I was just expecting someone more . . . mature.' She raised an eyebrow. 'I mean,' he went on, 'someone older.'

'Ah,' she said. 'No, Mr Barclay, you are not senior enough to merit someone . . . older.'

'*Touché*,' he murmured, raising his glass to his lips.

Now it was Dominique Herault's turn to smile.

'So,' he went on, having swallowed the ice-cold beer, 'now that you've ransacked my room, I suppose that puts us on a footing of mutual trust and cooperation.'

'I was only—'

'Waiting for me. Yes, you said. Forgive me, but in Britain we normally wait *outside* a person's room. We don't break and enter.'

'Break? Nothing was broken. Besides, MI5 is famous for its breaking and entering, isn't it so?'

'Once upon a time,' Barclay replied coolly. 'But we draw the line at sinking Greenpeace ships.'

'That was the DGSE, not the DST,' she said, rather too quickly. 'And it too was a long time ago. What do you say . . . water under the bridge?'

'Ironic under the circumstances, but yes, that's what we say. Your English is good.'

'Better than your French, I think. I saw the grammar book in your room. It is for children, no?'

He shifted a little, saying nothing.

Her finger drew a circle on the tabletop. 'And do you think,' she said, 'you can find anything in Calais which we might have overlooked ourselves?'

'I didn't know you were interested.'

'French people were killed, Mr Barclay. Killed by a bomb, a terrorist bomb, we think. Naturally we are interested.'

'Yes, I didn't mean—'

'So now you will answer my question: do you think you can find anything we might have overlooked?'

He shook his head.

'No,' she agreed. 'And let me make some guesses. You have been talking to . . . sailors. Just as the Special Branch agent did. You have been interviewing all the people *he* interviewed. You have read the local police report. You have been concentrating on the boat, on the people who died on it, on people who might have seen it. Yes?'

'Basically correct.'

'Yes. We made the same mistake. Not me, I was not involved at the beginning. But now I am here to . . .'

'Assist?' he offered.

'Assist, yes, I am to assist you. So, what I say to you is . . .' She leaned forward and lowered her voice. 'You are not thinking about this the right way.'

'I'm not?' He tried to keep the acid out of his voice. She was shaking her head, deaf to nuance.

'No. The way to work is backwards, backwards from the departure of the boat.'

'Yes, that's what I've been—'

'*Further* back. Much further.'

'I'm not sure I understand.'

'I will tell you.' She checked her watch. 'You are dressed to go out. You're eating out?'

'Yes.'

She was on her feet. 'I know a good restaurant. Not here, out of town a few kilometres. We can take my car.' She called over to the hotelier. 'I've told him to put my drink and yours on your bill.'

'Thank you. So kind.'

She stared fixedly at him through narrowed eyes. 'Irony?' she guessed at last.

'Irony,' he admitted.

She had a Citroën 2CV, not a recent model. The sides of the car were dented and scraped from years of Parisian lane-discipline. The suspension was like nothing Barclay had ever experienced, and she drove like a demon. The last time he'd been thrown about like this had been on a fairground ride. She yelled to him over the noise from the motor, but he couldn't make out a word. He just nodded, and smiled whenever she glanced towards him. His responses seemed enough.

By the time they arrived at what looked like someone's cottage, deep in the middle of nowhere, he felt that he would never eat again. But the smells wafting from the kitchen soon changed his mind.

'My employers' treat,' she said as they took their seats at a cramped table for two. Menus the size of the table's surface were handed to them, and she immediately ordered two Kirs before gazing over her menu at him.

'Shall I order?' she asked. He nodded his head. Her eyelashes were thick but not long. He was still trying to work out whether she dyed her hair. And her age, too, he wondered about. Somewhere between twenty-one and twenty-eight. But why not twenty or twenty-nine? She kept her head hidden behind the menu for a full minute, while he looked around him at the diners occupying every other table in the place. There had been no sign that their table had been reserved, and she'd said nothing to the waiter about a reservation, but he wondered all the same . . .

At last she put down the menu. 'You eat meat?' she asked.

'Yes.'

'Good, here in France we are still a little . . . recidivist about vegetarianism.'

'Recidivist?'

She looked appalled. 'That is not the right word?'

He shrugged. 'No idea,' he told her. 'Not only is your French better than mine, I'm beginning to wonder about your English, too.'

This remark seemed to cheer her enormously. She straightened her back and gave another red-lipped smile.

'For that,' she said, 'I order the *second* cheapest bottle of wine rather than the cheapest.'

'Your employers are very generous.'

'No, they are very literal-minded, like security organisations all over the world. Do you enjoy Thomas Pynchon?'

'I don't even *understand* Thomas Pynchon.'

Barclay was remembering that, foreign territory or not, he had the ability to charm if nothing else. She was still smiling. He thought she probably was charmed.

'Do you ever read Conan Doyle?'

'What, Sherlock Holmes? No, but I've seen the films.'

'The books, the stories, they are very different to these films. Sherlock Holmes has an exaggerated power of deductive reasoning. He can solve any case by deductive reasoning alone. To some extent, Mr Conan Doyle has a point.' She paused, suddenly thinking of something. 'The Mr Doyle from Special Branch, do you know him? Is he perhaps related to Mr Conan Doyle?'

'I don't know him, but I shouldn't think so.'

She nodded at this, but seemed disappointed all the same. 'You know,' she said, 'Mr Conan Doyle was interested in deductive reasoning, yet he also believed deeply in spiritualism.'

'Really?' said Barclay, for want of anything better to reply. He couldn't see where any of this was leading.

'Yes,' she said, 'really. I find that strange.'

'I suppose it is a little.'

The waiter had appeared, pad and pen at the ready. To Barclay's mind, it seemed to take a lot of talking for the meal to be ordered. There was much discussion, backtracking, changing of mind. And glances from both Dominique and the waiter towards him; even, at one point, a conspiratorial smile. The waiter bowed at last and retreated, accepting Barclay's unused menu from him with exaggerated courtesy. A new waitress had arrived with two glasses of Kir.

'Cheers,' said Dominique, lifting hers.

'*Santé*,' replied Barclay. He sipped, sounded his appreciation, and put the glass down. A basket of bread now arrived, courtesy of the original waiter. At a nearby table, something sizzling was being served on to two plates. The diners at surrounding tables looked eagerly, unashamedly, towards the source of the sound, then exchanged remarks about the quality of the dish. When Barclay looked back at her, Dominique was staring at him from behind her tall glass.

'So,' he said, shifting his weight slightly in the solid wooden chair, 'what were you saying about Conan Doyle?'

'Not Conan Doyle, Sherlock Holmes. Deductive reasoning. This is my point. We should be working backwards, asking ourselves questions, and deciding on probabilities. Don't you agree?'

Lateral thinking, following an idea all the way through . . . that was how Dominic Elder had put it. Barclay nodded. 'So what would *you* do?'

She leaned forwards, resting her elbows on the tabletop. 'The assassin, we think probably she is a woman, yes?'

'Agreed.'

'Now, think of this: how did she come to arrive in Calais?'

'By train or by road.'

'Correct. Which is the more probable? Road. *Perhaps* she came from Paris. But trains are very public, aren't they? While assassins are not. So, it is *more* probable that she arrived by road. Yes?'

He shrugged. 'If you say so.'

'Then either she drove or she was driven. She is said to enjoy working alone. An independent woman, self-sufficient.' She paused, waiting for his nodded agreement that she had chosen her words correctly. 'Probably therefore,' she went on, 'she did not have an accomplice. She may have hitch-hiked, or she may have driven to Calais by herself. Yes?'

'Yes.'

'Now, the easiest hitch-hiking is by lorry. Lorry drivers will more probably pick up hitch-hikers than will car drivers. I know this from experience.' A flickering smile at this, but she was too busy concentrating on her English for the smile to last. 'So,' she said, 'this woman probably either hitch-hiked by lorry or else drove here herself.'

Barclay, slow at first, was picking it up quickly. 'So we shouldn't be talking to fishermen,' he said, 'we should be talking to lorry drivers?'

'Freight terminals, haulage firms, yes. And also, we should check for abandoned vehicles. Cars left in car parks or set fire to in fields, that sort of thing. There is always the chance she arrived here by other means . . .'

'But the laws of probability dictate otherwise?'

She took a second or two translating this. 'If you say so,' she said finally, just as the tureen of soup was arriving.

Wednesday 10 June

The fair had yet to open for the day, but the front of Barnaby's Gun Stall had been unlocked and drawn back. The machine-gun had been connected to its compression pump, and it had been loaded with pellets too. Keith was now fixing a three-inch square target (half the size of the usual scorecards) to the heart of the life-size metal figure. He glanced back warily to where she was standing, balancing the gun's weight in her hand, finding its fulcrum. Rosa's girl: that's who she'd always been, Rosa's girl. Little was ever said about her. There were shrugs, and the acceptance that she had once been part of the fair. Keith couldn't remember that far back. But he knew he fancied her now. Which was why he didn't mind opening the gun range for her, even though the locals might complain about the noise this early in the day. She'd even put her two one-pound coins down on the counter.

'Don't be daft,' he'd said. But she'd shaken her head.

'Keep it, I'm quite well off at the moment.'

'Lucky for some.' So Keith had pocketed the money.

He stuck the last pin into the last corner of the target. She was already lining up the gun. He could feel its sights on him like a weight pressing the back of his head. The compressor was hissing somewhere behind him.

'Okay,' he cried. 'That's it.' And he stumbled backwards away from the silhouette.

But still she did not fire. She stood there, her eye trained along the sights, the barrel of the gun barely wavering by a millimetre. Then she pulled the trigger. There was furious noise for ten seconds, then blessed silence. Keith stared at where dust was rising from in front of the silhouette figure. The edges of the paper target were still intact, like a window-frame. But everything inside the frame had been reduced to a haze in the air.

He gave a loud whistle. 'I've never seen shooting like—'

But when he turned around she had vanished. The machine-gun was lying on its side on the counter. Keith whistled more softly this time, grinning at the target and rubbing his chin. Then he stepped forward and began carefully removing the tacks from the corners of the target. He knew exactly what he was going to do with it.

Thinking back on the evening, running the dialogue through his head, Barclay saw that there had been a great deal of competitiveness during the meal. Which wasn't to say that it hadn't been fun.

He was breakfasting – milky coffee and croissants in the hotel bar – while he waited for Dominique. She'd driven him back last night with beady determination. She was probably half his weight, yet she'd drunk the same as him during dinner. She'd dropped him off outside the hotel, waving and sounding her horn as she sped off. And he'd stood there for a moment, searching for his door-key and wondering if he should have said something more to her, should have attempted a kiss.

'Not on a first date,' he'd muttered before dragging the key out of his pocket.

A shower before breakfast, and he felt fine. Ready for the day ahead. He even noticed how a Frenchman, eating breakfast standing at the bar, dunked his croissant into his coffee. So when Barclay's croissants arrived without butter, he knew just what to do with them, and felt unduly pleased with himself as he ate.

The door opened and in breezed Dominique. Having met the hotelier yesterday, she was now on hailing terms with him, and uttered a loud '*Bonjour*' as she settled into the booth.

'Good morning,' she said.

'Hello.'

She looked as though she'd been up for hours. She had clipped a red woollen head-square around her throat with a gold-coloured brooch. The scarf matched her lipstick, and made her mouth seem more glistening than ever. White T-shirt, brown leather shoulder-bag, faded blue denims turned up at bared ankles, and those same sensible laced shoes. Barclay drank her in as he broke off a corner of croissant.

'Thank you for last night,' he said. He had rehearsed a longer speech, but didn't feel the need to make it. She shrugged.

'Come on,' she said, looking down meaningfully at his cup, which was still half full. 'We've got a lot of work ahead of us.'

'Okay, okay.'

'Now listen, I've been thinking.' She took a deep breath before continuing. 'I'm looking for my sister. That's the story I will tell to the drivers. She has run away from home and I think maybe she is heading for England.'

'That's good, we'll get their sympathy if nothing else.'

'Exactly, and they may like the idea of two sisters. It may make them remember something.'

'You're speaking from experience?' She narrowed her eyes and he nodded. 'Yes,' he admitted, 'irony, sort of.'

'Well, anyway, it's true.'

'And what role do I play?'

'You are like The Who's Tommy: deaf and dumb.'

'And blind?'

'No, but just let me do all the talking. Yes?'

'Fine by me.'

'Now *hurry up*.' And to help, she seized the last piece of croissant, drowned it in his cup, then manoeuvred the whole dripping concoction across the tabletop and into her mouth.

'Shall we take my car?' he suggested.

'I'm from Paris,' she snapped. 'Why would I be driving a British car?'

'I won't say another word,' he said, following her to the café door.

It was every bit as tiring and frustrating as the previous day, but with the bonus that *she* was doing all the work while he loitered in the background.

Dominique took the freight-men's comments and double entendres in good part, even though Barclay himself felt like smashing some of them in the mouth. But though she listened, there didn't seem much to learn. No driver knew anything. If she had a photograph of her sister, perhaps, a picture they could keep . . . ? Maybe something of the both of them in their swimming costumes . . . ?

General laughter and guttural speech, slangy, spoken at furious speed. Barclay caught about a quarter of it and understood less than that. They ate at the French equivalent of a greasy spoon: a dingy bar which, hazy with smoke, still served up a more than passable five-course meal. Barclay ate three courses, pleading that he was still full from the previous evening. From a booth in the post office in town, Dominique made several telephone calls, paying the counter staff afterwards and asking for a receipt.

Then there were more firms to check, more fake questions to ask, always to more shakes of the head and shrugs of the shoulders. He saw her spirits flag, and suddenly he knew her. He knew her for what she was. She was young and hungry like him, keen to succeed, keen to show up the flaws and weaknesses of others before her. She wasn't here to 'assist' him: she was here to make her mark, so that she could climb the rungs of the promotion ladder. Watching her work, he saw an emptiness at his own core. Watching her fail to get results, he became more determined that they shouldn't give up.

Until suddenly, at five o'clock, there were no people left to ask. They had exhausted the possibilities. Or rather, they had exhausted one seam; but there was another seam left to mine, so long as her spirits were up to it.

Over a glass of wine in a bar, he gave something equating to a pep talk. It half-worked. She agreed to give it another hour or so. Then he would take her to dinner – on *his* firm this time.

They made for the police station, and there asked at the desk about abandoned vehicles. Inspector Bugeaud, who had already spent more time than he cared to remember helping the DST, Special Branch, and Barclay, groaned when he saw them. But he was persuaded to look in the files. He came up with only two possibilities. A motorbike stolen in Marquise and pushed off a cliff several kilometres out of town, and a car stolen in Paris and found by a farmer in some woods, again several kilometres out of town.

'Stolen in Paris?' Dominique said, her eyes glinting. The Inspector nodded.

'This car,' said Barclay, 'where is it now, Inspector?'

Bugeaud checked the paperwork. 'Back with its owner,' he said.

'Was it checked for fingerprints?' Dominique asked. She had risen onto her tiptoes. Barclay got the feeling that in another location, she might actually have been jumping up and down with excitement. But here she managed to retain a measure of composure.

The Inspector shrugged. 'Why bother? It wasn't damaged, except for some paint scraped off by the trees. The owner was happy enough to know its whereabouts. End of story.'

'I don't think so,' said Dominique with a slow shake of her head. 'I don't think it's the end of the story at all, Inspector.' She turned towards Barclay. 'I think it's just the beginning.' She slapped the file. 'Can I please have a photocopy of the relevant details, Inspector? *Two* photocopies.' (Another glance in Barclay's direction.) 'No, best make it three. My superiors will want to take a look. I'll see that your help is reported back to them, too.'

'Don't bother,' said Bugeaud, retreating back upstairs to turn on the photocopier. 'I prefer the quiet life.'

That night, after another large meal, Barclay telephoned London from his room. His call was transferred to a private house – there were sounds of a loud dinner party in the background – where he was able to speak to Joyce Parry. He gave her what news he had, playing down Dominique's role, feeling only a little like a snake as he did so. She sounded thoughtful rather than enthusiastic.

'It's an interesting idea,' she said, 'a car stolen in Paris . . .'

'Yes, ma'am.'

There was silence. 'What do the DST think?' Joyce Parry asked at last.

'They're heading back to Paris to do some checking.'

'Fair enough. So you'll be back here tomorrow?'

He swallowed, ready with his story but still nervous. 'I'd rather stick close to this, ma'am,' he said. 'It seems to me that we and DST are coming at this from different angles. They're worried that Witch may have had help in France. They want to cut any future aid-route. They're not bothered by the fact that she's now in England. Left to themselves, they may not ask the right questions.'

An excruciating pause, background laughter, then: 'I see. Well, all right then, off you go to Paris. Call me from there.'

'Yes, ma'am.' *Just* keeping the excitement out of his voice.

'And don't play silly buggers with your expenses. I don't want to see receipts from the Moulin Rouge. Okay?'

She was making a joke of it. She'd believed him. Well, and why not? Dominic Elder had said it might work. Elder had called only twenty minutes ago, while Barclay and Dominique had been drinking and scheming in the hotel bar.

'Understood,' said Barclay, ringing off before she could change her mind. Dominique was waiting for him downstairs.

'Well?' she said.

He was very casual, shrugging his shoulders as he slid into the booth. 'It's settled.' He picked up his beer. 'I'm coming to Paris.'

She nodded, managing to seem neither pleased nor displeased.

'Now,' he said, 'what about a nightcap?'

She looked at him strangely. 'Nightcap?' she repeated.

'A final drink before retiring,' he explained.

'Oh.' She nodded thoughtfully. 'Yes, why not? But remember, Michael, we are not celebrating . . . not yet. These are still—'

'Probabilities, I know. But whatever they are, they're better than nothing. They're certainly better than being stuck in an office in London.' He found himself believing this, too. The office was no longer a safe haven. It seemed boring, a place without possibilities. Besides, he *had* to go to Paris, didn't he? He'd found a lead, something Doyle had missed. Who knew what else he might find if he stuck close to Dominique? It was difficult work, but someone had to do it.

'Have you ever been to Paris before?' she asked.

'Once or twice.'

'With lovers?'

'That's classified information.'

She laughed. 'I will show you Paris. You will love it.'

Barclay was signalling to the barman. 'Is that your deductive reasoning again?'

'No,' she said, finishing her drink, 'just instinct.'

Thursday 11 June

The first meeting between the two Special Branch detectives and Dominic Elder could not be considered a success. It wasn't helped by the attendance, for part of the time, of Joyce Parry and Commander Trilling, who looked to be conducting their own personal Cold War.

But it was Doyle who really set the tone. Introduced to and shaking hands with Elder, his first question was: 'So, Mr Elder, and how long have you been on the pension?'

Elder ignored this, but Doyle just couldn't let it go. His contributions to the discussion were peppered with references to 'the retired gentleman', 'the ex-agent', 'the man from the country' and so on. The more he went on, the more fixed became Elder's smile. Greenleaf tried jolting Doyle's mind on to another track, getting him to talk about Calais, about the Folkestone operation, but nothing could deter Doyle. Nothing could rob him of his simple pleasures. He even, as Elder had judged he would, came up with a crack about Elder's name: 'Perhaps,' Doyle began one loud sentence, 'I shouldn't say this in front of my *elders*, but—'

Dominic Elder had been waiting. 'Elders and betters, Mr Doyle. I believe that's the phrase.'

He wasn't smiling any more.

Greenleaf twisted in his seat as though trying to avoid a shrewdly placed drawing-pin. He had spent most of the previous evening boning up for this meeting, ensuring he was word perfect. He had learned the casenotes off by heart, wanting to look good in front of Parry and Elder. But now he seemed the unwilling referee in a tag-team wrestling match, trapped between Parry and Commander Trilling grappling in one corner of the ring, and Doyle and Elder in the other. He knew he wouldn't make any friends if he attempted to make the peace, so he sat quiet in his chair, reciting inwardly his litany of dates, times, officers' names, interviewees . . . Until finally it was too much for him. He thought he was going to burst. He did burst.

'As you know,' he began, 'we've got officers on the ground around Folkestone, stopping drivers and asking questions. Nothing as yet, but it's early days. While we're waiting, the least we could do is study the security procedures for, say, the top three targets on the list, by which I mean next week's nine-nation summit, the Houses of Parliament, and Her Majesty the Queen.'

'God bless her,' said Doyle.

'Since security is in place, and is constantly monitored and tightened around the last two, perhaps we can concentrate our efforts on the summit. I know there has already been considerable liaison between Special Branch, the security services, and the secret services of the countries taking part. But maybe if we put our heads together and study the available commentaries, we can decide a) whether the summit is a likely target for the assassin, and b) *how* she might strike. If we know how she's going to strike, we can work out *where* she's going to strike, and perhaps even *when*. As you may know, I've already done some work on the summit security arrangements, but as you also know nothing is ever the last word. In some ways, I'd even say the summit is *too* tempting a target. On the other hand, we've got this.' He waved in front of him an artist's impression of the man George Crane had met, the man described by McKillip. The others in the room had an identical xerox. 'We could concentrate our efforts on finding this customer. Maybe he'd lead us to Witch.'

Suddenly, the flow ceased. Greenleaf was himself again, and found himself looking at the intent faces around him. He swallowed. 'I . . . uh . . .' He looked to Trilling. 'That's how I see it, sir.'

'Thank you, John,' said Trilling quietly. Doyle was sitting arms folded, lips pursed, eyes on his own navel. He looked like he might laugh, might shoot his 'partner' down, but he didn't get the chance.

'They're as good as any ideas I've heard so far,' commented Elder, 'and better than most.' He nodded in Greenleaf's direction.

'Agreed,' said Joyce Parry.

'What about Khan's bodyguard and the woman?' Elder asked.

Doyle answered. 'They were interviewed in Perth.'

'Are they back in London?'

Doyle shifted a little in his seat. 'They've left Perth.'

'You can't find them?' Elder suggested.

Now Doyle sat up straight. 'The bodyguard's okay.'

'The woman then?'

Now Doyle nodded. 'She gave a false address. We're on to it though, don't worry.'

Joyce Parry saw that Elder had no more questions. 'I've another meeting to go to,' she said. 'I'd better say my piece before I go. We've got a man in Calais, Michael Barclay.'

Doyle started. 'I've already covered Calais.'

Joyce Parry ignored the interruption. 'He telephoned last night with new information.'

(Greenleaf noticed how Dominic Elder perked up at this, enjoying Doyle's discomfort. If truth be told, Greenleaf himself enjoyed it just a little, too.)

'Rather than confining himself to the details of the woman's *departure* from Calais,' Parry went on, 'Barclay concentrated on her mode of arrival at Calais.'

'I checked that,' snapped Doyle.

Again, Parry ignored him. 'He went to the local police and asked about vehicles which had been abandoned or destroyed in and around the town. The police came up with two possibilities, and one of these was a car stolen in Paris several days before and found hidden in a patch of woodland. Barclay is now on his way to Paris to . . .' (consciously, she chose Doyle's own word) '. . . to *check* the details of the theft. That's all. Now, if you'll excuse me, gentlemen.'

'Yes,' said Trilling. He rose to his feet and collected his things together. He too was due in another meeting.

Greenleaf was studying Dominic Elder. An impassive face, not old, certainly not past it despite Doyle's jibes. The problem with Doyle was, there was too much on the surface. He presented far too much of himself, or his image of himself, to the outside world. Which was dangerous, since it made him easy to 'read'. Greenleaf was willing to bet Elder could 'read' Doyle. Look at how quickly he'd come back over the elder jibe. Anticipation. He wondered just what Elder made of *him*, especially after that outburst. He didn't know what had made him do it, but he had a sneaking feeling it was all Shirley's fault. He'd been trying to concentrate all last night, concentrate on learning his facts. And she'd had the telly on – louder than necessary. He'd pleaded with her to turn it down, and she'd had a go at him.

'What's the point of all that swotting? Trying to impress the teachers, is that it, John? Give up, you're too old. That sort of stuff is for schoolboys. You're a grown man. Initiative, that's what impresses people in a grown-up. Memory-men are freaks, the sort of thing you might see at Blackpool or on the telly.' Then she'd subsided, touching his arm. 'John, love, you're not in Special Branch because you're good at studying. You're there because you're good, full stop. Now take a break from that and come and sit with me. Come on.'

It was the most she'd said to him in days, ever since the picnic really. They'd talked themselves hoarse the rest of the evening. God, what a relief it had been. But he'd lain awake long after Shirley had drifted off to sleep. He could hear her words. And he was afraid, afraid that the only thing he *was* good at was the learning and spouting of facts and figures. He'd been called a 'copper's copper' in the early days. But initiative . . . when had he ever really shown any of that? He was a 'company man', and initiative was for lone wolves like Doyle, the sort who got into all sorts of trouble but usually ended up with a result along the way. So he'd been sitting there, alternately bursting to recite his facts and desperate to show his initiative. Initiative had won, for a change . . . and no one had minded. It sounded like this Barclay character – the one who'd contacted Special Branch in the first place – it sounded like *he* was showing initiative too . . .

As Parry and Trilling left the room – not together but one after the other, with a decent pause between – Doyle handed him a scrap of paper. He unfolded it. It read: 'What are you looking so fucking smug about?'

He looked back at Doyle and shrugged his shoulders. There was no malice in the note, and no necessity for it. It was a public gesture, meant for Elder. The message to Elder was clear. It was two against one now, Doyle and Greenleaf were a team. Greenleaf didn't want this. It wouldn't help to isolate Elder. So, dropping his pen and stooping to retrieve it, he scraped his chair a little further along the table, away from Doyle, making the seating arrangement slightly more triangular. Elder noticed, but his face showed nothing. As the door closed, leaving the three of them together, there was another silence until Doyle broke it, directing his words at Greenleaf.

'Come on then, Sherlock, you seem to know all about it. What's the game plan?'

'We could start by taking a look at the Conference Centre and surrounding area.'

'Join the queue, you mean? The place is already swarming with Anti-Terrorist Branch, sniffer dogs, bomb experts . . .'

'Not to mention a few dozen ... delegates from the other countries,' added Elder.

'Yes,' agreed Doyle, 'we've already got security men checking the security men who're checking security. What more can *we* do?'

'I didn't mean to imply,' said Elder, 'that we shouldn't get involved. Everyone should be notified that Witch may pay a visit.'

'What, work them up good and proper?' Doyle was dismissive. 'They'd start shooting at shadows. The American lot are edgy as it is. Someone sent a threat to their embassy: the President gets it, that sort of thing.'

'We needn't alarm them,' said Elder quietly. 'But they should be informed.'

Greenleaf was about to agree when there was a knock at the door. It opened, and a woman announced that there was a telephone call for Mr Doyle.

'Won't be a minute,' he said, getting up and leaving the room. Only then did Greenleaf notice that the conference room itself contained no telephones. On cue, Elder seemed to read his mind.

'Phones are receivers,' he explained. 'They can be bugged.'

Greenleaf nodded at this. He did not know what he had been expecting of the building. It appeared much the same as any other civil service admin block ... or police admin block come to that. Yet it was, as Doyle had commented on the way there, CDHQ – Cloak & Dagger Headquarters.

'So,' said Elder conversationally, 'whose idea was the name?'

'The name?'

'Operation Broomstick.'

'Oh, that. Commander Trilling.'

Elder nodded. 'Bill Trilling's a tough old bull, isn't he?'

Greenleaf shrugged.

'When did he stop smoking?'

'About seven months back.'

'Remind me to buy some shares in whoever manufactures those mints of his.'

Greenleaf smiled, then checked himself. He didn't want to appear disloyal. 'The Commander's all right,' he said.

'I don't doubt it. Not slow to take offence though, wouldn't you agree?'

'Unlike Mrs Parry, you mean?'

'Oh, no, I wasn't ... never mind.'

There was quite a long pause. Elder had turned to his case-file and was browsing through it.

'How long have you been retired?' Greenleaf asked.

'Two years.' Elder's eyes were still on the file.

'Enjoying it?'

'Yes, thanks.'

'So why are you here?'

Now Elder looked up. 'Because I'm interested. I wrote the original Hiroshima summary ...'

'Yes, I know. And you've been interested in Witch ever since. If I didn't know better, I might even say you're a fan.'

Elder nodded. 'Oh, I'm a fan all right. Look at the Khan hit. Don't you find it in some way admirable? I mean, as a *professional*. There is something to admire in perfection, even when it's the perfection of the enemy. Somehow, I can't see Mr Doyle planning and executing anything with the same degree of . . . élan.'

'His bark's worse than his bite.'

'I sincerely hope not. If we *do* locate Witch, his bite will have to be very fierce indeed.' Elder wagged a finger. 'And so will yours, Mr Greenleaf. It doesn't do to ignore the facts of the Khan assassination. Witch is utterly ruthless.'

'Not *so* ruthless. She didn't kill the bodyguard and the girlfriend.'

'No, quite. I've been wondering about that.'

'Oh?'

'Leaving the bodyguard alive is the only evidence we have that the assassin *was* a woman.'

'You think she wanted us to know? That wouldn't make sense, would it?'

'I suppose not. But then blowing up both those boats hardly "makes sense".'

'Tying up loose ends? Maybe the crews knew something we don't.'

'Possibly.' Elder didn't sound enthusiastic.

'Well,' said Greenleaf, 'why *does* she want us to know she's here?'

'Maybe she's issuing a challenge.'

'To you?'

'Yes.'

'You think she knows about you?'

'Oh, she knows all right, believe me.'

'How?'

Elder shrugged.

'Then how can you be so sure?' Greenleaf persisted.

Another shrug. 'I just am, Mr Greenleaf. I just am. What you said about the summit being almost *too* tempting . . . there may be something in that.'

Another knock at the door. Someone opened the door from the corridor, and someone else bore in a tray of mugs.

'Mrs Parry said you'd likely be needing some tea,' the man announced. He placed the tray on the table. The tea was already in the mugs, but the tray also held a bowl of sugar, jug of milk, and plate of biscuits.

'Thanks, Derek,' said Elder. The man smiled.

'Didn't think you'd remember me.'

'Of course I remember you. How're things?'

'Not so bad.' The man lowered his voice a little and wrinkled his nose. 'It's not the same these days though,' he said. 'Not like it was.' His partner, waiting in the corridor with his hand still on the door handle, gave an impatient cough. The man winked at Elder. 'I'll leave you to it then,' he said, closing the door after him.

'Anyone would think you'd been retired twenty years,' Greenleaf said.

'All the same,' said Elder, lifting one of the mugs, 'he's got a point. I've only been back one full day and I've noticed changes. More machines and less staff.'

'You mean computers?' Greenleaf poured milk into his chosen mug. 'They're a boon. All the sifting that Profiling had to do to produce the target list, it only took a few hours.'

'The problem is that the operatives tend to speed up too, making errors or creating gaps, where patience and plodding really *are* necessary virtues.' Elder thought of a comparison Greenleaf could relate to. 'It's like running a murder inquiry without the door-to-door. Nothing beats actually talking to someone face-to-face. You get an inkling, don't you, whether they're telling the truth or not? I've seen people beat lie-detector tests, but I've never seen them get past a shrewd interrogator.'

'I'll take your word for it,' said Greenleaf, raising the mug to his lips.

The door burst open. This time it was Doyle. His eyes darted around excitedly, eventually alighting on the last mug of tea.

'Great,' he said. He lifted the mug and gulped from it, not bothering with milk or sugar.

'What is it?' said Greenleaf, recognising in Doyle the symptoms of some news. But knowing Doyle, it would take an age to extract the actual information.

And indeed, he shook his head as he drank, until he'd finished the tea. He went to his chair and gathered up his papers. Only then did he pause, studying the two seated figures.

'Come on then,' he said.

'Where?'

'You can stay here if you like,' Doyle said.

'For Christ's sake, spit it out, will you?'

Doyle's eyes twinkled. 'Say please.'

'Please,' said Greenleaf. Somehow, Elder was managing to stay calm and silent, nibbling on a biscuit between sips of milky tea.

Doyle seemed to consider. He even glanced over towards Elder who certainly wasn't about to say 'please'. Then he placed his papers back on the desktop and sat down again, but resting on the edge of the chair only.

'That phone call was Folkestone. They've traced a driver who says he gave a lift to a woman.'

Elder put his mug down on the table.

'Really?' said Greenleaf. 'That night? What time?'

There was a scraping sound as Dominic Elder pushed back his chair and stood up, collecting together his own sheaf of paper. 'Never mind questions,' he said authoritatively. 'We can ask those on the way. Come on.' And with that, he strode to the door and out of the room. Doyle grinned at Greenleaf.

'Thought that might get him going.'

For one stomach-churning second, Greenleaf thought Doyle had just played some monstrous practical joke. It was a hoax, there was no driver, no sighting. But then Doyle too got to his feet. 'What are you waiting for?' he called back to Greenleaf as he made for the door.

Sitting in the police station, smoking his sixteenth cigarette, Bill Moncur was regretting ever opening his mouth. It was like his mate Pat had told him: say nowt at no time to no one. When he was a kid, there'd been a little china ornament on the mantelpiece at home. It was called The Three Wise Monkeys. They sat in a row, one seeing no evil, one hearing no evil, one speaking no evil. But one day Bill had picked the ornament up, and it had slipped out of his hand, smashing on the tiles around the fireplace. When his mother came through from the kitchen, he was standing there, hand clamped to his mouth just like the third monkey, stifling a cry.

He thought of that ornament now, for some crazy reason. Maybe the same crazy reason he'd said 'yes' to the policeman's question.

'Hello, sir. We're just asking drivers about a woman who might have been hitching along this way a couple of weekends back, late on Sunday the thirty-first or early Monday the first. Don't suppose you were along this way then, were you?'

Why? Why had he opened his big mouth and said, 'Yes, I was.' Why? It was just so . . . stunning. He'd never felt important like that before, included like that. He'd been stopped before by similar checkpoints, usually trying to find witnesses to a crash or a hit-and-run. He'd never been able to help in the past. He'd never been able to involve himself. Not until now.

Say nowt at no time to no one.

See no evil, hear no evil, speak no evil.

'Yes, I was. I picked up a hitch-hiker, too. Young woman. Would that be her, do you think?'

The constable had said something like, 'Just wait there, sir,' and then had retreated, off to have a word with his superior. Right then, right at that precise moment, Bill Moncur knew he'd said the wrong thing. He'd a load to deliver to Margate, and after that he'd to head for Whitstable and Canterbury before home. A busy schedule. Why hadn't he just shaken his head and driven on? Another van, which had been stopped in front of him, now started off again. His boss would give him hell for this. Why didn't you just keep your trap shut, Bill? His van was still revving. He could scarper while the copper was out of sight. But not even Bill Moncur was *that* stupid. They were looking for a young woman. Maybe she'd gone missing, been raped. Couldn't have been the woman he picked up, could it? Must be somebody else. Oh Christ, but what if it *was* her? What if she'd been found dead in a ditch somewhere, and here he was saying he'd given her a lift. He'd be a suspect, the sort you heard about on the news. A man is helping police with their inquiries. Well, that's what *he* was trying to do, but out of public-spiritedness, not because he had anything to confess or anything to be guilty about. Okay, so he skimmed a bit off his company. He might use the van for a bit of business at nights and weekends, but never anything outrageous. Not like Pat, who'd taken *his* van over the Channel one weekend and used it for smuggling back porn mags, videos, fags and booze. It was like one of those old mobile shops in the back of Pat's van, but he'd shifted the lot before Monday morning, and with four hundred quid clear profit in his pocket. But Jesus, if he'd been caught . . . caught using the firm's van . . .

'Hello, sir.' There were two of them standing there, the constable he'd spoken to before and now this plain-clothes man, reeking of ciggies and CID. 'My colleague tells me you may have some information for us?'

'Yeah, that's right, but I'm a bit pushed just now, see. Deliveries to make. Maybe I could come into the station later on, like. Tomorrow morning, eh?'

The CID man was gesturing with his arm, as if he hadn't heard a word Bill had been saying. 'You can park just over there, sir. In the lay-by, other side of the police car. We'll have a little chat then, eh? Don't want to hold up the vehicles behind.'

So that was that. He'd shoved first gear home and started off. Even as he moved slowly forwards, he thought: I could still run for it. He shook the thought aside. He had absolutely nothing to hide. It wouldn't take him five minutes to tell them his story, and after that he could bugger off again. Maybe they'd take his name and address, maybe they'd get back to him later, but for today he'd be back on the road. With luck, he could push the speedo to 70 or 80 on some stretches, make up the time easy. Wouldn't it be funny if he got stopped for speeding? Sorry, officer, I was helping your colleagues with their inquiries and I sort of got behind on my deliveries.

He pulled into the lay-by at quarter to eleven. Now, as he sat in the police station and lit his seventeenth cigarette – seventeenth of the day – it was quarter past one. They'd brought him a filled roll, egg mayonnaise, disgusting, and a packet of spring onion crisps. By dint of putting the crisps *in* the roll, he managed to force it all down. He thought, not for the first time: On a normal run I'd be in the Feathers by now, supping a pint and tucking in to one of that big bird Julie's home-made stews. Full of succulent carrots and little bits of onion. No gristle on the meat either. Beautiful. Egg mayonnaise and bloody crisps. Bill Moncur and his big bloody mouth.

They'd let him call the office. That hadn't been much fun, even though the CID man had explained that everything was all right, that he wasn't in any trouble or anything, but that he'd have to stay at the station for a little while longer. The firm were sending someone else out, some relief driver (it might even be Pat). The van keys were at the desk. The relief would pick them up and do the run for him. The relief driver would stop at the Feathers to chat up Julie and watch the way she pulled a pint with her manicured, painted fingernails on the pump.

How much fucking longer? he said to himself. There were four empty polystyrene cups in front of him as well as the empty crisp packet, cellophane from the roll, brimming ashtray, ciggies and lighter. He used the tip of his finger to pick up a few crumbs of crisp from the desktop, transferring them to his mouth. They'd be along in a minute to ask him if he wanted more coffee. He'd tell them then: 'I'm not waiting any fucking longer. You can't keep me here. If you want me, you know where to look. I'm in the phone book.'

That's what he'd say. This time. This time he'd really say it, and not just think it. Bonny girl they'd sent in last time to ask about the coffee, mind. Took his mind off it for a moment, so that he forgot to ask in the end. No, not ask, *demand*. It was his *right* to walk out of there whenever he felt like it. He'd only been in a police station twice in his life. Once when he was thirteen, and they found him staggering pissed out of his head along the main road. They took him back to the station, put him into a cell, stood him up, and kneed him in the nuts until he threw up. Then they left him for an hour before kicking him out. Could hardly walk straight for days after that . . . which was ironic, as Pat said, since they'd picked him up in the first place for not walking straight.

That was once. The second time, they raided a pub during a brawl, and though he'd taken hardly any part in it he was dragged down to the station with the rest of them. But the barman, Milo, had put in a word for him, so they'd let him go with a caution.

That was twice. Hardly premier league, was it, hardly major crime? Were they holding him so they could look him up in their records? Maybe they were seeing if he had any priors for rape or murder or abduction or anything. Well, in that case he'd walk when they'd finished checking. How long could it take?

Of course, he did have *something* to hide. For a start, if it got back to his boss that he was out in the van on a Sunday night . . . well, bosses tended to have inquiring minds in that direction. But his boss wouldn't find out, not unless the police said anything. He could always tell them he was in his car rather than the van anyway . . . but no, it didn't do to lie when the truth wouldn't hurt. If they caught him lying, they might wonder what else he was hiding. No, he'd tell them. He was using the van to help out a friend. And indeed this was the truth. His neighbour Chas played keyboards in a sort of country and western band. They'd been playing a Sunday night gig at a pub in Folkestone, and he'd been acting as Road Manager, which meant picking up the PA from Margate and taking it back to Folkestone. It was all a fuck-up in the first place, that's why he'd had the drive to do. The band's own PA had blown half a dozen fuses or something, and a friend of Chas's who had a residency in Margate had said the band could borrow *his* band's gear on the proviso that they brought it back the same night.

Stupid, but the gear was good stuff, a few thousand quid's worth, and the guy didn't want it out of his sight overnight. So, for fifty quid and a few drinks, Bill had driven to Margate, picked up the gear, brought it to Folkestone, sat through the gig, then hauled it back to Margate again before returning to Folkestone, absolutely knackered. It was a lot of work for fifty quid, but then Chas was a mate, and besides Bill liked being a Road Manager. He'd have liked to play in a band himself had he been what you would call musical. Musical he was not. He'd tried auditioning as a vocalist once – not in Chas's band, in another local outfit – but the ciggies had shot his voice to hell. Like the band's leader said, his timing and pace were superb, and he'd plenty of emotion, but he just couldn't 'hold a tune'. Whatever that meant.

The door opened and in walked the same CID man who'd spoken to him in the lay-by.

'Well about bloody time,' said Bill. 'Listen, I can't hang around here any longer, and I'm—'

They kept filing into the room, three of them as well as the CID man. The room, which had been so empty before, now seemed overfull.

'These gentlemen have driven down from London to see you, Mr Moncur,' said the CID.

'Bit pokey in here, innit?' said one of the men. He looked to Bill Moncur like an old boxer, semi-pro. The speaker turned to the CID man. 'Haven't you got an office we could use?'

'Well . . .' The CID man thought about it. 'There's the Chief's office. He's not around this afternoon.'

'That'll do us then.'

The other two Londoners were silent. They seemed happy enough to let their colleague do the talking. They all trooped out of the interview room and along to a more spacious, airier office. Extra chairs were carried in, and the CID man left, closing the door behind him. The oldest of the three Londoners, craggy-faced and grim-looking, had taken the chair already behind the desk, a big comfortable leather affair. Moncur was sitting in the other chair already in place on the other side of the desk. He kept looking to

Craggy Face, who seemed like the boss, but he still wasn't speaking. The one who'd done all the speaking, and who now remained standing, started things off.

'We're Special Branch officers, Mr Moncur. I'm Inspector Doyle, and this' – with a nod to the third man, who had taken a seat against the wall – 'is Inspector Greenleaf. We're particularly interested in what you told Detective Sergeant Hines. Could you go through your story again for us?'

'You mean I've been kept in here waiting for you lot to arrive from London? You could have asked me over the phone.'

'We could have, but we didn't.' This Doyle was a short-fuse merchant, Moncur could see that. 'The sooner we have your story, the sooner you'll be out of here. It's not as if you're in any trouble . . .'

'Tell that to my gaffer.'

'If you want me to, I will.'

The third Londoner, Greenleaf, had picked up a briefcase from the floor and rested it on his knees. He now brought out a twin cassette-deck, an old-fashioned and unwieldy-looking thing. The other one was speaking again.

'Do you mind if we record this interview? We'll have it transcribed, and you can check it for mistakes. It's just a record so we don't have to bother you again if we forget something. Okay?'

'Whatever.' He didn't like it though. The man with the briefcase was plugging in the deck. Positioning it on the desk. Checking that it worked. Testing, testing: just like Chas at a sound-check. Only this was very different from a sound-check.

'You were out on a run in your van, Mr Moncur?' asked Doyle, almost catching him off-guard. The interview had started already.

'That's right. Sunday night it was. Last day of May.'

'And what exactly were you doing?'

'I was helping a mate. He plays in a band. Well, their PA had broken down and I had to fetch another from Margate, see. Only, after the show, the guy who owned the PA wanted it delivered back to him. So off I went to Margate again.'

'Were you alone in the van, Mr Moncur?'

'At the beginning I was. Nobody else in the band could be bothered to—'

'But you weren't alone for long?'

'No, I picked up a hitch-hiker.'

'What time was this?'

'Late. The dance the band were playing at didn't finish till after one. Then we had a few drinks . . .' He caught himself. 'I stuck to orange juice, mind. I don't drink and drive, can't afford to. It's my livelihood, see, and I don't—'

'So it was after one?'

'After two more like. After the gig, we'd to load the van, then we had a drink . . . yes, after two.'

'Late for someone to be hitching, eh?'

'That's just what I told her. I don't normally pick up hitch-hikers, no matter what time of day it is. But a woman out on her own at that time of night . . . well, that's just plain bloody stupid. To be honest, at first I thought maybe it was a trap.'

'A trap?'

'Yeah, I stop the van for her, then her boyfriend and a few others appear from nowhere and hoist whatever I'm carrying. It's happened to a mate of mine.'

'But it didn't happen to you?'

'No.'

'Tell me about the woman, Mr Moncur. What sort of—'

But now the man behind the desk, the one who hadn't been introduced, now *he* spoke. 'Before that, perhaps Mr Moncur could show us on a map?' A map was produced and spread out on the top of the desk. Moncur studied it, trying to trace his route.

'I was never much good at geography,' he explained as his finger traced first this contour line, then that.

'These are the roads here, Mr Moncur,' said the man behind the desk, running his finger along them.

Moncur attempted a chuckle. 'I'd never make it as a long-distance driver, eh?' Nobody smiled. 'Well, anyway, it was just there.' A pen was produced, a dot marked on the map.

'How far is that from the coast?' asked Doyle.

'Oh, a mile, couple of miles.'

'All right.' The map was folded away again. The questioning resumed as before. 'So, you saw a woman at the side of the road?'

'That's right.'

'Can you describe her?'

'Long hair, dark brown or maybe black. I didn't have the lights on in the cab, so it wasn't easy to tell. Sort of . . . well, I mean, she was quite pretty and all, but she wasn't . . . she wasn't anything out of the ordinary.'

'What about height?' This from the one behind the desk.

'I dunno, average. Five-seven, five-eight.'

'A little taller than average, maybe,' he suggested. 'What was she wearing?'

'Jeans, a jacket. She looked cold.'

'Did she seem wet?'

'Wet? No, it wasn't raining. But she looked cold. I turned the heating up in the cab.'

'And what was she carrying?'

'Just a bag, a haversack sort of thing.'

'Anything else?'

'No.'

'Was the haversack heavy?'

A short nervous laugh. 'I don't know. She heaved it into the van herself.'

The man behind the desk nodded thoughtfully.

'Okay, Mr Moncur,' Doyle continued. 'Is there anything else you can tell us about her appearance? Her shoes for example.'

'Never noticed them.'

'Was she wearing make-up?'

'No. She could have done with a bit. Pale face. I suppose it was the cold.'

'And her accent, was it local?'

'No.'

'But English?'

'Oh, yeah, she was English. Definitely.'

'Right, so you picked her up. You've given us her description. What did you talk about?'

'She wasn't all that talkative. I got the idea she was doing a runner. Well, that time of night . . .'

'Running from whom exactly?'

'Boyfriend probably. She wasn't wearing any rings, not married or anything. I reckoned boyfriend. She looked like she'd been crying.'

'Or swimming,' from behind the desk.

'At that time of night?' Bill Moncur laughed again. Again, nobody laughed with him. 'We didn't talk that much really. I thought that if she got to talking about it, she'd burst into tears. That was the last thing I wanted.'

'So would you describe her as . . . what? sullen?'

'No, not sullen. I mean, she was pleasant enough and all. Smiled a few times. Laughed at one of my jokes.'

'Where was she headed?'

'She said Margate would do. At first, anyway.'

'She didn't specify her destination?' asked Doyle, but now the quiet man, Greenleaf, the one with the cassette-deck, spoke.

'What did you mean, "at first"?'

'Well, when we got a bit closer, she asked if I was going through Cliftonville. To be honest, I wasn't, but she looked washed out. So I asked her if that was where she wanted dropping off, and she nodded. It wasn't much out of my way, so I took her there.'

'Cliftonville. Somewhere specific in Cliftonville?'

'No, anywhere along the front seemed to suit her. She wasn't bothered. I thought it was funny at the time. I mean, saying where you want to go, then not really minding whereabouts you're dropped off once you get there. Maybe she was going to run away with the circus, eh?'

'Maybe.' This from behind the desk again. 'I'd like to hear anything she said to you, Mr Moncur, anything you can remember. It doesn't matter how trivial you think it was, whether it was just yes or no to a question or whatever. *Any*thing she said to you, I'd like to hear it.'

So he'd to go over the whole journey. It took the best part of half an hour. They'd to put in fresh tapes at one point. He noticed that they were making two copies of the interview. Finally, he asked a question of his own.

'What's she done then? What's so important?'

'We think she's a terrorist, Mr Moncur.'

'Terrorist?' He sounded amazed. 'I don't hold no truck with that sort of—'

'You might not *hold* any truck,' said Doyle, 'but you had one *in* your truck.' And he grinned. Bill Moncur found himself unable to smile back. 'Get it?' Doyle asked Greenleaf.

'I get it, Doyle,' said Greenleaf.

'You said she had long hair,' the man behind the desk interrupted. 'How long?'

Moncur tapped his back with a finger. 'Right down to here,' he said.

'Could it have been a wig?'

Moncur shrugged.

Now Doyle came up to him, leaning down over him, grinning. 'Just between us, Bill, man to man like, we all know what it's like driving a lorry . . . picking up a woman. Did you . . . you know . . . did you . . . ?' Doyle winked and leered. But Moncur was shaking his head.

'Nothing like that,' he said.

Doyle straightened up. He looked disappointed. He looked at Moncur as if he might be gay.

'Not that I wouldn't have or anything,' Moncur protested. 'But that time of night . . . I was absolutely shattered. I couldn't have got it up for a centrefold.'

Doyle still looked dubious.

'Honest,' said Moncur.

'Well,' said the one behind the desk, 'no need to dwell on that.'

Then came the crusher.

'Mr Moncur,' he continued, 'we'll have to go to Cliftonville. We need to know exactly where you dropped her off.'

'Fine, okay.' Bill Moncur nodded enthusiastically. They were leaving! He'd be out of here in a minute. 'When you go into the town,' he said, 'you head straight for—'

'You don't understand, Mr Moncur. Directions won't do. We need you there with us to show us the spot.'

'What?' It dawned on him. 'Cliftonville? *Now?* Aw, for Christ's sake.'

They busied themselves with locating a detailed map of Cliftonville, ignoring Bill Moncur's protestations. The CID man, DS Hines, appeared again to see if they needed a car. No, the one car they already had would be enough. And then the pretty WPC put her head round the door, smiling at Moncur. He blessed her for that smile.

'Need any tea or coffee here?' she asked.

'Not for us, thanks. We've got to be going. Come on, Mr Moncur. We'll take the same route you took that night. That way, you can show us where you picked up Witch.'

'Picked up which what?'

The one from behind the desk smiled for a moment. 'A slip of the tongue,' he said, motioning towards the doorway with his arm. 'After you.'

Eventually, at the end of his gruelling day, a police car took Bill Moncur back to Folkestone.

Elder, Doyle and Greenleaf remained in Cliftonville, their unmarked car (Doyle's car, still messy from his French trip) parked in the forecourt of a small hotel. They'd booked rooms for the evening, despite having brought nothing with them, no change of clothes, no toothbrushes . . . It was Elder's decision, but the Special Branch men were happy to go along with it, Greenleaf despite the facts that a) he'd have to call Shirley to tell her, and b) he'd be sharing a room with Doyle. They visited a chemist's and bought toiletries, before rendezvousing in the hotel lounge. It was just the right side of salubrious, with a tropical theme to the furnishings which extended to an island mural on one wall. A long time ago someone had painted white seashells on the dark green linoleum floor. They had the place to themselves. Greenleaf couldn't imagine why.

'It's important,' said Elder, 'not to let the trail grow colder than it already is. That means working through this evening.'

'Fine,' said Doyle, 'but am I being stupid or was the last sighting of Witch in Auchterwhatsit, six hundred miles north of here?'

Elder smiled. 'You're not being stupid, Mr Doyle, but there's something we've got to ask ourselves.'

Doyle said nothing, so Greenleaf provided the answer.

'Why did she specifically want to come to Cliftonville?'

'Exactly, Mr Greenleaf. I mean, look at the place. It's quiet, anonymous. It's perfect for her.'

Now Doyle spoke. 'You think she's got a contact here?'

Elder shrugged. 'It's possible her paymaster met her here with final instructions.'

'You don't think she's *here* though?'

'Mr Doyle, as my old Aberdonian tailor used to say, discount nothing.'

Doyle thought about this for a moment, realised a joke had been made, and laughed. Greenleaf didn't: his mother had come from Aberdeen.

'So what do we do this evening?'

'We cover as much ground as possible. That means splitting up. I'd suggest one of us makes contact with the local police, one asks around in the pubs, and one asks taxi drivers and so on. We're talking about the wee sma' hours of a Monday morning. A woman dropped off and having, presumably, to walk to some destination. A late-night patrol car may have spotted her. Taxi drivers may have slowed to see if they had a fare. Were there any nightclubs emptying around the time she arrived? Someone may, without knowing it, have seen something. Perhaps she'd prearranged her late arrival with a hotel or boarding-house. Or maybe some early-day fisherman saw her – we can't possibly cover all the angles, that's where the local police will come in.'

'We should set up a Portakabin on the front, put up posters: have you seen this woman, that sort of thing. Ask everybody who passes . . .'

But Elder was shaking his head. 'No, Doyle, that's precisely what we don't want.'

'Because,' Greenleaf added, 'if she *is* still around here, we don't want to chase her away.'

'Precisely. Softly softly, as the saying goes. Now, sitting here like this, we're already losing valuable time. Let's get down to some *real* work.'

Walking through the blowy streets that night, his feet swelling in his shoes, Dominic Elder was worried. It wasn't Greenleaf and Doyle who worried him. They seemed capable sorts, if slightly curious as a twosome. Well, perhaps not. It was the old interrogation two-step: bad guy and nice guy. It could be a useful combination.

Elder did something he hadn't done in years. He bought some cod and chips. The meal came on a polystyrene tray with a small wooden fork, the whole wrapped in a custom paper bag. Different to the way Elder remembered it: greasy newsprint coming off on his hands, picking at the fish-flesh with his fingers. The cod had texture but no flavour at all. And the chips tasted mass-produced. There was a regularity about their size which depressed him, but it did not worry him.

Witch worried him.

He could almost smell her, almost taste her behind the seaside flavours and aromas. She had been here. And not long enough ago for her taint to have left the place. Was she still here? He didn't think so. But if the hunt started to close in on her, she might just come back. A safe port in a storm. This had been her first lair on arriving in England. It would have meaning and resonance for her. Wounded, she might come crawling back. It would do no harm for Elder to learn the ground, her home-ground. So he walked, stopping to talk with people. Was the bakery all-night? It was, but the shift didn't come on till eleven. He could come back and ask his questions then. As he walked, he became more comfortable with his story. She was his daughter. She'd run away, and he wanted to find her. Doyle and Greenleaf were to tell similar tales in the pubs and clubs, with the necessary alteration turning Witch into their sister rather than daughter.

Elder knew he was getting old. Despite living in the country, tonight was as much walking as he'd done in a year or more. Doyle and Greenleaf were younger, fitter and faster than him. They'd be fast making a life or death decision. Would he be too slow? Say he came up against Witch, came up against her again. Would she be so much faster than him? Or was she ageing too? No, not judging by the Khan assassination. If anything, she was sharper than ever, damn her. He'd been rusty at the police station, interviewing the lorry driver. He'd asked leading questions rather than waiting for Moncur to tell his version. That was bad. *That* worried him.

Something else worried him, too. She wouldn't have come to Britain unless she was after very big game indeed. He didn't know why he felt this, but he did. Britain was enemy territory to her, Elder's territory. He couldn't help but think of the whole thing on the personal level. Which was dangerous. Things might start getting out of perspective. He might start reading too much or not enough into certain situations. He wished he knew who her target was. It crossed his mind – it had crossed his mind all week – that maybe *he* was her target. But, really, this was nothing but ego. It didn't make sense. He was no threat to her. He was in retirement, off the scene. Unless . . . unless there was something in his file on her, something he'd overlooked and which could be dangerous to her. Well, Barclay had the file now; maybe *he* would see something, something Elder couldn't see.

Her target had to be the summit. But wasn't it at the same time just too obvious, as Greenleaf had hinted? All those heads of state . . . But look at the challenge it presented to her. The security services of nine countries would be there, protecting their leaders. Over seven hundred and fifty security personnel in total (the majority supplied, of course, by the host nation), and more if you counted the uniformed police officers who would line the routes, holding back traffic and the public. Oh yes, it was a challenge all right, but then challenges had never been Witch's thing. She worked on a smaller scale. Yes, there was the Pope, but they'd scared her off there with fewer personnel. Besides, that was Wolf Bandorff's plan, not hers. Kidnappings, peace campaigners . . . these were her arena. Would she bother, these days, with a head of state?

God alone knew. God, and the woman herself.

Dominic Elder. A priest's name. You should have been a priest. That's what she'd told him. Remembering, he rubbed his back.

He had come to the outskirts of the town. The wind was sharp and salty, the sea a distant clash. Maybe a storm was coming. The wind, though sharp, was warm. Clouds moved fast against the sky. He paused to rub at his back, and stared at the spotlit frontage of a small pub. Pubs were Doyle's and Greenleaf's territory. But all the same, the vinegary chips had left him with a dry throat. He stared at the pub's name.

The Cat over the Broomstick.

The name decided him. He pushed open the door and entered smoke and noise. It was a young people's pub. Jukebox, video games, loud conversations peppered with swearing, and necking in the few dark corners available. He hesitated, but walked up to the bar anyway. The youth in front of him, being served with seven pints of lager, wore a denim jacket with its arms shorn off, and beneath it a leather jacket, arms intact. Elder recognised biker gear when he saw it. A biker pub then, the dull offspring of the original Hell's Angels. Someone behind him called out 'Hey, Grandad!' to snorts of laughter. Elder stood his ground. The pints had been loaded onto a tray, the tray taken away. The barman was Elder's age, and sweating. He wore an apologetic look for his new customer, a look which said, 'It's business. If they weren't spending money here they'd be doing it somewhere else.'

'Whisky, please,' said Elder, 'a double.'

He wondered if Doyle and Greenleaf had made it out this far yet. Somehow he doubted it. They'd most probably have a drink in every pub they visited . . . He gave the barman a fiver and, while waiting for his change, added plenty of water to his drink from a jug on the bar.

'I'm looking for my daughter,' he told the barman. But as he started to speak, a particularly thunderous track started on the jukebox, gaining a roar of approval from the drinkers.

'What?' said the barman, leaning his ear towards Elder.

'My daughter!' Elder yelled. 'I'm looking for her.'

The barman shook his head, and then jerked it towards one of the loudspeakers. The message was clear: We'll talk when the music stops. He went off to serve another customer. Another tray was needed. At one point, the barman twiddled with a knob mounted on the wall behind the optics. He did this as the song was ending. Another started up, but not so loud any more.

'Turn it up, Joe!'

'Come on, Joe, we can hardly hear it!'

'Crank it up!'

He shook his head and smiled. 'In a minute,' he called. 'Just give me a minute's rest, eh?'

There were groans but nothing more. Joe the barman came back to Elder.

'Now then, you were saying . . . ?'

'I'm looking for my daughter. She's run off and I think maybe she . . . she might have come down this way.'

'Are you Mr Elder?'

Elder's knees almost collapsed under him. 'What? How . . . yes, yes, I'm Dominic Elder.'

The barman nodded and moved back to the optics. On a shelf sat a letter, which he lifted and handed over the bar. Elder's hand didn't quite tremble as he accepted it.

'She left it for you.'

On the white envelope was printed MR DOMINIC ELDER. Elder knew the score. He knew he shouldn't touch it. It should go straight into a polythene bag for forensic analysis, for checks on fibres, saliva used to stick the envelope down . . . the arcana of the forensic arts. But then Elder was a retired member of the security services. He might forget procedures, mightn't he? He tore open the envelope. Inside was a single folded sheet of lined writing-paper on which was scribbled a handwritten message. He looked around him. Joe the barman had gone off to serve yet another thirsty client. Then he read.

'Don't bother. When it's time, I'll find you. W.'

He read it again . . . and again . . . and again.

'Don't bother. When it's time, I'll find you. W.'

The 'I'll' and the 'you' had been double-underlined. *I'll* find *you*. Yes, but only when it was time. There was something else to be done first. The Khan assassination? Or something on a grander scale? He managed a wry smile. Oh, she was clever. She'd known Elder might well become involved . . . she'd even guessed that he might track her as far as Cliftonville. So she'd gone into an aptly named pub and left a note for him. She couldn't know it would reach him of course. But if it did . . . Yes, it seemed her style all right. But she'd slipped up, too. The note was handwritten. It wasn't much, but it was something. He looked about for the telephone, and found that there was a booth next to the toilets. He slipped the letter back into its envelope, put the envelope in his pocket, and made for the booth.

Doyle and Greenleaf weren't yet back at the hotel, so he tried the police station. No, the two gentlemen had called in, but there'd been no one available to help them. They'd arranged a meeting with Inspector Block in a pub somewhere . . . probably the Faithful Collie. Yes, he had the telephone number.

So he tried the Faithful Collie. Calling to a pub from a pub: talk about a noisy line! *I'll* find *you* . . . Eventually he got the barman in the Faithful Collie to understand. There was a yell, another yell, and finally Greenleaf answered.

'Is that you, Mr Elder?'

'She's left a message for me in a pub.'

'What? I didn't make that out.'

'Witch has left me a message.'

A burly biker roamed past on his way to the toilets. Another came out. They exchanged handslaps.

'How do you know?' Greenleaf was asking.

'Because a barman just handed it to me.'

'What does it say?'

'It says I'm not to look for her, she'll find me when she wants.'

'We've got to get it down to a lab . . .' The fact suddenly struck Greenleaf. 'Oh,' he said, 'you've opened it.'

'Obviously.'

'You shouldn't have done that.'

'I realise . . .'

'Still, not much we can do now. Which pub?'

'The Cat over the Broomstick.'

'You're kidding. You think she's guessed about Operation Broomstick?'

'I don't know. She knows we call her Witch.'

'We'll be right over.'

'Is Doyle sober?'

'He will be. Give us . . . I don't know, depends how far we are from you.'

'Is Inspector Block still with you?'
'Yes, I'll bring him along too.'
'Fine. But be warned, this is a Hell's Angels' watering-hole.'
'Funny pubs you choose, Mr Elder. Is it the leather you like or what?'
Elder smiled but said nothing. He put down the receiver and went back to the bar, where his whisky was still waiting. Joe the barman was waiting too.
'Can you tell me anything about her?' Elder asked.
Joe shrugged. 'Came in about a week ago. Said she was on the move, keeping away from an older man.'
'How did she look?'
'Fine. Tired maybe. And she had a sprained wrist. That's why she got me to write it.' He looked along the bar to his right. 'Coming, Tony.' He went off to serve the customer. But Elder followed him.
'What do you mean?'
'I mean she'd sprained her wrist. She had a bandage on it. So she couldn't write. She thought for some reason you'd come looking for her in here. I told her we didn't usually cater to . . . older men. Well, you can see that for yourself. But she seemed to know . . . well, you're here, so it looks like she was right.'
'She didn't write the note then?'
Joe shook his head. 'One pound thirty-five please, Tony. No, like I say, I'd to write it for her. She told me what to put. Looks like she doesn't want to be found, Mr Elder, not yet any road.'
'Yes,' he said, 'looks like.'
A sprained wrist . . . couldn't write. She was cunning all right, and at the same time she was playing with him. If he found the note, she must know he would talk to the barman. And if he talked to the barman, he would find out the handwriting wasn't hers. If she'd *really* wanted to lead him a dance, she'd have asked someone else to write the note, so Elder wouldn't know that it *wasn't* her writing . . . Yes, she was playing games. This was so different to the Witch of old. What had happened to her? Had she gone mad? Was she on a suicide mission? What had happened? This wasn't the old Witch at all.
And yet, obviously it *was* the old Witch – as shrewd and as deadly as ever.
'I'll have another whisky when you're ready,' he told Joe the barman. 'And have one yourself.'
'Thanks, I will,' said Joe, making for the optics and once more turning up the volume. He received the cheers from the bar with a little bow from the waist.

Looking back on a startling day, it still seemed to Barclay that the most startling thing of all had been Dominique's driving in central Paris.
They set off from Calais in her car, leaving his in the police station car park, his packed bag locked in the boot. He brought to Dominique's car a single change of clothes, the Witch file, and a couple of opera tapes. During the drive, and above the noise of the engine and the rather extraordinary ventilation system (a single flap between dashboard and windscreen), they planned their next moves.
'His name,' Dominique yelled, 'is Monsieur Jean-Claude Separt. I know of him actually. He is a cartoonist. He draws stories.'

'You mean strip cartoons?'

'Cartoons in a strip, yes.'

'For a newspaper?'

'No, he makes books. Books of strip cartoons are very popular in France.'

'What sort of stuff does he do?'

'Political cartoons, or cartoons with a political point. He is left-wing. More than that I can't tell you until we get to Paris. There will be information on him when we get there.'

'What about his car?'

'It's curious, he reported it missing only *after* it was found. Doesn't that sound strange to you?'

'A bit. What's his story?'

She shrugged, pulling out to overtake a lorry. The 2CV barely had enough power to pull past the long, fuming vehicle. A car bore down on them, but Dominique shot the 2CV back into the right-hand lane with two or three seconds to spare. The blood had vanished entirely from Barclay's face.

'I don't know yet,' she continued, as though nothing had happened. 'We shall have to ask him ourselves . . .'

The car didn't have a tape-deck, but it did have a radio. Dominique found a jazz station and turned the volume all the way up, so the music was just about audible above the engine. She beat her hands against the steering-wheel.

'In your room,' she yelled, 'I saw your cassettes – classical music.'

'Opera,' he corrected.

She wrinkled her nose. 'Jazz,' she said. 'Jazz is the only music in the world, and Paris is the capital!' She signalled, slipped the gear down into third, and roared out to pass another lorry.

In Paris, she first headed for her office, Barclay remaining in the car while she sprinted to the building, and, moments later, sprinted out again. She threw a file on to his lap, slapped his hand away from the radio (he'd been trying to find a classical station), and slammed shut the driver's-side door. Then she indicated and screeched back into the traffic again, horns sounding all around them.

'They had it waiting at reception for me,' she said of the file. 'Read it out while I drive.'

So, in his stilted French, he read from the report, thankful for it since it served to take his eyes off the madness all about him. Lunchtime in Paris. He'd been here for weekends before, and even then had marvelled at the ability of the local drivers to squeeze five-abreast into a three-lane road without scraping up against each other. Meanwhile, as he read, Dominique translated some of the more difficult sentences into English, until at last he'd finished the report on the life and career of the cartoonist Jean-Claude Separt and they were pulling into a narrow street, the buildings tall on either side, blocking out the light and a good deal of the city's noise. There were shops and offices at ground level, dingy-looking things with unwashed windows. But the storeys above were apartments, some with small verandahs, all with dusty shutters, the paint flaking off, some slats missing or hanging loose. Dominique double-parked the 2CV alongside a venerable-looking low-slung Citroën.

'Come on,' she said.

'Where?'

She motioned upwards. 'This is where I live . . . my home. I have to change my clothes.' She pulled at the material of her jacket. She was smiling. 'Coming?'

He nodded. 'Sure,' he said. His heart started pumping a little faster. 'Sure,' he repeated, getting out of the car.

'Stairs only,' she warned him. 'No elevator.'

The place smelled a bit like the London Underground. He couldn't think why. It was a smell like burnt oil, and lurking beneath it dampness and rot. He got the feeling that if he touched the dark green walls, a residue would come off on his fingers.

He was behind Dominique, carrying her small suitcase. He watched her body as she climbed the winding stairs.

'Next floor,' she said, a little breathlessly.

'Right, okay.' But it wasn't okay. Her case was heavier than he'd expected. What did she have in there, a couple of sub-machine guns?

And then they were standing facing one another outside an ornate front door. She smiled, catching her breath. He smiled back, concentrating his eyes on hers, trying not to show how hard he was breathing after the climb. She brought a key out of her bag and opened the door.

He looked into a well-kept if old-fashioned hall. The carpet was faded. So were the furnishings. Was there a radio playing in the distance?

'Mama,' called Dominique. *'C'est moi.'*

Briskly, she took the case from him and walked up the hall.

'C'est toi, Dominique?' came a wavering voice from behind one of the doors. Barclay still stood in the hall, drinking in this unexpected reality. Dominique waved for him to follow her, then opened a door at the end of the hall.

In the living-room sat Madame Herault. But she stood to receive her foreign visitor, and switched off her radio too. She looked like her daughter, but was between thirty and forty years older. She patted her hair and said something about how Dominique should have warned her. To which Dominique replied that if she had warned her mother, her mother would merely have tired herself out cleaning and making cakes and dressing herself up, when they were only staying for fifteen minutes or so. Then Dominique said she had to go to her room and change. Barclay was made to sit on the huge springy sofa which reminded him unnervingly of the 2CV's suspension.

'Keep Mama company, will you?' Dominique asked in English. 'I won't be long. Oh, and if she offers you some of her calvados . . . refuse it.'

And with that she was gone. Madame Herault, still standing, asked him if he would like something to drink? He didn't, but nodded anyway, since Madame Herault fixing him something to drink was preferable to Madame Herault sitting expecting him to make conversation with her. Then he remembered the warning about the calvados.

'Pastis, s'il vous plaît,' he said.

But a drink was not enough. He would have something to eat, too, wouldn't he? Barclay shook his head, patting his stomach.

'Complet,' he said, hoping it was the right word.

She persisted, but he persisted too. Just a drink, a drink would be very good.

'Calvados?' Madame Herault asked.

Barclay shook his head. *'Pastis, s'il vous plaît,'* he insisted.

So off she went to fetch him a pastis. He released a great intake of air, and smilingly chastised himself for his original thoughts regarding Dominique's intentions. The room was comfortably old-fashioned, exuding what seemed to him a particularly French sort of genteel shabbiness. The ornaments were too ornate, the furniture too bulky. The dresser was enormous, and should have stood in a chateau entrance hall rather than a second-floor Parisian apartment. He wondered how they'd got it into the room in the first place. The obvious answer seemed to be: through the large windows. A block and tackle job from street level. Yes.

God, he thought, what am I doing here? I should have stayed in the car. She's been teasing me, hasn't she? She could have said it was her mother's place. She could have told me her mother would be home. Instead of which, Dominique had let him think his own thoughts, teasing him. Little vixen.

Madame Herault carried a tray back into the room. Barclay had risen from the sofa and was examining some framed photographs on top of an upright piano. There was one of a man in police uniform.

'Mon mari,' explained Madame Herault. *'Il est mort.'*

She placed the tray on a footstool. There was a long slim glass containing an inch of pastis and a single ice-cube. There was also a jug of water, and a saucer on which sat some plain biscuits. She motioned with the jug and poured until he told her to stop. Then she handed him the glass and picked up the photograph, giving him some long story of which Barclay made out probably most of the relevant facts. Monsieur Herault had been a policeman in Paris, a detective. But a terrorist bomb had blown him up ten years ago. He'd been helping to evacuate shoppers from a department store where a bomb was said to be hidden. But it had gone off sooner than expected . . .

She gave a rueful smile and picked up another photograph, a beaming schoolgirl.

'Dominique,' she said, quite unnecessarily. Barclay nodded. She looked up at him. *'Très belle.'* He nodded again. For want of anything else to add, he gulped at the drink. Mother of God, it was strong! He lifted a biscuit to disguise his discomfort. But the biscuit disintegrated in his hand, falling like bits of bomb-blast to the floor.

Madame Herault apologised and went to kneel to pick the pieces up, but Barclay was already down on his knees, his fingers trying to lift the tiny pieces without them splintering further.

And that was the scene which presented itself to Dominique when she entered the room. The crumbs collected, more or less, Barclay got to his feet and helped Madame Herault to hers. Dominique had changed into a knee-length skirt, showing off legs which, even in the dim light of the apartment, Barclay could see were tanned and smooth. She had a jacket slung over her shoulder, and wore a crisp white blouse with a small gold cross on a chain around her neck.

'Drinking in the middle of the day?' she chided him. 'We've still got a lot of work to do, Michael, remember?' Then she said something in a rush of French to her mother, and her mother replied in an even faster rush, her cadences soaring and plummeting. He finished his drink while the conversation went on, noticing Dominique glancing towards him from time to time. When he made to replace the empty glass on the tray, she signalled, with the slightest jerk of her head, that it was time to go. This was actually hard to achieve, since Madame Herault seemed to have a lot she still wanted to say to him, and there were hands to be shaken, cheeks to be kissed.

'Oui, Mama, oui,' Dominique kept saying, her exasperation increasing. Finally, they were at the front door, and with a final push from Dominique herself Barclay found himself on the stairs and starting his descent. But Madame Herault came to the stair-head and continued to call down instructions to her daughter.

'Oui!' Dominique called back. *'Bien sûr! D'accord. A ce soir, Mama! Ce soir!'*

The street, the dull claustrophobic street, seemed suddenly a huge and necessary release, a refuge. Even Dominique sighed and fanned her face with her hand before getting back into the car. She didn't say anything as she keyed the ignition, checked behind her, and started off along the street. But, edging out into the traffic at the end of the road, she remarked simply, 'That was my mother.'

'Really?' replied Barclay.

His irony escaped her. 'Yes, really.'

'She was charming, so like her daughter.'

She pursed her lips. 'I should have warned you.'

'Yes, you bloody well should.'

She laughed. 'Tell me, Mr Michael Barclay, what were you thinking?'

'When?'

'When I led you up the stairs.'

'I was wondering why the stairwell smelled like the London Underground.'

The answer surprised her. She glanced at him. 'Really?' she asked.

He nodded. 'That's what I was thinking,' he said. And he kept his eyes on the windscreen, well away from her bare tanned legs as they worked brake, clutch and accelerator.

'Mama kissed you twice,' Dominique mused. 'I think you made an impression of her.'

'An impression *on* her,' Barclay corrected.

'Well, anyway,' Dominique added with a smile, 'you made an impression.' And she laughed, suddenly and brightly.

By a strange twist of fate, Jean-Claude Separt's apartment-cum-studio was the sort of place Barclay had imagined Dominique's apartment would be. It was obvious that cartoonists, even (especially?) left-wing cartoonists, could live very comfortably in France. The apartment took up the whole top storey of a sandblasted block near Odeon.

'Très cher, très chic,' Dominique kept saying as they made their way up in the lift to the penthouse. They'd spoken about Separt on the way to Paris, talking about the garret he would inhabit, vermin-ridden and with unsold tracts and pamphlets piled to the ceiling. Preconceptions were there to be broken. Here was the second (only the second?) shattered preconception of the day.

Barclay knew his place. He was Dominique's colleague, a police officer from England (but not London; nowhere as important as London) on an exchange programme and spending the day with Dominique, who was herself a lowly police officer, a trainee in one of the administrative departments. They were here to interview Monsieur Separt regarding the theft of his motor vehicle, for a scheme called, as far as Barclay could work it out, the Vehicle Repatriation Register Survey. Well, something like that. Dominique had prepared some questions, and had written them down on a sheet of paper attached to a clipboard. She looked the part, he decided. Her clean, efficient clothes were just a bit *too* clean and efficient – the sort of outfit a trainee would wear when wanting to impress with the notion that they wouldn't stay a trainee forever. And she'd got rid of her lipstick, so that her face was a little plainer. It was perfect.

So was Separt's apartment. He was fat and greying with cropped hair and a grizzled beard. He wore faded denims, baggy at the knees and ankles, but tight at the stomach. He wore a short-sleeved striped shirt, and his eyes glinted from behind thick-lensed glasses. A strong yellow-papered cigarette either hung from his mouth or else from his fingers. And he lit a new cigarette with the dying embers of each old one.

Having ushered them in, Separt flapped back to his working-desk. 'I won't be a second,' he said. 'Just the finishing touches to a face . . .'

The bulk of the apartment was taken up by a single, huge thick-carpeted room. At one end stood a series of architect's tables over which hung anglepoise lamps. Here, Separt worked on his cartoons. On shelves behind him along the walls were various tools, old comic books, magazines, disparate newspaper cuttings. Pinned to the walls were photographs of politicians, some of them subtly and tellingly altered by the cartoonist. Barclay laughed at one of his country's own Prime Minister, showing the premier emerging from a bowl of soup. Written at the bottom was 'Prime Minestrone'.

Separt seemed inordinately pleased at Barclay's response. He chuckled and went back to inking some wild hair on his latest caricature.

There was a computer close by, which Barclay studied too. He thought maybe it would be a Paintbox, one of those extraordinary machines used by some artists and graphic designers. But it was just a plain old personal computer.

At the other end of the room, Dominique had already settled on the extremely long sofa. Empty wine bottles and beer bottles were strewn around the floor, and ashtrays brimmed with cigarette ends and the roaches from several joints. Separt, who had known from their intercom conversation that two police officers were on their way up, didn't seem bothered in the slightest. Two walls of the room were made up of windows, one side opening onto a small rooftop patio. The view of the city was breathtaking.

'How can he work with a view like that in front of him?' Barclay marvelled. Dominique translated the question, and Separt, who had thrown down his pen with a flourish, beamed again before saying something.

'He says,' Dominique replied, 'that he no longer sees the view. It is something for visitors, that's all.' Separt and Barclay shared a smile, and Separt motioned for his English guest to sit on the sofa beside Dominique. Barclay did so, and Separt, ignoring the spare chair, flopped on to the floor in front of his visitors, resting with legs out, one foot over the other, hands stretched behind him so he sat up. He had an impish look, as though every moment of his life was both revelation and opportunity for humour. But Barclay noticed that Dominique pressed her knees together and kept them like that, and he wondered if there were some more sordid reason for Separt's choice of seat . . .

His French was coming on fast, and he understood most of the dialogue which followed.

'Your car was stolen, monsieur,' Dominique began, her pen held above the clipboard.

'Of course, otherwise you would not be here.' Separt beamed again.

'Of course,' said Dominique. She was a good trainee police officer. But Barclay wondered how she would have talked her way out of it if Separt had asked for identification. They'd considered the question on the way over here. Considered it, and come to no solution.

'We'll handle it when the time comes,' she had said, leaving it at that.

'But you are one of the lucky few,' she was saying now, 'who not only have their car stolen, they also have it recovered.'

'So I understand. But it's an old car.' He shrugged. 'It would not have been a catastrophe if the car had disappeared from my life for ever!'

'You reported the car missing quite late, I believe?'

'No, not late, just before midday I think.' He chuckled again.

Dominique managed the faintest of official smiles. 'I meant, monsieur—'

'Yes, yes, I know what you meant.' Another shrug. 'I reported it stolen when I realised it had been stolen. You've seen the parking around here, mademoiselle. A nightmare. I had parked the car around the corner in Rue des Fêtes. It was not visible from the apartment.' He laughed, gesturing towards the huge windows. 'Unlike most of the motor vehicles in Paris.'

She smiled a cool smile, scratched on the pad with her pen. 'You were ill, is that correct?' This much they had read in the Calais police report.

Separt nodded. 'I wasn't out of the apartment for four days. Some sort of bug, I don't know exactly.'

'What did the doctor say?'

'Doctors?' He wrinkled his face. 'I can't be bothered with doctors. If I get better, I get better; and if I die, so be it. I'd rather give my money to tramps on the street than hand any over to a doctor.'

'And the tramps might give you a more accurate diagnosis,' added Dominique, causing Separt to collapse into a laughing fit, which then became a coughing fit. He rose to his feet, shaking his head.

'You are making my day, believe me,' he said. 'I must write that down. It's a good idea for a cartoon. Give the money to the beggars instead of the doctors, and the beggars give you a diagnosis – on the state of society's health.'

Barclay and Dominique sat silently while he went to his work table and wrote something on a sheet of paper, which he then tore from its pad and pinned to the wall.

'You know,' he called, 'my best ideas come this way – from other people. I feel a little guilty sometimes, I do so little work myself.'

When he returned, he chose the chair rather than the floor, sinking into it and crossing his ankles. Now that he was seated on a level with her, Dominique relented and released the pressure on her knees.

'So the car could have been taken any time during those four days?' she asked.

'That's right. I went outside on the fifth day, and I was puzzled at first, I wondered if I'd parked it where I thought I had. I walked around all the neighbouring streets. No sign. So I called the police.'

'This was on the first of June?'

'Was it? I'll take your word for it.'

'According to the records it was.'

'Then it was.'

'But your car's outside now?'

'And as rusty as ever. There are a few scratches on it that weren't there before. Well, to be honest maybe they *were* there before – it's hard to tell.'

'Nothing missing from the car?'

'No.'

'And nothing there that wasn't there before?'

He laughed again. 'You mean, did the thief *leave* me anything? No, not a sou.'

'Why do you think someone would steal a car from this arrondissement and take it to Calais?'

Separt shrugged. 'Joy riding. They may have been all over the place, and just run out of petrol there. Or maybe they were considering a trip to England, but changed their minds. Something like that, I imagine.'

Dominique nodded. 'On the whole, monsieur, you're happy to have your car returned?'

Separt gave this a little thought. 'On the whole, I suppose I am. Not that it would bother me unduly if someone stole it again . . . Listen, I'm being rude, can I get you a glass of wine?'

'That's very kind, but we've already taken up enough of your time. We appreciate your talking to us like this.'

'Not at all.'

Dominique rose to her feet. Barclay rose too. He was glad they didn't have to drink anything. His head still ached from the pastis. Separt seemed disappointed that they were leaving so soon.

'When the survey is complete,' Dominique said, 'I may have to return with a few final follow-up questions . . . without my colleague here, I'm afraid.'

'Oh, yes?' said Separt. 'You'll be welcome any time, believe me.'

Barclay had never seen anyone chatting up an on-duty policewoman before. Trust the French. Separt took Dominique's hand and brushed his lips against it. Then he shook Barclay's hand warmly. A few words of English came to the cartoonist.

'Urrr . . . good luck, chum. Have a nice day.'

'Merci,' said Barclay. He waved a hand around him. 'You have a beautiful home.'

Nodding, grinning, laughing to himself now and then, the cartoonist showed them out of the apartment. When Dominique and Barclay were alone in the lift, and it had started its descent, he turned to her.

'Seemed like a nice chap,' he said.

'And genuine?'

'Not entirely.'

'A complete fake. He was worried as hell, that's why he kept laughing like that. Nervous laughter.'

'You think he knows something? So what do we do now? Keep a watch on him?'

She bit her bottom lip. 'Better than that, I would like to bug him. But I don't think my superiors would allow it.'

'Why not?'

'Separt's politics. If a bug was discovered, the left would have a . . . what do you say?'

'A field day?'

She nodded. 'A field day.'

Barclay had a thought. 'What if you *didn't* bug him?' he said.

'What do you mean?'

'Do you know how to make a listening device?'

'No.'

He nodded. 'What if someone created a bug of their own? Not the French security service. Maybe the British.'

She gasped. 'You're mad. If it got back to your superiors . . .'

'Or if it got back to *your* superiors that you'd helped me . . .'

They were both silent for a moment, considering these thoughts. Then Dominique turned to him. 'What would you need?'

'A shop selling electronic parts, an enthusiast's shop. And entry to Separt's apartment, preferably when he's out.'

'We can find such a shop,' she said. 'As for entry to the apartment, did you notice, he does not have a burglar alarm?'

'I didn't notice, no.'

She nodded. 'And only two locks on the door. It shouldn't be difficult. After all, I got into your hotel room, didn't I?'

'I thought you said . . . ?'

'The manager? No, he told me your room number. I went upstairs to see if you were in. You weren't, so I opened your door.'

'Where did you learn tricks like that? Part of the training?'

She shook her head. 'My father taught me,' she said quietly. 'A long time ago.'

One phone call to a friend who was a 'buff', and Dominique had the address she needed. The shop was a wonderland of chips and processors and wiring and tools. The assistant was helpful too, even though Dominique had trouble translating some of Barclay's requests into French. She wasn't sure what a soldering-iron was, or what it might be in French. But eventually Barclay had just about everything he needed. It wouldn't be craftsmanship, but it would do the job.

'And maybe some computer disks too,' he said. He inspected the available stock and picked out the type he needed. 'A couple of these, I think.'

They returned to Dominique's apartment where the spare bedroom was handed over for his use.

'My very own workshop,' he said, getting down to work. Work stopped quite quickly when he found they'd forgotten to buy a plug for the soldering-iron. He removed the two-pin plug from the room's bedside lamp and attached it to the soldering-iron. Then he had to borrow a pair of tweezers from Dominique, and a small magnifying-glass (which she used for reading) from Madame Herault.

As he worked, he could hear Dominique and her mother talking in the living room. Whenever Madame Herault spoke too loudly, her daughter would 'shush' her, and their voices would drop to a whisper again. It was as if he were the surgeon and this some particularly difficult operation. It wasn't really. It was the sort of stuff any teenage kid could accomplish with the aid either of inspiration or the plans from a hobby magazine. It took Barclay just over an hour. The wire he was using was no thicker than thread. He feared it would snap. Using runs of shorter than a centimetre, he dropped countless pieces and then couldn't find them, so had to cut more tiny lengths.

'A kid would have a steadier hand,' he muttered. But at last he was finished. He washed his face, splashing water into his bleary eyes, then had tea with Dominique and her mother. Then, with Dominique in her room and Barclay outside the front door, they tested the two small devices. Their range was not great. He hoped it would be enough. A neighbour passed him as he was standing in the stairwell with the receiver. He smiled at her, and received a mighty and quizzical frown in return.

'All right,' he said at last, after Dominique had hugged him briefly for being a genius, 'now it's your turn.'

But before they left, he tried telephoning Dominic Elder at his London hotel. He didn't know why exactly. Maybe he just wanted the assurance he felt Elder would give. But Elder wasn't there.

They drove back to Separt's block and squeezed the car into a parking space, then Dominique went to the phone-box on the corner and tried Separt's number. She returned quickly.

'An answering machine,' she said. 'And I don't see his car anywhere.'

'That doesn't mean he's out. He may just be working. Did you see his car when we were here earlier?'

'To be honest, no. It may be parked in another street.'

'So what now?'

'We'll have to try the intercom. If he answers, that's too bad.' So they walked to the front door and tried the intercom. There was no reply. 'So now we know he's out,' she said.

'Which doesn't get us *in*.'

He looked up and down the street. A woman was heading in their direction, pausing now and again to chastise her poodle about something it either had or had not done. 'Back to the car,' he said. They sat in the car and waited. 'When I call you, don't come,' he ordered. While Dominique puzzled over this, the woman stopped finally at the front door to the block, and then opened the door. Barclay sprang from the car and held the door open for the woman, who was having trouble persuading her poodle to enter the building.

'Merci, madame,' Barclay said. Then he called towards the car: *'Dominique, ici! Vite!'* Dominique sat still and looked at him. She had changed, back at her apartment, into faded denims and T-shirt, and she was wearing her lipstick again. She now checked her lipstick in the rearview mirror, ignoring his calls.

Barclay made an exasperated sound and shrugged to the woman. But now the woman was inside the building and making for the lift. *'Ici, Dominique!'* Barclay glanced behind him, saw the lift doors close with the woman and her dog inside, and now gestured for Dominique to join him. She lifted the plastic bag from the back seat and got out of the car. He gestured her through the door, and it locked behind them. They waited for ages while the lift took its cargo to the third floor, paused, then started down towards them. After their own ascent, the lift opened on to Separt's private floor. There were two doors, one unmarked, the other belonging to Separt's apartment. Dominique got busy on this door. She had brought some old-fashioned-looking lock-picks with her from her apartment. No doubt they had belonged to her father before her. Barclay had his doubts whether they would be up to handling modern-day locks. But within two minutes, the door was open.

'Brilliant,' he said.

'Quick, in you go.'

In he went. It was his job now. Hers was to stand by the lift. If it was called for, if it started back up from ground level, then she'd call to him and he'd clear out. What they would do after that was unclear to him. 'We'll think of something,' she'd said. 'Don't worry.'

Don't worry!

Well, after all, what was there to worry about? He was only bugging someone's private home, having broken into it. That was all. And in foreign territory, too. And without permission from Joyce Parry. That was all. It was a breeze . . .

The telephone was on the floor beside the desks, next to the answering-machine. He unscrewed the receiver and fixed the small transmitter in place, screwing the receiver shut again and shaking it to check it didn't rattle before replacing it in its cradle. Then he placed another transmitter down at the other end of the room, stuck to the underside of the sofa. Recalling how Separt liked to sit on the floor, he slouched on the floor himself. No, the bug wasn't visible. He'd no way of knowing if either bug would work. In theory they would, but in practice? And as for getting them out again afterwards . . .

Now he went to the computer. It was switched on, which saved a bit of time, but also indicated that Separt wouldn't be gone for long. He opened the box of computer disks beside the terminal. There were half a dozen disks, none bearing helpful markings. He pulled his own disks out of his pocket. The shop assistant had formatted them already, and Dominique had given him some French computer commands. The keyboard was slightly different from British models, but not so different. It didn't take long to copy a couple of Separt's disks.

A hiss from Dominique at the open door. 'Lift's coming!'

He closed the disk box and checked the screen display. There was no indication that he'd accessed the computer. Dominique was calling out floor numbers as he took a last look around. It might be another resident. The lift might stop before the penthouse. But it didn't look like it was stopping.

'Two . . . three . . .'

He was out now. She closed the door and did what she had to do with her pick-lock. Just the one lock needed reworking, the other being a Yale-type which had locked itself on closing.

He looked at the lift. 'Four,' he said. 'Five. Christ, Dominique, it's this floor next!'

She swivelled from the door and pushed him backwards. His back hit the landing's other door, which opened, and suddenly he was on the emergency stairwell, his kidneys colliding with the banister. He gasped while Dominique pushed the door closed again, just as the ping of a bell from the landing signalled the arrival of the lift. They both held their breath and listened as Separt unlocked his door. He closed it behind him, and all was quiet again.

'He didn't notice anything,' she hissed, leaning her head against Barclay's shoulder. 'He's gone inside. Come on.'

They crept stealthily down one flight of stairs, entered the fifth floor landing, and summoned the lift from the floor above to take them to ground level. Back in the 2CV they smiled at one another, releasing the tension.

'That was *too* close,' Barclay said.

Dominique shrugged. 'I have been in tighter places.'

'Tighter spots,' Barclay corrected. But when she asked him what was wrong with the way she'd phrased it, he couldn't think of an answer.

Then came the moment of truth. He switched on the receivers. There were two, each with its own local frequency. One would pick up the telephone, one the bug under the sofa. They might jam or feed back on one another, but he didn't think so. A more real problem was that they might pick up other frequency-users: local taxis, CB radios . . . The signal was weak. A hiss, nothing more. Then the sound of a cough. Dominique thumped him on the shoulder in triumph.

'That's him!' she said. Then she clamped her hand over her mouth. Barclay laughed.

'He can't hear you, don't worry,' he said. Now came the sound of music. Classical music. Separt hummed along to it. Actually, it occurred to Barclay that there was a chance Separt *could* hear them if he happened to put his ear close enough to the microphones while they were talking: these things had a way of working in both directions. Headphones were microphones, too.

'Now,' Dominique was saying, 'all we can do is wait.'

'And hope,' added Barclay.

'Hope?'

'That he doesn't find the bugs.'

She was dismissive. 'Don't worry about that,' she said. 'If he finds them, we'll . . .'

'I know, I know: we'll think of something.' He turned to her. 'Tell me,' he said, 'did you *know* there were stairs behind that door?'

She smiled. 'Of course.'

'You might have—'

'Warned you? Yes, I forgot. Pardon me.'

'I'm not sure I can,' said Barclay. She leaned over and gave him a peck on the cheek. She was wearing perfume. He hadn't really noticed before. He looked in the rearview mirror and saw lipstick on his cheek. He smiled, and did not wipe it off.

After an hour, Dominique got bored. 'Nothing's happening,' she said.

'I can see you're not a cricket fan.'

'Cricket? You mean the English game?'

'Surveillance requires patience,' he said.

Well, so he would guess at any rate. He'd never actually been on a proper surveillance operation, had never been active 'in the field'. He'd always been what could be called a backroom boy. But he'd read about 'the field' in novels. He supposed the novelists must know. Besides, he was quite enjoying the music Separt was playing. Ravel.

Dominique opened her door. 'I'll get us some coffee and a sandwich,' she said.

'What happens if there's some action while you're away?'

'You'll still be here.'

'Yes, but I don't understand French. If anyone telephones . . .'

She thought about this, then collapsed back into her seat with an exasperated sound and slammed shut her door.

'I'll fetch us something to drink if you like?'

She gripped the steering-wheel. 'I'd get even *more* bored on my own. Besides, I'm not really thirsty.' Her pout turned her into a teenager again. What was her age? 'Listen,' she said suddenly, springing forward. Separt's phone was ringing. Barclay sat up straight in his seat. This was his bug's first trial. The music was being turned down. Barclay placed a finger to his lips, warning Dominique not to speak. The phone stopped ringing.

'*Allo?*' Separt's voice.

'*C'est Jean-Pierre.*' The caller was loud and clear – much to Barclay's relief. Dominique was listening intently to the conversation, mouthing the words silently as though learning them off by heart. She signalled for a pen and paper. He took his pen and diary from his inside pocket and handed them over. She opened the diary at November and began to write. After a few minutes of pretty well one-sided conversation, the call was terminated. But Dominique wrote on for another minute or so, reaching December, then read back through what she'd written, altering some words, adding others.

'*Eh bien,*' she said. 'That was lucky.'

'How?'

'When Separt went out, he was trying to find the caller. But the caller was not at home, so he merely left a message asking him to call back. This he has done.'

'And?'

She smiled. 'I don't think we fooled him completely. He wanted to tell the caller all about us. Why would the police do such a survey? What could it mean? The caller was very interested.'

'Did they say anything specific about Witch?'

'Do not rush me. No, nothing about Witch. They were very . . . careful. A care that is learned over years. You might even say a *professional* care. They talked around the subject, like two friends, one merely telling his story to the other.'

'You think Separt knows about the bug?'

She shook her head. 'If he knew, he would have warned the caller, and the caller would not have given away his location.'

'You know where he is?'

She nodded. 'Pretty well. He said Separt had just missed him. He'd been across the street in Janetta's.'

'Janetta's?'

'It sounds like a bar, yes? Perhaps Janetta's is not the name of the bar but of the woman who runs the bar. We will find out, but it might take some time. I think this Jean-Pierre knows something.'

'Such as?'

'Monsieur Separt reported his car missing *after* the assassin landed in England. I think someone persuaded him to . . . to turn the other cheek while the car was taken. He was not ill. He was waiting until it was safe to report the vehicle stolen. Why do you smile?'

'You mean turn a blind eye, not turn the other cheek.'

'Do I?'

He nodded slowly. 'Okay, so now we track down Janetta's.' He paused, wriggling in his seat. 'Or do you want to stick around here?'

'No.' She checked her watch and turned towards him. 'Tonight, you will sleep with me.' The look on Barclay's face alerted her. 'I mean,' she said quickly, 'you will sleep at the apartment. Mama will insist that we dine with her. Don't worry, she is a very good cook. And after dinner . . .'

'Yes?'

'Maybe you will show me your file on Witch. We are partners now after all, aren't we?'

'I suppose we are,' said Barclay, wondering what he would elect to tell Joyce Parry about all of this. She'd be expecting him back soon, maybe as soon as tomorrow morning. He'd have to think up a story to tell her, something convincing. Dominique seemed to read his mind.

'Your employers will allow you another day in Paris?' she asked.

Barclay slapped a confident look onto his face and said nonchalantly, 'Oh, yes.'

But inside, he couldn't help wondering.

Friday 12 June

Elder telephoned Joyce Parry just before breakfast. Smells of bacon-fat and frying tomatoes wafted up to his room as he made the call.

'Joyce? Dominic here.'

'Who else would have the . . . consideration to call at this hour?'

She sounded sleepy. 'Sorry,' he said, 'did I wake you?'

'Just give me the news.'

He wondered idly whether she'd spent the night alone, as he had. 'I've been sent a note,' he said.

'From whom?'

'Witch.'

'What?'

'Not what, who: Witch.'

'Don't get smart, Dominic. Tell me.'

'Just that. A note warning me to stay away.'

'You personally?'

'Me personally.'

'Was it delivered?'

'She left it at a pub, The Cat over the Broomstick.'

'What?'

'That's the name of the pub. I think she left it on the off-chance.'

'You don't think she's following you?'

'No.'

'But she knows you're after her.'

'I'm not even sure about that. Could just be a shrewd guess. She may not know I've retired.'

'Have forensics had a—'

'They're checking it this morning. I don't expect they'll find anything. She left the note with a barman. Doyle and Greenleaf are interviewing him this morning. We had a word with him last night, but today they're really going to put him through it. For what it's worth.'

'Meaning?'

'Meaning she got *him* to write the note for her. Pretended her wrist was sprained.'

'Clever girl.' Joyce Parry almost purred the words.

'Few more like her on our side,' Elder conceded, 'and we might still be an Empire.'

There was a choked sound as Joyce Parry stifled a yawn. 'Description?' she asked at last.

'Come on, Joyce, wakey wakey. She could have changed her looks a dozen times since then. No description the barman can give is going to be valid.'

'You sound disheartened.' She almost sounded concerned.

'Do I?' He managed a smile. 'Maybe it's because I haven't had breakfast yet.'

'What's stopping you?'

'I thought you'd want to—'

'And now I *do* know. So go and have your breakfast. And Dominic . . . ?'

'Yes?'

'Don't do too much. Rely on Greenleaf and Doyle, that's what they're there for.'

'You mean I should ask them to push my bath-chair?'

'I mean it isn't all on *your* shoulders. You're not a one-man band.'

'I have a strange feeling of déjà vu . . .'

'Don't joke about it! I warned you at the start of—'

'Operation Silverfish, I know.'

'And I'm warning you now. You didn't listen then. But listen now, Dominic: if I get any hint that you're going solo on this, I'll send you back to the valleys. Understood?'

'Jesus, next time I'll phone *after* we've both had breakfast.'

'Do you understand me?'

He punched his pillow before replying. 'Yes, Joyce,' he said sweetly, 'loud and impeccably clear.'

'Good. Now go and eat, there's a good boy.'

'Yes, Joyce. Thank you, Joyce. Oh, one last thing. How's the kid doing?'

'I take it you mean Barclay. He's in Paris, following a lead.'

'Really?'

'You sound surprised.'

'I am. Pleasantly so. Field experience, Joyce. There's no substitute for it.'

'I don't recall it doing *you* much good on Silverfish.'

There was a moment's silence. He was waiting for her to apologise. She didn't.

'Goodbye, Joyce,' he said. 'Oh, hold on. Did you ever find out where Ms Capri found Khan's tongue?'

'Between her thighs,' Joyce Parry said quietly.

'Exactly. Remember the rough trade NATO General? Same modus operandi. It goes all the way back, Joyce, just like I told you.'

He put down the receiver. Then, going over the conversation again as he knotted his tie and slipped on his jacket, he smiled to himself. Same old Joyce. Prudent and cautious. She hadn't got where she was today by going out on a limb. He'd always been the limb-creeper. And damn it, some things just didn't and couldn't change. He'd spoken to Barclay quarter of an hour ago. He knew what Barclay had done; he'd have done the same himself. Elder was smiling as he left his room, locking the door after him.

He was impressed to find that Greenleaf and Doyle had already eaten and were on their way to the police station, where Joe the barman had agreed to meet them. So he took breakfast alone, staring out of the window at the early sunshine, thinking about his garden. A drinking companion, Tommy Bridges, had agreed at short notice to water the garden as necessary. But Tommy's memory wasn't so hot these days – too many bottles of rum had cascaded down his throat; perhaps Elder should phone and remind him. But according to the paper, it had rained in south-west Wales yesterday, with more to come today. He hoped his seedlings wouldn't be drowned.

After a filling breakfast and too much weak coffee, he headed back on to the streets, stomach swilling, and decided to concentrate his efforts on the town centre. Witch's note had been a nice shortcut in one respect, in that they now knew she'd been here, had spent at least a little time here. But exactly *where* had she stayed? Doyle was to spend today organising door-to-door enquiries of the resort's hotels and guest houses. Officers were being drafted in from Margate, but Elder doubted they'd be enough. They might have to start recruiting further afield. The problem with that was that it increased the visible presence, and while it was unlikely Witch *was* still here, it might be that too many coppers suddenly appearing on the streets would scare off accomplices or witnesses.

He'd stressed to Doyle that it had to be low-key. Doyle in turn had argued that low-key was slow, and speed was of the essence. In a hostage situation, Doyle would not hesitate to kick the door down and go in shooting. Megaphone diplomacy, waiting it out, these were not his style. And it niggled Elder, for maybe Doyle was right at that. Greenleaf, the quiet one, had made no comment. He'd been fairly docile ever since his outburst at that first meeting in London. If careful Greenleaf, rather than wham-bam Doyle, had been sent to Calais in the first place, perhaps there would have been no new lead for Barclay to find. Now that he thought about it, Joyce hadn't said what was happening in Paris. Keeping it close to her chest, in case nothing came of it: prudent and cautious. And he, Elder, hadn't asked, hadn't probed. Another slip-up on his part, and Joyce would doubtless realise it.

He'd been too long out of the game, it was true. Whatever his failings, someone like Barclay at least had youth on his side. Elder stopped on the pavement and considered this. Yes, he'd wanted Barclay sent to France because he'd thought it would teach the young man a lesson. But what kind of lesson: the useful kind, or the cruel kind? He wasn't sure now. It seemed so long ago. He was standing outside a butcher's shop, busy despite the early hour. Inside the large plate-glass window was displayed an array of red, glistening meat, grey sausages, pink pork loins. The butcher and his young assistant were working speedily, chatting all the time with the customers, who were also passing the time talking among themselves. Pleasures of the flesh-ing.

Then his eyes focused on the window itself. There was a small poster advertising a craft exhibition. And on the glass door to the shop, a door wedged open, there was a larger poster advertising a travelling fair. He'd passed similar flysheets last night during his walk, but he hadn't actually seen the fair itself. He recalled someone saying, 'Maybe she was going to run away with the circus . . .' Moncur the lorry driver had said it. A travelling fair. Night-people. Maybe one of them would have seen something. She'd been making for Cliftonville, and there'd been a fair here. Now she'd gone, and so it seemed had the fair. Elder walked briskly into the shop.

The women stared at him suspiciously as he failed to join the queue. Instead, he leaned over the counter.

'Excuse me, that fair . . .' He pointed to the poster on the door. 'Is it still in town?'

The butcher, busy wrapping a package, glanced at the door. 'Don't know, sorry,' he said, taking a pencil from behind his ear. 'Now, Mrs Slattery, is that it?' The woman nodded, and he began totting up figures on a scrap of paper. 'That's four pounds and fifty pence then,' he said.

'Cleared out at the beginning of the week,' said a voice from the queue. Elder turned towards it.

'Do you know where they were headed next?'

Mutters and shakes of the head. 'Someone down on the front might know. A landlord, someone like that.'

'Yes,' said Elder. 'Thank you.' A woman was coming into the shop.

'Hello, Elsie,' said a voice from the queue. 'Here, any idea where that fair was off to?'

'Same as every year,' said Elsie authoritatively. 'Brighton.'

She wondered why the man beamed at her before rushing out of the shop. 'You get some funny types,' she said, 'this time of year. Some right funny types.' Then she sniffed and joined the end of the queue, where there was valuable gossip to be exchanged and the man was soon forgotten.

Madame Herault and Barclay were getting along like the proverbial house on fire. Despite the language barrier, despite barriers of age and culture, they knew one thing: they both liked to dunk their croissants in their coffee.

They sat together at the table in the kitchen. Now and then Madame Herault would call for Dominique, and Dominique would call back that she'd be there in a moment. There was a news programme on the radio, the presenters talking too fast for Barclay to make much sense of any of the stories. Madame Herault commented from time to time before shrugging her shoulders and returning to her coffee. She pushed the basket of croissants and chocolatines closer to him, exhorting him to eat, eat. He nodded and smiled, smiled and nodded. And he ate.

He'd spent a restless night in the spare room. Dominique's bedroom was through the wall from his, and he could hear her old bed creaking and groaning. His own bed was newer, more solid. It was also short, so that he couldn't lie stretched out unless he lay in a diagonal across the bed. His feather-filled pillow smelt musty, as did the sheets and the single blanket. Finally, he shrugged off sleep altogether and got up. He still had a lot of bits and pieces left over from his shopping trip to the electronics store. He plugged in the soldering-iron and hummed an aria or two from *The Marriage of Figaro*, waiting for it to warm . . .

Now here she came, into the kitchen. Madame Herault gave an insulted gasp. Barclay almost gasped too. Dominique was dressed in winkle-picker black-buckled boots, black tights, black leather mini-skirt, a white T-shirt torn at the armpits and spattered with paint, and more jewellery than Barclay had seen outside a department store. Her eyes were surrounded by thick black eyeshadow and her face was dusted white, making her lips seem redder than ever before. She'd teased her hair up into spikes, brittle with gel or hairspray, and she wore three earrings in either ear.

Her mother said something biting. Dominique ignored her and leaned past Barclay to grab a chocolatine. With it in her mouth, she went to the stove and poured coffee from the ancient metal percolator, then dragged a chair out from beneath the table and sat down between her mother and her guest. Barclay tried not to look at her. He kept his eyes on the tabletop, on her mother, on the pans and utensils hanging from the wall in front of him. He could smell patchouli oil. He could feel his heart pounding. She really did look incredible. It was just that she wasn't Dominique any more.

She was wearing her disguise.

'I telephoned a colleague,' she informed Barclay in English. 'He's checking on possible Janettas. With luck there won't be more than one or two.'

He nodded. 'I've made a wire,' he said.

'A wire?' Flakes of pastry escaped from her mouth.

'A bug for you to wear, so I can listen.'

She swallowed some coffee. 'When did you make it?'

'During the night. I couldn't sleep.'

'Me neither. I was reading your file. It was interesting. I would like to meet Mr Dominic Elder.'

Madame Herault, who had been muttering throughout and averting her gaze, now said something aloud, directed at her daughter. Dominique replied in similarly caustic tones then turned to Barclay. 'My mother says I am insulting her in front of a guest. I've told her all the women dress like this in London. She's waiting for you to agree.'

Barclay shrugged and nodded. Madame Herault pursed her lips and stirred her coffee-cup, shaking her head. The rest of breakfast was passed more or less in silence. After breakfast, Dominique and Barclay retired to the spare room.

'We need some tape,' he said.

'I'll bring some.'

She was back within a minute, holding a roll of thick brown packing tape.

'Just as well your T-shirt's baggy,' said Barclay. 'Otherwise, anyone could see you're wearing a wire.'

She stood with the transmitter in her hand. There wasn't much to it – a length of wire connecting a small microphone at one end to a transmitter at the other. It was bulkier than Barclay would have liked, and at the same time it was more delicate, too. His soldering wasn't perfect, but it would hold . . . he hoped.

'Lift your shirt at the back,' he ordered. She did so, and he stood behind her. Her skin was very lightly tanned, smooth, broken only by a pattern of variously-sized brown moles. She was not wearing a bra. This is work, he told himself. Just work.

He tore off a length of tape with his teeth and placed it over the wire, pushing it on to her back so that the transmitter hung free below the tape itself. Then around to her front, the T-shirt lifted still higher so that he could make out the swelling shadowy undersides of her breasts. Work, work, work. He ran the wire around to her smooth stomach, wondering whether to place the microphone just above her belly-button, or higher, in the hollow of her sternum.

'Having fun down there?' said Dominique.

'Sorry, I'm considering placements.' He touched her stomach then her sternum with the tip of his forefinger. 'Here or here?'

'Ah, I see. High up, I think. Unless the man is a midget, the microphone will be closer to his mouth.'

'Good point.' He tore off more tape and secured the microphone in the cleft just below her breasts. Then he used more tape to attach the wire to her side. 'Okay,' he said at last. 'Just try not to wriggle or bend over. He might hear the tape crinkling.'

She dropped her T-shirt and examined herself in the mirror, twisting to see if the wire was visible through the cotton. She stepped over to the window, then walked back slowly towards Barclay. He shook his head.

'Can't see a thing,' he said.

'What if I stretch myself?' She thrust back her shoulders and stuck out her chest. Barclay still couldn't see any sign either of brown tape or of black wire. And as for the slight bulge of the microphone itself . . .

'If you do that,' he said, 'I don't think Jean-Pierre's eyes are going to rest *between* your breasts so much as *on* them.'

She thumped his shoulder. 'You are teasing,' she said. He was about to deny it when there was a sound from the hall: the telephone was ringing. Dominique dashed out of the room to answer it, spoke excitedly, then dashed back.

'The fifth arrondissement,' she said. 'A street in the Latin Quarter. There is a bar called Janetta's.'

'Sounds good. Lift your T-shirt again. After all that running around, I want to check the tapes are still fast.'

'Fast?'

'Still stuck down.'

'Okay.' She lifted the T-shirt. 'But listen,' she said, 'there's more. In the same street lives an Australian, an anarchist. Called John Peter Wrightson. He's lived in France for years. You see?'

'John Peter, Jean-Pierre.'

'Yes! It makes sense, no?'

'Separt's caller didn't sound Aussie to me.' She shrugged. The tape had held fairly well. He just hoped she didn't sweat. 'Okay,' he said, 'you can drop the shirt. It looks okay.'

'You sound like a doctor.'

He smiled. 'Your . . . colleague, he sounds as if he's on the ball. I mean, he sounds efficient.'

'It was easy for him. The bar was in the directory. Then he entered the street name into the computer just to see if there was any further information. Monsieur Wrightson's name came on to the screen.'

'Speaking of computers . . .'

'Everything is being printed out at my office. We can pick up copies later today. That was a clever trick you played.'

He shrugged. 'A computer makes it easy.' Not that he imagined Separt would keep anything important on the disks. Dominique looked ready to go. 'We haven't tried out the transmitter yet.'

'They worked yesterday. This one will work today. I trust you.'

'That's another thing. We've got to go back to Separt's apartment and get those two—'

'Later, later.' She grabbed his hand. 'Now let's hurry, otherwise Mama will wonder what we're doing in here.' And she giggled as she led him down the hall, yelling a farewell to her mother. Then she stopped. 'Wait a moment,' she said returning to her bedroom. When she appeared again, she was pinning an Anarchy badge to her T-shirt.

'Nice touch,' he said.

The punk driving the 2CV certainly attracted stares from male drivers whenever she stopped at lights or was caught in a jam. Barclay had to give her credit. If – when – Separt and Jean-Pierre spoke again, their descriptions of the two women who visited them would be difficult to reconcile into a single individual. The winkle-picker heels even made her a good inch taller. Her hair was the same colour as yesterday, but that was the only area of comparison. In all other details, she was a different person.

They'd agreed that she would visit Jean-Pierre alone: Barclay would stick out like a sore thumb. Dominique could disguise herself, but there was no disguising Barclay. She would visit alone, but Barclay insisted that she would wear a wire, so that he could listen from the car. He didn't want her getting into trouble.

They went over Dominique's story again on the way there. The fact that Jean-Pierre might well be the anarchist John Wrightson gave them a new angle to work from. They added it to her story, making slight alterations. The street they finally entered was squalid and incredibly narrow, or rather made narrow by the lines of parked cars either side, leaving a single lane with no passing places. A car in front of them – and thankfully travelling the same direction as them – hesitated by a gap between two of the parked cars, considered it but moved on. It was a gap just about big enough for a motorbike or a moped, but not for a car.

'We're in luck,' said Dominique, passing the gap and then stopping. 'Here's a space.'

'You've got to be kidding.'

But she'd already pushed the dashboard-mounted gear-stick into reverse, and craned her neck around to watch through the rear window as she backed the car in towards the kerb, turning the steering-wheel hard. Barclay watched through the front windscreen and saw that they were a centimetre from the car in front. Then there was the slight jolt of a collision: they had hit the car behind. But Dominique just kept reversing, pushing against the car behind, then easing down on the clutch and turning the steering-wheel hard back around. This time, edging forwards, her front bumper touched the car in front and pushed it forward a couple of centimetres.

'In Paris,' she said, 'we park with the handbrake off.'

'Right,' said Barclay. The 2CV was now parked, kerbside, a couple of inches from the car in front, and the same distance from the car behind. He tried not to think about how they would make a fast getaway.

'That's Janetta's,' said Dominique. 'You see? With the PMU sign.'

Barclay saw. 'It doesn't look particularly open.'

'It's open,' she said. With nice timing, the door of the bar was pulled from within, and a fat unshaven man wearing blue workman's clothes and a beret came sauntering out. He looked like he'd had a few drinks. It was quarter to ten. The door jangled closed behind him.

'So it's open,' he said.

'Monsieur Wrightson lives this side of the street, across from the bar. Number thirty-eight. Oh, well.' She took a deep breath. She did look a little nervous. It struck Barclay that maybe she too was getting out of her depth.

'Be careful,' he said as she opened the door.

'I'll be careful,' she said, closing the door after her. She came round to his side of the car and opened the door to say something more. 'If anything *does* happen to me . . .'

'Yes?'

'Please, look after Mama.' Then she closed the door again, gave him a big grin and threw him a kiss, before turning on her noisy heels and making for number thirty-eight. He wondered if that extra wiggle of her leather-clad bum was for him, or whether she was just getting into her part. Then he reached for his receiver, switched it on, and waited.

She had to climb two flights to the door marked WRIGHTSON, J-P. She spoke in a low voice as she climbed.

'I hope you can hear me, Michael. This is a very dirty stairwell, not at all like Monsieur Separt's. It makes me wonder what the two men could have in common, one living in luxury, the other in squalor. What do you think? Their politics, perhaps? Ideals can bridge gulfs, can't they?'

She paused outside the door, then pressed the buzzer. She couldn't hear anything from inside, so she knocked with her closed fist instead. And again. And again. There was a noise from within, a creaking floorboard, someone coughing. The door was unlocked.

'*Qui est* . . . ? Jesus Christ!' The man who stood there was scrawny, no fat at all on his body. He wore only tight grey underpants, and had a cigarette hanging from one corner of his mouth. He stared hard at every inch of the girl in front of him. 'Jesus Christ,' he said again. Then he lapsed into French, and Dominique was sure in her mind. When she spoke, she spoke in English.

'Ah . . . I am looking for Diana.'

'You speak English?' He nodded, scratching himself. Then he frowned. 'Diana? Never heard of her.'

'Oh.' She looked crestfallen. 'She told me she lived here.'

'*Here?*'

She nodded. 'I think so. She told me her address and I forgot it. I was drunk a little, I think. But this morning I wake up and I think I remember it. I dreamed it, maybe.'

'You mean this building?'

She shook her head, earrings jangling against each other. 'This floor.'

'Yeah? Well, there's old Prévost across the hall . . . but he hasn't set foot outside since '68.' Wrightson smiled. He was still studying her, appraising her. 'Anyway,' he said, 'come in. Can't remember when I last saw a punk.'

'Is it not still the fashion in England?'

'I wouldn't know, *chèrie*. I'm not English, I'm Australian.'

Dominique looked excited. 'Yes!' she said. 'Diana told me there was an Australian!'

'Yeah?' He frowned again. 'Beats the hell out of me.'

'You do not know her?'

He shrugged. 'Describe her to me.'

He had led her through a hall resembling a warehouse. There were boxes of flysheets, teetering piles of books, and the walls were covered with political posters. One of the posters showed a scrawled capital A over a circle.

'Anarchy,' she said, pointing to it. 'Just like my badge.'

He nodded, but didn't say anything. Maybe she'd been a bit too heavy-handed. She tried to slow her pulse-rate, keeping her breathing regular. She stared at another poster, another artfully scrawled circle but this time with a capital V on the top of it.

'*V for Vendetta*,' he explained. 'It's a comic book.'

'It looks like the anarchy symbol upside down.'

'I suppose it does.' He seemed pleased by the comparison.

The room they entered was stuffy, and seemed to double as living room and bedroom. There were more boxes here, more books, more mess. A woman, not too young, was sitting up inside a sleeping-bag on the floor, long brown hair falling down over her naked chest. She looked like she was in the process of waking up.

'Dawn, go make some coffee, girl.'

'Jesus, J-P, I made it yesterday.' Her accent was American. Wrightson growled at her. 'What time is it anyway?'

'Nearly ten,' Dominique answered after Wrightson had shrugged his shoulders.

'Middle of the damned night.' The woman looked about her until she found some tobacco and a paper, rolled herself a cigarette, then stepped from the sleeping-bag and walked through to the kitchen. Wrightson watched her depart.

'No shame, these Yanks,' he said. 'Speaking of which . . .' He wandered over behind the sofa and pulled a pair of jeans from the floor, shaking them free of dust before putting them on. Then he sat down again, resting on the arm of the sofa. Dominique was still standing. 'You were describing Diana to me,' he said.

'Oh, well, she's tall, short dark hair. English, I think. She has very . . . uh, piercing eyes.'

He thought for a moment, then shrugged. 'You say her hair's short? Pinned up maybe?'

'Pinned up, yes.'

Another moment's thought. 'Where did you meet her?'

'Outside the Louvre, beside the pyramid. She was sitting by herself, watching the fountains. I was bored. We talked a little. I liked her.'

He drew on his cigarette, blowing the smoke out through his nose. He was studying her very closely. 'What was she wearing?'

Dominique made show of remembering. 'Black jeans, I think. A T-shirt, I don't remember what colour.'

'Sunglasses?'

'No. Maybe she had some in her pocket.'

'Mm-hmm.'

The woman, Dawn, had come back and was pulling on her clothes. She examined Dominique, saw the badge. 'Anarchy,' she said, nodding.

'What's your name, *chèrie*?' Wrightson asked.

'Françoise.'

'Like Françoise Sagan?'

'Yes, I suppose so.'

'Are you an anarchist, Françoise?'

She nodded. He gestured towards the boxes.

'Take some literature with you. Maybe you'll have read it before, maybe not. And leave an address and phone number. If Diana comes here, I can tell her where you are.'

'You know her then?'

He shrugged. 'Maybe. Maybe not.'

'I already gave her my phone number, outside the Louvre. She never got in touch. She said she would. We had a drink together . . . I liked her.'

She hoped she sounded and looked in as much despair as she felt. Wrightson was suspicious, of course he was. He was also very careful. She should have realised that from his telephone conversation with Separt. Only that one word – Janetta's – had given him away. She had another thought, too: maybe there was another Janetta's in another street with another Jean-Pierre living across the road. Maybe, but she didn't think so. This *felt* right. She walked across to the boxes and pulled out a pamphlet – wordy, written in slightly imperfect French.

'Make Françoise some coffee, too,' Wrightson said to Dawn, who was making for the kitchen again. Then he came over towards Dominique and put an arm around her shoulders. She flinched. What if he felt the transmitter?

'Easy,' he said. 'It'll be all right. You'll find other . . . women friends. I know lots of girls like you, Françoise, believe me.' His proximity disgusted her. She could smell his sweat, the rancid nicotine breath. Then she saw some cartoon books and moved away from him, picking one up. It was by Separt.

Wrightson followed her. 'You like his stuff?'

She shook her head. 'Too tame.'

He looked disappointed. Obviously, he'd just been about to claim friendship with the great cartoonist. Below the cartoon book there was a newspaper. She picked it up, too.

'You read the London *Times*?' she said.

'Just the crossword. I enjoy a challenge.'

'The pages are torn.'

He winked. 'It saves on toilet paper.'

She gave a small laugh.

'That's more like it,' he said. 'How old are you, Françoise?'

Barclay had told her on the way that she would pass for eighteen. 'Nineteen,' she said, just to be safe.

'It's a good age to be. Have you got a job?'

'No.'

'Where do you live?'

'With friends. Some HLM housing . . .'

'Do *you* enjoy a challenge, Françoise?'

She frowned. 'I don't understand.'

Wrightson waved some of his pamphlets at her. 'I need help distributing my . . . literature. It's late-night work, you understand? Not much pay, but maybe you'd be interested.'

'Maybe.'

He nodded. She saw him for what he was, a cunning man but also stupid. A user of women, hiding his true feelings and desires behind political slogans. She'd met his type before.

'Leave me your phone number,' he said.

'We don't have a phone.'

The eyes narrowed. 'You said you gave it to Diana?'

She was ready for this. She nodded. 'The number of a club where some of us go. Everybody knows me there.'

'Okay, which club?'

She was ready for this too. Her night had been busy with plans, with dress rehearsals. 'L'Arriviste,' she said. 'Rue de la Lune, second arrondissement.'

He nodded. 'I'll remember that.'

Dawn appeared with three filthy mugs, brimming with black coffee. 'There's no sugar,' she said.

'Then we drink it black and bitter,' said Wrightson, taking a mug, 'like our thoughts.'

Dawn thought this over, then smiled towards Dominique, a smile full of admiration for Wrightson. But she was also warning the young pretender, the arriviste: 'He's *my* property.' Dominique drank to it.

They talked politics over the coffee, and she managed to sound less knowledgeable than she actually was. She also made sure to express her naivety, leading Wrightson to give speech after speech. The more he spoke, the less he asked, and the less he asked the more comfortable she felt. Yes, his ego was his fatal flaw. It had made him blind to the motives of others. All he cared about was himself. She had heard better speeches in the bars of schools and polytechnics.

The coffee finished, she said she had to go. He pressed her to stay but she shook her head. So he put together a bundle of stuff, photocopied single sheets, folded pamphlets, a couple of posters, and thrust it into her hands. The paper everything was printed on was cheap scratchy stuff, some of it off-white, some yellow. She thanked him.

'Just read,' he said. 'And pass on the message.'

'Message?'

He tapped the pamphlets. 'Tell your friends.'

'Ah, yes, yes, of course.'

She said goodbye to Dawn, and Wrightson saw her to the door, his hand rubbing her shoulder again, creeping down to graze against the bare skin of her arm. Then, as he opened the door, he put his hand on the back of her head and pulled her to him. With her hands full of paper, she couldn't push away. He planted a kiss on her lips, his tongue probing against her gritted teeth. Then he pulled away, leaving her gasping.

As she ran (as best she could in her heels) down the stairs, she could hear him laughing. Then he slammed shut the door, and it boomed and echoed like cannon-fire all the way out to the street.

Barclay could see that she was in a furious temper. She threw the bits of paper on to his lap, got behind the steering-wheel, and shunted her way out of the parking space and into the road.

'You were in there for hours,' he said into the silence. 'What happened?'

'Didn't you hear?'

'Only up to where he had Dawn go make you coffee.'

'He put his arm around me.'

'Probably pulled loose a connection. You'll have to tell me the rest.'

'First I need a drink. I need to get rid of the taste in my mouth.' She reached under her T-shirt and ripped off the transmitter, tossing it on to Barclay's lap beside the bits of paper.

She was quiet all the way to her favoured corner bar, where she collapsed into one of the terrace chairs and ordered a *pression*. What the hell, it had just gone eleven. Barclay ordered one too. She still didn't seem to want to talk, so he glanced through the literature she'd thrown at him, and which he had brought with him to the cafe.

'Well, well, well,' he said, holding one pamphlet up for her to see. It was concerned with 'European Freedom Fighters'. There was mention of the Italian group Croix Jaune, and of the German Wolfgang Bandorff. There was, to Barclay's eyes, a *lot* about Wolfgang Bandorff, with a final call to all 'lovers of freedom' to follow Bandorff's dicta, to motivate and mobilise and to let 'actions speak where the mouths of the oppressed are gagged'.

'Interesting,' said Barclay. He'd got Dominique's attention. She read through the pamphlet, but didn't speak until the beer had been placed in front of her, demolished, and another one ordered.

'Bandorff was mentioned in the Witch file,' Barclay reminded her.

'Yes, he was in Scotland when the Pope visited.'

'It can't be just coincidence.'

Dominique didn't say anything. She was running her tongue over her gums, as though washing them clean of something.

'So what happened up there?' he asked.

Her second beer arrived, and this time she drank it slowly, taking her time as she told him all about John Peter Wrightson.

Roadworks impeded Elder's progress on the route to Brighton. There were times when it seemed to him the whole road network of England was being coned off and dug up. He was sure he could remember a time when there'd been no contraflows. But of course there'd been less traffic then, too. It was taking him a little while to get used to Doyle's car. It was fast and certainly nippy in traffic, but the clutch seemed to have a mind of its own. Doyle had complained when Elder asked for his car. But it was only reasonable. They'd travelled down in the one car – Doyle's – and now that car was needed. Besides, as Elder pointed out, Doyle was staying in the town. What did he need his car for? And if a car *were* needed, he could always borrow one from the police.

'So what's stopping you doing that, too?' Doyle had said.

'I'm in a hurry.'

'I can't see there's any rush.'

Elder had already filled both Doyle and Greenleaf in on his planned trip, and the reasoning behind it, so he stayed silent and let Doyle have his grumble. As ever, Greenleaf wasn't saying much. The silent type.

They looked like they'd been working together on interrogations for years. They looked confident, successful. They looked like a team.

'If you scratch it,' Doyle said at last, digging his hand into his trouser pocket, 'if you so much as fart on the seat-fabric . . .' He held the keys in the air for an instant, not letting Elder have them.

'Understood,' he said. 'It'll get a full valet service before I bring it back.'

Doyle spoke quietly, spacing each word. 'Just bring it back.'

Elder nodded. 'Will do.' He reached out his hand and took the keys from Doyle.

There was nothing for him to do in Cliftonville anyway. The note was already in the forensic lab. The paper and envelope would be analysed, since Witch rather than the barman had provided them. Sometimes you could tell a lot from a sheet of paper: brand used, batch number, when produced, where stocked. Same went for fibre analysis. They would take the envelope apart with surgical precision, just in case there was a fibre or anything similar inside, anything that could tell them anything about Witch.

Joe the barman had been little help. And so far no one they'd spoken to had seen or heard anything that Sunday night. The thing to do was get the local police involved and have them do the leg-work. Time was pressing. They needed to be in London. The summit would start on Tuesday; hardly any time at all to recheck security. A few of the delegations, Elder knew, had already arrived. Most would arrive over the weekend. The last to arrive, the Americans, would touch down on Monday morning. Thirty secret servicemen would protect the President. But they couldn't protect him from a single sniper's bullet, from a well-placed bomb, from most of the tricks Witch had learned.

Sitting in a slow-moving queue, Elder leaned forwards the better to scratch his back, just where it itched. He'd had the itch for a long time. It hadn't really bothered him in Wales, not often, but now it had started up again. There was just something about a traffic jam that set it off. At least, he kidded himself it was the traffic jam.

Finally, he reached the outskirts of Brighton. He knew the town well, or had known it well at one time. He used to have a friend just west of the town in Portslade, beyond Hove. A female friend, the partner in a veterinary practice. He remembered her bedroom faced on to the sea. A long time ago . . . He made friends with difficulty, kept them with even more difficulty. His fault, not theirs. He was a slovenly correspondent, forgetful of things like birthdays, and he found friendship at times a heavy baggage to bear. That was why he hadn't made a good husband: he didn't make a good friend in the first place. He sometimes wondered what kind of father he'd have made, if Susanne hadn't been taken from him.

He drove through Brighton until he hit the seafront. There was no sign of a travelling fair. He couldn't see any posters, either. Nothing to say whether it had been and gone, or was still to arrive. Nothing. But what he did notice were kids – kids lounging about, kids with nothing to do. School-leavers, probably, their exams over. Or the unemployed youth of the town. There were tramps too, and younger men, somewhere between school-leaver and tramp. They tried begging from passers-by, offering swigs from their bottle as trade. Living in rural Wales, Elder was accustomed to the occasional hippy convoy, but nothing like this. The unemployed men he knew in his local village had been hard-working men who wanted to get back into hard work.

He drove slowly all the way along the front and back, studying the faces he saw. The world was changing; time was slipping into reverse. It was like the 1920s and 30s, or even the Victorian world described by Dickens. In London, he'd seen teams of windscreen washers, something he'd only before seen on American TV dramas. Young men – predominantly black – would wait at traffic lights and, when the lights turned red, would wash windscreens, then ask to be paid. One group Elder had seen had brought a sofa to the kerbside, so that they could relax in comfort between shifts. He wondered how much they made. He'd arrived in London without his car. A car would have protected him from the worst of it, from the beggars waiting for him in underpasses, the buskers in the Underground, the cardboard boxes which had become people's homes. That hopeless, toneless cry: 'Spare change, please, any spare change. Spare change, please, any spare change.' Like rag and bone men expecting society's leftovers.

Finally, having twice driven the length of the promenade, he pulled in at the kerb, near a group of teenagers, and wound down his window.

'Oi, oi!' cried one. 'Here's a punter looking for a bit of bum action! Go talk to the man, Chrissy!'

The one called Chrissy spat on the ground and gave Elder a baleful look.

'I'm looking for the fair,' Elder called from the car. 'Is there a fair in town?'

'You're after kids, is that it? We know your sort, don't we?' There were grins at this. Elder tried to smile back, as though he too were enjoying the joke.

'I'm just looking for the fair,' he said, making it sound like a not unreasonable request.

'Marine Parade,' said one of the crowd, waving a hand holding a can of beer in the direction of the Palace Pier.

'Yes,' said Elder, 'but that's a permanent fairground, isn't it? I'm looking for a *travelling* fair.'

'Sorry I spoke. Here, give us five quid for some chips, guv.' The youth was slouching towards him, hand held out. Elder didn't see anything dangerous in the young man's eyes; just an idiot vacancy. He knew pressure points which would have the youth dancing in agony within seconds. He knew how much pain the body could stand, and how much less the mind itself could stand. He knew.

Then he sighed and handed over a five-pound note.

'The fair,' he said.

The youth grinned. 'There's a fair up on The Level. Know where that is?'

Yes, Elder knew where it was. He'd practically driven past it on his way down to the shore. He didn't recall seeing a fair, but then he hadn't really been looking.

'Thank you,' he said, driving on. Behind him, the youth was fanning himself with the banknote. Already his friends were gathering round like jackals.

The front at Brighton was all pebblestone beach and inescapable breeze, fun-rides and day-trippers. But further up the town's hill, past the Pavilion and the shops, was a large, flat, grassy park called The Level, crisscrossed with paths. Locals walked their dogs here, children shrieked on swings. And every year there came a fair. He wondered that he'd been able to miss it, but then he'd presupposed any fairground would be stationed along the promenade, where the pickings were richest. There weren't as many stalls and rides as he'd been expecting. The usual waltzers and dodgems and rifle-ranges, ghost train, kiddies' rides, hot dog stalls. But no big wheel or dive-bombers, nothing that he would call a big attraction. Marine Parade had stolen a march on the travelling fair.

And everything was closed, save a couple of the kiddies' rides which were doing desultory business. A monkey swung down over the children on one ride, operated by a sour-looking woman. The trick seemed to be that if a child pulled the tail off the monkey, the child got a free ride. Something like that. The fair proper would no doubt open up later on in the day. He parked Doyle's car at a safe distance from The Level itself – he didn't want errant hands wiping candy floss on it – and walked back. One ride was discharging its cargo. The woman who operated both ride and monkey came out of her stall to collect the money from the few kids waiting for the ride to start up again. She wore a leather bag slung around her neck, the sort conductors still used on some London buses. Elder noticed that the rides were old, certainly older than their cargo. There was a horse, a racing car with a horn, a tiny double-decker bus, a sort of ladybird from which most of the paint had flaked, a jeep with moveable steering wheel, and a spaceship. There was heated competition for both the spaceship and the racing car.

'Excuse me,' he said to the woman, 'where can I find whoever's in charge?'

'That's me.' She went on taking money, dispensing change.

'No, I mean in charge of the fair as a whole.'

'Oh?' She gave him the benefit of a two-second glance, then sighed. 'What's wrong now?'

'Nothing.'

'Are you council?'

'No, nothing like that.'

'What then?'

He paused. 'If you'd just tell me where I can find . . .'

Having collected all the fares, she moved past him. 'Mind yourself,' she said. 'If you stay on there, you'll have to pay same as the rest.' Back in her perspex-fronted booth, she turned on a tape-recorder. A pop song blasted out of the speaker overhead. Then the carousel started to turn, and she tugged her left arm, jiggling the monkey up and down, comfortably out of reach of the squealing children. Elder stood his ground by the open door. The children were waving at their parents as they spun slowly past them. One of the kids looked petrified, though he was trying not to show it. He gripped on to the steering wheel of his jeep, hardly daring to take a hand off to wave, despite the cajoling of his mother. Fear, Elder was reminded, was utterly relative, a shifting quantity.

As the allotted time of the ride came to its end, the woman lowered the monkey so that a girl could whip off its tail. Then she pulled the monkey up again and hooked her end of its line over a nail on the wall of her booth, holding it there. The music was turned down, but not off, the ride came to a stop, the parents collected their children. The boy from the jeep looked pale. The woman looked at them through the perspex window, then turned to Elder.

'Still here?'

He shrugged. 'I've nothing better to do.'

'Sure you're not council?' He shook his head and she sighed again. 'Try the caravan behind the waltzers,' she said. 'The long caravan, mind, not the little one.'

'And who am I looking for?'

'His name's Ted. That's all, just Ted.'

And indeed it was.

'Just call me Ted,' the man said when Elder appeared at the caravan door and asked for him. They shook hands.

'I'm Dominic Elder.'

'Pleased to meet you. Now, Mr Elder, what seems to be the problem?'

'No problem, I assure you.'

'Good, pleased to hear it. In that case, why don't you come in?'

The caravan was large but cramped, the result of too many ornaments on too many occasional tables. Glass clowns seemed to predominate. There was a small two-seater sofa, and two armchairs, re-covered in an orange-coloured flowery print. Ted nodded towards a chair.

'Take a pew, Mr Elder. Now, what can I do for you?'

It wasn't until Elder was seated that he saw it was Ted's intention to continue standing, arms folded, ready to listen. Elder admired the man's grasp of psychology. Standing, he had authority over the seated Elder. They were not equals. That, at least, was the ploy. Ted might not be the man's real name. He was in his 50s, and wore his hair slicked back, his sideburns long: a Teddy Boy look. Perhaps the name had stuck. There was doubtless a comb in the back pocket of his oily denims.

'I'm looking for my daughter,' Elder said.

'Yes? In Brighton is she?'

'I don't know. I *think* she was in Cliftonville.'

'We were there the other week.'

Elder nodded. 'She's keen on fairs, I thought maybe somebody might have seen her wandering around . . .'

'How old is she, Mr Elder?' There was sympathy in Ted's voice, but not much. He was still suspicious.

'She's twenty-nine,' Elder said. Ted looked suitably surprised.

'So it's not a case of the kid running away with the fair?' he said, more to himself than to Elder. 'Twenty-nine, eh? Got a photo of her?'

'Not on me, no. I was in Cliftonville, and when I heard about your fair, well, I rushed down here without thinking.'

'Twenty-nine . . . and she likes fairs, you say?'

'I'm afraid she's . . . well, she's a little *backward*, Ted. An accident as a child . . .'

Ted raised a hand. 'Say no more, Mr Elder. Understood. Well, I can certainly put the word about. You'd better give me a description.'

'Of course. She's slim, five foot ten inches.'

'Tall then?'

'Tall, yes.'

'Go on.'

'Well, the problem is . . . she may have disguised herself. You know, dyed her hair, bought a wig. Her hair's usually short, dark brown.'

'Doesn't matter really. A woman her age, hanging around the rides, someone'll have clocked her. Are you sticking around Brighton, Mr Elder? Only, there's a few more fairs on the go – Eastbourne, Guildford, Newbury – I could give you the names of some people to talk with . . .'

'That's very kind of you, Ted.'

'Hold on, I'll get a bit of paper.'

He went through to another room, probably his office. Elder thought about getting to his feet but decided that his best bet was to stay seated, that way he could be fairly sure of maintaining the sympathy vote. The standing/sitting psychology only worked if, when you were standing, the person who was seated was trying to be your equal. But Elder, in confessing to having a 'backward' daughter, had relinquished such a role, placing the burden of responsibility on the 'stronger' Ted.

It was the sort of stuff you learned early on in Elder's profession. Another trick of the tradecraft.

The door to the caravan opened and a woman clambered aboard. She seemed surprised to see Elder. He took her for Ted's wife until she spoke.

'Sorry, is Ted about?'

'Here, Rosa,' called Ted, emerging from his office. He pointed a biro at Elder. 'This is Mr Elder. His daughter's run away. Last seen in Cliftonville. He was wondering if we'd come across her.'

'Oh dear,' said the woman. She perched herself on the edge of an armchair. 'What's her name, lovey?'

'Diana,' said Elder.

Ted laughed. 'Trust Rosa to get down to nuts and bolts. I clean forgot to ask you what she was called. Mr Elder, this is Gypsy Rose Pellengro, mistress of the crystal ball.'

Elder nodded his greeting towards Gypsy Rose, and she smiled back.

'Diana,' she said. 'It's a lovely name, sir. Your wife's choice or yours?'

Elder laughed. 'I can't honestly remember. It was a long time ago.'

'Mr Elder's daughter is twenty-nine,' Ted informed Gypsy Rose. He had settled at a table, slipped on a pair of half-moon glasses, and was scratching on a piece of notepaper with his pen.

'Twenty-nine?' said Gypsy Rose. 'I thought she was—'

'Me, too,' said Ted. 'Preconceptions, Rosa. You see, Mr Elder, we get a lot of parents coming to us. Oh, yes, a lot. Their kiddies have gone missing and they're desperate to find them. One woman . . . up in Watford, I think it is . . . she's been coming to see me for six or seven years. Very sad, clinging to hope like that.'

'Sad,' echoed Gypsy Rose.

'Diana's tall and slim,' Ted informed Gypsy Rose, 'and she's maybe got short dark hair. I don't suppose she came to you for a consultation while we were in Cliftonville?'

'No.' Gypsy Rose shook her head. 'No, I'd have remembered someone like that.'

Like what? thought Elder. The description was vague to the point of uselessness.

'Well, ask around the other stalls, will you, Rosa?' Ted had taken off his glasses and risen from his chair. He handed Elder the slip of paper, which Elder read. Four different fairs in four locations, with dates and a contact name for each.

'Thank you very much,' Elder said, pocketing the note. 'They're not as big as this, mind. We all join up for the bigger events. Tell them Ted sent you, they should see you right.'

'Thanks again,' Elder said. He reached into his pocket and brought out a small notebook and a pen. 'I'm staying at a hotel in Cliftonville. I may have to move on, but they can forward any messages to me.' He wrote down the telephone number, tore out the page, and handed it to Ted.

'If I hear anything, I'll let you know,' said Ted.

'I'd be very grateful.' Elder rose to his feet. 'It's been nice to meet you,' he said to Gypsy Rose.

'Likewise.'

Ted saw him to the door. The two men shook hands.

'Mind how you go, Mr Elder,' said Ted. 'And good luck.'

'Thanks,' said Elder. 'Goodbye.'

He walked with care across the snaking lengths of power-cable, squeezed between two closed stalls, and was back on the road again. He wandered the length of the fair, and stopped beside the caravan belonging to Gypsy Rose Pellengro, reading the citations pinned to the board beside her door. He peered in through the window. The interior looked neat and plain.

'She'll be back in five minutes!' someone yelled from further along. Elder walked towards the voice. A middle-aged man was unhooking chains from in front of the ghost train. Already, two young children, brother and sister, stood waiting for the ride to open. Elder nodded a greeting at the man. 'Thanks,' he said, 'maybe I'll come by later.'

'Please yourself.' The man looked at the children and jerked his head towards the carriages. 'On you go then, hop in.' They fairly sprinted for the train's front carriage. The man smiled, watching them go. Then he headed for his booth, leaning into it. 'Hold tight,' he warned. 'Or the goblins'll grab you.' He grinned towards Elder. 'And being grabbed by the goblins,' he said, 'is no laughing matter.'

Elder obliged with a laugh, then watched as the train jolted forwards, hit the doors, and rattled its way through them into darkness. The doors swung shut again, showing a picture of a leering demon.

'Your two, are they?' the man asked.

'No,' said Elder, listening for shrieks from the interior.

'No?' The man sounded surprised. 'I thought they were. If I'd known, I'd have had the money off them first.'

Elder brought out some coins from his pocket. 'They can have this ride on me anyway,' he said, handing over the money. Then he moved off again, passing rides and booths and Barnaby's Gun Stall. Outside the Gun Stall, which was locked shut, there was a wooden figure, its sex indeterminate. Pinned to the centre of its chest was what remained of a small paper target, only the four right-angled edges left. Above this, taped to the figure's head, was a crudely written message: 'A young lady did this. Can YOU do better?' Elder smiled.

A voice came from behind him. 'Well, could you?'

He turned. A young man was standing there, head cocked to one side, hands in the greasy pockets of his denims. Elder looked at the target.

'Probably not,' he said.

'Come back in an hour, guv, and you can see if you're right. Only two quid a go.'

'The young woman . . . she must have been quite something.'

The man winked. 'Maybe I'm lying, eh? Maybe I just tore the middle out myself.' And he snorted a short-lived laugh. 'Open in an hour,' he repeated, moving away. Elder watched him go.

A travelling fair. What connection could Witch possibly have with a travelling fair? None that he could think of. *I'd have remembered someone like that.* Rosa Pellengro had sounded very sure of herself. Very sure. But then she *was* supposed to be a clairvoyant. He wondered if it was worthwhile keeping a watch on the fair. Maybe Witch had been here. If so, she might come back or she might not.

He was in a thoughtful mood as he reached Doyle's car. Two gulls cackled somewhere in the distance. They had left generous gifts on the windscreen and bonnet. Elder sighed. Time to find a car-wash.

'I'm glad you've called,' Michael Barclay said into the receiver.

'And who was that delightful French lady?' Dominic Elder asked.

'My colleague's mother.' Just then Dominique herself came into the hall and handed Barclay a glass of cold beer, with which he toasted her. It had been another long day.

'Since you're glad I called,' Elder went on, 'I take it you're either in trouble or you're on to something.'

'Maybe both,' said Barclay. 'When I bugged Separt's apartment, I copied some of his computer disks.'

'Clever boy.'

'I bet Mrs Parry would say something different. Anyway, we've been reading through them. Mostly ideas for cartoon strips, but there's a lot of personal correspondence too, including a couple of letters to Wolf Bandorff.'

'Well well.'

'Discussing some project of Separt's, a cartoon book about Bandorff's career.'

'The world is a strange place, Michael. So what does this tell us?'

'It connects Separt to Witch's old teacher.'

'It does indeed. It's almost as if she's living her life again backwards.'

'Sorry?' Barclay had finished the beer. He held the cold glass against his face, like a second telephone receiver.

'She started her life in Britain, but early on joined Bandorff's gang. The link seems still to be there.'

Barclay still wasn't sure what Elder was getting at. 'You told me,' he said, 'always work the idea all the way through.'

There was a pause. 'You're thinking of taking another trip?'

'Yes. Do you think I could get it past Mrs Parry?'

Elder considered this. 'To be frank, almost certainly not. It's getting too far out of our territory.' He paused. 'Then again, maybe there's just a chance.'

'How?'

Elder's voice seemed to have faded slightly. 'You've lied to her before, haven't you . . . ?'

Dominique had already made *her* necessary telephone calls, and now all Barclay had to do, before taking her to dinner, was make one call himself. To Joyce Parry.

Elder was right, he'd lied to her before. Well, he'd been economical with the truth, say. But this time he was going to deliver a whopper. He went over his story two or three times in his head, Dominique goading him into making the call right now and getting it over and done with. At last he picked up the phone.

'Joyce Parry speaking.'

'It's Michael Barclay here.'

'Ah, Michael, I wondered where you'd got to.'

'Well, there's a bit of a lull here.'

'You're on your way home then?'

'Ah . . . not exactly. Any progress?'

'Special Branch and Mr Elder are still in Cliftonville. A lorry driver picked up a hitchhiker and dropped her there, did you know? Anyway, it seems a note was left for Mr Elder at a pub in the town.'

'A note?'

'Vaguely threatening, signed with the initial W.'

'God, that must have shaken him up a bit.' He swallowed. He'd almost said, He didn't tell me.

'He seemed very calm when I spoke to him. Now then, what about you?'

He swallowed again. 'DST are keeping watch on a couple of men. One of them, the one who had his car stolen, he's a left-wing sympathiser. He didn't report the car stolen until *after* the explosions on the two boats. DST think that's suspicious, and I tend to agree with them.'

'Go on.'

'This man has made contact with an anarchist. We . . . that is, DST . . . think the anarchist may know Witch. They think maybe the anarchist persuaded the other man to turn a blind eye while his car was taken.'

'Not to say anything, you mean?'

'Yes, until *after* Witch was home and dry . . . so to speak.'

'You sound tired, Michael. Are they treating you all right?'

He almost laughed. 'Oh yes, no complaints.'

'So what now?'

'As I say, they're keeping a watch on both men. I thought I'd give it until Monday, see if anything happens.'

'A weekend in Paris, eh?'

'A working weekend, ma'am.'

'I don't doubt it.' Her tone was good-humoured. Barclay hated himself for what he was doing. But it had to be done. No way would she sanction a trip to Germany, especially when explaining the trip would mean explaining how he'd come upon Separt's correspondence and Wrightson's leaflets.

'Okay, take the weekend,' Joyce Parry was saying. 'But be back here Monday. The summit begins Tuesday, and I want you in London. God knows, we'll be stretched as it is.'

'Yes, ma'am.'

'And let me know the minute you learn anything.'

'Of course.'

'And Michael . . . ?'

'Yes, ma'am?'

'You've already proved a point. You found something Special Branch missed. Okay?'

'Yes, thank you, ma'am. Goodbye.'

He noticed that his hand was shaking as he replaced the receiver.

'Well?' asked Dominique. Barclay wiped a line of perspiration from his forehead.

'I can stay on till Monday.'

Dominique grinned. Somehow, Barclay didn't share her enthusiasm. 'Good,' she said, 'we can start for Germany in the morning. The interview is arranged for two o'clock on Sunday.' She noticed his pallor. 'What's wrong, Michael?'

'I don't know . . . It's not every day I put my career on the line.'

'How will your boss find out? She won't. If we find nothing, we *say* nothing. But if we find *some*thing, then we are the heroes, yes?'

'I suppose so.'

'Cheer up. You are taking me to dinner, remember?'

He gave a weak smile. 'Of course. Listen, any chance that I can wash these clothes?' He picked at his shirt. 'Remember, I only brought the one change with me.'

She smiled. 'Of course. We will put them in the machine. They will be dry by morning. All right?'

He nodded.

'Good, now I will get changed. You, too.' She skipped down the hall to her room, calling back after her: 'Rendezvous in twenty minutes!'

After a moment, Barclay walked slowly back to his own room, his feet barely rising from the floor. Behind Dominique's door, he could hear her humming a tune, the sound of a zip being unfastened, of something being thrown on to the bed or a chair. In his own room, he fell onto the bed and stared at the dusty ceiling, focusing on one of its dark cobwebbed corners.

How did I talk myself into this?

Perhaps Witch *had* been in touch with Bandorff recently. But why should Bandorff admit it or say anything to them about it? Although he knew what he was doing, and knew that Dominique and he were making the decisions, he couldn't help feeling that Dominic Elder was an influence too, and not entirely a benign one. He wished he knew more about the man. He knew almost nothing about him, did he? All he knew was that Elder had pulled him into this obsession – an obsession Barclay himself had recently termed a psychosis.

'I'm mad,' he said to the ceiling.

But if he was, Dominique was mad too. *She'd* been the first to phone her office, securing clearance for herself and Barclay to go to Germany. He'd missed most of that call actually: he'd been busy in the toilet. He'd emerged again as she was dialling Germany, dialling direct to the Burgwede Maximum Security Prison, just north of Hanover.

'It's fixed,' she said after dialling, waiting for an answer. 'My office has given me clearance. I just have to . . .'

And then she lapsed into German, talking to the person on the other end of the phone. Barclay heard her mention the Bundesamt für Verfassungsschutz, Germany's security service, the BfV. Even in German, she was able to charm whoever she was speaking with. She laughed, she apologised for her accent and her lack of vocabulary (not that either, to Barclay's ear, needed apologising for). And eventually, after some quibbling, she had a day – Sunday – and a time – two in the afternoon.

For a meeting with the terrorist Wolfgang Bandorff, Witch's old lover.

She looked distinctly pleased with herself when she came off the phone, and hummed a little triumphant tune.

'What was that about the BfV?' asked Barclay.

'Michael, you are so . . . astute. That was my one little white lie. I told Herr Grunner I had liaised with the BfV. I think this means he takes me more seriously.'

'Don't tell me, when we turn up there, I'm going to pretend to be a German secret agent?'

'Of course not, Michael. But sometimes bureaucracy has to be . . .' She sought the word.

'Got around?' he suggested.

She liked that, and nodded. 'Yes,' she said, 'like swerving to avoid another car, yes?'

'Bobbing and weaving, ducking and diving.'

As now, hours later, staring at the cobwebbed ceiling above his bed, he feels his stomach diving. He might not be able to keep anything down at dinner. Maybe he'll have to cry wolf on the whole thing. Let Dominique cover herself with glory; he could ship out on the first hovercraft or cross-Channel ferry. But he knows he won't. He can't. He's already told Joyce Parry too many white lies.

So they're going to Germany, driving there in the awful 2CV. Hanover wasn't just across the border either. It is hard driving. And both of them out of their territory – even Elder had said as much. He didn't think they'd learn anything from Bandorff. And they'd have to be careful, too. If he found out how keen they were to track down Witch, he might start throwing them off her scent, laying false trails.

Jesus, what if this whole thing was an extended false trail? No, no, best not to think about that. She couldn't be that clever, could she? No one was *that* clever, clever enough to lay a trail backwards through Europe, a trail with a trap lying at the end of it.

Jesus, don't think about it!

Dominique came in unannounced. She looked sensational, in clinging woollen red dress and black tights. She wasn't wearing shoes or make-up yet.

'I thought you were being quiet,' she said. She closed the door, before settling herself on the edge of his bed. 'What's the matter?'

'Pre-match jitters.'

'What?'

'It's a football term. The nerves you get before a game.'

'Ah.' She nodded understanding and took his hand in hers. 'But I am nervous, too, Michael. We must plan carefully what we will say to Herr Bandorff. We must . . . like actors, you know?'

'Rehearse.'

'Yes, rehearse. We must be word perfect. We will set off in the morning, and stay overnight at a hotel. We will rehearse and rehearse and rehearse. The leading man and leading woman.' She smiled, and squeezed his hand.

'It's all right for you,' said Barclay, 'your department's behind you. I've lied through my teeth to mine.'

'Because you want to stay with me, yes?'

He stared into her eyes and nodded. She stood up, dropping his hand.

'And you are right to stay with me,' she said. 'Because I am going to find out about this Witch woman, I am going to discover all about her from Herr Bandorff. Just you wait and see. Besides, Mr Elder is behind you.'

'Yes, and pushing hard.'

She was at the door now, opening it. She turned back to him. 'Rendezvous in five minutes,' she said, 'whether you're ready or not.'

And with a final carefree smile, she was gone. Barclay sat up on the bed, clasping his arms around his knees. From the living room came the sound of an accordion. Madame Herault was listening to her radio. Madame Herault, who had already lost a husband to the terrorist threat, and whose daughter now might be in danger. He got up off the bed and stood in front of the dressing table, where the Witch file sat surrounded by bits of wire and solder, unused diodes and broken bits of circuit-board. He touched the cover of the file for luck.

Back in her room, Dominique studied herself in her mirror. Her employers had attached her to Michael Barclay because she was persistent. She had been brought up to be stubborn in pursuit of her goal, and her goal had been an assignment. She wanted to prove herself. How could you prove yourself in an office? She touched a framed photograph of her father. He had proved himself on the streets of the city, not behind a desk. He was her hero, and always would be, his life snuffed out by terrorists. And now she was in pursuit of terrorists, of people like those who had murdered her father. She kept her mind focused on that fact.

She didn't mind cutting corners. She didn't mind lying to her employers. She gave them daily reports on the British agent's actions and whereabouts. As long as he was around, she was to stick close to him, nothing more than that. They did not know how fascinated she had become, fascinated by this creature called Witch, conjured up from scattered events and rumours. It was as though the creature stood for all the terrorists in the world. Dominique wanted to get closer to it still. She examined her hair, her face, her body, and she smiled. She knew she was just about beautiful.

She knew too that Witch, not she, was the real *femme fatale*.

She had spent much of the past few days in London, watching. At times she had been a tourist, clutching her street-map and her carrier bag from Fortnum's, her head arched up to take in the sights, while those around her kept their eyes either firmly straight ahead or else angled downwards, checking the paving stones for cracks to be avoided.

At other times, she'd been a busy office worker, rushing with the best of them, with only enough free time for a lunch of a takeaway burger. And she'd been unemployed, too, with too much time on her hands, sitting against a wall with her knees hugged to her beneath her chin. All these things she had been. Nobody paid much attention to her several incarnations. To passers-by, the tourist was merely another obstacle in their way as they manoeuvred past her while she stood in Victoria Street, staring up in the direction of Westminster Abbey. And as the office worker ate her burger, seated in the plaza between Victoria Street and Westminster Cathedral, only one young man attempted to chat her up. But he was in a hurry, too, and so a single shake of her head was enough to deter him.

While the unemployed girl, the pale and tired-looking girl – well, everybody chose to ignore her existence. She was moved on once or twice by doormen and police officers. The police asked her where she stayed.

'Lewisham.'

'Well, bugger off back there then. And don't go hanging around Victoria Station either. We'll be along there in an hour, and if you're still there we'll take you down the nick. All right?'

She sniffed, nodded, picked up her cheap blue nylon shopping-bag. There were tears in her eyes as the policemen moved away. An old man took pity on her and handed her a one-pound coin. She took it with muttered thanks. She wandered off towards Victoria Station, where, in a toilet cubicle, she stripped down and swapped her clothes for another set in the shopping-bag. Then the shopping-bag itself was folded and slipped into a better-quality bag, along with the clothes. At the wash-basin, she combed the snags out of her hair, washed her face, dried it, and applied make-up. Girl about town again. In the station concourse, true to their word but half an hour ahead of schedule, the two police constables were passing through. She smiled at one as she passed them. He smiled back, and turned to watch her go.

'Thought you'd cracked it there,' his colleague said.

'Some of them just can't resist the uniform.'

Girl about town went back to Victoria Street, walked its length, pausing only outside the building which was 1–19 Victoria Street, headquarters of the Department of Trade and Industry. She had a momentary feeling of claustrophobia. She was within a five-minute walk of the Houses of Parliament, Westminster Abbey, Westminster Cathedral, New Scotland Yard, the Queen Elizabeth II Conference Centre. Not much further to Whitehall, Downing Street, Buckingham Palace even . . . So many targets to choose from, all so convenient. One really *huge* device and you could wreak mayhem.

It was an idle thought, an idle moment, the stuff of crank anarchists' dreams, anarchists like John Wrightson. She let it pass and checked her watch. Quarter to six. Friday evening at quarter to six. The offices had started their weekend evacuation at four-thirty. Pubs and wine-bars would be filling. Train carriages would be squeezing in just one last body. The discharge of the city. It was hard to tell, but she thought she probably had another ten minutes. She didn't like the thought of loitering, not in her girl about town disguise. But of course, if anyone should ask, she was waiting for a boyfriend who worked for the DTI. She was respectable. She wasn't suspicious. She rose onto her tiptoes then rocked back onto her heels. Waiting for her boyfriend. A few drinks after work, then a meal, maybe a film . . . no, not a film: she didn't know what films were on where. A meal, one of the little Chinese restaurants off Leicester Square. Then back to his place . . . The perfect start to the weekend.

Another five or ten minutes. She hoped to God she hadn't missed her quarry. It was unlikely. The first day Witch had spotted her, she'd worked till six-thirty, the next day six-fifteen. She would knock off early on a Friday, of course she would. But not that early. She had an important position. Let the others in the office leave her behind, she'd be the last out, feeling virtuous, another hard professional week over. Maybe a last-minute task would keep her. Maybe she'd been taken ill and had gone home early . . .

Witch had spent some time choosing. She was a fussy shopper. There had been false starts: one woman was perfect in build and face, but too junior.

Witch needed someone with a modicum of clout, the sort of person the security guards would look up to. Another woman had seemed senior enough for the purpose, but she was also too striking, the sort of person people would notice, so that they'd notice, too, if she went missing for a few days or if someone else brandished her security pass.

Security. She'd wandered into one of the DTI buildings at lunchtime one day. There were seats in the reception area, tedious-looking literature to pass the time. A businessman sat leafing through the contents of his briefcase. A young man stepped from an elevator and called to him. The businessman shook hands with the young man, the young man signed him in at the desk, a chitty was given to the businessman, and both headed for the elevator again.

'Yes, miss?' the security man called from behind his large desk.

There were two of them seated behind the desk. The one who had called to Witch, and another who was talking with another colleague, a black woman. Witch approached the desk and smiled.

'I'm meeting my boyfriend for lunch.' She looked at her watch. 'I'm a bit early. Is it all right if I wait?'

'Of course, miss. If you'll just take a seat. You can call up to him if you like, maybe he can knock off early.'

She smiled gratefully. 'No, he's always complaining I'm too early for things.'

'You're not like my wife then,' said the security man, laughing, turning to share the joke with his colleagues.

'I'll just wait for him,' said Witch.

So she sat in the reception area, watching the civil servants come and go. Most were going – it *was* lunchtime – but a few were already returning with sandwiches and cans of soft drinks. As they passed the security desk, heading for the elevators, some merely smiled and nodded in the direction of the guards, some showed passes, and some just glided by without acknowledging the guards' existence – which was also the guards' response to the flow: they barely looked up from their desk. The legitimate workers had a breeziness about them. Yes, breeziness was the word. It was the feeling that came with a certain power – the power to move past an official barrier which kept others out, the power of belonging.

If she moved breezily, holding her pass out like every other day, would the guards look up? And if they did, would they go any further? Would they frown, ask her to step over to the desk, scrutinise her pass? She doubted it. They'd blink. She'd smiled at them so she must know them. They'd return to their telephone call or their tabloid newspaper or the conversation they were having.

What alerted them to strangers were the movements of the strangers themselves. Someone pushed open the glass door slowly, uncertainly. They hesitated once inside, looking around, getting their bearings. And they walked almost reluctantly towards the desk, where the guard, who had caught these signs, was already asking if he could help. Yes, visitors gave themselves away. If they knew the layout, if they breezed towards the elevators rather than staring dumbly at the desk . . . *anyone* could walk into the building. Anyone could take the elevator to any floor they liked, floors where ministers and senior civil servants might be meeting.

Oh, how Witch loved a democracy. They took their freedoms too easily, treated them too casually. This wasn't security; it was the opposite of security. It was a soft job, and the guards were happy to acknowledge this. She got up from her seat and walked one circuit of the reception area, then stood by the glass door. When the guards were busy, she pushed the door open and walked back out on to the street, sure that they would have forgotten her existence by the time the next tea-break came.

How long had she been waiting now? Maybe her fears of an illness were well-founded . . . Ah, but no . . . here came the woman now. Calling back over her shoulder to the security guard. Then pushing open the heavy glass door. Outside, she stopped and took a deep invigorating breath. Her weekend started here, started now. She held two briefcases, one a plain brown attaché case – her own – the other looking like an expensive school satchel, made from black leather and bearing a small crown insignia above the name-plate. This was government property, and a sign that she wasn't just some clerical worker. She had achieved a good grade, not quite senior but certainly on her way there. She was vivacious, full of life and hope. She made friends quite easily. The security guard would know her name. Yet she didn't seem to go out much. She shared a house with two other young professional women in Stoke Newington. Perhaps the house was rented, or perhaps they'd clubbed together and bought it between them before the government had changed the law on mortgage tax relief. Some things, even Witch couldn't be sure of.

She travelled to work by overland railway and tube. She travelled home the same way. It was a fairly hellish journey, and the later she worked or stayed on in town, the less teeming the crowds were on the trip home. So, one night, she'd hung around for an hour in a nearby wine-bar, having a drink with some of the other office staff. They were celebrating someone's birthday. But she hadn't stuck around for the Indian vegetarian meal. She'd kept looking surreptitiously at her watch. She'd made her apologies at half-past seven.

No boyfriend to meet, despite the nods and winks and oohs of her colleagues, just the tube and train and the short walk home. To stay in all the rest of the evening, as all her other evenings, watching TV.

Wondering what her weekend plans would be, today, after all three women had left for work, Witch had entered their house. Inside, she'd found a pleasant surprise: the other residents were going away for the weekend. There were signs of planned departure: packed and half-packed bags, raids on the bathroom toiletries. They'd tried to pack this morning before leaving for work, but had blearily only half succeeded. Only Christine Jones's room was tidy. No luggage there.

In the kitchen was the brochure for a Welsh campsite. Its telephone number had been ringed. Obviously it was there in case Christine needed it: Christine's idea probably. She seemed so much more organised than her housemates. And on a wall calendar was marked a time this evening when 'Garry and Ed' would be calling. Another look in the housemates' bedrooms confirmed that Garry and Ed were the boyfriends. The four of them were off to Wales on a camping expedition. Lovely.

Witch wondered how Christine Jones would spend her weekend. There didn't seem any clues that she was planning to go away, or to have someone over, or to hold a party, even a dinner party. She was doing German at night school, and it looked like part of her time would be spent catching up on her assignments. There were also three fat and newly borrowed library books to be read, and a video club membership card was handy on the coffee table in the living room, in case she wanted to rent a film or two . . .

There'd be a spot of shopping on Saturday morning. Not having transport, she tended to use the local shops – though someone in the flat had access to a car, since there had been supermarket buying in bulk, shown in the contents of the refrigerator. Christine Jones wouldn't go hungry, not for food. But it wasn't party food, not social food; it was fast food, the stuff of days spent doing homework and nights spent watching TV.

One of her housemates, Tessa, kept a diary, and recent entries, when not running on about Garry and his physique and his bedroom athletics, showed concern for 'Chris', who had split up with a boyfriend several months before and seemed to have just lost interest . . .

'Hope she'll be okay this weekend,' the entry ended. Witch was tempted to take up a pen and add: 'She'll be fine, honest.'

She didn't.

When the mail arrived, she glanced at it, leaving it untouched on the hall floor. Then, having satisfied herself with the layout of the house, she left it as neatly as she had entered it, and walked back to the railway station, a lazy stroll, nothing better to do, just whiling away the hours . . .

Until now. As she follows Christine Jones along Victoria Street, she's thinking, ticking things off on a list in her mind. Christine knows the guard, but that probably doesn't matter. Another of the DTI buildings further along Victoria Street would do just as well, once Witch has a security pass. She's studying the way Christine moves, the way she walks, how far she places one foot in front of the other, the way she turns her head when she wants to cross the road. None of this is necessary – she doesn't intend to impersonate Christine Jones after all – but it is useful and it is interesting. Witch is learning to move like a professional woman, a woman on the way up in the civil service. She's thinking too of the evening ahead, of what must be done immediately, and what can be left till later. And, briefly, she's thinking of Khan, of how pleased her employers were, how generous. And she spares a thought, too, for Dominic Elder and all the other people who may be chasing her shadow just now. She's thinking all these things, but her walk is that of the girl about town, making her way home.

Home to Stoke Newington. Directly home. Poor Christine Jones, her eyes fixed on yet another book, a fat paperback this time. (She's almost finished it. Probably she's already looking forward to the three fat library books waiting for her at home.) No after-work drinks for her. Probably she wants to make it back to the house before her housemates leave. Sending her best wishes with them. Yes, better to return to a few minutes of chaotic farewell than to an absolute forty-eight-hour emptiness. Poor Christine Jones.

She stops in at a newsagent on the way home. She buys a couple of magazines, and then, biting her lip guiltily, adds several chocolate bars to her purchases. Comfort food. The newsagent puts the whole lot into a white paper bag. It is awkward to carry. She might stop for a moment, open her satchel, and place the magazines and sweets inside, but she's hurrying now. Bloody London bloody public bloody transport. The bane of her existence.

Late home as usual. It's nearly seven. The girls will be leaving soon. Yes, the car is parked outside the house. A tanned young man is carrying out two suitcases.

'Hello, Garry,' says Christine.

Garry lifts the cases higher. The action shows off his physique. 'Look at this,' he says. 'You'd think we were off for a fortnight on the QE2. I wish now I was staying behind with you, Chris. We could get nice and cosy, eh?'

'Leave my flatmate alone!' yells Tessa from the front door, half-jokingly at least.

The other housemate emerges with more bags. Behind her, her boyfriend is manoeuvring a large suitcase out of the door.

'We'll never get it all in!' calls Garry.

'As the actress said to the bishop,' retorts his friend. The girls laugh, the way they're supposed to. This is fun. Christine's smile is fixed. Witch can see that she is in a quandary. She's holding the paper bag to her, while she wonders whether to offer the chocolate to the foursome for their journey, or whether to say nothing about it. Witch is surprised, but pleased too, to see that self-gratification wins. Christine keeps the chocolate to herself.

Witch has passed the scene now, eyes on the cracks in the pavement ahead. She's on the other side of the street from them, but not quite invisible enough. Garry gives her a half-hearted wolf whistle, almost drawing unwanted attention. But no one seems to pay him any heed. The cases *will* all go in, but only if some of the bags sit on the floor in the back and under the driver's and front-passenger's seats, and even then it's going to be tight.

'As the actress said—'

A thump silences the end of the sentence. Witch has turned the corner now. She stops, pretending to rummage in her bag for something. The car doors are opening, closing, opening again. Kisses and hugs are exchanged.

'It's only for the weekend,' complains Garry as the housemates make their farewells. 'It's not like a fortnight on the QE2 or anything . . .'

The doors close. All four of them. The engine starts with a throaty roar. Not one to hang about, the driver lets the tyres squeal as he releases the handbrake, and he fairly races to the end of the road, signalling left, turning left, and revving away in the opposite direction from Witch.

Moments later, the front door of the house closes, leaving Christine Jones indoors on her own.

Witch waited at the corner for a few minutes, not looking in her bag any more but waiting for a gentleman friend. She peered up this road and down along that, searching for him. And glanced at her watch, for the benefit of anyone looking from their windows. Not that anyone did. They minded their business and got down to the proper work of the evening: watching the television.

A few people hurried past, refugees from the latest train, she guessed. They looked worn out and glanced at her, nothing more. Nobody smiled, nobody offered a chat-up line or a joke or a 'Can I help you?' The time passed without incident.

She walked back around the corner then started into a brisk run, clutching her carrier bag to her to stop the contents from spilling out. She ran up to the gate, pushed it open, climbed the steps noisily, and rang the doorbell.

Christine Jones had hardly had time to start her first chocolate bar of the evening. She'd taken off jacket and shoes, nothing more. She opened the door wide, then looked disappointed.

'Have I missed her?' said Witch, panting, trying to catch her breath.

'Who?'

'Tessa, only there was something I wanted to give her.' She winked. 'For the weekend, if you know what I mean.'

'You just missed her,' said Christine. 'Funny, I thought maybe that was her coming back to say she'd forgotten something.'

'Oh shit!' Witch threw back her head and exhaled noisily. 'Shit, shit, shit.' Then she caught herself, grinned. 'Sorry, you must be Chris. She's told me about you. I'm Anna.'

'Hello, Anna. Do you work beside—? God, listen to me.' Christine rolled her eyes. 'Do you want to come in? You look like you could use a drink.'

'Too right I could.'

'Me too. After all, it *is* the weekend.'

Christine Jones stepped back so Witch could walk into her home. Then Christine closed the door. Witch was standing, waiting. 'Along here,' said Christine, signalling with the chocolate bar, leading her towards the living-room. 'You didn't say, do you work beside Tessa?'

'Well, sort of, yes.'

As Christine pushed open the door to the living room, Witch hit her at the base of the skull. Christine froze for a moment, then fell forwards, turning sideways as she did so, so that her left shoulder hit the rug first, her head following it with an almighty thump.

She was aware that she couldn't move, aware too of a heat-source near her face. She opened her eyes to agony, the blood beating in her head. Immediately she opened her eyes, a hand descended on to her mouth, the thumb hooking itself under her chin. The side of the hand left just enough room below her nose to allow her to breathe. She looked up into the eyes of the woman who had tricked her way indoors. And she knew why she couldn't move.

Witch had tied Christine Jones to her own bed, using pairs of grey tights. There was an electrical socket just beside the bed, hidden behind the bedside cabinet. A clock-alarm and a reading-lamp had been plugged into the double socket. She'd unplugged the lamp and plugged in the iron, turning the heat all the way up. Now, while one hand gagged Christine Jones, the other gripped the handle of the iron and held it close to her face. Witch turned away from Christine and spat on to the dull metal face of the iron. Her saliva sizzled and bubbled.

'A nice hot iron,' she said quietly. 'You've got to be careful with a hot iron. Place it on the wrong kind of material and you can do terrible damage. Place it on *delicate* material, and you can ruin the material forever.' Christine's nostrils flared as she fought for breath, hyperventilating.

'Now,' said Witch, 'I'm going to take my hand away from your mouth. You could scream if you wanted to, but I'm not sure anyone would hear. There's no one else in the house, your windows are double-glazed and shut tight, and your room's on the end of the house. A good solid end wall rather than a connecting wall. No neighbours to hear. You understand what I'm saying? If you scream, nobody will hear, and you might startle me. I might drop the iron. I don't think you'll scream. I don't want to hurt you. It's not necessary to hurt you. I just need you to answer a few questions about your work.' She paused. 'Now, do you want me to repeat anything I've said?'

Beneath the pressure of her hand, Witch felt Christine Jones try to shake her head. She brought the iron down until it was inches above Christine's face, causing the young woman to screw shut her eyes. The iron went 'click' occasionally, its light coming on to show that it was heating up again, then another 'click' as maximum heat was achieved and the light went off, the iron starting to cool . . .

Witch lifted away her hand. Christine gulped in air, licked her lips. There was sweat on her face. She suddenly started thrashing, but Witch had expected this and sat still on the edge of the bed, waiting for the thrashing to stop. The bonds were holding. Christine calmed down.

'Oh God,' she said, trembling. 'Oh God, I'm sorry. I didn't mean to do that.'

Witch smiled. 'It's all right, Christine. It's only natural. Chain up any animal and it'll do the same thing . . . for a moment or two, until it realises it really is chained.'

'How do you know who I am?'

'I've been watching you. I'm interested in where you work.'

She seemed confused. 'DTI?'

'Yes, all those buildings along Victoria Street.'

'What about them?'

'I want you to tell me about them, anything you know, no matter how trivial.'

'What? Is this some kind of—' But of course it wasn't a joke. She could feel the heat of the iron. No, whatever else this was, it wasn't a joke.

'Take it floor by floor,' said Witch, 'starting with the ground.'

'Why? I don't understand.'

'You don't *need* to understand. All you have to do is tell me.'

'About the buildings?'

'Yes, about the buildings.' Another click from the iron. 'Take it floor by floor,' Witch repeated.

Christine Jones took it floor by floor.

After a while, Witch saw that she didn't need the iron. She rested it on its end on the bedside cabinet. She even left the room long enough to fetch water and paracetamol from the bathroom. It didn't look as though Christine had struggled at all during her absence, but of course she had. Witch merely smiled.

'I know how to make a knot,' she said.

'Why do you want to know all this?' asked Christine.

'Open wide,' said Witch. She held a tablet above Christine's mouth, and, when the mouth with its good solid teeth opened, she dropped the tablet in, placing the cup of water against her bottom lip and pouring some in. Christine swallowed the tablet, and Witch repeated the process.

'You're bound to have a sore head,' she said. 'It'll wear off in time. No lasting effects, I promise. I know how to hit people, too.'

'You know a lot,' said Christine, refreshed by the water. She'd been talking for over an hour.

'Knowledge is power,' said Witch quietly. Then she smiled. 'And I'm power-crazy, Christine. You're an intelligent woman. By now you're beginning to guess *why* I might want to know so much about Victoria Street. You won't say anything, because if you did, you think *I* might think I'd have to silence you. Permanently. Am I right?' Christine said nothing: answer in itself. 'Well, don't worry. I don't kill people for pleasure, only for profit.' She paused, seeming to think of something. Then she came to herself. 'And there's no profit in killing you, Christine. But I can't have you telling anyone either.'

'I wouldn't tell, I'd keep my mouth—'

Witch shook her head. 'So I'm going to have to hide you somewhere until this is all over. Probably Wednesday. It's not a long time, Friday night until Wednesday. It'll be uncomfortable, but no more than that. Now, because of this, because you're going to be my . . . guest over the next few days, I need some more information, different information this time.'

'Yes?'

'Who's your doctor, Christine?'

'My doctor?' Witch nodded. 'Doctor Woodcourt.'

'Male or female?'

'Female.'

'With a practice where?'

'Ebury Road . . . just at the end of the street.'

'And does Doctor Woodcourt know you?'

'Know me?'

'Do you visit regularly? Would she know you to look at?'

'I went a year or so ago for some jabs, holiday vaccinations. But now that I think about it, some locum saw me. I can't think when I last saw Doctor Woodcourt . . . maybe two years ago, when I was going on the pill.'

'Two years is a long time. I don't think she'd recognise you, do you?'

'Probably not. I don't see what—'

'On Monday morning, I'm going to call in sick to your office on your behalf. You're allowed several sick days before you need notification from your doctor.'

'A sick-line, yes.' And then Christine Jones saw. 'You'd pretend to be me? Just to get a sick-line?'

'It shouldn't come to that. Three days should suffice. What about your housemates?'

'What about them?'

'They'll be worried if you suddenly disappear.'

'Not them. I don't think they'd bother. I go away with my boyfriend all the time without saying anything.'

'But you've split up with your boyfriend.'

'How do you know that?'

Witch smiled. 'And you're lying about your housemates. They'll be worried if they don't hear from you.' She reached into her bag and produced a card of some kind. Christine saw it was a postcard. There were four separate views on the front and some writing: 'Greetings from Auchterarder'. Witch untied Christine's right hand. 'I want you to send them a postcard.' The card, which had been sitting on the bed, slipped off on to the floor. Before she realised the enormity of her mistake, Witch had leaned halfway towards the floor to retrieve it.

Christine's free hand shot to the bedside cabinet and snatched at the iron, stabbing at Witch with it. But Witch was too quick. She leapt from the bed and stood at a safe distance.

'Get out!' screamed Christine. 'Go on, get out of here!' Then she started to yell at the top of her voice. 'Help! Someone, please! Help!'

There was no time for indecision. Witch turned and left the room, closing the door after her. Christine might stop yelling for a moment to listen for sounds of her leaving. At the bottom of the stairs, Witch walked along the hall, opened the front door, checked that no one was in the street, then slammed it shut. On tiptoe, she walked back along the hall to the cupboard beside the living-room door, the cupboard under the stairs. Christine would have put the iron down so that, with her one free hand, she could untie her other bonds. They were difficult knots. It would take her some seconds.

The switch on the fusebox went from On to Off. The lights went off. The noisy fridge clunked to a halt. The display on the bedside clock went blank. Christine realised what was happening and started yelling again. Witch was climbing the stairs, her eyes cold and hard. She opened the door to Christine's room. The evening was still light, even though Witch had closed the curtains. There was the beginning of an orange glow from the street-lighting. They stared at one another, Witch utterly silent, Christine almost hoarse from shouting, and crying too. Of course, Christine knew that the iron she was again holding, the only thing that held Witch at bay, was cooling and would not get hot again. If she put it down, she could untie the knots, but if she put it down . . .

She did what Witch had hoped she would. She grew frustrated. And she tried to throw the iron not at Witch – Christine was cleverer than that – but at the window. But the plug held in the socket and the iron fell to the floor with a dull thud. It took two seconds for Witch to reach the bed, raise a fist, and strike Christine Jones back into unconsciousness.

Stillness. Peace. She peered out through the curtains. Someone in the house across the street was staring from their window. Someone else joined them, then they gave up and turned away. She had to act fast now. Things were becoming dangerous. She went to the fusebox and turned it back on. Then, in the living room, she made a telephone call.

'It's me,' she said into the receiver.

'I was wondering when you'd call.' He pronounced the final word as 'gall'.

'I need a package picked up,' Witch said. 'A large package. I'll give you the address. The package needs to be stored for a few days. Can you do that?'

'It's in one piece, is it? Damaged goods might be a problem.'

'It's in one piece.'

'All right, give me the address.'

She did so.

'We need to meet,' said the voice, a European voice, Dutch perhaps.

'Monday,' she said. 'I'll call you. The package needs to be picked up within the hour, sooner if possible.'

'To Stoke Newington? Twenty minutes.'

'Good.' She put down the telephone. She returned to Christine's room and opened the wardrobe. On top was a small suitcase, which she lifted down. She began to pack clothes, enough for a few days' travel. Good clothes, too, including the smartest-looking dress. She also packed make-up, and a few toiletries from the bathroom. Christine seemed to keep her things in a wash-bag. The wash-bag and its contents went into the case. Shoes, too. And one of the fat new library books.

She took her own carrier bag downstairs and placed it next to the front door. Beside it she left Christine's attaché case and satchel, having first checked that her security pass was in the satchel, along with other documentation allowing access to canteens, clubs, sports facilities. She stared for a moment at the photograph on the security pass. The photo showed head and shoulders only, as these things always did. Another lapse: anyone with similar facial features could use another person's card, even if, like Witch and Christine, one of them was a good four inches taller than the other.

With make-up and a little hairdressing, she could pass for Christine Jones. She felt sure of it. She looked again out into the street. No signs of police or even curious neighbours. If anyone had heard the cries, they were ignoring them. Witch lifted the postcard from beside Christine's bed, took up a pen, and printed the message: HARD WORK BUT FUN. SEE YOU SOON. C. She then also printed the address of the house, leaving the space for names blank. An envelope on Christine's study-desk gave her the correct postcode. She reread the card. It was by no means perfect, but it would have to suffice . . . under the circumstances. The card had already been stamped with a Scottish-issue stamp, the lion rampant in one corner. She'd been so careful in Auchterarder. So careful. The card was delicious. Elder and company wouldn't see it till afterwards, till long after she'd gone.

The case was all packed. Time to tidy up. She put the iron back where she'd found it, and plugged the lamp back in. She reset the time on the clock-alarm, and went through to the other bedrooms to do the same. There was a humming from one bedroom. It was a computer, its screen white and blank and flickering, sitting on a large table. It had been left on. She ejected the disk, found the start-up disk, and rebooted the system. Then she put the original disk back in. Had it been set at the menu screen? That would make sense, nobody would leave it halfway through a file when they were going off for the weekend. Unless . . . She looked down the file names on the menu. One caught her eye: CHRIS. BYE. She opened the file. It was a message, short and to the point:

WHAT ARE YOU DOING IN HERE? DON'T YOU DARE READ MY LETTERS!!

Witch smiled. It was a message left for Christine. She began typing, her fingers efficient.

WOULDN'T DREAM OF IT! ANYWAY, GOT A CALL THIS EVENING. SOMEONE'S DROPPED OUT OF A CONFERENCE AT GLENEAGLES, AND DTI WANT ME TO GO!

She pondered the exclamation marks: were they Christine's style? Yes, probably. A woman on the way up in the civil service, and now a chance to shine at an important conference . . . yes, they were excusable. Witch typed on.

OFF TOMORROW MORNING, BACK LATER IN THE WEEK, CHRIS.

She saved, and considered leaving the screen on. But Christine wouldn't, not all weekend with no one in the house. So Witch ejected the disk and switched off the computer. She reset the room's clock-alarm and, with a last look around, headed for the stairs. There was a soft knock at the door.

'Yes?'

'Come to pick up a package,' called the voice. Witch opened the door and stood back so that the two men could enter the hall. One of them carried a long, flat-packed section of cardboard.

'Upstairs on the right,' said Witch. 'And listen . . .' She handed one of the men the postcard. 'This has to be posted by Monday morning in Scotland, to arrive here Tuesday or Wednesday morning.'

'No problem,' said the man, taking the card from her and slipping it inside his shirt. 'Might even manage it tomorrow.' Then the two men went upstairs. Minutes later, they appeared at the top of the stairs grappling with a large cardboard box, no longer flat-packed. Inside, Christine Jones would be trussed like a Christmas bird, knees tucked up into her chest, plastic restraining cords wrapped around her, arms tied against her sides. The human body, positioned just right, could make a smaller package than might be imagined. The box was barely four feet long.

They brought her downstairs slowly, careful not to topple or trip. Witch held open the door for them, and held the suitcase out towards the man at the back. 'This too,' she said. 'It can stay with her.' The man took the case with difficulty by its handle, but said nothing. Witch closed the door after the men. She watched from the upstairs bedroom window as they loaded the van, got in, and drove off. The street still did not stir. It took more than odd comings and goings to produce a reaction here. Now, alone in the house, Witch went about her final tidying-up. She untied the tights from the bedposts and put them back in Christine's drawer, then straightened the bed. Having made sure things looked neat and tidy, she went back downstairs and picked up her bags. She let herself out and closed the door behind her. Then she took out Christine's bunch of keys and locked the mortice. There, just the way Christine would have left the place. Yes, she'd been in a hurry. Yes, the conference had come as a surprise. But she'd still left the house without fuss or undue mess. A very proper young woman.

Then Witch remembered the trick with the iron, and the way Christine had screamed the place down. She didn't blame her; she blamed herself. Next time, she'd have to do better. Get everything ready *before* loosing the knot around the hand.

Preparation, that was the secret. Be prepared. She'd learned her lesson. She was just glad she hadn't had to learn it the hard way. Christine Jones was still alive. Witch was still unscarred. She knew why she'd made the mistake, too. Her mind was running along two parallel roads, with occasional jolts from one road onto the other. In those moments, she was weak. She knew she couldn't afford any weakness. She was taking a risk this time, bigger than any she'd taken before. The deceit was greater, the sense of treachery more impending. If she double-crossed them . . . *when* she double-crossed them, they would be far from pleased. They'd perhaps send another assassin after her. She smiled at that. Who would they hire? Who would take the job? The answer to the second question was obvious: if the price was right, *anyone* would take the job, no matter how dangerous.

Witch closed the gate. A police car was drawing up on the other side of the road. One of the officers called to her. She crossed the road towards the car. The policeman sat with his elbow resting on the sill of his wound-down window.

'Sorry to trouble you, miss. There's been a report of some screaming or yelling. Heard anything?'

Witch thought for a moment. 'I don't think so,' she said. Then she smiled. 'Hard to tell in this street though. They're always yelling at each other.'

The policeman smiled back and turned to his colleague. 'It was number twenty-seven made the call, wasn't it? Better go have a word.' He turned back to Witch and nodded in the direction of Christine Jones's house. 'You live there?' Witch nodded slowly. 'Well, that's one to cross off the list then, eh?'

'Yes,' said Witch. 'I've just locked the place up. I'm going away for a few days.'

'Lucky you. Anywhere nice?'

'Scotland.'

'Locked all your windows?'

'Of course.'

'Burglar alarm?'

'We don't have one.'

He puckered his lips. 'Think about getting one, that's my advice. Well, thanks anyway.'

'You're welcome,' Witch answered politely, crossing the road again and walking on steady legs in the direction of Stoke Newington railway station.

The policeman turned to his companion. 'Travels light, doesn't she?' he said.

Saturday 13 June

'What are we looking for?'

Joyce Parry was not best pleased at being summoned to her own office on a Saturday morning, and all because Elder didn't like using computers. She sat at her desk in front of the terminal while Dominic rested his hands on the back of her chair and leaned his head close to her right shoulder.

'Someone this end helped her enter the country,' he answered. 'She's travelling, she's hiding, she's already had help on the Khan hit. There *has* to be someone else, however loose a tie they might be.' He checked that he wasn't about to give away more than he should know. 'Your man Barclay has found a link between Witch and two men in Paris.'

'DST found it, he's just tagging along.'

Elder looked at the back of her head. 'Whatever,' he said. 'I'm wondering if there's another terrorist loose over here, someone she knows she can call on for help.'

'You want to access MI6's files?'

'Yes.'

'How wide a search?'

'I'm still thinking about the American woman, Khan's lover.'

Parry nodded. 'It's a starting point.' She half-turned to him. 'Could be a long day.' She didn't sound angry with him any more. He squeezed her shoulder and she began tapping in her security code. Then she had a thought, and swung her chair towards the telephone. 'I'd better just clear this with my oppo.'

After a short conversation, she was back at the screen. Moments later, the first file appeared – a brief description and history with a head and shoulders picture. Elder wanted to study every one of them as they came up. After a dozen or so, Joyce smiled at the screen. He saw the reflection of her face there.

'What's so funny?'

She shook her head. 'Nothing. It's just a bit like old times.'

A few dozen files later, Elder made her go back a couple of files. It wasn't a woman's face on the screen, it was a man's, going bald.

'Someone we should know?' Joyce asked.

'Someone we *do* know.'

The phone rang, and she swivelled towards it, leaving him staring at the picture on the screen.

'It's for you,' she said.

He tore his gaze away and took the receiver from her. 'Hello?'

'It's Doyle here.'

'Good, I think I've got something for you.'

'Me too.' There was a pause. He was waiting for Elder to ask, so Elder obliged.

'And what would that be?'

'Khan's tart, Shari Capri. I know who she is.'

It was oppressively hot in Trilling's office. Outside there was a generous summer's day. The building was quiet, it being the weekend. Yet here they were – Dominic Elder, Doyle and Greenleaf, and Trilling himself – stuck in darkness behind a firmly shut door and closed venetian blinds.

'It's the bleedin' black hole of Calcutta,' Doyle said, shifting on his chair. Doyle, Greenleaf and Elder sat on a row of three stiff-backed chairs facing the wall behind Trilling's desk where a white screen had been erected, the sort used for slide-shows and home movies. Not that anyone bothered with Super 8 any more; it was all videos these days.

'When does the usherette come round?' Doyle asked, changing his metaphor but not the irritation in his voice. He had something to say and he wanted to say it, but first there was all this to be gone through. Trilling was behind them, fiddling with a slide projector which had been set up on a tripod. Its piercing beam shot between Greenleaf's left and Doyle's right shoulder and wavered against the screen as Trilling made adjustments to height and attempted to level the slightly askew – 'pissed' was Doyle's word – beam.

'Can I help you with that, sir?' asked Greenleaf, not for the first time.

'Perfectly capable myself,' muttered Trilling, also not for the first time. He was grinding a peppermint to powder between his teeth.

Elder was thinking of Joyce Parry. They were dining out together tonight, a celebration of their morning's work and, as Elder put it, a chance to relax before the storm came. He'd chosen a small, intimate restaurant near Kew Gardens, and he'd been in luck: a booking had just fallen through, there was a spare table.

He wondered now why he'd chosen *that* particular restaurant. The answer, of course, was its intimacy. It was a restaurant for seduction. The fact that it was run by an apparently brilliant young chef had little to do with it. He wanted Joyce to get his message, loud and clear, which meant soft lighting and low music . . .

'That looks about right,' said Trilling.

'Maybe move the tripod an inch to the left, sir,' commented Greenleaf.

Lab analysis of Witch's letter to Elder had thrown up nothing, not even saliva on the flap: Barman Joe told them she'd dabbed her finger into her drink and wet the seal with that. The lab confirmed that the drink had been neat tonic water with a slice of lemon. Joe's session with the two Special Branch men had been long, but totally unproductive. She'd only come into the bar the once, and he hadn't seen her around before or since. An artist drew up a sketch from Joe's description, and this had been run off for the officers whose job it now was to check hotels, boarding-houses, taxi-ranks, and so on. The sketch had been turned into a small wanted-style poster. Information wanted on the whereabouts of this woman. Details were given beneath the drawing itself: approximate age, height, what she'd been last seen wearing.

The van driver, Bill Moncur, who'd given her the lift from Folkestone to Cliftonville said all she'd had with her was the one rucksack of stuff, and it hadn't looked full, yet already she'd worn two outfits – the one described by Moncur and the one described by Barman Joe. Maybe she'd done some shopping in Cliftonville. Shops, too, would be shown the artist's impression. The poster would go up in clubs and pubs, on the off-chance that some pissed late-night punter had seen her.

The drawing had been shown to Moncur, who had shrugged. 'Hard to tell,' he'd said. 'Maybe it's the same woman, maybe not.'

More copies had been made, too, of the drawing of the man Mike McKillip had seen his employer talking to in the bar. To be shown around Cliftonville at the same time as the Witch drawings. Yes, they were going through the procedures, the correct and proper routine. But Elder thought he had something better than an artist's impression.

Greenleaf had suggested yet another line of inquiry: travel. She'd travelled from Cliftonville to Scotland. How? She wouldn't still be hitching, not now that the hunt was on for her. Too open, too public. Which left several options: public transport, a bought or hired car, or an accomplice. Train stations were being checked, booking clerks questioned. Bus company offices would be next, then car-hire firms, then car dealers. She would need fake documents for these last two, and Elder reckoned there was a better chance that she was actually using train or bus or plane or, most likely, a combination of these. He didn't think she'd be using an accomplice to chauffeur her around. She liked working alone too much.

Auchterarder did not have a railway station. However, buses passed through it, and nearby Gleneagles *did* have its own small railway station, an echo of the days when visitors would arrive by train for their holiday there. Maybe some still did.

It was true that they hadn't given Auchterarder much thought. They'd been too busy further south. But the town wasn't populous, and Elder knew the Scots to be a curious race, in the sense that they liked to know all about strangers. So now a team was being despatched north – a proper team, not just local CID and the like. They knew what questions to ask, and where to ask them. In a town that small, Elder reckoned Witch wouldn't have opted for staying at a hotel or B&B. She just about had the cheek to check in to Gleneagles itself, and this option would be checked. But he thought the likeliest bet was that she'd slept rough, out in the countryside around the town. Which meant checking camp-sites, showing her sketch to farmers . . . She'd travelled further afield than anticipated. The Fablon she'd used was only available in that part of the world, according to the makers, from a store in Perth. The store had been visited. Yes, they did sell that particular design, but no, no one remembered serving anyone with it, let alone someone of Witch's description.

Another dead end, but it opened other routes. How had she travelled to Perth? Had she bought any other materials there? Had she stayed there for any time? The local CID were now busy finding answers to these questions. Patience and manpower were the necessities. But they were already stretching things to the limit and beyond. This close to the summit, they should be focusing in, instead of which the hunt seemed to be spreading wider and wider. He thought for a moment of Barclay. He hoped he would be all right. No, that wasn't exactly true: he hoped he would get results.

The summit started on Tuesday, meaning Witch was probably already in town calculating her plan of attack and her escape routes. She'd have more than one escape route. Unless this really was to be her swansong, her kamikaze trip. Elder was beginning to wonder. He'd stared long and hard at the drawing of her conjured up by the police artist's hand and Barman Joe's memory, trying to place the face . . . failing . . .

'Here we are,' said Trilling. There was no longer white on the screen in front of them, but colour. Greenleaf adjusted the focusing before sitting down. 'Thank you, John.'

In focus, the slide showed a man leaving a building. It had been shot with a powerful zoom, looking down from an angle. Probably taken, thought Elder, from the second or third storey of the building across the road from where the man was emerging. There was a car standing at the kerbside and he was heading purposefully for it, his lips pursed. In the second slide he was looking to his right, and in the third to his left, checking both ways along the street as he stooped to get into the passenger seat. A careful man, quite a nervous man. He had blond hair, but was mostly bald. What was left of his hair he wore quite long, in strands which fell down around his ears and over the back of his neck. His face was pale, cheekbones prominent. He didn't have much in the way of eyebrows.

'We don't know his name,' said Trilling. 'Or rather, we know too many of them – at least a dozen aliases in the past three or four years, and those are only the ones we know about.'

'So who is he?' asked Doyle, wanting Trilling to get on with it. Trilling did not reply. Instead, the projector clicked its way to slide number four. Same man, at a café table, enjoying a joke with an olive-skinned man.

'The Arab gentleman is known as Mahmoud. He works for an arms dealer. Or should I say, he works for the owner of an import-export business located in Cairo.'

'I went there once on holiday,' commented Doyle. 'You think the traffic's bad here . . .'

Cli-chack, cli-chack. Slide five. A street scene. The camera had just about managed to focus on a conversation between two men who looked to be arguing about something. The bald blond, and this time a small fat Asian-looking man.

'Spokesman for a now-defunct terrorist group. This is a rare photo of him, made more rare by the fact that he died last year. *Not* natural causes.'

Cli-chack. Slide six. Cli-chack. Slide seven. And so it went. In a few of the photos, the bald blond had disguised his appearance. There was a particularly risible hairpiece. There were sunglasses, of course, and what looked like an authentic moustache. Eventually, the slides came to an end.

'So he doesn't mix with royalty,' said Doyle. 'But, with respect, sir, who the hell is he?'

Trilling switched off the projector. Greenleaf went to the window and tugged up the venetian blinds. Elder walked to the projection screen and stood in front of it.

'He's a go-between,' he said. 'Just that. He has made a profession and a reputation out of liaising between people – terrorist groups and arms suppliers, crooked politicians and drug dealers, all sorts of organisations. He's worked in India, Czechoslovakia, Beirut, Austria, Egypt, Colombia . . .'

'A one-man United Nations.'

'I think *divided* nations would be nearer the mark, Doyle. He's Dutch, that much we're sure of. These slides came courtesy of MI6, who were given them by the Dutch authorities. There was, and still is, a long-term operation to arrest this man.' He paused.

'But not,' suggested Trilling, 'until his usefulness is past.'

'I can't comment on that,' said Elder.

'What do you mean, sir?' Greenleaf asked Trilling.

'I mean,' Trilling was happy to explain, 'just now they keep a watch on him, and they learn what he's up to. They amass information about all these groups he seems to work for. He's more useful as an unwitting source of information than he is behind bars.'

'The old story,' Doyle said simply.

'The old story,' Elder agreed.

'Like with Khan,' Doyle added.

'I can't comment on that either,' said Elder with a smile.

'So anyway,' said Greenleaf, 'what about him?'

'Two things,' Elder said. 'One, he's in Britain. That, at any rate, is what the Dutch think. His trail's gone cold, and they'd quite like to pick it up again.'

'As if we don't have enough on our plates,' said Doyle.

'I don't think you quite see,' Elder told him.

'Oh? What don't I see? We're up to our arses in the summit and Witch and everything . . .'

'And so,' said Elder quietly, 'is the Dutchman. My second point. Think back to the description of the man Crane was seen having a drink with. Do you remember?'

Ever-ready Greenleaf supplied the answer. 'Fair and balding, according to Mr McKillip.'

Elder nodded, while Doyle took it all in.

'It does seem a mighty coincidence,' said Trilling. He handed a copy of the McKillip drawing to Doyle so that Doyle could take in the resemblance for himself.

'It could well be that this Dutchman is the link between the assassin and her paymasters,' said Elder.

'You mean her paymasters on the Khan hit?'

Elder shook his head. 'Nobody brings an expensive assassin like Witch into the country for a hit like that. There's another job, and *those* paymasters will have supplied the Dutchman.'

'I thought,' said Greenleaf, 'she did one paid hit to finance her own private vendettas, isn't that what you told us?'

'Yes, but aspects of this operation make it unique. It doesn't quite fit her previous profile.'

Doyle was pinching the skin at the bridge of his nose. 'So now you're saying we change tack completely? Leave Witch and start looking for this Dutchman? New posters made up, more questions at hotels and boarding-houses . . .'

'Starting here in London,' Greenleaf added. 'It's the obvious place.'

'Which is probably precisely why he'll be based elsewhere,' said Elder. 'Somewhere out in the suburbs, pretending to be the rep for a Dutch company or something.'

Doyle counted on his fingers. 'Saturday, Sunday, Monday. Three days before the summit opens. It's too much ground even to *start* to cover.'

'So what should we do? Ignore the information?'

'You know that's not what I'm saying.'

'I *know* what you're saying, Doyle. You're saying you object to the workload, you object to grafting all weekend – again. You're tired and you need a break. Am I right?'

Doyle shifted his weight on the chair.

'We all need a break,' Trilling said quietly. Then he smiled. 'Maybe our Dutch friend will be *precisely* the break we need.'

Only Greenleaf laughed at the pun, and then not for long.

'Find the Dutchman,' said Elder levelly, 'and we find who Witch's target is. He's almost bound to know. We may even catch Witch herself.'

Trilling nodded. After a moment, Doyle nodded too. He looked around at the three faces.

'Well?' he said, rising to his feet. 'What are we waiting for? I'll just phone my bird and tell her I'm not available for lechery this weekend.'

Greenleaf sighed. 'And I suppose *I'd* better phone Shirley. I've hardly seen her recently. She'll go spare.'

'And I,' said Trilling, 'have to cancel a race meeting I was supposed to be attending. You see, we all make sacrifices.'

Elder was pleased, but didn't let it show. He was wondering how he would break it to his colleagues that he had to make a progress report to Joyce Parry this evening, a briefing he just couldn't cancel. Then Doyle remembered something.

'Oh,' he said, 'I know who the American bird is. An old mate of mine, Pete Allison – I used to work with him in CID, he runs his own security firm these days. He phoned me to say he'd been working for Khan, trying to find out about Shari Capri.'

'Why did he want you to know?'

Doyle shrugged. 'He was a bit sweaty about Khan being bumped off like that. He thought it through and decided he'd better come clean.'

'So what did he find?'

'She's a hooker, not a cheap one. That was all crap about her being a model. The story Pete heard is that another security firm had hired her to sniff around Khan.'

'Commercial espionage?'

Doyle nodded. 'Women and money, that's what it boils down to in the end. Another bank wanted to know what Khan's bank was up to, so they hired themselves a spy.' He turned to Elder. 'You still think she was working with Witch?'

Elder shrugged. 'Maybe not. But Witch *did* know a lot about Khan's movements. Maybe she had the Dutchman put a bit of money about, ask a few questions.'

'The security firm?'

'That'd be my guess. Someone there would have known what Ms Capri knew. Any idea where she is?'

'Not a clue. Want me to push it a bit further?'

Elder shook his head. 'It's a dead end. I'm sure she only took the job because she knew it would stretch us, lead us away from the real action. No, she's *here* now. Let's remember that and act on it.'

They left the office as a team.

The first thing to be done was to distribute photos of the Dutchman to police stations in central and greater London. The weekend wasn't really the time to accomplish this, but they did their best. A computer was used to create an A4-sized poster containing a description of the Dutchman and his photograph. The quality of reproduction of the photo left a little to be desired, and Elder doubted that, faxed, it would remain recognisable.

'The woman who really knows this machine is on holiday,' was the excuse offered.

'Then bring her back.'

They brought her back, and she sharpened the image to Elder's satisfaction, after which they laser-printed a few dozen copies. As well as police stations, the first target remained the Conference Centre itself. The description would go to every delegation, and to the various security organisations involved in the summit. The Dutchman probably wouldn't risk getting close to the summit itself, but the warning was worth making. Here was someone tangible for everyone to keep an eye open for. Here was something to keep them on their toes. Here was, at the very least, a *photograph*.

The day passed quickly. Doyle was sent to have a word with his snitches and least salubrious contacts.

'Bit out of their league,' he said, 'but you never know.'

There were Dutch-style pubs and Dutch restaurants in the capital. Greenleaf went to talk with owners, staff and regular clients. Again, they could be pretty sure that the Dutchman would steer clear of such places. Again, it was still worth a try.

Elder thought of his own contacts in London . . . and came to the conclusion that none of them was left; none, at least, who could be of any possible use. Apart from Charlie Giltrap. He wondered if Charlie was still around. He wasn't in the phone book, and a check showed that he wasn't unlisted either. Not that either of these meant anything. It was over two years since he'd seen Charlie, over two years since Charlie had given him his last, near-fatal tip-off.

'Just popping out for a minute,' he said. He made for the nearest newsagent's where he flicked through a listings magazine, concentrating on 'Events'. Sure enough, there was a record buyers' mart in London today, and ironically it was taking place at Westminster Central Hall, within spitting distance of the Conference Centre and not a five-minute walk from where he was standing. He put the magazine back on the rack and set off. It was just another long-shot . . . either that or fate.

At the Central Hall, he paid his entrance money and squeezed into a mayhem of noise and too many people crammed into the narrow aisles. Most of the music seemed to be heavy metal, not what he'd been expecting. The clientele was young and bedenimed and greasy-haired. They were listening to tapes on personal cassette-players before deciding whether to buy. Rare LPs were displayed against walls, some of the asking prices reaching three figures. A young woman, a heavy metal fan by the look of her, was attracting attention and comment as she browsed, apparently unaware of the hungry stares behind her. She was wearing a tight red leather skirt, zipped up both sides, and a black leather jacket. Elder found himself examining her too. He was looking for someone he knew beneath all that make-up and dishevelled hair. He failed to find her.

A few old-timers, and he put himself in this category, did their best to move through the crush, seeking out stalls selling older stuff: 50s and 60s music. He did one circuit of the hall without seeing Charlie Giltrap. And then, in a corner, stooped as he rifled through a cardboard box full of LPs, there he was. Grinning, Elder tapped him on the shoulder.

Charlie Giltrap turned around, his fingers still keeping his place in the box. Then his eyes opened wide and he let the records fall back, both his hands coming round to clasp Elder's.

'Dom! Where the hell did you spring from?' He was pumping Elder's right hand with both of his own, his grin near-toothless, cheeks slightly sunken where the extractions had been made. His eyes were dark-ringed, nose red-veined. Typically, he wore clothes too young for him: faded, patched denims, cheesecloth shirt, and a leather thong around his neck. His long grey hair was tied back in a ponytail.

'You never did send me your address, you bastard,' he said.

'I didn't have an address for *you*, remember,' replied Elder. 'But as it happens, I *did* send you a note.'

'Yeah?'

'Care of your father.'

A snort. 'That explains it then. Mind like a sieve. He probably chucked it out without telling me.'

'How is he?'

'Six feet under, God rest his soul. Went last Christmas.'

'I'm sorry.'

'Comes to us all, Dom. Maybe if I start smoking forty a day I'll live to be eighty-six like him. He used to say he'd smoked so much he'd been *cured*.' Charlie's laughter spluttered out of him.

'Yes, I remember,' said Elder.

'How are you doing anyway? What brings you back to the Smoke?'

'Work brings me back, Charlie.'

'Yeah, didn't think you'd just want to talk over old times.'

'Still get out and about, do you?'

'Not as much as before, but I keep my hand in.' Charlie winked. 'Let me settle up here and we'll go for a drink, yeah?'

Charlie turned back to the stall-holder. Elder noticed that half a dozen LPs had been lifted from the box and placed flat down on top of another box. Charlie picked them up and handed them over. The stall-holder totted up the prices and put them in a plastic carrier.

'Thirty quid, mate,' he said. Charlie handed over a fifty and, waiting for his change, turned to Elder.

'This place has gone right downhill, Dom. All hip-hop records and thrash bootleg tapes.'

'So I noticed.'

'Thing is, it's about the only place in London where you can still buy LPs. The shops all sell CDs, bigger mark-up, see. Phasing out vinyl. It's a catastrophe.' He took his change and his albums. 'Cheers, mate. See you next time.'

'Right you are, Charlie.'

Charlie and Elder squeezed back through the crowds in the aisles until they reached the doors to the lobby. Elder noticed that the heavy metal girl was standing chatting to some friends. As she laughed, he saw she was about ten years too young to be Witch . . .

'What a relief,' said Charlie, glad to be out of the crowd. 'My motor's parked round the side of the cathedral. Come on.'

'Where are we going?' asked Elder. Charlie looked at him.

'We're going to find you a pint of Young's best,' he said.

Elder laughed. 'I haven't had any of that in over two years.'

'You used to knock it back.'

'So where do we find Young's round here?'

'It's in a few places. The best I've tasted's in Soho.'

They drove into the middle of Soho and, the car park being full, cruised until they found someone pulling away from a parking meter.

'God bless you,' Charlie called to the departing car, slipping his own resprayed Escort into the space. Elder noticed that Charlie hid his LPs under the driver's seat, and then unslotted his radio and did the same with it.

'These days . . .' he said, simply, locking the car. He put some more money in the meter and led Elder into the dark interior of a pub. No jukebox, no television, no video games, and only a single fruit-machine.

'It's an oasis,' commented Elder, who thought such pubs no longer existed in London.

'It gets noisy at night,' said Charlie, ordering two pints of Young's Special. The beer when it came was dark and rich. 'Just like my landlord,' said Charlie. They perched on stools at the bar and exchanged histories of the past two years. Charlie had cut down on cigarettes and also on drugs and drink.

'Doctor's orders,' he said. He thumped his chest. 'Dodgy bellows, plus high blood pressure.'

Meantime, his album collection had risen from three thousand to nearer five, most of the records bought secondhand, few of them more contemporary than 1972.

The conversation was stilted, awkward. They were at the same time recalling past events and attempting to evade making mention of them. They both knew they were doing this, and smiled a few times in embarrassment as the conversation lapsed into silence.

'So,' Charlie said at last, 'what can I do for you, Dom?'

Dominic Elder ordered two more pints and a couple of filled rolls. 'I'm looking for a Dutchman,' he said.

'Uh-huh.'

'I thought maybe you could do your sniffer-dog routine.'

'Long time since anyone's said that to me: sniffer-dog. Private matter, is it?'

'No, strictly company business.'

'Uh-huh.' Charlie sipped his drink thoughtfully, then shook his head. 'I'm not sure, Dom. I mean, after that last time . . .'

'This is a team effort.'

'Yeah, but so was *that*. Didn't stop you going off and . . . I don't know. I'd be worried, that's all.'

'About me?' Elder smiled. 'I'm touched, Charlie, but I meant what I said, this time it's a team effort.'

'No individual skills, eh? Playing for the team.'

'That's right.'

'Yeah, well . . .' He straightened his back, scratched his nose, slumped again, studying his glass. 'All right then, can't do any harm. Mind, I don't have the eyes and ears I once had.'

'Just do what you can.' Elder handed over one of the descriptions of the Dutchman. Charlie read through it.

'Dutch pubs?' he said.

'We're already covering them.'

'Clubs, restaurants?'

'Those too.'

'Wonder if he's hired a car while he's here . . .'

'We'll check.'

Charlie nodded. He refolded the piece of paper and put it in his back pocket. 'Like I say, Dom, I'll do what I can.'

'What's the going rate these days, Charlie? I'm a bit out of touch.'

'You and me both. We'll sort the money out later. Don't worry, there's a discount for friends. Where can I find you?'

Elder gave the name of his hotel.

'Using your own name?' asked Charlie. Elder nodded, then thought: I shouldn't be, though. I shouldn't be using my own name. How long would it take her to find him, phoning all the hotels alphabetically, asking for him at reception? A day, two at most . . . if she wanted to, if she didn't have anything else to keep her busy.

'Have another?' said Charlie. Elder shook his head.

'Better get back,' he said. 'I want a clear head for tonight.'

'Oh, yes? Still up to your old tricks, eh? Who is she?'

'Never mind.'

'Dinner, is it?' Elder nodded. 'Listen, do me a favour. After you've bought the forty-quid bottle of wine and you're tasting it, just ask yourself this: does it taste any better than the pint I had this afternoon? I can tell you now what the answer'll be.'

Elder laughed. 'You're probably right, Charlie.'

'That's me, Dom, a right Charlie. Come on, I'll give you a lift back.'

Joyce Parry came naked from her bathroom into her bedroom and stood there again, hands on hips, staring at the clothes laid out on her bed. She just couldn't make up her mind. Two dresses and a skirt and blouse: she could not for the life of her choose between them. And until she'd decided that, she couldn't decide on her colour of tights or stockings, which meant she couldn't yet choose her shoes, never mind her accessories.

She was used to dressing to suit the occasion. Perhaps that was the very problem: she wasn't sure just what the occasion tonight actually *was*. She wasn't sure of Dominic's intentions, of how he felt. Was her confusion his fault or her own? She was nervous as a cornered rat, and afraid of coming to wrong conclusions. If she dressed one way, perhaps *he* would come to some wrong conclusion, too.

It was so easy usually. For the office, she dressed hard and efficient, because that was what the office required. For a dinner party, she would be elegant and intelligent. Receiving friends at home, she was just slovenly enough so that they felt comfortable in her house.

And for an intimate dinner with a man . . . ? That depended on what she thought the man felt about her, and what she felt – if anything – in return. There was her long ice-blue dress, covering most of her body like a shield. Then there was the jersey dress, which came to her knees and showed a lot of her arms and shoulders too. Or there was the skirt and blouse. The blouse could be worn open-necked, or else clamped shut and tied at the neck with a bow.

Decisions, decisions. She turned and went back into the bathroom. If she left the choice of outfit until the last minute, she'd *have* to make a snap judgement. So be it. God, he'd laugh to see her getting in such a state. The unflappable Joyce. She'd flapped all right, the first time she'd met him. They'd become lovers only several years later, and then for a matter of weeks. He'd still been married then – though only just. It didn't work. It could never have worked. But that hadn't stopped it being good at the time.

She cleaned her teeth, rinsed, spat. Turned off the tap and stared at herself in the mirror, her hands on the rim of the washbasin.

Silverfish had aged Dominic, but she wasn't looking so young herself. She patted her hair self-consciously. She still wasn't sure whether bringing Dominic to London had been such a good idea. He certainly seemed full of energy and ideas, his mind sharp. He'd covered good ground in Folkestone, Cliftonville, Brighton. He got results from people, mainly because he looked like he was there to be obeyed and impressed. Even the Special Branch pair worked well with him. Not *under* him, but *with* him. That was another thing about Dominic, he consciously underplayed his role. He didn't need to brandish his authority in anyone's face. Yet all the time he was manipulating them.

Maybe there were still a few things she could learn from him, a few of his strengths that she'd forgotten all about. But she knew his weaknesses of old, too. The way he bottled things up, always thinking more than he said, not sharing. And now Witch had threatened him: what must the shock of finding that note have done to him? She'd find out tonight, she'd sit at the table and ask him outright, and she'd go on asking until he told her.

She'd considered putting a guard on him. After all, he was the one real and actual person so far threatened by Witch. But Dominic wouldn't have agreed to a bodyguard. Besides, he was working most of the time alongside two bodyguards of a sort – Doyle and Greenleaf. But she'd phoned Trilling anyway, and had asked him to have a quiet word with his men, telling them to keep an eye open for Elder's safety. Trilling had been sympathetic, and had given her a progress report.

Too many fish, all of them possible red herrings. They were heading towards confusion rather than clarity. It wasn't Joyce Parry's way. The phone rang in the bedroom. Maybe Barclay and another of his too-vague reports. Maybe Dominic to say there was a fresh lead and he was cancelling dinner. She sat on the edge of the bed and picked up the receiver.

'Joyce Parry speaking.'

She listened for a moment, frowned, shifted a little on the bed. She pulled the corner of the duvet over her lap, as though her nakedness suddenly embarrassed her.

'What?' she said. She listened to more. 'I see,' she said. 'Yes, I quite understand. Thank you.' But the conversation lasted for several more minutes before she hung up.

Half an hour later, Dominic Elder rang the doorbell. She was dressed for travel, and knew she looked flustered and angry. Still, she opened the door to him. He was beaming. She swallowed before speaking.

'Dominic, I tried ringing you but you'd already left. Sorry, I've got to call off tonight.'

'What?' She stood at the door, holding the door itself by its edge. There was to be no invitation in.

'I know, I know. Somewhere I've got to be, cropped up less than half an hour ago. I really am sorry.'

He looked pitiable. His shoulders had collapsed forwards. He stared at the doorbell as though trying to make sense of the conversation. 'But . . . where? What's so important it can't—'

She raised her free hand. 'I know, believe me. But this can't wait. A car's picking me up in ten minutes and I haven't finished packing.'

'Packing?'

'Just overnight.' A pause. 'It's Barclay.'

'What's happened to him?'

'Nothing, he's just . . .' Her eyes narrowed. 'Tell me this is nothing to do with you.' He stood there, saying nothing. 'Well, thanks for the vote of confidence.' She pulled the door open wide. 'Get in here and tell me. Tell me *everything.*'

The schnapps before bed was probably not necessary. Barclay would have slept on a street of broken glass, never mind between the clean white sheets provided by the Gasthof Hirschen. It had been a hell of a drive. Dominique was of the let's-press-on school of travel, so that stops were few and far between, and what stops they made were perfunctory. Then a tyre went on the 2CV and the spare turned out to be in a distressed condition. And when a new tyre had been found and fitted, at what seemed to both of them major expense (whether converted into francs or sterling), a small red light had come on on the dashboard, and wouldn't go off, despite Dominique's attempts at tapping it into submission with her finger.

'What is it?'

'Just a warning light,' said Dominique.

'What's it warning us *of*?'

'I don't know. The owner's manual is under your seat.'

Barclay flicked through it, but his French wasn't up to the task. So Dominique pulled over and snatched the book from him.

'You're welcome,' Barclay muttered, but she ignored the jibe. He was dying for a cup of tea, and for the simple pleasures of Saturday in London: shopping for clothes and new classical CDs, reading a book or the newspaper with the CD playing on the hi-fi, preparing for a dinner party or drinks . . .

'Oil,' Dominique said.

'Let's take a look then,' said Barclay, getting out of the car. But the bonnet was almost impossible to open and he had to wait for Dominique, who was in no hurry to assist, to come and unhook the thing for him. There was less to the motor than he'd imagined.

'Do you have a rag or something?'

She shook her head.

'Fine.' He tugged a handkerchief from his pocket, pulled out the dipstick, wiped it, pushed it back into place again, and lifted it out again. Dominique consulted the owner's manual.

'Yes,' she said. 'The oil level is low.'

'Practically non-existent.' Barclay's voice was furiously calm. 'And do we have a can of oil with us?'

She looked at him as if he were mad even to ask.

'Fine,' he said again.

They were parked by the side of the autobahn. The road itself looked, to Barclay, like some old airstrip, short, pitted concrete sections with joins every few yards. The sound of the 2CV rumbling over each join had become monotonous and infuriating, but even that was preferable to this.

Then it started to rain.

They sat together in the front of the car, not even bothering with the windscreen-wipers. Drops of rain thudded down on the vinyl roof, trickling in at a few places where the vinyl had either perished or been breached. Inside the damp car, not a word was exchanged for several minutes.

'Well?' Barclay said at last. 'Maybe we could make it to the next petrol station.'

'The last sign was a couple of kilometres back. The next station is sixty kilometres away. We wouldn't make it, the engine would seize.'

Barclay did not want the engine to seize. 'So what do you suggest?'

Dominique did not reply. A car was slowing to a stop behind them. A man hurried out and started urinating on to the verge. Dominique watched in her wing-mirror and, when he was finished, dashed out and ran towards him, asking in German whether the man by chance had any spare oil.

'Ja, natürlich,' Barclay heard the man reply. He opened the boot of his car and brought out a large can and a plastic funnel. And even though this man was their saviour, Barclay saw why it was that some people disliked the Germans. Their efficiency in the face of one's own shortcomings merely intensified those shortcomings. And nobody liked to be shown up like that. Nobody.

'What a nice man,' said Dominique, cheered by the encounter. She turned the ignition. The red light came on but then went off again. She signalled out into the autobahn and drove off, sounding her horn at the man still parked by the side of the road. She was chatty after that, and eventually succeeded in talking Barclay out of his sullenness. The rain stopped, the clouds cracked open, and there was the sun, where it had been hiding all the time. They rolled back the vinyl roof and, only thirty or forty kilometres further on, stopped in a town for a good hour, grabbing a bite at a café and then simply walking around.

The men stared at Dominique. During the drive, she had become ugly to him, but now Barclay saw her again, petite and full of life, the sort of woman who got noticed even when there were taller, more elegant or more glamorous women around: not that there were many of those in the town. Refreshed, the rest of the drive was a bit easier on the nerves if not on the body. The Gasthof Hirschen, when they'd stumbled upon it, looked just the place to Barclay, more than adequate for an overnight stop. Dominique wasn't so sure. She'd thought maybe they could press on a little further . . . But Barclay had insisted. They were only fifty kilometres, if that, from Burgwede. Fifty kilometres from Wolf Bandorff. It was close enough for Barclay. The manager had asked if they would want just the one room. No, they wanted two. And dinner? Oh yes, they definitely wanted dinner.

But first Barclay had taken a bath, lying in it until Dominique had come thumping at his door, trying the doorhandle.

'I'm starving!' she called. So Barclay got dressed and met her in the restaurant. After half a bottle of wine, his eyes had started to feel heavy. Then he'd decided to take a schnapps to his room. He'd telephoned Dominic Elder's London hotel, knowing Elder expected to be back there sometime today. But he wasn't around, so Barclay left a message and his telephone number. Then he'd fallen asleep . . .

The first thing he was aware of was a weight on him. The sheets were tight around him, constricting him. He tried to tug them free, but weight was holding them down. What? Someone sitting on the edge of the bed, halfway down. He tried to sit up, but the weight held him fast. He struggled for the lamp, switched it on. It was Dominique. She was wearing only a long pink T-shirt. It fell, seated as she was, to just above her knees.

'What is it?' he said. He was thinking. That door was locked. She's brought her lockpick's tools with her. Then he looked at his watch. It was one-fifteen.

'I couldn't sleep,' she said. She rose from the bed, padded barefoot to the room's only chair, and sat down quite primly, knees together and the T-shirt clamped between them. 'I thought maybe we could talk about Bandorff.'

'We've talked about him.' Barclay sat up, wedging a pillow between him and the headboard.

'I know, but I'm . . .'

'Nervous? So am I.'

'Really?'

He laughed. 'Yes, really.'

She smiled for a moment, staring at the carpet. 'I don't know whether that makes me feel better or not.'

'Dominique, don't worry. Like you say, either we find out something or we don't. Is it me? Are you worried about my superiors finding out? *I'm* not worried,' he lied, 'so it's stupid for *you* to be.'

'Stupid?'

'Well, no, not stupid. I mean, it's very . . . I'm *glad* you worry about me. It's nice of you to worry, but you shouldn't.'

She came over to the side of the bed and knelt down in front of it. Barclay shifted uneasily beneath the sheets. She stared hard at him.

'Michael,' she said, 'there's something I want to tell you.' She paused. The spell seemed to break, and she shifted her gaze to the headboard. 'Tomorrow,' she said. 'Tomorrow will be time enough.' She got back to her feet. 'I'm sorry I woke you up.' She smiled again and bent down to kiss his forehead. 'Try to sleep.' After the view he'd just had down the front of her T-shirt, he doubted he would.

Then she padded to the door and was gone. Just like that. Barclay didn't move for a couple of minutes, and then when he did move it was merely to sit up a little higher against the headboard. He drew his knees up in front of him and rested his arms on them. He stared at the bedroom door, willing Dominique to walk back through it. She didn't. Eventually, he slid back down beneath the sheets and turned off the bedside lamp. Etched on the insides of his eyelids were supple shadowy bodies, hanging breasts, shapes concave and convex. His forehead tingled where she'd kissed him. The birds were starting to sing as he eventually drifted off to sleep.

Sunday 14 June

There was a big meeting at the Queen Elizabeth II Conference Centre. Central London was deserted except for the tourists, the security people, and some of the 2,500 media representatives who would cover the summit. Before the meeting, there was a photo session. Most of the security people, for obvious reasons, didn't want to become involved in the photo shoot, which seemed to suit the Home Secretary just fine. Jonathan Barker had been Home Secretary for just under a year, his political career having been steady rather than meteoric. There had been a rough few months at the beginning, with calls for his resignation after several prison escapes, a mainland terrorist attack, and a police scandal. But for the moment he could do little wrong, his second wife, Marion, having died two months back. She had been a tireless worker for charity, especially children's charities, as all the obituaries had pointed out. And it was as if some of her polish had rubbed off on her handsome widower.

Watching the photo opportunity take its course, Elder smiled. Only one of the obituaries had mentioned Marion Barker's crankier side, her belief in spiritualism. And no one had mentioned how she'd been Barker's secretary while he'd still been married to his first wife. There had been gossip about that at the time. Then the first wife had died, and slowly, without unseemly haste, Marion and Jonathan had begun to appear together in public.

It wasn't even close to a scandal. Nothing of the sort. Yet Elder wondered how significantly it had slowed Barker's political progress. He wondered as he watched the Home Secretary smiling again, this time shaking hands with yet another dignitary. They all stood in a line off-camera, all the people who still had to have their photo taken. They preened, straightened ties, flicked a stray hair back behind an ear. They were all men. An underling gave them instructions, sending them on their way when each photo was taken. It was a real production line. And all for half a dozen photographers. The media wasn't really interested, not yet. The real scrum would begin when the summit got underway. This was a day of dress rehearsals and final checks. That was why the Home Secretary was on the scene, to give a very public thumbs-up to the security arrangements.

'Thank you, gentlemen,' the underling said at last to the photographers, who had already turned away and were winding back rolls of film, chatting in huddles. Elder stood in another huddle, a huddle of security chiefs. Trilling was there, and was in whispered conversation with an American. There were two Germans, a tall and dapper Frenchman, a Canadian, and many more . . . a real United Nations of secret agents and policemen. Elder had been introduced to them all, but they were names to him, little more. They were simply in his way.

But then he, of course, shouldn't be here at all. Joyce had only sent him because there was no one else available at such short notice. Her fury the previous evening had been tempered only by the arrival of her chauffeur. She'd still managed to make known her views. Elder was not to speak to Barclay 'under any circumstances'. In fact, he wasn't to do anything at all. But then she'd remembered this meeting . . .

The Home Secretary, sweeping back his hair as he walked, was approaching. His underling was telling him something, to which Jonathan Barker did not appear to be listening. He stuck out a hand towards Trilling.

'Commander, nice to see you.' They shook hands. Barker smiled and half-nodded towards Elder, as if to say 'I know you', when in fact he couldn't even be sure of Elder's nationality.

'Mr Elder,' explained the underling, 'is here as Mrs Parry's representative.'

'Ah,' said Barker, nodding and frowning at the same time. 'Thought I didn't see her.' His tone, to Elder's ears, was slightly ominous.

'Mrs Parry sends her apologies,' said Elder. 'Something came up last night, very last-minute, very important.'

Barker looked as though he might have something to say about this, but he was already being introduced to the Canadian, to the Germans . . . Elder had to give the underling his due: the guy knew all the names and faces. Trilling's voice was a peppermint murmur beside him.

'What's Joyce up to?'

'I don't know.'

'Barker didn't sound too pleased.'

Elder nodded slowly. Not too pleased at all . . . Well, he wasn't in such a good mood himself. If Barker wanted to pick a fight, that was fine by Elder. He'd spent a sleepless night in his room, a piece of paper by his telephone. On the paper was a note of Barclay's phone number in Germany. Joyce had warned him not to speak to Barclay. And hadn't Barclay let himself in for it? Elder had requested that no calls be put through to his room.

But this morning he'd cracked. He'd placed a call to the Gasthof Hirschen, only to be informed that Herr Barclay had already checked out. Well, that was that.

'If you'll come this way, gentlemen,' said the Home Secretary, taking charge. Introductions over, they were on their way into the Conference Centre proper.

'First stop,' said the Home Secretary, 'screening unit.' They had stopped in front of a doorway the edges of which were thick metal, painted bright orange. Two guards stood this side of the doorway, two the other. This was the start of the tour which, conducted by the Home Secretary, was supposed to reassure everyone that the security precautions were, well, more than adequate. Elder believed it; he knew they were more than adequate. He still wasn't impressed.

'Anyone entering has to pass through this metal detector. It's a special design, extremely accurate, not yet, I believe, in place in any airports due to the costs involved. Cost has not been a factor at this summit. But before even this, a body search takes place. Nothing too distracting or disruptive, and of course the heads of state will not be subject to this particular search.' A smile. 'We think we can trust them.' There were a few laughs, Trilling's amongst them. 'Any baggage is checked by hand and by a hand-held detector, before being passed through this X-ray machine.' Barker patted the machine itself. 'Again, it's British-designed and British-built and it's more sophisticated than similar devices found in airports. An inbuilt computer, for example, points out anomalies to the operator. Now, can I ask you all to submit to a search then walk, one at a time, through the doorway?'

'What happens if two people pass through at the same time?' questioned an American voice.

'They're sent back,' answered the underling quickly. 'The scanner won't accept two people. They *both* go back, just in case one has passed something to the other. Then they walk back through the detector individually.'

The Home Secretary beamed. 'Any more questions?' There were none. 'Then I suggest we proceed.'

The tour was brisk, but Elder noticed that the underling had to field more questions than was comfortable. The Home Secretary, it seemed, had not been properly briefed; or if he had, he'd not remembered it. Well, this was only PR after all. It wasn't important.

They saw the hall where the nine-nation summit itself would take place; the interpreters' boxes; the rest-rooms; the smaller, more intimate conference rooms; the 'suites' which had been set aside for the individual delegations – all with computer terminals, photocopying machines, fax machines; the toilets; the press facilities; the monitoring room. There was even a small gymnasium. They passed technicians who were busy checking for listening devices. A policeman dressed clumsily in a suit wandered past them reining in a sniffer-dog on a leash. Cleaners seemed to be re-cleaning every spotless surface in the place, and behind them came more technicians checking for more unwanted devices.

'Tremendously impressive, I'm sure you'll agree,' said the Home Secretary. There were nods, mumbled agreement. The Home Secretary, it seemed to Elder, like most politicians equated effort with success. The more you did to secure a place, the more secure it became. Elder didn't agree. Elder didn't agree at all. The more sophisticated the security, the more loopholes it contained; the more people were involved, the greater the possible access for a stranger; and the more you relied on technology . . . Well, the word 'relied' gave it away, didn't it? You shouldn't have to rely on *anything*. They only needed to take such huge precautions in the first place because central London had been chosen as the location for the summit. And the reason London had been chosen had little to do with security and everything to do with prestige.

Elder would have chosen an isolated castle, or the top of Ben Nevis, or an underground bunker. But that would never do. These were statesmen. They didn't hide away, not at summits. Summits were events; media events, the pictures beamed around the world, photo opportunities and sound-bites of the grandest kind. No statesman wanted to hide from all that good publicity. Summits would soon be run by ad agencies.

The tour was winding up. It had taken a little over an hour and a half. Drinks and canapés were being provided in another part of the building, outside the 'secure zone'.

'I'm sorry I can't stay,' said Barker. 'I hope you'll understand that my schedule is busier even than usual.' He managed by tone and intonation to turn this into a joke of sorts, so that no one minded that they were being shuffled off to a hot little room somewhere. Not Trilling and Elder, though: they were tagged by the underling and told to come with the Home Secretary. Another underling escorted the larger group away from the scene. There were backwards glances from a few of the men. They looked like they would prefer to stay with Barker, Trilling and Elder.

'This way, please,' said the underling.

They followed the route they'd just come until they reached one of the small conference rooms. It contained a round table, eight chairs, and a water-cooler, which looked newly installed. The Home Secretary drank two beakerfuls of spring water before sitting down. Three men were already seated at the table: a senior armed forces commander whom Elder recognised straight away, a representative from the SAS, and an Intelligence officer. The Home Secretary shook hands with them, then motioned for Trilling and Elder to be seated. The underling remained standing till last.

'Right,' said Jonathan Barker, looking towards Trilling, 'now what's all this about a Dutchman?'

'Mr Elder found the connection.'

'Then Mr Elder can tell me.'

So Elder explained about the intelligence which had come from The Netherlands, while the Home Secretary nodded, his eyes making a tour of the other men round the table, as though ensuring that they were paying attention. They were certainly paying attention. The underling, whom Elder had expected to take notes with a fountain pen, unfolded a small case, turning it into a laptop computer. He tapped away at the keys while Elder spoke, like the stenographer in some courtroom drama.

Barker was staring at Elder. 'And Witch?'

'A female assassin, sir. Known to be in this country. The summit would seem a likely target of her attentions.'

'How does she operate as a rule?'

'At close range.' The question, which had surprised Elder, was a fair one and also astute.

'Then we've no problems,' said the Home Secretary. 'She's not going to get within spitting distance of anyone attending the summit.'

'We can't know that for sure, sir,' countered Elder. 'And besides, while the available evidence points to close range, there are plenty of possible hits she's made at longer range: bombs, shootings . . .'

'Well then, Mr Elder, perhaps you can suggest possible ways of tightening up security?'

All eyes were on him. A couple of hours ago he would have taken up the gauntlet. He would have revelled in pointing out all the mistakes. But they were basic mistakes – such as choice of location, for example – and couldn't be changed at this late stage. So he shrugged. The gauntlet remained on the ground.

'I've been over the security arrangements with some of Commander Trilling's men. We haven't made any recommendations.'

'Yes,' said Barker, 'but that's rather an ambiguous answer, Mr Elder, isn't it? You may not have made any recommendations, but did you see any flaws?'

Elder swallowed. 'No, sir,' he said.

Barker seemed satisfied. 'Thank you, Mr Elder. Mrs Parry sees flaws.'

Elder's heart sank. He'd walked straight into a trap. The underling was handing the Home Secretary a sheet of paper.

'She thinks,' Barker went on acidly, '*in retrospect* that London was a poor choice of location for the summit. She *feels* security is difficult to maintain in a city of ten million inhabitants.' He placed the sheet of paper on the table. Elder saw that it was a letter of sorts, a memo. He'd guess, by Barker's pique, that it had been sent to the Prime Minister direct, bypassing Barker himself.

'I have to agree with Mrs Parry,' Trilling said quietly, 'that London is far from ideal from a purely security point of view.'

'Well, it's a bit bloody late to tell us now, isn't it?' said the Home Secretary coldly. 'It looks to me, from where I'm sitting, as though MI5 and Special Branch are attempting to cover their arses in the event that an assassination attempt *does* take place, and maybe even, God forbid, succeeds. That smacks to me of panic and impotence. Panic and impotence, Commander.' His eyes found Elder's. 'Panic and impotence, Mr Elder.'

'I'm sure Mrs Parry is only pointing out—'

'Why isn't she here today?' The Home Secretary's voice had risen enough for his underling to glance up. 'I'll tell you why, Mr Elder, because she didn't have the guts to face me on this. So she sent *you* instead. And who are you, Mr Elder?' The finger pointing at him was long and thick with a gleaming, manicured nail. 'You're in retirement. You're in London on a consultancy basis. What the hell is going on in Joyce Parry's department, that's what I'd like to know? And believe me, I intend asking her.'

'What Mrs Parry means,' said Elder, 'is that you can't cordon off central London. The IRA learned that a long time ago. You can't be secure in London.'

'This assassin, though, she's not IRA, is she?'

'She doesn't belong to a group.'

'People hire her?'

'Sometimes, not always. Look, people like Witch don't want peace. They're not the types to sit in hotel rooms and around conference tables. Look at Hamas in Palestine – the PLO were getting too much like the establishment. Witch is a one-woman splinter group.'

'Then what is her ideal?'

Elder smiled. 'People keep asking me that. Why does she have to have one?' He paused, aware that Trilling's foot was touching his beneath the table. It was a warning. It was telling him not to explode.

Barker sat for a few moments in silence, his face implacable. His voice when he spoke again was cool, not quite objective.

'We're going to go through the security arrangements again. Step by step. Don't bother looking at your watches because we'll be in this room as long as it takes.' He slipped out of his jacket and hung it over the back of his chair. He began to roll up his shirtsleeves. 'Sandwiches will be brought in, as will tea and soft drinks. There's water available whenever required. You may know that the Foreign Secretary has urgent business in the Middle East, so I'm going to be attending more of his bloody summit than was the intention. This being the case, I don't want any fuck-ups.' He paused, glancing from man to man to man. 'So, gentlemen . . . perhaps we'd better begin?'

Elder looked down at the table. He knew that several pairs of accusing eyes were on him. The Army, the SAS, Intelligence. Stuck in here because of his department, because of a letter sent by *his* boss. Elder knew why Joyce had written the letter. She'd written it because, having checked security at the Conference Centre and beyond, having read Greenleaf's impressive report on the security arrangements, Elder had warned her to. He just hadn't expected she would take his advice.

'Let's cover ourselves,' had been his exact words. 'Let's cover ourselves from criticism.'

Yet now he felt naked as the day he'd been born.

Herr Grunner of the Burgwede Maximum Security Prison was far too polite a man to tell the two young people in front of him that their request for an interview with Wolfgang Bandorff had upset his whole weekend. His wife and he had been due to visit their son in Geneva. The son was a physicist and worked at the huge CERN project beneath the Swiss-French border. Herr Grunner knew that the letters CERN stood for Conseil Européen pour la Recherche Nucleaire. He also knew that 'nucleaire' in this case had nothing to do with nuclear bombs or anything military. The people on the project were scientists, and they were trying to probe the secrets of particle physics – hence 'nucleaire', the nucleus.

The proud parents had been taken before on a tour of the CERN complex, their heads dizzied by the size and complexity of the underground machines. But, though Herr Grunner had listened closely to Fritz's explanations, he hadn't really understood much of anything. So this trip was to be pleasure only: a trip to the mountains, a few meals, a chance to meet Fritz's Swiss ladyfriend Cristel.

And now he'd had to make telephone calls, to explain matters to his wife. The trip was put back until the following weekend. Herr Grunner's wife was not at all amused. Which was perhaps why he had brooded on the visit to his prison by a member of the French internal security agency, accompanied by a member of British internal security. It was curious after all, wasn't it? Curious that those two countries' very adequate external intelligence agencies shouldn't be involved. Curious enough certainly to merit a call to his country's own internal security agency, the BfV.

Still, when Mademoiselle Herault and Mr Barclay arrived, Herr Grunner was polite, obliging, deferential. They had to take tea in his office while he told them something of the prison's history. Not that he wanted to keep them from their appointment, you understand; this was a matter of courtesy alone, and the young couple seemed to acknowledge this.

All the same, Mr Barclay had questions for Herr Grunner.

'Has Bandorff had any visitors lately?'

'Visitors are kept to a minimum.'

'Lately though?'

Herr Grunner looked as though he might become difficult, then relented. He pressed two digits on his telephone and repeated Barclay's question in German, then waited. After a moment he began to scribble on a notepad, then gave a grunt of acknowledgement and put down the receiver.

'His mother and his sister.'

'On the same day?'

'No, on different days.'
'When did the sister visit?'
'March the twentieth,' Herr Grunner looked up from the notepad, 'at ten o'clock.'
'I take it you check the identities of visitors?'
'Of course.' Herr Grunner looked at his watch. 'Now, if we are ready . . . ?'
They were ready.

Bandorff's cell was large, more like a hospital room than part of a prison. Bandorff was allowed, as Herr Grunner had explained, a lot of his own things: books, tapes, a cassette-player, his own clothes even. There was a typewriter and plenty of writing paper, and even a portable colour TV. The walls had been painted sunflower gold, and then decorated with maps and posters, including a smiling photograph of the Pope.

Two warders entered the cell first, and would remain there throughout. Wolf Bandorff was watching television. He lay on his bed, hands behind his head, legs stretched out, feet crossed at the ankles. He seemed to be watching a quiz show. Herr Grunner bowed towards Bandorff – who nodded his head slightly in response – then left for his office. Two chairs had been placed on the same side of a small desk, both the chairs facing Bandorff. It did not look as though the terrorist was about to shift either his body or his gaze.

But as Dominique sat down, she saw Bandorff's eyes move to just below the level of the desk. He was staring at her legs. Instinctively, she tugged her skirt down a little further. He looked up at her, light glinting from his round wire-framed spectacles, saw that her wriggling was his doing, and grinned. He was in his early fifties, his hair long and silvered and swept back. Had it been thicker, it might have been described as a 'mane', but it was thin and unwashed. He was thinner than the photos – those old photos in the Witch file – had intimated. He no doubt kept in shape in the prison gymnasium. He was a good-looking man who had not gone to seed.

'You're beautiful,' he told Dominique in German.
'Thank you,' she said crisply in English.
'You're French?' he asked her in French.
'Yes,' she said, still in English.
'But you want to conduct this interview in English,' he said, nodding. He turned his attention to Barclay. 'Therefore I take it you, my friend, are either American or British?'
'I'm English,' said Barclay.
'And I,' said Bandorff, 'am German.' He began watching the quiz show again. 'And this,' he said, waving a hand towards the TV, 'is as good a theory of terrorism as I've ever seen.' His hand curled into a fist, index finger extended like a pistol barrel. The hand bucked, an imaginary bullet finding the all-too-real target.
'You miss guns, Herr Bandorff?'

Bandorff didn't reply. Barclay looked at Dominique. He was trying hard to phrase another question, but his mind was not cooperating; all it could think of was the bombshell Dominique had dropped as they were leaving Herr Grunner's office.

'Michael,' she'd said to him in an undertone, 'you know there was something I wanted to tell you last night? Well, it's this. None of this is sanctioned by my superiors.'

He'd almost passed out. 'What?'

'I'm not authorised to be here. I telephoned a colleague and got him to give me the prison details and phone number. I didn't tell my superiors I was coming.'

His walk had slowed. If he moved any faster, he felt his legs would buckle under him. 'Why not?'

'They wouldn't have let me. This is a big job. And I'm not that big. Remember, I told you back in Calais: you weren't important enough to merit someone more senior. My superiors don't know anything about anything . . . not yet. They think I've been following you these past days while *you* made your investigations. I haven't told them anything more.'

'Jesus Christ!'

'I'm sorry.'

'Why tell me now?'

She shrugged. 'Maybe because now you can't back down and leave me all by myself . . .'

'You seem engrossed.'

Barclay snapped out of it. Bandorff was talking to him. He became aware that he'd been staring at the TV screen. He took a deep breath. 'My name is Michael Barclay, Herr Bandorff. This is Mademoiselle Herault. We'd like to ask you a few questions.'

'Do I win any prizes?'

Barclay just smiled. He took a photograph from his pocket, got up and walked over to Bandorff. The warders looked bored. Barclay stopped a foot or so from Bandorff's bed and held the photograph towards him.

'She's beautiful too, Herr Bandorff.'

Bandorff peered short-sightedly at the photo. 'I can't . . . my eyes aren't what they were.'

One of the warders said something in German.

'He says Herr Bandorff can see fine,' translated Dominique.

Barclay held his ground. The hand holding the photo was remarkably steady. Well, after all, what had he to lose? He was here because Dominique had played a trick on him. They'd run fast and loose, ignoring all the laws of the game. Rugby had been invented that way, but careers had come to a speedy end that way too. What had he got to lose?

'The photo was taken some time ago. It shows you and a young woman. For want of her real name, we in the security service call her Witch.'

'Witch?'

'*Die Hexe,*' translated Dominique. Bandorff glanced towards her.

'Thank you,' he said crisply, 'I do *know* what the word means.' He paused, watching for her reaction, then chuckled. 'Witch. I like the name.'

'The photo,' Barclay went on, 'shows you with a young woman, Herr Bandorff. You're in a crowd in the city of Edinburgh. You're watching the Pope.'

'Are we?'

'We're interested in the woman.'

'Why?' Bandorff was still staring at the photo.

'She's become a very proficient terrorist over the years. I believe she gained her earliest training at your hands?'

'Oh no, not her earliest training.'

A breakthrough! He'd acknowledged he knew her. Barclay had to press on. 'Do you know much about her early life?'

'Nothing at all, my friend. She came, she stayed, she left. I knew less about her when she left than I did when she arrived. While she, on the other hand, knew quite a lot about me.' He took a deep breath, sighed. Barclay could smell pork sausage, garlic, caries. 'Ah, the good old days. I'd like to know what happened to her. Can you tell me?'

'I thought maybe you could tell me. She visited you quite recently, didn't she?'

'Did she?'

'Posing as your sister. Witch is good at disguise, it wouldn't have been difficult. What did you talk about?'

Wolf Bandorff stared into Barclay's eyes and laughed. 'So young and yet so wise.' Then he turned back to the TV. Barclay stood his ground. From this close, he could see the musculature beneath Bandorff's grey T-shirt, the veins and tendons in his arms.

'She needed help, didn't she? You must have been surprised to see her after all this time.'

Bandorff spoke quietly, his words evenly spaced. 'Do you know how long they intend keeping me here?' Barclay waited for him to answer his own question. 'Another sixteen years, my friend. Another sixteen years of books, music, magazines.' He nodded towards the TV. 'When I am released, I shall make my fortune by appearing on general knowledge quiz programmes, always supposing my memory holds up.' He paused, his eyes fixed on the photograph.

'I must thank you for showing me this,' he said. 'It has reinforced one of my memories.' He looked past Barclay to Dominique. 'She *is* beautiful, isn't she?'

Barclay didn't think he meant Dominique. 'She was,' he said.

'She still is, believe me. You never forget those eyes.'

'What did she want?'

Bandorff shrugged and returned to the TV.

'She needed help,' Barclay replied, 'and you gave it. You were able to introduce her to two people in Paris who could help her.'

Bandorff looked back to Barclay and smiled. He smiled back. 'I'm fed up calling her Witch,' he said. 'What did you call her?'

Now Bandorff was chuckling. Barclay went back to his chair and sat down. He caught Dominique's eye. She seemed to be urging him on.

'Can you leave me that photograph?' Bandorff asked casually.

'Maybe,' said Barclay. But he slipped the photo back into his pocket.

'Shall I tell you something, my friend?' Barclay waited. 'I may be the only man alive who has ploughed his way through Balzac's *Comédie humaine*. Yes, all ninety-one volumes. Here's my advice: don't bother.' He smiled to himself, then lowered his head so that he could scratch his nose just beneath his glasses. 'I shouldn't think Herr Grunner is happy about your visit,' he said at last, straightening. 'He enjoys his Sundays at home. Sunday . . . strange choice of day to pay your respects.'

'We're not going to get anything here,' Dominique said to Barclay, just loud enough for Bandorff to hear.

'Tell me, Herr Witchfinder,' said Bandorff, 'what are you doing here really?'

'Her most recent assassination was in the United Kingdom.'

Bandorff nodded. 'The banker, Khan?' He smiled at the surprise on Dominique's face. 'The newspapers here printed the story. I am not clairvoyant, I only read words. Clairvoyants, though, read faces, don't you think? I knew of Khan. His bank was said to sponsor terrorist groups . . . but never mine. We had to find our backers elsewhere. That photograph . . . how do you know it is Witch?'

Barclay shrugged. 'Personally I don't.'

'Personally? Personally I? But someone else, eh? Someone who has seen her since, and then saw the photograph, and who made the connection. He would be the Witchfinder General, eh?'

Barclay tried to think of Dominic Elder in such a role. It fitted all too easily.

'One thing I learned about the woman you call Witch . . .'

'Yes?'

'She changes allegiances.'

'That's hardly news, Herr Bandorff. She's been involved with several terrorist groups.'

'Still, it was one of the things I learned about her. She might also appreciate being given a sort of codename . . . this "Witch" that you call her. She was fascinated by word games and crosswords.' He tilted his head to one side, remembering. 'She would lie in bed puzzling over them . . . Ah, then there was the third thing.'

'Yes?'

'Sex, Herr Barclay. She didn't like sex. No sex for *Die Hexe*.' A smile.

'That must have disappointed you,' said Dominique coolly.

'Oh yes,' said Bandorff reflectively. 'A grave disappointment. But it went further. I felt she didn't like *men*.'

'She was a lesbian?' Dominique sounded disbelieving. Bandorff laughed.

'No, no, all I mean is that she hated men. Now tell me, you're a woman, why might that be?'

'I can think of a few reasons,' said Dominique.

'Me, too,' said Bandorff. 'I wonder if they're the same? Perhaps psychoanalysis could explain it.'

'And you've no idea where she came from?' asked Barclay.

'Oh, well, she was passed along the line. One activist passed her to another . . . and so on. Each time a little more radical, a little more committed. But all those people are gone now. You won't trace her history that way. All I knew was that she wanted to change the world. That was good enough for me back then, and good enough for her. When she left, she left without warning. She'd brought no baggage, and she took none, except for her tarot pack and her teddy bear.' He was reminiscing. It sickened Barclay. 'She's become a myth, hasn't she? Who am I to tamper with myths?'

He returned to his television. A new quiz show was about to replace the old one. 'Ah, now this one is my favourite. It contains a nice element of chance.'

Barclay stood up, followed by Dominique. Was this it? Was this what they'd come so far for? Barclay tried to think of other things to say. He turned to Dominique, who nodded merely. It was time to leave. But Barclay paused, reaching into his pocket again for the photograph. He placed it silently on the desk.

'Thank you, Herr Witchfinder,' said Bandorff.

Barclay and Dominique walked back the way they'd come. 'You were brilliant, Michael,' she told him. 'Have you forgiven me yet?'

'For what?'

'For lying to you . . . and then for telling you the truth?'

He smiled. 'It was a shock, that's all.'

'Yes, and look what it did to you.'

Which was true. Something had galvanised him. He'd actually interviewed Wolf Bandorff and had come away with information on Witch – useless information in itself, but something to be added to the file.

'So what now?' he asked.

'Back to Paris, I suppose. Then back to London for you.'

He nodded. There was nothing keeping him on the Continent any more. Time to head back and confess that he'd come away from France with not a great deal. They were passing Herr Grunner's office.

'Should we look in and say goodbye?' asked Barclay.

'He's probably already gone home,' said Dominique. But the office door opened and Herr Grunner stood there, gesturing to them.

'Would you be so kind . . . ?' He held the door open and motioned for them to enter. Past him, a man was standing in front of Herr Grunner's desk, his raincoat still on, arms folded. Dominique gasped.

'Who is it?' asked Barclay.

'Not my boss,' she said. 'But *his* boss!'

They were at the door now, crossing the threshold, the door closing with a quiet click after them. A figure stood staring from Herr Grunner's rain-dappled window. It turned around and spoke in a voice which chilled Barclay all the way down to his feet.

'Good afternoon, Mr Barclay,' said Joyce Parry.

The trip back to London was the least comfortable of Barclay's life. Despite the chauffeured car, the airplane waiting on the tarmac, coffee and biscuits on board.

'My car's still in Calais,' he said. 'And I've some clothes in Paris.'

'They'll be picked up,' Parry said coolly. She had her glasses on and was browsing through the big fat Witch file, Dominic Elder's file. She didn't seem to be in much of a mood for talking, which worried Barclay all the more. Not much had been said in Herr Grunner's office. Dominique had been given a few curt words of French and then had followed her superior's superior out of the room, without so much as a backward glance at Barclay. Barclay had steeled himself for similar treatment from Parry.

It hadn't come. She'd thanked Herr Grunner – in fluent German – and they'd left. He saw Dominique being driven away in a large black Citroën, while an official-looking person got into her 2CV, started it, and rolled out of the prison car-park.

'Come on,' said Parry. She led him to a white Rover 2000 where a driver was waiting. He had an embassy look about him which Barclay translated into MI6. 'Straight to the airport,' Parry informed the driver.

'Yes, ma'am,' he said. Barclay heard humour in his tone, the joke being that Barclay was in for it and he, the driver, was not.

'How did you know?' Barclay asked Joyce Parry. He was thinking of Dominic Elder. He had tried phoning the hotel again first thing, but they said they couldn't put through his call. He hadn't understood at the time. He thought maybe he did now. Parry turned her head towards him.

'Don't be stupid. How could we *not* know? I've heard of cavalier, but this little stunt . . .' She exhaled noisily. ' "How did you know?" ' she echoed, mockingly. She shook her head slowly. By the time they'd reached the airport, she'd decided to explain it to him anyway. 'Herr Grunner contacted the BfV, who contacted the DGSE and SIS. What do you think SIS did?'

'Contacted you?' hazarded Barclay.

'You can imagine my surprise, being told that one of my agents, who had told me he was in Paris, was actually in Germany. Perhaps you can also imagine my humiliation at having to be told your true whereabouts by bloody SIS!'

Yes, thought Barclay, there was little love lost between MI5 and SIS – the Secret Intelligence Service, also known as MI6. The French DGSE was the equivalent of the SIS, an external intelligence service. They'd no doubt contacted the DST. Dominique was no doubt receiving a similar lashing. Dominique . . .

'You're as bad as Dominic bloody Elder,' said Parry. 'This is just the sort of stupid trick *he'd* have played.' She paused. 'I know he's been in touch with you throughout. Tell me, did he tell you to come here?'

Barclay stayed silent. No point defending himself. It was best just to let her get on with it; let all the anger roll out of her. But in fact she said nothing more until the airport, where they boarded their plane. As she was fastening her seatbelt, she looked up at him.

'Why did you lie?'

He'd been preparing for this very question. 'Would you have let me go?'

'Certainly not.'

He shrugged. 'That's your answer then. You saw Dom . . . Ms Herault. *She* was going. If I'd called you for permission and you'd turned me down flat, how would that have made me look?'

'It would have made you look like a junior agent who's still got to be kept on a tight leash. Which is the truth. But I suppose that wouldn't have done, would it? It would hardly have . . . impressed Ms Herault.'

'It would have made me look like a fool.'

'So you lied to me instead.'

'I'm sorry, I know I shouldn't have.'

'No, you shouldn't. Believe me, Mr Barclay, you shouldn't. As for conspiring with Dominic Elder behind my back, it's intolerable!'

'I did what I did because I thought it was in our best interests.' He paused. 'Ma'am.'

'And you think that's an excuse?'

There was no more dialogue between them until after take-off. Barclay felt a sudden crushing fatigue, despite the sour airplane coffee. It was days since he'd had an unbroken night's sleep. Adrenaline had kept him going, but now the adventure had come to an abrupt end and his body just wanted sleep. Only fear of his boss's reaction should he doze off kept his eyes open.

Joyce Parry kept tapping the Witch file which lay across her lap. 'For your information,' she said at last, 'I learned of your little escapade *yesterday*. I arrived in Germany late last night.'

'What? Then why did—'

'I had some trouble persuading Monsieur Roche that we should let you and Ms Herault go ahead with the interview.'

'You let it go ahead? But why?' He was wide awake now.

She shrugged. 'Why not? What did we have to lose? Tell me, why were you there?'

'It's a long story.'

'And this is a long flight. I expect a report from you, and I mean a *full* report. If you leave anything out . . .'

'I understand.'

'I'll want it by tomorrow morning, first thing, on my desk. Meantime I want to hear it from your own mouth. Did you learn anything from Bandorff?'

Barclay shrugged. 'Tidbits.'

'But something?'

'Maybe, yes.'

'Well, at least there's *something* to show for all your bungling.'

'It's not much. He told me she hated men. He wondered what could have caused that. He said maybe psychoanalysis would provide an answer. What do you think he meant?'

'Families?' Parry answered.

'So it goes back to her parents? He also mentioned two things she carried with her: a teddy bear and a pack of tarot cards.'

Parry considered this. 'Maybe Profiling can make something of it.'

'They're both signs of insecurity, aren't they? A teddy bear brings past security, a tarot is supposed to reassure for the future.'

She stared at him, eyebrows raised a fraction. 'Maybe you've been in the wrong department all along.'

Barclay gave her just a hint of his winning smile. 'He also mentioned clairvoyance at one point, just in passing. Maybe it was a reference to the tarot.'

'Elder visited a fairground in Brighton,' Parry stated.

'Really? Coincidence?'

She shrugged. 'We'll see.'

Barclay had trouble forming his next question. 'She left a message for Mr Elder, and Bandorff hints that she hates her father.'

'What are you saying?'

'It's just, when I was at Mr Elder's, there was a photograph there of his daughter.'

Joyce Parry went very still. 'Did he talk about her?'

'He just said she was dead. "Deceased" was his word.'

Joyce Parry nodded. 'She is.'

'What happened?'

'Her name was Susanne, and she was on a school trip to Paris. There was an explosion in a shopping arcade. No group ever claimed responsibility. Three children were among the dead.'

Barclay recalled how Dominique's father had died. 'He thinks Witch did it?'

Joyce Parry was staring from her window. 'He doesn't know. He *can't* know.' She turned to him. Barclay supplied her thoughts.

'Unless he asks her himself?'

She nodded. 'That's his obsession, Michael. He's got a question he needs to ask her, a question only she can answer.'

He thought of Dominique who had lost a father, of Elder's lost daughter. It would mean nothing to people like Bandorff and Witch. He saw now why Dominique, who had been so full of action before, had said almost nothing in Bandorff's cell. She had been facing a ghost, a terror with her since childhood.

'Get some sleep,' Joyce Parry was saying. 'You look exhausted.'

She was right, he was exhausted. Yet he doubted he would sleep.

Enterprise & Initiative

Monday 15 June

They were arriving. Or had already arrived. Mostly, they touched down in their national jets at an RAF base outside London. A few chose to helicopter into the city itself, the rest travelled by way of a huge police escort. These were the heads of state, heading for the summit.

They came with full and impressive entourages, almost as if one-upmanship were the game. Several brought with them personal hair-stylists. All of them brought 'gofers': anonymous individuals whose job it was to find and fetch whatever was needed during the stay in London. The gofers tended to be ex-diplomats who had spent time in England and built up a network of contacts in London itself. There were some who said the gofers were the most important people of all. It was they who kept the heads of state happy.

The real show of one-upmanship, as it turned out, was to bring your own chef with you. And the chef brought with him his *équipe*, his pots and pans and utensils. Ingredients from the various homelands were brought, too, all slipping quietly through as diplomatic baggage so that no customs people need declare them illegal. Arms were brought too, of course. More diplomatic baggage, arriving in well-packed crates. High-tech equipment was packed in separate cases: scramblers, decoders, debuggers, communications systems . . .

Watching it all arrive, there were those who were glad the summit was only lasting a week. Vans were provided at the base, to be loaded and driven by members of each entourage. Some of the vans made for the Queen Elizabeth II Conference Centre, others for the embassies of the countries concerned, where the delegations were staying for the week. There was fun to be had from sorting out the secret servicemen from the rest of each delegation. Sometimes they made it easy, donning the near-mandatory dark glasses even though the day was overcast and showery. Perfect summer weather, and due to last for the whole week. The hot spell had been just that – a spell. Now someone had cast another spell, and storms were rumbling inland from the west.

So far the movement of the eight delegations into London had been accomplished without a hitch. There were several small demonstrations to contend with outside certain embassies, but these passed off with a minimum of bother. And they gave the secret servicemen a chance to try out their discreet photographic equipment. The Metropolitan Police had drafted several hundred extra officers into the capital for the week. The mood in the ranks was buoyant: there'd be plenty of overtime, plenty of holiday money made over the next seven days.

But the mood elsewhere was verging on panic. There had been a catastrophe at a large nursery garden in Cornwall: an invasion of cows. As a result, several thousand fresh flowers, just ready to be picked, had been crushed or beheaded. The flowers had been ordered to decorate the Conference Centre itself. A 'floral decorist' had been hired, and Monday afternoon was when he and his own *équipe* had intended to start their work, finishing late on Monday night. But now there were no flowers for them to work with.

A senior civil servant spent several panicky hours making various telephone calls, until at last four new and willing suppliers were located. Between them, they had just about enough spare flowers to save the day: two hundred carnations short of the original plan, but so be it. However, this in turn led to problems with security, since the new firms needed clearance before delivering the flowers. Once more, the civil servant picked up her telephone.

In a sticky, overworked office on the second floor of a building in Victoria Street, the telephone rang. Judy Clarke picked it up. Judy was in a panic too. Her boss hadn't come in yet, and it was already quarter past ten. She hadn't heard of any train disputes or hitches on the underground. Mind you, you only heard of hold-ups on the underground *after* they'd happened. Still, it wasn't like her boss. And there was so much to do! She was breathless as she picked up the receiver.

'Hello?' she said.

'Oh, hello,' said the female voice at the other end. 'My name's Tessa. I share a house with Chris . . . Christine Jones.'

'Oh, yes?' Judy's heart sank. She knew what a call like this meant. Then she brightened. 'Tessa, yes, hello. Remember me? Judy Clarke. We met at Christine's birthday party.'

'Judy . . . ? Oh yes, hello again, how are you?'

'Not so bad. Is Christine ill?'

'Not exactly. But she's had a bit of bad news, a bereavement.'

'Oh dear.'

'Family, an aunt. I think they were very close.'

'An aunt? Oh dear, I am sorry.'

'Well, these things . . .'

'So Christine's not coming in today?'

'Well, that's the thing. She's gone off. The funeral's not till Wednesday.'

'Wednesday! God, I need to speak to her. There are things that need—'

'She said she thought you could cope.'

'Yes, well, maybe we can but it's still . . .'

'If I hear from her, shall I tell her to call you?'

'Could you get in touch with her? Is she at her mum's in Doncaster? Maybe if you gave me the phone number . . . ?'

'She didn't leave one.'

'That's not like—'

'She was a bit distraught. She's not in Doncaster anyway. The aunt lived somewhere in Liverpool.'

'Yes, I see.' Liverpool? Christine hadn't mentioned an aunt in Liverpool.

'Shall I get her to call you?'

'Yes, please, Tessa. I really need to know about Dobson's and about the MTD meeting.'

'Hold on, I'll write that down. Dobson's . . .'

'And the MTD meeting. Management Training Directive. Just tell her MTD, she'll know what it is.'

'Okay.'

'And if you do hear from her, please tell her I'm sorry.'

'Yes, thank you, I will.'

'Oh, and Tessa?'

'Yes?'

'Have you got a cold or something? Your voice sounds hoarse.'

'Must be the anabolic steroids. 'Bye, Judy.'

''Bye, Tessa,' said Judy, putting down the phone. She sighed. Oh, hell. No Christine till Thursday. No one to steer the ship for the next three days. Three days off for a bereavement. She wondered how Mrs Pyle in personnel would react to that. She didn't like you taking off three consecutive days for major surgery, never mind a funeral. Liverpool? An aunt in Liverpool? Oh well, it came to us all, didn't it? Maybe she'd phone Christine's house tonight . . . talk to Tessa again, see if Christine had been in touch.

Then again, maybe she wouldn't. Derek was supposed to be taking her out to the pictures. That was typical of him, choosing Monday night. He knew the cinemas were half-price on a Monday . . .

'There goes another one,' said her colleague Martin, coming into the room.

'What?'

'A motorcade.' He walked to the window. She joined him, peering down. Four growling motorbikes preceded the slow-moving convoy of long black cars.

'Wonder who it is this time?' she said.

'I can't see. Usually there's a flag on the front of the chief's car. Can you see one?'

She craned her neck. 'No,' she said.

'Me neither.'

'I feel we should be throwing down confetti or something.'

He laughed. 'You mean tickertape. Except these days, we'd have to use the leftovers from the paper-shredder instead.'

She laughed at this, at the idea of tipping a binful of shredded documents out of the window. Martin could be really funny at times. If he took off his glasses, he wasn't bad-looking either. Nice bum, too. He seemed to sense what she was thinking and turned towards her, taking off his glasses to wipe them with his hankie. There were red marks either side of his nose where the frames pinched.

'So,' he said, 'what are you doing tonight, Judy?'

She thought for a moment, swallowed, and said: 'Nothing.'

Witch put down the receiver. Shit, *merde, scheisse*. Trust her to end up speaking to someone who *knew* Tessa. A girl called Judy . . . who sounded concerned about Christine Jones. Concerned enough to pick up the phone and make some enquiries? Concerned enough to telephone the *real* Tessa this evening? Witch bit her bottom lip. Dispose of the girl Judy? No, it would be too suspicious. Two people disappearing from the same office . . . a laughable idea. No, this would have to be one of those rare occasions where she was forced to trust to luck. That's all there was to it. Maybe she should read her tarot again, see what it had planned for her. Maybe she shouldn't. What good would it do if the news were bad? She'd still have to go through with it. Too late to back out now.

She had time to kill. Her meeting with the Dutchman wasn't till lunchtime. She took her hand-mirror out of her shoulder-bag and looked at herself. She'd cut and dyed her hair, plucked her eyebrows, dusted her cheeks. She felt she resembled the photo of Christine Jones on her security pass almost *more* than Christine Jones herself did. After all, the photo had been taken some time ago. Christine's hair had grown out since it was taken. But Witch's was just the right length. And Christine had let her eyebrows grow out, too. Sensible woman. It was an unnecessary and painful chore. All to attract the male . . .

She placed the mirror back in her shoulder-bag. She was also carrying Christine's office-issue satchel, containing a few of her files but also some bits and pieces which were specifically, unquestionably Witch's own. She came out of the phone-booth and, in less than ten steps, was back on Victoria Street. Just in time to see the tail-end of the convoy. A policeman, who had been holding back traffic at the intersection, now told pedestrians they could cross the road.

'Just a bloody nuisance, this conference,' muttered one elderly lady, wheeling her shopping-trolley off the pavement and on to the road, making it rattle noisily as she pushed it.

A driver, stuck in line and awaiting permission to move, opened his car door and leaned out.

'How much longer, guv?' he called to the policeman.

'Couple more minutes,' the policeman called back. He shook his head at Witch. 'Some people got no patience.'

'Patience is a virtue,' she agreed. For some reason, he laughed at this. Witch walked on. She wasn't headed for 1–19 Victoria Street. She was making for another DTI building closer to Victoria Station. It was a very short walk. Not enough time for her to become nervous. She went to push open the glass door to the building, but a man, just leaving, held it open for her.

'Thank you,' she said with a smile. She strode through the lobby, her security pass held out in her hand as she passed the guard-desk. The man on duty looked at her dully, blinked, and returned to his reading. She waited for the lift to descend, and at the same time checked out the ground floor, especially the stairs. Entrances and exits were important. The stairs actually kept on going down. She wondered what was downstairs. In the lift, there was a button marked B for Basement. So she pressed it and headed downwards. The doors shuddered open, and she found herself staring at another entrance lobby – the back entrance to the building – and another guard, who was staring at her. She smiled at him.

'Pressed the wrong button,' she called, before pushing the button for level 2. It took a moment longer for the doors to close. She saw two grey-liveried drivers coming into the lobby. Their cars were parked just outside the doors. Now she remembered. She'd walked around the back of this building before. There was a slope down from street-level to the back entrance, and on this slope the chauffeurs left their cars while they waited for their ministers or other 'important people' to finish their meetings. So: back entrance, front entrance, two lifts and one set of stairs. She nodded to herself.

At the ground floor, the doors opened and two men in pinstripe suits got in, giving her a moment's glance, deciding they didn't know her, and continuing their conversation.

'Spurrier's doing a good job,' said one of them. 'That office was a shambles . . .'

Witch got out at the second floor while the men continued upwards. She was standing in a small entrance area from which led, to left and right, narrow green-carpeted halls. She chose to go right, and passed several offices. Green seemed the predominant colour: she saw lime green chairs in some of the offices, and olive green curtains. In some of the offices stood a single desk and chair. Other rooms were larger, with a staff of secretaries working away on word processors, or clerical-looking people rushing around with sheaves of paper or large manila envelopes under their arms. Telephones did not ring; rather, they buzzed, quite annoyingly. In the corridor ahead, two shirt-sleeved men were having an intense discussion. One stood with arms folded, resting most of his weight on his forward foot. The other had his hands in his pockets. Both wore pale shirts and dark ties. They looked senior. The one with arms folded turned and watched Witch approach.

'Can I help you?' he said.

Damn! She was supposed to look as though she belonged here. She swallowed.

'I'm looking for Mr Spurrier,' she said.

He grinned. '*Mrs* Spurrier, you mean.'

'Oh yes, Mrs Spurrier.'

'Next floor up,' said the man. 'You're new, aren't you?' He was almost purring. His colleague was staring fixedly, nervously, at the tips of his shoes.

She managed a coy smile. 'No, I work at Number One.'

'Ah.' Folded-arms nodded as though this explained everything. 'Back along here, lift to the next floor, corridor on the left.'

'Thank you,' she said, turning away. Another close call. What if he'd said, 'I'm Spurrier, how can I help you?' It was bad enough that Spurrier had turned out to be a woman. She was beginning to take risks. The game was becoming difficult. Difficult, but not dangerous. It would turn dangerous if she were *forced* to take risks . . . She took the stairs, not the lift. Just to experience them. At the top of the stairwell, two girls were giggling together.

'What's the joke?' said Witch, conversationally.

They looked around before confiding in her. 'The hunky policemen,' one said.

'We're wondering which one we'll get outside our window,' explained the other.

'Ah,' said Witch, nodding. Yes, she'd been wondering about that. Police marksmen on the roofs along Victoria Street: it was bound to happen. There would be times when all the heads of state would be driving along Victoria

Street towards Buckingham Palace. Police marksmen on the roofs . . . and in the buildings? There were ledges outside the windows of this building. Witch had spent a long time in her several disguises checking the look of the DTI buildings on Victoria Street. Staring up at them . . . sometimes taking a photograph. Just a tourist, eating her burger lunch or killing time. The marksmen would be sited on the ledges. But did they . . . ?

'Do you ever get the chance to talk to them?' she asked. The girls giggled again.

'Not enough,' said one.

'Not *nearly* enough,' said the other.

'God, there was one . . . when was it? Back in April.'

'March,' her friend corrected.

'March was it? Yes, when that whassisname was in town. He visited just along the road. They had policemen on the ledges then. The one outside our office . . .'

'God, what a hunk!'

Witch laughed with them, asked them to describe the man. They did, then they all laughed again. The two girls hugged their files to their chests.

'I hope we get him again.'

'I'll keep my fingers crossed for you,' said Witch. 'How do they get out on to the ledges?'

'Oh, some of the windows open. You know, like in the minister's office. You can get out that way.'

'I've never been in the minister's office,' Witch admitted.

'No? We're in there all the time, aren't we, Shelley?'

'All the time,' she agreed. 'He's got his own telly and everything in there.'

'Drinks cabinet, *all* the papers, and paintings on the wall, supposed to be really valuable.'

'Yes?' said Witch.

'Oh yes,' said Shelley. 'And if he doesn't like them, they fetch him some more.'

'I don't know about paintings. Give me a big poster of that police hunk any day!'

Witch left them to their giggles and walked along the third-floor corridor. She was keeping an eye out for Folded-arms. Maybe he'd follow her, try another chat-up line. She did *not* want him directing her personally to Mrs Spurrier's office.

She came to a solid wooden door with a plate reading Conference Room. Pinned to the door was a sheet of typed paper with dates, times and names on it. Presumably bookings for use of the room. There was no booking for just now. She turned the doorhandle. The door, though it had a lock, was open. She slipped inside and closed the door again. The room had a stuffy, unused smell. There was a plain oval table, five lime green chairs, a single uninspired painting on one wall. Two glass ashtrays sat on the table, and on the floor by the window sat an empty metal wastebasket.

Utilitarian; Witch quite liked it. She went to the window and stared out, resting her hands on the inner sill. The window was not the opening kind. It was swathed in yards of off-white gauze curtaining, the kind popular in public offices because, the popular wisdom went, the curtains would catch shards of glass exploding inwards after a blast. Witch's blurred view was of the traffic and the pedestrians below in Victoria Street. The hold-up for the VIP convoy had led to frayed tempers and congestion. She thought for a moment of the drive she was going to take tomorrow or Wednesday. She had to get her routes right. She had to find a car tonight and make a test-run. She had to find *two* cars tonight. There was so much still to do. The ledge, she noted with pleasure, was hardly wide enough to accommodate a man. The ledges on the next floor down, she knew, *were* wide enough. What was more, the ledge outside her window had crumbled a little, rendering it unsafe. Good. Very good. She examined the face of the building across the road, then spent a little time looking down on to the road itself, her lips pursed thoughtfully.

Back at the door, she examined the keyhole. An uncomplicated affair, as easy to lock as it would be to unlock. Better and better. She opened the door again and stepped out into the corridor, closed it behind her and checked the list on the door. There were no scheduled meetings tomorrow at all, and only two on Wednesday, one at 10 and the other at 4.15. A nice gap between. Excellent. Witch was in no doubt. At last, she'd found her bolt-hole, her assassin's perch. Sometimes it happened like that, you just wandered into a place or up to a place and you saw it straight away, the perfect position. Other times, you had to search and scour and scratch your head and maybe even make other plans, look at other sites. She'd lost weeks of her life changing initial plans, executing – apt word – new ones. But today it had come easy. Perhaps her luck was changing. She turned around and saw, coming towards her, Folded-arms. Only his arms weren't folded any more. They were spread out, palms towards her.

'You see,' he said, 'you see? I just knew if I left you alone you'd get lost again.'

'I'm not lost,' replied Witch crisply. 'I was checking the time of Wednesday's meeting.' Then she bit her lip. Risk, risk, risk.

Folded-arms looked both delighted and amazed. 'What? The four-fifteen? But *I'm* going to that. Are you going to be there, too?'

She shook her head. 'The ten o'clock.'

'Pity,' he said. 'Still, we must have coffee afterwards. What do you say?'

'Great.'

'My name's Jack by the way. Jack Blishen.'

'Christine,' she said. She shook the proffered hand. Afterwards, he held on to her hand just a little too long, his eyes wolfing her. She managed a smile throughout.

'Room two-twenty-six,' he said.

'Two-twenty-six,' she repeated, nodding.

'Have you time for a drink just now? Canteen's—'

'No, really. I've got to get back. There are some papers I forgot to bring.'

'Dear, oh dear, not very bright today, are we?'

'Monday morning,' she explained.

'You don't need to tell me, love,' he said, grinning with wolf's teeth. Witch had an image of herself ramming the heel of her hand into his nose, thrusting upwards, of bone and cartilage piercing the brain. It took no more than a second. She blinked the image away. Or slice his fat gut open. She blinked again.

'You haven't seen Madam yet then?' he was saying.

'Madam?'

'Spurrier.'

'No, not yet.'

'I shouldn't bother if I were you. Not unless you're bringing her *good* news. She's brutal, Christine, believe me. Have you met her before?'

'No.'

He sucked in his breath. 'Careful how you go then. She'll tear your throat out. I've seen her do it.'

'Look, sorry, Jack, but I really must . . .'

'Sure, don't mind me. Spurrier's not so bad really. I was exaggerating. Didn't mean to . . . here, I'll walk you back to the lift.'

'Thank you,' she said. Then he put his hand on her shoulder, and she felt a fresh wave of revulsion. Fight it, she thought to herself. Fight it. She had to be strong for her meeting with the Dutchman. She had to *look* strong, more than strong – invincible. She had to keep him fooled. By Wednesday at the latest, nothing would matter any more. She clung to that thought, pulled it to her, embraced it the way the secretaries had embraced their cardboard files. Two more days at most. She would last. She would.

She had to.

There were times when the Dutchman subscribed to the notion that 'public was private'. In London, he certainly subscribed to it. What was suspicious about two people having a lunchtime drink in a Covent Garden pub, crammed with other people doing exactly the same thing? Answer: nothing. What was suspicious about two people meeting clandestinely in some locked room or on some tract of wasteland? Answer: everything.

So it was that he had arranged the meeting in Covent Garden, just outside the tube station entrance in James Street. So it was that he took her into the heart of Covent Garden itself, past the piazza with its jugglers and musicians, past the racks and the stalls with their glittering clothes and jewellery, and down some stairs to a wine-bar. Witch eventually baulked when he suggested they sit at a table outside. People on the level above could lean on the guard-rails and watch them, as they were watching the other people at the tables.

'I'd feel like an animal in a zoo,' she spat.

'And which animal would you be?' the Dutchman asked wryly.

She considered this, thinking of Jack Blishen, but did not answer. The Dutchman patted her back as he ushered her through the doors of the bar and into cool gloom. They found a table in a quiet corner.

'What would you like to drink?' he asked, expecting her to say orange juice or mineral water or . . .

'Chablis or Meursault, very cold.'

'Sure,' he said. 'Just the glass, or a whole bottle?'

'Are you having some?'

'It sounds good.'

'Better make it a bottle then.'

The Dutchman went off to the bar. 'Yes, sir?' asked the barman.

'A bottle of Chablis, please. Chilled.'

'Of course, sir.' The barman stared at him as though he had taken 'chilled' as a snub of sorts. The Dutchman took a twenty-pound note from his wallet.

He was in a mood of nervous excitement. He knew the feeling well, and loved it. The feeling got even better afterwards, after a successful operation. So far this was a successful operation, but it was all out of his hands now, or nearly so. The initial planning, the various and copious briefings, all but one of them by mail, the heaping up of necessary and unnecessary detail, the contact with Crane . . . Ah, the contact with Crane. That had been sublime, almost as though fate were in charge. He'd seen the advert in a newspaper, advertising the boat *Cassandra Christa* for sale. He'd made enquiries of the boat's owner. He'd found in Crane the perfect fool. These were *his* successes. These were what he was being paid for. Not even *he* knew who was actually doing the paying. Anonymity all round. What did the British say? No names, no pack drill.

'Here you are, sir.'

'Thank you.' He handed over the note, then, when the barman's back was turned, touched the side of the bottle with his palm. It was cold. He ran a finger down the condensation.

'Your change, sir. And how many glasses?'

The Dutchman accepted the change. 'Two glasses,' he said. At that moment the waiter who was managing the outside tables came into the bar. He leaned his elbows on the bartop, as though wilting with exhaustion.

'With you in a second, Terry,' said the barman, reaching into the rack above him for two long-stemmed glasses.

'Hectic?' the Dutchman asked the waiter.

'As usual,' he replied.

'There you go, sir, two glasses.'

'Many thanks.'

The Dutchman headed off with his bottle and his glasses. When he'd rounded the corner of a stone wall, the barman and waiter stopped staring at him and looked at one another instead.

'Looks like him,' said the barman.

The waiter nodded. 'Foreign, too, just like Charlie said.'

The barman lifted a telephone from beneath the bar, picked up the receiver, took a scrap of paper from his back trousers pocket, and started to dial, reading the number from the note.

'Can't you do that after?' complained the waiter. 'I've a big order here. Look like good tippers.'

'Don't worry, Terry. I'll give you a tip personally if this comes good.' The barman listened to the dialling tone. 'Nobody at home,' he muttered. 'Trust Char— Hello? Who's that? What? Christ! Hello, Chris. Where you working? Yeah, I know it, up Charing Cross Road. Used to be a good pub.' He listened, laughed. 'All right, all right, *still* is a good pub, especially now you're there. Listen, is Charlie Giltrap there?' His face darkened. 'Oh, that's a pity. He wanted me to look out for— Oh, great, can I have a word?' The barman put his hand over the mouthpiece. 'He's just walked in,' he told the waiter. 'Talk about luck.'

'Yeah, and my customers'll be walking *out* at this rate.'

The barman held up his hand for silence. The waiter turned as three new customers came in through the front door. 'Hello, Charlie? Andy here. Fine, listen, got to make this quick. You know I was to keep a lookout for a likely lad? Got one here.' He stared towards the corner around which the

Dutchman had disappeared. 'Yeah, fits the bill, Charlie. He's here just now. Right, cheers.' He put down the receiver and tucked the phone back beneath the bar. 'Now then, Terry, what's the order?'

'Two bottles of Chablis.'

The barman shook his head. 'Try me with something else, son. I just sold the last one.'

Back in their little corner, Witch and the Dutchman were talking. Witch had chosen a spot close to one of the wall-speakers. The bar's music was not loud, but it would mask their conversation should anyone happen to be listening.

She paused to savour the wine. 'Nice,' she said. 'So, is my little package safe?'

'The one my men picked up from the house? Oh yes, it's safe all right. Safe and well. I've stored it in a garage.'

'I don't want to know. I just want to know it's safe.'

'Rest assured.'

Witch nodded. She remembered the iron, hot in Christine Jones's hand. The first mistake.

'Do you need anything else?' asked the Dutchman.

Witch shook her head. 'I'm ready.'

'Really?'

'Really.'

'So when will you . . . ?' He raised a hand, apologising. 'Sorry, I don't need to know that, do I?'

'No, you don't.'

'And you're clear in your mind? I can't be of any more assistance?'

'No.'

'Well, I'll be at my telephone number until . . . well, until the job's done.'

She nodded, drank more wine. Her glass was nearly empty. The Dutchman filled it again. Then he lifted his own glass.

'Here's to the free world,' he said.

She smiled. 'Here's to love.' And she took a sip of her wine.

'I'll drink to that,' said the Dutchman. He couldn't keep his eyes off her. She was incredible. The first time they'd met – the only other time they'd met – had been in Paris. The initial briefing. He'd suggested working closely, but she'd turned him down. She preferred working alone. When he learned a little more about her – most of it hearsay, but accurate – he knew this for the truth. She was a loner, a mystery. She almost didn't exist at all, but then, once a year or so, would come some atrocity, some murder or bombing, a disappearance or a jailbreak, and 'she' would be mentioned. That was all anyone called her: *she*. 'She's been active again.' 'Who did it?' 'We think probably *she* did.' Stories were whispered, the myth grew.

And now here he was with her for their second and final meeting. And she'd changed so much since Paris. He hadn't recognised her at the tube station. She'd been standing against a wall, fretting, checking her watch. He hadn't seen through her disguise, until, after five minutes, he too checked his watch. Then saw her grinning in his direction. He looked to left and right, but she was grinning at *him*. And walking towards him. Christ, even her walk was different; every single thing about her was different. And yet it was her. It was her. He shivered at the thought.

'What about your exit?' he asked her now, trying to show that he cared.

'It'll happen.'

'I can help if you need any—'

'You've done your work.' She paused. 'And done it well. Now it's my turn. Okay?'

'Yes, yes, fine.'

'Tell me, why did we need to meet?'

'What?'

'Today, why did you need to see me?'

He was flustered. 'Well . . . for the . . . for your final briefing.'

She smiled. 'Unnecessary.'

'And to wish you luck,' he blurted out.

'Also unnecessary.'

'And because . . . well, I'm *interested.*'

'Don't be.' She finished her second glass of Chablis and rose to her feet, picking up her shoulder-bag and satchel. 'Enjoy the rest of the bottle,' she said. 'Stay here at least five minutes after I've gone. Goodbye.'

'See you,' he said, knowing even as he said it that it wasn't true. He would almost certainly never see her again. He looked at the bottle, then at his glass. Well, if his work really *was* over, why not? He poured a generous measure, and toasted the wall in front of him.

Witch walked on. The Dutchman was like all the others: weak. All the men she'd met in her life, all the ones she'd worked with. The left-wing terrorists who agreed with radical feminism then got drunk or stoned and tried to sleep with her. The leaders of the various groups who used too many words, filling a huge void with them, but had no conception of anything beyond the 'word' and the 'idea'. The anarchists: political shoplifters. She'd seen them all, spent time with them. In the early days, maybe she'd even believed in them for a time. It was easy to believe when you were sitting in a stinking garret passing round a joint of middling-quality Moroccan.

Why had she drunk that wine? The Dutchman would worry about her now. He'd think maybe she wasn't as coldly perfect as people said. Was that why she'd done it? No, she'd done it because she felt like it. She felt like a drink. Chablis and Meursault were her father's favourite wines. It said so in the book she'd read about him . . .

She felt queasy suddenly. There were too many people around her. She ducked into an alley and felt better. The air was cooler in the alley. She began to walk along it. It was a narrow street, the backs of tall brick buildings backing on to it. Emergency exits, steel-barred and openable only from within. There was litter in the gutter. Dirty city. Cramped, crammed city. She despised it. She despised them all.

Shuffling footsteps behind her. She half-turned. Two youths, shambling along. One black, one white. The black massive for his age, bare arms taut and bulging. The white youth pale and wiry. They wore ludicrously large training-shoes, and metal medallions jangled round their necks. They weren't talking. And they were looking at her. The wine dissipated through her; she was ready for them. They still didn't say anything as they snatched her shoulder-bag. She held it beneath her elbow and struck out. Her right hand went for the black youth first. He represented the real physical danger. She chopped at his windpipe, and jerked a knee up into his groin. The white youth half-turned to look at his friend, and she caught him with the side of her forehead on his nose. Blood burst across his face. One hand went to cover his nose, the other scrabbled for the pocket of his denims. No, she couldn't allow that, no knives. She caught the hand and twisted it, all the way around and up his back, breaking the wrist for good measure.

The black youth, who had fallen on all fours, caught an ankle in his vice-like grip and tugged, trying to pull her down. She kicked him in the ribs, then in the temple. The white youth was howling now, and running for the end of the street. She looked past him, at the busy thoroughfare, but no one was paying any attention. That was the city for you. She could be mugged, assaulted, and no one would dare help. She looked down on the black youth. She had backed four feet from him, and he was pushing himself to his feet. She allowed him to stand up. He presented no threat any more.

'Go find your friend,' she said.

But he had other ideas. There was a loud k-schick as the blade sprung open. She raised her eyebrows. Couldn't he *see*? Where was the intelligence? Where was the basic survival instinct? She hadn't broken sweat yet. She hadn't even warmed up. There was a shout from the far end of the street.

'Oi! What's going on?' The youth turned. Two police constables stood in the mouth of the alley. He looked at Witch, brandishing the knife.

'Next time, bitch.' Then he ran in the same direction as the white youth, while the policemen came jogging from the opposite direction. Witch composed herself. She took several deep breaths, let her shoulders slump, and forced a few tears up into her eyes. She raised her fingers to her hair, rubbing it slowly, tousling it.

'You all right, miss?' asked the first policeman.

She nodded, but said nothing.

The second policeman ran to the end of the alleyway and looked around, then started back, shrugging.

'Never catch them now,' he said. 'These roads are like a bloody warren. How you feeling, love?'

'I'm all right,' she said faintly, nodding. 'Yes, I'm fine, really.'

'Course you are. Did they get anything?'

She looked at her left arm, with the shoulder-bag tucked beneath it, her left hand still clutching her satchel. 'No,' she said.

'Looked to me like you was holding your own,' said the first policeman.

'I went to some self-defence classes.'

'Very wise. Not so wise coming down a street like this.'

'It's the middle of the day,' she complained.

'They don't bother about that, not these days. Morning, noon and night. Mugging's a full-time occupation now.'

She smiled a little.

'That's better, love. Come on, let's get you down the station.'

'The station?'

'It's only two minutes' walk. Or we could radio for a car?'

'No, I can walk.'

'We'll get you a cup of tea, and let the doc have a look.'

'But I'm fine.'

'Could be in shock though, see. And then after that, we'll get a description from you, eh? See if we can catch those bastards before they pick on someone else . . . some woman who's *not* done self-defence. Okay?'

Witch nodded slowly. 'Okay,' she said, searching in her shoulder-bag for a tissue with which to wipe her eyes.

Down at the station, they really were very kind, very sympathetic. They asked her if there was anyone she'd like them to phone. A friend? Or her work maybe, to say she'd be back late from lunch? No, there was no need, she explained, thanking them. A WPC brought her some sweet tea, and a doctor took a look at her and said she'd had a fright but she was all right now. The constables looked like they were glad of an excuse to be back in their station. They sat with their helmets off, drinking tea and chatting. She gave a description – a detailed and accurate description. After all, they had a point: why shouldn't she help catch the two thugs? The thought of them attacking someone else infuriated her. If she'd thought of it at the time, she would have disabled them more thoroughly.

'And the white one,' she said, 'he sort of stumbled and I think he hurt his wrist. He said something about it cracking.'

'Broken wrist, eh? That would be handy. We could check with the local hospital casualties.'

The other constable was laughing. 'Broken wrist . . . handy,' he explained.

There was excitement elsewhere in the station. One of the constables disappeared to find out what was going on. He returned and shrugged.

'Just brought in some Dutch geezer, according to the Sarge. The Yard are on their way to fetch him, Anti-Terrorist Branch or something.'

'Yeah?' His colleague seemed to lose interest in Witch. Now this was action. But the blood had drained from Witch's face.

'Excuse me,' she said, 'is there a toilet I could use?'

They directed her along the corridor. She wandered along it, glancing into offices. Some men pushed open a set of swing-doors and marched a dishevelled man into an office. The door closed after them. Oh Christ, it *was* the Dutchman. How the . . . ? Who . . . ? Elder? Dominic Elder? Was he clever enough . . . ? She knew she needn't fear the Dutchman. He might not hold out forever, but he would certainly say nothing until after the operation was complete. If he wanted to save his skin, that was, and she thought probably he would want to save his skin. He'd rather face interrogation and a prison sentence than the thought that his ex-employers might put a contract out on *him*. And that's just what they'd do if he said anything. No, he'd keep his mouth shut. Tightly shut.

But all the same, it was another setback. The swing-doors were pushed open again. A man came through them carrying two large polythene bags. Behind him, another man brought a single bag. They held them carefully, as though they contained eggs, and both men disappeared into the office, the office which held the Dutchman.

She knew what those plastic bags contained. Not eggs: two wine glasses and a bottle. So they'd have her fingerprints now. Not that it mattered. Her prints had been altered before, they could be altered again. Painful and expensive, but an option. She wondered if she should . . . if she *dare* creep closer to the door so she could listen.

There was a call from behind her. 'You've gone past it, love. It's that door behind you.'

She turned. One of the constables was standing in the doorway, pointing behind her. She smiled in apology: sorry, still a bit shocked. He nodded back. Then she pushed open the door to the ladies' toilets. She sat in a cubicle for a few minutes, working things out. Only one thing really stood out: the Yard were on their way here. Which meant, in all probability, that Dominic Elder was on his way here. Would he recognise her after all this time? If anyone could, *he* could. It was too risky. She had to get out of this police station.

She flushed the toilet, looked at herself in the soap-splashed mirror over the wash-basin, and composed her victim's face again. She'd given them Christine Jones's name and Christine's address, but had stressed that she was leaving London later today and would be out of town till tomorrow night. They hadn't bothered asking for her out-of-town address. As she walked back down the corridor, she knew, too, that she could not afford to wait. The hit must take place tomorrow, Tuesday. It would not wait till Wednesday.

Tomorrow.

'Feel better, love?' asked the constable.

'Yes, thank you. I'd like to go now.'

'No problem there. If you do think of anything else, anything you could add to your description of the two assailants . . .'

'I'll let you know.'

He scribbled his surname and the station's telephone number on to a pad of paper, tore off the page, and handed it to her.

'Normally,' he said, 'it'd be a CID matter. Maybe it will be, but they've got their hands full at the moment.'

'Yes, you said . . . something about a Dutchman?'

'That's right. Don't ask me what though. I only work here.'

She smiled. 'If I do think of anything, I'll let you know.'

'Appreciate it. Now, can we get you a cab?'

'That's all right, I'll walk I think. Some fresh air.'

'Fresh air? Round here? Some hope.'

She shook hands with both constables (they seemed embarrassed by the gesture), and even said a polite goodbye to the desk sergeant. She was about to pull open the main door when it was pushed from outside with sudden force. She took a couple of steps back.

'Sorry,' said the man, coming in. He didn't sound sorry. She shook her head, saying nothing. He paused, taking her silence as reproof, and held the door open for her.

'Thanks,' she said, brushing past him.

Outside, she felt giddy. She crossed the street quickly and melted into a queue at a bus shelter. She watched the entrance of the police station, but he didn't come out again. He hadn't recognised her.

He'd grown old. Not weak, but certainly old. Older than his years. She smiled, knowing the cause. Ah, but it was him all right, recognisably him. Dominic Elder. She wondered if he'd got her note, the one she'd left at that pub in Cliftonville. She was sure he had. He might even have gone after the fairground, talked to the boss, Ted. A dead end. Nobody there would tell him anything. And now he'd be busy with the Dutchman, interrogating him, tracking his history through Interpol. Yes, Elder would be busy, which suited her. It left her free to get on with her work. She'd best get busy. She had to steal a vehicle . . . *two* vehicles . . . and she had to drive some routes.

She only had until tomorrow. Tomorrow, some time around noon, the cavalcade of world leaders would drive slowly along Victoria Street, heading for lunch at Buckingham Palace. Right past her nose.

A bus arrived and she took it, for no other reason than that she had some thinking still to do, and time to kill before evening. She climbed to the top deck and found a seat to herself near the front. Two things bothered her, both out of her hands now. One was that she had given the police Christine Jones's name and address. It had seemed prudent at the time. They only had to look in her handbag or at the label on her satchel to know who she was supposed to be. But now they had the Dutchman, and if they connected him to the assault in the alley, they would have a name and an address.

The second thing, well, the second thing wasn't nearly so important. Even so, she couldn't help wondering, with the Dutchman in custody, would anyone be feeding and watering Christine Jones?

Elder was nursing a mug of tea and chatting to CID when Greenleaf arrived.

'Hello, John.'

'Sorry I'm late,' said Greenleaf. 'Couldn't track down Doyle.'

'Then we'll just have to do without him, won't we? Let's call it, using our own initiative. Now, using your initiative, John, did you manage to get in touch with Mr McKillip?'

Greenleaf nodded. 'I said we'd send a car to fetch him, but he'd rather make it up here under his own steam. His train gets into Victoria Station.'

'Handy for the Yard then.'

'Which is why I said I'd meet him there.'

'What time does he get in?'

'Five-ish.'

'So, by six we'll have a witness that our Dutch friend met with George Crane in Folkestone.'

'Hopefully. Speaking of the Dutchman . . .'

'He's in a holding cell. They'll bring him to an interview room when we're ready.' Elder looked at Greenleaf above the rim of his mug. 'Can I take it we're ready?'

Greenleaf nodded. 'Good and ready.'

So the Dutchman was brought up to one of the interview rooms. He was complaining all the time: he was a tourist, was this how they treated visitors to their country? He demanded to contact his consulate, his embassy, anyone. He was just a tourist . . . they'd no right.

'No right at all, treating me like a criminal.'

Elder and Greenleaf, seated impassively at the small metal-framed table, let him have his say. From the way his eyes refused to meet theirs, they knew *he* knew they were trouble. They both liked that. For a few moments more, they thrived on his discomfort.

'Look,' he said, 'look!' And he raised a shoe in the air, the tongue of leather flapping loose where the shoelaces had been removed. 'They take away my shoelaces, my trouser-belt, my necktie. In case I *injure* myself, they say. Why in God's name should I injure myself? I am a tourist. I don't . . .'

Elder reached into a large manila envelope which he'd brought with him. He drew out a black and white photograph and threw it on to the desk, so that it faced the Dutchman who glanced at it, then looked away again, addressing his words to the police officers behind him, all four of them, standing massively between him and the door.

'I am treated like a common criminal . . . British justice, law and order, a farce, I tell you! A farce! We in The Netherlands have more respect for the . . .'

Another photograph landed on the desk, then another. They were the photographs supplied to Commander Trilling by SIS, the ones which had accompanied the slides. The Dutchman saw himself again and again, in different places, different situations, in conversation with different people, and all during different operations.

Then Elder spoke.

'We want to know what she's planning, and we want to know where she is. We want to know quickly.'

The Dutchman met Elder's eyes for a dull second.

'What are you talking about?' he said. 'I'm a tourist.'

'No, you're not. We both know what you are. The authorities in several countries would like to speak with you. Most of them are less law-abiding than we are. They wouldn't hesitate to use . . . well, whatever means they see fit, to prise information from you.' Elder paused to let this sink in. 'If you don't tell us where she is and what she's intending to do, I'll see to it that you're handed over to the least . . . the least *hesitant* country possible. Speak to us now, and you'll be kept here in the UK. Do you understand?'

'I demand my rights. I demand a lawyer, I demand to see someone from the Dutch Embassy. This is illegal.'

'Under the Prevention of Terrorism Act, very little is illegal. But then, I'd have thought you'd have read up on that particular document.'

Elder rose to his feet, had a word with the guards, and left the room. Greenleaf followed him in silence. The guards stayed.

'Will anyone give me a cigarette, please?' asked the Dutchman.

'We don't smoke,' said one policeman.

Outside, Elder was talking in an undertone. 'We'll have him transferred to Paddington Green. The security here isn't good enough.'

'You think they may try to spring him?'

Elder shook his head. 'Not spring him, no. He's a gofer, a go-between. It's late on in the operation now. He's probably expendable. But they may try to kill him.'

'What?'

Elder nodded. 'He won't know much in any case, but these people, whoever it is who's hired Witch, I shouldn't think they like loose ends. And *that's* what we need to play on.'

'Get him scared?'

'Right, not scared of us, scared of his bosses – present and past. So that *we* become his only protection.'

Greenleaf was impressed. 'You sound like you've done this sort of thing before.'

Elder smiled. 'That's because I have, John. We sweat him, then, if he hasn't told us anything, we tell him we're going to put out an announcement that he's singing like a bird. Singing in return for his freedom. We tell him the announcement's gone out, then we say we're—'

'Letting him go.'

Elder nodded. 'Funny, they never want to go, given the chance. They'd rather stay. But the price of staying, the price of protection, is that they tell us everything anyway.'

'Nice.'

Elder shrugged. 'He's been around. He may not fall for it. We may actually *have* to issue the announcement. And it all takes time.'

'Time we may not have.'

'Exactly. So let's get him over to Paddy Green straight away, before Witch learns we've got him.'

'One thing, Dominic.' Greenleaf only called him Dominic when Doyle wasn't around. 'What did he have on him in the wine-bar?'

'Good point. Let's take a look.'

The Dutchman's possessions were in an envelope in the desk sergeant's locked drawer. The desk sergeant himself tipped the contents on to the surface of his desk.

'Not much,' he said.

No, not much. Cash . . . just under a hundred pounds in notes, plus some small change. The notes were crisp and clean.

'Better check they're not forgeries,' said Greenleaf.

Passport in the name of Hans Breuckner, occupation: schoolteacher. No visas.

'We'll check that, too,' said Greenleaf. 'See what the Dutch think of it.'

'I can tell you now what they'll think of it, John. It'll be a forgery. Either that or stolen, but a forgery's my bet.'

'Do we know where he was living?' asked Greenleaf.

'He hasn't said.'

'Maybe this will tell us.' Greenleaf was pointing to a small key.

'It's not a room-key or house-key though, is it?' said Elder. 'Looks more like the sort you use to lock a petrol-cap.'

'Bit too big for that,' said Greenleaf. 'Not a car-key though. My guess would be a lock-up.'

'A lock-up?'

'You know, a garage. I used to live in a block of flats, we all had a garage down near the road. And we all opened our garages with a key like this.'

Elder examined it more closely. 'It's British, by the look of it. You think he's got a flat then?'

'No, or he'd have a key for it, too. I think he's rented a garage. Maybe he's been holing up in it, maybe he's just using it for storage while he lives elsewhere.'

'Storage . . . now what would he be storing in a garage?' Elder looked up. 'I'm glad you came, John.'

Greenleaf shrugged. 'Doyle would've told you the same thing.'

'But he didn't. *You* did.'

There wasn't much else of interest: a one-day travelcard, a tube-map, and two pages pulled from an *A–Z*, showing the centre of London from Bloomsbury to Victoria to the Elephant and Castle to Farringdon.

'Can't see any markings,' said Greenleaf. 'Can you?'

'No,' said Elder. 'But maybe there are pressure points where a pencil or something's been pressed against the page. Better get it into a poly bag and let forensics take a look. You know we got some glasses?'

'Glasses?'

'And a bottle. Our Dutch friend was nabbed in a wine-bar.'

'That much I knew.'

'He'd been drinking with a young woman. The barman's given us a description.'

'Witch's latest incarnation?'

'Maybe. Anyway, there were two glasses on the table. We've got them.'

'So maybe we'll end up with Witch's prints?'

'If nothing else, yes. Not that we've got anything to match them against.' Elder turned to the desk sergeant. 'Can we have a poly bag for this map?'

'Right away, sir.'

Elder turned back to Greenleaf. 'Give me an educated guess,' he said. 'How long to check every lock-up in the London area?'

'An educated guess?' Greenleaf did some calculations. 'About four and a half months.' Elder smiled. 'That's always supposing,' Greenleaf went on, 'we were given the manpower, which is doubtful anyway. All the time I'm on Operation Broomstick, the caseload's just growing higher and higher on my desk. It's not going to go away.'

'It'll soon be over,' Elder said quietly. 'One way or the other, it'll soon be finished.'

The desk sergeant, returning with a clear plastic bag, was chuckling and shaking his head.

'What's the joke?' asked Greenleaf, taking the bag from the desk sergeant. He held it open so Elder could drop the map inside.

'Oh, nothing really. Just some of the lads. Two would-be muggers, big bastards by the sound of them, they picked on this slip of a girl near Covent Garden. Only, she'd been to self-defence classes. Gave them a terrible pasting the way the lads are telling it.' He chuckled again, not noticing the fixed way in which Elder and Greenleaf were staring at one another.

'Did you happen to speak with her?' Elder asked, calmly.

'Speak to her? She was here in the station till half an hour ago.' He saw the look on Dominic Elder's face. 'What's the matter? You look like you've seen a ghost.'

Barclay sat that afternoon at his old desk in his old office. It seemed like an eternity since he'd last been there. He found it hard to believe that in the past he'd been satisfied with just his information base and his computer console. He was itching to be elsewhere, to be in the thick of things. But he knew Joyce Parry wouldn't let him out of her sight. So he'd spent the morning trying to be professional, trying not to let it worry him or niggle at him or scoop away at his insides. He'd tried. At least he could say he'd tried.

He'd handed his report to Joyce Parry first thing. Not that there was anything in it she hadn't heard on the trip back last night. He hadn't left anything out: bugging Separt's apartment, Dominique disguising herself and going to see the Australian, wearing a wire which Barclay had made for her. And then the journey to Germany, and Dominique's revelation that nothing they'd done had been sanctioned.

He felt like a shit as he typed it all in, felt he was somehow letting Dominique down. But she was probably doing exactly the same thing, thinking much the same thoughts. Neither of them wanted to lose a good job. Besides, doubtless Joyce Parry would cross-check Barclay's testimony against that given by Dominique. If he left anything out, anything she'd admitted to . . . well, that would only count against him.

Joyce Parry had listened to him in silence mostly, with only the occasional shake of the head or disbelieving gasp. And she accepted the report from him with a slight nod of the head and no words. So now he had to wait. He had to sit at his desk and wait to see if his resignation would be asked for, or a demotion agreed, or whatever. Maybe he'd end up sweeping the corridors. He hadn't felt as nervous as this since he'd been a schoolboy, caught playing truant and left waiting outside the headmaster's door. What he'd dreaded then was a letter home to his parents. The guilt and shame of having been caught. But now, uneasy as he was, he was pleased too. He'd had a few days of real adventure, and if he could go back, he'd do the same again. He allowed himself a private smile. Maybe Mrs Parry was right, maybe Dominic Elder was the kind of person who used those around him then tossed them away. It didn't bother Barclay.

He'd tried phoning Dominique three times this morning, with no reply. The international operator couldn't help. He wondered if the phone was off the hook, and if so why. He'd also forwarded a copy of his report to Profiling, as Joyce Parry had told him to do. See what the mind doctors could make of it. Something was niggling him, something he knew he'd been going either to tell Joyce Parry or to ask her. It had been at the back of his mind for several days – before Germany, maybe even before Paris. As a result, it had now slipped from his mind altogether. Something he'd been going to say. But what?

He shook it away. If he left well alone, it would come back to him. He stared at the wall above his desk: the venomous Valentine, the Fire Drill, and the quotation he'd pinned there on a piece of memo paper – this fluke called life.

He plunged a hand into his full in-tray. Reports to be read, classified, passed on. His daily bread. He'd been given a sod of a job, collating 'trigger words'. It was a little known fact that the technology existed not only to monitor telephone calls but to zero in on calls containing certain words – trigger words. It was a miracle of computer technology, but also highly fallible. The word 'assassination' for example was unlikely to crop up in a conversation between two terrorists, whereas it might in a chat between two gossipy neighbours. And the word 'summit' posed problems too, being a homonym shared with the abbreviated form of 'something'. Yes, highly fallible but potentially invaluable.

Currently, specifically, there was another problem, in that 'Witch' sounded like 'which' . . . and people on the telephone said 'which' an awful lot of times. Dominic Elder had requested that Witch become a trigger word, clutching at yet another straw.

Barclay's task was to deal with the information handed on to him by the trigger system, which meant checking the details of callers who had used a trigger word. It was a lot of work, but he was not alone. Others, too, were feeding telephone numbers into computers, seeing whether any of the callers were known terrorist sympathisers or suspect aliens, or even just suspect. A lot of work and a lot of futile effort. Somehow, from what he knew of her, Barclay couldn't imagine Witch picking up a receiver and saying, 'Hello, Witch here. It's about that assassination I'm carrying out at the summit . . .' He started to tap the first set of details into his computer.

'Barclay.'

It was Parry's voice. By the time he turned, she'd already retreated back into her office. Ah well, this was it then. He took a deep breath and got to his feet, surprised to find his legs so steady beneath him. He walked to her office doorway and knocked once on the door. She motioned him in. She was reading something on her desk, one of many reports that would pass through her hands that day, as every day. She took off her glasses before speaking.

'Mr Elder wants you down at the Conference Centre,' she said casually.

'What? Why?'

'His argument runs that you know as much about Witch as anyone, so why waste your – talents – here when you could be helping him.' She made the word 'talents' sound like it was something rotten on her tongue. 'Let me make one thing clear.' She looked up at last. 'You're not off the hook. *Neither* of you is off the hook. This is strictly a short-term reprieve, and it can be terminated at a moment's notice.'

'Understood, ma'am.'

She nodded, slipped her glasses back on, and returned to her report. 'What are you waiting for then?'

'Yes, ma'am.'

Joyce Parry waited a full sixty seconds after he'd gone before she allowed herself a smile.

Elder was waiting for him in the Conference Centre foyer. 'Come on,' he said, moving away as Barclay approached. 'Let's get you some official ID.'

Elder moved briskly. He seemed very different to the person Barclay had met in a Welsh cottage garden. He looked like a man who'd discovered his purpose in life . . . or, perhaps, *re*discovered it. He was a little disappointed though. He'd been expecting more of a welcome. Hadn't they worked together throughout the French adventure? And hadn't they both received dressings down for it?

They went to a small room where forms had to be filled in. A glowering woman then asked a few questions before transferring the details from the forms on to a card, typing the details quickly but meticulously. Then Barclay had to sign the card before moving to a booth where his photograph was taken.

'It's just like matriculation,' he said to Elder. But Elder, leaning against a desk, said nothing in reply. At last, the camera disgorged a small plastic-coated card containing the typed details, Barclay's signature, and a tiny photograph of him. Elder handed him a red and blue striped ribbon attached to a clip at one end and a safety-pin at the other.

'Clip it on to your lapel,' he ordered.

Barclay did so. 'Why the ribbon?'

'Red and blue means security. There are different ones for media, general staff, delegates . . .'

'You've seen my report?'

At last Elder gave a grim smile. 'Joyce gave me the highlights over the phone.'

Barclay swallowed. 'And?'

'And what?'

Barclay waited. 'Nothing,' he said.

Elder looked at him. 'Look, number one, I wouldn't have got caught. Number two . . .'

'Yes?'

'Never mind. Come on.'

Elder led the young man back through the corridors. He'd 'sprung' Barclay to keep him out of Joyce Parry's way. She was angry, and with good reason. But then Elder had done her a favour, taking the force of Jonathan Barker's heat and spending a long Sunday in a fuggy room talking about defending the indefensible. So she was letting Elder have Barclay. He knew he was in a strong position anyway; *he* could always shuffle back to Wales. But he was also in a very weak position, because he wanted very much to stay put. Joyce was allowing him a lot of rope, more even than he'd expected.

After all, if the shit really did hit the fan, Joyce would be closest.

He saw that Barclay was bursting to talk to him. That was why it wasn't a good time for them to talk. He'd wait till the young man calmed a little. He knew that Barclay's career was hanging by a thread, but that had been Barclay's decision, not his. All the same . . . It was true that Elder would have done exactly the same as Barclay all along the line. He'd done as much before. And as for never getting caught . . . well, that wasn't entirely accurate. Several times he'd come close to disaster; closer than he liked to admit . . .

A message on the already-overworked Tannoy system.

'Call for Mr Elder. Call for Mr Dominic Elder.'

They made for reception. The place was chaotic. Flowers were being delivered, and nobody seemed to know where they were to go. One-day security passes were being made up for half a dozen sweating florists. The switchboard was jammed with incoming calls, and someone had arrived to fix the malfunctioning baggage X-ray machine. Tomorrow, the summit would begin, and on the surface all would be placid. But underneath they'd be kicking like hell.

'I'm Dominic Elder,' he said to a receptionist.

'What?' she said, cocking a hand to her ear.

'Dominic Elder,' he said, more loudly. 'There's a call for me.'

'Yes, hold on.' She picked up a receiver and handed it across the desk to him, then flipped a switch. 'You're through.'

Elder listened for a moment. 'Can't hear a thing,' he said into the mouthpiece. 'It's pandemonium here. Can you speak up?'

He listened again. Barclay, standing behind him, looked around the foyer. Some people were just entering the building. Instinctively, he knew they were French: their clothes, their gestures, the way they moved. There were two women, one a tall redhead and the other shorter, wearing a red beret and round sunglasses. As she entered the dim interior, she slipped off the sunglasses.

Barclay nearly collapsed. It was Dominique. She saw him, pointed, and laughed. Then she bounced over and kissed him right cheek, left cheek, right and left again.

'Hello, Michael. What are you doing here?'

'Never mind me, what are *you* doing here?'

Elder turned around. 'Keep the noise down!'

Barclay took Dominique's arm and led her away from the reception desk. He was trembling and couldn't control it.

'I'm here with the French delegation,' said Dominique.

'I was expecting you to be in chains in the Bastille.'

She laughed again. 'There is no Bastille, not for a long time.'

'Well, you know what I—'

'Yes, but your superior, the woman . . .'

'Joyce Parry?'

'Parry, yes. She told Monsieur Roche all about the threat posed by Witch. Our own President could be her target. So now Monsieur Roche is worried. And guess who is the French expert on Witch?'

Barclay nodded, understanding.

'There may be a punishment for me when I go back to Paris, but for now . . .' She opened her arms wide. 'Here I am!'

One of her crowd called to her.

'*Oui*,' she called back, '*j'arrive*!' She turned back to Barclay. 'I must go with them.'

'Yes, but where are you staying? When can I see you? What about tonight?'

'No, tonight I have to work. But you are attending the summit, so we will meet.'

'Yes, but—'

There was a sudden tug at his arm. It was Dominic Elder.

'Come on,' Elder said, 'things to do.'

'Yes, just a—' But Dominique was waving a farewell as she headed back to the French group.

'That was Doyle on the phone,' insisted Elder, still tugging a reluctant Barclay towards the exit. 'They've located Breuckner's hotel. Let's go take a look.'

'What?' Barclay twisted his neck for a final glimpse of Dominique. She was in conversation with a tall, long-faced man. The man was looking towards Barclay. Dominique was not. 'Who's Doyle?' he said. 'Who's Breuckner?'

'Christ, you *are* out of touch, aren't you? Hasn't Joyce told you anything?'

'No.' They were out of the building now.

'Then I'll bring you up to date on the way. By the way, was that . . . ?'

'Yes, that was her.'

'Pretty girl,' Elder said, pulling Barclay further and further away from her. She reminded him a little of the woman he'd opened the police station door for, the woman he was sure had been Witch. He kept hold of Barclay's arm. 'By the way, you've got lipstick on both cheeks.'

The hotel in Bloomsbury was every bit as upmarket as Elder had been expecting, this being the age of expense-account terrorism, of *legitimised* terrorism. You could bomb a place of worship, strafe a busful of women, then a few months later be sitting down to peace talks with a posse of well-known politicians and negotiators, your photo snapped for front-page posterity and the six o'clock news.

'Very strict about his privacy,' said the manageress, leading them upstairs. She had her hair swept into a beehive, revealing large ears and a bulbous forehead. 'Only wanted his room cleaned once a week.'

'How long has he been a guest, Mrs Hawkins?'

'Almost a month now. Prompt with payment, beginning of each week.'

'He paid cash?'

'Yes, cash. Along here.' She led them to the room, and produced a key from the folds of her skirt. 'Very quiet man, but secretive. Well, I always try to mind my business . . .'

'Yes, Mrs Hawkins, thank you. A policeman will be along shortly to take your statement.'

She nodded with sharp jolts of her head. 'Always happy to help the authorities.'

'Thank you, Mrs Hawkins. Leave the key, and we'll lock up afterwards.'

'Right you are.'

'And remember, nobody else is to enter before the forensics team gets here.'

'Forensics . . .' She jabbed her head again, then giggled, the tremor running all the way through her large frame. 'It's just like on the television, isn't it?'

Elder smiled. 'Just so, Mrs Hawkins, just so.'

He pushed Barclay into the room then followed him, closing the door softly but determinedly on the hotelier. Then he swivelled Barclay round to face him.

'You'll see her tomorrow,' he said. 'Now snap out of it. You're no good to me like this. I'd be as well sending you back to the bloody office.'

That did it. Barclay straightened up, and his eyes seemed to come into focus.

'Sorry,' he said.

'Okay, now let's see what we've got here. Remember, don't touch if you don't need to. We might find some prints when forensics get here – *if* they ever bother to turn up.'

'Whose prints?'

'Witch's maybe. Or – outside chance – whoever's paying her. But that really *is* an outside chance.' He paused. 'You did a good job in that cartoonist's apartment, let's see you do it again now.'

Breuckner wasn't messy. The bedclothes had been pulled back and straightened, his clothes were hanging neatly in the wardrobe, and on the bedside table sat a copy of the previous day's evening paper, a travel alarm, and a used ticket to Madame Tussaud's.

'Travels light, doesn't he?' said Elder. 'To say he's been here a month.'

'For a holidaymaker, he certainly hasn't collected many souvenirs.' Barclay reached down and lifted a shoe. 'Shall I check the heel for a radio transmitter?'

Elder smiled. 'Radio transmitters are more *your* line.'

'You know I left a couple of bugs at the cartoonist's?'

'Don't worry, someone'll take care of them.'

'Really?' The relief in Barclay's voice was all too evident.

'But don't tell Joyce I told you. She'll want you to sweat for a bit.'

'Understood.'

The search continued, throwing up nothing out of the ordinary except the sheer lack of the usual traveller's detritus: no used travel tickets, used carrier bags, stamps, foreign change, no guide books or souvenirs.

Barclay squatted down and angled his head to peer beneath the bed. 'Something under here.' He looked around him, then got up and went into the small bathroom adjoining the room. He came back with, of all things, a loo-brush, which he used to manoeuvre out from under the bed whatever was there.

'No fingers, you said,' he informed Elder, who stood over him smiling.

'I just hope that brush was clean,' said Elder.

Magazines. Glossy magazines. Dutch writing on their covers. There were three of them. Still using the loo-brush, Barclay awkwardly turned some of the pages.

'Yes, I get the gist,' said Elder.

'S and M,' said Barclay, closing the magazines. 'Heavy duty stuff.'

'Really? You have some expertise in this area?'

'I know what's legal, and this stuff isn't.'

Elder clapped his hands together. 'Bloody good point, Michael. If we nab friend Breuckner for nothing else, we can have him under the Obscene Publications Act. Importation of material likely to offend. Anything else under there?'

Barclay had another look. 'Over the other side,' he said. 'Looks like a paperback.' He walked round the bed, crouched again, and swept from beneath the bed an *A–Z* book of London streets.

'I'll bet the pages for the city centre are missing,' said Elder. 'He had them in his pocket.'

'There's a piece of card.' Barclay pointed to where a cardboard edge protruded from the book. Elder took a pen from his pocket and eased it between the pages marked by the card. Then slowly he used the pen to open the book. The piece of card was a one-day travelcard, nearly a month old. The pages opened were those showing Hackney, Leyton and Clapton.

'Interesting,' said Elder. His first thought was of the address given to the police by the woman calling herself Christine Jones. It had been around this area. But no, not quite . . . her address was just off this particular map, one page back in the book in fact. So, rule that out.

'What do you think, sir?' asked Barclay. They were both crouching now, with the book between them on the floor.

'There was a key in the Dutchman's pocket.'

'Yes, so you said.'

'Greenleaf—'

'Doyle's partner?'

Elder nodded. 'Greenleaf reckoned it might be the key to a lock-up.'

'Plenty of lock-ups round there,' Barclay said, nodding towards the map.

'Really?'

'Yes. Lots of tower blocks. Well, at least there used to be in Hackney. I had a friend lived on the top floor of one.'

'Well, it's worth a try. At least it gives us a starting-point. I'd better get on to Special Branch and tell Greenleaf. What time is it?' He checked his watch. 'No, he'll still be out at Christine Jones's address. Not that *that'll* take long. My guess is, nobody at that address will even have heard of anyone called Christine Jones. The lock-up idea is more interesting though.'

'Maybe we should get some copies made, help speed up the search.'

Elder nodded. 'Copies are being made.' He looked around the room. 'Nothing else for us here, is there?'

'We haven't checked the bathroom or under the carpets or . . .'

'Not really our department. The police'll do all that. I just wanted a quick look at the place before they started. Hold on though.' He walked up to the bedside cabinet and looked at the evening paper. 'Open at the crossword, but he's hardly even started it.' Elder stared at the clues and the answers entered in the grid. 'Mmm, no, nothing there.'

'You thought maybe a code?'

'It's a handy way of leaving a message for someone if you're in a hurry. Stick the message in a crossword grid, no one gives it a second look.'

'Unless they like crosswords.' The thought struck Barclay . . . what was it Wolf Bandorff had said? *'She was fascinated by word games and crosswords.'* Word games and crosswords.

'Did I ever tell you what Dominique and I found at the Australian's?'

'Pamphlets about Wolf Bandorff?'

'Yes, but there was a crossword too, from the *Times*. Strange paper for an Australian anarchist to be reading in Paris.'

'Go on.'

'Well, the crossword had been done. The Australian said *he* liked crosswords.'

'But we know from Bandorff that Witch likes word puzzles. You think the crossword belonged to Witch? It's possible she spent time at the flat before taking away the cartoonist's car. Still, it's a bit late in the day to be any help.'

'No, hold on, something else. There was a page torn out of the paper. The Australian said something about it saving on toilet paper. But why only the one page? And why wasn't the newspaper in the toilet if that was its function?'

Elder smiled. 'You're learning,' he said. 'So what you're wondering is, what was on the torn-out page?'

Barclay nodded. 'Maybe it was something to do with the summit, or with her particular target. We don't *know* who her target is yet. There could have been some clue in that newspaper.'

'Well, which day was it? Which edition?'

Barclay shook his head. 'I don't know.'

'But Dominique might.'

'And she's at the Conference Centre.'

'Come on then,' said Elder. 'Let's go find her.'

There was a knock at the door. It was the fingerprint team. 'All yours, gentlemen,' said Elder. He was now as anxious to be back at the Conference Centre as he had been to leave it in the first place.

But when they got to the foyer and asked at the desk, they were told that the new additions to the French security retinue had already left the building, and no one knew where they were headed.

Greenleaf and Doyle returned to the house in the evening, just after seven. They'd tried in the late-afternoon, but no one had been home. So then they'd hared off back to Victoria Station to meet McKillip off his train and deposited him at Paddington Green, where he was delivered into the hands of other Special Branch men. And now they were back in Stoke Newington again.

'Wild goose chase,' muttered Doyle, pressing the doorbell. 'Have you noticed how Elder's started giving orders? I mean, who the fuck is he to give orders?'

'He's all right,' said Greenleaf.

Doyle turned to him. 'Oh, yes? You *would* think that, wouldn't you? Very pally, the two of you.'

'We're *all* together on this. It doesn't help if personalities become the issue.' Greenleaf pressed the bell.

Doyle feigned amazement. 'When did your Chair come through?'

'What?'

'Your Chair in Psychology, when did it come through?'

'Don't talk daft.'

As Doyle was reaching yet again for the bell, the door flew open. A frazzled-looking young woman stood there. Behind her, along the entrance hall, lay a trail of dirty clothes issuing from a rucksack.

'Yes?' she said.

'Good evening, miss,' said Doyle, showing his ID. 'We're police officers. We're looking for Christine Jones. Does she live here by any chance?'

'Yes, Chris lives here.' The woman frowned. 'I'm Tessa Briggs. Has anything happened to Chris?'

'Not that we know of, miss. Could we come in for a minute?'

'Yes, of course.' She left the door open for them, and started back down the hall. 'Come into the living room. Sorry everything's such a state. We just got back from a short holiday. It was supposed to be a weekend away, but we couldn't drag ourselves back.'

'I can appreciate that,' said Doyle.

There was a yell from upstairs. 'Tess, have you started that wash yet? I can't hear the machine. Who was that at the door?'

'Two policemen,' Tessa yelled back. 'Asking about Chris. Come downstairs!'

In stepping over the threshold, Doyle and Greenleaf had to step over some mail still lying on the carpet where it had dropped through the letterbox. Greenleaf stooped to pick it up. Two letters for C. Jones, one for T. Briggs, and a postcard. There was a small table in the hall, and he dropped the mail on to it before following Doyle into the living room.

Doyle, already seated on the sofa, was asking Tessa Briggs about her weekend.

'It was great,' she said. 'We went canoeing. First time I've been. Scared the life out of me, but I'd do it again.'

'We being . . . ?'

'Oh, Rachel and me and our two boyfriends.'

'Not Miss Jones then?'

'No, Chris stayed here. Only she's not here just now, she's gone off for a couple of days . . . she left a note on my computer.'

The two policemen looked at one another. This seemed to tally with the story given to the constables by the person calling herself Christine Jones. Doyle raised an eyebrow. The meaning to Greenleaf was clear: wild goose chase. There was a framed photo on the mantelpiece: three young women, arms around shoulders, grinning towards the camera. Greenleaf picked it up.

'Which one's Miss Jones?'

'In the middle,' said Tessa Briggs.

Yes, he'd have known that: her photo pretty well matched the description of her given by the two constables and by Elder, who apparently had seen her leave the police station. Greenleaf handed the photo to Doyle, who looked at Christine Jones and nodded, handing it back. Even to Greenleaf, it was beginning to look like a dead end.

'When did Miss Jones leave?'

'No idea.'

'You didn't contact her over the weekend?'

Tessa Briggs shrugged, as though the thought had never crossed her mind. Now another woman came into the room. She looked red-faced from exertion.

'It's all right,' she said with a big smile, 'I've hidden the crack beneath the arms cache.'

Greenleaf managed a wan smile; Doyle just stared at her.

'Only joking,' she said. 'I'm Rachel Maguire. What's up?'

Greenleaf noticed how Doyle reacted to the name – Maguire. An Irish name, as Irish a name as Doyle. And suddenly it came to Greenleaf: terrorists had Irish names, *that's* why Doyle was so defensive about his own name.

'Yes,' Tessa was saying. 'What *is* up? You haven't said.'

'It's Miss Jones,' said Doyle, recovering. 'She was mugged this morning.'

'Mugged?' The two women spoke in horrified unison. 'Is she all right?'

'She's fine,' Greenleaf said, calming them. 'Not a scratch on her. The attackers ran off. They didn't get a thing.'

'God, that's horrible. Where did it happen?'

'Near Covent Garden,' said Doyle.

'In broad daylight?'

'It's when most crimes occur, miss.'

'Where does Miss Jones work?' asked Greenleaf.

'She's a civil servant,' said Tessa.

'DTI,' said Rachel. 'On Victoria Street somewhere.'

'Right at the start of Victoria Street,' Tessa added.

'Number 1–16 or 1–18, something like that.'

Again, Greenleaf and Doyle exchanged a glance. Victoria Street . . . that was a bit close to the Conference Centre.

'How has she seemed lately?' asked Greenleaf. 'I mean, has she been worried about anything?'

The women shrugged. 'What's that got to do with her being mugged?' asked Tessa.

'Nothing,' said Greenleaf. 'I was just wondering, that's all.'

'Look,' said Rachel, 'if she was mugged but she's all right . . . just what *exactly* are you doing here?'

There was no answer to that, so Greenleaf supplied one.

'Just routine, like I say, miss, in cases like this. We like to check afterwards to see whether the victim's remembered anything else.'

'Oh, like a description?'

'That's it, yes.'

Doyle rose to his feet. 'Anyway, we *would* like to talk to Miss Jones when she gets back.' He took a card from his wallet. 'Maybe she could give us a call. Or if she gets in touch with you . . .'

'Yes, we'll let you know,' said Tessa, accepting the card.

'We'd appreciate it,' said Doyle. 'Goodbye, Miss Maguire. We'll leave you to get on with your laundry and your crack dealing.'

Rachel Maguire managed a weak smile.

'Bye, miss,' said Greenleaf. Tessa accompanied the two policemen to the door. 'Oh,' said Greenleaf, 'I put your mail on the table there.'

'Thanks, bills probably.'

'Probably,' agreed Greenleaf. 'And a postcard, too.'

'Oh?' She glanced towards the table.

'Goodbye, Miss Briggs.'

'Yes, goodnight,' said Tessa Briggs. 'Sorry we couldn't be' – the door closed – 'more help.'

Doyle put both hands to his eyes and rubbed. 'And so,' he said, 'another long day comes to an end. Time for you to buy me a drink.' He started off towards the front gate.

'I told Elder I'd phone him,' said Greenleaf.

'Why?'

'To let him know if we found anything.'

'It can wait till tomorrow.'

'The summit *starts* tomorrow.'

'Really? Somehow that'd slipped my mind.'

Greenleaf closed the gate after them. 'She works on Victoria Street.'

'I know.'

'It's a bit of a coincidence.'

'Look, a woman called Christine Jones gets mugged near Covent Garden. Elder's so paranoid he sees Witch round every corner. We've checked, and as far as we can tell, her story's straight.' Doyle unlocked the passenger door, then went round to the driver's side, unlocked it, and got in.

'She beat off the attackers,' added Greenleaf. 'We should've asked her housemates if she had any training. Maybe I'll just—'

'You go back there and you're walking home.' Doyle waited until Greenleaf had settled in the passenger seat and closed his door. 'I'll say one thing for Elder,' he murmured, 'he really did get the car cleaned.' Not that this impressed Doyle: he liked his car to smell like a car, which in his mind meant cigarette smoke, fumes, and old bits of discarded chewing gum. Now, the interior smelt of air-freshener and polish. He lit a cigarette. Greenleaf wound down his window.

'Come on,' complained Doyle, 'we'll freeze.'

'Shirley complains when I go home smelling like an ashtray.'

'Jesus,' said Doyle. He took two long drags on the cigarette, then opened his own window long enough to flick it out. 'Satisfied?' he said. 'Now wind your window back up.'

Greenleaf did so, and Doyle started the car. 'There's a pub in Islington, you won't *believe* the beer.'

'We should call into Paddy Green, see if they've put together a line-up for McKillip.'

'After we've had a drink,' Doyle insisted. He sounded irritated; maybe it was the phrase Paddy Green . . . The car pulled away from the kerb.

'What's that?' said Greenleaf.

'What's what?'

Greenleaf had caught sight of something in the wing mirror. There was a noise, like a yell. He turned around and looked out of the rear windscreen. Tessa Briggs was leaning over the gate, calling something, waving something.

'Stop the car,' he said.

'What's up?'

'It's Tessa Briggs.' Greenleaf wound his window back down and Tessa, having opened the gate, ran to the car.

'God, I thought you weren't going to stop!'

'What is it, Miss Briggs?'

'This.' She handed a postcard through the window. 'It's supposed to be from Chris. Postmarked Saturday.'

'Supposed?' said Greenleaf.

'That's nothing like her writing,' said Tessa. 'Now tell me, please, what the hell is going on?'

Greenleaf read the card and handed it to Doyle, who read the greeting out aloud.

'"Hard work but fun. See you soon. C." ' He turned the card over, then back again. 'And it's printed.'

Tessa was shaking her head. 'Nothing like Chris's writing,' she said. 'And she wouldn't *print* a message anyway.'

'Wild goose chase?' Greenleaf asked. '"Greetings from Auchterarder". She's got some nerve.'

Doyle studied the card yet again, then looked up at his partner.

'Better phone Elder,' he said.

'Where are you phoning from?' asked Dominic Elder into the mouthpiece.

'From home, Doyle just dropped me off.'

Elder was lying on his bed in his hotel room, an arm over his eyes. There were no lights on in the room, but the orange glare of the street-lighting penetrated the curtains, exacerbating his migraine. He was tired, dog-tired. He knew he needed rest. For the first time, he felt real homesickness for his little cottage, its cosy den, his slumber-chair.

'So what do you think?' asked Greenleaf. He'd already told Elder about the postcard.

'It's such a giveaway, obviously we weren't supposed to find it until the end of the mission. Meaning the mission must be soon.'

'Think she knows we're on to her?'

'That depends on whether she needs to get in touch with our friend the Dutchman. Someone's monitoring the hotel switchboard. The two constables who brought her in say they didn't mention anything about a Dutchman being arrested, but then they could be lying.'

'You're suggesting my colleagues might be covering themselves rather than telling the truth?'

'If they didn't say anything, chances are she doesn't know. She wasn't anywhere near CID, which is where our Dutchman was. All the same, if she was so close to him, I can't help feeling she'll know.'

'Then she'll know how close we are to her?'

'And how close is that, John?'

'We know who she's pretending to be. Key to a lock-up, missing civil servant. We'll find Christine Jones in a garage somewhere.'

'Somewhere around Hackney.'

'If your hunch about the *A–Z* is right, yes.'

'Don't forget, Barclay found the *A–Z*.'

'I won't forget. But whose snitch was it found the Dutchman in the first place?'

Yes, Charlie Giltrap. Elder owed Charlie rather a large drink for that.

Greenleaf was still talking. 'Is Barclay your . . . is he some kind of protégé?'

'Not exactly. Meantime, the key is being copied tonight. Inspector Whitlock is going to coordinate the search.'

'Whitlock?'

'Stationed in Hackney. I'm told he's a good man for this sort of job.'

'So the Dutchman grabbed Christine Jones . . .'

'And now Witch has assumed her identity. I hear McKillip was able to identify our Dutch friend.'

'Pointed straight to him.'

'Good, we can hold him a bit longer then. Bit late all the same. His part in the operation has almost certainly finished.'

'You think she'll try a hit from this building in Victoria Street?'

'Yes, 1–19 Victoria Street.' Elder paused. 'Or maybe one of the other DTI buildings along the route.'

'There are details already assigned to every one of them.'

'Yes, and she'll no doubt realise that.'

'But you still think she'll try? It's suicide.'

'I know, I can't really understand what she's playing at.'

'How do you mean?'

Elder sighed. 'Oh, nothing probably. It just seems . . . she's just making too many mistakes, John.'

'Maybe she's getting old, eh?'

Elder smiled in the darkness. 'Maybe.' There were sounds at the other end of the line. A clinking of china. A muffled 'Thanks, love, won't be long', presumably from Greenleaf to his wife. Elder felt cold and empty, he felt a longing for something he daren't quite put into words.

'We'll place guards on the doors,' Greenleaf was saying.

'And inside the buildings,' suggested Elder.

'I don't know, Dominic, we're stretched as it is.'

'Just a suggestion,' said Elder, hoping Greenleaf would take his meaning: It may be just a suggestion, but I've made it and so that puts it in your hands. If you *don't* put men inside the buildings and she *does* succeed in killing someone my conscience is clear . . . how about yours? It was just like his warning to Joyce Parry, the one she in turn had passed on to the PM, bypassing the Home Secretary.

'I'll see what Commander Trilling says,' Greenleaf said after a long pause. Yes, he'd taken Elder's meaning, and he would pass the buck along.

'Every security man on that route,' Elder went on, screwing up his eyes with effort, 'must have a recent description of Witch and a photograph of Christine Jones. All passes must be checked. It's obvious that Witch now looks like Miss Jones; it's just as obvious she'll use Miss Jones's pass to get past DTI's own security.'

'Even though she knows we know?' Greenleaf persisted.

'It sounds crazy, but I've got a feeling she'll try. We'll have to be ready for her, which means we'd all better get some rest tonight.'

'I could do with it. You sound like you could, too.'

'Me?' said Elder. 'I'm just about to go for my evening run. A quick sprint around Hyde Park.'

Greenleaf laughed tiredly. 'Give me five minutes and I'll join you there. See you in the morning, Dominic.'

'Goodnight, John.'

With eyes still closed, Elder managed to place the receiver back in its cradle. It rang again almost immediately. He groaned and groped for the still-warm receiver.

'Elder here.'

'Mr Elder, it's Barclay.' The young man sounded frantic, or maybe just frustrated. 'I've hunted all over . . . restaurants, bars, clubs . . . no sign of her. All anyone at the embassy said was she's out on the town with the other new arrivals. But at last they've come up with the name of her hotel. Do you think I should—'

'Michael,' said Elder gently, 'I think you should go home and get some sleep. Tomorrow morning will be time enough.'

'Yes, but if I find her tonight I could take her to *The Times* offices and—'

'Michael, answer me one question.'

Barclay's breathing was fast and ragged. From the background noise – drunken yells, music blaring, teeming life, car horns – he was calling from a phone-booth somewhere in the West End. 'Sure,' he said, 'go ahead.'

'Why do you want to find Dominique so urgently? Is it maybe because you feel left out of her life all of a sudden?'

There was a long silence. 'That's two questions,' Barclay said at last.

'Rhetorical questions, too, I think. Go home, get some rest, and be at the Conference Centre early. We know Dominique will be there.'

'Yes.' Barclay sounded as if all the air had been let out of him. 'Yes, okay.'

'Goodnight then.'

Elder hung up the phone. It rang again. 'Oh, for Christ's sake.' He picked it up. 'Elder,' he snapped.

'Dominic?' It was Joyce Parry. 'Are you all right?'

He softened his voice. 'Oh, hello, Joyce. Yes, yes, I'm fine. Sorry about that.'

'Been a long day, huh?'

'Yes,' he agreed, 'it's been a long day.'

'And a successful day too, by all accounts. Congratulations.'

'Premature, I'd say. You know we actually had Witch *inside* a police station?'

'And she got away, yes. Hardly your fault, Dominic. And we *do* have the Dutchman. People on the Continent are very pleased about that.'

'Good for them.'

Joyce Parry laughed. 'It helps us with SIS. After Barclay's German escapade, we need it.'

'But will it help mend the rift between you and the Home Secretary?'

'Who knows. He can be a spiteful little sod.' She paused. 'How about a nightcap? I thought we could have a drink at the—'

'That's sweet of you, Joyce, and any other time, I'd be . . .'

'But tonight you're whacked? Fair enough. How did Barclay bear up today?'

'More than adequately.'

'Really? You're not just covering for him?'

'He's just called me. He's still busy working.'

'I *am* impressed. He's always been first out of the office here, soon as five-thirty comes.'

'Maybe he's changed.'

'Maybe. Just so long as you haven't taught him too many of your tricks.'

He smiled. 'Joyce, about that drink. Might room service be available?'

She considered her answer. 'It might.'

'On one condition.'

'What's that?'

'Bring some paracetamol as well. Either that or massage oil.'

'Alcohol, drugs and baby oil . . . sounds just like the old days.'

Elder laughed. 'I think the relevant word there is "old", Joyce. Definitely old.'

He put the receiver down again and counted to ten. No more calls came. He knew he should get up, tidy the room a bit, and tidy himself too. But still he lay, the arm across his eyes, thinking of an encounter he knew must come, and come soon. Just like Operation Silverfish. He wriggled on the bed, rubbing the itch in his back. Silverfish. *You should have been a priest.* Maybe she had a point. Finally, he got up and turned on the bedside lamp, squinting into the light as he opened the wardrobe and took out his case. There was a shirt in the bottom, rolled up. It was torn and tattered, and stained a dull brown, almost the colour of rust. It was the shirt he had worn . . . And wrapped up inside it was a gun, a Browning nine-millimetre pistol. He lifted out the gun and put the shirt back in the case. The pistol felt icy and unnatural in his hand, but the longer he held it the warmer it became and the more natural it felt, until he was hardly aware of it there at all.

'This time,' he whispered to himself, running his eye along the sight. 'This time, Witch. That's a promise.'

The Shooting Gallery

Tuesday 16 June

Barclay was at the Queen Elizabeth II Conference Centre almost before it had opened for the day. But the foyer was already buzzing with security and the media. Everyone was handed a sheet detailing the day's itinerary. Supposedly, this had been held back until the day itself for 'security reasons'. But in fact most of the delegations, in pre-summit chats with the press, had given away the details anyway. A large section of the Conference Centre had been set aside for representatives of the media, and they wouldn't be allowed to linger in the foyer. A restless young woman was already weaving through the bodies, seeking out media-coloured ribbons. She looked at Barclay, seemed to think he *must* be a reporter, and was about to tell him that breakfast was available in the . . . But then she saw that he was wearing a security-coloured red-and-blue ribbon, so she veered away at the last moment.

Some German security personnel were sharing a German joke. One of them, seeing the colour of Barclay's ribbon, nodded a greeting towards him. Barclay nodded back. His cheeks were tingling: he wondered if the joke was the one about the British secret agent and the German terrorist. A couple of the Germans kept placing a hand against their chest and running it down the front of their buttoned suit-jacket. It was clear to Barclay that they were armed. In fact, as more security personnel appeared, he began to wonder if he alone was unarmed. Still there was no sign of Dominique. He read through the itinerary again, already knowing it by heart. The first session was to be short, a sort of official welcome. A couple of speeches, then a photo-shoot. The real business would begin in the afternoon, after an 'informal' lunch at Buckingham Palace. He wondered how informal 'informal' was. Not very, he thought.

'Morning, Michael.'

It was Elder. He had heavy bags under his eyes, which were red at their corners. Having spoken, he stifled a yawn.

'Good morning, sir.' Barclay examined Elder's suit for bulges, and found none. Well, at least someone else around here wasn't toting a gun.

'Bright and early, eh?'

'Well, early anyway.'

Elder nodded, stifling another yawn. 'I could do with some coffee,' he said at last. A room had been set aside for the British security contingent, and in it sat a steaming coffee-machine. Elder made straight for a large polythene bag full of beakers, tipped some 'creamer' into one, then poured himself coffee. Barclay refused. 'Creamer,' muttered Elder. 'What in God's name's that?'

'Something with no milk products in it,' guessed Barclay. Elder shuddered, but drank the drink anyway, screwing shut his eyes for the first couple of gulps.

He exhaled noisily. 'Hit the spot,' he said. 'Now listen, we've had some more news.'

'Oh?'

'A civil servant called Christine Jones. She's missing. We think Witch has abducted her and is using her identity.'

Barclay whistled. 'Where does she work?'

'1–19 Victoria Street.'

Barclay nodded. 'Makes sense.'

'So today, and every day if it comes to it, Victoria Street's our priority.'

'When did you find all this out?'

'Last night.'

'Why didn't you tell me when I phoned?'

'Michael, you were overheated as it was. I didn't want you to explode. Besides, we know a lot, but we still don't know who Witch's target is.'

'So you don't think my idea about *The Times* is a lost cause?'

'Absolutely not.' Elder, having finished the coffee, poured himself another cup, not bothering to add creamer this time. 'Absolutely not,' he repeated. 'I want you and Dominique to follow it up.'

'Speaking of which . . . I should be in the lobby in case she arrives.'

'Fine, I'll come with you. I'm going to take another wander along Victoria Street.' He finished the second cup.

'Feel better for that, sir?'

Elder nodded, stifling yet another yawn.

'You obviously didn't get much sleep last night,' said Barclay, solicitously.

'No,' said Elder with a smile. 'Not much.'

Barclay saw that the smile was in memory of something. It didn't take him long to work out what that memory might be.

Dominique, entering the foyer unaccompanied, was yawning too. She looked like she'd had a heavy night of it. Barclay, who'd just been thinking about Elder and Joyce Parry, didn't want to consider what Dominique had been doing.

'Dominique,' he said, approaching.

She raised a hand to her forehead. 'Michael, please, I am dying. English beer . . . how do you manage to drink it?'

Barclay smiled. 'Dominique, this is your near-namesake Dominic Elder.'

She tried to brighten a little. She looked very pale, and hadn't bothered with the morning chore of make-up. But her eyes sparkled as she smiled. 'Monsieur Elder, I am pleased to meet you.' She put out a small red-gloved hand for Elder to take. 'The famous author of the Witch file.'

Elder swallowed another yawn and made a non-committal sound.

'Listen, Dominique,' said Barclay, 'something's come up. It might be a clue to Witch's intended victim.'

'Oh yes?' She just failed to sound interested.

'Remember the Australian anarchist? His flat?'

She rolled her eyes. 'Monsieur Wrightson and his apartment. Ugh, how could I forget?'

'There was a copy of *The Times* there.'

'Yes.' She seemed puzzled now, but her interest was growing.

'With the crossword done.'

'Yes.'

'And remember what Bandorff said . . . Witch liked to do crosswords.'

She nodded slowly. 'So you add one to the other,' she said, 'and you assume the crossword was done by Witch and not by Mr Wrightson?'

Barclay shrugged. 'It's a theory.'

She considered this, acknowledged with a shrug of her own that it was possible. 'So what?' she said.

'The thing is,' Elder broke in, 'there was a page torn out of that newspaper, according to Mr Barclay here.'

Another shrug. 'A page, maybe several pages. Used for toilet paper, according to—'

'Perhaps *Witch* tore the page out,' continued Elder.

'You see,' said Barclay, warming to the subject, 'it could be some clue to her chosen victim, a profile of them or something.'

'Oh, yes, I see.'

'So can you remember which day's *Times* it was?'

She laughed. 'I cannot even remember which *month* it was.' She saw that they looked crestfallen. 'I'm sorry,' she said.

'Don't be,' said Elder. But Barclay's dejection moved her to remember.

'There was a photograph,' she said. 'A large black and white picture on one of the inside pages. I recall it because it attracted me. A photograph of New York from the air, and lots of *ballons*.'

'Balloons?' said Elder.

'Yes, the big ones with baskets beneath them.'

'Hot-air balloons?'

'Yes, lots of those, rising over New York.'

'The Picture Editor's *got* to know when that one appeared,' said Barclay, brightening again.

Elder was nodding. 'Off you go,' he said. 'And be lucky.'

Barclay looked to Dominique. 'Coming?'

She looked undecided. 'I should . . . my colleagues . . . I am supposed to be the expert, you know.' Then she made up her mind. 'Oh God, yes, of course I am coming.'

A broad smile spread across Barclay's face. 'Good,' he said.

Elder watched them leave. A nice young couple, but he wouldn't want to have to depend on them. He patted his chest, and let his hand slide down the front of his suit. Then he walked outside. The morning was overcast, threatening rain. The forecast for the rest of the week was even worse. Wet weather seemed to exacerbate his back problem. God knows, after last night he felt achy enough as it was.

'You look rough,' said a voice to his left. It was Doyle, accompanied by Greenleaf.

'Maybe fragile is a better word,' Elder admitted.

Doyle laughed, and patted his jacket ostentatiously. 'Well, don't worry about a thing, Mr Elder, we'll look after you.' His voice fell to a dramatic whisper. 'Tooled up.'

Elder stared at the bulging jacket. 'I'd never have guessed.'

'It makes me nervous,' said Greenleaf. He looked nervous, wriggling at the unaccustomed weight strapped to his side, beneath his left arm. Neither Special Branch man wore a suit really fitted for carrying a gun. Not like Elder's suit, which was unfashionably roomy to start with. Elder many years before had given the suit to a tailor in Shoreditch who had eased it out a little to the left-hand side. The result was that he could have worn a .44 Magnum without any hint of a bulge, never mind his favoured pistol.

'I picked up itineraries for you,' said Elder. He took from his pocket two folded sheets of A4-sized paper, and gave one to each of them. Doyle glanced down the list.

'Not much here we didn't know already. When d'you think she'll make the hit? Lunchtime?'

Elder nodded. 'That would be my guess. After this morning's handshakes and champagne. The cars are supposed to leave for Buck House at noon, but I suppose it depends on how long the photo opportunity takes.'

'They won't keep Her Maj' waiting,' said Doyle knowledgeably.

'You're probably right,' said Elder.

'Speaking of photo opportunities . . .' Greenleaf reached into the plastic carrier bag he was holding and came out with a xeroxed sheet. 'We've had these distributed to everyone.' On the sheet was a picture of Christine Jones and a description. The picture wasn't terribly good.

'I got it last night,' Doyle said proudly. 'Went back to the house. There weren't many snaps to choose from. We had to crop that one as it was.' He reached into his jacket pocket. 'Here's the original.'

Elder studied the photo. It showed Christine Jones and a female friend posing on a beach. Christine was wearing a one-piece swimsuit, her friend a very brief bikini.

'Mmm,' said Elder. He looked up at Doyle, who was looking at the photo, then he glanced towards Greenleaf, who smiled. Yes, they both had their ideas as to why Doyle had chosen this particular photograph.

'And,' added Greenleaf meaningfully, 'there are extra men on guard inside 1–19.'

'Not inside the other buildings?'

'We couldn't stretch to it.'

'No way,' said Doyle, retrieving the picture. 'We're like india-rubber men as it is.'

Greenleaf was rummaging in the bag again. 'We thought these might come in handy.' He lifted a walkie-talkie out of the bag and handed it to Elder. It was heavier than it looked. 'They've not got much range, but . . .' Another walkie-talkie was handed to Doyle. When Greenleaf lifted out the third, the bag was empty. He crumpled it and stuffed it into his pocket.

'Not exactly unobtrusive,' commented Elder.

'True,' said Doyle. 'Carry one of these and every bugger knows what your game is.'

Greenleaf said nothing but looked slighted. Elder guessed the walkie-talkies had been his idea. 'I'm sure they'll be invaluable,' Elder said.

'Here they come,' said Doyle. Which was, in a sense, true. Cordons had been hastily erected, traffic stopped. Uniformed policemen were suddenly in greater evidence than ever. Motorbikes arrived with their indicators flashing, the drivers had a word with someone, then they turned and headed back the way they'd come.

'Yes,' said Doyle, 'here they come.'

The three men stood well out of the way as they watched the delegations arrive. Doyle was not impressed. 'Why do they need all these cars and all this razzmatazz? Be a lot cheaper if they just flew the big cheeses in – first class, natch – and had them all sit round a table. Look at all these bloody hangers-on.'

'I believe,' said Elder, smiling, 'the term is aides.'

'Hangers-on,' Doyle insisted.

One car deposited the Home Secretary and his private secretary. Jonathan Barker fastened a button on his suit jacket as he emerged, smiling for the cameras. A gust caught the parting in his hair, and he swept the stray locks back into place. He glanced towards where Elder and the others stood, and frowned slightly, bowing his head so the newsmen wouldn't catch the look.

'"Shagger" Barker we call him,' said Doyle from the side of his mouth. Elder laughed, quite loudly, further discomfiting the Home Secretary. The private secretary scowled openly at the trio as he followed his minister into the building.

'Why "Shagger"?'

Doyle shrugged. 'He just looks the type, doesn't he?'

'He was happily married until a couple of months ago.'

'Yeah, to his secretary. Says a lot about him, doesn't it?'

'Does it?'

When the last delegation had entered the Conference Centre, Greenleaf expelled a long whistle of air between his teeth.

'The collective sigh of relief,' said Elder. The police and other security people all looked a bit easier now that everyone was safely inside.

'To think,' said Greenleaf, 'we're going to be doing this at least twice a day for the rest of the week.'

'Well, let's hope we are,' said Elder. 'I'd rather breathe a sigh of relief than a gasp of panic.'

Doyle chuckled. 'I wish I could say clever things like that.'

'I take that as a compliment, Doyle, coming from the man who invented "Shagger" Barker.'

Doyle made a little bow. 'Now what?' he asked.

'Victoria Street,' said Elder. 'Fun's over here. Let's see how security's shaping up.'

Witch had been in the Victoria area since daybreak. Just after midnight, she'd stolen a car. It was her second car theft of the night, her first being a four-year-old Peugeot 305. For the second, she wanted something similar – fast but unshowy – and finally settled on a three-year-old Alfa Romeo. She'd gone outside London to accomplish this. A car stolen in London and then driven around London could be spotted by police. A car stolen in East Croydon and driven around central London might not. She had brought the first car, the Peugeot, back into the city and parked it on the corner of her chosen cul-de-sac off the King's Road. Then she'd returned to East Croydon by the late train, a train full of drunk commuters and even drunker youths, and found the Alfa Romeo. Back in London, she had driven one particular route three times, with slight detours and amendments, memorising the final, chosen route until she felt she could drive it blindfolded.

Then she'd slept for an hour or two in an all-night car park, slouched in the front seat of the Alfa, awaking to a tingling feeling in her gut, a feeling that told her it was time. Time to put theory into practice. Time for the final day.

She'd watched the various entourages arrive at the Conference Centre, headphones clamped to her head. Her personal hi-fi's radio news told her that the morning session would be short. Yes, because they were going to lunch at Buckingham Palace; she'd read that in one of the briefs prepared by the Dutchman.

The Dutchman was another unreliable factor, now that Elder had his hands on him. That was why she was here early, just to check what extra security precautions they'd taken.

As the sleek black cars had arrived, while she was listening to her radio, she'd been watching Dominic Elder. No chance of his spotting her of course. She was just one of a crowd who had stopped on their way to work to watch, from behind the metal barriers, the famous people arriving. She'd tucked herself in between two large men. And she watched Elder, watched him talking to two other men – they looked like police to her, probably Special Branch, MI5's dogsbodies. One of them made a big show of the fact that he was armed. The other was quiet, almost sleepy in comparison. Elder looked tired and alert at the same time. Like her, he wouldn't have been getting much sleep recently. Like her, he'd been waiting for this day. Beneath the shabby suit he would be carrying his own gun, the Browning. It was typical of him to buy British. Typical of him to keep faith with something which had failed him before . . .

She'd watched for a few moments, and she'd looked up occasionally to spot the marksmen, armed only with binoculars thus far, as they examined the scene from their lofty heights. Then she drifted away. Her car was parked outside a mansion block in a street behind Westminster Cathedral, tickets on the windshield showing she'd paid for three hours' parking. Three hours was the limit. She'd toyed with the idea of breaking into another car and taking a resident's parking permit to stick on the Alfa's windscreen. But any traffic warden worth the name would pause to compare licence plate details.

She was playing a cassette on her personal hi-fi: an Ohm mantra repeated over the sound of a human heartbeat. It calmed her as she walked back to the car, got into it, and rummaged beneath the passenger seat for her civil service satchel and a green Harrods carrier bag. She glanced around her before opening the satchel and peering inside, seeming happy with what she found there. Her own choice of pistol was an Italian-made Beretta nine-millimetre 92F, a link to her days in Bologna as a member of Croix Jaune. She'd first handled a Beretta during the Gibson kidnapping. Christ, she'd been the only one of them who knew how to handle a gun. She'd practically had to teach them. Still, despite the clumsy trap laid for them, they'd all managed to escape with the ransom money. It had come in useful, that money . . .

She slipped the gun out of her satchel and into her jacket. She'd stitched a special pocket into it, hanging loose from the jacket by two straps. It was funny how often the authorities would want to search your baggage, but not your clothes. She had a feeling this might be one of those days at the DTI.

She closed the satchel again and got out of the car, this time taking satchel and carrier bag with her. She had a little time to kill. She noticed as she passed that there were men hanging around outside some of the buildings on Victoria Street itself, and especially outside the DTI Headquarters. It was only to be expected. She walked to a small supermarket and bought two large fresh chickens, two packs of fresh sandwiches, and a catering-sized tin of cheap instant coffee, then retreated to Victoria Station and locked herself in a toilet cubicle, where she did what she had to do. An attendant knocked eventually and asked if everything was all right.

'Everything's fine,' Witch called back. 'Bad curry last night, that's all.'

The attendant chuckled and moved away. Witch flushed the toilet and came out. The attendant, a small brown-skinned woman, was waiting.

'Sorry,' the woman said, 'it's just that you've got to be careful. We get all kinds coming in . . . injecting themselves, that sort of thing.'

'I understand,' said Witch, washing her hands. 'Like you say, you've got to be careful.'

She walked around the back of Victoria Street, to where her car was, and from there to the back entrance of 45 Victoria Street. There was a guard with a dog outside the door. The dog barked as she approached, rearing up on hind legs, causing the guard to rein it in on its leash.

'It's all right,' he told her.

'I've some chickens here,' she said.

'That'll be it then, not that he doesn't get fed enough.'

She walked past him. She wasn't concerned, there was nothing for her to be concerned about. She was a government employee, she made this trip every day. Nothing to worry about. She entered the building and showed her security pass to the guard who stood in front of his desk. He looked at it a bit more carefully than usual, and thanked her.

'I don't often forget a pretty face,' he said.

'I usually come in the front way,' she explained, 'but it's pandemonium out there.'

'I'll bet.'

Witch slipped the pass back into her handbag. She had altered the name on Christine Jones's card to Caroline James, knowing they would be on the lookout for poor starving Christine. She made to move past him.

'Sorry, miss, I need to check all bags today.'

'Yes, of course.'

'It's pandemonium in here too.' He looked through her handbag first, then her official bag. 'I'm on my own. They've sent my partner up the road to Number One.'

'Really?' She allowed herself a small smile.

He was looking at her shopping.

'Chicken's on special offer at Safeway,' she said.

'Really? I like a bit of leg myself.' And he gave her a wink, to which she responded with her most winning smile. He glanced towards the other items: it was obviously her turn to provide the office coffee, and lunch today consisted of nothing more than a sandwich.

In her Harrods bag were some clothes, a pair of shoes.

'Partying tonight, eh?'

'That's the plan,' said Witch.

'Thank you, miss,' the guard said.

'You're welcome.'

She walked to the lifts, pressed the button and waited.

The lift arrived. She got in and pressed the button for the third floor. On the way up, she did not blink. She just stared ahead, even when the lift stopped at the ground floor and some people got in. There were guards pacing the space outside the lifts. They did not look at her. She looked through them. Then the lift was ascending again. She got out at the third floor and made for the Conference Room. God, wouldn't it just be her luck to bump into that slimeball from yesterday, Blishen, Mr Folded-arms? But she didn't. She looked up and down the corridor, saw that no one was paying her any attention, and opened the door of the Conference Room.

Inside, she worked quickly. She took out both chickens and reached inside them, where the plastic bags of giblets had been until she'd flushed them down the toilet in Victoria Station. Now the hollow chickens housed small soft packages wrapped in grey polythene and black tape. She dumped the chickens in the wastepaper bin, and reopened the packs of sandwiches, which she had closed herself using tiny strips of clear tape. Inside were thin coils of copper wire and small connectors, plus a tiny screw-driver. She joined the two packages by runs of wire, working quickly and calmly. She held one foot wedged up against the door, preventing anyone from opening it while she worked.

At last she was satisfied. Time for a break, she thought. She lifted out the large tin of coffee and prised off its lid. The toilet at Victoria had taken a lot of punishment: giblets, sandwich fillings, and an awful lot of instant granules. The blonde wig inside the tin still smelled of bitter coffee. She shook it free of brown specks, then dumped the tin in the basket beside the chickens.

She lifted the clothes and shoes from her bag, stripped and changed. With lipstick and the aid of a hand-mirror she turned her lips vermilion. Make-up is the beginning of disguise. She'd learnt that early in life at the fairground: she could be virgin or whore to order, twelve or sixteen, above or below the age of consent. She could smile and be unhappy; or weep while she was overjoyed. She'd been playing a game of dressing-up with her life until the Irishman had come . . .

She looked at herself now and blinked. A question had framed itself in her mind. Who am I? She shook it away as she brushed out her wig. She knew who she was. She knew what she was. And she knew why she was here.

Wasn't that more than most people knew?

When she turned the Harrods bag inside out, it was just a plain white cloth bag with green handles. She placed her cassette recorder on the floor near the door, unplugging the headphones. The recorder came with its own built-in speaker, and, more unusually, included automatic rewind and repeat functions. Witch swapped her Ohm and Heartbeat cassette for another tape and switched the machine on.

In the lower ground floor of the building, the guard was tuning his radio to something musical when there were steps on the stairwell. A man appeared. The guard knew him. He was from the police. The police were all over the place, on window-ledges and in corridors, patrolling the foyer and the main entrance. He half-expected to see one of them hiding beneath his desk. The policeman was waving something, a notice or leaflet.

'Here, George,' the policeman said, 'has anyone given you one of these?'

The guard slipped his spectacles back on. 'What is it? No, nobody's given me nothing.'

'Typical,' said the policeman. 'If you want a job doing, do it yourself. Well, you can keep that one anyway.'

A bell sounded once as the lift doors opened. A couple got out, a man in a pinstripe suit and a tall, big-boned woman.

'Back in ten minutes,' the man said.

'Right you are, sir,' said the guard. The policeman watched the couple leave.

'Dirty sods couldn't wait till knocking-off time, eh?'

The guard was laughing as he turned his attention to the sheet of paper. He recognised the name, he'd been told to look out for it. But now there was a photo, too.

'I don't know,' he said.

'What's up, George?'

The guard tapped the photo with a finger yellow from cigarettes smoked to the nub. 'I think I've seen her this morning, about twenty minutes ago.'

'You sure?'

'Christine Jones, that wasn't the name on her pass. I've been on the lookout for Christine Jones.'

The policeman was already slipping a radio out of his pocket. 'This is Traynor,' he said into the mouthpiece. 'I'm in number 45. Suspect is inside the building. I repeat, suspect is inside the building.'

There was silence, then crackle and a disembodied voice. 'It's Doyle here, Traynor. Secure all exits, and I mean *all* exits. Start searching the floors. We're on our way.'

Traynor made for the stairs then paused. 'You heard him, George. No one in or out of here, okay? Anyone wants out, send them to the ground floor.' He turned, then stopped again, turned back. 'George, what was she wearing?'

'Mmm . . . blue jacket, dark blue . . . white blouse, dark skirt.'

'Right.' This time Traynor started climbing the stairs. George switched his radio back on and began fiddling with the dial again. He looked out of the window, but the pinstripe man and lipstick woman had gone. Ah, Radio Two, he'd found it at last. Manuel and his Music of the Mountains, lovely. George settled back in his chair.

Doyle and Greenleaf put together reinforcements and brought them into the building. They were both a little breathless, but ready for anything. The news had been circulated, more men would be on their way.

'Any sign?' Doyle asked Traynor.

'Not yet. She's dressed in a dark-coloured two-piece and white blouse, but then so are half the women in the place.'

'Which floor was she headed for?'

Traynor shook his head.

'We've just got to be methodical,' said Greenleaf.

Doyle looked at him. 'Methodical, right. How long have we got before the bigwigs go to lunch?'

Greenleaf checked his watch. 'Quarter of an hour.'

'Right then,' said Doyle, 'we can afford to be methodical for about five minutes. After that, we start screaming and kicking down doors.'

'Progress report, gentlemen.' This was said in brisk, clipped tones by Commander Trilling, almost at marching-pace as he entered the foyer and joined them.

'She's in here somewhere, sir,' said Doyle.

'But we don't know where,' admitted Greenleaf.

'Well, I'll tell you one place she's not – she's not standing here with us!' Trilling tossed a mint into his mouth. 'Let's start from the roof down. Snipers like height, don't they?'

'Yes, sir.' Doyle turned to Traynor. 'What are you waiting for? Roof and the top floor down!'

'Yes, sir.' Traynor started giving orders to his unit.

'You start at the top, Doyle,' said Greenleaf, 'I'll start at the bottom. Keep in touch by walkie-talkie and we'll meet halfway.'

'Right,' said Doyle.

'Where's Elder?' asked Trilling. Greenleaf shrugged.

'I think he was headed for the lower ground floor.'

'Let's try to keep him there, eh? He'll only get in the way.'

Doyle grinned at this, so Greenleaf swallowed back a defence.

'Right, sir,' he said instead, heading for the stairs. The last thing he heard Doyle saying was: 'And check the lift-shaft, too. Remember that film with the cannibal . . .'

Doyle stood outside the third-floor conference room. Traynor was with him. So was a civil servant who worked on the third floor.

'It's usually open,' she said. 'I can't think why it would be locked.' She was young and blonde and chewing gum.

Doyle nodded, then put a finger to his lips and tried the doorhandle quietly, trying to turn it one way and then the other. It was definitely locked. He put his ear to the door and listened. Silence. Then a shuffling sound. He thought about knocking, then thought better of it. He motioned for them to follow him further down the corridor.

'I'm lost,' he whispered. 'Is this the front of the building or the back?'

'The front, sir,' Traynor whispered back.

'Can we get someone on the ledge to take a peek inside?'

'I'll go check.' And off Traynor tiptoed.

'Back to your office,' Doyle whispered to the girl. 'It's too dangerous here.'

He thought she was going to swallow her gum. He gave her hand a reassuring squeeze in his and nodded along the corridor. Off she walked, on silent tiptoe. Doyle went back to the door and listened again. Silence. He put his eye to the keyhole, but it was the wrong type. He couldn't see into the room. There was a gap between the bottom of the door and the floor. He lay down, but again could not see into the room. Traynor was coming back.

'No can do,' he said when they'd moved away from the door. 'The ledge isn't wide enough or something.'

'What about across the road? Can anyone see anything from across there?'

'I'll radio and check.'

'And get some more men up here. We may have to storm the place.'
'Don't we have the SAS to do that sort of thing?'
'Don't be stupid, Traynor. It's only a hardwood door, not the Iranian bloody Embassy.'
Greenleaf appeared. A distance behind him, Doyle could see Trilling.
'Is she in there?' Greenleaf hissed.
Doyle shrugged and nodded towards the Commander. 'Do me a favour,' he whispered to Greenleaf, 'keep the old man away from here. He'll only be in the bloody way, and you know he can't keep his voice down.'
Greenleaf nodded, moved back along the corridor, and stopped in front of Commander Trilling, talking to him softly.

Elder was questioning the guard called George. He was beginning to get a sour feeling in his stomach about all of this, the whole set-up.
'I'm not even sure it was her,' George was saying now. 'I mean, it's hard to tell with some women, isn't it?'
'Well, has there been anyone else, anyone new to you?'
The guard shook his head. From Elder's walkie-talkie came information that the procession of cars was leaving the Conference Centre, moving in slow convoy past the building he was standing in. He felt like screaming.
'Look,' said the guard, 'I've got to get back to work.' He walked over to the outside door, where a police officer was stopping a man in a pinstriped suit from entering the building.
'He's all right,' said the guard to the policeman. 'It's Mr Connaught from the third floor.'
'I only went out to get these,' Mr Connaught was explaining, waving some documents. 'I'd left them in my boot.'
The policeman looked to Elder, who nodded assent. The officer moved aside, letting Connaught into the building.
'What's going on?'
'Security,' the guard explained. 'Some woman they're after.' This reminded him of something. 'Who was that blonde lady you were with?'
Connaught shook his head. 'Met her at the lift. Don't know who she was exactly.'
'Oh, Christ!' said Elder, making for the stairs.

There was that shuffling sound again, like someone who was seated moving their feet on the floor. Doyle took a deep breath and knocked, keeping his back hard against the wall to the side of the door, rapping with his fist and then removing it from any line of fire. Silence.
He knocked again, a little harder. 'Anyone in there? We've got a meeting starting in five minutes. Hello, anyone there?'
Silence. From their distance, Greenleaf and Trilling were watching him. When Greenleaf spoke, he spoke in an undertone which Doyle couldn't catch. Trilling's idea of an undertone, however, would not have gone unheard in a football stadium.
'I see . . . Yes, of course . . . As you see fit . . .' Then a message came over Greenleaf's radio (Doyle had switched his off: it sat on the ground beside him). Greenleaf listened and mumbled something into the radio.
Doyle licked his lips. No use pretending any longer; no time left in which

to pretend. Traynor was returning, pushing past Greenleaf and Trilling. He had four men with him.

'Net curtains are in the way,' Traynor whispered. 'Nobody across the street can see anything. No movement at all.'

Doyle nodded. 'I can hear somebody though.' Patches of sweat were spreading from beneath his arms. And now Greenleaf was creeping forwards.

'They're passing the building right this second.'

'Can't hang around any longer then,' said Doyle. He withdrew his pistol, raising it high above him, gripped in both hands and pointed ceilingwards. He closed his eyes for a moment. 'Right,' he said to the men around him. 'We're going in.' They were all withdrawing their weapons now, a series of quiet snicks as safety catches were slipped off. Doyle looked at Traynor. 'You keen to kick down that door?' Traynor nodded. 'Okay, two of you behind me, two of you other side of the door. Soon as the door opens, we're in. My side low, other side aiming over our heads. Take the diagonals. Got that?'

They nodded, assumed their positions. Doyle, back to the wall, crouched low. Traynor stood in front of the door, took a moment to size it up. Greenleaf, who had gone back along the corridor to let Trilling know the score, had withdrawn his own weapon and was now advancing again, walkie-talkie gripped in his free hand, watched by Trilling. Doyle gave Traynor the nod. Traynor took a step back, both hands around the butt of his gun, aiming it straight at whatever was behind the door. He raised his right knee, so that the sole of his shoe faced the door, just below the handle. And took a deep breath.

Dominic Elder ran up the stairs, across the reception area, and out of the glass doors on to Victoria Street. He ran into a crush of people, waving, some of them cheering, held back by metal-grilled barriers from the road. There was a dull slow roar from the motorcycle escorts. And then there was glitter in the sky, and a net-curtain, blown out from its window and wafting in the breeze.

And then there was the explosion.

A dull boom. Not a large explosion by any means, but enough to panic the crowds. The motorbikes suddenly speeded up, as did the cars. Front fenders dented back fenders as the cars behind put their foot down. They were speeding away from the scene, and the security men on the street had guns in their hands and were trying to see what had happened. But it was raining glass. That was what was happening. Large and small shards and splinters, landing at velocity. And the screams were no longer solely of fear.

'What happened?' he yelled into his walkie-talkie. 'John, what the hell happened?' He was jostled by people fleeing the scene. Doors were kicked open as people attempted to find shelter. Anywhere but on the street. Barriers clattered to the ground as people scrambled over them.

The walkie-talkie crackled. He struggled to hear it. 'Bomb inside the door. Hair-trigger.'

'Anybody hurt?'

'Traynor, leg blown off. Doyle . . .'

'What about Doyle?'

'Concussion.'

'The room, John . . . is there anyone in the room?'

A pause. 'Negative, Dominic. The room's empty. Repeat, the room is empty.' Then: 'Jesus Christ.'

'What is it?'

'Chickens, two supermarket chickens.'

They'd walked straight into a bloody trap! If Witch had left nothing else, she'd left yet another warped calling card. Which meant what? That the real attempt would take place elsewhere? Up ahead maybe? The motorcade was moving off in disarray. Christ, a trap . . . he couldn't believe . . . couldn't take it in. Why? What was the point? Suddenly, a hand gripped his arm. He reached inside his jacket, turning towards the— But it was only Barclay.

'Jesus, you gave me a fright.' His grip on the pistol relaxed. Barclay saw what had been about to happen.

'Sorry,' he said. 'What's going on?'

Elder nodded upwards, where the curtain still fluttered like a flag. It didn't look like a flag though; it looked like a shroud. 'Bomb,' he said. 'Witch led us into a trap.'

Sirens were nearing, ambulances. Uniformed police officers were attempting to comfort the prone and wounded bodies. A helicopter surveyed the pandemonium from on high. The convoy had disappeared from view. Barclay was yelling something above the noise.

'What?' Elder yelled back.

'I said we know who she's—'

The ambulances were drawing to a squealing halt in front of them. Barclay put his hand out towards Dominique, palm upwards, only to find that she wasn't there. She was ten feet away, tending to a woman's cuts. He walked over, opened the flap of her shoulder-bag, and took something from it, then came back to Elder, handing him a folded page from *The Times*. Elder looked at it. A full-page advert for British Aerospace.

'Other side,' yelled Barclay. Elder turned the page over. The obituaries column. There were four, a couple of churchmen, head of an Oxford college, and . . . Marion Barker, the Home Secretary's wife.

Elder's face creased into a huge frown. He looked at Barclay, who was nodding. Dominique, looking paler than ever, was coming back to join them. An ambulanceman had taken over from her. She watched as he worked on the woman. The woman caught Dominique's eye and smiled at her, mouthing 'thank you'.

'You think her target's the—'

'The Home Secretary,' said Barclay. He shrugged. 'Unless you think it's the Oxford don's widow.'

A police sergeant was approaching, his arms stretched out like a barrier. 'Clear the area, please. Please clear the area.'

'Yes, sergeant, we're just going,' said Dominic Elder quietly, not really aware of what he was saying. Then his eyes came back into focus. 'Come on then,' he said. 'Back to the Centre.'

They joined the evacuation of Victoria Street. More ambulances and fire engines were blocked in a traffic jam, the traffic having been halted to allow the motorcade sole access to Victoria Street in the first place. Sirens blared, blue lights circled, but the drivers in front complained that there was nothing they could do till the barriers were moved. One ambulance mounted the pavement, only to find itself firmly wedged between the vehicle in front and a concrete lamppost.

At the Conference Centre, a crowd of people stood on the steps, wondering what had happened. Elder pushed past them and into the foyer. He walked quickly to the reception desk. 'The Home Secretary,' he said, 'I need to know . . . did he go to Buckingham Palace with the rest of them?'

'I'll just check.' The receptionist made an internal call. 'Jan, what was Mr Barker doing this lunchtime?' She listened. 'Thank you,' she said, cutting the connection. 'He went home,' she said. 'Car collected him ten minutes ago.'

'Thank you,' said Elder. Barclay and Dominique were waiting just inside the door. 'He's gone home,' Elder told them. 'I know his address.' He was outside again, the young couple following him. He started to descend the steps, looking about him. 'What we need now is a car.'

Dominique continued past him and perused the line of cars parked outside the building. 'How about this one?' she said. It was a marked Metropolitan Police Rover 2000. 'It's even got the keys in.' She was already opening the driver's door. 'You can direct me, come on.'

Elder got into the back, Barclay into the passenger seat. Dominique had started the ignition, but was now looking at the controls around her.

'What's the problem?' said Barclay.

'My first time in a right-hand-drive car.' She pulled the big car out of its parking-space. 'See if you can find the siren, Michael.' After a few false attempts, he did so. People looked at them as they pulled out into the main road. 'Which way?' she called back to Elder.

'Keep going along here,' he said. 'I'll tell you when to turn.'

Dominique nodded, shifted up a gear, then thought better of it, shifted down again, and slammed her foot on the accelerator. Barclay was thrown against the back of his seat. He looked around, but Elder didn't seem at all fazed. He was yelling into his walkie-talkie.

'John? John?'

'Dominic, where are you? I can hardly—' The signal broke up.

'I'm heading towards Jonathan Barker's home. We think he's Witch's target. Over.'

He listened to a lot of crackle and static. Then: 'Sorry, Dom . . . signal's break . . . didn't catch a . . . please rep—'

'We're out of range,' said Barclay.

'Yes,' said Elder, throwing the walkie-talkie on to the seat beside him. It bounced off the seat and on to the floor, where it erupted into static before dying. Elder looked out of the window. 'Right here!' Dominique slammed on the brakes and sent the car whipping around the corner. Barclay was desperately trying to fasten his seatbelt.

'You don't trust me, Michael?' she called. 'I am a Parisian driver. *C'est facile!*'

Elder reached between them for the police radio.

Jonathan Barker, Home Secretary, had a town house in Belgravia's Holbein Place. It was one of his three UK residences, the others being a converted vicarage in Dorset and an old hunting-lodge on Speyside. His address in London wasn't quite public knowledge, but neither was he a low-key minister – he'd given several early-morning doorstep interviews to the media during his short time in office. The parking-space in front of the house was kept free, courtesy of two bright red traffic-cones which sat in the road whenever Barker's chauffeured car was elsewhere. It was an arrangement which worked, mostly. The most frequent transgressors were workmen and tourists, who would shift the cones on to the pavement so as to have room to park their vans or BMWs.

Today, it was an Alfa Romeo.

The chauffeur swore under his breath and stopped the minister's car in the road, a little way behind the Alfa, giving the driver room to move it. Always supposing the driver was anywhere around. The chauffeur sounded the car-horn, just in case the driver was in one of the houses near the minister's.

The minister's bodyguard spotted something from his passenger seat. 'There's somebody still in the car,' he said. And so there was, a woman. She appeared to be consulting a map. The driver sounded his horn again.

'Come on, you dozy bint.'

'She must be deaf.'

'Come on.'

Throughout this exchange, Jonathan Barker sat in the back of the car with his private secretary. They were discussing an afternoon meeting, with the aid of an agenda on which the minister was scratching with a slim gold fountain-pen. Suddenly, the minister seemed to realise it was lunchtime. He handed the agenda to his private secretary and slipped the pen into his breast pocket.

'Sort it out, will you?' he said to the men in the front of the car. 'I'm going inside.'

And with that, he got out of his car. So did the private secretary. And so, with a muttered, 'I'll sort it out all right,' did the bodyguard.

And so did the woman. The chauffeur couldn't believe it. He rested his hand on the horn again and called out: 'Come on, darling, you can't park there!' But she appeared not to have heard him. The bodyguard was just behind her as she bent down, looking as though she was locking her car door. The minister and his private secretary were mounting the pavement behind the Alfa Romeo.

'Excuse me, miss, that's a private parking bay, I'm afraid.' The guard didn't think she'd heard him. Bloody foreigner. He touched her shoulder.

Witch, crouching, slammed her elbow back into the bodyguard's groin, then clasped the hand on her shoulder and twisted her whole body, taking the man's arm with it, turning it all the way round and up his back. He sank to his knees in pain. The butt of the Beretta smashed against the back of his neck. He slumped unconscious to the ground.

Now her gun was on the minister.

'Into the car!'

He hesitated.

'You,' she said to the blanching secretary, 'back into the minister's car. You,' to Jonathan Barker again, 'into *this* car.'

'Now look here . . .'

But the private secretary was already shuffling back to the Rover where the driver sat motionless, trying to decide whether to try ramming her or merely blocking her escape or even reversing to a safe distance. She settled his mind for him by swivelling and expertly shooting one front and one rear tyre. The driver yelped and ducked beneath the level of the windscreen. The private secretary had fallen to his knees and was crawling on all fours. Witch turned her eyes on Jonathan Barker.

'You're dead.'

People were looking out of their windows now. A few pedestrians had stopped and were watching from a safe distance. Jonathan Barker decided he'd stalled long enough. She walked around the car towards him. He opened the passenger door.

'No, the back,' she said. Her aim with the pistol looked steady as he opened the car's rear door and leaned down to get in.

'I think you must be making a—' The sentence went unfinished as Witch flipped the pistol and smashed the butt down on Jonathan Barker's skull. He fell into the car and she pushed his legs in after him, closing the door and running to the driver's side. Then she started the car and sent it hurtling out of the parking space. It would be a short drive. Her other car was parked and waiting.

As she drove off, the private secretary opened the Rover's passenger door.

'A lot of help you were,' he squealed at the chauffeur.

'I didn't notice you exactly *leaping* into action.'

'No, but at least I got the licence plate. Here, hand me that phone. We'll have the cunt in five minutes.'

But in five minutes, all they had was a general alert and the arrival of a single police car . . . which didn't even contain police.

'Who are you?' asked the private secretary. Neighbours had come out of their houses and were milling around. The bodyguard sat on the edge of the pavement, holding his head. A woman was trying to give him an aspirin and some water.

Elder took it all in with a single sweep: the flat car-tyres, the empty parking-space, the sickly looks on the faces of the three men.

'What happened?' he asked, ignoring the private secretary's question.

'Where are the bloody police?' asked the private secretary, ignoring Elder's. 'I called them.'

'They're a bit busy at Victoria Street. I suppose all available units have rushed down there.'

The man's interest was deflected for a moment. 'What happened?'

'A bomb. Nothing serious. It was just a . . .' A what? A flanker? Yes, that's what it was. A tactic to shift attention solidly and completely on to Victoria Street, so that *this* could happen. She'd bought herself valuable time. Five minutes already, and still no police had arrived. Too late to go chasing her now, though Elder could see Dominique was keen. She was still sitting in the police car's driving-seat, ready for the off. Barclay was getting the story from one of the neighbours who'd seen everything.

'It's a mess,' Elder said, more to himself than anyone else. 'A shambles. She led us all the way up the garden path and in through the front door. Only we were in the wrong house, the wrong garden, the wrong bloody street!'

What he still couldn't work out was the one simple question: why

Jonathan Barker? Why go second division when the premier league were there for the taking?

Why?

The question bothered him, and others, for the rest of the afternoon. He talked it through with Barclay and Dominique. He talked it through with Joyce Parry, and with Trilling and Greenleaf. Doyle was in hospital, though unwillingly. They were keeping him in overnight, if such were possible. Trilling, shaken by the bomb, had developed a stammer, but Greenleaf seemed fine. Certainly, he was up to the task of re-interviewing the Dutchman and informing him of Witch's devastating double-cross. Would the Dutchman's employers believe that he *didn't* know anything about it? Or would they suspect he must have been in on it with Witch?

Always supposing it *was* a double-cross. It was. The Dutchman was evidence of that.

The Dutchman was scared. They allowed him to watch the news reports on TV, just so he would know this was no bluff. He did not blink as he watched. And afterwards, with the tape recorders turning, he talked. But he had little enough to say. He told Greenleaf about Crane, told him where to find Christine Jones (they were close to finding her anyway, thirsty and frightened but otherwise unharmed). He wouldn't say anything about the men who'd employed him in the first place, the men who'd paid him to liaise with Witch. But he did admit to meeting her in Paris, at the Australian's apartment.

He did not, however, know the answer to the question: why Barker? He kept shaking his head disbelievingly. 'They paid her a million,' he kept saying, 'a million to kill the US President . . . and she pulls a stunt like this.' He looked up at Greenleaf. 'She must be crazy.'

Greenleaf tended to agree.

The media, of course, had their own ideas. First reaction was that the double-blow was the work of the IRA, of at least *two* active service units, one attacking the motorcade while the other abducted the Home Secretary. This made sense to the reporters: who else but the IRA would go to so much trouble to kidnap the Home Secretary? Then the speculation started, all about IRA 'cells' in London and how there might be more of them, about safe houses where the gang (numbering at least a dozen) could be hiding. There was a blackout on the real story, of course. None of Jonathan Barker's neighbours had been allowed to speak to the media, and those who had had been disbelieved. One woman? No news editor was going to believe that. So the idea of the gang stuck, and Londoners were asked to keep their eyes open for anything suspicious.

London, thought Elder: that's the last place she'll be. He was sitting in Joyce Parry's office. Outside, Barclay was showing Dominique around. It looked as though MI5 had adopted her, which didn't bother Elder: a friend in the DST camp would no doubt be welcome at the department, and especially one who might rise through the ranks . . . There had been a potential spot of bother earlier on, when some furious policemen had tried to arrest her for taking their car, but Elder had calmed them.

He was calm himself now; well, calmer. Again, they'd come so close and yet were back to square one. For a couple of naive, undisciplined cavaliers,

Barclay and Dominique hadn't done so badly. He took *The Times* obituary column from his pocket and read it again. Had this started the whole thing rolling in Witch's mind? Had this somehow persuaded her that instead of fulfilling her objective she should run away with the Home Secretary? It still didn't make sense. Marion Barker, *née* Rose. Secretary to Jonathan Barker . . . then his first wife died and later on he married Marion. Nothing so unusual about that. Tireless worker for various charities and so on. Lifelong interest in spiritualism . . . What else did he know about her? What did he know about Jonathan Barker? Not much.

'Dominic, sorry I've been so long.' Joyce Parry came into the room, went to her desk, and began lifting files out of her briefcase.

'How did it go?'

'PM's furious, of course. He doesn't know what's worse, the scratches on the delegates' limos or someone buggering off with Jonathan Barker.' She looked down at him. 'You got close.'

'Not close enough. If I'd let Barclay go on digging last night instead of sending him off to bed . . .'

'Don't blame yourself. I don't know anyone who's done more on this.'

'Barclay has. So has Miss Herault.'

'And whose idea was it to involve Barclay in the first place?'

He smiled. 'As you know, my motives at the time were not exactly . . .'

'Honourable?'

He nodded.

'Well, honourable or not, we came bloody close.'

'Is that what you told the PM?'

'Of course. No doubt Commander Trilling will tell him something else entirely, but we'll see.' She sat down at last, leaning back in her chair, arms falling down over its sides. A brief smile passed between them, a shared memory of the previous night. Then it was back to business. 'So what now?'

Elder sat forwards. 'Joyce, I need to see the file on Barker. I mean the *real* file, warts and all.'

She formed her lips into an O. 'Absolutely not.'

'Joyce . . .'

'Do you know how restricted that is? *I* hardly get access to those files.'

'Joyce, you've got to understand. His wife's obituary set Witch off. The answer's got to lie somewhere in Barker's past, or somewhere in his wife's. Jonathan Barker's life is at stake here. I think *he'd* want me to see that file.'

She was shaking her head. She was still shaking it as she sighed and said, 'I'll see what I can do.'

'Now, Joyce, it's got to be now.'

'Dominic, it's not that simple.'

'Yes it is. Get the file, Joyce. Please.'

She looked at him, considering. 'You always have to take shortcuts, don't you?'

'Always.'

'You want her badly.'

'Very badly,' he agreed.

Joyce Parry sat for a moment, her eyes on her desk. 'I'll get the file,' she said at last.

Sitting in Joyce Parry's office a little later, Michael Barclay looked decidedly grumpy. And not without cause. Everything he'd shown Dominique, from his computer to his wastepaper-bin, had been received with a shrug and five short words: 'We have better in France.' She'd been impressed by none of it. She sat beside him now, one leg crossed over the other, her foot waggling in the air, and looked around the room. Inwardly, she was still crackling. Her drive through the London streets had been exhilarating. They'd come so close to confronting the assassin. And yet in the end, it was reduced to this: sitting around in an office waiting for something to happen. She felt she would *explode* with the energy inside her. Why didn't someone *do* something?

Dominic Elder knew what she was thinking. It was the sort of thing he'd have been thinking twenty-five years ago. Who needs patience? Let's get out there and *hunt*. Only just over two years ago, that same instinct had led him straight to retirement and a scar that would never disappear.

'The gang's all here,' said Joyce Parry, walking through the ever-open door. She paused inside the room, turned, and closed the door behind her. Then she went to her desk and sat down. She did not have a file with her.

'Nobody told me there was going to be a party,' she said to Elder, having first smiled a greeting towards Dominique.

'I thought, after what they've been through, Mr Barclay and Miss Herault deserved not to be left out of anything at this late stage.'

It smacked of a prepared speech. Parry didn't reply to it. Instead she said, 'I've changed my mind.'

'Yes, so I see.'

'I've read the file, Dominic. There's a lot in there that isn't relevant to this case.'

'How can you be sure?'

'I can't. So instead of reading the file, you can question me. I'll answer anything. That way, whatever isn't touched upon isn't touched upon. It stays secret. Agreed?'

Elder shrugged. 'It seems a long-winded way of—'

'Agreed?'

'Agreed,' he said. Barclay and Dominique were paying attention now, their own problems forgotten. Dominique burst in with the first question.

'Is the Home Secretary suspected of being a double agent?'

Joyce Parry smiled. 'No,' she said.

'I think you're on the wrong track,' Elder told Dominique gently. 'What we have here is something altogether more . . . personal.' He turned to Parry. The idea, growing in his mind these past hours, was monstrous, almost unthinkable. Yet it had to be tested. 'Did Jonathan Barker have an affair with his secretary?'

'Which secretary?'

'Marion Rose.'

Joyce Parry nodded. 'That's my understanding.'

'This was before his first wife died?'

'Yes.'

'Long before she died?'

'Probably, yes. A number of years.'

Elder nodded thoughtfully. Doyle had known something about it, had heard some rumour. Hence his nickname for Barker. 'Did his wife know?'

'I shouldn't think so. She wasn't the type to keep that sort of knowledge to herself.'

Now Barclay interrupted. 'There's no suspicion surrounding her death?'

'No, the post-mortem was meticulous. She died from natural causes.'

'To wit?'

'Lung cancer. She was a heavy smoker.'

'Yes,' said Elder, 'so I seem to remember. What about Barker during this time?'

'What time?'

'The time he was having an affair with Marion Rose. How was his career shaping up?'

'Pretty well. He wasn't quite in politics then, of course. But he was in the running for a candidacy. He got it, won the seat, and that was him into parliament.'

'At quite a young age.'

'Twenty-nine.'

'Yes, twenty-nine. No children by the first marriage?'

'No.'

'Did the first marriage have its problems then?'

'Not that we know of. Apart from the glaring fact that Barker was having at least one affair.'

'This was his second marriage – Marion's first?'

'That's right.'

'A quiet woman?'

'Yes, until recently. I mean, her profile increased.'

'Mmm, the image-men got their hands on her. Charitable good works and so on, but unassuming with it . . . the model MP's wife.'

'I suppose you could say that.'

'He didn't get into parliament at the first attempt, did he?'

'No.'

'Why not?'

'Because he lost.'

'Yes, but *why* did he lose?'

A shrug. 'Swing to the—'

'But *why*, Joyce?'

She paused, swallowed. 'There was a rumour he was a bit of a ladies' man. A localised rumour, but it put enough voters off.'

'But by the second by-election?'

'He was cleaner than clean.'

'And has been since?'

'Yes.'

'And he's risen and risen.'

'Not exactly meteoric though.'

'No, slow, meticulous, I agree with you there. And there've been no scandals?'

'Not in parliament, no.'

'But outside parliament?'

'Just the one you referred to, and that was never public.'

'What? His fling with Marion? Mm, wouldn't have gone down well though, would it? Wouldn't go down well even now, even as ancient history – MP sleeping with secretary while wife's dying of cancer. Bit of a black mark. He was a millionaire?'

'By the time he was twenty-one.'

'Father's money?'

'Mostly, yes, but he put it to good use.'

'A wise investor.'

'A chain of record shops, actually, just in time to clean up on the Beatles and the Stones.'

'Like I say, a wise investor.' Elder rubbed at his forehead. 'To get back to his affair with Marion, what do we know about it?'

'You tell me.'

'All right,' said Elder, 'I will. What happened to the child?'

'Child?'

'There *was* a child, wasn't there?'

Joyce Parry looked down at the desk. 'We don't know for sure.'

'No? But there were "localised rumours", yes?'

'Yes.'

'Dear me, a pregnant secretary, a wife dying of cancer, and he's put himself forward as a constituency candidate. Maybe for the second and potentially the last time. I mean, the last time if he didn't win.' Elder tutted and turned to Barclay. 'What would *you* do, Michael?'

Barclay started at the mention of his name, then thought for a second. 'If I was a millionaire . . . pay off the secretary. She could go and look after the kid in secret, a monthly allowance or something.'

'Mmm . . . what about you, Miss Herault?'

'Me?' Dominique looked startled. 'Oh, I don't know. I suppose I would perhaps persuade my lover to abort.'

Elder nodded. 'Yes, that's probably what I'd do. What about you, Joyce?'

'An abortion, yes, if she'd agree to it.'

'Ah . . .' Elder raised his index finger. 'If she'd agree to it. What if she wouldn't?'

'Tell her it's finished between us?' suggested Barclay.

'That would break her heart, Michael,' said Elder. 'She *loves* you. She'd do anything but leave you. It would turn her against you if you spurned her. She might go to anybody with her story, the papers, the TV, anybody.'

'Then we're back to square one,' said Joyce Parry.

'If she loves this man,' said Dominique, 'surely she will agree eventually to the termination, no?'

'Yes,' said Elder. 'Yes, she'd agree all right. The question is: would she go through with it?'

Dominique gave a big shrug. 'We cannot ask her, she is dead . . . isn't she?'

'Oh yes, she's dead all right.'

'Then who can we ask? I do not understand.'

'It's not as though we've got a crystal ball,' said Barclay.

'Michael,' said Elder, turning to him and slapping a hand down onto his knee, 'but that's precisely what we *have* got. And that's exactly what we'll use . . .'

With Trilling's blessing, Greenleaf took a breather long enough for him to visit Doyle in hospital. Doyle's head had been bandaged, and his face was bruised. He was awake, but kept his eyes tightly shut for most of the short visit and complained of a thumping headache. A nurse had warned Greenleaf of this, and he had been told not to spend too long 'with your friend'.

Walking towards the bed, Greenleaf wondered about that word 'friend'. *Were* Doyle and he friends? Certainly they were closer than they had been a scant fortnight before. They worked well enough together, but that was only because they were so utterly different in outlook and temperament. The shortcomings of each were made up by the other.

The hospital was hectic. Victoria Street victims, being treated for cuts and shock. In some operating theatre, they were working on what remained of Traynor's leg. But Doyle's ward was quiet enough. He was lying with his head propped on a single white pillow. They'd changed him out of his suit and into regulation pyjamas, thick cotton with vertical stripes the colour of uncooked liver. The nurse had asked Greenleaf what they should do with Mr Doyle's handgun. Greenleaf carried it with him now, inside a rolled-up white carrier. Doyle's shoulder-holster was in there too.

Greenleaf still hadn't handed in his own gun. Somehow he was getting used to it, nestling beneath his jacket there.

'Hello, Doyle.' He dragged a chair over to the bedside. The cabinet was empty save for a jug of water and a plastic beaker. Greenleaf placed the carrier beside the water-jug. Doyle opened his eyes long enough to watch this happening.

'Is that my gun in there?'

'Yes.'

'Thank God for that. Thought maybe I'd lost the bloody thing. Bet they'd have taken it out of my wages.'

'There's these too.' Greenleaf produced a packet of mints. 'From Commander Trilling.'

'It's the thought that counts, so they say.'

Greenleaf smiled. 'How are you feeling?'

'Chipper. Can you get me out of here?'

'They're holding you overnight.'

Doyle groaned. 'I was seeing my bird tonight.'

'Give me her number and I'll send your apologies.'

Doyle grinned, showing stained teeth. 'I'll bet you would, John-boy. No, it's all right, let her sweat. She'll be all the keener tomorrow. Have we caught that bitch yet?'

'Not yet.'

'Leading us a merry dance, isn't she?'

'Have you heard about Barker?'

'Yeah, couldn't happen to a nicer bloke. What does she want with him?'

Greenleaf shrugged. 'Nobody seems to know.'

'We were set up, weren't we?'

'It looks like she set *everybody* up, Doyle.'

'Yeah, everybody. What does Elder say?'

'I don't know.'

'You don't know much, do you, pal? Where is he?'

'Back in his office, I suppose.'

Doyle tried to sit up, though the effort cost him dear. He gritted his teeth and levered himself on to his elbows. Greenleaf rose from his chair to help, but Doyle growled the offer aside. 'Listen,' he said, 'stick close to Elder, John. He knows something we don't, believe me. If anyone catches her, it's going to be him. Stick close, and *we'll* get a pop at her too. Savvy?'

Greenleaf nodded, then saw that Doyle's eyes were closed again. 'I savvy,' he said. Doyle nodded back at him, and let his head fall back on to the pillow.

Greenleaf was remembering . . . remembering the note Witch had left for Elder. What special bond was there between them? Maybe Doyle had a point.

'Last time I had a head like this,' Doyle said, 'was the morning after that party in the boxing club. Remember it?'

'I remember it.'

Doyle smiled faintly. 'Good night that, wasn't it? Knew back then that you were a good man, John. Knew it even back then.' Doyle's voice grew slurred and faint. 'I've still got that French booze. When I get out we'll have a bit of a party. Good man . . .'

Greenleaf waited till he was asleep, the breathing regular, then he got up, moved the chair away, and lifted the carrier bag from the bedside cabinet. He touched Doyle's shoulder lightly, smiling down on the sleeping figure.

'You're not so bad yourself,' he said quietly, almost too quietly to be heard.

Barclay's car had been brought back from Calais, so they drove south in that. Barclay did the driving, while Dominique sat beside him thumping his leg and demanding that he go faster.

'Either that or we swap places. And turn off that noise.'

'Noise?' Barclay bristled. 'That's Verdi.'

Elder sat alone in the back seat. He wasn't in a mood for conversation, so he stared from the window and kept his responses brief whenever a question was asked of him, until both Barclay and Dominique seemed to take the hint.

He had seen it suddenly, crystal clear. Barker's second wife, so recently deceased, had been a spiritualist. When Elder had visited the fairground, the palm-reader had been too direct in her denial of having seen Witch. It had jarred at the time, but there'd seemed no real connection until now. His back was burning, and he had to sit forward in his seat so as not to graze it against the car's rough fabric. Have patience, Susanne, he thought to himself. Have patience. He knew he was addressing not his daughter but himself.

This time when they reached Brighton he knew exactly where to go. A few of the bigger rides had already been packed away and transported elsewhere. He still had Ted's list in his diary, all the other fairs taking place in the region.

As they headed for The Level, he sat right forward, his head between Dominique's and Barclay's. 'Now listen,' he said, 'hopefully I'm going to have a word with a ball-gazer. If she's still around, that is. I want you two to take a look around . . . a *good* look around.'

'You think Witch may be here?'

'It's possible.'

'Shouldn't we have some back-up?'

'Does she know what you look like?'

'No.'

'Then why do we need back-up? Anyway, there'll be back-up. Turn left here.'

Barclay turned left. It was early evening and the fair was doing some business, but not much. A late-afternoon downpour had drenched the spirits of the holidaymakers. Elder knew where Gypsy Rose's caravan was. It was near the ghost train. Only the ghost train had gone, and in its place was a stall of some kind. But the palmist's caravan was still there, hooked up to an estate-car. He could see it from the road. 'Drop me here,' Elder ordered. The car slowed to a stop, and he got out. 'Park at the end of the road and walk back. Remember, you're on holiday. You're just having a look. Don't go behaving like snoopers or coppers or anything else. Just behave . . . naturally.' The door closed, and Elder watched the car move off. Dominique seemed to put her hand to Barclay's hair, ruffling it. He watched a moment longer before walking across the grass towards Gypsy Rose Pellengro's caravan.

'Mr Elder?'

The man who confronted him was heavy-built, balding. He had his hands deep in the pockets of a windcheater beneath which he wore a white T-shirt. He looked like a manual worker, maybe a carpenter or builder, but respectable. He was one of Special Branch's best.

Elder nodded, looking around. 'Anything?'

'Quiet as the grave. I don't know how she affords that Volvo of hers.'

'Her kid has money.'

Late on Sunday night, Joyce Parry had reported to Elder Bandorff's mentions of tarots, clairvoyance and psychoanalysis. First thing Monday morning, Elder had briefed the man supplied by Special Branch. Not that he thought Witch would creep back to the fair, but there was always the chance.

Even so, he'd still not been sure of the connection between a gypsy palm reader and a female assassin. Marion Rose, he now knew, was the connection.

'Don't wander off,' he warned the undercover officer. Then he paused before the caravan door and knocked twice.

'It's open.'

Elder turned the rickety handle and let himself in.

It took her a moment to recognise him. 'I thought you'd be back.'

'Second sight?'

'No, I just got a feeling from you . . . a bad feeling.'

'You know why I'm here?'

She was seated on a bench at a table, and motioned for him to sit opposite her. A tarot deck lay on the table. She gathered the oversized cards up.

'No,' she said, 'I've no idea.'

'I don't know what you call her . . . what you christened her . . . but *we* call her Witch.'

'Witch?' She frowned, shuffling the cards slowly. 'Funny name. Nothing to do with your daughter then?'

'You know it's not.'

'Yes, I know.'

'You knew that day too. Do you know what she's done?'

'What?'

He looked around the caravan. There was a small portable TV on the floor in one corner, and a radio on the edge of the sink. 'You really don't know?' he asked.

She shrugged. 'Why should I?'

'Surely someone at the fair has said *something*?'

'What has she done?' she asked, rather too quickly.

'She's abducted her father.'

Rose Pellengro flinched. A few of the cards fell from her hands to the table. Elder picked up one of them. It was the High Priestess. He picked up another. It was Strength.

'Linking the Abyss to the Centre,' Rose Pellengro murmured, looking at the two cards. She paused. 'Abducted? I don't know what you're talking about.'

'I thought I was talking to someone with *vision*,' said Elder disappointedly. 'Very well, I'll make it a bit clearer. She has kidnapped Jonathan Barker.'

The cards fell to the table in a heap. The woman's cheeks reddened.

'Was Marion Rose one of your . . . clients?' Elder asked softly.

Rose Pellengro seemed deep in thought. Then she nodded. 'Oh yes, she was a regular. We seemed to have an affinity. She'd travel miles to come and see me.'

Elder nodded. 'This affinity, she felt it, too, didn't she? So much so that she confided in you.'

Pellengro smiled. 'This was in the days *after* priests but before psychiatrists. Yes, she told me all about her . . . her problems.'

'One particular problem, I think.'

'Ah yes, one problem. A large one.'

'She was pregnant by Jonathan Barker, and he wanted her to get rid of the child.'

Rose Pellengro eyed him shrewdly. 'You know a lot.'

'But not all of it.'

She nodded slowly, thoughtfully. 'Yes,' she said. 'His career had to come first. He twisted her round.'

'What happened?'

'Marion didn't want to lose the child. She was very religious in her own way. She was a *believer*. I decided to help her.'

'You took the child, fostered it?'

'As far as Barker was concerned, Marion had gone to a clinic. Actually, she stayed here with me. When the baby was born, I kept it.'

Elder released a long-held breath. This was what he had suspected, the truth of Witch's identity. 'Did she . . . did the mother keep in touch?'

'Oh yes.' Pellengro sifted through the cards. 'At first she kept in touch all the time. I thought maybe Barker would become suspicious, but not him.' She tapped her head. 'He was too stupid, his mind only on himself.'

'Then what?'

'Then?' A shrug. 'Marion started visiting less and less. By that time,

Barker's wife had died. They were to be married. More children arrived . . . born in wedlock. *Proper* children. She stopped coming altogether. She never came again.'

'And the child? The girl?'

A faint smile. 'You call her Witch, but to me she's Brigid Anastasia. Brigid, the Celtic goddess of fire, Anastasia, resurrection. Brigid Anastasia . . . A real mouthful, isn't it? I always used to call her Biddy. I brought her up, mister. I educated her as best I could. She was always wild. Wild like fire.' Her eyes were glistening. 'She once stabbed a boy who was bothering her. Then at fourteen she ran off with an Irishman. He'd been hanging around the fair for weeks. We were in Liverpool. When she went, I thought he'd killed her or something. But she sent me a letter from Ireland. She sent a lot of letters in the early days. Then she didn't send any at all. Instead, she'd just turn up at my door. I never even recognised her half the time.'

'But this time . . . this trip . . . it was different?'

'Different, yes. Because she'd found out who her mother was.'

'How?'

The woman shrugged again. 'She had vague memories of a lady visiting her when she was a toddler, picking her up and hugging her and crying and making her cry, too.' A tear slid down Rose Pellengro's left cheek. 'And when she was a bit older, I told her a little. Not much, but enough.' She sniffed. 'Enough so that when she read the death notice . . . One of the papers had a photo of Marion. Biddy wasn't daft. She remembered all right. And she knew now who her father was and what he'd done.'

She reached into the cuff of her cardigan and tugged out a small lace handkerchief with which to wipe her eyes and blow her nose.

'Did she tell you what she was going to do?'

Pellengro shook her head. 'Oh no, nothing like that. She just said she wanted to hear the story. Well, she's old enough, isn't she? So I told her the whole thing. I thought maybe she'd . . . well, I didn't think she'd . . . Oh God, what does she want him for?'

'What do you think?'

'*I* don't know.'

'Tell me, what do you think she's been doing all these years?'

'She's never said.'

'And you've no idea?'

'I thought maybe a prostitute?'

Elder shook his head.

'What then?'

'Never mind. Where will she take him?'

'God in heaven, how would I know that?'

'We've got to find her, you know that, don't you? If we're too late, she may be charged with murder.'

'Oh, she wouldn't kill him, would she? Little Biddy? I know she's been a bit wild in her time, but she's a woman now.'

He gripped her hands in his own. 'Rosa, tell me what you told her. Tell me *everything* you told her.'

She stared at him wide-eyed. 'Who are you? What are you? Are you the police?'

'I'm a father,' he said.

She blew her nose again, staring at him. Then she began to gather up the tarot, and as she did so, she started to speak.

Almost half an hour later, he made his way out into the evening air. His legs were stiff, and he rubbed them. He gestured to the Special Branch man, who came over to him.

'Stick around,' Elder ordered. 'She might come back.'

There was no sign of Barclay and Dominique. He had choices now, several choices, and he was keen to get away from this place. He passed Barnaby's Gun Stall.

'Here, guv, have a go?' cried the young man. He didn't recognise Elder. The wooden cut-out was still there, the target destroyed with such accuracy. *A young lady* . . . The whole fair was Witch's cover, because she was part of it and always had been.

Where were they? Then he heard a shriek, and he saw them. Dominique was on the dodgems, Barclay watching from the sidelines and smiling. She shrieked again and tried to avoid a collision, but too late. Elder could not help but be affected by the scene. He stood, leaning against a rail, and watched. Barclay saw him at last and joined him.

'Sorry, sir,' he said.

'No need to apologise, Michael. Let's call it necessary R and R. Listen, there's something I want to get from the car. Just point me in the general direction and give me the keys.'

Barclay dug the keys out of his pocket. 'The car's parked on Islingword Road. Top of Richmond Terrace and turn right.'

Elder nodded. 'Thanks,' he said, turning away.

'You're coming back, aren't you, sir?'

Elder nodded again. He wanted to say, It's not your fight, it's not worth the risk. Instead, he glanced towards Dominique. She made up his mind for him.

He wondered what they would do. Maybe a train back to London. Or stay the night in Brighton. Elder had never seen himself as a matchmaker. He didn't see himself as one now. All he knew was that he had to do this alone. The young couple represented too much baggage, too much of a responsibility. And besides, there was a score he had to settle. Silverfish.

Wolf Bandorff had said Witch hated men. In fact, she hated only the one man. Aged thirteen, she had asked Rose Pellengro about her parents. Rose had told her some of the story, enough to fuel hatred but not enough to identify the people involved. Witch had pressed, but Rose Pellengro would say no more. But the obituary of Marion Barker had struck a chord, and this time, confronted with the name, Rose had admitted the truth. The man who had forced Witch's mother into discarding her was Jonathan Barker. Suddenly, there was someone for her to focus her vague, long-held hatred on. The Home Secretary.

The young Brigid Anastasia had run away with an Irishman. It was a short sea-crossing from Liverpool to Ireland. Maybe the man himself was a terrorist, or maybe she had drifted into the company of terrorists afterwards. Female and a teenager she would have proved useful to the IRA, running cross-border errands. Perhaps they had even sent her as far as Germany to liaise with Wolfgang Bandorff and his group. From Germany, she'd drifted south to Italy. In a sense, she'd been drifting ever since. She had no cause, no real set of ideals. All she'd had was anger, an anger she could do little to assuage. Until now.

Elder didn't doubt that she had taken on the London job before discovering her father's identity. But when she did discover his identity from the newspaper in the Australian's apartment, she had come to a decision. Instead of going ahead with the assassination, she would carry out a stunning double-bluff, fooling both her employers *and* the security forces. It was no mistake that she'd made such a noisy and messy entry into the country. She'd wanted them to know she was there. And while security had been tightened around the summit, while all that effort and manpower had been focused on the gathering of world leaders, Witch's real target had gone unnoticed and underprotected. She'd taken her employers' money, doubtless with thoughts of retirement and disappearance after this last task: dealing with her father.

The Alfa Romeo had been found abandoned off the King's Road. No doubt she'd switched cars. The Alfa had been stolen the previous night in Croydon. There was no way of knowing from where the second car had been stolen, or what make it was. Police were now on the lookout for any one of forty-six reported stolen vehicles from in and around the London area. Elder had the list with him. Roadblocks had been set up, but only on major roads, a stupid and wasteful procedure only set in motion because it would mean the police were doing *something* to stop her getting away with it.

Well, Elder was doing something too. From his talk with Rose Pellengro, he had noted six possible locations, six places where Witch might take her father before . . . before what? Killing him? Would that be enough for her? Whatever, Elder knew she would not linger over her task, so he dare not linger over his.

Joyce Parry was in a meeting in her office when the telephone buzzed. She picked it up.

'Hello?'

'Mrs Parry? Barclay here.'

'Michael, are you still in Brighton?'

'Well . . . yes, actually.'

She knew from his tone that something was wrong. She sat forward in her seat. 'What is it?'

'It's Mr Elder. He's gone off in my car.'

'Gone off where?'

'We don't know. He said he had to go and fetch something . . .'

Joyce Parry rose to her feet, taking the telephone apparatus with her, holding the body of the telephone in one hand, the receiver in the other.

'Has he talked to the palm reader?'

'Yes.'

'What did he find out?'

'He didn't say.'

Parry let out a sharp hiss of breath.

'Sorry,' said Barclay, sounding despondent.

'Michael, go talk to the palm reader, find out what she told him.' She looked at her visitor, as though only now remembering that he was there. 'Hold on a second,' she said into the receiver, before muffling the mouthpiece against her shoulder. 'Elder,' she said. 'He's gone haring off in Barclay's car.'

Greenleaf got up from his chair. 'We need a description of the car.' He came to the desk and took a notebook and pen from his pocket.

'Michael?' Parry said into the mouthpiece. 'What kind of car is it?' She listened. 'White Ford Fiesta, okay. And registration number?' Barclay gave it to her, and she repeated it for Greenleaf. 'Right,' she said. 'Go talk to Madame Whatever-her-name, and call me straight back.'

'Will do,' said Barclay's voice. 'Just the one thing. There's something I've been meaning to ask. It's just come back to me. What was Operation Silver—'

But Joyce Parry was already severing the connection. Greenleaf took the receiver from her and pressed some numbers home, pausing for his call to be answered.

'Inspector Greenleaf here,' he said. 'I've got a car needs tracing. Notify every force in the country. As soon as anyone sees it, I want to be the first to know. Understood?'

Joyce Parry slumped back down on to her chair and rubbed her face with her hand. Dominic, Dominic. Where the hell are you? *And why don't you ever learn?*

He drove first to Salisbury, where, according to Marion Rose, Jonathan Barker had first held her hand, first planted a kiss on her cheek. He had done so as they came out of the cathedral after attending a choral concert. Elder drove up to the cathedral, got out, walked around, got back into the car, cruised around the town for twenty minutes, then headed off. Second stop: a hotel in Henley-on-Thames. Pellengro told him this was where Marion and Barker had first made love. The fortune teller even recalled the hotel's name.

'In my business, a good memory helps. You sometimes get a client coming back after two or three years. Helps if you can remember what you said to them last time.'

He parked in the hotel car park, and checked the other parked cars for any on the stolen list. None. The hotel itself was busy, but there was no sign of Witch. Tired, he stopped at a burger drive-in and bought coffee, then bought more later when he filled the car with petrol. He was headed north, doing this because, as with the roadblocks, there was nothing else to do. He had no leads, no real ideas. He didn't have anything.

And no one would thank him for any of this anyway. Running off on his own, just like in the old days. Barclay would tell Joyce, and Joyce would not be pleased. She would not be pleased at all. Last night, she had massaged his back.

'It hasn't healed,' she said. 'I thought by now it would have.'

'Sometimes it clears up, then it starts again.'

She had traced the outline with her finger. 'Is it sore?'

'More itchy than sore, but then if I scratch it . . . yes, it's sore. And I know what you're thinking: serves me right. Which is true. I learned my lesson.'

'Did you, Dominic? I wonder. I wonder if Silverfish taught you anything.'

Silverfish, stupid name for a stupid operation. A terrorist cell in London. Kept under surveillance. The mention of a meeting to take place in the city between senior members of four European terrorist organisations. But the whole thing had been botched, the terrorists escaping. Including a woman, a woman Elder thought he knew. There was an immediate clampdown: checks on airports, ferry terminals, fishing ports. One of the terrorists, a Spaniard, was arrested at Glasgow Airport. Then came Charlie Giltrap's phone call.

'Might be something or nothing, Mr Elder. Just that there's this woman been sleeping rough on a bit of waste ground near all that building work in Docklands. She don't talk, and she don't look right, if you know what I mean. I mean, she don't fit in.'

Which had been enough to send Elder down to Docklands, to an area of scrapyards, building-sites and derelict wastes. It was late evening, and he hadn't told anyone he was going. He'd just do a recce, and if back-up was needed he'd phone for it.

Besides, he had his Browning in his pocket.

After half an hour's hunting, he saw a crouched figure beside what remained of a warehouse wall. It was eating sliced white bread from a bag, but scurried off mouse-like at his approach. So he followed.

'I only want a word,' he called. 'I'm not going to move you on or anything. I just want to talk.'

He cornered her in the shell of another building. It had no roof left, just four walls, a gaping doorway, and windows without glass. She was crouched again, and her eyes were fearful, cowed. But her clothes weren't quite ragged enough, were they? He came closer.

'I just want to talk.'

And then he was close enough to stare into her eyes, and he knew. He knew it was all pretence. She wasn't fearful or cowed or anything like that. She was Witch. And she saw that he knew.

And she was fast. The kick hit his kneecap, almost shattering it. He stumbled, and the flat edge of her fist chopped into his throat. He was gagging, but managed somehow to get the gun out of his pocket.

'I know you,' she said, kicking the gun cleanly out of his hand. 'You're called Elder. You've got a nice thick file on me, haven't you?' Her next kick connected her heel to his temple. Fresh pain flared through him. 'You call me Witch.' Her voice was calm, almost ethereal. A kick to the ribs. Christ, what kind of shoes was she wearing? They were like weapons. 'You're called Dominic Elder. Even *we* have our sources, Mr Elder.' Then she chuckled, crouching in front of him, lifting his head. It was dark, he couldn't make out . . . 'Dominic Elder. A priest's name. You should have been a priest.'

Then she rose and he heard her footsteps crunch over gravel and glass. She stopped, picked up his pistol. He heard her emptying the bullets from it. 'Browning,' she mused. 'Not great.' Then the gun hit the ground again. And now she was coming back towards him. 'Will you put this in your file, Mr Elder? Or will you be too ashamed? How long have you been tracking me?'

She was lifting his arms behind him, slipping off his jacket.

'Years,' he mumbled. He needed a few moments. A few moments to recover. If she'd give him a few more moments, then he'd . . .

'Years? You must be my biggest fan.' She chuckled again, and tore his shirt with a single tug, tore it all the way up his back. He felt his sweat begin to chill. Christ, what was . . . ? Then her hand came to within an inch of his face and lifted a piece of broken glass. She stood up, and he thought she was moving away again. He swallowed and began to speak.

'I want to ask you something. It's important to me.'

Too late, he felt her foot swinging towards him. The blow connected with his jaw, sending him spinning out of pain and into darkness.

'No interviews,' she was saying. 'But I'd better give my biggest fan an autograph, hadn't I?'

And then, with Elder unconscious, she had carved a huge letter W into his back, and had left him bleeding to death. But Charlie Giltrap had decided Elder might need help. It was a rough area down there; a man like Mr Elder . . . well, he might need a translator if nothing else. Charlie had found him. Charlie had called for the ambulance. Charlie had saved Elder's life.

One hundred and eighty-five stitches they gave him. And he lay on his front in a hospital bed feeling each and every one of them tightly knitting his skin. His hearing had been affected by one of her kicks – affected temporarily, but it gave him little to do but think. Think about how fast she'd been, how slow he'd been in response. Think of the mistake he'd made going there in the first place. Think maybe it was time for an easier life.

But, really, life hadn't been easier since. In some ways it had been harder. This time he'd shoot first. Then maybe his back would heal, maybe the huge scar wouldn't itch any more.

His next stop was another hotel, this time near Kenilworth Castle, the probable site of Witch's conception. Barker, usually so cautious, had one night drunk too many whiskies, and wouldn't let his secretary say no later on, after closing time, up in their shared room. The hotel was locked and silent for the night. There were only two cars in the car park and neither was on the stolen list. Three more to go: York, Lancaster and Berwick. If he pushed on, he could have them all checked by late-morning. If he pushed on.

Dominique booked them into the hotel, pretending that Barclay also was French and could speak no English. The receptionist looked disapproving.

'Any luggage?' she sniffed.

'No luggage,' said Dominique, barely suppressing a giggle. The woman stared at her from over the top of her half-moon glasses. Dominique looked back over her shoulder to where Barclay stood just inside the hotel door. She motioned for him to join her, but he shook his head, causing her to giggle again before calling to him: 'I need some money!'

So at last, reluctantly, he came towards the desk. He was worried about Dominic Elder. He'd argued that they should go back to London, but Dominique, pragmatic as ever, had asked what good that would do? So instead they'd had a few drinks and eaten fish and chips out of paper. And they'd played some of the machines in the pier's amusement arcade.

'This is a family hotel,' warned the receptionist.

They both nodded towards her, assuring her of their agreement. So she gave them a key and took their money and had them sign their names in the register. When Barclay signed himself Jean-Claude Separt, Dominique nearly collapsed. But upstairs, suddenly alone together in the small room with its smells of air-freshener and old carpet, they were shy. They calmed. They grew sober together, lying dressed on the top of the bed, kissing, hugging.

'I wonder where Elder is,' Barclay said at last.

'Me, too,' murmured Dominique drowsily.

He continued to stroke her hair as she slept, and he turned his head towards the large window, through which seeped the light and the noises of night-time. He thought of Susanne Elder, and of Dominique's father. He hoped Dominic Elder would get an answer to his question. Later still, he closed his own eyes and prayed for restful dreams . . .

It wasn't quite dawn when Elder reached York. The streets were deserted. This was where Marion had told Barker she was pregnant, and where he'd insisted she have an abortion. Poor Marion, she'd chosen the time and the place to tell him. She'd chosen them carefully and, no doubt to her mind, well. A weekend in York, a sunny Sunday morning. A stroll along the city walls. Radiant, bursting to tell him her news. Poor Marion. What had she thought? Had she thought he'd be pleased? She'd been disappointed. But where on the city wall had she told him? Pellengro hadn't known, so neither would Witch. Elder, many years ago, had walked the circuit of York's protective city wall. He knew it could take him an hour or more. He parked near Goodramgate, a large stone archway. There was a flight of steps to the side of the 'gate' itself leading up on to the ramparts. A small locked gate stood in his way, but he climbed over it. It struck him that Witch would have trouble dragging a prone body over such a gate. But on second thoughts, he couldn't imagine the Home Secretary would have much trouble climbing over it with a gun pointing at his back.

Parts of the wall were floodlit, and the street-lighting was adequate for his needs. The sky was clear and the night cold. He could see his breath in the air in front of him as he walked. He could only walk so far in this direction before the wall ended. It started again, he knew, a little further on. He retraced his steps and crossed Goodramgate, this time walking along the wall in the direction of York Minster itself. He hadn't gone ten yards when he saw the body. It was propped against the wall, legs straight out in front of it. He bent down and saw that it was Jonathan Barker. He'd been shot once through the temple. Elder touched Barker's skin. It was cool, slightly damp. The limbs were still mobile however. He hadn't been dead long. Elder stood up and looked around him. Nobody, obviously, had heard the shot. There were houses in the vicinity, and pubs and hotels. It surprised him that no one had heard anything. A single shot to the temple: execution-style. Well, at least it had been quick.

There was a sudden noise of impact near him, and dust flew from the wall.

A bullet!

He flattened himself on the wall, his legs lying across Barker's. He took his pistol from its shoulder-holster and slipped off the safety. Where had the shot come from? He looked around. He was vulnerable up here, like a duck on a fairground shooting-range. He had to get back to the steps. She was using a silencer. That's why nobody had heard anything. A silencer would limit her gun's range and accuracy, so probably she wasn't *that* close. If she'd been close, she wouldn't have missed. She was somewhere below, in the streets. He decided to run for it, moving in an awkward crouch, pistol aimed at the space in front of him, in case she should appear. She did not. He scrambled back down the steps and over the gate. The city was silent. Outside the walls, a single car rumbled past. He knew he'd never reach it in time. His own car was less than fifty yards away in any case. But he'd no intention of returning to it. He had come this far. He wasn't going to run.

A sound of heels on cobblestones. Where? In front of him, and fading. He headed into the narrow streets of the old city, following the sound. The streets were like a maze. He'd been lost in them before, unable to believe afterwards that there were so few of them . . . just as those lost in a maze cannot believe it's not bigger than it is.

He couldn't hear the footsteps any more. He stood for a moment, turning his head, listening intently. Then he moved on. The streets grew, if anything, narrower, then widened again. A square. Then more streets. Christ, it was dark. Back-up. He needed back-up. Was there a police station anywhere nearby? Noise, voices . . . coming into the square. Three teenagers, two girls and one boy. They looked drunk, happy, heading home slowly. He hid his gun in its holster and ran up to them.

'Have you seen a woman?'

'Don't need to, I've got two here.' The boy gave the two girls a squeeze.

Elder attempted a sane man's smile. 'Is there a police station?'

'No idea.'

'Are you in trouble?' asked one of the girls. Elder shook his head.

'Just looking for my . . . my wife. She's tall, younger than me. We managed to get separated, and . . .'

'On holiday are you? Thought so.'

'Here, we did see that woman . . . where was she? Stonebow?'

There were shrugs.

'Down that way,' said the girl, pointing.

'Thanks,' said Elder. As he moved off, he heard the boy say 'Silly sod' quite loudly. The girls giggled.

Down this way. Hold on though . . . He stopped again. What was he doing? Witch had already taken a shot at him. She knew he was here. So why not let *her* find *him*? Was she behind him, following, watching patiently as he ran himself ragged? That would be typical of her, biding her time until he was exhausted, then catching him off-guard. Yes, he could run this maze for hours and never find her. Not unless she wanted to be found. He walked back the way he'd come, glancing behind him. What he needed was a dead end, and he found one: an alleyway leading from The Shambles. He staggered into it, tipping over a litter-bin, and leaned against the wall, breathing hoarsely, coughing. One hand was against the wall, supporting him, the other was inside his jacket, as though holding his ribs or rubbing away a stitch. Whenever he paused in his loud breathing, there was silence around him, almost oppressively heavy. And inside him, a pounding of blood.

'Hey, priest.' Her voice was quiet. He had not heard her approach. He turned his head slowly towards the mouth of the alley. It was dark in the alley itself, but the street was illuminated. He knew he could see her better than she could see him. But she knew it too. Perhaps that's why she was standing to one side of the alley's mouth, partly hidden by the corner of the wall. She was aiming a pistol at him.

She looked different. Not just physically different – that was to be expected – but somehow calmer, at peace.

'Are you satisfied now?' he asked between intakes of breath. 'Now that your father's dead?'

'Ooh, Mr Elder, and there I was thinking age had slowed you down. Yes, I'm satisfied.' She paused. 'Just about.' The gun was steady in her hand. She had made no attempt to enter the alley itself. Why should she? It was a dead end. He was not going to escape.

'What now? Retirement?' he asked. 'Your Dutch friend tells us you were paid a million dollars for the assassination.'

'A million, yes. Enough to buy a lot of retirement. What about you, Mr Elder? I thought *you* were retired, too.'

'I was, but how could I turn down the chance of finding you?'

He saw her smile. 'Finding me *again*,' she corrected. 'Tell me, Mr Elder, how's your back?'

'Good as new.'

'Really?' She was still smiling. 'You must be ready for another autograph then. Something a bit more permanent.'

'Do you remember,' he said, 'in Docklands, just before you gave me that final kick . . . ?'

'You started to ask me a question.'

'That's right. I want to ask it now. It's important to me.' He paused. 'It's the reason I've been hunting you so long.'

'Go ahead and ask.'

He swallowed drily, licked his lips. His mouth felt coated with bad coffee.

'Paris, eight years ago, in June. A bomb went off in a shopping arcade. Was it you?'

She was silent for a tantalising moment. 'You'll have to be more specific.'

'No, it was either you or it wasn't.'

'No interviews allowed.' Her finger began to squeeze the trigger.

Elder called out: 'Biddy, no!'

The use of her real name froze her for a second. A second was all Elder needed. The hand inside his jacket was already gripped around the Browning's butt. He swung and fired, diving further back into the darkness as he did so. He fired off three shots, stumbling backwards all the time, seeking safety in the shadows and the dustbins and the stacks of empty boxes. Three shots. None of them returned. He waited, listening. Some dogs had been startled awake and were barking in the distance. A window opened somewhere nearby.

'What the hell was that?' he heard a voice say. 'Sounded like guns. Call the police, love.'

Yes, call the police. Slowly, Elder got to his feet and walked to the mouth of the alley, keeping close to the wall, his gun-hand hanging at his side. Then he stuck his head out into the street.

And the cold metal mouth of a pistol touched his forehead.

Witch was standing there, smiling unsteadily. Her grip on the gun wasn't steady either. She was wounded. He daren't take his eyes off hers, but he could see a dark stain spreading across her right side. She placed the palm of her hand against it, then lifted the hand away, her fingers rubbing slickly against each other. Elder could smell the blood.

'Biddy,' he said, 'you don't hate me.' His whole head felt numb from the touch of the pistol against his brow. He felt dizzy, giddy. Witch's smile grew wider.

'Hate you? Of course I don't hate you. It's just that I don't want to . . .' she swallowed '. . . to disappoint you.' She fell against the shopfront, her gun-arm dropping to her side. Elder took hold of her and eased her down so that she was sitting on the ground, legs in front of her, back resting against the shopfront, the same rag-doll posture in which she'd left her father. Only then did he remove the pistol from her hand. From the lack of resistance in her fingers he knew she was dying, if not already dead. He heard feet running, several pairs of feet, and calls.

'Down this way?'

'No, down here.'

'The car's parked at Goodramgate.'

'Try The Shambles.'

'Take that street there . . .'

And then someone was standing in front of him.

'Found him!' the voice called. It belonged to a uniformed constable. The constable looked young, still in his teens. He stared in horror at the bloody bundle nestling against Dominic Elder.

'Is she . . . ?'

And now more footsteps. 'Dominic! Are you all right?'

Joyce crouched down in front of him, her eyes finding a level with his. He nodded.

'I'm fine, Joyce. Really.' He looked up. Greenleaf was standing there too now, pistol in his hand, not looking at Elder but at Witch.

'Here she is, John,' said Elder, still holding the unmoving body. 'Here's what all the fuss was about. A kid who didn't like her dad.'

'Her dad?'

'Jonathan Barker. He's on the wall between Goodramgate and the Minster.'

'Not alive, I presume?'

'Not alive, no.' Elder looked down at Witch again. She looked like Christine Jones. Now, she would always look like Christine Jones in his mind, just as for two years she'd looked like a down-and-out. He wondered what she looked like really. He wondered if even she knew.

Greenleaf holstered his gun. 'We call them "domestics" on the force,' he said. 'Family fallings-out . . .'

'That's what this was then,' said Elder, letting the body go and rising slowly to his feet. 'A domestic.'

Joyce Parry slipped her arm around his waist. Her fingers spread out across his back. His back had no feeling at all.

Departure

Doyle kept his head bandaged for a few days, even though the doctors had told him he needn't bother. But he said he liked the way it made him look, and so did his girlfriend.

'She says I look like a war hero.'

'Or a lobotomy patient,' added Greenleaf.

Elder laughed. They were standing in the East End boxing club, which again had been hired for one of Doyle's by now notorious parties. The French lager was piled high in cardboard boxes of forty-eight bottles per box. The punch-bags were in use, as were the parallel bars.

'He's sharp, isn't he, Dom?' said Doyle, nodding towards Greenleaf.

Elder nodded. 'But how do you feel really, Doyle?'

'Oh, I'm fine. Just a spot of amnesia.'

'Oh?'

'I seem to have forgotten all my character defects. Ay-ay, here comes lover boy.'

They turned towards the door. Barclay was walking tall, having just arranged by phone with Dominique that he'd be spending next weekend in Paris with her.

'Mama's idea,' she'd said, but he hadn't believed it.

Doyle had turned away from Barclay and towards the table. When he turned round again, he was holding a bottle of beer.

'There you go, Mikey. You don't need a bottle-opener, just twist the top.'

'Right, cheers,' said Barclay. Greenleaf knew what was coming. As Barclay twisted the bottle-top, a welt of foam burst from the bottle and sprayed his shirt.

Doyle tutted. 'Still a bit lively from the trip.'

Later, while discussion raged as to which curry house should receive the party's late-night custom, the one they'd used last time having said never again, Elder slipped away. He was going to hunt down a black taxi, but saw in the distance a seedily-lit cab office, so started walking towards it.

'Stealing my car again?'

He turned and saw Barclay following him. And when he looked, he was indeed standing next to the white Ford Fiesta. Barclay unlocked the passenger door.

'Hop in, I'll give you a lift.'

'You don't know where I'm headed.'

'I'll give you a lift there anyway.'

The trip took the best part of half an hour. At the end of it, Joyce would be waiting for him. Like last night and the night before. Tonight was their final night together: Tommy Bridges was going off on holiday and Elder's garden needed him. But Joyce had some holiday-time owing, too, and she was making plans to visit before the month was out. They'd see how it went. Now that Witch was behind him, maybe Dominic could relax a little. Maybe.

'A penny for them,' said Barclay.

'I'm wondering whether to envy you or not.'

'Why's that?'

'It's hard to put into words without an overload of clichés.'

'Try anyway.'

'You're just beginning, Michael.' Elder stopped abruptly. He couldn't say it. Barclay nodded anyway.

'I get the message,' he said.

Elder smiled. 'I hope so.'

'By the way, how's the patient?'

How indeed. Earlier today Elder had travelled to the hospital in Leeds. Witch was on a life-support system, her brain activity still sluggish. Without the machines . . . The doctor had shrugged. He couldn't see the point of keeping a killer alive.

Elder could . . . well, sometimes he could. He sat by her bed for half an hour, alternately staring at her face, at the tubes running from nose and mouth, and at the machinery itself with its constant bleep and the slow hiss of pumped air.

'You never did answer me,' he said quietly. He turned from her, the better to examine the workings of the machines around them. He followed the snaking line the cables took to the electrical sockets at the bottom of the cream-painted wall. He glanced now and then at the plugs, at the machinery's several on/off switches, so clearly marked.

So, so clearly marked.

And finally, he rose to his feet, quietly, softly, so as not to disturb. There was a flutter from her eyelashes, movement behind the eyelids themselves: REM, they called it, Rapid Eye Movement. She was dreaming. He wondered what she was dreaming of. He touched her bare arm, feeling its delicate warmth. Her face was ghostly pale, her lips almost colourless. Elder leant down over her and planted a kiss on her forehead. The machine gave a sudden double-blip, as though somewhere inside her the kiss had registered. Elder smiled and stepped away from the bed, placing the chair back against the wall, and finally standing in front of the machines themselves, his fingertips just touching the cool painted metal.

Bleeding Hearts

For Elliott and Fawn

Part One

1

She had just over three hours to live, and I was sipping grapefruit juice and tonic in the hotel bar.

'You know what it's like these days,' I said, 'only the toughest are making it. No room for bleeding hearts.'

My companion was a businessman himself. He too had survived the highs and lows of the 80s, and he nodded as vigorously as the whisky in him would allow.

'Bleeding hearts,' he said, 'are for the operating table, not for business.'

'I'll drink to that,' I said, though of course in my line of work bleeding hearts *are* the business.

Gerry had asked me a little while ago what I did for a living, and I'd told him export-import, then asked what he did. See, I slipped up once; I manufactured a career for myself only to find the guy I was drinking with was in the same line of work. Not good. These days I'm better, much cagier, and I don't drink on the day of a hit. Not a drop. Not any more. Word was, I was slipping. Bullshit naturally, but sometimes rumours are difficult to throw off. It's not as though I could put an ad in the newspapers. But I knew a few good clean hits would give the lie to this particular little slander.

Then again, today's hit was no prize: it had been handed to me, a gift. I knew where she'd be and what she'd be doing. I didn't just know what she looked like, I knew pretty well what she'd be wearing. I knew a whole lot about her. I wasn't going to have to work for this one, but prospective future employers wouldn't know that. All they'd see was the score sheet. Well, I'd take all the easy targets going.

'So what do you buy and sell, Mark?' Gerry asked.

I was Mark Wesley. I was English. Gerry was English too, but as international businessmen we spoke to one another in mid-Atlantic: the lingua franca of the deal. We were jealous of our American cousins, but would never admit it.

'Whatever it takes, Gerry,' I said.

'I'm into that.' Gerry toasted me with whisky. It was 3 pm local time. The whiskies were six quid a hit, not much more than my own soft drink. I've drunk in hotel bars all over the western world, and this one looked like all of them. Dimly lit even in daytime, the same bottles behind the polished bar, the same liveried barman pouring from them. I find the sameness comforting. I hate to go to a strange place, somewhere where you can't find any focus, anything recognisable to grab on to. I hated Egypt: even the Coke signs were written in Arabic, and all the numerals were wrong, plus everyone was wearing the wrong clothes. I hate Third World countries; I won't do hits there unless the money is particularly interesting. I like to be somewhere with clean hospitals and facilities, dry sheets on the bed, English-speaking smiles.

'Well, Gerry,' I said, 'been nice talking to you.'

'Same here, Mark.' He opened his wallet and eased out a business card. 'Here, just in case.'

I studied it. Gerald Flitch, Marketing Strategist. There was a company name, phone, fax and carphone number, and an address in Liverpool. I put the card in my pocket, then patted my jacket.

'Sorry, I can't swap. No cards on me just now.'

'That's all right.'

'But the drinks are on me.'

'Well, I don't know—'

'My pleasure, Gerry.' The barman handed me the bill, and I signed my name and room number. 'After all,' I said, 'you never know when I might need a favour.'

Gerry nodded. 'You need friends in business. A face you can trust.'

'It's true, Gerry, it's all about trust in our game.'

Obviously, as you can see, I was in philosophical mood.

Back up in my room, I put out the Do Not Disturb sign, locked the door, and wedged a chair under the handle. The bed had already been made, the bathroom towels changed, but you couldn't be too careful. A maid might look in anyway. There was never much of a pause between them knocking at your door and them unlocking it.

I took the suitcase from the bottom of the wardrobe and laid it on the bed, then checked the little Sellotape seal I'd left on it. The seal was still intact. I broke it with my thumbnail and unlocked the suitcase. I lifted out some shirts and T-shirts until I came to the dark blue raincoat. This I lifted out and laid on the bed. I then pulled on my kid-leather driving-gloves before going any further. With these on, I unfolded the coat. Inside, wrapped in polythene, was my rifle.

It's impossible to be too careful, and no matter how careful you are you leave traces. I try to keep up with advances in forensic science, and I know all of us leave traces wherever we are: fibres, hairs, a fingerprint, a smear of grease from a finger or arm. These days, they can match you from the DNA in a single hair. That's why the rifle was wrapped in polythene: it left fewer traces than cloth.

The gun was beautiful. I'd cleaned it carefully in Max's workshop, then checked it for identifiers and other distinguishing marks. Max does a good job of taking off serial numbers, but I always like to be sure. I'd spent some time with the rifle, getting to know it, its weight and its few foibles. I'd practised over several days, making sure I got rid of all the spent bullets and cartridge cases, just so the gun couldn't be traced back to them. Every gun leaves particular and unique marks on a bullet. I didn't believe that at first either, but apparently it's true.

The ammo was a problem. I didn't really want to tamper with it. Each cartridge case carries a head stamp, which identifies it. I'd tried filing off the head stamps from a few cartridges, and they didn't seem to make any difference to the accuracy of my shooting. But on the day, *nothing* could go wrong. So I asked Max and he said the bullets could be traced back to a consignment which had accompanied the British Army units to Kuwait during the Gulf War. (I didn't ask how Max had got hold of them; probably the same source as the rifle itself.) See, some snipers like to make their own ammo. That way they know they can trust it. But I'm not skilled that way, and I don't think it matters anyway. Max sometimes made up ammo for me, but his eyes weren't so great these days.

The ammo was .338 Lapua Magnum. It was full metal-jacket: military stuff usually is, since it fulfils the Geneva Convention's requirements for the most 'humane' type of bullet.

Well, I'm no animal, I wasn't about to contravene the Geneva Convention.

Max had actually been able to offer a choice of weapons. That's why I use him. He asks few questions and has excellent facilities. That he lives in the middle of nowhere is a bonus, since I can practise all day without disturbing anyone. Then there's his daughter Belinda, who would be bonus enough in herself. I always take her a present if I've been away somewhere. Not that I'd . . . you know, not with Max about. He's very protective of her, and she of him. They remind me of Beauty and the Beast. Bel's got short fair hair, eyes slightly slanted like a cat's, and a long straight nose. Her face looks like it's been polished. Max on the other hand has been battling cancer for years. He's lost about a quarter of his face, I suppose, and keeps his right side, from below the eye to just above the lips, covered with a white plastic prosthesis. Sometimes Bel calls him the Phantom of the Opera. He takes it from her. He wouldn't take it from anyone else.

I think that's why he's always pleased to see me. It's not just that I have cash on me and something I want, but he doesn't see many people. Or rather, he doesn't let many people see him. He spends all day in his workshop, cleaning, filing, and polishing his guns. And he spends a lot of his nights there, too.

He had a Remington 700, pre-fitted with a Redfield telescopic sight. The US Marines use this military version of the 'Varmint' as sniper rifles. I'd used one before, and had nothing against it. More interesting though was a Sterling Sniper Rifle. Most people I'd met thought only cars were made in Dagenham, but that's where the Sterling was crafted. It was user-friendly, down to the cheek-rest and the grooved receiver. You could fit it with any mounting-plate you wanted, to accommodate any telescope or night-sight. I admit, it was tempting.

There were others, too. Max didn't have them, but he knew where he could get them: an L39A1, the ugly Mauser SP66, a Fusil Modele 1 Type A. I decided I wanted British; call me sentimental. And finally Max handed over the gun we'd both known I'd opt for: a Model PM.

The manufacturers, Accuracy International, call it the PM. I don't know what the letters stand for, maybe Post-Mortem. But the British Army know it as Sniper Rifle L96A1. A mouthful, you'll agree, which is why Max and I stick to calling it the PM. There are several versions, and Max was offering the Super Magnum (hence the .338 Lapua Magnum ammo). The gun itself is not what you'd call a beauty, and as I unwrapped it in my hotel room it looked even less lovely, since I'd covered its camouflage with some camouflage of my own.

The PM is olive green in colour, fine if you are hiding in the trees, but not so inconspicuous when surrounded by the grey concrete of a city street. So in Max's workshop I'd wound some grey adhesive tape around it, wearing my gloves all the time so as not to leave prints on the tape. As a result, the PM now looked like the ballistic equivalent of the Invisible Man, all bandaged except for the bits I needed left open to access. It was a neat job of binding; the wrapping around the stainless-steel barrel alone had taken a couple of hours.

The PM is a long rifle, its barrel nearly four inches longer than the Remington. It's also heavy, to say that it's mostly plastic, albeit high-impact plastic: double the weight of the Remington, and over four pounds heavier than the Sterling. I didn't mind though, it wasn't as if I'd be carrying it through the jungle. I made it even longer by fitting a flash hider of my own construction. (Max smiled with half of his face as he watched me. Like me, he is an admirer of beauty and craft, and the best you could say of my finished product was that it worked.)

All the guns Max had offered me were bolt-action, all were 7.62mm, and all had barrels with four grooves and a right-hand twist. They differed in styles and muzzle velocity, in length and weight, but they shared one common characteristic. They were all lethal.

In the end, I decided I didn't require the integral bipod: the angle I'd be shooting from, it would hinder rather than help. So I took that off, minimally reducing the weight. Although the PM accepts a 10-round box, I knew I'd have two bullets at most, preferably only one. With bolt-action rifles, you sometimes didn't have time for a second shot. While you were working the bolt, your quarry was scuttling to safety.

I picked the gun up at last, and stood in my bedroom staring into the full-length mirror on the wardrobe door. The curtains were closed, so I was able to do this. I'd already fitted the telescopic sight. Ah, Max had made things *so* difficult. He could give me a Redfield, a Parker-Hale, the Zeiss Diavari ZA . . . even the old No. 32 sniping telescope. But the PM wasn't geared up for these, so instead of fussing and having to make my own special sight-mounting plate, I opted for a Schmidt and Bender 6×42 telescopic sight, all the time telling myself I was maybe, for once, going to too much trouble.

I was ready to pick off a flea from a cat's whisker at 600 yards, when all I had to do was hit a human target, out in the open, at something like a tenth of that. What was I doing buying all this lavish craft and expertise when something bashed together in China would achieve the same objective? Max had an answer.

'You like quality, you like style.'

True, Max, true. If my targets were suddenly to depart this world, I wanted them to have the best send-off I could give them. I checked my watch, then double-checked with the clock-radio.

She had just over two hours to live.

2

Everything was waiting for Eleanor Ricks.

She'd woken that morning after a drugged sleep, knowing yet another day was waiting out there, ready to bite her. Breakfast and her husband Freddy were waiting in the kitchen, as was Mrs Elfman. When Eleanor and Freddy were both working, Mrs Elfman came in and got breakfast ready, then cleaned everything away and tidied the rooms. When they weren't working, she did the cleaning but no cooking. Freddy insisted that one or other of them *had* to be capable of preparing cereal or sausage and eggs and a pot of coffee, so long as their minds weren't on work. Funny, usually Eleanor ended up cooking if Mrs Elfman wasn't around, even if she'd to go to work while Freddy was 'resting'. Today, however, was a work day for both of them.

Freddy Ricks was an actor, of consequence (albeit in TV sitcoms) in the early 80s but now squeezing a living from 'character' parts and not many of them. He'd tried some stage acting but didn't like it, and had wasted a good deal of their joint savings by spending fruitless time in Hollywood, trying to call up favours from producers and directors who'd moved on from British TV. Today, he was starring in a commercial for breakfast cereal. It would be head and shoulders only, and he'd be wearing a yellow oilskin sou'wester and a puzzled expression. He had two lines to say, but they'd dub another actor's voice on later. Freddy couldn't understand why his own voice wasn't good enough for them. It had, as he pointed out, been quite good enough for the 12 million viewers who'd tuned in to *Stand By Your Man* every week of its runs in 1983–4.

He sat at the table munching cornflakes and reading his preferred tabloid. He looked furious, but then these days he always looked furious. The radio sat on the draining board, volume turned down low because Freddy didn't like it. But Mrs Elfman liked it, and she angled her head towards the transistor, trying to catch the words, while at the same time washing last night's dishes.

'Morning, Mrs E.'

'Morning, Mrs Ricks, how did you sleep?'

'Like a log, thanks.'

'All right for some,' Freddy muttered from behind his cereal spoon. Eleanor ignored him, and so did Mrs Elfman. Eleanor poured herself a mug of black coffee.

'Want some breakfast, Mrs Ricks?'

'No thanks.'

'It's the most important meal of the day.'

'I'm still full from last night.' This was a lie, but what else could she say: if I eat a single morsel I'm liable to be throwing up all morning? Mrs Elfman would think she was joking.

'Is Archie up?'

'Who knows?' growled Freddy.

Archie was their son, seventeen years old and the 'computer player' in a pop group. Eleanor had never heard of anyone 'playing' the computer as a musical instrument, until Archie had shown her. Now his band were making their second record, their first having been a success in local clubs. She went to the bottom of the stairs and called him. There was no answer.

'He's like bloody Dracula,' complained Freddy. 'Never seen in daylight hours.' Mrs Elfman threw him a nasty look, and Eleanor went through to her study.

Eleanor Ricks was a freelance investigative journalist who had somehow managed to make a name for herself without recourse to the usual 'investigations' of pop stars, media celebrities, and royalty. But then one day she'd found that magazines wanted to send round journalists to profile *her*, and she'd started to rethink her career. So now, after years of newspaper and magazine articles, she was finally going into television – just, it seemed, as Freddy was moving out of it. Poor Freddy: she gave him a moment's thought, then started work.

Today she was interviewing Molly Prendergast, the Secretary of State for Social Security. They were meeting at a central hotel. They wouldn't be talking about anything concerning the Department of Social Security, or Molly Prendergast's position there, or even her standing in her own political party. It was much more personal, which was why they were meeting in a hotel rather than at the Department's offices.

It was Eleanor's idea. She reckoned she'd get more out of Molly Prendergast on neutral ground. She didn't want to hear a politician talking; she wanted to hear a mother . . .

She went through her notes again, her list of questions, press clippings, video footage. She spoke with her researchers and assistant by phone. This was an initial interview, not intended for broadcast. Eleanor would take a tape recording, but just for her own use. There wouldn't be any cameras or technicians there, just two women having a chat and a drink. Then, if Prendergast looked useful to the project, there'd be a request for a proper on-screen interview, asking the same or similar questions again. Eleanor knew that the Molly Prendergast she got today would not be the one she'd get at a later date. On screen, the politician would be much more cautious, more guarded. But Eleanor would use her anyway: Prendergast was a name, and this story needed a name to get it some publicity. Or so Joe kept telling her.

The batteries for her tape recorder had been charging up overnight. She checked them, taping her voice then winding it back to listen. The recorder, though small, had a stereo microphone built into it and a tiny but powerful external speaker. She would take three C90 tapes with her, though it was expected to be an hour-long interview. Well, it might overrun, or a tape might snap. What was she thinking of? It wouldn't overrun. Two C90s would do it. But she'd best take a lot of batteries.

She rewound the video compilation and studied it again, then went to her computer and tweaked some of her questions, deleting one and adding two new ones. She printed off this new sheet and read it over one more time. Then she faxed it to her producer, who phoned back with the okay.

'You're sure?' Eleanor asked.

'I'm sure. Look, don't worry about this, Lainie.' She hated him calling her 'Lainie'. One day, she'd tell him to his face . . . No, that wasn't true, was it? It was a small price to pay for Joe Draper's backing. Joe was an excellent producer, if, like so many of his television colleagues, a bit of a prima donna. He'd earned his money doing a cop drama series and a couple of sitcoms (one of them with Freddy playing the errant next-door neighbour), then had set up his own production company, which specialised in documentaries and docu-dramas. These were good days for independent producers, so long as you knew your market and had a few contacts in the TV broadcasting companies. Joe had plenty of friends: his weekend coke parties at his home in Wiltshire were *very* popular. He'd invited her along a couple of times, but had neglected to invite Freddy.

'You forget, Joe, I'm new to this, I can't be laid back like you.' Okay, so she was fishing for a compliment, and of course, Joe knew it.

'Lainie, you're the best. Just do what you're best at. Talk to her, open her up, then sit back and look interested. That's it. You know, like you were a . . .' Here it came, another of Joe's tortured similes. 'A lion tamer. You go in there, crack your whip, and when she starts to do the trick, you can relax and take the applause.'

'You really think it's that simple, Joe?'

'No, it's hard work. But the secret is, don't make it *look* like hard work. It should be smooth like the baize on a snooker table, so smooth she doesn't know she's been potted till she's falling into the pocket.' He laughed then, and she laughed with him, amazed at herself. 'Look, Lainie, this is going to be good TV, I can feel it. You've got a great idea, and you're going about it the right way: human interest. It's been a winning formula since TV had nappies on. Now go to it!'

She smiled tiredly. 'All right, Joe, I will.' Then she put down the phone.

Satisfied, Eleanor phoned for a bike messenger. She wrote a covering note, put it with a copy of the questions into a large manila envelope, and wrote Prendergast's name and her home address on the front of it. When the bike arrived she hesitated before letting him take the envelope. Then she closed the door and exhaled. She thought she might throw up, but didn't. That was it. Those were the questions she'd be running with. There was little else to do until five o'clock but panic and take a few pills and try on clothes. Maybe she'd go out for a little while to calm herself down, walk to Regent's Park and along the perimeter of the Zoo. The fresh air and the grass and trees, the children playing and running or staring through the fence at the animals, these things usually calmed her. Even the jets overhead could have an effect. But it was fifty-fifty. Half the time, after they calmed her she had to sit on a park bench and cry. She'd bawl and hide her face in her coat, and couldn't explain to anyone why she was doing it.

She couldn't explain, but she knew all the same. She was doing it because she was scared.

In the end she stayed home. She was soaking in the bath when the phone rang. Mrs Elfman had already gone home, having once more informed

Eleanor that she would not touch Archie's room until he'd sorted the worst of it out for himself. Freddy had left for his sou'wester cereal slot, not even saying goodbye or wishing her luck. She knew he wouldn't be home again. He'd stop in one of his many pubs to talk to other embittered men. It would be seven or eight before he came back here. As for Archie, well, she hadn't seen him in days anyway.

She'd let the phone ring for a while – what could be so important? – but then realised it might be Molly Prendergast querying or nixing one of the new questions. Eleanor reached up and unhooked the receiver from the extension-set on the wall above the bath. It had seemed mad at the time, a phone in the bathroom, but it came in useful more often than they'd thought.

'Hello?'

'Eleanor?'

'Geoffrey, is that you?'

'Who else?'

'You always seem to catch me in the bath.'

'Lucky me. Can we talk?'

'What about?'

'I think you know.'

Geoffrey Johns was Eleanor's solicitor, and had been for fifteen years. Occasionally, her journalism had landed her with an injunction, a libel suit or a court appearance. She knew Geoffrey very well indeed. She could imagine him seated in his grandfather's chair in his grandfather's office (also at one time his father's office). The office was stuffy and gloomy, the chair uncomfortable, but Geoffrey wouldn't make any changes. He even used a bakelite telephone, with a little drawer in the base for a notepad. The phone was a reproduction and had cost him a small fortune.

'Humour me,' she said, lying back further in the water. A telephone engineer had told her she couldn't electrocute herself, even if the receiver fell in the water. Not enough volts or something. All she'd feel was a tingle. He'd leered as he'd said it. Just a tingle.

'I think you know,' Geoffrey Johns repeated, drawling the words out beyond their natural limits. Eleanor had a feeling he spoke so slowly because he charged by the hour. When she didn't say anything he sighed loudly. 'Are you doing anything today?'

'Nothing much. I've an interview this afternoon.'

'I thought we might meet.'

'I don't think that's necessary.'

'No?' Another silence, another pause. 'Look, Eleanor—'

'Geoffrey, is there something you want to say?'

'I . . . no, I suppose not.'

'Look, Geoffrey, you're one of the dearest people I know.' She halted. It was an old joke between them.

'My rates are actually very reasonable,' he supplied, sounding mollified. 'What about next week? I'll buy you lunch.'

She ran the sponge between her breasts and then over them. 'That sounds heavenly.'

'Do you want to fix a date now?'

'You know what I'm like, Geoffrey, I'd only end up changing it. Let's wait.'

'Fine. Well, as the Americans say, have a nice day.'

'It's gone two, Geoffrey, the best of the day's already over.'

'Don't remind me,' said Geoffrey Johns.

She reached up to replace the receiver in its cradle, and wondered if Geoffrey would try charging her for the call. She wouldn't put it past him. She lay in the bath a little longer, until there was just enough hot water left in the tap to let her shower off. She ran her fingers through her hair, enjoying the sensation, then towelled briskly and set off naked to the bedroom for her clothes.

She'd had her yellow and blue dress cleaned specially, and was glad the day was sunny. The dress worked best in sunlight.

3

I took a cab from the hotel.

My destination was only a ten-minute walk away, but I knew I'd be less conspicuous in a taxi. London cab-drivers aren't, in my experience, the all-knowing and inquisitive individuals they're often made out to be. They nod at you when you tell them your destination, and that's about it. Of course, mine had one comment ready as I got into his cab.

'What you got there then, a bazooka or something?'

'Photographic equipment,' I answered, though he showed no interest. I had manoeuvred the long metal box into the back of the cab, where, angled between the top corner of the rear window and the bottom front corner of the door diametrically opposite, it afforded me scant space for myself. It was longer than it needed to be; but it was also the shortest adequate box I could find.

It was silver in colour, with three clasp-locks and a black carrying-handle. I'd bought it in a specialist shop for photographers. It was used for carrying around rolls of precious background paper. The shop assistant had tried to sell me some graduated sheets – they were on special offer – but I'd declined. I didn't mind the box being too big. It did anything but announce that there was a gun inside.

In the movies, the local assassin tends to carry a small attaché case. His rifle will be inside, broken down into stock, fore-end and barrel. He simply clips the parts together and attaches his telescopic sight. Of course, in real life even if you get hold of such a weapon, it would not be anything like as accurate as a solid one-piece construction. Normally, I'd carry my rifle hanging from a special pouch inside my raincoat, but the PM was just too long and too heavy. So instead of walking, I was taking a taxi to the office.

I'd been watching the weather for a couple of hours, and had even phoned from the hotel for the latest Met Office report. Clear, but without bright sunshine. In other words, perfect conditions, the sun being a sniper's worst enemy. I was chewing gum and doing some breathing exercises, though I doubted they'd be effective in my present cramped condition. But it was only a few minutes until the driver was pulling into the kerb and dropping me outside the office block.

This was a Saturday, remember, and though I was in central London my destination wasn't one of the main thoroughfares. So the street was quiet. Cars and taxis waited for the lights to change further down the road, but the shops were doing slow business and all the offices were closed. The shops were at street level, the usual mix of ceramics studios, small art galleries, shoe shops, and travel agents. I paid the driver and eased the carrying-case out on to the pavement. I stood there until he'd driven off. Across the street were more shops with offices above, and the Craigmead Hotel. It was one of those old understated hotels with overstated room rates. I knew this because I'd toyed with staying there before opting for a much safer choice.

The building I was standing outside was a typical central London office complex, with four steps up to an imposing front door, and a façade which in some parts of the city would hide a huge family home broken up into flats. Indeed, the building next-door had been converted to flats on all but its ground and first floors. My chosen site, however, was currently being gutted and reshaped to offer, as the billboard outside put it, Luxury Office Accommodation for the 21st Century.

I'd been along here yesterday and the day before, and again earlier today. During the week, the place was busy with workmen, but this being Saturday the main door was locked tight, and there was no sign of life inside. That's why I'd chosen it over the flats next door, which offered the easier target but would probably be in use at weekends. I walked up to the main door and worked the lock. It was a simple Yale, not even permanently fixed. The real locks would come later on in the renovation. Meantime, there being little inside worth pinching, the contractors hadn't bothered with a quality lock.

They hadn't got round to installing the alarm system yet either: another reason for my choice. Wires led out of the front wall into fresh air. Later, they'd be hooked up to the alarm and a casing put over the whole. But for now security was not the main concern.

I'm not the world's greatest locksmith, but any housing-estate teenager could have been into the place in seconds. I walked into the entrance hall, taking my carrying-case with me, and closed the door behind me. I stood there for a minute listening to the silence. I could smell drying plaster and wet paint, planed wood and varnish. The downstairs looked like a building site. There were planks and panels of Gyproc and bags of cement and plaster and rolls of insulation. Some of the floorboards had been lifted to allow access to wiring ducts, but I didn't see any fresh rolls of electrical cable: the stuff was probably too valuable to be left lying around. The electrical contractor would take it away with him every night in his van and bring it back again next day. I knew a few electricians; they're careful that way.

There were also no power-tools lying around, and very few tools of any description. I guessed they'd be locked away somewhere inside the building. There was a telephone on the floor, one of those old slimline models with the angular receiver resting over the dial. It was chipped and dotted with paint, but more surprisingly was attached to a phone-point on the wall. I lifted the receiver, and heard the familiar tone. I suppose it made sense: this was going to be a long job; there'd have to be some means of communication between the gang and their base. I put back the receiver and stood up.

Since I hadn't been in the place before, I knew I had to get to know it quickly. I left the case in the reception area and headed upstairs. Some doors had been fitted, but none were locked, except one to a storage area. I presumed that was where the tools were kept.

I found the office I needed on the second floor.

The first floor was too close to ground level. There was always the chance of some pedestrian glancing up, though they so seldom did. The third floor, on the other hand, made the angle a little too difficult. I might have accepted its challenge, but I knew I needed a good hit. No time for games today, it had to be fast and mundane. Well, not *too* mundane. There was always my calling card.

My chosen office was as chaotic as any other part of the building. They were fitting a false ceiling, from which fell power points, probably for use with desktop computers. The ceiling they were putting up, a grid of white plastic strips, would be hiding the real ceiling, which was ornately corniced with an even more ornate central ceiling-rose, presumably at one time surrounding the room's main light fitting, a chandelier perhaps. Well, they're fucking up old buildings everywhere, aren't they?

I checked my exits: there was only the front door. It looked like they were working on a fire exit to the rear of the building, but meantime they'd left all their ladders and scaffolding there, effectively barricading the door. So when I left, I'd have to leave through the front door. But that didn't worry me. I've found that just as attack is the best form of defence, so boldness can be the best form of disguise. It's the person slinking away who looks suspicious, not the one walking towards you. Besides, attention was going to be elsewhere, wasn't it?

The window was fine. There was some ineffective double glazing, which could be slid open, and behind which lay the original sash-window. I unscrewed the window lock and tried opening it. The pulleys stuck for a moment, their ropes crusted with white paint, and then they gave with an audible squeak and the window lifted an inch. With more effort, I opened it a second and then a third inch. This wasn't ideal. It meant the telescopic sight would be pointing through the glass, while the muzzle would be stuck into fresh air. But I'd carried out an assassination before under near-identical conditions. To be honest, I could probably have forced the window open a bit further, but I think I was looking for just a *little* challenge.

I peered out. No one was looking back at me. I couldn't see anyone in the shops over the road, and no one staring from the hotel windows further along. In fact, some of the shops looked like they were closing for the day. My watch said 5.25. Yes, some of them, most of them, would close at 5.30. The tourists and visitors at the Craigmead Hotel wouldn't be in their rooms, they'd still be out enjoying the summer weather. By six o'clock, the street would be dead. I only had to wait.

I brought the case upstairs and opened it. I couldn't find a chair, but there was a wooden crate which I upended. It seemed strong enough, so I placed it by the window and sat on it. The PM lay on the floor in front of me, along with two bullets. I sat there thinking about cartridges. You wouldn't think something so small and so fixed in its purpose could be quite so complex. Straight or bottleneck? Belted, rimmed, semi-rimmed, rimless or rebated? Centre-fire or rim-fire? Then there was the primer compound. I knew that Max mixed his own compound using lead styphnate, antimony sulphide and barium nitrate, but in a ratio he kept to himself. I picked up one of the bullets by its base and tip. What, I wondered, is it like to be shot? I knew the answer in forensic terms. I knew the kinds of entrance and exit wounds left by different guns at different ranges and using different ammunition. I had to know this sort of thing, so I could determine each individual hit. Some snipers go for the head shot; some of them call it a 'JFK'. Not me.

I go for the heart.

What else did I think about in that room, as the traffic moved past like the dull soothing roll of waves on a shore? I didn't think about anything else. I emptied my mind. I could have been in a trance, had anyone seen me. I let my shoulders slump, my head fall forward, my jaw muscles relax. I kept my fingers spread wide, not clenched. And with my eyes slightly out of focus, I watched the second hand go round on my watch. Finally I came out of it, and found myself wondering what I would order for dinner. Some dark meat in a sauce rich enough to merit a good red wine. It was five minutes to six. I picked up the PM, undid the bolt, pushed home the first bullet, and slid the bolt forward. Then I took a small homemade cushion from my jacket pocket and placed it between my shoulder and the stock of the rifle. I had to be careful of the recoil.

This was a dangerous time. If anyone saw me now, they wouldn't just see a man at a window, they'd see the barrel of a gun, a black telescopic sight, and a sniper taking aim. But the few pedestrians were too busy to look up. They were hurrying home, or to some restaurant appointment. They carried bags of shopping. They kept their eyes to the treacherous London paving slabs. If a cracked slab didn't get you, then the dog shit might. Besides, they couldn't look straight ahead; that was to invite a stranger's stare, an unwanted meeting of eyes.

The sight was beautiful, it was as if I was standing a few feet from the hotel steps. There was a central revolving door, and ordinary push-pull doors to either side. Most people going into or coming out of the hotel seemed to use the ordinary doors. I wondered which one she would use. It was six now, dead on the hour. I blinked slowly, keeping my eyes clear. One minute past six. Then two minutes past. I took deep breaths, releasing them slowly. I'd taken my eye away from the telescope. I could see the hotel entrance well enough without it. Now a car was drawing up outside the hotel. There was a liveried chauffeur in the front. He made no effort to get out and open the back doors. The man and woman got out by themselves. He looked like a diplomat; the car carried a diplomatic plate below its radiator grille. They walked up the three carpeted steps to the revolving door. And now two women were coming out.

Two women.

I put my eye to the telescopic sight. Yes. I pulled the gun in tight against my cushioned shoulder, adjusted my hands a fraction, and put my finger on the trigger. The two women were smiling, talking. The diplomat and his wife had moved past them. Now the women were craning their necks, looking for taxis. Another car drew up and one of the women pointed towards it. She started down a step, and her companion followed. The sun appeared from behind a cloud, highlighting the yellow and blue design on her dress. I squeezed the trigger.

Straight away, I pulled the gun in from the window. I knew the hit had been good. She'd fallen backwards as if pushed hard in the chest. The other woman didn't realise for a moment what had happened. She was probably thinking, fainting fit or heart attack. But now she'd seen the blood and she was looking around, then crawling down the steps on her hands and knees, taking cover behind the diplomat's car. The driver was out of the car and looking around. He'd pulled a pistol from inside his jacket and was screaming at the diplomat to get indoors. The driver in the other car seemed to have ducked down in his seat.

And now there were sirens. You were always hearing sirens in central London – ambulances, fire engines. But these were police cars and they were screaming to a stop outside the hotel. I stood up and moved away from the window. It was impossible, they couldn't be here so quickly. I took another look. Some of the police were armed, and they were making for the block next to this one, the block with all the flats in it. Passers-by were being ordered to take cover, the woman was yelling and crying from the cover of the car, the armed chauffeur was crouching over the lifeless body. He put his hands up when the police took aim at him, and started to explain who he was. It might take them a little while to believe him.

I knew I had seconds to get out. They'd turn their attention to this building next. I put the gun back in its box along with the unused bullet, closed the box, and left it there. Normally I'd take the gun away with me and break it up, then dispose of it. Max never wanted my guns back, and I couldn't blame him. But I knew I couldn't risk walking out with that carrying-case.

As I walked downstairs, the idea came to me. There was a hospital just a few blocks away. I picked up the telephone and dialled 999, then asked for an ambulance.

'I'm a severe haemophiliac, and I've just had a terrible accident. I think there's haemorrhaging to the head.' I gave them the address, then put the phone down and went in search of a brick. There were some just inside the front door. I picked one up and smashed it into my forehead, making sure the edge of the brick made the initial contact. I touched my forehead with the palm of my hand. There was blood.

And then from outside came the sound of a muffled explosion: my calling card.

I'd planted the device in the morning. It was at the bottom of a dustbin in an alley behind some restaurants. The alley was about five hundred yards from the Craigmead Hotel. It was a small bomb, just big enough to make a noise. The alley was a dead end, so I doubted anyone would be hurt. Its purpose was to deflect attention while I walked away from the scene. I knew it would still deflect attention, but I doubted I'd be able to walk away without being spotted by the police.

Now there was another siren, not a police car but an ambulance. God bless them, the emergency services know that when a haemophiliac phones them up, it has to be priority. I unlocked the main door and looked out. Sure enough, the ambulance had drawn up outside. One of the ambulance-men was opening the back door, the other was climbing out from the driver's side.

Together they pulled a stretcher from the back of the ambulance, manoeuvred it on to the pavement, and wheeled it towards the front door. Someone, a policeman probably, called out to them and asked what they were doing.

'Emergency!' one of them called back.

I held the door open for them. I had a hand to my bloody forehead, and an embarrassed smile on my face.

'Tripped and fell,' I said.
'Not surprised with all this rubbish lying around.'
'I was working upstairs.'
I let them put me on to the stretcher. I thought it would look better for the audience.
'Do you have your card?' one of them asked.
'It's in my wallet at home.'
'You're supposed always to carry it. What's your factor level?'
'One per cent.'
They were putting me in the ambulance now. The armed police were still in the apartment block. People were looking towards the source of the explosion from a few moments before.
'What the hell's happened here?' one ambulanceman asked the other.
'Christ knows.' The second ambulanceman tore open a packet and brought out a compress, which he pressed to my forehead. He placed my hand on it. 'Here, you know the drill. Plenty of pressure.'
The driver closed the ambulance doors from the outside, leaving me with his colleague. Nobody stopped us as we left the scene. I was sitting up, thinking I wasn't safe yet.
'Is this your card?' The ambulanceman had picked something off the floor. He started reading it. 'Gerald Flitch, Marketing Strategist.'
'My business card. It must have fallen out of my pocket.' I held out my hand and he gave me back the card. 'The company I'm working for, they're supposed to be moving into the new office next week.'
'It's an old card then, the Liverpool address?'
'Yes,' I said, 'our old offices.'
'Are you factor eight or nine, Mr Flitch?'
'Factor eight,' I told him.
'We've got a good Haematology Department, you'll be all right.'
'Thank you.'
'To tell you the truth, you'd have been as quick walking there.'
Yes, we were already bumping through the hospital gates and up to the Emergency entrance. This was about as far as I could take the charade. I knew that behind the compress the bleeding was already stopping. They took me into Emergency and gave a nurse my details. She went off to call someone from Haematology, and the ambulancemen went back to their vehicle. I sat for a few moments in the empty reception area, then got up and headed for the door. The ambulance was still there, but there was no sign of the ambulancemen. They'd probably gone for a cup of tea and a cigarette. I walked down the slope to the hospital's main entrance, and deposited the compress in a waste-bin. There were two public telephones on the wall, and I called my hotel.
'Can I speak to Mr Wesley, please? Room 203.'
'Sorry,' said the receptionist after a moment, 'I'm getting no reply.'
'Can I leave a message? It's very important. Tell Mr Wesley there's been a change of plans, he has to be in Liverpool tonight. This is Mr Snipes from Head Office.'
'Is there a number where he can contact you, Mr Snipes?' I gave her a fictitious phone number prefixed with the Liverpool code, then put down the phone. There was a lot of police activity on the streets as I walked back to my hotel.

The thing was, the police would find the PM, and then they'd want to speak to the man who'd been taken away in the ambulance. The nurse in Emergency could tell them I'd given the name Gerald Flitch, and the ambulanceman could add that my business card had carried a Liverpool address. From all of which, they could track down either Flitch's Liverpool home or his employers and be told he was on a trip to London, staying at the Allington Hotel.

Which would bring them to me.

The Allington's automatic doors hissed open, and I walked up to the reception desk.

'Any idea what's going on? There are police all over the place?'

The receptionist hadn't looked up yet. 'I heard a bang earlier on,' she said. 'I don't know what it's about though.'

'Any messages for me? Wesley, room 203.'

Now she looked up. 'Goodness, Mr Wesley, what happened to you?'

I touched my forehead. 'Tripped and fell. Bloody London pavements.'

'Dear me. I think we've got some plasters.'

'I've some in my room, thanks.' I paused. 'No messages then?'

'Yes, there's a message, came not ten minutes ago.' She handed it to me, and I read it.

'Shit,' I said in exasperation, letting my shoulders slump for the second time that day. 'Can you make my bill up, please? Looks like I'll be checking out.'

I couldn't risk taking a cab straight from the Allington to another hotel – the cabbie would be able to tell police my destination – so I walked about a bit, lugging my suitcase with me. It was lighter than before, about fourteen pounds lighter, and too big for the purpose. Having used nearly all my cash settling my bill, I drew two hundred out of a cash machine. The first two hotels I tried were both full, but the third had a small single room with a shower but no bath. The hotel sold souvenirs to guests, including a large holdall with the hotel name emblazoned front and back. I bought one and took it upstairs with me. Later that evening, I took my now empty suitcase to King's Cross. Luggage lockers are hard to find in central London, so I deposited the case in the left luggage room at King's Cross station. Seeing the size of the case, the man behind the desk braced himself before attempting to lift it, then was caught off-balance by how light it was.

I took another cab back to my hotel and settled down to watch the news. But I couldn't concentrate. They seemed to think I'd hit the wrong person. They thought I was after the diplomat. Well, that would help muddy the water, I didn't mind that at all. Then they mentioned that police had taken away a large box from a building across from the hotel. They showed the alley where my little device had gone off. The metal bin looked like torn wrapping. Nobody had been injured, though two kitchen assistants in a Chinese restaurant had been treated for shock and cuts from flying glass.

They did not, of course, speculate as to how police had arrived on the scene so quickly. But I was thinking about it. I was tumbling it in my mind, and not coming up with any clever answers.

Tomorrow, there'd be time for thinking tomorrow. I was exhausted. I didn't feel like meat and wine any more. I felt like sleep.

4

There was little love lost between Freddy Ricks and Geoffrey Johns, despite which, the solicitor was not surprised to receive Freddy's call.

Freddy was half cut, as per usual, and sounded dazed.

'Have you heard?'

'Yes,' Geoffrey Johns said, 'I've heard.' He was seated in his living room, a glass of Armagnac trembling beside him on the arm of the sofa.

'Jesus Christ,' wailed Freddy Ricks, 'she's been *shot*!'

'Freddy, I'm . . . I'm so sorry.' Geoffrey Johns took a sip of burning liquid. 'Does Archie know?'

'Archie?' It took Freddy an understandable moment to recognise the name of his son. 'I haven't seen him. I had to go down to the . . . they wanted me to identify her. Then they had to ask me some questions.'

'Is that why you're phoning?'

'What? No, no . . . well, yes, in a way. I mean, there are things I have to do, and there are about fifty reporters at the garden gate, and . . . well, Geoffrey, I know we've had our differences, but you *are* our solicitor.'

'I understand, Freddy. I'll be straight over.'

In Vine Street police station, Chief Inspector Bob Broome was deciding what to say to the press. They were clamouring around the entrance to the gloomy station. Even on sunny days, Vine Street, a high narrow conduit between Regent Street and Piccadilly, got little light, though it managed to get all the available traffic fumes and grime. Broome reckoned the station had affected him. He thought he could remember days when he used to be cheerful. His last smile had been a couple of days ago, his last full-throated laugh several months back. Nobody bothered trying to tell him jokes any more. The prisoners in the cells were a more obliging target.

'So what've we got, Dave?'

Detective Inspector Dave Edmond sat opposite Broome. He had a reputation as a dour bugger, too. People seeing them together usually gave the pair a wide berth, like you would a plague ship. While Broome was tall and thin with an undertaker's pallor, Edmond was round and tanned. He'd just returned from a fortnight in Spain, spent guzzling San Miguel on some beach.

'Well, sir,' he said, 'we're still taking statements. The gun's down at the lab. We've got technicians in the office building, but they won't be able to report before tomorrow.'

There was a knock at the door and a WPC came in with a couple of faxes for Broome. He laid them to one side and watched her leave, then turned back to Edmond. His every action was slow and considered, like he was on tranquillisers, but Edmond for one knew the boss was just being careful.

'What about the gun?'

'Sergeant Wills is the pop-pop guru,' Edmond said, 'so I've sent him to take a look at it. He probably knows more than any of the eggheads in the Ballistics section. From the description I gave him, he said it sounds military.'

'Let's not muck about, Dave, it's the Demolition Man again. You can spot his m.o. a mile away.'

Edmond nodded. 'Unless it's a copycat.'

'What are the chances?'

Edmond shrugged. 'A hundred to one?'

'And the rest. What about the phone call, did we take a recording?'

Edmond shook his head. 'The officer who took the call has typed out what he remembers of the conversation.' He handed over a single sheet of paper.

The door opened again. It was a DC this time, smiling apologetically as he came in with more sheets of paper for the Chief Inspector. Outside, there were sounds of frenzied activity. When the DC had gone, Broome got up, went to the door, and pulled a chair against it, jamming the back of the chair under the knob. Then he walked slowly back to his desk.

'Shame we didn't get it on tape though,' he said, picking up Edmond's sheet of paper. 'Male, English, aged between twenty and seventy-five. Yes, very useful. Call didn't sound long distance.' Broome looked up from the report. 'And all he said was that there was going to be a shooting outside the Craigmead Hotel.'

'Normally, it would be treated as a crank, but the officer got the impression this one wasn't playing games. A very educated voice, quite matter-of-fact with just enough emotion. We couldn't have got men there any quicker.'

'We could if we hadn't armed some of them first.'

'The man who called, who do you think it was?'

'I suppose it could have been the Demolition Man himself. Maybe he's gone off his trolley, wants us to catch him or play some sort of cat-and-mouse with him. Or it could be someone who spotted him, but then why not warn those people on the steps?' Broome paused. His office wasn't much bigger than an interview room; in some ways, it was even less inviting. He liked it because it made people who came here feel uncomfortable. But Dave Edmond seemed to like it too . . . 'The people on the steps, that's another thing. We've got a journalist, a Secretary of State, and some senior bod from an East European embassy.'

'So which one was the target?' Edmond asked.

'Exactly. I mean, did he get who he was going after? If not, the other two better be careful. Remember, he's shot the wrong bloody person before.'

Edmond nodded. 'It'll be out of our hands soon anyway.'

This was true: Scotland Yard and the Anti-Terrorist unit would pick over the bones. But this was Bob Broome's manor, and he wasn't about to just hand the case over and catch a good night's sleep.

'Bollocks,' he said. 'What about this other phone call, the one to the Craigmead?'

'We're talking to the receptionist again. All she knows is that a man called wanting to speak to Eleanor Ricks. Ricks was paged, but she ignored it.'

'She hadn't left?'

'No, the receptionist says she walked past the desk while her name was being put out over the loudspeakers.'

'Was the Secretary of State with her?'

'Yes. But she says she didn't hear anything.'

'So maybe Eleanor Ricks didn't hear anything either?'

'Maybe.'

'But if she'd taken the call . . .'

'Molly Prendergast would have walked out of the hotel alone.'

'And we'd have a clearer idea who the intended target was.' Broome sighed.

'So what's our next step, Bob?'

Broome checked his watch. 'For one thing, I've a transatlantic call to make. For another, there's the media to deal with. Then I'll want to see those buggers at the hospital.'

'They're being brought in.'

'Good. Nice of them to help him escape, wasn't it?'

'Think he might've had an accomplice?'

'I think,' said Bob Broome, getting to his feet, 'he might've just lost one of his nine lives.'

'That phone call, sir.'

'Oh, right.' Broome sat down again. Someone was trying the door, but the chair was holding. He picked up the phone. He knew one man who'd want to know the Demolition Man was back in London. 'I want to place a call to the United States,' he said into the receiver.

5

Hoffer hated flying, especially these days when business class was out of the question. He hated being cooped up like a factory chicken. He was strictly a free-range cockerel. The crew didn't like it if you strayed too far for too long. They were always getting in the way, squeezing these damned tin trolleys down aisles just wide enough for them. Those aisles, they weren't even wide enough for *him*. You were supposed to stay in your seat to make the trolley-pushers' jobs easier. Screw them, he was the customer.

There were other problems too. His nose got all blocked up on long-haul flights, and his ears bothered him. He'd yawn like a whale on a plankton hunt and swallow like he was choking down a lump of concrete, but his head got more and more like a pressure cooker no matter what he did. He waited till the better-looking stewardess came along and asked her with a pained smile if she had any tips. Maybe there were tablets these days for this sort of thing. But she came back to his seat with two plastic drinks cups and said he should clamp them over his ears.

'What is this, a joke? I'm supposed to wear these things all the way to London?'

He crunched the plastic cups in his beefy fists and got up to use the bathroom. There was a guy four rows back who kept laughing at the in-flight movie, some Steve Martin vehicle which had left the factory without wheels or any gas in its tank. The guy looked like he'd have laughed at Nuremberg.

The bathroom: now there was another problem. A Japanese coffin would have been roomier. It took him a while to get everything set out: mirror, penknife, stash. They'd been sticky about the knife at airport security, until he explained that he was a New York private detective, not a Palestinian terrorist, and that the knife was a present for his cousin in London.

'Since when,' he'd argued finally, 'did you get *fat* terrorists? Come to that, when did you last see a pocket-knife terrorist? I'd be better armed with the in-flight knife and fork.'

So they'd let him through.

He took a wrinkled dollar bill from his pocket and rolled it up. Well, it was either that or a straw from the in-flight drinks, and those straws were so narrow you could hardly suck anything up. He'd read somewhere that eighty percent of all the twenty-dollar bills in circulation bore traces of cocaine. Yeah, but he was a dollar sort of guy. Even rolled up, however, the dollar was crumpled. He considered doing a two-and-two, placing the powder on his pinky and snorting it, but you wasted a lot that way. Besides, he was shaking so much, he doubted he'd get any of the coke near his nose.

He'd laid out a couple of lines. It wasn't great coke, but it was good enough. He remembered the days of great coke, stuff that would burn to white ash on the end of a cigarette. These days, the stuff was reconstituted Colombia-Miami shit, not the beautiful Peruvian blow of yore. If you tried testing it on a cigarette tip, it turned black and smelt like a Jamaican party. He knew this stuff was going to burn his nose. He saw his face in the mirror above the sink. He saw the lines around his mouth and under his eyes, coke lines. Then he turned back to the business at hand and took a good hit.

He wiped what was left off the mirror with his thumb and rubbed it over his gums. It was sour for a second before the freeze arrived. Okay, so he'd powdered his nose. He doubted it would put wheels on the movie, but maybe he'd find something else to laugh at. You never could tell.

Hoffer ran his own detective agency these days, though he managed to employ just two other tecs and a secretary. He'd started in a sleazy rental above a peep show off Times Square, reckoning that was how private eyes operated in the movies. But he soon saw that clients were put off by the location, so he took over a cleaner set of offices in Soho. The only problem was, they were up three flights of stairs, and there was no elevator. So Hoffer tended to work from home, using his phone and fax. He had one tec working for him; he'd only met the guy twice, both times in a McDonald's. But the clients were happier now that Hoffer Private Investigations was above a chi-chi splatter gallery selling canvases that looked like someone had been hacked to death on them and then the post mortem carried out. The cheapest painting in the shop covered half a wall and would set the buyer back $12,000. Hoffer knew the gallery would last about another six months. He saw them carry paintings in, but he never saw one leave. Still, at least Hoffer had clients. There'd been a while when he'd been able to trade on his name alone, back when the media exposure had been good. But stories died quickly, and for a while the name Hoffer wasn't enough.

$12,000 would buy about eight weeks of Hoffer agency time, not including expenses. Robert Walkins had promised to deposit exactly that sum in the agency's bank account when Hoffer had spoken to him by phone. It was funny, speaking to the man again. After all, Walkins had been Hoffer's first client. In some ways, he was Hoffer's *only* client, the only one that mattered.

The Demolition Man was in action again, and Hoffer badly wanted to be part of the action. He didn't just want it, he *needed* it. He had salaries and taxes to pay, the rent on his apartment, overheads, and money for his favourite drugs. He needed the Demolition Man. More crucially, he needed the publicity. When he'd started out for himself, he'd hired a publicity consultant before he'd hired an accountant. When he'd learned enough from the publicist, he'd kicked her out. She had a great body, but for what she was costing him he could *buy* a great body, and it wouldn't just talk or cross its legs either.

When he'd got the call from London, he'd been able to pack his bags in about thirty minutes. But first he'd called to get a ticket on the first available flight, and then he'd called Robert Walkins.

'Mr Walkins? This is Leo Hoffer.' On the force, they'd all called him Lenny, but since he'd left the force and recreated himself, he'd decided on Leo. The Lion. So what if he was actually Capricorn?

'Mr Hoffer, I take it there's news?' Walkins always sounded like he'd just found you taking a leak on his carpet.

'He's in London.' Hoffer paused. 'London, England.'

'I didn't think you meant London, Alabama.'

'Well, he's there.'

'And you're going to follow him?'

'Unless you don't want me to?'

'You know our agreement, Mr Hoffer. Of course I want you to follow him. I want him caught.'

'Yes, sir.'

'I'll transfer some funds. How much will you need?'

'Say, twelve thou?' Hoffer held his breath. Walkins hadn't been tight with money, not so far, though he'd nixed Hoffer travelling club class.

'Very well. Good luck, Mr Hoffer.'

'Thank you, sir.'

Then he'd packed. It didn't take long because he didn't own a lot of clothes. He checked with Moira at the office that she'd be able to control things for a week or so. She told him to bring her back a souvenir, 'something royal'.

'What about a pain in the ass?' he'd suggested.

He finished packing and called for a cab. He didn't have any notes to take with him. All the notes he needed were firmly lodged inside his head. He wondered if he should take a book with him for the journey, but dismissed the notion. There were no books in the apartment anyway, and he could always buy a couple of magazines at the airport. As a final measure, he stuck his penknife in his carry-on luggage, and his mirror and stash in his inside jacket pocket. The knife, of thick sharp steel, was purposely ornate and expensive: that way people believed him when he said it was a gift for his cousin. It was French, a Laguiole, with mahogany handle and a serpent motif. In emergencies, it also had a corkscrew. But the real quality of the thing was its blade.

He knew the cab was on its way, which left him only a few minutes to make his final decision. Should he carry a gun? In the wardrobe in his bedroom he had a pump-action over-under shotgun and a couple of unmarked semi-automatic pistols. He kept the serious stuff elsewhere. Ideally, he'd go get something serious. But he didn't have time. So he grabbed the Smith & Wesson 459, its holster and some ammo from the wardrobe. He packed it in his suitcase, wrapped in his only sweater. The door buzzer sounded just as he was closing his case.

At London Heathrow, he phoned a hotel he'd used before just off Piccadilly Circus and managed to get a room. The receptionist wanted to tell him all about how the hotels were quiet for the time of year, there just weren't the tourists around that there used to be . . . Hoffer put the phone down on her. It wasn't just that he felt like shit. He couldn't understand what she was saying either.

He knew he could claim for a cab, so schlepped his stuff down to the Underground and took a train into town. It wasn't much better than New York. Three young toughs were working the carriages, asking for money from the newly-arrived travellers. Hoffer hadn't taken the Smith &

Wesson out of his case yet, which was good news for the beggars. London, he decided, was definitely on its way down the pan. Even the centre of town looked like it had been turned over by a gang. Everything had been torn up or sprayed on. Last time he'd been in London, there had been more punks around, but there'd been more life to the place too, and fewer street people.

The train journey took forever. His body knew that it was five hours earlier than everyone around him thought it was. His feet were swollen, and sitting in the train brought on another bout of ear pressure. Plastic cups, for Christ's sake.

But the receptionist smiled and was sympathetic. He told her if she really felt sorry for him he had a litre of Scotch in his bag and she knew his room number. She still managed to smile, but she had to force it. Then he got to his room and remembered all the very worst things about England. Namely, the beds and the plumbing. His bed was way too narrow. They had wider beds in the concentration camps. When he phoned reception, he was told all the beds in the single rooms were the same size, and if he wanted a double bed he'd need to pay for a double room. So then he'd to take the elevator back down to reception, get a new room, and take the elevator back up. This room was a little better, not much. He switched the TV on and went into the bathroom to run a bath. The bath looked like a child might have fun in it, but an adult would have problems, and the taps were having prostate trouble if the dribble issuing from them was anything to go by. There wasn't even a proper glass by the sink, just another plastic tumbler. He unscrewed the top from his Johnny Walker Red Label and poured generously. He was about to add water from the cold tap, but thought better of it, so he drank the Scotch neat and watched the water finally cover the bottom of the bath.

He toasted the mirror. 'Welcome to England,' he said.

He'd arranged to meet Bob Broome in the hotel bar.

They knew one another from a conference they'd attended in Toronto when both had been Drugs Squad officers. That was going back some time, but then they'd met again when Hoffer had been in London last trip, just over a year ago. He'd been tracking the Demolition Man then, too.

'You mean Walkins is still paying you?' Broome sounded awed.

'I'm not on a retainer or anything,' Hoffer said. 'But when we hear anything new on the D-Man, I know I can follow it up and Walkins will pay.'

Bob Broome shook his head. 'I still can't believe you got here so quickly.'

'No ties, Bob, that's the secret.' Hoffer looked around the bar. 'This place stinks, let's go for a walk.' He saw Broome look at him, laughed and patted his jacket. 'It's okay, Bob, I'm not armed.' Broome looked relieved.

It was Sunday evening and the streets were quiet. They walked into Soho and found a pub seedy enough for Hoffer's tastes, where they ordered bitter and found a corner table.

'So, Bob, what've you got?'

Broome placed his pint glass carefully on a beermat, checking its base was equidistant from all four edges. 'There was a shooting yesterday evening at six o'clock, outside a hotel near the US Embassy. A minute or two after the shooting, a bomb exploded in a rubbish bin nearby. We had an anonymous call warning us, so we sent men over there. We arrived just too late, but in time to start a search for the assassin. But he'd been a bit too clever. We went for the building directly in front of the hotel, and he'd been holed up in the office block next-door. He must have seen us coming. He called for an ambulance, gave them some story about being seriously ill, and they whisked him away to hospital from right under our noses.'

Hoffer shook his head. 'But you've got a description?'

'Oh, yes, a good description, always supposing he wasn't wearing a wig and coloured contact lenses.'

'He left the weapon behind?'

Broome nodded. 'An L96A1 Sniper Rifle.'

'Never heard of it.'

'It's British, a serious piece of goods. He'd tweaked it, added a flash hider and some camouflage tape. The telescopic sight on it was worth what I take home in a month.'

'Nobody ever said the D-Man came cheap. Speaking of which . . . ?'

'We don't even know who his target was. There were four people on the steps: a diplomat and his wife, the Secretary of State for the DSS, and the journalist.'

'How far was he away from the hotel?'

'Seventy, eighty yards.'

'Unlikely he missed his target.'

'He's missed before.'

'Yeah, but that was a fluke. He must've been after the reporter.'

'We're keeping an open mind. The diplomat seems sure he was the intended victim.'

'Well, *you* have to keep an open mind, I don't. In fact, I'm famous for my *closed* mind.' Hoffer finished his drink. 'Want another?' Broome shook his head. 'I need to see anything you've got, Bob.'

'That's not so easy, Leo. I'd have to clear it with my—'

'By the way, something for your kids.' Hoffer took an envelope from his pocket and slid it across the table. 'How are they anyway?'

'They're fine, thanks.' Broome looked in the envelope. He was looking at £500.

'Don't try to refuse it, Bob, I had a hell of a job cashing cheques at the hotel. I think they charged me the same again for the privilege, plus they had an exchange rate you wouldn't accept from a shark. Put it in your pocket. It's for your kids.'

'I'm sure they'll be thankful,' Broome said, tucking the envelope in his inside pocket.

'They're nice kids. What're their names again?'

'Whatever you want them to be,' said the childless Broome.

'So can you get me the info?'

'I can do some photocopying. You'll have it first thing in the morning.'

Hoffer nodded. 'Meantime, talk to me, get me interested. Tell me about the deceased.'

'Her name is Eleanor Ricks, 39, freelance journalist. She covered the Falklands War and some of the early fighting in ex-Yugoslavia.'

'So she wasn't just puffing fluff?'

'No, and lately she'd made the move into television. Yesterday she had a meeting with Molly Prendergast, that's the DSS Minister.'

'What was the meeting about? No, wait, same again?' Hoffer went to the bar and ordered two more pints. He never had to wait long at bars; they were one place where his size lent him a certain authority. It didn't matter if he wasn't wearing great clothes, or hadn't shaved in a while, he had weight and he had standing.

That was one reason he did a lot of his work in bars.

He brought the drinks back. He'd added a double whisky to go with his beer.

'You want one?' But Broome shook his head. Hoffer drank an inch from the beer, then poured in the whisky. He took two cigarettes from one of his packs of duty free, lit them and handed one to Broome.

'Sorry,' he apologised, 'bad habit.' It wasn't everyone who wanted him sucking on their cigarette before they got it. 'You were telling me about Molly Prendergast.'

'It was an interview, something to do with Ricks's latest project, the one for TV. It's an investigation of religious cults.'

'And this MP has something to do with them?'

'Only indirectly. Her daughter was involved in one for a while. Prendergast and her husband had to fight like mad to get her back. In the end, they virtually had to kidnap her.'

'And that's what Ricks wanted to talk about?'

'According to Mrs Prendergast.'

'You don't sound too sure.'

'I've no reason to suppose she'd lie. Besides, her story is backed up by the programme's producer.'

'What's his name?' Hoffer had taken a notebook and pen from his pocket.

'Joe Draper. One strange thing, somebody called the hotel. They asked for Eleanor Ricks and said it was urgent. She was paged, but she didn't take the call. Not many people knew she was going to be there. Draper's one of the few.'

'Which TV company is it?'

'It's a small independent production company. I think it's just called Draper Films or Draper Vision, something like that.'

'You work too hard, Bob, you know that? I mean, you're a seven-day man, am I right? Of course I'm right. You've got to rest your brain some time.'

'It's not easy.'

'But if you don't rest your brain, you start forgetting things, like whether it's Draper Films or Draper Vision. I mean, little things, Bob, but little things can be the important things. You're a cop, you know that.'

Broome didn't look happy at this little lecture. In fact, he finished his drink and said he had to be going. Hoffer didn't stop him. But he didn't hang around the pub either. It reminded him of a few bad Irish bars he knew in and around the other Soho. He headed across Shaftesbury Avenue and into Leicester Square, looking for interesting drugs or interesting whores. But even Leicester Square was quiet. Nobody worked a patch these days. It was all done by mobile phone. The telephone kiosks were full of whores' business cards. He perused them, like he was in a gallery, but didn't find anything new or exciting. He doubted there was anything new under the sun, though apparently they were doing mind-boggling things with computers these days.

There were some kids begging from their doorway beds, so he asked them if they knew where he could find some blow, then remembered that over here 'blow' could mean boo. They didn't know anyway. They hardly knew their own damned names. He went on to Charing Cross Road and found a taxi to take him to Hampstead.

This was where the D-Man had carried out his other London hit, at an office on the High Street. As usual, he'd kept his distance. He'd fired from a building across the street, the bullet smashing through a window before entering and leaving the heart of an Indian businessman who'd been implicated in a finance scam involving several governments and private companies.

The D-Man always kept his distance, which interested Hoffer. Often, it would be simpler just to walk up to the victim and use a pistol. But the D-Man used sniper rifles and kept his distance. These facts told Hoffer a lot. They told him that the D-Man was a real pro, not just some hoodlum. He was skilled, a marksman. He gave himself a challenge with every hit. But he was also squeamish the way hoodlums seldom were. He didn't like to get too close to the gore. He kept well away from the pain. A single shot to the heart: it was a marksman's skill all right, hitting dead centre every time.

He'd planted a bomb in Hampstead too, though he hadn't needed one. The police had thought they were dealing with an IRA device, until they linked it to the assassination. Then Hoffer had come along and he'd been able to tell them quite a lot about the Demolition Man. Few people knew as much as Hoffer did about the D-Man.

But Hoffer didn't know nearly enough.

He took another cab back to the hotel, and got the driver to give him half a dozen blank receipts, tipping him generously as reward. He'd fill the receipts in himself and hand them to his client as proof of expenses.

'Anything else you want, guv?' said the driver. 'An escort? Bit of grass? You name it.'

Nostrils twitching, Hoffer leaned forward in his seat.

'Get me interested,' he said.

6

Mark Wesley was dead.

It was a shame, since it meant I'd have to close a couple of bank accounts and get rid of a bunch of expensive counterfeit identity cards and an even more expensive counterfeit passport with some beautifully crafted visas in it.

More drastic still, it was the only other identity I had in the UK, which meant that from now on I'd have to be me. I could always arrange to create another identity, but it took time and money.

I'd spent a long time not being me. It would take a while to get used to the name again: Michael Weston. The first thing I did was rent a car and get out of London. I rented from one of the big companies, and told them it might be a one-way rental. They explained that one-way rentals are more expensive, but since I was guaranteeing it with a credit card they didn't seem to mind.

It was a nice car, a red Escort XR3i with only 600 miles on the clock. I drove to a shopping complex just off the North Circular Road and bought, amongst other things, a hat. Then I headed north. I didn't phone ahead. I didn't want Max expecting me.

I'd spent a lot of time thinking, and I kept coming up with the same answer: someone had tipped off the police, someone who had wanted me caught. There were only two possibilities: Max, or my employer. I never like to know who I'm working for, just as I never like to know anything about the person I'm being paid to kill. I don't want to be involved, I just want the money. The work I get comes from a variety of middlemen: a couple in the USA, one in Germany, one in Hong Kong, and Max in England. It was Max who'd contacted me with the job I'd just done. He was the only other person apart from my employer who knew the details of the job.

Like I say, I'd given it a lot of thought, and still it came down to Max or my employer. This still left the question of why. Why would Max want me arrested? Was the money suddenly not enough to salve his conscience? He could get out any time he wanted to, but maybe he didn't realise that. If he wanted out, but thought I wouldn't like such an idea, maybe he also thought I'd want to kill him. Was he just getting his retaliation in first?

Then there was my employer. Maybe he or she had got cold feet at the very last, and phoned for the cops. This seemed the more likely answer, though there was one other consideration: what if the whole thing had been a trap from the start? I was sure I could come up with other theories, but they all led in the same direction: I was going to have to talk to Max. Then maybe I'd have to find out who my employer was, and ask them a few questions, too.

It bothered me. I hate to get involved. I hate to know. But this time there might be no other way. I might have to find out *why* I'd been paid to assassinate Eleanor Ricks. I'd seen the papers and the news. It was in my favour that the authorities were baffled. They still didn't know who my target had been. But I knew, right down to her name and the details of her dress. The diplomat had been there by pure chance, though not the politician. Whoever had known Eleanor Ricks would be coming out of the hotel at six knew her very well. So they almost certainly also knew the politician would be with her. Was I scaring off the politician? Was I sending a message?

Maybe you begin to see why I don't like getting involved.

I didn't rush my journey. I wanted my arrival to surprise Max. If I turned up straight away, he would probably be less surprised. But I broke my journey quite near him in Yorkshire, so I could walk in on him early the following morning. Max was a careful man, but he didn't go armed to the breakfast table. He was also surrounded by fields and hills. No one would hear a shot, no one would hear a burial.

No one except Belinda.

I booked into a small hotel, wearing my cap at the reception desk. Then I went out and had a haircut, quite a severe one.

'You sure about this?' the barber asked.

'I'm sure,' I said. 'It's for the summer. Gets too hot otherwise.'

'True enough,' he said, picking up the scissors.

I wore the cap again on my way back to my room, then washed my hair and used some of the dye I'd bought on it, turning it from dark brown to inky black. I looked at my eyebrows too, but reckoned I could get away with not dyeing them. The cropped hair didn't take long to dry. The cut on my forehead was healing quickly, though there was still bruising around the scab.

I unpacked my bag. I'd bought some new clothes at the shopping centre and ditched the ones I'd worn for the hit. This wasn't a special precaution: I always wear cheap clothes on a hit, then discard them afterwards. If you've used a gun, forensic scientists will find traces of the primer compound on your hands and clothes. Incredible, isn't it? When I tell Max these things, he doesn't believe me. He says they make it all up to scare people off using guns. Maybe he's got a point. In the bag I also had my standby, a .357 Magnum, not bought from Max this time but from a friend in France. It was a Colt copy, and not a very good one. On the firing range, it seemed to want to aim everywhere but at the bull. Its saving grace was that, like all revolvers, it scared people. That was its job. I didn't think it would scare Max; nevertheless, I wanted him to know I was armed.

There wasn't much else in the bag except for a manila envelope, a few bottles of fine white powder, some larger bottles of sterilised water, and a couple of packs of disposable syringes. I always kept them in the bag, ever since a hotel maid had spotted them in my bathroom and informed the manager that I was dealing heroin from my room. Poor girl, she'd been so embarrassed afterwards. But I'd left her a tip anyway.

I lay on my bed for a while, running one finger through what was left of my hair and stroking the cat with the other. The cat belonged to the hotel. I'd seen it in the lobby on arrival and made a clicking noise to attract it.

'Don't bother,' the receptionist had said. 'Geronimo's very timid.'

Maybe, but I have a way with animals. Geronimo had padded meekly to my room unsummoned, and had miaowed at the door until I let him in, after which he'd twined himself round my legs a few times, then rubbed his jaw along my proffered knuckles, leaving his scent on me. I didn't have anything for him to eat, but he forgave me. So we lay, the pair of us, our eyes closed, somewhere between thought and nothingness, until I went down to the bar for some supper.

Back in my room, having drunk an indifferent half-bottle of Montrachet, I opened the manila envelope. This contained all the details of the hit, everything my employer had wanted me to know about Eleanor Ricks. I'm not a forensic scientist or a descendant of Sherlock Holmes, but I could tell the stapled sheets of paper had been word processed. The print quality was good, and the printing itself nice and regular. The paper was heavy and had a watermark. There was no handwriting anywhere; even the envelope had been typed. All it said was 'Private & Confidential'.

I read through the information again, searching for clues to my employer's identity. There was a photo of the target, too. It was a head and shoulders shot. She was smiling, her head tipped to one side so the hair fell and rested on her shoulder. It looked to me like a professional job, a publicity shot. For a start, it was black and white, and how many people use monochrome film these days? Plus it was obviously posed, definitely not a snapshot.

Who would have access to publicity shots? The photographer of course, plus the model. The model's employers, and probably members of her immediate family ... plus fans, the housekeeper, and anyone who happened to snatch one off a desk. I wasn't exactly narrowing things down.

I've said I don't like knowing about my targets, but my employer this time had sent me a lot of information, much of it extraneous. The amount of background they knew, they had to be close to the target. I mean, this wasn't the sort of stuff you could glean from press cuttings alone. They had to have known her pretty damned well. Either that or they'd been extremely thorough in their research.

None of which explained how they'd known the sorts of colours she'd be wearing on the day. I was back to family and the people she worked with. I had the idea I was going to have to go back to London and do some digging ... but that would all depend on what Max had to say.

I settled my bill that night, since in the morning I intended starting off before breakfast. But the manageress wouldn't hear of this, and was up at six to cook me bacon and scrambled eggs and boil some tea. She even sat with me as I ate, though I'd have preferred to be alone.

'Long drive ahead of you?'

'Not really. Just a busy day.'

'I know all about that, sweetie.'

I smiled, but doubted this. As I left, Geronimo came out to the car with me, but then caught the scent of something better and trotted away. There was a heavy dew on the car, and the morning was raw, with cloud low and thick in the valleys and the roads wet. But the XR3i started at the first turn of the ignition. I had the .357 on the passenger seat, covered with the local freesheet which I'd picked up in the bar last night. As I drove off, I knew I had a long walk ahead.

Max's house sat in nine acres of moorland, the monotony broken only by the dry-stone dykes which divided the land into unused enclosures. The dykes had been built to give local employment during the hardest years of the 1920s. They were never intended to be put to any use. Max used those nearest his house as firing ranges, and had converted a long Dutch-style barn into an indoor range. The rest of the farm buildings had either been knocked down or left to fall in their own good time. Piles of rocks dotted what had been the farmyard. Max had graded them into large, middling and small, for no good reason that I could see. But then he was always methodical, even with debris.

I stopped the car about a mile from the house and left it on the grass verge, then climbed over one of the walls and started walking. The grass was wet underfoot, and I wished I'd bought some boots. But better this than driving up to the house. You could hear a car from hundreds of yards away. Though I could see the house, I knew the kitchen faced on to the interior farmyard, not out over the moors. I counted fewer than a dozen trees in the whole expanse, and wondered how Bel could live here.

I'd pushed the Magnum into my trouser waistband, but the ground was so uneven I transferred it to my jacket pocket. I kept a hand on it as I walked. I'd noticed in the car that brown spots of rust were appearing on the barrel. That was the problem with a cheap gun, it wasn't worth the maintenance.

Halfway across the first field, I stopped dead. I didn't know if I was ready for this. It was a long time since I'd used a handgun, even as a means of threat. Besides, if Max didn't have anything to do with it, I had a favour to ask of him . . . and of Bel.

Max no longer kept a dog. He thought animals belonged in the wild. There were no pets at all on the farm, though Bel was soppy about cats and dogs and horses. Everything was quiet as I clambered over the last wall on to the track. If Max kept to his regular schedule, he'd be in the kitchen just now, probably eating something macrobiotic. He was on a weird diet which he swore was keeping the cancer at bay. I walked around the side of the house and peered round the wall. The farmyard was silent. I could see Max's Volvo estate parked in the barn, and behind it one of the human-shaped targets belonging to the indoor range. I took the Magnum from my pocket and walked to the kitchen door, turning the handle.

The kitchen had been gutted and redone about a year ago. It was all gleaming white tile and white units. Kept fanatically clean, it reminded me more of a hospital lab than a kitchen. And at its centre, seated at a foldaway table, was Max. He was already dressed and had strapped his mask across his maimed cheek and jaw. He was trying to eat something brown and sludgy with a teaspoon, and listening to the 'Today' programme on Radio Four.

'I wondered when you'd get here,' he said, not looking up. He had one hand on his bowl, the other holding his spoon. He was showing me both hands so I wouldn't get nervous. I wasn't aiming the gun. It was hanging almost casually from my hand. 'Want some breakfast?'

'You don't sound surprised to see me, Max.'

Now he looked up at me. 'That's some serious haircut, boy. Of course I'm not surprised. I heard what happened. They said the police were on the scene just too late to stop the shooting. I knew what you'd think.'

'What would I think, Max?' I leaned against the sink, keeping my distance.

'Do you want some breakfast?'

'I've had some, thanks.'

'Tea?'

'All right.' He got up to fetch a mug from the rack. 'You haven't answered my question.'

'That's because it's a stupid question. I was waiting for you to come up with a cleverer one.' He shuffled back to the table with the mug. 'Sit down, why don't you? And put away that bloody awful revolver. It embarrasses me having to look at it. Bloody cheap Asian copy, you'd probably miss me even at six feet. How far out of alignment is it?'

'About half an inch at twenty yards.'

Max wrinkled his nose. 'And it's rusting. If you tried popping me with that, I'd more likely die of shame than anything.'

I smiled, but didn't put the gun away. Max sighed.

'If not for me, then for Bel.'

'Where is she?'

'Sound asleep in her bed, lazy sow. Here, do you want this tea?'

I took the mug from the table and placed it on the draining board, leaning against the sink again.

'So,' said Max, 'someone knew you were doing the hit, and they tipped off the police. Stands to reason it must have been me or whoever was paying you in the first place.' I nodded. He looked up at me again. 'Well, it wasn't me. I don't blame you for being cagey, but it wasn't. So all I can do is tell you how the job came about. A man phoned me, a greaseball called Scotty Shattuck. Do you know him?' I shook my head. 'He was regular Army, but got a fright or something in the Falklands. Collected a few ears as souvenirs, and when the Army found out they dumped him back into society. He's tried his hand at mercenary work since, trained some of the fighters in Sarajevo. He doesn't have much of a rep, spends more time bouncing for night clubs than doing short-arms practice.'

'Where does he live?'

'Don't rush me, Mark. Shattuck said he had a client who was interested in having a job done. What he meant was someone had slipped him a few quid to find an assassin.'

'Why didn't he just take the job himself?'

'Maybe he pitched for it but the client knew his rep. Anyway, I said I'd need a few details, and we met in Leeds. He handed over a sealed envelope, giving me the gen I gave to you when I phoned you.'

'How much did he know about the hit?'

Max shrugged. 'The envelopes weren't tampered with, but he could always have torn open the original envelopes, read the gen for himself, and put it in a fresh envelope after.'

'Would he be curious enough to do that?'

'I don't know, maybe. Shattuck would like to play with the big boys. He seemed to think I was some sort of pimp with a stable of snipers, asked if I'd give him a trial. I told him to behave. And he did behave, too, except when payment time came.'

'Yes?'

'At our final meet, again in Leeds, he handed over the case. The final details were there, but the cash was short. Two hundred short. He said it was his cut. I told him that was fine by me, but the person the money was going to wouldn't be pleased. I asked him if two hundred was worth having to look over his shoulder the rest of his life and not go near windows.'

I grinned. 'What did he say?'

'He didn't say anything, he just sort of twitched and sweated. Then he took the money out of his pocket and handed it over.' Talking was thirsty work for Max. He had a straw in his mug of tea and took a long suck on it.

'So where can I find him, Max?'

'I don't know.'

'Come on, you must know.'

'I never needed to know. It was always him that contacted me.'

I raised the gun ever so slightly. 'Max,' I said. I didn't bother saying anything else. I was too busy looking at the kitchen doorway, the one leading to the hall and the rest of the house. Bel was standing there. She was wearing a short nightdress, showing very nice legs.

She was also pointing a shotgun at me.

'I know how to use it, Mark. Put away the gun.'

I didn't move. 'Let's get one thing straight,' I said. 'If you're going to be working for me, my name's not Mark Wesley any more. It's Michael Weston.'

Max leapt from his chair.

'Jesus, Bel! That's a Churchill *Premier*!' He ran to the doorway and took the shotgun from her. 'Do you know how much one of these is worth?'

'About ten grand,' she said.

'Ten grand is right. Less if it's been fired.' He broke open the barrels to show that Bel hadn't bothered loading the thing. I put my Magnum down on the draining board.

'Look,' said Max, 'let's all calm down. I'll tell you what I can about Shattuck, Mark.'

'Michael.'

'Okay, Michael. I'll tell you what I can. But let's sit down. All this Gunfight at the OK Corral stuff makes me nervous, especially in the kitchen. Do you know how long it took me to do this tiling?'

So Max put the kettle on and we sat down. Bel gave me a lopsided smile, and I winked back at her.

'Black suits you,' she said, meaning my hair. 'Even if that haircut does make you look like a copper.' She touched my foot with her own under the table. We'd played this game before, enjoying the fact of having a secret from Max. I tried to remember that only a few minutes ago, she'd been aiming a shotgun at me, albeit unloaded. Bel had the face of a sixth-form schoolgirl, but I knew there was much more to her than that.

'Sorry,' I said, 'I haven't brought you a souvenir this trip.'

She attempted a pout. 'I'm hurt.'

I put my hand in my pocket and pulled out the hat I'd bought. 'Unless you want this.'

She took it from me and looked at it. 'Gee, thanks,' she said, her voice heavy with irony. 'I'll keep it under my pillow.'

Max was massaging his jaw. Usually he didn't say much, understandably. He'd said more in the past twenty minutes than he would over the course of a normal day.

'What was that about me working for you?' Bel asked, folding her arms.

'More properly, working *with* me.' I was looking at Max as I spoke. 'I'm going to have to go back to London, there are questions I need to ask. I'd look less conspicuous with a partner. Plus maybe there are some people I can't talk to myself. But Bel could talk to them.'

'No,' Max said.

'I pay well, and I'd look after her. I'd play it straight. First sign of danger, I zoom back up here with her.'

'What am I, a ventriloquist's dummy?' Bel had risen from the table and was standing with hands on hips. 'Why not ask me yourself? You sound like you're asking to borrow a car or a bike, not a person.'

'Sorry, Bel.'

'You're not going,' said Max.

'I haven't said anything yet!' she protested, slapping the table with her hand. 'I want to hear about it first.'

So I told her. There was no point leaving anything out. Bel wasn't stupid, she certainly wasn't naïve. She'd have rooted out a lie. It isn't easy telling someone what you do for a living, not if you're not proud of your work. I'd never minded Max knowing, but Bel . . . Bel was a slightly different proposition. Of course, she'd known all along. I mean, I was hardly coming to the farm, buying guns, firing them, customising them, I was hardly doing any of this as a weekend hobby. Still, her cheeks reddened as I told my story. Then a third round of tea was organised in silence, with the radio switched off now. Bel poured cereal for herself and started to eat. She'd swallowed two spoonfuls before she said anything.

'I want to go.'

Max started to protest.

'A few days, Max,' I broke in, 'that's all. Look, I need help this time. Who else can I turn to?'

'I can think of a dozen people better qualified than Bel, and always keen to make money.'

'Well, thanks very much,' she said. 'Nice to know you have such a high opinion of me.'

'I just don't want you—'

She took his hand and squeezed it. 'I know, I know. But Michael needs help. Are we supposed to turn our backs? Pretend we've never known him? Who else *do* we know?'

It hit me then for the first time. They lived out here in the wilds through necessity not choice. You couldn't run a gun shop like Max's in the middle of a town. But out here they were also lonely, cut off from the world. There were twice-weekly runs into the village or the nearest large town, but those hardly constituted a social life. It wasn't Max, it was Bel. She was twenty-two. She'd sacrificed a lot to move out here. I saw why Max was scared: he wasn't scared she'd get hurt, he was scared she'd get to like it. He was scared she'd leave for good.

'A few days, Max,' I repeated. 'Then I'll bring Bel back.'

He didn't say anything, just blinked his watery eyes and looked down at the table where his hands lay, nicked and scarred from metal-shop accidents. Bel touched his shoulder.

'I'll go pack a few things.' She gave me another smile and ran from the room. Only now did I wonder why she was so keen to go with me.

We were awkward after she'd gone. I rinsed out the mugs at the sink, and heard Max's chair scrape on the floor as he stood up. He came to the draining board and picked up the revolver.

'Do you need anything?' he asked.

'Maybe a pistol.'

'I think I've got something better than a pistol. Not cheap though.'

'Money's no object this time, Max.'

'Mark . . . Sorry, I mean Michael. Funny, I'd just got used to calling you Mark.'

'I'll be another name soon enough.'

'Michael, I know you'll take care of her. But I wouldn't like . . . I mean, I don't want . . .'

'This is strictly business, Max. Separate rooms, I promise. And besides, Bel can look after herself. She's had a good teacher.'

'Don't patronise me,' he said with a smile, putting down the Magnum and reaching for a dishtowel.

7

'You're not a reporter, are you?'

It was first thing Monday morning and Hoffer wasn't in the mood. The ambulance was parked in a special unloading bay directly outside Casualty, and the ambulanceman was in the back, tidying and checking.

Hoffer stood outside, one hand resting on the vehicle's back door. He had a sudden image of himself slamming the ambulanceman's head repeatedly against it.

'I've told you, I'm a private investigator.'

'Only I told the police everything I know, and then the bleeding newspapers start hassling me.'

'Look, Mr Hughes, I've shown you my ID.'

'Yeah, anyone can fake an identity card.'

This was true, but Hoffer wasn't in a mood for discussion. He had a head like a St Patrick's Day parade in Boston. Plus his ears still weren't back to normal. Every time he breathed in through his nose, it was like he was going to suck his eardrums into his throat.

'Talk to me and I'll go away,' he said. That usually worked. Hughes turned and studied him.

'You don't look like a reporter.'

Hoffer nodded at this wisdom.

'You look like a cardiac arrest waiting to happen.'

Hoffer stopped nodding and started a serious scowl.

'All right, sorry about that. So, what do you want me to tell you?'

'I've seen the transcript of your police interview, Mr Hughes. Basically, I'd just like to ask a few follow-up questions, maybe rephrase a couple of questions you've already been asked.'

'Well, hurry up, I'm on duty.'

Hoffer refrained from pointing out that they could have started a good five minutes ago. Instead he asked about the phony patient's accent.

'Very smooth,' said Hughes. 'Polite, quiet, educated.'

'But definitely English?'

'Oh, yes.'

'Not American? Sometimes the two can sound more similar than you'd think.'

'This was English. I couldn't tell you which county though. He wasn't a Yank, I'm sure of that.'

'Canadian possibly?' Hughes shook his head. 'Okay then, you've given a fairly good description of him, what he was wearing, his height, hair colour and so on. Do you think his hair might have been dyed?'

'How am I supposed to know?'

'Sometimes a dye job doesn't look quite right.'

'Yeah? We must meet a different class of women.'

Hoffer tried to laugh. The door handle felt good in his hand. He kept looking at Hughes's head. 'And it couldn't have been a toupee?'

'You mean an Irish?' Hoffer didn't understand. 'Irish jig, wig. No, I'm sure his hair was his own.'

'Mm-hm.' Hoffer had already spoken to the nurse in Emergency, the one who'd taken the man's details and then gone to call a haematologist. She'd been as much help as codeine in a guillotine basket. He rubbed his forehead. 'He told you he was a haemophiliac.'

'He *was* a haemophiliac.'

'You sure?'

'Either that or he has one in the family. Or maybe he just went through medical school.'

'He knew that much about it?'

'He knew about factor levels, he knew haemophiliacs are supposed to carry a special card with them, he knew they get to call the emergency number and order an ambulance if they hurt themselves. He knew a lot.'

'He couldn't just have been guessing?'

Hughes shook his head. 'I'm telling you, he *knew*.'

'Who's your haematologist here?'

'I don't know, I just act as chauffeur.'

'That's being a bit harsh on yourself.'

Hughes's look told Hoffer flattery wasn't going to work. 'What about the business card, it fell out of his pocket?'

'Yes. He said it was his, but the police tell me it wasn't. They had me take a look at Gerald Flitch, I mean the real Gerald Flitch. It wasn't him.'

'Mm, I want a word with him myself.'

The Casualty doors crashed open as the ambulance driver pulled a wheelchair out and down the ramp. Hughes jumped out of the ambulance. There was a woman in the wheelchair so ancient and still she looked like she'd been stuffed.

'Here we are again, Mrs Bridewell,' Hughes yelled at her, as they prepared to hoist her into the ambulance. 'Soon have you home.'

'Is it worth the trip?' Hoffer muttered to himself. He turned away from the ambulance, but Hughes called to him. The driver was already getting into his seat and starting the engine. Hughes had an arm on the back door, ready to close it.

'I meant it about the cardiac. You really should lose some weight. We could do our backs in rolling you on to the stretcher.'

'You're all heart, pal!' Hoffer called, but he called it to a slammed door as the ambulance revved away. He walked back up the hill to Emergency. The same nurse he'd spoken to was still there. She didn't look like she'd been pining.

'Just one more thing,' Hoffer said, raising a crooked index finger. 'Who do I speak to about haemophilia?'

'It means love of blood, literally.'

Dr Jacobs was a small man with one of those English-actor voices that make American women wet their drawers. It was like Jeremy Irons was behind the scenes somewhere and Jacobs was his dummy. He also had the hairiest arms Hoffer had seen outside a zoo, and he only had ten minutes to spare. He was explaining what the word haemophilia meant.

'That's very interesting,' said Hoffer. 'But see, the man we're dealing with here, he's a hired killer, a gunman. He also uses explosives. Does that sound like a suitable occupation for a haemophiliac?'

'No, it doesn't. Well, that's to say, not for a *severe* haemophiliac. You see, there are three broad levels of haemophilia. You can be severe, moderate, or mild. Most registered haemophiliacs in the UK are severe – that is, they show less than two percent factor activity.'

'What's factor activity?'

'Haemophiliacs, Mr Hoffer, suffer from a clotting deficiency in the blood. Clotting is a complex event, involving thirteen different factors. If one thing happens, then another happens, and we get a knock-on effect. When all thirteen things have happened, we get blood clotting. But haemophiliacs lack one of the factors, so the knock-on can't happen and clotting can't take place. Most haemophiliacs suffer from a factor eight deficiency, some from a factor nine deficiency. There are a few even rarer conditions, but those are the main two. Factor eight deficiency is termed Haemophilia A, and factor nine Haemophilia B. Are you with me so far?'

'Reading you like braille.'

Dr Jacobs leaned back in his black leather chair. He had a small cluttered office, all textbooks and test results and piles of unanswered mail. His white coat was hanging up behind the door, and there were a lot of framed certificates on the walls. His arms were folded so he could run his hands over his monkey arms. Hair sprouted from the collar of his shirt. Naked, Hoffer bet you could use him as a fireside rug.

'Severe haemophiliacs,' the doctor said, 'make up over a third of all haemophilia cases. They can suffer spontaneous internal bleeds, usually into soft tissues, joints and muscles. As children, they're advised to stay away from contact sports. We try to make them get a good education, so they can get desk jobs rather than manual ones.'

'They don't go into the armed forces then?'

Dr Jacobs smiled. 'The armed forces and the police won't recruit from haemophiliacs.'

Hoffer frowned. If there was one thing he'd been sure of, it was that the D-Man had been either a soldier or a cop. 'No exceptions?'

'None.'

'Not even if they've got the milder form?'

Jacobs shook his head. 'Something wrong?' he said.

Hoffer had been tugging at his ears. 'Flying does things to my ears,' he said. 'Say, can you help? Maybe take a look?'

'I'm a haematologist, Mr Hoffer, not ENT.'

'But you can prescribe drugs, right? Some painkillers maybe?'

'Consult a GP, Mr Hoffer.'

'I can pay.'

'I'm sure you can. Did you catch your cold on the plane?'

'Huh?' Hoffer sniffed so much these days, he was hardly aware of it. He blew his nose and reminded himself to buy more paper handkerchiefs. Damned nose was always itchy too. 'It's this lousy weather,' he said.

The doctor looked surprised and glanced out of his window. It was another beautiful day outside. He looked back at Hoffer.

'The police have already asked me about this assassin. It seems from what I hear that he does possess some knowledge of haemophilia, but as I told them, I just can't visualise a severe haemophiliac being an assassin. He told the ambulanceman that he was one per cent. I think he was lying. I mean . . . well, this is guesswork.'

'No, go on.' Hoffer stuck his shred of handkerchief back in his pocket.

'Well, it seems to me that these weapons he uses, they would have a recoil.'

'Believe it.'

'You see, any recoil might start a severe haemophiliac bleeding. It wouldn't be long before he'd start to suffer problems with his shoulder. After which he wouldn't make much of a marksman at all.'

'What about a moderate sufferer?'

'Even with a moderate sufferer, there would be dangers. No, if this man suffers from haemophilia, then he is a mild case.'

'But he'd still know about the disease, right?'

'Oh, yes. But he'd also be able to injure himself without needing medical aid afterwards. Simple pressure on the cut would be enough to stop it.'

Hoffer chewed this over. 'Would he be registered?'

'Almost certainly.'

'I don't suppose those records . . . ?'

Jacobs was shaking his head. 'If the police wish to apply to see them, then of course there might be a chance, especially if it's a case of catching a murderer.'

'Yes, of course. Dr Jacobs, how many mild sufferers are there?'

'In the UK?' Hoffer nodded. 'About fifteen hundred.'

'Out of how many?'

'Roughly six and a half thousand.'

'And how many of those fifteen hundred can we discount?'

'What?'

'You know, how many are kids, how many are pensioners, how many are women? It's got to bring the number down.'

Jacobs was smiling. 'I have some pamphlets here you should read, Mr Hoffer.' He opened a desk drawer, hunting for them.

'What? Did I say something funny?'

'No, it's just that haemophilia affects only men. It's passed on from the mother, not the father, but it is only passed on to the sons.'

Hoffer read the pamphlets as he sat in the bar of the Allington Hotel.

He found it all unbelievable. How could a mother do that to her son? Unbelievable. The women in the family could carry the disease, but they almost never suffered from it. And if they passed it on to their daughters, the daughters could fight it. It was all down to chromosomes. A boy got his mother's X and his father's Y, while a girl got two X chromosomes, one from each parent. The bad genetic information was all in the X chromosome. A man with haemophilia passed his bad X to his daughter, but the good X she got from her mother cancelled the bad X out. So she became a carrier but not a sufferer. Each female had two X chromosomes, while males had an X and a Y. So boys had a fifty-fifty chance of getting the bad X passed on to them from their mothers. And they couldn't override it because they didn't have another good X chromosome, they had a lousy Y which wasn't any use in the battle.

There was other stuff, all about Queen Victoria and the Russian royal family and Rasputin. Queen Victoria had been a carrier. There didn't have to be a history of haemophilia in the family either, the thing could just spontaneously occur. And a mild haemophiliac might never know they had the disease till it came time for a surgical operation or tooth extraction. The more Hoffer read, the more he wondered about going for a blood test. He had always bruised easily, and one time he'd been spitting blood for days after a visit to his dentist. Maybe he was a haemophiliac. He wouldn't put anything past his mother.

He wasn't sure what difference it made, knowing the D-Man was probably a sufferer. It could just be that his family had a history of haemophilia; he could just be an interested onlooker. Hoffer wasn't going to be given access to any records, and even if he did get the records, what would he do with them? Talk to every single sufferer? Drag them here and let Gerry Flitch take a look at them?

Ah, speaking of whom . . .

'Mr Flitch?'

'Yes.'

Hoffer offered his hand. 'Leo Hoffer, can I buy you a drink?'

'Thank you, yes.'

Hoffer snapped his fingers, and the barman nodded. The first time Hoffer had done it, the barman had given him a stare so icy you could have mixed it into a martini. But then Hoffer had given him a big tip, and so now the barman was his friend. Hoffer was sitting in a squidgy armchair in a dark corner of the bar. Flitch pulled over a chair and sat down opposite him. He flicked his hair back into place.

'This has all been . . . I don't know,' he began, unasked. 'It's not every day you find out you've had drinks bought for you by an international terrorist.'

'Not a terrorist, Gerry, just a hired gun. Do you mind if I call you Gerry?'

'Not at all . . . Leo.'

'There you go. Now, what'll it be?' The barman was standing ready.

'Whisky, please.'

'Ice, sir?'

'And bring some water, too, please.'

'Certainly, sir.'

Hoffer handed his empty glass to the barman. 'And I'll have the same again, Tom.'

'My pleasure, Mr Hoffer.'

Gerry Flitch looked suitably impressed, which had been the plan all along. Hoffer gathered up his haemophilia pamphlets and stuck them down the side of the chair. It was a great chair, plenty big enough and damned comfortable. He wondered if he could buy it from the hotel, maybe ship it back.

'You said you're a private detective, Leo.'

'That's right, Gerry.'

'And the police tell me you're very well known.'

'In the States, maybe.' Good. As suggested, Flitch had called Bob Broome to check Hoffer's credentials. 'So tell me about Saturday, Gerry. No rush, I just want to listen.'

Tom the barman arrived with their drinks, and Hoffer gave him another tip. 'Let us have some nuts or something, Tom, huh?'

'Surely, Mr Hoffer.'

The nuts and crisps arrived in small glass bowls. Hoffer helped himself to a fistful. He'd had a mellowing-out joint half an hour ago, and was now hungry.

'Well,' said Flitch, 'what is there to tell? I was drinking at the bar, sitting on one of those stools there. This guy came in for a drink, and sat a couple of stools away. He was drinking some soft drink, grapefruit and lemonade I think.'

'It was tonic, not lemonade. We know that from his bar tab.'

Flitch nodded. 'Yes, tonic, that's right. Anyway, we got talking.'

'Who started?'

'I think I did.'

'And did this guy, did he speak sort of grudgingly?'

'No, not at all, he seemed very pleasant. You wouldn't think he had murder on his mind.'

'Maybe he didn't. These guys have a way of blocking it out when they want to. So what did you talk about?'

Flitch shrugged. 'Just general stuff. He told me he was in import-export, I told him I was a marketing strategist. I even gave him my card.' He shook his head. 'What a mistake *that* was. Next thing I know, armed police are at the door of my room.'

'You're the biggest break we've had, Gerry. It was the Demolition Man who made the mistake, accepting your card.'

'Yes, but now he knows who I am, who I work for, where I live. And here I am talking to you.'

'But he won't know you've talked to us until he's arrested. Besides, he's not stupid. He won't come near you.'

'He won't have to come near me though, will he? From what I've heard, a few hundred yards would be close enough.' Flitch finished his drink. Hoffer knew the man was nervous, but he suspected Flitch was a heavy drinker anyway. The guy was young, late-twenties, but he had a face that was hardening prematurely, losing its good looks and gaining jowls. Only a big man, a man like Hoffer himself, could carry jowls and not look like a drunk. Flitch was a drunk in the making, and the pattern was just about complete.

'Tell me something, Gerry, you ever do coke?'

Flitch's eyes widened. 'I take it you don't mean the soft drink?'

'I do not.'

Flitch shrugged. 'I might've done a little at parties.' He narrowed his eyes. 'Why?'

Hoffer sat forward. 'Know where I could get some?'

Flitch smiled. 'In Liverpool I could help you, but not down here.'

Hoffer sat back again and nodded slowly, then craned his neck. 'Another round here, Tom.' Flitch didn't say no. Hoffer rubbed a hand across his nose. 'So what else did you talk about? Family? Background? That's what businessmen talk about in strange bars, isn't it?'

'Not us, it never became personal. We talked about how easy things had seemed in the mid-80s, then how tough they'd become, and how tough they still were. He said something like, "There's no room for bleeding hearts in our line of work".' Flitch shivered at the memory.

'The guy's got a sense of humour,' Hoffer remarked. Tom arrived with the drinks. 'Gerry, I'm not going to ask you what this guy looked like. You've already given the cops a good description, and he'll have changed his appearance by now anyway. I'm going to ask for something more difficult.' Hoffer sat forwards. 'I want your impressions of him as a man. Just close your eyes, think back on that day, fix it in your mind, and then say anything you want to say. No need to feel embarrassed, the bar's empty. Go on, close your eyes.' Flitch closed them. 'That's right. Now, to get you warmed up, I'll ask a few questions about him, okay?'

'Okay.' Flitch's eyelids fluttered like young butterflies.

'Tell me about his movements, were they stiff or fluid? How did he pick up his glass? Did you see him walk?'

Gerry Flitch thought for a moment and then started to speak.

Afterwards, Hoffer washed his face and hands in the men's room and looked at himself in the mirror. He felt tired. He'd have to phone Walkins tonight with a preliminary report. There'd be plenty to tell him. Walkins was greedy for information about the Demolition Man. It was like he wanted to build up a good enough picture so he could then tear it to shreds. Hoffer couldn't really figure Walkins out. There were no photographs of his daughter in Walkins' house, though there were plenty of his wife, who'd died of lung cancer. The man was loaded, a fortune made in politics. When he was a senator, Walkins had tucked the money away, probably most of it legit. You didn't have to be crooked in politics to make a small fortune. But when he'd left politics, Walkins must have done something to turn his small fortune into a large one, large enough to pay for Hoffer's obsession and still leave plenty over.

He thought about doing a couple of lines. They'd keep him awake and alert. But he had one more job to do yet, and besides, he was perilously close to the end of his stash. He left the men's room and sweet-talked the receptionist, who let him take a look at Room 203. The police had given it a good going over. There was still fingerprint powder on the dressing table, wardrobe and television. But it looked like 'Mark Wesley' had spent some time before checking out engaged in a bit of dusting. He'd left a couple of dry bath-towels on the floor of his room, and why else would they be there if he hadn't been using them as dusters? However, the police reckoned they had half a palm print from the inside of the door, and an index finger from the courtesy kettle. They could not, of course, be sure whose prints they were. They might belong to a maid or a visitor or a previous occupant. They'd only know when they arrested Mark Wesley, or whatever he was calling himself now. They'd also dusted the ambulance, but Wesley had been helped in and helped out. He hadn't touched a thing.

The room didn't tell Hoffer anything. Gerry Flitch hadn't told him much either. He was building up his own picture of the D-Man, but didn't know where that would get him. He was no psychologist, no specialist in profiling. He had a friend at the FBI who might make more sense of it all. He went back to reception and found that the receptionist had his print-out and photocopies all ready. He handed her the promised twenty. He'd already been given the information by Bob Broome, but he wanted to check that Broome was playing straight with him. The information was all here. He'd used a credit card to reserve his room, but had paid cash when he checked out. The police had run tests and serial number checks on all the cash taken by the hotel on Saturday. The potential big break, though, was the credit card. The home address Mark Wesley had given to the hotel was false, but the credit card had turned out to be genuine.

It had taken a while to wring the information out of the credit card company, but now they knew all the lies Wesley had told them: occupation, date of birth, mother's maiden name . . . Well, maybe it was all a fabrication, but maybe there were a few half-truths and little slips in there. It would all be checked out. The credit card company sent its statements to an address in St John's Wood, and that's where Hoffer was headed, as soon as his chauffeur arrived.

Broome arrived only five minutes late, so Hoffer forgave him.

'Had a productive morning?' Broome asked, as his passenger got in.

'I think so, what about you?'

'Ticking over.'

On the way to St John's Wood, Hoffer told Broome some of what he'd found out about haemophilia.

'If we could get a list of registered haemophiliacs, I bet we could narrow it down pretty fast.'

'Maybe. I'll see what I can do. It could be a dead end.'

'Hey, we won't know till we've got our noses pressed against the wall, will we?'

'I suppose not. But maybe we can take a short cut. We're just passing Lord's, by the way.'

'Lord who?'

'Just Lord's. It's the home of cricket.'

'A sports field, huh? Cricket's the one that's like baseball, only easier?' Broome gave him a dark look. 'Just kidding. But did you ever watch a game of baseball? Greatest game on earth.'

'That must be why so many countries play it.'

They arrived at a block of flats and parked in the residents' only parking area. When they got to the right door, Broome made to ring the bell, then noticed Hoffer slip the Smith & Wesson out from his waistband.

'Christ, Leo!'

'Hey, our man may be in there.'

'It's a mail service, that's all. An accommodation address. Remember, they're expecting us, so put that gun away.'

Reluctantly, Hoffer tucked the pistol back into his waistband and buttoned his jacket. Broome rang the doorbell and waited. The door opened.

'Mr Greene?'

'Chief Inspector Broome?'

'That's right, sir.' Broome showed his ID. 'May we come in?'

'Of course.'

They were led down a short dimly-lit hall and into a living room. It was a ground-floor flat, as small as any Hoffer had been in. One bedroom and a bathroom, but the kitchen was part of the living room. It was well-finished though, if you liked your home decorated according to fashion rather than personal preference. Everything had that just-bought-from-Habitat look.

Desmond Greene was in his 40s, wiry and slack-jawed with hands that moved too much and eyes that wouldn't meet yours. When he talked, he looked like he was lecturing the pale yellow wallpaper. Hoffer marked him straight away as gay, not that that meant anything. Often Hoffer met men he was sure were gay, only later to be introduced to their pneumatic wives. Not that that meant anything either.

Broome had made a point of not introducing Hoffer. It wasn't exactly Metropolitan Police policy to drag New York private eyes around with you on a case. Maybe Broome was hoping Hoffer would keep his mouth shut.

'How long you been running this set-up, Mr Greene?' Hoffer asked.

Greene's fingers glided down his face like a skin-cream commercial. 'Four and a half years, that's quite a long time in this business.'

'And how do potential clients find you?'

'Oh, I advertise.'

'Locally?'

A wry smile. '*Expensively*. I run regular advertisements in magazines.'

'Which magazines?'

'My Lord, you *are* curious.'

Hoffer tried out his own wry smile. 'Only when I'm hunting a cold-blooded killer and someone's standing in my way.'

Greene looked giddy, and Bob Broome took over. Hoffer didn't mind, he reckoned he'd scared Greene into telling the truth and plenty of it. He didn't even mind the way Broome looked at him, like Hoffer had just asked a boy scout to slip his hand into his trouser pocket and meet Uncle Squidgy.

'How long have you been handling mail for Mr Wesley?'

'You understand Chief Inspector,' Greene said, recovering slightly, 'the purpose of a mailing address is confidentiality?'

'Yes, sir, I understand. But as I told you over the phone, this is a multiple murder inquiry. If you do not cooperate, you'll be charged with obstruction.'

'After which we'll take your chintzy flat apart,' added Hoffer.

'Gracious,' said Greene, having a relapse. 'Oh, goodness me.'

'Hoffer,' said Broome quietly, 'go and put the kettle on. Maybe Mr Greene would like some tea.'

What am I, the fucking maid service? Hoffer got up and went to the kitchenette. He was behind Greene now, and Greene knew it. He sat forward in his chair, as though fearing a knife between the shoulder blades. Hoffer smiled, thinking how Greene would react to the feel of a cold gun muzzle at the back of his neck.

'So,' Broome was saying, 'are you willing to assist us, sir?'

'Well, of course I am. It's not my job to hide murderers.'

'Maybe if you told me a little of the service you offer Mr Wesley?'

'It's the same as my other customers. There are forty-odd of them. I receive mail, and they can contact me by telephone to find out what's arrived, or they can have the mail forwarded to them monthly. I also operate a call-answering and forwarding service, but Mr Wesley didn't require that.'

'How much mail does he receive?'
'Almost none at all. Bills and bank statements.'
'And does he have the stuff forwarded?'
'No, he collects it in person.'
'How often?'
'Infrequently. Like I say, it's just bank statements and bills.'
'What sort of bills?'
'Credit cards, I'd guess. Well, he doesn't need a credit card statement to pay off the account, does he? A simple cheque and note with his account number would do it.'
'That's true. He never has the stuff forwarded to him?'
'Once he did, to a hotel in Paris.'
'Do you remember the name of the hotel?'
Greene shook his head. 'I'm sorry, it was well over a year ago.'
'Maybe two years ago?' Hoffer added.
Greene half-turned to him. 'Could be.'
Hoffer looked to Broome. 'That Dutchman, the heroin pusher. The D-Man took him out in Paris a couple of years back.'
Broome nodded. The kettle came to the boil and Hoffer picked it up, then thought better of it.
'Does anyone *really* want tea? Me, I could murder a drink.'
'I've some gin,' Greene said. 'Or a few cans of lager.'
'It's your party, Des,' Hoffer said with a grin.
So Broome and Hoffer had a can of lager each, and Greene sat with a gin and tonic. He loosened up a little after that. The lager was fine, even though a couple of months past its sell by.
'Okay,' said Broome, 'so mail gets sent here and Wesley phones up and you tell him what's arrived?'
Greene nodded, stirring his drink with a finger and then sucking the tip.
'Does he ever get you to open mail and read it to him?'
Greene smacked his lips. 'Never.'
'And he's never received anything other than bills?'
Hoffer interrupted. 'No fat brown envelopes full of banknotes? No large flat packages with photos and details of his next hit?'
Greene quivered the length of his body.
'Can you give us a description of him?' Broome asked, ignoring Hoffer. The description Greene gave was that of the man Gerry Flitch had given his card to.
'Well, that's about all for now, Mr Greene,' said Broome. He placed his empty can on the carpet.
'But there's one other thing,' said Greene.
'What's that?'
'Aren't you going to ask if there's any mail waiting for him?'
'Well, is there?'
Greene broke into a huge wrinkle-faced grin. 'Yes!' he squealed. 'There is!'
But having got both men excited, he now seemed to want to stall. It was a crime, after all, to open someone else's mail without their express permission. So Broome had to write a note to the effect that he was taking away the letter, and that he was authorised to do so. Greene read it through.
'Can you write that I'm exonerated from all guilt or possible legal action?'

Broome scribbled some words to that effect, then signed and dated the note. Greene studied it again. Hoffer was close behind him, breathing hard.

'Fine,' said Greene, folding the note but leaving it on the breakfast bar. He went off to fetch the letter. When he was out of the room, Hoffer tore a fresh sheet of paper from the writing pad, folded it, and put it down on the breakfast bar, then lifted Broome's note and scrunched it into a ball before dropping it into his pocket. He winked at Broome. Greene came back into the room. He was waving a single, slim envelope.

'Looks like a bank statement,' he said.

It was a bank statement.

The bank was closed when they got to it, but the staff were still on the premises, balancing the day's books. The manager, Mr Arthur, ushered them into his utilitarian office.

'I can't do anything tonight,' he said. 'It's too late to get anyone at head office. You realise that there are channels that must be gone through, authorisations, and even then a really thorough check could take some considerable time.'

'I appreciate all of that, sir,' said Bob Broome, 'but the sooner we can get the ball rolling, the sooner we'll be near the goal. This man has murdered over half a dozen individuals, two of them in this country.'

'Yes, I do understand, and tomorrow morning we'll do everything we can, as quickly as we can, it just can't be done tonight.'

They were in the Piccadilly branch of one of the clearing banks. It was, naturally, a busy branch, perfect for someone like the Demolition Man, who needed to be anonymous.

'If we could just talk about his account for a few minutes, sir,' Broome said. The manager glanced at his wall clock and sighed.

'Very well then,' he said.

Broome produced the bank statement. There wasn't much to it. It referred to the previous month, and showed a balance of £1,500 on the 1st, with cheque and cashpoint withdrawals through the month totalling £900, leaving a closing credit balance of £600. Arthur typed in the account number on his computer.

'Mm,' he said, studying the screen, 'since that statement was drawn up, he's withdrawn another £500.'

'In other words,' said Hoffer, 'he's all but emptied the account?'

'Yes, Friday, Saturday and Sunday. He withdrew money on each day.'

Hoffer turned to Broome. 'He's shedding Mark Wesley.' He turned to the bank manager. 'Mr Arthur, I think you'll find that account stays dormant from now on.'

'Can we find out where he took the cash from?' Broome asked.

Arthur studied the screen again. 'Central London,' he said.

'What about old cheques?' Hoffer asked. 'Do you hold on to them?'

'Yes, for a while at least.'

'So we could look at his returned cheques?'

Arthur nodded. 'After I've had authorisation.'

Broome looked at Hoffer. 'What are you thinking?'

'He has to pay people, Bob. Maybe he doesn't always have the cash on him.'

'You think he pays for his guns and explosives *by cheque*?'

Hoffer held his hands up, palms towards Broome. 'Hey, maybe not, but we need to check. Could be there's something he's paid for, or *someone* he's paid for, that can lead us right to him. He'll be underground now, busy making himself a new identity. All we have to go on is the old one. I say we dig as far as we can.' He turned to Arthur, who was looking dazzled by this exchange. 'We need old cheques, old statements, and we need to know the site of every auto-teller he's used. There could be a pattern that'll tell us where he's based.'

'Auto-teller?' said Arthur.

'Cash machine,' explained Broome.

8

I sat in my hotel room, counting out my money.

I had $4,500 in cash, money I'd been keeping safe at Max's farm. I had another $5,000 in cash in a safe deposit box in Knightsbridge, and $25,000 cash in another safe deposit box at the same location. I reckoned I'd be all right for a while. I'd all but emptied the Mark Wesley bank account, and had disposed of his credit cards. I still had my Michael Weston account and credit cards, and no matter how far the police probed into 'Mark Wesley', I couldn't see them getting close to Michael Weston.

The hotel I was in had asked for a credit card as guarantee, but I'd paid upfront instead. I put some of the money back in my holdall, and put some in my pocket, leaving a couple of thousand still on the bed. I had more money in New York, and some in Zurich, but I definitely wouldn't need to touch that.

I rolled up the final two thou and stuck it in the toe of one of my spare shoes, then put the shoes back in the closet. I'd had to take everything out of the holdall. The stiff cardboard base was loose, and I'd slipped the money under it. There was a soft knock at the door. I unlocked it and let in Bel.

'How's your room?' I asked.

'All right.' She'd taken a shower. Her hair was damp, her face buffed. She was wearing jeans and a T-shirt. We were in a new hotel, the Rimmington. It wasn't central, but I didn't mind. I knew returning to London so soon was dangerous. I didn't want to be anywhere near the Craigmead or the Allington. So we were in a much smaller hotel just off Marylebone Road, handy, as the receptionist said, for Madame Tussaud's, the Planetarium, and Regent's Park. We were supposed to be on holiday from Nottingham, so we looked interested as she told us this. Actually, Bel had more than *looked* interested.

'There won't be much time for sightseeing,' I warned her now.

'Don't worry,' she snapped back, 'I'm here to work. What's that?' She was pointing to my 'works'. They were lying on the bed, syringes and all. I started loading them back into the holdall.

'Are you on drugs?'

'No, I just . . . sometimes I need an injection. I'm a haemophiliac.'

'That means you bleed a lot?'

'It means when I bleed, sometimes it won't stop without help.'

'An injection?' I nodded. 'But you're all right?'

I smiled at her. 'I'm fine.' She decided she'd take my word for it.

'So where are you taking me for dinner?'

'How about a burger?'

'We had burgers for lunch.'

This was true. We'd stopped at a motorway service area, where the burgers had looked the most appetising display. Bel deserved better, especially on her first night in London. That makes her sound naïve, a country bumpkin, which she wasn't. But she hadn't been to London in five years, hadn't been out of Yorkshire for the best part of a year. I wondered if I'd been right to bring her. How much of a liability might she become? I still didn't think there'd be any real danger, except of arrest.

'Well, you decide: Italian? Indian? Chinese? French? Thai? London can accommodate most tastes.'

She flopped down on my bed and assumed a thoughtful pose.

'So long as it's between here and Tottenham,' I added, 'but then you can find most things between here and Tottenham.'

I was all for taking a cab to Tottenham, but Bel wanted to ride on the tube. We'd dropped the XR3i back at its shop, and I'd settled for it in cash. There was no point hanging on to it; I thought we'd be in London for a few days. One thing about Bel, she surely did look like a tourist, wide-eyed and unafraid and ready to meet a stranger's eyes, even to smile and start a conversation. Yes, you could tell she was new in town. I couldn't help but be a bit more worldly, even though I was a tourist too. We got off the tube at Seven Sisters and ate at a Caribbean restaurant, where Bel had to have a second helping of the planter's punch and was nearly sick as a result. She didn't eat much though, apart from the dirty rice and johnny cakes. The fish was too salty for her, the meat too rich.

There was an evening paper in the restaurant, and I flicked through it until I found the latest on the Ricks assassination. The diplomat from the Craigmead was causing a stink, talking about lax security and an MI5 plot against him. According to his version, MI5 and some country neighbouring his own were in cahoots.

'Keep muddying the water, pal,' I told his grainy photograph. There was a more interesting snippet further down the page, added almost as an afterthought. It talked about a 'mystery call' to the Craigmead Hotel, a summons Eleanor Ricks had ignored. It intrigued me. Had my paymaster got cold feet and tried to warn her? And being unable to reach her, had he then phoned the police instead? I'd heard stories about employers changing their minds. I wouldn't mind if they did, so long as they weren't looking for a refund. If they wanted their money back, well, that was a different proposition entirely.

We walked up the long High Road, looking into a few of the less salubrious pubs. I'd already explained to Bel who I was looking for, and she seemed glad of the fresh air and exercise. The traffic was blocked all the way up the High Road to Monument Way, and all the way down Monument Way too. We stopped in at the Volley, but there was no one there I knew. I always had to be careful in Tottenham. There were people I might meet here who might assume I was either after something or being nosy. For example, sometimes I bought plastic explosives and detonators from a couple of Irishmen who lived here. They weren't really supposed to sell the stuff on, and they were always nervous.

Then there was Harry Capaldi, alias Harry Carry, alias Andy Capp, alias

Harry the Cap. It was true he sometimes wore a cap. It was true, too, that he was always nervous. And if Harry got the fright and went into hiding, I wouldn't be very happy. So I was being careful not to ask for him in any of the bars. I didn't want word getting to him before I did. Somewhere in the middle of the Dowsett Estate, Bel started complaining about her feet.

'We'll take a rest soon,' I said. I led her back to the High Road and the first pub we went into, she sat down at a table. So I asked what she was drinking.

'Coke.' I nodded and went to the bar.

'A coke, please, and a half of bitter.' While the barmaid poured our drinks, I examined the row of optics. I'd been close to ordering a brandy. Close, but not that close. Harry the Cap wasn't in the bar. Maybe he stayed home on a Monday night. I didn't want to go calling on him. I knew he owned a couple of guns, and the people in the flat upstairs from him were dealers. It would only take one shot, and the whole building might turn into *Apocalypse Now*. I took the drinks back to our table. Bel had taken off her shoes and was rubbing her feet. The men at the bar were so starved of novelty that they were watching her like she wasn't about to stop at the shoes. When she took her jacket off I thought one of them was about to fall off his stool.

'New shoes,' Bel said. 'I knew I shouldn't have brought them.'

'And they say townies are soft.'

She glared, then smiled. 'Cheers,' she said, lifting her glass. She crunched on a piece of ice and looked around the bar. 'So this is the big bad city? How do we find your friend?'

'We keep looking. You'd be surprised how many pubs there are between here and White Hart Lane.'

'And we go into every one of them?'

'That's the idea.'

'Couldn't you just phone him instead?'

'He's not on the phone.'

'Then I suppose we keep walking.' She took another drink.

'Speaking of phoning, have you called Max?'

'Give me a break, I only left him this morning.'

'He'll be worried.'

'No, he won't. He'll be watching reruns of *Dad's Army* and laughing his head off.'

I tried to visualise this, but failed.

'Look, Michael, do you mind me saying something?'

'What?'

'Well, we're supposed to be together, right? As in a couple. Look at you, you look more like my minder.'

I looked down at myself.

'I mean,' Bel went on, 'you're sitting too far away from me for a start. It's like you're afraid I'll bite. And the way you're sitting, you're not comfortable, you're not enjoying yourself. You're like a flick knife about to open.'

'Thanks,' I said. I slid closer to her on the bench-seat.

'Better, but still not great,' she said. 'Relax your shoulders and your legs.'

'You seem to know a bit about acting.'

'I watch a lot of daytime TV. There, that's better.' We were now touching shoulders and thighs. I finished my drink.

'Right, we better get going.'
'What?'
'Like I say, Bel, a lot of pubs still to go.'
She sighed and slipped her shoes back on. The men at the bar turned their attention to the television. Someone by a riverbank was gutting a fish.

We were in a pub on Scotland Green, the one people use after they've signed on at the dole office across the road. It was always busy, and was all angles and nooks. It might be small, but that didn't mean you couldn't hide in it. Harry the Cap was hiding round the corner beside the fruit machines. He was seated on a high stool, wearing a paisley-patterned shirt intended for someone three decades younger, jeans ditto, and his cap. It struck me I should have brought him the one I'd bought; he'd have appreciated it more than Bel.

He wasn't playing the machines, and in fact was staring at the cigarette dispenser.

'Hello there, Harry,' I said. He stared at me without recognition, then laughed himself into a coughing fit. Three gold chains jangled around his neck as he coughed. There were more gold bands on his wrists and fingers, plus a gold Rolex on his right wrist.

'Dear God,' he said at last, 'that nearly killed me.' He wiped his eyes. 'Did you beat him up afterwards?'

'Who?'

'The blind fella who gave you that haircut. It's diabolical. I won't even tell you what I think of the colour.'

'Why not take out an ad?'

'Sorry, son.' He lowered his voice and cleared his throat. 'Do I need an invite or are you going to introduce me?'

'Sorry, Harry, this is Belinda. Belinda, Harry.'

'What're you drinking, girl?'

She looked to me first and I nodded. 'Coke, please.'

'Needs your permission, does she? And you'll be wanting a double brandy, I take it?'

'Not tonight, Harry. A half of bitter's fine.'

He shook his head. 'My hearing must be going.'

'Let me get these,' I said. 'Are you still TJ?'

'That I am.' Bel looked puzzled, so he spelt it out. 'Tomato juice. I can't drink any more, it makes my hands shake.'

She nodded, understanding everything. I got the drinks in while Harry tried his usual chat-up lines. I needn't have worried; Harry was okay. He was stone cold sober and he wasn't dodging police or warrant-servers or his ex-wife's solicitors. He was fine.

When I got back, Bel was playing one of the bandits.

'She's had four quid out of it already,' Harry said.

'And how much has she put back?'

Harry nodded sagely. 'They always put it back.'

Bel didn't even look at us. 'Who's "they"?' she said. 'Women in general, or the women you know in general? I mean, there's bound to be a difference.'

Harry wrinkled his nose. 'You see,' he said in a stage whisper, 'things haven't been the same since women's lib. When my Carlotta burnt her bra, I knew that was the end. Cheers.'

'Cheers.' I sipped my beer and managed to catch Bel's eye. She gave me a wink. 'Harry,' I said, 'we need something.'

'We?'

'Bel and me.'

'What do you need? A wedding licence?'

'No, something that'll get us through a few doors, something with authority stamped on it.'

'Such as?'

'I was hoping you'd have a few ideas.'

He rubbed his unshaved jaw. 'Yes, I could maybe do you something. When would you need it?'

'Tonight.'

His eyes widened. 'Jesus, Mark, you've given me tough ones before, but this . . .'

'Could you do it though?'

'I wasn't expecting to work tonight . . .' From which I knew two things: one, that he *could* do it; and two, that he was wondering how much he could charge.

'It would be cash?' he said. I nodded. 'It's cash I like, you know that.'

'I know that.'

'Jesus, tonight. I don't know . . .'

'How much, Harry?'

He took off his cap and scratched his head, forgetting for a moment his psoriasis. Huge flakes of skin floated on to his shoulders. 'Well now, Mark, you know my prices are never unreasonable.'

'The difference is, Harry, this time *I'm* not getting paid.'

'Well, that may make a difference to you, Mark, it doesn't make a difference to *me*. I charge what's fair.'

'So tell me what's fair.'

'Five hundred.'

'What do I get for five hundred?'

'Two identity cards.'

'That's not much to show.'

He shrugged. 'At short notice, it's the best I can offer.'

'How long would it take?'

'A couple of hours.'

'All right.'

'You've the money on you?' I nodded, and he shook his head. 'Running around Tottenham with five hundred on him, and I bet he's not even carrying a knife.'

Behind us, the bandit began coughing up another win for Bel.

'This is definitely your lucky night,' said Harry the Cap.

'Make yourselves at home.'

It wasn't easy in Harry the Cap's first-floor flat. For one thing, what chairs there were were piled high with old newspapers and magazines. For another, half the already cramped living room was taken up with a rough approximation of a photographer's studio. A white bedsheet had been pinned to the wall to provide a backdrop, and there was a solitary bruised flash-lamp hanging from a tripod. Harry gave the back of the lamp a thump.

'Hope the bulb's not gone, bleeding things cost a packet.' The bulb flashed once, then came on and stayed on. 'Lovely,' said Harry. There was a plain wooden dining-chair which seemed to be the tomcat's regular perch, but Harry tipped the reluctant beast on to the floor and placed the chair in front of the bedsheet, angling the lamp so that it hit an imaginary spot just above the back of the chair. 'Lovely,' he said again.

Then he started tinkering with his pride and joy. It was a special camera which in the one unit could take a photo (slightly smaller than passport size), develop it on to an ID card, and then laminate the card. Harry patted the machine. 'Bought it from a firm that went bust. They used to do identity cards for students.'

Bel was standing in front of a mirror, combing her hair into place. The mirror was large and old and hexagonal, and in its centre was a posed photograph of a bride and groom with their best man and bridesmaid.

'Your parents?' Bel asked.

'Nah, picked it up down Brick Lane. A lot of people make your mistake. Sometimes I don't own up.'

'Where's that music coming from?'

'Upstairs, some black kids.'

The constant bass was like a queasy heartbeat. It seemed to envelop the flat.

'Can't you complain?' said Bel. Harry laughed and shook his head.

'Right,' he said, 'I'll just get the cards typed up.'

He had an old manual typewriter, the sort they'd thrown from offices on to the street in the 70s. It was solidly built, but the keys needed realigning. Or maybe they just needed a clean.

'You'll never notice once the machine's reduced it.'

This, I knew from previous experience, was true. Once the card had been filled in, it was placed inside the unit, a suitcase-sized object attached to the camera, and a reduced-size copy was made, only now with photograph in place. Normally, I didn't bother too much. People seldom really scrutinised an ID card of any make or variety. If they saw that the photo was you, they were satisfied. But this time was different.

'Remember, Harry, some of the people I'll be dealing with might just give my ID more than a cursory glance. Don't go making any typing errors.'

'Do me a favour, I did a secretarial course at night school. Seventy words a minute.'

'I didn't know there were seventy two-letter words.'

I left him to get on with it. Bel flicked a final hair into place and turned to me. She offered me the comb, but I shook my head. I looked in the mirror and saw a hard-looking bloke staring back. He had cropped black hair and a professional scowl. He looked just like a policeman.

'Which area do you want?' Harry asked from the typewriter.

'Better make it Central.'

'Central,' he acknowledged. 'Good, I know how to spell that.'

A good forger's art, of course, does not lie in making up the fake ID. Anyone can fake an ID. The forger's art lies in having to hand authentic or authentic-looking blank ID forms. Harry would never tell anyone where his blanks came from, or even if they were the genuine article. I reckoned he'd got his hands on a real ID form a while back, and had a friendly printer run up a few hundred. There were other things he could do, like put an official stamp on something. Those he made himself, and they were beautiful. He'd done a US visa for me once that was incredibly lifelike. Only, without me knowing, he'd made it a *student* visa. The questions at Immigration had almost given me away. Next time I'd seen Harry, I'd been able to get a fake passport at a reduced rate.

'I'll need both your signatures,' he said. He'd switched on an anglepoise lamp and put on a pair of John Lennon-style NHS glasses, the kind you hate to have to wear as a kid, but often crave as an adult. I'd never needed glasses. People said it was a sign of having lived a pure life.

I was using the name Michael West on my ID, while Bel was Bel Harris. She said she'd rather stick with her own Christian name. They say that the best lies have a nugget of truth in them, and these names were just different enough from our real names that they wouldn't help the police. I'd sometimes called myself Michael West in the USA, but never before in England. Bel was having enough trouble as it was remembering my name was now Michael and not Mark. She didn't need another name to confuse her.

'Right, sweetheart,' said Harry, 'if you'll sit on that chair . . .'

Bel turned to me. 'Is he talking to you?'

'I think he means you.'

'Oh dear,' said Harry, 'I forgot for a moment there. Women's lib, eh? Don't mind me, love, just sit down anyway.'

Bel eventually sat down, and Harry stuck the ID form he'd just typed into the suitcase-machine.

'Don't smile or frown,' he told Bel, 'just look natural. That's about as natural as a performing seal. Better, better.' There was a flash, and Harry stood up straight. 'Lovely. Takes about half a minute. Sit yourself down, Mark.'

We changed places.

'By the way, Harry, you'd better take a few extra shots of me. I want you to set up a whole new identity.'

'That takes time, Mark.'

'I know. What shall we say, four days?'

'Make it five. What do you need: passport, driving licence, National Insurance number?'

'They'll do for a start.'

'We're talking serious money.'

'I know. I'll give you two hundred on account.'

'Now, just think bland thoughts. Mushy peas, liquor, the Spurs midfield. Look at him, he's a natural.'

There was a flash, then Harry switched to his everyday SLR camera and plugged it into the flash-lamp. He fired off a few more shots, asking me questions while he did.

'What name?'

'How about Michael Whitney?'

'Date of birth?'

'Same as mine. No, make it a month earlier. Place of birth: London. You can make the rest of it up as you like.'

'I will then.'

When he peeled the paper from my card and handed it to me, the clear plastic laminate was still warm. Behind the plastic, I wore that same policeman's scowl. Bel wasn't happy with her card. She reckoned she looked like a frightened animal. I studied her card but had to disagree.

'Look on the bright side, Bel. At least it'll give them a laugh when they arrest us. Harry, have you got any of those—'

But he was already coming back into the room, waving two small black leather wallets.

'Put them in here,' he said. 'You can fill the spare pockets with anything you like.' He crumpled one in his hand. 'Give them a bit of a seeing to first though, otherwise they look like they've just come from the sweatshop. He smiled at me. 'No extra charge.'

Which was my cue to hand over the cash.

We took a mini-cab from the office at the corner of Harry the Cap's road. Our driver didn't even know where Marylebone was, and mention of Baker Street and Regent's Park didn't ring any of his rusted bells. So I gave him some directions, and kept giving them all the way back to the hotel. He radioed his office to see how much he should charge.

'Depends whether they look loaded or not,' said the crackly voice. The driver looked at me in his rearview, and I shook my head at him. I gave him the money, but no tip, seeing how I'd have been better driving myself and letting him sit in the back.

I'd got him to drop us a couple of streets from the hotel. If anyone got to Harry the Cap, they might ask questions at the cab office, and the cab office wouldn't forget a fare from Tottenham to Marylebone Road. I didn't want anyone coming any closer to me than that. And yes, I *did* have someone specific in mind.

'Hang on,' said Bel, 'I want a pizza.' So we went to a takeaway and stood with the delivery riders while Bel's deep-pan medium seafood was constructed. Then it was back to the hotel. I took her to her room. She lifted the pizza box to my nose.

'You want to help me with this?'

Which was, however innocent its intention, an invitation to her bedroom, where we'd have to sit on the bed to eat.

'Not hungry, thanks,' I said. But I'd paused too long.

'I won't tell my dad.' She was smiling. 'Shouldn't we talk anyway? Go through the plan for tomorrow?'

She had a point. 'Over breakfast,' I said.

'Cold pizza maybe?'

'Don't be disgusting.'

I went to my room and called Max. He'd been sitting right by the phone.

'Everything's fine,' I said. 'I'll give you the number here, you can call Bel any time you like.'

'Thanks,' he said grudgingly. He then found a pen and some paper. I gave him the hotel number and Bel's room number. 'She'll probably be calling you herself,' I said.

'If she hasn't already forgotten me.'

'Don't be daft, Max, she talks about you all the time.' This was a lie; she hadn't mentioned her father all day until I'd brought up the subject in the pub. *I won't tell my dad.* ''Night, Max.' I put down the phone.

I'd known Bel for a few years now, and naturally sex had never . . . well, it wasn't that I didn't like her. It wasn't that we didn't flirt. It wasn't even that I was scared Max would bury me in one of his walled fields. It was mostly that I didn't, as the Americans say, 'do' sex any more. It didn't exactly go with the lifestyle. The women I met in my life I met infrequently and for necessarily short periods. If I wanted to get to know any of them, I had to construct a set of lies and half-truths. You didn't get too many ads in the lonely hearts columns from women looking to meet 'tall okay-looking assassin, 30–35, interested in ballistics, cuisine, international travel'. So I'd given up on women. I didn't even use hotel whores often, though I liked to buy them drinks and listen to their own constructed stories.

Speaking of which, I knew I had one more call to make. It had taken me a while to get round to it. I picked up the receiver and pressed the digits from memory. I have a good memory for numbers. The call was answered.

'Allington Hotel, can I help you?'

'Yes, I'd like to speak to a Mr Leo Hoffer, please.'

'Hoffer? One moment, please.' A clack of computer keys. 'I'm sorry, sir, we don't appear to have a guest with that name.'

'I'm sure he's staying there,' I persisted. 'He was there today, or maybe he's booking in tomorrow?'

'Hold on, please.' She muffled the phone with her hand and asked a colleague. The colleague took the receiver from her.

'Hello, sir? I think there must be a misunderstanding. Mr Hoffer did visit the hotel earlier today, but he isn't a guest here.'

'Damn,' I said. 'I must have got a crossed line. You don't happen to know where he's staying, do you?'

'I'm sorry, sir. At least you know Mr Hoffer's in town.'

'Yes, that's true. At least I know that. You've been very helpful.' I put down the phone. After a minute or two, I allowed myself a small smile. It was good to know Leo was here. Where he was, the circus would surely follow, by which I mean the media circus he seemed always to attract . . . and to covet. I always knew when Leo was on my trail, no matter how far behind.

I only had to pick up a paper and let the interviewer tell me about it.

I'd seen Leo on TV in the States. Frankly, I wasn't flattered. They say it's nice to feel wanted, but Leo looked like the one who should be in the slammer.

There was a soft knock at my door. Two short, one long: our agreed signal. I sighed, got off the bed, and unlocked the door.

'Got anything for indigestion?' Bel said.

'Okay,' I said, letting her in, 'let's go through tomorrow.'

And we did. I had us stand in front of the mirror and showed Bel how to act like a police officer, how to stand, how to speak, what to say. She smiled too much at first, so we got rid of that. And she had a natural slouch, the result, so she said, of always being taller than her girl friends and trying to bring herself down to their level.

After an hour, she got bored and started making mistakes again.

'Listen,' I said. 'We'll get one or two shots at this. After that it'd be too risky. The police are bound to find out there are impostors going around. So we've got to make the most of it, understood?' I waited till she nodded. 'Remember, these IDs weren't cheap. Now, look at yourself in the mirror, you're slouching again.'

She straightened up.

'Better.' I was standing close behind her. 'Now do one last thing for me.' She turned to me.

'What?'

'Go phone your father.'

She narrowed her eyes. 'Yes, boss,' she said.

I locked the door after her.

9

The hardest work Hoffer had done so far in London was find a dealer who didn't think he was an undercover cop or the vigilante father of some teenage addict.

There was crack around, but not much actual cocaine. The stuff he'd ended up buying was far from premium grade, probably five parts lidocaine and three parts baking soda, but there was no way he was going to start doing crack or free-basing, he'd seen too much hurt result from those particular by-ways. He'd been a New York street cop when crack first hit town. In a matter of months the drug had swamped the housing schemes. Earlier in the 80s he'd been friends with another cop who'd started free-basing. That cop had gone downhill like a well-oiled skateboard, careering all the way.

Hoffer had got into drugs the same way. He spent his days busting pushers and users, living so close to drugs that it was like the fucking things were whispering to him, even in his sleep. One day he'd confiscated some bottles of rock cocaine, only he'd handed them in one short. He soon found that there was an underclass of police officer that used a lot of drugs. Some of them just took drugs off one pusher and resold to another, keeping a little back along the way. Others had deep habits and pinhole eyes, real smack heads. You were in a privileged position, being a cop. You didn't have to look far or try hard to score a baggie of white shit, and you so seldom had to pay. But free-basing, that was a nightmare. Someone had tried to introduce him to it, recycling their smoke into a balloon and offering him the used smoke. Hoffer had never enjoyed the more social aspects of drug use, and drew the damned line at breathing somebody else's high.

So here he was in London, doing what he did.

He added a couple of hundred milligrams of speed to his purchase, and to offset the speed asked about quaaludes or 'bennies', but ended up with Librium and a bit more boo.

'Packing heat,' he said to himself afterwards. Soho had still failed to provide a night's fun, so he'd prowled the West End, sitting in a fag bar for quarter of an hour before realising his mistake, and finally locating a hooker who wouldn't accompany him to his hotel, but could provide relief in her own quarters. Hoffer couldn't agree to this; he'd gone to a hooker's greasy bedroom before, only to have her pimp try to roll him. So they made do with a back-alley blow job, for which she charged a twenty. That put her on £240 an hour, which was decent money. It was even more than Robert Walkins was paying.

In the morning he had a shower, the bath being too narrow for anything like a soak, put on a sober blue suit, and went to see his bank manager.

Mr Arthur looked like *he* was the one begging a loan for his daughter's life-saving surgery.

'Events will take their course, Mr Hopper.'

'That's Hoffer.'

'Of course, Hoffer.' Arthur gave a smile like a toad at mating time. 'But it's a bit early yet to expect any results, as I say.'

'Say whatever you like, shithead, but listen to this.' Hoffer leaned forward in his cramped chair. 'I don't have to play by any rules, so if you want to be able to leave your office every lunchtime and evening without having to check both ways for baseball bats, I suggest you give events a kick along the course they're taking.'

'Now look here—'

'I *am* looking, and all I see is something I try not to tread in on the sidewalk. And I don't mean manholes. Now get hassling head office for all you're worth, and meantime let me see what you've got here behind the scenes.'

Arthur's top lip was glistening with sudden perspiration. He looked like he'd lost about twenty pounds in stature.

'I've got an appointment at eleven.'

'Cancel it.'

'Look, you can't just—'

'I thought I already was.' Hoffer stood up, keeping his hands in his pockets. With his elbows jutting from his sides, he knew he looked like something from the jungle. Arthur would have clambered up the cheese-plant in the corner if he'd had any motive power. 'Now go fetch me the files.'

He sat down again, trying to look comfortable. The bank manager sat there for a few moments, just to show he wasn't intimidated. Hoffer allowed this with a shrug. They both knew the truth. Mr Arthur got up slowly, his hands gripping the edge of the desk. Then he walked out of the office.

He came back with a couple of files and some sheets of photocopier paper. 'This is all I can find just now. Most of our records get sent to head office eventually.'

'Tell them you want them back here pronto. What about the check on Wesley's current account transactions?'

'It's being carried out. We have to go through all the old cheques. They're not kept in neat little piles.'

Hoffer reached out a hand for the files. There was a knock at the manager's door.

'Ignore it,' said Hoffer.

'I certainly shan't.' Arthur walked briskly to the door and pulled it open. 'This is the man, officers.'

Hoffer turned his head lazily. At the door stood two uniformed policemen. So Arthur hadn't just been seeking out the files. Hoffer peeked at them anyway. They contained only blank sheets of typing paper.

'You sonofabitch,' he said. The policemen then asked him to accompany them, and he rose from his chair. 'Certainly,' he said. 'No problem here,' he assured them.

But all the time he had eyes only for Mr Arthur.

'Never again! Do you hear?'

Hoffer heard. He was bored of hearing it. Bob Broome didn't seem to have any other words in his vocabulary.

'Can we turn the record over, Bob?'

Broome slapped his desk. 'It's not funny, Hoffer. It's not a game. You can't go around threatening bank managers. Jesus Christ, they run the country.'

'That's your problem then. Still, it could be worse.' Broome waited for an explanation. 'At least Arthur didn't look Jewish.'

Broome collapsed on to his chair. 'You're slime, Hoffer.'

Hoffer didn't need that. 'Yeah, I'm slime, but I'm slime that *pays*. So what does that make you?'

'Hold on a second.'

'No, shut up and listen. Remember, I've been a cop, I know what it's like. You try to look busy, but most of the time you're treading water waiting for somebody to come tell you who it is you're looking for. I can't do that any more. I don't have that luxury. What I've got is a head and a pair of fists, and if you don't like that, then just keep out of my way.'

'I just saved you from a barrow-load of manure.'

'And I thank you for that, but I've walked away from shit before without needing a pitchfork up my ass.'

Broome shook his head sadly. 'I don't want you around, Hoffer.'

'Tough titty.'

'I mean it. I don't want you anywhere near.'

'I can handle that, Chief Inspector.' Hoffer stood up. 'But remember, *you're* the one who called me, *you're* the one who took my money.' Hoffer walked out of the office. He didn't bother closing the door.

On his way out of Vine Street, he saw DI Dave Edmond going in. They knew one another through Broome.

'Hey . . . Dave, right?' said Hoffer, the bright smiling American.

'That's right,' said Edmond.

'Are you busy?'

'Well, I was just . . .'

'I thought maybe I could buy you a drink?'

Edmond licked his lips. It had been a whole eleven hours since he'd last touched a drop. 'Well, that's very kind.'

Hoffer put a hand on his shoulder. 'Ulterior motive, Dave. I've got a couple of questions, and Bob thought maybe you wouldn't mind . . .'

'What sort of questions?' Edmond was already being steered back the way he'd come.

'Oh, just background stuff. You know, ballistics, scene of crime, that sort of thing. And anything you have on the deceased.'

Edmond had said that if they were going to talk about guns, maybe he should invite Barney along. Sergeant Barney Wills was the station's arms aficionado. So they took Barney with them to the pub.

It was another of those 'olde worlde' interiors which bored Hoffer stupid. In America, a bar looked like a bar, a place where you went to drink. He couldn't see the point of horse brasses and framed prints of clipper ships and shelves of books. Yes, *books*, like people might suddenly mistake the place for a library and decide to have a drink anyway while they were there.

It was all a joke too, hardly any of it authentic. The prints were fresh and framed in plastic, the books bought by the yard. Often he despaired of the English. They were too easy to con. Edmond and Barney were perfect material for a *real* con artist, perfect because they thought they were putting one over on *him*. He was just a loud Yank with money to spend and a lot of daft notions. They'd play him along, laughing at him, taking his drinks, and they'd tell him a few stories along the way.

Hoffer didn't mind this game. He knew who was screwing who. If the scene had been a porn movie, the two policemen would have had their cheeks bared in submission.

Barney told him what the lab had discovered about the sniper rifle. Namely that it had indeed fired the fatal shot, and that it was a specialist weapon, in use in the armed forces but not in general circulation. Arms weren't easy to come by in Britain anyway, though recently the crack dealers hadn't been having any problems. The Army and the Royal Marines used the L96A1, but civilian target shooters wouldn't use one.

'It was a Super Magnum,' Barney said, between gulps of Scotch. '.338 Lapua Magnum ammunition. Christ knows where he got it.'

'There must be a few bent gun dealers around,' Hoffer suggested.

'Yes, but even they wouldn't deal in an L96. I mean, half of them wouldn't even know how to begin getting hold of one. This thing fires a thousand yards, who needs that? And the sight he had on it, this was quality gear, must've cost a fortune.'

'Someone must've been paying a fortune,' Edmond added.

'Question is, who?' Hoffer got in another round. 'I've looked into assassins, guys, I mean the whole tribe of them. Leaving out the one-off crazies who go blast their local burger joint with an Uzi, they tend to come from a military background. Makes sense, right? I mean, that's where they get the training, that's where they first taste what a gun can do.'

Both men nodded, too busy drinking to interrupt.

'But this guy is a haemophiliac, or at least we think he is, and the doctors assure me the military won't accept haemophiliacs.' Hoffer's own words hit him: *military background*. Maybe he was on to something. He thought about it for a minute. Edmond and Barney didn't seem to notice. They started up a conversation about some cricket match. Eventually Hoffer drifted back to the real world. It was the tap of empty glass on wooden table that did it. Not that his companions were hinting or anything.

'This'll have to be the last round, guys. We're all busy people.' So he got them in again, and decided the balance was all wrong. He was shelling out, and not getting back much of a dividend.

'So, Barney, what about these gun dealers? The bent ones, I mean. Are they on a list or anything? I'd appreciate a look-see.' What else could Barney do but nod and say he'd see what he could do? Hoffer turned to Edmond.

'Now, Dave, you were going to tell me about Eleanor Ricks . . .'

The Army camp wasn't such a bitch to find after all.

Hoffer had been expecting a hellhole in the middle of nowhere, but this was just north of London, on the edge of a commuter town and slap next-door to a housing estate.

When he'd spoken to the camp by telephone, they'd said he could take a mainline train up there, it only took half an hour. So that's what he did. The people were kidding themselves if they thought they lived in the 'country'. They weren't living *in* anything, they were living *on* something, and that something was borrowed time. London was snapping at their shoelaces. They worked there, earned their living there, and London wanted something back in return. It wanted *them*.

They tried to look prosperous and talk differently, but they were pale, almost ill-looking, and their cars only made traffic jams. Hoffer, who had considered taking a cab all the way, was relieved he'd gone by train. The roads he saw were crammed. Someone mentioned a nineteen-mile tailback on the M25. They called the road an 'orbital'. You could orbit the globe in less time. The train wasn't quite perfect though. It had been late leaving London, and it hadn't been cleaned or aired since depositing its rush-hour cattle in London. It smelt bad and there was trash on the floor.

The cab Hoffer took from the station didn't smell much better, and there was only slightly more room in the back than in a British Rail seat. He stuffed his legs in a diagonal and made do like that. He got the cab to drop him at the camp entrance. He was surprised to see armed guards on the gate. One nodded him in the direction of the gatehouse.

'What's the problem, chief?' Hoffer asked, as the guard on the gatehouse phoned him in.

'Terrorists,' the guard said. 'We're on constant alert.'

'I thought they'd stopped bothering you guys, started bothering the rest of us instead?'

'You never know.'

Armed with this philosophical nugget, Hoffer was pointed in the direction of the office he wanted.

He was met halfway by a young soldier whose face looked to have been pressed the same time as his shirt and pants.

'Mr Hoffer? The Major's expecting you.'

'It's good of him to see me at short notice.' Hoffer almost had to jog to keep up with the man. Somewhere along the route, Hoffer was supposed to catch the guy's name, but he was too busy catching his own breath. He was led into a building and told to take a seat. He was glad to. He tried focusing his eyes on the recruiting posters and glossy brochures. You'd think you were booking a holiday for yourself rather than a bruising career. The soldiers in the brochures looked tough and honest and Christian. You just knew democracy and the free world would be safe in their hands, even if you were dropping them into a country where they couldn't speak the language and the distant hills were full of mortar and Mullahs.

Hoffer caught himself whistling 'God Bless America' and checked it just in time.

A door opened along the hall. 'Mr Hoffer?'

Hoffer walked along the hall to meet the Major. His name was Major Drysdale, and he had a cool dry handshake, a bit like a Baptist minister's. 'Come in, please.'

'I was telling your . . . ah, I was saying I appreciate you seeing me like this.'

'Well, your call was intriguing. It's not every day I get to meet a New York detective. Speaking of which, there are certain formalities . . . Could I see your identification?'

Hoffer reached into his pocket and produced his detective's ID, which had been unfortunately mislaid at the time of his resignation from the force. It came in useful sometimes. People in authority would often prefer to speak to a real police officer than a shamus. Hoffer reckoned this was one of those times. Drysdale took down a few details from the ID before handing back the wallet. That worried Hoffer, but not much. He might go on to an Army file, but he doubted they'd go so far as to phone his supposed employers in the States. He kept reading about military cutbacks, and phone calls cost money.

'So,' said Major Drysdale, 'what can I do for you, Detective Hoffer?'

It was a small plain office, lacking any trace of personality. Drysdale might have just moved in, which would explain it. But Hoffer thought the man looked comfortable here, like he'd sat in the office for years. He wasn't much more than PR, a public face for the Army. The camp's real muscle was elsewhere. But Hoffer didn't need muscle, he just needed a few questions answered. He needed a friendly ear. He was on his best behaviour and in his best suit, but Drysdale still treated him with just a trace of amusement, like he'd never seen such a specimen before.

As to the Major himself, he was tall and skinny with arms you could have snapped with a Chinese restaurant's crab-crackers. He had short fair hair and blue eyes out of a Nazi youth league, and a moustache which could have been drawn on his face with ballpoint. He wasn't young any more, but still carried acne around his shirt collar. Could be he was allergic to the starch.

'Well, Major,' Hoffer said, 'like I said on the telephone, it's a medical question, and a vague one at that, but it's in connection with a series of murders, assassinations to be more accurate, and as such we would appreciate any help the Army can give.'

'And you're working in tandem with Scotland Yard?'

'Oh, absolutely. I have their full backing.'

'Could you give me a contact name there?' Drysdale poised his pen above his notepad.

'Sure. Uh, Chief Inspector Broome. That's B-r-o-o-m-e. He's the man to talk to. He's based at Vine Street in central London.'

'Not Scotland Yard?'

'Well, they're working together on this.'

'Orange, isn't it?'

'Sir?'

'Vine Street.' Hoffer still didn't get it. 'On the Monopoly board.'

Hoffer grinned, chuckled even, and shook his head in wonder at the joke.

'Do you have a phone number for the Chief Inspector?'

'Oh, yessir, sure.' Goddamned Army. Hoffer gave Major Drysdale the number. His skin was crawling, and he had to force himself not to scratch all over. He wished he hadn't taken some speed before setting out.

'Maybe before we start,' Drysdale was saying now, not stonewalling exactly, just following procedure, 'you could tell me a little about the inquiry itself. Oh, tea by the way?'

'Yes, please.'

Drysdale picked up his phone and ordered tea and 'some biccies'. Then he sat back and waited for Hoffer to tell him all about the D-Man.

It took a while, but eventually, two cups of strong brown tea later, Hoffer got to the point he'd wanted to start with. Drysdale had asked questions about everything from the assassin's first error to the sniper rifle he'd used in London. And he'd kept on scribbling notes, though Hoffer wanted to say it was none of his goddamned business, tear the pad from him, and chew it up with his teeth. He was sweating now, and blamed tannin poisoning. His throat was coated with felt.

'So you see,' he said, 'if the man we're looking for hasn't exactly been *in* the Army, well, maybe he's been or still is connected to it in some way. The most obvious connection I can think of is family.'

'You mean a brother or sister?'

'No, sir, I mean his father. I think it would have to be his father, someone who might have instilled in him a . . . relationship with weapons.'

'We don't normally allow children to train with live ammo, Detective Hoffer.'

'That's not exactly what I'm saying, sir. I mean, I'm sure the Army's probity is above . . . uh, whatever. But say this man was good with firearms, well, wouldn't he want to pass that knowledge and interest on to his son?'

'Even if the son could never join the Army?'

'The kid could've been a teenager before anyone found out he was a haemophiliac. Mild sufferers, sometimes they don't find out till they're grown up. It takes an operation or something before anyone notices they have trouble getting their blood to clot.'

'This is all very interesting,' said Drysdale, flicking through his copious notes, 'but I don't see where it gets us.'

'I'll tell you, sir. It gets us a kid who's diagnosed haemophiliac by an Army doctor, sometime in the past, maybe between twenty and thirty years ago. You must have records.'

Drysdale laughed. 'We may have records, but do you know what you're asking? We'd have to check every Army base here and abroad, every medical centre. Even supposing they held records from so long ago. Even supposing the child was treated by an Army doctor. I mean, he might easily have gone to a civilian doctor. Putting aside all this, he would have taken his records with him.'

'What?'

'When you change doctors, your new doctor requests from your old doctor all your medical notes. You don't keep them yourself, your doctor keeps them. Your *present* doctor.'

'Are you sure? Maybe if I spoke to someone from your medical—'

'I really don't think that's necessary.'

Hoffer considered his options. He could whack the guy. He could wheedle. He could offer some cash. He didn't think any of these would work, so he decided to be disappointed instead.

'I'm real sorry you can't find it in yourself to help, Major. You know how many innocent people this man has murdered? You know he'll keep on doing it till he's caught? I mean, he's not going to give it up and move jobs. I can't see him waiting tables at IHOP or somewhere.'

Drysdale smiled again. 'Look, I know what you're saying. I appreciate that you—'

Hoffer got to his feet. 'No, sir, with all due respect I don't think you do know. I won't waste any more of your time.' He turned to the door.

'Wait a minute.' Hoffer waited. He turned his head. Drysdale was standing too now. 'Look, maybe I can initiate a few general inquiries.'

Hoffer turned back into the room. 'That would be great, sir.'

'I can't make any promises, you understand.'

'Absolutely. We're all just trying to do what we can.'

Drysdale nodded. 'Well, I'll see what I can do.'

'I really appreciate that, sir.' Hoffer took Drysdale's hand. 'I'm sure I speak for us all.'

Drysdale smiled a little sheepishly. Then he said he'd get someone to escort the detective back to the gate.

'I'll be in touch,' said Hoffer.

While he waited back in the reception area for his 'escort' to appear, he spotted a drinking fountain and flew towards it, filling his mouth with water, gargling, spitting it back, and finally swallowing a few mouthfuls.

'How can they drink that stuff?' he asked himself as he wiped his mouth.

'It's only water,' his escort said from behind him.

'I meant the goddamned tea,' said Hoffer.

10

I knocked again.

'Come on,' I said, 'let's get busy. We're not tourists any more.'

Not that Bel had seen many of the sights of London, unless 'sights' was broad enough to encompass Tottenham and a couple of low-class restaurants. I listened at her door until I could hear her getting out of bed.

'I'll meet you downstairs,' she called.

I went back to my room and tried phoning again. This time I got through. I was calling someone at British Telecom. His name was Allan and he didn't come cheap.

'It's me,' I said. 'Have they started tapping your line yet?'

'No, just everybody else's. I can give you the latest royal dirt if you like.'

He didn't sound like he was joking. 'No thanks,' I said. 'I'm after a couple of numbers.'

'I take it you mean unlisted, or you'd be calling Directory Enquiries.'

'I've checked, they're unlisted. The first is a woman called Eleanor Ricks.'

'The one who got shot?'

'Could be.'

'You've got to be careful, man. Sometimes Scotland Yard or MI5 stick keywords into the system. If you say the word and they catch it, they record your whole conversation.'

Allan was always trying to impress me – or scare me, I didn't know which – with this sort of comment.

'Her husband may be the subscriber,' I carried on. 'He's called Frederick Ricks. According to the tabloids, they live in Camden. I'll need their address, too.'

'Got it.' He paused. 'You said a couple of names?'

'Joe Draper, he heads a TV production company. He's got a house in Wiltshire, the phone number there would be useful, plus any address for him in town, apart from his office. His office is in the book.'

I could hear Allan writing the information down. I gave silent blessing to the British media, who had provided me with the information I had.

'I see inflation's in the news again,' he said at last.

'Not another hike, Allan. You're pricing yourself out of the game.'

'As a special offer to regular subscribers, the increase has been held to ten percent for one month only.'

'Generous to a fault. Same address?'

'Who can afford to move?'

'Tens and twenties all right?'

'Sure.'

'Oh, one more name . . .'
'Now who's pushing it?'
'Call it my free gift. Scotty Shattuck.' I spelt it for him. 'Somewhere in London probably, always supposing he's got a phone.'
'Right, I'll do my best. Later today, okay?'
'I'll stick your fee in the post. If I'm not here, leave the details with reception. Here's the number.'
I gave it to him and terminated the call. Downstairs, Bel was already seated in the small dining room, pouring cereal from a one-portion pack.
'I see you're not one of these women who takes forever to dress.' I sat down beside her.
'Know a lot about that, do you?'
'What do you mean?'
'Oh, nothing.' She poured milk and started to eat. I knew what she meant. She meant she was good-looking and I hadn't made a pass at her, so what did that make me? She was wearing trousers and a blue blouse and jacket. They were the plainest items in her luggage. I tried to see her as a police officer. I couldn't. But then I'd be the one doing the talking; I'd be the one they'd be looking at. And examining myself in the mirror this morning, I'd seen a hard-nosed copper staring back at me. He looked like he wanted to take me outside.
'Aren't you eating?' Bel asked.
'I never eat much in the morning. I'll just have some coffee.'
'You will if anyone turns up to serve you. I haven't seen a soul since I came in. The stuff's all on that sideboard, but there's no coffee.'
I went to the sideboard to take a look. A thermos flask turned out to contain hot water, and there was a jar of instant coffee in one of the cupboards.
'Yum yum,' said Bel.
The coffee tasted the way thermos coffee always tastes. It reminded me of sports fields, of games watched with my father, the two of us sheltering beneath a tartan travelling-rug or umbrellas and hoods, depending on the weather. There'd be coffee and sandwiches at half-time. Thermos coffee.
'So the schedule for today,' said Bel, scraping up the last of the cereal, 'is a visit to Testosterone City, yes?' I nodded. 'And I provide the decoration while you ask your questions?' I nodded again. 'Are you quite sure you need my expensive skills, Michael? I mean, performing monkeys come cheap these days.' Then she touched the back of my hand. 'Only teasing. Drink your coffee and let's get out of here. This dining room's like something out of a horror film. I keep thinking all the other guests and staff have been murdered in their beds.' She started to laugh, but stopped abruptly, and her look was somewhere between embarrassment and fear. I knew exactly what had struck her: that there was only one murderer around here.

I didn't know where to find Scotty Shattuck, but wasn't prepared to sit around the hotel waiting for Allan to get back to me. So we got a taxi on Marylebone Road and headed for Oxford Street, where, above a shop selling what can be best described as 'tat', there was a gym and health centre called Chuck's.
Max had been able to offer a good physical description of Shattuck, and it

pointed to a man who did more than jog around the park to keep himself in shape.

'He's like a cross between a Welsh pit-pony and a brick shithouse,' Max had said.

There were a lot of gyms in London, a lot of places where sweaty males pushed weights, goaded by other musclebound lifters. Some of them no doubt took a few drugs to aid muscle development and performance. They were the sorts who have gaps between their upper arms and their torsos when they walk, and can't do anything to close those gaps.

A lot of gyms, but only one or two like Chuck's. Chuck's was more than a gym, it was a place to hang out, a haven for those who need to keep fit between assignments. You didn't get the grossly over-muscled at Chuck's. You got authentic hard men, men who'd been in the armed forces, or who had come out but still kept fit. Men sometimes recruited for work overseas, work they talked about in Chuck's, but seldom outside. I'd been introduced to Chuck's by an ex-Royal Marine who'd been my contact on an earlier job. He wasn't there when we walked in, but Chuck himself was.

He was about fifty, hair like steel wool, and he wore a green combat-style T-shirt, straining across his chest. The men on the machines behind him whistled appreciatively at Bel as Chuck came towards us. Bel's face reddened with anger.

'What can I do for you?'

'Are you the owner of this establishment, sir?'

He got a bored look on his face. One question had established in his mind who he was dealing with. I knew he wouldn't recognise me; I'd changed a lot since Brent Storey had brought me here.

'That's right,' he said warily.

'I'm looking for someone called Scotty.' Chuck's face stayed blank.

'As in "Beam me up?"' he hazarded. I didn't smile.

'Scotty Shattuck,' I went on. I had one hand in my pocket. I was wearing tight black leather gloves, as was Bel. We'd bought them on the way here. Her idea. They shouldn't have worked, but in fact they did make us look more like police officers. 'He works weights,' I went on. 'Little guy, but well-built. He's ex-Army.'

'Sorry,' said Chuck, ignoring all this, 'I didn't catch your name.'

'West, Detective Inspector West.'

'And this is . . . ?' He meant Bel.

'DC Harris,' she said, stony-faced. Chuck gave her a good long examination, not caring if I noticed or not. The two customers using the apparatus had stopped and were sauntering this way, rubbing their necks with towels. Another three men were squatting by the window. The noise of traffic was a low persistent growl, with vibrations from the buses shaking the mirrors on the walls.

'Well,' Chuck said at last, turning back to me, 'can't help, I'm afraid.'

'Look, we don't want any trouble. It's just that I need to talk to Mr Shattuck.'

'I don't think so.' Chuck was shaking his head, hands on his hips.

'He's not in trouble or anything, Mr . . .'

'People just call me Chuck. Know why? Because if I don't like someone, I'm liable to chuck them out of that window over there.'

'Ever tried a policeman?'

'Funny you should say that. Just tell me what you want to talk to Scotty Shattuck about.'

'You know him then?'

'Maybe I'm just curious.' He was checking the floor between us.

'Come on,' said Bel, 'let's go.'

Chuck looked up. 'All I want to know is why you want him.'

The last time I'd been here with Brent, the atmosphere had been very different. But then I'd been with a member, with someone everyone knew. I hadn't been a policeman then either. I'd misjudged this place. It looked like Chuck had a score to settle with law and order.

'Afraid not,' I said, shaking my head. 'But I can assure you it's nothing serious.'

'No?'

The two hard men were flanking Chuck now. They knew they didn't need to say anything. Their voices would only have spoiled the picture they made.

Suddenly Bel flipped open her ID the way she must have seen actors do on the television. 'If you don't tell us where to find Mr Shattuck, you'll be hindering our inquiries. That could be construed as obstruction, sir.'

Maybe she'd been watching too much daytime TV.

Chuck smiled, first at one of his men, then at the other. He seemed to find something interesting on the tips of his shoes, and studied them, talking at the same time.

'I've nothing to say. I don't know anyone called Scotty Shattuck. End of story. Goodbye, adios, au revoir.'

I stood my ground for a moment longer, knowing I didn't believe him. We could back off, or we could try another tactic. We didn't have time to back off. Besides, if we left now, word could get back to Shattuck, causing him to disappear. There was one option left.

So I drew the gun.

It's not easy to conceal a Heckler & Koch MP5, but it's always worth the effort. It was why I'd borrowed a Barbour jacket from Max. It was roomy, and he'd sewn a pocket into it so the gun could be carried more easily. So what if I sweated in the heat?

At twenty inches long and six pounds weight, the MP5 can be carried just about anywhere without creating a stir. It only created a stir when you brought it out and pointed it at someone. I held it one-handed and pointed it directly at Chuck.

'This thing's got a fifteen-round mag,' I said, 'and I've set it on a three-round burst. You've been around, Chuck, you know what that'll do to you. You'll be lying in two pieces on the floor, and so will everybody else. Whole thing'll take just a couple of seconds.'

Chuck had taken a couple of steps back and raised his hands slightly, but otherwise seemed fairly calm under the circumstances.

'I want to know where he is,' I said. 'When you tell me, I'm going to go talk to him. That's all, just talk. But if he's not there, if someone's warned him, then I'm coming back here.'

Chuck's minders couldn't take their eyes off the gun. To be honest, I didn't think I could aim the thing properly, never mind fire it. I wasn't used to sub-machine guns, far less ones so short you could use them one-handed like a pistol. I was brandishing it for two reasons. One, I knew it would scare the shit out of everyone. Two, I didn't have time to take 'no' as the answer to any question I needed to ask.

'I didn't think you were a cop,' Chuck sneered.

'I only want to talk to him.'

'Go fuck yourself.'

The men who'd been crouching by the window had risen to their feet. I could hear Bel breathing just half a step behind me. I should have known a pretty face wouldn't have been enough for people like Chuck. They'd gone way beyond pretty faces in their time.

He wasn't going to speak, so I waved the gun around a bit. One of his minders spoke for him, maybe for all of them.

'Scotty lives in Norwood, near Crystal Palace.'

'I need an address.'

He gave me one. 'But he hasn't been in for a while. I haven't seen him around either.'

'You think he's got a job?'

The gorilla shrugged.

'Okay,' I said, 'sorry for any inconvenience.' I started backing towards the door. Bel was already on her way. 'I'll let you get back to your weight-gain. Looks like a few of you have lost a pound or two into your underwear.' I looked at Chuck again and waved the gun a final time. 'They call it the mercenary's life-support.'

Then we were gone.

The taxi took us south of the river.

Bel said she felt drunk, with the excitement at the gym and then our brief jog to the traffic lights where a taxi was just unloading. I didn't want to talk about it, not in a taxi, so she waited till the driver dropped us off. We were standing on Church Road, a busy two-lane street of large detached houses. The area must have been posh at one time, but most of the buildings had fallen into disrepair to a lesser or greater degree. The house we were standing outside definitely fell into the category of 'greater degree'. It was a huge monstrous affair, all angles and gables and windows where you'd least expect to see them. Paint had faded and peeled from it, and some of the windows were covered with blankets for curtains, or with boards where the glass should be. The even larger house next to it had been added to and converted into a hotel. I imagined the cheapest rooms would be those to the side.

Bel wasn't looking at the house, she was looking at me, wanting me to say something.

'I wouldn't have used it,' I offered.

'Really?'

'Really.'

She broke into a nervous laugh. 'The look on their faces.' It was one of those laughs which can easily turn to sobbing. 'I was scared, Michael, and I was *behind* the bloody gun!'

An elderly lady was wheeling her shopping-trolley past us. She smiled a greeting, the way some old people do.

'Keep your voice down,' I cautioned. Bel quickly took my meaning.

'Sorry.'

'Look, Bel, I don't want to stick around London any longer than I need to. That's why I used the gun. I can't hang around being pleasant and polite and waiting for answers. I need them fast.'

She was nodding. 'Understood.' She turned at last to the house. 'God, it's ugly.'

'Let's make this short and sweet,' I said, heading for the front door.

The expansive front garden had been concreted over some time before, but weeds and grass were pushing their way through. There were huge cracks and swells in the concrete, doubtless caused by the roots of several mature trees nearby. A car sat on the concrete, covered by a black tarpaulin which itself now sported a covering of wet leaves, moss and bits of rubbish. It was sitting so low to the ground, it either had flat tyres or none at all. Past it, a dozen steps led to the front door, rotten at its base. There was an intercom next to the door, complete with buzzers for eight flats. Only three had names attached. None of them was Shattuck. I pressed one anyway. There was no reply. I pressed another, then another. Still no reply. Bel placed her hand against the door and gave it the slightest push. It swung inwards.

'Shall we?' she said.

There was a lot of mail in the entrance hall, along with litter which had blown in over time, and an untidy mouldering heap of free newssheets. Someone had left a bicycle frame against the wall. There was no sign of any wheels.

Some mail sat on an upturned cardboard box. Most of the letters were for Scotty Shattuck, some identifying his address as Flat 5. I checked the postmarks. They went back almost a week.

'Doesn't look good,' I said.

We climbed the creaking stairs, hearing no sounds from the other flats, and encountering not a soul. Flat 5 was three storeys up, near what had to be the top of the house, though the stairs kept winding. The door was cheap and newish, a wooden frame with thin panelling over it. A single Yale had been fitted. The door had no handles or nameplate. There were scrapes on the jamb near the lock.

'Looks like someone kicked the old door in.'

'Maybe he locked himself out.'

'Maybe. Since when he's had this new one fitted, but hasn't got round to adding decent locks yet.'

'That's handy,' said Bel. She pulled a small kit of tools from her pocket. 'I brought this along, thought it might be useful.'

She got to work on the Yale. It took her less than a minute to open it. Not fast, but quieter than a burst from the MP5.

'I knew there was some reason I wanted you with me,' I said.

She smiled. 'My dad taught me how to do it years ago. We only had one front-door key back then. He said this would save him having to get one cut for me.'

'That sounds like Max all right.'

Bel put away her lockpicker's kit and we entered Scotty Shattuck's flat. You could tell straight away he hadn't been there for some time. The place felt lifeless. It was a bachelor pad, sloppily decorated with nude mags, beer cans and empty containers from Indian takeaways. There was one chair, separated by a footstool from the TV and video. In the only bedroom, the bedclothes were messed up. The magazines here were a mix of middling porn and specialist titles for arms collectors and users. A few empty cartridge cases had been lined up like ornaments on the mantelpiece. Mirror tiles had been fixed to the ceiling above the bed.

'Ugh,' said Bel.

The room was dark, its walls lined with large cork tiles to which Shattuck had pinned pictures from his magazine collection. Women and guns. Sometimes he'd cut carefully around the guns and Sellotaped them on to the women so it looked like the nude models were carrying them.

'Ugh,' Bel said again.

I started opening drawers. What was I looking for? I didn't think I'd find a forwarding address, but I might find something. I'd know it when I found it.

What I found were packets of photographs. I sat on the bed and went through them. They were mostly of Scotty and his colleagues in action: firstly in what I took to be the Falklands, then later in what might have been Yugoslavia. The soldiers were fully kitted, but you could tell Scotty was regular Army in the Falklands, and mercenary by the time of Sarajevo. In the later shots, he wore camouflage greens, but no markings. His smiling colleagues looked like nice guys to do business with. They liked to wear green vests, showing off biceps and triceps and bulging chests. Actually, most of them were going to seed, showing beer guts and fat faces. They lacked that numb disciplined look you see in the regular Army.

I knew Scotty from Max's description. I knew him, too, because he was in a few photos by himself. He was dressed in civvies, and photographed at ease. These photos were taken by the sea, and on some parkland. Probably they'd been taken by a girlfriend. Scotty flexed his muscles for her, posing at his best. Bel took one look at him.

'Ugh,' she said.

He didn't look that bad. He had a long drooping moustache which Max hadn't mentioned, so had probably been shorn off. He was square-jawed and wavy-haired, his shape not quite squat, but definitely not tall enough for his girth. I stuck one of the photos in my pocket – it showed Shattuck with some girlfriend – and put the rest back in the drawer.

'Anything else?' I asked Bel, who'd been roaming.

'Nothing,' she said.

There was a squeal of braking tyres outside. No uncommon sound in London, but I went to the window and peered out anyway. A car had stopped outside the house. It was an old Jaguar with a purple paint job. The driver was still wearing his white work-out vest. He probably had his towel with him too. There was somebody else in the passenger seat, and Chuck was fuming in the back.

'Time to go,' I told Bel. She didn't hang around. I'd seen a back door on the ground floor, and just hoped we'd have time to make it that far. I took out the MP5 as we descended, but held it beneath my coat. Either Chuck and his men were so incensed at the way they'd been treated that their pride had compelled them to follow us or else they were making a rational move. If the latter, then they had to be tooled up. If the former, I'd be in for a beating anyway.

And I'd always tried to avoid contact sports.

We were in luck. They were sitting it out in the car, waiting for us to emerge. The back door was locked by means of a bolt top and bottom, easily undone. I pulled the door open and we found ourselves in a garden so overgrown it hardly justified the term. We waded through it to the side fence and clambered over into the rear car park of the hotel. The MP5 jabbed my gut as I climbed the fence. I double-checked that its safety was still on.

From the car park, we climbed over a low brick wall on to a piece of waste ground. Past this, we found ourselves emerging from behind a public toilet on to a completely different road, busy with traffic and pedestrians. A bus had pulled up at its stop, so we jumped aboard. We didn't know where it was going, and the driver who was waiting to be paid didn't seem about to tell us, so I reached into my pocket for some coins.

'Two to the end of the line,' I told him.

Then we climbed to the top deck and took the empty back seat. A purple Jag would be easy to spot if it tried following us, but it didn't.

'I wonder how long they'll sit there?' Bel asked.

I told her I couldn't care less.

We ended up taking a train back over the Thames, and a taxi from the station to our hotel. The receptionist had a message for me, two telephone numbers and their corresponding addresses. As I'd already seen, Scotty Shattuck didn't possess a phone. But now I had addresses and numbers for the Ricks's household and Joe Draper's Barbican flat.

While Bel took a shower, I started phoning. It was probably late enough in the police inquiry for me to be asking follow-up questions. All I needed was gumption and one hell of a lot of luck. Chuck wouldn't go to the police, he wasn't the type. But I knew things were going to get increasingly dangerous the closer we got to the real police inquiry, which was why I didn't give myself time to think. If I'd thought about it, I might not have made the calls.

As it was, I stumbled at the first fence. My call to the Ricks's Camden home was intercepted by the operator, who told me all calls were being rerouted. Before I had time to argue, I was back to the ringing tone, and my call was answered by a secretary.

'Crispin, Darnforth, Jessup,' she said, as though this explained everything.

'I've just been rerouted by the operator,' I said. 'I was trying to get through to—'

'One moment, please.' She cut the connection and put me through to another secretary.

'Mr Johns's office, how can I help you, sir?'

'I was trying to reach Mr Frederick Ricks.'

'Yes, all calls to Mr Ricks are now being dealt with by this office. You understand that his wife was killed recently.' She gave the news with relish. 'And Mr Johns, as the family's solicitor, has taken on the task of dealing with all enquiries.'

'I see. Well, this is Detective Inspector West, I've just been brought into the inquiry and I wanted a few words with Mr Ricks.'

'Mr Ricks and his son have gone away for a few days. Someone on the inquiry should be able to give you the details you need.'

She was boxing me into a corner. I could either throw in the towel or box myself out again.

'Would it be possible to speak to Mr Johns?'

'I'm sure that could be arranged.'

'I meant just now.'

She ignored this. 'Three-thirty this afternoon, all right?' Then she gave me the address.

I put down the phone and thought, not for the first time, of leaving London, leaving the whole mess behind. It was madness to keep on with this. But then what was the alternative? If I didn't find out why I'd been set up and who was behind it, how could I take another job? I went down to Bel's room and she let me in. She was dressed, but wearing a towel wrapped turban-style around her head.

'So what are we up to this afternoon?' she asked.

'Doing our police act for Eleanor Ricks's solicitor.'

She took off the towel and let it fall to the floor. Already she'd become a seasoned hotel guest. Next she'd be requesting more shampoo and teabags.

'I'm enjoying this,' she said. I looked surprised. 'Really, I am. It beats staring at sheep and dry-stone dykes all day.'

'I thought you watched daytime TV.'

'It beats that, too.' She sat down on the bed and, taking my hand, guided me to sit beside her. She didn't let go of my hand.

'Have you phoned Max lately?' I asked.

'That's a low punch.'

I shrugged. 'It's the only punch I've got.'

'Good.' She leaned towards me and touched her lips to mine. I was slow responding, so she opened her eyes. 'What's wrong?'

I pulled away from her, but slowly and not too far. 'We don't seem to be getting anywhere. It's all dead ends.'

'No, Michael,' she said, 'not *quite* all dead ends.' Our next kiss lasted a lot longer. By the end of it, her hair was all but dry, and this time she pulled away first.

'Can I just say one thing, Michael?'

'What?'

'In that gymnasium . . .'

'Yes?'

'You were holding the MP5 all wrong.'

'I was?' She nodded. 'Don't tell me you've actually fired an MP5?'

She looked surprised at the question. 'Of course I have. I get to fire most of my dad's guns eventually. Want me to give you some tips?'

I blinked. 'I'm not sure.'

She laughed at the look on my face. 'You thought you were getting Little Red Riding-Hood, is that it?'

'Well, I certainly didn't think I was getting the wolf.'

This time when we kissed, we used our hands to unbutton one another's clothes . . .

11

'You weren't entirely truthful, were you, Mr Hoffer?'

The speaker was DI Dave Edmond. He was in the same pub he'd been in before with Hoffer. And as before, Hoffer was buying him a drink.

'A couple of large Scotches, please.' Hoffer turned to the policeman. 'How do you mean?'

'You didn't tell me you'd had a blow-up with my boss. He's not very pleased with you, Mr Hoffer.'

'Did you tell him we'd had a drink?' Edmond shook his head. 'What he doesn't know can't hurt him, right?'

'It can hurt me, if he ever finds out.'

'Why should he, Dave? Besides, you can look after yourself.' Hoffer sniffed and scratched his nose. The drinks arrived and he proffered a twenty. 'Keep five for yourself,' he told the barman, 'and keep these coming till the change runs out.' He then handed a whisky to Edmond, who dribbled water into it.

'Come on,' said Hoffer, 'let's sit down.'

The just-the-one-after-work commuter drinkers had departed, so there were tables free. Hoffer liked Edmond less than he liked Bob Broome, but he smiled anyway. He needed a friend in the police investigation, and if Broome could no longer be bought, others like Edmond could. Broome would return to the fold. They'd fallen out before and then made things up. But meantime Edmond would suffice.

'I like your style, Dave. You're not showy. You're the sort of guy who gets things done, who doesn't make a song and dance number out of it.' Hoffer lit a cigarette, then slid the pack towards the policeman.

'Cops are cops,' Edmond said.

'God, that's true.'

'I hear you left the force.'

Hoffer opened his arms. 'I failed the physical. I was fine once I'd caught the bad guys. I could sit on them till they 'fessed up. But I just couldn't catch them.' Hoffer laughed and shook his head. 'No, it was the Walkins case. I got obsessed with it. So much so, my chiefs decided to move me to some other investigation. I couldn't take that, so I resigned and set myself up as a private dick. Only, the only case I was interested in was the Walkins one.'

'There was something about it in the papers.'

'Hey, the media *loved* my story. They brought it flowers and chocolates. I'd given up a good career to make a life of hunting this mystery gunman. And the millionaire father of one of his victims was paying me. Are you kidding? It made great copy. Plus of course I was a fat ugly bastard, they loved that too. They like anything but *normal* in their photographs.'

Edmond laughed. Hoffer liked him even less.

'They still love me,' he went on. 'And I don't mind that. See, some people think I'm pandering to them, I mean to the press, and maybe they're right. Or maybe I'm on some ego trip. All this may be true, but consider.' He raised a finger. 'The Demolition Man knows I'm out there. He knows I'm not going away. And I really get a kick out of *that*. Maybe he's not worried, but then again maybe he is.'

'You don't think he'd take a pop at you?'

Hoffer shrugged. 'I never think about it.' He'd told this story many dozens of times, always leaving out just a few truths. Such as the fact that his employers had *requested* his resignation when they'd decided he was doing a bit too much obvious nose talc. It was Hoffer's story that he'd resigned so he could follow up the Walkins story in his own way and his own time, but really he'd been given an ultimatum. Of course, once he'd explained to a reporter that he now had only one mission in life, then he'd had to do something about it, just to show willing. And then old man Walkins had come along and offered to pay him, and the story had expanded until he was trapped. Now he had his office and his employees and his reputation. He couldn't just walk away from the D-Man, even if he wanted to.

And he often thought that he wanted to.

'So how much do you make?' Edmond asked, the way serving policemen always did, sooner or later.

'Think of a number and double it,' Hoffer said. Then he laughed. 'No, I'm a businessman, an employer, I've got overheads, salaries to pay, taxes and shit. I don't come out so far ahead.'

'Walkins must be rich though.'

'You kidding? He's loaded.'

'Is it right that his daughter was a mistake?'

Hoffer nodded. She was just about the only mistake the D-Man had ever made. He had eleven, maybe twelve clean hits to his name, plus Ellen Walkins.

'She was eighteen, standing in the doorway saying goodnight to some people after a dinner party. They were all government people, plus wives, family. She wasn't the target. They reckon the target was a congressman with very strong views about certain foreign policies. Any number of dictators and crooked governments would have paid to have him shut up. But the step was icy and the fucker slipped. The bullet had been going straight through his heart, but it hit Ellen instead. The investigation got taken off our hands pretty fast. I mean, it was too big for just the police to handle. I couldn't let them do that.'

'Why not?'

The barman had appeared with two more whiskies, plus a bottle of water, giving Hoffer time to consider the question. It was one he'd asked himself a few times. Why couldn't he just let it go?

'I don't know,' he said honestly. 'I just couldn't.' He sniffed again and shook himself up. 'Jesus, you don't want to hear all this. *You* should be the one doing the show and tell. So what have you got?'

Edmond pulled an envelope from his jacket pocket. Inside were several folded xerox sheets. There were photocopies of bank statements and old cheques, together with a run-down of cash machines Mark Wesley had used.

'It's not complete yet,' Edmond explained. 'This is just the first tranche. I could get into a lot of trouble for this.'

'You could,' agreed Hoffer, slipping an envelope across the table. 'But this might cheer you up.'

Edmond counted the money into his pocket, crumpling the envelope into their ashtray, then sat waiting. Hoffer didn't say anything for a while.

'Guy does a lot of travelling,' he said at last, reaching for his whisky.

'We'll check the travel companies mentioned, see if they can give us details.'

'Of course you will. What about these cash withdrawals? Any pattern you can see?'

Edmond shook his head. 'Except that some of them are in Yorkshire, according to Vine Street's geography A-level. Not in cities either, in country towns.'

'Maybe he lives there?'

Edmond shrugged. 'He's bought a whack of traveller's cheques too, by the look of it. One of those cheques to Thomas Cook isn't for travel.' He pointed to the photocopy. 'See? They've written on the back what it's for, purchase of traveller's cheques.' Hoffer nodded. 'We'll see if we can take it any further. If we can get the numbers of the traveller's cheques, might be we can find where he's used them. There's just one thing . . .'

'What's that, Dave?'

'Well, all we seem to be doing is tracking *backwards* through an identity he's already shed. Where will that get us?'

'Use your head, Dave. We can't track him forwards, so what else can we do? This way, we tie down accomplices, contacts, maybe we find patterns, or even a clue to his next hit. This for example.' Hoffer was tapping a cheque.

'Ah, I was coming to that,' said Edmond.

'So,' said Hoffer, 'Here's a cheque made out to someone called . . . what is that name?'

'It says H. Capaldi,' said Edmond.

'Right, so who is he?'

'He's a counterfeiter.' Now Edmond had Hoffer's full attention.

'A counterfeiter?'

Edmond nodded. 'Harry the Cap's been around for years, done some time, but when he comes out he goes back to what he's best at.'

'What does he forge?'

'Documents . . . anything you want really.'

'Where can I find him?'

Edmond licked his lips. 'About four hundred yards up the road.'

'What?'

'We've brought him to Vine Street. Bob Broome's got him in an Interview Room right this minute.'

Hoffer waited for Edmond to come back.

It took a while, and he was starving, but he daren't leave the pub and miss the policeman's return. Instead, he ate potato chips and peanuts and then, as a last resort, a toasted sandwich. It was alleged to be cheese and ham. If you'd served it up in a New York bar, your client would have returned at dead of night with a flame thrower.

After all the whisky, he took it easy and went on to beer. The stuff was like sleeping with a severe anorexic: warm and dark and almost completely flat. Barney hadn't come up with a list of bent gun dealers yet, so he'd nothing to read but Edmond's photocopies. They didn't throw up much apart from Yorkshire and this guy called Capaldi, who didn't live in Yorkshire. Hoffer guessed that the bank was for convenience only, and that the D-Man kept the bulk of his money in stashes of ready cash. The travel stuff didn't interest him, though if they found he'd been cashing traveller's cheques in Nicaragua or somewhere, that would be a different story.

Edmond shrugged as he came to the table.

'He's not saying anything. Bob tried an obstruction number on him, but Harry's been around too long for that. His story is that he met a guy in a pub and the guy needed cash.'

'And this Harry, being the trusting sort, gave the stranger £500 and accepted a cheque?'

'Well, he says he got the cheque *and* a Rolex as security.'

'Did the mystery man ever come back for his watch?'

'Harry says no. He says he flogged the watch and cashed the cheque.'

'Did Bob ask him why he hung on to the cheque so long? It took him nearly six months to cash it.'

'Bob did mention it. Harry said something about mislaying it and then finding it again.'

'This guy's wasted as a counterfeiter, he should be on the improv circuit. I know comedians in New York couldn't make up stories that fast.' He paused. 'Or that full of shit either.'

'What can we do?'

Hoffer's eyes widened. 'You mean that's it? You can't lean on him a little? What about the trusty British truncheon? You guys are purveyors of torture equipment to the world, you can get this slob to talk.'

Edmond shook his head slowly throughout.

'You're right we can lean on him, but only so far. Harry knows the score. If he doesn't want to talk, he won't.'

'Jesus.' Hoffer sat back. 'I don't believe this. All right, where is he?'

'Who?'

'Perry Mason. Who the fuck d'you think I mean? I mean Capaldi!'

'He's probably on his way home by now.'

'Where does he live?'

Edmond looked like a cricketer who suddenly finds he's walked on to a baseball diamond. 'Wait a minute,' he said.

'Tell me where the fuck he lives!' Hoffer reached around his back to scratch it. Or maybe he was tampering with the stitches on the ball.

'He lives in north London,' Edmond said. Then he gave the American the address.

Tottenham seemed a pretty sleepy place. Though it was a warm summer's night, there weren't many people on the streets. What people there were on the streets were black, which didn't bother Hoffer one bit. He didn't have a racist bone in his body. He'd take on *anyone*.

He was running up some good cab receipts for Walkins. He got a couple more blanks from his driver and gave the guy a healthy tip. The house where Harry Capaldi lived was a narrow three-storey building, its third storey no more than an attic. But from the doorbells, it had been sliced and diced into three apartments. Hoffer rang Capaldi's bell. There wasn't any answer. He looked around him. The street was quiet and dark. It was like they'd turned down the juice; the street-lamps were a puny glow most of which was obscured by insect life.

Hoffer charged the door with his shoulder. He kept low, putting his weight against the keyhole. The door gave a little, but then resisted. At the second attempt, it flew open. He walked quickly to the first floor. There was no use knocking at Capaldi's door. The guy was either in and not answering, or else not in, and the only way to answer it one way or the other was to keep on going. This time it took a good four attempts before the door gave. When it did, it brought Hoffer into a hallway smelling of cooking fat and stale beer.

'I only want to talk,' he called, pushing the door closed. 'I'm not the cops, I'm just a guy. Mr Capaldi? Hey, anyone home?'

There was a light on in the room at the end of the hall, and the sound of a TV or something. But Capaldi could have left it on when the police had come to take him to Vine Street. Or maybe he left it on all the time whatever, so nobody'd think the place was empty. Hoffer eased the Smith & Wesson out of his pocket and felt a little more comfortable.

'Mr Capaldi?' he repeated. Then he pushed the door at the hall's end. It was a cramped room, mostly due to the large piece of photographic equipment sitting in the middle of it. Edmond had mentioned this. It was for taking reduced-size photos and fixing them on ID cards and the like. As Edmond had said, you couldn't prosecute; Capaldi was legitimate owner of the equipment. And he was always too clever to let them find anything else, no fake IDs or blank forms, nothing incriminating.

There was an old dining table by the window, the sort with legs which folded beneath it and wings which folded down so it didn't take up space. Something was making a noise beneath it, a cat or dog. Hoffer crouched down and took a look, then walked forward a couple more steps to get a better fix on it. He crouched down again and pocketed the gun.

'I think,' he said, 'we'd talk more comfortably if you came out of there, Mr Capaldi.'

Capaldi came out stiffly from beneath the table. He was shaking, and had to be helped to a chair.

'Who are you?' he said. But Hoffer was busy pouring Irish whiskey into a used glass. He handed it to Capaldi.

'Drink this. Sorry if I gave you a fright.' He looked over at the table. 'You'd hardly believe a full-grown man could squeeze into there, would you?' Then he turned back to Capaldi and grinned. 'You must've been scared shitless. Who'd you think was ringing your bell, aliens? Think I was going to suck your heart out? Nope, all I want to do is have a little talk . . . Jesus, what's wrong with your head? It's like a fucking snowstorm.'

'Who are you?' Capaldi repeated. He found his cap and placed it firmly on his head.

'Doesn't matter who I am, Mr Capaldi. What matters is, I want to know about Mark Wesley.'

'I already told the police, I only met the guy—'

'I know, in a bar. But between you, me, and the police, that's a crock of shit. Now, they can't do much but tut-tut and send you off with a warning. Me, I can do better than that.' He produced the gun again. 'I can shoot you.' Capaldi looked like someone had stuck him to the chair with superglue – head, arms, legs, the lot. 'Now, I don't want to shoot you. I don't know anything about you, it may be you're a very nice man, generous to a fault, friendly with the neighbours, all that jazz. To be frank, that doesn't mean squat to me. I still might have to shoot you, unless you start telling me what you wouldn't tell the police.'

Hoffer leaned forward and lifted the whiskey glass from Capaldi's unresisting hand. He turned the glass around to drink from the clean side, and finished the whiskey in a single gulp. Now that he was calmer, he could hear a thudding bass sound from upstairs, shaking the ceiling and walls.

'Ten seconds,' he said quietly. 'And I'm not counting aloud.'

He always believed in giving people time to consider their next move, especially when they were scared senseless. He'd been that scared himself once or twice in the past, and you really did lose your senses. You could eat, but not taste. You couldn't smell anything, except maybe your sweat. Your sense of touch was restricted to the cooling damp of your trouser legs, or the gun nuzzling your head. You certainly couldn't see straight, or hear rational arguments.

It was good to have some time to adjust.

'Nine, ten,' Hoffer said. 'Shame it has to end like this, Mr Capaldi.' He touched the gun to the counterfeiter's head.

Capaldi started to speak, sort of. It took him five or six goes to utter the single word 'Jesus', and a few more tries before he could manage 'Don't shoot me.'

'Why not?'

'What?'

'Why not?'

'Because I'm not . . . because I . . . Jesus, all I did was . . .' He came to a dry stop.

'All you did was what? Make him up a new ID? *What?*' Then Hoffer too stopped, his mouth gaping. 'You son of a bitch,' he said at last. 'You've *seen* him, haven't you? I mean recently, in the last day or two?' He glanced towards the photographic equipment, all set up with a flash-lamp and a chair for the sitter.

'He's still in town, isn't he?' Hoffer could hardly believe it. 'Why's he still here? No, wait.' He knew there were other questions to ask first, so many of them it was a matter of getting the order right. Capaldi was staring past Hoffer's shoulder. When Hoffer turned his head, he saw why. There were two big black men standing in the hall, looking in on the scene. They had their mouths open, lower lips curled.

'No problem here, guys,' Hoffer called.

But there certainly *was* a problem. They'd probably seen the busted main door, and now Capaldi's door in the same state. And whoever they thought Hoffer was, he wasn't police. Even the cops in Tottenham didn't pack a .459 with their handcuffs.

They ran for the front door, yelling out someone's name. He could hear them climbing the stairs, heading for the second floor. Hoffer looked back at Capaldi, seeking an explanation.

'They deal a bit of dope,' Capaldi said. 'They don't like strangers.'

'Oh, shit.' Hoffer started pulling Capaldi to his feet. 'You're coming with me.'

But Capaldi resisted. More than that, he was still too scared to operate his legs, and Hoffer couldn't carry him, not with dope dealers on his ass.

'We'll finish our chat later,' he promised, then ran for the door. He could hear loud voices upstairs, not just two of them but three or four or five. He started down the stairs for the front door. He could hear footsteps pounding after him. Finish it now or keep running? He wondered if they'd fire on him out on the street? If yes, then it was better to make a stand here. But some instinct told him to get his fat self outside. There were houses on one side of the street only, the other being wall and embankment leading to a railway line. He didn't know which way to run. There didn't seem an obviously busier road in either direction. So he took a left and ran.

There were more houses, then some lock-ups, and then a corner shop. The street met another one at a T-junction, and he made the junction just as four figures came cautiously out of Capaldi's building. One of them pointed at him, and another raised a pistol. It could have been anything, airgun, starting-gun, even a water pistol. Hoffer wasn't taking any chances.

As far as he could aim, he aimed over their heads, but not so far over their heads that they'd think he didn't mean business. A couple of them dove back indoors again, but the one with the pistol kept cool and fired off two shots. The first hit some harling on the wall of the corner shop, while the second went through its display window, leaving large radial fractures around the hole.

'Fuck this,' said Hoffer, letting off a couple more and not caring where they went. He turned the corner into the new road, ignoring the people who were coming to their windows and doors. They seemed to go back inside pretty damned quick, but at least they came to look, which was more than would've happened in New York. At the bottom of the street, he saw a busy well-lit road, buses passing along it. He thought he recognised it from the cab ride. He kept turning around, but no one seemed to be following him. He knew they'd probably get a car first and follow him in that. Gun-toting drug dealers were so lazy these days.

'Damn,' he said, 'I could do with some dope, too.' Maybe they'd sell him some before taking off the top of his head. He'd known dealers kill their victims by ODing them. Well, let them try that trick on him with a mountain of opalescent coke, he'd put them out of business before he died.

He'd tucked the gun into his waistband and closed his jacket. He wasn't running any more, just walking very briskly. There were sirens ahead. Yes, he'd passed a police station on the way here. He walked into a pub as the sirens approached, looked around the interior as though searching for someone, then stepped out again when the sirens had passed. There was an Indian restaurant coming up. It was curtained from the road, nobody could see in or out.

If he kept moving, someone would stop him, be it police or irate dealers. There were no cabs to be seen, and the buses didn't move fast enough to be havens. He could walk, or he could hide. And if he was going to hide, why not hide somewhere he could get a meal and a drink? He pushed open the door of the Indian place and found another door which he had to pull. The restaurant was quiet, and he got the table he asked for: in a corner, facing the door. Anyone coming into the restaurant had to close the first door before opening the second. For a second or two, they'd be trapped between the two. He'd be able to pick them off while still spooning up the sauce, like a scene out of *The Godfather*.

'Quiet tonight,' he said to the young waiter.

'It's always quiet midweek, sir.'

After the meal, he had a couple of drinks in what seemed to be an Irish bar, not a coloured face in the place. There was a sign on the door saying 'Sorry, No Travellers'. He almost hadn't gone in, but then the barman explained that it meant tinkers, gypsies, not visitors. They all had a good laugh about that.

He took a taxi back to Capaldi's flat and made the driver go straight past it. Now that he thought of it, Capaldi would be long gone. He might not come back till all the heat had died. He might never come back at all. He'd either talk to Hoffer, and the D-Man would kill him, or he'd stay quiet and Hoffer might kill him. It wasn't much of a life, was it?

'Piccadilly Circus, please,' Hoffer told the driver.

'You're the guv'nor.'

It was unfortunate they'd been interrupted. All Hoffer knew now was that the D-Man had stayed in town after the assassination, when normally he'd have taken off. Why? That was the question. What was there for him here?

The tip-off, it had to be the tip-off to the police. The assassin was mad about it, and maybe he was going to do something about it. He'd be tracking down his paymasters. He'd be seeking out whoever set him up.

'I'll be damned,' Hoffer said to himself. At this rate, even in a city of ten million people, they might end up bumping into one another by accident.

He spent the rest of the drive wondering what his opening line would be.

12

Bel and I sat waiting for our meeting with Joe Draper. His production company had a set of offices on the top floor of a building near Harrods. We'd arrived early so Bel could do some window-shopping. I offered to buy her anything she liked, but she shook her head, even when I said I'd dock it from her pay.

Actually, we hadn't stayed long in the store. She'd looked a bit disgusted with it all after a while. She'd hooked her arm through mine as we'd walked to Draper Productions.

'Relax,' she'd told me.

We'd spent last night in bed together, Bel asking questions about my life, and me deciding how to answer them. I'd deflected her for a while by talking about guns. She knew a lot about guns and ammo, but that didn't mean she liked them. They scared the hell out of her.

Now we sat in Draper's offices, pretending to be CID. We were wearing the same clothes as yesterday, down to the black leather gloves. We weren't leaving fingerprints anywhere. Bel flicked through a trade mag, while I watched Teletext. There were three monitor-sized TVs in reception, all with the sound turned down. One of them was showing a looped montage of recent Draper output. The secretary kept deflecting calls to Draper's assistant.

'I did that,' I said. Bel looked up from her magazine. Teletext was running a news page, all about how two East European countries were about to close their shared border. Tensions had been high between the neighbours since the break-up of the Soviet Union, but a recent perceived assassination attempt on a diplomat based in London had brought things to a head.

'Maybe you should do something about it,' she whispered. The whisper wasn't necessary, the secretary having put on headphones so she could start some audio-typing.

'Like what?'

'I don't know, own up or something, say the diplomat was never your target.'

'But that would mean telling them who my *real* target was. I quite like it that they're not sure.' I was smiling, but Bel wasn't.

'You could start a war, Michael.'

I stopped smiling. 'You're right. Maybe I could offer Draper the exclusive.'

She slapped me with the magazine, then went back to reading it. Teletext flipped to its News Directory. There was some story near the bottom about a shoot-out on a north London street. It was coupled with another story, some get-tough-on-drugs speech the Home Secretary had made. I didn't think it meant anything, but I got up and went over to the secretary. She stopped her tape.

'Yes?'

'Do you have a handset for the TV?' She looked disapproving. 'I don't want to change channels, I just want to check a story on Teletext.'

Without saying anything, she opened a drawer and brought out a couple of remotes.

'One of these has Teletext,' she said, restarting her tape.

'Thanks a million,' I muttered. I aimed one of the remotes and pressed three digits. Up popped the story. There was a bit about the Home Secretary first, then a slim paragraph about gunshots fired in a street in Tottenham. It was the street where Harry the Cap lived. Maybe some people believe in coincidence. I'm not one of them. I knew Hoffer was getting too damned close.

Just then Draper's door opened and a young man and woman came out. They were dressed like students, but carried briefcases. The boy had a ponytail, while the girl's blonde hair was cropped short and tipped with red dye. They shook hands with Draper, then headed for the door. Draper checked something with the secretary, then came towards us.

'Sorry to keep you, Inspector West.'

'That's all right, sir, we appreciate your finding time to see us.'

He was ushering us into his office. 'The gloves are a nice touch,' he said. I didn't get it. 'I used to produce a cop show called *Shiner*, maybe you know it?'

'I used to watch it,' said Bel. Draper looked pleased.

'Only,' he said, 'the Inspector in that used to wear gloves like yours.'

'I see,' I said. Draper saw that he hadn't scored any points, and shifted in his swivel-chair.

'I'm not sure how I can help. I've already told your colleagues everything I can think of.'

'Just a few follow-up questions, sir. A fresh perspective.'

'Well, okay then.' He clasped his hands in front of him. 'Tea or coffee?'

'No, thank you, sir. This is DC Harris, by the way.'

Draper had been staring at Bel. 'We're thinking of pitching a police documentary series,' he informed her. 'Ever wanted to be on television?'

She smiled professionally. 'I don't think so, sir. Bright lights make me nervous.'

Draper laughed. 'Too much like the interrogation room, eh?' Now he turned to me. 'Shoot.'

I suppose he meant I could start asking questions.

'We'd like to know a little more about Ms Ricks, her family, colleagues, any possible enemies she may have had.'

'Well, none of her colleagues was an enemy. Lainie had a first-rate reputation. All her fellow journalists admired her. I dare say a few TV people were preparing knives, but only in the figurative sense.'

'How do you mean?'

He opened his hands. 'She was going to be a star. She was a natural on TV.' He looked at Bel again. 'Know why? Because she didn't trust the medium. And that came over, that honesty, that sense that she wasn't going to put up with any manure.'

'But she hadn't actually made any programmes?'

'That's true, I'm talking about the mock-ups we do beforehand, especially with a tyro. Lainie breezed it. It was like she was walking on water. I knew when we got her on the screen, she'd start to make . . . not enemies exactly, but there'd be jealousy from other presenters, because she was going to show them how the job should be done.' He shook his head and calmed a little. 'She's a big loss.'

He sounded like he was thinking of her in financial terms.

'What about her family?' I asked. 'Did you know them?'

'Oh yes, I suppose I knew them as well as anyone can.'

'Meaning?'

Draper sighed, like he didn't gossip normally, but since we were the police how could he refuse?

'Freddy's not an easy man to like, Inspector. I mean, his star's so low it's sweeping up leaves. And that doesn't sit easy with Freddy. He still wants to act the soap star. Did you ever see him in *Stand By Your Man*? It wasn't exacting stuff. Also, it was ten years ago, something Freddy doesn't seem to realise. He sees all this "vintage" comedy being repeated on the box, and his stuff isn't there. No surprise to anyone else, believe me. Meanwhile he sees his wife breaking into TV and there I am telling her how wonderful she's going to be. You can see it's not easy for him.'

'Yes, I can imagine. Did they have arguments?'

'All the time.'

'What about?'

'Everything under the sun. You want an example?' I nodded. 'Okay, Freddy blew their savings on a trip to Hollywood. He was out there looking for work, but all he came back with were a tan and some books of matches from expensive restaurants. Lainie was furious with him.' He paused. 'Look, there's no way Freddy would put out a contract on Lainie, that's not what I'm saying here. They had arguments, but they were never physical. They didn't even really have screaming matches. They just smouldered and wouldn't communicate for weeks on end. All I'm saying is, they did not have the perfect marriage. But then who does?'

Bel had a question. 'Did you like Ms Ricks as a person, Mr Draper?'

'Like her? I loved her. I'd've liked nothing better than . . .' He stopped and shook his head. 'I don't know.' His eyes were growing moist, but then he'd been around actors all his working life. Some tricks must have rubbed off.

'She had a son,' I nudged.

'That's right, a useless streak of sham called Archie. I say that, watch this, he'll be a millionaire at twenty-one.'

'What does he do?'

'He's in a band, programmes music samples, that sort of thing.'

'Electronics.'

'Yeah, I can't see the band doing much. I listened to their stuff as a favour, in case we could use any of it as backing to our programmes. Forget it. But Archie's a genius, in a limited sort of way. I see him moving into production, and *that's* where he'll make his pile.'

'Mr Draper, I know you've been asked this question before by my colleagues, probably by the media too, but can you think of anyone who would have wanted Eleanor Ricks dead?'

He shook his head. 'It had to be a mistake. The bastard was obviously after Prendergast or the foreigner. Got to be.'

'You sent Ms Ricks to interview Molly Prendergast?'

'No, it was Lainie's idea. I mean, she was running the whole show. It was her story right down the line, minimum input from me. She'd say she wanted to go in a certain direction, we'd talk about it, and she'd go off and do it. She was the driver, me, I was somewhere in the boot, like luggage. I hardly saw the light of day.'

'And what direction was she travelling in?'

He sighed. 'It'll probably never get made now.'

'We've spoken with Ms Ricks's solicitor, a Mr Johns. He mentioned something about religious cults?'

Draper nodded. 'Prendergast's kid was in a cult for over a year. In the end, Prendergast mounted a commando-style raid to snatch her back. This was a couple of years back, it made the news at the time. The daughter's not too bad now, it was *her* we wanted for the programme, but her mother said no, if we wanted to speak to anyone it would have to be her. Lainie set up the meeting partly to get Prendergast's story, and partly to make her change her mind. We thought once Prendergast met Lainie, she might melt a bit.'

'So it was a programme about Prendergast's daughter?'

'God, no, she was just a sentence, a phrase, in a much bigger book. No, Lainie was looking at the cult itself.'

'Which one?'

'The Disciples of Love. Sound like a band out of the 60s, don't they? You can see them opening the show at Monterey.'

'What sort of . . . tone was the documentary going to take?'

'It was basically an exposé of how the group is run. They've got one of these charismatic leaders, you know, like at Waco or the Children of God. But most sects go for your wallet before they try to snatch your soul, and the Disciples aren't like that. They take in poor people.'

'I don't see the problem.'

'Well, they won't say how they're funded. Lainie reckons it takes thousands, maybe hundreds of thousands a year to keep them operating, and their total income can't even be half that. So where does the money come from?'

'Did she try asking them?'

'They didn't so much stonewall her as put up the Great Wall of China. She got some financial wizards to do some sniffing. We got a bill from them that nearly killed us budget-wise, but they couldn't tell us anything about the Disciples.'

'Do you have anything here about the project? I mean, something I could take away with me?'

'Sure, I've got a few copies of the Bible.'

'Bible?'

He smiled again. 'That's what we work from, it's a sort of blueprint of the shape the documentary's going to take. We use it to get backers interested.' He opened a cupboard. It was full of bulging files and reams of typed paper, scripts and the like. It took him a few seconds to find what he was looking for.

'Here we go, take one each.'

The Bible was loosely bound with a cardboard cover and a thin plastic sheet protecting it. There were holes in the cover through which appeared the name of the project, Draper's and Ricks's names, and a few other details. The project was just called *Disciples of Love*, but with a question-mark.

'I appreciate this, Mr Draper. I'll see these get back to you.'

He shrugged. 'Keep them. The whole thing's history without Eleanor Ricks.'

'One last thing, did she have any favourite colour of clothing?'

The question threw him, so I smiled reassuringly. 'We're still wondering if maybe the assassin mistook her for Mrs Prendergast.'

'I see what you mean, Lainie wearing the kind of clothes Prendergast would normally wear.' He nodded to himself. 'Well, I know one thing, she did like to empathise with her interviewees, and that could sometimes mean dressing like them. As to favourite colours . . .' He shook his head. 'The best I can come up with is bright colours, reds, blues, yellows. Primary colours.'

I nodded. I'd been told to look for yellow and blue. I stared at Draper, trying to see something behind his eyes, some inkling of guilt. But where was his motive? No, there was nothing there.

'What about Mrs Prendergast?' Bel inquired suddenly.

'What about her?' Draper asked back.

'She's a public figure, and she's tough, plus she's got an interest in the cult.' Draper still didn't get it. 'She might be persuaded to take over where Ms Ricks left off.'

Draper leapt to his feet. I thought he was going to vault the desk, but he just leaned over it towards Bel.

'Brilliant!' he shrieked. 'That's fucking brilliant!' He slapped the desk with both hands and shook his head wildly. He was somewhere in the hinterland between laughter and tears. 'That is just *so* brilliant. Why didn't I think of it?'

Bel's look towards me confirmed she thought this a tautology. Draper couldn't get us out of there quick enough, but all the time trying to be polite. He had his hand on Bel's shoulder and one on my back. He was telling her to think about fronting his documentary series.

'All right,' she said, 'I'll think about it.'

'You'd be a great loss to the force,' I told her as we left.

Outside, I headed for the first newspaper kiosk I saw, and bought up several of the dailies. I wanted more on the Tottenham shoot-out. I didn't think Harry would have said anything, but how could I be sure? Without a trip to Tottenham, the answer was, I couldn't.

I told Bel she deserved some time to herself, and managed to press £50 on her, which in Knightsbridge would just about pay for a passable lunch. Then I headed north. I knew this was one of the most stupid things I'd ever done, but I couldn't talk myself out of it. One thing I did know was that if I was going to meet Hoffer, I didn't want Bel around. No matter that she was my best form of camouflage, I'd promised she wouldn't be in danger.

Before we separated, she made me make a phone call. Afterwards, I said I'd see her back at our hotel. She kissed my cheek, and I pressed a finger to her chin. She didn't tell me to be careful, but I knew what she was thinking.

All the way to Tottenham, I found myself doing something I never ever do. I thought of the past. Not the distant past, I don't mind that, but the more recent past, and my life as an assassin. Well, what else was I going to do with my life? I'd never fancied being deskbound, but the Army weren't going to have me. As a teenager I was clever but easily bored, and I was frustrated that I couldn't play football or rugby. I did try to take part in games sometimes, but the other kids knew about me, and they wouldn't come near. They were being kind in their way, I suppose, but I couldn't see it at the time. All I saw was that I was different. I started to spend more time on the gun range, and I acquired a marketable skill.

My father had started me off, despite my mother's warnings. He was a top-class target shooter himself. He started me with air pistols and air rifles, then we moved up to real ammo, small calibre at first. Funny to think those afternoons of bonding had led me here.

Here, thinking about my victims.

I had never had much of a conscience. Like I say, everyone bleeds. But then I'd missed a target and killed an innocent girl. That was when word started to go round that I was losing it. I'd cried about that girl. I'd sat by a hotel swimming pool in the Bahamas and played it through in my head, over and over again, the New York cold, that icy step, that single slip . . .

They called me the Demolition Man, but all I'd ever really demolished were lives. You could buy a new dustbin, new windows, you could repair walls with fresh bricks and mortar. But I'd noticed something in Draper's office, I'd noticed his pain. He'd lost someone, and the loss, for all my glibness at the time, was not merely financial. He'd lost someone he loved. He might be a hard-nosed businessman, a schemer, a ruthless capitaliser on rumour and grief. I'd seen the clips from some of his programmes; they concentrated on the tearful close-up and the hounding of interviewees. But he was human too. He could feel what his victims felt. He was feeling it now.

See, that's why I like to get away from the scene. I never go back. I don't buy the papers or anything, I don't read about myself and cut out my exploits to stick in some scrap album. I do the job and I get the hell away. I never think about it afterwards. I drown the memories in alcohol and travel.

Well, here I was stone-cold sober, and travelling towards something, not away from it. I wasn't even armed, and I knew Hoffer would be.

I got the cab to drop me on the High Road, and walked the few hundred yards to Harry's street. The front door was still waiting to be repaired. I could see where the lock had been wrenched open, but there were no signs of leverage, no marks left by a crowbar. No footprints on the door either, which meant it had been a shoulder charge.

There was noise on the stairs. A black man came down, on his way out. He glared at me.

'What happened here?' I asked. He ignored me. 'I'm a friend of Harry's.'

He gave me a look brimming with distrust. 'He ain't in, man.'

'What happened to the door?'

'Some big white fucker rammed it.' If he'd been a dog he'd have been sniffing me. 'Cop?' I shook my head. He looked around him, up and down the street. A train which had been sitting at the station started to move past us, way up the embankment. 'Some big guy, right? Kicked the door in, kicked in Harry's door. We came back and thought someone was ripping us off, right? So in we go, and this guy's got a gun out and he's standing over Harry. Harry's looking like he's going to croak, right? So we chased the fucker off.'

I whistled. He shifted his weight, looking pleased at the part he'd played in the drama.

'Is Harry all right though?'

'Dunno, man, he took off. Cops wanted to talk to him, but Harry was gone.'

'I don't blame him.'

'Yeah.'

'No point trying his door?'

'The place is picked clean. Cops didn't put a lock on it, so kids went in and ripped off everything. We had to chase them off, too.'

I nodded, though suspecting that the bulk of Harry's goods were now sitting in a pile in the flat above his.

'Thanks for helping him out,' I said.

'Hey,' he shrugged, 'what are neighbours for, right?'

Back in my room, I lay on the bed and read the *Disciples of Love?* project. Eleanor Ricks had been planning little less than an assassination of her own. The cult had its roots in the Pacific north-west of the USA, an area I knew, but its branches stretched all around the world. There were more than a dozen communes in Europe, but only one in Great Britain. Prendergast's daughter had actually belonged to a commune in south-west France, but the focus of Ricks's investigation was the British enclave on the Scottish west coast.

According to some notes added at the back of the file, she'd twice visited Scotland, but was planning a much longer visit once she'd completed what she called her 'primary research'. Only she'd never been allowed to finish that research.

The funding of the sect seemed to be the key. So long as no one would explain it, you could guess any way you liked: drugs, prostitution, blackmail, coercion. There were press cuttings in the file referring to stories about other cults, not just the Branch Davidian in Texas but the Children of God in Argentina and some Southern Baptist splinter groups in Louisiana and Alabama. As far as I could see, cults in general provided a useful service: they kept the arms dealers in business. Koresh's group in Waco had stockpiled enough weapons for Armageddon and beyond. I'd visited Texas. To buy a gun, any gun, all you needed was a state driver's licence and a form you completed yourself stating you'd never been in an asylum and you weren't a drug addict. They have about four guns in Texas for every man, woman and child. And those are the *legal* ones. I knew there were plenty of gun dealers who didn't require any ID from their buyers, just a wad of cash. I'd once bought a night-vision scope from a man with a military haircut after I got talking to him in a bar in Lubbock. I paid half the market price. It was the only good thing that happened to me in Lubbock, until I met Spike. Spike was, Max and Bel apart, the closest thing I had to a friend in the whole overpopulated world.

And Spike was crazy, gun crazy.

Bel gave her knock and came into my room. She was red-cheeked as she flopped on to the bed beside me.

'I must've walked for miles,' she said. 'How did it go?'

'I don't think we can hang around much longer.'

'Well then, that makes it easy.'

'What do you mean?'

She rolled on to her side and propped her head on one hand. 'I've just spent an hour in a cafe reading through the file.' She nodded at my copy. 'And the way I see it, the Disciples of Love are as likely suspects as anyone.'

'How would they know what clothes she'd be wearing?'

'They must have had someone watching her, otherwise they couldn't have compiled all that information they gave you. Maybe the watcher spotted that she wore similar clothes every day, or every interview she did.'

Yes, I'd thought of that myself. 'Maybe,' I said.

'Look,' said Bel, 'there's the jealous husband, the misunderstood teenage son, the producer who wanted to jump into bed with her, the lawyer who might have been just behind him in the queue.'

It was true that the solicitor, Geoffrey Johns, had professed a more than merely professional interest in Eleanor Ricks when we'd talked to him.

'So we've got a lot of possible paymasters,' I said.

'Agreed, but none as strong as the Disciples of Love. Look at what she was saying about them. I mean, from those American press clippings these aren't people to toy with.'

Bel had another point. The Disciples of Love had been in trouble in the USA after a journalist had been beaten up and another pummelled with his own camera.

'We don't know they'd go as far as assassination.'

'We don't know they wouldn't. Besides, there's my final point.'

I smiled. So far, we'd been thinking along such similar lines that I knew what was coming.

'The need to get out of London,' I said. Bel nodded agreement.

'We've got two choices,' she said. 'We either wait it out here until Shattuck comes back, since he's the only one who can tell us for sure who hired you. Or we scarper. We can always come back later, and meantime we could be doing something useful like checking on the Disciples of Love.'

'You took the words right out of my mouth,' I said. 'And I can always drop you off at Max's on the way.'

'What?' She sat up. 'What do you mean?'

'Bel, I needed you here to give me some cover. I don't need any cover in Scotland.'

'How do you know?'

'I just do. They're not combing the streets for an assassin up there.'

'But there's this man Hoffer. If he's figured things out this far, what's to stop *him* going to Scotland?'

'What if he does? Are you going to shield me from him?'

I was smiling, but she wasn't. With teeth gritted she started to thump my arms. 'You're not leaving me behind, Weston!'

'Bel, see sense, will you?'

'No, I won't.' She was still thumping me. 'I'm going with you!'

I got off the bed and rubbed my arms. Bel put a hand to her mouth.

'Oh my God,' she said, 'I forgot! Michael, are you all right?'

'I'm fine. There'll be bruises maybe, but that's all.'

'Christ, I'm sorry, I forgot all about . . .' She got off the bed and hugged me.

'Hey, not *too* hard,' I said. I was laughing, but when I looked at Bel she had tears in her eyes. 'It's okay,' I said. 'I'm a haemophiliac, not a paper bag. I won't burst.'

She smiled at last, then embraced me again.

'I'm coming with you,' she said. I kissed both her eyes, tasting salt from her lashes.

'We'll talk to Max,' I said.

13

'Come in, Mr . . . ah . . .'

'Hoffer.'

'Absolutely. Take a seat, won't you?'

Geoffrey Johns's office was everything Hoffer loathed and loved about England. It was old-fashioned, a bit dusty, and fairly reeked of centuries of history and family and tradition. There was something upright and solemn and confidential about it. You couldn't imagine Johns in red braces and Gekko-slick hair, doing billion-dollar deals on the telephone. He was more father-confessor than lawyer, and though he wasn't so old, he put on a good act of being wise, benign and endearingly fuddled. Like making Hoffer introduce himself, even though he knew damn fine who he was. Hoffer wanted to flick the man's half-moon glasses into the wastebin and slap him on the head, try to wake him up. The twentieth century was drawing to a close, and Geoffrey Johns was still working in the Dickens industry.

'Now then, Mr . . . ah . . . Hoffer.' He'd been shuffling some papers on his desk. They were little more than a stage-prop, so Hoffer bided his time, sitting down and smiling, arms folded. The solicitor looked up at him. 'Some tea perhaps? Or coffee, I believe you Americans prefer coffee.'

'We prefer, Mr Johns, to cut through all the shit and get down to business.'

Johns didn't peer through his spectacles at Hoffer, he dropped his head and peered *over* them. 'There are courtesies to be observed, Mr Hoffer. Mrs Ricks's family is still in mourning. I myself am still in a state of some shock.'

'She was a good client, huh?'

Johns wasn't slow to get the meaning. 'I regarded her as a *friend*, one I'd known for many years.'

Hoffer's attention had been attracted to the bakelite telephone. It made him smile. The solicitor misunderstood.

'Good God, man, what is there to smile about?'

'Your phone,' Hoffer said. 'It's a phony, isn't it? I mean a fake.'

'I believe it's a replica.'

'Lot of fakes about these days, Mr Johns. I'll have tea, please, milk and two lumps of sugar.'

Johns stared at him, deciding whether or not to let the brash American have his tea. Politeness won the argument. Johns buzzed his secretary and asked for a pot of tea.

'I believe,' Hoffer said, 'your principal duty lies with your clients. Would you agree, Mr Johns?'

'Of course.'

'Well, one of them's been murdered. And her family have asked you for your help. Now, way I see it, they want her killer found, *she* would want her killer found, and probably you do too.'

'Of course I do,' fussed the lawyer. 'No "probably" about it. I think they should bring back hanging for terrorists.'

'Terrorists? What makes you say that?'

'What?'

'That the assassin was a terrorist?'

'Well, who was his intended victim?'

'I've no reason to believe it wasn't Mrs Ricks.'

'Really? But the MP and the diplomat . . . ?'

Hoffer shook his head. 'The Demolition Man usually gets who he aims for.'

'Ah, but the papers say he shot the wrong person in New York. They say that's where *your* story starts.'

Hoffer accepted this. He'd been interviewed yesterday and this morning by a couple of papers and a radio station. No television yet, which was surprising. The story had a new angle with the two East European countries closing their mutual border. The Demolition Man was still news, and Hoffer always gave good copy.

'As I see it, Mr Hoffer,' Johns went on, 'my duty is to aid the official police investigation any way I can. I don't believe you form part of that investigation, therefore I'm not *obliged* to grant you an interview at all.'

'If you know anything,' Hoffer said, 'you'll know that if anyone's going to catch this man, that person is me.'

'Really? And how long have you been tracking him? Quite a while, I believe.'

Hoffer was getting to like the solicitor better all the time.

'Have you spoken to the police much?' he asked.

'Practically every day, *twice* yesterday.' Johns shook his head. 'I try to help where I can, but some of the questions . . .'

A tray of tea arrived. Hoffer gave the secretary a good look as she stood beside him and leaned over to put the tray down on the desk. Great legs, nice ass, but a face so thin and sharp you could use it as an awl.

'Thank you, Monica,' said Johns. After the secretary had gone, he started pouring milk and tea with the grace of a duchess.

'I'll let you help yourself to sugar.'

Hoffer helped himself. 'What sort of questions?' he asked casually.

'Well, the one that got me was: what colours did she like to wear? I couldn't see the point of that at all, but the officer said he had his reasons for asking.'

'Didn't tell you what those reasons were though?'

'No, he didn't. A typical policeman, I'm afraid.'

'Her favourite colours, huh?' Hoffer pondered the question himself, seeking the point behind it, while he stirred his tea. It was one of those elegant little china cups with a handle so overelaborate and undersized that he ended up with his hand around the cup itself, ignoring the handle.

Johns seemed to be having no trouble with his own handle. They probably taught tricks like that in law school.

'I should tell you, Mr Johns, that I'm working pretty closely with the

London police. They know I'm on the right side. I mean, we've all got the same objective, right?'

'Yes, I understand.'

'So don't misunderstand me.' Hoffer smiled humbly. 'The press don't always paint the real picture of me. I'm not after glory or anything, I'm not some obsessed crazy guy with a mission from on high. I'm just a cop doing my job.' Sincerity was easy. 'And I'd appreciate your help.'

Johns put down his cup. 'And you shall have it, so far as I can give it.'

The telephone interrupted them. It might be a replica, but it had a nice old tinny ring which faded only slowly after Johns picked up the receiver.

'Monica, I wanted all calls held. All right, put him on. Hello, Ray, what can I do for you? No, I haven't had the news on this morning. What's that?' He looked at Hoffer and kept looking. 'That's interesting. When was this? Mm, well, I don't know what to think. No, no comment at this time. Thank you, goodbye.'

He put down the phone but left his hand on the receiver.

'That was a reporter,' he informed Hoffer. 'He says a local radio station has been contacted by someone claiming to be the assassin.'

'Some crank,' said Hoffer. 'What's he saying?'

'He says he wants the two East European countries to know he wasn't hired to assassinate the diplomat. He says he got who he was aiming at.' Johns looked very pale as he lifted his hand from the receiver. 'I think I need something stiffer than tea.'

There was a drinks cabinet beneath the window. Johns poured a dark liquid into two tiny stemmed glasses. There was about a shot's worth in the glass he handed to Hoffer, who sniffed it.

'Sherry,' said Johns, gulping his down.

Hoffer, who'd only come across the stuff in English trifle, knocked it back, rolling it around his mouth before swallowing. It was sour to start with, but quickly got mellow as it warmed his gut.

'Not bad,' he said.

'You still think this was a crank call?' asked the solicitor.

'I don't know.'

'Maybe your man has just found himself a conscience.'

'Some conscience.' Hoffer still didn't get the question about Ricks's clothes. 'The policeman you spoke to yesterday, the one who asked what Mrs Ricks normally wore, can I ask who he was? Was it Chief Inspector Broome maybe? Or DI Edmond?'

'No, neither of those, though I've spoken to them before. This was someone new to the inquiry. He apologised for asking questions I'd probably been asked before.'

'Was he on his own?'

'No, he was with another officer.'

'He didn't have brown hair, did he?'

'Black hair, cut short as I recall.'

Hoffer was beginning to wonder. Mark Wesley had got some fake ID from Harry Capaldi . . .

'Did they show you any identification?'

'Oh, yes. The man was called Wes . . . no, hold on.' Hoffer had nearly leapt from his chair, but the solicitor was fussing on his desk again, trying to find a scrap of paper or something. 'Here it is. Inspector West.'

'No first name?'

'No. His assistant was a woman, a Detective Constable Harris.'

Hoffer shook his head slowly. 'I don't know them,' he said, not convinced he was quite telling the truth.

Bob Broome wasn't thrilled to see him. Vine Street was its usual chaos and gloom. Broome wouldn't let Hoffer past the front desk, so Hoffer waited for Broome to descend.

'I'm busy,' he said curtly, when he finally arrived.

'You'll find time for me, Bob, when you hear what I've got.'

Broome narrowed his eyes. 'I've got enough cranks around here as it is.'

'You don't think that call was a crank, do you?'

'I don't know.'

'Have you got a recording or just a transcript?'

Broome narrowed his eyes further. 'Is that all you're here for, to try pumping me about the phone call?'

Hoffer shook his head defiantly. 'Just tell me this: DI West and DC Harris, do you know them?'

'First names?' Hoffer shook his head. Broome gave it another couple of seconds. 'Never heard of them.'

'West sounds a bit like Wesley, doesn't it?'

'Come on, Hoffer, what's your story?'

'Can we go upstairs and talk about it? I feel like a victim stuck down here.'

Broome decided to give the American the benefit of his very grave doubts.

'Come on then,' he said. On the way up, they passed Barney coming down. He winked at Hoffer.

'I'll have it for you tomorrow,' he said.

'Thanks,' Hoffer said, trying to sound guilty or embarrassed as Broome gave him a long dirty look.

When they got to the office, Broome made a show of checking the time. 'You've got five minutes,' he told Hoffer. Then he sat down and looked like he was waiting for a show to begin.

'I don't pay dues to any acting union, Bob.' Hoffer sat down slowly, taking a while to get comfortable. 'I'll put it to you straight, but stop acting like you're in a sulk.'

'*Sulk?* You're going around like *you're* the Chief Inspector and I'm just some office-boy who gets in your way. I'm not sulking, Hoffer, I'm bloody furious. Now, what have you got for me?'

A Detective Constable came into the room and placed a small packet on Broome's desk. Broome ignored it, waiting for Hoffer to speak. Hoffer pointed to the packet.

'Is that the tape, Bob?' Broome didn't say anything. 'Come on, let's listen to it.'

'First tell me what you know.'

'Well, "know" is a bit strong. But there's this solicitor, Geoffrey Johns. Know what johns are in the States? Well, never mind.'

'I know Mr Johns.'

'Yes, you do. But you don't know anyone called West or Harris. West's in his mid-thirties, tall and lean, with short black hair. He's with a young woman, pretty tall with short fair hair. I'll let your guys go get more detailed descriptions from Johns and his secretary.'

'Good of you. So you think West is Wesley?'
'Yes.'
'And he's posing as a police officer?'
'With ID faked up by Capaldi.'
'Why?'
Broome had asked one of the questions Hoffer couldn't answer.
'And who's his partner?'
Now he'd asked the other. Hoffer shrugged. 'I don't know, but he was asking questions about Ricks. The important thing is, he's still in town and he's asking around. By rights he should be miles away, but he's here under our noses.' The image made Hoffer think of something. He sniffed the thought away. 'He's *here*, Bob, and the only reason I can think of why he's still around is that he's on to something.' He paused. 'I think he's going after his employer.'
'What?'
'The anonymous phone call, the one that nearly got him caught, he's after whoever made it. Stands to reason it must have been someone close to the deceased, otherwise how would he know where to find her?' He clicked his fingers. 'That's why he's asking about her clothes.'
'Her clothes?'
Hoffer's mind was racing. 'He must've been told what she'd be wearing! Christ, could that be it?'
'I'm not really getting this, Hoffer.'
Hoffer slumped back as far as he was able in his chair. 'Me neither, not all of it. Just pieces, and the pieces don't all make sense.'
Broome fingered the packet, but didn't seem in a hurry to open it. 'Hoffer,' he said, 'there was some shooting in north London last night.'
'Yeah, I read about it.'
'We've got a description of a fat man seen running away.'
'Uh-huh?'
Broome pinched the bridge of his nose. 'There's also been a mugging, except that no money was taken from the victim.' Broome looked up. 'You're supposed to ask me who the victim was.'
Hoffer blew his nose before asking. 'So who was it?'
'Mr Arthur, the bank manager.'
Hoffer threw his used tissue into the bin beside Broome's desk.
'You wouldn't know anything about it, Hoffer?'
'Give me a break, Bob. I haven't mugged anyone since I quit the NYPD. You get a description of the assailants?'
Broome was staring at Hoffer. 'He was hit from behind. He's got concussion.'
Hoffer shook his head. 'Nice guy, too. Nobody's safe these days.'
Broome sighed and rubbed his eyes. 'All right,' he said, 'let's listen to the tape.'
He had a DC bring in a portable cassette player and set it up.
'This local station must be on their toes,' said Hoffer.
'They tape all calls to the news desk, partly as a favour to us.'
'Why?'
'Because the IRA often call a local radio station to take responsibility for a bombing. That way the news gets on the air faster, plus it doesn't look like they're cooperating with us.'

'So the radio station's a kind of go-between?'

'Sort of, yes.' Broome loaded the tape and pressed Play. There was some soft hissing, which became louder until someone spoke.

'News desk, Joely speaking.'

'This is the Demolition Man, do you understand?'

'Dem . . . ? Oh yes, yes, I understand.'

'Listen then. Tell everyone I hit my intended target, got that? I wasn't after the diplomat. He just happened to be there. Understood?'

'Mm, yes.' Joely was obviously writing it all down. 'Yes, I've got that. Can I just ask—'

'No questions. If anyone thinks this is a hoax, tell them Egypt, the Cairo Hilton, twelfth of December two years ago.'

'Hello? Hello?' But the Demolition Man had put down the phone. Broome listened to the silence for a few moments, then stopped and rewound the tape.

'The original's gone to the lab boys,' he said. 'We'll see what they say.'

'Sounded like he was in a callbox, and not long distance. He's English, isn't he?'

'Sounds it. Sounded like he was trying to disguise his voice too.'

Hoffer smiled. 'You weren't taken in by the Jimmy Durante impression?'

'Maybe he's got a cold.'

'Yeah, maybe.'

Broome looked at Hoffer. 'Egypt?'

Hoffer nodded. 'Yeah, it's not one everyone knows about. Nobody's been able to say it was the D-Man, so it never makes the papers. It was a precision hit, long-range, but he didn't leave a bomb. Either that or the bomb didn't detonate.'

'Who did he kill?'

'Some Arab millionaire with big gambling debts which he was unwisely ignoring.' Hoffer shrugged. 'The gambler was a Mr Big, didn't think anyone could touch him. He had an armoured Mercedes and four bodyguards a grenade launcher couldn't've budged. They used to huddle round their boss when he went anywhere, like he was Muhammad Ali going into the ring. Then, pop, a bullet hits the guy smack in the heart, and they're all looking around, only they don't know where to look because there's nothing there to look at. They reckon it was a hit from six, maybe seven hundred yards.'

'You know a lot about it.'

'I've had a lot of time to look things up. I've got a file of more than sixty assassinations going back fifteen years. He could be behind any number of them.'

'Would anyone else know about it?'

'Only someone as obsessed as me.' Hoffer paused. 'It's him on the tape, I know it's him.'

'We'll see if the boffins can come up with anything.'

'Such as?'

'You'd be surprised. We've got linguistic people who might pin down his accent, even if you and I can't tell he's got one. We could get it down to a region or county.'

'Wow, I'm impressed.'

'It's slow and methodical, Hoffer, that's how we do things. We don't go shooting our mouths off and our guns off.'

'Hey, I make the jokes around here.'

'Just don't become a joke, all right?'

'Whoa, Bob, okay, you got me, I yield to your sharper wit. Now what say I get a copy of that tape?'

'What say you don't?'

'Still sore at me, huh?'

'What's Barney got for you?'

'Just a few names, gun dealers.' Hoffer shrugged. 'You're not the only one who can be slow and methodical. Gumshoes do a lot of walking, Bob, a lot of knocking on doors.'

'Just don't come knocking on mine for a while, Leo.'

'Whatever you say, Bob.' Broome had gone back to calling him Leo; it was going to be all right between them. Hoffer got slowly to his feet. 'What about Inspector West?'

'I'll have someone talk to Mr Johns, get a description circulating.' Hoffer nodded. 'Don't expect a bunch of roses, Hoffer, you just did what you're supposed to do *all* the time. If you get anything else, come back and see me.'

Hoffer fixed a sneer to his face. 'You can fucking well go whistle, Bob.' He opened the door, but turned back into the room. 'You know how to whistle, don't you?'

And then he was gone.

Hoffer sat next morning, lingering over the hotel breakfast. The hotel he was in had a restaurant which opened on to the street, and was open to the public as well as to residents. Something inside Hoffer didn't like that. Anyone could walk in off the street and sit down next to you. There was a guy sitting by the window who looked like Boris Karloff had donated to a sperm bank and Bette Davis had picked up the jar. He wore little round Gestapo-style glasses which reflected more light than there was light to reflect. He was reading a newspaper and eating scrambled eggs on toast. He gave Hoffer the creeps.

Hoffer wasn't feeling too well to start with. He didn't have earache any more, but he had a pain in his side which could be some form of cancer. Through the night he'd woken in agony with a searing pain all down one side of his back. He'd staggered into the bathroom, then out again, and was about to phone for an ambulance when he discharged a sudden belt of gas. After that he felt a bit better, so he tried again and got out another huge belch. Someone hammered on the wall for a couple of moments, but he ignored them. He just sat there bare-assed on the carpet until he could stop shaking.

Christ, he'd been scared. The adrenaline had kept him awake for another hour, and he'd no pills left to knock him out.

He put it down to nervousness. He'd called Walkins, and Walkins hadn't been too happy with Hoffer's report.

'Mr Hoffer, I wish you wouldn't sound so excited all the time.'

'Huh?'

'I don't know what you think you're doing. I mean, you call me with news of great import, and say you're getting close, and you sound so thrilled at the prospect. But Mr Hoffer, we've been here before, *several* times before, and each time you get my hopes up, the next thing I know your lead has proved false or the trail has grown cold. I want more than your hope, Mr Hoffer. I want a result. So no more acting, no more milking me for money. Just find him, and find him fast. The media would love me to tell them you've been a fake all along.'

'Hey, stop right there! I'm busting a gut here, I'm working round the clock. You think you pay me too much? You couldn't pay me *half* enough for what I go through for you.'

'For me?'

'You bet it's for you! Who else?'

'Yourself perhaps, your reputation.'

'That's a crock of shit and you know it.'

'Look, let's not get into a fight.'

'I didn't start it.' Hoffer was standing up in his room, facing the dressing-table mirror. He was hyperventilating, and trying to calm down. Walkins was thousands of miles away. He couldn't hit him, and he didn't want to hit a stand-in. He took deep slow breaths instead.

'I know you didn't, Mr Hoffer, it's just that . . . it's just we've been here before. You've sounded so close to him, so excited, so *sure*. Do you know what it's like at this end, just waiting for your next call? You can't possibly know. It's like fire under my fingernails, knives stuck between my ribs. It's . . . I can hardly move, hardly bear to do anything except wait. I'm as housebound as any invalid.'

Hoffer was about to suggest a portable phone, but didn't think flippancy was in order.

'Sir,' he said calmly, 'I'm doing what I can. I'm sorry if you feel I build up your hopes without due cause. I just thought you'd want to know how it's going.'

'I do want to know. But I'd rather just be told the sonofabitch was dead.'

'Me, too, sir, believe me.' Hoffer stared at the gun lying on his bedside cabinet. 'Me, too.'

And here he sat next morning, awaiting his order of Full English Breakfast with orange juice, toast and coffee. His waitress was a crone. She was probably in the kitchen grinding up wormwood to add to the egg-mix. He wondered if maybe she had a sister worked in the porn cinema where he'd wasted more money than time last night. There were three movies on the bill, but he'd lasted only half the first one. The stuff they were showing was as steamy as a cold cup of coffee, and the 'usherette' who'd waddled down the aisle selling ices had looked like she was wearing a fright-mask. She'd still managed to exude more sex than the pale dubbed figures on the unfocused screen. The film was called *Swedish Nymph Party*, but it started with some cars drawing up outside a mountain chalet, and the licence plates were definitely German, not Swedish. After that, Hoffer just couldn't get into the film.

London was definitely getting shabby.

A few more hungry clients wandered in off the street. There was no one about to show them to a table, so some wandered back outside while others sat down and then wondered if they'd maybe walked into Tussaud's by mistake.

'Mr Hoffer.'

'Hey, Barney, sit down.' Hoffer half rose to greet the policeman. They sat opposite one another. 'I'd ask you to share my breakfast, only I don't have any yet, and the speed they're serving you could probably come back after work and they'd be pouring the coffee.'

'I'm fine, thanks.'

'I'm glad someone is. Thanks for coming.'

'I think it suits us both. You're not exactly this month's centrefold at Vine Street.'

'Yeah, Bob really holds a grudge, huh? Just because I took him off the payroll. Speaking of which . . .' Hoffer handed over two twenties. 'This ought to cover your expenses.'

'Cheers.' Barney put the notes in his pocket and produced a folded-up piece of lined writing paper. It looked like he'd saved it from a wastebin.

'This is a class act, Barney.'

'You wouldn't have been able to read my typing, and names are names, aren't they?'

'Sure, absolutely.' Hoffer unfolded the paper gingerly and laid it on the table. It was a handwritten list of names. There were two columns, one headed 'London/South East' and the other 'Other Areas'. But there were only names, no addresses or other information.

'Maybe I pay too much,' said Hoffer.

'What's the matter?'

'This tells me less than Yellow Pages, Barney. What am I supposed to do, scour the phone book for these guys or what?'

'You said you wanted their names.'

'What did you think I would do with them? Find one I liked and name my first son after it?' The policeman looked uncomprehending. He couldn't understand why Hoffer wouldn't be pleased.

'This is all hush-hush info. I mean, on the surface these guys are clean. This isn't the sort of gen you could just get anywhere.'

'I appreciate that, really I do. I hear what you're saying. But Jesus, Barney, I expected a little more.'

Barney took the list back and studied it. 'Well, I could give you some addresses off the top of my head.'

'That would help. I'd be real grateful.' Hoffer took the list back and got a pen from his pocket. He looked around in vain for his breakfast. 'Two more minutes, I swear, then I'm going into that fucking kitchen and cooking it myself.'

A new waitress had appeared at the front of the restaurant and was handing menus to customers who'd come in, and taking the orders from others. Then Hoffer's waitress appeared with a tray full of food, but took it to another table.

'That fuck came in after me!' Hoffer hissed. 'Hey! Excuse me!' But the waitress had dived back into the kitchen.

'These first three are south London,' Barney was saying, his finger on the list. 'He lives in Clapham, that one's Catford, and the third one is Upper Norwood. Actually, Shattuck's not a dealer so much as a buyer, but he sometimes tries selling stuff on.' Hoffer was scribbling the information down. 'Now as for these others . . .'

'Hey, wait, you said addresses.'

So Barney screwed shut his eyes and concentrated like he was the last man left in the quiz show. He came up with three streets, but only one positive house number.

'They're not big streets though.'

'I am duly thankful,' Hoffer said dubiously. The waitress appeared bearing another tray, this time laying it on Hoffer's table.

'I've got to tell you, honey,' he said, 'the starving in Africa get fed faster than this.'

She was unmoved. 'We've got staff problems.'

'Right, it takes them longer than other people to fry ham. Tell them to turn the gas on next time.'

'Very droll.' She turned away with her empty tray. Hoffer attacked a small fat sausage, dipping it in the gelatinous yellow of his solitary egg.

'This is one sad-looking breakfast,' he said. It looked almost as lugubrious as Barney, and had all the charm of the guy in the Gestapo glasses, who was now having a third cup of coffee. The toast felt like they'd lifted it from a pathology lab, where it must have lain not far from the deep-frozen pats of butter.

'These others,' Barney was saying, 'the other London names, they're north of the river or a bit further out. That one's Clapton, that one's Kilburn, he's Dagenham and the last one's Watford.'

'Addresses?'

Barney shrugged. 'Then there are these ones outside London. One's near Hull, there are two in Yorkshire, a couple in Newcastle, one in Nottingham, and one in Cardiff.' He paused. 'I'm not exactly sure which one's which though, not off-hand.' He brightened and stabbed at a name. 'He's definitely Bristol though.'

'Bristol, huh? Well, thanks for your help. Thanks a heap.' He tried the coffee. By this stage of the meal, it could hold few surprises. Hoffer was suitably laconic. 'Shit,' he said. 'You know, Barney, a lot of people complain about the food in the States. They say it's beautifully presented, you know, great to look at, but that it doesn't taste of much. Either that or it's all fast food, you know, burgers and pizza, and there's no real *cuisine*. But I swear, compared to the stuff I've eaten in London, a poor boy sandwich from some mosquito-filled shack in the Everglades is as foie gras and caviar.'

He stared at Barney. Barney stared back.

'You don't much go for it then?'

Hoffer was still staring. 'Did you say Yorkshire?'

'Pardon?'

'Two of these guys live in Yorkshire?'

'Yeah, Yorkshire . . . or Lancashire, thereabouts.'

'This is important, Barney. Yorkshire? Think hard.'

'I don't know . . . I think so, yes.'

'Which ones?'

Barney could see this meant a lot to Hoffer. He shook his head like a pet pupil who's failing his mentor. 'I don't know. Wait a minute, Harrison's in Yorkshire.'

Hoffer studied the list. 'Max Harrison?' he said.

'Yes, he's Yorkshire, but I think he's retired. He got cancer or something. It rotted all his face.'

'Terrific. I'd still like an address.' Hoffer was speaking slowly and carefully.

'I can find out.'

'Then find out. It's *very* important.'

'Why Yorkshire?'

'Because the Demolition Man has spent some time there, and some money there.' Hoffer went down the list again, picking between his teeth with one of the tines of his fork. None of the names set any bells ringing. 'I need to know about the Yorkshire dealers, Barney, I need to know about them soonest, *capisce*?' Barney looked blank. 'Understood?' Now Barney nodded. 'Good man. How soon?'

'Later today, maybe not till tomorrow.'

Which meant Barney couldn't get them till tomorrow, but didn't want to admit it straight out.

'I mean,' he went on, 'I've got my real job, you know. I can't suddenly go off and do other stuff, not without a good reason.'

'Isn't my money reason enough?'

'Well, I won't say it isn't welcome.'

'A hundred if I get them today, otherwise it's another forty.'

Barney thought about haggling. He was London-born and bred, and Londoners were famed for their street wisdom, their deal-doing. But one look at the New Yorker told Barney he wasn't going to win.

'I'll do what I can,' he said, getting to his feet.

'And Barney, typed this time, huh? Bribe a secretary if you have to. Use your old charm.'

'Okay, Mr Hoffer.' Barney seemed relieved to be leaving. He sought a form of farewell, and waved one arm. 'Enjoy your breakfast.'

'Thank you, Barney,' said Hoffer, smiling a fixed smile. 'I'll certainly try.'

He stuck with the coffee and toast. After all, breakfast was included in the price of his room. The toast put up some resistance to the notion of being gnawed to bits and swallowed, but the coffee seemed to have a fine corrosive quality. So engaged was he in the battle, that Hoffer didn't notice the Karloff-Bette Davis test-tube baby leave his table and start walking back through the dining area towards the hotel proper. But he noticed when the man stopped at his table and smiled down on him.

'What am I, a circus act?' Hoffer said, spitting flecks of bread on to the man's burgundy jacket. It was one of those English-style jackets that the English seldom wore, but which were much prized by Americans.

'I couldn't help hearing you try to . . . ah, summon the waitress,' the stranger said. 'I'm American myself.'

'Well,' Hoffer said expansively, 'sit down, pardner. It's good to see another patriotic American.'

The man started to sit.

'Hey,' snapped Hoffer, 'I was being ironic.'

But the man sat down anyway. Close up, he had a thin persistent smile formed from wide, meatless lips. His face was dotted with freckles, his hair short and bleached. But his eyes were almost black, hooded with dark bags under them. He wasn't tall, but he was wide at the shoulders. Everything he did he did for a specific purpose. Now he planted his hands on the table.

'So, how're things going, Mr Hoffer?'

'I get it, another fan, huh? No autographs today, Bud, okay?'

'You seem nervous, Mr Hoffer.'

'As of right now I'm about nervous enough to bust you in the chops.'

'But you're also curious. You wonder who I am really. On the surface you affect disdain, but beneath your mind is always working.'

'And right now it's telling my fists to do the talking.'

'That would be unwise.' There were long regular spaces between the words.

'Persuade me.'

The man looked at the cold food still left on Hoffer's plate. 'The food here is appalling, isn't it? I was disappointed when you booked into this hotel. I was thinking more the Connaught or the Savoy. Have you ever eaten at the Grill Room?'

'What are you, a food critic?'

'My hobby,' the man said. 'How's your mission going?'

'Mission?'

'Locating the Demolition Man.'

'It's going swell, he's upstairs in my room watching the Disney Channel. Who are you?'

'I work for the Company.'

Hoffer laughed. 'You don't get any points for subtlety, pal. The *Company*? What makes any of my business the CIA's business?'

'You're looking for an assassin. He has murdered United States citizens. Plus, when he kills, he often kills politicians.'

'Yeah, scumbags from sweatshop republics.' Hoffer nodded. 'Maybe they're all friends of yours, huh? How come you haven't introduced yourself before?'

'Well, let's say we're *more* interested now.'

'You mean now he's almost started World War Three? Or now he's killed a journalist? Let's see some ID, pal.'

'I don't have any on me.'

'Don't tell me, you left it in your other burgundy jacket? Get out of my face.'

The man didn't look inclined to leave. 'I'm very good at reading upside down,' he said.

Hoffer didn't understand, then saw that Barney's sheet of paper was still spread open by the side of his plate. He folded it and put it away.

'Arms dealers?' the man guessed. When Hoffer didn't say anything, his smile widened. 'We know all about them, we had that information days ago.'

'Ooh, I'm impressed.'

'We even know what you told Chief Inspector Broome yesterday.'

'If you know everything, what do you want with me?'

'We want to warn you. You've managed to get close to the Demolition Man, but you need to be aware that we're close to him too. If there should come a confrontation . . . well, we need to know about you, and you need to know about us. It wouldn't help if we ended up shooting at one another while the assassin escaped.'

'If you're after him, why not just let me tag along?'

'I don't think so, Mr Hoffer.'

'You don't, huh? Know what I don't think? I don't think you're from the

Company. I've met Company guys before, they're not a bit like you. You smell of something worse.'

'I can produce ID given time.'

'Yeah, somebody can run you up a fake. There used to be this nifty operator in Tottenham, only he's not at home.'

'All I'm trying to do here is be courteous.'

'Leave courtesy to the Brits. Since when have we ever been courteous?' Hoffer thought he'd placed the man. 'You're armed forces, right?'

'I was in the armed forces for a while.'

Hoffer didn't want to think what he was thinking. He was thinking Special Operations Executive. He was thinking National Security Council. The CIA was a law unto itself, but the NSC had political clout, friends in the highest and lowest places, which made it infinitely more dangerous.

'Maybe we're beginning to see eye to eye,' the man said at last.

'Give me a name, doesn't matter if it's made up.'

'My name's Don Kline, Mr Hoffer.'

'Want to hear something funny, Don Kline? When I first saw you I thought, Gestapo-style glasses. Which is strange, because normally I'd think John Lennon. Just shows how prescient you can be sometimes, huh?'

'This doesn't get us very far, Mr Hoffer.' Kline stood up. 'Maybe you should lay off the narcotics, they seem to be affecting your judgement.'

'They couldn't affect my judgement of you. *Ciao*, baby.'

For something to do, Hoffer lit a cigarette. He didn't watch Kline leave. He couldn't even hear him make a noise on the tiled floor. Hoffer didn't know who Kline was exactly, but he knew the species. He'd never had any dealings with the species before, it was alien to him. So how come that species was suddenly interested in the D-Man? Kline hadn't answered Hoffer's question about that. Did it have to do with the journalist? What was it she'd been investigating again? Cults? Yes, religious cults. Maybe he better find out what that was all about. Wouldn't that be what the D-Man was doing? Of course it would.

He foresaw a triangular shoot-out with the D-Man and Kline. Just for a moment, he didn't know which one of them he'd be aiming at first.

His waitress was back.

'No smoking in this section.'

'You're an angel straight from heaven, do you know that?' he told her, stubbing out his cigarette underfoot. She stared at him blankly. 'I mean it, I didn't think they made them like you any more. You're gorgeous.' These words were obviously new to the waitress, who softened her pose a little. The brittle beginning of a smile formed at the corners of her mouth.

'So what are you doing this evening?' Hoffer went on, rising to his feet. 'I mean, apart from scaring small children?'

It was a low blow, but no lower than the one she gave him.

Part Two

14

We took a train from Euston to Glasgow.

I'd decided against renting a car in London. Rentals could always be checked or traced. By now, I reckoned there was a chance the police – or even Hoffer – would be finding out about DI West and DC Harris. Plus they had the evidence of my phone call to the radio station. They knew I was still around. They'd be checking things like hotels and car hire.

So I paid cash for our train fares, and paid cash to our hotel when we booked out. I even slipped the receptionist £20, and asked if she could keep a secret. I then told her that Ms Harrison and I weren't supposed to be together, so if anyone should come asking . . . She nodded acceptance in the conspiracy. I added that even if she mentioned my name to anyone, I'd appreciate it if she left Bel's name out.

Bel had phoned Max and told him of her plan to go north with me. He hadn't been too thrilled, especially when she said we'd be passing him without stopping. She handed the phone to me eventually.

'Max,' I said, 'if you tell me not to take her, you know I'll accept that.'

'If she knows where you're headed and she's got it in her head to go, she'd probably only follow you anyway.'

I smiled at that. 'You know her so well.'

'I should do, she gets it all from me. No trouble so far?'

'No, but we're not a great deal further forward either.'

'You think this trip north will do the trick?'

'I don't know. There should be less danger though.'

'Well, bring her back without a scratch.'

'That's a promise. Goodbye, Max.'

I put Bel back on and went to my room to pack.

On the train, I reread all the notes on the Disciples of Love.

'You must know it by heart by now,' Bel said, between trips to the buffet. We were in first class, which was nearly empty, but she liked to go walking down the train, then return with reports of how packed the second-class carriages were.

'That's why we're in here,' I said. It's a slow haul to Glasgow, and I had plenty of time for reading. What I read didn't give me any sudden inspiration.

The Disciples of Love had been set up by an ex-college professor called Jeremiah Provost. Provost had taught at Berkeley in the 70s. Maybe he was disgruntled at not having caught the 60s, when the town and college had been renamed 'Berserkeley'. By the time he arrived at Berkeley, things were a lot tamer, despite the odd nudist parade. The town still boasted a lot of strung-out hippies and fresher-faced kids trying to rediscover a 'lost

California spirit', but all these incomers did was clog the main shopping streets trying to beg or sell beads and hair-braiding.

I was getting all this from newspaper and magazine pieces. They treated Provost as a bit of a joke. While still a junior professor, he'd invited 'chosen' students to his home at weekends. He'd managed to polarise his classes into those who adored him and those who were bored by his mix of blather and mysticism. One journalist said he looked like 'Beat Poet Allen Ginsberg before the hair went white'. In photos, Provost had long frizzy dark hair, kept parted at the front, a longish black beard and thick-lensed glasses. It's hard to get kicked out of college, especially if you're a professor, but Provost managed it. His employers didn't cite aberrant behaviour, but rather managed to dig up some dirt from his past, showing he'd lied in his initial application form and at a later interview.

Provost stuck around. He was busted for peddling drugs, but it turned out he'd only given them away, never sold them. He was fast turning into a local underground hero. His shack-style house in a quiet residential street in Berkeley became a haven for travellers, writers, musicians and artists. The outside of the house boasted a huge paste-and-wire King Kong climbing up it until the authorities dismantled it. The house itself was painted to resemble a spaceship, albeit a low-built cuboid one. Inside the house, Jeremiah Provost was slowly but surely leaving the planet Earth.

Out of this home for strays emerged the Disciples of Love. It was a small enterprise at first, paid for, as investigative journalism revealed, by a legacy on which Provost had been living. His family was old Southern money, and as the elders passed away their money and property kept passing to Provost. He sold a couple of plantation houses, one of them to a museum. And he had cash too, as aunts and uncles found he was their sole surviving heir.

An article in a Californian magazine had gone farther than most in tracing Provost back to his childhood home in Georgia. He'd always been pampered as a child, and soundly beaten too, due to a doting mother and a disciplinarian father (whose own father had financed the local Ku Klux Klan). At school he'd been brilliant but erratic, ditto at college. He'd landed a job at a small college in Oklahoma before moving to Nebraska and then California.

He found his vocation at last with the Disciples of Love. He was destined to become leader of a worldwide religious foundation, built on vague ideals which seemed to include sex, drugs and organic vegetables. The American tabloid papers concentrated on the first two of these, talking of 'bizarre initiation rites' and 'mandatory sexual relations with Provost'. There were large photos of him seated on some sort of throne, with long-haired beauties draped all around him, swooning at his feet and gazing longingly into his eyes, wondering if he'd choose them next for the mandatory sexual relations. These acolytes were always young women, always long-haired, and they all looked much the same. They wore long loose-fitting dresses and had middle-class American faces, strong-jawed and thick-eyebrowed and pampered. They were like the same batch of dolls off a production line.

None of which was my concern, except insofar as I envied Provost his chosen career. My purpose, I had to keep reminding myself, was to ask whether this man's organisation could have hired a hit-man. It seemed more likely that they'd use some suicide soldier from their own ranks. But then that would have pointed the finger of the law straight at them. The Disciples of Love were probably cleverer than that.

The Disciples really took off in 1985. Trained emissaries were sent to other states and even abroad, where they set up 'missions' and started touting for volunteers. They offered free shelter and food, plus the usual spiritual sustenance. It was quite an undertaking. One magazine article had costed it and was asking where the money came from. Apparently no new elderly relations had gone to their graves, and it couldn't just be a windfall from investments or suddenly accrued interest.

There had to be something more, and the press didn't like that it couldn't find out what. Reporters staked out the Disciples' HQ, still the old Spaceship Berkeley, until Provost decided it was time to move. He pulled up sticks and took his charabanc north, first into Oregon, and then Washington State, where they found themselves in the Olympic Peninsula, right on the edge of Olympic National Park. By promising not to develop it, Provost managed to buy a lot of land on the shores of a lake. New cabins were built to look like old ones, grassland became vegetable plots, and the Disciples got back to work, this time separated from the world by guards and dogs.

Provost was not apocalyptic. There was no sign in any of his writings or public declarations that he thought the end of the world was coming. For this reason, he didn't get into trouble with the authorities, who were kept busy enough with cults storing weaponry like squirrels burying nuts for the winter. (These reports were mostly written before the Branch Davidian exploded.) The Revenue people were always interested though. They were curious as to how the cult's level of funding was being maintained, and wanted to know if the whole thing was just an excuse for tax avoidance. But they did not find any anomalies, which might only mean Provost had employed the services of a good accountant.

Lately, everything had gone quiet on the Disciples news front. A couple of journalists, attempting to breach the HQ compound, had been intercepted and beaten, but in American eyes this was almost no offence at all. (The same eyes, remember, who were only too keen to read new revelations of the sex 'n' drug sect and its 'screwball' leader.)

All of which left me where precisely? The answer was, on a train heading north, where maybe I'd learn more from the cult's UK branch. Bel was sitting across from me, and our knees, legs and feet kept touching. She'd slipped off her shoes, and I kept touching her, apologising, then having to explain why I was apologising.

We ate in the dining car. Bel took a while to decide, then chose the cheapest main dish on the menu.

'You can have anything you like,' I told her.

'I know that,' she said, giving my hand a squeeze. We stuck to non-alcoholic drinks. She took a sip of her tonic water, then smiled again.

'What are we going to tell Dad?'

'What about?'

'About us.'

'I don't know, what do you think?'

'Well, it rather depends, doesn't it? I mean, if this is just a . . . sort of a holiday romance, we're best off saying nothing.'

'Some holiday,' I joked. 'He'd work it out for himself, no matter what we said.'

'But if it's something *more*, then we really should tell him, don't you think?'

I nodded agreement, saying nothing.

'Well?' she persisted. 'Which is it?'

'Which do you think?'

'You're infuriating.'

'Look, Bel, we've not known each other . . . I mean, not like this . . . for very long. It hasn't been what you'd call a courtship, has it?'

She grinned at the memories: producing the gun in Chuck's Gym, fleeing his men in Upper Norwood, making false documents in Tottenham, pretending to be police officers . . .

'Besides,' I said, 'the sort of work I'm in doesn't exactly make for a home life. I've no real friends, I'm not sure I'd even know how to *begin* the sort of relationship you're suggesting.'

Now she looked hurt. 'Well, that's very honest of you, Michael. Only it sounds a bit feeble, a bit like self-pity.'

My first course arrived. I ate a few mouthfuls before saying anything. Bel was looking out of the window. Either that or she was studying my reflection. It struck me that she knew so little about me. The person she'd seen so far wasn't exactly typical. It was like she'd been seeing a reflection all along.

'Once you get to know me,' I confided, 'I'm a really boring guy. I don't do much, I don't say much.'

'What are you trying to tell me? You think I'm looking for Action Man, and I'm not.' She unfolded her napkin. 'Look, forget I said anything, all right?'

'All right,' I said.

I thought about our relationship so far. There'd been some kissing and hugging, and we'd spent two nights together. We hadn't done anything though, we'd just lain together in the near-dark, comfortable and semi-clad. It wasn't that I didn't want to make love with her. I don't know what it was.

Part of me wished I'd left her behind in London, or insisted on dropping her off in Yorkshire. It was hard to concentrate with her around. I knew it was harder to take risks, too. I'd taken them in London, then regretted them afterwards. In Scotland, I wouldn't take any, not with her around. I'd be like one of those Harley Davidson riders, forced by circumstance to wear a crash helmet. But when I looked across the table at her, I was glad she was there looking back at me, no matter how sulkily. She kept my mind off Hoffer. He was in danger of becoming an obsession. He'd come close to me once before, last year, after a hit in Atlanta, not far from the World of Coca-Cola. I'd visited the museum before the hit, since my target would visit there during his stay in the city. But in the end I hit him getting out of his limo outside a block of offices. He was being fêted in the penthouse suite while he was in Atlanta. The bastard was so tough, he lived a few hours after my bullet hit home. That doesn't normally happen with a heart shot. It's the reason I don't shoot to the head: you can blast away a good portion of skull and brain and the victim can survive. Not so with a heart shot. They took him to some hospital and I waited for news of his demise. If he'd lived, that would have been two fails from three attempts and my career would not have been in good shape.

After the news of his death, I moved out of my hotel. I'd been there for days, just waiting. Across the street was an ugly windowless edifice, some kind of clothing market. 'A garment district in a box' was how a fellow drinker in the hotel bar described it. It was so grey and featureless, it made me book a ticket to Las Vegas, where I didn't spend much money but enjoyed seeing people winning it. The few winners were always easy to spot; the countless losers were more like wallpaper. Hoffer looked like a loser, which was why despite his bulk he was hard to notice. But then he made a mistake. He had himself paged in the hotel casino. I'm sure he did it so people might recognise him. I recognised his name, and watched him go to the desk. Then I went to my room and packed. I could have taken him out, except no one was paying me to. Plus I'd already disposed of my armoury.

I still don't know how he tracked me. He has a bloodhound's nose, as well as a large pocket. So long as Walkins is paying him, I'll have to keep moving. Either that or kill the sonofabitch.

What sort of a life was that to share with someone?

I found out in Vegas that my victim had been a prominent businessman from Chicago, down in Atlanta for the baseball. In Chicago he'd been campaigning to clean up the city, to bring crooked businesses to light and reveal money laundering and bribery of public officials. In Vegas the saloon consensus was that the guy had to be crazy to take that lot on.

'You see a sign saying "Beware – Rattlesnakes", you don't go sticking your head under the rock. Am I right or am I right?'

The drinker was right, of course, but that didn't make me feel any better. I felt bad for a whole two hours and five cognacs, after which I didn't feel much of anything at all.

And then Hoffer had come to town, as welcome as a Bible salesman, sending me travelling again.

No, mine was definitely not a life for sharing, not even with someone like Bel.

We stuck around Glasgow long enough to rent a car. Now I was clear of London and the immediate investigation, I didn't mind. It was another Ford Escort, white this time and without the options. Driving out of the city was not the happiest hour of my life. The centre of the city was based on the American grid system, but there were flyovers and motorways and junctions with no route signs. We found ourselves heading south, and then west, when what we wanted was north. The directions the man at the rental firm had given us proved useless, so I pulled into a petrol station and bought a map book. Although we were on the road to Greenock, we could cut over a bridge at Erskine and, with any luck, join the A82 there.

We cheered when the roadsign informed us we'd found the A82, and the drive after that was beautiful. The road took us winding along the westernmost side of Loch Lomond, Bel breaking into half-remembered songs about high roads and low roads and people wearing kilts. After Loch Lomond we stopped at Crianlarich for food, then cut west on to the A85, the country wild and windswept. It had been raining on and off since we'd crossed the border, but now it became torrential, the wind driving the rain across our vision. We hit the tip of another forbidding loch, and soon reached the coast, stopping in the middle of Oban to stretch our legs and sniff out accommodation.

There were No Vacancy signs everywhere, till we asked at a pub on the road back out of town. Bel had wanted to stay near the dockside, and I told her that was fine by me, I just hoped she'd be warm enough sleeping out of doors. When she saw our two rooms at the Claymore, though, she brightened. The woman who showed us up said there'd be a 'rare' breakfast for us in the morning, which I took to mean it would be very good rather than hard to find or undercooked.

The rooms smelt of fresh paint and refurbished fittings. Bel had a view on to fields next to the pub. There were sheep in the fields and no traffic noises. It was just about perfect. The rain had even stopped.

'And I could understand every word she said,' she claimed with pride, referring to our strained conversation with the car hire man in Glasgow, and the local in Crianlarich who had tried engaging Bel in conversation about, so far as either of us could make out, trout-tickling.

We ate in the bar, and asked casually if our hostess knew where Ben Glass was.

'It's out past Diarmid's Pillar. Hillwalkers, are you?'

'Not exactly.'

She smiled. '*Beinn Ghlas* is a summit between Loch Nell and Loch Nant.'

'That doesn't sound what we're looking for. It's more of a . . . commune, a religious community.'

'You mean the New Agers? Yes, they're off that way.'

'You don't know where, though?'

She shook her head. 'How was the Scotch broth?'

'It was delicious,' Bel said. Later, we asked if we could borrow a map of the area. Most of the roads were little more than tracks. The only Ben Glass I could see was the summit.

'I don't suppose they'd be in the phone book?' Bel suggested.

'We could try Yellow Pages under cults.'

Instead, we went back into Oban itself. It was too late in the day to start our real business, so we became tourists again. The wind had eased, and there was no more than a marrow-chilling breeze as we traipsed the harbour area and the shops which had closed for the day. Bel huddled into my side, her arm through mine. She had the collar of her jacket up, and the jacket zipped as high as it would go. There were other holidaymakers around us, but they looked used to the climate.

'Let's go in here,' Bel said, picking a pub at random. I could see straight away that it was a watering-hole for locals, and that strangers, while tolerated in the season at least, couldn't expect a warming welcome. The customers spoke in an undertone, as though trying to keep the place a secret. Bel ignored the atmosphere, or lack of one, and asked for a couple of malts.

'Which malt?' the red-cheeked barman asked back.

'Talisker,' she said quickly, having just seen a bottle displayed in a shop window.

The barman narrowed one eye. 'What proof?'

That got her. She thought he must mean proof of age.

'Seventy, I think,' I said.

'And double measures,' said Bel, trying to recover. As the barman stood at his row of optics, she saw there were three grades of Talisker: seventy, eighty and one-hundred proof. She nodded at me and smiled, giving a shrug. We paid for our drinks and went to a corner table. The bar grew silent, waiting to eavesdrop. They were out of luck. The door swung in and a laughing group of teenagers stormed the place. They couldn't be much over the legal drinking age, and a few of them might even be under it. But they had confidence on their side. Suddenly the bar was lively. Someone put money in the jukebox, someone else started racking up for a game of pool, and the barman was kept busy pouring pints of lager.

They kept looking over at us, probably because Bel was the only woman in the bar. One of the pool players, awaiting his turn, came over and drew out a chair. He didn't look at us, but returned to the seat after he'd played. This time he gave us the benefit of his winning grin.

'I don't know why I bother,' he said. 'He beats the pants off me every time.'

I watched the other pool player potting his third ball in a row. 'He does seem pretty handy.'

'He's lethal. Look at him covering that pocket.' He got up to play, but was quickly back in his seat. 'On holiday?'

'Sort of.'

'It's all right, I don't mind tourists. I'm a carpenter. I work for this other guy who sculpts lamps and stuff from bits of old wood. The only people who buy them are tourists.'

'Maybe we'll look in,' I said. 'Where's his shop?'

'He doesn't have a shop. He's got a workshop, but he sells the stuff through shops in the town. Souvenir shops, fancy goods.'

'We'll look out for them,' Bel said. 'Meantime, could you do me a favour?'

He licked his lips and looked keen. Bel leaned across the table towards him. They looked very cosy, and his friends were beginning to exchange comments and laughter.

'We were told there's a sort of religious commune near here.'

He looked from Bel to me. I tried to look meek, harmless, touristy, but he seemed to see something more. He got to his feet slowly and walked to the pool table. He didn't come back.

We drove into town next morning and bought a map of our own. It was newer than the hotel's map, but still didn't help. We sat poring over it in a coffee shop. The other customers were all tourists, their spirits dampened by another cool, wet day. The rain was as fine as a spraymist, blowing almost horizontally across the town. Bel bought a bottle of Talisker to take back to Max.

An old van puttered past the cafe window where we were sitting. It was an antiquated Volkswagen bus, most of its body green but the passenger door blue. It squeezed into a parking place across the street and the driver cut the engine. He got out, as did his passenger. The driver pulled open the sliding side-door, and three more passengers emerged. They all seemed to be holding scraps of paper, shopping lists maybe. They pointed in different directions and headed off.

'Stay here,' I said to Bel.

By the time I left the coffee shop, they had disappeared. I crossed to the Volkswagen and walked around it. It was twenty-four years old, two years older than Bel. There was a lot of rust around the wheel arches and doors, and the bodywork was generally battered, but the engine had sounded reliable enough. I looked inside. The thing was taxed for another three months. It would be interesting to see if it passed its MOT this time round. There were some carrier bags and empty cardboard boxes in the back of the bus. The rows of seats had been removed to make more space. There was a dirty rug on the floor and a spare can of petrol.

The passengers had looked like New Agers: pony tails and roll-up cigarettes and torn jeans. They had that loose gait which hid a post-hippy sensibility. The few New Agers I'd come across were a lot tougher than their 1960s ancestors. They were cynical, and rather than escape the system they knew how to use it to their advantage. Aesthetics apart, I had a lot of time for the ones I'd met.

'Something wrong?'

I turned. The driver was standing there, lighting a cigarette from a new packet.

'The way you were looking,' he went on, 'I thought maybe we had a bald tyre or something.'

I smiled. 'No, nothing like that.'

'Maybe you're thinking of buying?'

'That's pretty close to the mark. I used to own one of these, haven't seen one in a while.'

'Where was this?'

'Out in the States.' I hadn't actually owned one, but the New Agers I'd met there had.

The driver nodded. 'There are a lot of them still out there, on the west coast especially.'

'Right,' I said. 'They don't use salt on the roads.'

'That's it. They last longer than this rust-bucket.' He gave the van a playful slap.

'The one I had blew up. I'd twin-carbed it.'

He shook his head. 'That was a mistake. You don't live around here, do you?'

'No, why?'

'You're talking. Not everybody does.'

'You're not a local yourself then?'

'I haven't lived here long.'

He inhaled on his cigarette and examined its tip. He was in his 20s, nearer Bel's age than mine. He had short wavy black hair and a week's growth of beard, and wore liver-coloured Doc Marten boots with stained jeans and a thick woodsman's shirt.

'I'm just visiting,' I said.

'Enjoy the trip.' He nicked his cigarette and put it back in the pack, then got into the van and put some music on. As far as he was concerned, I had already left.

I walked back across to the cafe and got Bel.

'I nearly yelped when I saw him coming out of the shop,' she said. 'I knew you couldn't see him. What did he say?'

'Not much. Come on.'

We got into the Escort and drove back the way the Volkswagen had come in. Once we were out of sight, I pulled over again.

'You think it's them?'

'I get that impression. We'll find out.'

So we waited in the car, until the bus announced itself with its high-turning engine. It could put on good speed, which was a relief. I hadn't had much experience in tailing vehicles, but I knew that out here, with so little traffic on the roads outside the town, I'd have trouble keeping my distance from a crawling VW. The thing didn't have side mirrors, which helped, since the driver probably couldn't see much from his rearview mirror other than the heads of his passengers. Habitations became sparser as we drove, and a sudden heavy shower slowed us down, though the driver didn't seem to worry. At last, the tarmac road ended, we went through a five-barred gate and were driving on a gravel track. I stopped the car.

'What's up?' said Bel.

'If he sees us behind him, he'll know we're headed the same place he is. How many houses do you think are up this road?'

'Probably just the one.'

'Exactly, so we can't really lose him, can we? We'll sit here for a minute, then move at our own pace.'

'What are we going to say when we get there?'

'Nothing, not this visit. We'll just take a look at the place, not get too close.'

I looked in my rearview mirror. Not that I was expecting any other vehicles.

The gate behind us was shut.

I turned in my seat, hardly able to believe the evidence in the mirror.

'What is it, Michael?'

There were figures outside the car. One of them pulled open the passenger door. Bel shrieked. The figure bent down to look at us. He was big, cold-looking and soaked, with a beard that looked like it could deflect blows.

'Keep on going up the trail,' he said, his accent English. 'It's another mile or so.'

'Can we give you a lift?' I offered. But he slammed the door closed. I counted four of them out there, all of them now standing behind the car. If I reversed hard enough, I could scatter them and maybe smash my way back through the gate. But it looked like a quality gate, and since we were where we wanted to be, we might as well go on.

So I moved forward slowly. The men followed at walking pace.

'Michael . . .'

'Just remember our story, Bel, that's all we need to do.'

'But, Michael, they were *waiting* for us.'

'Maybe they always keep a guard on the gate.' I said this without much confidence. The man hadn't asked us what we wanted or whether we'd taken a wrong turn. It was true, we were expected.

Well, they might be expecting us, but I doubted they'd be expecting what I had in the car-boot.

The MP5.

The commune sat in a glen with a stream running through it. It reminded me of one of those early American settlers' communities, just before the bad guys rode into town. The houses, little more than cabins, were of wooden construction. There were a few vehicles dotted about, only half of them looking like they were used, the rest in a process of cannibalisation. Solar heating panels sat angled towards a sun that wasn't shining. A large patch of ground had been cleared and cultivated, and some lean black pigs were working on clearing another patch. I saw goats and chickens and about thirty people, some of whom, all women, were helping unload the VW bus. The VW's driver nodded at us as we stopped the car. I got out and looked at him.

'You want to make an offer on it after all?' he said, slapping the van.

An older man emerged from the largest cabin. He gestured for us to follow him indoors.

The cabin's interior was spartan, but no more so than a lot of bachelor flats or hotel rooms. It was furnished with what looked like home-crafted stuff. On one table sat a lamp. I ran my hand over the gnarled wooden base.

'You're the carpenter?' I said, knowing now why we were expected.

The man nodded back. 'Sit down,' he said. He didn't sit on a chair, but lowered himself on to the floor. I did likewise, but Bel selected a chair. There was a large photograph of a beneficent Jeremiah Provost on the wall above the open fireplace. He looked younger than in some of the newspaper photos. There was a tapestry on another wall, and a clock made from a cross-section of tree.

'You've been asking about our community here,' the man said, eschewing introductions.

'Is that a crime?' Bel asked. He turned his gaze to her. His eyes were slightly wider than seemed normal, like he'd witnessed a miracle a long time ago and was still getting used to it. He had a long beard with strands of silver in it. I wondered if length of beard equated to standing within the commune. He had the sort of outdoors tan that lasts all year, and was dressed for work right down to the heavy-duty gloves sticking out of the waistband of his baggy brown cord trousers. His hair was thin and oily, greying all over. He was in his 40s, and looked like he hadn't always been a carpenter.

'No,' he said, 'but we prefer visitors to introduce themselves first.'

'That's easily taken care of,' Bel said. 'I'm Belinda Harrison, this is a friend of mine, Michael Weston. Who are you?'

The man smiled. 'I hear anxiety and a rage in your words, Belinda. They sound like they're controlling you. Their only possible usefulness is when *you* control *them*.'

'I read that sort of thing all the time in women's magazines, Mr . . . ?'

'My name's Richard, usually just Rick.'

'Rick,' I said, my voice all balm and diplomacy, 'you belong to the Disciples of Love, is that right? Because otherwise we're in the wrong place.'

'You're where you want to be, Michael.'

I turned to Bel. 'Just ask him, Belinda.'

She nodded tersely. 'I'm looking for my sister, her name's Jane.'

'Jane Harrison? You think she's here?'

'Yes, I do.'

'What makes you think that?'

'Because when she ran away, I went through her room, and she'd cut pieces from newspapers and magazines, all about the Disciples of Love.'

'One of them,' I added quietly, 'mentioned yours as being the only British branch of the sect.'

'Well, Michael, that's true, though we're about to start a new chapter in the south of England. Do you know London at all?'

'That's where we've come from.'

'My home town,' Rick said. 'We're hoping to buy some land between Beaconsfield and Amersham.'

I nodded. 'I know Beaconsfield. Any chance that Jane might be there, helping set up this new . . . chapter? I take it she's not here or you'd have said.'

'No, we've got nobody here called Jane. It might help if I knew what she looked like.'

Bel took a photograph from her pocket and handed it over. I watched Rick's face intently as he studied it. It was the photo I'd taken from the flat in Upper Norwood, the one showing Scotty Shattuck and his girlfriend.

'That's her,' said Bel, 'about a year ago, maybe a little less.'

Rick kept looking at the photo, then shook his head. 'No, I've never seen this woman.'

'She may have cut her hair shorter since,' Bel pleaded. She was turning into a very good actress.

'Take another look, please,' I urged. He took another look. 'She ran off with her boyfriend, that's him in the photo.'

'I'm sorry, Belinda.' Rick handed the photo back.

'And you're sure she couldn't be helping start off your new branch?'

'They're called chapters, Michael. No, there's no possibility. We haven't bought the land yet, there's another bid on the table. None of our members are down there at present.'

I saw now that in a corner of the room beyond Rick sat a fax machine and telephone.

'The estate agent contacts you by phone?'

Rick nodded. 'Again, I'm sorry. Bel, why does it worry you that Jane has left home? Isn't she allowed to make her own choices?'

Maybe the acting had proved too much for her. Whatever, Bel burst into tears. Rick looked stunned.

'Maybe if you fetch her some water,' I said, putting an arm around her.

'Of course.' Rick stood up and left the room. When I looked at Bel, she gave me a smile and a wink.

I stood up too and went walkabout. I don't know what I was looking for, there being no obvious places of concealment in the room. The fax and handset gave no identifying phone numbers, but the fax did have a memory facility for frequently used numbers. I punched in 1 and the liquid crystal display presented me with the international dialling code for the USA, plus 212 – the state code for Washington – and the first two digits of the phone number proper. So Rick kept in touch with the Disciples' world HQ by fax. The number 2 brought up another Washington number, while 3 was a local number.

Bel was rubbing her eyes and snuffling when Rick returned with the water. He saw me beside the fax machine.

'Funny,' I said, 'I thought the whole purpose here was to cut yourselves off from the world.'

'Not at all, Michael. How much do you know about the Disciples of Love?'

I shrugged. 'Just what Belinda's told me.'

'And that information *she* gleaned from magazines who are more interested in telling stories than telling the truth. We don't seduce young people into our ranks and then brainwash them. If people want to move on, if they're not happy here, then they move on. It's all right with us. We're just sad to see them go. The way you've been skulking around, you'd think we were guerrillas or kidnappers. We're just trying to live a simple life.'

I nodded thoughtfully. 'I thought I read something about some MP who had to . . .'

Rick was laughing. 'Oh, yes, that. What was the woman's name?' I shrugged again. 'She was convinced, despite everything her daughter told her, that the daughter was being held prisoner. None of our missions is a prison, Michael. Does this look like a cell?'

I conceded it didn't. I was also beginning to concede that Rick had never laid eyes on Scotty Shattuck in his life. He'd looked closely at the photograph, and had shown not the slightest sign of recognition. Meaning this whole trip had been a waste of time.

'Prendergast,' said Rick, 'that was the woman's name. You know, I wouldn't be surprised if she's done irreparable harm to her daughter. And from what *I've* read, the daughter is now a prisoner in her home. She can't go out without some minder going with her. So who's the villain of the piece?' Lecture over, he turned to Bel. 'Feeling a little better?'

'Yes, thanks.'

'Good. You've had a long trip from London, I'm sorry it's not been helpful to you. Can I show you around? If Jane is interested in us, it may be that she'll find her way here eventually. I can't promise to contact you if she does . . . that would have to be *her* decision. But at least maybe I can reassure you that we won't have her in a ball and chain.'

'We'd like that.'

He led us outside. He stood very erect when he walked, and his arms moved slowly at his sides. I reckoned he'd been meditating this morning, either that or taking drugs. Outside, the VW driver was resting his hand on the boot of our Escort. I sought his face for some sign that he'd opened it, but I'd locked the boot myself, and he didn't look as handy with a picklock as Bel.

'I'm just going to give Belinda and Michael the tour,' Rick told him. 'Is anyone earthing up the potatoes?'

Understanding, the driver went off to find a spade.

Our tour didn't take long. Rick explained that Jeremiah Provost believed in balance between wilderness and civilisation, so a lot of the land had been left uncultivated. He took us into the woods to show us how they harvested trees for fuel and materials, but did not disturb trees which had fallen of their own volition.

'Why not?'

'Because they nourish the soil and become a place where other things can grow.'

I could see Bel had had enough of this. She might start forgetting soon that she was supposed to have a sister, whereabouts unknown.

'We'd better be getting back,' I said. Rick walked us to the car and shook my hand.

'Belinda's lucky to have a friend like you,' he said.

'I think she knows that.'

Bel was in the passenger seat before Rick could walk round the car. She waved, but didn't smile or roll down her window. Rick touched his palm to her window, then lifted it away and retreated a couple of steps.

'He gave me the heebie-jeebies,' Bel said as we drove back down the track.

'He seemed okay to me.'

'Maybe you're easily led.'

'Maybe I am.'

We didn't see any sign of the welcoming committee on the track, but when we reached the gate someone had left it open for us. I pushed the car hard towards Oban, wondering what the hell to do next.

15

Hoffer didn't see Kline again, which was good news for Kline. Hoffer was nursing the biggest headache since the US budget deficit. He'd tried going to a doctor, but the system in London was a joke. The one doctor who'd managed to give him an appointment had then suggested a change of diet and some paracetamol.

'Are you kidding?' roared Hoffer. 'We've *banned* those things in the States!'

But he couldn't find Tylenol or codeine, so settled for aspirin, which irritated his gut and put him in a worse mood than ever. He'd asked the doctor about a brain scan – after all, he was paying for the consultation, so might as well get his money's worth – and the doctor had actually *laughed.* It was obvious nobody ever sued the doctors in Britain. You went to a doctor in the States, they practically wheeled you from the waiting room to the surgery and back, just so you didn't trip over the carpet and start yelling for your lawyer.

'You're lucky I don't have my fucking gun with me,' Hoffer had told the doctor. Even then, the doctor had thought he was joking.

So he wasn't in the best of moods for his visit to Draper Productions, but when Draper found out who he was, the guy started jumping up and down. He said he'd read about Hoffer. He said Hoffer was practically the best-known private eye in the world, and had anyone done a profile of him?

'You mean for TV?'

'I mean for TV.'

'Well, I've, uh, I'm doing a TV spot, but only as guest on some talk show.' It had been confirmed that morning, Hoffer standing in for a flu-ridden comedian.

'I'm thinking bigger than that, Leo, believe me.'

So then they'd had to go talk it through over lunch at some restaurant where the description of each dish in the menu far exceeded in size the actual dish itself. Afterwards, Hoffer had had to visit a burger joint. Joe Draper thought this was really funny. It seemed like today everyone thought Hoffer was their favourite comedian. Draper wanted to come to New York and follow Hoffer around, fly-on-the-wall style.

'You could never show it, Joe. Most of what I do ain't family viewing.'

'We can edit.'

Early on in their relationship, Draper and Hoffer had come to understand one pertinent detail, each about the other. Maybe it was Hoffer's sniffing and blowing his nose and complaining of summer allergies. Maybe it was something else. Draper had been the first to suggest some nose talc, and Hoffer had brought out his Laguiole.

'Nice blade,' Draper said, reaching into his desk drawer for a mirror . . .

So it was a while before Hoffer actually got round to asking about Eleanor Ricks.

'Lainie,' Draper said in the restaurant, 'she was a lion tamer, believe me. I mean, in her professional life. God, this is the best pâté I've ever tasted.'

Hoffer had already finished his *salade langoustine*. He poured himself a glass of the white burgundy and waited.

'She was great, really she was,' Draper went on, buttering bread like he was working in the kitchen. 'Without her, three of my future projects just turned to ashes.' He squashed pâté on to the bread and folded it into his mouth.

'How much would I get paid for this documentary?' asked Hoffer.

'Jesus, we don't talk money yet, Leo. We need to do costings, then present the package to the money men. *They're* the final arbiters.'

'What was Eleanor working on when she died?'

'The Disciples of Love.'

'I think I saw that movie.'

'It's not a film, it's a cult.' So then it took a while for Draper to talk about that. 'I've got some info in my office, if you want it. I should be selling it, not giving it away. I had two detectives took copies away, on top of the half dozen I'd already handed over. It was worth it though. One of them suggested Molly Prendergast take over from Lainie on the Disciples project.'

'That's the woman she was with when she got shot?'

'The same.'

'What about these two detectives?'

'The man was called Inspector Best.'

'West?' Hoffer suggested. 'His colleague was a woman called Harris?'

'Oh, you know them?'

'It's beginning to feel that way,' said Hoffer. 'Did they ask you what colour clothes Ms Ricks liked to wear?' Draper was nodding.

'Uncanny,' he said.

'It's a gift, my grandmother was a psychic. Joe, I'd appreciate it if you could give me whatever you gave them.'

'Sure, no problem. Now let's talk about you . . .'

After lunch and the post-prandial burger, they went back to Draper's office for the *Disciples of Love?* folder and a final toot. Hoffer gave Draper his business card, but told him not to call until the producer had some figures.

'And remember, Joe, I charge by the hour.'

'So do all the hookers I know. It doesn't mean they're not good people.'

The TV show was a late-afternoon recording to go out the following morning. Hoffer went back to his hotel so he could wash and change. He'd bought some new clothes for the occasion, reckoning he could probably deduct them for tax purposes. He looked at himself in the mirror and felt like a fraud. He looked perfect. The suit was roomy, a dark blue wool affair. Even the trousers were lined, though only down to the knees. These London tailors knew their business. Fuckers knew how to charge, too.

With a white shirt and red paisley tie he reckoned he looked reputable and telegenic. It wasn't always easy to look both. They had a cab coming to pick him up, so all he had to do was wait. The burger wasn't agreeing with him, so he took something for it, then lay on his bed watching TV. His phone rang, and he unhooked the receiver.

'Yep?'

'Mr Hoffer, there's a letter in reception for you.'

'What sort of letter?'

'It's just arrived, delivered by hand.'

'Okay, listen, I'm expecting a cab to the television studio.' He couldn't help it, though he'd already told the receptionist this. 'I'll be leaving in about five minutes, so I'll grab the letter when I'm going out.'

'Yes, sir.'

Hoffer put down the phone fast. His guts were telling him something as he rushed for the bathroom.

Sitting in his cab, he told himself it was the langoustine, had to be. Unless he was getting an ulcer or something; it was that kind of pain, like a cramp. It clamped his insides and squeezed, then let go again. Some colonic problem maybe. No, it was just the food. No matter how lavish a restaurant's decor, its kitchen was still just a kitchen, and shellfish were still shellfish.

He tore open the brown envelope which had been waiting for him at reception. He knew from his name on the front that the letter was from Barney. There was a single typed sheet inside. God help him, the man had done the typing himself, but only two lines mattered: the two addresses in Yorkshire. The gun dealer called Darrow lived in Barnsley, while the one called Max Harrison lived near Grewelthorpe.

'Grewelthorpe?' Hoffer said out loud, not quite believing the name.

'What's that, guv?'

'It's a town or something,' Hoffer told the driver. 'Grewelthorpe.'

'Never heard of it.'

'It's in North Yorkshire.'

'That explains it then, I've never been north of Rickmansworth. Yorkshire's another country, you see them down here for rugby finals and football matches. Strange people, take my word for it. Do you work on the telly then?'

So far this trip, Hoffer had merited only five short newspaper interviews, one piece in a Sunday 'Lifestyle' supplement, a magazine article which he had to share with some new private eye movie that was coming out, and half a dozen radio segments. But now TV had picked up on him, and he made the production assistant promise he could have a recording to take away with him.

'It won't operate on an American machine,' she warned him.

'So I'll buy a British video recorder.'

'Remember, we're 240 volts.'

'I'll get a fucking adaptor!'

'Only trying to help.'

'I know, I'm sorry, I'm just a bit nervous.'

She then explained as she led him along corridor after corridor that he would be on with three other guests: a fashion designer, a gay football player, and a woman novelist. She smiled at him.

'You represent the show's harder edge.'

'If I ever survive this goddamned route march,' Hoffer complained. Then he had an idea. 'Do you have a library in the building?'

'Sort of, we've got a research unit.'

Hoffer stopped in his tracks, catching his breath. 'Could I ask you a *big* favour?'

'You mean *another* big favour.' The assistant checked her watch and sighed. She'd probably had guests ask her for blow jobs before. Compared to which, Hoffer reasoned, his was not such an unreasonable demand.

'Go on,' she said, 'what is it?'

So Hoffer told her.

The show itself was excruciating, and they all had to sit in chairs which were like something Torquemada would have had prisoners sit on when they went to the john. All of them except the host, naturally. Jimmy Bridger, as the gay soccer player explained to Hoffer in the hospitality lounge, had been an athlete and then a commentator and now was a TV presenter. Hoffer had a few questions for the soccer player, like whether anyone else would go in the post-match bath the same time as him, but he might need an on-screen ally so instead told the guy how lots of macho American football and baseball players were queens, too.

Then they went on to the set. The audience were women who should have had better things to do at four o'clock in the afternoon. Jimmy Bridger was late, so late Hoffer, already uncomfortable, was thinking of switching chairs. Bridger's chair was a vast spongy expanse of curves and edges. It sat empty while the show's producer did a warm-up routine in front of the audience. He told a few gags, made them clap on cue, that sort of stuff. TV was the same the world over, a fucking madhouse. Hard to tell sometimes who the warders were.

Jimmy Bridger looked mad, too. He had a huge wavy hairstyle like an extravagant Dairy Queen cone, and wore a jacket so loud it constituted a public nuisance. He arrived to audience cheers and applause, some of it unprompted. Hoffer knew that the hosts on these shows usually liked to meet the guests beforehand, just to lay ground rules, to check what questions might not be welcome, stuff like that. By arriving so late, Bridger was guilty of either overconfidence or else contempt, which added up to much the same thing. Before the taping began, he shook hands with each guest, apologised again for his tardiness, and gave them a little spiel, but you could see that his main concern was his audience. He just *loved* them. He kissed a few of the grandmothers in the front row. Hoffer hoped they had stretchers standing by for the cardiac seizures.

At last the recording got underway. As Hoffer had hoped he would, Bridger turned to him first.

'So, Mr Hoffer, what's one of New York's toughest private detectives doing here in England?'

Hoffer shifted in his seat, leaning forward towards Bridger. 'Well, sir, I think you're confusing me with this gentleman beside me. See, *I'm* the gay NFL player.'

There was a desperate glance from Bridger to his producer, the producer shaking his head furiously. Then Bridger, recovering well after a slow start off the blocks, started to laugh, taking the audience with him. They were so out of it, they'd've laughed at triple-bypass surgery. The interview went downhill from there. They'd probably edit it down to a couple of minutes by tomorrow.

Afterwards, Hoffer didn't want to bump into Bridger. Well, that was easily arranged. Bridger stuck around the studio, signing autographs and kissing more old ladies. Hoffer moved with speed to the 'green room', as they called their hospitality suite. It was a bare room lined with chairs, a bit like a surgery waiting room. Those still waiting to do their shows were like patients awaiting biopsy results, while Bridger's guests had just been given the all-clear. Hoffer tipped an inch of Scotch down his throat.

'I thought he was going to pee himself,' said the gay footballer of Hoffer's opening gag.

'That audience would have lapped it up,' Hoffer said. 'I mean, *literally*.' He downed another Scotch before collaring the production assistant.

'Forget the video,' he told her. 'You can spring it on me when I'm on *This is Your Life*. What about the other stuff?'

'I've got Mandy from Research outside.'

'Great, I'll go talk to her.'

'Fine.' And don't bother coming back, her tone said. Hoffer blew her a kiss, then gave her his famous tongue-waggle. She looked suitably unimpressed. This was in danger of turning into an all right day.

Mandy was about nineteen with long blonde hair and a fashionably anorexic figure.

'You could do with a meat transfusion,' Hoffer said. 'What've you got there?'

He snatched the large manila envelope from her and drew out a series of xeroxed map grids.

'I've run over it with green marker,' she said.

Hoffer could see that. Grewelthorpe: marked in green. The hamlets nearest it were Kirkby Malzeard and Mickley. These were to the south and east. To the west, there were only Masham Moor and Hambleton Hill, some reservoirs and stretches of roadless grey. Further south another hamlet caught his eye. It was called Blubberhouses. What was it with these comedy names? More relevantly, the nearest sizeable conurbations to Grewelthorpe were Ripon and Thirsk, the Yorkshire towns where Mark Wesley had made cash withdrawals.

'Any help?' Mandy said.

'Oh, yes, Mandy, these are beautiful, almost as beautiful as you, my pale princess.' He touched a finger to her cheek and stroked her face. She began to look scared. 'Now, I want you to do one more thing for me.'

She swallowed and looked dubious. 'What?'

'Tell Uncle Leo where Yorkshire is.'

It wasn't really necessary to clean the Smith & Wesson, but Hoffer cleaned it anyway. He knew if he got close enough to the D-Man, it wouldn't matter if the assassin was state-of-the-art armed, Hoffer would stick a bullet in his gut.

With the gun cleaned and oiled, he did some reading. He'd amassed a lot of reading this trip: stuff about haemophilia, and now stuff about the Disciples of Love. He didn't see anything in the Disciples' history that would unduly ruffle the red, white and blue feathers of the CIA or NSC. Yet Kline was over here, so someone somewhere was very worried about *some*thing. He imagined the assassin reading the same notes he was reading. What would he be thinking? What would be his next step? Would he take up the investigation where his victim had left off? That sounded way too risky, especially if the Disciples were the ones who'd set him up in the first place.

But then again, the D-Man had taken a lot of risks so far, and every risk brought him closer to the surface. Hoffer had a name and a description, and now he had Max Harrison. He knew Bob Broome wasn't stupid; he'd make the connection too before long. But Hoffer had a start. The only problem was, it meant driving. There were no rail stations close to his destination, so he'd have to hire a car. He'd booked one for tomorrow morning, and had asked for his bill to be made up. He knew that really he should make a start tonight, but he wasn't driving at night, not when he was heading into the middle of nowhere on the wrong damned side of the road.

He needed a clear head for tomorrow, so confined himself to smoking a joint in his room and watching some TV. Then he took a Librium to help him worm his way into the sleep of the just. After all, no way should he be there on merit.

'Don't be so hard on yourself, Leo,' he muttered. 'You're the good guy. You're the hero, you must be . . . Jimmy Bridger told you so.' He finished the glass of whisky beside his bed and switched off the TV.

On his way to the john, he got a sudden greasy feeling in his gut, and knew what it was. It wasn't cancer this time, or liquefaction of the bowel. It wasn't something he'd eaten or something he hadn't, a bad glass of tap-water or too much hooch.

It was the simple realisation that another day or two would see this whole thing finished.

The car rental firm had the usual selection of cramped boxes, each with as much soul as a fast-food carton.

'So which is the cheapest?'

'The Fiesta, sir.'

Hoffer tried to haggle over the Fiesta, but the assistant couldn't oblige. There wasn't even the chance of a blank receipt, since the whole system was computerised, so Hoffer couldn't hike his expense sheet. He quickly got the hang of driving on the left: it was easy if you stuck to one-way streets. But getting out of London was more pain than he'd bargained for. Twice he had to get out of his car at traffic lights and ask the driver behind for help, then suffer the drivers behind sounding their horns when the lights changed.

He got lost so often that after punching the steering wheel a few times he just stopped caring. He didn't study roadsigns, he just took whichever route looked good. When he stopped for lunch, he yielded to temptation and asked somebody where he was.

'Rickmansworth.'

So he'd reached his cab driver's northern frontier. Cheered by this, he reneged and bought a map book, finding that he would have to cut across country a bit to get on to the right road. The whole UK road network looked like a kid had taken a line for a walk. There seemed no order, no sense to it.

Driving was easy in the States, once you'd negotiated the cities. But here the cities didn't seem to end, they just melted each into the other, with preserved blobs of green inbetween.

As he moved north, however, he changed his mind a little. There was *some* green land between London and Yorkshire; it was boring green land, but it was definitely green. He relaxed into the driving, and even remembered to ask for petrol and not 'gas'. It was late afternoon before he got past Leeds. He came off the A1 and into Ripon, where he stopped for a break and a mental council of war.

If Max Harrison was like any gun dealer Hoffer knew, then he would have an arsenal like something from Desert Storm. And what did Hoffer have? A .457 and a pocket knife. All he had going for him was the element of surprise. That meant he'd have those few initial moments to size the situation up. If Harrison was toting heavy artillery, it was no contest. Likewise, if the man was not alone, Hoffer would be compelled to hold back. He realised too late that he'd drunk a whole pot of tea while mulling this over. The caffeine started its relentless surge through his bloodstream. He took a downer to balance things out, and regretted it immediately: he'd need to be sharp, not dopey.

So he took an upper as well.

But Max Harrison didn't actually live *in* what there was of Grewelthorpe. He lived somewhere on the outskirts. It was almost dark by the time Hoffer made his approach to the farm. Foresight had warned him to bring a torch, and he stuck it in his pocket after killing the engine. There was no other sign of habitation, and Hoffer had stopped the car half a mile from the house. He was going to walk that final half mile . . . Or was he? If Harrison had already heard or seen him, then why make himself an easy target? Better to arrive wrapped in steel than leave wrapped in a coffin. He turned the ignition back on and drove sedately up the track and into the yard.

He killed the engine and looked around. There was no sign of life. He sounded the horn tentatively, but got no response. Maybe the guy was a real farmer, out somewhere with his favourite sheep or cow. He opened his door and eased himself out. He couldn't hear any animals, not even a dog.

'Hello, anyone home?' he called. Only the wind whistled a reply. Hoffer walked to the house and peered in through a couple of windows. He was looking into a large clean kitchen. He tried the door and it opened. He went inside and called out again.

The house didn't feel empty. There was a television or radio on somewhere. He touched the kettle, but it was cold. He came out of the kitchen into an L-shaped hallway. At the other end of the hall was the front door of the house, obviously not much used. A rug had been pushed against it to stop draughts. Halfway along the hall were stairs up. But the sounds were coming from behind a door in the hall. There were two doors. The first was wide open, leading into an empty dining room. Three chairs sat around a four-cornered table. The second was closed, and must presumably lead to the living room. Hoffer's fingers tightened around the butt of his gun. Harrison couldn't have fled: where was there to go? Just the barns or the fields beyond. But he could be hiding. He touched the door handle, then turned it and let the door fall open.

Max Harrison had been beaten to a pulp.

His face was almost featureless, just a mess of blood and clots and tissue, like red fruit after a kid had been playing with it. Barney had told him Harrison was suffering from face cancer. A sort of cutaway plastic mask lay on the floor, and there was a large blackish hole cut deep into one of Harrison's cheeks. Sure, beat up a dying man, why don't you? Hoffer felt rage inside him, but then Harrison wasn't his problem.

He was seated on a dining chair in the centre of the room. His hands had been tied behind him and around the back of the chair, and his feet had been tied to the chair-legs.

'Hey, you Max Harrison?' Hoffer said.

The room was messy too. There'd been a fight here, or some serious ransacking, or more probably both. A lot of broken ornaments and glass were lying underfoot. Hoffer went over to the chair to take a pulse. As he touched the body, the head rolled from the shoulders and fell on to the carpet.

'Son of a bitch!' Hoffer roared, half-turning his head to spew up tea and cake and scones. He spat and wiped his mouth with the back of his hand. 'Damn,' he said, 'I paid good money for that meal.' He coughed a couple of times and turned back to the headless corpse. He was no pathologist, but he'd seen a few autopsies during his time on the force. The dead man's throat had been cut through so deeply and thoroughly that practically nothing had been holding it on. Whoever had left Harrison sitting like that had known what would happen when someone finally touched the corpse.

'Nice touch, dude,' Hoffer muttered. He thought of his own knife: it wouldn't do to be caught here by the police. He had some quick thinking to do. He took another look at the corpse, then around the room. He couldn't glean much here, so headed upstairs. Could it have been the D-Man's work? Maybe the gun dealer had double-crossed him in some way, and the D-Man had murdered him.

The first bedroom Hoffer walked into belonged to a man. There were no women's things lying around, no dresses in the wardrobe. But there were a lot of framed photos, mostly of a man Hoffer assumed to be Max Harrison with a girl Hoffer took to be his daughter. There were photos of her as a baby, and all the way up to what looked like her 20s. Not a bad looker either. Fair hair, prominent cheekbones, beautiful eyes.

There were two other bedrooms, one of them obviously a guest room, which didn't stop Hoffer looking around for any signs of weapons. The other belonged to a woman, a young woman judging from the magazines and make-up and a few of the cassette tapes lying around.

So Harrison's daughter lived at home . . .

'Whoa!' Hoffer said, sitting down on the bed. 'Hold on there.' He was thinking of the description he'd been given of 'DC Harris', the D-Man's accomplice. He went back to Harrison's bedroom and picked up the most recent-looking photo. Too close to be coincidence.

'Son of a bitch,' he said quietly.

This changed things. Because if the D-Man had killed Harrison, then he'd also taken the daughter with him. Had he taken her under duress? If so, then she was hostage rather than accomplice, which would make a difference when it came time to confront the assassin.

Harrison's bedroom showed no signs of having been searched, and the daughter's bedroom was tidy too. There were paperback books on a shelf above her bed. Hoffer opened one and found her name written in the corner of the prelim page: Bel Harrison. Bel, short for Belinda. Hoffer spent a little more time in her room, trying to find out more about her. She hadn't taken away many clothes; her drawers and wardrobe were more than half full. As he usually did given access to a woman's bedroom, he lingered over the underwear drawer. You could tell a lot about a woman from her underwear. They should turn it into a police discipline, like psychological profiling. He picked up various items, sniffed their detergent smell, then put them back.

There were no posters on the walls, no clues to any hobbies. Her room gave away less than most. He looked under the bed and even under the carpet, but didn't find any dope. There didn't seem to be any contraceptives around either.

'A clean-living country girl,' he said to himself. 'Except, sweetheart, that your daddy dealt in illegal firearms, and now you're running around with the enemy.'

Downstairs again, he checked the cellar. It contained a few bottles of wine and spirits, plus a deep freeze and some DIY tools and materials. He selected a bottle of Scotch and brought it up to the kitchen. He poured from it, then wiped it clean with a cloth, and he held his glass with a piece of kitchen towel. After he'd had the drink, he went around wiping the doorhandles and all the other surfaces he'd touched with his fingers. Then he switched on his torch and headed for the outbuildings. He found the indoor range straight away. From the length of it, it could be used for both rifles and handguns. He still hadn't found any weapons. There had to be a cache somewhere. If he could find it, he could help himself. He looked for twenty minutes without success, and returned to the kitchen.

He had another drink and sat down at the table. The extravaganza in the living room was not the D-Man's style. The D-Man liked to keep his distance. He'd never killed at close range. And for a skilled shot suddenly to revert to a knife or a razor or whatever had been used . . . No, it hadn't been the D-Man. Which left two questions. Who'd done it? And what was Bel Harrison doing with the D-Man?

There was a telephone in the kitchen, hooked to an answering machine. He played the tape but there were no messages. Several choices presented themselves. He could phone for the police, then wait for them. He could phone them anonymously and then get out. He could get the hell out without telling anyone. Or he could hang around and see if either the killers or the D-Man came back. It stood to reason that the daughter would return some time. Maybe the body would have been found by then. There had to be a mail service, even to this outpost of civilisation. The body was still fairly fresh. Hoffer didn't like to think about Bel Harrison stumbling upon it a few days or even weeks hence.

Then again, did he really want another police force involved? What if they scared off the D-Man?

Hoffer didn't know what to do, so he let another drink decide for him. Then he drove back towards Ripon, seeking a bed for the night.

16

The first thing I saw after breakfast was Leo Hoffer.

That may sound crazy, but it's true. When I got back to my room to do some final packing, I must have left the TV on. I'd been watching the early-morning news. Now there was a chat show on, and one of the guests was Hoffer. Not that he stole much airtime, a few minutes, but he was omnipresent, coughing offscreen, twitching and interrupting when other guests were speaking. I told Bel to come and see. They'd got round to the question and answer segment. The host was moving around the audience, his mike at the ready.

'That's Jimmy Bridger,' said Bel. 'I watch this sometimes.'

A middle-aged lady was standing up to ask her question. 'Is Mr Hoffer married?' The camera cut to Hoffer, who was wearing an expensive suit but wearing it cheaply. The cloth shone but he didn't.

'No, ma'am,' he said. Then, creasing his face: 'Was that an offer?' Everyone thought this very funny. Someone else asked him if he found his weight a problem. He agreed that it was.

'I've got to put on a few more pounds before I can Sumo wrestle, and you know those last few pounds are the toughest.'

This had them practically rolling in the aisles.

'A question for another of our guests,' said the host, making it plain that he wasn't going to let Hoffer hog proceedings. It looked to me like they must have had a disagreement along the way.

'And this is the man who's chasing you?' Bel commented.

'That's him. My shadow. I sometimes think the only reason he hunts me is so he can appear on shows like this.'

'Why would he do that?'

'His ego for one thing. But also, he's in business, and I'm a good advert for him. As far as I can see, I'm the only advert he's got.'

'He doesn't look like he could catch a cold.'

'That,' I said quietly, 'is why he's so good.'

I sent Bel off to do her packing, and then finished my own. We'd take the car back to Glasgow, I'd buy us train tickets south and let Bel make the connections to take her home. As for me, I'd go back to London. What else could I do? I'd wait it out till Shattuck crept out of the woodwork. I'd waited for victims before.

Bel wasn't happy.

'Does this mean the engagement's off?'

'It's the way it was always going to be.'

She couldn't help but notice a change of tone. 'What's up, Michael?'

'Nothing. Just phone Max and tell him with any luck you'll be back tonight. Tell him you'll call from Glasgow with train times.'

So she made the call. It took Max a few moments to answer. Listening, Bel rolled her eyes, meaning it was the answering machine.

'Hi, Dad, it's me. Stick by the phone when you get in. I'm headed home, probably tonight. I'll call again when I know my arrival time. 'Bye.'

We checked out of the hotel, but Bel wanted to go back into town.

'What for?'

'A few souvenirs. Come on, Michael, this is the last day of my holiday.'

I shook my head, but we went anyway. While she was shopping, I walked by the harbour. A ferry was leaving for Mull. The island was about six miles away, beyond the smaller isle of Kerrera. The sun was out, and a few boatmen were going about their business, which mostly comprised posing for the tourists' video cameras. There was a hotel near the harbour we'd tried to get into, with a low wall alongside it. I lifted myself on to the wall and just enjoyed the sunshine. Then Bel was in front of me, thrusting a large paper bag into my hands.

'Here,' she said.

'What's this?'

'It's *your* souvenir.'

Inside the bag was a thick Fair Isle sweater.

'Try it on,' she said. 'I can always take it back if it doesn't fit.'

'It looks fine.'

'But try it on!'

I was wearing a jacket and a shirt, so took the jacket off and laid it on the wall, then pulled the sweater over my head and arms. It was a good fit. She ruffled my hair and pecked my cheek.

'Perfect,' I said. 'But you shouldn't have. It must've cost—'

But she was heading off again. 'I just wanted to make sure it was okay. I've got to get something for Dad now.' She gave me a wave and was gone.

I didn't dare take the jumper off again. She'd expect me to wear it for a little while at least. Well, it kept out the breeze, but I had the feeling it made me look less like a local and more like a tourist. I took my sunglasses from my jacket pocket and slipped them on.

A car had drawn up nearby. It rose perceptibly on its axles when its driver got out. I nearly tipped backwards off the wall.

It was Hoffer.

He stretched, showing an expanse of shirt and a belt on its last notch. He also showed me something more: that he didn't have a holster beneath his jacket. He did some neck stretches, saw me, and came walking over.

'It's been a long drive,' he said with a groan.

'Oh, aye?' If he'd just come north, maybe he wouldn't know mock-Scots from the real thing.

He wasn't looking at me anyway. He was taking in the harbour, and talking more to himself than to anyone else. I thought he'd been taking drugs. 'This is some beautiful place,' he said.

'No' bad.'

He looked up at the hotel. 'What about this place, is it no' bad too?' I shrugged and he smiled. 'A canny Scot, huh?' Then he turned away and made to enter the hotel. 'See you around, bud.'

The moment he'd gone, I slid from the wall, grabbed my jacket, and walked away. I didn't know which shop Bel would be in, and had half a mind to go to the car instead and get the MP5. But she was coming out of a fancy goods emporium, so I took her arm and steered her with me.

'Hey, what's up?'

'The TV tec is in town.'

'The fat man?' Her eyes widened.

'Don't look back, just keep walking. We're going to the car and we are getting out of here.'

'He *can't* be here,' she hissed. 'He was in a TV studio only an hour ago.'

'Have you ever heard of videotape? They record these shows, Bel. You think anyone would have the balls to put Hoffer on *live*?'

'What are you going to do?'

I looked at her. 'What do you think I should do?'

'Maybe . . .' she began. Then she shook her head.

'What were you going to say?'

'I was going to say . . .' her cheeks reddened. 'I was going to say, maybe you should take him out.'

I looked at her again. We were at the car now. 'I take it you don't mean I should date him?'

She shook her head. 'Michael, did you hear him on TV this morning? All those questions they asked: was he armed, would he think twice about killing you?'

I unlocked her door and went round to the driver's side. 'I get paid to do jobs. I don't do it for fun.'

'There are other ways to make a living,' she said quietly.

'What? Work behind a desk? That's what they like haemophiliacs to do. That way we're *safe*. To hell with that.'

'Don't you think becoming a hired assassin is a bit extreme, though?'

'Jesus, Bel, you're the one who just said I should bump off Hoffer!'

She smiled. 'I know, but I've changed my mind. I think you should stop. I mean, stop altogether. I think you want to.'

I started the engine. 'Then you don't know me.'

'I think I do.'

I let off the handbrake and started us rolling out of Oban. Maybe it was Hoffer, or Hoffer added to the conversation I'd just had. Whatever, I wasn't being very careful. All I knew was that Hoffer's car was still parked when we passed it.

I spotted them just outside town. To be fair, they weren't trying very hard. They didn't mind me knowing about them. There were two cars, one a smart new Rover and the other an Austin Maestro.

'Don't do anything,' I warned Bel. 'Just keep looking ahead. We're being followed.'

She saw them in her wing mirror. 'One car or two?'

'Both of them, I think.'

'Who are they?'

'I don't recognise any faces. They're clean shaven, the one I can see best is smartly dressed, jacket and tie. I don't think they're the Disciples.'

'Police maybe? That could be why the fat man's in town.'

'Why not just arrest us?'

'Do they have any evidence?'

She had a point. 'They could do us for impersonating police officers. That would keep us in the cells till they found something. The police'll always find a way to stitch you up if they need to.'

I accelerated, knowing the Escort couldn't outrun the pursuers. We were heading down the coast, since we'd agreed to take a different route back to Glasgow. When we reached a straight stretch with no other traffic in sight, the Maestro signalled to overtake. The way it pulled past, I knew there was a big engine lurking inside it. There was no need for pretence, so I gave the driver and passenger a good look as they cruised past, trying to place them. Both were young and fair-haired and wearing sunglasses. They pulled in sharply in front of us and hit the brakes, so that we'd have to slow down, or else overtake. The Rover was right behind, making us the meat in the sandwich.

'What are they doing, Michael?'

'I think they want us to stop.' I signalled that I was pulling over, and hit the brakes so fast the Rover's tyres squealed as the driver stopped from ramming us. I couldn't see the road ahead, but shifted down into second and pulled out into the oncoming lane. There was nothing coming, so I tore alongside the Maestro, which was already accelerating. There was a bend approaching, and neither car had the beating of the other. Suddenly a lorry emerged from round the bend, and I braked hard, pulling us back into the left lane, still sandwiched.

'I don't think policemen play these kinds of game,' I told Bel. She was looking pale, gripping the passenger door and the dashboard.

'Then who are they?'

'I'll be sure to ask them.'

The front car was braking again. The driver had put on his emergency flashers. He was obviously coming to a halt on the carriageway. A stream of traffic had been trapped behind the lorry, so there was no chance of us pulling past the Maestro. The Rover behind was keeping its distance, but I knew once we stopped that would be it. One would reverse and the other edge forward until there was nowhere for us to go.

I stopped the car.

'What's going to happen?' Bel said.

'I'm not sure.'

Traffic heading in the other direction was slowing even further to watch. Whoever our pursuers were, they didn't seem to care about having an audience. A normal person might be relieved, thinking nothing serious was going to happen in front of witnesses. But I saw it another way. If they weren't worried about having an audience, maybe they weren't worried about *anything*.

I slid my hand back between the driver's and passenger's seats. On the floor in the back, wrapped in my old blue raincoat, was the MP5. I don't know what made me switch it from the boot when we were loading the car, but I said a silent thank you to whichever bad angel was watching over me.

'Oh God,' Bel said, seeing the gun. I opened my driver's door and stepped out, leaving raincoat and contents both on the floor beside the pedals. The Maestro had backed up to kiss my front bumper, and the Rover was tucked in nicely behind. Three cars had never been closer on a car transporter or parked on a Paris street. I decided to take the initiative and walked to the car at the back. I reckoned the front car was the workhorse; the person I wanted to speak to would be in the nice car, probably in the back seat. Electric windows whirred downwards at my approach. The windows were tinted, the interior upholstery cream leather. All I could see of the driver was the back of his head, but the man in the back of the car was smiling.

'Hello there,' he said. He was wearing ordinary glasses rather than sunglasses, and had short blond hair. His lips were thin, his face dotted with freckles. He looked like his head hadn't quite grown up yet. He was wearing a suit, and a white shirt whose cuffs were slightly too long for the jacket. The shirt was buttoned to the neck, but he didn't wear a tie.

'Good morning,' I said. 'Is there a problem?'

He acted like there wasn't. 'We'd appreciate a few minutes of your time.'

'Pollsters aren't usually so determined,' I said. I was thinking: *he's American*. Was he working for Hoffer? No, I didn't get that impression at all.

'If you and your friend will get in the car, I'd appreciate it very much.'

'You mean, get in your car?'

I didn't even dent his smile. 'That's what I mean.'

I shrugged. 'What's this all about?'

'It can be explained in five minutes.' He held up a hand, palm spread wide to show fingers and thumb.

'You could have talked to us in town.'

'Please, just get in the car.'

At last another vehicle appeared coming from Oban. It was a Volkswagen estate pulling a caravan. The car had a German licence plate.

'Oh oh,' I said, 'here comes an international incident.'

The bastard just kept on smiling. He didn't seem to mind if he held up the traffic for the rest of the day.

'I'll go fetch my friend,' I said.

As I walked back to the car, a van driver idling past asked what was happening. I just shook my head. I stuck my head into the Ford Escort.

'Bel,' I said, 'I want you to be calm, okay? Here, take the keys. I want you to grab the map book, then get out of the car, unlock the boot, and get our stuff. We're changing cars.'

Then I picked up the raincoat and walked forward towards the Maestro. The driver and passenger were watching in their mirrors. When I started towards them, they opened their doors. I came to the passenger side, away from the oncoming traffic, and showed the passenger my raincoat. He could see the gun barrel.

'You've seen one of these before,' I told him. 'Now tell your partner.'

'He's packing heat,' the passenger said. He was American too.

'We're going to see your boss,' I told him, and motioned with the gun for him to move. They walked in front of me. When we reached the boot of the Escort, I told them to keep walking. The German motorist was out of his car and was talking in broken but heated English with the Rover driver, who didn't look to be answering.

Bel had lifted out our two bags. I took one and she the other, and we walked to the Maestro again and got in. I started the ignition and we roared away, leaving the mess behind. Bel screamed with relief and kissed me on the cheek.

'I nearly wet myself back there!'

'Have you got the Escort keys?' I asked, grinning. She shook them at me.

'Then they'll be stuck there till they either push it off the road or learn the German for "back your caravan up".' I tried to relax my shoulders. I was hunched over the steering-wheel like a racing driver. 'It was a close one though,' I said. 'Twice in one day is too close.'

'You think they were something to do with Hoffer?'

I shook my head. 'Too smooth. They had a sort of government smell about them. There's a kind of smugness you get when you know you've got everything on your side.'

'Then they're to do with Prendergast?'

She'd misunderstood me. 'No, they had American accents.'

'The *American* government?'

I shook my head slowly, trying to clear it. 'Maybe I'm wrong. But they were definitely Americans.'

'More men hired by that girl's father?'

'I really don't know. I think it all ties in with the Disciples of Love.'

She looked startled. 'You're not going back there?'

'No, don't worry.'

'I thought you'd ruled out Rick and his gang.'

Now I nodded. 'Maybe it goes higher, Bel.' I didn't bother explaining what I meant.

We'd no hire car to return, so I decided to hang on to the Maestro. I could drop Bel off in Yorkshire then dump the car somewhere. We kept moving, stopping only to fill up with petrol, buy sandwiches and drinks from the filling-station shops, and try getting through to Max.

'Maybe he's had to go somewhere?' I suggested.

'Maybe. He'd have said, wouldn't he?'

'Short notice. I know I've been in a tight spot once or twice and dragged him away with no notice at all.'

She nodded, but stared at the windscreen. To take her mind off Max, I got her round to talking about the men from that morning, what they could have wanted from us, how they'd known where we were.

'What would you have done,' she asked, 'if one of them had drawn a gun?'

'Taken the drawing from him and torn it up.'

'But seriously.'

'Seriously?' I considered. 'I'd probably have gone along peacefully.'

'Really?'

'It's hard to know, but I think so.'

I assumed it was the answer she wanted to hear.

We reached the farm before dark.

I got a bad feeling about the place straight away, and was glad I had the MP5 with me. As soon as I stopped the car, Bel was out and running. She'd felt something too. I called out for her to wait, but she was already opening the kitchen door.

I left the car idling and followed her, holding the sub-machine gun one-handed. With its stock fully retracted, the thing was just like an oversized pistol. I pushed the safety catch past single-shot and on to three-round burst.

Then I went in.

Bel's scream froze my blood. I wanted to run to her, but knew better than that. There could be many reasons for her screams. I peered into the hall but saw no one. Holding the gun in front of me, I walked forward, brushing the wall all the way. I passed the open door of the dining room and noticed that one of the chairs was missing from around the table. Then I saw the living room, things scattered over the floor, and Bel kneeling in the middle of it all, her hands over her face. Finally I saw Max.

'Christ Almighty.'

His headless torso sat on the missing dining-chair, like some ventriloquist's dummy gone badly wrong. Flies had found the body, and were wandering around the gaping hole which had once been a neck. A false glimmer struck me: maybe it wasn't him. But the build was right, and the clothes seemed right, though everything had been stained dark red. The blood on the skin had dried to a pale crust, so he'd been here a little while. There was a sour smell in the room, which I traced to a pool of vomit on the carpet. A tea-towel from the kitchen was lying next to this pool, covering something the size of a football.

I didn't need to look.

I squeezed Bel's shoulder. 'We can't do any good here. Let's go to the kitchen.'

Somehow I managed to pull her to her feet. I was still holding on to the gun. I didn't want to let go of it, but I pushed the safety back on.

'No, no, no, no,' Bel was saying. 'No, no, no.' Then she started wailing, her face purple and streaked with tears. I sat her on a chair in the kitchen and went outside.

I'm no tracker. There were tyre marks on the ground, but they could have belonged to Max's car. I took a look around, finding nothing. In the long barn, I flicked the lights on and stood staring at one of the distant human-shaped targets on the range. I switched the MP5 to full auto and started blasting away. It took about fifteen seconds to empty the magazine. Only the legs of the target remained.

Bel was standing at the kitchen door, yelling my name.

'It's okay,' I said, coming out of the barn. 'It's okay.' She put her arms around me and wept again. I held her, kissed her, whispered things to her. And then found myself crying too. Max had been . . . I can't say he'd been like a father; I've only ever had the one father, and he was quite enough. But he'd been a friend, maybe the closest I'd ever had. After the tears I didn't feel anger any more. I felt something worse, a cold creeping knowledge of what had to be done.

Bel blew her nose and said she wanted to walk about a bit, so I went back into the house. They hadn't left many clues. The vomit and the dishtowel were curious, but that was about it. Why cover the head? I couldn't understand it. I went upstairs and looked around. The bedrooms hadn't been touched. They hadn't been burglars.

Of course they hadn't. I knew who they'd been. The Americans. And either Max had talked, or they'd worked it out for themselves anyway, or someone from the Oban Disciples of Love had contacted them. I considered the first of these the least probable: Max wouldn't have talked, not when talking would mean putting Bel in danger. As for working it out for themselves, well, if Hoffer could do it so could they.

Bel still hadn't come back by the time I went downstairs. I walked out into the yard but couldn't hear her.

'Bel?'

There was a noise from the long barn, something being moved around.

'Bel?'

I had to go to the car for a fresh cartridge-box. When I pushed it home, I had thirty-two rounds ready for action. I moved quietly towards the barn.

When I looked in, someone had cleared an area of straw from the concrete floor, revealing a large double trap-door, which now sat open. The trap-door led to a bunker. There were wooden steps down into it, and a bare lightbulb inside. Bel was coming back up the steps. She had a rifle slung over each shoulder, a couple of pistols stuck into the waistband of her denims, and she was carrying an MP5 just like my own.

'Going to do some practice?' I asked her.

'Yes, on live targets.' She had a mad look in her puffy eyes. Her nose was running, and she had to keep wiping it with the back of her hand.

'Fury is the enemy, Bel.'

'Who taught you that?' she sneered. 'Some Zen monk?'

'No,' I said quietly, 'my father . . . and yours.'

She stood facing me, then I saw her shoulders sag.

'Don't worry,' I went on, 'you'll get your revenge. But let's plan it first, okay?' I waited till she'd nodded. 'Besides,' I added, 'you've forgotten something.'

'What?'

'Bullets.'

She saw that this was true, and managed a weak smile. I nodded to let her know she was doing okay.

'You don't need guns just now,' I went on. 'You need your brain. Your brain . . . and your passport.'

'My passport?'

'Just in case,' I said. 'Now go pack yourself some clothes. Are there any more sub-machine guns down there?'

'I'm not sure. Why do you ask?'

'I need some practice, that's all.' I started down the steps until I was surrounded by guns, cocooned in oiled black metal. It was like being in a chapel.

It took us some time to straighten things out. We knew we couldn't call the police, inform the proper authorities, anything like that. I did propose that Bel stay behind, a proposal she angrily rejected. So we did what we had to do. The soil in the field nearest the farmhouse was workable. Even so, it took until dark and beyond to dig the grave. It wasn't a very adequate hole. I knew the reason you dug down six feet was that much short of this and you'd get soil disturbance, the ground above the body rising eventually rather than staying flat. But we'd dug down only three or four feet. We could always rebury him later.

'Sorry, Dad,' Bel said. 'I know you were never much of a Christian, but you probably wanted something better than this.' She looked at me. 'He fought that cancer for years. He was ready for death, but not the way it happened.'

'Come on,' I said, 'let's keep busy.'

It wasn't hard. We had to finish packing and then lock up the house. We couldn't do much about the living room, so just left it. Bel couldn't think of anyone who'd come to the house anyway. Their mail was held by the post office and picked up whenever they were in town.

'It might be a while before we're back,' I warned.

'That's fine.'

I was never far from the MP5. I knew they could come back at any minute. I would be ready for them. I'd considered stocking up from Max's cache, but knew it didn't make any sense. So I locked the cellar again and covered its doors with straw. The house was locked now, a timer controlling the lights. I walked through the yard to the field wall, and found Bel there, standing over the closed grave.

'Time to go, Bel,' I said.

'He hated this place,' she said quietly. I put a hand on her shoulder. She took a deep breath and exhaled. ''Bye, Dad. I'll be home again soon.' Even to my ears, she didn't sound like she meant it.

We got on to the A1 and stopped at the first hotel we found. I didn't suppose either of us would get much sleep, but we were exhausted and dirty and our sweat-stained clothes needed changing. We shared a room, as we'd known we would. Bel took the first bath. I soaped her back and shoulders in silence, then towelled her dry. She went through to the bedroom while I changed the bathwater. I was lying back, eyes closed, when she came back.

'Hurry up, Michael, I need you,' was all she said.

We made love hungrily at first, and then with more tenderness than I'd ever thought possible. She cried a bit, but when I tried to ease away from her she held me tight, not wanting to let me go. The only light drifting into the room came from a lamp outside the hotel. I ran my hands over Bel's back, feeling her vertebrae. For a little while there, my hands didn't feel like the hands of a killer.

We rose early and didn't bother with breakfast.

On the road south, she asked me what we were doing. I told her. She didn't know if it made sense or not, but she wasn't in a state to offer ideas of her own. The traffic into London was like sludge easing into a drain. Bel was wearing a scarf and sunglasses. I knew her eyes were red, like she was suffering hay fever. Hay fever could be the excuse if anyone asked. When we got to London, we left the Maestro in a long-stay car park and got our cases out of the boot.

I left the MP5 in the boot but took my raincoat.

We took a taxi with our luggage to Knightsbridge. 'I'll be about five minutes,' I told the driver when we arrived. Then, to Bel: 'Wait here.'

She watched me go into the bank like she'd never see me again.

Inside the bank there were the usual security procedures before I was led into a small room. The room contained a table and two chairs. There were framed prints on the wall showing Victorian London, and a few brochures to read. These offered further bank services. Eventually, the employee who had led me into the room returned with my safe deposit box. I let him leave again before opening the box.

Inside were a passport, a bundle of cash, and some traveller's cheques, about $25,000 in total. I scooped the lot into my pockets, then took out a pen and piece of paper. Hurriedly I scribbled a note outlining events so far. It wouldn't make sense to anyone outside the case. I folded the note and addressed it to the one man I knew *could* make sense of it: Leo Hoffer at Hoffer Investigations, New York City. Then I placed the letter in the box.

As insurance policies go, it was among the worst and most hastily conceived and executed. But it was all I had.

I thanked the assistant, left the bank, and got back into the taxi.

'Where to now?' the driver asked.

'Heathrow Airport,' I told him. Then I sat back, took Bel's hand, and gave it another squeeze.

17

The problem was, Hoffer couldn't find a room in Ripon, or anywhere else for that matter. So he'd decided to keep driving. Then he'd pulled into a parking area to relieve his bladder, and found three lorries there, their drivers having a break and thinking about sleep. Hoffer got talking to them and one of them broke out a bottle of whisky. After which he'd returned to his car, put the seat back as far as it would go, and fallen asleep.

He slept badly, and woke up with stiffness, headache and raging thirst. He was also freezing, and had certainly caught a cold, if not something more serious. He drove to the nearest service station to chow down and have a wash. Then he got back in the car and started driving again.

The map book was a Godsend, without it he wouldn't have stood a chance in hell of finding Oban. He parked by the dockside, got out feeling like shit, asked a local about accommodation, then went into the hotel, where they didn't have any rooms left but the bar was open and boasted an open fire.

Hoffer sat beside it with a large malt and wondered how he'd find the Disciples of Love. He asked the barman, but the barman said he'd never heard of them.

'Well, they live here, a whole posse of them.'

But the barman stuck to his story. So, revived by the drink, Hoffer went walkabout. He found a shopkeeper who did business with the Disciples and drew him a map on an empty brown-paper bag. Hoffer got so far, but then found his way barred by a padlocked gate. He looked around him, then fired off a couple of shots at the padlock, busting it open. He was damned if he was going to walk any further.

He'd been annoyed by a sudden realisation that he'd missed his TV appearance. And it looked like everyone in Oban had missed it too, judging by the lack of interest in him.

'Fucking backwoods,' he complained, driving up the track.

After nearly a mile, he came upon habitation, a series of shanty-town shacks more suited to animals than people. There were people about. They stopped what they were doing and stared at him as he drew up. When he got out, they kept on staring. A big bearded man came out of one of the shacks.

'Who are you?' he said.

'Name's Hoffer, sir, Leo Hoffer. I was wondering if I might have a word. I'm looking for a couple, man and woman, they might have been here recently.'

'There's been nobody here.'

Hoffer looked around him. 'This place was started by an American, wasn't it?' The man nodded. 'Only, we Americans have a reputation for hospitality to strangers. I'm not seeing much of that here.'

'How did you get past the gate?'

'Huh? The thing was standing wide open. I mean, it had a chain and all, but it was just hanging there.'

The man told an underling to go check. The underling nodded and jumped into an old hippy van.

'There's nothing here for you,' the man told Hoffer.

'Hey, maybe I want an application form. This looks like my kind of living.'

'I don't think so.'

'You don't?' Hoffer rubbed his chin. It felt raspy. He needed a shave and a soak. 'You know, I could make a habit of this, dropping in on you, asking the same question.'

'You'd get the same answer.'

The man turned his back on Hoffer and walked back into the shack. Hoffer considered following him and introducing the man to the holy rite of pistol-whipping. What the hell, there'd be other times. So he got into his car and left. The VW van was beside the gate. Hoffer tooted his horn and waved as he passed. The VW driver was standing there holding the chain, watching Hoffer leave.

Back in town, Hoffer asked at a couple of places about two tourists called Weston and Harrison. He didn't think they'd keep up their police act, not when it wasn't necessary. The names didn't mean anything, but one shop assistant recognised the photograph of Bel Harrison.

'She was in here this morning. She bought a Fair Isle jumper. It was funny, she was so excited. She rushed out of the shop so her husband could try it on.'

Hoffer started. 'What sort of sweater was this?'

The assistant showed him one just like it. She mistook the look of pain on Hoffer's face.

'We've got it in different colours if you'd prefer.'

He was groaning as he left the shop. He'd actually *talked* to the D-Man, and had been too hungover and crashed to know it. But at least one thing was clear: Bel Harrison wasn't under duress. Captives didn't often buy sweaters for their captors.

More crucially, they might still be around, he had to remember that . . . No, who was he fooling? The assassin knew who he was. He'd be out of town by now and putting miles on the clock.

Either that, Hoffer considered, or he'd be hiding somewhere, wondering how best to hit the detective. Hoffer looked around him at all the windows, large and small. He didn't feel very comfortable.

He went back to the lounge bar and ordered another whisky. There was some gossip being passed around, something about a traffic jam. Hoffer snorted into his drink. A traffic jam, around *here*? Three cars had been left stationary in the road while their drivers had a confab, holding up the traffic behind and providing a sideshow for cars heading north towards Oban.

Something about the story started to niggle Hoffer. He walked up to the storyteller and proffered the photo of Bel.

'I've no idea,' the man said. He held a pint in one hand and a cigarette in the other, so that Hoffer had to stand with the photo held out for his inspection. 'One of the cars, the middle one, it had a woman in it right enough. You couldn't see into the car ahent, and I don't remember the one in front.'

'It had two men in it,' piped up another drinker. Hoffer moved on to this man. He was wearing wellingtons, a check cap and green jacket, and his cheeks and nose were red. 'We were stuck behind Bert McAuley's lorry, bloody old thing that it is.'

'The man and woman were in the middle car?' Hoffer prompted.

'Aye, with a posh car ahent, and a car and caravan ahent that. The front car had his flashers on. They'd either had a bit of a knock, or else the front car had broken down.'

'What about the man and woman?'

'What about them?'

'Remember, Hughie,' said a third drinker, 'the man went and spoke to the people in the front car and they got out.'

'I didn't see that,' said Hughie. Hoffer moved on to the third drinker.

'What happened?'

'It was funny. The man and woman got their stuff out of the boot and took it to the other car, then drove off while the driver and passenger were back at the *third* car.'

Everyone looked at everyone else. It was obvious this story would run and run. Nothing so exciting had happened in weeks.

'Where was this?' said Hoffer.

'Just after the Cleigh turn-off.'

While Hoffer bought everyone a drink, the third drinker drew a map on the other side of the brown-paper bag.

It didn't take him long to find the car.

It had been pushed none too daintily up on to the verge. Though the Escort was practically brand new, someone had scored a line all down one side. It looked like the kind of scar kids made with a key, coin or knife.

'Temper, temper, guys,' Hoffer said, giving the car a good lookover. He'd bet it was rented, just like his own. There'd be prints on it belonging to the assassin and Bel Harrison. Fingerprints would be worth having, so Hoffer went to look for the nearest phone. He found a campsite a few miles further south. There was an information kiosk, locked up tight for the day, and a telephone booth outside it. He stood in the booth and called Vine Street. He couldn't get through to Broome, but Edmond finally accepted the call.

'Take your time,' said Hoffer, 'this is costing me a fucking fortune and I'm doing you a favour!'

'What favour?'

'I've got a car near here with the D-Man's prints all over it, plus his girlfriend's.'

Edmond took a bit more interest. 'Where are you?'

'I'm in the Scottish Highlands, south of a place called Oban on the A816.'

'Where's the car?'

'Parked roadside just south of a place called Cleigh.' He spelt the word for Edmond.

'I'll get on to the local constabulary.'

'They probably know about the car already. It's been abandoned after the D-Man got into trouble. There could be a lot of other people's prints on it, but some of them will definitely be his.'

'Wait a minute, what sort of trouble?'

'Money's running out, be seeing you.'

Hoffer put down the phone. There was a standpipe nearby, and a girl was filling a plastic jerry-can with water. He went over to her.

'On holiday with your folks?' She nodded. 'I'm looking for a friend, honey. He arrived earlier today towing a caravan.'

'The caravans are over there.' She pointed him in the direction.

'Thanks,' he said. 'Can I carry that for you?'

'My parents wouldn't like it. You're a stranger.'

Hoffer smiled. 'Take care, honey-pie.'

He watched her go. She had to work hard to keep the jerry-can off the ground. She'd be about eleven or twelve, he guessed. He knew twelve-year-olds in New York more grown up than he hoped she'd ever need to be. He liked kids on principle, the principle being that a day would come when he'd be old and they'd be in their prime. He might need their help then. He wouldn't be able to smack them in the head or pull his knife on them. You had to have respect for the future, otherwise it might kick away your stick and punch your dentures down your throat.

It took him a couple of questions to hit lucky. Another caravaner told him the Germans weren't here just now, they'd gone into town. But their caravan was here, and they'd be back. When they'd arrived the man had still been outraged, and had told his story about the traffic jam he'd been stuck in.

'I think I'll wait for them,' Hoffer said. Then the caravaner said his wife and children were out walking and was Hoffer by any chance American? The family had gone to Florida last year and loved it, Disney and the beaches and everything. This year they were on a tighter budget, with the recession and everything and him losing his job. He asked if Hoffer wanted a beer? Hoffer reckoned he could bear to listen to a few stories about Florida, so long as the price was right.

'Sure,' he said, 'why not?'

Then the man said something that warmed Hoffer's heart. 'You know,' he started, handing over a can, 'I can't help thinking your face looks familiar. Have you ever been on TV?'

The Germans weren't late. They were a couple in late middle age, showing signs of having earned well and saved well over their lives. They wore pension fund clothes and drove a pension fund car. When Hoffer told them what he wanted, they unlocked their caravan and took him inside. There wasn't much room, but Hoffer managed to look comfortable as he wedged his legs under the table and sat down.

They were bemused by his questions at first. The woman said she just wanted to forget all about it, but her husband had drunk a beer or two and got back in the mood pretty quickly. His English wasn't great, but it was better than Hoffer's delicatessen German. Hoffer eventually focused in on the back car of the three.

'The driver,' said the German, 'large man, not very happy. He would not speak to me a word just. There is some resentment here still, but I do not excuse.'

'Uh, right,' said Hoffer, 'absolutely. Was there a passenger?'

'On the back chair, yes. He talked to the other driver—'

'You mean the driver of the middle car?'

The German nodded. '—and then the other driver went away, but the man on the back chair would not talk with me. He was smile, smile all the time.'

'Smiling,' Hoffer said.

'This is how I say. And I am telling him what is the problem here? But he is smile only.'

'Smiling,' his wife corrected.

'Can you describe this man, sir?'

'Um . . . he wore a suit, shirt, but no tie I don't think. He was not large like the other men. Glasses he wore, round ones, and his hair it was white.'

'Blond,' his wife said. 'White is for old people.'

'What happened?' Hoffer asked. The couple probably hadn't noticed how his attitude had changed.

'It was very confusing. The people from the middle car drove away in the front car. The people from the front car talked to the men in the third car. Then three men pushed the second car out of the way.'

'The blond man stayed in his car?'

'Oh, yes, in his car he stayed. Then all together they drove off, no apology to me.' The man's cheeks had reddened furiously. He was beginning to drift back into his mother tongue. His wife stroked his arm, calming him.

'You've been very helpful,' Hoffer said.

'Something to drink?' asked the woman.

'*Nein, danke,*' said Hoffer. He might have had no training in the language, but it was surprising what you could pick up from a few war films and sandwich bars. He unwedged himself from beneath the table and said his farewells, then got back into his car and lit a cigarette. Kline had confronted the D-Man, and the D-Man had escaped, which either made Kline very stupid or the assassin very clever. No one had been shot, that was the really surprising thing. It warmed Hoffer's heart. If the D-Man was not a close-range performer, then all Hoffer had to do was get close enough to him. The further away he stayed, the more danger he was in. But then again, the closer he got, the more chance there was that he'd come slap bang up against Kline and his commandos.

And he'd already seen what *they* would do at close range. They'd saw your fucking head off and leave it for a surprise.

'What kind of shit am I getting into?' he asked himself, starting his car up and heading towards the south.

Part Three

18

We flew into Boston. I always try to do that, avoid JFK. The place is more like a cattle market than an airport, and they do more checks there than anywhere else. We flew as Michael Weston and Belinda Harrison, since our real passports were the only ones we had. I knew we'd taken a calculated risk. Airlines keep computer records, and anyone can access computer data. That was another reason for flying into Boston: it was a long way from our ultimate destination.

At the airport, I found us a hotel room in town, and we took a taxi. Bel was still disoriented from the flight. It was tough on a beginner, flying backwards through time. We hadn't touched any alcohol on the flight; alcohol stopped you retuning yourself. We watched the films and ate our meals and took any soft drink we were offered. Bel was like a child at first, insisting on a window seat and peering out at the clouds. She made me tell her some things about the USA. She'd never been there before, and only had a passport at all because Max and she had taken a couple of foreign holidays. He never took her with him on business trips.

'His wasn't a very honourable profession, was it?' she said suddenly, causing me to look up from my newspaper. I thought of a lot of answers I could give her, the standard one being something about guns never killing anyone, it was only people who did that.

'More honourable than mine,' I said instead. Then I went back to my reading. Bel was coping in her own way. We'd talked about Max, of course, edging around the actual discovery of his mutilated corpse. Bel had gone through a few transitions, from hysterical to introspective, hyperactive to catatonic. Now she was putting on a good act of being herself. It *was* an act though. When we were together in private, she was different. I tried not to show how worried I was. If I needed her to be anything this trip, I needed her reliable.

It was a good flight. There were a couple of babies on board, but they were up at the bulk-head and didn't cry much anyway. Some children nearer us went through a bored stage, but their parents and the aircrew were always prepared with new games, toys, and drinks.

It would have been a good time for me to do some thinking, but in the event I didn't think too much about what we were doing. I had a very vague plan, and maybe if I thought it through too hard it would begin to look mad or full of holes. So instead I read old news, and did some crosswords, showing Bel how you worked out the answers from cryptic clues. That part was easy: the flight, getting past customs and immigration (tourists didn't even need proper visas these days), finding a hotel . . . it was all easy.

But by the time we reached the hotel, just off Boston Common, I realised I was mentally exhausted. I needed rest and relaxation, if only for a few hours. So I closed the curtains and undressed. Bel had slept a little on the plane, and wanted to go out exploring. I didn't argue with her.

She woke me up a couple of hours later and told me how she'd walked around part of the Common, and seen where they used to make some TV series, and then walked up and down some beautiful cobbled streets, and seen inside a gold-domed building, and wandered into the Italian part of town . . .

'You must walk fast,' I said, heading for the shower. She followed me into the bathroom. I hadn't heard half of it. I'd given her fifty dollars and she'd used some of it to buy herself a meal and some coffee.

'I had a hot dog and some Boston baked beans.'

'Yum yum.'

She deflated only slowly. When I came back from the shower she was flicking channels on the remote TV, finding episodes of *Star Trek* and other old reruns, plus the usual talk shows and sports, and the cable shopping and Christ channels.

'Can you turn the volume down?'

'Sure.' She seemed to enjoy the shows just as much without the sound. 'There are a lot of adverts, aren't there? I mean, they even put them between the end of the programme and the closing credits.'

I looked at her and tried out a sympathetic smile, but she was back watching TV again. I knew what she needed; she needed a period of calm, reflective mourning. The problem was, we couldn't afford that luxury. We had to keep moving.

I was making a phone call. Somewhere in Texas, I got an answering machine. I decided to leave a message.

'Spike, it's Mike West. I'm here on a brief trip. This is just to warn you I have another shopping list. I'll be there in a couple of days, all being well.' I didn't leave a contact number.

'Spike?' Bel said.

'That's his name.'

She went back to her TV stupor. A little later she fell asleep, lying on the bed, her head propped up on the pillows. The remote was still in her hand.

I felt a little better, though my nose was stuffy. I went out and walked around. My brain told me it was the middle of the night, but in Boston it was mid-evening. I found a bar with the usual shamrocks on the wall and draught Guinness. Everyone was watching a baseball game on the large-screen TV. There was a newspaper folded on the bar, so I read that and sipped my drink. Drive-by shootings had gone out of fashion; either that or become so prolific they weren't news any more. News so often *was* fashion. Car-jackings were still news, but it had to be a particularly nice model of car to make a story.

Gun stories were everywhere. People were trying to ban them, and the National Rifle Association was giving back as good as it got. Only now even the President was pro-legislation to curb gun ownership, and a few states had made it an offence for minors to carry handguns. I had to read that sentence twice. In some cities, it turned out, one in five kids took a gun to school with them, along with their books and lunch-box. I closed the paper and finished my drink.

I knew what Spike would say: Welcome to gun heaven.

The barman was asking me if I wanted another, and I did want another. He took a fresh glass from the chiller and poured lager into it, only here it was called beer, and dark beer – proper beer – existed only sparsely, usually in trendy bars near colleges. I couldn't remember how easy it was to buy beer in Boston. I didn't know whether off-licences existed and were licensed to sell at night. Legislation differed from state to state, along with rates of tax and just about everything else. There were no off-licences, for example, they were called package stores and were government run. At least, that seemed right when I thought it. But my brain was shutting down transmissions for the night. I was trying to think about anything but Bel. In seeing her grief, I was face to face with a victim. I'd killed so many people . . . I'd always been able to think of them without humanising them. But they were drifting around me now like ghosts.

I drank my drink and left. There was a beer advert pinned to the door of the bar as I opened it. It read, 'This is as good as it gets'.

I thought about that on the way back to the hotel.

Next morning we went to the Amtrak Station and took a train to New York. Bel got her window seat and became a child again. She was actually well prepared for some aspects of 'the American experience', since back in the UK she watched so much American TV. She knew what 'sidewalk' and 'jay-walking' meant. She knew a taxi was a 'cab', and that chips were 'fries' while crisps were 'chips'. She even knew what Amtrak was, and squeezed my arm as, nearing the end of the trip, she started to catch glimpses of the Manhattan skyline behind the dowdier skyline of the endless suburbs. Upstate New York had just been countryside, and she could see countryside anywhere. She couldn't always see Manhattan.

Our hotel in Boston was part of a chain, and I'd already reserved a room at their Manhattan sister. We queued for a boneshaker yellow cab and tried not to let it damage our internal organs. The hotel was on 7th and 42nd Street. Outside, spare-change hustlers were being told where to get off by merchants trying to sell cheap trinkets, scarves and umbrellas. The sun was hazy overhead. More men shuffled around or stood in doorways, oblivious to the traffic and pedestrians speeding past. I practically had to push Bel through the hotel door.

The reception area was like a war zone. A coach party had just arrived and were checking in, while another consignment of tourists attempted to check out. The two groups had converged, one telling the other useful tips and places of interest. We took our luggage through to the restaurant.

'Two coffees, please,' I told the waitress.

'You want coffee?'

'Please.'

'Anything with that?'

'Just milk for me,' said Bel. The waitress looked at her.

'Nothing to eat, thanks,' I told her. She moved off.

'Remember,' I said to Bel, 'we're only here the one night, so don't start going tourist on me. If you want to see around, fine, I'll do my bit of business and we can go sight-seeing together. What do you fancy: museums, galleries, shopping, a show, the World Trade Center?'

'I want to take a horse and carriage around Central Park.'

So we took a ride around Central Park.

But first, there was my business. My safe deposit box was held in discreet but well-protected premises on Park Avenue South, just north of Union Square. I telephoned beforehand and told them I'd be coming. Bel insisted that we walk it, either that or take the subway. We did both, walking a few blocks and then catching a train.

At Liddle Trusts & Investments, we had to press a door buzzer, which brought a security guard to the door. I told him who I was and we were ushered inside, where my passport was checked, my identity confirmed, and we were led into a chamber not unlike the one in Knightsbridge. Bel had to wait here, while the assistant and I went to the vault. It took two keys, his and mine, to open my safe. He pulled out the drawer and handed it to me. I carried it back through to the chamber and placed it on the table.

'What's inside?' Bel asked.

The drawer had a hinged top flap, which I lifted. I pulled out a large wad of dollar bills, fifties and twenties. Bel took the money and whistled softly. I next lifted out a folded money-belt.

'Here,' I said, 'start putting the money into this.'

'Yes, sir. What else have you got?'

'Just these.'

The box was empty, and I held in my hand a bunch of fake American documents. There was a passport, social security card, medical card, various state gun and driving licences, and a few other items of ID. Bel looked at them.

'Michael West,' she said.

'From now on, that's who I am, but don't worry about it, you won't have any trouble.' I smiled. 'My friends still call me Michael.'

She packed some cash into the belt. 'No guns or anything? I was expecting at the very least a pistol.'

'Later,' I said.

'How much later?'

I looked at her. 'Not much.'

'Good.'

I sat down beside her. I could see that Manhattan's charms had failed to take her mind off the fact of Max's murder. I took her hands in mine.

'Bel, why don't you stay here?'

'You think I'd be safer?'

'You could do some sightseeing, have a bit of a break. You've been through a lot.'

Her face reddened. 'How dare you say that! Somebody killed my father, and I want to look them in the face. Don't think you can leave me behind, Michael, because you can't. And if you try it, I'll scream your name from the chimney-pots, so help me.'

'Bel,' I said, 'they don't have chimney-pots here.'

She didn't grace this remark with a reply.

We took a cab back towards Central Park. The driver reckoned we could find a horse and carriage near Columbus Circle. Bel had bought a tiny foldaway map of the island. She kept looking at it, then at the real streets, her finger pointing to where we were on the map.

'It's all so crammed in, isn't it?'

This was before she saw Central Park.

The park was looking at its best. There were joggers, and nannies pushing prams, and people walking their dogs, and throwing frisbees or baseballs at one another, and arranging impromptu games of baseball and volleyball, and eating hot dogs while they sat on benches in the sunshine. She asked me if I'd ever walked all the way round the park.

'No, and I doubt anyone else has. Further north, the park hits Harlem.'

'Not so safe?'

'Not quite.'

Our coach-driver had asked if we wanted a blanket or anything, but we didn't need one. Our horse didn't scare easily, which was a blessing, considering the number of cars and cabs crossing town through the park. Bel squeezed my hand.

'Tell me something, Michael.'

'What sort of thing?'

'Something about yourself.'

'That sounds like a line from a film.'

'Well, this is like living in one. Go on, tell me.'

So I started talking, and there was something about the sound the horse's hooves made on the road, something hypnotic. It kept me talking, made me open up. Bel didn't interrupt once.

I was born near an Army camp in England. My father was an Army officer, though he never rose as far as he would have liked. We moved around a lot. Like a lot of forces kids, I made friends quickly, only to lose them again when either they or I moved. We'd write for a little while, then stop. There was always a lot to do on the camps – films, shows, sports and games, clubs you could join – but this just set us apart from all the other children who didn't live on or near the camp. I used to bruise easily, but didn't think anything of it. Sometimes if I bumped myself, there'd be swelling for a few weeks, and some pain. But I never told anyone. My father used to talk about how soldiers were taught to go 'through the pain barrier', and I used to imagine myself pushing against it, like it was a sheet of rubber, until I forced my way through. Sometimes it would take a few plasters before a cut knee or elbow would heal. My mother just thought I picked off the scabs, but I never did. My father had to take me to the doctor once when I bit the tip off my tongue and it wouldn't stop bleeding.

Then one day I had to have a dental extraction. The dentist plugged the cavity afterwards, but I just kept on bleeding, not profusely, just steadily. The dentist tried putting some sour stuff on my gums, then tried an adrenaline plug, and finally gave me an injection. When that didn't work – I was on my fourth or fifth visit by now – he referred me to a specialist, whose tests confirmed that I was a mild haemophiliac. At first this gave me a certain stature within my peer group, but soon they stopped playing with me. I became an onlooker merely. I read up on haemophilia. I was lucky in two respects: for one thing, I was a mild sufferer; for another, I'd been born late enough in the century for them to have made strides in the treatment of the disease. Factor VIII replacement has only been around since the early 1970s, before that you were treated with cryo. Acute sufferers have a much harder time than me. They can bleed internally, into joints, the abdomen, even the brain. I don't have those problems. If I'm going for an operation or for dental treatment, they can give me an injection of a clotting agent, and everything's fine. It's a strange sort of disease, where women can be carriers but not sufferers. About one man in 5,000 in the UK is a haemophiliac, that's 9,000 of us. Not so long ago, nobody bothered testing blood donors for HIV. That led to over 1,200 haemophiliacs being treated with a lethal product. Over 1,200 of us, men and boys, now HIV positive and doomed.

A similar thing happened in France. They gave contaminated clotting factors to children, then tried to hush it up. I was in such a rage when that happened, such a black rage. I almost went out and picked off those responsible . . . only who was responsible? It was human error, no matter how sickening. That's one reason I won't do a hit in a Third World country, not unless the money is very good. I'm afraid I might be injured and treated with contaminated Factor VIII. I have dreams about it sometimes. There are rigorous checks these days, but does every country check, does every country screen and purify? I'm not sure. I can never be sure.

I carry my works with me everywhere, of course, my syringes and powdered clotting factor and purified water. I'm supposed to visit a Haemophilia Centre when I need a doctor or dentist, and for a yearly check-up. The blood products we haemophiliacs use can contain all sorts of contaminants, leading to liver damage, hepatitis, cirrhosis . . . Then there's the bleeding, which can lead to severe arthritis. (Imagine an assassin with arthritis.) Between five and ten percent of us develop inhibitors, antibodies which stop the Factor VIII from working. Like I say, it's a strange disease. We can't have intramuscular injections or take aspirin. But things are always getting better. There's DDAVP, a synthetic product which boosts Factor VIII levels, and now there's even properly synthetic Factor VIII, recombinant Factor VIII they call it. It's like 8SM and Monoclate P, but created in the lab, not from blood. No contaminants, that's the hope.

Meanwhile, there *is* a cure for haemophilia: liver transplant. Only at present it's more dangerous than the disease itself. There will come a cure; it'll come by way of genetic research. They'll simply negate the affected chromosome.

As you can tell, haemophilia has had a massive impact on my life. It started as soon as the disease was diagnosed. My parents blamed themselves. There was no family history of the disease, but in about a third of cases there never is; there's just a sudden spontaneous mutation in the father's sperm. That's how it was with me. My parents, especially my mother, treated me like a china wedding present, as though I could only be brought out on special occasions. No more rough games with the other boys – she made sure the other parents knew all about haemophilia. My father spent more time away from me, at the shooting range. So I followed him there and asked him to teach me. A pistol first, and later a rifle. To stop me bruising my shoulder, he had my mother make a little cushion to wedge behind the stock. I still use that cushion.

My mother was opposed to the whole enterprise, but could never stand up to my father. It was a couple of years before I could beat him. I don't know whether his eyes were getting worse, or his aim less steady, or it was just that I was getting better. When I finally left home, I left it as a marksman.

I'd always been clever at school, and ended up at a university, but I didn't last long. After that there were dead-end jobs, jobs which gave me a lot of time to myself. I worked in a library, then in a couple of bookshops, and eventually got a great job working with kayak rentals in the Lake District. Only that fell through when my employers discovered I was a haemophiliac. They said the job was too risky, I'd become a liability.

Was it any wonder I couldn't hold down a job? The only place I wanted to be was on the range. I joined gun clubs and shot competitively. I even went hunting on a few occasions, looking for a new challenge. Then I met a disarming man called Holly MacIntyre. He swore this was his real name. Friends of his called him 'Mad Dog' MacIntyre. He was huge and bull-headed with cropped hair silvering above the ears. His eyes were bulbous and red-rimmed, like he spent too long in chlorinated swimming pools. He was always ready for aggro, and sometimes initiated it for its own sake. He reminded me of a rugby league forward.

Holly had known my father, and he'd seen me shoot a few times. He was by this time long out of the armed forces and working in what he called a 'security capacity' for a number of countries, though he couldn't name them. In fact, he was a mercenary, leader of a gang of about a dozen men who could be bought, who would go anywhere in the world and train any rag-tag rabble for a price. Mad Dog was on the lookout for fresh blood.

I told him he couldn't have mine, and explained why.

'Is that all that's stopping you?' he said. 'Christ, you could still be useful to me.'

I asked him how.

'Sniper, my boy. Sniper. Put you up a tree and leave you there. You'd be nice and cosy, no cuts or bruises, nobody'd know you were there. All you'd do is pick 'em off as they came into sight.'

'Pick off who?'

'The fucking enemy, of course.'

'And who would they be?'

He leaned close to me and hissed whisky. 'Whoever you like!'

I turned down his offer, but not before he'd introduced me to a few people who were later to prove useful. See, at this time I was a military groupie. I liked to hang around with squaddies and old soldiers, with anyone who shared my background and belief system. I knew which pubs and clubs to go to, which gyms. I knew where some weekend shoot was going to be. These shoots, they weren't paintball or grouse or a few hoary old foxes. They were held in secret, far away from humanity, where you could make a big noise and nobody'd hear you. I used to take bets. They'd place a coin upright on the bonnet of a car, and there'd be someone in the car with his hand by the bonnet-release. At a given signal, I'd have to hit the coin before the bonnet sprang open.

Everyone loved me. But I knew I was turning into a sideshow. Worse than that, I was becoming a freak. So I did something about it. I made myself a life plan. It didn't happen overnight; I read books and went travelling. I knew three things: I was bored, I was poorer than I wanted to be, and I had a skill.

I started small, shooting a few rats I bought from a pet shop. That wasn't very satisfactory: I'd nothing against the rats, and nothing to gain from shooting them. I found I actually liked them better than I liked most of the people around me. I don't like people really, I'm just very good at pretending. I did some hunting in the USA, and that was better than shooting rats. Then one night in New York, I picked off a junkie from my darkened hotel room. They were standing in an alley six floors below me. I reasoned that they didn't have long to live anyway, the life expectancy of a junkie on the New York streets being slightly less than that of your average rat. From then on, it got easier.

I went back to see Mad Dog, only he was somewhere in Africa, and this time he didn't come back. But I knew other people I could talk to, other people who knew what I needed to know. It was six months before I got my first contract. They were expecting me to hit the victim on the head and bury him in Epping Forest. Instead, I took him out from four hundred yards and created an immediate news story. My employers decided this was okay, too. I was paid, and my name was passed along. I knew I wouldn't be working for the Salvation Army. But then I wasn't killing any nuns and priests either. It was only after a few hits that I decided anyone was fair game. It isn't up to the executioner to pronounce guilt or innocence. He just makes sure the instruments are humane.

I noticed that Bel was sitting like a block of stone beside me.

'Sorry,' I said. 'But I'm not telling you anything you didn't already know.'

'Michael, you've spoken for so long, and yet you've said almost nothing.'

'What?'

'Can we go get something to drink?'

'Sure.'

I told the driver to take us back now. We passed another carriage on the way. There were some Japanese tourists in the back. While the drivers exchanged bored looks, the Japanese videoed us, waving and grinning as they did. We looked like a couple weary of their life together, and reeling from yet another spat.

'You know,' Bel said, 'you've never asked me about myself. That's strange. When I've gone out with men before, they've always ended up asking me about myself. How old are you, Michael?'

'My passports say thirty-five.' We were lying in bed together. We hadn't made love, our bodies weren't even touching. The silent TV was playing.

'And you've never been married, never had a steady girlfriend?'

'There've been a few.'

'How many?'

'I don't know.'

'A few hundred? A few dozen?'

'Just a *few*. Christ, Bel.' I threw off the cover and stood up. The air conditioning was whirring away, blowing cool air over me.

'Look,' I said, 'I'm not . . . I never said I was much good at this . . . this sort of thing.'

'Do you hear me complaining?'

'Okay, I'll ask you something about yourself.'

She smiled sadly. Her eyebrows were beautiful. Her lips were beautiful. 'Don't bother,' she said. 'Ask me some other time when I'm not expecting it.'

Then she sat up and started watching TV, disappearing back into herself.

The next morning we flew to New Mexico.

I wasn't going to buy a car in New York. Nobody buys a car second hand in New York if they can help it. The cars are rustier than elsewhere, with more miles on the clock (even if they show *less* miles) and steeper price tags. You either buy on the west coast or you buy in New Mexico, Texas, somewhere like that. We bought in Albuquerque.

Bel was right: the blond man and his team might have no trouble picking up our trail again. From flight and hotel information, they could trace us as far as New York. But Michael West, not Michael Weston, had paid for the flights to Albuquerque, and the name on his companion's ticket was Rachel Davis. I was taking all these precautions when all the blond smiler from Oban had to do was head directly to the Olympic Peninsula and wait for us there. That was okay; I just didn't want him intercepting me. This way, I might get at least one good shot in first.

We didn't linger in Albuquerque. My New Mexico ID and a bundle of cash bought us a fast car. It was a Trans-Am, just right for the trip ahead. I'd picked up a few small ads and car ads magazines from the first newsagent's in town, and we sat in a diner while I scoured them. I ringed half a dozen and went to the pay-phone. The first number I called, the owner was at work and his wife said I'd have to see the car when he was around. I hit the jackpot with the second number. I was talking to a drawling mechanic called Sanch who was mad about 'shit-kickers' (his term for fast cars) and was selling this Trans-Am because he wanted to buy a beautiful old Firebird with a paint job 'to die for, man'.

He was so keen to sell, he picked us up outside the diner in a pickup truck and took us back to his three-storey house along a dirt road in what seemed a nice middle-class neighbourhood.

'I fix all the neighbourhood cars, man, they bring them all to me.'

It looked like half the neighbourhood cars were parked right outside Sanch's house, mostly in bits. He kept his best models in the garage, including another, highly-tuned Trans-Am. I'd rather have had this one, but the one he was selling sounded sweet too. I looked at the engine, and we took it for a spin. It was white, and the interior was a bit grotty, plus it was missing quarter of a fender. The engine was clean though, and it had a hi-fi. He brought the price down another $1,000 for cash and I asked if I could use his bathroom.

While Bel enjoyed a cold beer and the collection of nude calendars in Sanch's kitchen, I unzipped my money belt and took out the notes. Back in the kitchen, Sanch had already filled in the relevant details on his ownership papers.

'Hey,' he said, handing me a beer, 'I meant to ask you, what you gonna use the car for?'

'Just some driving.'

'That's the way to see America.'

'Yes, it is,' I said, handing over the money. He examined it, but didn't count it.

'Looks about right. Here, I got something for you.' It took him a little while to find what he was looking for. It was a Rand-McNally Road Atlas, its covers missing, corners curled and oily. But the pages were all there. 'I got about half a dozen of these things laying around. After all, you don't want to get lost between here and there.'

I thanked him, finished the beer, and put my part of the ownership document in my pocket.

Then we drove to Lubbock.

It served as a nice introduction to American driving. Long straight roads, the occasional shack planted in the middle of nowhere, and sudden towns which disappeared into the dust you left behind. The car was behaving, and, lacking a TV, Bel was communing with the radio. She liked the preachers best, but the abrasive phone-in hosts weren't far behind. One redneck was praising the gun.

'Guns made America, and guns will *save* America!'

'You're loon-crazy, my friend,' said the DJ, switching to another call.

Albuquerque is only about 250 miles from Lubbock. We could do it inside a day easy, but we weren't in any particular rush. When we stopped at a place called Clovis and I still got an answering machine in Lubbock, we decided to check into a motel. The place we chose was choice indeed, twenty dollars a night and decorated in 1950s orange. Orange linoleum, orange lampshades, orange bedspread. We looked to be the only guests, and the man in the office could have given Norman Bates some tips. He rang up our fee on an ancient till and said he was sorry about the swimming pool. What he meant was, the swimming pool wasn't finished yet. It was a large circular concrete construction, waiting to be lined. It was unshaded and sat right next to the road. I couldn't see many holidaymakers using it. There was a hot wind blowing, but the motel boasted an ice machine and another machine dispensing cold cola.

'The TV hasn't got cable!' Bel complained, already a seasoned traveller in the west. Along the route we'd been offered water beds and king-size beds and adult channels and HBO, all from noticeboards outside roadside motels. Bel wasn't too enamoured of our bargain room, but I was a lot more sanguine. After all, the owner hadn't made us fill in a registration card and hadn't taken down the number of our licence plate. There would be no record that we'd ever stayed here.

'Let's go do the sights,' I said.

We cruised up and down the main and only road. A lot of the shops had shut down, their windows boarded up. There were two undistinguished bars, another motel the other end of town with a red neon sign claiming No Vacancies, though there were also no signs of life, a couple of petrol stations and a diner. We ate in the diner.

There was a back room, noisy from a party going on there. It was a fireman's birthday, and his colleagues, their wives and girlfriends were singing to him. Our waitress smiled as she came to take our order.

'I'll have the ham and eggs,' Bel said. 'The eggs over easy.' She smiled at me. 'And coffee.'

I had the chicken dinner. There was so much of it, Bel had to help me out. Since there was no phone in our room, I tried Lubbock again from the diner, and again got the answering machine. After the meal, we stopped at the petrol station and bought chocolate, some cheap cola, and a four-pack of beer. I had a look around and saw that the station sold cool-boxes too. I bought the biggest one on the shelf. The woman behind the till wiped the dust off with a cloth.

'Fill that with ice for you?'

'Please.'

Then I added another four-pack to our bill.

Next morning we filled the cool-box with ice, beer and cola, and had breakfast at the diner. The same waitress was still on duty.

'Good party?' Bel asked.

'Those guys,' clucked the waitress. 'Practically had to hose them down to get them out of here.'

It was ten o'clock and already hot when we headed out of town. One thing Sanch hadn't told us about the Trans-Am, its air conditioning wasn't a hundred percent. In the end, I turned it off and we drove with the windows down. At another service station, Bel bought some tapes, so we didn't have to put up with the radio any more. The drivers on these long two-lane stretches of Texas were kind to a fault. If you went to overtake someone, the car in front would glide into the emergency lane so you could pass without going into the other carriageway. Even lorries did it, and expected you to do the same for them. Not that many people passed us. We cruised at between 70 and 80 and I kept an eye open for radar cops. Every time we passed a car or lorry, Bel would wave to it from her window.

This was the most relaxation I'd had in ages. I'd driven part of the way across the USA before, and had enjoyed it then too. As Bel said, you became your favourite film star in your own road movie. More importantly from our point of view, no one could trace your route.

Lubbock, birthplace of Buddy Holly, was a prairie sprawl with a museum dedicated to ranching. The museum boasted a large collection of types of barbed wire, plus a rifle display that took the breath away. That was all I could tell you about Lubbock. The last time I'd been here, I had failed to find a centre to the place, but that's not so surprising in American cities. Last time, I stayed in a run-down motel near the Buddy Holly statue. But after last night, I reckoned Bel would object, so we found a new-looking hotel just off the highway and registered there.

American hotels and motels used to ask for your ID, but these days all they did was ask you to fill in a registration card. So it was easy to give fake names, fake car details and fake licence. Bel liked the room: it had Home Box Office on cable, plus in-house pay-movies. It also had a king-size bed and a telephone. I called the number one last time, then decided to head out there anyway.

'So do I get to know now?' Bel said as we got back into the Trans-Am.

'What?'

'Who you've been trying to call.'

'A guy called Jackson. Spike Jackson. You'll like him.'

Spike lived not far from Texas Tech and the Ranching Heritage Centre. He'd taken me there on my previous visit. There was a dual carriageway, with single-storey shops along one side, and a couple of lanes off. Up one of these lanes, at the end of the line, was Spike's place. I hoped he wasn't out of the country on business. I knew he did most of his business from home.

We came off the dual carriageway and drove alongside the shops. Bel spotted a western-wear emporium, and wanted us to stop. I dropped her off and said I'd be back in five minutes, whatever happened. She disappeared through the shop door.

There were a couple of cars parked outside the two-storey house, but that didn't mean anything. Like all 'good old boys', Spike usually had a few cars hanging around. He owned at least two working cars, and sometimes bought another dud, which he'd tinker with for a while before towing it to the junk yard. I revved the Trans-Am a couple of times to let him know he had a visitor. I didn't want him nervous.

But there was no sign of life as I walked up the steps to the front door. There was a screened-in porch either side of the door, with chairs and a table and a swing-bench. Spike hadn't had the maid in recently; there were pizza boxes and beer cans everywhere. I rang the bell again, and heard someone hurtling towards the door. It flew open, and a teenage girl stood there. Before I had a chance to say anything, she waved for me to follow her, and rushed back indoors again.

'I'm about three thou off the high score!' she called. I followed her upstairs and into a bedroom. It looked like a radio shack. There were electronics everywhere. Sprawling across a makeshift table (an old door laid flat with packing-cases for legs) was a computer system.

The girl could have been anywhere between fifteen and eighteen. She was thin and leggy, her black denims like a second skin. She'd tied her thick red hair carelessly behind her head, and wore a black T-shirt advertising some rock band. She was back in front of the computer, using the joystick to fire a killing beam at alien crustaceans. Two speakers had been wired to the computer, enhancing the sound effects.

'Who are you anyway?' she asked.

'I'm a friend of Spike's.'

'Spike's not here.'

'When will he be back?' As the screen went blank and a fresh scenario came up, she took time to wipe her hands on her denims and look at me.

'What are you, Australian?'

'English.'

'Yeah? Cool.'

I was tempted to pull the plug on her game, but you could never tell with teenagers. She might draw a gun on me. I had to attract her attention somehow.

'Spike never used to like them so young.'

'Huh?'

'His girlfriends.'

She smirked. 'Not!' She had dimples and a faceful of freckles, a pale face which seldom saw the sunshine outside. The curtains in her room were drawn closed. She'd stuck photos on them; film stars mostly. 'I'm not Spike's girlfriend.' She rolled her eyes at the thought. 'Jee-zuss!'

I sat down on her unmade bed. 'Who are you then?'

'I shouldn't have let you in, should I? I mean, you could be any-fucking-body, right? You could be a rapist, or even worse a cop.'

'I'd have to be an English cop, wouldn't I?'

'Not. I *know* who you are. Spike's told me about you.'

'Who am I then?'

'He calls you "Wild West".'

I smiled. This was true. She was looking at me again. 'Am I right?'

'Yes, you're right. I need to see Spike.'

'Well, he's not here. Look at that, eight million seven hundred thou.'

'The high score?'

'You bet.'

'I'm a great believer in quitting while you're ahead.'

'Uh-uh, bud.' She shook her head. 'I'm headed all the way to annihilation.'

'Where is Spike?'

'You're getting boring, man. He's on a shoot.'

'A shoot?'

'Down towards Post. It's an hour's drive.'

'Can you give me directions?'

'Sure, head south-east out of town—'

'On a piece of paper?'

She smirked again. 'I'm an American teenager, we don't *write*.'

'I'm going to pull the plug on your little game.'

'Do that and you'll be sorry.' There was no humour in her voice, but I'd run out of patience. I found a four-way adaptor on the floor and picked it up, my hand clenched around the first cable.

'Okay, man, you win.' She hit a button on the keyboard and the screen froze. 'This thing's got a sixty-second pause.' She looked for paper, found a paperback novel, tore the back cover from it, and drew a map on the blank side. She threw the map at me and jumped back into her seat.

'Thanks for the hospitality,' I said.

'How hospitable would you be if your parents kicked you out?'

She was asking me to ask her something. My only weapon was to walk away, and that's what I did.

Back at the store, Bel had bought a pair of boots for herself. They had shiny metal tips and ornate red stitching on black leather. She'd bought a new pair of denims to go with them. She almost looked like a native, which was no bad thing. Maybe that was the reason she'd bought the stuff. Or maybe she was just trying to shed her old clothes, her English clothes. Clothes from a home she no longer wanted.

I handed her the map as we drove off. She looked at the drawing, then at what it was written on.

'"Mainframe bandits",' she read, '"are on the loose in hyperspace, and only you can stop them, playing the role of Kurt Kobalt, Innerspace Investigator, with your beautiful but deadly assistant Ingress".' She looked at me. 'Is that us, do you think?'

'Not.'

19

It wasn't that easy to find the shoot.

The map wasn't wrong in itself, but some of the roads were little more than dirt tracks, and we doubted we were ever going to end up anywhere. As a result, we lost our bottle once or twice and headed back to the main road, only to find we'd been on the right road all the time.

At last we came to a lonely spot, a wilderness of hillocks and valleys. There was no habitation for miles, yet cars and vans had gathered here. Men and women were standing around guzzling from cans. That worried me straight off: guns and alcohol – the worst marriage.

As soon as we stepped out of the car we could smell it: the air was thick with cordite. We couldn't tell if there was smoke or not, we'd kicked up so much dust along the track. I was glad I'd bought the Trans-Am and not some anonymous Japanese car. These were Trans-Am people. There were a couple more parked nearby, along with Corvette Stingrays and Mustangs and a couple of Le Barons.

Somebody yelled 'The line is hot!' and there was a sudden deafening fusillade from behind the nearest rise. Instinctively, Bel ducked, raising a knowing smile from the beer-drinkers. The sound of firing continued for fifteen seconds, then died. There were whoops and sounds of applause. A man came up to us, beer can in hand.

'It's six bucks each, buddy.' I was handing over the money when I heard an unmistakable voice.

'You old dawg, what in the hell are you doing here?' It was Spike Jackson. He had a baseball cap on his head, turned so the shield was to the back. He took it off and ran a hand through his hair. He had thick wavy brown hair swept back to display a high prominent forehead. He wore steel-rimmed glasses, sneakers and old denims, and a T-shirt with the sleeves ripped off, showing rounded muscular shoulders and thick upper arms. He stopped suddenly, arched his back to the sky and threw open his arms.

'This is gun heaven, man! I died and went to gun heaven. Didn't I always used to tell you that, Wild West? That's what this country is, man.'

His audience voiced their agreement. Now he came up to us and, arms still open wide, closed them around me in a hug that lifted me off the ground.

'Wild West, man, how in the hell are you doing?' He let me down and gave Bel a smile, touching his crotch for luck, then turned back to me. 'You old *dawg*, you! Come on, let's go where the action is.' He went to a stack of beer cans and pulled off a few, tossing one to me, but opening Bel's and handing it to her with a bow from the waist.

'Name's Spike Jackson, ma'am, and this one's for you.'

Bel took the beer but didn't say anything. Spike led us around to where, as he'd put it, the action was. In another clearing people milled around examining the damage the latest fusillade had done to a couple of wrecked cars, a lean-to shack, and an array of crates and bottles and cans. Fresh targets were being set up by sweating volunteers.

I knew what this was, of course. Spike had taken me to a Texan shoot before. Forty or fifty enthusiasts would gather together and fire off a range of weapons. You could spectate, or you could participate. A couple of arms dealers, who supplied much of the arsenal, would then take orders. I could see the dealers. They were short and dumpy and wearing holsters under drenched armpits. The day was fiercely hot, and I half wished I'd bought a stetson; or at the very least a baseball cap.

Spike never *officially* organised these shoots, because he wasn't officially a gun dealer. He worked the black market, and got a lot of his stuff from Army bases throughout Texas. He bought from overseas too, though. He just didn't do any of this legally.

'Look at this,' he told me. He had led us to where today's arms were displayed, spread on sheets of plastic on the ground. It looked like an arsenal captured from the Iraqis. Spike had picked up a Browning anti-aircraft gun. It showed off his bronzed arm muscles. 'Something for the lady,' he said, laughing.

I laughed back, and Bel gave me a disgusted look.

'We got your M16s, your AK-47s and 74s.' Spike pointed out the most interesting items. 'Look here, we even got something from Finland or Sharkland or someplace, a Varmint.'

'Valmet,' I corrected. 'The M62.'

'Whatever. We got armour-piercing ammo you wouldn't believe, man. Look here, the M39B. Use it in a handgun, it'll go through a bullet-proof vest. Get 'em while you can. Black Talon bullet here, you ever hear of it?'

'It expands on impact,' Bel said coolly, 'and has these sharp little edges.'

Spike opened his eyes and mouth wide. 'Lookee here, we got us an expert! It's the quiet ones you have to watch out for!' Then he went back to his inventory. 'It's all cute stuff, and believe me we got *everything*.'

'So what would you suggest?'

Spike stopped his spiel and looked at me. He was wavering, but it was an impersonation of a drunk rather than an effect of drink. His blue eyes were clear.

'Well now, depends what you need it for.'

'We need a variety of things. A sniper rifle, a couple of pistols, and maybe an assault rifle, something serious.'

Spike nodded thoughtfully, then counted off on his fingers. 'Sniper rifle for long range, pistol for close range, and assault rifle for taking on the Seventh Cavalry.'

'You might not be far off.'

He finished his beer and crushed the can, throwing it on to the ground. 'What's this "we" shit, man?'

I nodded in Bel's direction. Spike stared at me, working out if I was serious, then he shook his head.

'Maybe we better discuss this,' he said.

I knew he wouldn't want to discuss anything out in the open. Texas had lax gun laws, but that didn't mean illegal dealers were encouraged. After the Waco siege, even Texans had started to ask questions about the amount of guns around.

We followed Spike's pick-up truck. Bel said she wanted to drive, so she drove the Trans-Am. I didn't mind her driving at all; two drivers would make the trip north all the faster. Back at his house, Spike yelled up the stairs that he was home, then went into the kitchen and brought out half a dozen refrigerated beers. We made ourselves comfortable on the porch. Bel said she needed the bathroom, and Spike told her where it was. We didn't see her for a while after that.

Spike drank his first beer in silence.

'So who is she?' he said at last.

'A friend.'

'What's her problem?'

'She's in mourning.'

'Mm-hm.' He opened the second beer and wiped sweat from his brow with his forearm. 'So, what's the story, Wild West?'

I shook my head, and he shrugged.

'That's up to you, of course, but if you're looking to buy so much hardware, people are going to be wondering.'

'That's not my problem. My problems start if you can't get the stuff.'

'Man, I can get anything. I just want to be right in my mind about why *you* want it.'

'What is this, new legislation? You have to have a clear conscience after each sale?'

He smiled and shook his head. 'Things are crazy though. We've got doctors telling us guns kill more teenagers than every known disease combined. We've got Clinton, man, the most anti-gun president we've ever *known*. That fucker got the Brady Bill through! We've got the NRA fighting its battle, but not always winning any more. I don't always agree with the NRA, man, you know that. It simply isn't right that minors can carry handguns, no way. But now some states are banning assault weapons, they're limiting how many guns you can buy . . . Forty deaths a day, man, forty a day. I know it's mostly gangs fighting each other, but it's a lot of blood.'

'Maybe you're just getting old, Spike. Either that or Democrat.'

'Wash your mouth, boy! No, I'll tell you what it is, it's ever since Jazz came to stay. Her real name's Jasmine, but she likes Jazz. There are kids she hangs around with, they carry guns, a boy in her class got himself shot. There was a shoot-out at some zoo someplace. She tells me all this, and I just . . .' He shrugged his shoulders and finished beer number two.

'Who is she?' I asked.

'Jazz? She's my niece, man, my sister's kid. Her mom and dad split up, and neither of them was ready to take her with them. Hell, I don't blame my sister, she's just mixed up just now, you know. So I said I'd let Jazz stay here for a while, see if I couldn't give her a less crazy environment, something stable, you know.'

I think I nodded.

'She's a great kid, man, clever too. She's got a computer up in her room, she can do *anything* with that pile of junk. She's some kind of genius, I guess.'

'Can you get me an assault rifle?' I said, smashing into his reverie.

'Hell, yes, just so long as you don't want an ownership licence. Know why they started licensing automatics?' He'd told me before, but I didn't say. 'To stop Dillinger, man, and gangsters like him. They reckoned you could stop those guys by getting the Bureau of Alcohol, Tobacco and Firearms to run background checks. Man, they can hardly check the baseball scores.'

Spike had drunk more than I'd thought. He could ramble on all night, trying to justify his existence and that of the other people around him, trying to make sense of his world. I knew the only place his world made sense was out on the gun range.

'You're staying tonight, right?'

'We've got a hotel.'

'Aw, you could stay here.'

'Thanks, but it's already bought and paid for.' I shrugged my shoulders.

'That's too bad.'

'We can talk more in the morning. How long will it take to get the stuff?'

'I can have it for you tomorrow, I guess. Cash, right?'

'Right.'

'We're talking big numbers here.'

'Let me worry about the money.'

'That's cool.' He looked around. 'Where's your woman?'

'She's not my woman.'

'Oh? Whose is she then?'

'Her own.'

'A ballbreaker?'

'That's not what I said.'

'It's what I hear in your voice. She must've got lost or something.'

We went inside. Bel wasn't lost, she was in Jazz's room, seated at the computer and playing a new game while Jazz gave instructions over her shoulder.

'Time to go, Bel.'

'Five more minutes, Michael.'

Jazz glowered at me. 'If you don't obey him, Bel, he might pull the plug.'

'He'll get a kick in the balls if he does,' Bel said quietly, bringing a spume of laughter from Jazz. Spike mouthed a word at me.

The word was ballbreaker.

We lay in bed naked, damp from our shower, and watched TV. Then Bel did something that surprised me. She turned the TV off and put down the remote.

'Jazz,' she said.

'What about her?'

She turned on her side to face me. 'She's got an incredible computer.'

'Yes?' I started stroking her spine.

'Maybe we could . . . *use* it in some way.'

'How?' I was interested now.

'Keep stroking,' she instructed. 'I don't know how exactly, but you can do things with computers these days, can't you? They're not just for games or glorified typewriting.'

'It's a thought. We'll put it to her.'

'Michael, tell me something. You love guns, don't you?'

'Yes.'

'Why?'

'I don't know. Maybe I can control them.'

'Or control other people with them.'

I shrugged. 'Maybe I should go on one of these chat shows and talk it out of my system.'

She smiled for a moment. 'I hated what was happening out there on that range. Those people were *having fun*. How can it be fun?'

I shrugged again.

'Michael, do you think you love them more than you've ever loved a woman?'

By 'them' she meant guns of course. I thought for a second. 'I wouldn't say that exactly.' She'd turned on to her back, trapping my arm beneath her. Our faces were close.

'Prove it,' she said.

This time when we made love she didn't cry, not on the outside. But there was a rage inside her, and she bucked, punching and clawing at me. Then she stopped suddenly.

'What is it?' I asked after a moment.

'We're going to kill them, aren't we?' Her voice was strangely calm. 'Promise me we're going to kill them.'

Kill them? Jesus, we didn't even know who *they* were.

'Promise,' I whispered. She wanted me to say it louder.

I said it louder.

Spike had invited us round for lunch, which meant barbecued steaks in his 'yard'. The yard was in fact a very long narrow garden, nearly all of it grass, with a wire pen at the bottom where Wilma lived.

'It's a pig,' Bel said when introduced. She was wearing her new denims and cowboy boots with a fresh white T-shirt.

'That's no pig,' said Spike, 'that's a *hawg*. Anyone I don't like, Wilma eats those suckers alive.' He was wearing a plastic cooking-apron and waving a wooden spoon, which he occasionally stuck in his mouth. Then he'd go and stir the barbecue sauce again and add another dash of Tabasco.

Spike's living room was no advert for the bachelor life. There were photos and magazine cuttings covering most of the walls, and you couldn't see the carpet for old engine parts, sports trophies, discarded clothes and memorabilia. Spike collected service-station signs, especially ones made of metal. He also seemed to be going in for full-sized cardboard replicas of his sporting heroes. There was a black basketball player I'd never heard of leaning against one wall, and a baseball pitcher behind the sofa.

'When he's watching a game,' Jazz confided, 'he actually talks to it like it was the real person.' Then she shook her head and went back to her room.

Muffled in black cotton cloth on the sofa were several items for me to look at. Spike, his lips coated orange with sauce, came back in and waved his spoon. 'Gimme a minute and I'll be with you. Bel's gone upstairs with Jazz.'

When he left, I unwrapped the first gun. It was the sniper rifle, a

Remington 700 'Varmint'. It wasn't the military version which Max had offered me, but the commercial version, which meant it was beautifully polished and didn't have a pre-fitted telescopic sight. I'd used one before, last time I'd been in Lubbock. Maybe it was the same gun. It was manufactured in Ilion, New York State, and I knew it was an accurate weapon. It wasn't the greatest sniper gun around, but it would do. The sight was a Redfield. I checked that it was compatible with the mounting plate. Then I opened the second package.

These were the handguns, one pistol and one revolver. The revolver was a Smith & Wesson 547, with the four-inch rather than three-inch barrel. I'd never had much time for revolvers, though I knew Americans loved them, more for what they represented perhaps – the past – than for their modern-day ability.

The pistol felt better. It was another Smith & Wesson, a 559 semi-automatic, steel-framed and heavier than the revolver. It took fourteen rounds of parabellum ammo, but wouldn't accept a silencer. Not that I thought I'd need a silencer, though the option would have been welcome.

I was opening the third package when Spike came in.

'Wait till you see,' he said.

I'd been expecting an M16, but this was a lot shorter, almost a foot shorter in fact. It didn't weigh much more than double the pistol, and I picked it up one-handed.

'It's a Colt Commando,' Spike said. 'It's close to the M16, but the barrel's half the length. The stock's adjustable, see, and there's a flash hider if you want it. It'll take anything from a twenty- to a thirty-round mag. Elite forces use them, man, so you know you're talking quality.'

'Spare me the sales pitch, Spike. It won't take sights.'

He grinned. 'That don't matter, see.'

'Why not?'

'Because they're shit long-range. They don't have the muzzle velocity of an M16. You need the muzzle flash, too, because this thing makes a noise like a Gatling gun. But for close-up action, you can't beat it. Tuck it into your shoulder with the stock retracted and you can fire one-handed, just like Big Arnie!'

'I like that it's compact.'

'Man, you can put it in an overnight bag, nobody's going to know. Shit, the steaks!'

He ran out of the room. I tucked the guns away again and checked what ammo he was giving me. I knew I was going to take everything except the revolver. Bel had shown some interest in being armed, but I wasn't about to encourage her. Whatever the NRA says, if you've got a gun, you're more likely to get shot than if you haven't.

I went upstairs and found Bel and Jazz busy on the computer.

'Go away!' Jazz screamed. So I went away.

Downstairs in the garden I opened another tin of Old Milwaukee. 'So how much?' I said. Spike turned another steak and basted it.

'Oh, well now, let me see . . .'

Which meant he already knew the exact figure he was going to ask. He started pretending to tot up numbers. Then he went into the kitchen and brought out a tub of potato salad Jazz had made earlier.

'She's a sweet little thing really,' Spike said. 'I know you didn't hit it off with her yesterday, she told me last night. She always sits and talks with me at night. Of course, then she hits me for a twenty and takes off till dawn.' He laughed. 'Only kidding. She's usually back home by two.'

'That's all right then.'

'Bel seems nice.'

'I know you didn't hit it off with her yesterday.'

'*Touché*, brother. You know me, I'm called Spike 'cause I'm spikey. You say the two of you aren't doing the devil's business?'

'I don't recall saying that.'

Spike smiled, then worked on the steaks again. 'I get the feeling . . . Man, I'm sorry, you know me, I don't pry or anything. But I get the feeling you're in deep shit.'

'I am.'

He nodded to himself. 'And are you going to get out of it all right?'

'I hope so.'

'Wild West, you shouldn't be taking a civilian along.'

'Bel's not a civilian, Spike. Her father was a casualty.'

'I guess that makes it her war too,' he admitted. 'Only, she don't look the type. But then, neither do you.'

'I've become the type.'

'Yeah, I can see that, partner, but I see something else too. I see you're tired of it. That's dangerous.'

'After this trip, I'm thinking of packing it in.'

'That may not be soon enough, Wild West.'

'Just tell me how much I owe for the guns.'

'Well, what do you want?'

'Everything except the revolver.'

He basted the steaks afresh. 'Need any help?'

I knew what he was offering, he was offering himself. He didn't look at me.

'I appreciate it, Spike, but I don't think so. Now, how much do I owe you?'

'Tell you what, come back and see me when it's over. I'll take the guns off you if you've still got them, and I'll relieve you of that car of yours.'

'The Trans-Am?'

'That's the deal.'

'What if I don't come back?'

'You wouldn't do that to me, man.' He stuck his free hand out, and I shook it. 'Only, I don't want no fresh dents in it, okay?'

'Immaculate,' I said. Then: 'Do you know anyone who fixes air conditioning?'

Spike called a friend, who could look at the Trans-Am that same day. The guy turned up with a friend, and they took the car with them. Spike had already called upstairs three times that the food was ready. It was more than ready by the time Jazz and Bel came downstairs. They looked shiny-faced and excited about something. Bel had her hand on Jazz's shoulder. Jazz was looking younger and prettier than yesterday. Bel had certainly done something to her.

Spike and I were halfway through our steaks.

'Outstanding potato salad,' he told his niece.

'Thanks, Unc.'

Jazz opened beers for Bel and her. They toasted one another.

'Okay, give,' said Spike.

'Wait and see,' said Bel. 'The printer could be busy for some time.'

After which all they wanted to talk about was the food, the car, and the drive which lay ahead. I tried giving Bel my long hard stare, but it didn't so much as nick her. We feasted on meat and beer, and then Jazz announced that there was something she wanted to show me. Bel came too, Spike staying behind to scrape the plates into Wilma's pen.

Upstairs in Jazz's room, paper had spewed from her printer. She started gathering it up, while Bel explained.

'This machine's fantastic, Michael. We got into an information network and asked for stuff about the Disciples. Where was it we went, Jazz?'

'Library of Congress to start with.'

'Yes, Jazz's computer talked to the one in the Library of Congress. Then we went to Seattle. What was the name of that place?'

'The U-Dub,' said Jazz.

'Short for the University of Washington. We talked to their information system, and to one at a newspaper, and lots of other places. It only took *minutes* . . . and see what we got.'

Jazz proudly handed me the pile of printed sheets. There were newspaper reports about the Disciples of Love, a whole bibliography of source material. I should have looked more impressed, but I knew none of this could tell me anything fresh.

'This is the guy,' Jazz said, tapping one sheet. It was a piece by a reporter called Sam T. Clancy.

'He's been looking into the Disciples,' Bel explained. 'And now he's disappeared.'

'Gone into hiding,' Jazz corrected. There was a story about this too. After a near-miss hit and run followed by a near-fatal malfunction of his car's braking system, Sam T. Clancy had gone to ground. His newspaper, the *Post-Intelligencer*, had made it front-page news. Being a newspaper, they'd also printed a photo of the journalist. I couldn't see that exactly helping him go to ground.

'I don't see where this gets us,' I said.

'Come on,' said Bel. 'Someone sets you up, someone gets rid of a reporter in England, now they try to bump off a reporter in Seattle. We need to find this Clancy and talk to him, see what he knows.'

'Do you know the north-west, Bel? The coastline, the islands, the wilderness, the mountains? What do we do, climb to the top of Mount Rainier and yell for him to come see us?'

'Jesus,' said Jazz, 'talk about no spine.'

'Look, I appreciate—'

'No forward planning,' Jazz went on. 'Think artillery's the answer to everything.'

Bel just stood there, lips slightly parted like a ventriloquist.

'Big macho guy, kick down a few doors, fire a few rounds, and suddenly everything becomes clear. *Wrong!*'

'Look, Jazz . . .' But she pushed past me out of the room and took the stairs three at a time. Bel was pouting now, her arms folded.

'She worked hard to get that information. She worked fast and well.'

'I know, Bel.'

'And how hard can it really be to find this reporter? Think about it, Michael. He's a *reporter*. If we turn ourselves into a story, he'll come to *us*.'

I had to admit, she had a point.

We got the car back in A-1 shape. The air conditioning worked. It had been a minor repair, no more. The mechanic had also retuned the car. It purred when I turned the ignition. And all for a hundred dollars cash. We celebrated with a trip to the Ranching Heritage Centre. Bel thought the whole thing was a bore, a distraction: the reconstructed plantation houses and windmills, the steam locomotive, the indoor exhibits.

Me, I went and paid my respects to the Winchesters.

We took Spike and Jazz out for a meal that night, but I didn't drink. There'd be a hard day's drive tomorrow, which was no place for a hangover. But I did have a shot of Jack Daniels to finish the meal, just to placate Spike. After all, I had several thousand dollars' worth of guns in the boot of the Trans-Am, and he hadn't even asked for a down payment.

I didn't ask him again about the chance that I wouldn't make it back. I didn't want to think about it.

Back at the hotel, Bel flaked out on the bed. I went for a walk, and ended up at the Buddy Holly statue. He held his guitar the way a marching man would hold his rifle. Well, almost. I'd settled up for our room, explaining that we'd be leaving at dawn and wouldn't require breakfast. I was glad now we'd booked into somewhere comfortable and clean, if utterly soulless. I didn't know how things would go from here on in.

I went to bed at 11.30, but didn't sleep. I lay there for an hour, ticking off the minutes and assuring myself that Bel was fast asleep. Then I got out of bed and went to the bathroom, where I'd left my clothes. We'd packed before dinner, and I picked my bags up on the way out of the room. I'd thought of leaving a note, but couldn't find the right words. Bel would know what was happening. She'd go to Spike's place. I'd phone her there in the evening.

Out in the car park, the streets were silent. I laid my bags on the ground and searched my pockets for the keys to the Trans-Am. I'd left them back in the room. I said a silent curse and hauled my bags back upstairs. We had a room key each, and I'd left mine at reception. Now I had to pick it up again and take the elevator to the third floor.

I left my bags in the corridor and let myself in. The keys had to be lying on the table next to the television, but I couldn't see them or feel them. Bel's breathing was still deep and regular.

'Looking for these?' a voice said.

I turned around. She was still lying with her head beneath the cover, but one arm was raised and she was waving the keys at me.

'I was just putting some stuff in the car,' I said.

'It can wait.'

'I couldn't sleep.'

'Liar. You were creeping off without me.' She pushed the keys back under her pillow. 'I'd've hated you forever if you'd done it. That's why I couldn't let you do it.'

'You'd be a lot safer here.'

'So would you.'

'Bel, it's not. . .'

'I *know* what it is, Michael.' She sat up in bed, drawing her knees up in front of her. 'And it's okay, I accept it. But I need to see those bastards blasted off the planet. I need to be there.'

I stood for a moment in the dark, trying to understand. Then I brought my bags back in from the corridor and got undressed again.

I woke again at five. Bel woke up too. She didn't complain or say anything more about last night. She just got up and showered, then got dressed.

Before she dressed, she gave me a hug, her eyes squeezed tightly shut.

We stayed that way for a long time.

20

Robert Walkins had a house overlooking Chesapeake Bay, between Washington DC and Baltimore and not too far from Annapolis. It was finished in clapboard which had been given a recent coat of brilliant white paint. The picket fence around the house was white too. You couldn't see much of the place from the road. You had to get out of the car and walk around to what should be the back of the house. In fact, the back of the house was what looked on to the road. The *front* of the house, naturally enough, looked on to the bay. The downstairs seemed to be mostly workshop, garage, play room. A flight of stairs led up to a columned balcony, and that's where the front door was. The Stars and Stripes was fluttering from one of the columns. Hoffer blew his nose again before knocking on the door.

While he waited, he turned and looked out across the long narrow lawn which was broken only by a few mature trees as it swept down to the edge of the bay. He knew erosion was a problem for a lot of these waterfront homes. Each year the Bay crept a little closer to your door. There was some wood lying around, either driftwood or part of some scheme to ward off nature's encroachment. And past it, stretching out on to the Bay, was a plain wooden deck. The day was fine and Hoffer had to squint against the water's reflections as he peered towards the deck.

There was someone there, sitting on a chair with their feet up on a circular wooden table. They lifted a glass to their lips, then placed the glass down on a smaller table next to the chair. From this distance, Hoffer couldn't be sure, but he reckoned it had to be Walkins.

As he walked back down the stairs, he didn't know whether to be relieved or not. He didn't like sitting in Walkins's house. The place gave him the creeps, what with there being no photos of the daughter anywhere, and all those photos and paintings of the wife. So he should feel better, more comfortable, talking to Walkins in the fresh air. Only, he wasn't the outdoors type. He'd sat on Walkins's deck for a few hours one time, the salt wind whipping across him, and afterwards his skin had stung for days and his lungs had tried rejecting the smoke he sucked into them.

He crossed the lawn, slipping his jacket off and slinging it across one shoulder. He was nervous too. Well, meeting your sugar daddy face to face. It was bound to make you nervous.

'Sit down,' Walkins said, eschewing greetings. 'Drink?'

There was a bottle of J&B on the table, along with a bucket of ice and a spare glass. But Hoffer shook his head. He gave a half-yawn, trying to unblock his ears. The flight had done for him again. Goddamned flying.

'How was England?' Walkins asked.

'Like it had just lost the war.'

'We took vacations there occasionally. I liked the people.'

There wasn't much to say to this, so Hoffer stayed quiet. He noticed that Walkins was looking old these days. Maybe it was just that he looked bored: bored of doing nothing all day but waiting for Leo Hoffer to call with news.

'Is he here?' Walkins asked.

'Yeah, he's here.' Hoffer was lighting a cigarette. Walkins didn't mind him smoking out here, so long as he took the stubs home with him. Hoffer never did figure it; the whole of Chesapeake Bay for an ashtray, and he had to take his goddamned stubs home with him.

'How do you know?'

'I'm paid to know, sir.' Hoffer tried to get comfortable on the chair. The thick wooden slats didn't make things easy. 'I've got contacts: airlines, travel companies, the airports . . .'

'Yes?'

'They flew into Boston. That part was easy. The woman was travelling under her real name, Belinda Harrison. There probably wasn't time or opportunity enough for them to arrange a fake passport for her.'

'And him?' Walkins was nothing if not singleminded.

'Her travelling companion was called Michael Weston. That's the third name he's used so far this time. I've got a contact in the FBI, I've got him keeping eyes and ears open. If they get into bother, we'll hear about it.'

'Good.'

'Meantime, I've sent one of my team up to Boston to check hotels, car rental, that sort of thing.'

Hoffer was on auto-pilot. It gave him a chance to check out Walkins while he filled him in. Walkins had steel-grey hair and deep grooved lines in his face. He was a handsome man, ageing well despite his tragedies. But his eyes were filled to the brim with liquid, the pupils not quite fixed on the world outside. He took another drink of Scotch, but really the whisky was drinking *him.*

'This is a damned big country, Hoffer,' Walkins said at last. He sounded like he was boasting.

'Yes, sir,' Hoffer replied.

'A man could hide forever in a country this size.'

'Not if someone wants him found.'

'You believe that?'

'Yes, sir, I do.'

Walkins stared at him, so Hoffer daren't blink. He felt his eyes getting as watery as Walkins's. At last the old man pulled himself to his feet and walked to the rail at the end of the deck, leaning on it as he spoke.

'What now?'

'I've got a few leads,' Hoffer said, half-believing himself as he spoke.

'A few leads,' Walkins repeated, as though exhausted.

'You might be able to help, sir.'

'Oh? How?'

'Well, I presume you still have friends in positions of seniority?'

'What if I have?'

'Maybe one of them could play with a name. The name's Don Kline. He was in London, and interested in the D-Man. He told me he was agency, but I'm not sure he was. That's K-l-i-n-e.'

'I can ask around.'

The state Walkins was in, Hoffer doubted he'd recollect the name half an hour after Hoffer had driven away. He wrote it on the back of one of his cards and walked to the table, where he weighed it down with the lid from the ice bucket. Walkins was watching from the corner of his eye. He nodded towards Hoffer as Hoffer went back to his seat. Then he turned from the rail to face the detective, and took a good deep breath. Ah, at last, thought Hoffer: the floor-show.

'I want that bastard dead,' said Walkins, 'do you hear? I want his ass as cold as a mountaintop, and I want it delivered to me here.' The voice was growing louder, trembling with anger. Walkins started to move towards Hoffer. 'And I don't want a quick death either, it's got to be slow . . . slow like cancer, and burning like a fire inside. Do you understand?'

'Loud and clear.' It struck Hoffer, not for the first time, but now with absolute conviction, that Robert Walkins was howl-at-the-moon mad. There were white flecks at the edges of the old man's lips, and his face was all tics and wriggling demons.

'You've got it, sir,' Hoffer said, trying to calm things down. He was in the employ of a lunatic, but a lunatic who paid the bills and the rent. Besides, rich lunatics were never crazy . . . they were *eccentric*. Hoffer tried to remember that.

Finally, Walkins seemed to grow tired. He nodded a few times, reached out a hand and patted Hoffer's shoulder.

'Good, son, that's good.' Then he went and sat down again, poured himself another whisky, and dropped some ice into the glass. He sat back, sipped, and exhaled.

'Now,' he said, 'how will you do it?'

It took Hoffer a minute to answer. He was still trying to imagine himself as the Good Son.

21

No sightseeing now, just concentrated travel. North on Interstate 27 to Amarillo, then the 287. We were going to be travelling west back in time, from Mountain to Pacific. But we were heading nowhere but north to begin with. It was over 500 miles from Lubbock to Denver. We skirted the peaks to the west of Denver and crossed into Wyoming just south of Cheyenne.

'Tell me again,' said Bel. 'Why aren't we flying?'

'Air travel's easy to check if you're someone with the clout of a government agency. Also, it's easy for them to have airports covered, or car rental facilities at airports. This way, we're sort of sneaking up on them.'

She nodded, but didn't look convinced. I could have added that I needed time to think, time to plan, time this drive would give me. The thing was, I didn't know what we'd do in Seattle. I hadn't a clear plan of attack. I was praying something would come to me between here and there.

We'd covered over 600 miles by early evening. I'd been thinking about a lot of things. One of them was that it was crazy to arrive at our destination wiped out. Just off the interchange we found a motel. Or it found us. We just cruised into the first forecourt of many on the road and booked ourselves a room.

Standing up and walking were strange. My whole body tingled. In my head I was still in the car, still driving. I'd been on automatic for the past hour or so. My left arm was sunburnt from leaning on the driver-side sill. Bel had done her share of the driving too, seeming to understand the car better than I did, at least at first. We had our differences about choice of music and choice of stops along the route, but otherwise hadn't said much really. Oh, at first we chattered away, but then we ran out of things to say. She bought a trashy novel in a service area and read that for a while, before tipping it out of the window on to the verge.

'I can't concentrate,' she explained. 'Every time I think I'm managing to block it out, I see it again . . . I see Max.'

She didn't have to say any more.

At the motel, we each took a bath. We phoned out and had a restaurant deliver ribs and apple pie. We stared at the TV. We drank Coke with lots of ice. And we slept. The beds were too soft, so I swapped mine for the floor. When I woke up in the night, Bel was lying beside me. I listened to her breathing and to the vibration of the traffic outside. Our room held a pale orange glow, like when my parents had left the landing light on and my bedroom door ajar. To keep away the monsters.

How come the monsters would only come at night? What were they, stupid?

In the morning, we ate at another diner. 'The coffee gets better out west,' I promised. But Bel took a proffered refill anyway.

We took I-80 west across the continental divide. This was high country, and there were tourists around, slowing us down sometimes. They travelled in state of the art vehicles which were like motor caravans only the length of a bus. And behind they usually towed the family car. They probably saw themselves as descendants of the pioneers, but they were just vacationers. It was hard not to get into conversation with them at stops along the route. But if we did, there were endless questions about Europe. One woman even insisted on capturing us on video. We tried to look lovey and huggy for the seeing-eye. It wasn't easy.

'Maybe drugs would help,' Bel suggested.

'Not in the long run. They'd keep us driving, but they only mask the symptoms, they don't cure them. We'd end up hospital cases.'

'You've been there before?'

I nodded and she smiled. 'I keep forgetting how much more *worldly* than me you are, Michael.'

'Come on, let's see if we can fill up the cool box.'

We stopped outside Ogden on I-84. Another motel room, another long soak, another diner.

Bel rested her head on the table top. 'Remind me,' she said, 'which state are we in?'

'Utah, I think. But not for much longer. It'll be Idaho soon.' The waitress took our order.

'Are you all right?' she asked Bel.

'I'm fine, thanks, just tired.'

The waitress moved off. 'She thinks you're on drugs,' I told Bel.

'Only adrenaline.'

'This isn't the best way to see the country. Actually, that's a lie. This is the *only* way to see America. We'll do it properly one day, if you'd like to.'

'I'd love to, Michael.' She rested her head on the table again. 'Say, in a decade or two.'

'I once spent a week in a car going across the country. I slept in that car.'

'You must have felt like shit.'

I smiled at the memory. 'I felt very, very alive.'

'Well, I feel half-alive at best, but that's better than nothing.' She took a long drink of iced water. 'You know, if I hadn't gone off with you, I mean to London and Scotland . . .'

'I know,' I said.

'Christ, Michael, I'd be dead now.' There were tears in her eyes. She looked away, staring out of the window, and put her hand to her mouth. The hand was trembling. When I made to touch her, she jumped up from the table and ran outside.

I ran out to join her. Our diner was a truck stop. There was a vast tarmac parking area, with only a couple of trucks at its farthest edge. Stadium-style lights shone down on us from the lot's four corners. Our waitress was peering out of the diner window.

Bel was walking in a rough circle, eyes to the ground, and she was wailing. She flapped her arms to keep me away, so I took a few steps back and crouched down on the ground. The tarmac was warm to the touch. I sat there with my legs out in front of me, watching the exorcism with little pleasure.

She was saying things, sometimes yelling them. Curses, swear-words, imprecations. Finally she got to her father's name. When it came out, it was stretched to breaking point, like she was tearing it out of her system. She repeated it over and over, then had a coughing fit. The coughing became a dry retch, and she fell over on to her hands and knees. A huge lorry was pulling into the car park, air-brakes wheezing. The headlights picked out the figure of a crazy woman. The driver made sure to park at a good distance.

Eventually, when Bel was taking deep uneven breaths, I got up and walked over to her and crouched down again to put my arm around her.

'Buy you a coffee?' I said.

Next morning we crossed into Idaho. The state licence plates all had 'Famous Potatoes' written on them.

'Potatoes?' Bel said.

'Potatoes. These are a proud people.'

We were about 800 miles from Seattle. I thought we should get as close as we could then stop for another night, so we'd arrive fresh in the city. Bel wanted to push on. The road really had become her drug. She could hardly relax when we stopped. Even in the motel she fidgeted as she watched TV, her knees pumping. Her diet now comprised hamburgers and milk shakes. Her skin and hair had lost some vitality, and her eyes were dark. All my fault, I kept telling myself. She'd seemed better since last night though, a bit more together. Her voice was hoarse from shouting, and her eyes were red-rimmed. But I didn't think she was going to fall apart again. She seemed more confident, tougher . . . and she was ready to rock.

'No,' I told her, 'we'll stop somewhere, pamper ourselves, take a little time off.'

Problem was, where did you pamper yourself in the wasteland between Salt Lake City and Seattle? A detour to Portland wouldn't make sense. The answer started as a sort of joke. We decided to stop at a place called Pasco, for no other reasons than that it was a decent size and Bel's mother's maiden name had been Pascoe. But on the road into town, alongside all the other cheap anonymous motels, there was a Love Motel, with heart-shaped waterbeds, champagne, chocolates, adult movies . . . Our room was like a department store Santa's Grotto, done in red velvet and satin. There were black sheets on the bed and a single plastic rose on the pillow.

'It's like being inside a nosebleed,' Bel said, collapsing on to the bed. When it floated beneath her, she managed a laugh, her first in a while. But after a bottle of something that had never been within five hundred kilometres of Champagne, everything looked better. And lying on the bed, as Bel pointed out, was a bit like still being in the car. We didn't watch much of the porn flick, but we did take a bath together. It was a spa-bath, and Bel turned the jets up all the way. We started making love in the bath, but ended on the waterbed. We ended up so damp, I thought the bed had sprung a leak. I'd not known Bel so passionate, holding me hard against her like she was drowning. It was the kind of sex you have before dying or going off to war. Maybe we were about to do both.

We fell asleep without any dinner, woke up late and went to an all-night store where we bought provisions. We sat on the floor of our room and ate burger buns stuffed with slices of smoked ham, washed down with Coke. Then we made love again and drowsed till morning. We still had over 200 miles to go, and decisions to make along the way, such as whether it would be safer to stay in a motel out of town or a big hotel in the centre. It made sense to have a central base, but it also made sense not to get caught.

Snow-tipped Mount Rainier was visible in the distance as we took I-90 into the heart of Seattle.

There were things I wanted to tell Bel. I wanted to tell her why I hadn't cried over Max's death. I wanted to tell her why I didn't do what she had done out on that parking lot. I wanted to tell her about bottling things up until you were ready for them. When I met Kline again, the bottle would smash wide open. But somehow I didn't find the words. Besides, I couldn't see how they would help.

It was another hot dry day, and the traffic was slow, but no one seemed to mind too much. They were just happy to be here and not in some other more congested city. The placement and layout of Seattle are quite unique. From the east, we crossed on to Mercer Island and off it again on to the narrow stretch of land which housed the city itself, squeezed between Lake Washington and Puget Sound. We came off the Interstate into the heart of the downtown grid system, Avenues running north to south, Streets east to west. Last time I'd been here, I'd taken a cab from Sea Tac, which took you through a seemingly unending hinterland of sleazy motels, bars, and strip joints advertising '49 Beautiful Women . . . and One Ugly One'. This was a much better route. There were a few prominent hotels, all outposts of known chains catering mostly to business travellers. The first one we tried had a vacancy, so we took it. It was a relief to garage the car and take our bags up, knowing we now had a base. We'd decided to stay central, since it would cut down travelling time. We checked in as Mr and Mrs West, since we'd bought pawnstore rings. Bel flicked through the city information pack while I made a phone call.

I spoke to someone on the news desk.

'Can I speak to Sam Clancy, please.'

'He's on a sabbatical.'

'That's not what I've read. Look, can you get a message to him?'

There was a pause. 'It's possible.'

'My name's Mike West and I'm staying in a hotel downtown. I'd like Sam to contact me. It looks like we've been following a similar line of inquiry, only I've been working in Scotland, near Oban.' I waited while he took down the details. 'That's O-b-a-n. Tell him Oban, he'll understand.'

'Are you a journalist?'

'In a way, yes.' I gave him our room number and the telephone number of the hotel. 'When can I expect him to get this message?'

'He calls in sometimes, but there's no routine. Could take a few days.'

'Sooner would be better. All I'm doing here is pacing the floor.'

He said he'd do what he could, and I put the phone down. Bel was still studying the information pack.

'I'll tell you what you do in Seattle,' I said. 'You go up the Space Needle on a clear day, you visit Pike Place Market any day, and you wander around Pioneer Square.'

'Michael, when you were here before . . . was it business?'
'Strictly pleasure,' I said.
'What sort of pleasure?' She wasn't looking at me as she spoke.
'Whale-watching,' I said. Now she looked at me.
'Whale-watching?'
'I took a boat up to Vancouver Island and went whale-watching.'
She laughed and shook her head.
'What's wrong with that?'
'Nothing, it's just . . . I don't know. I mean, you're so *normal* in a lot of ways.'
'You mean for a hired killer?'
She had stopped laughing now. 'Yes, I suppose I do.'
'I'm still a killer, Bel. It's what I do best.'
'I know. But after this is over . . .'
'We'll see.'
The phone rang, and I picked it up. It was Sam Clancy.
'That was quick,' I said.
'I have to be careful, Mr West. The desk downstairs tells me you only checked in twenty minutes ago.'
'That's right.'
'You're not losing any time.'
'I don't think either of us can afford to.'
'So tell me your story.'
He didn't sound far away at all. He had a soft cultivated accent, which just failed to hide something more nasal and demanding, a New York childhood perhaps. I told him my story, missing out a few details such as my profession and my true involvement in the whole thing. I said I was a journalist, investigating the murder of one of my colleagues. I told him about Max's death, and how the gun dealer's daughter was with me in Seattle. I told him about the Americans we'd met on the road out of Oban, just after a visit to the Disciples of Love. I probably talked for twenty or thirty minutes, and he didn't interrupt me once.
'So what's your story?' I said.
'I think you already know most of it. There have been two attempts on my life, neither of them taken very seriously by the police. They couldn't find any evidence that someone had tampered with my car brakes, but I found a mechanic who showed me how it could be done without leaving any trace. Never buy an Oldsmobile, Mike. Anyway, since Seattle's finest weren't going to do anything about it, I thought I would. Then the paper ran my story, and that merely confirmed for the police that I was seeking publicity, nothing more.'
'You think the Disciples were responsible?'
'Well, I asked my ex-wife and it wasn't her. That doesn't leave too many enemies. Jesus, it's not like I wrote *The Satanic Verses* or anything, all I was doing was asking questions.'
'About funding?'
'That's right.'
'What did you find?'
'I'm still finding. It's just not so easy when I have to walk everywhere with my head in a blanket.'

'I could help you.'
'I've got people helping me.'
'At your newspaper?'
'No names, Mike. I still don't know that I can trust you.'
'Could we meet? I want to talk about the Disciples.'
'I don't know . . . Do you have any proof you could give me? I mean proof of anything you've said, of who you are?'
I thought about this. The answer was, no. 'I think you'd find the murdered man's daughter proof enough, Sam.'
He sighed. 'Is she there with you?'
'She's right here.'
'Put her on.'
I passed the phone to Bel. 'He needs convincing we're genuine.'
'Mr Clancy?' said Bel. 'You've got to help us. If you saw what they did to my father. I mean, they didn't just kill him, that wasn't enough for them. I want them caught . . . whatever it takes. With you or without you, we're going after them.' She handed me the receiver.
'All right,' said Clancy, 'let's have dinner.'
'Where?'
'There's a little Mexican place near Green Lake. Do you know where that is?'
'I can find it.' He gave me the name and address of the restaurant. We agreed eight o'clock, and the call ended there.
'Sounds promising,' I told Bel, giving her a kiss. 'Is there a street map in that pile of stuff?'
'Only a downtown one.'
'Then let's go do some shopping.'

It's very hard to get lost in American cities, so long as you stick to the grid system. You'll nearly always find the right road, though you may then have trouble finding the right building, since there doesn't always seem to be much sense to the way street numbers run.

That evening, we got on to Aurora and followed it for miles. I don't think Bel had ever seen a street so long, and when we came off at Green Lake, Aurora still had a long way to run. Green Lake was busy with joggers and walkers, skateboarders and roller-skaters, and people just enjoying the air.

We'd had a good afternoon, walking the streets, sitting in coffee shops, making new friends. As I'd promised Bel, the coffee here was definitely a class above the stuff they doled out in diners. She'd already had three cups of Starbuck's, and the caffeine was showing. Every café we sat in, when people heard our accents they wanted to talk to us. So we learned a bit more about the city. Ballard was the district where the descendants of the Norsemen lived. The streets east of the Kingdome were to be avoided. The Mariners were having another lousy season, and were now owned by Nintendo. We'd missed the annual Folklife Festival. There was a drought. A couple of local micro-breweries were producing excellent dark beers . . . Some of this I already knew, but some of it was new to me, and I appreciated all the information I could get. Jeremiah Provost, after all, was on home ground. It was important to know as much about the city as he did. That way, we'd be less likely to fall into any traps.

So far, Seattle had looked distinctly free from traps. I showed Bel Pike Place Market, pointed out the bicycle cops in Pioneer Square, and steered her around the street people and panhandlers milling around the streets near the waterfront. The pawnshops were doing good business in Seattle. They had guns and guitars in their windows, but I didn't stop to look. I wasn't carrying a gun with me, but when we headed off for dinner with Sam Clancy, I hid the pistol under the Trans-Am's front seat.

The car was sounding ropey. It needed another tune, oil change, and maybe a new exhaust. Probably it also needed a complete rest. We'd pushed it hard, and it had served us well, but we needed it healthy for a while longer.

We'd overestimated the weight of traffic and were early at the restaurant, so we parked the car and walked back down to the lake. Bel pulled off her cowboy boots to walk barefoot on the grass. She looked okay, not tired or stressed out. She was keen for something to happen, for some showdown to arrive, but she managed not to look too impatient.

By the time we got back to the restaurant she declared herself ready for a drink. There was still no sign of Clancy, but a table had been reserved in the name of West, so we took it. It was laid out for three diners. The waiter asked if we wanted a margarita while we waited. Bel nodded that we did.

'Large or small?'

'Large,' she stated, before ploughing through the menu. 'What's the difference between all these things?' she asked me. 'Tacos, burritos, fajitas, tortillas . . . ?'

'Ask the waiter.'

But instead she took her very large margarita from him and ran her finger around the rim.

'It's salt,' I said.

'I knew that.' Having wiped a portion of the rim clean, she sipped, considered, then took another sip.

There was a man at the front of the restaurant. He'd been studying the takeaway menu when we'd come in, and he was still studying it. I got up from the table and walked over to him.

'Why don't you join us?' I said.

He tried to look puzzled, then gave up and smiled. 'Have you known all the time?'

'More or less.'

I led him to the table. Sam Clancy was tall and thin with a cadaverous face and sunken eyes. He was in his late 20s or early 30s, with thinning brown hair combed across his forehead. From his voice, I'd imagined he'd be older. He took Bel's hand before sitting down. The waiter arrived, and Clancy nodded towards her drink.

'Looks good,' he said. The waiter nodded and moved off. 'So, I guess I wouldn't make a career working undercover, huh? Do you want some introductory conversation, or shall we get down to work?'

'Let's consider ourselves introduced,' said Bel.

'Right. So, you want to know what I know. Well, here goes. Jeremiah Provost takes a bit of a back seat these days as far as the day-to-day running of the Disciples is concerned. You know a bit about his background?'

'Rich family,' I said, 'bad college professor.'

'That's not a bad precis. Also completely mad. He's been in and out of expensive clinics. No sign that he does heavy drugs or booze, so there has to be some other reason, like pure mental instability.'

'So if he's in the back seat,' asked Bel, 'who's behind the wheel?'

'On the business side, a man called Nathan. I don't even know if that's his first or second name, he's just called Nathan. You know a couple of reporters got hit on by the Disciples? That was Nathan. He didn't like them, so he whacked them.'

'He's a bit handy then?' I said.

'He's a tough mother. Then there's Alisha, she's an earth mother type with just a streak of junta. She runs the people, makes them do what needs to be done.'

'And this is all out on the Olympic Peninsula?'

Clancy nodded. 'The most beautiful spot on the continent. But Provost isn't there much. He's taken on a Howard Hughes existence in a brand new house up on Queen Anne Hill. Terrific view on to downtown, a few thousand square feet and a swimming pool. Rumour has it Kiefer Sutherland wanted to rent the place when he was here filming *The Vanishing*. Anyway, that's where Provost spends his time, surrounded by phones and fax machines and computers, so he can keep in touch with his minions overseas.'

'There was a fax machine in Oban,' I recalled, 'it had at least two Washington State numbers on its memory.'

'Olympic Peninsula and Queen Anne,' Clancy stated with authority.

'Have you ever spoken to Provost?' Bel asked him.

'I've tried, but he's ringed with steel.'

'But who runs the show really, him or his lieutenants?'

'Now that's a good question.'

Clancy broke off so we could order. Bel took his advice when her turn came, and we ordered another round of drinks to go with the meal. Some tortilla chips and dips had been placed on the table, so we munched as we spoke.

'The men who killed my father,' said Bel, 'if they were the same men who stopped us on the road out of Oban, then they were Americans.'

'They didn't look like cult members though,' I told Clancy. 'They seemed more like government types.'

'Which brings me to my research,' Clancy said, beginning to enjoy himself. 'You know that the Disciples suddenly took off late in 1985? I mean, they started buying land and real estate. Which means Provost had money to spend. Where did it come from? Nobody knows. Did a bunch of rich relatives suddenly and conveniently die? No. Did he win some state lottery? No. A lucky week at Vegas? Uh-uh. It's been driving people nuts, wondering where that money suddenly came from.'

'You've found out?' Bel asked.

'Not exactly, not yet. But I think I was getting close.' So maybe Eleanor Ricks had been getting close too. 'I do know this.' Clancy made a melodramatic point, glancing around the restaurant then leaning forward across the table. I wondered if he could always differentiate between gossip and fact. 'Provost went to Washington DC. Please, don't ask how I know this. I have sources to protect and my . . . uh, techniques weren't always strictly legit. He was in DC for a meeting with some lawyers and other fat cats. But while he was there he had a couple of visitors, two men called Elyot and Kline. They visited him on more than one occasion. This was in January 1986, a few months after Provost started spending.

'Now, I think I've tracked down who Elyot and Kline were and are. There's an agent called Richard Elyot works for the CIA. And at the NSC there used to be a cat called Kline.'

'Used to be?'

'He resigned officially in 1986. Since then he's been on the fringes, only his name's not on the books any longer. Nobody knows why he resigned, whether he was forced out or what. I'm going to describe Kline to you.'

He did. I nodded halfway through and continued nodding. 'Sounds familiar,' I conceded.

'The guy in the rear car, right?' Clancy surmised.

'Right,' I confirmed. 'What about Elyot?'

'Elyot's posted in some overseas embassy just now, not a very prestigious one. He's been getting shitty assignments for about the past five years. I even hear that he was in the US consulate in Scotland for a couple of months.'

'Interesting.'

'It's *all* interesting,' said Bel, finishing her second margarita. 'But where does it get us?'

'The Disciples,' Clancy said, 'are somehow connected to the CIA and the NSC. How come? What could they possibly have in common?'

'And whatever it is,' I added, 'does it add up to Provost being in their pay?'

'Absolutely,' said Clancy, sitting back.

'I wouldn't mind a word with Jeremiah Provost.'

Clancy laughed. 'Get in line, fella.'

'Michael has ways,' Bel said quietly, staring at me.

'Oh, yeah?' Clancy was interested.

'But his techniques,' she went on, 'aren't *ever* strictly legit.'

Clancy looked more interested. 'Bel,' I said, 'it's been a long day.'

'A long day's journey,' she agreed.

'Maybe we should get the bill?'

She didn't say no. I asked Clancy how he wanted to play it. He shrugged, so I made a couple of suggestions. We agreed he'd meet us at our hotel in the morning. I settled the bill with cash. On the back of the check there was a little form asking for comments. We'd seen them before in diners. Bel had filled one of them in. She'd put, 'Service overfriendly, food big but tasteless, have a nice day.' This time she got a pen from Clancy and wrote: 'I love tequila.'

At the bottom she drew a little heart, broken into halves.

22

We met Clancy next morning in the hotel lobby. His first words were, 'I made a few calls to England. Nobody I spoke to has heard of you.'

'Michael does magazine work,' Bel said. 'Let's go get some coffee.' We ordered three *caffè lattes* at a nearby coffee shop and sat at a table inside, even though the proprietor assured us we'd be better off sitting at one of the sidewalk tables. We had a view across the street to the Seattle Art Museum. Clancy just called it 'Sam'.

'There's a porno theatre one block down,' he said. 'It used to advertise Sam exhibitions on its awning. Only in Seattle, friends.'

He told us that Seattle's main industries were Boeing, fish processing and Microsoft, and that things at Boeing were extremely shaky just now. 'We used to be world leaders in grunge music. You know what that is? Torn jeans, drug habits and sneers.'

'Didn't Keith Richards patent that?'

Clancy laughed and looked at his watch. I knew he didn't altogether trust us yet, and I didn't like it that he'd been asking about us in London. Word there could get to anyone. 'Come on,' he said, 'time to rock 'n' roll.'

We took the Trans-Am to a mechanic Clancy knew near the U-Dub. 'He's a Christian mechanic,' Clancy said. 'Every job he does comes with a blessing and a guarantee from above.'

The man was young, stocky and bearded. He reminded me of the Amish. He said the car would take a day or so, and meantime we could have a VW Rabbit. It was a small brown car, perfect for the trip we were about to make. There was a plastic litterbag hanging from the dashboard. It had Uncle Sam's hat on one side, and the Pledge of Allegiance on the other. I took my bag from the Trans-Am and locked it in the boot of the Rabbit. Nobody asked what was in it, and I wouldn't have answered if they had.

Bel sat in the back of the car, and I let Clancy drive. We drove south on Aurora into Queen Anne Hill. This was a prime residential area, mostly bungalow-style housing. A precious few lots sat on the very edge of the hill, looking down on to the city. This was where Jeremiah Provost had his house.

It was big, even by the standards of the area, and it was on an incline so steep it made you giddy.

'I wouldn't fancy walking back from the shops,' Bel said.

Clancy looked at her. '*Walk?* Nobody walks, Bel. Nobody ever walks.'

We parked across the road from Provost's house. Even with the handbrake on and the car left in gear, I wasn't sure I trusted the Rabbit not to start careering downhill. We all wore sunglasses, and as further disguise

Clancy was wearing a red baseball cap. There was a sheen of nervous sweat on his face. We knew we were taking a big risk coming here. But the time had come to take risks. We were parked outside a house with its own turret. We couldn't see much of Provost's house though. Steps led up through a bristling garden to a white concrete wall, showing no windows or doors.

'There's only one entrance,' said Clancy, 'round the side of the house. There are French windows leading on to the pool and patio, so I suppose that makes it two entrances really.'

'And two exits,' I added. 'Where are the security cameras?'

He looked at me, perhaps wondering how I knew. 'Just as you round the corner.'

'Is there an infra-red trip?'

'I don't know, could be.'

'It's just that on the surface, there looks like there's no security at all. So I take it what security there is is high-tech.'

'Sure, plus the muscle-man on the door.'

'Just the one?'

'Hey, Provost's a religious nut, not a Middle East guerrilla.'

'What about at night? He's got approach lights?'

'Yeah, if a hedgehog so much as inspects the lawn, the place lights up like the Fourth of July.' Clancy was still looking at me. 'You're asking all the right questions, only I'm not sure they're questions a reporter would think to ask.'

'I'm not your everyday reporter,' I said. 'He spends most of his time in there?'

'Yeah. There's a house out on Hood Canal belongs to Nathan. That's hot real estate too. Sometimes Provost goes there for the weekend. He doesn't do much, digs clams, picks oysters at low tide. Mr Microsoft has a compound a few houses down.'

'How much do you know about Nathan?'

'Not much. I got a name and a face.'

'When did he join the Disciples?'

'I don't know. The problem is, only having one of his names, I can't even begin to do a trace back.'

'He handles the business, does that mean the money?'

'Yeah, there's an accountant too, but Nathan does the day to day balance sheet. Thing is, there's very little on the profit side. Very little income compared to the outgoings.'

'Maybe we should talk to Nathan rather than Provost.'

'He's no easier to get to, Mike. And he wears this look like he's just waiting to break someone's face open. These cults, they're always suspicious. I mean, someone comes sniffing around them for a story, chances are it isn't going to be a panegyric.'

I looked out at Provost's house. 'Can we see it from another angle?'

'Yeah, if you walk downhill and take a left. But frankly, you won't see much more than you can from here. More concrete and the top of a window, that's about it. It's a smart design, completely open but totally private. He doesn't even have a fence, but he could be filming hard-core in his pool and none of the neighbours would know.'

'Some of these cult leaders like to initiate new recruits,' said Bel, who'd done her reading.

Clancy shrugged. 'I don't know if Provost shafts the women in the cult. I mean, with a name like Disciples of Love, and starting off where it did and how it did, it's got to be a good bet. But he's never gone public on humping politics.'

'That sounds like a quote from one of your own stories.'

He grinned. 'It is, only the paper spiked it as defamatory.'

'Okay,' I said, 'I've seen enough. Let's go buy what we need.'

The shop we wanted was on Aurora, way north of Green Lake. It was called Ed's Guns and Sporting Goods and was run by a man named Archie with a trace of a Scots accent. I knew pretty much what we needed: camouflage jackets, overtrousers, boots, a couple of tents, a small stove and pot, plates, mugs and cutlery, binoculars, and a couple of rucksacks to put everything in.

The binoculars he showed me were small but powerful. 'Bird watchers love them,' he said, like this was a recommendation.

I handed them back. 'Got anything with a night vision facility?'

'You're talking major expense.'

'So let me talk.'

He went off to find a night-scope. Bel was picking out thick socks to go with her boots. 'We want to look like tourists, right?'

'Right.'

'Then we'd probably have too much gear, all of it brand new.'

'Right again.'

'So I want some new sunglasses.' I nodded and she went to choose some. Meantime I picked out a compass, and studied a few of the available knives. The survival knives looked good. There was one with a hollow handle, inside which were fishing-line, hooks and a needle, a tiny compass, stuff like that. Another was so versatile you could turn it from knife into axe or shovel or even a torch. It was big too. I reckoned it was big enough to scare most people.

'I'll take that,' I said, pointing it out to Archie, who had come back with a plain cardboard box. He was licking his lips, excited at the total sale but nervous about the ease with which we were spending money. Maybe he thought we were going to pull a gun or even one of his own combat knives on him. Instead I pulled out a wad of cash and waved it in his face. He nodded and relaxed a little.

I checked the night-scope. It was perfect. I could use it like a telescope or, with a couple of adjustments, fit it to my sniping rifle.

'How discreet are you, Archie?' I asked.

'That depends.'

'Well, I want to buy all this, and I want to pay cash. But I've a job I'd like to do. Do you have a workshop back there?' He nodded. 'Could I borrow it for, say, fifteen minutes?'

He shrugged. 'You buy that lot, you can bunk in the back for all I care.'

'That won't be necessary.'

Bel was asking Archie about maps when I left the shop. She'd slid a survival knife into the top of her right boot to see how it felt. Clancy stared at the knife for a moment, then followed me out. Clancy wasn't a country boy or a born-again backwoodsman. Seattle still had something of the frontier town about it, but he was strictly *latte* and art museum. He told us the only times he'd been out to the Olympic Peninsula had been to visit the hot springs resort. He'd driven past the Disciples' compound, but only on day trips, and he'd hardly budged from the car.

But a lot of the Olympic Peninsula was wilderness, mountains and first-growth temperate rainforest. I knew there was no such thing as being underprepared. Clancy stood watching as I unlocked the boot and lifted out my bag.

'Come on, Mike, who the fuck are you, man? You're security, right? I mean, a secret agent or something. Reporters I know, they wouldn't have the expenses to claim for that hotel you're staying in, never mind leaving the room empty for a night. Even if they *could* claim it, they'd stay someplace ratty and cream the cash. And they'd never *ever* have so much cash on them. Strictly plastic, and a receipt every time you spend.'

I locked the boot. 'So I'm not a journalist. All you have to know is, if you stick around I'll give you a story. This is better for you, Sam. See, I don't represent any competition. It's your exclusive.'

He was shaking his head. 'I'm not going.'

'Sam, we don't need you any more. You want to stay here, fine. Maybe it'll take us an hour or two longer to find the compound. But we'll find it. I'm not going to beg you to come with us.'

'I could blow you wide open, man. All it would take is a call to Provost.'

I smiled. 'We're not your enemies, Sam. Why would you do that?'

He thought about this. 'I wouldn't do it. Forget I said it.' He followed me into the shop. Bel was trying on a red and black check lumberjacket. Archie gestured for me to follow him. Sam was still on my tail. We entered a back room full of equipment and work benches. There was even a metal-turning lathe. And there were bits and pieces from gun-cleaning kits. I put the bag down on a bench and unzipped it.

'I just want to know,' Sam was saying. 'See, people have been trying to kill me, and I can't afford not to be choosy about my friends. Someone comes up to me with a chickenshit story about being a journalist, and it turns out he's not, then I've got to wonder what he really is.'

The words died in his throat as he saw the Varmint being unwrapped, then the pistol and finally the Colt Commando.

'Sweet Lord Jesus,' he said quietly. I started seeing if I could fit the night-scope to the Varmint.

'Sam,' I said, not looking up, 'you're safe with us.'

'I hear that.'

'I'm a friend of Bel's. I was a friend of her father's. He sold me guns from time to time. I saw what those bastards did to him, and I intend finding out just why they did it. That's the whole story, except for one thing.' Now I looked at him. 'I don't care what it takes.'

His mouth was suddenly dry. There was an open can of beer on the bench, and he took a swig from it.

'Why don't you go get us a pack of those things from the grocery?' I suggested. 'Think things out while you're there. If you want out, we'll get your camera from the car and you can catch a cab back into town.' I made to hand him some money.

'I don't need your money, Mike. I can stretch to a few beers.'

'Okay then.'
And he was gone. Archie put his head round the door.
'Sorry to interrupt, but that lady out there is going to put you in the poorhouse.'
'We'll be the best dressed paupers there.'
He laughed. This was turning into a more interesting day than usual for him. He looked at what I was doing. 'Nice gun. Give you some help there?'
'I might just need it. The receiver and the sight-mounting are all wrong.'
'Well, let me take a look. No extra charge.'
'It's all yours, Archie.'
It took us a little while, but Archie had a few bits and pieces in the back, and one of them seemed to be what we needed. It made the gun look like something from *Man from UNCLE*, but it seemed okay.
'I never ask customers what they're planning to shoot,' said Archie.
'Maybe an animal or two,' I said.
'Yeah, maybe, but that other gun you've got there, that's strictly terror.'
I grinned. 'I hope so, Archie. I really do.'
When we went back out front, there were no new customers and Clancy hadn't come back.
'Where's the nearest place to buy beer?' I asked.
'There's a grocery on the corner,' Archie answered. I nodded to myself. It looked like Clancy had just walked away.
'Better start adding this lot up, Archie.'
'And then maybe I better close for the day for restocking.' He got to work on his calculator.
Bel was back in her ordinary clothes. She hadn't worn anything on her feet but the cowboy boots since she'd bought them. 'Where's Sam?' she said.
'I think we're on our own.'
'He didn't even say goodbye. Will he tell anyone?'
'I doubt it.'
'What did you say to him?'
'I admitted I wasn't a reporter.'
'Did he see the guns?' I nodded. 'No wonder he ran. They have that effect on me, too.'
Archie had paused in his addition so he could fill a few carrier bags with goods already totted up.
'Just put them straight in the rucksacks, Archie, we'll sort them out later.' I added another torch to the total.
'Listen,' he said, 'I know you may not need it, but I'm giving you a first aid kit and some mosquito repellant. Plus all my cash customers receive a ten percent discount.'
'Thanks.' I turned back to Bel.
'So we're going on our own?' she said.
'I suppose so. I think we can find the ferry terminal, don't you?'
'We can also save some money.'
'How's that?'
'We don't need two tents now, and one big sleeping bag would do us.'
'You've got a point.' But just then the door opened and Clancy staggered in. I thought he was hurt, and moved forward, but he was only staggering under the weight of the shopping bags he carried.

'A few provisions for the trip,' he said, putting down the bags. 'Beer, potato chips, tinned chilli, tuna, franks, and beans.' He put his hand into one bag. 'Look, I even packed the tin opener.'

We all laughed except Archie, who was too busy on his calculator. When he'd finished, it was his turn to laugh. I counted out the money, and Clancy snatched the receipt.

'If you can't claim, maybe I can.'

'Then you can pay for the boat tickets,' I said, hoisting a rucksack on to my shoulder.

'It's a deal.'

The ferry was busy with families heading off on holidays.

'Where are they all going?' I asked Clancy.

'The same place as us,' he said. 'The Olympic Peninsula's popular this time of year.'

'I thought it was wilderness.'

'Mostly it is. The folks you see here probably won't get more than a couple of hundred yards from their vehicles all the time they're away. There's a highway circuits the Peninsula, but almost no roads at all in the National Park itself. Here, I brought a map.'

It was the map the National Park Service handed out to visitors. As Clancy had said, there were almost no roads inside the park, just a lot of trails and a few unpaved tracks. The one good road I could see led to the summit of Hurricane Ridge. We were headed west of there, to Lake Crescent. Clancy pointed it out on the map. Outside the National Park boundaries, the rest of the peninsula was considered National Forest. The National Park ended just north of Lake Crescent.

'See, what Provost did, he took over a house that was already there. They're very cautious about new building inside the park, but there's nothing they can do about homes that were there before the area was designated a National Park. He didn't have too much trouble getting permission to add a few log cabins of the same style. He even had the timber treated so it looked weathered.'

'I bet he's kind to dumb animals too.'

We were part of a slow-moving stream coming off the ferry. There were backpackers trying to hitch a ride with anyone who'd take them. Bel smiled at them and shrugged her shoulders. Everybody took the same road out of Bremerton along the southern shore of Hood Canal. There were no stopping places, other than pulling into someone's drive, so Clancy just pointed out Nathan's house to us as we passed. It had a low front hedge, a large neatly cut lawn, and was itself low and rectangular, almost like a scale model rather than a real house, such was its perfection. Beyond it we could see the canal itself, in reality an inlet carved into the land like a reverse J. We kept along Hood Canal for a long time, then headed west towards Port Angeles.

'From what I've heard,' said Clancy, 'as well as what I've seen today, I think our first priority should be to find a campsite.'

He was right. Fairholm was the closest campsite to the Disciples' headquarters, but by the time we got there it was already full. We retraced our route and called in at Lake Crescent Lodge, but it was fully booked. So then we'd to head north towards the coast where, at Lyre River, we found a campground with spaces. It was less than a mile from the Strait of Juan de Fuca, beyond which lay Vancouver Island, Canadian soil. The air was incredible, intoxicating and vibrant. You felt nobody'd ever breathed it before. It wasn't city air, that was for sure.

Clancy had been telling us that there was bad feeling in the Pacific north west about logging. A lot of loggers were losing their jobs, a lot of logging towns were going broke. They'd asked if they could go into the National Forest and 'tidy up' fallen trees, but this request had been rejected. There were other forests they couldn't touch because of a protected species of owl. They were getting desperate.

'One man's paradise . . .' I said.

At the campground, there was a box full of envelopes. We put our fee in the envelope and pushed it through the posting slot. Then we stuck our receipt in a little display case on a post next to our own little site.

'Isn't this cosy?' I said. Bel looked dubious. She'd been sleeping in too many real beds recently to relish a night under the stars. It was about fifteen miles from here to the Disciples' HQ, so we pitched our tents. Or rather, Clancy and I pitched the tents while Bel walked by the river and chatted to a few other campers. Then, happy with the state of our accommodations, we got back in the car and headed off. We were on the wrong side of Lake Crescent, as we soon found. No road went all the way around the lake. The main road went round the south, and to the north it was half unpaved road and half trail. We were the trail end, which meant we couldn't take the car anywhere near the Disciples without going all the way around the lake and heading in towards them from the west along the unpaved road. We took the car to the trail-head past Piedmont and got out to think. It looked like it was about a three-mile walk. Driving around the lake might save a mile of walking.

'Well,' I said, 'we might as well get our money's worth from all this gear we've brought.'

So we got ourselves made up to look like hikers, Clancy carrying the only rucksack we'd need, and I locked the car.

'You're not carrying heat?' he inquired.

'You've been watching too many gangster flicks.'

'But are you or aren't you?'

'No.'

'Good.'

We walked for about half a mile, till Bel suddenly stopped. I asked what was wrong. She was looking all around her.

'This,' she said, 'is the most beautiful place I've ever been. Listen: nothing. Look, not a soul around.'

She'd barely got these words out when a party of three walkers emerged on the trail ahead of us. They nodded a greeting as they passed. They hadn't spoilt things at all for Bel. She looked the way I'd seen girls in my youth when they were stoned at parties. She was an unfocused, all-encompassing smile.

'It's the lack of toxins in the atmosphere,' Clancy explained. 'If your system isn't used to it, weird things start to happen.'

We walked on, and she caught us up. Clancy had the map.

'There's a picnic area at North Shore,' he said, 'but we'll see the cabins before that. They're between this trail and the one leading up Pyramid Mountain.'

We came upon them sooner than expected. It was a bit like the set-up at Oban, but a lot less obtrusive. No signs or fences or barriers, except that the very existence of the cabins, here where there should be nothing, was a barrier in itself. I couldn't see the Disciples getting many casual visitors.

'So what do we do now?' Bel said.

'We keep walking,' I told her. 'We're just out for a hike. We'll soon be at North Shore. We'll have our picnic and we'll talk. Just now, we're walking.'

But from the corner of my eye I was taking in the cabins, the small vegetable plot, the boat on its trailer. I couldn't see any signs of life, and no cars, no pick-ups or vans. No smoke, but then the cabins didn't have chimneys, with the exception of what I took to be the original structure, slightly larger than the others. Instead, there were solar panels on the roofs, and a couple more on the ground. There was plenty of tree and bush cover around the cabins, and no sign of any pets. I wasn't even sure you were allowed to keep pets inside the park.

There were boats out on Lake Crescent. They looked like they'd come from Lake Crescent Lodge. I could see fathers wrestling with the oars while spouses caught the antics on video and the children rocked the boat further to discomfit 'pop'. We sat down at the picnic site and gazed out over the lake.

'It is beautiful,' said Bel.

'Almost as pretty as a baseball game,' Clancy agreed. Bel ignored him.

'So that was it?' I said.

'That was it.'

'I was expecting more.'

'The Disciples are small-time, Mike. I could show you a dozen cults bigger than them in the US, including the cult of the Sainted Elvis. They're not big, they're just rich and obsessed with their privacy.'

Bel turned away from the view. She had been bitten already, and sprayed more gunk on her bare arms. I'd bought a dark blue baseball cap at Archie's, and was now glad of it. The sun beat down with a sizzling intensity. Clancy opened the cooler and handed out beers.

'So now we go and knock at their door,' said Bel, 'ask them what the hell they were doing murdering my father?'

'Maybe not straight away,' I cautioned.

'But I thought that was the whole point?'

'The point is to play safe. Sam, have you ever heard of anyone leaving the Disciples?'

He shook his head and sucked foam from the can. 'That was my first line of inquiry. If you'd been a real reporter, it's about the first thing you'd've asked me. I was desperate to find someone with inside info, but I never found a soul.'

'Ever talk to any existing members?'

'Oh, yes, lots of times. I'd strike up conversations with them when they went into Port Angeles for supplies. I have to tell you, those were very one-sided conversations. Hamlet's soliloquies were shorter than mine. I got snippets, nothing more.'

Bel was sorting out the food. We had ham, crackers, cold sausage and potato chips.

'Bel,' I said, 'how's your acting?'

'I think I played a policewoman pretty well.'

'How about playing a very stupid person?'

She shrugged. 'It'd be a challenge. What sort of stupid person did you have in mind?'

'One who's on vacation and has gone for a walk on her own. And she comes across these cabins and thinks they must be a restaurant or something, maybe a ranger station or some souvenir shops.'

Clancy was looking at me. 'You're crazy.'

Bel opened a packet of chips. 'Are you saying, Michael, that I'd be going in there on my own?'

'That's what I'm saying.'

'Why?'

'I think they'd suspect you less if you were on your own.'

'Yes, but why do I need to go there at all?'

'Reconnaissance. I want you to learn as much as you can about the lay-out, memorise it. Are there locks on the doors and windows? Are there any alarms or other security precautions that you can see? Any skylights, loopholes, chinks in the armour?'

'You're thinking of paying a night-time visit?'

I smiled at her and nodded. She wasn't fazed at all by my intention. She just ate some crisps and thought about it.

'I'd have to go into the cabins,' she said at last.

I shook my head. 'Just the one, the main cabin. That's the one I want to know about.'

'You're both crazy,' Clancy said, gripping his beer with both hands.

Bel finished her crisps and stood up, wiping her hands on her legs. 'I need a pee,' she said. 'I'll see you back at the trail-head.'

'We'll be waiting.'

I watched her walk away. I'd promised Max she wouldn't be in any danger. I'd been breaking that promise time and time again.

'She's got guts,' Clancy admitted.

I nodded but didn't say anything. Clancy couldn't get a word out of me the rest of the makeshift meal.

We walked back along the trail quite slowly, nodding to people who passed us. Again, we didn't look at the cabins as we passed within a hundred yards of them. They were built on a fairly serious slope. Slopes and night-walking did not make good companions. But if I stuck to the path by the lake, there'd be more chance of being spotted. I had a lot on my mind as we walked the rest of the route. We sat in the car for a while. Clancy switched the radio on and retuned it, and I got out and walked about a bit.

It was over an hour before we saw Bel. She was hurrying towards us, her cheeks flushed with what I took to be success. When she gave me a grinning thumbs-up, I hugged her, lifting her off the ground. Then we got back into the Rabbit and on the way back to the campsite she told us all about it.

Not that there was a whole lot to tell. She'd found a young woman first of all, who'd turned out to have studied in England for several years. So she'd wanted to ask Bel all about how England was these days, and then Bel had asked to use the toilet, and only then had she asked the woman what this place was exactly. At which she got the story and even a brief tour. Because she and the woman appeared to be friends, no one else batted an eye at first. Then a man came up and asked who she was, and after that everything was distinctly cooler. She'd lingered over a cup of herbal tea the woman had prepared, but then had been asked politely but firmly by the man if she would leave.

She hadn't gotten to see the inside of the old cabin, just its outside. But there were no alarm boxes, and none of the windows she'd seen had boasted anything other than the most superficial locks. There was more, and at the end of it I felt like hugging her again. Instead we celebrated back at the campsite with a meal cooked on our stove: franks and beans, washed down with black coffee. Clancy had bought a pack of filters and some real ground coffee. It smelt great and tasted good. The insects by this time were out in force, hungry for a late supper before bed.

'Oh, one other thing,' Bel said. 'In a couple of days, Provost himself is visiting the HQ.'

'Really?' I looked at Clancy. 'Any significance?'

He shrugged. 'It's rare these days, but not exactly unknown.'

'It'll mean his house in Seattle is empty,' I mused.

'Yeah, as empty as a high-security bank.'

I smiled. 'I get your drift.'

Later, Clancy hinted at taking Bel into Port Angeles to check out the night life. They could drop me off first, then pick me up again on the way back. But Bel made a face. She just wanted to crawl into her sleeping bag with a torch, another beer, and her latest cheap paperback. I was pleased she didn't want to go with Clancy. I sat outside with him for a while longer. He asked if I wanted him to drive me to Piedmont, but I shook my head.

'I'll do this one alone.'

When it was properly dark, I was ready.

23

I drove back to Piedmont and parked a little way from the trail-head. I was wearing a camouflage jacket and dark green combat trousers, plus hiking boots. I had the night-scope with me. If anyone stopped me, my excuse would be that I was out looking for nocturnal animals, maybe the rare Roosevelt Elk.

Firearms weren't allowed in the park, but I had the 559 with me too, fully loaded. I reckoned that, laws or not, the Disciples would have an armoury.

There was half a moon, appearing now and then from behind slow-moving clouds. The cloud cover wasn't thick, so there was a welcome glow, and as my eyes got used to the night, I found I could pick my way forwards without falling arse over tit.

I hadn't done much of this sort of thing before, though of course I'd recced my hits. There was silence in the camp. Bel hadn't heard any radios or seen any TV aerials. It looked like the Disciples were early-to-bed early-to-rise types, which suited me fine. Maybe they were busy making love under their patchwork quilts.

The old original cabin faced the newer ones, so I would be at my most vulnerable if entering by the front. I looked in through the rear and side windows, but couldn't see anyone. The windows were locked though, and I'd no tools with me. I knew Bel could have used her skill here, but no way was I going to bring her with me. In the silence, the sound of breaking glass would be like a foghorn. So I went around to the front of the cabin. Then I saw the torch. I saw the beam first, scanning the ground. Someone had left one of the other cabins. If I moved, I'd be heard, so I stood still, my face averted, hoping I'd blend in with the cabin walls. If they shone the torch right at me, of course, they'd see me instantly. I held my breath and waited.

Someone cleared his throat. Then I heard water pouring on to the ground. He'd come outside to urinate. Yes, I'd seen a compost heap over where he was standing; no doubt he was peeing on to that. I could hear the blood rushing in my ears, my heart thumping. Then the man turned and retraced his steps. I heard a cabin door close, though I hadn't heard it open.

Quickly, I went to the front door of the old cabin and turned the handle. It wasn't locked. I slipped inside and closed the door again slowly. I didn't want to use my torch. It would be too obvious. Anyone stepping out to the compost heap would see its glow reflected in the windows.

As far as I could make out, I was standing in an office. There were two desks, and another table with office machines on it. I saw the outlines of computers and file-boxes, what looked like a photocopier, and several large filing-cabinets. I went to these and tried a drawer. It too was unlocked. I knew I really needed some light, so took the handkerchief from my pocket and wrapped it over the torch. Now when I switched the torch on, there was a faint illumination, just enough to read by. I started working my way through the papers in the first cabinet.

Though the night was cool, there was sweat on my back and my brow. The third drawer down was full of details about cult members. I checked out Nathan and Alisha. Alisha had joined in early '86, having come west from Raleigh NC. Nathan had joined later the same year. His file gave scant details of any life before joining the Disciples, which was unusual. I knew which high school Alisha had attended, when she was born and where, what she had studied at college. All I really knew about Nathan after reading his file was that Nathan was his first name.

His second name was Kline.

It couldn't just be coincidence. I tucked his file back in place and closed the cabinet. I tried a few other drawers, but didn't turn up much. There was certainly nothing about the finances of the cult, other than the daily outgoings. The only way Provost could be financing the set-up was if he had a mountain of cash back in his Queen Anne house. I also found no evidence of conspiracy to murder, though any such documents were unlikely to be kept here. Nathan's house on Hood Canal would be an infinitely better bet, and suddenly I was keen to return there and take a closer look.

But I had other things to do first. Beyond the front office there was a narrow hallway with doors leading off. More offices, by the look of things. I tried a door, opened it, and looked in. Yes, if the front desks were manned by underlings, then these two offices most probably belonged to Nathan and Alisha. One of them might even be Provost's. There were no clues to the owner of either office, and the desk drawers and filing-cabinets were locked. It wasn't very trusting, was it? It told me something about the Disciples. So open on the surface – witness the unlocked front door – yet with secrets which had to be kept locked up. I decided against forcing any of the locks. I didn't want them to know how close I was.

Out in the hall again, I noticed a staircase. It was right at the end of the hall, and led up into the roof-space. I hadn't thought about the roof-space. There were no windows up there, so I hadn't considered it used. Yet here was a stair leading up.

I'd climbed three steps when I saw the figure standing at the top.

'Who the hell are you?' he said.

But I was already running. He took the stairs quickly, but not quickly enough. I was out of the front door and running. I didn't think he would follow, but he did. He must have been wearing shoes, or the forest floor would have cut his feet open in seconds.

I didn't have any plan other than flight, but of course my pursuer knew the woods better than I did. He hadn't yelled out for help, so it was one-on-one. What's more, I had a gun and a knife. I was feeling a little more confident when he appeared suddenly in front of me. I went for the knife, but he slammed a fist into my face and a foot into my leg. I knew he was trying for the kneecap, which told me he'd been trained. But he landed high, numbing my thigh but not paralysing me. He was quick, no doubt about that. But now I had the gun in my hand. He snatched at it, his hand snaking out of the dark, and twisted my wrist until it nearly broke. I let the gun fall and went for the knife with my left hand. This gave him all the time in the world to land another punch and kick. The punch caught me on the side of the head, and the dark suddenly became fifty shades of stunning blue. His kick was Kung-Fu style and just missed my heart. It had enough power to throw me back through the trees. I kept my balance, God knows how. I knew I had to get the damned knife into play.

The moon appeared, lighting his bare torso. It was criss-crossed with cuts from branches, but that wasn't going to slow him down. There was a snarl on his face as he launched himself at me, hurling himself forward, arms outstretched. He knew all about close-quarters combat, knew I couldn't use the knife once he got me in a hug.

I dived sideways, falling as I did. I heard him grunt as he missed me. There was a cracking sound. I got to my feet as quick as I could. He wouldn't miss a sitting target. But when I looked, he was standing very still, his arms hanging by his sides. Then I saw why. There was a low branch sticking out through his back. He'd speared himself on a hemlock.

'Thank Christ for that,' I said. Then I switched on the torch and found my pistol, sticking it back into my trousers. I considered burying the body, but knew it wouldn't be easy. At least leaving him here, any coroner might be persuaded of a bizarre accident. It certainly didn't look like murder. I shone the torch into his face, and saw the resemblance to his brother immediately.

'Hello, Nathan,' I said.

I was shaking as I drove back to the campsite. I hadn't been so close to death before. I'd never seen that much fresh blood close up. I'd seen Max of course, but Max's corpse hadn't been warm. The picture of Nathan Kline would stay with me long after my victims' had faded. I didn't think liquor and a holiday would ever wipe out Nathan's staring face.

Clancy and Bel were still awake, awaiting my return. When they saw me, they knew something had gone badly wrong. One side of my face was swollen, bruising nicely. My chest hurt, and I was still limping from the kick to my thigh. My hair was tangled with sweat, and my clothes were smeared with earth.

'I need to get to a hospital,' I said.

'There might be something at Port Angeles.'

'This is sort of specialised,' I said.

'Michael's got haemophilia,' Bel explained.

'It'll have to be Seattle or Tacoma,' Clancy decided.

So we packed everything up by torchlight. Or rather, they did while I stayed in the car. A couple of campers complained about the noise, until Bel explained that we had an emergency and had to get someone to hospital. I'd been hoping she wouldn't say anything. Now we had campers out looking at me like I was a zoo exhibit. I kept my head bowed so they wouldn't see the bruises. I knew most of the campers would be gone by morning, when Nathan's body would be found. But the police could find them elsewhere in the park and ask them about tonight. And now they'd be able to tell all about a man with his head hidden from them, a sudden need to break camp in the middle of the night.

Things, I thought, had taken a very bad turn.

We got out of there and Bel apologised.

'I just didn't think,' she said.

'That's okay.'

Clancy was driving. There were no ferries that he knew of, not this late, so we headed south on 101 and picked up I-5 through Tacoma to Seattle. There was a hospital not too far from our hotel. We had to go through the usual American bureaucracy, details taken, disclaimers and waivers signed, and of course they wanted to know how they'd get paid, before a doctor took a look at me. He wasn't a haemophilia specialist, his first few questions were all about what had happened.

'A fight outside a bar,' I told him.

'You're not supposed to get into fights.'

'That's what I told the guy who hit me.'

Eventually he gave me a dubious all-clear, but told me to come see a specialist in the morning. I paid cash back at the desk and Clancy drove us back to the hotel.

The night staff didn't say anything when Bel asked for the room key. Maybe they'd seen wasted-looking people before, turning up in the wee small hours wearing hiking outfits.

We broke into a bottle of tequila Bel had bought, and I put some ice into a towel for my bruises.

'I still don't get it,' said Clancy. 'You say his name's Nathan *Kline*?'

'That's what it said on his file.'

'You think he's some relation of Kline's?'

'There were facial similarities.'

He shook his head. 'Jesus,' he said.

'And whatever he was, he wasn't my idea of a "disciple of love". He knew unarmed combat like I know rifles. I'm lucky we were fighting at night. In daylight he'd have killed me.'

'So what does that make him?'

'Ex-military, something like that. Maybe CIA or NSC. All I know is that it makes him dead.'

Bel was staring at me, so I turned to her.

'I don't feel great about it, Bel, but this time it was him or me. And I didn't kill him, a tree-branch did. But I *would* have killed him. And he'd have killed me.'

'I know,' she said quietly. 'I'm glad he's dead.' Then she went back to her drink.

Clancy didn't go home. He slept in a chair, while Bel and I took the beds. We talked some more, and finally settled down to sleep as the sun was rising. I probably slept for an hour, maybe a little more. Then I went into the bathroom, closed the door and turned on the light. I looked like I'd been in an accident with a timber-lorry. My chest and thigh were purple with shades of mauve and black. My eye had closed up a little as the flesh below it swelled. It was tender to the touch, but at least I hadn't lost any teeth.

I didn't think I was going to die. Haemophiliacs rarely die these days, not if they look after themselves. But I'd go back to the hospital anyway and have a proper check done.

I went down to the lobby and out into the fresh air of a new day. Only in my head it was still the middle of the night and I was out in the woods, being taken apart by a crazed jungle-fighter. I tried not to limp as I walked. I'd changed into some clean clothes. There were a few early risers about, driving to work, or shuffling through the streets examining garbage. I headed for the waterfront to do some thinking.

I didn't doubt that Nathan was Kline's brother, which tied the Disciples of Love very closely to the NSC. But a question niggled: did anyone at the Disciples know Nathan's real identity? And come to think of it, what was so important that Nathan would go undercover for nearly eight years to protect it? They might have discovered his body by now. They might be contacting the police. If they *didn't* contact the police, that would be a sign of the whole cult's complicity. I knew I had to go back to the peninsula to be sure.

I also wanted to investigate Nathan's house on Hood Canal. If I wanted to do it, I'd have to do it fast, before Kline got to hear of his brother's all-too-suspicious demise.

'Great day for it,' a woman told me as she pushed a supermarket shopping-trolley over the train lines. A train had just crept past, holding up the few cars. It carried wood, thousands of planks coming south from Canada. We'd both watched it roll inexorably past.

'Great day for it,' she said again, waving to me as she moved away.

We went out for breakfast and ate huge blueberry muffins, washed down with strong coffee. I told Clancy and Bel I wanted to go back to the peninsula.

'You're out of your mind,' Clancy said.

We'd listened to the early-morning radio news, and there'd been nothing about Nathan's death. And only a few minutes ago, Clancy had phoned a colleague at the newsdesk and asked if any reports had come in of 'anything' happening in the park. The colleague's reply had been negative.

'First,' Bel said, 'you're going to go back to that hospital. I don't want you keeling over on me, Michael.'

'And we need to change cars,' Clancy added. He had a point. It would be a lot safer heading back to the peninsula in a new car. The campers had seen me sitting in a VW Rabbit, which was a world away from a Trans-Am. 'Look,' he said. 'Why don't I drop the two of you off at the hospital, go fetch the Trans-Am and pick you up again afterwards?'

'Sounds good to me,' said Bel.

So that was agreed. We checked that the car was ready and that my hospital appointment was confirmed. I checked we'd left nothing in the Rabbit before we left the hotel.

The car worried me. All it needed was for one camper to remember the licence plate and reel it off to the police, and they would track it instantly by computer to the repair shop, where the owner knew Clancy. And once they knew about Clancy, that would be the end of it.

I had to trust to luck that no one would remember the plate. And I hated trusting to anything other than myself.

Bel and I sat in the hospital for a while. She remarked how bright and new it seemed, how well equipped. She was just making conversation, that was all.

'Wait till you see what they charge,' I told her, 'then you won't be surprised.'

We were getting through the money. I didn't like to think about how I'd go about earning some more.

'I wish I'd been there when you killed him,' Bel said quietly.

'I didn't kill him,' I reminded her. 'And for God's sake, why would you want to be there?'

She turned to me and smiled a humourless smile.

I saw the doctor and everything seemed to be all right. He insisted on a few blood tests, since he wanted to be 'on the safe side', even though I objected I'd be flying back to England in a few days.

After all of which, I parted with some cash. The person behind the desk pointed out that they couldn't know yet how much everything would cost, since the blood tests were done at an independent lab, so they'd bill me later. I gave my fake address again, the same one I'd given the previous night, and walked out of the hospital knowing I'd saved a few dollars at least.

Then we waited for Clancy. We waited a long time. At last we gave up and took a cab back to the hotel.

The receptionist remembered something as Bel and I stood waiting for the elevator.

'Oh, Mr West? Did your friends get in touch?'

'Sorry?'

'There were a couple of calls for you yesterday evening. I said you were out.'

'Did they leave a name?'

'I'm sorry, sir, they just said you were expecting them to call.'

Well, in a way this was true. I walked back to the desk.

'We'll be checking out,' I said.

She looked surprised. 'Nothing wrong, I hope?'

'I've got to go back to England. You can see I've been in an accident . . .'

'Well, I wasn't going to say anything, but—'

'And the medical costs here are too high. We're just going up to our room to pack. Could you make up our bill?'

'Yes, of course.'

The elevator had arrived. I followed Bel into it. She waited till the doors had closed before she asked what was wrong.

'Everything,' I said. 'Someone knows we're here. It had to happen, we're just lucky we got this warning.'

We packed quickly. I kept the Colt Commando near the top of my bag, and put the pistol in my waistband. If you see someone in the US with his shirt hanging outside his trousers, think gun.

I paid our bill and the receptionist hoped she'd see us again. I wasn't laying bets on it as I went outside and found a cab. Only when he'd pulled up to the hotel door did I signal for Bel to come out. We loaded our bags into the boot, as well as a carrier bag belonging to Clancy. Inside it were a camera, film, and a small cassette recorder.

'Sea Tac?' our driver asked. But I gave him the address of the car repair shop instead.

We passed close by the hospital and stuck to the main route. But the road ahead was cordoned off, and a police officer was waving traffic on to other streets.

'Musta been an accident,' the driver said.

'Can you pull over?' I asked him. He did. 'Wait here, I'll only be a minute.' I told Bel to stay put. I think she knew what was going through my mind. She bit her lip but nodded.

I walked back towards the cordon. There were sightseers standing beside it. A car was standing at traffic lights, officials milling around it. An ambulance was there, but mostly I saw people who looked like detectives. Some of them were taking photographs.

The stalled car was our white Trans-Am. There were splashes of blood on the windshield. A sightseer asked what was going on. A veteran at the scene was eager to supply details.

'A drive-by shooting. Probably pushers, it's getting as bad here as LA. Guy's dead. They sprayed him all over the inside of the car. Looks like strawberries in a liquidiser, the cops told me.'

'Strawberries, huh?'

I walked away with deadened feet. Bel didn't need to ask. I told the driver there was a change of destination. He took us out on to Aurora until we found a cheap motel with a red-neon vacancy.

It reminded me of the first motel we'd stayed in after buying the Trans-Am: gaudy colours and infrequent maid-service. I went out to the ice machine while Bel unwrapped the 'sanitised' plastic tumblers she'd found in the bathroom.

We drank tequila. Bel finished her second one before collapsing on the bed in tears. I stood at the window and looked out through the slats in the blind. I'd specified a room round the back of the motel, not sure how much safer this made things. My view through the window was of the parking area, strewn with litter, and behind it a narrow street with junkyard housing, hardly meriting the description 'bungalows'.

'What do we do now?' she said.

'Same as we would have done,' I replied. 'Only now we know they're close to us. Forewarned is forearmed.'

'Yes, and cleanliness is next to godliness. It doesn't *mean* anything, Michael.'

'Bel.' I went to the bed and pulled her up, hugging her close. I ran my hands down her hair. I kissed her wet cheeks. I didn't know how long we'd be safe in this motel. A couple of days maybe, but it could be less. There were dozens, maybe hundreds of motels on Aurora. But I was sure Kline or his men would search each one. The quicker we went to work the better.

'Stay here,' I said. 'Switch the TV on. They've got HBO.'

'I don't want HBO! I want this to end!'

'Bel, it's ending, believe me.' I just didn't trust myself to script the finale.

I did something not many people do on Aurora. I walked. There wasn't much in the way of pavement, and the drivers looked at me like I was roadkill. I didn't have far to walk though. Our motel hadn't been entirely chosen at random. It happened to be close to half a dozen used-car lots. I walked into the first one and browsed. There were some serious cars here, highly-polished numbers from the 50s and early-60s, all chrome and fin and leather. But I wanted something a lot more prosaic. Most important of all, I wanted local plates. We needed to merge with the scenery.

'Hi, can I help you?'

He was exactly what you'd expect: ill-chosen clothes and a grinning cigar. He walked with splayed feet and was shaped like a rugby ball: all stomach, tapering off top and bottom. I asked about a couple of the cars, and said I might be back. I also told him I'd be paying cash.

The next lot I tried was full of dodgems, not a roadworthy car in the place. They had a good mechanic though. He'd done a few tricks to make the cars look and sound nice. You had to study the trick twice or even three times to see how he'd done it. The Americans have a love affair with their cars, as a result of which there are a million products on the market for the home mechanic. You can pour gunk into your car which will temporarily stop an oil leak, or make the engine sound smoother, or stop the thing sounding like a cancer patient. They weren't even remission, these cures. They were quack.

The next place along had some nice newer models. There was a Volvo I liked the look of, and an older Mercedes. A Ford Mustang was an expensive option I toyed with for a couple of minutes, but then I saw the VW Camper. I knew it was by no means perfect. It wouldn't outrun a bicycle, was slow on hills, and was noisy. In its favour, we could get out of town and sleep in it instead. The guy was asking $4,000 for it, but when we had trouble sliding open the side door, he came down to three and a half. I studied the engine. It had been twin-carbed, and not by an expert. I told him I didn't want anything twin-carbed.

'Brings the life span and the resale down.'

I walked away from the vehicle, then turned and looked at it again, ready to banish it from my thoughts.

'Oh, did I mention I'd be paying cash?'

He came down to three and told me he was cutting his throat.

'Just don't splash blood on the hubcaps,' I said. I shouldn't have: it made me flash back to the Trans-Am and Sam Clancy's death.

We settled the paperwork and I drove out of the lot. The steering felt slack, but not too slack to be fatal. The indicators weren't working either, so I didn't make many friends crossing the traffic into the motel. I parked right outside our room. Bel was standing at the door, hugging herself, bouncing on her toes. I didn't imagine the sight of the VW had got her so excited.

'He's alive!' she said. I got her inside and shut the door.

'What?'

'He's okay, he's not dead. It was on the TV news.'

I sat down on the bed. 'Clancy?' I said. She nodded, biting back tears. We watched the TV together in silence, holding hands. It took a while till we got another news bulletin. There was a reporter at the hospital.

'That's the same hospital I went to.'

The reporter said that the driver of the vehicle, Sam Clancy, a local journalist who had been in hiding after what he claimed at the time were attempts on his life, had been shot four or five times, once in the head, once in the neck, and at least twice in the shoulder. He was in a stable condition, but was still unconscious. Police were at his bedside and were on armed guard outside his room.

'I'll be damned,' I said.

There was an interview with a senior police officer. They asked him about the previous attempts on Sam Clancy's life, but the cop had nothing to say at this juncture. Then they spoke to Sam's editor and to a colleague. It could have been the man I spoke with the first time I phoned the paper. And finally they showed pictures of the Trans-Am and the repair shop.

'Shit.'

So they would have talked to the owner, who would tell them that it wasn't Sam Clancy's car, no sir, it belonged to a couple of English friends of his . . . Which would set the police wondering: where were those friends now? And if they were *really* clever, or really lucky, they'd connect Sam and his friends with the late-night disappearance of three people, one of them injured, from a campground near where a man had died.

Bel saw it all too, of course, and she squeezed my hand all the tighter. 'We've got to move,' she said. 'Before this starts falling around our heads.'

I nodded slowly, and she smiled at me. 'He's alive, Michael. He's alive.' We hugged one another, then I pulled her off the bed. 'Come on, places to go, people to see.'

'By the way,' she said, 'what were you doing in that rattle-wagon?'

That rattle-wagon took us back over to Bremerton and into the Olympic Peninsula. The gearbox had a habit of springing back into neutral, but apart from that there were no problems. The van didn't have air conditioning of course, or a radio. But Bel lolled in the back and opened all the little cupboards and took the cover off the sink, and seemed to like it well enough in the end.

It was true there wasn't anywhere to park on the road along Hood Canal. I suppose they'd done it on purpose so tourists wouldn't stop and gawp at the nice houses. However, you couldn't always see the house from the driveway, and vice versa, so I stopped in a driveway across the road from Nathan's house and a couple of houses down. Effectively, I was blocking the access, but the only people likely to complain were the occupants of the house, and they might never know. Clancy had pointed out that a lot of the homes here were used only at weekends and vacation time. I went round the back of the VW and propped open the engine, so we could claim mechanical trouble if anyone asked us. I'd tell them we were waiting for the triple-A.

We seemed to sit in the van for a long time. We hadn't brought anything with us, nothing to eat or drink or read. Bel found a pack of cards in the glove compartment, but there were only thirty-three of them. She found a few other bits and pieces too. A soiled dollar bill, a cushion-cover, the whistle from a steam-kettle, an unused stick of Wrigley's, and a bicycle pump.

'If we had a boot,' she said, 'we could have a car-boot sale.'

'Hey, come and look at this.' She came forward and peered through the windscreen. A car was coming out of Nathan's drive. It hadn't been there earlier when we'd passed, so must have been parked in the garage. It was smart, long at the front and squat at the back. I guessed it to be a Buick sedan. We'd seen enough cars on the road to make us expert.

'It's a Lincoln,' Bel said.

'Is it?'

As it passed our drive, I caught a glimpse of the figure in the back. All I could make out was platinum hair and a suit, but by this time that was enough.

'You want to break into the house?' Bel asked.

I'd been thinking this over, and now I shook my head. 'The house is just a meeting place. I don't think we'd find anything there.'

'So what now?'

'Now,' I said, 'we follow Kline. Here, you drive.'

'What?' We started to change places.

'He doesn't know you,' I said. 'At least, he hasn't met you. If we're going to tail him, it better be you in the front seat and me in the back.'

'He saw me when I got out of the car that time outside Oban.'

'He didn't see much more than the back of your head. Besides, you weren't wearing sunglasses then.'

Bel squeezed into the driver's seat. 'He's probably halfway to Seattle by now.'

'Doesn't matter,' I said. 'I think I know where he's headed.'

The problem was the ferry, or it could have been. But we stayed in the van, sitting in the back, pretending to play cards with our incomplete pack.

'Snap,' Bel said. We didn't look up much from the table, just in case Kline happened to stroll past and glance in. To the outside world, we must have appeared as engrossed as any poker fiends. We needn't have worried. Kline's sedan was in a different line, and about eight vehicles ahead of us. He stayed in his car, while his driver went for a smoke on-deck. I saw the driver very briefly, and recognised him as the same man who'd been driving for Kline that day in Oban.

We followed them off the boat, but lost them on the steep streets up near the Seattle Centre. It didn't matter. I directed Bel up into Queen Anne and then over to the big houses off Bigelow. The second street we tried was the right one.

'How's the handbrake?' Bel asked as she parked roadside.

'I haven't needed it yet,' I answered.

Jeremiah Provost's house boasted a cellar garage with a slope running down to it from the pavement. This was where Kline's car was parked, its nose almost touching the garage's closed door. Bel had taken us a bit further down the hill, which was fine. We couldn't afford to be obvious; it was still daylight. But I decided to take one risk anyway.

'Stay here,' I said.

'That's what you always say.'

'This time I mean it.' I left the van and stuck my hands in my pockets, whistling like a regular Joe on his way home from work. I climbed back up the hill and passed Kline's car. Bel had been right, it was a Lincoln. I didn't suppose the licence would help me, but I memorised it anyway. I passed the path which led around to the side of the house. I looked up and down the street, but there was no one about, no one to see me dive into the shrubbery and begin crawling my way around to the front door. Clancy had mentioned night-lights, but this was still daytime. I was hoping the system would only work at night.

I could hear voices, and slowed my pace accordingly. I could hear Kline's voice, then another man's. It seemed, amazingly, that they were holding a conversation – and a heated one at that – on Provost's doorstep. I could hear snatches. Kline kept his voice low, the other voice was the angry one.

'I told you not to come back here! You never did listen, did you?' This was the other voice talking.

Then I found myself nose to a prickly bush, and looking through its foliage across a postage stamp lawn to the open front door. A man stood in the doorway, looking down on to where Kline and his driver stood. The driver had his hands behind his back. Kline stood with hands in pockets, head bowed. He started to make a speech I couldn't hear. Above the three men, I could see a lamp high on the wall of the house. It was pointing in my direction and it was on. I must have triggered a beam. I prayed they wouldn't look up and see it. There was no point worrying anyway.

So instead I concentrated on Jeremiah Provost.

It was my first sight of him, and he was impressive in a mad professor sort of way. He looked like he'd gained weight since the most recent newspaper photos. His beard was longer and greyer, his frizzy hair swept back and out from his forehead, like he had electricity searing through him. He was wearing denims and a T-shirt and an old cardigan. There was a strand of thick round beads around his neck, and he touched them as he spoke. His stance made it clear he had no intention of letting Kline over the threshold.

That was the most puzzling thing of all.

Kline's speech over, Provost looked to the sky for guidance. 'Look,' he said, his voice an educated drawl, 'just stay the fuck away, okay? Is that too much to ask?'

More undertones from Kline.

'I *know* he's dead,' Provost snarled. He meant Nathan. Nathan's gory end still hadn't been on any news I'd seen. No doubt Kline and his men had been busy covering it up. Provost was still talking. 'As yet,' he said, 'we don't know anything other than that he *is* dead. What're you saying?'

I almost whistled: Provost didn't know the connection between Kline and Nathan. I even felt a moment's pity for Kline, who had just lost a brother. Then I smiled to myself.

The light overhead was still on. I wondered what kind of timer it had. And I thanked God it wasn't wired into any alarm. There was a camera, but it was aimed at the path, just in front of the main door. Kline was shuffling his feet. He said a few more words, then turned to go.

'Yeah,' said Provost, 'and don't forget to take your fucking gorilla with you.' I could see the gorilla clench his fists behind his back. Oh boy, he wanted to swipe Provost. But all he did was give him the surreptitious finger instead.

I waited till they'd gone and Provost had closed and locked his door, then worked my way around the rest of the perimeter towards where the shrubbery ended just before the swimming pool. 'Swimming pool' was actually stretching things; it was more an outsized bath. The French windows were open, curtains wafting through them. There was a big white open-plan living area, and a dumpy woman standing in the middle of the floor. She was stroking Provost's hair and kissing his neck, whispering to him. I squinted against the glare from the sinking sun. On the other side of the house, I could hear Kline's car pull back on to the street and drive off. The woman had long lifeless hair and was wearing a floaty kaftan which caught the breeze from the French windows. I guessed she might be Alisha. She stepped back from Provost, who was rubbing his hands over his face, a man carrying the weight of the world. He started flapping his arms, shouting something, near to frenzy or madness or something.

'What's on your mind, Jerry?' I said to myself, hoping he might yell out an answer.

But instead the woman hiked the kaftan over her head and let it fall to the floor. She was naked underneath. It wasn't a bad move. Provost stopped fretting and started looking. There was a lot to look at, including a wondrously large pair of breasts. He walked forward to meet her, and she took his head and rested it against her. He seemed like a child then, as she spoke quietly to him and stroked his hair and soothed him. When he broke away from her long enough to start taking off his own clothes, I back-pedalled through the shrubbery and on to the street.

My knees and elbows were black with earth, and with my bruised face I knew anyone seeing me now would have little hesitation calling the cops. So I fairly jogged back to the VW and got in.

'I saw them leave,' said Bel. 'When you didn't come back straight away, I thought—'

I stopped her panic with a kiss. What do you know, it worked, just as it had with Provost. In fact, she took another kiss and then another, this time with eyes closed.

I told her what I'd found out, but she couldn't make much out of it.

'Things seem to be getting more confused all the time.'

She had a point. It took us a while to find a road down on to Aurora, where we found ourselves part of the evening rush-hour. There was a drive-in burger bar, so we stopped there for dinner. The burgers were huge and delicious. Then Bel dropped her bombshell.

'I want to see Sam.'

24

New York, New York. Hoffer was back in his element.

He loved all of it, from Brooklyn and Queens to downtown Manhattan. He *belonged* here, along with all the other movers and shakers, the trick operators and cowboys and scammers. New York made sense to him, he knew its rules, knew when to play and how to play. Other cities, other countries: fuck 'em.

He stood outside the splatter gallery and felt so euphoric, he almost climbed the stairs to his office. Then he crossed to the diner and phoned his secretary instead.

'Moira baby, I'm down here if anybody wants me.'

'Sure. Constantine's here.'

'Send him down in five minutes.'

'Okay. Did you bring me a souvenir?'

'Hah?'

'A souvenir,' she persisted. 'I wanted something royal.' She sounded petulant.

'Give me a break,' Hoffer told her, putting down the phone. He didn't recognise any of the waitresses. The one who came to his table told him it was vacation time, everyone waiting tables this week was relief.

'And do you *give* relief as well, honey?' Hoffer said, grinning. She stopped chewing her gum and gave him a look. You couldn't have called the look 'interested'. 'Just coffee,' Hoffer said, dismissing her.

He glanced at his watch. Five minutes gave him time for one quick coffee. He didn't intend staying here, not with Constantine. That fuck always had an appetite, and never seemed to have money enough of his own with which to satisfy it.

Constantine was one of Hoffer's three employees. He'd just come back from Boston, and Hoffer wanted the lowdown. Meantime, he drank his coffee and stared out of the window. The street was noisy with cabs and drunks and what looked like a few tourists. Someone who looked like a prospective buyer even walked into the splatter gallery. That had to be a first. Then he saw Constantine come out of the building. The guy was young, mid-20s. He was always sharply dressed. Hoffer reckoned he had a side job. He sure as hell didn't buy all those clothes on what Hoffer paid him. Constantine was a shrewd guy, despite his years. He'd grown up on the street, or not far from it, and had a good way with words. He usually got people to talk.

Hoffer was at the diner door waiting for him. He put an arm round Constantine's shoulder and led him away from the diner.

'Let's walk, get some air.'
'I was gonna have some cheesecake,' Constantine complained.
'Sure, kid, later. First, tell me about Boston.'
What was there to tell? Armed with the information that the D-Man and Harrison had touched down there, all Constantine had done was find their hotel.
'They only stayed one night,' he told his employer. 'Staff hardly saw them. Crashed out, I'd guess.'
Hoffer was only half-listening. Between his friend in the FBI and Robert Walkins's contacts, he'd been able to find out a little about Don Kline. This past day or so, he'd found himself thinking more about Kline than about the D-Man. After all, the D-Man had never had the bad grace to disturb Hoffer at breakfast.
Kline was ex-NSC. Nobody seemed to know why he'd resigned; at least, nobody was telling. This niggled Hoffer, because now he couldn't be sure who was paying Kline. Somebody had to be paying him. That trip to the UK must have cost something, plus he had men to feed. Kline was beginning to worry Hoffer more than the D-Man himself was. Maybe he was just nervous that Kline might track the D-Man down before he did. Maybe there was more to it than that . . .
'What's that you said?' Hoffer said suddenly.
'The sister hotel,' Constantine repeated. 'That's where they headed after Boston. They booked from their hotel.'
'Sister hotel where?'
'Here,' Constantine said, opening his arms wide. 'That's what I've been telling you. Here in Manhattan.'
'Where in Manhattan?'
'The corner of 42nd and 7th.'
Hoffer was already waving down a cab.

The hotel was a typical tourist place, lacking style but clean enough to suffice. They'd booked in as Weston, and again they'd stayed just the one night. Hoffer handed a twenty to the desk clerk, as agreed.
'Any idea how they spent their time?'
'Sir,' said the desk clerk, pocketing the money, 'to be honest, I don't remember them at all.'
'You don't, huh?' The clerk shook his head.
'Well, thanks for your time. Rate you charge, I'd've been cheaper renting a hooker.' Hoffer turned away and found himself face to face with Constantine. 'I don't like it,' he said.
'What?'
'The fact that the D-Man's been *here*. This is my fucking town!' Then he stuffed his hands into his pockets and charged out of the hotel, nearly toppling two elderly tourists in his wake. Constantine followed him into the street. Hoffer turned so suddenly, the two almost collided.
'Right,' he said, 'look at flights, trains, coaches, car rental, the lot. Leave nothing out. Names to check: Weston, West, and Wesley, pre-names Michael or Mark. And remember there'll be a female companion.' Hoffer turned away again and faced the traffic. He wasn't seeing it.
'What was he doing here?' he asked. 'What did he come here for? He must've had someone to see, maybe something stashed away.'

'You don't think he's still here, chief?'

'What am I, fucking Sitting Bull? Don't *ever* call me "chief", understand?'

'Sure.' Constantine swallowed. He'd never seen his boss like this. Come to that, he'd seldom seen his boss *period*. But the guy paid, always on time and always the amount owing, and you had to respect that. Money: it was practically the only thing, excepting the Giants, his mother, and the pairing of Cary Grant with Katharine Hepburn, that Constantine *did* respect.

'So what're you waiting for?' Hoffer said. 'A gratuity?'

Then he turned away from Constantine and walked away. Constantine watched him go. There was room in his heart for a moment's pity. He wouldn't like to be Leo Hoffer, not for a day, not for a hundred thousand dollars (which was what he reckoned Hoffer earned in a year). There couldn't be many years left inside Hoffer's oversized body, maybe ten at most. Guys his size never lasted; they were like dinosaurs that way, neither species meant to last.

Eventually, Constantine's attention was diverted by a burger bar across the intersection. He dug into his pocket and started counting his change.

Back in his apartment that evening, Hoffer took a shower, then wished he hadn't.

His ears still hadn't recovered from the flight, and he got some water and soap in one of them, making it worse. It was like the wax was moving in there, like it was alive, crackling. Maybe the stuff was evolving or mutating. He stuck a match in, but that hurt, so he let the wax be. Maybe it was more than wax, some infection or something. He took some painkillers and had a hit of his duty free. Then he slumped on his sofa and took a look around him.

The apartment didn't have much to it. No personality or anything like that. It was a place to sleep, to ball sometimes, a place to cook up a meal if he could be bothered. He didn't have hobbies, and he wasn't about to waste his time decorating or anything like that. He never brought friends back here, because he didn't have any friends. There were a few guys he might go to a ball game with or play poker with, but that was always someplace else, not here. They were men he'd known on the force. Actually, these days, he hung out with more old hoods than old cops. A sign of the way his life had gone.

He couldn't remember the last woman he'd brought back here. Why should he? They were always one-night stands, the woman was usually drunk, and so, come to that, was Hoffer. He had plenty to waste his self-pity on. He could sit here all night bawling inside like a baby. Or he could go get ripped at the bar down the street. Instead, he pulled out the file Joe Draper had given him. And he wondered again, what am I doing here when I could be in Seattle? He knew that's where the D-Man would head, maybe not straight away, but eventually. So what was Hoffer doing hanging around New York? He reckoned he had half the answer: he wanted the D-Man to do his thing. Because Hoffer too wanted to know who had set the D-Man up, and why. He wanted to know who else wanted the D-Man as badly as Hoffer himself did. Part of him didn't like the competition. It was like someone was trying to steal his pet mutt.

But there was more to it than that. There was Kline. He still couldn't see where Kline fitted in, but he knew Kline would be on the lookout for him. Since arriving back in the States, he'd been watching for tails, checking for bugs. Kline would be keeping tabs somehow. Hoffer didn't want to look too keen. He'd hit Seattle soon, but on his own terms. And by then maybe Kline and the D-Man would be out in the open. That would be interesting. That would be very interesting.

'Yeah,' he said, nodding to himself. Then he got up and put his jacket back on. All of a sudden he wanted two things: a drink, and not to be alone.

'Simple needs,' he muttered, locking the door behind him.

25

It was time Bel had a disguise.

So we dyed her hair dark and I helped her with a haircut. Her hair had been short to start with, now it made her head look like a hedgehog. Not that I told her this. She quite liked the cut, and ran her hand over her head, enjoying the feel of the bristles. She used an eyelash-brush to dye her eyebrows. Then she started playing with the make-up we'd bought in the supermarket next to the motel.

Bel trimmed my hair. She was good at it, she'd gone on a course once. My own choice of dye wasn't so successful, and left my hair streaky. I didn't bother with the eyebrows.

'How do I look?' said Bel. The truth was, she looked stunning. It was just that she didn't look like Bel any more. Her eyes were heavily made up, black, and incredibly sexy. It was hard to look at them without looking away again quickly. She'd dusted her cheeks and applied cherry lipstick to her mouth. She'd bought some cheap jewellery, and now wore earrings and bangles and a gold chain around her throat.

'You look different.'

'Different is what we want.' She pouted. 'Now, Mikey, do I get to go to the hospital?'

'Just don't try an American accent, all right?'

'You got it, Mikey.'

Actually, to my ears her accent was pretty good. Its only flaw was that it sounded like an actress doing it rather than the real thing. I guessed she'd picked it up from TV and films rather than from our travels.

She seemed confident, so I drove her downtown. Part of me was hoping she'd walk into Clancy's room and be arrested on the spot. I didn't think she'd tell them anything, but at least she'd be safely locked away. I considered phoning the cops from a callbox and tipping them off, only she'd know who'd done it.

So I dropped her off near the hospital steps and drove the VW around the block. There was a visitors' car park, and since I couldn't find a space anywhere else, I ended up there. The problem was, I couldn't see the hospital entrance, so I got out of the van and walked about, kicking my heels like I was waiting for someone. I wasn't alone. There were a couple of other men doing the same thing, plus a cab driver chewing gum and leaning his arm out of his cab to beat a tattoo with his fingers on the roof.

It was a warm evening, but not sticky. It had been about this time of year that I'd come here whale-watching. I'd been lucky. I'd seen several pods of Orcas. I couldn't remember now why I'd wanted to watch whales, but I was glad I'd done it.

'I hate hospitals.' I turned towards the speaker. It was the cabbie. I walked over towards him. 'I mean, I could wait inside, right? But I prefer to wait in the car. Inside, I could maybe get a coffee, but then there'd be that smell wafting up at me. You know that smell?' He waved his hands beneath his nose. 'That damned doctor smell, things in bottles. That sort of smell.'

'I know what you mean.'

'You need a cigarette?' He offered me one, and for some reason I took it. He decided this had broken sufficient ice for him to get out of the car. Once out, he lit both our cigarettes. He had an ex-boxer's face and a few faded blue tattoos on his arms. He was wearing a short-sleeved shirt with a row of pens in the breast-pocket. 'You ever wonder how many people are dying in there while you're waiting outside, huh? How many are throwing their guts up or haemorrhaging? You get in a fight or what?'

I touched my face. 'Yeah, sort of.'

'Jesus, what did he hit you with, a tyre-iron?'

'Actually, it was his fist.'

The cabbie whistled. 'Big fuck, huh?'

'Huge.'

He flexed his shoulders, wondering if he could have made a better job of my opponent.

'Have you ever boxed?' I asked him.

'Yeah, I used to do some.'

'I thought so.'

'You?'

'I'm a man of peace.'

'Well, in my estimation, everyone's a man of peace until he gets steamed up about something. I had a lot of aggression in my youth. What was I going to do, be a public nuisance or step into a ring? Step into a ring, all that aggression is licensed. It's entertainment.'

'You enjoyed it, huh?'

'I didn't much enjoy getting beat.'

I wasn't listening any more. I was watching the entrance. A few people had just come out of the hospital and were standing on the steps. I recognised Kline first. It took me another moment to recognise Bel.

Kline was looking up and down the street. At first I thought he was looking for me, but in fact they were waiting for a car. One of his men, the passenger from the front car in Oban, spoke into a radio. Bel was staring at the ground. Kline had a hand on her arm.

'Hey, you okay?'

The cigarette had dropped from my mouth. I turned away from the cabbie and walked quickly to the van. I went into the back, opened a cupboard, and brought out the Colt Commando. It was pre-loaded and ready for action. Then I got into the driver's seat and started the van. The cabbie was wide-eyed as I passed him, one hand on my steering-wheel and the other gripping the gun.

Kline's car was just arriving. They'd brought Bel down to the kerbside. I speeded up and hit the kerb, bouncing the van on to the pavement. Kline and his men looked surprised, then scared. They dived out of the way as I let rip with a few rounds. Bel didn't need to be told what to do. She opened the passenger door and clambered in.

'Hey, Kline!' I roared. 'We need to talk.'

He was crouching behind the car. 'Fuck you!'

I fired another burst to keep them down, then reversed back on to the road, hit first gear again, and roared forward.

'Get down!' I yelled. I fired a burst up into the air, but they weren't scared any more. The initial shock had worn off and they'd found their pistols. I felt rounds thumping into the side and rear of the van. But they missed the tyres. We took a hard right into another street, ran a red light and took a left. I didn't know where the hell we were, but I knew we were out of range.

'We don't seem to be having much luck with our vehicles,' I said. I was thinking: at the very least now they'd know that I was seriously armed and driving a VW van. They might even have got the licence number. It was only three letters and three numbers, easily memorised. I kept checking in the rearview, but there was no sign of pursuit. I slowed down a bit until I'd got my bearings. Soon we were back on 99 and heading north.

'Don't you want to hear what happened?' Bel said. She was shivering. I wound my window back up, then realised that wasn't why she was shivering.

'So what happened?' I was more than angry with her, I was furious. I'd told her not to go, I'd known it was a stupid idea. Yet I hadn't stopped her. I was furious with myself.

'They must have been in the reception area, only I didn't see them. I asked where I could find Sam Clancy, and the woman on the desk pointed me along a corridor. Only, halfway along they grabbed me. They had a good look at me, and then Kline told me to say something.'

'You tried your American accent?'

'Yes. The bastard hit me. So I started swearing at him, and all he did was smile. Then he told me he knew who I was and he asked me where you were.'

'What did he call me?'

'Weston.'

'Not West?'

'No, Weston. Or maybe West. I don't know. Jesus, I was petrified, Michael.'

'Did you say anything else?'

'I told him I knew he killed my father and I was going to kill him for that.'

'Well then, you've told him pretty much all he needs to know. He can't let either of us live now.'

She bit her lip. 'Thanks for bailing me out.'

I managed to smile at her.

I passed the motel without stopping, turned at a fast food place, and waited for a minute by the roadside. No one was following us.

'Tomorrow we have to move again. For tonight, we sleep in shifts. The other one keeps watch from the window. Okay?'

'Okay.'

As it turned out, I didn't have the heart to wake her. It was all my fault she was here in the first place. What had I been doing taking her to London with me? Of course, if I hadn't taken her with me, they'd probably have killed her when they killed Max. This thought pushed away the guilt. I sat in a chair by the window, and went out to the vending machine occasionally for ice-cold Coke and chocolate bars. I crunched a few caffeine tablets until my heart rate sounded too high. I knew every inch of the parking lot, every scrap of trash blowing across it. The sodium glare hurt my eyes. I wanted to close them, to wash them out. Then I closed them for a second too long.

I slept.

It was morning when I woke up, and not early-morning either.

Through the window I saw the maid's cleaning cart. She was looking at me, so I shook my head and she pushed the cart along to the next room, knocked, and then went into it.

My watch said 10.15. I got up from the chair and stretched, shrugging my shoulders free of their stiffness. I needed a shower.

'Bel,' I said. 'Time to wake up.'

She rolled over, exhaled, and then lifted her head from the pillow. Like me she was almost fully dressed.

'What time is it?'

'It's gone ten. Come on, get up. You can take first shower.'

I watched her as she slunk into the bathroom and closed the door. I knew our options now had narrowed considerably. We were no longer the hunters but the hunted. Worst of all, I still didn't know what was going on. I could think of one man who knew: Jeremiah Provost. But Kline would have Provost covered. Kline would have *everything* covered.

I had enough quarters left to buy us a couple of breakfast Cokes. I had a head full of mud and my body felt like it was dragging weights. The vending machine was next to the ice-box in a little connecting alley between the back of the motel and the front. There was a concrete stairwell up to the rooms on the first floor. I'd sat there last night for a while, listening to traffic. Now, as I got the second can from the machine, I heard tyres squeal out front. I looked around the corner and saw a car sitting next to the motel office. A man was getting out of the passenger side, buttoning his jacket as he walked to the office. He wore sunglasses and looked around him. I didn't recognise the man, but he didn't look like a typical resident. He looked official. I ducked back into the alley and flew to our room.

'Got to go!' I called. Bel came out of the bathroom dressed and rubbing her hair with a towel. 'Got to go,' I said. When she saw me throwing stuff into a bag, she took the hint, threw down the towel, and started packing.

'What's the problem?'

'Bad guys at the office. They could be asking about VW vans.' I took hold of the Smith & Wesson. 'Here,' I told her, 'take this.'

She didn't say anything. It took her a moment to make up her mind, then she snatched the pistol from me. She checked the clip, slapped it home and made sure the safety was on. I didn't have time for a smile.

They say discretion is the better part of valour, but we were anything but discreet leaving the room. We ran to the van, heaving bags into the back. Bel was toting the pistol, and I had the Colt Commando by its carrying handle. I'd taken off the flash-hider. When I'd used the Commando last night, the noise without the hider had been impressive. It had made people duck. So the hider stayed off.

Now we were in the van, I hesitated for a second. What were we supposed to do? Cruise past the car with a nod and a smile? Play hide and seek around the motel? Or leave the van and take to the streets? I certainly didn't want to leave the van, not just yet. So the only thing to do was drive . . . drive, and see what happened. I knew I could tell Bel to split, to run off on her own, or stay holed up in the room. It was me they wanted. But of course they'd want her too. We were a package now; she knew everything I did. Besides, she wouldn't stay behind. It wasn't her style. I turned to her.

'Tell me about yourself.'

'What?'

'You said I should ask you some time when you weren't expecting it.'

'You're crazy, Michael.' But she was grinning. I realised she was probably readier for this than I was. I started the engine.

'It's just, it'd be nice to have known you before we die.'

'We're not going to die.' She raised the pistol. 'I love you, Michael.'

'I love you, too. I always have.'

She flipped the safety off the semi-automatic. 'Just drive,' she said.

I drove.

We took it slow out of our parking bay and around the side of the motel, then speeded up. I saw that the car was still parked. Worse, it had reversed back to block the only ramp into and out of the car park. I brought the van to a stop. The passenger came out of the office and saw us. He pointed us out to the driver, then took a radio from his pocket. With his other hand, he was reaching into his pocket for something else. And when the driver got out of the car, I saw he was holding a machine-gun. I risked a glance over my shoulder, but all I could see were walls.

'Come on, Michael, let's do it.'

'Do what?'

'What do you think?' She pushed open her door, readying to get out. The driver was taking aim against the roof of the car. I opened my door and steadied the Commando.

Then I saw it.

It was a flat-bed pick-up with a cattle bar on the front and searchlights on top of the cab. I don't know where it came from, but I could see where it was going. It mounted the pavement and kept on coming. Hearing the engine roar, the car driver half-turned, saw what was happening, and pushed himself away from his vehicle, just as the cattle bar hit it from behind. The pick-up's back wheels lifted clean off the ground from the force of the collision, but that was nothing compared to the car. It jumped forward and then spun, looking like a wild horse trying to throw off its rider. Its boot crumpled and then flew open, its rear window splintering. Both driver and passenger had hit the ground. Now a shotgun appeared from the pick-up's passenger-side window and blasted two rounds over the heads of the men, shattering the office window. Then the pick-up reversed back down the short ramp and out on to the road, stopping traffic.

'He's waiting for us!' Bel yelled. She was back in the van now, and slammed shut her door. I drove out past the wrecked car, keeping the Commando aimed out of my window in case the two men decided to get up. The pick-up was already moving, so we followed it, stalled cars complaining all around.

'Who is it?' Bel was shouting. 'Who's in the truck?'

I had a grin all over my face. 'Who do you think it is? It's Spike, of course.'

26

The pick-up seemed to know where it was going.

We followed it east on to I-5 and then south through the city till we connected with the I-90 east out of town.

We were headed for the interior.

'Why doesn't he stop?' Bel said.

'I don't know.' I'd flashed my lights a couple of times, but all I'd received in return was a wave from the window. We crossed over Mercer Island, retracing the route we'd taken into Seattle when we'd arrived. Soon we were on a wide road with wilderness either side. This really was frontier country. Few tourists or holidaymakers ventured into the interior. It was hot and dry, and if you didn't like hills and trees there wasn't much in the way of scenery. That this was logging country was reinforced by crudely made roadside signs denouncing government policy, foreign timber imports, owls and environmentalists. Not always in that order.

We came off the Interstate at Snoqualmie. I was wrong about the tourists. A lot of cars had come to see the Snoqualmie Falls. The pick-up signalled into the car park and we followed. The only space left was a dozen cars away from the pick-up. I could hardly turn the ignition off quick enough.

I sprinted back to the pick-up. There was no one in the cab. Then I saw Spike. He was crouched in front of the vehicle, examining the damage to his cattle bar. He stood up and grinned at me, showing gorgeous white teeth.

'You look like hell,' I said.

'I've been driving all night, what's your excuse?'

We met and hugged, and this time it was me who lifted him off the ground.

'Damn it, Spike, I don't know where you came from, but you're an angel straight from heaven.'

'Man, you know where I come from: Lubbock, Texas. And the only angel I ever was was a hell's angel. Oo-ee!' He touched the bruise on my face. Then Bel came running up, and there was a hug and a kiss for her.

'Why didn't you stop before now?' she asked.

'I wanted to be sure those chimpanzees weren't on our tails.'

'Are you kidding? Did you see what you did to their car?'

'Oh, but they've got friends. And you folks, looks like you've got enemies.'

'And not many friends,' I conceded.

'But we only needed one.' And Bel pecked Spike's cheek again and squeezed his arm. He blushed, but covered it up by wiping his face with a red bandana. He had dark eyes and greasy hair and three days of beard growth.

'Man,' he said, 'I been living in these clothes.'

'Yeah, we can tell.'

He punched me in the chest. It was a playful punch, but it hit a raw spot. I winced and doubled over.

'Jesus, Wild West, I'm sorry.'

Bel helped me upright and explained, 'Michael got into a fight with one of the bad guys.'

'I see you've got a story to tell me.'

'We have,' I said, now recovered. 'And we've a few questions for you.'

Spike shrugged. 'Let's find a bar in town, somewhere to take the weight off.' He thought of something. 'You didn't swap my Trans-Am for that Nazi shit, did you? The thing's full of bullet holes!'

I thought of an answer. 'Let's get a beer first.'

'Follow me.'

It turned out that Spike knew the Snoqualmie and North Bend area pretty well.

He'd hunted out here, he had old friends here, and he'd once crashed a car here, which put him on crutches for a month.

'Good people,' he said in the bar, 'but some of them can be a bit strange. I don't know, inbreeding or something. You know they filmed *Twin Peaks* here?'

My face remained blank, but Bel looked interested.

'So what made you follow us?' I asked.

Spike took a mouthful of Rainier. 'Figure it out. I knew you were in trouble, Wild West. Jazz told me some of what Bel had told her. I got the kid to tap back into her computer and print me the same stuff she printed for you. I knew then why you were headed for Seattle, and I knew it could get serious. These cults are bad news. I had a friend got mixed up in one. He's still in therapy. And don't forget, I have a Trans-Am riding on this. So I thought maybe I'd tail along.

'I got to tell you, though, it was coincidence I was there this morning, not inspiration or anything. I hit town first thing this morning, and I was cruising up and down Aurora looking for a motel I liked the look of. I have to tell you, I passed yours twice and never even considered it. What's wrong, man, your credit no good in this town or what?' He sniffed and leaned back in his seat. He'd crossed a foot over one leg, showing off scuffed silver-toed shitkicker boots. Very clearly, he was enjoying telling the story. 'Anyway, as I was going up and down I was seeing these cars with suits in them. They didn't look like Aurora types at all. They looked like the worst kind of normal. They were checking all the motels, not looking for rooms, that was obvious. They were asking for someone. I followed one of them into an office and got to hear the description he gave to the clerk: man and woman, English, in a Vee-Dub. Well, apart from the car, that seemed to fit. So I stopped looking for a room and started following. When I saw your Volkswagen, man, I knew I'd done something right.'

'You can say that again,' said Bel.

'The Trans-Am got shot up,' I said. 'That's why we're in the camper.'

'What happened to it?'

'A man called Kline had his men spray it with bullets. A journalist who'd been helping us was driving at the time.'

'Is he . . . ?'

'He's okay, we think. He's in hospital.'

'So those sonsabitches shot up my car, huh?' Spike had a determined look on his face. It was the sort of look he got every time he picked up an assault rifle. 'We've got to total them, man.'

'Not so fast,' I said. 'You haven't heard our story yet. Maybe when you have, you won't be so enthusiastic.'

'Then let's get some more beers in and tell me all about it.'

We got in more beers.

'This guy called Kline,' said Spike, 'I've got to waste him, man. I've never met him, he doesn't know me from shit, and yet I just *know* I've got to waste him. I won't rest easy till I do.'

It wasn't just the beer talking; it was all the drugs he'd been taking on the road, drugs to keep him awake, drugs to push the accelerator harder, and drugs to hold it all together. I could see that in anywhere between five minutes and a couple of hours he was going to come crashing down.

'I need some sleep,' I said. 'My brain's stopped working. I was awake all night. Why don't we head out into the country, find a quiet spot, and recharge a little?'

'Hey,' said Spike, 'I know just the place.'

He led us out of Snoqualmie on the North Bend road, but then turned off and up a forest track. He was kicking up so much dust I thought our engine would die on us, but the VW just kept on going. The track got narrower, then narrower still. At first it had been a logging track, wide enough for a transporter, but now the trees were scraping both sides of the van, and there was grass growing through the gravel. I counted eight miles of this before we emerged into a clearing. So far since coming off the main road we hadn't seen a single signpost, and no signs of habitation: no electricity pylons or phone lines or mailbox or anything.

But here was a big log house, fairly new and with a lawn surrounding it, beyond which lay impenetrable forest. Spike sounded his horn a few times, but no one came out of the house. We went up to the front door together. There was a note taped there, which Spike read out.

'"Dear Friend, If you've travelled this far, then you probably know us, so you also probably won't be surprised that we're not here. We're in Portland for a few days and will be back Thursday or Friday. You're welcome to camp. There's a stream if you know where to find it. Love and peace, Marnie and Paul."'

'Friends of mine,' Spike said. There were potted plants all around the outside of the house, and he tapped a few playfully with his toe. 'We go back a long way.'

'This is fine,' I said. 'We've got tents in the van, and the van itself is good for sleeping in.' He was bending down, lifting the plants and looking at them, sniffing them. 'We even have a stove . . .' My voice died away as he turned a small plant pot upside down and eased the earth and shrub out on to the palm of his hand. There, embedded in the soil and the thin white roots of the plant, was a house-key. Spike winked at me.

'Friends know where to find the key.'

Inside, the house was fantastic, almost too bright for my liking. Sun streamed through huge louvred windows in the roof. There was unpainted pine everywhere. The walls and furniture were made of it, and the ceiling was panelled with pine tongue-and-groove. There was one large living room, complete with a central stove. Then there were doors off to bedrooms, bathrooms and a kitchen.

'The bathroom has a whirlpool spa,' Spike informed us. He flopped on a white sofa. 'Man, this is the life.'

I didn't want to sit down. I didn't want to touch anything for fear of contaminating it. I was amazed to see that when Spike got up again he hadn't left black smudges on the white material.

Bel had examined the place like a sceptical would-be buyer. She picked up a wastepaper basket and showed it to me.

'They've cleaned the inside of it,' she said. And so they had.

'Hey,' said Spike, 'you want trash, you come back to my place. This is perfect for our purpose.'

'And what is our purpose?' I asked.

'Follow me and find out.'

He led us back down to the pick-up. I noticed it had a rifle rack behind the bench-seat, but the rack was empty. Spike had opened the door of the cab so we could see in. It wasn't a pretty sight. The ashtray was brim-full, with cigarette ends lying on the floor where they'd been stubbed out. There was enough lettuce and tomato to make a family a salad. I guessed Spike had been fuelled by service-station subs. There were empty cans and dirty socks and a begrimed T-shirt and maps and cassettes lying everywhere.

'Nice,' I said, 'we'll take it.'

Spike just smiled and swept everything off the bench-seat on to the floor.

'Put some carpet down there and it'll all look spick and span.'

He was still smiling as he unhooked a couple of catches underneath the seat. Then he pulled at the bench-seat, sliding out the actual part you sat on. He pulled the whole thing out and stood it against the pick-up.

'Well, well,' I said.

There was a lot of storage space underneath the seat. Spike had filled the space with a lethal array of arms.

'I think I thought of everything,' he said.

Bel stuck in a hand and pulled out a cartridge belt. It was full of very long brass cartridges. She held it up like it was a python which had wrapped itself around her wrist.

'Heavy artillery,' I said.

'The time for tiptoeing through the tulips is long past,' Spike said, pulling out what looked like an Ingram, maybe a Cobray. Beneath it I could see some M16s. My mind boggled at what else he might have in there. 'No dynamite,' he said ruefully. 'Otherwise I couldn't have taken a chance on ramming that asshole. But I've some *plastique* if you're in the mood.' He put his face close to mine. It was a good-looking face, typically American in being well-fed but still hungry. He was wearing one of his sleeveless black T-shirts with black denims. 'Gun heaven, Wild West, pure gun heaven.'

I hesitated for all of five seconds.

'Let's do it.'

We slept the rest of the daylight away. I emerged to find Spike dressed only in fresh T-shirt and shorts, chopping onions in the kitchen. He'd found a marijuana plant in the main bedroom and pinched off a few leaves. The aromas in the kitchen weren't just cooking herbs. He held up the chopping-knife for me to see. It was a rubber-handled combat knife with a fat nine-inch blade, the last three inches of which were saw-toothed.

'Chops vegetables great, Wild West.'

'I'll take your word for it.' I looked in the fridge and pulled out a carton of orange juice. I was a lot more comfortable about the place. The condemned man tends to worry less about the state of his cell. I shook the carton and drank from it.

'Oh, man, cooties!' Spike complained. 'Glasses are in the cupboard over the sink.'

So I poured the rest of the juice into a glass, filling it to the brim. I'd drunk half the juice when Bel came in, wearing a long trucker's T-shirt and not much else that I could see. She'd bought the shirt at a service station. It showed a chrome-fronted truck blowing out smoke like steam from a cartoon bull's nose. There was a Confederate flag in the background and the legend 'Ain't No Chicken!'

Spike was trying not to look at her legs as she stood in front of the fridge, bending from the waist to see what there was.

'Any juice?'

'Here.' I handed her my glass. 'We're on cootie-sharing terms,' I told Spike.

'Cosy,' he said, still chopping. He scooped the onion into a pan and added oil. Bel went to watch. 'Uncle Spike's Texas-Style Chilli,' he revealed. 'So long as I can find all the ingredients.' He opened a tin of tomatoes and poured the lot in, along with half a tube of puree. Then he added chilli powder and some other herbs, and finished with a drained tin of red kidney beans.

'Can't find any meat, but what the hell. How hot do you like it?' He offered Bel a spoonful of the juice. She thought it was hot enough already.

'Chicken,' he said to her.

'Well, Spike, why don't you pour some into another pan, that can be my pan? Then you two boys can add as much fire as you like to your share. I'll just sit and watch you tough it out when it comes time to eat.' She patted his back. 'It's food, remember, not an arm-wrestling contest.'

Spike waited a few moments, then howled with laughter.

'Bel, you've got more balls than half the guys I know. Move down to Texas and marry me.' He got down on one knee and grabbed her hand. 'I'm proposing right now, proposing to the woman of my dreams.'

She pushed him away with her bare toe and he sat back on the floor, arms behind him.

'The Good Lord spare me from rejection!'

'Sorry, Spike. Maybe one day when you're older.'

'Come on,' I said, leading her through to the living area. There was a breakfast bar between it and the kitchen. We flopped on to the sofa while Spike sang a few bars of some country song, then decided to whistle it instead.

'Bel,' I said quietly, 'I want you to stay here while Spike and I—'

She leapt back up. 'No way, José! I come this far and now you want to dump me?'

'Sit down, please.'

She sat down. 'Listen, before you try any other speeches or tactics, Michael, I know why you said what you said, and I appreciate it. It shows you care. But you couldn't stop me coming with you if you put a gun to my head, not even one of those M16s. If you leave me here, I'll wave down a car, cosh the driver, and come after you. And I *won't* be in a good mood.'

'Bel, I only want to—'

'I know you do, sweetheart.' She stood up, then bent over me and planted a kiss on my forehead. Then she went over to the hi-fi and searched for something suitable.

Well, I thought, that went pretty much as predicted. I'd tried, which didn't mean I could now progress with a clear conscience. What I'd been about to tell Bel was that if she came along, she'd only be a liability. She might get in the way, or she might cause us to make a critical misjudgement. I knew if I was wounded and there was heavy fire, Spike would leave me . . . and he'd be right. But would either of us leave Bel under the same circumstances? Spike had already confided that he didn't want Bel along.

'I'm not being sexist, man, but this won't be any party for a lady. Nobody's going to be eating sausage-on-a-stick and drinking Californian white. There won't be nice dresses and urbane conversation. It's going to be expletives and explosives, and that's pretty much all. What if she freezes? What if she chokes, man? What then?'

I hadn't an answer for him. It was a question, really, that had to be put to Bel.

Bel put Springsteen on the hi-fi, which met with a roar of approval from the chef. It was early Bruce, and even I knew the record. We sang along where we could, and Spike even sang along where he couldn't. Bel disappeared back into the bedroom and reappeared wearing jeans and boots. Spike had worked up a sweat in the kitchen, and guzzled from a bottle of red wine. He saw me looking at him.

'Hey,' he said, 'not a touch after this, okay?'

'That's okay,' I said, 'we're not going out there tonight.'

'Why not, Wild West?'

'Lots of reasons. They're almost certainly expecting us, we're not ready, we're still all a bit zonked or a bit hyper. Lots of reasons.'

'Not ready? Man, how ready can we be?'

'Readier than this. We want to be fully rested. Tomorrow is better.'

'What? Tomorrow at dawn?'

'Tomorrow night.'

'Why wait, man?'

'Because Jeremiah Provost's supposed to be visiting HQ tomorrow.'

Bel sat down beside me. 'You think he still will?'

'I don't know, maybe.' Spike had come out of the kitchen. He handed round glasses and poured wine into them from the bottle he'd been swigging from.

'It's safe, Wild West, no cooties on me.'

'He means germs,' I told Bel.

'I knew that,' she said coolly.

'Spike,' I said, 'we need this extra time. You've still got to show us how to use that arsenal you've provided.'

'Yeah,' he conceded, 'that's true. I was just itching to do it tonight.'

'Relax, calm down. Take a slow drink and we'll eat a lazy meal. Tomorrow we'll fire off some guns, check their action.'

Bel shook her head. 'If we're going to the peninsula tomorrow night, surely it makes more sense to try out the guns tonight, when conditions are the same?'

Spike whistled through his teeth. 'That is a *good* point.'

'I do have my good points,' Bel said, accepting more wine.

Twenty minutes later, we sat down to the meatless chilli. We ate it with rice and nothing else. It was fine, but Spike kept complaining about how tame it was and splashing pepper sauce over his. His forehead was all perspiration as we talked.

'That Commando is pretty good,' I said. 'Kicks a bit.'

'You're using it one-handed, of course it kicks. Wait'll you try the Ingram, that thing is like somebody's standing there jostling your arm all the time. We are *not* talking pinpoint accuracy, but it's a nine-point-five on the mayhem scale.' He scooped up another spoonful of beans. 'Have you tried the Varmint yet?'

'Haven't needed to.'

'Been one of those weeks, huh? Well, here's my plan. I'll fire an Ingram up into the air and flush them out, then spray the fuckers, while you sit up a tree and pick off the clever ones who're hiding in the cabins. How does that sound?'

'Lousy,' I said, reading Bel's mind. Me, I didn't think it was such a bad plan.

But Bel threw her spoon into her bowl. 'You could be shooting innocent people. We don't know that they're *all* involved. So far as the cult goes, we don't know that *any* of them are involved.'

'That's true, Spike,' I said quickly. I didn't want to give him a chance to say something that would really get Bel angry. 'From what I heard and saw of Provost's conversation with Kline, they're not exactly buddies. Kline couldn't have been treated worse if he'd been selling Bibles in hell.'

'Hell's full of Bible salesmen,' Spike said, and I smiled a wide smile at his joke. Bel was still stony-faced, but he had one weapon to throw at her.

'Bel,' he said, lobbing it without looking, 'now don't get me wrong, but I don't want you along tomorrow night.'

'Tough,' she said. Spike looked to me for support, but I was busy trying to get the last few beans on to my spoon.

'See,' he went on, 'Wild West and me, we've been there before in our different ways. Never as a team exactly, but we know the situation and we know the ground.'

'No,' she said to him, '*you* don't, *I* do. I've been out there, I've been in the fucking compound! And you expect me to sit here knitting you scarves for winter while you go scurrying off to play your little game? No way.'

'Bel,' he said, 'I know you *know* about guns, but can you actually use one?'

There was a silent stare between them. Bel was first to speak. 'You son of a bitch.' She turned it back into four words, where for most Americans it was one. Not sumbitch but son of a bitch. Then she stood up, left the table, and went outside.

I followed, curious to see what she'd do. What she did was find a switch on the wall outside. I suppose she'd noticed it before. Bright white light filled the clearing. I thought I caught a glimpse of a young deer melting back into the woods. There were lamps at ground level and up in the trees. It was like watching a stage-set. Spike joined me on the porch, handing me my wine glass. Bel got into the pick-up and started its engine.

'What's she up to?' he said.

'I think I've got an idea.'

She drove the pick-up to the far edge of the clearing and parked it. Then she started looking around her. I took the empty wine bottle from Spike and headed down the stairs. By the time I reached her, she'd found a couple of large stones and an empty Coke can. I handed her the wine bottle. She smiled and placed it on the bonnet of the pick-up. Then she reached into the cab and emerged with some weapons.

Spike had come down the stairs too. Even he knew what was going on. Bel walked back towards the house and turned to face the pick-up. It was standing side-on to her, the targets all in a row along its bonnet. She chose a handgun first. Expertly she checked and reloaded the clip, then held it out one-handed, closed her left eye, and let off three shots. She hit the can and two of the stones, sending them sliding across the bonnet. I replaced the stones and the can, by which time she'd got to know the small service-style revolver. Three more shots from that, all finding their target.

Spike started clapping, spilling wine from his glass. 'Okay,' he said, 'another good point. Message received.'

But she wasn't about to take that. She got the Varmint from the camper and loaded it, then fired off six elegant shots, each one on target. She hadn't nicked the pick-up's paintwork. For her final shot, she smashed the wine bottle to pieces.

Spike was clapping and whistling again. She turned to face him.

'I can shoot,' she said. 'I just don't like it. And I especially don't like it when innocent people get hurt.'

'Okay,' said Spike, arms open in conciliation. 'Give us another plan.'

'I've got a plan for you,' I said. 'It's in the form of a question. How do you sort out the good guys from the bad?'

They both shook their heads, so I supplied the answer.

'You see who runs away. Now come on, the next drink is on the house.'

But we had coffee instead of wine, and we sat on the ground outside while Spike spread out his wares. He laid everything out on a couple of old blankets.

'You ever see that film,' he said, 'where all the guns are laid out on the bed, and De Niro's buying? Man, I can't wait to see their faces when we turn up toting this little package.' Spike's grin was halogen-white.

I thought I saw Bel shiver, but then it was getting late. I felt a little shivery myself.

27

And still there were decisions.

For instance, should we check Provost's house, see if he really had gone to Lake Crescent?

Should we visit the house on Hood Canal first? That way, we might take out possible reinforcements. We didn't want to lay siege to the cabins only to have a vanload of newly-summoned heat creep up on us from behind.

Should we take the pick-up, the V-Dub, or both? They'd be looking out for the camper, but then they'd also be on the lookout for a crazy pick-up driver with dents in his cattle-bar.

One thing we knew: it was too dangerous to cross on to the peninsula by ferry. They'd almost certainly be watching Bremerton. In fact, there weren't nearly enough roads into the Olympic Peninsula for my liking. For an area measuring roughly ninety miles by sixty, it boasted only two routes into it. There was just the one main road, the 101, circling the perimeter of the National Park and National Forest. Using as few as maybe half a dozen men, they'd have advance warning of any approach we might make.

There were other possibilities, but they were time-consuming. One had us take a boat to Victoria, British Columbia, and then another boat back from there to Port Angeles. The two crossings would take a total of several hours, and as Spike pointed out, Kline would already have considered this. If he was agency or government, he'd have an order put out for all sailings to be watched.

'What you're saying,' said Bel, 'is that there's no way in there without them knowing about it?'

Spike nodded, but I had an idea. It was just about my craziest notion yet, but my partners went for it. After that, things started slotting into place.

Since the authorities weren't on the lookout for Spike, we rented a car in his name in North Bend. It was a bland family model, and Spike decried the loss of his beloved stick-shift. But it gave us the confidence to head back into Seattle. We stopped at Ed's Guns and Sporting Goods. I asked Archie if anyone had been asking questions. He shook his head.

'What're you looking for this time, son?'

'Balaclavas and warpaint,' I informed him.

It was when I said this that it all hit home, the sheer madness of it all. I was way out of my league; I was playing a different game altogether. I should have been scared shitless, and I was. I could hardly stop my hands shaking – not exactly a good sign in a professional sniper. My heart was thumping and I kept thinking I was going to be sick. But at the same time it was like being a little drunk, and Bel and Spike felt the same. We kept grinning at each other and collapsing into fits of nervous giggling. I burst out laughing in Archie's shop. He gave me a look, and smiled like he got the joke.

'There's no joke,' I told him. And there wasn't. There was just the euphoria of fear. I was pushing myself towards the confrontation as though each step had to be taken in thicker and deeper mud. It was the slowest day of my life. For all the activity and movement, it was slower than all the days I'd spent in hotel rooms, waiting for my hit to arrive in town, all the days I'd sat by windows, working out firing angles and distances. Archie seemed disappointed at the size of the sale.

'I see your friend's going to be all right.'

'What?'

He smiled. 'Don't worry, I won't tell anybody. They had a photo of him on TV. I recognised him straight off.'

'What's the latest?'

'He's awake. The police are talking to him. So far it's as one-sided as staging *The Price is Right* in a convent.'

I nodded, relieved. 'Archie,' I said, 'could you go to the hospital, say you're a friend of his?'

'You want me to go see him?'

'If you give your name and address, I think he'll agree to see you.'

'Well, hell, what am I supposed to say?'

'Tell him we're fine. Tell him today's the day. It might help cheer him up.'

He screwed shut one eye. 'Does this make me an accessory?'

'What's the crime?'

'Well . . .' He scratched his head. 'I can't close up the shop till six.'

'This evening would be fine. It'd be perfect.'

I tried handing him a twenty for his trouble, but he wouldn't take it.

'Be careful out there,' he told me.

'I will, Archie, I will.'

'I hate this car,' said Spike. 'This is the most boring car I've ever sat in in my life. Period.'

We were parked at the top of the hill, a hundred yards from Provost's house. We'd been sitting watching for a while, Spike drumming his fingers on the steering-wheel.

'I say we switch to my plan.' Spike's plan was simple. He'd walk up to Provost's front door and ring the bell.

'Just like the Avon lady,' he said.

The plan depended on two things: the fact that Provost, Kline and the others didn't know Spike, and that Spike could manufacture some bullshit excuse as to why he was ringing the bell in the first place.

We took a vote: it was two to one in favour. I was the lone dissenter. So Spike got out of the car and jogged his way down the hill.

'What's wrong?' Bel asked.

'I can't help feeling we're playing our joker a bit early.' She didn't get it, so I explained. 'Spike's our secret weapon. If they rumble him, we're back to square one.'

She smiled. 'Aren't you mixing your card games and your board games?'

I gave her a sour look, like I'd just bitten on something hard and was checking my molars for damage. Then I watched through the windscreen for Spike's return.

It wasn't long before he came jogging back up the hill again. He cast a look back to see if anyone was watching him, then got into the car and turned the ignition.

'The place is empty,' he said. 'I took a look around, nothing. They've got curtains over the windows, but even then I could tell nobody was home.'

'Then he's gone to the peninsula,' said Bel.

'Looks like. Either that or he's off to Costco for his month's groceries.'

This was it then. We were headed out to confront Provost and Kline. I felt weary, and leaned my head against the back of the seat, happy to let Spike do the driving. He turned on the radio and found a rock station. Springsteen: Born in the USA. Spike turned the volume up all the way and sang his heart out to the distorted song.

We already knew we were taking the long route to the peninsula, south through Tacoma and then north again.

'Spike,' I said, 'we really appreciate you helping us.'

'Man, I'm not helping you, I'm on *vacation*.'

'How's it been so far?'

'More fun than EPCOT, I'll tell you that.'

'I'm not sure that's a recommendation.'

He was grinning with his near-perfect teeth. 'It is, believe me. We should all go to EPCOT when this is over.'

'Who knows?' I said quietly. We drove into Port Angeles and then out again in the direction of Pioneer Memorial Museum.

We stopped on the southern edge of town, not far from the Park Headquarters. Then we put my plan into action.

Bel managed to get the attention of two park wardens who'd just driven their car out of Park HQ. She brought them over to our car, where Spike and I smiled and nodded a greeting.

'What's the problem here?' the first of them asked pleasantly.

'This,' said Spike, pointing the Ingram at the man's chest. The man, to give him credit, saw the problem immediately. It wasn't our problem, it was *his*. We took him and his partner in the Chrysler, while Bel drove the Park Service car. A little further out of town, we pulled off the road on to a track in the woods and stripped the wardens of their clothes.

'Jesus, why did you have to pick on Laurel and Hardy?' Spike complained to Bel. He was having trouble getting his uniform on, while mine fell off me like washing on a clothes-horse. We'd already tried swapping, but it had been worse.

We tied the wardens up thoroughly, and left one of them lying in the front of the Chrysler, the other in the back. We transferred our stuff to their car, and Bel got into the back, lying down across the seat and covering herself with a tartan travel-rug.

'National Park Service,' said Spike, getting into the driving seat. 'Here to serve and protect the wildlife.' He laughed. 'We'll show them what a wild life really means.'

Then he reversed all the way back on to the road. We took the 101 west. Five miles out of town, the road forked, but we kept heading west on 112. Just after the branch-off, we saw them.

There was a 4×4 parked by the side of the road, and two men standing beside it. They were as obvious a lookout as we could have hoped for. We debated stopping and confronting them – Spike said it would be a test of our disguises if nothing else. But I prevailed, and we drove past. If we'd put them out of action, their absence might be spotted. And we needed time to set things up. So we left them there, knowing that if they were summoned to the Disciples' HQ, it would still take them half an hour to get there. I didn't think we'd need more than half an hour. The way Spike saw it, if we went along with *his* plan we wouldn't need more than five minutes.

If you've ever seen the napalm attack in *Apocalypse Now*, you'll get some idea of the scale he was thinking on.

I crouched in the woods and watched the world through my night-vision scope. Strange things were happening in the Disciples' compound.

Or rather, *nothing* was happening.

And that was strange.

It wasn't that everyone had retired for the night. I got the feeling that most of the cabins were devoid of life. Spike and Bel had gone on a recce and come back with the news that they couldn't see any vehicles anywhere. Well, I could see one: Kline's Lincoln. It was squeezed in between two cabins, supposedly out of sight. But I couldn't see any other cars.

Only one explanation made sense: someone had sent the Disciples away. Now why would they do that? Obviously, because they weren't wanted. It meant one thing to me: the Disciples didn't know what was going on, and Kline and his men didn't *want* them to know what was going on.

I was concentrating not on the original cabin, the one where I'd been disturbed by Nathan, but on the smaller cabin next to it. This was where the light was burning. It looked like an oil-lamp or something powered by gas, and gave off a halo of yellow light. The pow-wow was taking place in this cabin. I was waiting for the braves to emerge.

Meanwhile I scanned the rest of the compound. It was pitch black, but to my right eye the world was a red filter with a black cross-sight. It was still and quiet. Sound carried a long way out here, and I actually heard a distant rattle as the cabin door opened.

I moved the scope back to the cabin and watched as a man appeared in the doorway. He was one of Kline's men, and he was smoking a cigarette. Other men filtered out on to the porch and lit up. Provost must be a non-smoker. They'd been in a room with him, and were now desperate. There were six of them. Three I thought I recognised from Oban, and three I didn't. Provost and Kline must still be in the cabin. The door opened again and someone stepped out.

A woman.

I recognised her by her shape. She was Alisha, Provost's lieutenant and lover. She accepted a cigarette and stood talking to the men.

They spoke in undertones, but even so I could hear the noise they made, even if I couldn't hear the words. The men were wearing suits. There would be handguns under the suits, but they were more prepared than that. Two of them had rested their M16s against the wall of the cabin while they smoked. They kept looking into the distance, mostly towards me. But from where they were, I knew they couldn't see anything. All they could see was movement, and the only things moving were the branches of the trees as the breeze passed over them.

I waited, but Kline and Provost didn't come out. Nor did they pass in front of the window. I adjusted the scope a fraction, and felt better. The scope was attached to the Varmint, and the Varmint was loaded with its full five rounds. I didn't have any padding against my shoulder. I didn't mind if I bruised. Bruising seemed the least of my problems.

I heard movement behind me.

'Well?' Spike whispered.

'I count six men so far. I haven't seen Provost or Kline, but there's one woman. So that's a total of nine.'

'And seven of those we can take out straight away,' Spike said.

'I'd like Kline alive . . . at least until he's talked to me.'

'Then we'd better get a car battery and a couple of electrodes. I mean, he's not going to talk for the fun of it.'

He had a point. Bel had moved more quietly than Spike. She was the other side of me. All three of us were wearing balaclavas and face-paint: green and black. Just in case they had a lighting system rigged up somewhere. So far, they were relying on darkness. But they could always change tactics and light the forest up. If they lit us up, of course, they also lit themselves up. And we'd be camouflaged. We were wearing green and black jackets and green trousers. We certainly looked the part, even if we didn't feel it. Spike was in his element, but the markings on Bel's face only hid the fact that she had lost all colour. Even her lips were bloodless.

As for me, I'd lost the shakes, but I still wanted to play it cautious. This was all new. I wasn't a mercenary, though I'd hung with them. I wasn't Action Man or GI Joe. I wasn't Spike.

'What about all the regular hippies?' he asked.

'They've shipped out.'

'That's perfect. That's beautiful.' He fixed his eyes on me. 'I got them here, man,' he whispered. He was holding four short, fat cylinders.

'So you keep saying.'

'When are we going to do it?'

I looked to Bel, who nodded. 'We're doing it now,' I said.

'Well, all right then,' said Spike, disappearing back into the gloom.

Bel and I stared at one another for a while. I wanted to kiss her, and I think she knew it. But she just smiled and nodded again, then squeezed my shoulder and started creeping away in the opposite direction from Spike.

It was my play now. I rested the Varmint's stock against my shoulder again and took a look. I knew I had to give Spike and Bel a minute or two. The guards had finished their cigarettes. They were kicking their heels. I liked the way they were lined up on the porch like targets on some fairground rifle-stall. I heard the static crash of a radio, and saw one of them lift a walkie-talkie out of his pocket. I was glad now that we hadn't hit the men at the checkpoint. It would have meant a welcoming committee.

But then at least a welcoming committee would have prompted action.

I counted up to thirty. Then I did it again.

When I reached twenty-nine for the second time, I started firing. I'm no speed-shooter, remember, but I knew I had to knock down as many of these guards as I could. I wasn't concentrating on any clever shots, I just aimed to hit the targets anywhere I could.

I'd fired off two shots before they located me. That's the problem with shooting at night with no flash-hider. They saw the second blast of fire from my barrel. Not that it helped them, not at this distance. They were still firing at shadows, and I was picking them off. Two bodies had gone down when the first of Spike's flares landed in the compound. To get it so near the cabin, he must've crept up suicidally close. He chucked a couple more flares. They burnt orangey-pink and let off a lot of smoke. I fired off the final three shots from my clip before the smoke got too bad. They'd tried retreating back into the cabin, but were being ordered to spread out across the compound.

Which was just what we'd expected. That's why Spike was way over one side of the compound and Bel, armed with two handguns, was over the other. The guards were firing now, spraying automatic rounds. From somewhere, I heard the unmistakable sound of Spike's Ingram firing back. I took off the night-sight, put down the Varmint, picked up my Colt Commando, and waded in.

The compound was all smoke and circus lights now, but the breeze was dispersing the smoke as rapidly as it formed. I decided to frighten whoever was left in the cabin, so let off a few rounds at it. The walls were thin wood planks over wood studding. In films, walls like that could stop bullets, but not in real life. I drilled into the walls until I could see light coming out through them. Then someone turned the lamp out. I'd been firing high, guessing anyone scared would be ducking or lying flat. I hoped I hadn't hit anyone I didn't want hit. Then I realised something.

I realised I was the only target the guards had. A bullet from a handgun flew past my head. I squatted down and let off a burst with the Colt. I hit the gunman three times across his chest, sending him flying backwards into the dirt. I could hear Bel now, firing in quick bursts the way she'd been taught. One-two-three, one-two-three, like dance steps. And Spike, Spike was back on the range in Texas, wasting bullets but making plenty of noise. They must've thought there was an army coming at them. And it was working, the guards were firing but retreating at the same time. If you fire a gun while you're moving, forget about accuracy. I held my ground and fired another burst from the Colt. It was fitted with a thirty-round clip. I had a few more clips in my pocket.

Then the cabin window shattered and someone started firing through it. I heard a dull thwump and realised they were firing grenades. I dived sideways, thudded into the ground, and started moving. The explosion was way behind me and over to one side, but it still lifted me off the ground. I felt the earth swell beneath my chest, like the planet was taking a deep breath, and the blast kicked my legs up into the air.

I lay flat facing the cabin and started firing, only to have the magazine die on me. It took a few seconds to reload, by which time another thwump had signalled a fresh grenade. I crawled again. The blast was a lot closer this time. It closed off my eardrums and rattled my head. I rolled and kept rolling, bits of earth and tree-bark raining down on me. There was nothing but a mute hissing in my ears, and somewhere behind it the distant firing of guns.

I tried to shake my head clear, and realised something had hit me. A rock or something. My left arm felt numb from the impact. I bit my fingers, trying to force some sensation back into them. Then got on to my feet and started firing again. There were bodies in front of me, three of them. They were lifeless. Two I had hit on the porch, and another hit since then, I couldn't say by whom.

Then I saw another figure darting through shadow. I put the night-sight to my eye and made out Spike. He knew I could see him, and gave an OK sign with thumb and forefinger. Not that he could see me, but he gave it anyway. I fired another spray towards the cabin. There were no more thwumps, which meant that Kline only had the two grenades. Now I could hear a woman shrieking, and hear two men shouting. I checked over to my right with the night-sight, but there was no sign of Bel.

Then the cabin door flew open, and Alisha came stumbling out.

'Don't shoot!' she yelled. 'I'm not armed or anything!' She was wailing, and holding her arm. It looked like she'd been winged.

'Everybody else out of the cabin!' I called. My voice sounded firm enough, from what I could hear of it. 'Out of the cabin *now*!'

Spike had come forward and was yelling Bel's name. There was no answer.

'Go find her,' I ordered, trying to keep the panic out of my voice. I took a slow-burn flare out of my pocket, stuck it in the ground, and lit it, moving away immediately. Spike was moving towards the side of the cabin. A man appeared at the cabin door. It was Jeremiah Provost. He had his hands up. Now that the flare was lighting up the scene, I saw he had blood on his white shirt. But it was a smear, nothing more, and I guessed it to be not his blood but Alisha's.

'Lie on the ground, Alisha,' I ordered. 'Why don't you join her, Provost?'

'Who are you?' He wasn't moving. 'What do you want?'

There was a sudden pistol shot, and Spike slumped to the ground. I moved towards him, then realised my mistake. I half-turned in time to see Alisha drawing a gun from beneath her. I shot her in the head with the Colt. One shot was all it took.

Then I turned again, and saw Kline stepping over Spike's body. He had his pistol pointed at my head. I ducked down, firing as I did so. His body fell forwards and landed on the ground. From behind him stepped Bel. Wisps of smoke were rising from the barrel of her pistol. The back of his head was matted with blood where she'd hit him.

She collapsed to her hands and knees and threw up on the ground.

'Are there any of them left, Bel?'

She managed to shake her head. I turned the Colt to Provost. He'd come down the cabin steps and was kneeling over Alisha.

'Why?' he said, repeating the word over and over again. I left him there and checked the cabin. It was empty. The back window Kline had climbed out of stood wide open. Smells of forest and cordite were mixed in the air. I walked back out, and found Bel sitting on the ground next to Spike. She was stroking his forehead.

'He's alive,' she said. 'Should we move him?'

'We may have to.'

I took a look. There was warm sticky blood all over his chest. He'd taken a clean hit in the front and out the back. If he'd been a little further away, the bullet might have stuck or burst open inside him. I didn't know whether he'd live.

'You got a stretcher here?' I said to Provost. He looked up at me with tears in his eyes, and mouthed the word 'Why?'

'I'll tell you why. Because she had a gun. Why did she have a gun? Because she wasn't a Disciple of Love, she was working for Kline, the way Nathan was. Did you know Nathan was Kline's brother? Did you know he was Nathan *Kline*? No?' Provost shook his head. 'It's in the files in your own office. How come your beloved Alisha didn't tell you? Work it out for yourself, but first tell me if you've got a first aid kit and a fucking stretcher!'

He stared at me. 'No stretcher,' he said. 'There's first aid stuff in the office.'

I turned to Bel. 'Go fetch it.' Spike was breathing in short painful gasps, but he was breathing. I went over to him again. His eyes were closed in concentration. He was concentrating on sticking around.

'Spike,' I said, 'remember, you can't afford to die. I suppose I better tell you the truth, Spike. There aren't *any* guns in heaven.'

He almost smiled, but he was concentrating too hard.

I went back to Provost and stood over him.

'Time to talk,' I said.

'Talk? We could have talked without *this*.'

'Not my choice, Provost, Kline's choice. Your man's choice.'

'My man?' He spoke like his mouth was full of bile. 'Kline wasn't my man.'

'Then who was he?'

'He used to work for the NSC. Have you heard of them?'

'A bit.'

'They retired him after an accident. *I* was the accident.'

'I don't understand.'

'You will.' He stood up. 'You really think Alisha was working for Kline?'

'It doesn't mean she didn't love you.'

He glowered at me. 'Don't patronise me, Mr West. Kline told me about you. He said you were coming after me. He failed to specify why.'

'Questions, that's all.'

He turned away from me and sat on the cabin steps, holding his head in his hands. 'Fire away,' he said without looking up.

Fire away? I hardly knew where to begin. Bel had returned with the first aid kit and was starting to staunch Spike's bleeding. I walked over to the steps and stood in front of Provost. I'd taken Sam Clancy's recording walkman from my pocket, and switched it on.

'A woman was killed in London,' I said. 'Her name was Eleanor Ricks. She was a journalist, investigating the Disciples of Love.'

'I don't know anything about it.'

'You didn't sanction her killing?'

'No.'

'Then Kline acted alone.'

Now he looked up at me. '*You* killed her?'

'Yes.'

'Then answer me a question. Why would Kline need to pay someone to do the job when he had his own hired army?'

It was a good question. So good, in fact, that I didn't have an answer . . .

'I don't know,' I said. 'You tell me.'

Provost smiled. 'I can't tell you. I can only tell you what Kline told me. He doesn't *know* why you've been snooping around. He didn't order any assassination, and he, too, was wondering who did. When you started asking questions, you became a threat.'

'He's had journalists killed, hasn't he? He had Sam Clancy shot.'

'Kline didn't have much of a conscience, if that's what you're saying.'

'But what was he trying to protect? Why was he shielding you?'

'Money, Mr West, what else? Oh, I don't mean I was paying him. I mean *he* paid *me*, and he's been paying for that mistake ever since.' He glanced down at Kline's body. 'He paid most dearly tonight.'

'I still don't get it.'

'Kline worked for a part of the NSC involved with funding the Nicaraguan Contras. This was back in the mid-80s. He managed to wheedle ten million dollars out of . . . I don't know, the Sultan of somewhere, some Middle Eastern country. At this time, I had a little money. Elderly relatives kept dying. I got bored attending so many funerals. I liked to keep my money my own business, so I held an account in Switzerland.'

'Go on.'

'It was quite a coup for Kline, getting so much money for the Contras, but he didn't exactly know what to do with it. Someone at the NSC, I'm not saying it was Colonel Oliver North, suggested holding it in a bank account until it could be disposed of as intended.'

'A Swiss bank account?'

'The NSC held just such an account. Only the gods of fate and irony stepped in. Kline copied the details of the account down wrongly. I can't recall now exactly why I decided to check the state of my account, but I telephoned Switzerland one Thursday morning their time, and was told the exact amount I had on deposit. It seemed larger than I remembered, about ten million larger. I asked my account manager how much notice I had to make of a large withdrawal.'

Provost stopped there.

'You took out the whole ten mil?'

'No, in the end I merely transferred it to a new account.'

'Christ.'

'It was Kline's mistake. He was sent to reason with me – no matter how discreet Swiss banks are, the NSC has ways of tracking people down. We came to a compromise. I handed back half the money. The other half I kept.'

'And he went along with that?'

'He didn't have much choice.'

'He could have killed you.'

Provost smiled. 'The NSC weren't mentioned in my will, Mr West. He still wouldn't have gotten the money. Besides which, his superiors were furious with him. They couldn't possibly sanction something so messy.'

'So they booted him out?'

'No, they booted him into the shadows. His remit was to make sure no one ever got to learn about the whole thing.'

'And that meant stopping reporters from snooping too deeply?'

'Exactly.'

'Which is why Eleanor Ricks had to be stopped.'

He shook his head. 'I've already told you, Kline denied it. And he went on denying it.'

'Then it doesn't make sense.'

'Maybe someone else hired your services.'

'Yes, but I've . . .'

He saw what I was thinking. 'You've come all this way and killed all these people, and you're no further forward?'

I nodded. My mind was reeling. I'd got most of my hearing back, but it didn't matter, I could hardly take any of it in.

'Two digits, that's what did it,' Provost was saying. 'Kline wasn't much of a typist. He transposed two of the digits on the account number. And in doing so, the NSC paid for the Disciples of Love. *That*, Mr West, is why they had to keep it quiet. They'd funded a religious cult, and the interest on their money is still funding it.'

'Where's the proof?'

'Oh, I have proof.'

'Where?' I wasn't sure I believed him, not completely. There had to be something more. He looked to be having trouble with his memory, so I tickled his chin with the Colt.

'Remember what I do for a living, Provost.'

'How can I forget? There are papers in my wall safe, and copies with my lawyer.'

Maybe it was the word 'lawyer' that did it. I almost felt something click in my head.

'You're going to open your safe for me.'

'It's not here, it's in my home in Seattle.'

'Fine, we'll go there.'

'I want to stay here. The combination's easy to find. I can never remember it myself, so I keep it written on a pad beside the telephone. It's marked as an Australian telephone number.'

I knew I had to see it for myself. I had to hold some proof of his story in my hands. Even then, it wouldn't be enough. I'd come through all this, and dragged Bel and Spike with me, and still there was no answer, not that Provost could provide.

A shot rang out. I spun round with the Colt. The guard had crawled from where Spike must have left him. There was blood all down his front. I didn't make things much worse by snuffing out what life he had left. I'd robbed him of a few minutes, that was all.

But when I turned back to Provost, I saw that he'd taken a shot to the heart. The guard had been aiming at him, not me. Suicide orders from Kline, no doubt. I eased the body on to the ground. Bel barely glanced up from her work. She'd patched Spike up as best she could.

'He's still losing blood,' she said. After feeling for Provost's pulse and finding none, I walked over to her. Then I saw the car between the cabins. It's rear windscreen had been shattered, but when I went to look, it had its tyres intact. I felt in Kline's pockets and drew out the keys, then reversed the car into the clearing.

With Bel's help we got Spike into the back of the car. He groaned and winced a little, so I repeated my warning to him about gun heaven. Then we got in the car and drove off.

'What are we going to do?' Bel asked.

'Get Spike to hospital.'

'But after that? I heard what that man said back there. He was telling us we'd come all this way for nothing. He was saying all those people died . . . and my father died . . . for *nothing*.'

I looked at her. She was crying. 'Maybe he was lying. Maybe . . . I don't know.'

We passed a car on the road, hurtling towards Crescent Lake. It was the lookout. They didn't even give us a second glance. I took a detour back to where we'd left the wardens. They seemed terrified to see us. I pulled them out of the Chrysler and left them propped back to back on the ground.

'You take Spike to hospital,' I said.

'Where are you going?'

'Provost's house.'

She looked at me. 'Do you think you'll find what you're looking for?'

'I don't know what I'm looking for, Bel. Look after Spike, eh?' Then I kissed her and got into the Chrysler.

On the road back into Seattle, I managed to put America out of my mind. Instead, I thought back to London, right to the start of this whole thing and to Scotty Shattuck. Why hadn't I hung around until he'd turned up again? He was the key to the whole thing. My impatience had led me the wrong direction. I'd been going wrong ever since.

Maybe I was still going wrong, but I kept on driving.

28

I was prepared to kick down Provost's door.

But it wasn't necessary. The door was unlocked. I eased the Smith & Wesson 559 out of my waistband and crept into the house. Someone had been there before me. The place had been turned over in what looked like robbery, except that nothing obvious was missing. The TV, video and hi-fi were still there, as was some women's jewellery scattered over the floor in the master bedroom. It had to be Alisha's jewellery. I didn't feel too guilty about killing her. She'd have killed me. But seeing the jewellery, plus her clothes, plus smelling her perfume . . . I had to rest for a moment and control my breathing.

And that's when he found me.

I felt the cold muzzle of the gun against the back of my neck. It froze my whole body for a moment.

'Toss the gun over there.'

I did as I was told, and then was frisked from behind.

'Walk into the living room.'

I did so. I recognised the voice. I knew who was behind me.

'Now turn around.'

I turned around and was face to face with Leo Hoffer.

'Sit down,' he said. 'Take the weight off. You look like you've had a heavy night.'

'It's been heavy.' I sat down on the sofa, but I rested on its edge, ready to spring up if I got the chance.

'Get comfortable,' he said. 'Go on, sit right back.'

I sat right back. The sofa was like marshmallow. I knew it was almost as good as restraints. I wasn't going anywhere in a hurry.

'Yeah, it's a bitch, isn't it?' Hoffer was saying. 'I sat in it earlier on while I was figuring out what to do. Took me five fucking minutes to get out of it. It's a regular Venus fly-trap. So, Mr Wesley-Weston-West, what're you doing here?'

'The same as you probably.'

'Well, I hope you've got some tools with you, because that safe isn't budging.'

He was pointing in the direction of the far wall. He'd taken down a large seascape painting to reveal a small wall safe. Even from here I could see he'd had a go at it. The wall all around it was scraped and gouged, and the metal surface of the safe was scratched and dented.

'I can open it,' I said.

'That's good. Because I want to stick your head in it then push my pistol up your ass.'

'That's class, Hoffer.'

'I'll tell you what class is, class is leading me on this fucking chase halfway across the world and back. That's so classy I'm going to blow you away.'

I felt tired suddenly. I mean, dog-tired. There was no steam left in me, no fight. I rubbed at my forehead.

'I want a drink,' I said.

'Provost hasn't got a damned drop in the house.' He reached into his jacket and pulled out a half bottle. 'That's why I had to go fetch this.' He tossed the bottle on to the couch beside me. It was Jim Beam, a couple of inches missing from the top. I unscrewed the cap and took a good deep gulp. Afterwards, I didn't feel quite so tired.

'How did you find me?'

He came close enough to me to take back the bottle, then retreated again. He took a slug, keeping his eyes and his Smith & Wesson 459 on me. He didn't bother recapping the bottle, but left it on the mantelpiece.

'Don't forget,' I said, 'your prints are on that.'

'And yours,' he said. 'I'll wipe it before I go. You look like you're ready for another shot already.'

But I shook my head. 'Any more and I'll fall asleep, no offence.'

He smiled. 'None taken. But I don't want you asleep. I've never killed a man while he's sleeping. In fact, I've never killed anyone, period, not even in anger, never mind anyone defenceless. I'm not like you, man. I don't kill the innocents. You fucked up big when you hit Walkins's daughter.'

'I know.'

'Yeah, and I bet you still lose sleep over it. I bet you lose sleep over all of them, man, all your victims. Well, I'm going to enjoy killing *you*.'

'Killing isn't as easy as you might think. Maybe you should hide me away till your client can come and help. I'm sure he wouldn't mind firing off a round or two.'

'You're probably right, but then he hasn't worked for that privilege the way I have. How did I find you? I didn't. *You* found *me*. I was waiting outside to see who turned up. I was expecting Provost or Kline.'

'You know Kline?'

'I've met him.'

'He's dead.'

'I'm pleased to hear it. He was about as evil a fuck as has ever given me indigestion. I hate indigestion at breakfast, it stays with me the rest of the day. Heartburn, you know.'

I nodded. 'Provost's dead, too.'

'You've been busy. So what the fuck was it all about?'

I shrugged. 'Listen,' I said, 'I want to thank you for something.'

He narrowed his eyes. 'What?'

'Covering up Max's head the way you did. His daughter found him.'

'Well, those sick fucks left the head teetering on the body.'

'I know, and thanks.'

'Is she still around?'

'She's . . . she's still around.'

'Don't worry,' he said, 'I've got no grudge with her.'

'Yes, I know.'

'This is you and me, Mikey, the way it was always supposed to be. Oh hey, your folks say hello.'

It was like a blow to the head. 'What?'

'I had this Army guy check haemophilia cases. It was a short list, and one of the names was Michael Weston. I found your mom and dad. They say hello. That's why I was so long getting here. Sidetracked, you might say. But I know a lot about you now, and that's nice, seeing how we're not going to be able to get acquainted the normal way.' He saw something like disbelief on my face. 'Your father's called John, he's retired now but he's still Army through and through. Your mother's called Alexis. They live in Stockport.' He smiled. 'Am I getting warm?'

'Fuck it, Hoffer, just kill me.'

'What's in the safe, Mike? Get me interested.'

'Huh?'

'You came here for whatever's in that safe. I want to know what it is.'

'Proof,' I said. 'This whole shitty deal is down to Kline and a bloody typing error.'

I had his interest now, which was good. It kept me from being killed. I told him the story, taking my time. I decided I didn't want to die. I didn't want anyone else to die. Not today, maybe not ever.

'That sounds,' Hoffer said, finishing the hooch, 'like a crock of twenty-carat gold-plated shit.'

'There are papers in the safe.'

'And you can open it?' I nodded. 'Go on then.'

He followed me to the telephone. There were a lot of scribbles on the message-pad, a lot of numbers and letters. I found what I wanted and tore the top sheet off, taking it with me to the wall-safe.

'Bullshit,' Hoffer sneered disbelievingly as I read from the sheet and started turning the dial. I pulled on the handle and opened the safe slowly.

I looked inside, knowing if he wanted to see, he'd have to come right up behind my back. I could feel him behind me. He was close, but was he close enough? If I swung at him, would I connect with anything other than air? Then I saw what was in the safe. There were papers there, and a tidy bundle of banknotes. But there was also a snub-nose revolver, a beautiful little 38. I took my decision, but took it too late. The butt of a gun connected with the back of my head, and my legs collapsed from under me.

I woke up cramped, like I'd been sleeping in a car. I blinked open my eyes and remembered where I was. I looked around. The pain behind my eyes was agony. I wondered if Hoffer had been in there and done some DIY surgery while I'd been out. Maybe a spot of trepanning.

I was in a bright white bathroom with a sunken whirlpool bath and gold taps. I was over by the sink, sitting on the cold tiled floor with my arms behind me. My arms were stiff. I looked round and saw that they were handcuffed round a couple of copper water pipes beneath the sink. My feet had been tied together with a man's brown leather belt.

Most disconcerting of all, Hoffer was sitting on the toilet not three feet away.

He had his trousers on though. And he'd put the toilet lid down so he'd be more comfortable. He had my money belt slung over one shoulder, and he was leafing through some documents.

'Well, Mike,' he said, 'looks like you were right, huh? Some fucking business, handed five mil by the government. Thank you very much and shalom. Jesus.' He patted his jacket pocket. 'Yet the scumbag only kept five thou in his safe. Still, it'll buy a few lunches. And thanks for your donation.' He tossed the money-belt towards me. 'I've left you the traveller's cheques. I don't want to get into any forgery shit. Not that they accept traveller's cheques where you're headed.'

I rattled the handcuffs.

'Good, aren't they? New York PD issue. Before they went over to plastic or whatever shit they use now. Look, I'll leave the key over here, okay?' He put it on the floor beside him. 'There you go. It'll give you something to do while you're dying. Of course, you may already be dying, huh? I whacked you pretty good. There could be some internal haemorrhaging going on. See, I know about haemophilia, I did some reading. Man, they're *this* close to a cure, huh? Genetics and stuff. Fuck all those liberals trying to stop laboratory experiments. Mike, we need *more* of those lab animals with holes drilled in their scrotums and wires running through them like they're circuit-boards or something.'

'Circuit-boards don't have wires, Leo. At least, not many.'

'Ooh, pardon me, professor.' He laughed and rubbed his nose. I knew he'd done some drugs since I'd last been conscious, but I couldn't tell what. He was feeling pretty good though, I could see that. Good enough to let me live? Well, he hadn't killed me yet. He stood up and opened the medicine-cabinet.

'All this organic shit,' he muttered, picking out bottles and rattling them. He half-turned towards me. 'I get fucking earache when I fly. And it's all your fault I've been doing so much flying of late.'

'My heart bleeds.'

Now he grinned. 'You can say that again. So Kline set you up, huh?'

'Provost says he didn't.'

'Well, somebody did. As soon as I heard you'd been asking the producer and the lawyer what clothes Eleanor Ricks usually wore, I knew the road you were going.'

'Then you're cleverer than me.'

'Whoever paid you knew what she'd be wearing, didn't they?'

'Yes.'

'Well, Mike, that kind of narrows things down, doesn't it?'

It struck me, the problem was I hadn't let myself narrow it down enough. Too late now, way too late . . .

'So,' I said, 'you know I'm a haemo. And you're right, a simple knock on the head might just do it.'

'But I know something that'd do it a lot better.' He stood up and came over, crouching in front of me. He had something in his hand. When he unfolded it, I saw a short fat blade. It was a damned pocket-knife.

'Beautiful, isn't it? Look, there's a serpent running down its back. That's the trademark. Talk about Pittsburgh steel, man, *this* is a piece of steel.'

'What are you going to do?'

'You know what I'm going to do, D-Man. I'm going to demolish you. The death of a thousand cuts. Well, maybe just a dozen or so.'

I started to wriggle then, pulling at the pipes, trying to wrench them away from the wall. Kicking out with my tied-together legs. He just crouched there and grinned. His pupils were pinpoints of darkness. He swiped and the first cut caught me across the cheek. There was nothing for a second, then a slow sizzling sensation which kept on intensifying. I felt the blood begin to run down my face. His second slice got my upper arm, and a short jab opened my chest. I was still wrestling to get free, but it was useless. He hit my legs next, more or less cutting and stabbing at will. He wasn't frenzied. He was quite calm, quite controlled. I stopped struggling, hard though it was.

'Leo, this isn't any way to settle it.'

'It's the perfect way to settle it.'

'Christ, shoot me, but don't do *this*.'

'I'm already doing it. Slice and dice. And . . . *voilà*!' He stood back to admire his work, wiping the blade on some toilet roll. I couldn't count the number of cuts on my body. There were over a dozen. They all hurt, but none was actually going to bleed me dry, not on its own. But all together . . . well, all together I was in deep shit. My shirt was already soaked in blood, and there was a smear of red beneath me on the tiles.

'Leo,' I said. Something in my voice made him look at me. 'Please don't do this.'

'The magic word,' Leo Hoffer said. Then he walked out of the bathroom.

'Leo! Leo!'

But he was gone. I knew that. I heard the front door close quietly. Then I saw the handcuff key. I stretched my feet towards it, but was a good ten to twelve inches shy. I slid down on to the floor, nearly taking my arms out of their sockets, and tried again, but I was still an inch or two away from it. I lay there, exhausted, pain flooding over me. Haemophiliacs don't bleed faster than other people, we just don't stop once we've started. I was a mild case, but even so there was only so much clotting my body could do for me. Leo must've known that. He knew so much about me.

'You son of a bitch!'

I sat up again and twisted the chain linking my cuffs. Every chain had its weakest link, but I wasn't going to find it, not like this. I looked up. Resting on the sink were a toothbrush and tube of toothpaste, and a small bar of soap, like something you'd lift from your hotel room. Soap: maybe I could grease my wrists and slip off the handcuffs. Except that there was no give at all in the cuffs. I've always had skinny wrists, much skinnier than my hands. No way this side of the grave was I going to be able to slip my hands out, soap or no soap.

I sat back against the wall and tried to think. I thought of a lot of things, all of them brilliant, and in the movies one of them would have worked. But this was a bathroom floor in Seattle, and all I was doing here was dying.

Then the front door opened.

'Hey!' I yelled. 'In here!'

Who did I expect to see? Bel, of course. I'd half expected she'd follow me here, once she'd got Spike to the hospital.

'In here!' I yelled again.

'I know where you are, dummy,' said Hoffer. He stood in the doorway, hands on hips. He was a big bastard, but not as big as he looked on TV. He gave me a good look, like I was a drunk cluttering up the hall of his apartment building. He was deciding whether to kick me or throw me a dime.

He threw me the dime.

Rather, he stepped on the key with the tip of his shoe and slid it closer to me.

'Hey,' he said, 'what's life without a bit of fun? Now I want you to do me a favour.'

'What?'

He was fumbling in his pocket, and eventually drew out a small camera. 'Look dead for me.'

'What?'

'Play dead. It's got to convince Walkins, so make it good. The blood looks right, but I need a slumped head, splayed legs, you know the sort of thing I mean.'

I stared at him. Was he playing with me? Hard to tell. His eyes were dark, mostly unfocused. He looked like he could burst into song or tears. He looked a bit confused.

I let my head slump against my chest. He fired off a few shots from different angles, and even clambered up on to the toilet seat to take one. The noise of the camera-motor winding on the film seemed almost laughably incongruous. Here I was bleeding like a pig while someone took snuff photos from a toilet seat.

'That's a wrap,' he said at last. 'Hey, did I tell you? Joe Draper's going to make a documentary of my life. Maybe we'll talk about my charity work, huh?'

'You're all heart, Leo.'

'Yeah, yeah.'

He turned to walk away, but then thought of something. He kept his back to me as he spoke.

'You going to come gunning for me, Mikey?'

'No,' I said, not sure if I meant it. 'I'm finished with that.' I found to my surprise that I did mean it. He glanced over his shoulder and seemed satisfied.

'Well,' he said, 'I've done some thinking about that, too. See, I could break your hand up a bit, take the fingers out of the sockets, smash the wrist. But the body has a way of repairing itself.'

'I swear, Leo, I'm not—'

'So instead of that, just in case, I'm putting contracts out on your parents. If I buy it, they buy it too.'

'There's no need for that.'

'And your friend Bel, too, same deal. My little insurance policy. It's not exactly all-claims, but it'll have to do.'

He made to walk away.

'Hoffer,' I said. He stopped. 'Same question: are you going to come gunning for me?'

'Not if you stay dead. Get a fucking day job, Mike. Stack shelves or something. Sell burgers. I'm going to tell Walkins I stiffed you. I'm hoping he'll go for it. I'm losing my best client, but this ought to help.' He patted his pocket again, where the money was. 'I may tell a few other people too.'

I smiled. 'You mean the media.'

'I've got a living to make, Mike. With you dead, I need all the publicity I can get.'

'Go ahead, Hoffer, shout it from the rooftops.'

'I'm going.'

And he went. I got the key, but even so it was hell unlocking the cuffs. How did Houdini do it? Maybe if you could dislocate your wrist or something . . . Eventually I got them off and staggered out of the bathroom, only to fall to my knees in the hallway. I was crawling towards the door when it opened again, very slowly. I saw first one foot, then the other. The feet were dressed in shitkicker cowboy boots.

'Michael!' Bel screamed. 'What happened?'

She took my head in her hands.

'Got a Band-Aid?' I asked.

29

Hoffer went back to New York with nine and a half grand in his pocket and Provost's papers in his case.

He didn't know if he'd ever do anything with those papers. They were worth something, no doubt about that. But they were dangerous too. You only had to look at the D-Man to see that.

The press were going to town on the Seattle story. Shoot-out at the home of the Disciples of Love. Hoffer could see there was a lot the authorities weren't saying. Even so, it didn't take long for the majority of the bodies to be identified as serving and ex-employees of the security services. The explanation seemed to be that Kline, an embittered ex-employee, had somehow persuaded some serving staff to work for him, and the whole lot of them were involved in some dubious way with the Disciples of Love. Sure, and the tooth fairy lives on West 53rd.

Nobody was mentioning the ten mil or the Middle East.

Hoffer didn't go to the office for a couple of days, and when he did he thought better of it after half a flight of stairs. After all, heights gave him earache. So he retreated instead to the diner across the street. The place was full of bums nursing neverending cups of coffee. They'd discovered the secret of life, and they were tired of it. A couple of them nodded at Hoffer as he went in, like he was back where he belonged.

Donna the waitress was there, and she nodded a greeting to him too, like he'd been there every day without fail. She brought him coffee and the phone, and he called up to his secretary.

'I'm down here, Moira.'

'Now there's a surprise.'

'Bring me the latest updates and paperwork, messages, mail, all that shit. We'll deal with it here, okay?' He put down the phone and ordered ham and eggs, the eggs scrambled. Outside, New York was doing its New York thing, busy with energy and excess and people just trying to get by if they couldn't get ahead.

'More coffee?'

'Thanks, Donna.'

She'd been serving him for a year, best part of, and still she never showed interest, never asked how he was doing or what he'd been doing. He'd bet she didn't even remember his name. He was just a customer who sometimes made a local call and tipped her well for the service. That was it. That was all he was.

Jesus, it was going to be hard getting by without the D-Man.

The parents, he should never have talked to the parents. They'd made the guy too real, too human. They'd stripped away all the cunning and the menace and had confronted him with photos of a gangly awkward youth with skinny arms and a lopsided grin. Photos on the beach, in the park, waving from the driving seat of Pop's car.

He should never have gone. He hadn't explained what he was doing there. He'd mumbled some explanation about their son maybe being witness to a crime, but now nobody could find him. They didn't seem to care, so long as he wasn't hurt.

No, he wasn't hurt, not much. But he'd done some damage in Washington State.

Hoffer knew the parents weren't the only reason, but they were an excusable one. He didn't really know why he hadn't killed the D-Man. Maybe he didn't want another death on his hands. He'd told Michael Weston he'd never killed anyone. That wasn't strictly true.

Hoffer had been killing himself for years.

The papers, of course, did not connect the D-Man to any of the stuff about Kline and Provost. Hoffer could have done that for them, but he chose not to. Instead he was biding his time. He was waiting for a lull in the news, when empty pages and screen time were screaming out to be filled. That was the time for him to step forward with his story and maybe even his photos, all about tracking down the D-Man and killing him. There was no body to show, of course, so Hoffer must've disposed of it in some way.

He'd think of something.

Meantime, he fed on the newspapers, on fresh twists about a man admitted to a local hospital with a gunshot wound. Of a mystery woman who dumped him there. Then there was Provost's luxury Seattle townhouse. How to explain the blood on the bathroom floor or the pair of metal handcuffs hanging around a water pipe?

'Better than the movies,' he said to himself, just as Donna arrived with his food.

'You say something?'

'Yeah,' said Hoffer, 'I said would you go to the movies with me some night?'

'In your dreams, sweetheart,' she said, 'in your dreams.'

Part Four

30

Not only did Spike walk out of that hospital having said nothing about how he came by his injuries, not only did he find that his bills had been taken care of, but he tracked down the authority holding on to the Trans-Am and managed to wheedle it out of them. He sent me a photo by the usual route. It showed Jazz and him leaning against the car. Scrawled over the photo were the words 'A little piece of heaven'.

Me, I claimed I was a tourist attacked by assailants who were after my traveller's cheques. Nobody really cared, they were too busy keeping an eye on the affair out on the Olympic Peninsula. Everyone had a theory. They were all far-fetched and they were all more feasible than the truth. Well, all except the one published in the *Weekly World News*.

A package arrived one day at Sam Clancy's hospital bed. It contained his walkman with a tape already inserted and ready to play. I didn't know what Sam would do with Jeremiah Provost's confession. It wasn't really my concern, not any more.

As soon as we could, Bel and I got out of the USA. Back in London, we spent a night in a hotel, then she headed back to Yorkshire. She had a lot of stuff to clear up. She wondered if I knew anyone who'd buy half a ton of unwanted weaponry.

Oh, I could think of a few people.

It was a drizzly London morning when I turned up at the offices of Crispin, Darnforth, Jessup. I shook rain out of my hair as I walked up the stairs. I knocked on the door before entering, and smiled as I approached the secretary's desk.

'Mr Johns, please.' She frowned and removed her spectacles.

'Is he expecting you?'

'I'm not sure.' She waited for me to say more, but I just stood there smiling and dripping water on to the pastel pink carpet.

'I'm afraid he can't see anyone without an appointment. He's very busy today.'

'He'll see me.' I could see my smile was beginning to irritate her. She stuck her glasses back on, pushing them up her nose.

'What name shall I give?'

'None.'

She picked up her phone and punched a number. 'Mr Johns, there's a Mr Nunn here. No, he's being very mysterious.' She looked at me. 'Well, he doesn't *look* like he's selling anything.' I shook my head in confirmation. 'Yes, sir.' She put her hand over the mouthpiece. 'If you'd like to make an appointment . . .'

I snatched the receiver from her and spoke into it.

'You know who I am. I came here before as a policeman.'

Then I slammed the receiver back into its cradle and waited, while the secretary gave me a look like I'd just tried to jump her. Johns opened the door of his office and stood there.

'Ah yes,' he said, 'do come in, won't you?'

I walked into his office and looked around. There was nobody else in there. It was just going to be the two of us.

'Take a seat, please,' he said. Then he sat down across the desk from me and put his hands together, as if in prayer. 'Yes,' he said. 'I remember you. As you say, you came here as a policeman. That, I take it, means you're not a policeman now.'

'I wasn't one then either.' It took me a little while to sit down. The bandages and plasters were tight across my body. Beneath them, the healing wounds were itching like hell.

Johns was nodding, as though I'd merely confirmed something. I wanted to damage his shiny face, the wealthy confidence in his eyes. He wasn't afraid of me. He'd seen worse than me before, if only in his dreams.

'I'm afraid I'm a bit in the dark,' he said.

'That makes two of us. Tell me about Mrs Ricks's death.'

'What? Again?'

'No, this time I want the truth. You weren't surprised she died, were you?'

'No.'

'Why was that?'

He pouted, his lips touching the tips of his fingers. Then he sat back in his chair, touching its sides with his arms. 'You killed her?' he said.

'Yes.' I didn't mind him knowing, not now. If he was going to be honest with me, he'd expect me to be honest too. In fact, he'd demand it.

'I see,' he said. 'In that case, I've something for you.' He stood up and went to his safe. It was a free-standing model, dark green with a brass maker's plate, like you see the bank robbers dynamite in old cowboy films. He unlocked it with a key and turned the handle. When he looked round at me, I was pointing a pistol straight at him. It didn't faze him, though last night it had fazed Scotty Shattuck when I'd relieved him of it.

'There's no need for that,' Johns said quietly. He opened the safe wide so I could see inside it. It was packed full of papers and large manila envelopes. He lifted the top envelope out and handed it to me. It didn't have a name or anything on it, and felt flimsy in my hand. I gestured for him to return to his chair, then sat myself down. I put the gun on the desktop and tore open the envelope. There were two typed sheets inside, written as a letter. The signature at the bottom read Eleanor Ricks.

I started to read.

'If you're reading this, you've done well, and you're sitting in Geoffrey's office. Maybe you've got a gun trained on him. Maybe you intend him some harm as vengeance for what you've been through. Please, believe me when I say he doesn't know anything. I'm leaving this with him as proof of that. If you're here, you probably intend him some harm. I wouldn't like anything to happen to Geoffrey, so please read this before you do anything.

'Another reason, I suppose, is that I feel this tremendous need to get it all down, to tell someone . . . even if it has to be you. Indeed, I can think of no better figure for my confessor.

'Actually, I say Geoffrey doesn't know anything, but by now he probably knows quite a lot. I didn't tell him anything, but he's not stupid, and I needed his help, so he knows a little.

'For example, I asked him to call the police at a certain time, some minutes before I would be walking out of the hotel with Molly Prendergast. That will be the hardest thing to do, walk out of there knowing you're waiting for me. I know that when I walk out of that hotel, dressed in the colours you're expecting, I'll be trembling. But I'd rather know why I'm afraid, and know something's going to stop me being scared and angry and in pain. Rather that than the slow, internal death.

'All the same, I'll be shaking. I hope I make it out of the door. I hope I make an easy target for you. Please, I hope I didn't linger. I found out several months ago that my condition is terminal. I didn't tell anyone. I didn't want that. But I felt this flow of frustration within me, anger that there would be so many projects left unfinished . . . including this one, my present one.

'I got the idea from Scotty Shattuck. Or, rather, thinking of Scotty, I came up with the idea. If you're reading this, you've probably spoken with Scotty.'

I paused and looked up at Geoffrey Johns. He was staring out of the window. Oh, I'd spoken with Scotty. I'd done a lot more than that, too. But he was alive, and it's amazing what they can do in hospitals these days, isn't it? I started reading again.

'Scotty helped me. I knew him from assignments in the Falklands, when he was a soldier, and later in ex-Yugoslavia, when he was a mercenary. I knew I could never commit suicide, not self-assisted suicide. My will to live, you see, is strong. It's the pain I can't stand. I asked Scotty if he thought he could kill someone for money. He rambled on in his usual way, then he mentioned you. An assassin. A good one, not cheap, but a very public success. And I got the idea. Because if my assassination was spectacular and public enough, then other journalists, the media, the police, maybe even Interpol or some other international group . . . they *all* might start asking who would want me killed. And that would lead them to investigate the Disciples of Love. Maybe then they'd uncover the cult's secret, whatever it is. I *know* there's something there. I weep to think I'll never know what it is . . . unless there's a heaven.

'I'm giving this to Geoffrey with instructions to keep it safe, just in case you ever come calling on him. I wonder if you will? I mean, I'm timing things just right. The police will be contacted a few minutes before I walk out on to the steps. There's a station not far from the hotel, but I'm not sure of the protocol. Maybe the police will have to be issued with firearms, delaying their arrival. Maybe they'll suspect a hoax and not turn up at all. You may be caught, or you may escape. If you're caught, the story becomes even bigger, with more media attention. If you escape, maybe you'll be driven to wonder why and how the police were tipped off. And by whom.

'God, you could end up doing my work for me, couldn't you? It's horrible not knowing how any of this has turned out. I've planned and arranged the whole thing, and I'm the only person who won't be around to see what comes of it. I want headlines, not an obituary. I hope I got them.

'I'm telling Geoffrey to tell the police there's an assassin in the apartment block across the street from the hotel. That's where you'll be, though I know I can't possibly stipulate anything like that in my instructions to you. I've had to be careful with those, so you won't suspect me straight away. I keep thinking of the wrong turnings the media could take. Maybe they'll suspect Freddy, or an enemy from my past. I wasn't exactly kind to the Bosnian Serbs, or to the mercenaries, come to that. Not that Scotty knows that; he's never read my piece. He says he never reads. I know that, for money, he'd probably kill me himself, but I prefer the thought of your anonymity. I want a stranger to kill me, and I want somebody more competent than Scotty.

'Forgive my typing. I'm getting a bit shaky. There are tablets I can take, but they deaden everything, and with so little time left, I want life, not a numb, hazy delusion of well-being. I see everything so vividly. A single blade of grass has more beauty than any painting, but any painting can make me weep.

'I hope my timing is right. I'm afraid the police may arrive too early and scare you off. I must wind my watch. These days, I often let it run down. But I'm determined that on my last day, everything will run the way *I* want it to run. I'll be in charge. I wonder if I have the power to stop you killing afterwards? I mean, maybe you'll be so shaken up that you'll retire. That would be good. I'd be saving lives and sacrificing none. Tell Geoffrey I'll miss him. Bless him, he always loved me.'

There was a signature, nothing more.

I looked up at the solicitor.

'She left two envelopes,' he confirmed. 'The first one was to be opened the day she . . . died. I opened it at the time stated, and it said to call the police anonymously and tell them a murder was taking place outside the Craigmead Hotel. I'd to put the other envelope in the safe until someone came for it.' There were tears in Johns' eyes. 'I phoned the police, but then I phoned the Craigmead and had Eleanor paged. They paged her, but she never came to the desk. She just walked outside, ignoring the call, and was shot.'

'She set the whole thing up herself,' I said. I'd known as much since last night, when Shattuck had admitted it. He'd known who was hiring me, but not that she was her own target. When he heard the news, he fled. Up until last night, he'd thought I killed the wrong person. But I'd put him right on that.

Who'd known what Eleanor Ricks would wear that day?

No one but herself.

Geoffrey Johns was blowing his nose. Then he got up and walked over to a cupboard, where he found a bottle of whisky and two glasses. He stood with his back to me, pouring.

'She said I'd know you when you came . . . I'd know to give you the envelope. Tell me, please, why did she do it?'

By the time he turned round again, I'd already left the room. I took her confession with me. I didn't owe Johns anything. The only debts I owed were to the dead.

31

The village was one of those Hollywood-style affairs, by which I mean it was so quintessentially English that you suspected it had to be fake.

Certainly the people seemed fake, like actors playing their given roles, be it bumpkin or squire or commuter. Everyone in the hotel bar was called George or Gerry or Arthur, a few of them wore cravats, and they drank from pewter tankards. The bar had wooden beams painted black. They looked like plastic, but weren't.

Bel loved it. Our room was all Laura Ashley, picked from a brochure or magazine feature and copied exactly. The bed was a new brass four-poster with a flower-print canopy. The walls boasted hand-painted wallpaper, so the manageress told us. It's just as well she mentioned it, for you'd never have guessed otherwise. It looked like wallpaper, and very plain wallpaper at that. It wasn't even signed.

I had to smile when the first thing Bel did in the room was switch on the TV. She lay on the bed with the remote, picking complimentary grapes out of a bowl and popping them into her mouth.

'Look at that,' she said.

She'd found the CNN news. Two East European nation-states were on a war footing.

'Looks like my phone call didn't do much good,' I said.

I was on my best behaviour throughout. I didn't complain. I was compliant, agreeing with everything Bel said. I've said before, I'm very good at looking like I fit in, like I'm normal, just like you are, standing at your bar with your tankard, or walking your dog around the golf course, or choosing yourself a new sweater or shirt. I can do all those things and show nothing but contentment.

It's an act, that's all.

Hoffer's a good actor too. He believes his role. He's all method. I get the feeling we'll meet up again, whether we like it or not. We're not two sides of the same coin; we're the *same* side of the same coin.

Not that Bel suspects any of this. She thinks it's all over. She thinks we came here for a lovers' weekend, a break from the past. From this day on, we'd be starting anew, putting the horror behind us. At lunch and dinner, I held her hand across the table and exerted the gentlest pressure. The light in her eyes was pure and radiant, almost unbearable in intensity. I kept swallowing back words, images, sentiments. I kept true to myself in the realm of thought.

We walked around the village. There wasn't much to it. Narrow streets, sloping up from the main thoroughfare on both sides. A train station, shops, five pubs, the one hotel, a churchyard with rose bushes all around it. Nobody poor seemed to live here. Bel didn't know that when I stopped to admire a particular house, I had an ulterior motive.

It was a large detached property with a low front wall and a well-tended garden. There was a gravel driveway, and a Volvo estate parked by the front entrance.

Bel squeezed my arm. 'Is this the sort of place you want to live?'

I thought about it. I wanted a penthouse in Manhattan, so I could look down on an entire city, like holding it in my open hand.

'Maybe,' I said.

There was a nameplate by the garden gate, but I deflected Bel's attention by pointing to some trees across the road. Maybe she wouldn't have noticed the name anyway, not that Ricks is *such* a common name.

They were Eleanor Ricks's parents.

This was where she'd been born. Just over forty years ago. I'd read that much in the papers. Her parents had been eloquent after her murder. They weren't in favour of the death penalty, even for terrorists. That was big of them.

Bel and I made love that night under our canopy. The room was costing £85 a day, including Full English Breakfast. My reserves were pretty low. Soon, I'd have to raid my Swiss account. Bel had posed the question of jobs. She thought she could get work as a secretary or something. And maybe I could . . . well, there'd be something I could do.

Sell burgers maybe, or stack supermarket shelves, like Hoffer had suggested.

We made love, as I say, and she went to sleep. I got dressed again and went down the stairs. The bar was still busy with Saturday night spenders, but nobody saw me as I passed into the night.

I walked through the village. Even at night it was picturesque, all hanging baskets and tile roofs, distant hills and low stone walls.

The walls around the cemetery were high though. The Real England had no place for death. Even so, I was coming here to pay my respects. The gate was unlocked, so I pushed it open. The wrought iron swung open in silence.

It didn't take me long to find what I was looking for. There were still fresh flowers on Eleanor Ricks's grave. I stood there for a while, shuffling my feet, hands deep in my pockets. I wasn't really thinking anything. After about five minutes, I left the cemetery again.

Her parents' place was just up the hill.

Acknowledgements

I'd like to thank The Haemophilia Society, and especially Alan Weir, for help with details of some aspects of haemophilia. Those who require more information should write to: The Haemophilia Society, 123 Westminster Bridge Road, London SE1 7HR. Thanks also to David in Edinburgh, Andrew Puckett, and my wife Miranda for helping with research.

Gerald Hammond was knowledgeable as ever about firearms, and I should also thank the Estacado Gun Club for taking me along on a shoot. In fact, so many people in the USA helped with this book that it would take a sizeable supplement to list them all. So a general thank you must suffice. But special honours must go to Becky Hughes and David Martin in Seattle, Jay Schulman in Arlington, Mass., and Tresa Hughes in New York, for putting up with me, Miranda and our son Jack for so long.

The Chandler-Fulbright Award made it possible for me to spend so much time (and money) in the United States. I owe a debt to the estate of Raymond Chandler and to the staff of the Fulbright Commission in London, especially Catherine Boyle.

The real unsung heroes of this book are probably Elliott Abrams and Fawn Hall. For those who don't know who they are, a two-part essay by Theodore Draper in the *New York Review of Books* serves as a good introduction, though you've really got to go to Draper's book *A Very Thin Line: The Iran-Contra Affairs* or to the full Congressional Hearings to get the bigger picture. I quote from part one of the essay, published in the edition of 27 May 1993:

> Unfortunately, Abrams didn't know how to set up a secret account in which to deposit the expected $10 million from Brunei [with which to fund the Contras]. He went to Alan Fiers of the CIA and Oliver North of the NSC staff for tutoring, and chose to follow North's advice. North gave him an index card with the number of a secret Swiss account, which North controlled; North's secretary, Fawn Hall, accidentally transposed two digits in typing out the number on another card; Abrams gave the erroneous information to the Brunei foreign minister; and $10 million went into the account of a stranger from whom it took months to get it back.

Blood Hunt

To Kit

Then you carried your ashes to the mountains: will you today carry your fire into the valleys? Do you not fear an incendiary's punishment?

— Nietzsche, *Thus Spake Zarathustra*

Part One

The Blooding

1

He stood on the edge of the abyss, staring down.

Not afraid, not feeling anything very much except the burning in his lungs, the damp ache behind his legs. He knew staring was never a one-way thing. It was reciprocal. Okay, he thought, get your staring finished, get it over and done with now. The fall, he thought – it isn't the fall that kills you, it's the ground at the end of it. It's gravity, the fatal pull of the planet. There was water at the bottom of the chasm, the tide rising, foam churning against the sheer sides. He could hear the water, but in what was left of the daylight he could barely see it.

He took a deep breath at last and drew back, stretching his spine. There was an hour left till dusk: not much time. They wouldn't find him now. He'd had one piece of luck about seventy-five minutes ago, but reckoned he was allowed one lucky break per mission.

At least they were quiet now, his pursuers. They weren't yelling ill-considered commands back and forth, their words carrying on the sweet still air all the way to where he lay listening. And they'd split into two-man patrols: also well-learned. He wondered whose idea that had been. They would know by now that time was against them, know too that they were tired, cold and hungry. They'd give up before he did.

That was the edge he had on them. Not a physical edge – some of them were younger, fitter, stronger than him – but a psychological one. The sharpest edge there was.

He looked up and listened, breathed in the wet bracken, the small dull buds, the charged air. There were thunderclouds in the distance, moving further away. A torrent of rain had swept the land yet again. There was nothing worse for the spirits than a periodical drenching. Their spirits, not his. They weren't within a mile of him. They weren't anywhere close. None of them would be blooded today.

He checked himself. Over-confidence. It had to be avoided. The most dangerous part of any mission, *any* mission, was the last part – those final few hours, or minutes, or even seconds. Your brain starts winding down, your tired body doing the same. And you start to make mistakes. He shook his head roughly; feeling the pain across his shoulders. He was carrying thirty-five kilos, which would have been nothing five or ten years before – he'd carried double that in the Falklands; some SAS missions in the Gulf War had carried even more – but now he'd been carrying the bergen for thirty-six hours, and the pack was wet and heavy.

He set off again after checking his map, walking backwards through the mud, sometimes circling so he crossed over his own tracks. He took a pride in all this confusion – a confusion his pursuers probably wouldn't even notice. They had, perhaps, turned back already. But this wasn't about *them* at all. It was about him. He'd never doubted it for a moment.

He started to climb again, with his back to the ground, heels pushing into the soil, his bergen transferred to his chest. Near the top of the ridge he paused, listened, and heard a sound he could identify all too easily: paper tearing, being crushed. The ball of silver foil bounced close to him and stopped. He could hear no footsteps; no advance, no retreat – and no conversation. A sentry, then; a lone lookout. Maybe part of an OP, which would mean two men. They had, after all, split into two-man patrols. He heard a bar of chocolate being snapped in two. He became certain he was dealing with a stand-alone; the other man must be out on recce.

The close of daylight being so near, it was tempting to take a prisoner, a hostage. But he knew it was only tempting because he was tired. Overconfidence again. He was trying to evade the enemy, not engage it. But if feet shuffled towards the overhang, if toecaps sent crumbled earth showering down, if a pair of eyes wondered what was below . . . The gun was ready.

He hugged the soil and grass, feeling the damp soaking into his back. To take his mind off it, he did a little mental check, ensuring he was ready for anything.

He was.

A sigh from above, barely ten feet away. Then: 'Sod this for a lark,' and the sound of feet shuffling away, a throat being cleared, phlegm hawked on to the ground. Minus points, he thought – traces left for any pursuer: a gob of spit, some silver foil. Plus speaking out loud. Very minus points.

One day, he thought, one day not so very long ago I'd have crept up behind you and dug my knife into your throat. Not a slit – a throat was tougher than you thought; a slit often wouldn't be enough – you went for maximum damage in minimum time, and above all you wanted to get the voicebox. So you stuffed the point of the dagger into the throat and hawked about with it.

Jesus.

He had that nightmare sometimes. Not so often these days. It worried him that he didn't dream about Joan and Allan. He never dreamed about them at all, yet they were his whole life – they were his saving.

He was wondering where the other man was, the one the chocolate-eater had gone to find. Last thing he wanted was for the bastard to stumble on him lying here, exposed, with the bergen on his chest getting in the way of his gun.

Go back down the slope, or head up over the rise? He gave it another minute, then wormed his way upwards, peering over the lip. Open countryside, a rounded dip to the land like a giant saucer; and a hundred yards away, stumbling along, the chocolate-eater. He recognised the young man, even from behind, even in this light and from this distance. He recognised his useful bulk, not too much of which was flab. A quick check of the map confirmed he was headed back to the enemy base. He wasn't looking for anyone. He just wanted to be indoors with a mug of something hot and wet. He'd had enough.

A final look at the map, committing it to memory. Soon it would be too dark to read, and the use of a torch, even the thinnest pencil-lead beam, was dangerous. So dangerous it was *verboten* during most active missions except in the direst emergency. There'd be no dire emergency this time.

He tracked the chocolate-eater, keeping a steady distance. After a while a tall thin man joined up with the chocolate-eater and they had a muted discussion, pointing their arms in various directions like windblown weather-vanes. Together they set off for camp, unaware that they were being watched by the very man they were supposed to capture at any cost.

Eventually, the 'camp' itself came into view: two olive-green Land Rovers with roofs that had once been white. There were three men already there, hovering around a steaming kettle on a Camping Gaz stove. They were shuffling their feet and checking their watches.

He knew this land fairly well by now, and decided to get closer. It would mean a hike of a couple of miles, round to the other side of the encampment where the ground cover was thicker. He set off, crouching low, crawling on his belly when necessary. Another two-man patrol was coming home, and passed within a hundred metres of him. He made himself part of the scenery. They weren't really concentrating any more – they were too close to home, not expecting anything. The most dangerous time.

At one point he heard a cry of 'Come out, come out!' followed by laughter. The laughter had an embarrassed edge to it. They'd be even more embarrassed if he walked into their camp, his gun trained on them.

He was where he wanted to be now, separated by the vehicles from the campfire and the men. They hadn't set guards; they hadn't done anything. Over-confidence. He lay his bergen on the ground and started to crawl in towards their position. He knew his target. He was going to crawl right under one of the Land Rovers and point his gun up at them as they drank their tea. Then he was going to say hello.

'Hello.'

The voice behind him, over him. A woman's voice, sounding amused, as well she might. He rolled over on to his back and looked up at her, at the gun she was carrying. In her free hand, she held his bergen. She was tutting now, shaking her head.

'Traces,' she said. She meant the bergen. He'd made no attempt to hide it. She glanced at her wristwatch. It was a man's chronometer with a time-lapse function.

'Thirty-six hours and three minutes,' she said. 'You almost didn't make it.'

They were close enough to the Land Rovers for her voice to carry. The men in their camouflage uniforms came round to the back of the vehicles to see what was happening. He stood up and looked towards them, finding the chocolate-eater.

'Traces,' he said, tossing the ball of silver paper. It landed in the young man's tin mug and floated in his tea.

They couldn't head back until everyone had returned to camp. Eventually, the last few stragglers came limping home. One of them, the car dealer, had twisted his ankle and was being supported by his two friends, one of whom – a school PE instructor – had badly blistered feet, the result of wearing the wrong kind of socks with nearly-new boots.

'I think I've caught pneumonia,' the man with the blisters said. He looked at the man they'd all been trying to catch for the past day and a half. Ten of them against one of him, within an area of six square miles outside which he was not allowed to operate. He was removing his belt-kit, always the last thing he shed. It comprised his survival kit, knife, compass, first aid kit, water bottle and chocolate bars. The PE instructor hobbled over and touched his arm, then his chest.

'How come you're not soaked like the rest of us?' He sounded aggrieved. 'There's not a bit of shelter out there, hardly a bloody tree. You been cheating, Reeve?'

Gordon Reeve stared at the man. 'I never need to cheat, Mr Matthews.' He looked at the other men. 'Anyone know how I kept my clothes dry?' Nobody spoke up. 'Try some lateral thinking. How can you keep your clothes dry if you've nothing to cover them with?' They still didn't answer. Reeve looked towards his wife. 'Tell them, Joan.'

She had placed his bergen against a Land Rover and was using it as a seat. She smiled towards Reeve. 'You take them off,' she said.

Reeve nodded at the men. 'You take them off and you stash them in your pack. You let the rain do its stuff, and when it stops you get dry again and you put your nice dry clothes back on. You've been cold and wet and miserable for a while, but you're dry afterwards. One final lesson learned, gentlemen.' He took a mug from the ground and poured a brew into it. 'And by the way, you were crap out there. You were absolutely crap.'

They drove back to the house for debriefing. The Reeves had turned the stables into an annexe that included a shower-room with a dozen spray-nozzles, a changing-room with metal lockers, so each man could store his civvy clothes and all the other paraphernalia of the life they were leaving behind for seventy-two hours, a well-equipped gym, and a small conference room.

The conference room was where Reeve did most of the initial teaching. Not the physical stuff – that was done in the gym, or outside in the courtyard and surrounding countryside – but the other lessons, the show-and-tell. There was a monitor and a video machine, a slide projector, various blackboards, wall-maps and diagrammatic charts, a big oval table and a dozen or so functional chairs. There were no ashtrays; no smoking was allowed indoors. Smoking, as Reeve reminded each new intake, is bad for your health. He wasn't talking about lung cancer; he was talking about traces.

After showering, the men dressed in their civvies and headed for the conference room. There was a bottle of whisky on the table, but none of them would sniff a drop until the debriefing – and then there'd be just the single glass apiece, as most of them were driving home after dinner. Joan Reeve was in the kitchen, making sure the oven had done its work. Allan would have laid the table, then made a tactical retreat to his room to play another computer game.

When they were all seated, Gordon Reeve stood up and went to the blackboard. He wrote the letter P seven times with lime-green chalk. 'The seven Ps, gentlemen. Not the seven dwarves, not the Magnificent Seven, and not the seven moons of Jupiter. I couldn't name the seven dwarves, I couldn't name the Magnificent Seven, and sure as shit sticks to your arse I couldn't name the seven moons of Jupiter. But I can tell you the seven Ps. Can you tell *me*?'

They shifted in their seats and offered up a few words. When they got a word right, Reeve chalked it on the board.

'Piss,' he said, writing it down. 'Planning . . . Poor . . . Proper . . .' He saw they were struggling, so turned away from the board. 'Proper Planning and Preparation Prevent Piss Poor Performance. I could add an eighth P today: Procedure. You were a shambles out there. A barefoot cub scout blind from birth could have avoided you these past thirty-six hours. An elephant looking for the graveyard could have avoided you. The British Ladies' fucking Equestrian Team and their horses could have given you a run for your money. So now it's time to evaluate exactly what went so bloody disastrously wrong.'

They exchanged sad glances; his captives. It was going to be a long time till dinner.

After dinner and goodbyes, after seeing them all off in their cars, waving them back to their real lives. Reeve went upstairs to try to convince Allan that it was bedtime.

Allan was eleven and 'bookish' – except that in his case the adjective referred to computers, computer games, and videos. Reeve didn't mind in the least that his son wasn't the outdoor type. Friends thought maybe Reeve would have preferred a musclebound son who was good at football or rugby. Friends were wrong. Allan was a lovely looking kid too, with a strawberry-cream complexion and peach-down on his cheeks. He had short fair hair which curled at the nape of his neck, and deep blue eyes. He looked like his mother; everybody said so.

He was in bed, apparently asleep, when Reeve opened the door. The room was still warm from computer-use. Reeve went over and touched the top of the monitor – it was hot. He lifted the plastic cover off the hard disk and found it was still switched on. Smiling, Reeve nudged the mouse and the screen came to life. A game screen was held on pause.

He walked over to the bed, crunching magazines and comics underfoot. The boy didn't move when he sat down on the bed. His breathing sounded deep and regular; too deep, too regular.

Reeve stood up again. 'Okay, partner, but no more games, right?'

He'd opened the door before Allan sat bolt upright, grinning.

Reeve smiled back at him from the doorway. 'Get some sleep . . . or else.'

'Yes, Dad.'

'How are you getting on with that game?'

'I'll beat it, just you wait. Uncle James always sends me games that're too hard.'

Uncle James was Reeve's brother, a journalist. He was working out in the States, and had sent Allan a couple of computer games as a very belated birthday-and-Christmas-combined present. That was typical of James; kids always forgave him his forgetfulness because he made it up to them once a year or so.

'Well, maybe I can help you with it.'

'I'll do it myself,' Allan said determinedly. 'There's one screen I can't get past, but after that it'll be okay.'

Reeve nodded. 'What about homework, is it done?'
'Done. Mum checked it this afternoon.'
'And do you still hate Billy?'
Allan wrinkled his face. 'I *loathe* Billy.'
Reeve nodded again. 'So who's your best friend now?'
Allan shrugged.
'Go to sleep now,' his father said, closing the door after him. He waited in the hall, listening for the crackle of footsteps on paper as Allan left the bed and headed for the computer. But he didn't hear anything. He stayed a little longer, staring along the passageway. He could hear Joan downstairs, watching television. The dishwasher was busy in the kitchen. This is home, he thought. This is my place. This is where I'm happy. But part of him was still crouching in the rain while a patrol passed nearby . . .

Downstairs, he made a couple of mugs of instant coffee and headed for the living room. This had been a farmhouse once, just a couple of rooms and an attic reached by a ladder. Reeve imagined that in the winters the farmer brought his animals into the house, keeping them warm and using them as central heating. The place had been uninhabited for eight years when they bought it. Joan had seen potential in the house – and Reeve had seen potential in the seclusion. They were close enough to civilisation, but they were on their own.

It had taken time to settle on this location. The Scottish Borders would have provided better communications; clients driving up from London could have done the trip in half a day. But Reeve had finally opted for South Uist. He'd been here on holiday once as a child and had never really forgotten it. When he persuaded Joan to come with him to see it again he pretended it was just a holiday, but really he'd been sizing the place up. There were a few villages nearby; but for the most part there was nothing at all. Reeve liked that. He liked the wilderness and the hills. He liked the isolation.

Most of his clients came from England, and didn't mind the travel. For them, it was part of the overall experience. They were a mixed lot: outward bounders looking for something more; gung-ho apocalyptic types, shaping up for the final showdown; trainee bodyguards; all-purpose masochists. Reeve provided intensive training that was partly outward bound, partly survivalist. His aim, he told them at the outset, was to get them to use their *instincts* as well as any skills they might learn along the way. He was teaching them to survive, whether it be in the office or on a wind-chilled mountaintop. He was teaching them to survive.

The final test was the pursuit. It was never a no-win situation for the weekend soldiers. If they planned, prepared and worked together, they could find him easily within the time allotted. If they read their maps, found themselves a leader, split into pairs, and covered the ground systematically, there was no way he could elude them. The area wasn't that big, and boasted few enough hiding places. It didn't matter if they couldn't find him, just so long as they learned their lesson, learned that they might have found him if only they'd gone about it the right way.

The chocolate-eater was going to be somebody's bodyguard some day. He probably thought being a bodyguard was all about being big and holding a clean driving licence; a sort of chauffeur with clout. He had a lot to learn.

Reeve had met a few heavyweight bodyguards, international types, political types. Some of them had been in Special Forces at the same time as him. Chocolate-chops had a long way to go.

He never told clients he'd been in the SAS. He told them he was ex-Infantry, and mentioned a few of his campaigns: Northern Ireland, the Falklands . . . He never went into detail, though he was often pressed. As he said, none of that was important; it was the past. It was just stories – stories he never told.

The living room was warm. Joan was curled up on the sofa, tending to the immediate needs of Bakunin the cat while they both watched TV. She smiled as she took the mug from him. Bakunin gave him a dirty look for daring to interrupt the stroking session. Reeve made a tactical withdrawal and sank into his favourite chair. He looked around the room. Joan had decorated it, doing her usual thorough job. This is what home is all about, he thought. This is fine.

'You slipped up today,' she said, her eyes still on the TV.

'Thanks for making me look good.'

'Sorry, I didn't know that was my job.'

Did she want an argument? He didn't need one. He concentrated on the coffee.

'Did you get all their cheques?' she asked, still not looking at him.

'They're in the drawer.'

'In the cash-box?'

'In the drawer,' he repeated. He couldn't taste the coffee.

'You gave them their receipts?'

'Yes.'

She didn't say anything after that, and neither did he, but she'd managed to get beneath his skin again. She could do it so easily. He'd been trained for most things, but not for this. Joan would have made a great interrogator.

This is home, he thought.

Then the phone rang.

2

The Co-World Chemicals building was situated on the corner of B Street and Fifth Avenue in downtown San Diego. That put it about sixteen miles north of the Mexican border, which was a lot closer than Alfred Dulwater liked. The place was practically a foreign country as far as he was concerned. He knew too that the city's Gaslamp Quarter started only a couple of blocks south of the CWC building and, though the city had cleaned the place up and now advertised it to tourists as 'historic', it was still as full of panhandlers and bums as it was overpriced restaurants and knick-knack shops.

Dulwater came from Denver. As a kid, he'd taken a map of the USA and drawn two diagonals through it, one from Seattle to Miami, the other from Boston to San Diego. In so doing, he'd managed to prove to himself that Denver, Colorado was just about at the heart of the blessed United States. Okay, Topeka had actually been nearest the cross-sights, but Denver was close too.

He didn't live in Denver these days, though. The private investigation company he worked for – indeed, was the newest junior partner in – operated out of Washington DC. The image a lot of people had of PIs was the usual fictional one: grubby men chain-smoking on motel stakeouts. But Alfred Dulwater's firm, Alliance Investigative, wasn't like that. Even its name made it sound more like an insurance company than some two-bit outfit. Alliance was big and prosperous and worked for only select clients, most of them big corporations like Co-World Chemicals. Dulwater didn't mind at all working for CWC, even on something which seemed so trivial, but he did mind that Kosigin kept bringing him to San Diego. Usually, a report would be delivered by trusted messenger service. It was very unusual for a client to demand that a junior partner deliver the report personally; in the present case it was not just one report, but several, requiring several trips to southern California – crazy economics, since the subject was living and working locally. It meant Dulwater had to fly out here, rendezvous with his team of investigators, read through their report, and then carry the same to San Diego, like he was a damned postman.

Still, Kosigin was paying. As old man Allerdyce at Alliance said, he who pays is king. At least for a day.

Mr Allerdyce was taking a close interest in this investigation. It seemed Kosigin had approached him personally and asked him to take on the case. This was a simple surveillance, with background biography and clippings. They were to look for the usual – dirt buried beneath the fingernails of the subject's past – but were also to report on his workday activities.

Which, really, as Dulwater had suggested to Mr Allerdyce, was a bit beneath them; they were *corporate* investigators. But Allerdyce had sat behind his huge oak desk and pouted thoughtfully, then waved his fingers in the air, dismissing the complaint. And now *he* wanted regular reports from Dulwater too. Dulwater wasn't stupid; he knew that if he kept in with the old man, did a good job, and kept quiet, then there might be advancement. And he lived for advancement.

No Mexicans seemed to work in the CWC building. Even the doorman, the security guard who checked Dulwater's identity, and the cleaner polishing the brass rails on the wall between the four elevators, were all male, all white. Dulwater liked that. That had class. And the air conditioning pleased him too. San Diego was warm-to-hot; it was like that all year, except when it got *real* hot. But there were sea breezes, you had to admit that. It wasn't a baking or steamy heat. It would've been quite pleasant if Dulwater hadn't been trussed into a blue woollen three-piece with a tie constricting his neck. Damned suit and shirt used to fit – but then he'd added some weight recently, since the injury to his knee stopped his weekly squash torture.

There was a gym in the CWC building. It was one floor below the lobby, and one floor up from parking. Dulwater had never been that far down, but he'd been right to the top, and he was going there again. The security guard came with him to the elevator and turned his key in the lock, pressing the button for the fourteenth floor. You couldn't simply press the button, you needed the key as well, like in some of the hotels Dulwater had stayed in, the ones with penthouse and executive levels. The doors closed, and he tried to stop seeming nervous. Kosigin wasn't the biggest fish within the multinational; he was maybe number five or six in the States, which made him seven or eight in the world. But he was young and arrogant with it, and Dulwater didn't like his attitude. In another life, he'd have punched him out and then given him a sharp-toed kick in the lumbar region for good measure.

But this was business, and Kosigin was king for the duration of the meeting. The doors opened, bringing Dulwater out on to the thick silent carpeting of the fourteenth floor. There was a reception area, with only three doors leading off. Each door led to an office, and each office covered several hundred square feet, so that they didn't feel like offices at all; they felt more like temples. The secretary, who was actually known as a Personal Assistant, smiled at him.

'Good morning, Mr Dulwater.' She still pronounced it dull-water, even though on his first visit he'd corrected it to doo-latter. In truth, the family back in Denver said dull-water too, but Alfred didn't like the sound of that, just as he'd hated all the jibes and nicknames at school and college. When he left for Washington, he'd decided to reject dull-water and become doo-latter. He liked doo-latter. It sounded like it had class.

'Mr Kosigin will be about five minutes. If you'd like to wait inside . . .'

Dulwater nodded and approached the door to Kosigin's office, which the secretary unlocked with a button beneath the lip of her desk. Then he walked in.

That was another thing. He'd looked at Kosigin's name and thought koss-eegin, like the Soviet guy in the 50s – or was it 60s? But the name was pronounced kossigin, rattled off in a single breath, all the letters short and hard. There was a hardness to Kosigin's office which matched both his name and personality. Even the works of art looked harsh and brutal: the paintings were full of squared-off objects, geometric shapes in dull colours; the sculptures looked like either disfigured people or things that had gotten too close to a heat source. And even the view, which should have been fantastic, was somehow harder, crueller than it merited. You couldn't quite see the waterfront, there were other, taller buildings in the way. He thought he could see the shiny Marriott through a gap in the downtown buildings, but the way it reflected light it could have been anything.

True to his investigator's skills, Dulwater didn't spend much time on the view but walked over to Kosigin's desk, just to see what was there. The answer as usual was disappointingly little. It was an ornate antique desk, maybe French, with bowed legs that looked like they'd snap if you put any weight on them. It was quite long but narrow, and didn't seem to square with Kosigin's chosen chair, a workaday swivel-model with red covers and black plastic armrests. Dulwater got the feeling Kosigin did his real work elsewhere. On the desk's surface were a blotter pad, a tray of pens and stuff, and a small anglepoise. It could've been a student's desk; it could have been *any*body's desk.

He took stock of the rest of the room. There was a lot of bare parquet floor between himself and the living area. This comprised a sofa and two chairs, all done in black crushed leather, a large and well-stocked drinks cabinet, with empty decanter and crystal glasses on top, and a couple of TV sets, one of which seemed to be switched on permanently. It was showing C-Span with the sound on mute.

Some of the wallspace was taken up with tall free-standing wooden cabinets, locked, and never opened in Dulwater's presence. He didn't know if they were empty or full, if they contained files or Kosigin's shoe collection. Hell, maybe they were secret doors to other offices. It didn't much matter. What mattered was that Kosigin was keeping him waiting. He put his briefcase – rigid, matt-black, almost impossible to open without both keys, official Alliance issue – on the low table next to the working TV and sat himself down on the sofa. There was no remote for the TV that he could see, but he found the control panel on the front of the set, eased its cover aside, and changed channels. There was a Rolling Stones tribute on MTV, so he left it at that and sat back to watch, not bothering with the sound.

He wondered again about the surveillance. Surely a corporation like CWC, one of the globe's chemical giants, could and would afford its own security operatives. Why hadn't Kosigin handed the piss-ant job to them? And why was old man Allerdyce taking such a close interest? It wasn't as though he was afraid Dulwater would screw up; he'd assured him of that. Why then? What was it about this guy James Reeve, this asshole Anglo with the boring personal habits and the peripatetic job? That wasn't Dulwater's concern, just like Mr Allerdyce had said. What was his phrase? 'We are the means, not the end.' It sounded great when he said it, but what the fuck did it mean?

He walked over to one of the windows and looked directly down on to the street below. One block south he saw an orange and green trolley-bus on its tourist route, one of the old city trolleys almost colliding with it. He hoped the tourists would have more sense than to get off in Gaslamp.

'Mr Dulwater.'

He hadn't even heard the door opening, but when he turned Kosigin was already half-way to his desk. He wasn't looking at Dulwater, though; he was looking over towards the TV and the briefcase. The briefcase wasn't supposed to leave Dulwater's hands. It made going to the john an interesting outing, but those were the explicit instructions. Dulwater went over to retrieve the case. By the time he got back to the desk Kosigin had unlocked a drawer and brought out a remote. He pointed it towards the distant TV and flipped back to its original channel. Dulwater almost apologised, but didn't. Apologies made you weak. Besides, what had he done wrong?

He sat down opposite Kosigin and watched the man put the remote back in the drawer and relock it with a key he tucked into his vest pocket. For a few seconds, all he had was a view of the top of Kosigin's head, with its thick salt-and-pepper hair, curling and luxuriant. Maybe he had it dyed like that to look older. When he looked up, he almost seemed like a teenager, with bright healthy cheeks and sparkling eyes with no wrinkles or creases. His burgundy silk tie shimmered with life. Then he slipped on his metal-rimmed glasses and changed again. He didn't need to harden his face; the glasses did that for him. And the voice – the voice was pure authority.

'Now then, Mr Dulwater.'

Which was Dulwater's cue to unlock the briefcase. He took one key from his jacket pocket and slipped off his left shoe to retrieve the second key from where he had taped it to the heel of his sock. The case was fireproof, bombproof, and tamperproof; if anyone attempted to open it without both keys, a small incendiary wiped out the contents. Dulwater opened the case with ease, Kosigin avoiding eye contact as he waited for the investigator to place the file on his desk. The first time they'd met, Dulwater had held out the file and Kosigin had sat like a dummy until Dulwater realised what was wanted of him: Kosigin didn't want any contact with the investigator, not so much as linkage by a document folder. So now Dulwater placed the file on the desk, and when he'd taken his hand away Kosigin slid the file a bit closer and opened it, leafing through the sheets of paper.

It was a thick report this time: further background, biographies of friends, colleagues, family. It had taken hundreds of man hours to compile, including use of investigators overseas. It was utterly thorough.

'Thank you, Mr Dulwater.'

And that was it – no small talk, no drink, no eye contact even. Alfred Dulwater was dismissed.

After the investigator had gone, Kosigin took the file over to one of the leather chairs and made himself comfortable. He glanced up at the TV whenever he turned to a new sheet, but otherwise had eyes only for the report. He didn't like Dulwater – the man was oversized and slow-witted – but he had to concede that Allerdyce ran an impressive operation.

He reread the report, taking his time. He didn't want to make the wrong decision after all, not when it might be such a *serious* decision. James Reeve the journalist was no longer just a thorn in CWC's side, and the man would not take a warning. Money had been attempted; threats had been attempted; physical threats, too. But the journalist was either very stupid or simply over-confident.

Kosigin read for a third time the updated biog. Several things caught his eye: a failed marriage which ended in acrimony and legal debts; a drinking problem; flirtation with narcotics – some speed and coke, plus grass, but then nearly everyone in California did grass – several unsuccessful relationships since the marital break-up. No children. And now a story that was going nowhere – a state of affairs which might just break Reeve. There was one brother, but no one of importance. And no powerful friends, no real allies.

He buzzed Alexis and asked her to bring him coffee, decaffeinated with one percent milk. Then he took out his leather-bound address book and made a telephone call to Los Angeles.

'It's me,' he said into the receiver. 'How soon can you get down here?'

3

James Reeve woke up that morning feeling the usual apprehension.

He'd really tied one on the previous night, but there was nothing so unusual in that. In the course of his life he'd been kicked out of more bars than he cared to remember. His motel room looked unfamiliar to him, until he caught sight of the large suitcase – his suitcase – its contents spewing out on to the olive-green carpet. Yes, that looked familiar all right. He'd seen that suitcase look the same way all over the USA, Europe and the Far East. The case had probably done more travelling than most of the world's population.

It took him a couple of minutes to reach the bathroom, what with getting dizzy and having to sit on the end of the bed for a moment, screwing shut his eyes against the headache and the white flashes. It was the kind of thing Vietnam vets should get: huge phosphor explosions across the glaze of his eyeballs.

'I'm not cut out for drinking,' he told himself, reaching for the first cigarette, knowing it was a mistake even as he did so, even as he placed it between his lips, even as he lit it and inhaled.

He almost had to pick himself off the floor after that. God, it hurt, and it tasted foul. But it was necessity. Sheer addiction, like with the drink. Some men were built for alcohol; they had large frames which soaked up the juice, and brains which rejected all thought of a hangover. On the other hand, he was lean and lanky – and by Christ he got hangovers. He guessed by now his liver must be about the size of a sheep's head. It was a wonder it hadn't pushed all his other organs aside, knocked them out of the game. He loved drinking but hated getting drunk. But of course by the time he was getting drunk, the defences were all down, so he kept on drinking. It was a problem. It surely was a problem.

So why did he drink?

'I drink therefore I am,' he reasoned, rising once more from the bed. He smiled through the pain. Maybe his brother would have appreciated the philosophy. Or maybe it was the wrong kind of philosophy. He'd never been able to figure Gordon out, not for a minute. He suspected – no, hell, he *knew* – Gordon had been in the SAS or one of those other quasi-secret branches of armed service. He knew it just as surely as he knew the bathroom was only another three hundred yards away. Maybe if I crawl, he thought, maybe everything would be easier if I resorted to all fours, returning to nature, communing with my fellow beasts. Hell, this is California, the idea might catch on. Every other idea in the world had. You could get tai-chi with your chilli or send your kids to satanist preschool.

Every looper in the world seemed to have landed here with their One Idea, some life-changing thing that might take off. You'd always find at least *one* sucker, one easy-to-dupe disciple.

I'm a journalist, he thought. I'm a persuader. I could have half of Beverly Hills crawling on all fours and talking to the dogs and cats in no time. What I can't do, right now, is find my way to the bathroom.

He was sweating when he finally crawled up to the toilet, the sweat cooling on his back and brow as he threw up down the pan. He hauled himself up and sat, resting his head against the cool porcelain sink. He was beginning to feel better, his heart rate slowing, even starting to consider the day ahead, his agenda, things that must be done. Like phone Eddie. Then he'd try and talk to that chemist again. But first he had to phone Eddie.

He pulled himself up and stared into the mirror. Most of the glass was covered with dried toothpaste. A woman he'd had back here a few nights before had left a message for him. She'd been gone by the time he got up. He'd stumbled through to the bathroom and leaned against the sink, rubbing his head against the cool mirror. When he'd finally looked up, he saw he'd smeared away whatever the message had been and had red and white stripes of toothpaste clogged in his hair.

When he went back into the bedroom he saw he'd plugged the laptop into the mains some time the previous night, which showed forethought; the batteries would be charged up by now. He couldn't live without his laptop. Just as some people had cats, and held them in their laps and stroked them, he had his computer. It was like therapy; when he picked it up and started to work the keys, he felt his worries evaporate. It felt stupid when he said it to people, but it made him feel immortal; he was writing, and that writing would one day be published, and once something was published it became immortal. People would store it, hoard it, keep it for reference, read it, devour it, cross-reference it, transfer it to other media like microfiche or CD-ROM. His laptop was a hangover cure, a panacea. Maybe that was the reason he wasn't afraid of Co-World Chemicals. Maybe.

He sat on the bedroom floor and went through his recent notes. The thing was shaping up – at least, he hoped it was. There was a lot of speculation in there, stuff that needed, as any editor would tell him, meat on its bones. And by meat they'd mean validation. He needed to get people to talk on the record. Hell, even *off* the record would do for the moment. He could still let an editor have a listen to off-the-record remarks. Then maybe that editor would have a cheque made out to him so he could bolster his flagging finances.

The catch was, he was in hock to Giles Gulliver in London, and the bugger was refusing to front him any more cash until he'd seen a story he could run with. Catch-22. He needed more money if he was going to be able to give Giles that story. So now he was looking for a spin-off, something he could sell elsewhere. Jesus, he'd already pitched at a couple of travel editors, pieces about San Diego, the border, Tijuana, La Jolla. He'd do the zoo or Sea World if they wanted it! But they didn't want anything from him. They knew his reputation. Knew several of his reputations. They knew he was bad with deadlines, and didn't write nice little travel articles to be read over the Sunday cornflakes and coffee. That wasn't journalism anyway – it was filler, an excuse for a cramming of adverts, and he'd told three travel editors exactly that. Also that they could go bugger themselves.

Which left him running out of money fast, and reduced to cheap motels where they cleaned the rooms once a week and skimped on the towels. He had to work faster. Either that or take CWC's money, use it to placate Giles, and buy a holiday with whatever was left. Everyone would be happier that way. Maybe even *he'd* be happier. But it didn't work like that. There was a story out there, and if he didn't get it it would nag him for months, years even. Like the time he had to give up on the Faslane story. He'd been working for a London paper then, and the proprietor had told the editor to rein him in. He'd fumed, then resigned, then decided he didn't want to resign – so they sacked him. He'd gone back to the story, working freelance, but couldn't get any further with it, and no one wanted to publish what he had except *Private Eye*, who'd given it half a page at the back of the mag.

God bless the Fourth Estate!

He had another cigarette, then pulled the phone off the bedside cabinet.

Once, he would have been living in a Hyatt or Holiday Inn, maybe even a Marriott. But times had changed, and James Reeve with them. He was meaner now; meaner in both senses. He left smaller tips (when he tipped at all: that guy in *Reservoir Dogs* had a point) and he was less pleasant. Poor people can't afford to be pleasant; they're too busy barely getting by.

Eddie's phone kept ringing and ringing, and Reeve let it ring until it was answered.

'What? What?'

'Good morning, sir,' Reeve said sweetly, smoke pouring down his nose, 'this is your requested alarm call.'

There were groans and hacking coughs at the other end of the line. It was good to feel you weren't alone in your afflictions.

'You scumbag, you loathesome string of shit, you complete and utter douchehead.'

'What is this?' said Reeve. 'Dial-a-Foulmouth?'

Eddie Cantona wheezed, trying to speak and laugh and light a cigarette all at the same time. 'So what's our schedule?' he finally said.

'Just get over here and pick me up. I'll think of something.'

'Thirty minutes, okay?'

'Make it half an hour.' James Reeve put down the phone. He liked Eddie, liked him a lot. They'd met in a bar in the Gaslamp district. The bar had a western theme and sold ribs and steaks. You ate at a long, hewn wooden bench, or at hewn wooden tables, and at the bar they served the tap beer in Mason jars. It was an affectation, yes, and it meant you didn't get a lot of beer for your money – but it was good beer, almost good enough and dark enough to be English.

Reeve had come into the dark cool bar after a hot, unprofitable walk in the sunshine; and he'd drunk too many beers too quickly. And he'd got talking to the man on the stool beside him, who introduced himself as Eddie Cantona. Reeve started off by saying there was a football player called Cantona, then had to explain that he meant soccer, and that the player himself was French.

'It's a Spanish name,' Eddie persisted. And it was too, the way he said it, turning the middle syllable into 'toe' and dragging the whole name out – whereas in England the commentators would try to abbreviate it to two syllables at most.

The conversation could only improve from there, and it did, especially when Eddie announced that he was 'between appointments' and owned a car. Reeve had been spending a fortune on cabs and other modes of transport. Here was a driver looking for short-term employment. And a big man at that – someone who just might double as bodyguard should the need arise. By that point, Reeve had figured on the need arising.

Since then he'd been offered money to quit the story. And when he'd turned the offer down, there had been a silent beating in a back alley. They'd caught him while Eddie was off somewhere. They hadn't said a word, which was the clearest message they could have given.

And still James Reeve wanted the story. He wanted it more than ever.

They drove out to La Jolla first to visit the retired chemist unannounced.

It was a white-painted clapboard house (Eddie pronounced the word 'clabbard'), a bungalow with not much land around it. It had a green picket fence, which was being freshly redecorated by a whistling workman in overalls. His van was parked with two wheels on the kerb, its back doors open to show a range of paintpots, ladders and brushes. He smiled and said 'Good morning to you' as James Reeve pushed open the stubborn gate. There were bells hanging from the latch, and they chimed as he closed it behind him.

He'd been here before, and the old man hadn't answered any of his questions. But persistence was a journalist's main line of attack. He rang the doorbell and took one pace back on to the path. The street wasn't close to La Jolla's seafront, but he guessed the houses would still be worth at least a hundred and fifty thou apiece. It was that kind of town. Eddie'd told him that Raymond Chandler used to live in La Jolla. To James's eye, there didn't seem much worth writing about in La Jolla.

He stepped up to the door again, tried the bell, then squatted to peer through the letterbox. But there was no letterbox. Instead, Dr Killin had one of those mailboxes on a post near the gate, with a red flag beside it for when there was mail. The flag was down. James went to the only window fronting the bungalow and looked in at a comfortable living room, lots of old photographs on the walls, a three-seat sofa with floral covers taking up way too much room. He remembered Dr Killin from their first, only and very brief meeting. Killin had reminded him physically of Giles Gulliver, a knotted strength beneath an apparently frail exterior. He had a shiny domed bald head, the skull out of proportion to the frame supporting it, and thick-lensed glasses behind which the eyes were magnified, the eyelashes thick and curling.

The old fart wasn't home.

He walked back down the path and wrestled with the gate again. The painter stopped whistling and smiled up at him from his half-kneeling position.

'Ain't in,' he informed James Reeve, like this was news.

'You might have said before I went three rounds with that damned gate.'

The painter chuckled, wiping his green fingers on a rag. 'Might've,' he agreed.

'Do you know where he is?'

The man shook his head, then scratched his ear. 'I was told something about a vacation. But how do you take a vacation when you live in paradise?' And he laughed, turning back to his task.

James Reeve took a step towards him. 'When did he leave?'

'That I don't know, sir.'

'Any idea when he'll be back?'

The painter shrugged.

The journalist cursed under his breath and leaned over the fence to open the mailbox, looking for something, anything.

'Shouldn't do that,' the painter said.

'I know,' said Reeve, 'tampering with the US Mail.'

'Oh, I wouldn't know about that. But see, you got green paint on your shirt.'

And so he had.

Dismissing the offer of white spirit, in need of another kind of spirit altogether, he stomped back to the car where Eddie was waiting for him. He got into the passenger seat.

'I heard,' said Eddie.

'He's been scared off,' Reeve declared. 'I know he has.'

'You could leave a business card or something, ask him to get back to you.' Eddie started the engine.

'I did that last time. He didn't get back to me. He never let me past the front door.'

'Well – old folks, they do get suspicious. Lot of muggings around.'

James Reeve turned as best he could in the seat, so he was facing Eddie Cantona. 'Eddie, do I look like a mugger?'

Eddie smiled and shook his head, pressing the accelerator. 'But then you don't look like the Good Humour man either.'

The painter watched them go, waved even, though they'd already forgotten about him. Then, still grinning, he wiped his hands as he walked to his van. He reached into the passenger side and took out a cellphone, holding it to his face. He stopped smiling only when the connection was made.

'They were just here,' he said.

That afternoon, Eddie dropped his employer off downtown, on the corner of Eighth and E. James Reeve had some work to do at the Public Library. He sometimes typed his notes into the laptop there, too – it was better than his motel room, a hundred times better. Surrounded by busy people, people with projects and ideas, people with *goals*, he found his own work, his own goal, became more focused.

Plus, the library was only four blocks from Gaslamp, which meant he could get a beer afterwards. Eddie had a couple of things to do, but said he might be in their regular haunt by six. If he still hadn't arrived by the time James felt like going home, the bar would call him a cab. It was an eight-dollar ride, including tip.

The story was slowing down, he decided. Here he was in San Diego, which should have been the heart of it, and he wasn't getting anywhere. He had Preece and the pesticide research, but that was years back. He had a rape, also ancient history. He had stories from two retired investigators. He had Korngold . . . but Korngold was dead.

He had Agrippa and the bank accounts. Maybe if he went back to England, concentrated on that particular corner of the puzzle, talked to Josh Vincent again; the union man's story was almost enough in itself. But he'd already pitched that at Giles Gulliver, who'd pooh-poohed it, saying the *Guardian* had run a similar story the year before. He'd checked, and the *Guardian* hadn't been following the same tack at all – but there'd been no persuading Giles, the stubborn old bastard.

So there was little enough for him to add to his files. He had other names, and had tried telephone calls, but no one wanted to meet him, or even talk on the phone. This was a shame, as he'd had his little recorder beside him, the microphone attached to the telephone earpiece. All his recordings showed so far was evasiveness on a grand scale, which didn't mean anything. Americans were wary of callers at the best of times. Blame all the cold-callers out there, interrupting lunch or dinner or a post-prandial snooze to drum up money for everything from the Republican Party to Tupperware parties. He'd even had someone call him in his motel room, trying to sell him language courses. *Language courses!* Maybe they tried every room in every motel. Barrel-scraping was what it was.

Barrel-scraping.

He sighed, turned off the laptop, folded it away, and decided he could use a beer, Mason jar or no Mason jar. As he pushed through the library's main door the heat hit him again. It was very pleasant; almost too pleasant. You could go crazy in a place like this, with only slight fluctuations in temperature all year. Almost no rain, and the streets clean, and everyone so polite to you; it could get to you.

He found himself in the dimly lit air-conditioned bar, sliding onto what had become his favourite stool. The barmaid was new and wore cut-off denims and a tight white T-shirt. Her hair was tied back with a red bandana, another one loose around her throat. Her legs, arms and face were tanned and smooth. You just didn't get girls like that in England – not with that all-over even tan and that unsullied complexion – yet here they were thick on the ground. Then he looked in the long mirror behind the bar, seeing not only his own reflection, but those of his fellow drinkers. Who was he kidding? Imperfections were staring him in the face. Men – men in love with beer – pasty-faced and thick-paunched, with greasy thinning hair and little stamina. Here's to the lot of us, he thought, draining his first jar.

The drinker on the stool along from him didn't look in the mood for conversation, and the barmaid needed everything repeated twice, unable to comprehend his accent. 'I haven't got an accent,' he told her, then had to repeat that too. So when Eddie hadn't turned up by 6.30, he thought about calling him. After all, he was Eddie's employer and Eddie's job was to ferry him around. But that wasn't exactly fair, he decided after a moment's thought. He was paying Eddie peanuts, and the guy was with him most of the day as it was – though he got the feeling Eddie hung around so he could pick up some free drinks and maybe even a free dinner.

He decided he wasn't hungry. He'd had enough. He just wanted to go back to his lousy motel and sleep for twelve or so hours. He asked if the barmaid could call him a cab, remembering to shorten the 'a' in cab so she'd understand the word.

'Sure,' she said.

Then the silent drinker next to him decided it was time to bow out too. He walked out of the bar without saying a word, though he did nod in James's general direction, and he left a couple of dollars on the bartop for the server, which was pretty generous. While she had her back to him, making the call, James slipped one of the dollars along to his own section of bartop and left it there. Times were hard.

A minute later, the driver stuck his head into the bar.

'Mr Reeve!' he called, then went back outside again. James Reeve slid off his stool and said 'so long' to the assembly. He'd only had the four beers, and felt fine – maybe a little depressed as he picked up his laptop, but he'd been worse. He *would* do something with the story, something lasting, something immortal. He just needed a little more money and a lot more time. He couldn't just let it go, not when it affected the whole damned planet.

There were a couple of panhandlers directly outside, but he brushed past them. They never really bothered him. They took one look at him – his height, his pallor – and decided there were better options. The driver was holding the rear door open for him. The cab was unmarked, that struck him as he got in. And something else struck him, just a little too late.

He hadn't given the barmaid his name.

So how did the driver know it?

Part Two

Ghosts

4

As he drove south, Gordon Reeve tried to remember his brother, but the phone call kept getting in the way.

He could hear the operator telling him he had a call from the San Diego Police Department, then the detective's voice telling him it was about his brother.

'Very unfortunate circumstances, sir.' The voice had betrayed no emotion. 'It appears he took his own life.'

There was a little more, but not much. The detective had wanted to know if he would be collecting the body and the effects. Gordon Reeve said yes, he would. Then he'd put the phone down and it rang again. He was slow to pick it up. Joan had been standing beside him. He remembered the look on her face, sudden shock and incomprehension mixed. Not that she'd known Jim well; they hadn't seen much of him these past few years.

The second phone call was from the British Consulate repeating the news. When Reeve told them he already knew, the caller sounded aggrieved.

Gordon Reeve had put down the phone and gone to pack. Joan had followed him around the house, trying to look into his eyes. Was she looking for shock? Tears? She asked him a few questions, but he barely took them in.

Then he'd got the key to the killing room and gone outside.

The killing room was a single locked room attached to the outbuildings. It was fitted out as a cramped living room. There were three dummies dressed in cast-off clothes – they represented hostages. Reeve's weekend soldiers, operating in teams of two, would have to storm the room and rescue the hostages by overpowering their captors – played by two more weekend soldiers. The hostages were to come to no harm.

Reeve had unlocked the killing room and switched on the light, then sat down on the sofa. He looked around him at the dummies, two seated, one propped upright. He remembered the living room of his parents' home, the night he'd left – all too willingly! – to join the Army. He'd known he would miss Jim, his older brother by a year and a half. He would not miss his parents.

From early on, mother and father had led their own lives and had expected Jim and Gordon to do the same. The brothers had been close in those days. As they grew, it became clear that Gordon was the 'physical' one, while Jim lived in a world of his own – writing poetry, scribbling stories. Gordon went to judo classes; Jim was headed to university. Neither brother had ever really understood the other.

Reeve had stood up and faced the standing dummy. Then he punched it across the room and walked outside.

His bag packed, he'd got into the Land Rover. Joan had already called Grigor Mackenzie who, hearing the circumstances, had agreed to put his ferry to the mainland at Gordon's disposal, though it was hours past the last sailing.

Reeve drove through the night, remembering the telephone call and trying to push past it to the brother he had once known. Jim had left university after a year to join an evening paper in Glasgow. Gordon had never known him as a serious drinker until he became a journalist. By that time, Gordon was busy himself: two tours of duty in Ulster, training in Germany and Scandinavia . . . and then the SAS.

When he saw Jim again, one Christmas when their father had just died and their mother was failing, they got into a fight about war and the role of the armed forces. It wasn't a physical fight, just words. Jim had been good with words.

The following year, he'd moved to a London paper, bought a flat in Crouch End. Gordon had visited it only once, two years ago. By then Jim's wife had walked out and the flat was a shambles. Nobody had been invited to the wedding. It had been a ten-minute ceremony and a three-month marriage.

After which, in his career as in his life, Jim had gone freelance.

All the way to the final act of putting a gun in his mouth and pulling the trigger.

Reeve had pressed the San Diego detective for that detail. He didn't know why it was important to him. Almost more than the news of Jim's death, or the fact that he had killed himself, he had been affected by the *means*. Anti-conflict, anti-Army, Jim had used a gun.

Other than stopping for diesel, Gordon Reeve drove straight to Heathrow. He found a long-term car park and took the courtesy bus from there to the terminal building. He'd called Joan from a service station and she'd told him he was booked on a flight to Los Angeles, where he could catch a connecting flight to San Diego.

Sitting in Departures, Gordon Reeve tried to feel something other than numb. He'd sometimes found an article written by Jim in one of the broadsheets – but not often. They'd never kept in touch, except for a New Year phone call. Jim had been good with Allan though, sending him the occasional surprise.

He bought a newspaper and a magazine and walked through Duty Free without buying anything. It was Monday morning, which meant he'd no business to take care of at home, nothing pressing until Friday and the new intake. He knew he should be thinking of other things, but it was so hard. He was first in the queue when boarding time came. His seat on the plane was narrow. He discarded the pillow but draped the thin blanket over him, hoping he would sleep. Breakfast was served soon after take-off; he was still awake. Above the clouds, the sun was a blazing orange. Then people started to pull down the shutters, and the cabin lights were dimmed. Headsets clamped on, the passengers started to watch the movie. Gordon Reeve closed his eyes again, and found that another kind of film was playing behind his eyelids: two young boys playing soldiers in the long grass . . . smoking cigarettes in the bathroom, blowing the smoke out of the window . . . passing comments on the girls at the school dance . . . patting arms as they went their separate ways.

Be the Superman, Gordon Reeve told himself. But then Nietzsche was never very convincing about personal loss and grief. Live dangerously, he said. Hate your friends. There is no God, no ordering principle. You must assume godhead yourself. Be the Superman.

Gordon Reeve, crying at 30,000 feet over the sea. Then the wait in Los Angeles, and the connecting flight, forty-five minutes by Alaskan Airlines. Reeve hadn't been to the USA before, and didn't particularly want to be here now. The man from the consulate had said they could ship the body home if he liked. As long as he paid, he wouldn't have to come to the States. But he had to come, for all sorts of jumbled reasons that probably wouldn't make sense to anyone else. They weren't really making sense to him. It was just a pull, strong as gravity. He had to see where it happened, had to know why. The consulate man had said it might be better not to know, just remember him the way he was. But that was just so much crap, and Reeve had told the man so. 'I didn't know him at all,' he'd said.

The car hire people tried to give him a vehicle called a GM Jimmy, but he refused it point blank, and eventually settled for a Chevy Blazer – a three-door rear-drive gloss-black wagon that looked built for off-roading. 'A compact sport-utility,' the clone at the desk called it; whatever it was, it had four wheels and a full tank of petrol.

He'd booked into the Radisson in Mission Valley. Mr Car Hire gave him a complimentary map of San Diego and circled the hotel district of Mission Valley.

'It's about a ten-minute drive if you know where you're going, twenty if you don't. You can't miss the hotel.'

Reeve put his one large holdall into the capacious boot, then decided it looked stupid there and transferred it to the passenger seat. He spotted a minibus parked in front of the terminal with the hotel's name on its side, so he locked the car and walked over to it. The driver had just seen a couple of tourists into the terminal and, when Reeve explained, said 'sir' could follow him, no problem.

So Reeve tucked the Blazer in behind the courtesy coach, and followed it to the hotel. He unloaded his bag and told the valet he didn't need any help with it, so the valet went to park his car instead. And then, standing at the reception desk, Reeve nearly fell apart. Nerves, shock, lack of sleep. Standing there, on the hotel's plush carpet, waiting for the receptionist to finish a telephone call, was harder than any 36-hour pursuit. It felt like one of the hardest things he'd ever done. There seemed to be fog at the edges of his vision. He knew it must be exhaustion, that was all. If only the phone call hadn't come at the end of a weekend, when his defences were down and he was already suffering from lack of sleep.

He reminded himself why he was here. Maybe it was pride that kept him upright until he'd filled in the registration form and accepted his key. He waited a minute for the lift, took it to the tenth floor, finding his room, unlocking it, walking in, dumping the bag on the floor. He pulled open the curtains. His view was of a nearby hillside, and below him the hotel's car park. He'd decided on this hotel because it was the right side of San Diego for La Jolla. Jim had been found in La Jolla.

He lay down on the bed, which seemed solid and floating at the same time. He closed his eyes, just for a minute.

And woke up to late-afternoon sun and a headache.

He showered quickly, changed his clothes, and made a telephone call.

The police detective was very obliging. 'I can come to the hotel if you like, or you can come down here.'

'I'd appreciate it if you could come here.'

'Sure, no problem.'

He took the lift back down to the ground floor and had some coffee in the restaurant, then felt hungry so had a sandwich. It was supposed to be too early for food, but the waitress took pity on him.

'You on vacation?'

'No,' he told her, taking a second cup of coffee.

'Business?'

'Sort of.'

'Where you from?'

'Scotland.'

'Really?' She sounded thrilled. He examined her; a pretty, tanned face, round and full of life. She wasn't very tall, but carried herself well, like she didn't plan to make waitressing a career.

'Ever been there?' His mouth felt rusty. It had been a long time since he'd had to form conversations with strangers, social chit-chat. He talked at the weekenders, and he had his family – and that was it. He had no friends to speak of; maybe a few old soldiers like him, but he saw them infrequently and didn't keep in touch between times.

'No,' she said, like he'd said something humorous. 'Never been outside south Cal, 'cept for a few trips across the border and a couple of times to the east coast.'

'Which border?'

She laughed outright. 'Which border? Mexican, of course.'

It struck him how ill-prepared he was for this trip. He hadn't done any background. He thought of the seven Ps, how he drilled them into his weekenders. Planning and preparation. How much P&P did you need to pick up the body of your brother?

'What's wrong?' she said.

He shook his head, not feeling like talking any more. He got out the map the car hire man had given him, plus another he'd picked up from a pile at reception, and spread them on the table. He studied a street-plan of San Diego, then a map of the surrounding area. His eye moved up the coast: Ocean Beach, Mission Beach, Pacific Beach, and La Jolla.

'What were you doing here, Jim?'

He didn't realise he'd spoken out loud until he saw the waitress looking at him. She smiled, but a little uncertainly this time. Then she pointed to the coffee pot and he saw that he'd finished the second cup. He nodded. Caffeine could only help.

'Mr Reeve?' The man put out his hand. 'They told me at reception I'd find you here. I'm Detective Mike McCluskey.'

They shook hands and McCluskey squeezed into the booth. He was a big fresh-faced man with a missing tooth which he seemed to be trying to conceal by speaking out of the other side of his mouth. There were shoots of stubble on his square chin where the razor hadn't done its job, and a small rash-line where his shirt-collar rubbed his throat. He touched his collar now, as though trying to stretch it.

'I'm hellish sorry, sir,' he said, eyes on the tablecloth. 'Wish I could say welcome to San Diego, but I guess you aren't going to be taking too many happy memories away with you.'

Reeve didn't know what to say, so he said thanks. He knew McCluskey hadn't been expecting someone like him. He'd probably been expecting someone like Jim; taller, skinnier, in less good all-round shape. And Reeve knew that if the eyes were the window on a man's soul, then his eyes were blackly dangerous. Even Joan told him he had a killer's stare sometimes.

But then McCluskey wasn't what Reeve had been expecting either. From the deep growl on the telephone, he'd visualised an older, beefier man, someone a bit more rumpled.

'Hell of a thing,' McCluskey said, after turning down the waitress's offer of coffee.

'Yes,' Reeve said. Then, to the waitress, 'Can I have the bill?'

'We call it a check,' McCluskey told Reeve when they were in the detective's car, heading out to La Jolla.

'What?'

'We don't call it a bill, we call it a check.'

'Thanks for the advice. Can I see the police report on my brother's suicide?'

McCluskey turned his gaze from the windscreen. 'I guess,' he said. 'It's on the back seat.'

Reeve reached round and picked up the brown cardboard file. While he was reading, a message came over McCluskey's radio.

'No can do,' McCluskey said into the radio, at the end of a short conversation.

'Sorry if I'm taking you away from anything,' Reeve said, not meaning it. 'I could probably have done this on my own.'

'No problem,' McCluskey told him.

The report was blunt, cold, factual. Male caucasian, discovered Sunday morning by two joggers heading for the ocean front. Body found in a locked rental car, keys in the ignition, Browning pistol still gripped in the decedent's right hand . . .

'Where did he get the gun?'

'It's not hard to get a gun around here. We haven't found a receipt, so I guess he didn't buy it at a store. Still leaves plenty of sellers.'

Decedent's wallet, passport, driving licence and so forth were still in his jacket pocket, along with the auto hire agreement. Hire firm confirmed that male answering the description of James Mark Reeve hired the car on a weekend rate at 7.30 p.m. Saturday night, paying cash upfront.

'Jim always used plastic if he could,' Reeve said.

'Well, you know, suicides . . . they often like to tie up the loose ends before they . . . uh, you know, they like to make a clean break.' His voice trailed off. Suicides; the next of kin. McCluskey was used to dealing with howling uncontrollable grief, or a preternatural icy calm. But Gordon Reeve was being . . . the word that sprang to mind was methodical. Or business-like.

'Maybe,' Reeve said.

Decedent's motel room was located and searched. No note was found. Nothing out of the ordinary was found, save small amounts of substances which tested positive as amphetamine and cocaine.

'We've had the autopsy done since that report was typed,' McCluskey said. 'Your brother had some booze in his system, but no drugs. I don't know if that makes you feel any better.'

'You didn't find a note,' Reeve stated.

'No, sir, but fewer suicides than you might think actually bother to leave a note. It looked like there'd been a message of some kind left on the mirror of the motel bathroom. He, uh . . . looks like it was written with toothpaste, but then wiped off again. Might indicate the state of mind he was in.'

'Any obvious reason why he would commit suicide?'

'No, sir, I have to admit I can't see one. Maybe his career . . . ?'

'I wouldn't know about that, I was only his brother.'

'You weren't close?'

Reeve shook his head, saying nothing. Soon enough they arrived in La Jolla, passing pleasant bungalow-type houses and then larger, richer residences as they neared the ocean front. La Jolla's main shopping street had parking both sides of the road, trees sprouting from the pavement, and benches for people to sit on. The shops looked exclusive; the pedestrians wore tans, sunglasses and smiles. McCluskey pulled the car into a parking bay.

'Where?' Reeve asked quietly.

'Two bays along.' McCluskey nodded with his head.

Reeve undid his seatbelt and opened the car door. 'I'll be fine on my own,' he told the detective.

There was a car in the second space along. It was a family model, with two kids playing in the back. They were boys, brothers. Each held a plastic spaceman; the spacemen were supposed to be battling one another, the boys providing sound effects. They looked at him suspiciously as he stared in at them, so he went and stood on the pavement and looked up and down the street. Jim's body had been found at six o'clock Sunday morning, which meant two o'clock Sunday afternoon in the UK. He'd been on the moor, chased by a group of weekend soldiers. Playing soldiers: that's how Jim had summed up his brother's life. At 2 p.m. it had been raining, and Gordon Reeve had been naked again, clothes bundled into his bergen – naked except for boots and socks, crossing the wetland. And he hadn't felt a thing; no twinge of forewarning, no sympathetic gut-stab at his brother's agony, no fire in the brain.

McCluskey was standing beside him. Reeve turned his back and rubbed at dry stinging eyes. The boys in the car had stopped playing and were looking at him too. And now their mother was coming back with a young sibling, and she wanted to know what was happening. Reeve walked quietly back to McCluskey's unmarked car.

'Let's go,' he said.

'Deal,' said McCluskey.

They drank one drink apiece in an overpriced hotel bar. Reeve insisted on paying. The detective wanted a beer and, though Reeve knew he wasn't supposed to touch alcohol, he ordered a whisky. He knew he must be careful; his medication was back in Scotland. But it was only one whisky, and he deserved it.

'Why La Jolla?' he asked.

McCluskey shrugged. 'I don't have an answer to that, except maybe why not. Guy hires a car, suicide on his mind. He drives around, and the world looks beautiful to him – so beautiful it makes him sad, which he hadn't been expecting. And he decides, fuck it, why not now?' He shrugged again.

Reeve was staring at him. 'You almost sound like you've been there yourself.'

'Maybe I have. Maybe that's why I take the suicides. Maybe that's why I like to spend some time with the still-living.' Then he shut up and sipped the beer.

'No note,' Reeve said. 'I can't believe it. The one thing in his life Jim ever loved was words, especially printed ones. I'm sure he'd've left a note; and a long one at that. A manuscript.' He was smiling. 'He wouldn't have wanted to go quietly.'

'Well, he created a news story in La Jolla. Maybe that was his way of saying goodbye, a final front page.'

'Maybe,' Reeve said, half-believing, wanting to believe. He finished the whisky. It was a large shot, easily a double. He wanted another, so it was definitely time to leave.

'Back to the hotel?' McCluskey suggested.

'The motel,' Reeve corrected. 'Jim's motel.'

The room was as it had been.

They hadn't bothered to clean it up and relet it, McCluskey said, because James Reeve had paid until the middle of the week, and they knew his brother was coming and would take all the stuff away.

'I don't want it,' Reeve said, looking at the clothes spilling from the suitcase. 'I mean, there may be a couple of things . . .'

'Well, there are charities who'll take the rest of it, leave that side of things to me.' McCluskey toured the room with hands in pockets, familiar with the place. Then he sat down on the room's only chair.

'Jim usually stayed in better than this,' Reeve said. 'Money must have been tight.'

'You'd make a fine detective, Mr Reeve. What line of work are you in?'

'Personnel management.'

But McCluskey wasn't fooled by that. He smiled. 'You've been in armed forces though, right?'

'How could you tell?' Reeve checked the bedside cupboard, finding nothing but a copy of Gideon's Bible.

'You're not the only detective around here, Mr Reeve. I know Vietnam vets, guys who were in Panama. I don't know what it is . . . maybe you all have the same careful way of moving, like you're always expecting a tripwire. And yet you're not afraid. I don't know.'

Reeve held something up. It had been lying beneath the bed. 'Mains adaptor,' he said.

'Looks like.'

Reeve looked around. 'So where's whatever goes with it?'

McCluskey nodded towards the suitcase. 'See that carrier bag there? Half hidden under those trousers.'

Reeve went over and opened the bag. Inside were a small cassette recorder, microphone, and some tapes.

'I listened to the tapes,' McCluskey said. 'Blank, mostly. There are a couple of phone calls, sounded like your brother wanted to talk to some people.'

'He was a journalist.'

'So it says on his passport. Was he here covering a story?'

'I don't know. Haven't you found any notes? There must be a notebook or something.'

'Not a damned thing. I wondered if maybe that was another reason for the trip to La Jolla.'

'What?'

'To ditch all those kinds of things in the ocean. Clean break, see.'

Reeve nodded. Then he held up the cable and the recorder. 'It doesn't fit,' he said. And he showed the detective that the adaptor wouldn't connect with the small machine. 'It just doesn't fit.'

After the detective had dropped him back at his hotel, Reeve went upstairs to wash. He thought of telephoning Joan, but checked himself. In Scotland, it was the wee small hours of the following morning. He could phone her at 11 p.m. his time, but not before. He wasn't sure he'd still be awake at 11 p.m. He turned on the TV, looking for news, and found everything but. Then he made his way back downstairs. He used the stairs rather than the lift, feeling the need for some exercise. At the bottom, he felt so good he climbed back up to the tenth floor and then descended again.

In the restaurant, he had soup, a steak and a salad. He looked in at the bar, but decided against a drink. The hotel's gift shop was still open though, and he was able to buy a detailed street map of San Diego, better than the tourist offerings he'd so far been given. Back in his room, he found a couple of bulky phone books in one of the dresser drawers, took them to the table, and started working.

5

Next morning Reeve woke up early but groggy, and went to the window to check. The strange car wasn't there.

He'd seen it yesterday evening, outside Jim's motel, and had the feeling it followed McCluskey's car back here to the hotel. He thought he'd spotted it in the car park; a big old American model, something from the 60s or early 70s with spongy suspension and faded metallic-green paint that looked like a respray.

It wasn't there now, but that didn't mean it hadn't been there before.

He showered and telephoned Joan, having fallen asleep last night without fulfilling his own promise to himself. They spoke for only a couple of minutes, mostly about Allan. She asked a few questions about the trip, about Jim. Reeve's replies were terse; Joan would call it denial – she'd read some psychology books in her time. Maybe it was denial, or at least avoidance.

But there wouldn't be much more avoiding. Today he had to look at the body.

He ate breakfast in a quiet corner of the restaurant. It was buffet-style, with the usual endless coffee. There didn't seem to be many overnight guests, but a noticeboard in the reception area warned that the hotel would be playing host to a convention and a couple of large-scale civic meetings during the day. After three glasses of fresh orange juice and some cereal and French toast he felt just about ready. Indeed, he felt so good he thought he might get through the day without throwing up.

He went out to the car park, not bothering to have the car brought out front for him. He wanted a good look around. Satisfied, he got into the Blazer and put his map on the passenger seat. He'd marked several locations – today's destinations. The biggest circle was around his own hotel.

The green car was sitting at the exit ramp of a car park next to the hotel's. It slid out behind him, keeping too close. Reeve tried to see the driver in his rearview, but the windshield was murky. He could make out broad shoulders, a bull's neck, and that was about it.

He kept driving.

The funeral parlour was first. It was out in La Jolla, not too far from where the body had been found. The vestibule was cream satin and fresh flowers and piped music. There were a couple of chairs, one of which he sat on while he waited to be shown through to the viewing room. That was what the quiet-spoken mortician had called it: the viewing room. He didn't know why he had to wait. Maybe they kept the bodies somewhere else and only hauled them up and dusted them off when somebody wanted to see them.

Finally, the mortician came back and flashed him that closed-lipped professional smile, no hint of teeth. Pleasure was not a factor here. He asked Reeve to follow him through a set of double-doors which had glass panes covered with more cream satin material. All the colours were muted. In fact, the most colourful thing in the place was James Reeve's face.

There was a single open coffin in the room, lined, naturally, with cream satin. It stood on trestles at the end of the red-carpeted walkway. The corpse was dressed only in a shroud, which made it look bizarrely feminine. The shroud came up over the corpse's scalp. Reeve knew his brother had swallowed the Browning, angling it up towards the brain, so probably there wouldn't be much scalp there.

They'd given James's face the only tan, fake or otherwise, of its life, and there looked like rouge on the cheeks, maybe a little colouring on the thick pale lips. He looked absurd, like a waxwork dummy. But it was him all right. Reeve had been hoping for a fake, a monstrous practical joke. Maybe Jim was in trouble, he'd thought, had run off, and had somehow duped everybody into thinking he'd killed himself. But now there could be no doubt. Reeve nodded his head and turned away from the coffin. He'd seen enough.

'We have some effects,' the mortician whispered.

'Effects?' Reeve kept walking. He didn't want to be in the viewing room a second longer. He was angry. He didn't know why, perhaps because it was more natural to him than grief. He screwed his eyes shut, wishing the mortician would stop whispering at him.

'Effects of your brother's. Just clothes really, the ones he was wearing . . .'

'Burn them.'

'Of course. There are also some papers to sign.'

'I just need a minute.'

'Of course. It's only natural.'

Reeve turned on the man. 'No,' he snarled, 'it's highly *un*natural, but I need that minute anyway. Okay?'

The man went paler than his surroundings. 'Why . . . uh, of course.' Then he walked back into the viewing room, and seemed to count to sixty before coming out again, by which time Reeve had recovered some of his composure. The pink mist was shifting from in front of his eyes. Jesus, and his tablets were back in Scotland.

'I'm sorry,' he said.

'Quite . . .' The man swallowed back the word 'natural', and coughed instead. 'Quite understandable. When will you want the body released?'

That had been taken care of. The coffin would travel to Heathrow on the same flight Reeve himself was taking, then be transported to the family plot in Scotland. It all seemed so ludicrous – burying a brother, travelling thousands of miles with the physical remains. How would Jim have felt? Suddenly Reeve knew exactly what his brother would have wanted.

'Look,' he said in the vestibule, 'is there any way he can be buried here?'

The mortician blinked. 'In La Jolla?'

'Or San Diego.'

'You don't want to take the remains back?'

'Back where? He left Scotland a long time ago. Wherever he was at any given point, that was his home. He'd be as well off here as anywhere.'

'Well, I'm sure we could . . . burial or cremation?'

Cremation: the purifying fire. 'Cremation would be fine.'

So they went through to the office to fix everything, including the expenses to date. Reeve used his credit card. There were forms to sign, a lot of forms. A bell sounded, signalling that someone else had come in. The mortician went to his office door and looked out.

'I'll be just one moment,' he called, 'if you'd take a seat . . .'

Then he came back to his desk and was briskly businesslike. First, he got the details from Reeve and cancelled the cargo reservation LAX-LHR. He called the transport company in England, and caught someone just as they were about to leave for the night, so was able to cancel that too. Reeve said he could take care of the rest when he got back to Scotland. The mortician was obviously used to having to do these things, or things like them. He smiled again and nodded.

Setting up the cremation was like setting up a dental appointment. Would he want the ashes in an urn, or scattered? Reeve said he'd want them scattered to the four winds, and let them blow where they may. The mortician checked the paperwork, and that was that.

Plastic made these financial transactions so much easier.

The mortician handed over a clear cellophane bag – Jim's effects.

They shook hands in the vestibule. Reeve noticed that the new client wasn't anywhere to be seen, then just as he was leaving the double doors to the viewing room opened and the man came out.

He was broad across the chest and neck, with legs that tapered to pencil-thin ankles. Reeve ignored him and stepped outside, then hugged the wall beside the door. He looked along the street and there was the green car, not twenty feet from him. It was an old Buick. He was still standing to one side of the door sixty seconds later when the man came out. Reeve grabbed for a hand, wrenched it up the man's back, and marched him across the pavement to the car, where he slammed him on to the bonnet.

The man made complaining noises throughout, even as Reeve started searching his jacket pockets. Then he made out a few words, punctuated by gasps of pain.

'Friend . . . his friend . . . Jim's . . . your brother's.'

Reeve eased the pressure on the arm. 'What?'

'I was a friend of your brother's,' the man said. 'Name's Eddie Cantona. Maybe he mentioned me.'

Reeve let the man's hand go. Eddie Cantona lifted himself slowly from the bonnet, as though checking the damage – to both himself and the car.

'How do you know who I am?'

Cantona turned towards him and started rubbing his elbow and wrist. 'You look like him,' he said simply.

'What were you doing out at La Jolla?'

'You saw me, huh?' Cantona kept manipulating his arm. 'Some gumshoe I'd make. What was I doing?' He rested his bulk against the wheel-arch. 'Same as you, I guess. Trying to make sense out of it.'

'And did you?'

Cantona shook his head. 'No, sir, I didn't. There's only one thing I know for damned sure: Jim didn't commit suicide. He was murdered.'

Reeve stared at the stranger, and Cantona returned the look without blinking.

'I liked your brother a hell of a lot,' he said. 'Soon as I saw you, I knew who you were. He mentioned you to me, said he wished you could've been closer. He was mostly drunk when he talked, but they say drunk men speak the truth.'

The words rolled out like they'd been rehearsed. This was what Reeve wanted, someone who had known Jim towards the end, someone who might help him make sense of it all. But what had Cantona said . . . ?

'What makes you think,' Reeve said slowly, 'my brother was murdered?'

'Because he'd no need to hire a car,' Eddie Cantona said. 'I was his driver.'

They sat in a bar two blocks from the funeral parlour, and Reeve told Cantona what McCluskey had told him; how suicides like to make a break.

'If he was going to commit suicide, he wouldn't've wanted to do it in your car,' Reeve said.

'Well, all I know is, he didn't kill himself.' Cantona shot back his second José Cuervo Gold and sipped from his iced glass of beer.

Reeve nursed his orange juice. 'Have you talked to the police?'

'Sure, soon as I heard about it on the news. That fellow you were with, McCluskey, he took a sort of statement from me. Leastways, he listened to what I had to say. Then he said I could go, and that was the end of it, haven't heard from the police since. Tried phoning a couple of times, but I never catch him.'

'Did my brother ever tell you what he was working on?'

Cantona shrugged his huge rounded shoulders. 'Talked about a lot of things, but not much about that. Usually when he was talking he was drunk, which meant I was drunk too, so maybe he did talk about his work and I just didn't take it in. I know it was to do with chemicals.'

'Chemicals?'

'There's a company out here called CWC, stands for Co-World Chemicals. It was to do with them. I drove Jim out to talk to someone who used to work there, a scientist sort of guy. But he wouldn't say anything, wouldn't let Jim over the door. Second time we tried, the guy wasn't at home. On vacation or something.'

'Where else did you take him?'

'Well, there was another scientist, only this one wasn't retired. But he wasn't talking either. Then I used to take him to the library downtown, that's where he'd do his research. You know, take notes, all that.'

'He took notes?'

'Yes, sir.'

'You saw his notebooks?'

Cantona shook his head. 'Didn't have anything like that. Had a little computer, used to fold open, with a little bitty screen and all. He'd put these disks in there, and that was him all set.'

Reeve nodded. Now the cable made sense: it was to recharge the battery on the computer. But there was no computer, and no disks. He ordered another round and went to use the telephone next to the toilets.

'Detective McCluskey please.' His call was put through.

'McCluskey here.' The voice sounded like it was stifling a yawn.

'It's Gordon Reeve. I've been talking with Eddie Cantona.'

'Oh yeah, him.' There was a pause while the detective slurped coffee. 'I meant to tell you about him.'

'Why didn't you?'

'You want the truth? I didn't know how you'd feel finding out your brother had spent his last few days on earth rattling around every seedy joint in San Diego with a bum at the steering wheel.'

'I appreciate your candour.' A rustling noise now; a paper bag being opened. 'And I apologise for disturbing your breakfast.'

'I had a late night; it's no problem.'

'Mr Cantona says my brother had a laptop computer and some diskettes.'

'Oh yeah?'

'The cable in his room was an adaptor so he could charge the battery.'

'Uh-huh?'

'Am I boring you?'

McCluskey swallowed. 'Sorry, no. It's just, like, what do you want me to say? I know what that old bum thinks, he says your brother was killed. And now he's got you listening to his story . . . and would I be right in thinking you're calling from the payphone in a bar?'

Reeve smiled. 'Good detective work.'

'*Easy* detective work. And would I further be right in thinking you've already laid a few drinks on Mr Cantona? See, Gordon, he'll tell you any damned story he can come up with if it keeps a glass of hooch in front of him. He'll tell you your brother met Elvis and they rode off together in a pink Cadillac.'

'You sound like you know something about that state of mind.'

'Maybe I do. I don't mean any disrespect, but that's how I see it. There's no secret here; there's no cover-up or conspiracy or whatever you want to call it. There's just a guy who gets tired of it all one day, so he tidies up his life and gets himself a gun. And he does it in private, away from family and friends, and doesn't leave a note. It's a tidy way to go.'

'Unless you're the hire company with a car that needs cleaning.'

'Yeah, agreed, but those fuckers can afford it.'

'All right, McCluskey. Thanks for listening.'

'Name's Mike. Let's talk again before you leave, okay?'

'Okay.'

'And don't go buying Mr Cantona too many more drinks, not if he's driving.'

Detective Mike McCluskey put down the receiver and finished his pastry, washing it down as best he could with the scalding liquid from the vending machine down the hall that passed for coffee. While he chewed, he stared at the telephone, and after he'd swallowed the last mouthful he tossed the paper bag into his bin (making eight first attempts out of ten for the week, which was not bad) then reached again for his phone, checking first that there was no one in earshot.

'Fucking Cantona,' he snarled, trying to recall the number.

Back in the bar, Reeve sat on his stool and took a mouthful of orange juice. He studied Eddie Cantona, who was studying the cocktail menu and looking like he was settling in for the day. Yes, Eddie looked like a boozer, but not a liar. But then a lot of people were real pros when it came to lying. Reeve knew; he was one of them. He'd had to lie to a lot of people about his real position in the Army; he never said SAS or Special Forces, not even to other Army careerists. He kept his mouth shut when he could, and lied when he couldn't. Lying was easy, you just said you were in the regiment you'd been in before you joined Special Forces. Some people took pride in their lies. But nothing Cantona had said so far struck Reeve as anything other than accurate. It made sense that Jim would own a portable computer. But then it also made sense that he might ditch it . . .

No, it didn't. He'd been writing a story. He'd have wanted that story published in some form, even after death. He'd have wanted his monument.

'Eddie,' Reeve said, waiting till the man had turned away from the menu, 'tell me about my brother. Tell me everything you can.'

Cantona drove them to the car hire firm. Reeve had memorised the salient details of McCluskey's report, and knew which firm to go to. He'd found their address in the telephone book. He was thinking about his own expensive hire car, the Blazer, and how it was spending more time at rest than in motion.

'You got a wife, Gordon?'

'Yes.'

'Kids?'

'A son. He's eleven.'

'Jim used to talk about a nephew, would that be him?'

Reeve nodded. 'Allan was Jim's only nephew.' He had the side window open, his head resting into the air-flow.

'You got any photos?'

'What?'

'Your wife and kid.'

'I don't know.' Reeve got out his wallet and opened it. There was an old photo of Joan, not much bigger than a passport shot.

'Can I see?' Cantona took the photograph from him and studied it, holding it between thumb and forefinger as he rested both meaty hands on the top of the steering-wheel. He turned the photo over, revealing a line of sellotape. 'It's been torn in two,' he said, handing the photo back.

'I get a temper sometimes.'

'Tell my arm about it.' Cantona rolled his shoulder a couple of times.

'They tried treating me,' Reeve said all of a sudden, not knowing why he was telling a stranger.

'Treating you?'

'For the violence. I used to get angry a lot. I spent some time in a psychiatric ward.'

'Oh yeah?'

'Now I have pills I'm supposed to take, only I don't take them.'

'They'll be mood controllers, man. Never take a tablet that screws with your mind.'

'Is that right?'

'Take it from one who knows. I was in Monterey in the sixties, then

Oakland. I was twenty, twenty-one. I saw some action. Chemical action, if you know what I mean. Came out of it with a massive depression which lasted most of the seventies, started drinking around 1980. It doesn't cure anything, but other drunks are better company than doctors and goddamned psychiatrists.'

'How come you still have a driving licence?'

Cantona laughed. 'Because they've never caught me, pure and simple.'

Reeve looked out through his open window. 'Drinking's one of the things that seems to start me off with the violence.'

Cantona said nothing for a minute. Then: 'Jim told me you were ex-military.'

'That's right.'

'Seems to me that might explain things. You see any action?'

'Some.' More than most, he might have added. *Row, row, row your boat, Gently down the stream* . . . He cut that memory off at the pass.

'I was in Vietnam for a tour,' Cantona continued. 'Took some shrapnel in my foot. By that time, I was just about ready to do *myself* an injury to get me out of there. So you still get these spells?'

'What spells?'

'The violence.'

'I've tried self-help. I've read a lot of books.'

'What, medical stuff?'

'Philosophy.'

'Yeah, Jim said you got to like that stuff. Castaneda's about my limit. What stuff do you read?'

'Anarchism.'

'Anarchism?' Cantona looked disbelievingly at him. 'Anarchism?' he repeated, as though trying the word out for size. Then he nodded, but with a quizzical look on his face. 'Does it help?'

'I don't know. Maybe.'

'What do the doctors say?'

'They say I'm on my last warning. One more outburst, they'll section me. I think they mean it.' He stared at Cantona. 'Why am I telling you this?'

Cantona grinned. 'Because I'm listening. Because I'm harmless. Besides, it's a damned sight cheaper than therapy.' Then he laughed. 'I can't believe I'm sharing my car with a goddamned anarchist.'

The hire place looked like a used-car lot, dusty cars ranked behind a high fence. There was a metal gate, a chain and padlock hanging off it, and behind it a single-storey prefabricated office. Reeve could tell it was the office because there was a big painted sign above it stating just that. Garishly-coloured notices in the window offered 'the best deals in town', 'extra-special weekend rates', and 'nice clean cars, low mileage, good runners'.

'Looks like Rent-a-Wreck before they went upmarket,' Cantona commented.

They knocked and opened the office door. There was a single room inside with a couple of doors leading off, both open. One showed a store room, the other a toilet. A man in shirtsleeves was seated behind the desk. He looked Mexican, in his 50s, and he was showing teeth around a long thin cigar.

'My friends,' he said, half-rising. 'What can I do for you?' He gestured for them to sit, but Reeve stayed standing by the window, occasionally looking out, and Cantona stayed there with him.

'My name's Gordon Reeve.'

'Good morning to you, Gordon.' The Mexican wagged a finger. 'I seem to know you.'

'I think you rented a car to my brother on Saturday night.'

The smile melted. The man slipped the cigar out of his mouth and placed it in the overspilling ashtray. 'I'm sorry. Yes, you resemble your brother.'

'Was it you who dealt with my brother?'

'Yes, it was.'

'Do you mind if I ask a few questions?'

The Mexican smiled. 'You sound like a policeman.'

'This is just for my peace of mind.' Then Reeve spoke to the man in Spanish, and the man nodded. Family, he was saying, I have to take these memories back for the family. The Spanish understood these things.

'See,' he said in English, 'I'm trying to understand my brother's state of mind on that night.'

The Mexican was nodding. 'I understand. Ask your questions.'

'Well, one thing I don't quite yet understand. My brother was last seen drinking in a downtown bar, then it seems he came here. A cab picked him up from the bar. But to get here, he had to pass three or four other car hire firms.' In his hotel room, with map and telephone book, Reeve had done his work.

The Mexican opened his arms. 'This is perhaps easily explained. For one thing, we have the lowest hire rates in town, you can ask anyone. Being blunt, if you only need a car so you can drive somewhere quiet and put an end to your life, you do not need a Lincoln Continental. For a second thing, I open later than the other places. You can check this. So maybe they were closed already.'

Why would I want to 'check this'? Reeve thought, but he nodded his head. 'My brother had been drinking,' he said. 'Did he seem affected by drink to you?'

But the Mexican's attention was on Cantona, who was leaning against the noisy air conditioner. 'Please,' he said. 'It breaks easily.'

Cantona got up from the unit. Reeve noticed that the machine was dripping water into a bowl on the floor. He repeated his question.

The Mexican shook his head. 'I would not have done business with him if I thought he'd been drinking. I have nothing to gain by seeing my cars wrecked or messed up.'

'Speaking of which, where is the car?'

'It is not in the lot.'

'That's not what I asked.'

'It has gone for repair and . . . valeting. The police smashed the driver's side window to effect entry. Remember, the car was locked from within.'

I know that, thought Reeve, but why are *you* telling me? 'Before renting the car to my brother,' he asked, 'did you take a look at his driving licence?'

'Of course.'

Reeve stared at the man.

'What is it?' the Mexican asked, his grin looking queasy.

'He held a UK driving licence, not valid over here.'

'Then I should not have rented him one of my automobiles.' The man shrugged. 'A mistake on my part.'

Reeve nodded slowly. 'A mistake,' he repeated. He asked a few more questions, trivial ones, just to put the Mexican more at ease, then thanked him for his help.

'I am truly sorry about your brother, Gordon,' the Mexican said, holding out his hand.

Reeve shook it. 'And I'm sorry about your car.' He followed Cantona to the door. 'Oh, you forgot to say which garage is fixing the car.'

The Mexican hesitated. 'Trasker's Auto,' he said at last.

Cantona started chuckling the moment they were outside. 'I thought he was going to swallow that cigar,' he said. 'You really had him going.'

'He wasn't a very good liar.'

'No, he surely wasn't. Hey, where did you learn to speak Spanish?'

Reeve opened the car door. 'There was a time I needed to know it,' he said, sliding into the passenger seat.

Daniel Trasker ran what looked like four parts wrecking operation to one part repair. When Reeve explained who he was, Trasker went wide-eyed with shock.

'Hell, son, you don't want to see that car! There's stains on the—'

'It's okay, Mr Trasker, I don't want to see the car.'

Trasker calmed a little at that. They'd been standing outside the wood-and-tin shack that served as Trasker's premises. Most of the work was done in the yard outside. Trasker himself was in his well-preserved early 60s, clumps of curling silver hair showing from beneath an oily baseball cap. His walnut face showed deep laugh lines around the eyes, with oil and dirt ingrained. He wiped his hands on a large blue rag throughout their conversation.

'You better come in.'

In the midst of the shack's extraordinary clutter, it took Reeve a while to work out that there was a desk and chair, and even a PC. Paperwork covered the desk like so much camouflage, and there were bits of engines everywhere.

'I'd ask you to sit,' said Trasker, 'but there's nowhere *to* sit. If someone's writing me a cheque, I sometimes clear some space for them, but otherwise you stand.'

'Standing's fine.'

'So what is it you want, Mr Reeve?'

'You know my brother was found in a locked car, Mr Trasker?'

Trasker nodded. 'We got the car right here.'

'Police smashed the window to get in.'

'That they did. We got the replacement part on order.'

Reeve stood close beside the older man. 'Is there any way someone could have locked the car afterwards? I mean, after my brother died?'

Trasker stared at him. 'What's your point, son?'

'I'm just wondering if that's possible.'

Trasker thought about it. 'Hell, of course it's possible. All you'd need's a spare set of keys. Come to think of it . . .' Trasker's voice trailed off.

'What?'

'Let me go check something.' He turned and left the shack. Reeve and Cantona followed him outside, but he turned back to them, holding up his hands. 'Now, let me do this by myself. That car's not something you should be seeing.'

Reeve nodded, and watched Trasker go. Then he told Cantona to stay where he was, and began to follow the old man.

Around the back of the shack, and past heaps of wrecked cars, Reeve saw that there was another low-slung building, double-garage size. Half a dozen tall gas cylinders stood like metal sentries outside a wide door, which stood open. There was a car jacked up inside, but Trasker squeezed past it. Reeve looked around him. He was five or six miles outside San Diego, inland towards the hills. The air was stiller here, not quite so fresh. He had to decide now, right now. He took a deep breath and made for the garage.

'What is it?' he asked Trasker.

The old man shot up from his crouching position and swivelled on his heels. 'Nearly gave me a damned cardiac,' he complained.

'Sorry,' Reeve came forward. Trasker had opened the door of the car and was studying it. The car James Reeve had died in. It was smarter than Reeve had expected, a good deal newer, as good certainly as anything in the Mexican's lot. He approached it slowly. The seats were leather or leatherette, and had been wiped clean. But as he bent down to peer inside, he could see stains against the roof. A rust-coloured trajectory, fanning out towards the back of the car. He thought of touching the blood, maybe it was still damp. But he tore his gaze away from it. Trasker was looking at him.

'I told you to stay put,' the old man said quietly.

'I had to see.'

Trasker nodded, understanding. 'You want a moment to yourself?'

Reeve shook his head. 'I want to know what you were looking at.'

Trasker pointed to the interior door-lock on the driver's side. 'See there?' he said, touching it. 'Can you see a little notch, low down on the lock?'

Reeve looked more closely. 'Yes,' he said.

'There's one on the passenger door-lock too.'

'Yes?'

'They're sensors, son. They sense a beam from a remote-control keyring.'

'You mean you can lock and unlock the doors from a distance?'

'That's right.'

'So what?'

'So,' said Trasker, digging into his overall pockets and pulling out a key on a chain, 'here's what came with the car. This is the key that was in the ignition when the police found the car. Now, this is obviously the spare key.'

Reeve looked at it. 'Because there's no button to activate the locks?'

'Exactly.' Trasker took the key back. 'You only usually get the one remote-control keyring with a car like this. The spare key they give you is plain, like the one I'm holding.'

Reeve thought about it. Then without saying anything he walked back to Cantona's car. Cantona was standing in the shade provided by the shack.

'Eddie,' Reeve said, 'I want you to do something for me.'

By the time Daniel Trasker caught up with Reeve, Cantona's car was already reversing out of the yard.

'I want to wait here a few minutes,' Reeve said.
Trasker shrugged. 'Then what?'
'Then, if I may, I'd like to use your phone.'

Carlos Perez was sucking on a fresh cigar when his telephone rang. It was the brother Gordon Reeve again.

'Yes, Gordon, my friend,' Perez said pleasantly. 'Did you forget something?'

'I just wondered about the car key,' Reeve said.

'The car key?' This Reeve was incredible, the way his mind worked. 'What about the key?'

'Do you give your customers a spare set, or just the one?'

'That depends on the model of vehicle, Gordon, and other considerations too.' Perez put his cigar down. It tipped from the edge of the ashtray and rolled off the desk to the floor. He walked around the side of his desk and crouched down, the telephone gripped to his ear.

'Did my brother's car have remote locking?'

Perez made a noise like he was thinking. The cigar was beneath his desk. He felt for it, and received a burn on the side of his hand. Swearing silently, he finally drew the cigar out and returned to his chair, examining the damage to his left hand.

'Ah,' he said into the telephone, a man who has just remembered. 'Yes, that vehicle did have remote locking.'

'And it had the key, the push-button?'

'Yes, yes.' Perez couldn't see where this was leading. He felt sweat glisten on his forehead, tingling his scalp.

'Then where is it now?' Reeve said coldly.

'What?'

'I'm at the garage. There's no such key here.'

Key, key, key. 'I see what you mean,' Perez improvised. 'But that key was lost by a previous client. I did not understand you at first. No, there was no remote by the time your brother . . .' But Perez was speaking into a dead telephone. Reeve had cut the connection. Perez put the receiver back in its cradle and chewed on his cigar so hard he snapped the end off.

He got his jacket from the back of his chair, locked the office and set the alarm, and got into his car. Out on the road, he stopped long enough to chain the gates shut, double-checking the padlock.

If he'd checked everything with the same care, he'd have seen the large green car that followed him as he left.

6

Kosigin walked down to North Harbor Drive. A huge cruise ship had just docked at the terminal. He stood leaning against the rail, looking down at the water. Sailboats scudded along in the distance, angled so that they appeared to have no mass at all. When they turned they became invisible for a moment; it was not an optical illusion, it was a shortcoming of the eye itself. You just had to stare at nothing, trusting that the boat would reappear. Trust standing in for vision. Kosigin would have preferred better eyesight. He didn't know why it had been deemed preferable that some birds should be able to pick out the movements of a mouse while hovering high over a field, and mankind should not. The consolation, of course, was that man was an inventor, a maker of tools. Man could examine atoms and electrons. He might not be able to *see* them, but he could examine them.

Kosigin liked to leave as little as possible to chance. Even if he couldn't see something with his naked eye, he had ways of finding out about it. He had his own set of tools. He was due to meet the most ruthless and complex of them here.

Kosigin did not regard himself as a particularly complex individual. If you'd asked him what made him tick, and he'd been willing to answer, then he could have given a very full answer indeed. He did not often think of himself as an individual at all. He was part of something larger, a compound of intelligences and tools. He was part of Co-World Chemicals, a corporation man down to the hand-stitched soles of his Savile Row shoes. It wasn't just that what was good for the company was good for him – he'd heard that pitch before and didn't wholly believe it – Kosigin's thinking went further: what is good for CWC is good for the whole of the Western world. Chemicals are an absolute necessity. If you grow food, you need chemicals; if you process food, you need chemicals; if you work at saving lives in a hospital or out in the African bush, you need chemicals. Our bodies are full of them, and keep on producing them. Chemicals and water, that's what a body is. He reckoned the problems of famine in Africa and Asia could be ended if you tore down the barriers and let agrichemical businesses loose. Locusts? Gas them. Crop yields? Spray them. There was little you couldn't cure with chemicals.

Of course, he knew of side effects. He kept up with the latest scientific papers and media scare stories. He knew there were kids out there who weren't being vaccinated against measles because the original vaccine was produced after research on tissue from unborn foetuses. Stories like that made him sad. Not angry, just sad. Humanity had a lot still to learn.

Some tourists wandered past, a young couple with two children. They looked like they'd been out for a boat-ride; rosy-cheeked, windblown, grinning. They ate fresh food and breathed clean air. The kids would grow up straight and strong, which might not have been the case a hundred and fifty years before.

Good chemicals, that was the secret.

'Mr Kosigin?'

Kosigin turned, almost smiling. He didn't know how the Englishman could sneak up like that every time. No matter how open the terrain, he was always nearly on Kosigin before Kosigin saw him. He wasn't built to hide or be furtive: he stood six feet four inches, with a broad chest and thick upper arms, so that his lower arms didn't quite touch his sides when he let them hang. His legs looked powerful too, wrapped in tight faded denim, with Nike running shoes on the feet. His stomach was flat, ripples of muscle showing through the stretched black cotton T-shirt. He wore foldaway sunglasses, with a little pouch for them hooked on to his brown leather belt, the buckle of which was the ubiquitous Harley Davidson badge. The man had wavy blond hair, cropped high on the forehead but falling at the back past the neck of the T-shirt. The tan on his face was pink rather than brown, and his eyebrows and eyelashes were as blond as the hair on his head. He seemed proud of the large indented scar which ran down his right cheek, as though a single blemish were needed to prove how perfect the rest of the package was.

To Kosigin, admittedly no authority, he looked like one of those TV wrestlers.

'Hello, Jay, let's walk.'

That's all the man had ever been to Kosigin: Jay. He didn't even know if it was a first or second name, or maybe even an initial letter. They walked south towards the piers, past the wares of the T-shirt and souvenir sellers. Jay didn't so much walk as bound, hands bunched in his denim pockets. He looked like he needed to be on a leash.

'Anything to report?'

Jay shrugged. 'Things are taken care of, Mr Kosigin.'

'Really?'

'Nothing for you to worry about.'

'McCluskey doesn't share your confidence. Neither does Perez.'

'Well, they don't know *me*. I'm never confident without good reason.'

'So Cantona isn't a problem any more?'

Jay shook his head. 'And the brother's flight is out of here tomorrow.'

'There's been an alteration,' Kosigin said. 'He's not taking the body back with him. There's to be a cremation tomorrow morning.'

'I didn't know that.'

'I'm sorry, I should have told you.'

'You should always tell me everything, Mr Kosigin. How can I work best if I'm not told everything? Still, the flight out is tomorrow afternoon. He hasn't changed that, has he?'

'No, but all the same . . . he's been asking awkward questions. I'm sure he doesn't believe the story Perez threw him.'

'It wasn't my idea to involve Perez.'

'I know,' Kosigin said quietly. Jay always seemed able to make him feel bad; and at the same time he always wanted to impress the bigger man. He didn't know why. It was crazy: he was richer than Jay would ever be, more successful in just about every department, and yet there was some kind of inferiority thing at play and he couldn't shake it.

'This brother, he doesn't exactly sound your typical grieving relative.'

'I don't know too much about him, just the initial search Alliance did. Ex-Army, now runs an adventure vacation thing in Scotland.'

Jay stopped. He looked like he was staring at the million-dollar view, only his eyes were unfocused and he had the hint of a smile on his lips. 'Couldn't be,' he said.

'Couldn't be what?'

But Jay stayed silent a few moments longer, and Kosigin wasn't about to interrupt again.

'The deceased's name was Reeve,' Jay said at last. 'I should have thought of it sooner.' He threw his head back and burst out laughing. His hands, however, were gripping the guardrail like they could twist the metal back and forth on itself. Finally, he stared at Kosigin with wide greeny-blue eyes, the pupils large and black. 'I think I know the brother,' he said. 'I think I knew him years ago.' He laughed again, and bent low over the rail, looking for an instant as though he might throw himself into the bay. His feet actually left the ground, but then came down again. Passers-by were staring.

I'm in the presence of a madman, Kosigin thought. What's more, for the moment, having summoned him from LA, I'm his employer. 'You know him?' he asked. But Jay was scanning the sky now, stretching his neck to and fro. Kosigin repeated the question.

Jay laughed again. 'I think I know him.' And then he pursed his lips and began to whistle, or tried to, though he was still chuckling. It was a tune Kosigin thought he half-recognised – a children's melody.

And then, on the seafront in San Diego, with tourists giving him a wide berth, Jay began to sing:

'Row, row, row your boat,
Gently down the stream.
Merrily, merrily, merrily, merrily,
Life is but a dream.'

He repeated the tune twice more, and then suddenly stopped. There was no life, no amusement in his face. It was like he'd donned a mask, as some wrestlers did. Kosigin swallowed and waited for more antics, waited for the giant to say something.

Jay swallowed and licked his lips, then uttered a single word.

The word was 'good'.

Reeve had got a cab to pick him up from the breaker's yard. It had taken him to the funeral parlour, where he picked up his hire car. He resisted the temptation of a final look at Jim. Jim wasn't there any more. There was just some skin that he used to live inside.

Back in his hotel bedroom, he sat at the window thinking. He was thinking about the missing laptop, the laptop's diskettes. He was thinking that *anyone* could have locked Jim's body in the car. It added up to something – or nothing. The Mexican had been lying, but maybe he was covering up something else, something trivial like the hire car's roadworthiness or his own business credentials. Well, Eddie Cantona was tailing the Mexican. All he could do now was wait for a phone call.

He took the cellophane bag out of his jacket pocket and scattered the contents on the round table by the window. Jim's effects, the contents of his pockets. The police had established his identity, then handed everything over to the funeral parlour.

Reeve flicked through Jim's passport, studying everything but his brother's photograph. Then he turned to the wallet, a square brown leather affair with edges curling from age. Twenty dollars in fives, driving licence, some small change. A handkerchief. A pair of nail-clippers. A packet of chewing gum. Reeve peered into the packet. There were two sticks left. A piece of paper had been crumpled into the remaining space. He tore the packet to get it out. It was just the paper wrapper from a used stick of gum. But when he unfolded it, there was a word written in pen on the plain side.

The word was Agrippa.

The call came a couple of hours later.

'It's me,' Cantona said, 'and I hope you feel honoured. I'm only allowed one phone call, pal, and you're it.'

They were holding Eddie in the same police station Mike McCluskey worked out of, so instead of trying to see the felon, Reeve asked at the desk for the detective.

McCluskey arrived smiling like they were old friends.

Reeve didn't return the smile. 'Can you do me a favour?' he asked.

'Just ask.'

So Reeve asked.

A little while later they sat at McCluskey's desk in the sprawling office he shared with a dozen other detectives. Things looked quiet; maybe there wasn't much crime worth the name in San Diego. Three of the detectives were throwing crunched-up paper balls through a miniature basketball-hoop into the waste-basket below. Bets were being taken on the winner. They glanced over at Reeve from time to time, and decided he was victim or witness rather than perpetrator or suspect.

McCluskey had been making an internal call. He put the receiver down. 'Well,' he said, 'looks straightforward enough. Driving under the influence, DUI we call it.'

'He told me he was stone-cold sober.'

McCluskey offered a wry smile rather than a remark, and inclined his head a little. Reeve knew what he meant: drunks will say anything. During the phone call, Reeve had been studying McCluskey's desk. It was neater than he'd expected; all the desks were. There were scraps of paper with telephone numbers on them. He'd looked at those numbers.

One of them was for the funeral parlour. Another was the Mexican car hire. Both could be easily explained, Reeve thought.

'You phoned the funeral parlour,' he said, watching the detective very closely.

'What?'

Reeve nodded towards the telephone number. 'The funeral parlour.'

McCluskey nodded. 'Sure, wanted to double-check when the funeral was.

Thought I'd try to come along. Look, getting back to this Cantona fellow, seems to me he palled around with your brother for a few drinks and maybe a meal or two. Seems to me, Gordon, that he's trying to shake you down the same way.'

Reeve pretended to be following the basketball game. 'Maybe you're right,' he said, while McCluskey slipped another sheet of paper over the telephone numbers, covering the ones at the bottom of the original sheet. That didn't matter – Reeve had already memorised them – but the action itself bothered him. He looked back at McCluskey, and the detective smiled at him again. Some would have said it was a sympathetic smile. Others might have called it mocking.

One of the basketball players made a wild throw. The rebound landed in Reeve's lap. He stared at the paper ball.

'Does the word Agrippa mean anything to you?' he asked.

McCluskey shook his head. 'Should it?'

'It was written on a scrap of paper in my brother's pocket.'

'I missed that,' McCluskey said, shifting more papers. 'You really would make a good detective, Gordon.' He was trying to smile.

Reeve just nodded.

'What was he doing anyway?' McCluskey asked.

'Who?'

'Cantona, Mr DUI. He telephoned you after his arrest, I thought maybe he had something to tell you.'

'Maybe he just wanted me to put up the bail.'

McCluskey stared at him. Reeve had become Cantona's accuser, leaving him the defender.

'You think that was all?'

'What else?'

'Well, Gordon, I thought maybe *he* thought he was working for you.'

'Have you spoken with him?'

'No, but I was just on the telephone doing you a favour by talking to cops who *have*.' McCluskey cocked his head again. 'You sound a little strange.'

'Do I?' Reeve made no attempt to soften his voice. It was more suspicious if you suddenly changed the way you were speaking to comply with the way you thought the listener wanted you to sound. 'Maybe that's because I'm cremating my brother tomorrow morning. Can I see Mr Cantona?'

McCluskey rounded his lips into a thoughtful O.

'A final favour,' Reeve added. 'I'm off tomorrow straight after the cremation.'

McCluskey took a little more time apparently considering it. 'Sure,' he said at last. 'I'll see if I can fix it.'

They brought Eddie Cantona out of the cells and up to one of the interview rooms. Reeve was already waiting. He'd paced the room, seeming anxious, but really checking for possible bugs, spyholes, two-way mirrors. But there were just plain walls and a door. A table and two chairs in the middle of the floor. He sat on one chair, took a pen out of his pocket and dropped it. Retrieving it from the floor, he checked beneath both chairs and the table. Maybe McCluskey hadn't had enough time to organise a surveillance. Maybe he didn't care. Maybe Reeve was reading too much into everything.

Maybe Eddie Cantona was just a drunk.

They brought him into the room and left him there. He walked straight over and sat down opposite Reeve.

'We'll be right out here, sir,' one of the policemen said.

Reeve watched the uniformed officers leave the room and close the door behind them.

'Got a cigarette?' Cantona said. 'No, you don't smoke, do you?' He patted his pockets with trembling hands. 'Haven't got one on me.' He held his hands out in front of him. They jittered like they had electricity going through them. 'Look at that,' he said. 'Think that's the DTs? No, I'll tell you what that is, that is what's called being afraid.'

'Tell me what happened.'

Cantona stared wild-eyed, then tried to calm himself. He got up and walked around the room, flailing his arms as he talked. 'They must've started following me at some point. They weren't at the car hire – I'd swear to that on a Padres season ticket. But I was too busy watching Mr Mex. First I knew, there was the blue light behind me and they pulled me over. I've *never* been pulled over; I told you that. I've been too careful and maybe too lucky.' He came back to the table and exhaled into Reeve's face. It wasn't very pleasant, but proved Cantona's point.

'Not a drop I'd had,' he said. 'Not a damned drop. They did the usual drunk tests, then said they were arresting me. Up till that point, I thought it was just bad luck. But when they put me in the back of the car, I knew it was serious. They were stopping me tailing the Mexican.' He stared deep into Reeve's unblinking eyes. 'They want me out of the way, Gordon, and cops have a way of getting what they want.'

'Has McCluskey talked to you?'

'That asshole I talked to about Jim's murder?' Cantona shook his head. 'Why?'

'I think he's got something to do with it, whatever "it" is. Where was the Mexican headed?'

'What am I, clairvoyant?'

'I mean, which direction was he headed?'

'Straight downtown, it looked like.'

'Did he seem like the downtown San Diego type to you?'

Cantona managed a grin. 'Not exactly. I don't know, maybe he was on business. Maybe . . .' He paused. 'Maybe we're over-reacting.'

'Eddie, did Jim ever mention someone or something called Agrippa?'

'Agrippa?' Cantona screwed his eyes shut, trying his hardest. Then he sighed and shook his head. 'Does it mean something?'

'I don't know.'

Reeve stood up and gripped Cantona's hands. 'Eddie, I know you're scared, and you've got cause to be, and it won't bother me in the least if you lie through your teeth to get yourself out of here. Tell them anything you think they want to hear. Tell them the moon's made of cheese and there are pink elephants under your bed. Tell them you just want a fresh start and to forget about the past few weeks. You've helped me a lot, and I thank you, but now you've got to think of number one. Jim's dead, you're still here. He'd want you to avoid joining him.'

Cantona was grinning again. 'Are we engaged, Gordon?'

Reeve saw that he was still holding Cantona's hands. He let them go, smiling. 'I'm serious, Eddie. I think the best thing I can do for you right now is walk away and *keep* away.'

'You still flying home tomorrow?'

Reeve nodded. 'I think so.'

'What're you going to do?'

'Best you don't know, Eddie.'

Cantona grudgingly agreed.

'There's one last thing I'd like from you.'

'What's that?'

'An address . . .' Reeve brought the map out of his pocket and spread it on the table. 'And some directions.'

He didn't see McCluskey again as he left the police station; didn't particularly want to see him. He drove around for a while, taking any road he felt like, no pattern at all to his route. He stopped frequently, getting out his map and acting the lost tourist. He was sure he hadn't been followed from the actual police station, but he wondered if that might change.

He'd had to learn car pursuit and evasion, so he could teach it to trainee bodyguards who'd be expected to chauffeur their employers. He was no expert, but he knew the ground-rules. He'd taken a weekend course at a track near Silverstone, a disused airfield used for controlled skids and high-speed chase scenarios.

The last thing he'd expected to need this trip were his professional skills.

He looked in the rearview and saw the patrol car draw up behind him. The uniform in the driver's seat spoke into his radio before getting out, checking his holster, adjusting his sunglasses.

Reeve let his window slide down.

'Got a problem?' the policeman said.

'Not really.' Reeve was smiling, showing teeth. He tapped the map. 'Just checking where I am.'

'You on vacation?'

'How could you tell?'

'You mean apart from the map and you being stopped where you're not supposed to make a stop and your car licence being a rental?'

Now Reeve laughed. 'You know, maybe I *am* a bit lost.' He looked at the map and pointed to a road. 'Is this where we are?'

'You're a few blocks off.' The officer showed him where he really was, then asked where he was headed.

'Nowhere really, just driving.'

'Well, driving's fine, it's the stopping that can be a problem. Make sure parking is authorised next time before you settle down.' The cop straightened up.

'Thank you, officer,' said Reeve, putting the car into gear.

And after that, they were tailing him. It looked to Reeve like a two-car unmarked tail with a few patrol cars as back-up and look-outs. He drove around by the airport and then took Harbor Drive back into town, cruising the waterfront and crossing the Coronado Bay Bridge before doubling back downtown and up First Avenue. The downtown traffic wasn't too sluggish, and he speeded up as he left the high towers behind, eventually following signs to Old Town State Park. He parked in a car park adjacent to some weird old houses which seemed to be a centre of attraction, and crossed the street into the park itself. He reckoned one car was still with him, which meant two men: one of them would probably keep watch on the Blazer, the other following on foot.

He stopped to take a drink from a water fountain. Old Town comprised a series of buildings – stables, blacksmith's, tannery and so on – that might be original and might be reconstructions. The buildings were swamped, however, by souvenir and gift shops, Mexican cafés and restaurants. Reeve couldn't see anyone following him, and went into the courtyard of one of the restaurants. He was asked if he wanted a table, but said he was looking for a friend. He crossed the courtyard, squeezing past tables and chairs, and exited the restaurant at the other side.

He was right on the edge of the park and skirted it, finding himself on a street outside the perimeter, a couple of hundred yards from where his car was parked. This street had normal shops either side, and at the corner stood two taxi cabs, their drivers leaning against a lamppost while they chatted.

Reeve nodded to them and slipped into the back seat of the front cab. The man took his time winding up the conversation, while Reeve kept low in the seat, watching from the back window. Then the driver got in.

'La Jolla,' Reeve said, reaching into his pocket for the map.

'No problem,' the driver said, trying to start the engine.

From the rear window, Reeve saw a man jog to the edge of the pavement across the street, looking all around. He was slack-jawed from running, and carried a holster under the armpit of his flapping jacket. He might have been one of the other detectives in McCluskey's office, Reeve wasn't sure.

The driver turned the ignition again, stamping his foot on the accelerator. The engine turned but didn't catch.

'Sorry 'bout this,' the driver said. 'Fuckin' garage told me they fixed it.' He got on to his radio to tell base that he was 'fucked again', and whoever he was speaking to started raving at him for cursing on the air.

The cop was still there, talking into a two-way now, probably liaising with his partner back at the Blazer. Reeve hoped the partner was saying that suspect was bound to return to his car, so they'd be as well sitting tight . . .

'Hey, man,' the driver said, turning in his seat. 'There's another cab right behind. You understand English? We ain't going nowhere.'

Reeve handed the man five dollars without turning from the window. 'This is for your time,' he said. 'Now shut up.'

The driver shut up.

The cop seemed to be waiting for a message on his radio. Meantime, he lit a cigarette, coughing hard after the first puff.

Reeve was hardly breathing.

The cop flicked the cigarette on to the road as the message came for him. Then he stuffed the radio back into his jacket, turned and walked away. Reeve opened the cab door slowly, got out and shut it again.

'Any time, man!' the driver called to him.

He got into the second cab. The driver was prompt to arrive.

'His engine fuckin' up again?' he asked.

'Yeah,' said Reeve.

'Where to?'

'La Jolla,' said Reeve. The map was still in his hand. He'd folded it so that his destination wasn't showing. It was something he'd learned during Special Forces training: if you were caught, the enemy couldn't determine from the way your map was folded your landing point or your final destination. Reeve was glad he still knew the trick and had used it without thinking about it, like it was natural, a reaction.

Like it was instinct.

They stopped a few streets away from the one where Dr Killin lived. It was only a matter of days since James Reeve had been driven there by Eddie Cantona. Reeve didn't think the ex-CWC scientist would have returned; though with Jim out of the picture permanently it was just possible.

Cantona had told him about the man who'd been painting the fence. Why get your fence painted when you were going to be away? More likely that you'd stay put to see the job was done properly. It wasn't like an interior job, where the smell of paint or the mess might persuade you to leave the house while the work was being done. Okay, maybe the painter had just been booked for that time, and wasn't going to rearrange other jobs just so Killin could be there to oversee the minor work. But as Cantona himself had noted, the fence hadn't really *needed* repainting.

The Mexican at the car hire had persuaded Gordon Reeve that there was something very wrong about Jim's death, something very wrong indeed. It wasn't just murder, there was more to it than that. Reeve was catching glimpses of a conspiracy, a wider plot. Only he didn't know what the plot was . . . not yet.

Reeve wanted to know if Killin was back. More, he wanted to know if the house was under surveillance. If it was, then either Jim posed a threat to someone from beyond the grave, or there were others who still posed that threat.

Others like Gordon Reeve himself.

So he had a route he wanted the driver to take, and he went over it with him. They would cross Killin's street at two interchanges, without driving up the street itself. Only then, if still necessary, would they drive past Killin's house. Not too slowly, not like they might stop. But slowly enough, like they were looking for a number on the street, but it wasn't anywhere near the number of Killin's house.

The driver seemed bemused by his request, so Reeve repeated what he could in Spanish. Languages: another thing he'd learned in Special Forces. He had a propensity for language-learning, and had specialised in linguistics during his Phase Six training, along with climbing. He learned some Spanish, French, a little Arabic. The Spanish was one reason they'd chosen him for Operation Stalwart.

'Okay?' he asked the driver.

'Is your money, friend,' the driver said.

'Is my money,' Reeve agreed.

So they took the route Reeve had planned for them. The driver went too slowly at first – suspiciously slowly – so Reeve had him speed up just a little. As they crossed the intersection he took a good look at Killin's street. There were a couple of cars parked on the street itself, even though most of the bungalows had garages or parking-space attached. He saw one freshly painted fence, the colour Cantona had said it would be. There was a car half a block down and on the opposite side of the road. Reeve thought he saw someone in it, and that there was a sign on the door of the car.

They drove around the block and came back through another intersection, behind the parked car this time. He still couldn't make out what the sign said. But there was definitely someone in the driver's seat.

'So what now?' the driver said. 'You want we should go down the street or not?'

'Pull over,' Reeve ordered. The driver pulled the car into the kerb. Reeve got out and adjusted the wing mirror on the passenger side. He got back into the back seat and looked at the mirror, then got out and adjusted it again.

'What's going on?' the driver asked.

'Don't worry,' said Reeve. He made another very slight adjustment, then got back in. 'Now,' he said, 'we drive down the street, just the way we talked about. Okay?'

'Is your money.'

As they neared the parked car with the man in it, approaching it from the front, Reeve kept his eyes on the wing mirror. He was just a passenger, a bored passenger staring at nothing while his driver figured out an address.

But he had a perfect view of the car as they passed it. He saw the driver study them, and seem to dismiss them. Nobody was expecting anyone to turn up in a cab. But the man was watchful. And he didn't look to Reeve like a policeman.

'Where now?' the driver asked.

'That car we passed, did you see what was written on the side?'

'Yeah, man, it was some cable company. You know, cable TV. They're always trying to get you to sign up, sign all your money away in exchange for fifty channels showing nothing but reruns of *Lucy* and shitty soaps. They been to my house three four times already; my woman's keen. They can smell when someone's keen. Not me. So, where now?'

'Turn right, go a block or two and stop again.' The driver did so. 'You better fix your wing mirror,' Reeve said, so the driver got out to change it back. Reeve had a couple of options. One was to confront the man in the car, give him a hard time. Ask him a few questions while he pressed the life out of him. He knew interrogation techniques; hadn't used them in a long time, but he reckoned they'd come back to him like riding a bicycle. Just like the map-folding had come back. Instinct.

But if the man was a pro, and the man had looked like a pro – not like a cop, but like a pro – then he wouldn't talk; and Reeve would have blown whatever cover he still possessed. Besides, he knew what he had come to find out. There was still a watch on Dr Killin's house. Someone still wanted to know whenever anyone went there. And it looked like there was nobody home.

His driver was waiting for instructions.

'Back to where you picked me up,' Reeve told him.

He paid the driver, tipped him a ten, and walked back the way he'd come.

Back into Old Town State Park. He was in a gift shop, buying a postcard and a stamp and a kite that Allan would probably never use – too low-tech – when he saw the cop from the street corner watching him. The guy looked relieved; he'd probably gone back to his partner and then gotten jumpy, decided to go walkabout. The park was full of tourists who had decamped from some trolley tour; it must've been a hard time for him. But now he had his reward.

Reeve left the shop and sauntered back to his car. He drove sedately back to his hotel, and only got lost once. He was assuming now that he was compromised; they'd be following him wherever he went. And if he lost them too often, they'd know *they'd* been compromised. And they'd either get sneakier – homing devices on his car, for example – or they'd have to gamble on direct assault. Maybe even an accident.

He didn't think it would be a simple DUI.

In his room he wrote the postcard home and stuck the stamp on, then went down to reception to mail it. One man was seated in the reception area. He hadn't brought any reading material with him, and had been reduced to picking out some of the brochures advertising Sea World, the San Diego Zoo, and the Old Town Trolley Tours. It was a chore to look interested in them. So Reeve did the man a favour: he went into the bar and ordered himself a beer. He was thirsty, and his thirst had won out over thoughts of a cool shower. He savoured the chill as he swallowed. The man had followed him in and ordered a beer of his own, looking delighted at the prospect. The man was round the other side of the bar from Reeve. The other drinkers had the laughing ease of conventioneers. Reeve just drank his drink, signed for it, and then went upstairs to his room.

Except it didn't feel like a room now; it felt like a cell.

7

Next day, Gordon Reeve saw the ghost.

Maybe it wasn't so surprising under the circumstances. It was a strange day in a lot of ways. He packed his things away when he woke up, then went downstairs for breakfast. He was the only guest in the restaurant. The breakfast was buffet-style again. He could smell bacon and sausage. He sat in his booth and drank orange juice and a single cup of coffee. He was wearing his dark suit, black shoes and socks, white shirt, black tie. None of the hotel staff seemed to realise he was on his way to a funeral – they smiled at him the same as ever. Then he realised that they weren't smiling *at* him, they were smiling *through* him.

He brought his bag downstairs and checked out, using his credit card.

'Hope you enjoyed your stay with us, Mr Reeve,' the smiling robot said. Reeve took his bag outside. There was no one watching him in the hotel lobby, so there'd be someone out here, maybe in the car park. Sure enough, as he approached his car, the door opened on a car three bays away.

'Hey, Gordon.'

It was McCluskey. He was wearing a dark suit too.

'What's up?' Reeve asked.

'Nothing. Just thought you might have trouble finding the . . . thought you could follow me there. What do you say?'

What could he say – I think you're a liar? I think you're up to something? And I think you *know* I think that?

'Okay, thanks,' Reeve said, unlocking the Blazer.

He smiled as he drove. They were tailing him from in front, tailing him with his own permission. He didn't mind, why should he mind? His business here was almost done, for the moment. He needed some distance. A good soldier might have called it *safe* distance. It was a perfect manoeuvre: look like you're retreating when really you're on the attack. He knew he wasn't going to learn much more in San Diego without wholly compromising himself. It was time to move camp. He'd been taught well in Special Forces, taught lessons for a life-time; and as old Nietzsche said, if you remained a pupil, you served your teacher badly.

Someone somewhere had once termed the SAS 'Nietzsche's gentlemen'. That wasn't accurate: in Special Forces you depended on others as thoroughly as you depended on yourself. You worked as a small team, and you had to have trust in the abilities of others. You shared the workload. Which actually made you more of an anarchist. In Special Forces there was less bull about rank than in other regiments – you called officers by their first names. There was a spirit of *community*, as well as a sense of individual worth. Reeve was still weighing up his options. He could work alone, or there were people he could call. People he'd only ever call in an emergency, just as they knew they could call him.

He knew he should be thinking of Jim at this moment, but he'd thought about Jim a lot the past few days, and he didn't see how another hour or two would help. It wasn't that he'd managed to detach himself from the reality of the situation – his brother was dead, maybe murdered, certainly at the centre of a cover-up – but that he'd accepted it so completely he now felt free to think about other things. Mr Cold Rationalist himself. He hoped he'd stay cool at the cremation. He hoped he wouldn't reach over and thumb McCluskey's eyeballs out of their sockets.

The ceremony itself was short. The man at the front – Reeve never did learn if he was a priest, some church functionary, or just a crematorium lackey – didn't know the first thing about James Reeve, and didn't try to disguise the fact. As he told Gordon, if he'd had more time to prepare he might've said something more. As it was, he kept things nice and simple. He could have been talking about anyone.

There was a coffin – not the one Reeve had been shown at the funeral parlour, some cheaper model with not so much brass and polish. The chapel had some fresh cut flowers which Reeve couldn't name. Joan would have known them – English *and* Latin tags. He was glad she'd stayed behind with Allan. If she'd come, he wouldn't have taken such an interest, would never have met Eddie Cantona. He'd have signed for the body, shipped it back, and gone back to life as before, trying now and again to remember two brothers playing together.

There were just McCluskey and him in the chapel, and some woman at the back who looked like a regular. Then there was the man at the front, saying his words, and someone behind the scenes working the piped music and, finally, the little electric curtain that closed over the coffin. The hum of the conveyor belt was just barely audible.

McCluskey held Reeve's arm lightly as they walked back up the aisle; an intimate gesture, like they'd just been married. The woman smiled at them from her pew. She looked to be sticking around for the next service. Guests were already arriving outside.

'You all right?' McCluskey asked.

'Never better,' Reeve said, swallowing back the sudden ache in his Adam's apple. He almost gagged, but cleared his throat instead and blew his nose. 'Shame Cantona couldn't have been here.'

'He should be out later today. We like to dry the drunks out before we release them back to their bars.'

'Did you see him?'

'No.'

'He wasn't drunk. He hadn't touched a drop.'

'Blood test shows different.'

Reeve blew his nose again. He'd been about to say, Why doesn't that surprise me? Instead he said, 'Let's get out of here.'

'Got time or inclination for a drink?'

'I'm afraid you'd pull me in for DUI.'

'Hell, I wouldn't do that,' McCluskey said, smiling, 'not to a tourist. So where to now? The airport?'

Reeve checked his watch. 'I suppose so.'

'I'll come with you. Maybe we can have that drink there.'

'Why not?' Reeve said, though it was the last thing he wanted. They went to their cars. Other vehicles were arriving, including two large black limos bearing the family of the crematorium's next client. Other cars had arrived early, and the drivers and passengers were waiting to emerge. It looked like a point of etiquette: the chief mourners should be the first to arrive. Reeve's eyes almost met those of one mourner, sitting in his car with his hands on the steering wheel. But the man had turned away a second before.

He was back out on the highway, following McCluskey, when he realised who the man had reminded him of. He nearly lost control of the Blazer, and braked hard. A pick-up behind him sounded its horn, and he accelerated again.

A ghost. He told himself he'd seen a ghost. It was that sort of day.

At check-in, Reeve got rid of his bag. He had a few small items of Jim's, but otherwise was taking back practically nothing he hadn't brought with him. Allan's kite was safely layered between shirts. Maybe he could get some perfume for Joan on the plane. Not that she ever wore perfume.

McCluskey was suggesting that drink when his pager bleeped. He went to a phone-point and called the station. He looked annoyed when he returned.

'I've got to go, Gordon. Sorry.'

'Not your fault.'

McCluskey put out his hand, which Reeve felt duty-bound to shake. McCluskey could feel it was of a different quality from their first handshake. Reeve wasn't putting anything into it.

'Well,' the detective said, 'have a nice flight back. Come see us again sometime.'

'Right,' Reeve said, turning away. He saw the board pointing him towards his gate, and headed for it. McCluskey waited till he was out of sight, then watched for another minute or so. Then he headed out to his car. He was worried about Reeve. He didn't think Reeve knew much, but he *did* know something was wrong. And now he had Agrippa. McCluskey had considered telling Kosigin that Reeve now held that one word, but that would mean admitting that he'd missed the scrap of paper in the dead man's pocket. Kosigin didn't like mistakes. McCluskey intended keeping quiet about the whole thing.

Jay was leaning against McCluskey's car like he owned not only the car but the whole car park, and maybe everything else in the city too.

'Scratch the paint, I'll kill your whole family.'

'My family are all dead,' Jay said, lifting his weight from the wheel-arch.

McCluskey unlocked his door but didn't open it. He squinted into the glare as an aeroplane lifted into the blue, hanging sky. 'Think we've seen the last of him?' McCluskey asked. 'I certainly fucking hope so. I didn't like him. I don't think he liked me. I wasted a lot of effort on that fuck.'

'I'm sure Mr Kosigin is grateful. Maybe you'll have a bonus this month.'

McCluskey didn't like Jay's insolent smile. But then he didn't like his reputation either. He pulled open the driver's door. 'You didn't answer my question.'

'I wasn't listening.'

'I asked if you thought we've seen the last of him.'

Jay grinned. 'I think *you've* seen the last of him.' He was waving something. It looked to McCluskey like an air ticket. 'Mr Kosigin thinks I should take a vacation . . . back to the old homeland.' He paused. 'I think he saw me.'

'What?'

'Back at the crematorium, I think he got a sideways glance. It would make things more interesting if the Philosopher knew I was around.'

McCluskey frowned. 'What the fuck are you talking about?'

But Jay just shook his head, still grinning, and walked away. He was whistling something, a tune the detective half-recognised.

It bugged him for days, but he never did place it.

Jeffrey Allerdyce was entertaining a corporate client in the penthouse dining room of Alliance Investigative in Washington DC.

This meant, in effect, that Alliance's senior partners were entertaining, while Allerdyce looked on from his well-upholstered office chair, which had been brought up one flight to the penthouse by a pair of junior partners (who naturally played no other part in the affair).

Allerdyce did not enjoy entertaining, and didn't see why it was expected of a company. To his mind, if you worked well for a client, that should always be enough. But as one senior partner and a host of accountants had told him, there needed to be more these days. Clients needed to feel wanted, cherished, cosseted. They needed, the senior partner had had the temerity to declare, to feel loved.

As if Allerdyce were entertaining them because he actually *liked* them. The only human being Jeffrey Allerdyce had ever loved was his father. The list of people he had *liked* in his long life wouldn't have filled an address label. He liked dogs – he owned two – and he liked an occasional gamble. He liked pasta with fresh pesto sauce. He liked *The Economist* and the *Wall Street Journal*, though neither as much as he once did. He liked *Inspector Morse* on TV, and the music of Richard Wagner. He would travel far for a live concert, if he could be assured of the quality of the artists involved.

He held the belief that his very distrust and dislike of people had made his agency the success it was. But success had bred the need for further success – bringing with it the necessity for corporate entertainment. He watched with a beady eye from his chair as the hired staff made sure plates were full. They were under instructions not to approach him. He would make his needs, if any, known to a senior partner, and food would be brought to him accordingly.

The affair had been arranged meticulously. A senior partner was allocated someone from the client company. They had to entertain that person, make any necessary introductions, check that glasses were replenished. Allerdyce almost sneered his contempt. One balding man in an expensive suit which hung from him like a dishrag from its peg was gulping at the champagne. Gulping it, swallowing it down, getting it while he could. Allerdyce wondered if anyone knew, or even cared, that it was Louis Roederer Cristal, 1985. The champagne of tsars, an almost unbelievably beguiling wine. He had allowed himself one glass, just to check the temperature was correct.

A senior partner, nominally in charge of 'the floor', came over and whispered into Allerdyce's ear. It gratified Allerdyce to see that members of the client company, even the CEO, glanced over at the conversation with something like fear – as well they might. The CEO called him J. Edgar behind his back. It was almost a compliment, but was probably said with a certain amount of nervous, defensive laughter. The nickname was apposite because, like Hoover, Allerdyce craved information. He hoarded the stuff, from tidbits to full-scale secret reports. Being at the hub of Washington, and especially at the hub of Washington's *secrets*, Allerdyce had collected a lot of information in his time. He used very little of it in any physical way. It was enough that he knew. It was enough that he could shake the CEO's hand, stare into his eyes, and let the man know with that stare that he knew about the male prostitute the CEO kept in a suite only four blocks from the White House.

That was why they glanced over nervily at the whispered exchange – all of them, all the ones with secrets to hide. When in fact the partner's message had been, 'Dulwater's outside,' and Allerdyce's reply had been, 'I'll be a few minutes.'

As he got up slowly from his chair feet shuffled forward, showing their owners were only too willing to help him to his feet should their help be needed. And when he walked across the floor, the various conversations lost their thread, or trailed off, or became more hushed. And when the door had closed behind him, they all felt the need for another drink.

Dulwater was sitting in a chair near the single elevator. Only one of the building's several elevators had access to the penthouse. The chair he sat in was reproduction Louis Quatorze, and looked like it might break at any moment. Dulwater was quick to rise when his employer appeared. Allerdyce pressed the button for the elevator, and Dulwater knew enough to be silent till it had arrived, they'd entered it, and the doors had closed again. Allerdyce turned his access key, quickly pressed some digits on the small keypad with dexterity, so Dulwater couldn't recognise the code, and stood back. They began the descent to the basement.

'Well?' Allerdyce asked.

'I'm not sure what it adds up to,' Dulwater began.

'That's not your concern,' Allerdyce snapped. 'I merely ask for your report.'

'Of course,' Dulwater swallowed. There was nothing on paper – his employer's instructions – but he knew it off by heart anyway, or hoped he did. There was perspiration on his upper lip, and he licked it away. 'Kosigin has brought in some muscle from Los Angeles, an Englishman. They twice had meetings outside the CWC Building: once in a downtown café, once on the waterfront. Even with the long-range mike I had trouble picking up the conversation.'

From the way he was speaking, Allerdyce knew Dulwater was curious to know why Alliance were now spying on their employers. He admired the younger man's curiosity. He knew, too, that no answer he could give would be satisfactory.

'Both were good choices,' Allerdyce mused. 'Café . . . waterfront . . . A babble of background noise, other voices . . .'

'And on the waterfront they kept moving. Plus there was tourist traffic.'

'So, you've told me what you did *not* learn . . .'

Dulwater nodded. 'There was a death, an apparent suicide of the reporter who'd been looking into CWC and whom we had been asked to investigate. The man's brother came to town. That seemed to bother Kosigin. You know Kosigin has a detective in his pocket?'

'Of course.'

'The detective tailed the brother. Looked like he was calling favours from half the department.'

'And the muscle from LA, as you so described him?'

Dulwater shrugged. 'I don't have a name, not yet. I'll get one.'

'Yes, you will.' The elevator reached the basement, which housed an underground car park. The limos the guests had arrived in were parked in neat rows, their liveried drivers enjoying a smoke and a joke.

'No smoking in the building!' Allerdyce barked before letting the elevator doors close again. He keyed in the penthouse. 'Interesting,' he said to Dulwater, his voice a dull ripple once more.

'Should I continue?'

Allerdyce considered this. 'Where is the brother?'

'Our agents report he's heading out today.'

'Do you think we'd learn anything more in San Diego now that he's gone?'

Dulwater gave the answer he thought was expected. 'Probably not, sir.'

'Probably not,' Allerdyce echoed, tapping a finger to his thin, dry lips. 'They were watching the brother because they perceived in him some threat. The threat of discovery. Now that he's flown home, does he still pose a threat?'

Dulwater was stuck for an answer. 'I don't know.'

Allerdyce seemed pleased. 'Exactly. And *neither do they*. Under the circumstances, Kosigin might just want to know more about the brother, more than we've already been able to tell him.'

'We weren't able to find out much about him,' Dulwater confessed.

'Kosigin is a careful man,' Allerdyce said. It was part of the man's attraction. Allerdyce had not managed to build up much of a dossier on Kosigin, though he knew just by looking at the man, just from a casual conversation with him, that there were secrets there to be discovered. He was a challenge.

And of course one day Kosigin might rise to the very pinnacle of CWC. He was already close, and still so young. 'I'm not a chemist,' he'd told Allerdyce, as though imparting some confidence, and so perhaps hoping to satisfy Allerdyce's celebrated curiosity. 'I don't have to be to know how to run a company. To run a company, I need to know two things: how to sell, and how to stop my competitors selling more than me.'

Yes, he was a challenge. That was why Allerdyce wanted him, wanted a nice fat dossier of secrets with Kosigin's name on it. Kosigin had made a mistake coming to Alliance again. Allerdyce had known that CWC employed its own security department. Why hadn't Kosigin used them? Why the need for an outside agency to follow the English journalist? Allerdyce was beginning to form an answer: Kosigin had something to hide from his superiors. And of course Alliance had worked for Kosigin once before. Allerdyce knew now that the two cases were connected, even if he didn't know why.

The elevator arrived at the penthouse. While Dulwater held the doors, Allerdyce keyed for it to return to the lobby. Then he stepped out, leaving the young man inside, still holding the doors, awaiting instructions.

'This intrigues me,' Allerdyce said. 'Is your passport up to date?'

'Yes, sir,' Dulwater said.

'Then come to my office tomorrow morning at seven. We'll have a further discussion.'

'Yes, sir,' said Dulwater, releasing the doors.

Allerdyce walked back to the dining room door but did not open it, not immediately. Instead he pressed his ear to the wood, the way he used to when he was a young boy, tiptoeing downstairs from bed to listen at the living room door or at his father's study. Listening for secrets, for things that could not be said in front of him. Happiest then – when nobody knew he was there.

Part Three

Main Lines

8

London seemed every bit as alien to him as San Diego.

He actually found himself carrying out evasion procedures at Heathrow. After depositing his single bag in Left Luggage, he went down to the Underground terminal and moved along the platform, watching, waiting. There were good reasons for not taking his car into London of course, reasons anyone would understand: he was only going into town for a short while; his destination was close to a tube stop; he'd have to be crazy to drive through London, especially jetlagged. But also he wanted to know if he was being followed, and this was more easily accomplished on foot.

When a train pulled in, he walked on to it, then came off again, looking to left and right along the platform. Then he stepped in again as the doors were closing. The other passengers looked at him like he was mad. Maybe he was. He looked out of the window. There was no one on the platform. No one was tailing him.

He'd been the same on the aeroplane. His fellow fliers must have thought there was something wrong with him, the number of times he got up to walk the aisles, visiting the bathroom, or going back to ask the stewardesses for drinks he didn't really want. Just so that he could study the passengers.

Now he was on his way into London, with keys in his pocket he had taken from his brother's motel room. The train ran on the Piccadilly Line and would take him all the way to Finsbury Park. But he came off two stops short on the Holloway Road and took his time finding a taxi, then watched from the back window as the driver talked football at him. He got the driver to take him past Jim's flat and drop him off at the end of the road.

The street looked quiet. It was nine-thirty in the morning. People had gone to work for the day. There was a line of cars one side of the street, and he looked into each one as he passed. Further along, workmen were digging a hole in the pavement. They were laughing and trading Irish-accented obscenities.

He dismissed them, then checked himself. Nobody could ever be dismissed entirely. The one-armed beggar could be hiding an Uzi up his sleeve. The innocent pram could be boobytrapped. Dismiss nothing and no one. He would stay aware of them, though they were a low priority.

He'd been to the flat before. It was carved from a four-storey house which sat just off the top of Ferme Park Road and almost had a view of Alexandra Palace. Jim had laughed about that when he bought the flat. 'The estate agent told me as part of his pitch – *Nearly* has a view of Ally Pally! Like that was somehow better than being five miles away! Those bastards'll turn anything into a selling point. If the roof was leaking, they'd say it was a safety feature in the event of a fire.'

Reeve tried the mortice key in its lock, but it was already unlocked. So he tried the yale, and that opened the door. The garden flat had its own front door at the bottom of half a dozen steps, but the ground floor and first and second floors were reached via the main door. In the vestibule, there were two more solid doors. Jim's was the ground-floor flat.

'This was probably a nice family house at one time,' he'd told Gordon when showing him around. 'Before the cowboys moved in and carved the place up.' He'd shown him how a large drawing-room to the rear had been subdivided with plasterboard walls to make the kitchen and bedroom. The bathroom would once have been part of the main hallway, and the flat's designer had taken an awkward chunk out of what was left of the living room, too.

'It's ugly now, see?' Jim had said. 'The proportions are all wrong. The ceilings are too high. It's like standing shoeboxes on their ends.'

'So why did you buy it?'

Jim had blinked at him. 'It's an investment, Gordie.' Then they'd opened the back door so that Jim could show him that the so-called 'garden flat' had no garden, just a concrete patio. 'Besides,' said Jim, 'this area is *in*. Pop stars and DJs live here. You see them down on the Broadway, eating in the Greek restaurant waiting for someone to recognise them.'

'So what do you do?' Reeve had asked.

'Me?' his brother had replied with a smirk which took years off him. 'I walk right up to them and ask if I can reserve a table for dinner.'

'Jesus, Jim,' Reeve said now, unlocking the flat door.

There were sounds inside. Instinctively, he dropped to a crouch. He couldn't identify the sounds – voices maybe. Could they be coming from the flat below or above? He didn't think so. And then he remembered the hall. There'd been no mail sitting there awaiting Jim's return. Jim had been gone a while; there should have been mail.

He examined the short hall in which he stood: no places of concealment; no weapons to hand. The floor looked solid enough, but might be noisy underfoot. He kept to one side, hugging the wall. Floors were usually strongest there; they didn't make so much noise. He clenched his hands into fists. Running water, a clatter of dishes – the sounds were coming from the kitchen – and a radio, voices on a radio. These were domestic sounds, but he wasn't going to be complacent. It was an easy trick, lulling someone with sound. He recalled a line from Nietzsche: shatter their ears, and teach them to hear with their eyes. It was good advice.

The kitchen door was open a fraction, as were the other doors. The living room looked empty, tidier than he remembered it. The bathroom was in darkness. He couldn't see into the bedroom. He approached the kitchen door and peered through the gap. A woman was at the sink. She had her back to him. She was thin and tall with short fair hair, curling at the nape of her neck. She was alone, washing her breakfast dishes. He decided to check the other rooms, but as he stepped back into the hall he hit a floorboard which sank and creaked beneath him. She looked round, and their eyes met.

Then she started screaming.

He pushed open the kitchen door, his hands held in front of him in a show of surrender.

'It's all right,' he said. 'I'm sorry I gave you a fright . . .'

She wasn't listening. She had raised her hands out of the water and was advancing on him. Soap suds fell from her right hand as she lifted it, and he saw she was holding a bread-knife. Her face was red with anger, not pale with fear, and her screams would bring people running if they could be heard above the workmen outside.

He waited for her to lunge at him. When she attacked, he would defend. But she seemed to know better. She stopped short, bringing the knife down and turning it from a hacking weapon into something she could stab with.

When she stopped screaming for a second to catch her breath he spoke as quickly as he could: 'I'm Jim's brother. Gordon Reeve. We look alike. Maybe he's mentioned me. Gordon Reeve. I live in Scotland. I'm Jim's brother.' He shook the keys at her. 'His keys. I'm his brother.' And all the time his eyes were half on her, half on the knife, and he was walking backwards into the hall as she kept coming forwards. He hoped he was getting through.

'His brother?' she said at last.

Reeve nodded, but said nothing. He wanted it to sink in first. One concept at a time. She was pumped with adrenaline, and her survival instincts had taken hold. There was fear there too, probably – only she didn't want him to sense it. And at the back of it all, there would be shock, just waiting for its chance to join the party.

'His brother?' she repeated, like it was a phrase in some new language she'd only just started learning.

He nodded again.

'Why didn't you ring the bell?'

'I didn't think anyone would be here.'

'Why didn't you shout? You sneaked up, you were spying on me.' She was working herself up again.

'I thought the flat would be empty. I thought you were an intruder.'

'Me?' She thought this was funny, but she wasn't lowering the knife. 'Didn't Jim tell you?'

'No,' he said.

'But you're telling me he gave you the keys? He gave you the keys and he didn't say I was living here?'

Reeve shook his head. 'The reason I'm here,' he said quietly, weighing up the effect this would have on her, 'is that Jim's dead. He died in San Diego. I'm on my way home from the funeral.'

San Diego seemed to click with her. 'What?' she said, appalled.

He didn't repeat any of it. He was dealing with porcelain now; knife-wielding porcelain, but fragile all the same.

'I'm leaving,' he told her. 'I'll sit outside. You can call the police or you can call my wife, verify who I am. You can do whatever you want. I'll be waiting outside, okay?'

He was at the door now. A dangerous moment: he'd have to half-turn from her to work the lock, providing her with a moment for attack. But she just stood there. She was like some awful statue as he pulled the door closed.

He sat in the vestibule for ten minutes. Then the door opened and she looked out. She wasn't carrying the knife.

'I've made some tea,' she said. 'You better come in.'

Her name was Fliss Hornby and she was an ex-colleague of Jim's – which was to say, she still worked for the paper from which he had resigned.

'He didn't really resign,' she told Reeve. 'I mean, he *did* resign, but then he reconsidered – only Giles Gulliver wouldn't unaccept his resignation.'

'I had a policeman friend that happened to,' Reeve said.

'Jim was furious, but Giles said it was for his own good. I really think he meant it. He knew Jim would be better off going freelance. Not financially better off, but his stuff wouldn't get spiked so often. He'd have more freedom to write what he liked. And to prove it, he commissioned a couple of pieces by Jim, and took a couple of stories from him which ended up on the inside news page.'

They were eating an early lunch in an Indian restaurant on Tottenham Lane. There was a special lunchtime businessmen's buffet: large silver salvers with domed covers, blue flames licking beneath each. But they were just watching their food, rearranging it with their forks, they weren't really eating. They simply needed to be out of the flat.

Reeve had told Fliss Hornby about Jim's death. He'd meant to keep it simple, lying where necessary, but he found the whole story gushing out of him, a taste of bile at the back of his throat, like he'd been puking.

She was a good listener. She had listened through her tears and got up only once – to fetch a box of paper hankies from the bedroom. Then it had been her turn to talk, and she told Reeve how she'd met up with Jim and a load of other journalists one night in Whitehall. She'd told him that things weren't going well with her, that her boyfriend had become her ex-boyfriend and had threatened her with violence.

'I mean,' she told Gordon. 'I can look after myself—'

'I've noticed.'

'But it was more the atmosphere. It was disrupting my work. Jim said he was going to the States for a month, and suggested I look after his flat. Lance might get bored knocking on the door of an empty flat in Camden. And in the meantime, I could get my head together.'

'Lance, that's the boyfriend?'

'Ex-boyfriend. Christ, *boyfriend* – he's in his forties.'

Fliss Hornby on the other hand was in her late 20s. She'd been married some time in her past, but didn't talk about it. Everyone was allowed one mistake. It was just that she kept making the one mistake time after time.

They'd demolished a bottle of white wine in the restaurant. Or Fliss had; Reeve had had just the one glass, plus lots of iced water.

She took a deep breath, stretching her neck to one side and then the other, her eyes closed. Then she settled back in her chair and opened her eyes again.

'So what are you going to do?' she asked.

'I'm not sure. I was planning to search the flat.'

'Good idea. Jim filled the hall cupboard with all his stuff, plus there are a couple of suitcases under the bed.' She saw the look on his face. 'Would you like me to do it?'

Reeve shook his head. 'He didn't tell you why he was going to the States?'

'He was always a bit hush-hush about his stories, especially in their early stages. Didn't want anyone nicking his ideas. He had a point. Journalists don't have friends – you're either a source or a competitor.'

'I'm a source?'

She shrugged. 'If there's a story . . .'

Reeve nodded. 'Jim would like that. He'd want the story finished.'

'Always supposing we can start it. No files, no notes . . .'

'Maybe in the flat.'

She poured the last of the wine down her throat. 'Then what are we waiting for?'

Reeve tried to imagine anyone threatening Fliss Hornby. He imagined himself hurting the threatener. It wasn't difficult. He knew pressure points, angles of twist, agonies waiting to be explored. He could fillet a man like a chef with a Dover sole. He could have them repeat the Lord's Prayer backwards while eating sand and gravel. He could break a man.

These were thoughts the psychiatrist had warned him about. Mostly, they came after he'd been drinking. But he hadn't been drinking, and yet he was still thinking them.

More than that, he was enjoying them, relishing the possibility of pain – someone else's; maybe even his own – sensations made you feel alive. He was probably never more alive than when consumed by fear and flight at the end of Operation Stalwart. Never more alive than when so nearly dead.

He telephoned Joan from the flat to let her know what was happening. Fliss Hornby was pulling stuff out of the hall cupboard, laying it along the floorboards so it could be gone through methodically. Reeve watched her through the open door of the living room. Joan said that Allan was missing his dad. She told him there had been potential clients, two of them on two separate occasions. He'd already had her cancel this weekend's course.

'Phone calls?' he asked.

'No, these were personal callers.'

'I mean have there been any phone calls?'

'None I couldn't deal with.'

'Okay.'

'You sound tense.'

He had yet to tell Joan what he'd just sat and told a complete stranger. 'Well, you know, I've got all his things to sort through . . .'

'I can come down there, you know.'

'No, you stay there with Allan. I'll be home soon.'

'Promise?'

'I promise. Bye, Joan.'

By the time he got through to the hall, the cupboard was half empty.

'You start looking through that lot,' Fliss said, 'while I haul the rest out.'

'Sure,' Reeve agreed. Then: 'Shouldn't you be at work or something?'

She smiled. 'Maybe I *am* at work.'

An hour later, they'd been through the contents of the cupboard and had found nothing relevant. Fliss Hornby had burst into tears just the once. Reeve had thought it best to ignore her. Besides, his mind was on his work. They drank herbal tea and then went into the bedroom. At some point, Reeve couldn't work out when, Fliss had tidied the room. When he'd first glanced into it, the bed had been strewn with clothes, the floor with books and magazines. Now everything had been hidden.

She pulled two suitcases out from beneath the bed and lifted the first one on to the bed. It wasn't locked. There were clothes inside. Reeve recognised some of them: a gaudy striped shirt, a couple of ties, a Scotland rugby shirt, saggy, the way all rugby shirts seem to go after the very first wash. The second case contained paperwork.

They spent a lot of time flicking through files, bundles of paperclipped news cuttings, an old-fashioned card index. Then Fliss found half a dozen computer disks, and waved them at Reeve.

'I may be able to read these here.'

Her PC was set up on the desk in the living room. Reeve studied the bookshelves while she booted up.

'These all yours?' he asked.

'No, most of them are Jim's. I didn't bring much from my flat, just stuff I didn't want burgled.'

There were a couple of philosophy books. Reeve smiled, picking one out. David Hume's *An Enquiry Concerning the Principles of Morals*. He flicked through, and found a couple of lines had been underlined on one page. He knew which lines they'd be, but read them anyway.

A man, brought to the brink of a precipice, cannot look down without trembling.

He'd spouted philosophy at Jim during a couple of their meetings. He'd quoted Hume at him, this very passage, comparing it with Nietzsche: *If you gaze into the abyss, the abyss gazes also into you*. More melodramatic than Hume, probably less factual – but much more powerful. Jim had been listening. He'd appeared bored, but all the time he'd been listening, and he'd even bought a couple of the books. More than that, he'd read them.

Fliss Hornby was sliding the first disk home. It contained correspondence. They read through some of the letters.

'This feels weird,' she said at one point. 'I mean, I'm not sure we should be doing this. It's almost like desecration.'

The other disks dealt with stories Jim Reeve had been working on at one time or another. Reeve was glad Fliss was there; she saved him time.

'Giles used that one,' she said of one story. 'This one I think turned up unattributed in *Private Eye* or *Time Out*. This one I haven't come across before, but it looks like he hit a dead end with it.'

'We're looking for a chemical company, Co-World Chemicals, headquarters in San Diego.'

'I know, you told me.' She sounded impatient. She tried another disk. It was labelled 1993 and proved to be all old stuff. The other disks were no more helpful.

'Nothing current,' she said. 'He probably took the current disks with him along with his laptop.'

Reeve remembered something she'd said, about journalists only having sources and competitors. 'He wouldn't have left any of his notes here anyway,' he stated. 'Not with another reporter on the premises.'

'Where else would he have left them?'

'Could be anywhere. A girlfriend's, a drinking mate's . . .'

'With his ex-wife?'

Reeve shook his head. 'She disappeared a while back, probably left the country. Jim had that effect on women.' He'd tried contacting her, to tell her the news. Not that she'd have been interested; not that he'd tried very hard.

Reeve remembered something. 'We're also looking for the name Agrippa.'

'Agrippa? That's classical, isn't it?' Fliss slid a CD into the computer's CD-ROM slot. 'Encyclopaedia,' she explained. She went to Word Search and entered 'Agrippa'. The computer came up with ten articles, the word coming up a total of twenty times. They scanned all ten articles, but remained none the wiser about what Agrippa had meant to Jim. Fliss tried a few reference books, but the only additional Agrippa she found was in the *Oxford Companion to English Literature*.

'Dead end,' she said, slamming shut the last book.

'What about mail?' Reeve asked. 'Has he had any letters while he's been away?'

'Plenty. He told me he'd phone and give me an address I could redirect them to, but he never did. Last I spoke to him was when he handed me the front door keys.'

'So where's the mail?'

It was in the cupboard above the sink in the kitchen. There was a teetering tower of it. Fliss carried it to the kitchen table while Reeve cleared a space, moving cups, sugar bowl and milk bottle. He couldn't hear the pneumatic drill any more. He looked at his watch, surprised to find it was nearly five o'clock – the best part of the day had gone, used up on a hunt which had so far failed to turn up anything in the least useful.

The mail looked similarly uninspired. Much of it was junk. 'I could have just binned it,' Fliss said. 'But when *I* come home after a trip, I like there to be a big pile of letters waiting for me. Makes me feel wanted.'

'Jim was wanted all right,' Reeve said. 'Wanted by double-glazing firms, clothes catalogues, the football pools and just about every fund management scheme going.'

There was a postcard from Wales. Reeve deciphered the spidery handwriting, then handed it to Fliss. 'Who's Charlotte?'

'I think he brought her to the pub once.'

'What about his girlfriends? Anyone come to the flat looking for him? Anyone phoned?'

She shook her head. 'Just Charlotte. She called one night. Seems he hadn't said he was going to the States. I think they were supposed to be going to Wales together.'

Reeve considered. 'So either he was an unfeeling bastard who was giving her the big hint she was being ditched . . .'

'Or?'

'Or something suddenly came up in the States. When did he tell you you could move in?'

'The night before he flew out.'

'So he crammed all his stuff into the cupboard in the hall and the suitcases under the bed and off he went.' Reeve gnawed his bottom lip. 'Maybe he knew they were going to move the scientist.'

'Scientist?'

'Dr Killin – he worked at CWC. Jim went to see him once. Next time he tried, Killin had gone on vacation and the house was under surveillance.'

'I got the feeling he'd only had a few days' notice that he was making the trip. He complained at the price of the air-fare. It wasn't APEX. What's the matter?'

Reeve was studying an envelope. He turned it over in his hands. 'This is Jim's handwriting.'

'What?' She gazed at the envelope.

'It's his handwriting. Postmarked London, the day before he flew to the States.' He held the envelope up to the light, shook it, pressed its contents between thumb and forefinger. 'Not just paper,' he said. He peeled apart the two glued flaps. He would never use ready-seal envelopes himself; they were too easy to tamper with. He pulled out a sheet of A4 paper, double-folded. A small key fell out of the paper on to the table. While Fliss picked up the key, Reeve unfolded the paper. The writing was a drunken scrawl.

'Pete's new address – 5 Harrington Lane.'

He showed it to Fliss. 'What do you reckon?'

She fetched her *A–Z*. There was only one Harrington Lane in London – just off the upper Holloway Road, near Archway.

'It's not that far,' said Fliss. Her car was being fixed at a garage in Crouch End, so they called for a cab.

'Yeah,' said Pete Cavendish, 'like Jim said, you can't be too careful. And I had the garage gutted out, sold my car and my motorbike. I've gone ecology, see. I use a bicycle now. I reckon everybody should.' He was in his late 20s, a photographer. Jim Reeve had put work his way in the past, so Pete had been happy to oblige when Jim asked a favour.

Reeve hadn't considered his brother's car. He'd imagined it would be sitting in some long-term car park out near Heathrow – and as far as he was concerned they could keep it.

Cavendish put him right. 'Those places cost a fortune. No, he reckoned this was a better bet.'

They were walking from 5 Harrington Lane, a terraced house, to the garage Pete Cavendish owned. They'd come out through his back door, crossed what might have been the garden, been shown through a gate at the back which Cavendish then repadlocked shut, and were in an alley backing on to two rows of houses whose rear gardens faced each other. The lane had become a dumping ground for everything from crisp packets to mattresses and sofas. One sofa had been set alight and was charred to a crisp, showing springs and clumps of wadding. It was nearly dark, but the alley was blessed with a single working streetlamp. Cavendish had brought a torch with him.

'I think the reason he did that,' Cavendish said, meaning Jim's letter to himself, 'was he was pissed, and he hadn't been to my new gaff before. He probably reckoned he'd forget the bloody address and never find me again, or his old motor. See, Jim had a kind of dinosaur brain – there was a little bit of it working even when he'd had a drink. It was his ancient consciousness.'

Pete Cavendish spoke with a roll-up in his mouth. He had a ponytail and grey wizened cheeks. The holes in his denims weren't there by design, and the heel was loose on one of his sneakers. Reeve had noticed some cans of Super Lager on the kitchen worktop. He'd seen Cavendish swig from one before they set off. Ecology and dinosaurs. If Cavendish kept drinking, he'd be seeing green dinosaurs in his dreams.

They passed seven lock-ups before coming to a stop. Cavendish kicked away some empty cans and a bag of bottles from the front of his own private garage, then took the key from Reeve that Jim had posted to his own home. He turned it in the lock, pulled the handle, and the garage door groaned open. It stuck half-way up, but half-way was enough. The streetlight barely penetrated the interior gloom.

Cavendish switched on the torch. 'Doesn't look as though any of the kids have been in here,' he said, checking the floor and walls. Reeve didn't ask what he'd thought he might find – glue, spraypaint, used phials of crack?

There was only the car.

It was a battered Saab 900 of indeterminate colour – charcoal came closest – with a chip out of the windscreen, the fixings for wing mirrors but no actual mirrors, and one door (replaced after a collision) a different colour from the rest of the body. Reeve had never let his brother drive him anywhere in the Saab, and had never seen Jim drive it. It used to sit outside the flat with a tarpaulin over it.

'He spent a grand getting it done up,' Cavendish said.

'Money well spent,' Reeve muttered.

'Not on the outside, on the inside: new engine, transmission, clutch. He could've bought another car cheaper, but he loved this old tank.' Cavendish patted it fondly.

'Keys?' Reeve asked. Cavendish handed them over. Reeve unlocked the car and looked inside, checking under the seats and in the glove compartment. He came up with chewing gum, parking tickets, and a book of matches from the same Indian restaurant where he'd eaten lunch.

'The boot?' Fliss suggested. Reeve was unwilling; this would be it, the very last option, their last chance to move any further forward. He turned the key and felt the boot spring open. Cavendish shone the torch in. There was something nestling there, covered with a tartan travelling-rug. Reeve pulled off the rug, revealing a large cardboard box advertising its contents to be twelve one-litre bottles of washing-up liquid. It was the kind of box you picked up from supermarkets and corner shops. He opened its flaps. There were papers inside, maybe half a box full. He pulled out the top sheet and angled it into the failing torchlight.

'Bingo,' he said.

He lifted the box out, and Fliss locked the boot. The box was awkward rather than heavy.

'Can we call for a cab from your phone?' Reeve asked Cavendish.

'Yeah, sure.' They left the lock-up, and Cavendish locked it tight. 'Just one thing,' he said.

'What's that?'

'What's going to happen to the motor?'

Reeve thought about it for all of two seconds. 'It's yours,' he told Cavendish. 'Jim would have wanted it that way.'

9

January 13th

I suppose if this turns into a story, I'll have to credit Marco with the genesis – though he'd probably stress he's more of a Pink Floyd fan. He wears a T-shirt which must date back to Dark Side of the Moon. *It's black with the prism logo on it – only he says it's a pyramid. Sure, but light doesn't enter a pyramid white and come out the seven colours of the rainbow. It only does that with prisms, so it must be a prism. He says I'm missing the point, maaann. The point is, the album's a concept album and the concept is everyday madness. Pure white light into a myriad of colours. The everyday gone mad.*

But then why is it a damned pyramid? Why not a teacup or a toaster or even a typewriter? Marco laughs, remembering that party of his and how I looked at a poster on his wall and thought it was sailing boats on a rippling blue sea, pictured near sunset with some heavy filtering.

And it wasn't. It was pyramids. It was the poster that came with Dark Side of the Moon *and I was sober when I mistook it. Sober as a judge. Later, I was drunk as a lord and trying to get my hand up Marco's girlfriend's kilt until she reminded me, her mouth shiveringly close to my ear, that Marco had done a bit of judo in his time and part of his left ear was missing. So, fair enough, I retracted my hand. You do, don't you?*

Where the fuck was I? The story. The story.

It's about madness too: that's why I used the Pink Floyd reference. I could use it as a lead into the story proper. Tales of Everyday Madness. Was that a book or a film? Did someone give me that at charades one time? Absolutely impossible. Yes, charades, at Marco's party. And Marco's team were making half their titles up. The bastard even dumped in some that were in Italian.

Marco is Italian, and that is also relevant to the story. This is a story he told me last night in the Stoat and Whistle. I said to him, why haven't you told me this before? Know what he said? He said, this is the first serious (not to mention intelligible) conversation we've ever had. And when I thought about it, he was probably right. What's more, he only got round to telling his story because we'd run out of Tottenham jokes. Here's the last one we told. What's the difference between a man with no knob and a Spurs player? A man with no knob's got more chance of scoring.

See, we were desperate.

'Anything?' Fliss asked. She had her own sheaf of paper in front of her, as well as a second mug of coffee.

'I think he was drunk when he typed this.'

'Full of spelling mistakes?'

'No, just full of shit.'

They were back in the Crouch End flat. They'd brought a carry-out back with them – Chinese this time, with some lagers and Cokes bought from the corner shop. The tin trays of food sat half-uneaten on the living room's coffee table.

'What about you?' Reeve asked.

'Photocopies mostly. Articles from medical and scientific journals. Looks like he was calling up anything he could find on Mad Cow Disease. Plus on genetic patents. There's an interesting article about the company that owns the patent on all genetically engineered cotton. Might not be relevant.' She gnawed on a plastic chopstick. The chopsticks had been 50p a pair extra. Reeve rubbed his jaw, feeling the need for a shave. And a bath. And some sleep. He tried not to think about what time his body made it; tried to dismiss the eight hours he'd wound his watch forward, and the sleep he hadn't taken on the plane.

He started reading again.

Marco is a journalist. He's over here for a year, more if they like his reports, as London correspondent for some glossy Milan rag. They keep faxing him to say they want more royal family, more champagne balls, more Wimbledon and Ascot. He's tried telling them Wimbledon and Ascot come once a year, but they just keep sending the faxes to their London office. Marco's thinking of chucking it. He used to be a 'serious' journalist, real hard copy, until he sniffed more money in the air. Moved from daily to weekly, newspaper to magazine. He said at the time he was just sick of journalism; he wanted easy money and a break from Italy. Italian politics depressed him. The corruption depressed him. He'd had a colleague, a good friend, blown up by a parcel bomb when they tried to zero in on some minister with mafia connections. Ba-boom, and up and away to the great leader column in the sky. Or maybe the elevator down to the basement, glowing fires and typing up the classifieds.

Marco told me about some of the scandals, and I was matching him conspiracy for conspiracy, chicanery for chicanery, pay-off for pay-off. Then he told me he covered the Spanish cooking oil tragedy. I recalled it only vaguely. 1981, hundreds died. Contaminated oil – yes?

And Marco said, 'Maybe.'

So then he told his side of it, which didn't quite tally with the official line at the time or since. Because according to Marco, some of the people who died hadn't touched the oil (rapeseed oil it was – memo to self, get clippings out of library). They hadn't bought it, hadn't used it – simple as that. So what caused the deaths? Marco's idea – and it wasn't original, he got it from other researchers into the area – was that these things called – Hold on, I wrote it down – Jesus, it's taken me ten minutes to track it down. Should've known to look first on my fag packet. OPs, that what it says. OPs were to blame. He did tell me what they are, but I've forgotten. Better look into it tomorrow.

'OPs,' Reeve said.

'What?'

'Any mention of them in the stuff you're reading?'

She smiled. 'Sorry, I stopped reading a while back. I'm not taking it in any more.' She yawned, stretching her arms up, hands clenched. The fabric of her jumper tightened, raising the profile of her breasts.

'Shit,' said Reeve, suddenly realising. 'I've got to get a room.'

'What?'

'A hotel room. I wasn't planning on being here this late.'

She paused before answering. 'You can sleep where you are. That sofa's plenty comfy enough; I've fallen asleep on it a few times myself. I'll just check out *Newsnight* if that's all right, see what I've missed today and what I can expect to read tomorrow, and then I'll leave you to it.'

He stared at her.

'It's all right, really it is,' she said. 'You're perfectly safe with me.'

She had blue eyes. He'd noticed them before, but they seemed bluer now. And she didn't smell of perfume, just soap.

'We can read the rest over breakfast,' she said, switching on the TV. 'I need a clear head to take in half of what I'm reading. Bovine Spongiform Encephalopathy: it doesn't exactly trip off the tongue, does it? And nor does it trip off the eyeballs. Bloody boffins just refuse to call it Mad Cow Disease. I hope to God that's not what this is all about, the beefburgers of the damned – and bloody John Selwyn Gummer stuffing one down his poor sodding daughter's throat. Do you remember that photo?'

'Why do you say that?'

She was engrossed in the TV. 'Say what?'

'That you hope it's not about Bovine Spongy Whatsit.'

She glanced at him. 'Because it's been covered, Gordon. It's old news. Besides, the public are physically repelled by scare stories. They'd rather not know about them. That's why they end up in the *Grauniad* or *Private Eye*. You've heard of the right to know? Well, the good old British public has another inalienable right: the right *not* to know, not to worry. They want a cheap paper with some cartoons and funny headlines and a good telly section. They do not want to know about diseases that eat their flesh, meat that makes them mad, or eggs that can put them in casualty. You tell them about the bow doors on ferries, they still troop on and off them every weekend, heading for Calais and cheap beer.' She turned to him again. 'Know why?'

'Why?'

'Because they don't think lightning strikes twice. If some other bugger has died that makes it so much less likely that *they* will.' She turned back to the TV, then smiled. 'Sorry, I'm ranting.'

'You have a low regard for your readers?'

'On the contrary, I have a very high regard for *my* readers. They are discriminating and knowledgeable.' She turned the sound up a little, losing herself in the news. Reeve put down the sheets of paper he was still holding. Sticking out from below the sofa was a newspaper. He pulled it out. It was the paper Fliss worked for.

'Isn't he a dish?' she muttered, a rhetorical question apparently. She was talking to herself about the news presenter.

Reeve went through to the kitchen to boil some more water. He knew he should phone Joan again, let her know the score, but the telephone was in the living room. He sat down at the kitchen table and spread out the paper which he'd brought through with him. He started examining each page, looking for the byline Fliss Hornby. He didn't find it. He went through the paper again. This time he found it.

He made two mugs of instant decaf and took them back through to the living room. Fliss had tucked her legs beneath her and was hugging them. She sat forward ever so slightly in her chair, a fan seeking a better view, though there was nothing between her and her idol. Then Reeve was in the way, handing her the mug.

'You work on the fashion page,' he said.

'It's still journalism, isn't it?' Obviously she'd had this conversation before.

'I thought you were—'

'What?' She glared at him. 'A *proper* journalist? An *investigative* journalist?'

'No, I just thought . . . Never mind.'

He sat down, aware she was angry with him. Tactful, Gordon, he thought. Nil out of ten for leadership. Had he told her he appreciated all she'd done today? She'd halved his workload, been able to explain things to him – bits of journalist's shorthand on the disks, for example. He might have been there all day, and spent a wasted day, instead of which he had something. He had the genesis; that's what Jim had called it. The genesis of whatever had led him to San Diego and his death. It was a start. Tomorrow things might get more serious.

He kept looking at Fliss. If she'd turned in his direction, he'd have smiled an apology. But she was staring unblinking at the screen, her neck taut. Reeve seemed to have the ability to piss women off. Look at Joan. Most days now there was an argument between them; not when Allan was around – they were determined to put up a 'front' – but whenever he wasn't there. There was enough electricity in the air to fuel a ring-main.

After *Newsnight* was watched in silence, Fliss said a curt goodnight, but then came back into the room with a spare duvet and a pillow.

'I'm sorry,' Reeve told her. 'I didn't mean to imply anything. It's just that you never said anything, and you've been acting all day like you were Scoop Newshound, the paper's only investigative reporter.'

She smiled. 'Scoop Newshound?'

He shrugged, smiling also.

'I forgive you,' she said. 'First one up tomorrow goes for milk and bread, right?'

'Right, Fliss.'

'Goodnight, then.' She showed no sign of moving from the doorway. Reeve had pulled off his blue cotton jumper and was wearing a long-sleeved white T-shirt. She appraised his body for a moment, and gave a smile and a noise that was half-way between a sigh and humming, then turned and walked away.

He found it hard to sleep. He was too tired; or rather, he was exhausted but not tired. His brain wouldn't work – as he discovered when he tried carrying on with Jim's notes – but it wouldn't be still either. Images flitted through his mind, bouncing along like a ball through a series of puddles. Snatches of conversations, songs, echoes of the two films he'd watched on the flight, his trip on the Underground, the taxi cabs, the Indian restaurant, surprising Fliss in the kitchen. Songs . . . tunes . . .

Row, row, row your boat.

He jerked from the sofa, standing in the middle of the floor in his T-shirt and underpants, trembling. He switched on the TV, turning the sound all the way down. Night-time television: mindless and bright. He looked out of the window. A halo of orange sodium, a dog barking in the near-distance, a car cruising past. He watched it, studied it. The driver was staring straight ahead. There were cars parked outside, solid lines of them both sides of the street, ready for tomorrow's race.

He padded through to the kitchen on bare feet and switched on the kettle again. Rooting in the box of assorted herbal teabags he found spearmint and decided to give it a try. Back in the hallway, he noticed that Fliss's bedroom door was ajar. More than 'ajar' in fact: it was half-way open. Was it an invitation? He'd be bound to see it if he used the kitchen or the bathroom. Her light was off. He listened for her breathing, but the fridge in the kitchen was making too much noise.

He waited in the hall, holding the steaming mug, until the fridge switched off. Her breathing was more than regular – she was snoring.

'Morning.' She came into the kitchen sleepy-faced and tousling her hair. She wore a thick tartan dressing-gown and fluffy pink slippers.

Reeve had been out and purchased breakfast and newspapers. She slumped into a chair at the table and grabbed a paper.

'Coffee?' he asked. He'd bought a packet of ground and some paper filters.

'How did you sleep?' she asked without looking up.

'Fine,' he lied. 'You?'

As she was folding a page, she glanced up at him. 'Soundly, thanks.'

He poured them both coffee. 'I've found out what OPs are.'

'Oh?'

'I've been doing some more reading.'

'You *were* up early. So, what are they?'

'Organo-phosphorous treatments.'

'And what are those when they're at home?'

'Pesticides, I think. Marco and others think the Spanish cooking oil thing was all to do with pesticides.'

She drank greedily from her mug and exhaled. 'So what now?'

He shrugged.

'Are you going to talk to Marco?'

Reeve shook his head. 'He's got nothing to do with it. He's just a catalyst. Jim wasn't researching the Spanish incident, he was looking at BSE.'

'Bovine Spongiform thingy.'

'Encephalopathy.'

'Right.'

'How did he make the leap from cooking oil to BSE?'

'He remembered something he'd heard.'

So I phoned Joshua Vincent, and told him he probably wouldn't know me. He said I was correct in that assumption. I explained that some time ago the paper had received a press release from his organisation, the National Farmers' Union, concerning BSE. He told me he wasn't working for the NFU any more. He sounded bitter when he said it. I asked him what had happened.

'They sacked me,' he said.

'Why?'

'Because of what I said about BSE.'

And I began to sniff my story. Now if only I can persuade Giles to fund me . . .

'So what are you doing today?' Fliss asked. She'd had a shower, dried her hair, and was dressed.

'Trying to find Joshua Vincent.'

'And if you can't?'

Reeve shrugged again; he didn't want to consider failure, though really it should be considered. With any plan, there should be a fallback position.

'You could talk to Giles Gulliver,' she suggested, dabbing crumbs of toast from her plate.

'That's an idea.'

'And then?'

'Depends what I learn.'

She sucked at the crumbs. 'Don't expect too much from Giles, or anyone like him.'

'What do you mean?'

She grabbed the newspaper and opened it to a full-page advertisement, placed by Co-World Chemicals. 'Don't bother reading it,' she said, 'it'll put you back to sleep. It's just one of those feelgood ads big corporations make up when they want to spend some money.'

Reeve glanced at the ad. 'Or when their consciences are bothering them?'

Fliss wrinkled her nose. 'Grow up. Those people don't have consciences. They've had them surgically removed to make room for the cash-flow implants.' She tapped the paper. 'But as long as Co-World and companies like them are throwing money at advertising departments, publishers will love them, and the publishers will see to it that their editors never print anything that might upset Sugar Daddy. That's all I'm saying.'

'Thanks for the warning.'

She shrugged. 'Will you be here this evening?'

'I don't know. Maybe. I'll have to see how it goes.'

'Well, I'll probably be late. There's a second Giannini's opening in Covent Garden and I'm invited.'

'Giannini's?'

'The designer.'

'Hold the front page,' he said. She scowled and he held up his hands. 'Just a joke.'

'I want to know what you find, no matter what. Even if it's only a phone call from Scotland, let me know.'

'Sure, it's the least I can do.'

She left the kitchen and returned again wearing a coat and carrying a briefcase. She made show of adjusting the belt on the coat. 'Just one thing, Gordon.'

'What's that?'

'What are you going to do about the flat?'

He smiled at her. 'It's yours for as long as you want it.'

Finally she looked at him. 'Really?' He nodded. 'Thanks.'

Maybe he'd found his fallback position. If he didn't get any further with Jim's story, he could always track down her ex-boyfriend and make a mess of the rest of his life. She came over and pecked him on the cheek.

Which was payment enough in itself.

He found a telephone number for the NFU; but nobody could give him a forwarding address for Joshua Vincent. A woman who had tried to be helpful eventually passed him on to someone who had more questions than answers, wanting to know who he was and what his connection was with Mr Vincent.

Reeve put down the telephone.

Maybe Vincent lived in London, but there were several Vincent J.'s listed in the phone book. It would take a while to talk to them all. He went to Jim's notes again. They were a hodge-podge of the detailed and the rambling, of journalistic instinct and alcoholic excess. There were jottings on the backs of some sheets. He hadn't paid them much attention, but laid them out now on the living-room floor. Doodles, circles and cubes mostly, and a cow's warped face with a pair of horns. But there were names and what looked like times too, and some telephone numbers. There were no names beside the numbers. He tried the first one and got a woman's answering machine. The second just rang and rang. The third turned out to be a bookmaker's in Finsbury Park. The fourth was a central London pub, the one Fliss and her journalist colleagues used.

The fifth was another answering machine: 'Josh here. Leave your message and I'll get back.'

An evasive message. Reeve severed the connection and wondered what to say. Eventually he dialled again.

'Josh here. Leave your message and I'll get back.'

He waited for the tone.

'My name's Gordon Reeve, and I'm trying to locate Joshua Vincent. I got this number from my brother's notes. My brother's name was James Reeve; I think Mr Vincent knew him. I use the past tense because my brother is dead. I think he was working on a story at the time. I'm hoping you can help me. I'd like to find out why he died.'

He gave the flat's telephone number and put down the receiver. Then he sat down and stared at the telephone for fifteen minutes. He made more coffee and watched it for another fifteen minutes. If Vincent was home and had listened to the message straight away, even if he wanted to check James Reeve *had* a brother, he would have been back by now.

So Reeve telephoned Fliss's paper, spoke to Giles Gulliver's assistant, and was put through to the editor at last.

'Good God,' Gulliver said. 'I can't believe it. Is this some sort of joke?'

'No joke, Mr Gulliver. Jim's dead.'

'But how? When?'

Reeve started to tell him, but Gulliver interrupted. 'No, wait – let's meet. Is that possible, Mr Reeve?'

'It's possible.'

'Just let me check my diary.' Reeve was put on hold for the time it took him to count to sixty. 'Sorry about that. We could have a drink at midday. I've a lunch appointment at one, so it would make sense to meet at the hotel. Would that suit you? I want to hear everything. It's quite ghastly. I can hardly take it in. Jim was one of—'

'Where's the hotel, Mr Gulliver?'
'Sorry. The Ritz. See you there at midday.'
'Goodbye, Mr Gulliver.'
And still Joshua Vincent didn't call.

In Jim's notes, Giles Gulliver had always been 'the old boy' or 'the old buffer'. Reeve was expecting a man in his 60s or even 70s, a newspaperman of the old school. But when he was shown to Gulliver's table in the Ritz bar he saw that the man half-rising to greet him from behind a fat Cuban cigar could only be in his early 40s – not much older than Reeve himself. But Gulliver's actions were studied, like those of a much older man, a man who has seen everything life has to throw at him. Yet he had gleaming eyes, the eyes of a child when shown something wondrous. And Reeve saw at once that the phrase 'old boy' was perfect for Giles Gulliver. He was Peter Pan in a pinstripe.

'Good man,' Gulliver said, shaking Reeve's hand. He ran his fingers through his slicked hair as he sat back down again. They had a corner table, away from the general babble of the bar. There were four things on the table: an ashtray, a portable telephone, a portable fax machine, and a glass of iced whisky.

Gulliver rolled the cigar around his mouth. 'Something to drink?' Their waiter was standing ready.

'Mineral water,' said Reeve.

'Ice and lime, sir?'

'Lemon,' said Reeve. The waiter retreated and Reeve waited for Gulliver to say something.

Gulliver was shaking his head. 'Hellish business. Surprised no one told me sooner. I've got a sub working on the obit.' He paused, catching himself. 'My dear chap, I'm so sorry. You don't want to hear about that.'

'It's okay.'

'Now tell me, how did Jim die?'

'He was murdered.'

Gulliver's eyes were hidden by the smoke he'd just exhaled. 'What?'

'That's my theory.'

Gulliver relaxed; he was dealing with a theory, not a story.

Reeve told him some of the rest, but by no means all of it. He wasn't sure of his ground. On the one hand, he wanted the public to know what had happened in San Diego. On the other, he wasn't sure whose life he might be endangering if he *did* go public – especially if he went public without proof. Proof would be his insurance. He needed proof.

'Did you know Jim was going to San Diego?' Reeve asked.

Gulliver nodded. 'He wanted three thousand dollars from me. Said the trip would be worth it.'

'Did he tell you why he was going?'

Gulliver's phone rang. He smiled an apology and picked it up. The conversation – the side of it Reeve could hear – was technical, something to do with the next day's edition.

Gulliver pressed the off button. 'Apologies.' He glanced at his watch. 'Did Jim tell me why he was going? No, that was one of the irritating things about him.' He caught himself again. 'I don't wish to speak ill of the dead . . .'

'Speak away.'

'Well, Jim liked his little conspiracy; and he liked to keep it his own secret. I think he thought it gave him more power: if an editor didn't know what the story might be, they couldn't come straight out and say no. That's how Jim liked to play us. The less he told, the more we were supposed to think he had to tell. Eventually, he'd give you the story, the story you'd shelled out for, and it was seldom as meaty as you'd been led to believe.'

Listening to Gulliver, especially as the whisky did its loosening, Reeve could hear hard edges and jagged corners that were a long way away from the public school image Gulliver presented to the world. There was street market in those edges and corners. There was street smart. There was city boy.

The fax bleeped and then started to roll out a page. Gulliver examined the sheet and got on the telephone again. There was another technical discussion, another glance at the Piaget watch, a tug at the crocodile wristband.

'He didn't tell you anything?' Reeve persisted, sounding like he didn't believe it.

'Oh, he told me snatches. Cooking oil, British beef, some veterinarian who'd died.'

'Did he mention Co-World Chemicals?'

'I think so.'

'In what connection?'

'My dear boy, there *was* no connection, that's what I've been saying. He'd just say a couple of words, like he was feeding an infant egg from a silver spoon. Thinking he was stringing one along . . .'

'Someone killed him to stop the story.'

'Then prove it. I don't mean prove it in a court of law, but prove it to *me*. That's what you want, isn't it?' Gulliver's eyes seemed clearer than ever. He leaned across the table. 'You want to finish what Jim started. You want an epitaph which would also be a revenge. Isn't that right?'

'Maybe.'

'No maybe about it. That is what you want, and I applaud you. I'll run with it. But I need more than you've given me, more than Jim gave me.'

'You're saying I should finish the story?'

'I'm saying I'm interested. I'm saying keep in touch.' Gulliver sat back and picked up his glass, washing the ice with the amber liquid.

'Can I ask a question?' Reeve said.

'We only have a minute or so.'

'How much does CWC spend a year on advertising in your paper?'

'How much? That's a question for my advertising manager.'

'You don't know?'

Gulliver shrugged. 'CWC's a big company, a multinational. They own several subsidiaries in the UK and many more in Europe. There's UK production and some importation.'

'A multi-million-pound industry, with a proportionate advertising budget.'

'I don't see—'

'And when they advertise, they do it big. Full-page ads in the broadsheets and – what? – maybe double colour spreads in the financial glossies. TV as well?'

Gulliver stared at him. 'Are you in advertising, Mr Reeve?'

'No.' But, he might have added, I was well briefed this morning by someone on your fashion page. The fashion page, apparently, was a sop to certain advertisers.

Another glance at the watch, a rehearsed sigh. 'I have to go, unfortunately.'

'Yes, that is unfortunate.'

As Gulliver rose, a hotel minion appeared and unplugged his fax. Fax machine and telephone went into a briefcase. The cigar was stubbed into the ashtray. Meeting most definitely over.

'Will you keep in touch?' Gulliver implored, touching Reeve's arm, letting his hand rest there.

'Maybe.'

'And is there any good cause?' Reeve didn't understand. 'A charity, something like that. You know, for mourners to make donations to, as a mark of respect and in memory.'

Reeve thought about it, then wrote a phone number for Gulliver on the back of a paper napkin. 'Here,' he said. Gulliver waited for elucidation. 'It's the number of a bookie's in Finsbury Park. They tell me Jim owed them a ton and a half. All contributions gratefully received.'

Reeve walked out of the hotel thinking he'd probably never in his life met someone so powerful, someone with so much influence, a shaper and changer. He'd shaken hands with royalty at medal ceremonies, but that wasn't the same.

For one thing, some royalty were nice; for another, some of them were known to tell the truth.

Giles Gulliver on the other hand was a born-and-bred liar; that was how you worked your way up from market-stall to pinstripe suit. You had to be cunning too – and Gulliver was so slippery you could stage ice-dancing on him and still have room for the curling-rink.

The phone was ringing as he barged into the flat. He willed it to keep ringing and it obliged. His momentum took him on to the sofa as he snatched the receiver. He lay there, winded, trying to say hello.

'Is that Gordon Reeve?'

'Speaking.'

'My name's Joshua Vincent. I think we'd better meet.'

'Can you tell me what my brother was working on?'

'Better yet, I think I can show you. Three stipulations.'

'I'm listening.'

'One, you come alone. Two, you tell nobody where you're going or who you're going to meet.'

'I can accept those. And number three?'

'Number three, bring a pair of wellies.'

Reeve wasn't about to ask questions. 'So where are you?'

'Not so fast. I want you to leave Jim's flat and go to a pay-phone. Not the nearest one. Try to make it a pub or somewhere.'

Tottenham Lane, thought Reeve. There are pubs along that stretch. 'Yes?'

'Have you got a pen? Take down this number. It's a callbox. I'll wait here no longer than fifteen minutes. Is that enough time?'

Reeve thought so. 'Unless the telephones aren't working. You're taking a lot of precautions, Mr Vincent.'

'So should you. I'll explain when we meet.'

The line went dead, and Gordon Reeve headed for the door.

Outside in the street, just before the corner where the quiet side-road connected with Ferme Park Road, there was a dull-green British Telecom box, a metal structure three feet high which connected the various home-lines into the system. A special key was used by technicians to open the box's double doors. The key was specialised, but not difficult to obtain. A lot of engineers kept their tools when they left the job; an ex-BT engineer could open a box for you. And if he'd moved to a certain line of work, he could fit a call-activated recorder to any of the lines in the box, tucking the recording device down in the base of the structure, so that even a normal BT engineer might miss it.

The tape kept spooling for a few seconds after the call had ended. Then it stopped, awaiting retrieval. Today was a retrieval day.

10

It was a two-hour trip from London. Reeve didn't bother going out to Heathrow to retrieve his car. For one thing, it would have taken time; for another, Vincent wanted him to travel by public transport. Reeve had never heard of Tisbury. As his train pulled in, he saw beyond the station buildings a country town, a narrow main road snaking uphill, a football pitch turning to mud under the feet of the children playing there.

It had been raining stair-rods the whole journey, but now the clouds were breaking up, showing chinks of early-evening light. Reeve wasn't the only one getting off the train, and he studied his fellow travellers. They looked tired – Tisbury to London was a hell of a distance to commute – and had eyes only for the walk ahead, whether to car park or town house.

Joshua Vincent stood outside the station with his hands in his Barbour pockets. He was quick to spot Reeve; no one else looked like they didn't know quite where to go.

Reeve had been expecting a farming type, tall and heavy-bodied with ruddy cheeks or maybe a sprouting beard to match the wild hair. But Vincent, though tall, was rake-thin, clean-shaven, and wore round shining glasses. His fair hair was thinning badly; more scalp showing than follicles. He was pale and reticent and could have passed for a sixth-form science boffin. He was watching the commuters.

'Mr Reeve?'

They shook hands. Vincent wanted them to wait there until all the commuters had left.

'Checking I wasn't followed?' Reeve asked.

Vincent gave a thin smile. 'Easy to spot a stranger at this railway station. They can't help looking out of place. I'm so sorry to hear about Jim.' The tone of voice was genuine, not overwrought the way Giles Gulliver had been, and the more affecting for that. 'How did it happen?'

They walked to the car while Reeve started his story. Through several tellings, he had learned to summarise, sticking to facts and not drawing conclusions. The car was a Subaru 4×4. Reeve had seen them around the farming towns in the West Highlands. He kept on talking as they drove, leaving Tisbury behind them. The countryside was a series of rises and dips with irregular wooded sections. They chased crows and magpies off the rough-finished carriageway, then rolled over the flattened vermin which had attracted the birds in the first place.

Vincent didn't interrupt the narrative once. And when Reeve had finished, they drove in silence until he thought of a couple of things to add to his story.

As he was finishing, they turned off the road and started bumping along a mud track, churned up by farm machinery. Reeve could see the farm in front of them, a simple three-sided layout around a courtyard, with other buildings dotted about. It was very much like his own home.

Vincent stopped in the yard. A snapped command at a barking untethered sheepdog sent it padding back to its lair. A lone lamb bounded up to Reeve, bleating for food. He had the door open but hadn't stepped out yet.

'I'd put your boots on before you do that,' Vincent warned him. So Reeve opened the bag he'd brought with him. Inside were all Jim's notes plus a new pair of black wellingtons, bought in the Army surplus store near Finsbury Park station. He kicked off his shoes and left them in the car, then pulled on the boots. Swivelling out of his seat, his feet landed in a couple of inches of mud.

'Thanks for the tip,' he said, closing the door. 'Is this your place?'

'No, I just stay here sometimes.' A young woman was peering at them through the kitchen window. Vincent waved at her and she waved back. 'Come on,' he said, 'let's catch a breath of air.'

In the long barn furthest from the house, two men were preparing to milk a couple of dozen cows, attaching clear plastic pumps to the teats. The cows' udders were swollen and veinous, and complaints filled the shed. Vincent said hello to the men but did not introduce them. The milking machine shuddered as Reeve passed it. The two men paid him no attention at all.

The other side of the milking-shed, they came to a wall beyond which were darkening fields, trees silhouetted in the far distance.

'So?' Reeve asked. He was growing impatient.

Vincent turned to him. 'I think people are trying to kill me, too.'

Then he told his story. 'What do you know about BSE, Mr Reeve?'

'Only what I've read in Jim's notes.'

Vincent nodded. 'Jim contacted me because he knew I'd expressed concern about OPs.'

'Organo-phosphorous materials?'

'That's right. Have you heard of ME?'

'It's a medical complaint.'

'There's been a lot of controversy over it. Basically, some doctors have been sceptical that it exists, yet people keep coming down with the symptoms.' He shrugged. 'The letters stand for Myalgic Encephalomyelitis.'

'I can see why it's called ME. The E in BSE stands for something similar.'

'Encephalopathy. Encephalon just means the brain, from the Greek *enkephalos*, meaning "within the head". I learned that a few years ago.' He stared out over the fields. 'I've learned a lot these past few years.' He looked back at the farm. 'This place is organic. Do you know how BSE is supposed to have started?'

'I read something in Jim's notes about animal feed.'

Vincent nodded. 'MAFF – that's the Ministry of Agriculture – relaxed their rules in the 1980s, allowing the rendering industry to take a few short-cuts. Don't ask me why it happened or who was responsible, but it happened. They removed two processes, saving time and money. One was a solvent extraction, the other a steam-heat treatment. You see, the rendering industry was rendering down sheep and cows to feed to other cows. Bits of meat and bone were going into the feed-cake.'

'Right.' Reeve buttoned up his jacket, still damp from a dash through the rain to catch the train. The evening was growing chill.

'Because those two processes had been removed, prions got into the feed-cake. Prion protein is sometimes called PrP.'

'I saw it in the notes, I think.'

'It causes scrapie in sheep.' Vincent raised a finger. 'Remember, this is the accepted story I'm giving you. So the feed-cake was infected and the cows were being given the bovine form of sheep scrapie, which is BSE.' He paused, then smiled. 'You're wondering what all this has to do with Spanish cooking oil.'

Reeve nodded.

Vincent started to walk, following the wall along the back of the milking-shed. 'Well, the Spanish blamed contaminated cooking oil and left it at that. Only, some of the victims had never touched the oil.'

'And some of the cows who hadn't eaten the infected feed still caught BSE?'

Vincent shook his head. 'Oh no, the point is this: some farms – organic farms – who *had* used the so-called infected feed didn't catch the disease at all.'

'Hang on a second . . .'

'I know what you're thinking. But organic farms are allowed to buy in twenty percent conventional feed.'

'So you're saying BSE had nothing to do with feed-cake, infected or otherwise?'

Vincent smiled without humour. 'Why use the past tense? BSE is still with us. The "infected" feed-cake was banned on the eighteenth of July 1988.' He pointed into the distance. 'I can show you calves less than six months old who have BSE. Vets from MAFF call them BABs: Born after the Ban. There've been more than ten thousand of them. To date, nearly a hundred and fifty thousand cows have died in the UK from BSE.'

They had come back to the farmyard. Vincent opened the Subaru. 'Get in,' he said. Reeve got in. Vincent kept telling his story as he drove.

'I mentioned ME a little while back. When it first came to be noticed, it was supposed to have its roots in everyday stress. They called it Yuppie Flu. It isn't called that nowadays. Now we call it Farmers' Flu. That's because so many farmers show symptoms. There's a man – used to be a farmer, now he's more of a campaigner though he still tries to farm when they let him – he's trying to discover why there's an increase in the occurrence of neurological diseases like ME, Alzheimer's and Parkinson's.'

'What do you mean, "when they let him"?'

'He's been threatened,' Vincent said simply. 'People helping him have died. Car crashes, unexplained deaths, accidents . . .' He turned to Reeve. 'Only four or five, you understand. Not yet an epidemic.'

They were winding down country lanes barely the width of two cars. The sun had gone down.

Vincent put the heater on. 'It may just be coincidence,' he said, 'that BSE started to appear around the same time that MAFF was telling farmers to protect against warble fly in their cattle by rubbing on an organo-phosphorous treatment. What some of us would like to know is whether OPs can cause prions to mutate.'

'So these OP chemicals are to blame?'

'Nobody knows. It sometimes seems to me hardly anybody *wants* to know. I mean, imagine the embarrassment if it turned out a government directive had started the whole thing off. Imagine the claims for compensation that would be put in by the farmers suffering from OP poisoning. Imagine the cost to the agrichemical industry if they had to withdraw products, carry out expensive tests . . . maybe even pay compensation. We're talking about a worldwide industry. The whole farming world is hooked on pesticides of one kind or another. And on the other side of the coin, if pesticides had to be withdrawn, and new ones created and tested, there'd be a gap of years – and in those years yields would decrease, pests would multiply, farms would go out of business, the cost of every foodstuff in the supermarket would rocket. You can see where that would lead: economic disaster.' He looked at Reeve again. 'Maybe they're right to try and stop us. What are a few lives when measured against an economic disaster of those proportions?'

Reeve shivered, digging deeper into his coat. He felt exhausted, lack of sleep and jet-lag hitting him hard. 'Who's trying to stop you?'

'Could be any or all of them.'

'CWC?'

'Co-World Chemicals has a lot to lose. Its worldwide market-share is worth billions of dollars annually. They've also got a very persuasive lobby which keeps the majority of farmers and governments on their side. Sweetened, as you might say.'

Reeve nodded, taking his meaning. 'So there's a cover-up going on.'

'To my mind undoubtedly, but then I would say that. I was suddenly fired from my job, a job I thought I was good at. When I began to be persuaded that the feed-cake explanation just wasn't on, I spoke twice about it in public, sent out a single press release – and next thing I knew my job was being "phased out".'

'I thought the National Farmers' Union was supposed to be on the side of farmers.'

'It *is* on the side of farmers – or at least, it's on the side of the majority of them, the ones with their heads in the sand.'

'Where are we going?'

'We're nearly there.'

Reeve had half-thought he was going to be returned to the railway station, meeting over. But if anything the landscape had grown less populous. They turned up a track and arrived at a high mesh gate topped with razor wire. A fence of similar height, similarly protected, stretched off either side. There were warning notices on the gate, picked out by the 4x4's headlamps, but nothing to say what the fence and razor wire were protecting.

When Reeve followed Vincent out of the Subaru, a smell hit the back of his throat and he nearly gagged. It lay heavy in the air; the smell of dead flesh.

'We have to walk around the perimeter to get a good look,' Vincent said. 'It's a good job of invisible landscaping. You'd really have to be keen before you got to see what's inside.'

'There's something I might as well ask you,' Reeve said. 'God knows I've asked everyone else. Does the word Agrippa mean anything?'

'Of course,' Vincent said casually. 'It's a small R&D company, American-based.'

'My brother had the word written on a scrap of paper.'

'Maybe he was looking into Agrippa. The company is at the forefront of genetic mutation.'

'Meaning what exactly?' Reeve recalled something Fliss Hornby had said: Jim had been reading up on genetic patents.

'Meaning they take something and alter its genetic code, to try to make a better product. "Better" being their description, not mine.'

'You mean like cotton?'

'Yes, Agrippa doesn't have the patent on genetically engineered cotton. But the company *is* working on crops – trying for better yields and resistance to pests, trying to create strains that can be grown in hostile environments.' Vincent paused. 'Imagine if you could plant wheat in the Sahara.'

'But if you produced resistant strains, that would do away with the need for pesticides, wouldn't it?'

Vincent smiled. 'Nature has a way of finding its way around these defences. Still, there are some out there who would agree with you. That's why CWC are spending millions on research.'

'CWC?'

'Didn't I say? Agrippa is a subsidiary of Co-World Chemicals. Come on, this way.'

They followed the fence up a steep rise and down into a valley, then climbed again.

'We can see from here,' Vincent said. He switched off his torch.

It was a single large building, with trucks parked outside, illuminated by floodlights. Men in protective clothing, some wearing masks, wheeled trolleys between the trucks and the building. A tall thin chimney belched out acrid smoke.

'An incinerator?' Reeve guessed.

'Industrial-strength. It could melt a ship's hull.'

'And they're burning infected cattle?'

Vincent nodded.

'Did you bring Jim here?'

'Yes.'

'To make a point?'

'Sometimes a picture is worth a thousand words.'

'You should never tell a journalist that.'

Vincent smiled. 'Burning the cattle isn't going to make it go away, Mr Reeve. That's what your brother understood. There are other journalists like him in other countries. I'd guess each one is a marked man or woman. If BSE gets to humans, it's called Creutzfeld-Jakob Disease. Believe me, you wouldn't wish it on your worst enemy.'

But Reeve could picture himself syringing a strain of it into the arm of whoever had killed his brother.

There were other neuro-degenerative diseases too – Motor Neuron Disease, Multiple Sclerosis – and they were all on the increase. Their conversation on the way back to the farm was all one-way, and all bad news. The more Josh

Vincent talked, the more zealous he became and the angrier and more frustrated he sounded.

'But what can you do?' Reeve asked at one point.

'Re-examine all pesticides, carry out tests on them. Use less of them. Turn farms into organic co-operatives. There *are* answers, but they're not simple overnight panaceas.'

They parked in the farmyard again. The dog came out barking. The lamb trotted over towards them. Reeve followed Vincent into the kitchen. Once inside the door, they took off their boots. The young woman was still at the sink beneath the window. She smiled and wiped her hands, coming forward to be introduced.

'Jilly Palmer,' said Vincent, 'this is Gordon Reeve.'

They shook hands. 'Pleased to meet you,' she said. She had a flushed complexion and a long braid of chestnut-coloured hair. Her face was sharp, with angular cheekbones and a wry twist to her lips. Her clothes were loose, practical.

'Supper's ready when you are,' she said.

'I'll just show Gordon his room first,' Vincent said. He saw the surprise in Reeve's face. 'You can't get back to London tonight. No trains.'

Reeve looked at Jilly Palmer. 'I'm sorry if I—'

'No trouble,' she said. 'We've a bedroom going spare, and Josh here made the supper. All I had to do was warm it through.'

'Where's Bill?' Vincent asked.

'Young Farmers'. He'll be back around ten.'

'Don't be daft,' said Vincent, 'pubs don't shut till eleven.'

He sounded very different in this company: more relaxed, enjoying the warmth of the kitchen and normal conversation. But all that did, in Reeve's eyes, was show how much strain the man was under the rest of the time, and how much this whole conspiracy had affected him.

He thought he could see why Jim had taken on the story, why he would have run with it where others might have given up: because of people like Josh Vincent, scared and running and innocent.

His room was small and cold, but the blankets were plentiful. He took off his coat and hung it on a hook on the back of the door, hoping it would dry. His dark pullover was damp too, so he peeled it off. The rest of him could dry in the kitchen. He found the bathroom and washed his hands and face in scalding water, then looked at himself in the mirror. The image of him injecting BSE into a tapped human vein was still there in the back of his mind. It had given him an idea – not something he could put into use just yet, but something he might need all the same . . .

In the kitchen the table had been laid for two. Jilly said she'd already eaten. She left them to it and closed the door after her.

'She never misses *Coronation Street*,' Vincent explained. 'Lives out here, but has to get her fix of Lancashire grime.' He used oven-mitts to lift the casserole from the oven. It was half full, but a substantial half. There was a lemonade bottle on the table and two glasses. Vincent unscrewed the cap and poured carefully. 'Bill's home-brew,' he explained. 'I think he only drinks down the pub to remind himself how good his own stuff tastes.'

The beer was light-brown, with a head that disappeared quickly. 'Cheers,' said Josh Vincent.

'Cheers,' said Reeve.

They ate in silence, hungrily, and chewed on home-baked bread. Towards the end of the meal, Vincent asked a few questions about Reeve; what he did, where he lived. He said he loved the Highlands and Islands, and wanted to hear all about Reeve's outward-bound courses. Reeve kept the description simple, leaving out more than he put in. He could see Vincent wasn't really listening; his mind was elsewhere.

'Can I ask you something?' Vincent said finally.

'Sure.'

'How far did Jim get? I mean, did he find out anything we could use?'

'I told you, his disks disappeared. All I have are his written notes from London.'

'Can I see them?'

Reeve nodded and fetched them. Vincent read in silence for a while, except to point out where he himself had contributed a detail or a quote. Then he sat up.

'He's been in touch with Marie Villambard.' He showed Reeve the sheet of paper. The letters MV were capitalised and underlined at the top. They hadn't meant anything to Reeve or to Fliss Hornby.

'Who's she?'

'A French journalist, she works for an ecology magazine – *Le Monde Vert*, I think it's called. Green World. Sounds like they were working together.'

'She hasn't tried contacting him in London.' There'd been no letters from France, and Fliss hadn't intercepted any calls.

'Maybe he told her he'd be in touch when he got back from San Diego.'

'Josh, why did my brother go to San Diego?'

'To talk to Co-World Chemicals.' Vincent blinked. 'I thought you knew that.'

'You're the first person to say it outright.'

'He was going to try and speak to some of their research scientists.'

'Why?'

'Why? Because of the experiment they had carried out.' Vincent put down the notes. 'They tried to reproduce BSE the way it had flared up in the UK, using identical procedures after consultations with MAFF. They brought in sheep infected with scrapie and rendered them down, taking the exact same shortcuts as were used in the mid-eighties. Then they mixed the feed together and fed it to calves and mature cattle.'

'And?'

'And nothing. They didn't exactly trumpet the results. Four years on, the cattle were one hundred percent fit.' He shrugged his shoulders. 'They've got other experiments ongoing. They've got consultant neurologists and world-class psychiatrists working on American farmers who show signs of neuro-degenerative disease. Bringing in the psychiatrists is a nice touch: it makes everyone think maybe we're dealing with psychosomatic hysteria; that the so-called disease is actually a product of the human mind and nothing at all to do with what we spray on our crops and stuff into and on to our animals.' He paused. 'You want any more casserole?'

Reeve shook his head.

'The beef's fine, honestly,' Vincent said, smiling encouragement. 'Reared organically.'

'I'm sure,' said Reeve. 'But I'm full up, thanks.'
Well, it was eighty-five percent truth.

After breakfast on Saturday morning, Josh Vincent drove Reeve to the station.

'Can I contact you on the farm?' Reeve asked.

Vincent shook his head. 'I'll only be there another day or so. Is there somewhere I can contact you?'

Reeve wrote down his home phone number. 'If I'm not there, my wife can take a message. Josh, you haven't said why you're hiding.'

'What?'

'All these precautions. You haven't said why.'

Vincent looked up and down the empty platform. 'They tampered with my car too. Remember I told you about the farmer?'

'The one who's been campaigning against OPs?'

'Yes. A vet was helping him, but then the vet died in a car crash. His vehicle went out of control and hit a wall; no explanation, nothing wrong with the car. I had a similar crash. My car stopped responding. I hit a tree rather than a wall, and crawled out alive. No garage could find any fault in the car.' Vincent was staring into the distance. 'Then they bugged the telephone in my office, and later I found they'd bugged my home telephone too. I think they opened my mail and resealed the envelopes. I *know* they were watching me. Don't ask me who they were, that I don't know. I could speculate though. MI5 maybe, Special Branch, or the chemical companies. Could have been any of those, could have been someone else entirely. So' – he sighed and dug his hands into his Barbour pockets – 'I keep moving.'

'A running target's the hardest kind to hit,' Reeve agreed.

'Do you speak from experience?'

'Literally,' said Reeve as the train pulled in.

Back in London, Reeve returned to the flat. Fliss had left a note wondering if he'd gone for good. He scribbled on the bottom of it 'Maybe this time' and put the note back on the table. He had to retrieve his bag and his car and then head home. But first he wanted to check something. He found the page of Jim's notes, the one headed MV. On the back were four two-digit numbers. He'd suspected they were the combination to some kind of safe, but now he knew differently. He found a screwdriver in the kitchen drawer and opened up the telephone: apparatus and handset both. He couldn't find any bugs, so replaced the screws and returned the screwdriver to its drawer. He got the code for France from the telephone book and made the call. A long single tone told him he'd reached a French telephone.

An answering machine; a rapid message in a woman's voice. Reeve left a short message in his rusty French, giving his telephone number in Scotland. He didn't mention Jim's fate. He just said he was his brother. This was called preparing someone for bad news. He sat and thought about what Josh Vincent had told him. Something had been telling Reeve it couldn't just be about cows. It was laughable, unbelievable. But Josh Vincent had made it both believable *and* scary, because it affected everyone on the planet – everyone who had to eat. But Reeve still didn't think it was *just* about cows, or pesticides, or cover-ups. There was more to it than that. He felt it in his bones.

He made another call, to Joan, preparing her for his return. Then he gave the rest of the flat a once-over and locked the door behind him.

An engineer was checking the telephone junction box outside. The man watched Reeve go, then lifted the tape out from the recorder and replaced it with a fresh one. Returning to his van, he wound back the tape and replayed it. A thirteen-digit number, followed by a woman's voice in French. He plugged a digital decoder into the tape machine, then wound back the tape and played it again. This time, each beep of the dialled number came up as a digit on the decoder's readout. The engineer wrote down the number and picked up his cellphone.

Part Four

Living Dangerously

11

Gordon Reeve had become interested in anarchism because he needed to understand the minds of terrorists. He had worked in the Counter-Revolutionary Warfare unit of the SAS. They were happy to have him – he wasn't the only one among them who'd specialised in languages during his early training, but he was the only one with so many.

'Including Scots,' one wag said. 'Could come in handy if the Tartan Army flares up again.'

'I've got Gaelic too,' Reeve had countered with a smile.

After he left the SAS, he retained his interest in anarchism because of its truths and its paradoxes. The word anarchy had Greek roots and meant 'without a ruler'. The Paris students in '68 had sprayed 'It is forbidden to forbid' on the street walls. Anarchists, *true* anarchists, wanted society without government and promoted voluntary organisation over rule by an elected body. The real anarchist joke was: 'It doesn't matter who you vote for, the government always gets in.'

Reeve liked to play the anarchist thinkers off against Nietzsche. Kropotkin, for example, with his theory of 'mutual aid', was advocating the opposite of Nietzsche's 'will to power'. Evolution, in Kropotkin's view, was not about competitiveness, about survival of the strongest *individual*, but about co-operation. A species which co-operated would thrive, and grow stronger collectively. Nietzsche on the other hand saw competitiveness everywhere, and advocated self-reliance and self-absorption. Reeve saw merit to both assertions. In fact, they were not separate, distinct arguments but parts of the same equation. Reeve had little time for government, for bureaucracy, but he knew the individual could go only so far, could endure only so much. Isolation was fine sometimes, but if you had a problem it was wise to form bonds. War created bizarre allies, while peace itself could be divisive.

Nietzsche, of course, could persuade almost no one of his philosophy – give or take a tyrant or two who chose to misunderstand the whole. And the anarchists . . . well, one of the things Reeve found so interesting about the anarchists was that their cause was doomed from its philosophical outset. To grow, to influence opinion, the anarchist movement had to organise, had to take on a strong political structure – which meant taking on a hierarchy, making decisions. Everyone, from players of children's games to the company boardroom, knew that if you took decisions by committee you came up with compromise. Anarchism was not about compromising. The anarchists' mistrust of rigid organisations caused their groupings to splinter and splinter again, until only the individual was left, and some of those individuals felt that the only possible road to power left to them was the bullet and the bomb. Joseph Conrad's image of the anarchist with the bomb in his pocket was not so wide of the mark.

And what of Nietzsche? Reeve had been one of 'Nietzsche's gentlemen'. Nietzsche had carried on the work of Descartes and others – men who needed to dominate, to control, to eliminate chance. But while Nietzsche wanted supermen, controllers, he also wanted people to live dangerously. Reeve felt he was fulfilling this criterion if no other. He *was* living dangerously. He just wondered if he needed some mutual aid along the way . . .

He was on a hillside, no noise except the wind, the distant bleating of sheep, and his own breathing. He was sitting, resting, after the long walk from his home. He'd told Joan he needed to clear his head. Allan was at a friend's house, but would be back in time for supper. Reeve would be back by then too. All he needed was a walk. Joan had offered to keep him company, an offer he'd refused with a shake of his head. He'd touched her cheek, but she'd slapped his hand away.

'I'll only be a couple of hours.'

'You're never here,' she'd complained. 'And even when you're here, you're not *really* here.'

It was a valid complaint, and he hadn't argued. He'd just tied his boots and set out for the hills.

It was Sunday, a full week since he'd had the telephone call telling him Jim had killed himself. Joan knew there was something he wasn't telling her, something he was bottling up. She knew it wasn't just grief.

Reeve got to his feet. Looking down the steep hillside, he was momentarily afraid. Nothing to do with the 'abyss' this time; it was just that he had no real plan, and without a plan there would be a temptation to rashness, there would be miscalculation. He needed proper planning and preparation. He'd been in the dark for a while, feeling his way. Now he thought he knew most of what Jim had known, but he was still stuck. He felt like a spider who has crawled its way along the pipes and into the bath, only to find it can't scale the smooth sheer sides. There was a bird of prey overhead, a kestrel probably. It glided on the air currents, its line straight, dipping its wings to maintain stability. From that height, it could probably still pick out the movements of a mouse in the tangle of grass and gorse. Reeve thought of the wings on the SAS cap-badge. Wings and a dagger. The wings told you that Special Forces would travel anywhere at any notice. And the dagger . . . the dagger told an essential truth about the regiment: they were trained in close-combat situations. They favoured stealth and the knife over distance and a sniper's accuracy. Hand-to-hand fighting, that was their strength. Get close to your prey, close enough to slide a hand over its mouth and stab the dagger into its throat, and twist and twist, ripping the voicebox. Maximum damage, minimum dying time.

Reeve felt the blood rush to his head and closed his eyes for a moment, clearing them of the fog. He checked his watch and found he'd been resting longer than he'd meant to. His legs had stiffened. It was time to start back down the hill and across the wide gully. It was time to go home.

'Jackie's got this really good new game,' Allan said.

Reeve looked to Joan. 'Jackie?'

'A girl in his class.'

He turned to his son. 'Playing with the girls, eh? Not in her bedroom, I hope.'

Allan screwed up his face. 'She's not like a girl, Dad. She has all these games . . .'

'On her computer.'

'Yes.'

'And her computer is where in the house?'

'In her room.'

'Her bedroom?'

Allan's ears had reddened. Reeve tried winking at Joan, but she wasn't watching.

'It's like *Doom*,' Allan said, ignoring his father, 'but with more secret passages, and you don't just pick up ammo and stuff, you can warp yourself into these amazing creatures with loads of new weapons and stuff. You can fry the bad guys' eyeballs so they're blind and then you—'

'Allan, enough,' his mother said.

'But I'm just telling Dad—'

'Enough.'

'But Dad—'

'Enough!'

Allan looked down at his plate. He'd eaten all the chips, and only had the cold ham and baked beans left. 'But Dad wanted to know,' he said under his breath. Joan looked at her husband.

'Tell me later, pal, okay? Some things aren't for the dinner table.' He watched Joan lift a sliver of ham to her mouth. 'Especially fried alien eyeballs.'

Joan glared at him, but Allan and Gordon were laughing. The rest of the meal was carried off in peace.

Afterwards, Allan made instant coffee for his parents – one of his latest jobs around the house. Reeve wasn't so sure of letting an eleven-year-old near a boiling kettle.

'But you don't mind fried aliens, right?' Joan said.

'Aliens never hurt anyone,' Reeve said. 'I've seen what scalding can do.'

'He's got to learn.'

'Okay, okay.' They were in the living room. Reeve kept an ear attuned to sounds from the kitchen. The first clatter or shriek and he'd be in there. But Allan appeared with the two mugs. The coffee was strong.

'Is milk back on the ration books?' Reeve queried.

'What's ration books?' Allan asked.

'Pray you never have to know.'

Allan wanted to watch TV, so the three of them sat on the long sofa, Reeve with his arm along the back, behind his wife's neck but not touching her. She'd taken off her slippers and had tucked her feet up. Allan sat on the floor in front of her. Bakunin the cat was on Joan's lap, glaring at Reeve like he was a complete stranger, which, considering he hadn't fed her this past week, he was. Reeve thought of the real Bakunin, fighting on the Dresden barricades shoulder-to-shoulder with Nietzsche's friend Wagner . . .

'A penny for them,' Joan asked.

'I was just thinking how nice it was to be back.'

Joan smiled thinly at the lie. She hadn't asked much about the cremation, but she'd been interested to hear about the flat in London and the woman living there. Allan turned from the sitcom.

'So what's it like in the USA, Dad?'

'I thought you'd never ask.' Reeve had spent some time deciding on the story he'd tell Allan. He painted a picture of San Diego as a frontier town, exciting enough and strange enough to keep Allan listening.

'Did you see any shootings?' Allan asked.

'No, but I heard some police sirens.'

'Did you see a policeman?'

Reeve nodded.

'With a gun?'

Reeve nodded again.

Joan rubbed at her son's hair, though she knew he hated it when she did that. 'He's growing up gun-crazy.'

'No, I'm not,' Allan stated.

'It's all those computer games.'

'No, it isn't.'

'What are you playing just now?'

'That game I told you about. Jackie copied it for me.'

'I hope it hasn't got a virus.'

'I've got a new virus checker.'

'Good.' At that time, Allan knew only a little more about computing than Reeve and Joan put together, but he was steadily pulling away from them.

'The game's called *Militia*, and what you do is—'

'No fried eyeballs,' Joan demanded.

'What happened to that game Uncle Jim sent you?' Reeve asked.

Allan looked embarrassed. 'I was stuck on screen five . . .'

'You've given it away?'

Allan shook his head vigorously. 'No, it's upstairs.'

'But you don't play it any more?'

'No,' he said quietly. Then: 'Mum said Uncle Jim died.'

Reeve nodded. Joan said she'd had a couple of talks with Allan already. 'People grow old and tired, Allan, and then they die. They make room for other younger people to come along . . .' Reeve felt awkward as he spoke.

'But Uncle Jim wasn't old.'

'No, well some people just—'

'He wasn't much older than *you*.'

'I'm not going to die,' Reeve told his son.

'How do you know?'

'Sometimes people get feelings. I've got the feeling I'm going to live to be a hundred.'

'And Mum?' Allan asked.

Reeve looked at her. She was staring at him, interested in the answer. 'Same feeling,' he said.

Allan went back to watching television. A little later, Joan murmured 'Thanks', put her slippers back on, and went through to the kitchen, followed closely by Bakunin, scouting for provisions. Reeve wasn't sure what to read into her final utterance.

The telephone rang while he was watching the news. Allan had retreated to his room, having given his parents over an hour and a half of his precious time. Reeve let Joan get the phone. She was still in the kitchen, making a batch of bread. Later, when he went through to make the last cup of coffee of the night, he asked who had called.

'They didn't say,' she offered, too nonchalantly.

Reeve looked at her. 'You've had more than one?'

She shrugged. 'A couple.'

'How many?'

'I think this was the third.'

'In how long?'

She shrugged again. There was a smudge of flour on her nose, and some wisps in her hair, making her look older. 'Five or six days. There's no one on the other end, no noise at all. Maybe it's British Telecom testing the line or something. That happens sometimes.'

'Yes, it does.'

But not more than once in a very blue moon, he thought.

They'd been in bed for a silent hour and were lying side by side staring at the ceiling when he asked, 'What about those callers?'

'The phone calls?' She turned her head towards him.

'No, you said some customers had turned up.'

'Oh yes, just asking about courses.'

'Two of them?'

'Yes, one one day, one the next. What's the matter?'

'Nothing. It's just we don't often get people turning up like that.'

'Well, I gave them the brochure and they went away quite happy.'

'Did they come in the house?'

She sat up. 'Only as far as the hall. It's all right, Gordon, I can look after myself.'

'What were they like? Describe them.'

'I'm not sure I can. I hardly paid them any attention.' She leaned over him, her hand on his chest. She was feeling his heart-rate. 'What's wrong?'

'Nothing's wrong,' he said. But he swung his legs out of bed and started to get dressed. 'I don't feel tired; I'll go down to the kitchen.' He stopped at the door. 'Anybody else come while I was away?'

'No.'

'Think about it.'

She thought about it. 'A man came to read the meter. And the freezer lorry turned up.'

'What freezer lorry?'

'Frozen foods.' She sounded irritated. If he kept pushing, the end result would be an argument. 'I usually buy chips and ice cream from him.'

'Was it the regular driver?'

She slumped back on the bed. 'No, he was new. Gordon, what the hell is this about?'

'Maybe I'm just being paranoid.'

'What happened in the States?'

He came back and sat on the edge of the bed. 'I think Jim was murdered.'

She sat up again. 'What?'

'I think he was getting too deep into something, some story he was working on. Maybe they'd tried scaring him off and it hadn't worked. I know Jim, he's like me – try that tactic and he'd just be more curious than ever, and more stubborn. So then they had to kill him.'

'Who?'

'That's what I've been trying to find out.'

'And?'

'And, because I've been doing just what Jim was doing, maybe they're targeting me. The thing is, I didn't think they'd come here. Not so soon.'

'Two potential clients, a meter-reader and a man with a van full of spuds and sprouts.'

'That's four callers more than we usually get. Four callers while I was out of the country.' He got to his feet again.

'Is that it?' Joan asked. 'Aren't you going to tell me the rest?'

He stared towards her, just able to make out her shape in the shadows of the curtained room – curtained despite the blackness outside and the isolation of the house. 'I don't want to make you a target.'

Then he padded downstairs as quietly as he could. He looked around, turning on lights, not touching anything, then stood in the living room thinking things over. He walked over to the TV and switched it on, using the remote to flick channels.

'Usual rubbish,' he said, yawning noisily for the benefit of anyone listening. He knew how sophisticated surveillance equipment had become. He'd heard of devices that could read computer screens from a distance of yards, without there being any physical connector linking them to the computer. He probably hadn't heard half of it. The technology changed so quickly it was damn near impossible to keep up. He did his best, so he could pass what he knew on to his weekend soldiers. The trainee bodyguards in particular liked to know about that stuff.

He first checked that there were no watcher devices in the house. These were not so easy to hide: after all, if they were going to view a subject, they couldn't be tucked away under a chair or a sofa. They also took a lot longer to fit. Someone would have had to access the house while Joan was out or asleep. He didn't find anything. Next he put his jacket on and went outside, circling the house at a good radius. He spotted no one, certainly no vehicles. In the garage, he slid beneath both Land Rovers and found them clean – well, not *clean*, but lacking bugs. Before going back indoors he unscrewed the front panel from the burglar alarm. The screws were hard to shift, and showed no signs of recent tampering – no missing paint or fresh-looking scratches. The alarm itself was functioning.

Joan had said she'd let the new clients in as far as the hall. And he would guess she'd probably let the van driver in as far as the kitchen. He took a lot of time over both areas, feeling beneath carpets and behind curtains, taking the cookery books off the bookshelf in the kitchen.

He found the first bug in the hall.

It was attached to the inside of the telephone.

He went into the kitchen and switched on the radio, placing it close to the phone extension. Then he unscrewed the apparatus and found another bug identical to the first one. Both had the letters USA stamped into their thin metal casing. He wiped sweat from his face, and went through to the living room. Despite an hour-long search, he found nothing, which didn't mean the room was clean. He knew he could save a lot of effort by getting hold of a locating device, but he didn't have the time. And at least now he knew – knew his family wasn't safe, knew his home wasn't secure.

Knew they had to get out.

He sat on the chair beside the dressing-table in their bedroom. A morning ray of sun had found a chink in the curtains and was hitting Joan's face, moving from her eyes to her forehead as she twisted in her sleep. Like a laser-sight, Reeve thought, like an assassin taking aim. He felt tired but electric; he'd spent half the night writing. He had the sheets of printer paper with him on the chair. Joan rolled over, her arm flopping down on the space where he should have been. She used the arm to push herself up, blinking a few times. Then she rolled on to her back and craned her neck.

'Morning,' she said.

'Morning,' he answered, coming towards her.

'How long have you been up?' She was blinking her eyes again in an attempt to read the sheet of paper Reeve was holding in front of her.

'Hours,' he said with a lightness he did not feel.

DON'T SAY A WORD. JUST READ. NOD WHEN YOU'RE READY. REMEMBER: SAY NOTHING.

His look told her he was serious. She nodded, sitting up further in bed, pushing the hair out of her eyes. He turned to the next sheet.

THE HOUSE IS BUGGED: WE CAN'T SAY ANYTHING IN SAFETY. WE'VE GOT TO PRETEND THIS IS JUST ANOTHER DAY. NOD WHEN YOU'RE READY.

She took a moment to nod. When she did so, she was staring into his eyes.

'So are you going to lie there all day?' he chided, turning the page.

'Why not?' she said. She looked frightened.

YOU'VE GOT TO GO STAY WITH YOUR SISTER. TAKE ALLAN. BUT DON'T TELL HIM. JUST PACK SOME THINGS INTO THE CAR AND GO. PRETEND YOU'RE TAKING HIM TO SCHOOL AS USUAL.

'Come on, get up and I'll make the breakfast.'

'I'll take a shower.'

'Okay.'

WE CAN'T SAY WHERE YOU'RE GOING. WE CAN'T LET ANYONE KNOW. THIS IS JUST AN ORDINARY MORNING.

Joan nodded her head.

'Will toast do you?' he asked.

I DON'T THINK WE'RE BEING WATCHED, JUST LISTENED TO.

He smiled to reassure her.

'Toast's fine,' she said, only the slightest tremble evident in her voice. She cleared her throat and pointed at him. He had foreseen this, and found the sheet.

I'LL BE FINE. I JUST NEED TO TALK TO A FEW PEOPLE.

She looked doubtful, so he smiled again and bent forward to kiss her.

'That better?' he asked.

'Better,' she said.

I'LL PHONE YOU AT YOUR SISTER'S. YOU CAN CALL HER ON YOUR WAY THERE, LET HER KNOW YOU'RE COMING. DON'T COME BACK HERE UNTIL I TELL YOU IT'S ALL RIGHT. I LOVE YOU.

She jumped to her feet and hugged him. They stayed that way for a full minute. Her eyes were wet when he broke away.

'Toast and tea it is,' Reeve said.

He was in the kitchen, trying to hum a tune while he made breakfast, when she walked in. She was carrying a notepad and pen. She looked more together now that she was dressed, now she'd had time to think. She thrust the notepad into his face.

WHAT THE FUCK'S THIS ALL ABOUT?

He took the pad from her and rested it on the worktop.

IT'D TAKE TOO LONG. I'LL EXPLAIN WHEN I PHONE.

He looked up at her, then added a last word.

PLEASE.

THIS IS UNFAIR, she wrote, anger reddening her face.

He mouthed the words 'I know' and followed them with 'sorry'.

'Had your shower already?' he asked.

'Water wasn't hot enough.' She looked for a second like she might laugh at the absurdity of it all. But she was too angry to laugh.

'Do you want tea or coffee?' he asked.

'Tea. Want me to cut some bread?'

'Sure, thanks. How's Allan?'

'Not keen on getting up.'

'He doesn't know how lucky he is,' Reeve said. He watched Joan attack the loaf with the breadknife like it was the enemy.

Things were easier when Allan came down. Both parents talked to him more than usual, asking questions, eliciting responses. This was safe ground; they could be less guarded. When Joan said maybe she'd have that shower after all, Reeve knew she was going to pack. He told Allan he was going to get the car out, and walked into the courtyard, breathing deeply and exhaling noisily.

'Jesus,' he said. He circled the property again. He could hear a tractor somewhere over near Buchanan's croft, and the drone of a light aeroplane overhead, though the morning was too overcast to see it. He didn't think anyone was watching the house. He wondered how far the transmitters carried. Not very far by the look of them. There'd be a recorder somewhere, buried in the earth or hidden under rocks. He wondered how often they changed tapes, how often they listened. The recorder was probably voice-activated, and whoever was listening was only interested in telephone calls.

Or maybe they just hadn't had time to bug the house properly.

'Bastards,' he said out loud. Then he went back into the house. Joan was coming downstairs with a couple of travelling-bags. She took them straight out to her car and put them in the boot. She motioned for him to join her. When he did, she just stared at him like she wanted him to say something.

'I think it's okay outside,' he said.

'Good. What are you going to do, Gordon?'

'Talk to a few people.'

'What people? What are you going to talk to them about?'

He looked around the courtyard, his eyes alighting on the door to the killing room. 'I'm not sure. I just want to know why someone has bugged our telephones. I need to get hold of some equipment, sweep the place to make sure it's clean apart from the two I found.'

'How long will we have to stay away?'

'Maybe just a couple of days. I don't know yet. I'll phone as soon as I can.'

'Don't do anything . . .' She didn't complete the sentence.

'I won't,' he said, stroking her hair.

She brought something out of her pocket. 'Here, take these.' She handed him a phial of small blue pills – the pills he was supposed to take when the pink mist descended.

The psychiatrist had wondered at 'pink'. 'Not red?' he'd asked.

'No, pink.'

'Mmm. What do you associate with the colour pink, Mr Reeve?'

'Pink?'

'Yes.'

'Gays, cocks, tongues, vaginal lips, little girls' lipstick . . . Will those do for a start, Doctor?'

'I get the feeling you're playing with me, Mr Reeve.'

'If I were playing with you, I'd've said red mist and you'd've been happy. But I said pink because it's pink. My vision goes pink, not red.'

'And then you react?'

Oh yes, then he reacted . . .

He looked at his wife now. 'I won't need these.'

'Want to take a bet?'

Reeve took the pills instead.

Joan had told Allan they were taking Bakunin to the vet. The cat had resisted being put in its travel-box, and Allan had asked what was wrong with it.

'Nothing to worry about.' She'd been looking at her husband as she'd said it.

Reeve stood at the door and waved them off, then ran to the roadside to watch them leave. He didn't think they'd be followed. Joan drove Allan to school every morning, and this was just another morning. He went back inside and stood in the hallway.

'All alone,' he said loudly.

He was wondering if they would come, now that he was alone. He was hoping they would. He had plans for them if they did. He spent the day waiting them out, and talking to them.

'She's not coming back,' he said into the telephone receiver at one point. 'Neither of them is. I'm on my own.' Still they didn't come. He went through the house, organising an overnight bag, making sure he had the list of emergency telephone numbers. He ate a slice of bread and butter for lunch, and dozed at the kitchen table for an hour (having made sure all the doors and windows were locked first). He felt better afterwards. He needed a shower or bath, but didn't like the idea of them coming in on him when he was in the middle of lathering his back. So he just had a quick wash instead, a lick and a spit.

By late afternoon, he was going stir crazy. He checked the windows again, set the alarm, and locked the house. He had his overnight bag with him. He went to the killing room and unpadlocked and unbolted both sets of doors. Those doors looked ordinary enough from the outside, but were panelled inside with beaten metal, an extra deterrent to intruders. In the small hallway outside the room proper, he knelt down and pulled at a long section of skirting-board. It came away cleanly. Inside, set into the wall, was a long narrow metal box. Reeve unlocked it and pulled the flap down. Inside was an assortment of small arms. He had large-bore weapons too, but kept those in a locked cabinet in what had been the farmhouse's original pantry. He picked up one of the guns. It was wrapped in oiled cloth. What use was a killing room without weapons? In his Special Forces days, they'd almost always trained with live ammo. It was the only way you came to respect the stuff.

Reeve had live ammo for the handguns. He was holding a 9mm Beretta. Guns were always heavier than people expected. He didn't know whether that was because most people equated guns with childhood, and childhood meant plastic replicas, or because TV and cinema were to blame, with their blithe gun-toting goodies and baddies, guys who could fire a bazooka and still go ten rounds with the world champion warlord – whereas in real life they'd be checking into casualty with a dislocated shoulder.

The Beretta was just heavy enough to warn you it was lethal. In the killing room they used blank ammunition. Even blanks could give you powder burns. He'd seen weekend soldiers scared shitless, frozen with the gun in their hand like someone else's turd, the explosion echoing in the chambers of their heart.

Maybe he needed a gun. Just to scare these people. But you could only scare someone if you were serious and if they could see exactly how serious you were by the look in your eyes. And he wouldn't be serious if the gun wasn't loaded . . .

And what use was a loaded gun if you didn't intend to use it?

'Fuck it,' he said, putting the Beretta back in its cloth. He rummaged around behind the other packages – he had explosives in there, too; almost every other soldier brought *something* with them back into civvy life – until he found another length of oiled rag. Inside was a black gleaming dagger, his Lucky 13: five inches of rubberised handgrip and eight inches of polished steel, a blade so sharp you could perform surgery with it. He'd bought it in Germany one time they'd been training there. Its weight and balance were perfect for him. It had felt almost supernatural, the way the thing moulded to his hand. He'd been persuaded to buy it by the two men on weekend leave with him. The knife cost just under a week's wages.

'For old time's sake,' he said, slipping it into his overnight bag.

He crossed by ferry to Oban, which was where the tail started.

Just the one car, he reckoned. To be sure, he led it a merry dance all the way to Inveraray. Just north of the town he pulled the Land Rover over suddenly, got out and went to the back, looking in as though to check he hadn't forgotten something. The car behind was too close to stop; it had to keep going right past him. He looked up as it drew level, and watched the impassive faces of the two men in front.

'Bye bye,' he said, closing the back, watching the car go. Hard to tell from their faces who the men were or who they might work for, but he was damned sure they'd been following him since he'd hit the mainland: most cars would have stuck to the main road through Dalmally and south towards Glasgow, but when Reeve had headed on the much less popular route to Inveraray, this one had followed.

He started driving again. He didn't know if they'd have organised a second car by now, or if they'd have to call someone to organise back-up. He just knew he didn't want to be driving anywhere much now that they were on to him. So he headed into the centre of town. Close combat, he was thinking as he headed for his revised destination.

The Thirty Arms had a car park, but Reeve parked on the street outside. They didn't hand out parking tickets after six o'clock. Locals called it the Thirsty Arms, but the pub's true name was a reference to the fifteen men in a rugby side. It was the closest this quiet lochside town had to a 'dive', which was to say that it was a rough and ready place which didn't see many female clients. Reeve knew this because he dropped in sometimes, preferring the drive via Inveraray to the busier route. The owner had a tongue you could strike matches on.

'Go get that red fuckin' carpet, will you?' he said to someone as Reeve entered the bar. 'It's been that long since this bastard bought a drink in here I was thinking of selling up.'

'Evening, Manny,' said Reeve. 'Half of whatever's darkest, please.'

'An ungrateful sod of a patron like you,' said Manny, 'you'll take what I give you.' He began pouring the drink. Reeve looked around at faces he knew. They weren't smiling at him and he didn't smile back. Their collective stare was supposed to drive away strangers and outsiders, and Reeve was most definitely an outsider. The surliest of the local youths was playing pool. Reeve had noticed some of his mates outside. They weren't yet old enough looking to fool Manny, so would wait at the door like pet dogs outside a butcher's shop for their master to rejoin them. The smell of drink off him was their vicarious pleasure. In Inveraray, there wasn't much else to kill the time.

Reeve walked over to the board and chalked his name up. The youth grinned at him unpleasantly, as if to say, 'I'll take anybody's money'. Reeve walked back to the bar.

Two more drinkers pushed open the creaking door from the outside world. Their tourist smiles vanished when they saw the sort of place they'd entered. Other tourists had made their mistake before, but seldom stayed long enough to walk up to the bar. Maybe these ones were surprisingly stupid. Maybe they were blind.

Maybe, Reeve thought. He still had his back to them. He didn't need to see them to know they were the two from the car. They stood next to him as they waited for Manny to finish telling a story to another customer. Manny was taking his time, just letting them know. He'd been known to refuse service to faces he didn't like.

Reeve watched as much as he could from the corner of his eye. From the distorted reflection in the beaten copper plate that ran the length of the bar behind the optics, he saw that the men were waiting impassively.

Manny at last gave up. 'Yes, gents?' he said.

'We want a drink,' the one closest to Reeve said. The man was angry already, not used to being kept waiting. He sounded English; Reeve didn't know which nationality he'd been expecting.

'This isn't a chip-shop,' said Manny, rising to the challenge. 'Drink's the only thing we serve.' He was smiling throughout, to let the two strangers know he wasn't at all happy.

'I'll have a double Scotch,' the second man said. He was also English. Reeve didn't know whether it was done on purpose or not, but the way he spat out 'Scotch' caused more than a few hackles in the bar to rise. The speaker purported not to notice, maybe he just didn't care. He looked at the door, at the framed photos of Scottish internationals and the local club side – the latter signed – and the souvenir pennants and flags.

'Somebody likes rugby,' he said to no one in particular. No one in particular graced the remark with a reply.

The man closest to Reeve, the one who'd spoken first, ordered a lager and lime. There was a quiet wolf whistle from the pool table, just preceding the youth's shot.

The man turned towards the source of the whistle. 'You say something?'

The youth kept quiet and made his next pot, chalking up as he marched around the table. Reeve suddenly liked the lad.

'Leave it,' the stranger's companion hissed. Then, as the drinks were set before them: 'That's a treble.' He meant the whisky.

'A double,' Manny snapped. 'You're used to sixths; up here we have quarters.' He took the money and walked back to the till.

Reeve turned conversationally to the two men. 'Cheers,' he said.

'Yeah, cheers.' They were both keen to get a good look at him close up, just as he was keen to get a look at them. The one closest to him was shorter but broader. He could've played a useful prop-forward. He wore cheap clothes and had a cheap greasy look to his face. If you looked like what you ate, this man was chips and lard. His companion had a dangerous face, the kind that's been in so many scraps it simply doesn't care any more. He might've done time in the Army – Reeve couldn't see Lardface having ever been fit enough – but he'd gone to seed since. His hair stuck out over his ears and was thin above his forehead. It looked like he'd paid a lot of money for some trendy gel-spiked haircut his son might have, but then couldn't be bothered keeping it styled. Reeve had seen coppers with haircuts like that, but not too many of them.

'So,' he said, 'what brings you here, gents?'

The taller man, Spikehead, nodded, like he was thinking: Okay, we're playing it like that. 'Just passing through.'

'You must be lost.'

'How's that?'

'To end up here. It's not exactly on the main road.'

'Well, you know . . .' The man was running out of lies already, not very professional.

'We just felt like a drink, all right?' his partner snapped.

'Just making conversation,' Reeve said. The edge of his vision was growing hazy. He thought of the tablets in his pocket, but dismissed them instantly.

'You live locally?' Spikehead asked.

'You should know,' Reeve answered.

Spikehead tried a smile. 'How's that?'

'You've been following me since Oban.'

Lardface turned slowly towards him, fired up for confrontation or conflagration. A pool cue appeared between them.

'You're up,' the youth said.

Reeve took the cue from him. 'Mind my drink, will you?' he asked Lardface.

'Mind it yourself.'

'Friends of yours?' the youth asked, beer-glass to his mouth as they walked to the pool table.

Reeve looked back at the two drinkers, who were watching him from behind their glasses the way men watched strippers – engrossed, but maybe a little wary. He shook his head, smiling pleasantly. 'No,' he said, 'just a couple of pricks. Me to break?'

'You to break,' the youth said, wiping snorted beer-foam from his nose.

Reeve never really had a chance, but that wasn't the point of the game. He stood resting his pool cue on the floor and watched a game of darts behind the pool table, while the youth potted two striped balls and left two other pockets covered.

'I hate the fuckin' English,' the youth said as Reeve lined up a shot. 'I mean, a lot of the time when you say something like that you're having a joke, but I mean it: I *really* fuckin' hate them.'

'Maybe they're not too fond of you either, sunshine.'

The youth ignored the voice from the bar.

Reeve looked like he was still lining up his shot; but he wasn't. He was sizing things up. This young lad was going to get into trouble. Reeve knew the way his mind was working: if they wanted to fight him, he'd tell them to meet him outside – outside where his pals were waiting. But the men at the bar wouldn't be *that* thick. They'd take him in here, where the only back-up worth talking about was Reeve himself. There were a couple of drunks playing darts atrociously, a few seated pensioners, Manny behind the bar, and the roadsweeper with the bad leg on the other side of it. In here, the two Englishmen would surely fancy their chances.

'You see,' the youth was saying, 'the way I see it the English are just keech . . .' He said some more, but Lardface must have understood 'keech'. He slammed down his drink and came stomping towards the pool table like he was approaching a hurdle.

'Now,' Manny said loudly, 'we don't want any trouble.'

Spikehead was still at the bar, which suited Reeve fine. He spun from the table, swinging his cue, and caught Lardface across the bridge of his nose, stopping him dead. Spikehead started forward, but cautiously. Reeve's free hand had taken a ball from the table. He threw it with all the force he had towards the bar. Spikehead ducked and the ball smashed a whisky bottle. Spikehead was straightening up again when Reeve snatched a dart out of one player's frozen hand and hefted it at Spikehead's thigh. The pink haze made it difficult to see, but the dart landed close enough. Spikehead gasped and dropped to one knee. Reeve found an empty pint-glass and cracked it against a table-leg, then held it in front of Lardface, who was sprawled on the floor, his smashed nose streaming blood and bubbles of mucus.

'Breathe through your mouth,' Reeve instructed. It barely registered that the rest of the bar had fallen into stunned silence. Even Manny was at a loss for words. Reeve walked over to Spikehead, who had pulled the dart from his upper thigh. He looked ready to stab it at Reeve until Reeve swiped the glass across his face. Spikehead dropped the dart.

'Christ,' gasped Manny, 'there was no need—'

But Reeve was concentrating on the man, rifling his pockets, seeking weapons and ID. 'Who are you?' he shouted. 'Who sent you?'

He glanced back towards Lardface, who was rising to his feet. Reeve took a couple of steps and roundhoused the man on the side of his face, maybe dislocating the jaw. He went back to Spikehead.

'I'm calling the polis,' Manny said.

Reeve pointed at him. 'Don't.'

Manny didn't. Reeve continued his search of the moaning figure, and came up with something he had not been expecting: a card identifying the carrier as a private investigator for Charles & Charles Associates, with an address in London.

He shook the man's lapels. 'Who hired you?'

The man shook his head. Tears were coursing down his face.

'Look,' Reeve said calmly, 'I didn't do any lasting damage. The cut isn't deep enough for stitching. It's just a bleeder, that's all.' He raised the glass. 'Now the next slash *will* need stitches. It might even take out your eye. So tell me who sent you!'

'Don't know the client,' the man blurted. Blood had dripped into his mouth. He spat it out with the words. 'It's sub-contracting. We're working on behalf of an American firm.'

'You mean a company?'

'Another lot of PIs. A big firm in Washington DC.'

'Called?'

'Alliance Investigative.'

'Who's your contact?'

'A guy called Dulwater. We phone him now and then.'

'You bugged my house?'

'What?'

'Did you bug my house?'

The man blinked at him and mouthed the word 'no'. Reeve let him drop. Lardface was unconscious. Reeve regained his composure and took the scene in – the prone bodies, the silence, the horror on Manny's face . . . and something like idolatry on the youth's.

'I could've taken them,' the youth said. 'But thanks anyway.'

'The police . . .' Manny said, but quietly, making it sound like a request.

Reeve turned to him. 'I'll see you all right about the breakages,' he said. He looked down at Spikehead. 'I don't think our friends here will be pressing charges. They were in a car smash, that's all. You might direct them to the nearest doctor, but that'll be the last you hear about this.' He smiled. 'I promise.'

He drove south until he reached a phonebox, and called Joan to check she was all right. She had arrived safely at her sister's, but still wanted to know what he was going to do. He remained vague, and she grew angry.

'This isn't just about you, Gordon!' she yelled. 'Not now. It's about Allan and me too. I *deserve* to know!'

'And I'm saying that the less you know the better. Trust me on this.' He was still trembling, his body pumping adrenaline. He didn't want to think about how good he had felt laying into the two private eyes.

It had felt wonderful.

He argued a few more minutes with Joan, and was about to plead that he was running out of money when she remembered something.

'I called an hour or two ago,' she said. 'I got the answering machine, so checked it for messages.'

'And?'

'There was one there from a woman. She sounded foreign.'

Marie Villambard! He'd forgotten all about her. He'd left his home telephone number on her machine.

'She left a number where you can reach her,' Joan said.

Reeve cursed silently. That meant whoever was bugging his phone would have her number too. He took down the details Joan gave, told her he had to go, and dug in his pockets for more change.

'Allo?'

'It's Gordon Reeve here, Madame Villambard. Thank you for getting back to me, but there's a problem.'

'Yes?'

'The line was compromised.' Two cars went past at speed. Reeve watched them disappear.

'You mean people were listening?'

'Yes.' He looked back along the dark road. No lights. Nothing. The only light, he realised, was the bare bulb in the old style phone-box. He pulled a handkerchief out of his jacket and used it to disconnect the bulb.

'It is a military term, "compromised"?'

'I suppose it is. I was in the Army.' The darkness felt better. 'Listen, can we meet?'

'In France?'

'I could drive overnight, catch a ferry at Dover.'

'I live near Limoges. Do you know it?'

'I'll buy a map. Is your telephone—?'

'Compromised? I think not. We can make a rendezvous safely.'

'Let's do it then.'

'Okay, drive into the centre of Limoges and follow signs to the Gare SNCF, the station itself is called Benedictins.'

'Got it. How long will the drive take from Calais?'

'That depends on how often you stop. If you hurry . . . six hours.'

Reeve did a quick calculation. If he didn't encounter congestion or roadworks, he might make it to the south coast in eight or nine hours. He could sleep on the boat, then another six hours. Add a couple of hours for sailing, embarkation and disembarkation, plus an hour because France was one hour ahead . . . seventeen or eighteen hours. He'd flown to Los Angeles in about half that. The luminous hands of his watch told him it was a little after eight.

'Late afternoon,' he said, allowing himself a margin.

'I'll be waiting in the station at four,' she said. 'I'll wait two hours, best look for me in the bar.'

'Listen, there's one more thing. They recorded your call, they know your name now.'

'Yes?'

'I'm saying be careful.'

'Thank you, Mr Reeve. See you tomorrow.'

His money was finished anyway. He put down the receiver, wondering how they would recognise one another. Then he laughed. He'd have driven a thousand miles straight; she'd recognise him by the bloodshot eyes and body tremors.

But he *was* worried that 'they' would know she'd called. He should have destroyed the transmitters as soon as he located them. Instead, he'd tried playing games, playing for time. These were not people who appreciated games. He pushed the lightbulb home and pushed open the iron-framed door.

One more thing worried him. The private eyes. They were working for an outfit called Alliance, an American outfit, and he had no idea who'd hired Alliance in the first place.

Plus, if Lardface and Spikehead hadn't planted those bugs . . . who had?

12

Jeffrey Allerdyce was lunching with one of the few United States senators he regarded with anything other than utter loathing. That was because Senator Cal Waits was the only *clean* senator Allerdyce had ever had dealings with. Waits had never had to call on Alliance's services, and had never found himself under investigation by them. He didn't appear to be in any corporation's pockets, and had little time – at least in public – for Washington's veritable army of slick besuited lobbyists.

Maybe that was because Cal Waits didn't need the money or the attention. He didn't need the money because his grandfather had owned the largest banking group in the southwest, and he didn't need the attention because his style in the Senate got him plenty of that anyway. He was a large middle-aged man with a store of homespun stories that he was keen on recounting, most of them very funny, most of them making some telling point about the subject under discussion in the Senate. He was always being quoted, soundbitten, edited into fifteen seconds of useable television for the mid-evening news. He was, as more than one newspaper had put it, 'an institution'.

They ate at Allerdyce's favourite restaurant, Ma Petite Maison. He liked the crabcakes there; he also had a ten percent share in the place (though this was not widely known), and so liked to keep an eye on business. Business wasn't bad, but at short notice Allerdyce had still been able to get a booth, one of the ones at the back usually reserved for parties of five or more. A journalist from the *Wall Street Journal* had been moved to one of the lesser tables, but would be kept sweet by seeing his eventual tab reduced by ten percent.

Allerdyce couldn't tell Cal Waits that he'd had someone bumped. Some luncheon companions would have been impressed, honoured – but not Waits. Waits would have protested, maybe even walked out. Allerdyce didn't want him to walk, he wanted him to talk. But first there was the other crap to be got through, the so-called excuse for their lunch engagement: catching up on family, mutual acquaintances, old times. Allerdyce noticed how some of the other diners stared at them, seeing two scarred old warhorses with their noses in the feedbag.

And then the main courses arrived – cassoulet for Waits, magret d'oie for Allerdyce – and it was almost time.

Waits looked at his plate. 'The hell with healthy eating,' he chortled. 'This health kick we've been on for the past – what? – twenty years: it's killing this country. I don't mean with cholesterol or whatever new bodily disaster or poison the scientists are coming up with, I mean people aren't eating for fun any more. Dammit, Jeffrey, eating used to be a pastime for America. Steaks and burgers, pizzas and ribs . . . fun food. Surf 'n' turf, that sort of thing. And now everybody looks at you in horror if you so much as suck on a drumstick. Well hell, I told my doctors – you notice you don't just need one doctor these days, you need a whole rank of them, same thing with lawyers – I told them I wouldn't diet. I'd do anything else they told me to do, but I would not stop eating the food I've been eating my whole goddamned life.'

He chewed on a fatty piece of ham to prove his point.

'How much medication are you on, Cal?' Allerdyce asked.

Cal Waits nearly choked with laughter. 'About a bottle of tablets a day. I got little pink ones and big blue ones and some capsule things that're white at one end and yellow at the other. I got red pills so small you practically need tweezers to pick them up, and I got this vast pastel tablet I take once a day that's the size of a bath-plug. Don't ask me what they do, I just gobble them down.'

He poured himself another half-glass of '83 Montrose. Despite hailing from California, Waits preferred the wines of Bordeaux. He was rationed to half a bottle a day, and drank perhaps twice that. That was another reason Allerdyce liked him: he didn't give a shit.

Allerdyce could see no subtle way into the subject he wanted to raise, and doubtless Cal would see through him anyway. 'You were raised in Southern California?' he asked.

'Hell, you know I was.'

'Near San Diego, right?'

'Right. I went to school there.'

'Before Harvard.'

'Before Harvard,' Waits acknowledged. Then he chuckled again. 'What is this, Jeffrey? You know I went to Harvard but pretend you *don't* know where I was born and raised!'

Allerdyce bowed his head, admitting he'd been caught. 'I just wanted to ask you something about San Diego.'

'I represent it in the Senate, I *should* know something about it.'

Allerdyce watched Waits shovel another lump of sausage into his mouth. Waits was wearing a dark blue suit of real quality, a lemon shirt and a blue silk tie. Above all this sat his round face, with the pendulous jowls cartoonists loved to exaggerate and the small eyes, inset like a pig's, always sparkling with the humour of some situation or other. They were sparkling now.

'You ever have dealings with CWC?'

'Co-World Chemicals, sure.' Waits nodded. 'I've attended a few functions there.'

'Do you know Kosigin?'

Waits looked more guarded. The twinkle was leaving his eyes. 'We've met.' He reached for another bread roll and tore it in two.

'What do you think of him?'

Waits chewed this question over, then shook his head. 'That's not what you want to ask, is it?'

'No,' Allerdyce quietly confessed, 'it isn't.'

Waits' voice dropped uncharacteristically low. His voicebox was the reason Allerdyce had needed a table away from other diners. 'I feel you're getting round to something, Jeffrey. Will I like it when we arrive?'

'It's nothing serious, Cal, I assure you.' Allerdyce's magret was almost untouched. 'It's just that Kosigin has hired Alliance's services, and I like to know about my clients.'

'Sure, without asking them to their face.'

'I like to know what people think of them, not what *they* would like *me* to think of them.'

'Point taken. Eat the goose, Jeffrey, it's getting cold.'

Allerdyce obeyed the instruction, and sat there chewing. Waits swallowed more wine and dabbed his chin with the napkin.

'I know a bit about Kosigin,' Waits said, his voice a quiet rumble seeming to emanate from his chest. 'There's been an investigation, not a big one, but all the same . . .'

Allerdyce didn't ask what kind of investigation. 'And?' he said instead.

'And nothing much, just a bad feeling about the whole operation. Or rather, about the way Kosigin's headed. It's like he's building autonomy within the corporation. The only person he seems to answer to is himself. And the people he hires . . . well, let's just say they're not always as reputable as you, Jeffrey. This Kosigin seems to like to hang around with minor hoods and shady nobodies.'

'You think CWC is in trouble?'

'What?'

'You think something's going to blow up.' It was a statement, not a question.

Waits smiled. 'Jeffrey, CWC is one of the largest chemical companies in the world. And it's American. Believe me, *nothing*'s going to blow up.'

Allerdyce nodded his understanding. 'Then the investigation . . . ?'

Waits leaned across the table. 'How can the authorities protect American interests unless they know what problems might arise?' He sat back again.

Allerdyce was still nodding. Cal was telling him that the powers – the FBI, maybe the CIA – were keeping tabs on CWC in general and Kosigin in particular; not to root out illegalities, but to ensure those illegalities – whatever shortcuts Kosigin was taking, whatever black economy he was running – never ever came to light. It was like having the whole system as your bodyguard! Jeffrey Allerdyce, normally so cool, so detached, so unflappable, so hard to impress . . . Jeffrey Allerdyce sat in Ma Petite Maison and actually whistled, something no diner there – not even his old friend Cal Waits – had ever seen him do. Something they might never see him do again.

He gathered his thoughts only slowly, picking at the goose. 'But,' he said at last, 'they wouldn't protect him from every contingency, surely? I mean, if he became a threat to the standing of CWC in the world, then he wouldn't—?'

'He'd probably lose their protection,' Waits conceded. 'But how far would he have to go? That's a question I can't answer. I just know that I keep out of the guy's way and let him get on with getting on.' Waits wiped his mouth again. 'I did hear one rumour . . .'

'What?'

'That Kosigin has agency *privileges*.'

'You mean he's special to them?' Allerdyce knew who Waits meant by 'agency': the CIA.

Cal Waits just shrugged. 'What was he asking you to do anyway?'

'You know I can't answer that, Cal. I wish I could tell you, but I'm bound by a vow of client confidentiality.'

Waits nodded. 'Well, whatever it is, just do a good job, Jeffrey. That's my advice.'

A waiter appeared at that moment. 'Mr Allerdyce? I'm sorry, sir, there's a telephone call. A gentleman called Dulwater, he said you'd want to speak to him.'

Allerdyce excused himself.

The telephone was on the reception desk. A flunkey held it out towards him, but Allerdyce just pointed to the receiver.

'Can you have that call transferred to the manager's office?'

The flunkey looked startled. He didn't want to say no, but didn't want to say yes either.

'Never mind,' Allerdyce snarled, snatching the telephone from a palm that was starting to sweat. 'Dulwater?'

'Some bad news, sir.'

'Better not be,' Allerdyce looked around. 'I'm in a public place, I'm sure cursing is frowned upon.'

'The UK operatives proved to be disadvantaged.'

'In plain English?'

'They weren't up to it.'

'You assured me they were.'

'I was assured they were.'

Allerdyce sighed. 'Should've sent our own men.'

'Yes, sir.'

Both of them were well aware that the decision had been Allerdyce's; he'd wanted to save money on flights. So they'd used some firm in London instead.

'So what's the damage?'

'They were confronted by the subject. They sustained a few injuries.'

'And the subject?'

'Apparently uninjured.'

Allerdyce raised one eyebrow at that. He wondered what sort of man this Reeve was. A grade-A tough bastard by the sound of it. 'I take it they lost him?'

'Yes, sir. I doubt he'll return home. Looks like he's packed his wife and son off.'

'Well, it's SNAFUed, isn't it, Dulwater?'

'We can try to pick up his trail.' Dulwater sounded unconvinced. He wasn't sure why Allerdyce was so interested anyway. To his mind it was a wild-goose chase.

'Let me think about it. Anything else?'

'Yes, sir. One of the men said Reeve asked him about his house being bugged, asked if our operative was responsible.'

'What?'

'Somebody bugged Reeve's domicile.'

'I heard you the first time. Who?'

'Do you want an educated guess?'

'Let's see if we agree.'

'Kosigin.'

'We agree,' said Allerdyce. He thought for a moment. 'Makes sense. He's a clever man, doesn't like loose ends, we already know that. Now he's got one, and it's unravelling fast.'

Allerdyce was intrigued. If he kept close to Kosigin's operation, he could well end up with information, with the very power he wanted over Kosigin. Then again, it might mean mixing it with some powerful agencies. Allerdyce didn't know everybody's secrets; there were some agencies he probably couldn't fix . . . Stay close, or take Cal Waits' advice and back off? Allerdyce had always been a careful man – cautious in his business, prudent in his personal life. He could see Cal sitting at the distant table, pouring yet more wine. A warhorse, unafraid.

'Keep close to this, Dulwater.'

'Sir, with respect, I advise we—'

'Son, don't presume to advise Jeffrey Allerdyce. You're not far enough advanced on the board.'

'Board, sir?'

'Chessboard. You're still one of my pawns, Dulwater. Moving forward, but still a pawn.'

'Yes, sir.' A hurt pause. 'Pawns aren't very flexible are they, sir?'

'They just inch their way forward.'

'But if they inch far enough, sir, isn't it right that they can turn into more important pieces?'

Allerdyce almost laughed. 'You've got me zugzwanged, son. I'm going back to my lunch.' Allerdyce dropped the receiver. He was beginning not to detest Dulwater.

Back at the table, Cal Waits was in conversation with a leggy blonde who'd paused to say hello. She was standing in front of the booth, leaning down over the senator. It was a gesture hinting at intimacy, carried out solely so the other diners would notice. It wasn't supposed to embarrass Waits, it was supposed to flatter *her*. She wore a blue two-piece, cut just about deep enough so Waits could see down the front.

She smiled at Allerdyce as he squeezed none too gently past her and resumed his seat. 'Well, I'll leave you to your meal, Cal. Bye now.'

'Bye, Jeanette.' He released a long sigh when she'd gone.

'Dessert, Cal?' Allerdyce asked.

'Just so long as it ain't jelly on a plate,' Cal Waits said before draining his wine.

13

Reeve made the call from the ferry terminal. It was either early morning or else the middle of the night depending on how you felt. He felt like death warmed up, except that he was shivering. He knew the time of day wouldn't matter to the person he was calling. When he'd been a policeman, Tommy Halliday's preferred shift had been nights. He wasn't an insomniac, he just preferred being awake when everyone else was asleep. He said it gave him a buzz. But then he resigned, changed his mind, and found the force wouldn't take him back – just like what had happened with Jim and his newspaper. Maybe the force had discovered Halliday's drug habit; maybe news had leaked of his wild parties. Maybe it was just to do with manning levels. Whatever, Halliday was out. And what had once been a recreation became his main source of income. Reeve didn't know if Tommy Halliday still dealt in quantity, but he knew he dealt in quality. A lot of Army-types – weekenders and would-be mercenaries – bought from him. They wanted performance enhancers and concoctions to keep them awake and alert. Then they needed downers for the bad time afterwards, times so bad they might need just a few more uppers . . .

Reeve had few feelings about drug use and abuse. But he knew Tommy Halliday might have something he could use.

The phone rang for a while, but that was normal: everyone who knew Tommy knew he let it ring and ring. That way he only ended up speaking to people who knew him . . . and maybe a few utterly desperate souls who'd let a phone ring and ring and ring.

'Yeah.' The voice was alert and laid back at the same time.

'It's Gordie.' All Tommy's callers used first names or nicknames, just in case the Drug Squad were listening.

'Hey, Gordie, long time.' Halliday sounded like he was lighting a cigarette. 'You know a guy called Waxie? Came to see you for one of your long weekends.'

Henry Waxman. 'I remember him,' Reeve said. This was typical of Halliday. You phoned him for a favour from a pay-phone and spent half your money listening to his stories. Through the terminal's windows, Reeve saw a greasy sky illuminated by sodium, a blustery wind buffeting the few brave gulls up there.

'He's become a good friend,' Halliday was saying. Which meant Waxman had become a serious user of some narcotic. It was a kind of warning. Halliday was just letting Reeve know that Waxman might not be as reliable as he once was. Halliday was under the misapprehension that Gordon Reeve trained mercenaries. Reeve had done nothing to correct this; it seemed to impress the dealer.

'Sorry to ring you so early. Or do I mean late?'

'Hey, you know me. I never sleep. I'm right in the middle of *Mean Streets*, trying to figure out what's so great about it. Looks like a home movie. I dunno.' He paused to suck on his cigarette and Reeve leapt into the breach.

'Tommy, I'd like you to get Birdy for me.'

'Birdy?'

'Can you do that?'

'Well, I haven't seen him in a while . . .' This was part of the Drug Squad game too. Birdy wasn't a person. Birdy was something very specialised, very rare.

'I've got something for him.' Meaning, I can pay whatever it takes.

'I dunno, like I say, he's not been around much. Is it urgent?'

'No, I'm going to be away for a few days. Maybe I'll call you when I get back.'

'You do that, I'll see if I bump into him, maybe ask around. Okay, Gordie?'

'Thanks.'

'Sure, and hey, do me a favour. Rent out *Mean Streets*, tell me what's so great about it.'

'Three words, Tommy.'

'What?' The voice sounded urgent, like it mattered.

'De Niro and Keitel.'

He slept for three-quarters of an hour on the ferry crossing. As soon as the boat came into Calais and drivers were asked to return to their vehicles, Reeve washed down some caffeine pills with the last of his strong black coffee. He'd made one purchase on board – a hard rock compilation tape – and he'd changed some money. The boat was nearly empty. They took the lorries off first, but within five minutes of returning to his car he was driving out on to French soil. Back at a garage outside Dover he'd bought a headlamp kit, so he could switch beam-direction to the other side of the road. Driving on the right hadn't been a problem to him in the USA, so he didn't think it would be a problem here. He'd jotted down directions so he wouldn't have to keep looking at the map-book he'd added to his purchases at the garage.

He headed straight for Paris, looking to take one of the ring-roads further out, but ended up on the *périphérique*, the inner-ring. It was like one of the circles of Dante's hell; he only thanked God they were all travelling the same direction. Cars came on to the road from both sides, and left again the same way. People were cutting across lanes, trusting to providence or some spirit of the internal combustion engine. It was a vast game of 'Dare': he who applied the brakes was lost.

Still hyped from the caffeine and loud music, and a bit dazed from lack of sleep, Reeve hung on grimly and took what looked like the right exit. The names meant nothing to him, and seemed to change from sign to sign, so he concentrated on road numbers. He took the A6 off the *périphérique* and had no trouble finding the A10, which called itself *l'Aquitaine*. That was the direction he wanted. He celebrated with a short stop for refuelling – the car and himself both. Another two shots of espresso and a croissant.

When he started hallucinating – starbursts in his eyes – still north of

Poitiers, he stopped to sleep. A cheap motorway motel looked tempting, but he stayed with his car. He didn't want to get *too* comfortable, but it didn't make sense to turn up for his meeting with Marie Villambard unable to concentrate or focus. He wound the passenger seat as far back as it would go and slid over into it, so the steering wheel wouldn't dig into him. His eyes felt gritty, grateful when he closed them. The cars speeding past the service area might as well have been serried waves crashing on the shore, the rumble of lorries a heart beat. He was asleep inside a minute.

He slept for forty deep minutes, then got out of the car and did some stretching exercises, using the car bonnet as his bench. He took his toothbrush to the toilets, scrubbed his teeth and splashed water on his face. Then back to the car. He was a hundred miles from his destination, maybe a little less. Despite his stops, he'd made good time. At the back of his map-book there was a plan of Limoges. It had two railway stations: the one he wanted – Gare des Benedictins – was to the east, the other to the west. He headed south on the N147 and came into Limoges from the north. Almost at once the streets started to hem him in. They either bore no signposts or identifiers, or else were one-way. He found himself shunted on to street after street, twisting right and left and right . . . until he was lost. At one point he saw a sign pointing to *gare SNCF*, but after following it didn't see another sign, and soon was lost again. Finally he pulled over, double parking on a narrow shopping street, and asked a pedestrian for directions. It was as if he'd asked the man to talk him through open heart surgery: Benedictins was difficult from here, he'd have to retrace his steps, the one-way system was very complicated . . .

Reeve thanked the man and started driving again, waving at the complaining line of drivers who'd been waiting to pass him.

Eventually he crossed a bridge and saw railway lines beneath him, and followed those as best he could. Then he saw it, a huge domed building with an even higher clocktower to one side. Benedictins. It looked more like an art gallery or museum than a city's railway station. Reeve checked his watch. It was half-past five. He found a parking space, locked the car, and took a few seconds to calm himself and do a few more exercises. His whole body was buzzing as though electricity was being passed through him. He walked on to the station concourse, looked over to the left, and saw the restaurant and bar.

He paused again outside the bar itself, looking around him as though for a friend. Actually, he was seeking out the opposite, but it was hard to judge from the people milling around. There were down and outs and students, young men in military uniform and business people clutching briefcases. Some stared anxiously at the departures board; others sat on benches and smoked, or browsed a magazine. Any one of them could be putting on an act. It was impossible to tell.

Reeve walked into the bar.

He spotted her immediately. She was middle-aged, wore glasses, and was chain-smoking. There was a fug of smoke in the bar; walking through it was like walking through mist. She sat in a booth facing the bar, reading a large paperback and taking notes in the margin. She was the only single woman in the place.

Reeve didn't approach her straight away. He walked up to the bar and settled himself on a stool. The barman had already weighed him up and was reaching for the wine bottle. He managed not to look surprised when Reeve ordered Perrier.

There were six other men in the bar, eight including the waiting staff. Reeve studied them all. They'd stared at him collectively on his arrival, but that was only natural in a French bar as in bars around the world. Mostly they were drinking short glasses of red wine, a couple of them nursed espressos. They all looked like they fitted right in; they looked like regulars. Then he saw that someone else was watching him. She'd put down her book and pen and was peering at him over the top of her glasses. Reeve paid for the water and took his glass to her booth.

'Mr Reeve?'

He sat down and nodded.

'A good journey?' There was irony in the question.

'First class,' Reeve replied. He would place her in her early 50s. She was trim and well dressed and had taken care of herself, but the lines around the neck gave it away. Her hair was salt-and-pepper, swept back over the ears from a centre parting and feathered at the back of her head. She had the word 'executive' stamped on her.

'So,' she said, 'now you will tell me about your brother?'

'I'd like to know a bit about you first,' he said. 'Tell me about yourself, how you came to know Jim.'

So she told him the story of a woman who had always been a writer, ever since schooldays, a story not dissimilar to Jim's own life. She said they'd met while she was on a trip to London. Yes, she'd known Marco in London, and he'd told her his suspicions. She had come back to France and done some research. In France the farming lobby was even stronger than that in the UK, with close ties between farm owners and their agrichemical suppliers, and a government – no matter whether left- or right-wing – which bowed to pressure from both. The investigation had been hard going; even now she wasn't much further forward, and had to leave the story for long periods of time so she could do work that would earn her money. The agrichem story was her 'labour of love'.

'Now tell me about Jim,' she said. So Reeve told his side of it, a seasoned performer by now. She listened intently, holding the pen as if about to start taking notes. The book she'd been reading was the biography of some French politician. She tapped the cover absentmindedly with the pen, covering the politician's beaming honest face with myriad spots, like blue measles. The barman came over to take another order, and tutted and pointed. She saw what she'd been doing, and smiled and shrugged. The barman seemed not much mollified.

'Do you know this man?' she asked Reeve. She meant the politician. Reeve shook his head. 'His name is Pierre Dechevement. Until recently he was responsible for agriculture. He resigned. There was a young woman . . . not his wife. Normally, such a thing would not be a scandal in France. Indeed, there was no trace of a scandal in Dechevement's case. Yet he still resigned.'

'Why?'

She smiled. 'Perhaps because he is a man of honour? That is what his biographer says.'

'What do you say?'

She stabbed the pen at him. 'You are shrewd, Mr Reeve. For years Dechevement took bribes from the agrichemical companies – well, no, perhaps bribes is too strong. Let us say that he enjoyed hospitality, and received *favours*. In my opinion one of those favours was the young lady in question, who turns out to have been a sometime prostitute, albeit high-class. Dechevement was quite brazen; she accompanied him to functions here and abroad. He even became her employer, giving her a position on his private staff. There is no record that she contributed any work, but she was paid a generous salary.'

Marie Villambard lit a fresh Peter Stuyvesant from the stub of the old one. Her ashtray had already been emptied twice by the barman. She blew out a stream of smoke.

'Dechevement's closest ties were to a company called COSGIT, and COSGIT is a French subsidiary of Co-World Chemicals.'

'So Dechevement was in CWC's employ?'

'In a manner of speaking. I think that's why he was told to resign, so no one would bother to backtrack and find that the young prostitute had been paid for by Co-World Chemicals. *That* might have created a scandal, even in France.'

Reeve was thoughtful. 'So you weren't working along the same lines as my brother?'

'Wait, please. We have not yet . . . scratched the surface.'

Reeve sat back. 'Good,' he said, as his second Perrier arrived.

'In a sense, Dechevement is only a very small part of the whole,' Marie Villambard said. The waiter had brought her a new pack of cigarettes, which she was unwrapping. Reeve noticed that all the customers who'd been in the bar on his arrival had now been replaced by others – which didn't necessarily mean there wasn't surveillance.

'I have become,' she went on, 'more interested in a man called Owen Preece. *Doctor* Owen Preece. Your brother was interested in him too.'

'Who is he?'

'He's dead now, unfortunately. It looked like natural causes. He was in his seventies – a cardiac crisis, it could happen to anyone that age . . .'

'Well then, who was he?'

'An American psychiatrist.'

Reeve frowned; someone else had mentioned a psychiatrist in connection with CWC . . .

'He headed what was supposed to be an independent research team, funded partly by government and partly by agrichemical companies, to look into BSE, what you call Mad Cow Disease.'

Reeve nodded to himself. Josh Vincent had mentioned something similar – research funded by CWC itself, using psychiatrists as well as scientists.

'This was in the early days of the scare,' Marie Villambard was saying. 'The team comprised neurologists, viral specialists, experts in blood diseases, and psychologists. Their initial reports were that the disease ME – "Yuppie Flu" as it was called at the time – was not a disease at all but was psychosomatic, an ailment brought on by the sufferer for some complex psychological reason.'

'They were working on prion protein?'

'That is correct, and they found no evidence to link prion proteins found in organo-phosphorous substances, or any pesticides currently in use, to any of the range of diseases that other scientists claim *are* closely linked to them.'

'They were got at by CWC?'

'Not exactly, but there is good reason to believe Dr Preece was in the employ of CWC, and he was head of the team. He gave the final okay to their results. He had access to all the data . . .'

'And could have tampered with it?'

'One member of the team resigned, claiming something along those lines. He was killed in a boating accident only weeks later.'

'Jesus. So Preece falsified tests and results? And all this was part-funded by the US government?'

Marie Villambard nodded throughout. 'The initial idea had come down from someone in the middle ranks of Co-World Chemicals. Some of us assume this man was responsible for putting Preece in charge. Dr Preece was in some ways an excellent choice – he was a psychiatrist of some renown. He is also thought to have carried out experiments for the CIA.'

'Experiments?'

'On humans, Mr Reeve. In the fifties and sixties he was part of a team which tested the effects of various hallucinogens on the human nervous system.' She saw something close to horror on Reeve's face. 'It was all perfectly legal, believe it or not. The subjects were patients in lunatic asylums. They had few rights, and no one to fight for what few rights they had. They were injected with all manner of chemicals; we can't even say which. Preece was a small part of this. It only came to light recently, after his death, when some CIA files were released. It made some of us wonder about his involvement with various committees and research projects post-1960. This man had something to hide, some shame in his past, and those with a past can always be bought.'

'And the CWC employee who suggested all this . . . ?'

'Kosigin,' said Marie Villambard. 'A Mr Kosigin.'

'How do you know?'

'Your brother found out. He interviewed a lot of people under the pretext of writing a book about Preece. He spoke to scientists, government agencies, he tracked down people who had been involved in the original project. He had evidence linking Preece to Kosigin, evidence of a massive cover-up, something concerning every person on the planet.' She lifted her cigarette. 'That's why I smoke, Mr Reeve. Eating is too dangerous, to my mind. I prefer safer pleasures.'

Reeve wasn't listening. 'Whatever evidence my brother had has gone to the grave with him.'

She smiled. 'Don't be so melodramatic – and for goodness' sake don't be so *silly*.'

Reeve looked at her. 'What do you mean?'

'Your brother was a *journalist*. He was working on a dangerous story, and he knew just how dangerous. He would have made back-ups of his disks. There will be written files somewhere. There will be *something*. In an apartment somewhere, or left with a friend, or in a bank vault. You just have to look.'

'Supposing the evidence has been destroyed?'

She shrugged. 'Then the story is not so strong . . . I don't know. Maybe it is impossible to find a publisher for it. Everywhere we look, in every country which uses these chemicals and pesticides, we find some government connection. I do not think the governments of the world would like to see this story published.' She stared at him. 'Do you?'

He stayed silent.

'I do not think the agrichemical conglomerates would like to see the story appear either, and nor would agencies like the CIA . . . Maybe we should all just get back to our ordinary lives.' She smiled sadly. 'Maybe that would be safer for us all.'

'You don't believe that,' he said.

She had stopped smiling. 'No,' she said, 'I don't. It has gone too far for that. Another good reason for smoking. I am like the condemned prisoner, yes?'

And she laughed, the terror showing only in her eyes.

She had some information she could give him – copies of documents – so he followed her in his car. They left the city travelling towards a town called St Yrieix. This is all I need, thought Reeve, more driving. The road was a succession of steep ups and downs, and a couple of times they found themselves stuck behind a tractor or horsebox. At last Marie Villambard's Citroën Xantia signalled to turn off the main road, but only so that they could twist their way along a narrow country road with nothing but the occasional house or farmstead. It was a fine evening, with an annoyingly low sun and wide streaks of pale blue in the sky. Reeve's stomach complained that he'd been shovelling nothing but croissants and coffee into it all day. Then, to his amazement – out here in the middle of nowhere – they drove past a restaurant. It looked to have been converted from a mill, a stream running past it. A few hundred yards further on, the Xantia signalled left and they headed up a narrower, rougher track made from hard-packed stones and sand. The track led them into an avenue of mature oak trees, as though this roadway had been carved from the forest. A couple of roads leading off could have been logging tracks. At the end, in absolute isolation, stood a small old single-storey house with dormer windows in the roof. Its facing stones hadn't been rendered, and the shutters on the windows looked new, as did the roof-tiles.

Reeve got out of his car. 'This is some spot,' he said.

'Ah, yes, my grandparents lived here.'

Reeve nodded. 'He was a timber man?'

'No, no, he was a professor of anthropology. Please, come this way.'

And she led him indoors. Reeve was dismayed to see that security was lax. Never mind the isolation and the fact that there was only one road in and out – the house itself was protected by only a single deadlock, and the shutters had been left open, making for easy entry through one of the windows.

'Neighbours?' he asked.

'The trees are my neighbours.' She saw he was serious. 'There is a farm only a couple of kilometres away. They have truffle rights. That means the right to come on to the land to search for truffles. I only ever see them in the autumn, but then I see them a *lot*.'

There was a bolt on the inside of the door, which was something. There was also a low rumbling noise. The rumble turned into a deep animal growl.

'Ça suffit!' Marie Villambard exclaimed as the biggest dog Reeve had ever seen padded into the hall. The beast walked straight up to her, demanding to be patted, but throughout Marie's attentions its eyes were on the stranger. It growled again from deep in its cavernous chest. 'His name is Foucault,' Villambard explained to Reeve. He didn't think it was time to tell her he had a cat called Bakunin. 'Let him smell you.'

Reeve knew that this was the drill – same with any dog – don't be a stranger. Let it paw over you and sniff your crotch, whatever it takes, until it has accepted you in its territory. Reeve stretched out a hand, and the dog ran a wet discerning nose over the knuckles, then licked them.

'Good dog, Foucault,' Reeve said. 'Good dog.'

Marie was rubbing the monster's coat fiercely. 'Really I should keep him outside,' she said. 'But he's spoilt. He used to be a hunting dog – don't ask me which breed. Then his owner had to go into hospital, and if I hadn't looked after him nobody would. Would they, Foucault?'

She started to talk to the dog – Reeve guessed part Alsatian, part wolfhound – in French, then led it back to the kitchen where she emptied some food from a tin into a bowl the size of a washbasin. In fact, as Reeve got closer he saw that it *was* a washbasin, red and plastic with a chewed rim.

'Now,' she said, 'my thinking is that you need a bath, yes? After your first-class journey.'

'That would be great.'

'And food?'

'I'm starving.'

'There is an excellent restaurant, we passed it—'

'Yes, I saw.'

'We will go there. You are in France only one night, you must spend the time wisely.'

'Thanks. I've some stuff in my car, I'll just go fetch it.'

'And I shall begin your bath.'

The bathroom was a compact space just off the hall. There was a small kitchen, and a small living-space that looked more like an office than somewhere to relax. It had a look of organised chaos, some kind of order that only the owner of such a room could explain.

'You live here alone?' Reeve asked.

'Only since my husband left me.'

'I'm sorry.'

'I'm not. He was a pig.'

'When did he leave?'

'October 11th, 1978.'

Reeve smiled and went out to the car. He walked around the house first. This was real Hansel and Gretel stuff; the cottage in the woods. He could hear a dog barking, probably on the neighbouring farm. But no other sounds intruded except the rustling of the oak trees in the wind. He knew what Marie thought – she thought the very secrecy of this place made her safe. But where she saw secrecy, Reeve saw isolation. Even if she wasn't in the telephone book, it would take just an hour's work for a skilled operative to get an address for her. An ordnance survey map would show the house –

might even name it. And then the operative would know just how isolated the spot was.

There were two small outbuildings, one of which had been a bakery at one time. The bread oven was still there, the large wooden paddles still hung on the walls, but the space was used for storage these days. Mice or rats had chewed the corners out of a tower of empty cardboard boxes. The other outbuilding was a woodstore, and maybe always had been. It was stacked with neat piles of sawn logs. Reeve peered into the forest. A covering of dry leaves on the forest floor wouldn't be enough to give warning of anyone approaching the house. He'd have had trip wires maybe. Or . . .

Sudden beams of light flooded the shade. He blinked up and saw that halogen lamps had been fastened to some of the trees. Something or someone had tripped them. Then he saw Marie Villambard standing beside the house, arms folded, laughing at him.

'You see,' she said, 'I have protection.'

He walked towards her. 'They're movement sensitive,' he said.

'That's right.'

He nodded. 'All connected to a single source?'

'Yes.'

'Then they'd be easy to disable. Plus, what do they do? They light up the trees. So what? That's not going to stop someone from advancing.'

'No, but it gives Foucault something to aim at. He stays out here at night.'

'He's just one dog.'

She laughed again. 'You are a security expert?'

'I used to be,' Reeve mumbled, going back into the house with his bag.

He changed into his spare set of clothes, wrapping his soiled shirt around Lucky 13. He wasn't planning on staying here. He'd head off after dinner, find a hotel somewhere on the route. So he took his bag back out to the car and put it in the boot, out of sight. Marie Villambard had put together a cardboard box's worth of papers.

'These are all copies, so I do not need them returned.'

'Fine,' he said.

'And I don't know if they will tell you anything I haven't.'

'Thanks anyway.'

She looked like she had something awkward to say, her eyes avoiding his. 'You know, you are welcome to stay here tonight.'

He smiled. 'Thanks, but I think I'll head off.'

'You are sure?' Now she looked at him. She didn't look like an executive any more, she looked lonely and tired, tired of solitude and stroking Foucault, tired of long wakeful nights wondering if the sky would suddenly burst open with halogen. Tired of waiting.

'I'll see how I feel after dinner,' he conceded. But he loaded the box of files into the boot anyway.

'Shall we take my car?' she asked.

'Let's take mine. It's blocking yours anyway.' He helped her on with her coat. 'It looked like a very nice restaurant.' Making conversation didn't come easily. He was still getting over the feeling of being flattered that she wanted him to stay. She locked the door after them.

'It is an excellent restaurant,' she said. 'And a very good reason for moving here.'

'It wasn't sentimentality then?' He opened the passenger door for her.

'You mean because the house belonged to my grandparents? No, not that. Well, perhaps a little. But the restaurant made the decision easy. I hope they have a table.' Reeve started the engine and turned the car around. 'I tried calling, but the telephone is acting up again.'

'Again?'

'Oh, it happens a lot. The French system . . .' She looked at him. 'You are wondering if my phone is tapped. Well, I don't know. I must trust that it is not.' She shrugged. 'Otherwise life would be intolerable. One would think oneself paranoid . . .'

Reeve was staring ahead. 'A car,' he said.

'What?' She turned to look through the windscreen. There was a car parked fifty or sixty yards away – French licence plate; nobody inside.

'*Merde*,' she said.

Reeve didn't hesitate. He slammed the gearshift into reverse and turned to navigate through the back window. There was a logging trail behind him, and another car darted from it and braked hard across the road.

'Gordon . . .' Marie said as he stopped the Land Rover. It was the first time she'd used his name.

'Run for it,' Reeve hissed at her. He released both their seatbelts. The men in the rear car were reaching into their jackets, at the same time opening their doors. 'Just get into the woods and run like hellfire!' He was shouting now, pumping himself up. He leaned across her, pushed open her door and thrust her out of the car. 'Run!' he yelled, at the same time hitting the accelerator with everything he had and pulling his foot off the clutch. The wheels spun and the car started to fly backwards, weaving crazily from side to side. The men were half-way out of the car when Reeve hit them with everything his own vehicle had. One of the men slipped and Reeve felt his back wheels bump over something that hadn't previously been on the track. The other man slumped back into the car, either dazed or unconscious.

Reeve looked out of his windscreen. Men had appeared beside the car in front. They'd been hiding in the woods. He checked to his left and saw Marie scurrying away. Good: she was keeping low. But the men in front were pointing towards her. One of them headed back into the trees, the other two took aim at Reeve's car.

'Now,' he told himself, ducking and opening his door. He slipped out of the car and started crawling towards the boot, just as the first shots went off. There was a body lying under the car, between the front and back wheels. Most of it was intact. Reeve patted it down but found no gun. It must have been thrown during the collision. He couldn't see it anywhere nearby. Another shot hit the radiator grille. Would they hear shots at the neighbouring farm? And if they did, would they think them suspicious? The French were a nation of hunters – truffles not their only prey.

The collision had thrown open the back of the Land Rover. He couldn't hope to carry the box of papers, but snatched his overnight bag. They were closing on him, walking forward with real purpose and almost without caution. He could try the other car, there might be guns there. He was on the wrong side of the track to follow Marie, and if he tried crossing over they'd have a clean shot at him. His first decision had to be right. He knew what Standard Operating Procedure was: get the hell away from the firefight and regroup. If you had to go back in, come from a direction the enemy would least expect.

It made sense, only it meant leaving Marie. I can't help her dead, he thought. So he took a deep breath and, crouching low, made for the trees. He was like a figure in a shooting gallery to the two gunmen, but they only had handguns and he was moving fast. He reached the first line of trees and kept running. It was nearly dark, which was both good and bad: good because it made it easier to hide; bad because it camouflaged his pursurers as well as himself. He ran jaggedly for three minutes and was still surrounded by oaks. He hadn't been trying to run stealthily or silently, he just wanted distance. But now he paused and looked back, peering between the trees, listening hard. He heard a whistle, then another – one way over to his right, the other to his left, much closer. Only two whistles; only two men. He was getting further and further away from Marie. It could take him hours to circle back around to her. He was doing something he'd vowed to himself he'd never do again: he was running away.

He held out his hands. They were shaking. This wasn't one of his weekend games; his pursurers weren't using blanks. This was *real* in a way that hadn't been true since Operation Stalwart. Return or retreat: those were the options facing him now. He had seconds to decide. He made the decision.

He looked down at his clothes. His pullover was dark, but the shirt beneath was white and showed at the cuffs and neck. Quickly he tugged off the pullover and took off his shirt, then put the pullover back on. Trousers, shoes and socks were dark, too. He put the shirt back in his bag, then unwrapped Lucky 13. He used the damp and mud beneath the leaves to cover his face and hands and the meat of the dagger's blade. They might have torches, and he didn't want a glint of metal to give him away. The dark was closing in fast, the tree cover all but blocking out the last light of day. Another whistle, another reply. They were far enough apart for him to walk between them. They'd hardly be expecting him to double back.

But he was going to do just that. He left the bag where it was and set off.

He took slow, measured paces so as not to make noise, and he went from tree to tree, using each one as cover so he could check the terrain between that tree and the next. He had no landmarks to go by, just his own sense of direction. He'd left no tracks that he could follow back to the road, and didn't want to follow tracks anyway: they might belong to a truffle hunter; they might belong to a pursuer.

But the whistled messages between his two pursuers were as good as sonar. Here came the first call . . . then the response. He held his breath. The response was so close he could hear the final exhalation of breath after the whistle itself had ended. The man was moving slowly, cautiously. And very, very quietly. Reeve knew he was dealing with a pro. His fingers tightened around Lucky 13.

I'm going to kill someone, he thought. Not hit them or wound them. I'm going to kill them.

The man walked past Reeve's tree and Reeve grabbed him, hauling him down by the head and gouging into his throat with the dagger. The pistol squeezed off a single shot, but it was wild. Still, it would have warned the others. Even dying, the man had been thinking of his mission. Reeve let the body slump to the ground, the gaping wound in the neck spurting blood. He took the pistol from the warm, pliant hand and looked at the man. He was wearing camouflage, black boots and a balaclava. Reeve tore off the balaclava but couldn't place the face. He did a quick search but came up with nothing in the pockets.

It was time to go. Another whistle: two sharp staccatos. Reeve licked his lips and returned it, knowing it wouldn't fool his adversary for longer than half a minute. He set off quickly now, hoping he was heading towards the cars. But he knew his direction was off when he came out into a clearing he knew. There was the house, sitting in darkness. He looked up but couldn't see any halogen lamps hidden in the trees. Maybe the enemy had disabled them.

Had they taken Marie back to the cottage? It looked unlikely, there were no lights in there. He walked forward to check . . . and now there was a burst of halogen, lighting the scene like a stage-set in a darkened theatre.

'Drop the gun!'

A shouted command, the first words he'd heard for a while. It came from the trees. Reeve, standing next to the cottage window, knew he hadn't a chance. He pitched the automatic pistol in front of him. It landed maybe six feet away. Near enough for him to make a dive to retrieve it . . . if there was anything to shoot at. But all he could see were the trees, and the halogen lamps pointing at him from high up in the oaks. Great security, he thought – works a treat. And then a man walked out from the line of trees and came towards him. The man was carrying a pistol identical to the one on the ground. He carried it very steadily. Reeve tried to place the accent. American, he thought. The man wasn't saying anything more though. He wanted to get close to Reeve, close to the man who had slaughtered his comrade. Reeve could feel the blood drying on his hands and wrists, dripping off his forearms. I must look like a butcher, he thought.

The man kept looking at those hands, too, fascinated by the blood. He gestured with the pistol and Reeve raised his hands. The man stooped to retrieve the other automatic, and Reeve swung an elbow back into the window, smashing the glass. The man stood up quickly, but Reeve stood stock-still. The man grinned.

'You were going to jump through the window?' he said. Definitely American. 'What, you think I couldn't've hit you? You think maybe the telephone's working? You were going to call for help?' He seemed very amused by all these suggestions. He was still advancing on Reeve, no more than three feet from him. Reeve had his hands held up high now. He'd cut his elbow on the glass. His own blood was trickling down one arm and into his armpit.

The man held his gun-arm out straight, execution-style, the way he'd maybe seen it done on the Vietnam newsreels. Then he heard the noise. He couldn't place it at first. It sounded motorised, definitely getting closer.

Reeve dived to his right as Foucault flew out through the window, sinking his jaws into the man's face. The force of the dog knocked him flat on his back, the dog covering his whole upper body. Reeve didn't hang around to watch. He snatched up the pistol and ran back towards the track. A few hundred yards would take him to the cars. He heard another vehicle in the distance, something bigger than a car. Maybe it's the cavalry, he thought, someone from the farm.

But now there was another whistled command. Three low and long, two higher and shorter. Repeated five or six times. Reeve kept on moving forwards. Van doors closing. Engine revving. As he turned a bend he saw the car he'd smashed into and his own vehicle. He couldn't see anybody lying under the Land Rover, and there was nobody in the smashed car.

There was a sudden explosion. It threw him backwards off his feet. He landed heavily but got up quickly, winded but still aiming his pistol at whatever the hell had happened. His Land Rover was in flames. Had they booby-trapped it maybe? Then he saw what they'd done. They were disabling it – that was all – so it would be here when the police arrived. The police would find evidence of a firefight, maybe bodies, certainly blood, and a missing journalist. They would also find a British car . . . a car belonging to Gordon Reeve.

'Sons of bitches,' Reeve whispered. He moved past the burning wreckage and saw that the front car had gone, along with whatever vehicle had turned up towards the end. He kept hearing that whistled command. It sounded like the opening of a tune he recognised . . . a tune he didn't want to recognise. Five beats. Dahh, dahh, dahh, da-da. It was the opening to 'Row, row, row your boat'. No, he was imagining it; it could have been another song, could have been random.

He wondered about checking the woods for Marie Villambard's body. Maybe she was alive, maybe they'd taken her with them. Or she was lying somewhere in the woods, and very dead. Either way, he couldn't hope to help. So he set off the other way until he recovered his bag. He had a landmark this time though. The corpse with the cut throat was still lying slumped on the ground.

Row, row, row your boat. He detested that song, with good reason.

Then he froze, remembering the scene outside the crematorium in San Diego: the cars turning up for the next service, and a face turning away from him, a face he'd thought was a ghost's.

Jay.

It couldn't be Jay. It couldn't be. Jay was dead. Jay wasn't alive and breathing anywhere on this planet . . .

It was Jay. That was the only thing, crazy as it seemed, that made sense.

It was Jay.

Reeve was shaking again as he headed back to the cottage. There was a body cooling on the ground next to the window, but no sign of Foucault. Reeve looked into Marie Villambard's Xantia and saw that the keys were in the ignition. Car theft probably hadn't been a problem around here. Nor had warfare and murder, until tonight. He got in and shut the door. He was turning the key when a vast bloodied figure pounced on to the bonnet, its face framed by pink froth, growling and snarling.

'Got a taste for it, huh?' Reeve said, starting the engine, ignoring the dog. He revved up hard and started off, throwing Foucault to the ground. He watched in the rearview, but the dog didn't follow. It just shook itself off and headed back towards the cottage and what was left of its supper.

Reeve edged the Citroën past the two wrecked smouldering cars. There was black smoke in the night sky. Surely somebody would see *that.* He scraped the Xantia against tree bark and blistered metal, but managed to squeeze past and back on to the track. He allowed himself a cold glint of a smile. His SAS training told him never to leave traces. When you were on a deep infiltration mission, you'd even shit into plastic bags and carry them with you. You left nothing behind. Well, he was leaving plenty this mission: at least two corpses, and a burnt-out Land Rover with British plates. He was going to be leaving a stolen car somewhere too, with blood on its steering-wheel. And these, it seemed to him, were the very least of his problems.

The very, very least.

He drove north, heading away from a horror he knew would surely follow.

His arms and shoulders began to ache, and he realised how tense he was, leaning into the steering-wheel as if the devil himself were behind him. He stopped only for petrol and to buy cans of caffeinated soft drinks, using them to wash down more caffeine tablets. He tried to act normally. In no way could he be said to resemble a tourist, so he decided he was a businessman, fatigued and stressed-out after a long sales trip, going home thankfully. He even got a tie out of his bag, letting it hang loosely knotted around his throat. He examined himself in the mirror. It would have to do. Of course, the driver of a French car should be French, too, so he tried not to say anything to anyone. At the petrol stations he kept to '*Bonsoir*' and '*Merci*'; ditto at the various *péage* booths.

Heading for Paris, he caught sight of signs for Orly. He knew either airport, Orly or Charles de Gaulle, would do. He was going to ditch the car. He figured the ports might be on the lookout for a stolen Xantia. And if the authorities weren't checking the ports, he reckoned his attackers almost certainly were. In which case they'd be checking the airports too. But he had a better chance of going undetected on foot.

He drove into an all-night car park at Orly. It was a multi-storey, and he took the Xantia to the top deck. There were only two other cars up here, both looking like long-stayers or cars which had been ditched. The Xantia would be company for them. But first of all he knew he needed sleep – his brain and body needed rest. He could sleep in the terminal maybe, but would be easy meat there. He reckoned there'd be no planes out till morning, and it wasn't nearly light yet. He wound the car windows open a couple of inches to help him hear approaching vehicles or footsteps. Then he laid his head back and closed his eyes . . .

He had a dream he'd had before. Argentina. Grassland and mountain slopes. Insects and a constant sea-breeze. Two canoes paddling for shore. In the dream, they paddled in daylight, but really they'd come ashore in the middle of the night, faces painted. Supposedly in silence, until Jay had started singing . . .

The same song he'd sung when they landed on the Falklands only a week before, taken ashore by boat on that occasion. Splashing on to the beach, meeting no resistance. And Jay humming the tune he'd been ordered to stop singing.

Row, row, row your boat
Gently down the stream.

Merrily, merrily, merrily, merrily,
Life is but a dream.

A dream? More like a nightmare when Jay was around. He was supposed to be a good soldier, but he was a firing-pin short of a grenade, and just as temperamental.

Just as lethal.

They'd sent for them after that firefight in the Falklands. They wanted to mount a two-man mission, deep surveillance. They were briefed onboard HMS *Hermes*. Their mission would be to keep watch on Argentinian aircraft flying out of Rio Grande. (Reeve was told only afterwards that another two-man unit was given the same brief with a different location: Rio Gallegos.) Nobody mentioned the words 'suicide mission', but the odds on coming back alive weren't great. For a start, the Argentinians on the Falklands had been equipped with Direction Finding equipment and thermal imagers; there was little to show that the same equipment wouldn't be available on the mainland.

Therefore, their radio signals out would be monitored and traced. Meaning they would have to stay mobile. But mobility itself was hazardous, and the possibility of thermal imagers meant they wouldn't even be able to rest at night. Getting in would be easy, getting out a nightmare.

Jay only demurred when his request for a few Stinger shoulder-launched anti-aircraft missiles was rejected out of hand.

'You're going in there to watch, not to fight. Leave the fighting to others.'

Which was just what Jay didn't want to hear.

Row, row, row your boat . . .

And in the dream that's what they did, with a line of men waiting for them on the beach. For some reason, the men couldn't locate them, though Reeve could see them clearly enough. But Jay's singing got louder and louder, and it was only a matter of time before the firing squad by the water's edge let loose at them.

Row, row, row your boat . . .

Reeve woke up in a sweat. Christ . . . And the true horror was that the reality had been so much worse than the dream, so awful that when he'd finally made it back to *Hermes* they'd refused to believe his version. They'd told him he must be hallucinating. Doctors told him shock could do that. And the more they denied the truth, the angrier he got, until that pink haze descended for the first time in his life and then lifted again, and a doctor and two orderlies were lying unconscious on the floor in front of him.

He sensed movement, something low to the ground and in shadow, over beside one of the other cars. He turned his headlamps on and picked out a thin, hungry-looking fox. A fox, scavenging on the top floor of a multi-storey car park. What was wrong with the fields? Had things got so bad for the foxes that they were moving into tower blocks? Well, Reeve could talk: he was *hiding* in a car park. Hiding because he was being hunted. Right now, he was being hunted by the bad guys; but all too soon the good guys – the so-called forces of law and order – would be hunting him too. He turned off the headlamps and got out of the car to exercise. Sit-ups and press-ups, plus some callisthenics. Then he looked in his travelling-bag. He didn't have much left in the way of clean clothes. At the first service station on the route he had scrubbed away the blood. There were dried stains on his jumper, but his white shirt was still clean. He was wearing it now. He'd tried cleaning his shoes, not very successfully. They looked like he'd been playing football in them.

In his bag he found Lucky 13. The dagger was a problem. He knew he couldn't hope to get it past airport security. It would have to stay here. But it was a murder weapon; he didn't want it found. He walked with the dagger over to the lift, and pressed the button for the lift to ascend. Then he wiped the dagger with his handkerchief, rubbing off fingerprints, and held it with the handkerchief. When the lift arrived, he leaned in, pressed the button for the floor below, and stepped out again as the doors were closing. He slipped the blade of the dagger into the gap between the doors and, as soon as the lift started to descend, used the blade to prise open the doors a couple of inches. Then he simply pushed the hilt and handle through the gap and let the dagger fall on to the roof of the lift, where it could lie until maintenance found it – always supposing these lifts *had* any maintenance.

It was still early so he sat in the car for a while. Then he got out and went over to the far wall, and leaned out so he could see the terminal building. There were two terminals, separated by a monorail, but this was the one he wanted, and he could walk to it. There were bright lights inside, and movement, taxis pulling up – the start of another day. He hadn't heard any flights leave in the past half hour, excepting a few light aircraft. But they would start leaving soon. During the night some larger planes had landed. At that hour, they had to be package operators or cargo.

Reeve made a final check on the contents of his bag, finding nothing immediately incriminating or suspicious. So he walked through the cool morning air towards the terminal building. He was starving, so he bought coffee and a sandwich first thing. He slung the bag over his shoulder so he could eat and drink as he walked. He walked amongst businessmen, all looking bleary-eyed and regretful, like they'd spent the previous night being unfaithful. He'd bet none of them had spent a night like his, but at least he was blending in better than expected. Just another dishevelled traveller up too early.

He felt a little more confident as he walked to the desk to buy a ticket. He just hoped they'd have a ticket to spare. They did, but the saleswoman warned him he'd have to pay full business rate.

'That's fine,' he said, sliding over his credit card. He was running up a huge bill on the card, but what did that matter when he might not be around come time to pay? Intimations of mortality bred a certain recklessness. Better financial recklessness than any other kind. He waited while the deal was done, looking for recognition in the woman's eyes as she took details of his name from his passport. But there was no recognition; the police weren't on to him yet. She handed back the passport and credit card, and then his ticket and boarding-card. Reeve thanked her and turned away.

There was a man watching him.

Or rather, he had *been* watching him. But now the man was staring at the morning headlines in his paper. Only he didn't look like he was reading them; Reeve would bet the man couldn't even read French. He could walk over and reassure himself of that with a couple of questions, but he couldn't cause a fuss here on the concourse, not when his flight was still some time away. So he walked casually in the direction of the toilets.

The toilets were up a passageway and around a corner, out of sight of the concourse. They faced one another, the Ladies and the Gents. There was a sign on a trestle outside the Ladies, saying the place was closed for cleaning and could customers please use the other toilets at the far end of the building. Reeve shifted the sign to the Gents and walked in.

He was lucky; there was nobody about. He set to work fast, looking around at the possibilities. Then he went to the sink nearest the door and turned the tap on full, stuffing the plughole with toilet paper. The sink started to fill. On the wall by the door there was an electric hand-drier. Perfect. On the far wall were some vending machines. Reeve dropped a ten-franc piece into one and pulled the drawer. The small package contained a tiny toothbrush, tube of toothpaste, Bic razor and comb. He threw the toothpaste and comb aside and got to work, smashing the head of the razor against the sink until he'd snapped off the plastic. He pushed half the blade's length into the head of the toothbrush until he was sure it was firmly lodged there. Now, holding the toothbrush by its handle, he had a scalpel of sorts.

Water was pouring on to the floor. He wondered how long it would be before his watcher would get suspicious and wonder what the hell was going on. Maybe he'd suspect another door, some sort of exit from the toilets. He would come to look. Reeve just hoped he wouldn't call in first, letting his boss or bosses know the score. He wanted one-on-one. He sat up on the edge of the sink, right in the corner of the room, and reached over to the hand-drier. An electric lead curled out from it and disappeared into the wall. Reeve pulled on the end of the flex nearest the drier, tugging it hard. Eventually it came away, but he kept on pulling. As he'd hoped, there was cable to spare inside the wall cavity. Electricians did that; it made it easier later if the unit had to be moved. He pulled out as much of the cable as he could. Then he waited. Water was still pouring on to the floor. He hoped the bastard would come soon, or maintenance might get nosy, or a businessman's breakfast coffee might work its way through . . .

The door opened. A man splashed into the water. It was the watcher. Reeve flicked the live end of the cable into his face, then hauled him into the room. With his hands up to his face, the man slipped on the wet floor and nearly fell. Reeve let the cable drop from his hand to the floor, connecting with the water, making the whole floor live. The man's face went into a rictus spasm and he fell to his knees, hands on the floor, which only made things worse. The electricity jerked him for another couple of seconds until Reeve hauled the flex away and rested it on the sinktops. Then he slid from his perch, crouched in front of the man, and held the blade to his throat.

The man was shaking all over, sparks still flying around inside. Some people got to like it, apparently. Reeve had been trained in interrogation techniques, and one of the instructors had told him that some prisoners got hooked on those jolts so that afterwards they kept plugging themselves into the mains, just for old time's sake . . .

'Who are you?' Reeve asked quietly. 'Who are you working for?'

'I don't know anything.'

Reeve nicked the throat, drawing a bead of blood. 'Last chance,' he hissed.

The man swallowed. He was big, and had probably been hired for that reason alone. But he was not smart – not really a professional to Reeve's mind – he'd fallen too easily. Reeve searched the pockets. The man was carrying cash, but nothing else, no papers, no ID, no telephone or radio.

'When's your RV?' Reeve asked.

'Noon,' the man said.

So he knew what RV meant; a lot of Americans would have taken the letters to mean Recreational Vehicle. So he'd served time in the armed forces.

'That's when your relief takes over?'

The man nodded. He could feel blood running down his throat but couldn't see any, not at the angle his face was at. Reeve would bet the cut felt worse than it actually was.

'What do you do if I'm spotted?'

'Watch you,' the man said, his voice unsteady. He was losing colour from his face. Reeve thought maybe the bastard was about to faint.

'And?'

'Call in to report.'

'Have you called?'

The man swallowed. 'Not yet.'

Reeve believed him, and was thankful. 'When you call in, what's the number?'

'It's in Paris.'

'Give it to me.'

The man recited the number.

'Who's on the other end of the phone?'

'I don't know.' More pressure with the blade, a fresh trickle of blood. 'He hired me in LA,' the man said quickly, 'at my gym. I don't know his name, I only know an initial.'

'Jay?'

The man blinked at him, then nodded. Reeve felt his own temperature plummet. It was true; of course it was true. Reeve drew back his fist and hit the man solidly on the side of the jaw. The head jerked, and all resistance went out of the body. Reeve dragged him into a cubicle and locked the door, then hauled himself up and over the door. He tossed the blade into a washbasin and pulled open the door. A man was standing outside, briefcase in hand. He wasn't sure about the sign. Reeve showed the man the floor.

'Flooding,' he said. 'Toilet's out of order.'

Then he walked back to the concourse and made straight for his departure gate.

Part Five

Birdy

14

Reeve tried to eat the proffered breakfast on the plane but found he had no appetite. Instead he asked for an extra orange juice, and then for another after that. Heathrow was busier than Orly had been, but he still couldn't spot anyone waiting for him. He went down to the tube station and made the call from the telephones there.

'Hello?' a voice answered.

Reeve waited.

'Hello?'

'Hello, Jay,' he said.

'I think you must have a wrong number.'

'Oh?'

There was a long pause at the other end. Reeve watched the units on his card click away. The voice came back on.

'Hey, Philosopher, is that you?'

'Yes.'

'What's new, pal?'

Like they'd spoken only last week and had parted the best of friends. Like Jay wasn't in charge of a band of mercenaries with orders to hunt Reeve down and terminate him. Like they were having a conversation.

'I thought you were dead,' Reeve stated.

'You mean you wish I was.'

'Every day,' Reeve said quietly.

Jay laughed. 'Where are you, pal?'

'I'm at Orly.'

'Yeah? Then you must have met Mickey.'

'He gave me your number.'

'I hope he charged you for it.'

'No, I charged him.'

'Well, I knew you'd be tough, Gordon.'

'You don't know how tough. Tell your paymasters that. Tell them I'm taking this personally. Not a job, not a mission, just personal.'

'Gordon, you're not really at Orly are you? Don't make me run all the way out there.'

'Maybe we'll talk again.'

'I don't think so, Philosopher.'

And Jay put the phone down first.

Reeve took the tube into central London.

He thought about Jay. Paddling ashore with him in darkness, hitting the coast just south of Viamonte. Their target, Rio Grande, was twenty miles to the north. They were on the Isla Grande de Tierra del Fuego, the western half of which belonged to Chile. If their escape route back to Viamonte was compromised, their best bet was to head west. A forty-mile walk from Rio Grande would take them into Chile.

Jay was carrying the transmitter, Reeve most of the rest of their kit. It was a 100lb load. Additionally, he carried his M16 rifle and 200 rounds. The M16 came fitted with an M203 grenade launcher. The other armaments consisted of 66mm anti-tank missile, fifteen HE grenades, 9mm Browning and an assortment of SAS flash-bangs more for cover than anything else.

He carried binoculars, night-sight and tripod-mounted 60× telescope, sleeping bag and quilted trousers, change of clothing, Arctic dried rations and 'compo' rations, plus a hexamine stove for cooking the latter.

And the song Jay had been singing had somehow stuck in his head, so he couldn't think straight.

They'd begun their march under cover of darkness, aiming to complete it before dawn. That first night, they knew they probably wouldn't reach a good spot for an OP. They'd just find a good hiding place, maybe making a scrape and lying doggo all the next day under their netting and camouflage. And that was what they did. They maintained radio silence throughout. If only Jay was as easy to shut up . . .

'Fucking Argies better not expect *me* to eat their scummy corned beef again. You know how they make that stuff? I read about it in the *Sun* or somewhere. Makes sausages look like best fillet steak, I swear to God, Philosopher.'

He was a good-looking man, a bit heavy in the face, but with short fair hair and bluey-grey eyes. His looks were his best feature. Reeve didn't like him and didn't know too many men who did. He was a braggart, cruel and bullying; he followed orders, but always with his own agenda hidden in there somewhere. Reeve didn't know if he was a good soldier or not; he just knew he didn't like him.

But there was something else about Jay. Early on in the conflict, he'd been part of a team dropped by Wessex helicopter on to the Fortuna Glacier. It was an important reconnaissance mission. They landed in near-whiteout conditions and 60 mph winds. Snow turned their guns to ice. They had somehow to cross the glacier. In the first five hours they progressed less than half a mile. To save them from freezing to death, they erected tents, but these blew away. Finally, the order came to abandon the mission. A helicopter sent in to lift the men out crashed in the blizzard conditions, killing three. A second chopper eventually succeeded in getting everyone out. Most of the survivors were suffering from exposure and frostbite. Jay's cheek had been slashed in the crash and required seven stitches.

He should have been out of action for days, weeks even, but insisted he wanted straight back in. The command applauded his readiness, and a psychologist could see no after effects from the ordeal. But Jay wasn't the same. His mind was on revenge, on killing Argentines. You could see it behind his eyes.

'You know, Philosopher,' Jay said in the scrape that first night, 'you may not be the most popular man in the regiment, but I think you're all right. Yes, you'll do me.'

Reeve bit off a question. He's just trying to wind me up, he thought. That's all. Let it go. The mission's all that counts.

Jay seemed to read his thoughts. There was a roaring in the sky east of them. 'Rio Grande's getting plenty of action tonight. Wasn't that a film, *Rio Grande?*'

'John Wayne and Dean Martin,' Reeve told him.

'Now Dean Martin, there's an actor for you.'

'Yes, a fucking awful one.'

'You're wrong. Ever see Matt Helm? Or those comedies he did? Great actor.'

Reeve just shook his head.

'Don't shake your head, I'm serious. You can't let anybody else have a say, can you? That's why you're not popular. I'm only telling you for your own good.'

'Fuck off, Jay.' He liked to be called Jay. Most of the Regiment were known by their first names, but not Jay. He liked people to use his surname. Nobody knew why. He called Reeve the Philosopher after finding him reading Nietzsche. The nickname had stuck, though Reeve hated it.

The second evening, they set up the OP proper with a half-decent view of the airfield. That night, they sent out their first signals, then moved again double-quick, an eight-man Argentinian patrol heading in their direction.

'They were fast,' Jay conceded, carrying the half-packed transmitter.

'Weren't they though,' said Reeve, almost slipping under the weight of his bergen. They must have picked up the transmission straight off. It had been no more than a burst of a few seconds. Whatever Direction Finding equipment they had down at the airport, it was earning its keep. Jay had sent a 'burst transmission': a coded message, its contents predetermined, which could be transmitted to sea in a split-second. Prior to transmission, he'd keyed the scrambled message on a machine which looked like a small electronic typewriter. In theory, the Argentines shouldn't have been able to DF them given the brevity of the transmission. Theory was a wonderful thing, but fuck all use on the ground. The Argentines obviously had some new bit of kit, something they hadn't been told about, something that Green Slime – the Intelligence Corps – had missed.

There was aircraft noise overhead as they moved. Skyhawks, Mirage jets. Earlier, there had been Pucaras too. The Argentine air force was keeping itself busy. Both men knew they should be noting the flights in and out, ready to send the information on. But they were too busy moving.

The main problem was the terrain. As with most airfields – and with good reason – there weren't many hills around. Flat grassland and brush with some outcrops, this was their territory. Hard territory in which to remain undiscovered for any length of time. They shifted a couple of miles and scraped themselves another hide. They were further away from the airfield, but still able to see what was flying out. Reeve stood guard – rather, *lay* guard – while Jay got some kip. They didn't dare brew up for fear of the steam being seen. Besides, you never knew what a heat-seeking device could find. So Reeve drank some cold water and ate raw rations. He was carrying out conversations in his head, all of them in Spanish. It might come in handy later. Maybe they could bluff . . . no, his Spanish wasn't that good. But he could use it if they were caught alive. He could show willing. Not that he was obliged to, not under the Geneva Convention, but then Geneva was a long way from here . . .

Reeve blinked his eyes. The tube compartment was full to bursting. He looked over his shoulder out of the grimy window and saw the station sign: Leicester Square. He got up and pushed his way out of the train, making for the Northern Line. Standing room only for the first couple of stops. He stood next to a very beautiful young woman, and stared at her reflection in the glass, using her to take his mind off the past.

He alighted at Archway, and after a couple of questions found Harrington Lane and Pete Cavendish's house. Cavendish was still in bed, but remembered him. When Reeve apologised and said what he wanted, Cavendish gave him the key and told him to bring it back when he was finished. He didn't need to ring the bell, just stick it through the letterbox.

'Thanks,' Reeve said. Cavendish nodded and closed the door again.

It took him a little while to figure out how to access the lane behind Cavendish's street, but eventually he found a road in, and walked down the lane until he found what looked like the right garage, empty cans and bottles and all. He unlocked the garage door and pulled it up. It took him a few goes, and a few gentle applications of a half-brick on to the rollers, but eventually the garage was open. Dogs were barking in a couple of the walled back gardens, making as much noise as he'd done.

'Arnie! Shuddup!' someone yelled. They sounded fiercer than any dog.

Reeve unlocked the car, fixed the choke on and turned the ignition. It took a while, reconditioned engine or not, but the car finally started, shuddering a little at first, then smoothing itself out. Reeve took it into the lane and kept it running while he went back to shut the garage door. This set the dogs off again, but he ignored them, relocked the garage, and got back into the Saab. He drove slowly to the end of the lane, avoiding glass and bricks and sacks of rubbish. A couple of lefts took him back into Cavendish's street, and he left the car long enough to put the garage key through the letterbox.

He searched for a London street-map, but didn't find one. The glove compartment didn't have one, and there was nothing under the seats. The car was what he'd call basic. Even the radio had been yanked out, leaving just wires and a connector. Basic maybe, but not as basic as his own Land Rover, its carcass somewhere in France. A lot had happened this past day and a half. He wanted to sit down and rest, but knew that that was the last thing he should do. He could drive to Jim's flat; maybe Fliss Hornby would be there. But he couldn't do that. He didn't want to put her in any danger, and he'd already seen what a visit from him could do to a woman on her own . . .

The tank was nearly empty, so he stopped in a station forecourt, filled up, and added a newspaper to his purchase. He sat flicking through, looking for a news story from France, finding nothing. He wondered how long it would take the French authorities to link the torched car to its owner. He guessed a couple of days max, which gave him today and maybe tomorrow. Maybe, but not for certain. He had to get moving.

He only had the one plan: advance. He'd tried a tactical retreat last night, and it had cost several lives, including, for all he knew, that of Marie Villambard. Now that he knew he was up against Jay, he didn't want to hide any more, and didn't think he *could* hide – not for ever. Not knowing Jay was out there. Therefore, the only tactic left was to advance. A suicide mission maybe, but at least it was a mission. He thought of Joan and Allan. He'd have to phone Joan; she'd be worried about him. Christ, what lies would he concoct this time? He couldn't possibly tell her about Marie Villambard. But not to tell her might mean that the first she'd hear of it would be the police knocking at her sister's door, asking his whereabouts. She'd hear their side of it, but not his.

Marie Villambard . . . Marie had said Jim would've kept copies of his working notes. He wouldn't have entrusted all his information to disks alone. He wondered if Marie herself had kept an extra set, maybe with another journalist. Would someone else pick up her baton? A safe place, she'd said: maybe a friend's flat or a bank vault. Reeve turned back and headed to Pete Cavendish's. Cavendish couldn't believe it.

'This is a nightmare,' he said. 'I told you to stick the key through the letterbox.'

'I did that,' Reeve said, pointing to the spot on the floor where the key lay.

'What then?'

'It's just, my brother trusted you with his car. I wondered if you were keeping anything else safe for him.'

'Such as?'

'I don't know. Some files, a folder, papers . . . ?'

Cavendish shook his head.

'Maybe he told you not to tell anyone, Pete, but he's dead and I'm his brother—'

'He didn't give me anything, all right?'

Reeve stared into Cavendish's eyes and believed him. 'Okay, sorry,' he said, starting back down the path.

'Hey!' Cavendish yelled after him.

Reeve turned. 'What?'

'How's the motor running?'

Reeve looked at the idling Saab. 'Sweet as a nut,' he said, wondering how soon he could ditch it.

Tommy Halliday lived in Wales, because he thought the air and drinking water there were better; but he didn't have much affection for the Welsh, so lived as close to the border with England as he could while remaining near a funny place-name. Halliday lived in Penycae; the funny place-name was Rhosllanerchrugog. On the map it looked like a bad lot of Scrabble tiles, except that there were way too many letters.

'You can't miss it on the map,' Halliday had told Reeve, the first time Reeve was planning a visit. 'They always like to put Rhosllanerchrugog in nice big bold letters, just to show what silly fuckers the Welsh are. In fact, everybody round here just calls it Rhos.'

'What does it mean?' Reeve had asked.

'What?'

'The word must mean something.'

'It's a warning,' Halliday had said. 'It says: The English are coming!'

Halliday had a point. Penycae was close to Wrexham, but it was also within commuting distance of Chester, Liverpool, even Stoke-on-Trent. Consequently, English settlers were arriving, leaving the grime and crime behind, sometimes bringing it with them.

All Halliday had brought with him were his drug deals, his video collection and his reference books. Halliday hated films but was hooked on them. Actually, more than the films themselves he was hooked on the film *critics*. Barry Norman was god of this strange religion, but there were many other high priests: Maltin, Ebert, Kael, *Empire, Premiere* and *Sight and Sound* magazines. What got Reeve was that Halliday never went to a cinema. He didn't like being with other people, strangers, for two darkened hours. He rented and bought videos instead. There were probably six or seven hundred in his living room, more elsewhere in the semi-detached house.

For Halliday, films were not entertainment. His tussle with the movie form was like a student tackling some problem of philosophy. It was as though, if Halliday could work out films – why some were good, others bad, a few works of genius – then he would have solved a major problem, something that would change his life for the better and for always. When Reeve turned up at the house, Halliday was in a tizz. He'd just found an old *Guardian* review by Derek Malcolm panning Tarantino's *Pulp Fiction*.

'You should see the reviews in *Empire* and *Premiere*,' he said irritably, 'they loved that film.'

'What did you think of it?' Reeve waited in the hall while Halliday triple-locked the reinforced front door. He knew Halliday's neighbours thought the reason his curtains were always closed was that Halliday was busy watching films. There was a rumour Halliday was writing a film of his own. Or that he was some English director who'd made a packet in Hollywood and decided to retire young.

He looked younger than his years, with thinning short red hair, a faceful of freckles, and tapering ginger sideburns plus dark red moustache. He was tall and lanky with arms that seemed to be controlled by someone else. He flapped them as he led Reeve down the short hall into the living room.

'What did I think of it? I agreed with *Empire*.'

Halliday seldom had an opinion of his own – only what he'd gleaned from the reviewers and the theorists. There was a homemade bookcase, precariously angled, which held his store of film knowledge. There were library books and books he'd bought or lifted from shops. There were bound volumes of magazines, scrapbooks full of reviews from newspapers and magazines. He had video recordings of several years' worth of Barry Norman and the other film programmes. He slumped into his large easy-chair and jerked a hand towards the sofa. There was, of course, a film playing on the TV.

'Going through your Scorsese period?' Reeve asked. He recognised the film as *Mean Streets*. 'How many times have you watched this one?'

'About a dozen. There are a lot of tricks he does here that he uses again in other films. Look, this slo-mo run through the bar. That's in *Goodfellas*. Later there's a good bit with Harvey Keitel pissed. How come Keitel plays Catholics so often?'

'I hadn't noticed he did.'

'Yeah, I read that somewhere . . .' Halliday's eyes were on the screen. 'Music, too, the way he uses music in this film, like he does in *Goodfellas*.'

'Tommy, did you get the birdy?'
Halliday nodded. 'You're not going to like it.'
'How do you mean?'
Halliday just rubbed his thumb and forefinger together.
'Not cheap, huh?'
'Not cheap. The Colombians I used to deal with, they aren't around any more. They worked for the Medellin cartel, but the Medellin people got shafted by the Cali cartel. So now I seem to be dealing with Cali, and they're not quite so – I don't know – friendly. Plus, as you know, this stuff is thick on the ground in Colombia but thin on the ground over here . . .' He looked at Reeve and smiled. 'Thank God.'
'So what did it cost?'
Halliday told him.
'What, did I buy the whole fucking crop?'
'You bought enough to get you into bed with the Dagenham Girl Pipers.'
Looking around the living room, or indeed the rest of the house, you would not suspect Tommy Halliday of being a dealer in everything from drugs to arms. That was because he kept absolutely nothing incriminating on the premises. Nobody knew where the cache was hidden, but Reeve guessed it was another reason for Tommy's choice of this part of Wales. There was a lot of countryside around, mountains and forests frequented by hillwalkers and picnickers – a lot of potential hiding places in those sorts of terrain.
No, the only things about Tommy's house that might make someone suspicious were the anti-surveillance devices and the mobile phone. Tommy didn't trust to British Telecom, and in the house he used the phone with a portable scrambler attached. The scrambler was US Intelligence Corps standard, and Reeve guessed it had been 'lost' during the Iraqi war. A lot of armed forces equipment had been lost during the campaign; a lot of Iraqi gear had been picked up quietly and tucked away for resale back in Britain.
Most of the arms Tommy dealt in, however, were eastern bloc: Russian and Czech predominantly. He had a consignment of Chinese stuff for a while, but couldn't give it away it was so unreliable.
Halliday glanced at his watch. 'Wait till this film's over, all right?'
'I've got all the time in the world, Tommy,' Reeve said. He didn't mean it, but he found that the time spent in the living room was time well spent. He cleared his mind and relaxed his muscles, did a little bit of meditation, some breathing exercises Joan had shown him. He gathered himself. And when he'd finished, there was still half an hour to go.
'Mind if I use the equipment?' he asked.
'You know where it is.'
So he headed upstairs into the spare bedroom, where Tommy kept his weights and a couple of exercise machines. Reeve worked up a sweat. Sweat was the quickest way to void toxins from your body, assuming you weren't in the mood for sticking two fingers down your throat. From now on there was a regime he would follow: exercise when he could, and eat well. Keep his mind and body pure. He would guess Jay had kept fit. He'd recruited from a gym: no mere accident. He probably frequented a few gyms. Reeve had to prepare as best he could. He considered taking steroids, but ruled

them out quickly: their effects were short-lived, the side effects long-lasting. There was no 'quick fix' when it came to fitness. Reeve knew he was pretty fit; family life hadn't completely destroyed him, it had just robbed him of a little will power.

Joan – he should call Joan. When he got downstairs the film was finished and Halliday was on his computer. The computer was new, and boasted CD-ROM. Halliday was studying some kind of film encyclopaedia, open at *Mean Streets*.

'Look here,' he said, pointing feverishly at the screen. 'Maltin gives it four stars; "a masterpiece"; Ebert gives it four, Baseline gives it four out of five. Even Pauline bloody Kael likes it.'

'So?'

'So it's a film about a couple of arseholes, one smarter than the other, but both of them plainly fucked from the start. This is supposed to be great cinema?'

'What did you think of De Niro?'

'He played it the same way he always plays those roles, eyes all over the place, demented smile.'

'You think he's like that in real life?'

'What?'

'What do you think his background is?'

Halliday couldn't see where this was leading, but he was prepared to learn. 'Street punk, a kid in Brooklyn or wherever, same as Scorsese.' He paused. 'Right?'

Reeve shook his head. 'Look up De Niro.'

Halliday clicked the cursor over the actor's name. A biography and photograph came up.

'See?' Reeve said, pointing to the relevant line. 'His parents were artists, painters. His father was an abstract expressionist. This isn't a street kid, Tommy. This is a well-brought-up guy who wanted to be an actor.'

'So?'

'So he made you believe in his *character*. You got no inkling of his background; that's because he submerged it. He became a role. That's what acting is.' Reeve watched to see if any of this sank in. 'Can I use your telephone?'

Halliday flapped an arm towards the window sill.

'Thanks.'

Reeve walked over to the window.

'So you know about films, huh?' Halliday called.

'No, Tommy, but I sure as shit know about acting.' He picked up the telephone and dialled Joan's sister. While he waited for an answer, he pulled the curtains apart an inch and looked out on to the ordinary lower-middle-class street. He'd parked the Saab outside another house: that was an easy rule to remember. Someone answered his call.

'Hi there,' he said, recognising Joan's voice. The relief in her next words was evident.

'Gordon, where are you?'

'I'm at a friend's.'

'How are you?'

'I'm fine, Joan. How's Allan?' Reeve watched Halliday get up from the computer and go to a bookshelf. He was searching for something.

'He's missing you. He's hardly seen you lately.'

'Everything else okay?'

'Sure.'

'No funny phone calls?'

'No.' She sounded hesitant. 'You think they'll find us here?'

'I shouldn't think so.' But how difficult would it be to track down the wife of Gordon Reeve, to ascertain that she had one brother and one sister, to locate addresses for both? Reeve knew that if they needed a bargaining chip, they'd resort to anything, including ransoming his family.

'You still there?'

'Sorry, Joan, what did you say?'

'I said how much longer?'

'I don't know. Not long, I hope.'

The conversation wasn't going well. It wasn't just that Halliday was in the room; it was that Reeve was fearful of saying too much. In case Joan worried. In case someone was listening. In case they got to her and wanted to know how much she knew . . .

'I love you,' she said quietly.

'Same goes,' he managed, finishing the call. Halliday was standing by the bookcases, a large red volume in his hand. It was an encyclopaedia. Reeve walked over and saw he had it open at Art History, a section about abstract expressionism. Reeve hoped he hadn't set Halliday off on some new tangent of exploration.

He touched Halliday's shoulder. 'The birdy,' he said.

Halliday closed the book. 'The birdy,' he agreed.

Birdy was their name for *burundanga,* a drug popular with the Colombian underworld. It used to be manufactured from scopolamine extracted from the flowers of the *borachero* tree, *Datura arborea*, but these days it was either mixed with benzodiazepine, or else it was one hundred percent benzodiazepine, this being safer than scopolamine, with fewer, less harmful side effects.

Reeve followed Halliday's car. Tommy Halliday was as cautious as they came. He'd already taken Reeve's money and left it at the house. Reeve had made a large withdrawal in a London branch of his bank. They'd had to phone his branch in Edinburgh for confirmation, and even then Reeve had taken the receiver and spoken to the manager himself. They knew one another pretty well. The manager had come on one of Reeve's tamer weekends.

'I won't ask what it's for,' the manager said, 'just don't spend it all in London.'

They'd had a laugh at that. It *was* a large amount of money, but then Reeve kept a lot of money in his 'sleeper' account; an account he kept hidden from Joan and from everyone else, even his accountant. It wasn't that the sleeper money was dirty, it was just that he liked to have it as a fallback, the way SAS men often took money with them when they went on missions behind enemy lines – gold sovereigns usually. Money for bribes, money for times of desperate trouble. That's what Reeve's sleeper fund was, and he judged this to be exactly the sort of time and occasion it was meant for.

He hadn't been expecting the birdy to cost quite so much. It would put a big dent in his bankroll. The rest of the money was for contingencies.

It would give the police something else to mull over, too, once they'd connected him to the mess in France. They might well find the account – his bank manager wouldn't lie about it – and they'd wonder about this large withdrawal, so soon after the killings. They'd be even more suspicious. They'd most definitely be 'anxious' to talk to him, as they put it in their press releases.

Well, Tommy Halliday had some of that money now. And once he'd handed over the powder, that would be goodbye. Reeve wouldn't be allowed to return to Halliday's house, not carrying drugs. So Reeve had asked his questions beforehand. Like, was it scopo, benzo, or a mix?

'How the fuck do I know?' Halliday had replied. 'It's tough to get scopo these days, so my guess is pure benzo.' He considered. 'Mind, these Colombians have good stuff, so maybe it's ten, fifteen percent scopo.'

'Enough to put someone in a psychiatric ward?'

'No way.'

The problem with scopolamine was, there was just the one antidote – physostigmine – and neither man knew how readily available it was to hospital casualty and emergency departments, supposing they were able to diagnose *burundanga* poisoning in the first place. The drug was little known and little used outside Colombia; and even when it was used outside that country, it was normally used by native Colombians. No one in the British Army would admit to ever having used it as an interrogation aid. No, no one would ever admit that. But Reeve knew about the drug from his days in the SAS. He'd seen it used once, deep undercover in Northern Ireland, and he'd heard of its use in the Gulf War.

'Is there any physostigmine with it?'

'Course not.'

Tommy Halliday drove into the hills. He drove for half an hour, maybe a little more, until he signalled to pull into the half-full car park of a hotel. It was a nice-looking place, well lit, inviting. The car park was dark though, and Halliday pulled into the farthest, gloomiest corner. Reeve pulled up alongside him. They wound their windows down so they could talk without leaving their cars.

'Let's give it a couple of minutes,' Halliday said, 'just to be on the safe side.' So they waited in silence, headlights off, waiting to see if anyone would follow them into the car park. No one did. Eventually, Halliday turned his engine on again and leaned out of his window. 'Go into the bar, stay there one hour. Leave your boot slightly open when you go. Does it lock automatically?'

'Yes.'

'Right, that's where the stuff will be. Okay?'

'One hour?' Reeve checked the time.

'Synchronise watches,' Halliday said with a grin. 'See you next time, Reeve.'

He backed out of the space and drove sedately out of the car park.

Reeve had half a mind to follow. He'd like to know where the cache was. But Halliday was too careful; it would be hard work. An hour. He'd guess the stuff was only ten minutes away. Halliday would take his time getting there though, and he'd take his time coming back. A very careful man; a man with a lot to lose.

Reeve locked the car, opened the boot, and walked in through the back door of the hotel, into warmth, thick red carpeting, and wood-panelled walls. There was a reception area immediately ahead, but the bar was to his right. He could hear laughter. The place wasn't busy, but the regulars were noisy as only regulars are allowed to be. Reeve prepared smiles and nods, and ordered a half of Theakston's Best. There was a newspaper on the bar, an evening edition. He took it with his drink to a corner table.

He was thinking about the long drive ahead, back to Heathrow, not much relishing the idea. It would be good to stay put for a night, tucked between clean sheets in a hotel room. Good, but dangerous. He checked the newspaper. On one of the inside pages there was a 'News Digest' column, seven or eight single-paragraph stories. The story he'd been dreading was half-way down.

> FRENCH FARMHOUSE MURDER MYSTERY
>
> French police confirmed today that a burnt-out car found at the scene of a murder had UK licence plates. Three bodies were discovered near a farmhouse in a densely wooded area of Limousin. One unidentified victim had been savaged by a dog, which belonged to one of the remaining two victims, a local journalist. The journalist was killed by a single bullet to the head, while the third victim was stabbed to death.

Reeve read the story through again. So they hadn't taken Marie – or if they had, they hadn't taken her far. The first thing the police would have done was shoot the dog. Reeve felt bad: Foucault had saved his life. And Marie . . . well, maybe she'd have died anyway. She was almost certainly on somebody's list. Police would have linked the deaths to the Land Rover. Maybe they'd think one of the other bodies was that of the owner. It depended on the other car, the one Reeve had backed into. He doubted they'd be able to track it down. It had probably been stolen. But they could track *his* car down.

He went into the lobby and found a telephone. There were three of them, each in its own booth with stool, ledge, writing-pad and pen. Reeve phoned Joan again.

'What is it?' she said.

'Something I've got to tell you. I was hoping I wouldn't have to so soon.'

'What?'

'The police may come asking questions. The thing is, I had to leave the Land Rover in France.'

'France?'

'Yes. Now listen, there were some bodies at the scene.' He heard her inhale. 'The police are going to come looking for me.'

'Oh, Gordon . . .'

'It may take them a few more days to get to you. Here's the thing: you don't know where I was going, you only know I said I had to go away on business. You don't know what I'd be doing in France.'

'Why didn't you tell me any of this before?' She wasn't crying, crying wasn't her style. Angry was her style – angry and let down.

'I couldn't. Last time I phoned, there was someone else in the room.'

'Yes, but you could have told me before now. Look, is this all about Jim?'

'I think so.'

'Then why not just tell the police your side of it?'

'Because my side of it, as things stand, doesn't amount to anything. I've no evidence, no proof; I've nothing. And the men who did it, the police would have trouble finding them.'

'You know who did it?'

'I know who's responsible.' Reeve was running out of money. 'Look, just don't tell the police any more than you have to. They may think one of the bodies is mine. They may ask you to identify the body.'

'And I just go along with it, like we haven't spoken? I have to look at this dead man?'

'No, you can say we've spoken since, so you know it can't be me.'

She groaned. 'I really think you should go to the police, Gordon.'

'I'm going to the police.' Reeve allowed himself a small smile.

'What?'

'Only not here.'

'Where then?'

'I can't tell you that. Look, trust me, Joan. You're safest if we play it this way. Just trust me, okay?'

She didn't say anything for a long time. Reeve feared his money would run out before she did say something.

'All right,' she said, 'but Gordon—'

The money ran out.

Back in the bar, no one had touched his drink or his paper. He'd left the paper folded at the crossword, but now opened it up again and read, or at least stared at the headlines. He didn't think they'd be watching the airports yet – well, the police wouldn't. Jay and his team might, but he thought they were probably gone by now. Regrouping, awaiting new orders. One mission was over for them; only a partial success. He guessed they'd be back in the States, maybe in San Diego.

Which was exactly where he was headed.

After sixty minutes, he went back out to his car. At first he couldn't see anything in the boot. Halliday had tucked it deep underneath the lip. It was nothing really, a small packet – white paper, folded over. Reeve got into the car and carefully unfolded the A4 sheet. He stared at some yellowy-white powder, about enough for a teaspoon. Even with the interior light on, the stuff didn't look pure. Maybe it was diluted with baking soda or something. Maybe it was just a benzo-scopo mix. There was enough of it though. Reeve knew how much he needed: just over two milligrams a dose. Three or four per dose to be on the safe side; or on the *un*safe side if you happened to be the recipient. He knew the stuff would dissolve in liquid, becoming only very slightly opalescent. He knew it had no flavour, no smell. It was so perfect, it was like the Devil himself had made it in his lab, or dropped the *borrachero* seeds in Eden.

Reeve refolded the paper and put it in his jacket pocket.

'Beautiful,' he said, starting the car.

On the way south, he thought about how Tommy Halliday might have stitched him up, or been stitched up himself. The powder could be a cold remedy, simple aspirin. Reeve could take it all the way to the States and find only at the last crucial minute that he'd been sold a placebo. Maybe he should test it first.

Yes, but not here. It could wait till America.

'Another bloody night in the car,' he muttered to himself. And another aeroplane at the end of it.

15

Allerdyce had taken what for him was a momentous, unparalleled decision.

He'd decided he had to tread carefully with Kosigin and Co-World Chemicals. As a result, there was to be no more discussion of either topic within the walls of Alliance Investigative – not in his office, not in the corridors, not even in the elevators. Instead, Dulwater had to report, either by telephone or in person, to Allerdyce's home.

Allerdyce had always kept his office and home lives discrete – insofar as he never entertained at home, and no Alliance personnel ever visited him there, not even the most senior partners. No one except the dog handlers. He had an apartment in downtown Washington DC, but much preferred to return daily to his home on the Potomac.

The house was just off an AAA-designated 'scenic byway' between Alexandria and George Washington's old home at Mount Vernon. If streams of tourist traffic passed by his house, Allerdyce didn't know about it. The house was hidden from the road by a tall privet hedge and a wall, and separated by an expanse of lawn and garden. It was a colonial mansion with its own stretch of riverfront, a jetty with a boat in mooring, separate servants' quarters, and a nineteenth-century ice-house which was now Allerdyce's wine cellar. It wasn't as grand as Mount Vernon, but it would do for Jeffrey Allerdyce.

Had he chosen to entertain clients there, the house and grounds would have served as a demonstration of some of the most elaborate security on the market: electronic gates with video identification, infra-red trip beams surrounding the house, a couple of very well-trained dogs, and two security guards on general watch at all times. The riverfront was the only flaw in the security; anyone could land from the water. So the security men concentrated on the river and let the dogs and devices deal with the rest.

The reason for all the security at Allerdyce's home was not fear of assassination or kidnap, or simple paranoia, but because he kept his secrets there – his files on the great and good, information he might one day use. There were favours there that he could call in; there were videotapes and photographs which could destroy politicians and judges and the writers of Op-Ed pages. There were audio recordings, transcripts, scribbled notes, sheafs of clippings, and even more private information: copies of bank statements and bounced cheques, credit card billings, motel registration books, logs of telephone calls, police reports, medical examination results, blood tests, judicial reviews . . . Then there were the rumours, filed away with everything else: rumours of affairs, homosexual love-ins, cocaine habits, stabbings, falsified court evidence, misappropriated court evidence, misappropriated funds, numbered accounts in Caribbean islands, mafia connections, Cuban connections, Colombian connections, wrong connections . . .

Allerdyce had contacts at the highest levels. He knew officials in the FBI and CIA and NSA, he knew secret servicemen, he knew a couple of good people at the Pentagon. One person gained him access to another person, and the network grew. They knew they could come to him for a favour, and if the favour was something like covering up an affair or some sticky, sordid jam they'd gotten into – well, that gave Allerdyce just the hold he wanted. That went down in his book of favours. And all the time the information grew and grew. Already he had more information than he knew what to do with, more than he might use in his lifetime. He didn't know what he'd do with his vast (and still increasing) store of information when he died. Burn it? That seemed a waste. Pass it on? Yes – but to whom? The likeliest candidate seemed his successor at Alliance. After all, the organisation would be sure to prosper with all that information in the bank. But Allerdyce had no successor in mind. His underlings were just that; the senior partners ageing and comfortable. There were a couple of junior partners who were hungry, but neither seemed right. Maybe he should have fathered some children . . .

He sat in the smaller of the two dining rooms and considered this, staring at a portrait of his grandfather, whom he remembered as a vicious old bastard and tight-fisted with it. Genes: some you got, some you didn't. The cook, a homely woman, brought in his appetiser, which looked like half a burger bun topped with salmon and prawns and a dollop of mayonnaise. Allerdyce had just picked up his fork when the telephone rang. Maybe two dozen people knew his home telephone number. More knew his apartment number, and he kept in touch by monitoring the answering machine there morning and evening. He placed his napkin on the brightly polished walnut table and walked over to the small antique bureau – French, seventeenth-century, he'd been told – that supported the telephone.

'Yes?' he said.

There was a moment's pause. He could hear static and echoes on the line, like ghostly distant voices, and then a much clearer one.

'Sir, it's Dulwater.'

'Mm-hm.'

'I thought I'd let you know the situation here.'

'Yes?'

'Well, I kept watch on the house, but nobody's been near. So I decided to take a look around.'

Allerdyce smiled. Dulwater was an effective burglar, he'd used the skill several times in the past. Allerdyce wondered what he'd found in Gordon Reeve's home. 'Yes?' he repeated.

'Looks like they've moved out for a while. There's a litter tray and a bunch of cat food, but no cat. Must've taken it with them. The cat's name's on the food bowl. Bakunin. I checked the name, thought it was a bit strange, turns out the historical Bakunin was an anarchist. There are books on anarchism and philosophy in the bedroom. I think maybe they left in a hurry; the computer was still on in the kid's bedroom. The telephones were bugged, sure enough – hard to tell who did it; the mikes are standard enough but they *are* US-sourced.'

Dulwater paused, awaiting praise.

'Anything else?' Allerdyce snapped. He sensed Dulwater was saving something.

'Yes, sir. I found a box of magazines, old copies of something called *Mars and Minerva*.' Another pause. 'It's the official magazine of the SAS.'

'SAS? That's a British Army unit, isn't it?'

'Yes sir, mostly counter-revolutionary warfare: hostage rescue, deep infiltration behind enemy lines in time of war . . . I've got some stuff from the libraries here.'

Allerdyce studied his fingernails. 'No wonder Reeve dealt so diligently with the two personnel. Have you spoken to them?'

'I made sure their boss got the picture. They've been kicked out.'

'Good. Is that everything?'

'Not quite. There was some action in France – a journalist was killed. Her name was Marie Villambard. I recognised the name because it was thrown up during our background search on James Reeve. He'd had some contacts with her.'

'What happened?'

'I'm not absolutely certain. Looks like a firefight. A couple of burnt-out cars, one of them British. The Villambard woman was shot execution-style, another guy had his face ripped off by a guard dog. Last victim had his throat cut. They found other bloodstains, but no more bodies.'

Allerdyce was quiet for a minute. Dulwater knew better than to interrupt the silence. Finally, the old man took a deep breath. 'It seems Kosigin has chosen a bad opponent – or a very good one, depending on your point of view.'

'Yes, sir.'

Allerdyce could tell Dulwater didn't understand. 'It seems unlikely Reeve will give up, especially if police trace the car back to him.'

'Always supposing it's his car,' Dulwater said.

'Yes. I'm trying to think if we have contacts in Paris . . . I believe we do.'

'I could go down there . . .'

'No, I don't think so. What is there to find? We'll have Paris take care of that side of things for us. So Reeve is ex-Army, eh? Some special unit. What some would call a tough nut to crack.'

'There's just one more thing, sir.'

Allerdyce raised an eyebrow. 'More? You've been busy, Dulwater.'

'This is conjecture.'

'Go on.'

'Well, the muscle Kosigin's using, the one from LA. He's supposed to be English.'

'So?'

'So, he's also supposed to have been in the SAS.'

Allerdyce smiled. 'That could be interesting. Dulwater, you've done remarkably well. I want you back here.'

'Yes, sir.'

'And Dulwater?'

'Sir?'

'Upgrade your flight to Club; the company will pay.'

'Thank you, sir.'

Allerdyce terminated the call and returned to the dining table, but he was too excited to eat. He didn't know where this story was headed, but he knew the outcome would be anything but mundane. Allerdyce could foresee trouble for Kosigin and CWC. They might have need of Alliance's services again; there might be a favour Kosigin would need. There might well be a favour.

Maybe he'd underestimated Dulwater. He pictured him in his mind – a large man, quiet, not exactly handsome, always well dressed, a discreet individual, reliable – and wondered if there was room for a promotion. More than that, he wondered if there was a necessity. He finished his water and attacked the food. His cook was already appearing, wheeling a trolley on which were three covered silver salvers.

'Is it chicken today?' Allerdyce asked.

'You had chicken yesterday,' she said in her lilting Irish brogue. 'It's fish today.'

'Excellent,' said Jeffrey Allerdyce.

Part Six

Closed Doors

16

Reeve had flown in to New York's JFK. It had been just about the only route open to him at such short notice. The good news was he'd been offered a cheap seat that had been cancelled at the last minute. The woman behind the desk had seemed to take pity on him. He put the flight on his credit card. He couldn't know if Jay and his men – or whoever they worked for – had access to his credit card transactions, or to flight information and passenger lists; if they did, it would take a day or two for his name to filter down to them. And by then he wouldn't be in New York any more.

The passport control at JFK had taken a while, lots of questions to be answered. He'd filled in his card on the plane. The officer at passport control stapled half of it back into his passport and stamped it. They'd done that last time too, but no one had checked his passport going home. The officer had asked him the purpose of his visit.

'Business and pleasure,' Reeve said.

The official marked that he could stay three weeks. 'Have a nice trip, sir.'

'Thank you.'

And Reeve was back in the US.

He didn't know New York, but there was an information booth in the terminal, and they told him how to get into town and that there was another booth offering tourist accommodation along the other end of the concourse.

Reeve changed some money before heading for the coach into Manhattan. The information booth had provided him with a little pocket map, and his hotel was now circled on it in red. So he'd asked for another map, clean this time, and had torn the other one up and thrown it away. He didn't want anyone knowing which hotel he'd be staying at – if someone so much as looked over his shoulder, it would have been easy with the marked map. He was gearing himself up, ready for whatever they threw at him. And hoping maybe he could throw something at *them* first.

He was wearing a roomy pair of trainers he'd bought duty free at Heathrow. He'd divvied the birdy up into halves, folded each in a torn section of paper towel, and secreted one in either trainer, tucked into the cushioned instep. He'd also bought a clean polo-shirt and sports jacket – again on the credit card. He wanted to look like a tourist for the authorities at JFK but, since he didn't want to look like a tourist on the streets of New York, he'd kept his old clothes so he could change back into them.

His hotel was on East 34th, between Macy's and the Empire State Building, as the man in the booth had informed him. He tried not to think about how much it was costing. It was only for one night after all, two at most, and he reckoned he deserved some comfort after what he'd been through. Christ alone knew what lay ahead. The coach dropped him off outside Penn-Central, and he walked from there.

It was morning, though his body clock told him it was mid-afternoon. The receptionist said he shouldn't really book in until noon, but saw how red his eyes were and checked her computer, then phoned maid service. It turned out she could give him a room after all, freshly cleaned – she'd just have to tweak a reservation. He thanked her and headed upstairs. He lay down on his bed and closed his eyes. The room spun around him in his darkness. It was like the bed was on a turntable set to 17 r.p.m. Jim's first record player had been a Dansette with a setting for 17 r.p.m. They'd played Pinky & Perky records on it. The pigs had sounded like ordinary people. It was just a matter of slowing them down.

Reeve got up and ran a bath. The water pressure was low. He imagined a dozen maids all rinsing baths at the same time, preparing the rooms for new guests, guests who came and went and left nothing behind.

He remembered a quote he'd read in one of his books: something about life being a river, the water never the same for any two people who walked through it. He'd remembered it, so it must have meant something to him at the time. Now he wasn't so sure. He studied his face in the bathroom mirror. It was getting ugly, all tensed and scowling. It had looked that way in Special Forces: a face you prepared for when you met the enemy, a permanently pissed-off look. He'd lost it over time as he'd let his muscles relax, but he was getting it again now. He noticed that he was tensing his stomach muscles too, as though readying to repel a punch in the guts. And his whole body tingled – not just from jet lag; senses were kicking in. You might call them a sixth sense, except that there was more than one of them. One told you if someone was watching you, one told you someone you couldn't see was near. There was one that told you whether to run left or right to dodge gunfire.

Some of his colleagues in Special Forces hadn't believed in the senses. They'd put it down to sheer luck if you beat the clock. For Reeve it was instinct, it was about picking open part of your brain normally kept locked. He thought maybe Nietzsche had meant something similar with his 'superman'. You had to unlock yourself, find the hidden potential. Above all, you had to live dangerously.

'How am I doing, old man?' Reeve said out loud, slipping into the bath.

In Queens, the fashion accessory of choice was the stare.

Reeve, though dressed in his needing-a-wash non-tourist clothes, still got plenty of stares. His map of downtown Manhattan wouldn't help him here. This was a place they told strangers to avoid. His cab driver had taken some persuading; the yellow cab had been idling outside the hotel, looking for a fare up to Central Park or over to JFK if he was on a roll, but when Reeve had asked for Queens, the man had turned to examine him like he'd just asked to be taken to Detroit.

'Queens?' the man had said. He looked Puerto Rican, a ribbon of black curly hair falling from his oily baseball cap. 'Queens?'

'Queens.'

The driver had shaken his head slowly. 'Can't do it.'

'Sure you can, we just need to discuss the fare.'

So they'd discussed the fare.

Reeve had spent a lot of time with the Yellow Pages, and when he couldn't find what he wanted in Manhattan he'd switched to the outer limits: the Bronx and Queens. The third store he tried had sounded about right, so he'd asked for directions and written them down on a sheet of hotel notepaper.

So he sat with them in the back of the cab, listening to the wild, angry dialogue on the two-way radio. Whoever was manning the mike back at HQ was exploding. He was still exploding as the cab crossed the Queensboro Bridge.

The cab driver turned round again. 'Last chance, man.' His accent, whatever it was, was so thick Reeve could hardly make out the words.

'No,' he said, 'keep going.' He repeated the words in Spanish, which didn't impress the driver. He was calling in, holding the mike close to his mouth.

The street they were looking for, the one Reeve directed the driver to, wasn't too deep into Queens. They stuck close to the East River, as though the cabbie didn't want to lose sight of the Manhattan skyline. When the cab stopped at lights, there were usually a few men hanging around, leaning down to peer into the back like they were at an aquarium. Or looking into a butcher's cabinet, thought Reeve. He preferred the idea of the aquarium.

'This is the street,' Reeve said. The driver pulled over immediately. He wasn't going to cruise looking for the shop, he just wanted to dump Reeve and get out of there.

'Will you wait?' Reeve asked.

'If I stop longer than a red light, the tyres'll be gone. Shit, *I'll* be gone.'

Reeve looked around. The street was run down, but it didn't look particularly dangerous. It was no Murder Mile. 'What about giving me your card,' he said, 'so I can call for another cab?'

The man looked at him levelly. Reeve had already paid and tipped him. It was a decent tip. He sighed. 'Look, I'll drive around. No promises, but if you're right here at this spot in twenty minutes, maybe I'll be back here to pick you up. No promises, you hear? If I catch another fare, that's it.'

'Deal,' Reeve said.

Twenty minutes might cover it.

He found the store on the other side of the street. Its window made it look like a junkshop – which in part it was – but it specialised in militaria and survivalist goodies. The hulk behind the padlocked counter didn't look like he was going to be mugged. Brown muscled shoulders bulged from a tight black T-shirt with some Nazi-style emblems and writing on the front. There were tattoos on the man's arms, variously coloured. The thick veins ran through them like roads on a map. The man had a bulbous shaven head but a full black beard and moustache, plus a large looped earring in one ear. Reeve immediately pictured him as a pirate, cutlass between his teeth in some old black and white movie. He nodded a greeting and looked around the shop. What stock there was was mostly boxed, but the display cabinet behind which the owner – Reeve presumed he was the owner – sat was full of just what he'd come here for: knives.

'You the one that phoned?'

Reeve recognised the man's voice and nodded. He walked towards the display case. The knives were highly polished combat weapons, some with extremely mean-looking serrated edges. There were machetes too, and butterfly knives – even a foreshortened samurai sword. There were older knives among the flashing steel; war souvenirs, collectables with dubious histories.

The man's voice wasn't as deep as his frame would suggest. 'Thought you must be; we don't get too many customers midweek. Lot of our stuff goes out mail order. You want I should put you on the computer?'

'What computer?'

'The mailing list.'

'I don't think so.'

'You see anything you like?'

Reeve saw plenty. He'd considered buying a gun, but wouldn't have known how to go about it. Besides, a knife was just about as good, so long as you got close. He was hoping to get *very* close . . .

'Nothing exactly like what I'm looking for.'

'Well, this is just a selection.' The man came from behind the counter. He was wearing grey sweat-pants, baggy all the way down to his ankles, and open-toed sandals showing one toe missing. He went over to the door and locked it, turning the notice to 'Closed'.

'Was it a bullet or shrapnel?' Reeve asked.

The man knew what he meant. 'Bullet. I was rolling, trying to get to cover, bullet went into the toe of my damned boot.'

'Through the steel toecap?'

'I wasn't wearing steel toecaps,' the man said, smiling. 'This didn't happen to me in the Army.' He was leading Reeve through the shop. The store was narrow but went back a long way. They came to a section of clothing: disruptive patterns, plain olive greens, stuff from all over the world. There were boots too, and a lot of equipment for wilderness survival: compasses and stoves and pup-tents, binoculars, reels of filament for making tripwires, rifle-sights, crossbows, balaclavas . . .

This, Reeve realised, was going to take more than the twenty minutes his cabbie had allotted him. 'No guns,' he said.

'I'm not licensed for them.'

'Can you get them?'

'Maybe if I knew you better. Where you from anyway?'

'Scotland.'

'Scotland? You guys invented golf!'

'Yes,' Reeve admitted, not sure why the hulk was suddenly so excited.

'Ever played St Andrews?'

'I don't play golf.' The hulk looked bemused by this. 'Do you?'

'Hell yes, got me a five handicap. I *love* golf. Man, I'd like to play some of those courses over there.'

'Well, I'd be happy to help you.'

'But you don't play.'

'I know people who do.'

'Well, man, I would surely love to do that some day . . .' He unlocked a door at the back of the store. It had three locks, one of them a padlock attached to a central bolt.

'Not the rest rooms?' Reeve said.

'Yeah, the head's back here, but then so is a lot of other stuff.'

They entered a small storeroom with barely enough room for the two of them. There were three narrow doors with piles of boxes in front of two of them. A box sat on the small table in the middle of the room.

'I already looked these out, thought they might be more your thing.' He lifted the lid from an innocuous brown cardboard box, the size of a shoebox. There were layers of oiled cloth inside, and between the layers lay the knives.

'Nice balance,' Reeve said, handling one. 'Bit too short, though.' After handling each knife, he handed it to the hulk for repolishing. Near the bottom of the box, Reeve peeled off another strip of cloth and saw what he'd been looking for: an eight-inch blade with five-inch handle. He tried it for weight and balance. It felt almost identical to his German knife, his Lucky 13.

'I like this one,' he said, putting it to one side. He checked the remaining knives out, but none came close. 'No,' he said, 'it has to be this one.'

'That's a good knife,' the hulk agreed, 'a serious knife.'

'I'm a serious person.'

'You want a scabbard for it?'

Reeve considered. 'Yes, a scabbard would be useful. And I want to check out some of your other lines too . . .'

He spent another hour in the front of the shop, adding to his purchases. The hulk had introduced himself as Wayne and said that he used to be a professional wrestler, on TV even. Then he asked if Reeve was still interested in a gun.

Reeve wasn't sure. It turned out all Wayne had to offer was a revolver, a pump-action, and an assault rifle, so Reeve shook his head, glad the decision had been taken for him.

Wayne handed him some leg-straps, so he could fasten the scabbard on to his leg if he wanted. 'On the house,' he said.

Then he added up the total and Reeve took out some cash.

'Running around Queens with a bankroll,' Wayne said, shaking his head, 'no wonder you need a knife.'

'Could you call me a cab?' Reeve asked.

'Sure. And hey, write down your address, just in case I ever do make that trip.' He pushed a pad of paper towards Reeve.

Reeve had already given a false name. Giving a false address was easy.

The rest of the day was quiet. Reeve stayed in his room, slept for as long as he could, and exercised when he couldn't. About midnight, feeling fine, he walked the streets around the hotel and up as far as Times Square. The city felt more dangerous at night, but still not *very* dangerous. Reeve liked what he saw. He liked the way necessity had reduced some of the people to something edgier, more primeval than you found in most British cities. They all looked like they'd stared into the abyss. More than that, they looked like they'd bad-mouthed it as well. Reeve was not offered drugs – he didn't look the type – but he was offered sex and other sideshows. He stood on the fringes watching a man play the three-card trick. He couldn't believe people were making bets, but they were. Either they had money they didn't need, or they needed money very badly indeed. Which just about summed up the people he saw.

There were tourists about, looking like tourists. They were getting a lot of attention. Reeve liked to think that after a day in the city, he was fitting in, picking up less attention, fewer stares. Here he was, behind enemy lines. He wondered if the enemy knew it yet . . .

Next morning, he took a coach south 235 miles to Washington DC. This was where Alliance Investigative had its headquarters, according to Spikehead. The private eye might have been lying, but Reeve didn't think so.

Reeve's own hotel in New York had a sister hotel in Washington, but that would have made him too easy to trace. Instead, he called a couple of other chains until he found one with a room in its Washington hotel.

He took a cab to the hotel itself, and asked at reception for a street-plan. In his room he got out the phone directory and looked up Alliance Investigative, jotting down the address and telephone number. Spikehead hadn't been lying. He found the address on his map but didn't mark it, committing it to memory instead. He looked up Dulwater next, but didn't find an entry. The man who had been Spikehead's contact at Alliance was ex-directory. Knowing what he was going to do, he heaved Yellow Pages on to his bed and looked at the list of Private Investigation Agents and Agencies. There were plenty to choose from. Alliance had a small, understated advert which only said that they specialised in 'corporate management'. He went for one of the small adverts, and steered clear of anything that boasted having been 'long established'. For all he knew, PIs were every bit as clubby as lawyers or accountants. He didn't want to contact a PI only to have that PI telephone Alliance with the news.

As it turned out, he chose remarkably well.

'You've come to the right person, Mr Wagner.'

Reeve was calling himself Richard Wagner. He was sitting in the rented office of a Mr Edward ('please, call me Eddie') Duhart. Duhart was interested to speak to a European. He said he'd been researching his name and was positive it was originally DuHart and that he was somehow related to a big Bordeaux distillery.

'I think you mean vineyard,' Reeve had said.

Eddie Duhart was in his late 20s, smartly enough dressed but not wearing the clothes with ease. He kept moving in his chair, like he couldn't get comfortable. Reeve wondered if the guy was a cokehead. Duhart had cropped blond hair, shiny white teeth and baby blue eyes. You could see the child in him peering out from a college-football body. 'Well, yeah, vineyard. Sure I mean vineyard. See, I think these Duharts came over here to further their, you know, trade. I think they settled here, and,' opening his arms wide, 'I'm the result.'

'Congratulations,' said Reeve. The office was small and looked impermanent. There was a desk and a filing cabinet, a fax machine, and a coatstand on which hung something looking suspiciously like a fedora. There was no secretary, probably no need for one. Duhart had already informed him that he was 'fairly fresh' to the business. He'd been a cop three years but got bored, liked to be his own operator. Reeve said he knew the feeling. Duhart said he'd always loved private eye stories and movies. Had Reeve ever read Jim Crumley or Lawrence Block? Reeve admitted the gap in his education. 'But you've seen the movies, right? Bogart, Mitchum, Paul Newman . . . ?'

'I've seen some movies.'

Duhart accepted this as a truism. 'So I decided to become a PI, see how I made out. I'm making out pretty good.' Duhart leaned back in his creaking chair, folding his hands over a gut that did not yet exist. 'That's why, like I say, you've come to the right person.'

'I'm not sure I follow.' Reeve had admitted that he wanted to know a little about Alliance Investigative.

'Because I'm not stupid. When I decided to set out in this game, I did some reading, some research. Foreknowing is forearmed, right?'

Reeve didn't bother to correct the quotation. He shrugged and smiled instead.

'So I asked myself, who's the best in the business? By which I mean the richest, the best known.' Duhart winked. 'Had to be Alliance. So I studied them. I thought I could learn from them.'

'How did you do that?'

'Oh, I don't mean I spied on them or asked them questions or anything. I just wanted to know how they'd gotten so big. I read everything I could find in the libraries, how old man Allerdyce started from nothing, how he cultivated friends in high *and* low places. Know his motto? "You never know when you'll need a friend." That is so true.' If he leaned back any further in his chair he was going to tip it. 'So, like I say, if you want to know about Alliance, you've come to the right guy. Only thing *I'm* wondering is, why do you want to know about them? They done you wrong, Mr Wagner?'

'Do you believe in client confidentiality, Mr . . . Eddie?'

'Sure, Rule One.'

'Well, then I can tell you that, yes, I think they may have done me wrong. If I can prove that . . . well, that might put both of us in an interesting position.'

Duhart played with a cheap biro, handling it like it was rolled-gold Cartier. 'You mean,' he said, 'that we could both use information about Alliance to our separate advantages?'

'Yes,' Reeve said simply.

Duhart looked up at him. 'Going to tell me what they did?'

'Not just now, later. First, I want to know what *you* know.'

Duhart smiled. 'You know, we haven't discussed my charges yet.'

'I'm sure they'll be fine.'

'Mr Wagner, you know something? You're the first interesting damned client I've had. Let's go get a coffee.'

As Reeve had feared, the fedora was not just an ornament. Duhart wore it as far as the coffee shop on the corner, then placed it on the formica-topped table, checking the surface first for grease marks and coffee spills. He touched the brim of the hat from time to time with his fingernails, like it was his talisman. He watched from the window as he talked about Alliance. Nobody, it seemed, had any dirt on the company. They operated cleanly and for a client-roll that included most of the city's top companies and individuals. They were the establishment.

'What about their structure?' Reeve asked. So Duhart told him a little about that. He *had* done his research, and he retained knowledge well. Reeve wondered if it was the police training.

'Have you ever heard of someone called Dulwater working for Alliance?'

Duhart frowned and shook his head. 'It'd only take two seconds to check though.' He slipped a portable telephone out of his pocket. 'You don't happen to know Alliance's number, do you?'

Reeve recited it. Duhart pressed some buttons and took another sip of coffee.

'Mm, yes,' he said at last, 'Mr Dulwater's office, please.' He waited, staring at Reeve. 'Is that right? No, there's no message, thank you, ma'am.' He cut the connection and put the telephone back in his pocket.

'Well?' Reeve asked.

'Seems he's not in the office today.'

'But he does work there?'

'Oh yeah, he works there. And one other thing she told me.'

'What?'

'The name's pronounced Doo-latter.'

'Let me put something to you,' Reeve said, after their second coffees had appeared, along with a slice of pie for Duhart.

'Shoot.'

'Say Alliance wanted some work done overseas. Say they hire a couple of PIs from another firm based overseas to do some surveillance work.'

'Mm-hm.' Duhart scooped pie into his mouth.

'Well, who'd have the authority to put that sort of operation together?'

Duhart considered, swallowing the pie with some sour black coffee. 'I get your question,' he said. 'I'd have to make an educated guess.'

'Go ahead.'

'Well, it'd have to be at senior partner level, and for that they might even have to go to the old man himself.'

'His name's Allerdyce, you said?'

'Yeah, Allerdyce. He plays his cards close, you know? He likes to keep tabs on everything the company's doing, every operation. I know the names of the senior partners; Dulwater ain't one of them.'

'So Allerdyce would have to sanction something like that?'

'That's my guess.'

'Even if he didn't actually originate the plan?'

Duhart nodded. 'That what happened to you, Mr Wagner? I mean, I notice your accent and all. You're British, right? Did they come and do a number on you?'

'Something like that,' Reeve said thoughtfully. 'Okay, Eddie, what about telling me everything you know about Allerdyce?'

'Where do you want me to start?'

'Let's start with where he lives . . .'

17

Working shifts, Reeve and Duhart kept a watch on the offices of Alliance Investigative.

It wasn't easy. For a start, parking outside was restricted to loading and unloading. Added to which, one person couldn't cover all the angles: the main entrance faced one street, but the entry/exit ramp for the underground car park was round the corner, on a different street altogether. It took them the best part of a day to figure that Allerdyce *never* entered or left the building on foot.

Additionally, Reeve worried that he might not recognise Allerdyce. All Duhart had shown him were newspaper and magazine photographs of the scowling figure. Plus, neither Duhart nor Reeve knew what Allerdyce's vehicle of choice would be. If a black stretch limo came crawling up the ramp, fair enough that was probably the boss. But it could just be a client. Tinted windows didn't mean anything either. Like Duhart said, if you were going to see Alliance and you were a Washington 'name', you probably didn't want people recognising you.

In the end, they switched tactics and kept watch on Allerdyce's apartment, but that was no more fruitful.

'Bastard's got a house somewhere on the Potomac,' Duhart conceded that night, 'looks like he prefers it to the apartment.'

'Where's the house exactly?'

'I don't know.'

'Could we go look?'

'It's pretty exclusive real estate.'

'Meaning?'

'Meaning several things. One, people don't have their name written on the mailbox or anything. They figure the postman *knows* who they are. Two, the houses are surrounded by lawns you could host Superbowl on. You don't just cruise past and peer in through the window.'

Reeve thought about this. 'It's on the river?' Duhart nodded. 'Then why *can't* we just cruise past? I mean literally.'

Duhart was wide-eyed. 'You mean a boat?'

'Why not?'

'I've never been on a boat in my life, excepting a couple of ferries.'

'I've been on boats a lot. I'll teach you.'

Duhart looked sceptical.

'It's worth a shot,' said Reeve. 'Besides, I'm paying, remember?'

Which was about as much argument as Eddie Duhart needed.

Next day, on their way to the boat hire, they passed the Watergate Hotel.

The 'boat hire' was actually a club, and not supposed to hire, but Eddie had promised quiet cash and the boat back within a couple of hours. The owner wanted a deposit, too, and that had to be negotiated. But eventually it was agreed. They had their boat.

It was a two-person motorboat, though the motor wasn't exactly powerful. There was a rowing club next door, and Reeve feared they'd be overtaken by scullers. They were in possession of a good map, which showed they were about fifteen miles from Mount Vernon. According to Duhart, they'd come to the house before that. Neither man discussed how they would actually *recognise* the house as belonging to Jeffrey Allerdyce. Reeve was trusting to instinct. And at least they were *doing* something. He didn't mind reconnaissance when there was something to reconnoitre, but so far they'd been staring at smoke.

It was a fine day of sharp sunshine and scudding thin wisps of high cloud. There was a stiff breeze at their back as they puttered down the Potomac. They passed Alexandria on their right, and Duhart said they'd be coming to the district soon where Allerdyce had his home. Reeve had brought a small pair of green rubberised binoculars. They were discreet but powerful. They hadn't been cheap but, as Wayne had said, they were Marine-standard. Reeve had them around his neck as he steered, giving the throttle an occasional twist to push up the revs on the engine. He was wearing his tourist clothes today, plus sunglasses purchased on the plane from London and a white sailing hat borrowed from the boat's owner.

After they'd left Alexandria behind, Reeve slowed the boat down. 'Remember,' he said, 'we'll get two stabs at this, so don't fret. Try to look casual.'

Duhart nodded. The breeze had kicked around and was rocking the boat a bit. Duhart hadn't gone green at the gills exactly, but he wasn't saying much, like he was concentrating on his breathing.

They came to a row of palatial houses, two- and three-storied, with pillars and porches, gazebos and landing-decks. Most carried polite signs warning boats against mooring. Reeve saw rectangular black arc lights dotted on lawns – movement-sensitive, he guessed. He saw an elderly man pushing a lawnmower across grass which looked like green baize. Duhart shook his head to let him know it wasn't Allerdyce, as if he needed telling.

On one of the wood-slatted sundecks, a man lazed with his feet up on a stool, a drink on the arm of his chair. Behind him on the clipped lawn, a large dog chased a punctured red ball tossed by another man. The dog's jaws snapped on the ball and shook it from side to side – your basic neck-break procedure. Reeve waved jauntily towards the man on the deck. The man waved back with three fingers, keeping one finger and a thumb around his glass, a very superior gesture. I'm up here, he was saying, and that's a place *you'll* never be.

But Reeve wasn't so sure about that.

He was still watching the two men and the dog when Duhart puked.

It came up pink and half-digested, a half-sub special and a can of cherry Coke. The $3.49 brunch floated on the surface of the water while Duhart rested his forehead against the side of the boat. Reeve cut the engine and shuffled forward towards him.

'You okay?' he said, louder than was necessary.

'I'll be fine – feel better already.'

Reeve was crouching close by him, his head angled as though staring at his friend's face. But through the thick black lenses he was studying the layout of the garden where the man and the dog still played. He saw another dog pad around the side of the house, sniffing with its nose to the grass. When it saw there was a game in progress, it bounded on to the lawn. The first dog didn't look too thrilled, and they snapped at one another's faces until the man with the ball barked a command.

'Be still!'

And they both lay down in front of him.

The man on the deck was still watching the boat. He'd made no comment, hadn't even wrinkled his face at the sudden jetsam. Reeve patted Duhart's back and returned to the back of the boat, restarting the outboard. He decided he had an excuse to turn back, so brought the boat round, bringing him closer to where the dogs were now playing together.

'Hey,' the man with the dogs called to his friend, 'your turn to check if Blood's crapped on the front lawn!'

It was the sort of confirmation Reeve needed. The two men weren't owners – they weren't even guests – they were guards, hired hands. None of the other houses seemed to boast the same level of protection. He'd been told that Allerdyce was a very private man, an obsessive – just the kind of person to have security men and guard dogs, and maybe even more than that. Reeve scanned the lawn but couldn't see any obvious security – no trips or cameras. Which didn't mean they weren't there. He couldn't explain it, but he got the feeling he'd located Allerdyce's house.

He counted the other homes, the ones between Allerdyce's and the end of the building land. There were five of them. Driving out from Alexandria, he would pass five large gates. The sixth gate would belong to the head of Alliance Investigative.

Reeve was looking forward to meeting him.

They set off back to the boat club, then drove back out towards Allerdyce's home. Duhart hadn't said much; he still looked a bit grey. Reeve counted houses, then told him to pull over. To the side of the gate was an intercom with a camera above it. Behind the gate, an attack dog loped past. The stone walls either side of the gates were high, but not impossible. There was nothing on the top of them, no wire or glass or spikes, all of which told Reeve a lot.

'You wouldn't go in for all the security we've seen, then leave the walls around your house unprotected,' he said.

'So?'

'So there must be some sensing devices.'

'There are the dogs.'

Reeve nodded. 'There are the dogs,' he agreed. But when the dogs weren't around, there would be other measures, less visible, harder to deal with. 'I just hope they're a permanent feature,' he said.

The inflatable dinghy was big enough for one fully-grown man, and a cheap buy.

That night, Duhart drove Reeve out to Piscataway Park, on the other side of the Potomac from Mount Vernon.

'Half of me wants to come with you,' Duhart whispered at water's edge.

'I like the other half of you better,' Reeve said. He was blacked up – clothes, balaclava and face-paint bought at Wayne's – not because he thought *he'd* need it, more for the effect he thought it might have on Allerdyce. And on anyone else for that matter. All he had to do was paddle across the river and upstream a mile or so – in silence, under cover of darkness, without anything giving him away. He hoped there were no garden parties in progress, no late-night drinks on the sundeck. He hoped there wasn't too much traffic on the Potomac this time of night.

He felt the way he had done at the start of so many missions: not scared at all, but excited, energised, ready for it. He remembered now why he'd loved Special Forces: he'd lived for risk and adrenaline, life and death. Everything had a startling clarity at moments like this: a sliver of moon in bristling reflection on the edge of the water; the moist whites of Duhart's eyes and the creases in his cheek when he winked; the tactile feel of the plastic oar, its grip grooved out for his four fingers. He splashed ankle deep into the water and eased into the dinghy. Duhart waved him off. The PI had his instructions. He was to go somewhere they knew him – a bar, anyplace. It had to be some way away. He was to stay there and get himself noticed. Those were his instructions. *If* anything went wrong, Reeve didn't want any of the shit hitting Duhart.

Which didn't mean he didn't want Duhart back here – or, more accurately, parked outside Allerdyce's gates – in three hours' time . . .

He paddled upriver, keeping to the bank opposite the houses. In darkness it was hard to differentiate one house from the other; they all seemed to have the same huge expanse of garden, the same jetty, even the same gazebo. He paddled until the dwellings ended, then counted back to the house he was betting belonged to Allerdyce. The homes either side looked to be in darkness. Reeve checked for river traffic. A boat was chugging upriver. He hugged the bank, trusting to darkness. There were a couple of people on the boatdeck, but they couldn't see him.

Finally, when all was quiet again, he paddled across the width of the river until he reached the house on Allerdyce's right. He got out of the dinghy and deflated it, letting it float away, pushing the paddle after it. He was next to the wall which separated the two estates. It was a high stone wall covered with creepers and moss. Reeve hauled himself up and peered into the gloom. There were lights burning in Allerdyce's house. He heard a distant cough, and saw wisps of smoke rising from the gazebo. He waited, and saw a pinpoint of red as the guard sucked on a cigarette.

Reeve lowered himself back into the neighbours' garden and produced a package from inside his jacket, unwrapping the two slabs of choice meat that he'd drugged using a mixture of articles freely available in any pharmacy. He tossed both slices over the wall and waited again. He was prepared to wait a while.

In fact, it took about five minutes for the dogs' keen noses to locate the titbits. He could hear them slobbering and slavering. There were no human sounds, the other guard wasn't with them. They were free to wander the estate. This was good news: it meant the movement-sensitive lights and other devices had almost certainly been kept switched off. They'd be for use only when the dogs weren't around. Reeve heard the eating sounds stop, the noise of sniffing – greedy things were looking for more – then silence. He gave it another five minutes, then hauled himself over the top of the wall and into Jeffrey Allerdyce's garden. There was no sign of the dogs. The sleeping draught would have taken its time to act. They'd be elsewhere. He hoped they were sleeping somewhere they couldn't be seen.

He stayed close to the wall, feeling it at his back, and moved towards the gazebo. The guard was sitting facing the water, his back to Reeve. Reeve moved quickly and quietly across the muffling lawn. He held the dagger by its scabbard, the handle showing, and swung it, clubbing the guard across the side of his head. The man was dazed, but not quite out. He was half-turning, opening his mouth, when Reeve's fist caught him full in the face. The second blow knocked him cold. Reeve got out tape and did the man's ankles, wrists and mouth, making sure the nose wasn't broken or blocked, making sure the guard wouldn't suffocate. He felt in the pockets for a gun but there wasn't one, just loose change and cigarettes. He didn't recognise the face; it figured – there had to be two shifts, maybe three.

He looked around. There were French windows to the back of the house. He wondered if they were locked. He also wondered where the second guard was. Indoors? He ran in a crouch towards the French windows. Lights shone inside. He was looking through the glass when he heard a growl behind him. One of the dogs. It looked very alert. Too alert. So only one of them had found the meat. The dog galloped towards him, and he pointed an arm at it.

'Be still!'

The dog stopped short, a little confused. It recognised the words but not the person uttering them, but then it was used to obeying more than one master . . . Reeve plunged the dagger two-handed into the top of its head, just behind the skull. The dog's legs buckled and it went down, Reeve maintaining the pressure. He glanced through the window to see if anyone had been roused. All he saw was the reflection of a man blacked up so that the brightest things about him were the whites of his eyes, his gritted teeth, and the blade in his hands.

He pulled the knife out and wiped it on the dog's coat. The French windows were unlocked. He took off his boots, left them hidden below the level of the porch, and let himself into the house.

His socks left no marks on the carpet, and the floor was solid, so his weight did not cause it to creak. The room was a dining room. He noticed that the small table had only one place setting, and there was only one chair. He was surer than ever that this was the right house.

He opened the door to a large octagonal hall with several doors off. A staircase led up to a landing, similarly octagonal with more doors off. Music was playing somewhere, behind one of the doors on the ground floor. Reeve walked over to the door, all too aware that if anyone stepped out of a room upstairs they would see him immediately. He had to be quick. He peered through the keyhole and saw a man sitting on a sofa, reading a magazine and nodding to the music. It was on a personal hi-fi, and must have been turned up all the way; even from here Reeve could recognise it: 'Don't Fear the Reaper'. The man was short and wiry: he didn't look like prime bodyguard material.

Reeve knew his best bet was to rush him. His hand tightened on the door handle. A clock in the room started to chime. Reeve burst in.

In a mirror above the fireplace, Reeve saw what the man could see: a massive snarling intruder with a bloodied knife so big you could quarter a buffalo with it. The man stood up, mouth gawping, the hi-fi dropping to the floor, the headphones falling from his ears.

'No noise,' Reeve said quietly over the chimes. 'Just lie down on the floor with your hands—'

Half a second before the man sprang into action Reeve saw the change in his face – saw that the surprise had worn off already and he wasn't ready just to lie down. The man's body twisted, sending a powerful leg towards Reeve's groin. Reeve twisted too, the blow landing on his thigh, almost dead-legging him.

Small: yes; wiry: yes – but this guy had some martial arts training. The second blow, a fist this time, was already coming, aiming to disable the dagger. Blue Oyster Cult was still erupting from the headphones. All that was left of the chimes was an echo. Reeve dodged the fist and lashed out a roundhouse of his own. He wished he'd kept his shoes on. The blow glanced off the man's chest. The heel of a shoe slammed down on to Reeve's unprotected foot. His opponent was fast *and* smart. Reeve dummied with the dagger and swung his free hand into the man's throat. That felt better. The man's face and neck reddened as the oxygen tried to get through. Reeve followed up with a kick to the right knee and was readying to use an elbow, but the man hurled himself over the sofa and got to his feet again quickly. They hadn't made much noise yet; you didn't when you were concentrating. You hadn't time to think about screaming. Reeve hoped Allerdyce wasn't pushing some panic button somewhere. He had to make this quick.

His opponent had other plans. He tipped the sofa over so that Reeve had to dodge it: he was hemming Reeve in, making it awkward for him to move. Reeve launched himself over the sofa and hit the man full in the stomach, knocking him backwards on to the carpet. Reeve stuck the tip of the dagger to the man's stomach, just below the rib cage.

'I'll gut you like a fish,' he spat. He was kneeling on the man's legs. 'Ask yourself, is he paying you enough?'

The small man considered this. He shook his head.

'Lie on your front,' Reeve ordered. 'I'm only going to tie you up.'

The man obeyed, and Reeve got out the tape. He was breathing hard, his hands shaking slightly. And he had eyes only for the man on the floor; he didn't want the bastard trying anything else. After he'd taped wrists, ankles and mouth – using double runs on the wrists and feet – he pulled the sofa upright and lifted the man's hi-fi by its headphones, bringing it over and clamping the 'phones to the man's head. He checked the pockets again. No gun.

But the man standing in the doorway had a gun.

'Who are you?' the man said. He was wearing a paisley dressing gown with frilled tassels hanging from the cord, pale pink pyjamas and burgundy slippers. He fitted the description Duhart had given.

'Mr Allerdyce?' Reeve said, like they were meeting over canapés.

'Yes.' It was a small-calibre revolver, the kind molls kept in purses in the books Duhart read. But Allerdyce was holding it steadily enough.

'My name's—'

'Let's get rid of the dagger first.'

Reeve threw the dagger on to the sofa. He didn't have his hands up yet, but Allerdyce gestured with the gun, so he raised them.

'My name's Reeve, Gordon Reeve. I wanted a word with you.'

'You could have come to my office, Mr Reeve.'

'Maybe. But this was personal, not business.'

'Personal? I don't understand.'

'Yes you do. Men hired by your organisation have been following me.' Reeve paused. 'Are you sure you want to talk about this in front of witnesses?'

Allerdyce seemed to see the guard for the first time. The music was still blaring but there was no telling what else he could hear.

'I should telephone for the police.'

'Yes, sir, you should,' Reeve agreed.

Allerdyce thought about this. Reeve stared at him levelly throughout.

'Upstairs,' Allerdyce said at last.

Reeve preceded him up the staircase.

They went to a small sitting room. Allerdyce motioned for Reeve to sit down.

'Is it okay if I take my sock off?'

'What?'

'The guy downstairs stomped me pretty hard, I want to check the damage.' Allerdyce nodded, keeping his distance. Reeve rolled down the sock. The foot wasn't that bad, some swelling, and there'd be a good bruise, but nothing was damaged. He made it look worse than it was, easing the sock off with infinite slowness, grimacing as he manipulated his toes.

'Looks sore,' Allerdyce agreed.

'That bastard knew his stuff.' Reeve put the sock back on. He saw bottles and glasses on top of a walnut-veneered cabinet. 'Can I have a drink?'

Allerdyce considered this, too. Then nodded.

Reeve hobbled over to the cabinet, whistling as he examined the bottles. 'Royal Lochnagar – you have good taste.'

'You're Scottish, Mr Reeve?'

'You know damned well I am. You've probably got a big fat file on me. I'd like to know why.'

'I assure you I don't know the first thing about you.'

Reeve turned his head and smiled. 'Do you want one?'

'Why not?'

Reeve fixed both drinks and turned towards Allerdyce.

'Leave mine on the cabinet,' Allerdyce said. He waited until Reeve had hobbled back to the sofa, then backed his way to the cabinet, keeping the revolver on Reeve. Maybe the thing wasn't even loaded, but Reeve didn't want to take that risk, not yet. Allerdyce picked up the glass and came back round to face Reeve.

'*Slainte,*' Reeve said, drinking deep.

'*Slainte,*' Allerdyce echoed, like he'd used the toast before.

'You going to call the police?' Reeve asked.

'I think I'd better, don't you? A man has broken into my house, overpowered my dogs and my guards; that sounds like a man the police should know about.'

'Will they allow me one phone call?'

'What?'

'In Britain, we get one phone call.'

'You'll get a phone call.'

'Good, I wonder which paper I'll call.'

Allerdyce seemed amused.

'See,' Reeve went on, 'those two deadbeats you had following me in Scotland, they didn't just tell *me* they were working for you, they told a whole pub. Witnesses, Mr Allerdyce. A precious commodity.' He worked his injured foot again.

Allerdyce took another sip of whisky. 'I don't know what you're talking about.'

'No? Are you quite sure? I mean, if you're sure then I owe you an apology. But you'll have to tell me about CWC first.'

'Excuse me?'

'Co-World Chemicals. They murdered my brother. Or maybe they hired *your* people to kill him.'

'Now wait a minute—'

'Or maybe all you did was compile a dossier on him. I believe that's your speciality. And then you handed it over and washed your hands. Don't you think you should have gone to the police? I mean, when my brother was found dead. Oh no, you couldn't have done that, could you? The police might have had you for conspiracy, or aiding and abetting. Not a very good advertisement for Alliance Investigative.' Reeve finished the whisky.

'Your brother . . .' Allerdyce choked off the sentence.

'What?' Reeve raised his eyebrows. 'You *did* know about him, didn't you?'

'Yes, I . . .' Allerdyce was perspiring. 'No, I've never heard of . . . your brother.' His face had lost its colour and he was having trouble focusing. 'I think I'm . . .'

Reeve stood up and went to fix another drink. Allerdyce didn't try to stop him. The gun was hanging by his side, the empty glass held loosely in his other hand.

'Hope I didn't give you too much,' Reeve said from the drinks cabinet.

'Too . . . much . . . what?'

Reeve turned towards him, smiling again. 'Too much birdy,' he said. 'I had a little packet of it in my sock.'

'Birdy?'

'Know what? Maybe you should know all about birdy. It could revolutionise your business.' Reeve raised his replenished glass. '*Slainte*.'

This time the toast was not returned.

The thing about *burundanga* is, it is not just a truth drug. It makes the victim completely compliant. Completely suggestible. The victim becomes a sleepwalker. Men and women have been gang-raped after being tricked into taking it. They return to their senses forty-eight hours later and have no recollection. Amnesia. They could have been holding up banks, or emptying their own accounts, or playing in porno movies, or carrying drugs across borders. They'll do what they're told, no qualms, and will wake up with little more than a bad feeling, a feeling like their mind's not their own. That was why you had to judge the doses just right, so as not to do too much damage to the victim's mind.

It wasn't simply a truth drug the way sodium pentothal was – it was so much better than that.

'Sit down,' Reeve told Allerdyce. 'Take the weight off. I'm just going to look around. Anywhere special I should be looking?'

'What?'

'Do you keep any files here? Anything about me or my brother?'

'All my files are here.' Allerdyce still looked confused. He was frowning like someone on a geriatric ward faced with their children, not recognising them.

'Can you show me where?' Reeve said.

'Surely.' Allerdyce got up again. He wasn't overly steady on his pins. Reeve hoped he hadn't given him too much. He hoped he hadn't just given this old man a massive dose of scopolamine.

They walked out of the room and took a left. Allerdyce slipped a hand into the pocket of his dressing gown.

'What have you got there, Mr Allerdyce?'

'A key.' Allerdyce blinked his moist yellow eyes. 'I keep this room locked.'

'Okay, unlock the door.' Reeve took a look over the guard-rail. The hall below was empty and quiet. Mr Blue Oyster Cult probably wasn't worrying about anything. He'd seen his employer train a gun on the intruder. He'd be waiting either for a shot or for the police to arrive.

Allerdyce pushed open the door. The room was part-library, part-office. There was a lot of shiny new plastic around – fax, photocopier, shredder – but also a lot of antique wood and leather. The chair behind the desk was immense, more throne than chair, and covered in buttoned red leather. There was a matching sofa. The walls were book-lined, floor to ceiling. Some of the shelves were behind glass, and these housed the most precious-looking volumes. There were no filing cabinets, but there were files.

A lot of files.

They stood in towers which threatened to topple at any moment, slewing paper everywhere. Some of the towers were six feet high, resting in the corners of the room, giving it a musty unventilated smell. There were more files on the sofa, and on the floor in front of it, and others beside the desk. Older files had been tidied away into big cardboard boxes – ordinary grocery boxes like you picked up in supermarkets, advertising chilli beans and dishwasher powder and Planter's peanuts.

'Have you never heard of computers, Mr Allerdyce?' Reeve said, looking around him.

'I don't trust computers. With the right equipment, you can tap into a computer from a distance. To get this lot, someone would have to get very close indeed.'

'Well, you've got a point. Where are the relevant files?'

'File singular. It's on the desk. I was browsing through it earlier tonight, doing some updating.'

'Why don't you sit on the sofa, Mr Allerdyce?'

But there was no space. Allerdyce just stared at the sofa like a pet who'd been given an impossible command. Reeve cleared off some of the files so Allerdyce could sit down. Then Reeve sat behind the desk.

'You know about my brother?' he asked.

'Yes.'

'Did your people kill him?'

'No.'

'Then who did?'

'There's no proof he didn't kill himself.'

'Take it from me, he was murdered.'

'I don't know anything about it.'

Reeve accepted this. He opened a grey folder and started separating the handwritten sheets. There were photographs there too. 'But you have your suspicions?'

'Surely.'

'CWC?'

'It's feasible.'

'Oh, it's feasible all right. Who's Dulwater?'

'He works for me.'

'Why did you have me followed?'

'I wanted to know about you, Mr Reeve.'

'Why?'

'To see what Kosigin was up against.'

'Kosigin?'

'You're reading his file.'

Reeve picked up one of the photographs. It showed a boyish young man with steel-rimmed glasses and salt-and-pepper hair. He turned the photo towards Allerdyce, who nodded slowly.

Marie Villambard had spoken about Kosigin, how he'd set up the rigged investigation involving Preece and the others. Reeve had expected him to be older.

'What can you tell me about Kosigin?'

'It's all there in his file.'

Reeve read it through.

'You've been following him,' he said.

'Yes.'

'Why?'

'I want him.'

'I don't understand.'

'I want him for my . . . collection.' Allerdyce looked around the room.

Reeve nodded. 'You're a blackmailer? That's your hobby?'

'Not at all, I just like to collect people, people who may be useful to me.'

'I get it.' Reeve kept reading. Then he came to the other photographs. One of them showed two men on a marina, sail-boat masts sticking up behind them. One of the men was Kosigin.

The other was Jay.

'Housey-housey,' Reeve said. He got up and took the picture over to the sofa. 'You know this man?'

'Kosigin has hired him to do some work. I think he's called Jay.'

'That's right. Jay.'

'I don't know much more. He's rumoured at one time to have been in the SAS.' Allerdyce's eyes seemed to focus for a moment. 'You were in the SAS too, Mr Reeve.'

Reeve breathed in. 'How do you know that?'

'Dulwater broke into your house. He found some magazines.'

'Mars and Minerva?'

'Yes, that's the name.'

'Did your man plant any bugs?'

'No, but he found some.'

'Who do you think was bugging me?'

'I presume Kosigin.' Reeve went back to the desk and sat down. 'Is Dulwater still watching my house?'

'No, he knew it was empty. Your wife and son are elsewhere.'

Reeve sucked in breath again. 'Do you know where?'

Allerdyce shook his head. 'They're of little concern to me. My concern in all this is Kosigin.'

'Well then, we're on the same side . . . as far as that goes.' Reeve checked his watch. 'What about you, Mr Allerdyce?'

'What about me?'

'Do *you* have any secrets? Any skeletons?'

Allerdyce shook his head slowly but firmly.

'Where's Dulwater now?'

'I'm not entirely sure.'

'You're not?'

'No. He's just returned from the UK. He's probably at home asleep.'

Reeve checked his watch again. 'Mr Allerdyce, I'd like you to do something for me.'

'Surely.'

'Could you switch on your photocopier and copy this file for me?'

Allerdyce got up from the sofa and went to switch on the machine. 'It takes a moment to warm up.'

'That's fine. I'll be back in a minute.'

Reeve went out on to the landing and looked down on Mr Blue Oyster Cult, who was wriggling his way across the hall. He stopped when he saw Reeve looking at him. Reeve smiled and started down the stairs. The man was moving with more urgency now, trying to get to the door. Reeve walked beside him for a foot or two, then swept a leg back and kicked him on the side of his head with the meat of his stockinged heel. He dragged the unconscious figure back into the room, used more tape to bind him to the heaviest-looking table, and picked up the dagger.

Outside, he pulled his boots on and went and found the drugged dog. It was lying in front of some bushes near the gates. Anyone walking past could have seen it, but then nobody walked around here. Reeve dragged it deep into the shadows and taped its legs together, then wound more tape around its mouth. It was breathing deeply throughout, almost snoring.

Around the back of the house again, the guard in the gazebo looked like he'd been struggling for a while. It was good tape; the US Postal Service used it for taping parcels. It had nylon crosspieces – you could cut it, or tear it with your teeth, but no way could you snap it. This hadn't stopped the guard from trying.

Reeve walked up to the man and punched him unconscious again.

Back in Allerdyce's den, the old man had nearly finished the copying. Reeve found an empty folder and put the warm copies into it.

'Mr Allerdyce,' he said, 'I think you better get dressed.'

They went to the old man's bedroom. It was the smallest room Reeve had seen so far, smaller even than the bathroom which adjoined it.

'You're a sad old bastard really, aren't you?' Reeve was talking to himself, but Allerdyce heard a question.

'I never consider sadness,' he said. 'Nor loneliness. Keep them out of your vocabulary and you keep them out of your heart.'

'What about love?'

'Love? I loved as a young man. It was very time-consuming and not very productive.'

Reeve smiled. 'No need to bother with a tie, Mr Allerdyce.'

Allerdyce hung the tie back up.

'How do the gates open?'

'Electronically.'

'We're walking out of the gates. Do we need a remote?'

'There's one in the drawer downstairs.'

'Where downstairs?'

'The Chinese table near the front door. In a drawer.'

'Fine. Tie your shoelaces.'

Allerdyce was like a child. He sat on the bed and worked on the laces of his $500 shoes.

'Okay? Let me look at you. You look fine, let's go.'

True to his word, Duhart had come back. The car was parked outside, blocking the gates. His jaw dropped when he saw the gates open and Reeve come walking out, dressed like something from a Rambo film, with Jeffrey Allerdyce following at his heels.

'Get in the back, Mr Allerdyce,' Reeve ordered.

'Jesus Christ, Reeve! You can't kidnap him! What the fuck is this?'

Reeve got into the passenger seat. 'I've not kidnapped him. Mr Allerdyce, will you please tell my friend that you've come with me of your own volition.'

'Own volition,' Allerdyce mumbled.

Duhart still looked like a man in the middle of a particularly bad dream. 'What the fuck is he on, man?'

'Just drive,' said Reeve.

Reeve cleaned up a bit in the car. They went to Duhart's apartment, where he cleaned up some more and put on fresh clothes. Allerdyce sat on a chair in a living room probably smaller and less tidy than anywhere he'd ever been in his adult life. Duhart wasn't comfortable with any of this: here was his idol, his god, sitting in his goddamned apartment – and Reeve kept swearing Allerdyce wouldn't remember any of it.

'Just go get the stuff,' Reeve said.

Duhart giggled nervously again, rubbed his hands over his face again.

'Just go get the stuff.' Reeve was beginning to wish he'd given Duhart a dose of birdy too.

'Okay,' Duhart said at last, but he turned at the door and had another look at the scene within: Reeve in his tourist duds, and old man Allerdyce just sitting there, hands on knees, like a ventriloquist's dummy waiting for the hand up the back.

While Duhart was away, Reeve asked Allerdyce a few more questions, and tried to work out where they went from here, or rather, *how* they went from here. Allerdyce wouldn't remember anything, but the two guards would.

Then there was the corpse of the dog to explain. Reeve didn't reckon Mr Blue Oyster Cult had heard much, if anything, of his short dialogue with Allerdyce. So all they'd know was that there'd been an intruder – an intruder who'd fucked with Allerdyce's mind. They'd be wondering what else he'd fucked with.

Duhart was back within the hour, carrying a shoebox. Reeve opened it. Smothered in cotton wool, like a schoolboy's collection of bird eggs, were listening devices of various shapes, sizes and ranges.

'They all work?'

'Last time I used them,' Duhart said.

Reeve rooted to the base of the shoebox. 'Have you got the recorders to go with these?'

'In the car,' Duhart said. 'So what about Dulwater?'

'I want *you* to keep tabs on *him*.'

Duhart shook his head. 'What am I into here?'

'Eddie, by the time you've finished, you'll have so much dirt on our pal here he'll have to give you a senior partnership. Swear to God.'

'God, huh?' Duhart said, staring at Allerdyce.

Duhart brought his car to a stop beside the entry/exit ramp of the Alliance Investigative building. Reeve told Eddie Duhart to stay in the car, but not to leave the engine idling. They didn't want him stopped by nosy cops. It was four in the morning: he'd have some explaining to do.

'Can't I come with you? Man, I never been in there.'

'You want to be the star of *Candid Camera*, Eddie?' Reeve turned in the passenger seat. Allerdyce sat so quietly in the back it was easy to forget him. 'Mr Allerdyce, does your building have security cameras?'

'Oh yes.'

Reeve turned back to Duhart. 'I don't mind them seeing me; Allerdyce is already going to have a grudge against *me*. Do you want him to have a grudge against you, Eddie?'

'No,' Duhart said sullenly.

'Well okay,' said Reeve, picking up his large plastic carrier bag and getting out of the car. He opened the back door for Allerdyce.

'Which way would you usually go in?'

'Through the garage and up the elevator.'

'Can you open the garage?'

Allerdyce reached into his coat and produced a chain of about a dozen keys.

'Let's do it,' Reeve said.

He briefed Allerdyce as they walked the few steps to the garage entrance. 'I'm a friend, in from England, if anybody asks. We've been up drinking half the night, tried but couldn't sleep. I asked you to show me the offices. If anyone asks.'

Reeve repeated all this.

'The only guard is in the lobby,' Allerdyce said, 'and he's used to me coming in at all hours. I prefer the building when it's empty; I don't like my staff.'

'I'm sure the feeling's mutual. Shall we?'

They stood in front of the garage's roller-door. There was a concrete post to one side with an intercom, a slot for entry-cards and a keyhole to override everything. Allerdyce turned the key and the door clattered open. They walked down the slope into the Alliance Investigative building.

Allerdyce was right: there was no guard down here, but there were security cameras. Reeve put an arm around Allerdyce and laughed at some joke the old man had just told him.

'The cameras,' he said, 'are the screens up in the lobby?'

'Yes,' Allerdyce said. Reeve grinned again for the cameras. 'And do they just show or do they record as well?'

'They record.'

Reeve didn't like that. When the elevator arrived and they got in, Allerdyce slotted another key home.

'What's that for?'

'Executive levels. There are two of them – offices and penthouse. You need a key to access them.'

'Okay,' Reeve said as the doors slid closed.

Reeve guessed the security man would be watching the elevator lights. At the second storey from the top the elevator opened and they got out. Allerdyce's office door was locked by a keypad. He pushed in four digits and opened it.

Reeve got to work. There were no security cameras up here – the senior partners obviously didn't like to be spied on. Reeve placed one bug inside the telephone apparatus and taped another to the underside of the desk. The phone rang suddenly, causing him to jump. He answered it. It was the front desk.

'Good evening,' Reeve said, drawing out each word, like he'd had a few.

'Mr Allerdyce there?' the man asked, pleasant but suspicious too.

'Would you like to speak to him? Jeffrey, there's a man here wants to speak to you.'

Allerdyce took the phone. 'Yes?' he said. He listened, Reeve listening right beside him. 'No, it's just an old friend. We've been drinking, couldn't sleep. I'm showing him around.' A pause to listen. 'Yes, I know you have to check. It's what I pay you for. No trouble, goodnight.'

Reeve took the receiver and put it back in its cradle.

'Nice one, Jeffrey,' he said.

'These security men,' Allerdyce said, yawning. 'I pay them too much. They sit on their asses all night and call it working.'

'We're finished in here,' Reeve said. Then he saw the headed letterpaper on the desk. 'No, wait – sit down, Mr Allerdyce. I want you to write something. Will you do that?' He lifted a pen and handed it to Allerdyce, then placed a sheet of the elegant paper in front of him. 'Just write what I tell you: "I invited Mr Gordon Reeve to my home, and took him on a tour of my business premises. I did these things of my own free will and under no restraint or coercion." That's all, just sign it and date it.'

Reeve plucked the paper from him and folded it in four. It wasn't much – he wasn't even sure it qualified as insurance – but if the cops ever *did* come asking, at least he could make things a bit sticky for Allerdyce . . .

They took the elevator down a couple of floors to where Alfred Dulwater shared an office. The door was locked, but Allerdyce had a key for it.

'Do you have keys to all the offices?' Reeve asked.

'Of course.'

'Do you ever come here at night and rifle everyone's drawers?'

'Not everyone's.'

'Jesus, no wonder you're a PI.'

Reeve opened his bag, took out the shoebox and toolkit, and got to work again. Another bug in the telephone, another under Dulwater's desk, and one for good measure under his colleague's desk. There was nothing in the room about either James or Gordon Reeve, nothing about Kosigin or CWC, which was what he'd expected. Like Allerdyce had said, Dulwater reported directly to him. As little in writing as possible.

They started downstairs again. Reeve had another idea. He told Allerdyce what to do, and then pressed the button for the lobby. The two of them marched up to the front desk. The guard there stood up and straightened his clothes; he was obviously in awe of Allerdyce. Allerdyce went to say something, but yawned mightily instead.

'Late night?' the guard said with a smile. Reeve shrugged blearily.

'Donald,' Allerdyce said, 'I'd like the video of tonight.'

'The recording, sir?'

'Alan here has never seen himself on TV.'

The guard looked to 'Alan'. Reeve shrugged again and beamed at him. Allerdyce was holding out his hand. 'If you please, Donald?'

The guard unlocked a door behind him, which led to a windowless room with nothing but screens and banks of video recorders. The man ejected a tape, put in a fresh one, and came back out, locking the door after him.

'Thank you, Donald,' Allerdyce said.

Reeve dropped the cassette into his bag. 'Thanks, Donald,' he echoed.

As they walked back towards the elevator, he heard the guard mutter: 'The name's Duane . . .'

Outside, Duhart was waiting for them.

'Any trouble?' Reeve asked.

'No. You?'

Reeve shook his head. 'I just hope those bugs are working.'

Duhart smiled and held up a cassette player. He punched the Play button.

'Good evening?' It was Reeve's own voice, tinny but clear.

'Mr Allerdyce there?'

'Would you like to speak to him? Jeffrey . . .'

Reeve smiled an honest smile at Duhart, who began laughing.

'I can't believe we just did it,' he said at last, wiping tears from his eyes. 'I can't believe we just bugged the buggers!'

Reeve shook the shoebox. 'There are a few left.' He turned to the back seat. 'Let's take Mr Allerdyce home . . .'

They were aware, of course, that the Alliance building was swept top to bottom for bugs quite regularly. They were aware because Mr Allerdyce told them so in answer to a question. The last debugging had been a week ago. The building would be swept again, of course, if Allerdyce discovered he'd paid this middle-of-the-night visit to his offices – but that would depend on the guard mentioning the visit. Allerdyce himself wouldn't remember a damned thing about it, wouldn't even know he'd left his own house. And the night-duty guard, Duane, might not mention the incident to anyone. It wasn't like it was going to be public knowledge around Alliance that Jeffrey Allerdyce had been drugged and used in this way.

No, Allerdyce wouldn't want *anyone* to know about that.

Reeve didn't want either of the guards at Allerdyce's home to see Duhart, but at the same time they couldn't leave the car outside for too long. A private police patrol cruised the vicinity once an hour, so Allerdyce said, so they took the car in through the gates and up the gravel drive. Duhart came with them into the house, and Reeve warned him not to go into one particular room downstairs, not to say anything, and not to leave his fingerprints. Duhart made the sign of zipping his lips.

They took Allerdyce upstairs to his bedroom.

'Mr Allerdyce,' Reeve said, 'I think you must be exhausted. Get undressed and put your pyjamas back on. Go to bed. Sleep well.'

They closed the bedroom door after them and went to the office, which Reeve unlocked. Inside, they bugged the telephone, the underside of the desk, the underside of the photocopier and the leg of the sofa.

Downstairs, they bugged the other telephones but none of the rooms – they'd run out of bugs. They got back into the car and started down the driveway.

'What the hell is that?' Duhart gasped.

It was a dog, its mouth, front and back legs taped, jerking across the lawn towards the driveway.

Reeve pushed the button on the remote and the gates swung silently inwards. After they'd driven out, he used the remote to close the gates, then rolled down his window and tossed the thing high over the stone wall.

He hoped it would miss the dog.

Part Seven

Confessional

18

Reeve didn't hang around for the aftershock.

He flew out to Los Angeles that morning, grabbed a cab at the airport, and told the driver he wanted a cheap car hire.

'Cheapest I know is Dedman's Auto,' the cabbie declared, enjoying showing off his knowledge. 'The cars are okay – no stretch limos or nothing like that, just clean sedans.'

'Dead man's?'

The cabbie spelled it for him. 'That's why he keeps his rates so low. It's not the sort of name would leap out at you from Yellow Pages.' He chuckled. 'Christ knows, with a name like that would *you* go into car hire?'

Reeve was studying the cabbie's ID on the dashboard. 'I guess not, Mr Plotnik.'

It turned out that Marcus Aurelius Dedman, the blackest man Reeve had ever seen, operated an auto-wrecking business, and the car hire was just a sideline.

'See, mister,' he said, 'I'll be honest with you. The cars I get in here ain't always *so* wrecked. I spend a lot of time and money on them, get them fit for battle again. I hate to sell a car I've put heart and soul into, so I rent them instead.'

'And if the client wrecks them, they come straight back for hospitalisation?'

Dedman laughed a deep gurgling laugh. He was about six feet four and carried himself as upright as a fencepost. His short hair had been painstakingly uncurled and lay flat against his head like a Cab Calloway toupee. Reeve reckoned him to be in his early 50s. He had half a dozen black kids ripping cars apart for him, hauling out the innards.

'Nobody strips a vehicle quite like a kid from the projects,' Dedman said. 'Damned clever mechanics too. Here's the current options.' He waved a basketball player's arm along a line of a dozen dusty specimens, any of which would be perfect for Reeve's needs. He wanted a plain car, a car that wouldn't stand out from the crowd. These cars had their scars and war wounds – a chipped windscreen here, a missing fender there, a rusty line showing where a strip of chrome had been torn off the side doors, a sill patched with mastic and resprayed.

'Take your pick,' Dedman said. 'All one price.'

Reeve settled for a two-door Dodge Dart with foam-rubber suspension. It was dull green, the metallic sheen sanded away through time. Dedman showed him the engine ('reliable runner'), the interior ('bench seat'll come in handy at Lovers' Point'), and the trunk. Reeve nodded throughout.

Eventually, they went to Dedman's office to clinch the deal. Reeve got the feeling Dedman didn't want the project kids, no matter what their mechanical skills, to see any money changing hands. Maybe it would give them ideas.

The office was in a ramshackle cinder-block building, but surprised Reeve by being immaculately clean, bright, air-conditioned and high-tech. There was a large black leather director's chair behind the new-looking desk. Dedman draped a sheet over the chair before sitting, so as not to dirty the leather with his overalls. There was a computer on the desk with a mini-tower hard disk drive. Elsewhere Reeve glimpsed a fax and answering machine, a large photocopier, a portable colour TV, even a hot drinks machine.

'Grab a coffee if you want one,' Dedman said. Reeve pushed two quarters into the machine and watched it deliver a brown plastic cup of brown plastic liquid. He looked around the office again. It had no windows; all the light was electrical. The door, too, was solid metal.

'I see why you keep it padlocked,' Reeve said. Dedman had undone three padlocks, each one barring a thick steel bolt, to allow them into the office.

Dedman shook his head. 'It's not to stop the kids seeing what's in here, if that's what you're thinking. Hell, it's the kids who bring me all this stuff. They get it from their older brothers. What am I supposed to do with a computer or a facsimile?' Dedman shook his head again. 'Only they'd be hurt if I didn't look like I appreciated their efforts.'

Reeve sat down and put the cup on the floor, not daring to sully the surface of the desk. He reached into his pocket for a roll of dollars. 'I'm assuming you don't take credit cards,' he said.

'Your assumption is correct. Now, there's no paperwork, okay? I don't like that shit.' Dedman wrote something on a sheet of paper. 'This is my name, the address here, and the telephone number. Anyone stops you, the cops or anybody, or if you're in a crash, the story is you borrowed the car from me with my blessing.'

'Insurance?'

'It's insured.'

'And if I break down?'

'Well,' Dedman sat back in his chair, 'for another thirty, you get my 24-hour call-out service.'

'Does it stretch as far as San Diego?'

Dedman looked at the roll of notes. 'I guess that wouldn't be a problem. That where you're headed?'

'Yes. So how much do I owe you?'

Dedman appeared to consider this, then named a figure Reeve found comfortably low. Reeve counted out the notes and made to hand them over, but paused.

'The Dart isn't hot, is it?'

Dedman shook his head vehemently. 'No, sir, it's above board and legal.' He took the notes and counted them, finding the sum satisfactory. He looked at Reeve and smiled. 'I never rent a hot car to a tourist.'

Dedman had warned Reeve that he might get lost a few times on his way out of Los Angeles, an accurate assessment of Reeve's first hour and a half in his new car. He knew all he had to do was follow the coast, eventually picking up I-5, but finding the coast was the problem initially, and keeping to it proved a problem later. The freeway system around Los Angeles was like a joke God was playing on the human brain. The more Reeve focused his mind, the less sense things made. Eventually he let his eyes and mind drift into soft focus, and found himself miraculously on the right road, heading the right way. He wasn't on the coast, he was inland on I-5, but that was fine. I-5 was fine.

He had both windows open and wished he had a radio. One of Dedman's mechanics had offered him one, installation included, for fifty bucks, but it would've meant hanging around the breaking yard for another hour or so, and Reeve had been keen to get going. Now he wished he'd taken the teenager up on the offer. Everything about the Dart was fine except the axles. The steering-wheel juddered in his hands at speeds above 50, and it felt like the problem led directly from the axles, either front or back. He hoped a wheel didn't spin off and roll away ahead of him.

Once on the interstate it was a quick run to San Diego. He came off near the airport and took Kettner Boulevard into the downtown district. He wanted a different hotel from last visit, and something more central, something much closer to the CWC building. His first choice, the Marriott, had rooms. Reeve swallowed hard when told the price, but was too tired to go looking anywhere else – the previous night had been a long one, after all. He took his bag up to the room, pulled open the curtains, flooding the room with light and a spectacular view of the bay, and sat down on the bed.

Then he picked up the telephone and rang Eddie Duhart.

He didn't identify himself. He just asked, 'What's happening?'

Duhart couldn't wait to tell him. '*Everything's* happening! Allerdyce is running around like there's cactus up his ass and all the proctologists are in Hawaii. He knows something happened to him last night, only he doesn't know what.'

'He's back to himself?'

'Seems to be. First thing he did was sack the bodyguards. Then he decided that was too lenient, so they're back on the payroll till he can find a worse fate. Next he phoned for a vet and a van to take away the carcass.'

'But he doesn't remember any details from last night?'

'Not a one. Man, I should get my hands on some of that stuff. He's spent all day trying to put together the pieces. You should hear him. Man is he wild! He dropped into a private hospital, checked in as an emergency. He wanted them to run tests on him. He's been doing everything. He thought maybe he's been hypnotised, so he's got a hypno-therapist coming over to the house to try to get him out of it.'

'Hmm, he may have stumbled on to something.'

'You think the hypnotists can help him remember?'

'I don't know. I've never heard of anyone trying it before.'

'Christ, I hope he *doesn't* remember. He's been to my apartment!'

'Don't fret, Eddie. Has he been in to the office?'

'No, and nothing from the bugs in Dulwater's office either, except that whoever he shares the space with has a flatulence problem.'

'Allerdyce hasn't tried contacting Dulwater?'

'Well, he's made some calls and not gotten an answer, maybe he's been trying to catch him.'

'And he hasn't contacted the police?'

Duhart clucked. 'No, sir, no cops.'

'Which tells you something.'

'Yeah, it tells me a man like Jeffrey Allerdyce doesn't *need* cops. He knows someone broke into his house last night; it won't be long before he gets a gang in to sweep for clues. They'll find the bugs.'

'Doesn't matter.'

'How are you doing anyway?'

'Fine.'

'Where are you?'

'Best you don't know. Remember, if . . . *when* the bugs are found, I want you to lie low, okay? That's the point at which you drop the investigation.'

'Yeah, you said.'

'I mean it. Allerdyce will be cagier than ever. He'll know he's being watched. Just step back and leave it alone.'

'And then what?'

'Wait for me to get back to you. You've got other clients, right? Other cases you could be working on?'

'Sure, but I could work till I was a hundred and seventy, I'd never get another case like this. Hey, what if I need to contact you?'

'I'll phone twice a day, morning and evening.'

'Yeah, but—'

Reeve broke the connection. He wasn't sure he'd ever call Duhart again.

There was a low late-afternoon sun beaming in on downtown San Diego, casting shadows between the blocks and lighting the windows of the buildings. The streets were busy with shoppers on their way home, standing sag-shouldered at bus- and trolley-stops. No office workers – this was Saturday. Reeve had an espresso in a coffee shop right across the street from the Co-World Chemicals building. There was an office supply store next door to the coffee shop. It sold computers and other machines, plus mobile communications equipment. A cheap sign in the window said that it rented, too.

Reeve had rented a cellular phone. It wasn't much bigger than the palm of his hand. He'd put it on his credit card and handed over some cash as a deposit. The man in the store hadn't been too bothered about Reeve's lack of credentials. Maybe that was because he dealt with a lot of foreign businessmen. Maybe it was because he knew he could always cancel Reeve's personal cellphone number, negating the little black telephone altogether. Hook-up to the system was immediate.

So Reeve sat in the coffee shop and punched in some numbers. He tried Eddie Cantona's home first, but there was no answer. With the coffee shop's phone book in front of him on the window-length counter, he tried a couple of the bars Cantona had said he used. At the second bar, whoever had answered the call growled Cantona's name. Eddie Cantona picked up the telephone.

'Hello?' It sounded like he'd said 'yellow'.

'So they let you out?'

Cantona sucked in breath and his voice dropped to a mumble. 'Soon as you left town. That nice detective said I could go, but not to go talking to strange men any more.'

'This was Mike McCluskey?'

'The same. Where the fuck are you?'

'You think anyone's keeping tabs on you?'

'Well, hell, it wouldn't be hard. I only knew *you* a coupla days first time round, and how long did it take you to find me?'

'Three calls. This is the third.'

'There you go. I got to tell you, Gordon, I've been drinking steadily and seriously for some days now. My excuse is that it's in memory of Jim – a one-man moveable wake. But maybe it's because I took a jolt myself.'

'I don't want to get you mixed up in anything. I just want to hire you for a day or so.'

'Oh, is that all?' Cantona said, slipshod voice full of sarcasm. 'Maybe you didn't hear what I just said.'

'I heard.'

The voice dropped low again. 'I was *scared* back there, Mr Reeve.'

'I'm not asking you to do anything dangerous.' Reeve had his free hand cupped around his mouth and the mouthpiece. Nobody in the coffee shop seemed interested in him; they were buying take-out cups for the walk to the bus-stop. Traffic rumbled past, and the air-conditioning rattled like teeth in a cup. Reeve was in no danger of being overheard. 'I just want you to sit in a coffee shop for a while. I want you to keep watch. If you see a man answering the description I give you, call me. That's it.'

'You want me to follow him?'

'Nope.'

'You just want to know when he leaves this building?' Cantona sounded far from convinced.

'Well, I'd rather know when he goes in. Come on, who else in this town can I trust? The only danger you'd be in is from caffeine poisoning, and they do a great decaf espresso here.'

'No liquor licence?'

'No liquor licence. Hey, I'd want you sober.'

'I don't work drunk!'

'Okay, okay. Listen, what do you say?'

'Can we meet? Maybe talk about it over a beer?'

'You know that's not a good idea.'

'In case they're watching me, right?'

'Watching you or watching me. Safer if we don't meet.'

'You're right. Okay, let's give it a stab.'

These would not have been Reeve's favoured choice of words.

He gave the details over the telephone to Cantona – once Cantona had located some paper and a pen that worked. He told Cantona the address of the coffee shop, gave him its opening hours, and then described Kosigin, closing his eyes and picturing the photographs in Allerdyce's file. On the off-chance, he described Jay too. Finally, he gave Cantona his mobile number, and checked for him – Cantona was sobering fast – not only that there was a public payphone in the coffee shop, but that it was working too.

'Monday morning seven-thirty,' Cantona said. 'I'll be in position. Guess I'd better go home now and dry out.'

'Thanks.'

'Hey, you'd do the same for me, right?'

Reeve wasn't sure about that. His next call was to the San Diego Police Department. McCluskey wasn't in the office, and they said they couldn't patch any calls through to him.

'Well, can you get a message to him? He'll want to hear it, believe me.'

'Go ahead, I'll see what I can do.' The woman had a high whining voice, utterly without personality.

'Tell him Gordon Reeve would like to speak to him.' He spelt his surname for her. It took her three goes. 'I'll keep trying.'

'Sure.'

'Thank you very much.'

The young woman in charge of the coffee shop was relieved by the next shift. She seemed furious about something, maybe the fact that she'd been working on her own and they'd been real busy. Two people her own age – one male, one female – took her place, and soon had a rhythm going. One of them took the orders and the money, the other worked the machine. When the queue had been served, the female walked over to Reeve with a pot of coffee and asked if he wanted a refill. Reeve smiled at her and shook his head, then watched her retreat, clearing a couple of the cramped tables as she did. He felt touched by her offer. He knew a lot of places in the US had the same policy, the offer of coffee refills, but it seemed an act of kindness, too, and he hadn't been close to much kindness recently. He could feel defences inside him, barricades he'd hastily erected. They tottered for a moment, but held. He thought of Bakunin and Wagner again, side by side on the barricades of Dresden. The anarchist Bakunin, and Wagner – the friend of Nietzsche. Nietzsche: the self-proclaimed 'first amoralist'. When necessary, when events dictated, they had fought alongside one another. The anarchists would call that proof of the theory of mutual aid. They would say it repudiated Nietzsche's own theory, that the will to power was everything. Opposites reconciled, yes, but momentarily. Look at the role of Russia in World War Two: what happened afterwards was a descent into mistrust and selfishness. Just because you were allies didn't mean you didn't hate one another's guts.

'Jay,' Reeve said quietly, staring at nothing beyond the smudged glaze of the window, the words 'Donuts 'n' Best Coffee' stencilled on it in muted red.

Then he tried McCluskey again, and got through to the same woman.

'Oh yes, Mr Reeve. He said for you to give me your number there and he'll get back to you.'

'No,' Reeve said, and broke the connection again. He got up to leave the coffee shop, and realised by the stiffness in his legs how long he'd been sitting there. As he passed the cash register, he saw a glass tumbler beside it, half-filled with tips, nothing bigger than a quarter. He reckoned the shifts here were college kids, and pushed a dollar into the glass.

'Hey, have a nice evening,' the young woman said. She was choosing some music for the tape machine.

'You too.'

Reeve crossed at the lights with the other pedestrians and checked his reflection in the windscreen of a stopped bus. He didn't look any different from anyone else. He kept pace with a short woman in clacking high heels, so it almost looked like they were together but didn't know one another real well. He was half a step behind her as they passed the steps up to the glass revolving door which led into the foyer of the CWC building. Above the revolving door the CWC symbol was etched into the glass. It looked like a child had taken a line for a walk, so that a single doodle managed to spell out the letters CWC, like the CNN logo on a bad night.

The woman scowled at him eventually, figuring he was trying to pick her up by mime alone, and at the next street crossing he took a right as she went straight ahead. It was another half a block before he realised someone was keeping half a pace behind *him*. He didn't look round, didn't make eye contact; he kept his gaze to the pavement, and that way could watch the man's feet: polished brown shoes with leather soles, charcoal suit-trousers above them. Reeve took another right, into a quieter street. The shoes and trousers kept with him.

Must have picked me up outside the CWC building, he thought. It had to be Jay or one of his men. Thing was, they were too close for it to be mere surveillance. They didn't just want to follow him, they wanted contact. Reeve started fast shallow breathing, oxygenating his blood, and loosened his shoulders, tightening his fists. He walked briskly, hoping he could get his retaliation in first. A couple of pedestrians were coming towards him. He stared hard at them as though trying to see into their souls. He was seeking accomplices. But all the couple saw was an angry man, and they moved out of his way.

It was as good a time as any. Reeve stopped abruptly and swivelled on his heels.

He hadn't noticed that the man in the charcoal suit had slowed his pace a few yards back, and was now standing still, seemingly at ease, his hands out in appeasement. He was a tall man with slick black hair, thinning at the temples. He had a sharp face and sallow cheeks and the slightly narrowed eyes of one who sported contact lenses.

'This is just where I'd have chosen,' the man was saying, 'for the showdown, the confrontation.'

'What?' Reeve was looking around upwards, looking for an assassin's gunsight, a slow-moving car with tinted windows, looking for danger. But all there was was this tall well-dressed man, who looked like he'd be comfortable trying to sell you a spare vest to go with your suit.

'Who the fuck are you?' Reeve snarled.

'I knew you'd come back here. That's why I flew direct, saved time. Don't ask me how I knew, I just felt it.'

'What are you, a clairvoyant?'

'No, Mr Reeve, I study personalities, that's all.'

Reeve blinked. 'Dulwater?'

The man made a small bow with his head. 'I've been watching outside CWC for three hours.'

'You should've stopped for a coffee.'

'Ah, you were in the coffee shop?'

'What do you want?'

'Well, you seem to know who I am. I'm guessing you know what I want.'

'Indulge me.'

Dulwater took a step forwards. 'I want to know what you did to my employer, Mr Reeve.'

Reeve frowned, trying to look puzzled.

Alfred Dulwater just smiled. 'Might *I* make a guess?' he said.

'Go ahead.'

Dulwater pouted thoughtfully. 'I think it's known as *burundanga*.'

Reeve tried not to look impressed.

'I've heard of it,' Dulwater continued, 'but this is the first occasion I've known someone to use it.'

'I don't know what you're talking about.'

'Mr Allerdyce caught up with me an hour ago, by telephone. He had a very strange story to tell. Did the two London operatives tell you my name?' Reeve said nothing, which seemed to be what Dulwater was expecting. 'They told me they hadn't, but I didn't believe them.'

Though Reeve had been looking Dulwater in the eye, his peripheral vision had all been for the man's clothes. Dulwater didn't look armed, and he didn't look particularly dangerous. He was tall, a head taller than Reeve, but while his face showed cunning and intelligence there wasn't anything else there, nothing physical. Reeve reckoned he could take him out. He didn't relax, but he felt a little better.

'I know what you're thinking,' Dulwater said,

'What?'

'You're thinking about violence. In particular, you're thinking of violence which might be perpetrated by you upon me. I shouldn't take that thought any further.' Dulwater smiled again. 'I've seen the psychiatric report.'

Reeve remembered that Dulwater had been in his house. He knew what the man was talking about. He was talking about the warning. Any more fits of violence and Reeve might well be sectioned.

'I mean,' said Dulwater, 'after that scene in the bar . . .'

'Your men started it. I've got witnesses.'

'Terrible mess those two are in – and you, Mr Reeve, you don't have a scratch on you. How's the foot by the way? Kaprisky says he stomped on the intruder's bare foot.'

Reeve stared levelly at Dulwater. 'Nothing wrong with either foot,' he said.

'I'm glad to hear it.'

'So, what now?'

'Now? Now we go somewhere and have a talk. You see, we have a lot in common. We're both after information on Kosigin. And more than that . . .'

'Yes?'

Dulwater smiled. 'Neither of us much likes Jeffrey Allerdyce.'

They went to a bar. It might've been a bar Jim Reeve used to drink in, Gordon Reeve couldn't remember. While Dulwater went to the men's room, Reeve tried the Police Department again. This time he got through to Mike McCluskey, who sounded out of breath.

'Hey, Gordon,' McCluskey said matily, 'where are you?'

'Near San Diego,' Reeve told him.

'Yeah? Any reason for that?'

'I never do anything without a reason, McCluskey. I want us to talk.'

'Sure, no problem. Let me take down your—'

'Later tonight.' A waitress was advancing with the beers they'd ordered. Dulwater, rubbing his hands, was right behind her. 'Say midnight.'

'Midnight? Well, that's a funny—'

'La Jolla, remember that place we went for a drink after you showed me where my brother was murdered?'

'Now, Gordon, you know there's not one shred of evidence—'

'Outside there at midnight. If you're not alone, I don't show.'

Dulwater sat down as Reeve cut the call. 'What was that?' he asked.

'A sideshow,' said Reeve, taking one of the glasses. He gulped an inch of liquid and licked his lips. 'So why are we having this good-natured drink, Mr Dulwater? How come you don't have me trussed up in a crate on my way back to Washington?'

Dulwater lifted his own beer but did not drink. 'I like my job, Gordon, I like it fine. But I have ambition just like anyone else.'

'You want to set up for yourself?'

Dulwater shook his head. 'I want promotion.'

'Well, if you take me back to Allerdyce, I'm sure you'd be well placed . . .'

'No, that's not the way Allerdyce works. He'd only want more. Besides, what are you to him? You're a one-night irritant, like a mild allergic reaction. You're not the prize.'

'Kosigin?'

Dulwater nodded. 'I get the feeling if I stick close to you, I'll get Kosigin.'

'And then you hand Kosigin to Allerdyce?'

'But not all at once. He wouldn't be grateful if I just handed that bastard over. One little piece at a time.'

Reeve shook his head. Everybody wanted something: Duhart wanted something on Allerdyce; Dulwater wanted something *over* Allerdyce; Allerdyce wanted Kosigin; Kosigin and Jay wanted Reeve.

And what did Gordon Reeve want? He thought of Nietzsche again: the will to power. Power was what most of these games were all about, the desire for power, the fear of loss of power. Reeve wasn't a part of that game. He was on another board with different pieces. He wanted *revenge*.

'You know,' he said, 'I'm not even sure I should be talking to someone who broke into my damned house.'

Dulwater shrugged. 'I wasn't the first. Alliance didn't plant those bugs, Kosigin's men did. Besides, what have you to lose by co-operating? You surely don't think you can do anything to harm Kosigin on your own.'

'I'm not on my own.'

'You've got help?' Dulwater thought for the merest second. 'Cantona?' Reeve's face failed to disguise his surprise. 'Cantona's a deadbeat. You think you can put him up against Kosigin?'

'How do you know about Cantona?'

'You forget, Kosigin hired Alliance to compile a dossier on your brother. We're very thorough, Gordon. We not only did a full background check, including family, we watched him for a couple of weeks. We watched him get to know Cantona.'

'Then you handed the lot over to Kosigin and he had my brother killed.'

'There's no evidence—'

'Everybody keeps telling me that!'

Dulwater still hadn't touched his drink. He ran his thumb around the rim of the frosted glass. 'A good argument for letting me help you. The courts aren't going to be any use. You're never going to have enough evidence to go to court with. The best you can hope for is that someone else makes Kosigin's life hell. Kosigin lives for power, Gordon. If someone else gains power over *him* it's the worst torture he could ever imagine, and it will last the rest of his life.' He sat back, argument over.

Reeve sighed. 'Maybe you're right,' he lied. 'Okay, what exactly do you propose?'

Dulwater stared at him, measuring his sincerity. Reeve concentrated on the beer. 'Why did you come back here?' Dulwater asked.

'I wanted to speak to a few people. I intend speaking to one of them tonight. You can help.'

'How?'

'Two things: one, I need a video camera, a good one, plus a couple of recorders, more if you can get them. I want to make copies of a videotape.'

'You need these tonight?' Reeve nodded. 'Okay, I don't foresee a problem. What's the other thing?'

'I need you to keep lookout for me.'

'Where?'

'In La Jolla.' Reeve paused. 'About two miles away from where I'll actually be.'

'I think you've lost me.'

'I'll explain later. You're sure you can get the equipment?'

'Pretty sure. It may take a few phone calls. It may have to be brought down from LA. Are you in a hotel here?'

'Same one I stayed in last time, the Radisson.'

'I'm in the Marriott,' Dulwater informed him. Reeve's face was a mask. 'It's more central. We'll set the gear up in my room if that's all right with you.'

'Fine,' Reeve said drily.

At last Dulwater took a sip of his beer. He pretended to savour it as he framed another question. 'What is it you're going to video exactly?'

'A confession,' Reeve said. 'One man unburdening his soul.'

'Film at eleven,' Dulwater said with a smile.

19

Reeve parked the Dart a couple of streets away from where he wanted to be.

There was a pizza delivery van parked kerbside, a little boxy three-wheeler which looked like it might use an electric motor. He hadn't seen anyone inside it as he'd driven past, and he didn't see anyone in it now. He gave it another couple of minutes – maybe the delivery boy was having trouble making change. But he knew there was no delivery boy really. What there was was an undercover cop, keeping watch on the bungalow, except he'd been called to another job just a couple of miles away. The electric motor wouldn't take him there, so his buddies had come and picked him up.

Reeve checked his watch. It was quarter to midnight. He didn't have much time. Having already noted the delivery van, he hadn't bothered bringing the video camera with him. It was still locked in the Dart's boot. He walked down the street then back up the other side. There was no one about, no neighbourhood patrol or crime watch. Reeve stopped for a moment beside the delivery van. It boasted a radio with hand-set attached. He saw now why they'd used a delivery van: there was nothing particularly odd about such a van having a radio. It might have been so the driver could keep in touch with base.

Indeed, that was just what it was for.

Lights were burning in the bungalow, but not brightly. A reading-lamp maybe. The curtains were closed, the light seeping out from around the edges of the window. Reeve opened the slatted wooden gate, hearing bells jangle from a string attached to the back of it. He walked up to the bungalow and rang the bell. He was hoping there would be someone home. With the journalist dead, he was betting they'd have let the scientist come home. He heard a chain rattle. A security chain. The door opened a couple of inches, and Reeve stepped back to give it the meat of his shoe-heel. It took two blows till the door burst open.

He had wanted the elderly man shocked, surprised, scared. He was getting all three.

'Dr Killin?' he said to the figure cowering in the short hallway, holding a book over his head. The title of the book was something to do with molecular biology.

The old man looked up, blinking spaniel eyes. Reeve hit him just hard enough to send him to sleep.

He left the body where it lay and went back outside. There was still no one about. The houses were separated by high hedges. Somebody might have seen him from the house across the way but it was in darkness and, besides, the pizza van hid Dr Killin's doorway from general view. Reeve jumped the gate rather than bothering to open it, and jogged back to his car. He brought it round to Dr Killin's house, parking next to the pizza van. The old man didn't weigh much and was easy to carry out to the car. Reeve dropped him on to the back seat, then went back to the house, switched off the lamp beside Killin's chair, and pulled the front door to. In the shadow of the covered porch, you could hardly notice the splintered wood of the surround. From out on the pavement, you couldn't see it at all.

Reeve got into the Dart and drove north on a local road that seemed to parallel I-5 but kept closer to the edge of the Pacific Ocean. Just south of Del Mar he pulled the car into a rest area sheltered from the road but with a view of the ocean. Not that you could see anything much, but with the window rolled down Reeve could hear the waves. He got out of the car and opened the boot, bringing out the video camera and the replacement for Lucky 13. Back in the driver's seat, he swivelled so he was facing Killin. Then he switched on the car's interior lights. Dulwater and he had discussed lighting, but this camera had a good low-light facility and even a spot-beam of its own – though using it would drain the batteries fast. Reeve switched the camera to ready, removed the lens cap, and put his eyes to the viewfinder. He watched the old man stirring. The needle on the viewfinder told him the lighting was poor, but not unusable. Reeve put the camera down again and picked up the dagger. It was the first thing Dr Killin saw when he woke up.

He sat upright, looking terrified. Reeve wondered for a moment if the knife would be enough to slice the truth from the man.

'What's going on?' the doctor asked shakily. 'Where am I? Who are you?'

'This knife,' Reeve said quietly, 'could bisect you from skull to scrotum and still have an edge on it.'

The doctor swallowed and licked his lips.

'I have some questions,' Reeve said. 'I want answers to them. You're being watched, round the clock protection. Why?'

'That's absurd. Why would anyone watch me?'

Reeve smiled without a trace of humour. 'You worked for Co-World Chemicals, didn't you? Did you ever meet Dr Owen Preece?'

'I'm sorry, I want to help you, but I don't know that name.'

Reeve angled the dagger so light glinted off the blade, causing Killin to squint. The doctor licked his dry lips again.

'Fear can do that,' Reeve told him. 'It stops the saliva getting to your mouth. Here.' He reached into his left-hand jacket pocket and handed Killin a small plastic bottle of mineral water. Killin took the bottle and stared at it. 'Can't answer questions with a dry mouth,' Reeve said. He drew out an identical bottle from his right-hand pocket. 'Can't ask them either.' He broke the seal and unscrewed the top. Killin was still staring at him. 'You don't want it?' Reeve said. 'Want mine instead?'

Killin thought about it then shook his head, broke the bottle's seal, and unscrewed the top. He sipped at the water, tasting it, then gulping a mouthful. Reeve put his own bottle on the passenger seat and lifted the video camera. To do so meant putting down the dagger.

'Now,' he said, 'I hope you've noticed this car has no back doors. Your only exit is past me, and I don't think you want to try that.'

'Look, I'll answer your questions if I can, but I want to know what's going on.'

Killin was growing either testier or more confident – confident that Reeve wasn't the type to kill him.

'I'll tell you,' Reeve said. 'I want to know about Co-World Chemicals. I want to know about Dr Owen Preece and the work he did for CWC. I want to know about a man called Kosigin who set the whole thing in motion. I want to know about pesticides, Doctor. I want to know what *you* know.'

Killin took his time answering. 'It's true,' he said, nursing the bottle, 'that I worked for CWC. I headed the R&D team for four years, but I'd worked for the company for fifteen years before that. You are correct that a man called Kosigin also works for CWC, though in what capacity I'm not sure. He may not still be there; I don't keep in touch with CWC, and I believe executives in most companies flit about from competitive salary to competitive salary. And that,' he said, 'is all I *do* know.'

'Did a man called Reeve ever come to see you?'

'I don't recollect.' Killin sounded impatient.

'A British journalist? He came to your house wanting to ask questions.'

'If he did, I didn't let him in.' He tapped his forehead. 'My memory's not what it . . .' His fingers stayed on his forehead, rubbing at beads of sweat which were appearing there. He blinked hard, as though trying to focus. 'I don't feel well,' he said. 'You should know that my heart has been giving me trouble. There are some tablets back at my home . . .'

'You're all right, Doctor. You're just drugged.' Reeve hadn't started the tape running yet, but he had his eye to the viewfinder. Even in colour, Killin's face looked grey, like he was acting in a black and white movie. 'You don't need to break the seal to inject something into a plastic bottle. You just need a dot of glue to seal the bottle up again.'

'What?' The doctor lost the faculty of speech for a moment. Reeve took the doped bottle from him and replaced it with his own.

'Here, drink this, it'll help.'

'I don't feel well.'

'You'll feel a lot better when you clear your conscience. The birdy will help with that. Now, where were we? Yes, Co-World Chemicals.' Reeve started the tape running. 'You were telling me, Dr Killin, that you worked for CWC – what was it – nineteen years?'

'Nineteen years,' Killin agreed, his voice dull and metallic.

'The last four of those heading the company's R&D?'

'That's right.'

'Did you know a man called Owen Preece?'

'Dr Preece, yes, he was a psychiatrist.'

'Well respected?'

'They might have invented the word "eminent" with him in mind.'

'Did he do any work for CWC?'

'Yes, he headed a research team looking into pesticides.'

'Specifically?'

'Specifically side effects.'

'And these pesticides were . . . ?'

'Organo-phosphorous.'

'So he was looking at PrPs?'

'Well, the *team* examined all aspects of a great many pesticides. Its conclusions were published in several journals.'

'And those conclusions were accurate?'

'No, they were faked.' The doctor stared out of the car's back window. 'Is that the ocean out there? Doesn't it sound angry?'

'Yes, it does,' Reeve said.

'It should be angry. We dump so much dangerous trash into it. Our rivers trickle mercury and other poisons into it. You wouldn't think you could kill an ocean, would you? But we'll do it one day. That's how negligent we are.'

'Is CWC negligent?'

'Monstrously so.'

'Why haven't you spoken out about it?'

'To protect my career, for one thing. I discovered early in my professional life that I was a coward, a moral coward. I might seethe inside, but I'd do nothing to upset the status quo. Later, after I'd retired, I could have done something, but that would have meant admitting my silence, too. You see, I'm just as culpable as anyone. Preece was a psychiatrist, not a scientist; it was easy for him to believe that the cause of certain diseases might lie in the mind itself. Even today there are people who refuse to acknowledge the existence of ME as a disease proper. They say it's psychosomatic. But Preece's group, the scientists – we had *proof* that pesticides and certain neurological diseases were causally linked.'

'You had proof?'

'And we let them cover it up.'

'Who's them?'

'CWC.' He paused, gathering himself. 'Kosigin primarily. I've never been sure whether those above him knew about it at the time, or are any wiser now. He operates within his own sphere. Those above him allow him this leeway . . . Perhaps they have an inkling of what he's like, and want to distance themselves from him.'

'What is he like, Doctor?'

'He's not evil, that's not what I'm suggesting. I don't even think he's power mad. I believe he thinks everything he does is in the genuine interests of the company. He is a corporation man, that's all. He'll do all he can – anything it takes – to stop damage being done to CWC.'

'Did you tell him about the journalist, James Reeve?'

'Yes, I did. I was frightened.'

'And he sent men to guard you?'

'Yes, and then he told me to take a short vacation.'

'There's still a man guarding your house, isn't there?'

'Not for much longer. The threat has disappeared.'

'Kosigin told you that?'

'Yes, he told me to put my mind at rest.'

'Do the guards work for CWC?'

'Oh no, they're policemen.'

'Policemen?'

'Yes. Kosigin has a friend in the Police Department.'

'Do you know his name?'

'McCluskey. If there's any trouble, any problem, I can always phone this man McCluskey. You know something? I live about half a mile from the ocean, but I've never heard it sound so angry.'

'They're just waves, Dr Killin.'

'You do them an injustice.' He sipped undoped water. 'We all do.'

'So let me get this straight in my head, Dr Killin. You're saying you were part of a cover-up instigated by Kosigin?'

'That's right.'

'And you're not sure whether anyone higher up in CWC knew about it at the time, or knows about it now?'

The old man nodded, staring out of the window. Reeve recorded his face in profile, the face of a sad old man who had little to be proud of in his life.

'We're poisoning everything. We're poisoning the very food we eat. All over the world, from the biggest agribusiness to the smallest share-cropper, they're all doing business with the chemical companies, companies like CWC. In the richest countries and the poorest. And we're all eating the results – everything from daily bread to a nice juicy steak. All tainted. It's like the sea: you can't see the damage with the naked eye. That makes it easy to hide the problem, easy to cover it up and just deny, deny, deny.'

Slowly, methodically, Killin started to beat his forehead against the side window.

'Whoa,' Reeve said, pulling him away. 'It's not your fault.'

'Oh, but it is. It is!'

'Look, everything's going to be all right. You're going to forget all about this.'

'I can't forget.'

'Well, maybe not, but trust me on this. What about Agrippa? What does it have to do with any of this?'

'Agrippa? Agrippa has everything to do with it, don't you see? Agrippa has several patents pending on genetically engineered crop strains, with many more patents to come in the future. Do you realise what those will be worth? I don't think it's an exaggeration to say billions. Genetics is the industry of the future, no doubt about it.'

Reeve nodded, understanding. 'And if Kosigin's dirty tricks came to light, the licensing authorities might take a pretty dim view?'

'CWC could lose existing patents *and* be banned from applying for others. That's why the cover-up is imperative.'

'Because it's good for the company,' Reeve muttered. He made to switch off the camera.

'Aren't you going to ask me about Preece?'

'What?'

'Preece. That's what the reporter wanted to talk about.'

Reeve stared at Killin, then put the viewfinder back to his eye and watched as the lens refocused itself on the old man. 'Go on, Doctor. What about Preece?'

'Preece had a reputation to think of. You think he'd have worked for Kosigin, covered everything up and signed his name to the lies if there had been an alternative?'

'There wasn't an alternative?'

'Kosigin had information on Owen. He'd had people do some digging. They found out about Preece and his patients. The ones at the hospital in Canada.'

'What about them?'

'Preece had for a time advocated a kind of sexual shock treatment. Sex as a means to focus the mind, to pull it back to reality.'

Gordon Reeve swallowed. 'Are you saying he raped patients?'

'He had sex with some of them. It was . . . it was experimental. He never published anything, naturally enough. Still it was never the best kept of secrets. These patients were unpredictable. Preece had to have orderlies in the room to hold them down.'

'Jesus Christ.'

'The psychiatric community got to know about it, and the stories spread out until even people like me heard them.'

'And no one kicked up a stink?'

'These patients were incarcerated. They were fair game for experiments.'

'So Kosigin found out and used the information as a lever?'

'Yes. He had a private detective work on Preece's history.'

'Alliance Investigative?'

'I don't know . . .'

'A man called Jeffrey Allerdyce?'

'The name sounds familiar.'

Reeve thought for a moment. 'My brother knew this?'

'Your brother?'

'The reporter.'

'Yes, he knew some of it.'

'How could he know?'

'I take it he'd talked to a few people. As I said, it was not the world's best-kept secret. If the reporter had been looking into Owen's past, he would have stumbled on it eventually. I mean, he would have known about Owen and his patients.'

And would have put two and two together, Reeve thought. Jim hadn't only been trying to blow the pesticide story open, he'd made things more personal. He'd been homing in on Kosigin as manipulator *and* blackmailer. Kosigin wasn't protecting CWC, he was protecting *himself*. Reeve turned the camera round so it was pointing at him, and waited for the auto-focus to pick out his face. Then he spoke.

'This is being kept nice and safe, a long way away from you,' he said. 'I drugged the old man, that's why he's been talking. The drug's called *burundanga*; it's Colombian. You can check on it. You might even want your R&D people to do something with it. But listen to this: if you do anything to Dr Killin I'll know about it, and a copy of this tape goes straight to the police. And I don't mean the San Diego PD. We know now how much of *that* outfit you own, Kosigin. Okay?'

Reeve sought the right button and turned the recorder off. He wound it back a little and pressed Play. Peering into the viewfinder again, he saw his own face, muddy but definable. His voice came from the small built-in speaker.

'You can check on it. You might even want your R&D people to—'

Satisfied, he switched off the camera and laid it on the passenger seat. 'Dr Killin,' he said, 'I'm going to take you back now.'

They drove in silence, Killin nodding off in the back seat, his head sliding lower and lower down the backrest. Reeve stopped the car three streets away from Killin's bungalow, opened the passenger door, and pulled the back of the passenger seat down. Then he shook Killin awake.

'Get out of the car, Doctor. You'll know where you are. Just walk home and go to bed. Get some sleep.'

Killin staggered out of the car like he was drunk. He stood up straight, staggered a little more, and looked around him like he was on the moon.

'Look at all the stars,' he said. There were plenty of them up there. 'So many,' he said, 'you'd never think you could poison them all.' He bent down to peer into the car. 'But give us a chance and we'll do it. There are hundreds of tons of space-junk flying around up there already. That's an excellent start, wouldn't you say?'

Reeve closed the passenger door and drove off.

Dulwater sat on his bed, watching the television. He'd boosted the brightness and adjusted the colour and contrast. There was nothing wrong with the sound. Dr Killin was on the screen, saying his piece. Dulwater was watching the performance for a third time, and saying 'This is fucking unbelievable' for the seventh or eighth.

The tape that was playing was simultaneously being recorded on to the third blank tape of a box of five.

'Fucking unbelievable,' Dulwater said.

Reeve watched the tape counter. Dulwater's room was three floors down from his own. He'd been nervous coming here, but none of the staff had recognised him. It was a big hotel after all, and he'd done nothing to make himself memorable.

'Of course,' Dulwater said, 'you could never use this in a court of law. Killin's obviously been drugged.'

'You already said we'd never get Kosigin into a courtroom anyway.'

'Well, that's true too.'

'I don't particularly *want* him to stand trial. I just want him to know I have this on record.'

They'd come to the bit where Killin asked if Reeve didn't want to hear about Preece.

'Anyway,' said Reeve, 'what do you care? You've got what you wanted right there. Your boss compiled one of his famous dossiers on the dark side of Owen Preece's history, and this opened Preece up to blackmail.'

'Yes.'

'You should be happy. You've got something on your boss.'

'I suppose so.' Dulwater swung off the bed and went to the table. He had a bottle of whisky there, and helped himself to another glass. Reeve had already refused twice, and wasn't going to be given a third chance. 'What about you?' Dulwater asked between gulps. 'What're you going to do with the tapes?'

'One for me, and one for Kosigin.'

'What's the point of sending him one?'

'So he knows I know.'

'So what? He'll only send that butt-fuck Jay after you.'

Reeve smiled. 'Exactly.'

'Doesn't that bastard have a surname?' Dulwater sounded three-fifths drunk.

'Jay is his surname.'

'You really know him then?'

'I know him. Tell me again about the bar.'

Dulwater smiled. 'Half the damned police department must have been there. You told McCluskey you wanted one on one? You got a hundred on one. Cars, vans, armed to the teeth. Man, he was ready for you and then some. You should have seen how angry he was when he figured it was a no-show. And his pals weren't too happy with him either.'

'He'll be worse when he finds out I've walked into Killin's house after he pulled the guard away.'

'Oh yeah, he'll pop some blood vessels. And then Kosigin'll pop *him*.'

'I hope so.'

The tape was coming to its end, Reeve's face on the screen. Dulwater finished his drink and crouched in front of the machine. 'You know, Gordon, I called the Radisson. I thought it was pretty dumb of you to stay the same place you stayed last trip. But you're not that dumb, are you?'

'No, I'm not,' Reeve said. He was right behind Dulwater, arms stretched out, when Dulwater stood up. As Dulwater turned, slowed by the alcohol, Reeve brought his hands together in what would have been a sharp clap, had Dulwater's ears not been in the way. Dulwater's face creased in sudden excruciating pain, and his balance went. He bounced off the bed and crumpled on to the floor, trying his best to rise again quickly.

Reeve kicked him once in the head and that dropped him.

'No, I'm not,' he repeated quietly, standing over Dulwater. He didn't think he'd hit him hard enough to burst an eardrum. But then it wasn't what you'd call an exact science. The Nietzsche quote came to him: 'Must one first shatter their ears to teach them to hear with their eyes?' Well, maybe he was one of Nietzsche's gentlemen after all.

He spent a few minutes getting everything ready. Then he called McCluskey.

'Hey, McCluskey,' he said.

'You sonofabitch, where were you? I waited hours.'

'Well, leastways you weren't lonely.'

There was a pause. 'What do you mean?'

'I mean all your boyfriends.'

Another pause, then a sigh. 'All right, Gordon, I admit it – but listen, and this is a friend speaking now, you're on Interpol's list, man. It came through after we spoke. The French police want to talk to you about some murders. Hell, when I read that I didn't know what to think.'

'Nice story, McCluskey.'

'Now wait—'

'I'm gone.'

Reeve dropped the receiver on to the bed. He could hear McCluskey asking if anyone was still there. To drop a bigger hint, Reeve put the TV volume up. It was the insomniacs' shopping channel. It would take McCluskey time to trace the call, once he figured the phone had been left off the hook. Time enough for Reeve to check out of the hotel and into another. He took three copies of the video with him, leaving just the one.

He knew that if McCluskey and Dulwater sat down to watch the video together, they might find out it was better all round to destroy it. Or rather, McCluskey would want it destroyed, and he'd tell Dulwater that if he didn't let him destroy it, then Mr Allerdyce might be appraised of the situation – such as what Gordon Reeve had been doing phoning from Dulwater's hotel room, and what part Dulwater had played in the videotaping . . .

So in all, Reeve felt he needed three copies. One for himself, one for Kosigin.

And one just to let Allerdyce know the score.

20

Reeve headed north out of town on I-5, citing a 'family crisis' as the reason he had to leave the Marriott at such an odd hour. On the way down from Los Angeles, he had picked out a number of dreary-looking roadside motels, just off I-5 on the coastal road which ran parallel with it. He checked the mileage as he drove, and came off the interstate near Solana Beach. He was twenty miles out from the Marriott. The motel had a red neon sign which was making a buzzing sound as he parked beneath it. The reception was all locked up, but there was a sign drawing his attention to the machine attached to the wall alongside. It looked like a cash machine, but was actually an Automated Motel Reception. Reeve slipped his credit card into the slot and followed the onscreen instructions. The key which appeared from another slot was a narrow plastic card with holes punched in it. The machine flashed up a final message saying it wished him a pleasant night's sleep. Reeve wished the machine a pleasant night, too.

The rooms were around the far side of the building. Reeve drove slowly and picked out his room number with his headlights. There were four cars parked, and about twenty rooms. Reeve guessed they weren't doing great business at the Ocean Palms Resort Beach Motel. He also guessed that 'Resort' and 'Beach' were misnomers; the motel was a motorist's tired overnight stop, nothing more. The 1950s cinderblock construction told its own story. The building was in a gulch, closer to I-5 than any beach. The Cinderblock Last Resort Motel would have been a more accurate name.

But the locks on the doors were new. Reeve slotted home his card, turned the handle, and pulled the card out. He had his bag with him and slung it over a chair. He checked the room over, tired as he was – just the one door and one window. He tried the air conditioner and wasn't surprised when it didn't work. The lightbulb in the lamp fixed into the wall over the bedhead was dead too, but he took out the dud and replaced it with a working bulb from the ceiling light. He went back out again, locking his door, and prowled the area. There was a small well-lit room at the end of the row. It had no windows and no doors and a bare concrete floor. There were humming machines in there, one dispensing cold drinks, another snacks, and the last one ice. When he lifted the lid he saw there was no ice, just a small metal paddle on a chain. He looked in his pocket for quarters, then went back to the Dart and found a few more. Enough for a can of cola, a chocolate bar, and some potato chips. He took his haul back to the room and settled on the sagging mattress. There was an ugly lamp on the table beside the TV, so he moved it where he couldn't see it. Then he switched on the TV and stared towards it for a while, eating and drinking and thinking about things.

When he woke up, the morning programmes were on and a maid was cranking a trolley past his door. He sat up and rubbed his head. His watch told him ten a.m. He'd been asleep the best part of six hours. He ran a tepid shower and stripped off his clothes. He stayed a long time in the shower, letting the water hammer his back and shoulders while he soaped his chest. He had fallen asleep thinking and he was thinking now. How badly did he want Kosigin? Did he want Kosigin at all? Maybe Dulwater was right: the proper torment for Kosigin was to give someone else – Allerdyce in this case – power over him. It was a right and just fate, like something Dante would have dreamed up for one of the circles of Hell.

But then Reeve liked Allerdyce little better than he liked Kosigin. He wished he had a solution, something that would erase them all. But life was never that simple, was it?

Checking out of the motel was as easy as dropping his key into a box. He'd been there the best part of eight hours and hadn't seen a soul, and the only person he'd even heard was the chambermaid. It was everything he could have asked for.

By now he guessed McCluskey would be tearing up every hotel room in the city. He'd want details of Reeve's car, but Dulwater wouldn't be able to help him, and neither would anyone else. If he checked the automobile registration details at the Marriott, he'd see that Reeve had put down a false licence plate attached to an equally fictitious Pontiac Sunfire. Reeve drove the Dart down to a stretch of beach and parked. He pulled off shoes and socks and walked across the sand to the ocean's edge. He walked the beach for a while, then started jogging. He wasn't alone: there were a few other men out here, mostly older than him, all of them jogging along the waterline. But none of them ran as far as Reeve did. He ran until he was sweating then stripped off his shirt and ran some more.

Finally, he fell back on to the sand and lay there, sky swimming overhead, waves pounding in his ears. There were toxins in the sky and in the sea. There were toxins in his body. So much for the Superman. So much for Mutual Aid. Reeve spent the rest of that Sunday on the beach, dozing, walking, thinking. He was letting McCluskey and Dulwater sweat. His guess was that they wouldn't go to Kosigin, not right away. They'd try to find Gordon Reeve first. At least McCluskey would. Reeve wasn't so sure about Dulwater; he was the more unpredictable of the two.

That evening he ate at a roadside diner, his waitress not believing him when he asked for soup, a salad, and some orange juice.

'That all you want, sweetheart?'

'That's all.'

Even then, he wondered about additives in the juice, chemicals in the soup stock, residues in the salad vegetables. He wondered if he'd ever enjoy a meal again.

After a good night's sleep in another motel, Reeve took the Dart back into San Diego. His face was still stinging from his day on the beach. The traffic was heavy heading into town. It was the start of another working week. Eventually Reeve hit the waterfront, parked in the first space he found, and went walkabout.

He found the Gaslamp Quarter. He accosted the first non-crazy-looking beggar who approached him and laid out his scheme. The beggar forced the fee up a couple of notches from the price of a drink to the price of dinner *and* a drink, but Reeve reckoned he had dollars to spare. The beggar walked with him up Fifth Avenue and west to the CWC building. Reeve handed him the package.

It was pretty crude: a plastic carrier bag sealed shut with Sellotape, and 'MR KOSIGIN: PRIVATE & CONFIDENTIAL' in felt-penned capitals.

'Now, I'm going to be watching, so just do what I told you,' he warned his messenger. Then he stood across the street, on the corner outside the coffee shop. He could see Cantona inside, dunking a doughnut. But Cantona couldn't see him, and Reeve kept it that way. He kept an eye open for Dulwater or anyone else, but Dulwater was probably still tied up sorting out his own problems. It was a risk, using the coffee shop. After all, Dulwater knew Reeve himself had used the premises and Dulwater knew what Cantona looked like. But Reeve reckoned he was safe enough. Meantime, the beggar had entered the CWC building.

Reeve waited a few minutes, then walked to another vantage point and waited a few more. Nobody left the CWC building. As he'd guessed would happen, an unmarked police car eventually screamed to a halt outside the entrance. McCluskey got out, and was met half-way up the steps by Kosigin himself.

It was Reeve's first real look at Kosigin, Allerdyce's photographs aside. He was a short, slim man who wore his suit like he was modelling in a commercial. From this distance, he looked as dangerous as a hamburger. But then after what Reeve had learned lately, he couldn't be sure any more just how safe a hamburger was.

Kosigin led McCluskey into the building. McCluskey looked tired, pasty-faced. He'd had a very long couple of days. Reeve wondered if the detective had slept at all. He hoped not. He knew the beggar was inside, probably sandwiched between two security men. They'd want to ask him questions. They'd maybe take the money away from him; or threaten to, if he didn't give a convincing description of his benefactor.

Reeve's mobile rang. He held it up to his ear. Unsurprisingly, Cantona's voice came over loud and clear.

'Hey,' he said, 'your man just came out of the building. But get this, only as far as the steps where he met up with that fucking detective. They've both gone back inside.'

Reeve smiled. Cantona was doing his job. 'Thanks,' he said into the mouthpiece. 'Keep watching.'

'Sure. Hey, do I get to take a lunch break?'

'What? After that doughnut you just ate?'

There was silence on the line. When Cantona next spoke, he sounded amused. 'You sonofabitch, where are you?'

'I'm just leaving.' Reeve put away the telephone, turned on his heels and headed into the shopping district.

The first thing he did was have a haircut. Then he bought some very plain clothes which all but made him invisible. The barber had given him a shave too. If he hadn't been in fear of his life, Reeve would have felt great. He found a nice restaurant on the edge of Gaslamp and had lunch with the other business people. His table was near the window, facing another table laid for two with a single woman eating at it. She smiled at him from time to time, and he smiled back. He had the sense that rather than flirting with him, she was acknowledging her right – and his, too – to dine alone. She went back to her paperback novel, and Reeve watched the street outside. During dessert, he saw his messenger slouch past, a dazed scowl on his face. The world had given him another punch in the teeth, and the man was trying to figure out how he'd walked into it. Reeve vowed that if he saw him later, he'd slip him a dollar without stopping.

Hell, maybe he'd make it two.

He gave Kosigin a couple of hours, then telephoned from his mobile. He was guessing they'd try to trace any calls made to Kosigin. Reeve sat on a bench in a shopping mall and made the call.

'Mr Kosigin's office, please.'

'Just one minute.' The switchboard operator transferred him to a secretary.

'Mr Kosigin, please.'

'May I ask who's calling?'

'Sure, my name's Reeve. Believe me, he'll want to talk to me.'

'I'll try his office, Mr Reeve.'

'Thanks.'

The secretary put him on to one of those annoying music loops. He started to time how long he was kept waiting. He could visualise them setting up an extra telephone set so McCluskey could listen in, could see McCluskey busy on another line trying to get a trace on the call. Reeve gave it thirty seconds before he cut the connection. He walked to a coffee stand and bought a double decaf *latte*. He peeled off the plastic cover until he had a hole big enough to sip through, and window-shopped the mall. Then he sat on another bench and made the call again.

'Mr Kosigin's office, please.'

'Just one minute.'

And then Kosigin's secretary again, sounding slightly flustered.

'It's Reeve again,' he said. 'I have an aversion to waiting.'

'Hold the line please.'

Fifteen seconds later, a male voice came on the phone. 'Mr Reeve? This is Kosigin.' The voice was as smooth as the suit Kosigin wore. 'How can I help you?'

'What did you think of the video?'

'Dr Killin was obviously drugged, delirious. I'd say he'd almost been brainwashed into telling that crazy story. Abduction is a very serious offence, Mr Reeve.'

'What did McCluskey think of it?'

That stopped Kosigin for a moment. 'Naturally, I sent for the police.'

'Before you watched the video,' Reeve stated. 'That's a bit suspicious, isn't it? Almost like you were expecting something. I take it you're recording this call, that's why you're acting the innocent. Fine, act away. But Kosigin, I've got the tape. I've got *lots* of copies of it. You don't know who's going to receive one in the mail one of these fine mornings. Maybe they'll believe your version, maybe they'll believe Killin's.'

Another pause. Was Kosigin taking instructions from someone? Maybe McCluskey.

Maybe Jay.

'Perhaps we should meet, Mr Reeve.'

'Yeah? Just the two of us, same as I was supposed to meet McCluskey? Only McCluskey turned up with his private personal army, and you, Kosigin, you'd turn up alone – right?'

'Right.'

'Apart from Jay, of course, training a laser-sight on my forehead.'

Another pause.

Reeve was enjoying this. 'I'll call back in ten minutes,' he told Kosigin, then hung up.

He walked out of the mall into bright afternoon sun and warm coastal breeze. He didn't think he'd ever felt more alive. He made the next call from outside the main post office.

'So, Kosigin, had any thoughts?'

'About what? I believe you're a wanted man in Europe, Mr Reeve. Not a very pleasant situation.'

'But you could do something about that, right?'

'Could I?'

'Yes, you could hand Jay over to the French authorities, you could tell them he set me up.'

'You two know one another, don't you?'

'Believe it.'

'There's some sort of enmity between you?'

'You mean he hasn't told you? Get him to tell you his version. It's probably so fake you could install it as a ride at Disneyland.'

'I'd like to hear *your* version.'

'I bet you would, and at length too, right?'

'Look, Mr Reeve, this is getting us nowhere. Why don't you just tell me what you want.'

'I thought that was obvious, Kosigin. I want Jay. I'll phone later with the details.'

Reeve walked back to the office supply shop and handed over the mobile, signing some more documents and getting back his deposit.

'Any calls will be charged to your credit card,' the assistant told him.

'Thanks,' Reeve said. He went next door to the coffee shop. Cantona was reading a crumpled newspaper. Reeve bought them both a coffee.

'Hell,' Cantona said, 'I didn't recognise you there.'

Reeve reached into his pocket and drew out a miniature of whisky. 'Here, something to pep you up.'

'I meant what I said, Gordon.' Cantona's eyes were bloodshot and he hadn't shaved in a few days. His stubble was silver and grey. 'I don't drink when I'm working.'

'But you're not working any more. I'm heading out.'

'Where to?' Cantona received no reply. 'Best I don't know, right?'

'Right.' Reeve handed over the money from his mobile deposit.

'What's this for?'

'It's for looking after Jim, and taking some shit on my behalf last time I was here.'

'Aw hell, Gordon, that wasn't anything.'

'Put it in your pocket, Eddie, and drink up.' Reeve stood up again, his own coffee barely touched. Cantona glanced out of the window. It had become a reflex.

'There's McCluskey,' he said.

Reeve watched the detective get into his car. He didn't look happy. Reeve kept watching. If Jay walked out of the building, Reeve would finish it now. He'd leave the coffee shop, sprint between the traffic, and take the bastard out.

But there was no sign of Jay.

'Go home,' Reeve told Cantona. It was like he was telling himself.

He drove to LA.

It took him a while to find Marcus Aurelius Dedman's Auto-Breakers. He'd phoned ahead and Dedman was waiting for him.

Dedman gave the car a cursory inspection. 'She drive all right?' he asked.

'Fine.'

'No problems at all?'

'No problems at all,' Reeve echoed.

'Well in that case,' Dedman said, 'I might as well use her to give you your ride.'

Dedman had agreed to drive Reeve out to the airport. He insisted on driving, Reeve quite happy to rest in the passenger seat. On the way, Dedman talked about cars, using a language Reeve only half understood. He'd done a course in car mechanics as part of his SAS training, but that had been on elderly Land Rovers, and had been cursory at best. It seemed a long time ago.

Reeve shook Dedman's hand at the airport and watched him drive off. He didn't think they'd be expecting him to leave so soon. Kosigin would be waiting for the next call. Reeve walked around the concourse until he found a noticeboard. He scribbled a note on the back of a napkin he'd taken from the coffee shop, then folded the note over, wrote a surname in large capitals, and pinned the napkin to the noticeboard.

Then he checked himself on to the next available flight and made straight for the departure gate. There wasn't much to do at LAX; it was no Heathrow – which these days was more department store than airport. Reeve ate a pizza and drank a Coke. He bought a magazine, which he didn't read. There was no duty free shop, so he sat by the row of public telephones until just before his flight was called.

Then he called Kosigin.

'Yes?' Kosigin said impatiently.

'Sorry to have kept you waiting.'

'I don't like games, Mr Reeve.'

'That's a pity, because we're deep in the middle of one. Have someone – Jay preferably – go to LAX. There's a public noticeboard in the departures hall, near the information kiosk. There's a note there.'

'Look, why can't we just—?'

Reeve cut the connection. His flight was being called over the Tannoy.

He had probably got one of the last places on the aircraft. He was seated by the aisle in a middle row of three. Next to him were an Australian couple heading over to Ireland to trace the wife's ancestors. They showed Reeve some photographs of their children.

'Old photos, they're all grown now.'

Reeve didn't mind. He smiled and ordered a whisky and watched the sharp blue sky outside. He was just happy to be away from San Diego. He was glad he was going home. When the in-flight movie programme started, he pushed his cushion down so it was supporting his lumbar, and then he closed his eyes.

Old pictures . . . He had a lot of those in his head: old pictures he would never forget, pictures he'd once dreamed nightly, the dreams breaking him out in a sweat.

Pictures of fireworks in Argentina.

Part Eight

Stalwart

21

It was the third night, and enemy activity was increasing still further. There were constant patrols, firing searing pink-burn flares into the sky. An order would be yelled, and a patrol would spray their designated area with bullets. Reeve and Jay knew the tactic. The Argentine soldiers were trying to rile them, flush them out. They were trying to break them.

Reeve understood the shouted orders and would shake his head at Jay, meaning there was nothing to worry about. But they were both nervous. They'd been kept so low by the patrols that sending any more data to the ship was impossible; it had been that way for the best part of the day. They'd been forced further inland, away from the air base, so that they could no longer see the runway or any of the buildings, and the planes taking off and landing were droning flies.

In fact, *not* transmitting was the only thing keeping them alive. The patrols were so close they'd have DF'd the two-man team in seconds. Reeve and Jay maintained complete silence throughout. Reeve couldn't remember the last time either of them had spoken. Muscles were seizing up from being kept still and rigid for hours at a time. The back of Reeve's neck ached terribly, and he daren't crack it. The fingers on his M16 felt arthritic, and he'd already had two bouts of cramp.

Whenever he glanced over towards Jay, Jay would be looking at him. He tried to read the look in those eyes. They seemed to be saying, quite eloquently, 'We're fucked', and they were probably right. But because Jay thought that, he was getting edgier and edgier, and Reeve suspected he might be on the verge of panicking. It was all about nerve now: if they lost theirs, the only possible outcome was 'brassing up', blasting away at anything and anybody until your ammo ran out or you copped one.

Reeve fingered the two syrettes of morphine which hung around his neck. They felt like a noose. He hoped he wouldn't need to use them. He'd rather put a bullet to his head first, though the regiment considered that the coward's way out. The rule was, you fought to the death, and if the enemy didn't kill you but captured you instead, then you did your damnedest to escape. Both men had been trained to withstand various interrogation techniques, but maybe the Argentines had a few tricks Hereford hadn't heard of. Unlikely, but then torture was a broad subject. Reeve reckoned he could withstand quite a bit of physical abuse, and even psychological wearing down. What he knew he couldn't cope with – what no one could cope with – were the various chemical forms of torture, the drugs that fucked with your mind.

The name of the game was beating the clock. On the regiment's memorial clock back in Hereford were written the names of all SAS men killed in action. As a result of the war in the Falklands, there were already a lot of new names to be added to the clock. Reeve didn't want his to be one of them.

When he looked at Jay again, Jay was still looking at him. Reeve gestured with his head for Jay to return to watch. They were lying side by side, but facing opposite directions, so that Jay's boots rested an inch or so from Reeve's left ear. Earlier, Jay had tapped a morse message with his fingers on Reeve's boot – 'Kill them all' – repeating the message three times. Kill them all.

The ground was cold and damp, and Reeve knew his body temperature was dropping, same as it had done the previous night. A couple more nights like this and they would be in serious trouble, not so much from the enemy as from their own treacherous bodies. They had eaten only chocolate and drunk only water for the past thirty-six hours, and what sleep they'd taken had been fitful and short-lived.

Even when planning their escape route and emergency rendezvous they had not spoken, but had lain head to head with the map on the ground in front of them. Reeve had pointed to a couple of possible routes – if they were forced to withdraw from the OP in the midst of a firefight, chances were they'd be split up – then had tapped the map at the ERV. Jay had then traced a line with his unwashed finger from the ERV to the Chilean border, leaving no doubt what his route would be after the ERV.

Reeve wasn't so sure. Would the Argentine command expect them to make for the border or for the coast? They were still a lot closer to the coast than the border, so maybe the border *was* the best plan. Besides, there was no point reaching the coast if no ship had been alerted of your plight. They wouldn't be able to radio that message in the middle of brassing up, and if forced to retreat they would lighten their load, which meant leaving the bergens and very probably the transmitter. Reeve had already mentally checked off the contents of his bergen, and had decided he needed nothing out of it but a few more rations. It was because he was thinking along these lines that he knew the mission was at an end. There'd be time later to wonder where and why it had gone wrong, always supposing he was still alive at the end of it all. The coast was closer: Reeve couldn't get that idea out of his head. He had an emergency beacon with him. If they could find a boat and head out to sea, they could switch on the beacon and then pray someone would pick up the signal. The problem with that was, it was as likely to be an Argentine plane returning to base as anyone else.

The sky turned pink again and started to fizz and crackle as the flare started its gentle parachute-borne descent. Reeve could see a four-man patrol five hundred metres off to his right. Reeve and Jay were lying beneath netting and local foliage, and the patrol would have to get a lot closer to see them, even with the help of the flare. There was a sudden shrill whistle, like one of the old tin-and-pea jobs football referees use.

'Half time,' Jay whispered. He'd broken the code of silence, but he'd also broken the tension. Reeve found himself grinning, stifling laughter which wrenched itself up from his gut. The way Jay's feet were quivering he was laughing too. It became almost uncontrollable. Reeve took a deep breath and expelled it slowly. The patrol was moving away at speed – and there was nothing funny about that.

Then the first rocket thudded into the ground several hundred metres to Reeve's left. The earth beneath tried to buck his body into the air, and his face slammed down hard into the dirt.

'Shit,' Jay said, not caring who heard him. Not caring because he knew, like Reeve knew, that there was no one around to hear: the patrols had been signalled to evacuate the area.

Another rocket landed, further away this time. Then another, and another. Finally, a flare went up. Two blows on the whistle. Reeve guessed patrols were being sent in to the freshly bombed area to look for bodies or fleeing survivors.

'What do you reckon?' Jay whispered.

'Lie doggo,' Reeve said. His mouth felt strange when it worked. 'A rocket's as likely to hit us up-and-running as lying still.'

'You think so?' Jay sounded unsure. Reeve nodded and resumed watch. There was sweat in the hollow of his spine, trickling down towards the trouser-line. His heart was beating ever more loudly in his ears. Then he heard a distant megaphone, a voice speaking heavily accented English.

'Surrender or we will kill you. You have two minutes to decide.'

The two minutes passed all too quickly. Reeve flipped open the cover on his watchface and followed the sweep of the luminous dial.

'Very well,' the megaphone said. Then another single blow on the whistle. Reeve could feel Jay trying to burrow deeper into the scrape, pressing himself hard against the ground.

Rockets whistled past to their left and right, causing deafening explosions on impact. Great clumps of earth fell on both men. More missiles, more gut-wrenching explosions. Between impacts, Reeve could hear nothing but a loud buzzing in his ears. He'd been too late putting his hands over them, and was now suffering the consequence. He felt fingers tapping his leg, and half turned to see Jay starting to rise on to his knees.

'Get down!' Reeve hissed.

'Fuck this, let's go!'

'No.'

More explosions caused them both to fall flat, but Jay scrambled up again straight after, dirt and grass and bits of bark falling like heavy dollops of rain.

'They send a patrol out to check this grid, they're bound to spot us,' he spat.

'No.'

'I say we go.'

'No. We can't lose our bottle now.'

The flare went up, the double whistle sounded, and Reeve pulled Jay to the ground. Jay started to struggle, giving Reeve two options: let him go, or slug him. Jay came to his own decision first, catching Reeve on the side of the head with his rifle butt. Reeve snatched at the rifle, letting go of Jay in the process, and Jay got to his feet, pulling the rifle out of Reeve's hands.

Reeve risked a glance around. The patrols would be on their way. Smoke was being blown all around them, but when it cleared they'd be as visible as targets at the fairground.

Jay was pointing his M16 at Reeve, finger just shy of the trigger. He was grinning like a monkey, his face blackened, eyes wide and white. Reeve noticed that there was a 40mm missile in the 203 grenade launcher. Jay raised the rifle above Reeve's head and fired the grenade into the sky. With the 203 there was no explosion or recoil, just a loud pop as the grenade was launched.

Reeve didn't use up precious seconds on watching the grenade's trajectory. He was up and moving. Jay had done it now; he'd let the enemy know they were there. They were fair game now for anything the Argentines threw at them. Reeve left his bergen. He didn't care whether Jay left his or not, or even if he left the transmitter. It was time to move – and quickly. Behind them, the grenade made impact and exploded.

With his rifle carried low in front of him, Reeve ran.

'Where are you going?' Jay yelled at him, pouring bullets from his M16 towards where the enemy would be hunkered down, waiting for him to expend the lot. Reeve knew his partner had cracked. He'd never been sure of Jay in the first place, now his worst fears were being realised. Everything Jay was doing was against the standard operating procedure . . . or any other procedure. Reeve wondered if he'd be justified putting a bullet into Jay himself. He dismissed the thought in less than a second.

'See you in Chile!' Jay yelled. Reeve didn't look back, but he knew from Jay's voice that he was moving too, taking a different line from Reeve.

Which suited Reeve just fine.

He knew the first few hundred metres, could have run them blind. He'd been staring at the route for the past twelve or so hours, since switching directions with Jay. They'd changed position so they would stay fresh and alert. Staring at the same spot for too long, you could lose your concentration.

But Reeve had focused his mind on the route, his escape route. He didn't know what was over the next rise, but the next rise was shelter from gunfire and night-sights, and that was his primary objective: shelter. He knew from an earlier compass reading that he was running north-east. If he kept going, he'd reach the coastal road north of Rio Grande. He was taking a risk, since this direction meant he would have to skirt the northern perimeter of the airfield. Well, they wouldn't be expecting him anywhere near *there*, would they? More crucially, he had two obstacles to cross: a main road, and the Rio Grande river itself.

He didn't know why he'd set his sights on the coast, and if Jay was headed for Chile so be it. Jay would wait for him an hour or so at the ERV, then move off. Bloody good luck to him, too.

The bastard.

Reeve went over the rise on all fours, keeping low in case there were any nasty surprises waiting for him. But the Argentine bombing had done him a distinct favour by clearing out all the patrols. He scurried down the other side of the escarpment, sliding over loose rocks and pebbles. It didn't seem to be man-made. It wasn't a quarry or a dump for unwanted stone and shale, it was more like the scree Reeve had come across on the glacial slopes of the Scottish mountains. He ended up going down the slope on his arse. Just when he thought there was no end to the drop he found himself on a track and crossed it hurriedly, remembering to turn round first, in case they came hunting him with torches. His footprints led back the way he'd just come. The other side of the track, he turned on his heels again, hit another uphill slope at a run and powered his way to the summit. There was gunfire behind him, gunfire and rockets and grenades. The sky was full of pink smoke, like a fireworks display. Gunpowder was in his nostrils.

That stupid bastard.

There was someone over to his right, about seventy or eighty metres away. It looked like Jay's silhouette.

'Jay!' Reeve called.

Jay caught his breath. 'Keep going!' he hissed.

So Reeve kept going. And the sky above him turned brilliant white. He couldn't believe it. Jay had let off a WP grenade. White phos made a good smokescreen, but you didn't use the stuff when you were already on your way out of a situation. Then Reeve realised what Jay had done, and his stomach did a flip. Jay had tossed the phos in Reeve's direction, and had headed off the other way. He was using Reeve as his decoy, bringing the Argentine troops over in Reeve's direction while he made his own escape.

Bastard!

And now Reeve could hear whistling, a human whistle. A tune he recognised.

Row, row, row your boat,

Gently down the stream . . .

And then silence. Jay was gone. Reeve could have followed him, but that would mean running straight through the smoke into God knew what. Instead, he picked up his pace and kept running the direction he'd been going. He wondered how Jay could have set off one way yet come back round to meet up with Reeve. It was crazy, Jay's sense of direction wasn't *that* bad . . .

Unless . . . unless he'd come back on purpose. The enemy had heard only one yelled voice, come under fire from just one rifle, one grenade-launcher.

They didn't know there were two men out here!

Reeve saw it all. The safest way out of this was to lie low and let the enemy catch your partner. But that only worked if your partner *was* caught. Jay was just making sure. Back at Hereford, it would be one man's word against the other's . . . always supposing they both made it home.

Over the rise the ground seemed to level out, which meant he could move faster, but also that he could be spotted more easily. He thought he could hear rotors behind him: a chopper, maybe more than one, probably with searchlights attached. He had to reach cover. No, he had to keep moving, had to put some distance between himself and his pursuers. Relieved of his bergen and most of his kit, it was as though weights had been taken off his ankles. That thought made him think of shackles, and the image of shackles gave him fresh impetus. His ears still seemed blocked; there was still a hissing sound there. He couldn't hear any vehicles, any commands or gunfire. Just rotors . . . coming closer.

Much closer.

Reeve flung himself to the ground as the helicopter passed overhead. It was over to his right and moving too quickly to pick him out. This was a general sweep. They'd carry on until they were sure they were at a distance he couldn't have reached, then they'd come back, moving more slowly, hovering so the searchlight could play over the ground.

He needed cover right now.

But there was no cover. He loaded a grenade into the launcher, got up and started running again. The rifle was no longer in both hands and held low in front of him: now it was in his right hand, the safety off. It would take him a second to swing the barrel into his other hand, aim and fire.

He could see the beam of light ahead of him, waving in an arc which would pick him out when the chopper was closer. Reeve dropped to one knee and wiped sweat from his eyes. His knees hurt, they were stiff. The chopper was moving steadily now, marking out a grid pattern. They weren't rushing things. They were being methodical, the way Reeve would have done in their situation.

When the helicopter was seventy-five metres in front of him Reeve took aim, resting one elbow on his knee to steady himself. As soon as the helicopter went into a hover, Reeve let go with the grenade. He watched the bomb, like an engorged bullet, leave the launcher and head into the sky, but he didn't wait to see the result. He was running again, dipping to a protective crouch as the sky overhead exploded in a ball of flame, rotor-blades crumpling and falling to the ground. Something hot fell on to Reeve's arm. He checked it wasn't phos. It wasn't – just hot metal. It stuck to his arm, and he had to scrape it off against the ground, taking burning flesh with it.

'Jesus Christ!' he gasped. The helicopter had hit the ground behind him. There was another explosion, which almost toppled him. More flying metal and glass hit him. Maybe bits of bodies were hitting him too. He didn't bother looking.

His arm wasn't sore; the adrenaline and fear were taking care of that for the moment, the best anaesthetics on the planet.

He'd been scared for a second, though, and what had scared him most was the fear that the heat on his arm had been white phos. The stuff was lethal – it would have burned straight through him, eating as it went.

Well, he thought, if Jay's smokescreen had hinted I was here, the helicopter was an open fucking invitation.

He heard a motor, revving hard: a Jeep, probably on the track he'd crossed a few minutes back. If it unloaded men, then those men would be that few minutes behind, no more. No time to stop, no time to slow. He didn't have time to pace himself, the way he knew he should so he'd have some idea how far he'd travelled when he got a chance to stop and recce. You did it by counting the number of strides you took and multiplying by length of stride. It was fine in training, fine when they told you about it in a classroom . . .

But out here, it was just another piece of kit to be discarded.

He had no idea where Jay was. The last he'd seen of him he was vanishing behind all that thick white smoke, like a magician doing a disappearing trick. Magicians always had trapdoors, and that's what Reeve was looking for now – a door he could disappear through. There was a small explosion at his back. Maybe it was the helicopter, maybe Jay launching another grenade, or the enemy redoubling its bombardment.

Whatever it was, it was far enough behind him to be of little concern. He couldn't hear the Jeep any more. He wondered if it had stopped. He thought he could hear other vehicles in the distance. Their engine drones were just the right timbre to penetrate his blocked ears. Heavy engines . . .

surely not tanks? Personnel carriers? He couldn't see any other searchlights. There had been only the one chopper. They might be ordering another from the airfield, but if the crew were sensible they would take their time getting here, knowing the fate of their comrades.

Reeve was thinking about a lot of things, trying to form some structure to the chaos in his mind. Above all he was trying to think of anything but his own running. On a gruelling route march you had to transcend the reality. That was the very word his first instructor had used: *transcend*. Someone had asked if he meant it as in transcendental meditation, expecting to raise a smile.

'In a manner of speaking,' the instructor had said in all seriousness.

That was the first time Reeve got an inkling that being a good soldier was more a state of mind, a matter of attitude, than anything else. You could be fit, strong, have fast reflexes and know all the drills, but those didn't complete the picture; there was a mental part of the equation, too. It had to do with spirit, which was maybe what the instructor had been getting at.

He came suddenly to the main road which ran from Rio Grande on the east coast all the way into Chilean territory. He lay low, watching Army trucks roar past, and when the route was finally clear scuttled across the road like any other nocturnal creature.

His next obstacle was not far away, and it gave him a choice: he could swim across the Rio Grande – which meant ditching more equipment, including maybe even his rifle – or he could cross it by bridge. There was a bridge half a mile downriver, according to his map. Reeve headed straight towards it, unsure whether it would be guarded or not. The Argentines had known for some time now that there were enemy forces around, so maybe the bridge would be manned. Then again, would they have been expecting Reeve and Jay to make it this far?

Reeve's question was answered soon enough: a two-man foot patrol guarded the two-lane crossing. They were standing in the middle of the bridge, illuminated by the headlamps of their Jeep. At this time of night there was no traffic for them to stop and check, so they were talking and smoking cigarettes. Their eyes were on the distance, the direction Reeve had just come. They'd heard the explosions, seen the smoke and flame. They were glad to be at this safe distance from it all.

Reeve took a look at the dark, wide river, the cold-looking water. Then he peered at the underside of the bridge, and made up his mind. He clambered down to the water's edge and made his way underneath the bridge. It was an iron construction, its struts a criss-crossed series of spars forming an arch over the water. Reeve slung his rifle over his shoulder and gripped the first two spars, pulling himself up. He climbed slowly, quietly, hidden from land but all too visible from the river, should any boat with a spotlight come chugging along. Where he could, he used his feet and knees for purchase, but as he climbed higher he found himself hanging over the water below by his hands, moving one hand at a time, his legs swinging uselessly in space. He thought of training courses where he'd had to swing this way across an expanse of water or mud – but never this distance, never under these conditions. His upper chest ached, and the rusty metal tore into his finger-joints. He thought his arms would pop out of their sockets. Sweat was stinging his eyes. Above him he could hear the soldiers laughing. He could pull himself up on to the bridge and open fire on them, then steal their Jeep or cross the rest of the bridge on foot. But he knew if he opted for this kind of action he'd leave traces, and he didn't want that, he didn't want the enemy to know which way he'd come. So he kept swinging, concentrating on one hand, then the other, squeezing shut his eyes and gritting his teeth. Blood was trickling down past his wrists. He didn't think he was going to make it. He started to fantasise about letting go, falling into the water, about letting the river wash him all the way to the coast. He shook his head clear. The splash would be heard; even if it wasn't, what were his chances? He had to keep on moving.

Finally, he found purchase with his feet. He was at the far side of the span, where the struts started curving downwards towards the riverbank. He mouthed a silent 'Jesus' as he took his weight on his feet and legs, easing the pressure on his shredded palms. He felt exhausted as he started his descent, and dropped when he reached solid ground, gasping and panting on all-fours, his head touching the dank earth. He gave himself thirty precious seconds to get his breath back. He pressed some strands of grass against his palms and fingers, as much of a compress as he could manage.

Then he got to his feet and moved away from the water, heading north-east. He couldn't follow the river: for one thing, it led back towards the airfield; for another, he was more likely to encounter civilians close to a water source. Stumbling across a fisherman was not high on his Christmas present list.

Reeve was running the way he'd been taught: not a sprint, because a sprint used up too many resources too quickly – this running was measured, paced, steady, more a jog than anything else. The secret was not to stop, not to falter – and that was the most difficult part of all. It had been difficult on the Brecon Beacons during those arduous training runs. Reeve had jogged past men he regarded as fitter and stronger than him. They'd be standing bent over, hands on knees, spewing on to the ground. They daren't sit down – with the amount of kit they were carrying they'd never get back up. And if they stopped too long they'd begin to seize up. It was something joggers knew. You saw them at traffic lights or pausing to cross the road, and they jogged on the spot.

Never stop, never falter.

Reeve kept running.

The terrain became much as it had been the other side of the river, steep ridges of loose shale with shallow valleys between. He didn't bother counting his steps, just kept moving, putting miles between himself and the river. He knew he couldn't outrun vehicles, but this terrain, inhospitable to a human, would be downright lethal for any vehicle other than the hardiest. No Jeep could take these slopes, and a motorbike would slew on the loose stones. A helicopter was the enemy's best bet, and he'd probably wiped that option out for the meantime. He took strength from that fact.

He was climbing again, trying not to think about the pain in his hands, crossing the ridge, then sliding. At the bottom of the slide, he picked himself up and ran forward four paces.

Then he stopped dead.

He couldn't really see anything, but some sixth sense had told him to stop. He knew why: it was the nothingness itself that had warned him. He couldn't see the ground ahead, not even ten feet in front of him. He shuffled forwards, toeing the ground, until one foot stepped off into space.

'Christ!'

He took two steps back and got down on his hands and knees, peering into the darkness. He was on the edge of a gully. No . . . more than a gully: sheer sides dropped he didn't know how far. A ravine, a deep chasm. Even supposing he could climb down into it, he'd no idea whether he could scale the other side. He might be trapped. He'd have to go *around* it, but that might take hours. Damn it to hell. He tried to see something, anything down there, something that might tell him what was waiting for him. He unclipped the night-scope from his belt and put it to his eye. Its range was limited, but he thought he could make out shapes at the bottom of the hole, rocks or boulders probably. The drop was pretty sheer, tapering off towards the bottom. In daylight, if he wasn't rushed, he could probably find enough hand-and-foot-holds to climb out the other side. But in darkness with the enemy behind him . . .

He took the night-scope away from his eyes and was confronted by the ravine's blackness again. It was taunting him. Everybody, no matter how good, needs luck, it was telling him. And yours just ran out.

'Fuck that,' he said, clipping the scope back on to his belt and standing up. His leg muscles complained. He had to make a decision soon, for all sorts of reasons. Turn left or right? Right, and he'd be heading vaguely in Jay's direction; left, and he might hit the coast. Was that correct? He screwed shut his eyes and concentrated. No: if he turned *right* he might hit the coast. He had to turn right.

He ran more slowly now, keeping close to the edge of the ravine so he'd know if and when it ended. The problem was, this close to the edge, he daren't pick up his pace. One stumble might send him over. The ground was dangerous enough as it was. He remembered the dirt track, and the scree, and the boulders at the bottom of the pit . . . It *was* a quarry! The landscape made sense now. And if he was right, then he could half-circle the pit without too much difficulty. Quarries weren't *that* big. There might even be places he could hide, or, as a last resort, a vehicle he could hijack.

He heard voices ahead of him and stopped again, unclipping the night-scope. A two-man patrol. Somehow they'd got ahead of him, which was very bad news. There could be any number of them between here and the coast road. One man had called to the other to let him know he was stopping to urinate. The other carried on. Both had their backs to Reeve. He walked forward in a silent crouch and, when he was near enough, reached down to lay his rifle on the ground. His right hand was already clutching Lucky 13.

The man was zipping himself up as Reeve came close. He'd had to lay down his own rifle while he was peeing. Reeve tensed and sprang, one hand over the man's mouth, the dagger chewing into the exposed throat below. The man's hands reached up from his fly too late. Reeve kept gouging at the neck, hot blood spilling over him. It splattered on to the ground like urine. He laid the body on the ground and retrieved his rifle. The other man was calling for his friend. Reeve made an affirmative sound and started jogging forward, like he had finished and was now catching up. His eyes burned into the enemy's back. The soldier was saying something about radioing in when Reeve grabbed him by the head and went to work with the knife. More steaming blood. Another body.

He'd killed them by the book. Quick and silent.

He rolled both bodies over the lip of the quarry then started jogging again. There was not time for analysis or shock; he simply stuck the dagger back in its scabbard and ran. He had maybe four more hours of darkness.

He reached the other side of the quarry without incident. He'd presumed from the casual attitudes of his two kills that nobody was expecting him to get this far. The patrol hadn't been primed for sudden contact. At the other side of the quarry he got out his compass. He'd start heading east now, a direct line to the coast. From what he remembered of the map, there were no settlements of any size for thirty miles north of the town of Rio Grande. There was the coast road to cross, and he hoped that would be his next and final obstacle. He heard a chopper approaching but it veered off again. Maybe there had been a sighting of Jay. He hoped the chopper hadn't found the bodies in the quarry, not so soon.

He felt good again. He gave himself a few seconds to think about the killings. They'd been necessary, he was sure of that. They wouldn't exactly trouble his conscience; he hadn't even seen the men's faces, just their backs. One of the trainers had said it was eyes that haunted you, that final stare before oblivion – when you kill, never look at the eyes: concentrate on some other part of the face if you have to, best if you don't look at all. Because the person you're killing is staring death in the face, which makes *you* Death. It was not a role any man should be happy with, but sometimes it was a fact of conflict.

The blood was sticky on Reeve's hands. He had to pry his fingers off the rifle barrel. He didn't think about it at all.

He hit the coast road before dawn, and let the feeling of elation have its way for a few moments while he rested and checked the road for guards, patrols or traffic. He could see nothing, but he could hear and smell the sea. He double-checked with his night-scope that the route was clear, then picked himself up and jogged across the paved surface, his rubberised soles making little sound. He could make out the edge of the sea before him, and a ribbon of sand and shale. Lights south of him told the story: he was only five or so miles north of Rio Grande, which put him maybe twenty to twenty-five miles south of the next decent-sized settlement. Reeve knew what he wanted now – he wanted a boat. He doubted he'd find many between here and the next settlement north. He'd have to walk towards Rio Grande and, this close to the ocean and the road, cover was limited to say the least.

He had to use what darkness there was.

And he had to get a move on.

He picked up his pace, though every muscle in his body complained and his brain told him to go to sleep. He popped two caffeine tablets and washed them down with the last water from his canteen. His luck was holding. After barely a mile he came across a small cove filled with paddle-boats. They were probably used for fishing, a single rower and lines or a net. Some of them bobbed in the water, attached by lines to several large buoys, others lay beached on the shale. An old man was putting his gear into one of the beached boats, working by the light of his lantern. Reeve looked around but saw no one else. It would be dawn soon, and the other fishermen would arrive. This old man was beating the rush.

The man looked up from his work as he heard Reeve crunch over the shale towards him. He prepared a glint of a smile and some remark about another early bird, but his eyes and mouth opened wide when he saw the soldier pointing a rifle at him.

Reeve spoke to the man quietly in Spanish, stumbling over the words. He blamed fatigue. The man seemed to understand. He couldn't take his eyes off the caked blood on Reeve's arms and chest. He was a man who had seen blood before, and even dried to the colour of rust he knew what he was looking at.

Reeve explained what he needed. The man begged him to take another boat, but Reeve needed the man with him. He couldn't trust him not to raise the alarm as soon as his fellow fishermen arrived.

What Reeve did not say was that he was too tired to row. That was another reason he needed the old man. There was not yet light in the sky, but the darkness was not as black as it had been. Reeve didn't have any more time to waste. He pointed the rifle at the man, guessing that a dagger wouldn't suffice to scare someone who gutted fish. The old man put up his hands. Reeve told him to start hauling the boat out into the water. The man did as he was told. Then they both got into the boat and the old man slid the oars back and forth, finally finding his rhythm and working them strongly. There were tears in his eyes, not just from the wind. Reeve repeated that he wasn't going to kill the man. He just wanted to be taken out to sea.

The further out they got, the safer Reeve felt on the one hand, and the more exposed on the other. He was beginning to have doubts that such a small boat could get far enough out into the ocean for any rescue ship to make a rendezvous. He took out the metal cylinder which contained the beacon and twisted off its cap. The beacon was simple to use. Reeve switched it on, watched the red light start to blink, and placed it on the tiny bench beside him.

The fisherman asked how far they were going. Reeve admitted he didn't know.

'There have been rumours of gunfire around the airport,' the old man said. He had a voice thick with tobacco use.

Reeve nodded.

'Are you invading us?'

Reeve shook his head. 'Reconnaissance,' he told the man, 'that's all it was.'

'You have won the war, you know,' the man said without bitterness. Reeve stared at him and found he believed him. 'I saw on television. It will all end maybe today, maybe tomorrow.'

Reeve found he was smiling, then laughing and shaking his head. He'd been out of contact for seventy-two hours. Some mission, he thought. Some bloody mission.

They began to chat quite amiably. Maybe the man did not believe a smiling man could kill him. The man spoke of his youth, his family, the fishing, about how crazy it was that allies like Britain and Argentina, huge wealthy countries, should fall to war over a place like the Malvinas. The conversation was pretty one-sided; Reeve had been trained to give away nothing. When he spoke, he spoke generally, and sometimes he did not answer the old man's questions.

'This is usually as far as I go,' the old man said at one point.

'Keep going,' Reeve ordered.

The old man shrugged. Later he said, 'The sea is getting rough.'

As if Reeve needed telling. The waves were knocking the little boat about, so that Reeve held on to the side with both hands, and the old man had trouble keeping hold of the oars. Reeve held the beacon securely between his knees.

'It will get rougher,' the old man said.

Reeve didn't know what to say. Head back into calmer waters? Or stay here and risk being capsized? He didn't know how long it would take for someone to pick up the beacon's signal. It could take all day, or even longer if some final massed assault were taking place on the Falklands. Nobody would want to miss out on that.

In the end the old man made up his own mind. They retreated to water that was choppy, but not dangerous. Reeve could see land in the far distance.

'Will other boats come out this far?'

'Boats with engines, yes.'

Reeve couldn't see any signs of activity on the water. 'When?' He was forming an idea. He would make it look like the little boat was in trouble, and when one of the motorised boats came to help, he'd use his rifle to take command and head out further into the South Atlantic.

'When?' The old man shrugged. 'Who knows? An hour? Two hours?' He shrugged again.

Reeve was feeling the cold. He was wet and seriously fatigued. His core temperature was dropping again. He asked if the old man had any clothing on the boat. There was an oilskin beneath Reeve's seat. He put that on, and immediately felt more sheltered from the stiff breeze. The old man signalled that there was food and drink in the canvas bag. Reeve rummaged and found bread, apples, chorizo sausage, and a bottle of something which smelt evilly of alcohol. The old man took a swig of this, and told Reeve he could eat what he liked. Reeve ate one apple and half a peppery sausage. The old man pulled the oars in and laid them on the floor of the boat, where they sat in two inches of water. Then he lifted up one of his rods and started to tie bait onto it.

'Might as well,' he said. 'While we're here. Do you mind me asking, what are we waiting for?'

'Friends,' Reeve told him.

The old man laughed for some reason, and baited another rod.

An old man fishing from two lines, and another man huddled in a tattered yellow oilskin. That was the sight that greeted the rescue party.

Reeve heard the engine first. It was an outboard. He scanned the waves, but it was behind him. He turned his head and saw an inflatable dinghy scudding across the foam. It had no markings, and none of the three men in it wore distinguishing uniforms or insignia.

Reeve aimed his rifle at the boat, and two of the men on board aimed their rifles back at him. When the two vessels were twenty feet apart, the man steering the dinghy asked a question in Spanish.

'What are you doing here?'

'Fishing,' the old man said simply. He had rolled and lit himself a cigarette. It bobbed in his mouth as he spoke.

'Who are you?' the man on the dinghy demanded.

'Fishermen,' the old man said.

Now the man commanding the dinghy stared at Reeve. Reeve held the stare. The man smiled.

'You look like hell,' he said in English. 'Let's get you back to the ship.'

The debriefing took place while the Argentine garrison formally surrendered, on the night of 14 June. Reeve had been given a thorough physical by a doctor, then was allowed to eat, sleep and clean up – in any order he liked. 22 Battalion's CO, Mike Rose, was not on the ship. Reeve was debriefed initially by three of his own officers, and again later by a couple of spooks. There would be a further debriefing next day.

They asked about Jay and he told them the truth. They didn't like that. They made him go over the story several times, probing at various details like dentists seeking a pinprick of decay. Reeve just kept telling them the truth. It didn't go any further. A senior officer came to see him, one on one.

'You'll be up for a commendation,' the officer said, 'probably a medal.'

'Yes, sir.' Reeve didn't care a damn.

'But the Regiment doesn't air its dirty linen in public.'

'No, sir.'

'No one's to know about Jay.'

'Understood, sir.'

The officer smiled and nodded, unable to keep the relief off his face. 'You'll be looking forward to a bit of R&R, Gordon.'

'I want out altogether,' Reeve told the officer, quietly but firmly. 'Out of the Regiment and out of the Army.'

The officer stared at him, then blinked. 'Well, we'll see about that. Maybe you should take some time to think about it, eh?'

'Yes, sir.'

But Reeve knew he wouldn't change his mind.

Days and weeks passed. Jay never appeared – in Chile or anyplace else. He was eventually presumed dead, though the Argentine military authorities denied capturing him or killing him. It was as if he really had vanished in that puff of smoke, leaving nothing behind but a snatch of a badly whistled children's song.

A song Reeve had hated ever since.

And a man he'd hated with it.

22

Jay wore his Armani-lookalike suit to LAX. He liked the way it was roomy: you could strap a holster to your ankle, tape a knife to your leg, and nobody would know. You could carry a small semi-automatic beneath the jacket, an Ingram or one of the folding-butt Kalashnikovs, especially if you had a special pocket and release-strap sewn into the lining, as Jay had. The tailor in Singapore had made the alterations after Jay had been measured for the suit. Jay had drawn a picture of what he wanted, and what he wanted it for. The tailor had been bug-eyed, and had knocked a few dollars off his original estimate. It was a tactic Jay had tried since, with similar success.

He toted a Heckler & Koch MP5 to the airport, its stock fully retracted. He had a little snub-nosed revolver around his ankle, and ammo in his pocket. He was chewing gum and wearing Harley Davidson sunglasses. He wore brown loafers and ice-blue socks with the yellow suit. He fitted right in.

He didn't carry his two-way radio or a telephone of any kind, but he was wearing a wire. He had three men in the terminal building and two more outside. Not that he was expecting trouble. He was grinning, the way he often did these days, though nobody but him got the joke. He tried to blow a bubble but it was the wrong kind of gum. It was hard to find the right kind of gum these days. Jay whistled a little tune, knowing the guys listening in wouldn't appreciate it. He was wondering what kind of stunt Gordon Reeve would pull. Should have finished the fucker off in France. Funny the way fate threw old shadows in your face, blotting out the sun. In – where was it? Yes, Singapore, same trip be bought the suit – in Singapore he'd bumped into a guy he'd known in 2 Para, before he'd joined Special Forces. Jay had been sinking dark rums at some bar, maybe three in the morning, and this guy had literally bumped into him. They'd sized one another up, both keening for a fight, then the man took a step back and dropped his arms.

'Jay,' he'd said. 'Fuck me, it *is* you.'

So they'd had a drink – a few drinks actually – then Jay had taken the guy, whose name was Bolter or Boulter or something like that, to a brothel he knew. It was just a small flat of two bedrooms above an electrical shop, but it did such good business they had to wait in the rank hallway, plied with beer laced with Christ knew what, for twenty minutes, until Jay kicked down a door and dragged a weary punter off one of the girls. The service got better after that; they had a bloody good time after that. Then Jay and his pal went for a walk down by the docks. You'd never seen so many little boats bobbing on the water. It was getting on for six in the morning, and though both men were bushed neither wanted to go to sleep.

'Here, this'll help,' Jay had said, sliding a narrow-bladed knife into the back of his old colleague's neck. He dragged the body behind some trash-cans, took a wristwatch and all the cash on the body, plus any papers he had with his name on. He got rid of the stuff on his way back to his own hotel. Thing was, he couldn't have anyone from the old days knowing he was still around – the SAS would want to talk to him about desertion. They'd be terrifically keen to talk to him, and not just to catch up on the good old days. He didn't know what story Reeve had given, whether he'd told the truth or not; he hoped he'd never have to know.

Funny thing was, next time he was in Singapore and went back to the brothel, one of the girls complained that his friend had given her herpes. So Bolter or Boulter had left something behind. Everybody did.

Jay liked the life he had now, a life he'd carved out for himself – sometimes literally – in America. It hadn't been easy. In fact, it had been fucking hard – especially those first weeks in South America. On the run, a one-man slaughter-house. He'd killed three Argentine soldiers that first night, one for each man who'd died on the glacier, but it hadn't been enough to erase the memory of that doomed mission. Jay had seen something on that glacier, his eyes peering into the white-out. He'd seen the bland white face of death. It was an absence, an uncaring void, and the more chilling for that, the more hypnotic. He'd stared at it for a long time, not bothering with goggles. When they'd lifted him on to the helicopter, he'd been snowblind. But when the blindness receded, there was a clearer vision in its place, a knowledge of helplessness and the will to power. It had taken him all the way through Tierra del Fuego and into Chile.

He'd killed one poor bastard because he needed civvy clothes, and another for his motorbike, which duly packed up after thirty miles, forcing him to walk for a while. Big fucking country Chile – north to south anyway. He'd stuck to the west coast, killing some bearded Australian backpacker for his passport. Jesus, backpacking in fucking Chile: that was asking for trouble.

He'd crossed into Peru, smiling for the border guards like the man in the picture in the passport, rubbing his chin and laughing, to show he'd shaved a lot of his beard off since the photo had been taken. They stayed sombre throughout but let him go. The backpacker's body would never be found, not while it had skin on it, though one day the skeleton might be found. He bypassed Ecuador and went into Colombia. People in Peru had told him not to do it, but he didn't see why not – and it was lucky he didn't heed their warnings, because Colombia turned out to be a great place, and the site of his first civilian job. He'd met up with some hard cases in Cali and ran a few errands for them. He got to know the kingpin, Edouard, and Edouard told him there was always work for those willing to undertake personal risk.

'I've taken more risks than you'll ever know,' Jay had said, though in fact he'd already told Edouard most of the Rio Grande story, exaggerating somewhat and turning Reeve into an early corpse.

Eventually, Edouard had given Jay a job which involved liaison with some Americans. The Americans took him with them to Venezuela and from there to Jamaica, where he decided to stay a while and was duly passed to yet another new employer. He was learning fast what his employers wanted, and how to know if a proffered fee was a rip-off or not. He stayed in Jamaica over a year and saved enough to buy an American identity. Later on, homesick, he bought himself a new British passport too, and now he had a Canadian one as well – all in different names of course, none of them his own.

When the Jamaican police started asking questions about a headless, handless corpse that had been dragged out of a rubbish dump on the edge of Kingston, Jay left the island, not without regrets, and headed to the USA, feeling immediately at home in Miami. Jesus, what a madhouse. It was in Miami that he found himself talking like an American, even though most people he spoke to still mistook him for an Australian. Jay set up his stall in Miami, but found work hard to come by. It was all organised, mostly along clan lines: he wasn't Cuban, so the Cubans didn't want him; he wasn't Puerto Rican so the PRs wouldn't take him. They had their own firepower, and if they needed freelancers, there were a hundred kids on the street, each one with something to prove and nothing to lose.

Jay got in touch with Edouard, who put him in touch with an old friend. Edouard had been good to Jay, and Jay had liked him. There was an affinity between them, two men who only ever liked to be called by a single name. The only hit Jay had ever turned down had been on Edouard.

Edouard's old friend brought Jay to LA. The man's name was Fessler, and Jay had worked for Mr Fessler – that was what you had to call him, Mr Fessler; Jay sometimes thought even Fessler's wife called him that – for three years before setting up on his own. He liked the regular income, but itched to be his own boss. It was tough at first, but got easier after the first couple of jobs. In fact, the money got so good, Jay developed a nose-talc habit which he broke only with the aid of a lot of booze. A *lot* of booze. The booze had put some weight on him which no amount of workouts seemed able to shift, but he thought he carried it well enough, and in a baggy suit no one noticed, right?

LA-LA Land, that was what Jay called Los Angeles. He'd come across it in a book about snuff movies. The appellation stuck in his mind, and he pretended he'd made it up, even to people who knew he hadn't.

He liked LA-LA Land. He liked being his own boss. Above all, he liked working for big companies. Big companies paid well and let you get on with it. They didn't want to know the details, the procedures – they just wanted the job done. And they paid on the nail. No fuss, no mess, minimum paperwork. Jay's cover was as a 'corporate restructuring advisor', and he'd even read books on the subject. Well, articles anyway. He bought the *Wall Street Journal* sometimes too, and he was an avid reader of some bits of *Time*. He had letterheaded paper and knew a guy who could type up an expense sheet or an account if the employer really wanted one. These pieces of paper were art forms, full of terms like 'workstation projection analyses' and 'capital fluidity advisement', stuff Jay didn't understand, but the guy who did the typing swore they meant something.

Kosigin wasn't like anyone Jay had ever worked for. For a start, he wanted to know *everything* – every detail. And he would make Jay tell the story several times over. Jay was never sure if Kosigin was looking for him to make a mistake in the retelling, or if the guy just got off on the stuff Jay told him. Certainly, no matter how exaggeratedly gruesome Jay made the details, Kosigin never winced, never showed any emotion. He'd just stand there at his office window, or sit at his desk with his hands together as if in prayer, the tips of his fingers just touching his chin. The fucker was creepy, no doubt about that. No doubt at all.

But Jay reckoned he could learn a few things about deportment from Mr Kosigin. He liked Kosigin's style. Kosigin was Brooks Brothers for work and L. L. Bean for casual moments, as buttoned-down as an Oxford shirt. He would never feel right in Armani, even if it was original. He was aloof, but that just made him seem stronger. Jay liked to visit him in his office. He liked to study him.

It was like a message, when Kosigin gave him the job which led to Reeve being delivered unto him. It was like a dream. Jay could have taken Reeve out a dozen times since, any number of different ways, but he wanted a face-to-face. He wanted to know what had happened to Reeve, and what he'd told the brass. Just for his own personal satisfaction.

Then he'd kill him.

And if Reeve wouldn't tell, or made any rash first move . . . well, Jay would drop him without a second's hesitation.

'Where's this fucking noticeboard?' he murmured, walking through the packed concourse. It was like a demolition derby of luggage-carts and parties of elderly couples, all with walking-frames and umbrellas and bags of golf clubs and mackintoshes folded over pencil-thin liver-spotted arms. Umbrellas in LA-LA Land! It was a madhouse, and the lunatics had been in charge so long that nobody bothered to question the system any more.

'I love this town,' he said out loud, manoeuvring past the latest obstruction. He finally saw the information kiosk, though it was doing its best to blend in with the scenery. He passed a couple of his guys without acknowledging their presence, but when he got to the board he stopped and turned on his heels, checking all around, studying the scene through the plate-glass window – a jam of cabs and minibuses and a frantic cop windmilling his arms at them. The cop had a whistle in his mouth, referee-style. Jay remembered that moment in the scrape, when he knew he had either to jump and fight or he'd implode, he'd been lying there so long and so quiet. He knew that in technical parlance, he had 'cracked' – but fuck that. Reeve was so tight-arsed he'd have lain there and let a bomb detonate between his cheeks. If Jay hadn't got up and run, very probably neither of them would still be alive. That was something else he wanted to tell Reeve; he wanted Reeve to thank him for getting him out of that situation. He reckoned he was owed a little respect.

He looked around him again, and up towards the ceiling, and nothing he saw looked like a trap.

So then he studied the noticeboard, both sides, and he smiled at the clerk on the information desk, just in case he had something to do with it. Then he turned his attention to the notices again, especially the folded paper napkin with the name JAY written on it. He touched it with a finger, ran the palm of his hand down it, feeling for a bump, maybe some tiny explosive device which would take off a couple of fingers or blind him in one eye. That sort of magnitude.

But there was nothing. He lifted one corner of the napkin but the layers started to peel, and he had to take off another layer before he could make out that there was writing there. So then he licked his lips and hauled the napkin off the board in a single swift movement, so that the clerk looked at him quizzically. 'All clear here,' Jay said, as if to himself. Then he unfolded the note, the note telling him to fly to London. It gave the name of a hotel, and said a message would arrive there for him in the name of Rowe.

Rowe: that was a nice touch.

One of his hired hands came up, removing his earpiece as he approached. 'So?'

'So nothing, just a fucking note.'

They'd been all wound up. They'd been told of Reeve's rep. Jay had wanted them ready for anything. They were going to go away frustrated, pent-up, needing to unwind.

'Everyone to the cars,' Jay said. 'We'll go back to the gym, maybe hit a bar later. I just got to make a call first.'

He went to the public payphones and called Kosigin.

'Well?' Kosigin demanded.

Jay read the note out to him. 'What do you want me to do?' he asked when he'd finished.

'Personally,' Kosigin said, 'I want you to follow the instructions.'

'And what if I'm walking into a trap?'

'I thought you were clever enough to avoid traps?'

'I am, but I also don't believe in walking into them in the first place.'

'Then what do you suggest?'

'I'll go, but I want to take some men with me. It won't be cheap.'

'It never is.'

'You want to come along for the ride?'

'Absolutely not.'

'You still want me to go?'

'Absolutely,' Kosigin said, before hanging up.

Their conversation had gone exactly as Jay had known it would.

He looked around him for a sales desk, then walked over to the information kiosk.

'Which carriers fly to London?' he asked. He might have to try more than one. Could be difficult to make a block booking at such short notice . . .

Part Nine

Blood Hunt

23

There were police on duty at Heathrow, a lot of uniforms. Reeve would bet there were some plain-clothes detectives around, too. Maybe they were looking for him. At this point, he could only trust to luck. Everyone deserved one lucky break per mission. They might have a description of him, but it would be pre-haircut. They couldn't have a recent photograph; ever since his days in the SAS, Reeve had been camera-shy. The weekend soldiers sometimes wanted photographs, and he didn't refuse. But before posing for their cameras, he would don a balaclava and dark glasses. The weekend soldiers loved it.

Reeve had a lot of planning to do. He wasn't too happy about returning to Jim's Saab, which he had parked in a long-term car park only a courtesy bus-ride away from the Heathrow terminals. He didn't know how clever the police would be; he didn't think they would trace him as far as the Saab, but he couldn't be sure. To add to this, the car was a liability, and might break down at any minute. But he had very little alternative. He didn't want to hire a new car. That would mean handing over his credit card, and he guessed the police would be tracking its use. (They probably didn't know about his secret bank account, and even if they did they might not want to freeze it: if he accessed cash or wrote a cheque they'd have another way of tracking his movements.)

The people at the long-stay, on the other hand, knew only the false name he'd given them. He'd paid cash up front – so probably there wouldn't be a problem. But Reeve didn't enter the single-storey office straight away. First he took a look around the lot. He could see the Saab. It wasn't hard for him to spot among the shiny new Jags and BMWs and Rovers. The company had hemmed it in behind more expensive cars, reckoning them a better advert to potential customers. Reeve didn't blame them – he was actually relieved the Saab had been hidden from view during his time away.

He walked into the office.

'Had a good trip?' the girl behind the desk asked.

'Yes, thanks,' he said. There was complimentary coffee on a table nearby, and he helped himself to a cup. There was powdered milk only, so he took it black. It was bitter but it woke him up a bit.

'Now, Mr Fleming, you didn't specify a return date, so we've not been able to valet your car.'

'No problem. The dirt is the only thing holding it together.'

She smiled and filled in the rest of the form, which he had to sign at the bottom. He couldn't recall what first name he'd given, but saw it printed at the head of the sheet. Jay. He'd called himself Jay Fleming.

'And here are your keys,' the receptionist said, handing them over.

'I think you'll need to move a few of the other cars.'

'Oh, you're blocked in. I'll get Tom to see to it.'

Tom was outside, drinking tea from a flask. He wore overalls, waterproofs and wellingtons, and was without doubt the valet. Reeve watched as he started up and moved a gleaming red BMW 635 and a silver Rover 200. He thanked him and trundled the Saab out of the parking lot and into the lanes of traffic. It was the start of what was going to be a long twenty-four hours.

He headed north, stopping only for petrol and coffee and to read all the newspapers. He cursed the Saab's lack of a radio – he needed to know whether the police had connected him to the Marie Villambard killing. McCluskey had mentioned Interpol interest, but that could have been a bluff. But when he stopped near the border and bought some Scottish newspapers, he caught his first mention of the story, relegated to an inside page. Police, it said, were 'anxious to contact Scots outward-bound instructor Gordon Reeve'. There was no description, but they could have published one in a previous day's edition. He stopped at a Little Chef to replenish his caffeine level, and telephoned Joan's sister. Joan herself answered the phone.

'Joan, it's Bob Plant here, any sign of Gordon?'

She recognised his voice immediately. There was a slight pause as she came to understand what was going on. (She'd had a crush on Robert Plant of Led Zeppelin at one time.) 'Bob,' she said, 'sorry, I'm not thinking straight.'

'Are you all right, Joan?'

'I'm fine. It's just been a shock, with the police and everything.'

'They've been asking you questions?' He sounded like a solicitous friend.

'Well, they just want to know where Gordon is. You know they found his car in France, near where three bodies were found, one of them a woman's.'

'Gracious.'

'They're keeping watch on the house here, just in case he shows up.'

'They think he had something to do with the murders?'

'Well, Bob, what would *you* think if you were them? Gordon's Land Rover burned out and no trace of him anywhere.'

'I suppose you're right.'

'Bob, I'm worried about him.'

'Gordon can take care of himself, Joan.'

'Yes, I know, but—'

'Might he go back to the island?'

'I don't know. There are police watching the ferries.'

'A real manhunt, eh?'

'They may even be watching the house.'

'Ach, unlikely he'd head back there.'

'Yes, I suppose so. But where else would he be? Where could he go?'

'You know him better than I do, Joan.'

'Well, I thought I knew him, Bob.'

Silence on the line.

'Joan,' Reeve said, looking in at the diners – families mostly, 'he'll be all right. I'm sure he's done nothing wrong.'

'Try telling the police that.'

'Maybe he needs evidence first, I mean before he can come back.'
'Evidence?'
'Of his innocence.'
Joan sniffed. He could tell she was crying.
'I'll phone again,' he told her.
'I'm sorry,' she said, wiping her nose.
'Maybe I shouldn't have called.'
'No, I'm glad you did. It's been a while, Bob.'
'Yes, it has. Is Allan all right?'
'Missing his dad. But at the same time – I know this is wrong – he seems to quite like the idea of having a father who's a wanted man.' She laughed.
Reeve smiled, and blinked back tears. At one table, a father was admonishing his son, who still had a full plate of food in front of him. The kid was nine, maybe ten. The man spoke in a low voice but his eyes were blazing.
'Bye, Joan,' he said.
'Goodbye, Bob.'
He kept the receiver to his ear after she'd put down the phone, and heard a double-click and what sounded like a stifled sneeze. The bastards were listening in, just as he'd suspected. Not Jay or Kosigin this time, but the police. He ran through the conversation again, satisfied he hadn't given anything away. And he'd learned so much.
'Thanks, love,' he said quietly, heading back to his table and a refill of coffee.

If they were watching the ferries, they'd be watching Oban and Tarbert on the mainland, both of which had direct sailings: Oban to South Uist and Tarbert to North Uist. The two islands were separated by the smaller island of Benbecula, and all three were linked by bridges. They might also be watching Uig, a small port on Skye. But to get to Skye he would have to take a short ferry-ride from Kyle of Lochalsh, the bridge to Kylerhea, or the much longer ferry-crossing from Mallaig. Unless there was manpower to spare, Reeve doubted anyone would be watching Mallaig.
Which was precisely why he ignored Oban and drove instead to Fort William and from there to Mallaig on the coast. There were no direct ferries from Mallaig to the Outer Hebrides.
At the same time, he couldn't afford to relax. His face was known in the town, and a few people even knew him by name. There would be police in the vicinity, maybe not in Mallaig itself, but nearby. And if his description had been in the papers . . .
He was there to seek out one of the people who knew him by name, an old rogue called Kenneth Creech. 'Creech short for creature,' Kenneth sometimes said in introduction – and he had a point. He reminded Reeve in particular of a lizard; all he was missing was the green skin.
Kenneth Creech had a narrow, jagged face that fell to two distinct points – his chin and the extruding tip of his nose. When you looked at him face on, his nostrils couldn't be seen at all. His eyes bugged from his face and his tongue, which slid a centimetre or two from his mouth between utterances, was thin and pointed like his face. He was known to cheat at cards, siphon petrol from any unlocked fuel tank (to which end he sometimes carried a

gallon drum with him, empty at the start of the evening), and be foul-mouthed in front of the opposite sex, while nary a curse passed his lips in the company of his fellow men.

People steered clear of Kenneth Creech. Reeve had got to know him when Creech had tricked him out of some money which was to pay for the transportation of some stuff between North Uist and the mainland. Creech owned a couple of small boats and some creels and lobster pots. He never actually used these, but somehow managed to be the recipient of a European Community 'Business Expansion Grant', which had paid for the second boat and kept Creech well enough off besides.

In the summer, Creech sometimes tricked tourists into going with him on one of the boats for what was supposed to be an all-day pleasure cruise around 'the beautiful Hebrides'. In fact, he'd head straight for the choppiest waters and most dangerous wind-torn straits, after which the tourists would beg to return to land. At this point, they'd be told there were no refunds. If they argued for their money back, Creech would pay them, then would drop them off somewhere on the far side of Skye, pretending they were a mile or so south of Mallaig.

Reeve liked Creech. He liked him so much he had eventually let Creech keep the money he'd been cheated of.

Creech hated mankind, but he surely did love money. Reeve was counting on this fact.

Kenneth Creech had a boathouse just north of the town. It was six in the evening when Reeve got there, having driven through town without stopping. The sky to the west, out over Skye and the Minch, was a palette of pinks and greys, thin threads of silver and softly glowing red. Reeve gave it all of a second of his time then kicked at the boathouse door, which rattled on its hinges.

The door was locked, but that didn't mean Creech wasn't inside. At last a bolt slid back and the door opened.

'You'll pay for any damage,' Creech snapped, examining his door first and his visitor second. His mouth made an O when he recognised Reeve.

'Well now, Gordon,' he said. 'What brings you here?'

'Money,' Reeve said, holding up a thickish fold of notes. 'To wit, my desire to give you some.'

Creech couldn't take his eyes off the cash. 'Well now, Gordon,' he said, the tongue darting in and out of his mouth, 'you must be wanting a boat.'

'How did you guess?'

Creech didn't say anything, just ushered him inside. The back of the boathouse opened on to the Sound of Sleat. Reeve could see the southern tip of Skye. The larger of the two boats was tied up in the water; it had bench seats both sides, and could carry a dozen passengers. In the middle of the deck stood the control console with a small steering-wheel, like that of a sports car. In fact, if you looked closer there was the MG insignia in the centre of the wheel. Creech had stolen it from a crashed car south of the town. By the time the insurance investigators reached the vehicle, there hadn't been much left but a shell.

Creech's other boat was smaller, but boasted an outboard motor and was a lot nippier as a result. It had been hauled out of the water and now hung by winches over the wooden floor. Old newspapers were scattered beneath the hull, which Creech was in the middle of repainting.

'You're painting over the barnacles,' Reeve told him. Creech was wiping his hands on a rag. The paint-tin looked to Reeve like ordinary vinyl silk emulsion. The colour, according to the lid of the tin, was taupe.

'Well, it's a sight easier than scraping them off.'

Reeve nodded, and smiled at Creech, who looked nervier even than usual. He kept jerking his head and blinking his bulbous eyes.

'You know about me?' Reeve said.

Creech started to deny it. Denial was an instinct, like breathing. But then he broke off, knowing Reeve knew.

'I've heard a few stories,' he said at last, sounding like it didn't bother him in the slightest.

Reeve looked around. 'You've no phone here, Kenneth?'

Creech shook his head slowly, then spoke carefully. 'I wouldn't turn you in, Gordon.'

'That's unusually friendly of you, Kenneth. What's wrong, isn't there a reward?'

The momentary look in Creech's eyes told Reeve he'd never considered the possibility until now.

'Don't,' Reeve warned him.

Creech got back some mobility and went over to the boat, picking up his paintbrush. He'd left it lying on the edge of the newspaper, and some paint had dribbled on to the floor. He wiped the spot with his rag, but that just spread the stain further.

'I'm painting this boat,' he said.

'I'd never have guessed.' Reeve paused. 'But that's the boat I want.'

Creech glanced towards him. 'Now?' Reeve nodded. 'Can't it wait till I'm finished?'

'Do I look like a man who can wait?'

'No.' The word took a long time coming out. 'But you surely don't want to take a boat out at night?' Creech paused. 'No wait, of course you do. There's less chance of them spotting you at night.'

'Well done, Kenneth. How many police are there?'

Creech considered lying, but looked at the money again, the money Reeve was still holding in his hand.

'There's more where this came from,' Reeve told him.

Creech wet his already glistening lips. 'Well, there's nobody in Mallaig,' he said, 'but I've heard tell there are a couple of strange faces on Skye.'

'Anywhere else?'

'Oh aye, they were in Oban yesterday.'

'And Tarbert?'

'I couldn't tell you about Tarbert.'

'And on South Uist?'

'Well, they've been to your house a couple of times, that much I've heard. You're big news around here, Gordon.'

'I didn't do anything, Kenneth.'

'I don't doubt it, I don't doubt it, but the police used to have a saying in Glasgow: you don't arrest an innocent man. If they take you in, they'll try their damnedest to find *something* against you, even if it means planting the evidence.'

Reeve smiled. 'You sound like you've been there.'

'I was in trouble enough in my early days. I'm from Partick, remember. One look at my face – I know it's no beauty – and the polis would stop me.' Creech spat into the water.

'You'll help me?'

Creech considered the question. The tension left his shoulders. 'Ach, maybe I'm too sentimental for my own good,' he said. 'Of course I'll help you.'

And he held out his hand for the cash.

Reeve helped him move the boat back over the water and lower it in, so that its side scraped that of the larger vessel, leaving smears of paint on the wood. Creech went to check that the boathouse doors were locked. When he turned again, Reeve was standing at the workbench, his back to him. Creech licked his lips again and moved forward quietly. When Reeve turned, Creech let out an involuntary gasp. Reeve was holding the biggest knife Creech had ever seen. He had it in his right hand, a coil of Creech's best rope in the other.

'What . . . what are you going to do?' Creech said.

Reeve showed him. He sliced through the thick braids like they were string, then let the most part of the rope fall to the floor. 'I'm going to tie you up,' he told Creech.

'No need for that, Gordon. I'll come with you.'

'And you'd wait in the boat for me? You wouldn't for example sprint off the minute I was on dry land and head for the nearest mainland telephone?'

'No,' Creech said. 'You know I wouldn't.'

But Reeve was shaking his head. 'This way we both know where we stand. Or in your case, sit.'

And he made Creech sit on the floor with his back to the workbench, tying his hands behind him around one thick wooden leg of the structure. For good measure, he cut another length of rope – 'That stuff costs a fortune,' Creech protested – and tied Creech's ankles. He thought of sticking the paint-rag in Creech's mouth, but he wanted to restrain the man, nothing more. He doubted anyone would come to see Creech during his absence. Creech had no friends, no one who'd miss him; he spent most of his time in the boathouse, and had even put up a partition so he could sleep there too. Reeve glanced into the 'bedroom' to make sure there *was* no telephone. He'd seen no cables outside, but it was best to check. All he saw was a mattress and duvet on the floor, a candlestick, an empty whisky bottle, and a pornographic magazine.

Satisfied, he brought his bag in from the car and got to work, changing into dark clothes and balaclava, donning face-blacking. Creech's face told him he had achieved the right effect. There was a good-sized moon in a clear sky. He wouldn't have any trouble navigating; he knew the islands and the potential obstacles pretty well. He had a choice of two routes: one would take him into the Sound of Eriskay so he could approach the western side of South Uist. The advantage of this route was that he'd have a shorter hike at the end of it, two or so miles, but it meant a lot more time spent in the boat than the second route, which would land him in Loch Eynort, a seawater loch. This way he would land further away from Stoneybridge, maybe as much as a six-mile hike away. It made for a longer time on land, more time for him to be spotted. Plus, of course, if forced to retreat, he'd have a lot further to run to reach the safety of the boat.

He decided in the end to head for Loch Eynort. If all went well it would cut hours off the mission time, being a much shorter boat crossing. He still doubted he'd complete his mission under the cover of darkness, but the sooner he started the better chance he'd have. He loaded spare fuel into the boat, and took one of Creech's better waterproof combinations, plus a torch and mooring rope. Then he cut himself a length of twine, and tied about a dozen knots in it, each one a couple of inches from its neighbour.

Finally he went back over to Creech, who'd been complaining throughout about aching arms. 'I could always amputate,' he said, showing Creech the knife. That shut him up. 'What's the water in the Minch likely to be like tonight?'

'Cold and wet.' Reeve inched the knife closer to Creech, who gave in quickly and told Reeve the prevailing winds and the forecast: it would be blustery, but far from unmanageable. Of course, he could have been lying, but Reeve didn't think so – it was in his interests for Reeve to return. For one thing, he might starve to death otherwise, since chances were nobody came near the boathouse from one week to the next. For another, he loved his boats too much. He wouldn't want one tipped and sunk in a gale, especially not the one with the expensive European Community outboard motor.

'Take care of her,' Creech begged.

'Thanks for your concern,' Reeve said, climbing down the ladder into the boat.

The crossing was worse than he'd anticipated, but that was typical of Little Minch: you thought it had done its worst, then it did a little more. He was glad he didn't have to tackle the sounds; Eriskay could be particularly hair-raising. He wondered no amusement park had sought to emulate it – talk about a white-knuckle ride. His own knuckles were quite white enough as he wrestled with the outboard. The only good news was that it wasn't raining. Still, he was glad he was wearing the waterproofs considering the amount of spray that was being washed over him. He kept close to the Skye coast for as long as he could before heading out into Little Minch proper. He was taking as direct a line as he could, hoping he would hit the coast in the right place. The way the wind was blowing, and without much in the way of navigation save his small compass, he knew he might be blown off course by as much as three or four miles, which would only add to the land trek if he decided to land the boat.

He saw a couple of boats, warning-lights flashing to let others know they were there, but they didn't see him, and they certainly couldn't hear him. He changed hands often on the outboard's throttle, but even so wished he'd thought to bring gloves. He used his breath to warm his fingers, then worked them in the waterproof's pocket, rubbing life back into them.

His mind was on nothing but the crossing itself. He couldn't afford not to concentrate his full attention on it.

Finally he saw land, and checking to the south could make out the small island of Stuley, which meant he was just south of Loch Eynort. He'd been adjusting direction to account for the winds, and was pleased to find he had corrected his course wisely. The water was already much less choppy, and as he entered the inlet he felt the wind drop. He took the boat as far into the loch as he could. Stepping on to land was a relief and a strange sensation. He felt his feet weren't wholly connected to the ground, as though gravity had lost its grip. He knew the feeling would not last long. It was a trick his brain was playing on him.

Reeve grabbed his bag and headed along the road.

There were a couple of crofts nearby, but no signs of life in them. At this hour, the only things awake might be a few sheep and the night birds and animals. The road he was on would soon cross the A865. If he stayed on the road, he'd round the southern side of Loch Ollay and come to a junction. Left would take him to Ormiclate; right would take him towards Stoneybridge and home. He'd checked the time upon landing: he wanted to know how long the hike took. He was also pacing it out. He had the twine in his hand, and was counting his steps. Every hundred steps he slid another knot through thumb and forefinger. At the end of the piece of twine, he could then multiply by length of stride to find roughly how far he'd gone, which would help him estimate how fast he was travelling.

He didn't really need this information. What he *did* need was to feel like a soldier again. Because soon he'd be coming up against Jay, one way or another, and he had to be mentally sharp. At short notice, there wasn't much he could do to bolster his fitness or physique – the years had taken their toll. From what he'd seen of Jay, the man would be stronger than him: fighting him physically would be a lost cause. What Reeve needed to do was become strong mentally; he needed to hone his attitude and his instincts. He needed proper planning and procedure, starting right now.

Knowing the roads as he did, he made good time to the house. He could have shaved minutes off by crossing country, but he'd have been more likely to get lost, and running on a road was easier on the muscles than running over rough terrain.

He took his time approaching the house.

He did one full circuit around it at a distance of half a mile, then closed in and circled it again. If anyone was watching for him, they were well concealed. He knew policemen, and knew they weren't trained that way. For one thing, they liked their creature comforts; for another, they didn't have the necessary patience. There might be a presence inside the house, but he'd swear there was no one out here with him.

Silently, he entered the compound, crouching low, keeping to the shadows along the walls. There was an added advantage to staying close by the walls: the drive itself was gravel and noisy underfoot, but there was a two-foot border of earth between the driveway and the walls, a concession to Joan, who had planted small flowers and climbers there. Reeve crushed them underfoot in silence.

He had the keys he needed in his free hand, the keys to the killing-room door. But the police had been there first. They'd taken a sledgehammer to the door, which looked like it had resisted their onslaught bravely. The door swung inwards to the touch. He wondered what they'd thought when they'd found the room, with empty cartridge-casings on the floor and shop-window dummies acting as hostages. He knelt down in front of the skirting board and shone the torch against it. It looked undisturbed. Reeve pulled it open and reached in, touching the oiled rags, feeling the metal bulk beneath their wrapping.

And he smiled.

He unwrapped the Beretta and found the right package of ammo for it, filling his pockets as well as the gun. Pushing his hand back into the wall, he pulled out a package of plastic explosive with all the trimmings. The explosive itself was fairly fresh; he'd been using it to rig up explosions some weekends, to keep his soldiers on their toes. Reeve checked for detonators, wire and wire-cutters; everything he needed was in the package, including the crocodile clips which acted as triggers. He put everything in his holdall, then replaced the skirting board and made sure he'd left no footprints.

He crossed the courtyard, moving slowly on the gravel and pebbles. Peering through the kitchen window, he saw nothing. He circled the house, looking in the windows on all four sides: still nothing. He couldn't tell about upstairs. It was just possible that a guard could be asleep in one of the bedrooms. The curtains in Allan's room were closed, but maybe he'd just forgotten to open them the morning they'd been cleared out.

Reeve unlocked the front door and entered the hall. He didn't need to disable the alarm: the police must already have done that. He wondered how long it had rung before they'd found a way to silence it. Not that it mattered out here; the nearest croft wasn't within hailing distance.

He double-checked the downstairs rooms then made for the stairwell. The second step from the bottom was the creaky one, so he avoided it, just as he avoided the middle of the third step from the top. He didn't use the banister for fear of a warning sound. On the landing, he held his breath and listened. There was no noise. He waited there three full minutes: when someone's asleep, they usually make some sort of sound every three minutes or so. Reeve suspected that a policeman would have *some* regard for property, so any guard would probably choose to sleep in the guest room. He opened the door slowly and pointed his pistol through the crack. The curtains weren't closed and moonlight filled the room. The bed was made up, with several throw pillows and costume dolls arranged on it. Joan's work. She'd spent a lot of time lovingly decorating a room nobody ever came to stay in.

He turned and crossed the landing, opening Allan's bedroom door. The room was a mess: bedclothes thrown onto the floor, pyjamas draped over the end of the bed, comics everywhere; the computer's power light shone lemon-yellow in the gloom. Either Allan had left it on, or the police had checked it and forgotten to turn it off. Reeve left the room again and quickly checked the main bedroom and even the bathroom.

Then he breathed a sigh of relief.

Downstairs he found milk in the fridge, but it was off. There was an unopened carton of orange juice, and he cut it open with scissors, then gulped from it. There was an unopened packet of ham in there too, so he peeled it open and lifted out two slices, rolling them up and stuffing them into his mouth. Back in the living room, he assessed the visit by the police. They had dusted. Probably they wanted his fingerprints for the file they were opening on him. It looked like they'd shifted everything and put it back not quite in the right place. Searching for clues, he supposed. He unscrewed the telephone handsets. The bugging devices had been removed. He suspected this had been done by Dulwater rather than the police.

He didn't suppose anyone would be listening in, so went upstairs and took a quick hot shower, thanking God for the instantaneous water heater.

He left the light off in the bathroom, though he couldn't say why. Perhaps it was because it felt like procedure.

He dried himself off and searched for clean and, above all, *warm* clothes. There were a few other things he needed, but they were in his workshop. He walked into Allan's room again, restless, unable to sit down. The yellow light caught his attention. The screen was black, but when he nudged the mouse it came to life, showing him the games menu from the hard disk. There were a couple of good games there, and some which must have been new from the last time he and Allan had played together.

Then Reeve saw the game Allan had loaded from the disk sent to him by Jim. The game Allan couldn't get on with. It was called Prion.

'Jesus,' Reeve whispered. Prion, as in PrP, as in the bad chemicals which had started this whole nightmare. His hand was fairly steady as he moved the pointer on to Prion, and double-clicked to load the game.

When the title screen came up though, it wasn't called Prion at all. It looked a fairly straight arcade game called Gumball Gulch, which is what Allan had called it, Reeve recalled. Which screen was it Allan had said he couldn't get past? Five? Six?

It took Reeve a while to follow the instructions and get into the game. As far as he could tell, he was a turtle in the wild west, just made sheriff of the town of Gumball Gulch. In screen one, he rode into town and was voted sheriff after killing the three bad guys who had just shot the sheriff to bust their comrade out of the jail. In screen two, there was a bank robbery to foil. The graphics, so far as Reeve could judge, were pretty good, as were the sound effects, complete with voices.

After maybe half an hour, he was in screen four. In screen three he'd had the option of taking as deputy a one-legged drunk. Reeve had accepted 'Stumpy', who now guarded the villains from the bank robbery.

Suddenly Reeve paused. 'What the hell am I doing?' he asked himself. But he kept on going.

Screen four was a difficult one. Re-election time was coming up, and Reeve's popularity was only forty percent, two of the bank robbers having escaped, and one innocent bystander having been gunned down during the shoot-out. Reeve granted a new licence to the Brawlin' Barroom, which pushed his popularity to fifty percent. But then the rowdiness factor increased, and soon the cells were bursting. Reeve opted to take another deputy, a fresh-faced young kid.

'This is *Rio Bravo*,' he muttered.

The real trouble started on screen five. There was a mass break-out attempt at the jail. Stumpy had the place locked tight with himself inside. He wasn't letting anyone in, the sheriff included, which left Reeve outside with one kid deputy, a restless populace, and a possible lynch mob. In a little while, the escaped bank robbers would be coming into town intent on revenge. Reeve's guns and ammo, of course, were in the jail.

And Stumpy was asking for the password.

Reeve tried a few obvious things, some only a *Rio Bravo* buff would know. Then he sat back, arms folded, and did some thinking. Jim had changed the name of the game to Prion. Why? Suddenly it became clear. As Marie Villambard had said, Jim was a journalist from his head to his toes. He would have kept files. He would have kept back-ups, and kept them well hidden.

Reeve knew now the purpose of the password. He typed in CWC, but it didn't work. He tried Co-World, then PrP, then Prion – to no avail. He tried Killin and Preece. Nothing.

So then he tried Kosigin.

And suddenly he wasn't in Gumball Gulch any more. The bottom of the screen told him he was reading page one of twenty-eight. The print-size was small, Jim had crammed a lot in. Single-spaced, too. At the top was a message in bold:

> **I'll let you get back to the game soon, Gordon. I'm assuming it's you reading this, and if you are reading it then I'm most probably dead. If I am dead and if you are reading this, then you've probably been sniffing around and I thank you for your concern. The following may be of help. I'd dearly love to get it published. A friend called Marie in France may help, I'll give you her address at the end. But first, I have a story to tell you . . .**

And what a story. Reeve already knew it, of course, but Jim had more information than anyone had suspected. There was the stuff about Preece's history, his 'revolutionary' shock-sex therapy, and Kosigin's hiring of Alliance Investigative to dig up the details. Kosigin's blackmail of Preece had been implicit, but Jim's report made it explicit by actually interviewing two ex-investigators at Alliance who had worked on the job, as well as members of the original research team headed by Preece.

Including a Dr Erik Korngold.

Jim had had two very cordial meetings with Korngold. It was Korngold who had admitted the blackmail. Preece had spoken to him about it at the time. But then Dr Korngold had turned up dead, leaving Jim pretty well stuck unless he could get corroboration. The only other scientist he knew of from the original research team was Dr Killin. So he'd started pestering Killin, and Killin had gone to Kosigin.

And Kosigin had decided the reporter had to be taken out of the game.

Jim's research was impressive – and scary. He detailed countries around the world where neurological diseases were on the increase, and showed how these increases correlated to the introduction of CWC herbicides and pesticides on to those countries' farms. There were snippets of interviews with farmers and doctors, agrichemical experts and environmentalists. Farmers everywhere were getting more and more ill. Stress, the sceptics had said. But Jim had found out different. And when the police *did* start to get curious about pesticide side effects, CWC simply shifted spheres, concentrating on third world countries.

Jim found a correlation with tobacco companies who, as western markets contracted after health scares, merely opened up new unsuspecting markets – Africa, Asia . . . CWC were doing the same thing with chemicals. What was more, Jim had at the time of writing been getting inklings of crooked deals to introduce pesticides into third world countries. Deals were done with governments, regimes and dictators, money slipped into secret bank accounts, and import barriers suddenly disappeared. Jim hinted at links between CWC and the CIA, since the CIA wanted a presence in countries that CWC was opening up. It was a global conspiracy, encompassing governments, the scientific community, and everyone who had to eat.

Jim had worked hard and fast building up his case. He did so for a simple reason, one he stated towards the end of the file: 'I think some people would kill to keep this secret, because while bits and pieces are well enough known, certainly among the environmental pressure groups, no one has really been able to link it *globally*. They say you are what you eat. In that case, we're poison.'

At the end, Jim gave Marie Villambard's address, and beneath that were some instructions. They told Reeve where he would find the 'hard evidence'. Jim had hidden all the documents – transcripts, notes, archive material, and tapes of interviews. They were in a box at Jilly Palmer's farm outside Tisbury. Jilly Palmer: Reeve remembered her long braid of chestnut hair, her rosy-red cheeks. Jim had been introduced to her by Josh Vincent, and had trusted her from the off. He'd asked her to store a large box for him, and to say nothing to anyone about it unless they told her they'd read about it on the disk.

'I'm keeping copies of some of the stuff with me,' Jim concluded, 'so that if any burglaries suddenly and mysteriously occur, they'll think they got what they came for.'

Then a final message: 'To access the next game level, press Ctrl + N. To quit, press Esc.'

Reeve hit the Escape button and shut down the computer. The story had been here all the time, here under his own roof. His legs weren't the steadiest as he got to his feet. He couldn't think, couldn't concentrate on anything but his brother. He got down to the kitchen somehow and made himself a hot drink, then sat at the table sipping it, staring at nothing.

The mug was one-third empty when he started to cry.

He planned to call Jay's hotel that evening, which gave him a full day to prepare. High on his list was sleep, but first he had to return to the boat.

The early-morning waters were calmer, and the dawn made navigation easier. He made good time back to Mallaig. He could tell Creech had been sleeping, but he was awake now, looking miserable. Even so, he studied the boat carefully as Reeve brought her home.

'Not a scratch on her,' Reeve said, clambering out with his stuff. He checked Creech's wrists. They were red-ringed, the skin broken at a couple of points. 'Trying to escape, eh?'

'Wouldn't you?' Creech snarled. Reeve had to agree. 'Man my age and condition, trussed like a Christmas turkey.' Reeve untied him and told him to put the kettle on. When Creech came back, Reeve was laying out banknotes on the workbench.

'What's that for?' Creech tried not to sound too interested.

'I need your help, Kenneth. I'm sorry I had to tie you up, but to be honest I'd very little option. If I'd taken you with me, you'd've had to walk from Loch Eynort to Stoneybridge and back. But now I'd like you to help me. If you do, you pocket this money for starters.'

Creech eyed the money. 'How do you mean, starters?'

'I'll give you some passengers. They'll pay you whatever you ask. They'll just want to take one of your boats, perhaps both. Like I say, you can name your price.'

The kettle was boiling. Creech didn't go to switch it off.

'What do I have to do?' he said.

There were old wooden boards lying around the place. It wasn't difficult to find two or three the right size, along with some fixing poles. They used the taupe paint to put a few words on the boards, and when it was dry used a hot-air gun to peel some of it back off. Creech got some earth and rubbed it into the boards. In the end, they looked fairly authentic.

Then Reeve dipped into his bag and brought out a packet of red powder he'd brought from his workshop. It was like powdered paint, but mixed with a little water produced a thick bubbly liquid which looked just like blood. He used it some weekends, laying a fake trail for his soldiers. He didn't tell Creech what it was, or what it was for.

They stopped for more tea. Creech kept asking about these men who'd want to hire his boats. How did Reeve know about them? When would they come?

'I'll tell you later,' Reeve said, standing up. 'First though, I'm going to borrow your mattress for an hour or two. Okay?'

Creech nodded vigorously. Reeve lifted the Beretta out of the bag, waved it at Creech, and took it and his tea with him to the mattress.

Creech decided not to move from the table until Gordon Reeve awoke, no matter how long that took.

Reeve took Creech with him when he went to make the telephone call. Not because he didn't trust Creech, but because Creech didn't trust *him*. Creech wanted to hear him make the call.

They squeezed into a telephone box at the end of a farm road, and Reeve made the call.

A hotel receptionist answered, and Reeve asked to be put through to Mr Rowe's room. Jay answered on the first ring.

'It's me,' Reeve said icily.

'Who else? I want to thank you, Philosopher. I've always wanted an excuse to come back home. And all expenses paid, too.'

'Kosigin's a generous man. You weren't worried I'd sic the regiment on to you?'

'I don't think that's what you want.'

'You're right.'

'So when and where do we meet?'

'An island. Not far from my home.'

'You want home advantage, eh? Well, I'd do the same. Give me the details.'

'Head to Mallaig.' Reeve spelt it out. 'Just north of the town, there's a boathouse with an old Saab parked outside. You'll see it easily enough. The boathouse is owned by a man called Creech.' He spelt this too. 'He'll hire you a boat.'

'A boat? Hey, do I get to row it, like in the song?'

Reeve ignored this. 'Will you need just the one boat?'

Jay laughed. 'It's just you and me, Philosopher.'

'I'll bet. Creech will know where you're to go. He'll give you directions. Naturally, he'll want paying for the hire.' Reeve watched Creech's tongue flick momentarily from his mouth.

'Naturally. I'm looking forward to seeing you again. We've got a lot to catch up on.'

Reeve blinked away the pink fog. Soon, he thought. Soon. But he mustn't let the anger get the better of him. He had to control it.

'Kosigin must really want those tapes,' he said.

Jay just laughed. 'Come on, Philosopher, we both know this isn't about the tapes. Screw the tapes. Screw Kosigin. This is about you and me, am I right?'

'You're a clever man, Jay.'

'Not as clever as you, Philosopher, but I've been trying.'

Reeve put down the receiver and pushed his way out of the box.

'Is he coming?' Creech asked.

'He's coming.'

'When?'

'As long as it takes him. Come on.'

'Where to?'

'The boathouse. I want you to drop me off somewhere.'

'An island?' Creech guessed.

'Yes.'

'Which one?'

So Reeve told him.

24

Jay and his men took three cars from London.

They drove steadily, without saying much. The front car had a map. All three cars were equipped with comms: two-way radios, cellphones, bleepers.

'And if those don't work,' one man had said, 'we'll just have to whistle.'

There were ten men altogether. Jay split them as two four-man patrols and one two-man patrol. His was the two-man patrol. His second-in-command was an ex-LA cop called Hestler. Hestler was very good; Jay had worked with him before. However, Jay hadn't been given much notice of the mission, had needed men in a hurry, and a few of the others in the group were unknowns. There were a couple who weren't much more than street kids, ex-gang members. They looked mean, but looks counted for very little. Reeve could sneak up from behind them and take them out. The first he'd see of their mean looks, their eyes would already be glazed over.

Jay and his squad hadn't flown direct to Heathrow. He knew Heathrow customs could be tough. They'd flown to Paris instead, and got a French operative to organise cars to take them across the Channel by ferry. It was slow, but it meant no one checked the contents of the large metal cases they'd brought with them from the French capital.

The cases were polished aluminium, the sort of rigid carrier camera equipment was often shipped in. There could have been video cameras inside, but there weren't. Instead, the cases were packed with the same equipment they'd taken on the Villambard mission.

Everyone was tired, Jay knew that. They'd hardly checked into the hotel before Reeve's phone call had come. Probably Reeve was playing on that factor. He would keep Jay moving, keep him from sleeping. Jay had considered staying put in London, getting some rest and setting off next morning. But he was keen to get this over and done with. He was good and ready. There'd be plenty of time for sleep afterwards.

He knew his own enthusiasm wasn't shared by everyone. The car passengers were trying to sleep. They'd switch drivers every hour, and stop every two hours for a stretch and some coffee. The map was a Collins road atlas, and it showed them that Mallaig was in the Scottish Highlands, a hell of a way from London but very close to Reeve's own home. Reeve wanted them on his territory. Mallaig was coastal, not quite wilderness. Jay didn't mind. When he wasn't working, he liked to take off east out of LA to the forests and mountains of San Gabriel and San Bernardino. There was no terrain he didn't know. He was an adept skier, climber and runner. Last fall he'd taken off into the wilds for fifteen days, not coming across another living soul for fourteen of them. He knew Reeve had been running outward bound courses, but doubted they could be anything near as arduous as his own survivalist training. Plus, of course, Jay had been through the same training as Reeve, the same gruelling marches over moor and mountain. He didn't think the Highlands would faze him.

But that was another thing about his troop – they were city dwellers for the most part, used to street-fighting and gun law. Only two, Jay apart, had served in armed forces. One of these was Hestler, the other was a big but paunchy native American called Choa whose main line of work these days was as a bouncer at a night club on Sunset Boulevard. Some actor had died there a while back, but Choa's name hadn't been mentioned . . .

Reeve had done all right so far. He'd handled himself pretty well. But he'd been operating swift strikes, vanishing again afterwards. Jay didn't think he'd cope with confrontation quite so well. The odds still favoured Jay, which was the only way he'd play them.

They reached Mallaig at ten in the morning. It had been raining ever since they'd crossed the border. The windscreen wipers were on full and still were barely coping. There wasn't much of a road north out of Mallaig, and the next settlement along, Mallaigvaig, was the end of the line. The only thing you could do when you got there was turn back to Mallaig itself.

But just before they reached Mallaigvaig, they saw the boathouse and the Saab.

'Hestler, with me,' Jay said. At the last service station, they'd opened the metal cases, and when the two men left the front car, each carried a Heckler & Koch MP5 set at three-round burst. They ran to the boathouse door and Jay banged on it with his shoe. Then they stood to either side of the door and waited for someone to answer.

When the door started to open Jay shouldered it inwards, throwing Kenneth Creech on to his back, from which position he peered up into the mouth of the sub-machine gun.

'Are you Creech?'

'Sweet Jesus.'

'Are you Creech?'

Creech eventually managed to nod that he was. Hestler had recced the shed and now said, 'All clear,' then went to the door to signal for the others to come in.

'You know someone called Reeve?'

Creech nodded again.

'What did he tell you?'

'He said you'd . . . you'd need a boat.'

'To go where?'

'Skivald. It's a small island off South Uist.'

Jay turned to Hestler. 'Tell one of them to bring the map.' He turned back to Creech. 'I notice you've wet yourself.' The stain on Kenneth Creech's trousers was spreading fast. Jay smiled. 'I like that. Now, Mr Creech, how big is Skivald?'

'About a mile and a half by three-quarters of a mile.'

'Small.'

'Aye.' Choa handed the map book to Jay, who put it on the floor and crouched down to flick its pages. The MP5 was still trained on a point between Creech's eyes. 'I don't see it,' Jay said at last. 'Show me.' Creech sat up and looked at the map. He pointed to where Skivald was, north of Loch Eynort.

'There's nothing there.'

'No,' Creech said, 'it's not marked. You won't find it on a map.'

Jay narrowed his eyes. 'What's going on, Mr Creech?' The tip of the gun touched the bridge of Creech's nose. Creech screwed shut his eyes, which were watering. 'Dear me, Mr Creech, you're leaking from every orifice.'

The men who had gathered around laughed at this. Creech didn't feel any better for them being there, but he could hardly feel worse about their massive presence either.

'He's ugly,' said one of the street-gang youths. He'd been wearing his uniform of sawn-off black T-shirt and sleeveless denim jacket for most of the trip, but had insisted they stop at a service station just south of Carlisle so he could find something warmer to wear. The others had stayed in their cars.

'I doubt the shops here will sell clothes,' Jay had murmured. But the street-youth had come out with a wool-lined brown leather jacket. Jay didn't ask where he had found it. He knew he should be angry; it was a very public announcement of their presence, ripping off someone's jacket. But he doubted the victim would run to the police, who would have to listen to a story about an American Blood on the loose in Carlisle . . .

'I fucking hate ugly people, man,' said the youth, shuffling his feet.

'Hear that, Mr Creech?' Jay asked. 'He hates you. Maybe you'd better help me pacify him, or you never know what he might do.'

As if in answer the youth, whose name was Jiminez, expertly flicked open a gold-coloured butterfly knife.

'Reeve made me take him to the island,' Creech spluttered.

'Yes? When was this?'

'Last night.'

'Does he have any way off the island?'

Creech shook his head.

'Are you sure?'

'Positive. He could always swim, but that's about it.'

'Anything else, Mr Creech?'

Creech licked his lips. 'No,' he said.

Jay smiled and stood up. 'Cut him,' he ordered. Jiminez had been waiting. The knife flashed across Creech's thigh and he winced, covering it with his hand. Blood squeezed out from between his fingers.

'We can do you a lot of damage, Mr Creech,' Jay said, walking around the boathouse. 'You have some nice tools here, any one of which could be turned on you. All it takes is a little . . . creativity.' He picked up the hot-air gun. 'Now, where's the socket?'

'I swear to God!' Creech said.

'What did he take with him, Mr Creech?' Jay asked. 'You say you took him to this island, you must at least have seen what he took with him.'

'He had a bag, a holdall sort of thing. It looked heavy.'

'And?'

'And he had . . . he had a gun.'

'Like this one?' Jay asked, waving the MP5.

'No, no, just a pistol.'
'A pistol? Is that all?'
'It's all I saw.'
'Mmm. You didn't see anything else? No traps?'
'Traps?'
'Yes, for catching animals.'
'I didn't see anything like that.'

Jay had finished his tour of the room. He crouched down again in front of Creech. This was *his* show. He wasn't performing so much for Creech – who had been terrified from the outset anyway – as for his own men. He wanted to impress those among them who didn't know him. He needed their respect, their loyalty, and even a measure of fear. That was how to command.

'Anything else, Mr Creech?'

He knew if he kept asking Creech would keep telling. He'd tell until he was telling the tiniest details, because he knew if he stopped he might start to bleed all over again.

'Well,' Creech said, 'he made some signs.'

'Signs?' Jay frowned. 'What sort of signs?'

'He made them so they'd look old. They were danger warnings, warning about the island.'

'Warning of what exactly?'

'That it was out of bounds. That it was infected with anthrax.'

Jay stood up again and laughed. 'That's crazy!' he said. He turned to Hestler, who was smiling without knowing what the joke was. Hestler had cropped black hair, a long black beard and a face whose blotchiness was disguised by a year-round tan. 'You know what he's doing?' Jay asked. Hestler admitted he didn't. 'He'll scatter those signs around half-hidden, like he's pulled them up. When we come across one, we're supposed to panic. And while we're panicking, he picks us off with his toy pistol.'

'What's anthrax?' the other Chicano asked.

'A poison,' Jay explained. 'A tenth of a millionth of a gram can kill you. The Army *did* experiment with it in the fifties.' He turned to Creech again. 'Isn't that right?'

Creech nodded. 'But the island you're thinking of is north of here.'

'And not on any map?' Creech nodded again. 'Yes, maybe that was his thinking. He chooses an island the map-makers haven't bothered with and makes it look infected. Too elaborate, Gordon. Way too elaborate.' He turned to Choa. 'Take Watts and Schlecht and start bringing the stuff in.' Choa led the two men outside. Watts was tall and as thin as a reed, but deceptively strong. Jay had come up against him in an arm-wrestling contest in the gym, and had bet $300 on himself to win inside half a minute. Watts had beaten him in eleven seconds flat.

Schlecht was someone Watts knew, and that was about as much as Jay knew. He was small, but with massive biceps and a bull neck, an Ollie to Watts' Stan Laurel. Schlecht even had Hardy's moustache, but his face was like an animal's, nicked and scarred and mean.

The other three in the team had been suggested by Hestler, which was good enough for Jay. They were brothers: Hector, Benny and Carl. For some reason, they didn't reveal their surname. They looked like the weakest links, wide-eyed during the flight from LA, amazed to be visiting hotels and Paris and car rental offices, like Europe was one giant theme park. One of them had even brought a camera with him, which Jay had confiscated straight off.

Hestler agreed that they acted like kids, but he'd seen them in fights. Once they got going, he said, they were real bastards. He thought they'd had their whole moral training from video games and spaghetti westerns.

It took a couple of trips to bring all the stuff in. Everyone was damp, and not liking it.

'Start unpacking,' Jay ordered.

Hestler looked at him. 'Are we going now?'

'Why not?'

'It's raining hard!'

'Hestler, we're going to be in a fucking boat. We'd get wet even if the sky was blue as a South Carolina morning. I bet you're the sort who runs out of the swimming pool when the rain starts.'

There was more laughter at this. Hestler didn't appreciate being its butt, but he stopped questioning Jay's decisions.

Jay turned to Jiminez. 'See if you can find any oilskins.'

Jiminez nodded and set to work. Choa, Watts and Schlecht were handing out armaments. Each man had a sub-machine gun, either the MP5 or a Cobray M11. They also received a pistol, ammo, and knife. Jiminez refused the knife, preferring his own blade. Hestler and Jay were the only two to be given grenades – Jay's orders. The other men could be professional baseball pitchers, he still wouldn't have trusted them with a grenade.

'We take those three bags with us,' Jay said, pointing to the ones he meant. 'If you have dry clothes with you, put them in a backpack.'

Watts and Schlecht handed out the backpacks. They were day-walker spec, big enough for a change of clothes and some provisions. Belts and holsters were next. Creech could hardly believe the evidence of his own eyes. He didn't feel so bad now about grassing on Reeve. After all, Reeve hadn't warned him what he was getting him into.

All Creech hoped now was that he'd get out of this alive. Jiminez had found some waterproof clothing, not quite enough to go round. Jay examined the two boats, only one of which was big enough to accommodate all of them. He decided they should take both: a back-up was always useful.

'Are these ready to go?' he asked Creech.

'Might need some fuel,' Creech said, trying to be helpful.

'Do it. Hector, you watch him. Benny and Carl, go move the cars, see if you can get them out of sight.'

The three brothers nodded. Jay still didn't know which of them was which. He bit his bottom lip thoughtfully. This mission was costing Kosigin dear; he didn't want one single fuck-up.

'Hey, Hestler, you ever skippered a boat?'

'Some,' Hestler said. Hestler had done most things in his life, one reason why he was so useful.

'Okay,' Jay said, 'you take the motorboat. You can take the three stooges with you. The rest of us will take the bigger boat.' He looked down on Creech, who was carrying a canister of fuel down the short metal ladder that led to both boats. 'You're in charge of the bigger boat, Mr Creech.'

Creech managed to nod. 'Er . . .' he said. But then he swallowed. He'd been about to ask about the hire fee, but looking into Jay's eyes it suddenly didn't matter any more.

It was a terrible day to be in a boat. The Minch was notorious anyway, and this was the sort of day which merely added to its reputation. The two boats kept in radio contact, for though they were only thirty feet apart there was no way a shout could be heard from one to the other, and even hand signals were difficult, since most of the men were holding on with both hands to stop from being pitched over the side.

'I think we should go back!' Jay had heard Hestler say more than once. He'd just shaken his head towards Hestler's boat, not caring whether Hestler saw him or not. The Chicano whose name Jay had forgotten was puking over the side, his face close to green. Jiminez didn't look too good either, but stared ahead, refusing to acknowledge he was having any problem. Watts and Schlecht had sailed before, 'but never when we weren't carrying dope'. Choa was staring at the sea like he could control it with his anger, the way he could control people. He was learning a very old lesson indeed.

'What happens if we capsize?' the Chicano squealed, wiping his mouth with the back of his hand. 'What happens then?'

Jay said something the youth couldn't make out. Jiminez repeated it for his friend.

'Fallback.'

'Fallback? What fallback?' The youth turned to spew again, and that ended the argument.

'The wind's easing,' Creech said. He was pale in the face himself, but not from the weather. 'Forecast said it would be better in the afternoon.'

'We should have waited,' growled Choa.

Jay stared at him, then looked at the sea again. It was the same shade of grey they painted navy ships, with great spumes of white where the waves clashed. Yes, he should have waited. This way, they would land on the island less than a hundred percent ready to do battle. He wondered if the Philosopher had worked that out . . .

Hestler wiped stinging water out of his eyes; he was thinking much the same as Jay.

Jiminez and his friend were staring at Jay, not sure what to think. 'What the fuck is he doing?' Jiminez's friend asked.

'He's singing,' Jiminez told him. Jay was singing *Row, row, row your boat* at the top of his voice.

Nobody joined in.

'There!' Creech said eventually. 'There's the island.' He was as relieved as anybody, though he was filled with a certain dread too. Hands tightened around guns, eyes peered at the coastline. 'There's only one real place for a landing, that wee bit of beach.'

The beach was a narrow strip of sand so dark it might have been coal dust. The land adjoining it had been worn away, so that there was little more than a steep step up from the beach on to earth and grass.

'What do I do?' Creech asked.

'Beach the boat.'

'She's not built for that.'

'Then get us as close as you can and drop anchor. We'll wade ashore. Boots off, everybody!'

Choa was studying the pocket handkerchief beach. Jay asked him what he thought.

'He's been here since last night,' Choa said. 'He'll be ready. If it were me, I'd pick us off as we go ashore.'

'I don't see him.'

'Like I say, he's had time to get ready.'

'You mean camouflage?' Jay accepted the point and brought his binoculars up to his eyes. He scanned the horizon slowly, carefully. 'He's not there,' he told Choa, handing him the binoculars. Choa peered through them.

'Maybe,' he said, 'we should circle the island in the boats, see if we can spot anything. He could've booby-trapped the beach. No footprints, but with this wind and rain that's no surprise. Any footprints would be erased in minutes.' Choa had a deep molasses voice, and looked like he knew his stuff; he came from a race of hunters and trappers after all.

But Jay shook his head. 'He won't play it that way.'

He couldn't say why he felt so sure.

They tied the motorboat to the larger vessel and dropped anchor. 'You're coming with us,' Jay told Creech. 'Don't want you buggering off and leaving us.' Creech seemed resigned.

With trousers rolled up, they waded ashore, boots tied around their necks, packs on their backs, the first men in the water keeping their guns aimed at the beach, the men to the rear carrying the three large cases.

The rain was blowing almost horizontally as Jay gathered his troops around. 'Remember,' he said, 'there are signs warning of anthrax. They're a bluff, so don't be surprised if you stumble across one, even if it's been well hidden. Okay? Let's get off the beach.' He looked around, his eyes finding the nameless Chicano. 'Stay here with Creech. Don't let him near the boats, understood?'

'Understood.'

The rest of them set off towards a narrow trail which snaked up from the beach. The trail divided into two, and Jay split his men into two units.

The Chicano waved his friend goodbye, and turned his gun on Creech. 'This is horrible country.'

'You get used to it,' Creech said, heading for the shelter of the step. It formed a nice wind-break, so that if you crouched down you were completely protected. The Chicano didn't sit beside him – he had to keep watch – but he didn't stray too far either. He paced the beach, alternating between keeping a look out for Reeve, and keeping an eye on Creech. He knew they'd finish off the man eventually, probably as soon as they got back to the mainland. The youth shivered and shrugged his shoulders. He'd discovered that the wool in his brown leather jacket was synthetic, useless. He noticed that Creech's jacket looked warm.

'Hey,' he said, 'you don't need that. Give it to me.' And he used his gun instead of 'please'. Creech shrugged off the brown cord jacket. The Chicano had to put his gun down to put the jacket on over the top of his leather one. 'Move and I kill you,' he told Creech, who held up his hands peaceably. The Chicano placed his gun on the sand and stood up.

As he stood, he saw something incredible. The earth at the top of the step opened up and a man sprang to life, for all the world like a zombie. The man sprang forward and leapt on the youth, knocking him backwards. The young man wrestled to get his pistol out of its holster then stopped suddenly, intent on the hilt of a dagger which was protruding from his chest.

Creech leapt to his feet, mouth open in a silent scream.

Gordon Reeve stood up and looked down at the youth, whose hands were fluttering around the grip of the knife like moths around a flame. Reeve placed a foot on the dying man's stomach and pulled out the dagger, blood spewing out of the slit. Creech turned away and threw up on the sand. The Chicano's eyes were starting to close when Reeve wiped the knife clean on Creech's jacket.

It had taken him some time to find the perfect spot, and then longer still to dig his foxhole. He'd used a collapsible spade, brought from his workshop, first scraping off a three-inch deep layer of topsoil and grass. And when the hole was finished, and Reeve installed in it, he'd placed the section of turf back, convinced he was invisible.

He'd been in that hole the best part of ten hours, fearing trench-foot as the water table rose and the rain kept coming down.

'One down,' he said now.

'There are ten altogether,' Creech stammered, wiping his lips.

'I know, I saw you arrive.' Reeve stared at him. 'And I heard Jay talking about those signs we made.'

'Ach, Mr Reeve, I had to say *something*. I was shite-scared, I admit it.'

'It's okay, Kenneth. I knew Jay would find out about them.'

'What?'

'He was expecting a trap, and you handed him one. He wasn't so ready for another. Come on.'

'Where?'

'Back to the boat.'

Creech managed to let out a yip of relief. They waded into the water and were half-way to the boat when there was a roar from the island. Jiminez had come back to check on his friend. Now he was sprinting towards the body, yelling something Spanish at the top of his voice.

'Hurry!' Reeve urged. As if Creech needed telling. They grabbed for the side of the larger boat and hauled themselves in, Creech finding an energy he hadn't used in years. There was a sudden explosion behind them, and Reeve turned his head to see smoke rising into the sky, and earth raining down all around.

'Looks like someone stumbled on one of my surprises.'

He'd run tripwires across both paths. The explosive charges were big enough to take out two, maybe three men if they were close enough together. Only one explosion though; the other party had stopped short of the tripwire. They must have heard the scream and turned back towards the beach. They were starting to appear. Two ran straight to the water's edge, firing as they ran.

Creech started the engine. It was still warm and started quickly. Reeve dealt with the anchor by slicing the rope with a single hack of his dagger.

'Let's go!' he yelled.

They went, the motorboat trailing after them. When they were out of the range of bullets, Reeve ordered Creech to cut the engine. Creech had to be told twice; even then he couldn't believe what he was hearing.

'Why?'

'Because I want to watch.' Reeve had a backpack of his own, and took from it a small pair of powerful binoculars. Jay seemed to be talking to his men as they stood around the cooling body. From the looks on their faces, Reeve knew he had scored an important victory. They didn't look angry or set on revenge; they looked horrified. Doubts would now start to enter their minds. There were four of them, including the Hispanic-looking youth who'd run on to the beach first. Four. Which meant the explosive had been tripped by a unit of the remaining five men. The Hispanic had recovered a little and was yelling at Jay, waving his arms at him accusingly. Tears were streaming down his face.

Reeve moved the binoculars and saw the survivors of his little trap come staggering down on to the beach. There were only two of them, both spattered with blood and badly wounded. One man had a branch sticking out of his leg, the other looked to have lost an ear. They were the only two to emerge.

Reeve took a moment to slip his boots back on before putting the binoculars back to his eyes. Jay was standing on the beach, his own binoculars trained on Reeve.

And he was smiling.

The smiled seemed to anger the Hispanic youth still further. He turned Jay round so they were face to face. Reeve saw what the young man, so close to Jay, could not. He saw Jay's hand go to the holster, saw him ease the gun out. Saw him take a step back, raising his gun hand, and blow a hole in the young man's forehead. Then Jay turned round again, so he was looking towards Reeve.

Reeve got the message.

'What're they doing?' Creech said. 'Shooting each other?'

'Getting rid of excess baggage,' Reeve corrected him grimly.

Through the binoculars, he watched Jay order the two uninjured men remaining to open one of the cases. The two others, the ones injured in the blast, were huddled together, seated on the sand. Jay looked towards them, but wasn't about to offer any comfort. He was more intent on the metal case. Then Reeve saw why, and saw, too, why Jay had been happy Reeve and Creech had stuck around.

A grenade launcher.

'Oh shit,' he said.

'What is it?' Creech came to the side to see. 'What are they doing?'

'Get us out of here,' Reeve said quietly. His voice fell away as he saw the contents of the other cases.

Two small dinghies, gas-inflatable, and the paddles to go with them.

Creech was at the wheel. The beach faced the South Uist coastline, and Creech was headed there in as straight a line as he could navigate.

'Can they hit us at this distance?' Creech yelled.

'Depends what model of launcher they've got. Knowing Jay, it'll be a good one.'

Reeve could do little but watch. It wouldn't help, but he wished he'd brought the dead man's Cobray with him. The success of his own 'trap' had led him to underestimate Jay. The bastard wasn't stupid.

'Proper planning,' Reeve muttered. Jay had taken charge of the grenade launcher. He was crouched by the water's edge, one knee on the sand, his eye busy at the sight's crosshairs.

'Here it comes,' Reeve said, watching the wisp of smoke as the first grenade was launched. It flew past the boat and hit the water a hundred yards ahead.

'That answers your question,' Reeve told Creech, who was now steering wildly, serpentining the boat and throwing Reeve about.

A second grenade came over, landing short of their boat but hitting the motorboat full on. There was an explosion, wood and metal rising into the sky above a pall of black smoke.

Creech let out a shriek. Reeve thought he was panicking, until he saw the jagged point of wood protruding from his shoulder. Reeve went to help him, but the boat started circling. He had to get them out of range. He pulled the splinter out of Creech's shoulder with no ceremony, then pushed Creech aside and gripped the wheel tight, setting them back on course.

Another grenade just reached the boat, hitting it aft and blowing a hole in the wooden structure. Water started pouring in.

'Can you swim?' Reeve asked Creech, who nodded, his teeth gritted against the pain. 'Even with one arm?'

'I'll be all right. How far are we from land?'

Reeve looked up. The answer was less than half a mile. He took his boots off again and put them in his backpack, zipping it tight. It was waterproof, and didn't weigh very much. As a last resort, he would ditch it and trust to his dagger, which was in its scabbard attached to his leg.

'Come on then,' he told Creech, 'let's go for a swim.'

They swam away from the sinking boat. Creech couldn't help but look back at it, watching the hull tip, seeing barnacles and wood that was in dire need of repainting.

They swam together. Reeve couldn't see, but he guessed Jay would be setting out in the dinghies by now, bringing his two remaining men with him. Reeve had taken seven men out of the game.

But at a price.

They were swimming across the current, which made half a mile seem like three times that. Creech grew quickly exhausted, and Reeve had to help him. This is great, he thought, just what I need. Lying in a foxhole all night, and now a half-mile swim pulling an injured man with me.

Meantime, Jay would be paddling, not straining himself. The odds were turning against Reeve all the time.

He eventually pulled Creech ashore. Creech wanted to lie down and rest, but Reeve hauled him to his feet and slapped his face a couple of times.

'You've got to get out of here!' he yelled. Creech's leg wound, the slice the Chicano had given him, had opened up again. They were six or seven miles shy of the nearest village, but Reeve knew there was a croft to the south, maybe three miles distant. 'Keep to the coast,' he told Creech. 'Don't try crossing the hills. Okay?'

He waited till Creech had nodded. The man made to stumble away, but Reeve grabbed his arm. 'Kenneth, I'm sorry I got you into this.'

Creech shrugged free and started to walk. Reeve watched him go, trying to feel something for him. But the soldier had taken over. Creech was a casualty; that didn't mean you had time for flowers and sympathy. Like everyone else, it was sink or swim. Really, Reeve shouldn't even have helped him ashore. He should have conserved his own energy, which was what he did now. He took off his wet clothes and wrung them out, then lay them out to dry. They wouldn't have time to get really dry, but the wind might help. The things in his backpack were almost completely dry, which was good fortune. He trained the binoculars on the dinghies. There were two men in the front one, only one in the second. The man with Jay looked grim with a large black beard, the man paddling alone looked American Indian. Reeve scanned the boats for armaments: pistols and sub-machine guns; no rocket launchers that he could see. Nothing heavy. But there was something on Jay's lap . . . He'd thought at first it was a transmitter, but saw now that it was a radio-cassette player.

'What the hell is that for?' he asked himself.

He examined his surroundings. He knew this area fairly well, which was to his advantage. The hill range had two peaks, Hecla to the north and Beinn Mhor to the south, each at about two thousand feet. Reeve had managed to go unnoticed for whole weekends when tracked by up to a dozen men, and he'd only had part of this wilderness to play with. But now he had to assume he was up against professionals.

This time, he was really playing for his life.

Creech was out of sight. Reeve knew Jay wouldn't bother with him anyway: he couldn't afford to lose one third of his force. But just in case, Reeve bided his time until Jay and his men could see him clearly. He pulled on trousers, socks and boots, and tied the arms of his shirt around his neck, so it flapped like a cape. It would dry quicker that way. Then he picked up his backpack and pistol and headed into the hills, making sure his pursuers could see the direction he was taking.

He heard the bullet crack behind him but didn't slow down. His pursuers were carrying MP5s; Reeve knew the things were as accurate as rifles up to about a hundred metres, but he was well out of that range. They were just wasting ammo, and soon realised it. Reeve came to the top of the first rise and turned his head to watch. They were close to the shore now. He had maybe four or five minutes on them.

He started running.

25

Jay waited till the last possible moment before leaping out of the dinghy on to land. He was still fairly dry, and wanted to stay that way. The others didn't mind splashing into the knee-deep water, clambering over the rocks on to land. They brought the inflatables with them, and weighed them down with rocks so they wouldn't be blown back to sea.

'Do we split up?' Choa asked.

'Let's stick together,' Jay said. 'If it becomes necessary later, we can split up.' He had torn a page out of their map book – the one showing the Western Isles – but it was a driver's map, not a walker's. It didn't tell him much about the terrain except that they were a long way from civilisation.

'Let's go,' he said, folding the map back into his pocket. 'Choa, check your ammo clip.'

Choa had been the one who had blasted away at Reeve, on the principle that if you could see your target, you were as well to have a go at hitting it. Choa had never used the MP5 before. He'd liked firing it so much he was itching to fire it again. He held it ready, safety catch off.

'Space out,' Jay told the other two. 'Let's not make any easy targets. Choa, you watch our backs, in case he comes around us.'

'You don't think he'll just run?' Hestler asked.

'It would make sense,' Jay admitted. 'He's wet and most probably tired. He knows the odds. But I don't think he'll run. He wants this over as badly as I do.'

'No matter who wins?'

Jay looked at Hestler. 'No matter who wins,' he said. 'It's playing the game that counts.'

They marched in silence after that, Jay using hand signals to show when he thought they were bunching up too much. They didn't march in a line, but spread themselves out, making a more random pattern which would be harder for an enemy to hit. Jay wondered if Reeve had a plan. Reeve's house was only five or so miles distant; it made sense that, running an outward bound centre, he'd know these hills better than they did. He might know them very well indeed.

Jay knew it was three against one, but taking everything else into account those weren't ideal odds. He wished he had an Ordnance Survey map of the area, something that would give him a better idea of what they were up against. But all he had were his eyes and his instincts.

And the knowledge that Gordon Reeve had almost got them both killed.

The rain started again, like mischievous needles jabbing the skin. They walked into it face-on. Jay knew Reeve wouldn't keep moving in a straight line; that direction would take him to civilisation too quickly. He'd be circling round at some point, either towards Hecla or Beinn Mhor. If there had been three men with him Jay would have split the group in half, a two-man patrol in either direction, but he only had two men left. He didn't regret killing the Chicano, not for an instant, but another man would have been useful. He had Benny and Carl's word for it that their brother Hector, plus Watts and Schlecht, were lying dead back at the scene of the explosion. Jay had promised to come back for the two injured men. He wasn't sure if it was a promise he would fulfil.

He'd been right about one thing: the phony anthrax signs *had* been crazy. The Philosopher had known what he was doing. Creech had been allowed to know about them, and had spilled his guts to Jay . . . and Jay had been tricked into thinking he knew something important. They'd been a ruse, nothing more, the *real* trick had been the tripwires. He guessed now that his own unit had stopped just short of encountering one.

Nice, Gordon – very nice.

Jay and his two men came to a high point and looked into the deep valley below. There was no sign of Reeve and no visible hiding place. But Choa, with his hunter's eyes, spotted something, a dark shape against the hillside. They approached cautiously, but it was just a groove in the earth, maybe a foot deep, six feet long and a couple of feet wide.

'It's a scrape,' Jay said.

'A what?' Hestler asked.

'A hide. You scrape away the earth then lie in the hole. Put some netting over you and you're hidden from a distance.' Jay looked around, realising. 'He uses this area for his outward bound courses. There must have been a manhunt at some stage. There could be dozens of these spread out across the hills.'

'So he could be hiding?'

'Yes.'

'So maybe we've walked right past him; maybe he's already behind us.' Hestler eased his catch off. 'I say we split up, that way we cover more ground. We could be here all night otherwise.'

'Maybe that's what he wants,' Choa offered. 'Get us cold and lost, wet and hungry. Stalking us, just waiting for concentration to lapse.'

'He's only one man,' Hestler growled. He was still looking around, daring anything to move. Jay noticed Hestler's MP5 was set to full auto.

'All right,' Jay said, 'you two head north, I'll head south. There are two peaks. We each circle one and RV back at the dinghies. Keep in touch by two-way. It might take a few hours. It won't be dark by the time we finish. If there's no result, we think again.'

'Sounds good to me,' Hestler said, setting off. 'Sooner we start, sooner we finish.'

Choa gave Jay a doubting look, but set off after his partner.

Jay decided after they'd gone to make straight for the summit of Beinn Mhor. He'd be more of a target, but on the plus side he could take in the country below with a single sweep.

'Just do it,' he told himself, beginning to climb.

'This is fucking unbelievable,' Hestler told Choa. 'There were ten of us at the start, how the fuck did we get to this?'

'Search me.'

'Ten against one. He's fucked us up nicely. I'd like to tear him a new asshole.'

'You think he needs two?'

Hestler turned to Choa. 'He's likely to be shitting himself so much, maybe he will at that.'

Choa said nothing. He knew words came free; as a result people talked too much. Sometimes people could talk themselves into believing they were superhuman. Talking could make you crazy.

The last they saw of Jay he was clambering on all-fours up a steep slope. Then they rounded the hillside and lost him.

'This weather is the pits,' Hestler said.

Choa silently agreed. The last time he'd known anything like it was up in Oregon, near the mountains there. Rain so thick you couldn't see through it. But afterwards, the trees had smelt so beautiful, pine and moss bursting underfoot. There weren't many trees here. There was practically nowhere to hide, except for these scrapes. He didn't like the idea of these invisible hides. 'We're a long way from Los Angeles,' he said quietly.

Hestler chuckled. 'Killing's killing,' he said. 'Doesn't matter where you do it or who you do it for.'

'Look,' said Choa, pointing. He had good eyes. He'd been the first to spot the scrape, and now he'd noticed another smallish patch on the ground. When they got up close, it was wet, greasy to the touch. It was blood.

'Bastard's winged!' Hestler said.

'Let's radio Jay and tell him.'

'Fuck that, the bastard could be round the next bend. Let's get him.'

Hestler set off, but Choa held back. He had the two-way hooked to his belt and now unclipped it.

'Got something here,' he said. Then, with Hestler almost out of sight, 'Hey! Hold on a minute!' But Hestler kept on going.

'What is it?' Jay's voice said. He sounded a little out of breath, but not much.

'Blood, very fresh.'

'No way.'

'I'm telling yo—'

'I don't think he's hurt.'

'One of the grenades maybe?'

'Not the way he swam to shore. I watched him, remember. He clambered up that first slope like a mountain goat.'

'Well, it's blood.' Choa rubbed some of it between thumb and forefinger. It was sticky and cold.

'Taste it,' Jay said.

'What?' Choa couldn't believe what he was hearing.

'Put some on your tongue,' Jay commanded.

Choa looked at his fingers.

'Do it!'

Choa put the tip of his tongue against the blood. He couldn't taste anything. He licked at it, tasted it, then spat.

'Well?'

Choa spoke into the radio. 'Tastes funny,' he said.

'Is it metallic, the way blood is?'

Choa had to admit it wasn't like that. 'Sort of chalky,' he said.

'Like paint?' Jay guessed.

'How did you know?'

'It's fake. He's laying a false trail.'

Choa looked ahead of him. There was no sign of Hestler.

'Hestler!' he shouted. 'Get back here!'

Then there was a single gunshot. Choa knew better than to run towards it but he didn't freeze either. He moved off downhill and circled around towards the noise. He'd switched off the radio so it wouldn't give away his position. He carried his sub-machine gun cocked and ready.

There was a body ahead of him, lying in a gully. It looked like Hestler had taken a short cut. Instead of rounding the gully, he'd headed down into it, which made him easy prey for anyone hiding just over the ridge. What was the phrase? Like shooting a pig in a tub.

Choa daren't descend into the gully. Besides, the hole in the back of Hestler's head was big enough and clear enough. He held the radio to his face.

'What?' Jay said quietly. He'd heard the shot.

'Hestler's down,' Choa said simply.

'What happened?'

'Someone tore him a new mouth, wrong side of his head.'

Choa cut the radio. He needed both hands for his gun. Reeve was nearby. He rounded the gully. There were so many dips and rises in the landscape, he couldn't see further than eighty feet in any direction. Reeve could be as close as eighty feet. Apart from the rain hitting him and the wind in his ears, there was no noise at all. No birds, no leaves rustling. The sky overhead was like a slab of stone.

Choa came to a decision which seemed immediately right to him: head back to the dinghies and take one, then paddle away from here. The thought made him feel better. This was Jay's fight, not his. He felt like Reeve was watching him, even though he couldn't see a damned thing. His excellent eyesight didn't work so well in driving rain. A storm was directly over the island. Choa dropped the MP5 and his pistol, then started walking with hands held high above him. He guessed he was heading the right way; away from here seemed *exactly* the right way.

Reeve saw him go.

He was naked apart from his boots. His clothes were in the backpack, staying dry. He watched for a full ten minutes, then went to pick up the armaments. He scrabbled down the side of the gully and quickly unloaded Hestler's weapons, leaving them with the body but taking the ammo. Then he found the two grenades, and he took those too. He liked these odds better now. He knew the Indian had simply walked away from the fight, which was entirely sensible.

Then he heard the music. It was a long way off, but between the squalls fragments of it drifted to his ears. It was Jay, and he was singing that damned song. Reeve made towards the sound, but he took his time. He knew it wasn't really Jay – it was the cassette recorder. Jay had recorded himself singing the song over and over again, his voice rising the longer the recording went on.

Reeve had to cross a wide valley between the two peaks, and knew he would be most vulnerable here. There was no sign of Jay, just the music, getting closer now. He edged around towards it, moving in a crouch, backwalking part of the way, staying to the shelter of slopes wherever he could. Until he came to the final slope. The music sounded just the other side of the ridge. Reeve crawled up the slope, hugging the ground.

There was a saucer-shaped dip beyond the ridge, and in the centre sat the cassette recorder. Reeve lay there for a few minutes, until he could stand the music no longer. He took aim with the MP5 and hit the fat black box dead centre.

The box exploded, flames shooting out radially from it. Booby-trapped. Maybe now Jay would come looking.

Suddenly there was another explosion, much closer to Reeve. The ground quivered, and divots showered down around him. For a split second he was back in the scrape in Argentina, and Jay was about to crack.

Now another explosion, very close. He realised what was happening. Jay was in hiding somewhere, and had guessed the direction of Reeve's burst of gunfire. Now he was tossing grenades in that direction, and they weren't landing far short of their target. Reeve stood up to see if he could spot the grenades in flight. Smoke from the explosions was being dispersed by the sharp breeze, but pungent tendrils still coiled up from the plastic remains of the cassette player.

Suddenly a figure stood up on the far side of the gully. Naked, body and face smeared with earth, white teeth grinning through the improvised facepaint.

Jay.

Sixty feet away and firing from the hip.

Two bullets thudded into Reeve, pushing him off his feet. He rolled back down the slope, just managing to keep hold of his gun. He came to a stop on the gully floor, but knew he had no time to check the damage. He had to get out of the gully. He scraped his way up the other side, cresting the rise before Jay came into view. He just made it. Rain stung his eyes as he ran, feet slipping in mud. Another narrow valley, across a stream . . . he knew where he was going, knew where he'd end up. One bullet had caught him in the left shoulder, the other between shoulder and chest. They burnt. The scabbard was still strapped to his right leg, but it slowed him down so he undid the straps and drew out the dagger, discarding the scabbard.

'Hey, Philosopher!' Jay called, his voice manic. 'You like hide and seek? You were always chicken, Philosopher! No guts.'

Reeve knew what Jay was doing: trying to rile him. Anger made you strong in some ways, but so weak in others.

But there was no pink mist now, nothing in Reeve's heart but cool procedure and searing pain. He crested two more rises before he found himself at the chasm, a rupture in the land which ran in a jagged tear to the sea. At high tide, the base of the cavity filled with gurgling, murderous water. But just now it was a damp bed of jagged rocks. It was dark down there, no matter what time of day, whatever the weather above. A place of shadows and secrets never brought up into the light. Reeve walked its edge. He wasn't scared of it – it was too familiar to him – but he'd seen his weekend soldiers cower in its presence. He picked his spot and waited, taking time to examine his wounds. He was bleeding badly. Given time, he could create makeshift dressings, but he knew time was short.

'Hey, Philosopher!' Jay yelled. 'Is this blood real?' A pause. 'Tastes real, so I guess it is! Want to know something, Philosopher? I've done a lot of thinking over the years about Operation Stalwart. I've been wondering why they chose us. I mean, I was fucked up after that fiasco on the glacier. I should never have been allowed off the ship, never mind sent behind enemy lines. I wanted to kill those bastards so badly. And you . . . well, you weren't popular, Philosopher. You had too many ideas in your head, including your own ideas. You were the Philosopher, reading too much, turning yourself on to anarchism and all that other stuff. As far as the brass were concerned, there was half a chance you were becoming the enemy. See, Philosopher, we were both of a kind – loose wires, expendable. That was always going to be a one-way mission, and it would've turned out that way if I hadn't saved our hides.'

The voice sounded maybe a hundred yards away. Two thirds of a yard per stride . . . Reeve started counting, at the same time snaking his way back up the slope, listening intently for any clue as to the line Jay was taking. He guessed he would simply follow the trail of blood.

Reeve was just below the crest now. Suddenly he heard a grunt as Jay started to climb. In a few seconds he would crest the rise, Reeve just the other side of it, hugging the land. Reeve stopped breathing. Jay was so close, not even six feet away.

Reeve concentrated all his energies, closing his eyes for a moment, finally taking a deep breath.

'Hey, Philos—'

He threw out his good arm with all his strength, plunging the dagger through Jay's boot and into his foot. As Jay started to scream, Reeve yanked his ankles away from him, hurling him down the slope. Jay could see what was at the bottom of the slide and tried digging his heels, elbows, and fingers in, but the ground was slippery and he just kept on sliding. Reeve was sliding too. The force of his momentum when he'd hauled Jay over the crest had sent him into a roll. His shoulder banged against the ground, almost causing him to pass out. Below him, he saw Jay slip three-quarters of the way over the precipice, his hands scrabbling for purchase. Reeve was rolling straight towards him. They'd fall into the ravine together.

Reeve struck out with his right hand, the hand which still held the dagger. The blade sank into the earth, but started to cut through it, barely slowing his descent. He twisted the blade so the meat of it was gouging into the wet soil. It was like applying a brake. He jolted to a stop, his legs hanging into space. He found the edge with his knees and started to pull himself up, but a hand grabbed one of his ankles. And now Jay's other hand let go of the lip of the ravine and he used it to gain a better grip on Reeve, hauling himself up over Reeve's slippery legs while their combined weight started the dagger cutting through the earth again, so that as Jay climbed, Reeve slid further over the edge.

He waited till Jay was preparing to slide further up; while he was unbalanced, Reeve rolled on to his side, shrugging Jay off and at the same time lashing out at him with his feet. For an instant they were side by side, the way they had been that final night in Argentina, their faces so close Reeve could feel Jay's breath against his cheek.

'Well,' Jay panted, trying to grin, 'isn't this cosy? Just the two of us, like it was always meant to be.'

'You should have died back in Rio Grande,' Reeve spat.

'If we'd stayed in that damned trench, we'd have died,' Jay hissed. 'You owe me, Philosopher!'

'Owe you?' Reeve was clawing at the ground with the fingers of his left hand, feeling pain shoot through his shoulder. When he had a good handhold he started to ease the dagger out of the ground.

'Yes, owe me,' Jay was saying, readying to pull them both over the edge and on to the rocks below.

Reeve raised the dagger and plunged it into Jay's neck. Blood gurgled from Jay's mouth as, his eyes wide in amazement, one hand went to the wound. He lost all grip and started to slide over the edge.

Reeve watched him go, the head disappearing last of all, eyes still wide open. He didn't hear the body hit the ground. Reeve let out a roar which echoed down the chasm walls and up into the sky. Not a roar of pain or even of victory.

Just a roar.

'All debts repaid,' Reeve said, digging the dagger back into the ground, and for some reason he saw Jim in his mind, content.

Then he started slowly, carefully, to climb back up the treacherous slope, not relaxing until he was at the top, his head and trunk hanging over the crest of the rise. He closed his eyes then and wept, not feeling the pain in his shoulder or the chill damp ground robbing him of his core temperature, degree by wilful degree.

26

There was a lot of mess still to be cleared up: Gordon Reeve knew that. The police might or might not accept his story. It sounded pretty far-fetched when he thought about it. But he had Jim's computer file, and soon he'd have the documents to go with it, as soon as he could arrange a trip to Tisbury.

As for CWC itself and Kosigin . . . he didn't know what would happen. He only knew that *something* would. The same applied to Allerdyce and Alliance Investigative. He didn't really care any more. He'd done what he could.

He made his way back home and staggered indoors. He knew he should clean his wounds, make fresh dressings, call a doctor. But he sat at the kitchen table instead. He wanted to phone Joan, wanted to tell her it was all right now, that Allan and she could come home. He wanted that most of all.

He wasn't sure what they'd do after that. Go back to the old routine? Maybe. Or maybe he'd dig up some of their land, turn it into a vegetable garden . . . go organic, and worry less that way. He didn't think so, though.

He started to laugh, resting his head on his forearms.

'I'm one of Nietzsche's gentlemen,' he told himself. 'I'll think of something.'